The Norton Anthology
of American Literature

SEVENTH EDITION

VOLUME D

1914–1945

VOLUME A

Beginnings to 1700 • FRANKLIN

American Literature 1700–1820 • GURA

Native American Literatures • KRUPAT

VOLUME B

American Literature 1820–1865 • LEVINE • KRUPAT

VOLUME C

American Literature 1865–1914 • REESMAN • KRUPAT

VOLUME D

American Literature 1914–1945

LOEFFELHOLZ

VOLUME E

American Literature since 1945

KLINKOWITZ • WALLACE

The Norton Anthology
of American Literature

SEVENTH EDITION

Nina Baym, *General Editor*

SWANLUND CHAIR AND CENTER FOR
ADVANCED STUDY PROFESSOR EMERITA OF ENGLISH
JUBILEE PROFESSOR OF LIBERAL ARTS AND SCIENCES
UNIVERSITY OF ILLINOIS AT URBANA-CHAMPAIGN

VOLUME D

1914–1945

Mary Loeffelholz

W • W • NORTON & COMPANY • *New York* • *London*

W. W. Norton & Company has been independent since its founding in 1923, when William Warder Norton and Mary D. Herter Norton first published lectures delivered at the People's Institute, the adult education division of New York City's Cooper Union. The Nortons soon expanded their program beyond the Institute, publishing books by celebrated academics from America and abroad. By mid-century, the two major pillars of Norton's publishing program—trade books and college texts—were firmly established. In the 1950s, the Norton family transferred control of the company to its employees, and today—with a staff of four hundred and a comparable number of trade, college, and professional titles published each year—W. W. Norton & Company stands as the largest and oldest publishing house owned wholly by its employees.

Editor: Julia Reidhead
Manuscript Editors: Kurt Wildermuth, Michael Fleming,
Katharine Ings, Candace Levy, Pam Lawson
Electronic Media Editor: Eileen Connell
Editorial Assistants: Ann Abrams, Catherine Spencer
Production Manager: Diane O'Connor
Permissions Manager: Nancy Rodwan
Permissions Clearing: Margaret Gorenstein
Text Design: Antonina Krass
Art Research: Neil Ryder Hoos
Managing Editor, College: Marian Johnson

Composition: Binghamton Valley Composition
Manufacturing: RR Donnelley

ISBN 10: 0-393-92742-3
ISBN 13: 978-0-393-92742-9

W. W. Norton & Company, Inc., 500 Fifth Avenue, New York, NY 10110
www.wwnorton.com

W. W. Norton & Company Ltd., Castle House, 75/76 Wells Street, London W1T 3QT

4 5 6 7 8 9 0

Contents

Preface to the Seventh Edition

In this Seventh Edition of *The Norton Anthology of American Literature*, we offer the most extensive revision in our long publishing history. Three new section editors have joined the team, working with each other and the General Editor to consider afresh each selection and rethink the entire apparatus, from headnotes to footnotes to section introductions to bibliographies. These editors are Robert S. Levine, Professor of English at the University of Maryland, College Park, who succeeds Hershel Parker as editor of "American Literature 1820–1865"; Jeanne Campbell Reesman, Ashbel Smith Professor of English at the University of Texas at San Antonio, who succeeds Ronald Gottesman as editor of "American Literature 1865–1914"; and Mary Loeffelholz, Professor of English at Northeastern University, who succeeds Nina Baym as editor of "American Literature 1914–1945." Each editor, new or continuing, is a well-known expert in the relevant field or period and had ultimate responsibility for his or her section of the anthology, but we have worked together closely from first to last. We are excited about the outcome of our collaboration and anticipate that, like the previous six editions, this edition of *The Norton Anthology of American Literature* will lead the field among American literature anthologies.

From the anthology's inception in 1979, the editors have had three main aims: first, to present a rich and substantial enough variety of works to enable teachers to build courses according to their own ideals (thus, teachers are offered more authors and more selections than they will probably use in any one course); second, to make the anthology self-sufficient by featuring many works in their entirety along with extensive selections for individual authors; third, to balance traditional interests with developing critical concerns in a way that points to a coherent literary history. As early as 1979, we anthologized work by Anne Bradstreet, Mary Rowlandson, Sarah Kemble Knight, Phillis Wheatley, Margaret Fuller, Harriet Beecher Stowe, Frederick Douglass, Sarah Orne Jewett, Kate Chopin, Mary E. Wilkins Freeman, Booker T. Washington, Charles Chesnutt, Edith Wharton, W. E. B. Du Bois, and other writers who were not yet part of a standard canon. Yet we never shortchanged writers like Franklin, Emerson, Whitman, Hawthorne, Melville, Dickinson, Hemingway, Fitzgerald, and Faulkner, whose work students expected to read in their American literature courses, and whom teachers then and now would not think of doing without.

Although the so-called "canon wars" of the 1980s and 1990s appear to have subsided, it is clear that the number and diversity of authors now recognized as contributors to the totality of American literature have expanded dramatically since 1979. The traditional writers look different in this expanded context; they also change according to which of their works are selected. Teachers and students remain committed to the idea of the literary—that writers strive to produce artifacts that are both intellectually serious and formally skillful—but believe more than ever that writers should be understood in relation to their cultural and historical situations. In endeavoring to do justice to these complex realities, we have worked, as in previous editions, with detailed suggestions from many teachers and, through those teachers, the students who use the anthology. Thanks to questionnaires, comment cards, face-to-face and phone discussions, letters, and email, we have been able to listen to those for whom this book is intended. For this Seventh Edition, we have drawn on the careful commentary of 101 reviewers.

Our new materials have thoughtfully broadened the canon by representing 34 new writers in depth, without sacrificing widely assigned writers, many of whose selections have been reconsidered, reselected, and expanded. Our aim is always to provide extensive enough selections to do the writers justice, including complete works wherever possible. To the 36 complete longer texts already in the anthology we have added Benjamin Franklin's *Autobiography* (restored by popular demand); Hannah Foster's *The Coquette*; Frederick Douglass's novella *The Heroic Slave* (never before in a survey anthology); Stephen Crane's *Maggie: A Girl of the Streets*; Abraham Cahan's novella of immigrant New York City, *The Imported Bridegroom*; Willa Cather's *My Ántonia*; Raymond Chandler's hard-boiled detective story *Red Wind*; Sam Shepard's play *True West*; Louise Glück's *October*; and more. The Seventh Edition has expanded and in some cases reconfigured such central figures as Emerson, Hawthorne, Melville, Dickinson, and Twain, emphasizing new approaches in the headnotes and section introductions. The Seventh Edition likewise expands its representation of women writers and writers of diverse ethnic, racial, and regional origins— African Americans, Native Americans, Latina/os, and Asian Americans—whose critically acclaimed works have contributed to the American literary record. Under Arnold Krupat's editorship, Native American materials throughout the Seventh Edition have been rethought. New writers such as Sarah Winnemucca and Jane Johnston Schoolcraft, more selections from writers such as Zitkala Ša, and two new clusters (described below) enable teachers to bring early Native American writing and oratory into their syllabus or, should they prefer, to focus on these selections as a free-standing unit leading toward the moment after 1945 when Native writers fully entered the mainstream of literary activity.

In an innovation new to the Seventh Edition, each editor has gathered short texts that illuminate the cultural, historical, intellectual, and literary concerns of the period. The resulting clusters bring together markedly diverse voices—48 new to the anthology—in selections that highlight the range of views on a key issue or topic. For example, in "Slavery, Race, and the Making of American Literature," texts by David Walker, William Lloyd Garrison, Angelina Grimke, Sojourner Truth, and Martin R. Delany speak to the great paradox of pre–Civil War America: the rupture between the realities of slavery and the ideals of freedom. Or, in an example close to our own experience, "Writing in a Time of Terror: September 11, 2001" gathers verse and prose— from an excerpt from the collaboratively written official account, *The 9/11 Commission Report*, to selections by John Updike, Kimiko Hahn, Naomi Shahib Nye, and others—that show the range of powerful responses, written and visual, evoked by times of terror. Designed to be taught in a class period or two, or used as context, each of the twelve clusters consists of brief, carefully excerpted primary texts (about 6–10 per cluster) and an introduction.

Visual media, so central in contemporary American culture as well as in the classroom, has a prominent place in the Seventh Edition, which features forty pages of color plates in five new color inserts. In selecting our color plates—from Charles Wilson Peale's *Exhuming the Mastodon* at the beginning of the nineteenth century to *The Gates* by Christo and Jeanne-Claude at the beginning of the twenty-first—the editors aimed to provide images relevant to literary works in the anthology while depicting arts and artifacts typical of each era. We have looked for visually striking images that will provoke discussion, and our captions draw attention to important details and cross-reference authors and related literary texts. In addition, new graphic works—segments from Art Spiegelman's canonical graphic novel *Maus* and from the colonial children's classic *The New-England Primer*, a facsimile page of Emily Dickinson manuscript, an original illustration from Twain's *Roughing It*—open possibilities for teaching visual texts.

Period-by-Period Revisions

Volume A, Beginnings to 1820. "Beginnings to 1700," edited by Wayne Franklin, continues to feature narratives by a range of early European explorers of the North American continent. Along with a cluster on the much-recounted story of Hannah Dustan's captivity—which intensified European fear of Native populations and was used to rationalize stern measures against them—the section adds material from *The Bay Psalm Book*, Roger Williams, Edward Taylor, Robert Calef, and *The New-England Primer*, and retains the complete text of Mary Rowlandson's captivity narrative. The heightened attention in this section to the combined religious and territorial aspirations of the Anglo settlers gives students a fuller sense of the conflicts that ensued when the North American continent was perceived, by Europeans, as a "New World." We note, too, the important role of the experiences of, and narratives by, women in the early European settlement of the future United States.

In "American Literature 1700–1820," edited by Philip Gura, we distinguish the eighteenth century as a period of consolidation and development in an emergent American literature. Work by the political Founders is augmented by Benjamin Franklin's *Autobiography*, included complete by teacher request, and Royall Tyler's play *The Contrast*. Newly added is the complete text of Hannah Foster's novel *The Coquette*, which uses a real-life tragedy to meditate on the proper role of well-bred women in the new republic and testifies to the formation of a female audience. A segment from Tabitha Tenney's satiric novel *Female Quixotism* helps extend student awareness of literary activity among women, as does the cluster "Women's Poetry: From Manuscript to Print," with verse by six poets—among them Mercy Otis Warren, Sarah Wentworth Morton, and Annis Boudinot Stockton—whose work contributed to the civil and political discourse of the early republic. A second new cluster, prepared by Arnold Krupat, "Native Americans: Contact and Conflict," highlights speeches and accounts by Pontiac, Samson Occom, Chief Logan (as cited by Thomas Jefferson), Red Jacket, and Tecumseh that underscore a centuries-long pattern of initial friendly contact mutating into bitter and violent conflict between Native Americans and whites.

Volume B, American Literature 1820–1865. Under the editorship of Robert S. Levine, this volume is now much more diverse. Teachers will still find Emerson's *Nature*, Hawthorne's *Scarlet Letter*, Thoreau's *Walden*, Douglass's *Narrative,* and Whitman's *Song of Myself* complete, as well as novellas by Melville, Davis's *Life in the Iron Mills,* and other frequently assigned works. But, aware of the important role of African American writers in the period and the omnipresence of race and slavery as literary and political themes, we have added two major African American writers, William Wells Brown and Frances E. W. Harper, as well as Douglass's novella *The Heroic Slave,* Thoreau's "Plea for Captain John Brown," more chapters from Stowe's *Uncle Tom's Cabin,* and the cluster "Slavery, Race, and the Making of American Literature." The section also includes two other new clusters: "Section, Region, Nation," in which writers from varying regions—Daniel Webster, William Gilmore Simms, Richard Henry Dana, John Louis O'Sullivan, Francis Parkman, Louise Amelia Clappe Smith, Mary Boykin Miller Chesnut—challenge the notion of consensus on a "national" literature while reflecting the extraordinary enlargement of territory included within the national boundaries; "Native Americans: Resistance and Removal," prepared by Arnold Krupat, gathers oratory and writings—by Native Americans such as Black Hawk, Petelasharo, Elias Boudinot, and the collective authors of the Cherokee Memorials as well as by whites such as Ralph Waldo Emerson—protesting Andrew Jackson's ruthless national policy of Indian removal.

New women writers in this period include Lydia Huntley Sigourney, Elizabeth Stoddard, and the Native American writer Jane Johnston Schoolcraft, who is represented by authoritative texts established in Robert Dale Parker's new edition of her complete works. Added prose fiction includes chapters from Cooper's *Last of the Mohicans,* Sedgwick's *Hope Leslie,* Kirkland's *A New Home—Who'll Follow?* and Melville's *Moby-Dick,* along with Poe's "The Black Cat" and Hawthorne's "Wakefield." Nonfiction prose offerings have been expanded with several of Lydia Maria Child's letters and new selections by Fanny Fern and Margaret Fuller. By instructors' request, we have increased the representation of poems by Emerson, Longfellow, and Whittier; poetry by Emily Dickinson has been reselected, using the newly established texts by Franklin (we retain the Johnson numbers in brackets for reference), and now includes a facsimile page from Fascicle 10. Finally, the section introduction has been entirely recast; author headnotes have been updated to reflect the latest biographies and critical discussions; and the selected bibliographies have been completely revised and updated.

Volume C, American Literature 1865–1914. Edited by Jeanne Campbell Reesman, this section has taken on a striking new look. To our well-received complete longer works—Twain's *Adventures of Huckleberry Finn,* Chopin's *The Awakening,* and James's *Daisy Miller*—we add complete texts of Stephen Crane's *Maggie: A Girl of the Streets* and Abraham Cahan's *The Imported Bridegroom,* as well as chapters from Theodore Dreiser's *Sister Carrie* and Twain's *Roughing It.* Also new is a selection from Twain's *Letters from the Earth.* Short fiction throughout the section has been reconsidered; new selections include James's "The Figure in the Carpet," Edith

Wharton's "The Other Two" and "Roman Fever," and works by Jack London, Sui Sin Far, Bret Harte (notably the ground-breaking "Miggles" and "Tennessee's Partner"), Zitkala Ša, Joel Chandler Harris, and Ambrose Bierce. New poets James Weldon Johnson and Paul Laurence Dunbar, Emma Lazarus (moved from Volume B to this volume, where she belongs chronologically), the anonymous authors of *corridos*, and new prose writers Maria Ruíz de Burton, Anna Julia Cooper, Pauline Hopkins, Sarah Winnemucca, Mary Austin (restored by instructors' request), and Ida Wells-Barnett underscore that writers—male and female—from diverse ethnic, racial, and regional origins assumed the right and felt inspired to represent the American scene in the late nineteenth century. Finally, two clusters take up important political and literary disputes from the era: "Debates over 'Americanization'" considers internal divisions on policy toward the huge number of immigrants, toward Native Americans in the path of "manifest destiny," on the education of African Americans after the Civil War, and on hemispheric ideas of "America" in an age of imperialist expansion. Texts by Frederick Jackson Turner, Theodore Roosevelt, José Martí, Charles W. Chesnutt, Jane Addams, and Anna Julia Cooper consider these issues as they relate to the perennial question, Who is an American? Literary movements attuned to these divisions are considered in "Realism and Naturalism," where critical writings by William Dean Howells, Henry James, Frank Norris, Theodore Dreiser, and Jack London illuminate the turn to realism and naturalism as styles developed to represent an era of rapid modernization.

Volume D, American Literature 1914–1945. Newly edited by Mary Loeffelholz, Volume D expands its offering of complete longer works—O'Neill's *Long Day's Journey into Night* (exclusive to the Norton Anthology), Larsen's eminently teachable *Quicksand*, Faulkner's *As I Lay Dying*—with Cather's *My Ántonia*, returned by popular demand, and Raymond Chandler's hard-boiled detective story *Red Wind*, which introduces students to the fact that stylish writing has long found a home among popular genres. Other new prose texts are "Hands" from Sherwood Anderson's *Winesburg, Ohio* and "The White Horses of Vienna" by Kay Boyle, an author new to the anthology. The poet Mina Loy also appears for the first time. Loy's experimental work, as well as reconsidered selections by Ezra Pound, T. S. Eliot, Marianne Moore, Hart Crane, and Langston Hughes, encourages students and teachers to contemplate the interrelation of modernist aesthetics with ethnic, regional, and popular writing. Two new clusters address central events of the modern period. In "World War I and Its Aftermath," writings by John Reed, Ernest Hemingway, Gertrude Stein, Jessie Redmon Fauset, and others explore sharply divided views on the U.S. role in World War I, as well as the radicalizing effect of modern warfare—with 365,000 American casualties—on contemporary writing. And in "Modernist Manifestos," F. T. Marinetti, Mina Loy, Ezra Pound, Willa Cather, William Carlos Williams, and Langston Hughes show how the manifesto as a form exerted a powerful influence on international modernism in all arts.

Volume E, American Literature since 1945. In Volume E, prose and poetry, previously separately edited by Jerome Klinkowitz and Patricia B. Wallace, have been brought together in a mutually reinforcing collaboration. The result is a richer representation of the period's literary activity, and a more accurate presentation of the writers themselves, many of whom write in multiple genres. The collaboratively rewritten period introduction and headnotes provide a more nuanced, vital picture of the postwar literary scene and individual writers' contributions to it. The section continues to feature complete texts of Tennessee Williams's *A Streetcar Named Desire* (exclusive to this anthology), Amiri Baraka's *Dutchman*, Arthur Miller's *Death of a Salesman*, David Mamet's *Glengarry Glen Ross*, and Allen Ginsberg's *Howl;* to this group we add Sam Shepard's *True West* and Louise Glück's long poem *October*. Poets Lucille Clifton, Fanny Howe, and Yusef Komunyakaa have been added, as have new poems by Lorraine Niedecker, Theodore Roethke, Frank O'Hara, Adrienne Rich, Gary Snyder, James Merrill, Billy Collins, Charles Simic, Joy Harjo, and Rita Dove. Prose fiction has been enriched with short stories by newly added contemporary authors Max Apple, Amy Tan, Julia Alvarez, and Jhumpa Lahiri and new selections by Richard Powers, Annie Dillard, and Sandra Cisneros. In addition, Louise Erdrich and Sherman Alexie, two writers who work in multiple genres, are represented by selections from their poetry and prose. Appearing for the first time, a freestanding segment from Art Spiegelman's prize-winning *Maus* opens possibilities for teaching the graphic novel. Another innovation is the introduction of teachable stand-alone segments from important novels by Saul Bellow (*The Adventures of Augie March*), Kurt Vonnegut (*Slaughterhouse-Five*), Rudolfo Anaya (*Bless Me, Ultima*), and Jack Kerouac (*Big Sur*). Two new clusters add literary and topical context to this diverse section: "Postmodernist Manifestos" by Ronald Sukenick, William H. Gass, Hunter S. Thompson, Charles Olson, Frank O'Hara, Elizabeth Bishop, A. R. Ammons, and Audre Lorde show how many literary artists saw experimentation in poetry and fiction as the best way to register politics and culture in the postwar era. Finally, in "Writing in a Time of Terror: September 11, 2001," ten prose and verse selections show the powerful literary responses evoked by times of terror.

Additional Resources from the Publisher

The Seventh Edition retains the paperback splits format introduced in the Sixth Edition, which was welcomed by instructors and students for its flexibility and portability. This format accommodates the many instructors who use the anthology in a two-semester survey, but allows for mixing and matching the five volumes in a variety of courses organized by period or topic, at levels from introductory to advanced. To give instructors even more flexibility, the publisher is making available the full list of 180 Norton Critical Editions, including such frequently assigned novels as Harriet Beecher Stowe's *Uncle Tom's Cabin*, Herman Melville's *Moby-Dick*, Edith Wharton's *The House of Mirth*, and William Faulkner's *The Sound and the Fury*, among many others. A Norton Critical Edition can be included with Package 1 or 2 of the Seventh Edition for free. Each Norton Critical Edition gives students an authoritative, carefully annotated text accompanied by rich contextual and critical materials prepared by an expert in the subject.

With the Seventh Edition of *The Norton Anthology of American Literature*, the publisher expands its already extensive online resource, Norton Literature Online (wwnorton.com/literature). Students who activate the free password included in each new copy of the anthology gain access to an array of general resources, among them a glossary of literary terms, advice on writing about literature and using MLA documentation style, study aids and quizzes, an author portrait gallery featuring 380 authors, more than 100 maps, and over 90 minutes of recorded readings and musical selections. With their passwords, students also gain access to a site specifically developed to support *The Norton Anthology of American Literature*. Redesigned for easier navigation, this student website (wwnorton.com/naal), prepared by Bruce Michelson, offers timelines, outlines of the period introductions, over 400 annotated links, resource pages for 160 of the writers in the anthology, and searchable "Explorations" with questions and research projects. Also on the site are new self-grading quizzes, prepared by Jason Coats, on thirty of the most widely taught works in the anthology.

Teaching with The Norton Anthology of American Literature: *A Guide for Instructors* has been expanded and updated by Bruce Michelson. This much-praised guide offers extensive help, from developing a syllabus to preparing exams. The guide entries suggest approaches to each author and provide questions for class discussion. Finally, the Norton Resource Library (wwnorton.com/nrl) offers instructors the Course Guide and student website content in PDF format as well as a WebCT/BlackBoard coursepack featuring tests and quizzes on the period introductions and individual works, lecture outlines, maps, and timelines, among other resources.

Instructors who adopt *The Norton Anthology of American Literature* have access to an extensive array of films and videos. In addition to videos of the plays by O'Neill, Williams, Miller, and Mamet in the anthology, segments of the award-winning video series *American Passages: A Literary Survey* are available without charge on orders of specified quantities of the Norton Anthology. Funded by Annenberg/CPB, produced by Oregon Public Broadcasting, and developed with the Norton Anthology as its exclusive companion anthology, *American Passages* contains sixteen segments, each covering a literary movement or period by exploring two or three authors in depth. A website (learner.org/amerpass), instructor's guide, and student guide are also available. For information about the videos, contact your Norton representative.

Editorial Procedures

As in past editions, editorial features—period introductions, headnotes, annotations, and bibliographies—are designed to be concise yet full and to give students necessary information without imposing an interpretation. For long-time users, the familiar format may obscure the breadth of revisions in this edition, in which the editors have updated all apparatus in response to new scholarship and new ways of thinking about the literature of the United States: period introductions have been entirely or substantially rewritten, as have dozens of headnotes. All Selected Bibliographies have been thoroughly updated and augmented with new general-resources bibliographies categorized by Reference Works, Histories, and Literary Criticism for each period. The Seventh Edition retains three editorial features that help students place their reading in historical and cultural context—a Texts/Contexts timeline following each period introduction, a map on the front endpaper of each volume, and a chronological chart, on the back endpaper, showing the lifespans of many of the writers anthologized.

Our policy has been to reprint each text in the form that accords, as far as it is possible to determine, to the intention of its author. There is one exception: we have modernized most spellings and (very sparingly) the punctuation in Volume A on the principle that archaic spellings and typography pose unnecessary problems for beginning students. We have used square brackets to indicate titles supplied by the editors for the convenience of students. Whenever a portion of a text has been omitted, we have indicated that omission with three asterisks. If the omitted portion is important for following the plot or argument, we give a brief summary within the text or in a footnote. After each work, we cite (when known) the date of composition on the left and the date of first publication on the right; in some instances, the latter is followed by the date of a revised edition for which the author was responsible.

With the three additions to our editorial team, we offer an editorial line-up of experienced, active, expert classroom teachers and scholars. All of us have benefited from commentary offered by hundreds of teachers throughout the country. Those teachers who prepared detailed critiques, or who offered special help in preparing texts, are listed under Acknowledgments, on a separate page. The editors would like to express appreciation for their assistance to Kenneth L. Baughman, Genevieve Burger-Weiser, John Bryant, Lawrence I. Berkove, Kirby Brown, Lawrence Buell, Brad Campbell, Russ Castronovo, Granville Ganter, Samuel L. Gladden, Ivy Goodman, Vince Gotera, Ezra Greenspan, Tim Gustafson, Katrina Huffman, Julie Huffman-Klinkowitz, Julie Husband, Daniel Heath Justice, Carolyn Karcher, Virginia Kennedy, Judith Kicinski, Maurice Lee, David Wei Li, Joseph R. McElrath Jr., Anne Myles, James O'Laughlin, Samuel Otter, Kenneth Price, Sally Promey, Julian Rice, Alan Shucard, Martha Nell Smith, Paul Sorrentino, Julia Stern, Jesse Swan, John Swope, Heidi Shira Tannenbaum, Karen Tracey, Jennie Wang, Edward Whitley, Thomas Wolfe, and Christina Zwarg. We also thank the many people at Norton who contributed to the Seventh Edition: Julia Reid-head, who supervised the Seventh Edition; Marian Johnson, Managing Editor, College; Kurt Wildermuth, manuscript and project editor; Mike Fleming, Katharine Ings, Candace Levy, and Pam Lawson, manuscript editors; Catherine Spencer and Ann Abrams, editorial assistants; Eileen Connell, electronic media editor; Diane O'Connor, production manager; Toni Krass, designer; Neil Ryder Hoos, art researcher; Debra Morton Hoyt, art director; Nancy Rodwan, permissions manager; and Margaret Gorenstein, who cleared permissions. We also wish to acknowledge our debt to the late George P. Brockway, former president and chairman at Norton, who invented this anthology, and to M. H. Abrams, Norton's advisor on English texts. All have helped us to create an anthology that, more than ever, is testimony to the continuing richness of American literary traditions.

NINA BAYM

Acknowledgments

Among our many critics, advisors, and friends, the following were of especial help toward the preparation of the Seventh Edition, either with advice or by providing critiques of particular periods of the anthology: Jose Amaya (Iowa State University); Marilyn J. Atlas (Ohio University); Debra Bailey (Brazosport College); Peter J. Bailey (St. Lawrence University); Craig Barrett (Brescia College); Dale M. Bauer (University of Illinois, Urbana-Champaign); Alfred Bendixen (Texas A&M University); Nancy Bentley (University of Pennsylvania); Jill Bergman (University of Montana, Missoula); Bruce Bickley (Florida State University); Sarah Blair (University of Michigan); Tamara Ponzo Brattoli (Joliet Junior College); Jennifer Brezina (College of the Canyons); Patricia Brooke (Fontbonne College); Lawrence Buell (Harvard University); Keen Butterworth (University of South Carolina, Columbia); Russ Castronovo (University of Wisconsin); Charles Chappell (Hendrix College); Jeff Cofer (Belleune Community College); Robert M. Como (Northern Virginia Community College); Marc Conner (Washington and Lee University); G. T. Couser (Hofstra University); Robert W. Croft (Gainesville College); Andrew Delbanco (Columbia University); Matthew DeVold (University of Alabama, Birmingham); Steven Fink (The Ohio State University); Granville Ganter (St. John's University); Richard Gaughran (James Madison University); James Gifford (Mohawk Valley Community College); Ivy Goodman; Lisa Gordis (Barnard College, Columbia University); Ezra Greenspan (Southern Methodist University); Jay Grossman (Northwestern University); Andrew Gutteridge (University College of the Fraser Valley); Sally Harvey (Yuba College); Stephen Hathaway (Wichita State University); Susan Henry (Glendale Community College); Avis Hewitt (Grand Valley State University); Andrew Higgins (Louisiana Tech University); Susanna Hoeness-Krupsaw (University of Southern Indiana); James Hutchinson (The Citadel); Maggie Jaffe (San Diego State University); Ben Jennings (Virginia Highlands Community College); Gwendolyn Jones (Clayton College and State University); Daniel Heath Justice (University of Toronto); Carolyn Karcher (Temple University); Carla Kaplan (Northeastern University); Virginia Kennedy (Cornell University); Christopher Knight (University of Montana); Denise D. Knight (State University of New York, Cortland); Bill Koon (Clemson University); Donald D. Kummings (University of Wisconsin, Parkside); Peter J. Kvidera (John Carroll University); John Lang (Emory and Henry College); Caroline F. Levander (Rice University); Anna Lillios (University of Central Florida); Helen Lojek (Boise State University); Steven Mailloux (University of California, Irvine); Michael Marzelli (Florida Atlantic University); Tim Melley (Miami University); Jon

Miller (University of Akron); Clay Motley (Charleston Southern University); Peter F. Murphy (Murray State University); Lance Newman (California State University, San Marcos); Michael North (University of California, Los Angeles); Patricia Okker (University of Missouri, Columbia); Samuel Otter (University of California, Berkeley); Jennifer Parchesky (Arizona State University); Jeanne Perreault (University of Calgary); Kenneth M. Price (University of Nebraska); Sally Promey (University of Maryland); Ken Rayes (University of New Orleans); Elizabeth Renker (Ohio State University); David Reynolds (The Graduate Center, The City University of New York); Todd R. Richardson (University of Texas, Permian Basin); Debby Rosenthal (John Carroll University); David Rota (University of Missouri, St. Louis); Elizabeth Sachs (Niagara County Community College); Charles Scarborough (Northern Virginia Community College); John Schaffer (Blinn College); Gary Scharnhorst (University of New Mexico); Bill Schlientz (Philander Smith College); Lissa Schneider (University of Miami); Richard Schneider (Wartburg College); Dorothy U. Seyler (Northern Virginia Community College); Mark Silverberg (Cape Breton University); Ernest Smith (University of Central Florida); John J. Smith (United States Military Academy, West Point); Martha Nell Smith (University of Maryland); Julia Stern (Northwestern University); Jenny Sullivan (Northern Virginia Community College); Carole S. Tabor (Louisiana Tech University); Cynthia Van Sickle (McHenry County College); Kathryn Van Spancheren (University of Tampa); Kenneth Warren (University of Chicago); Cindy Weinstein (California Institute of Technology); Norman Weinstein (Boise State University); John Wenke (Salisbury University); Patrick Allen Wright (Lamar University); Dale G. Yerpe (Jamestown Community College).

The Norton Anthology
of American Literature

SEVENTH EDITION

VOLUME D

1914–1945

American Literature
1914–1945

THE TWO WARS AS HISTORICAL MARKERS

The conflict known as World War I broke out in Europe in 1914, with Great Britain and France fighting against Germany. The United States that belatedly entered the war in 1917, on the side of Britain and France, was still in the main a nation of farmers and small towns. Although several waves of immigration from southern and eastern Europe had altered the makeup of the population, and about one American in ten was of African descent, the majority of Americans were of English or German ancestry. This majority was deeply distrustful of international politics, and after the war ended, many Americans attempted to steer the nation back to prewar modes of life. In 1924 Congress enacted the first exclusionary immigration act in the nation's history, hoping thereby to control the ethnic makeup of the American population (and the proportion of Americans born outside the United States did decline markedly from 1910 to 1940). The immediate postwar years also saw the so-called Red scare, when labor union headquarters were raided and immigrant radicals deported by a government fearful of the influence of the newly Communist Soviet Union (formerly tsarist Russia).

For other Americans, however, the war helped accelerate long-sought changes in the forms of political and social life. The long struggle to win American women the vote—given a final push by women's work as nurses and ambulance drivers during the war—ended in 1920 with the passage of the Nineteenth Amendment to the Constitution. The National Association for the Advancement of Colored People (NAACP), founded in 1909, successfully argued during World War I for the commissioning of black officers in the U.S. armed forces; as they would after World War II, African Americans who fought abroad returned to fight for their rights at home. Despite the government's restrictions on leftist political activity, many Americans—among them writers and intellectuals as well as labor activists and urban immigrants— looked to the Soviet Union and the international Communist movement for a model in combating inequality and fostering workers' rights in the United States. Other Americans went abroad, for shorter or longer stretches of time, in order to taste the expatriate life (made cheaper in war-ravaged economies by the solid American dollar) in Europe's battered but still vibrant cities and countryside. Some Americans traveled physical and social distances almost as great within the boundaries of the United States, as African Americans began to migrate in large numbers out of the segregated South and young people everywhere increasingly attended college away from home and moved to the cities. African Americans, emancipated urban women, and the restless young faced off against rural and urban traditionalists over the question of who, exactly, was truly "American."

Thus the 1920s saw numerous conflicts over the shape of the future, which acquired new urgency when the stock market crashed in 1929 and led to an economic depression with a 25 percent unemployment rate. Known as the Great Depression, this period of economic hardship did not fully end until the United States entered World War II, which happened after the Japanese attacked the American fleet at Pearl Harbor on December 7, 1941. Because Japan and Germany were allies, Germany declared war on the United States, thus involving the country in another European conflict. The war unified the country ideologically; revitalized industry, which devoted itself to goods needed for the war effort; and put people to work. Indeed, with so many men away at war, women went into the work force in unprecedented numbers. Germany surrendered in the spring of 1945. The war ended in August 1945 following the detonation of two atomic bombs over the Japanese cities of Hiroshima and Nagasaki. Europe was in ruins and—regardless of the wishes of its citizens—the United States had become both an industrial society and a major global power.

The two wars, then, bracket a period during which, no matter how internally fractured it was, the United States became a modern nation. In fact, the internal fractures can be understood as diverse responses to the irreversible advent of modernity. American literature in these decades registers all sides of the era's struggles and debates, while sharing a commitment to explore the many meanings of modernity and express them in forms appropriate to a modern vision. Some writers rejoiced while others lamented; some anticipated future utopias and others believed that civilization had collapsed; but the period's most influential voices believed that old forms would not work for new times, and were inspired by the possibility of creating something entirely new.

The totality of the literary output produced during this period is called American literary modernism. Among literary conflicts, perhaps three issues stand out, all of them related to the accelerating transformations and conflicts of modernity. One conflict centered on the uses of literary tradition. To some, a work registering awareness and appreciation of literary history—through allusion to other literary works, or by using traditional poetic forms and poetic language—seemed imative and old-fashioned. To others, a work failing to register such awareness and appreciation was bad or incompetent writing. For still others, literary history was best appreciated oppositionally: modernist works often allude to previous literature ironically, or deliberately fracture traditional literary formulas. A related conflict involved the place of popular culture in serious literature. Throughout the era, popular culture gained momentum and influence. Some writers regarded it as crucial for the future of literature that popular forms be embraced; to others, good literature by definition had to reject the cynical commercialism of popular culture.

Another issue was the question of how engaged in political and social struggle a work of literature ought to be—of how far literature should exert itself for (or against) social transformation. Should art be a domain unto itself, exploring universal questions and enunciating transcendent truths, or should art participate in the politics of the times? For some, a work that was political in aim counted as propaganda, not art; others thought that apolitical literature was evasive and simplistic; for still others, the call to keep art out of politics was covertly political, in conservative directions, even if it did not acknowledge itself as such.

CHANGING TIMES

The transformations of the first half of the twentieth century were driven both by ideas and by changes in the economic and technological underpinnings of daily life. Much social energy in the 1920s went into enlarging the boundaries for acceptable self-expression. Adherents to small-town, white, Protestant values such as the work ethic, social conformity, duty, and respectability, clashed ideologically not only with internationally minded radicals but also with newly affluent young people who argued for more diverse, permissive, and tolerant styles of life. To some extent this debate recapitulated the long-time American conflict between the individual and society, a conflict going back to the seventeenth-century Puritans and epitomized in Ralph Waldo Emerson's call, in the 1840s: "whosoever would be a man, must be a non-conformist."

The 1920s saw significant changes in sexual mores, as was to be expected when young people were no longer under the watchful eyes of their small-town elders. These changes found their most influential theorist in the Austrian psychiatrist Sigmund Freud (1858–1939), inventor of the practice of psychoanalysis. According to Freud, many modern neuroses could be traced to repression and inhibition. Freud developed the idea of the self as grounded in an "unconscious," where forbidden desires, traumas, unacceptable emotions, and the like—most of these sexual in nature—were stored. Freud hoped that trained analysts could help people become aware of their repressed feelings, so that they would be able to control them productively. The American version of psychoanalysis—more utopian than Freud's cautious claim that individuals could learn to cope with their own personalities more effectively—held that emotional wholeness could be attained at once if people recognized and overcame their inhibitions. Americanized Freudian ideas provided the psychological underpinning for much literature of the interwar era, whether the focus was the individual trapped in a repressive culture or the repressive culture itself.

The middle-class double sexual standard had, in fact, always granted considerable sexual freedom to men; now, however, women—enfranchised and liberated by automobiles and job possibilities away from home—began to demand similar freedom for themselves. Women's demands went well beyond the erotic, however, encompassing education, professional work, mobility, and whatever else seemed like social goods hitherto reserved for men. Female dress changed; long, heavy, restricting garments gave way to short, lightweight, easily worn store-bought clothing. The combination of expanding urban life with new psychologies oriented to self-expression also brought into being new social possibilities for women and men whose sexual desires did not conform to traditional patterns. Freud was only one of a number of thinkers in the period who urged a measure of toleration for sexual minorities, especially homosexuals—a term that entered specialized English usage in the 1890s and came into wider circulation in the years following World War I. Although the legal risks and social stigma born by homosexuals remained very much in force, gay enclaves became more visible in American life and gay lives became more imaginable as a theme in American literature.

African Americans, like women, became mobile in these years as never before. Around 1915, as a direct result of the industrial needs of World War I, opportunities opened for African Americans in the factories of the North, and the so-called Great Migration out of the South began. Not only did migration give the lie to southern white claims that African Americans were content with southern segregationist practices, it damaged the South's economy by draining off an important segment of its working people. Even though African Americans faced racism, segregation, and racial violence in the North, a black American presence soon became powerfully visible in American cultural life. Harlem, a section of New York City, attained an almost wholly black population of over 150,000 by the mid-1920s; from this "city within a city," African Americans wrote, performed, composed, and painted. Here as well they founded two major journals of opinion and culture, *The Crisis* (in 1910) and *Opportunity* (in 1923). This work influenced writers, painters, and musicians of other ethnicities, and became known collectively as the Harlem Renaissance.

The famous black intellectual W. E. B. Du Bois had argued in *The Souls of Black Folk* (1903) that African Americans had a kind of double consciousness—of themselves as Americans and as blacks. This doubleness contributed to debates within African American cultural life. The Harlem Renaissance sparked arguments between those who wanted to claim membership in the culture at large and those who wanted to stake out a separate artistic domain; between those who wanted to celebrate rural African American lifeways and those committed to urban intellectuality; between those who wanted to join the American mainstream and those who, disgusted by American race prejudice, aligned themselves with worldwide revolutionary movements; between those who celebrated a "primitive" African heritage and those who rejected the idea as a degrading stereotype. African American women, as Nella Larsen's novel *Quicksand* testifies, could experience these divisions with special force. Women were very much called upon in efforts to "uplift," advance, and educate the black community, but these communal obligations could be felt as constraints upon individual freedom and exploration; meanwhile the white social world, given to exoticizing or sexualizing black women, offered few alternatives.

Class inequality, as well as American racial divisions, continued to generate intellectual and artistic debate in the interwar years. The nineteenth-century United States had been host to many radical movements—labor activism, utopianism, socialism, anarchism—inspired by diverse sources. In the twentieth century, especially following the rise of the Soviet Union, the American left increasingly drew its intellectual and political program from the Marxist tradition. The German philosopher Karl Marx (1818–1883) located the roots of human behavior in economics. He claimed that industrializing societies were structurally divided into two antagonistic classes based on different relations to the means of production—capital versus labor. The Industrial Revolution arose from the accumulation of surplus capital by industrialists paying the least possible amount to workers; the next stage in world history would be when workers took control of the means of production for themselves. Because, to Marx, the ideas and ideals of any particular society could represent the interests of only its dominant class, he derided individualism as a middle-class or "bourgeois" value that could only discourage worker solidarity.

Marx's ideas formed the basis for communist political parties across Europe. In 1917, a Communist revolution in Russia led by Vladimir Ilyich Lenin (1870–1914) overthrew the tsarist regime, instituted the "dictatorship of the proletariat" that Marx had called for, and engineered the development of Communism as a unified international movement. Americans who thought of themselves as Marxists in the 1920s and 1930s were usually connected with the Communist party and subjected to government surveillance and occasional violence, as were socialists, anarchists, union organizers, and others who opposed American free enterprise and marketplace competition. Although politics directed from outside the national boundaries was, almost by definition, "un-American," many adherents of these movements hoped to make the United States conform to its stated ideals, guaranteeing liberty and justice for all.

Where writers were concerned, a defining conflict between American ideals and American realities in the 1920s was the Sacco-Vanzetti case. Nicola Sacco and Bartolomeo Vanzetti were Italian immigrants, not Communists but avowed anarchists; on April 15, 1920 they were arrested near Boston after a murder during a robbery. They were accused of that crime, then tried and condemned to death in 1921; but it was widely believed that they had not received a fair trial and that their political beliefs had been held against them. After a number of appeals, they were executed in 1927, maintaining their innocence to the end. John Dos Passos and Katherine Anne Porter were among the many writers and intellectuals who demonstrated in their defense; several were arrested and jailed. It is estimated that well over a hundred poems (including works by William Carlos Williams, Edna St. Vincent Millay, and Carl Sandburg) along with six plays and eight novels of the time treated the incident from a sympathetic perspective.

Like the Sacco-Vanzetti case in the 1920s, the Scottsboro case in the 1930s brought many American writers and intellectuals, black and white, together in a cause—here, the struggle against racial bias in the justice system. In 1931 nine black youths were indicted in Scottsboro, Alabama, for the alleged rape of two white women in a railroad freight car. They were all found guilty, and some were sentenced to death. The U.S. Supreme Court reversed convictions twice; in a second trial one of the alleged victims retracted her testimony; in 1937 charges against five were dropped. But four went to jail, in many people's view unfairly. The Communists were especially active in the Scottsboro defense; but people across the political spectrum saw the case as crucial to the question of whether black people could receive fair trials in the American South. The unfair trial of an African American man became a literary motif in much writing of the period and beyond, including Richard Wright's *Native Son*, William Faulkner's *Intruder in the Dust*, and Harper Lee's *To Kill a Mockingbird*.

SCIENCE AND TECHNOLOGY

Technology played a vital, although often invisible, role in all these events, because it linked places and spaces, contributing to the shaping of culture as a national phenomenon rather than a series of local manifestations. Indeed, without new modes of production, transportation, and communication, modern America in all its complexity could not have existed. Electricity for lights and appliances, along with the telephone—nineteenth-century inventions—expanded into American homes during these years, improving life for many but widening the gap between those plugged into the new networks and those outside them. The phonograph record and the record player (early devices for recording and playing music), the motion picture (which acquired sound in 1929), and the radio made new connections possible and brought mass popular culture into being. Although the nineteenth-century dream of forging a scattered population into a single nation could now be realized more instantaneously and directly than was ever possible with print media, many intellectuals suspected that mass culture would create a robotic, passive population vulnerable to demagoguery.

The most powerful technological innovation, however, encouraged activity not passivity: this was the automobile, which had been developed by the end of the nineteenth century, but remained a luxury item until Henry Ford's assembly-line techniques made cars affordable. Automobiles put Americans on the road, dramatically reshaped the structure of American industry and occupations, and altered the national topography as well. Along with work in automobile factories themselves, millions of other jobs—in steel mills, parts factories, highway construction and maintenance, gas stations, machine shops, roadside restaurants, motels—depended on the industry. The road itself became—and has remained—a key powerful symbol of the United States and of modernity as well. Cities grew, suburbs came into being, small towns died, new towns arose, according to the placement of highways. The United States had become a nation of migrants as much as or more than it was a nation of immigrants.

It is impossible fully to dissociate technology from science, and certainly one of the most important developments in the interwar period was the growth of modern "big" science. At the turn of the century and soon afterward scientists discovered that the atom was not the smallest possible unit of matter, that matter was not indestructible, that both time and space were relative to an observer's position, that some phenomena were so small that attempts at measurement would alter them, that some outcomes could be predicted only in terms of statistical probability, that the universe might be infinite in size and yet infinitely expanding; in short, much of the common-sense basis of nineteenth-century science had to be put aside in favor of far more powerful but also far less commonsensical theories. Among many results, scientists and literary intellectuals became less and less able to communicate with each other and less respectful of each others' worldviews. Scientists saw literary people as careless thinkers; literary people, especially the more conservative among them, deplored the loss of authority for traditional, humanistic explanations of the real, concrete, experienced world and the felt human life. Poets like Ezra Pound, T. S. Eliot, Wallace Stevens, and William Carlos Williams reacted spiritedly to the increasingly prevalent assumption that nonscientific thinking, because it was imprecise and value laden, could not explain anything. They questioned the capacity of science to provide accounts of the things that matter, like subjective experience and moral issues. Art, to them, became the repository of a way of experiencing the world other than that offered by science. Their approach put a heavy burden of "meaning" on art and was a sign, if not a contributing cause, of the increased specialization of intellectual activity and the division of educated people into what the British novelist and physicist C. P. Snow was later to call the "two cultures"—science versus letters.

THE 1930s

The Great Depression was a worldwide phenomenon, and social unrest led to the rise of fascist dictatorships in Europe, among which were those of Generalissimo Francisco Franco in Spain, Benito Mussolini in Italy, and Adolf Hitler in Germany. Hitler's program, which was to make Germany rich and strong by conquering the rest of Europe, led inexorably to World War II.

In the United States, the Depression made politics and economics the salient issues and overrode questions of individual freedom with questions of mass collapse. Free-enterprise capitalism had always justified itself by arguing that although the system made a small number of individuals immensely wealthy it also guaranteed better lives for all. This assurance now rang hollow. The suicides of millionaire bankers and stockbrokers made the headlines, but more compelling was the enormous toll among ordinary people who lost homes, jobs, farms, and life savings in the stock market crash. Conservatives advised waiting until things got better; radicals espoused immediate social revolution. In this atmosphere, the election of Franklin Delano Roosevelt to the presidency in 1932 was a victory for American pragmatism; his series of liberal reforms—social security, acts creating jobs in the public sector, welfare, and unemployment insurance—cushioned the worst effects of the Depression and avoided the civil war that many had thought inevitable.

The terrible situation in the United States produced a significant increase in Communist party membership and prestige in the 1930s. Numerous intellectuals allied themselves with its causes, even if they did not become party members. An old radical journal, *The Masses*, later *The New Masses*, became the official literary voice of the party, and various other radical groups founded journals to represent their viewpoints. Visitors to the Soviet Union returned with glowing reports about a true workers' democracy and prosperity for all. The appeal of Communism was significantly enhanced by its claim to be an opponent of fascism. Communists fought against Franco in the Spanish Civil War of 1936 and 1937. Hitler's nightmare policies of genocide and racial superiority and his plans for a general European war to secure more room for the superior German "folk" to live became increasingly evident as European refugees began to flee to the United States in the 1930s, and many believed that the USSR would be the only country able to withstand the German war machine. But Soviet Communism showed another side to Americans when American Communists were ordered to break up the meetings of other radical groups; when Josef Stalin, the Soviet dictator, instituted a series of brutal purges in the Soviet Union beginning in 1936; and when in

1939 he signed a pact promising not to go to war against Germany. The disillusionment and betrayal felt by many radicals over these acts led to many 1930s left-wing activists' becoming staunch anti-Communists after World War II.

AMERICAN VERSIONS OF MODERNISM

Used in the broadest sense, "modernism" is a catchall term for any kind of literary production in the interwar period that deals with the modern world. More narrowly, it refers to work that represents the transformation of traditional society under the pressures of modernity, and that breaks down traditional literary forms in doing so. Much modernist literature of this sort, which critics increasingly now set apart as "high modernism," is in a sense antimodern: it interprets modernity as an experience of loss. As its title underlines, T. S. Eliot's *The Waste Land*—the great poem of high modernism—represents the modern world as a scene of ruin.

Modernism began as a European response to the effects of World War I, which were far more devastating on the Continent than they were in the United States. It involved other art forms—sculpture, painting, dance—as well as literature. The poetry of William Butler Yeats; James Joyce's *Ulysses* (1922); Marcel Proust's *Remembrance of Things Past* (1913–27); Thomas Mann's novels and short stories, including *The Magic Mountain* (1927)—these were only a few of the literary products of this movement in England and on the Continent. In painting, artists like Pablo Picasso, Juan Gris, and Georges Braque invented cubism; in the 1920s the surrealistic movement known as dadaism emerged. The American public was introduced to modern art at the famous New York Armory Show of 1913, which featured cubist paintings and caused an uproar. Marcel Duchamp's *Nude Descending a Staircase*, which, to the untrained eye, looked like no more than a mass of crudely drawn rectangles, was especially provocative. Composers like Igor Stravinsky similarly produced music in a "modern" mode, featuring dissonance and discontinuity rather than neat formal structure and appealing tonal harmonies. His composition *The Rite of Spring* provoked a riot in the Paris concert hall where it was premiered.

At the heart of the high modernist aesthetic lay the conviction that the previously sustaining structures of human life, whether social, political, religious, or artistic, had been destroyed or shown up as falsehoods or, at best, arbitrary and fragile human constructions. Order, sequence, and unity in works of art might well express human desires for coherence rather than reliable intuitions of reality. Generalization, abstraction, and high-flown writing might conceal rather than convey the real. The form of a story, with its beginnings, complications, and resolutions, might be an artifice imposed on the flux and fragmentation of experience. To the extent that art incorporated such a false order, it had to be renovated.

Thus a key formal characteristic typical of high modernist works, whether in painting, sculpture, or musical composition, is its construction out of fragments—fragments of myth or history, fragments of experience or perception, fragments of previous artistic works. Compared with earlier writing, modernist literature is notable for what it omits: the explanations, interpretations, connections, summaries, and distancing that provide continuity, perspective, and security in traditional literature. A typical modernist work may seem to begin arbitrarily, to advance without explanation, and to end without resolution, consisting of vivid segments juxtaposed without cushioning or integrating transitions. There will be shifts in perspective, voice, and tone. Its rhetoric will be understated, ironic. It will suggest rather than assert, making use of symbols and images instead of statements. Its elements will be drawn from diverse areas of experience. The effect will be surprising, shocking, and unsettling; the experience of reading will be challenging and difficult. Faced with the task of intuiting connections left unstated, the reader of a modernist work is often said to participate in the actual work of making the poem or story.

Some high modernist works, however, order their discontinuous elements into conspicuous larger patterns, patterns often drawn from world literature, mythologies, and religions. As its title advertises, Joyce's *Ulysses* maps the lives of its modern characters onto Homer's *Odyssey*; Eliot's *The Waste Land* layers the Christian narrative of death and resurrection over a broad range of quest myths. The question for readers lies in the meaning of these borrowed structures and mythic parallels: do they reveal profound similarities or ironic contrasts between the modern world and earlier times? For some writers and readers, the adaptability of ancient stories to modern circumstances testified to their deep truth, underlying the surface buzz and confusion of modernity; for others, such parallels indicated Christianity to *be* only a myth, a merely human construction for creating order out of, and finding purpose in, history's flux.

If meaning is a human construction, then meaning lies in the process of generating meaning; if meaning lies obscured deep underneath the ruins of modern life, then it must be effortfully sought out. Modernist literature therefore tends to foreground the search for meaning over didactic statement, and the subject matter of modernist writing often became, by extension, the poem or literary work itself. While there have long been paintings about painting and poems about poetry, high modernist writing was especially self-reflexive, concerned with its own nature as art and with its questioning of previous traditions of literature. Ironically—because this subject matter was motivated by deep concern about the interrelation of literature and life—this subject often had the effect of limiting the audience for a modernist work; high modernism demanded of its ideal readers an encyclopedic knowledge of the traditions it fragmented or ironized. Nevertheless, over time, the principles of modernism became increasingly influential.

Though modernist techniques were initiated by poets, they transformed fiction in this period as well. Prose writers strove for directness, compression, and vividness. They were sparing of words. The average novel became quite a bit shorter than it had been in the nineteenth century, when a novel was expected to fill two or even three volumes. The modernist aesthetic gave a new significance to the short story, which had previously been thought of as a relatively slight artistic form. (Poems, too, became shorter, as narrative poems lost ground to lyrics and the repetitive patterns of rhyme and meter that had helped sustain long poems in previous centuries lost ground to free verse.) Victorian or realistic fiction achieved its effects by accumulation and saturation; modern fiction preferred suggestion. Victorian fiction often featured an authoritative narrator; modern fiction tended to be written in the first person or to limit the reader to one character's point of view on the action. This limitation accorded with the modernist sense that "truth" does not exist objectively but is the product of the mind's interaction with reality. The selected point of view is often that of a naïve or marginal person—a child or an outsider—to convey better the reality of confusion rather than the myth of certainty.

The contents of modernist works may be as varied as the interests and observations of their authors; indeed, with a stable external world in question, subjectivity was ever more valued and accepted in literature. Modernists in general, however, emphasized the concrete sensory image or detail over abstract statement. Allusions to literary, historical, philosophical, or religious details of the past often keep company, in modernist works, with vignettes of contemporary life, chunks of popular culture, dream imagery, and symbolism drawn from the author's private repertory of life experiences. A work built from these various levels and kinds of material may move across time and space, shift from the public to the personal, and open literature as a field for every sort of concern. The inclusion of all sorts of material previously deemed "unliterary" in works of high seriousness involved the use of language that might previously have been thought improper, including representations of the speech of the uneducated and the inarticulate, the colloquial, slangy, and the popular. Traditional realistic fiction had incorporated colloquial and dialect speech, often to comic effect, in its representation of the broad tapestry of social life; but such speakers were usually framed by a narrator's educated literary voice, conveying truth and culture. In modernist writing like William Faulkner's As I Lay Dying, these voices assume the full burden of the narrative's authority; this is what Ernest Hemingway had in mind when he asserted that the American literary tradition began with Huckleberry Finn.

"Serious" literature between the two world wars thus found itself in a curious relationship with the culture at large. If it was attacking the old-style idea of traditional literature, it felt itself attacked in turn by the ever-growing industry of popular literature. The reading audience in America was vast, but it preferred a kind of book quite different from that turned out by literary high modernists: tales of romance or adventure, historical novels, crime fiction, and westerns became popular modes that enjoyed a success the serious writer could only dream of. The problem was that often he or she did dream of it; unrealistically, perhaps, the Ezra Pounds of the era imagined themselves with an audience of millions. When, on occasion, this dream came true—as it did for F. Scott Fitzgerald and Ernest Hemingway—writers often accused themselves of having sold out.

Nevertheless, serious writers in these years were, in fact, being published and read as writers had not been in earlier times. The number of so-called little magazines—that is, magazines of very small circulations devoted to the publication of works for a small audience (sometimes the works of a specific group of authors)—was in the hundreds. Poetry: A Magazine of Verse began in 1912. The Little Review followed in 1914. Then came the Seven Arts in 1916, the Dial in 1917, the Frontier in 1920, Reviewer and Broom in 1921, Fugitive in 1922, This Quarter in 1925, Transition and Hound and Horn in 1927, and many more. The culture that did not listen to serious writers or make them rich still gave them plenty of opportunity to be read and allowed them (in such neighborhoods as Greenwich Village in New York City) a freedom in lifestyle that was quite new in American history. In addition, such major publishers as New Directions, Random House, Scribner, and Harper were actively looking for serious fiction and poetry to feature alongside bestsellers like *Gone with the Wind* and *Anthony Adverse*.

Some writers in the period were able to use these opportunities to cross over the hierarchies separating high modernism from middlebrow and popular culture—and they crossed them in both directions. Kay Boyle's early short stories and poems appeared in little magazines like *Broom* and *Transition* in the 1920s; in the 1930s, however, as she began writing of the rise of fascism in Europe, she found a receptive larger audience in the *New Yorker* and *Harper's Magazine*. Raymond Chandler began his career in the early 1930s writing crime fiction for cheap popular magazines, moved into authoring film scripts and full-length novels issued by mainstream publishers, and by the 1950s had earned enough respectability to be interviewed about his artistic principles in *Harper's*. Where writers like William Faulkner and F. Scott Fitzgerald experienced Hollywood as a graveyard of serious literary ambition, Chandler found in the film industry not only financial rewards but also a powerful new medium for his distinctive popular modernism—a modernism as elliptical and innovative, in its own terms, as Hemingway's.

MODERNISM ABROAD AND ON NATIVE GROUNDS

The profession of authorship in the United States has always defined itself in part as a patriotic enterprise, whose aims were to help develop a cultural life for the nation and embody national values. High modernism, however, was a self-consciously international movement, and the leading American exponents of high modernism tended to be permanent expatriates like Gertrude Stein, Ezra Pound, H. D., and T. S. Eliot. These writers left the United States because they found the country lacking in a tradition of high culture and indifferent, if not downright hostile, to artistic achievement. They also believed that a national culture could never be more than parochial. In London in the first two decades of the twentieth century and in Paris during the 1920s, they found a vibrant community of dedicated artists and a society that respected them and allowed them a great deal of personal freedom. Yet they seldom thought of themselves as deserting their nation and only Eliot gave up American citizenship (sometimes, too, the traffic went in the other direction, as when the British-born poet Mina Loy became an American citizen). They thought of themselves as bringing the United States into the larger context of European culture. The ranks of these permanent expatriates were swelled by American writers who lived abroad for some part of the period: Ernest Hemingway, Sherwood Anderson, F. Scott Fitzgerald, Claude McKay, Katherine Anne Porter, Nella Larsen, Robert Frost, Kay Boyle, and Eugene O'Neill all did so, as did many others including Sinclair Lewis and Djuna Barnes.

Those writers who came back, however, and those who never left took very seriously the task of integrating modernist ideas and methods with American subject matter. Not every experimental modernist writer disconnected literary ambitions from national belonging: Hart Crane and Marianne Moore and

William Carlos Williams, for example, all wanted to write "American" works as such. Some writers—as the title of John Dos Passos's *U.S.A.* clearly shows—attempted to speak for the nation as a whole. Crane's long poem *The Bridge* and Williams's *Paterson* both take an American city as symbol and expand it to a vision for all America, following the model established by Walt Whitman. F. Scott Fitzgerald's *The Great Gatsby* is similarly ambitious, and many writers addressed the whole nation in individual works—for example, E. E. Cummings's "next to of course god america i" and Claude McKay's "America." And a profoundly modern writer like William Faulkner cannot be extricated from his commitment to writing about his native South.

Like Faulkner, many writers of the period chose to identify themselves with the American scene and to root their work in a specific region, continuing a tradition of regionalist American writing that burgeoned in the years following the American Civil War. Their perspective on the regions was sometimes celebratory and sometimes critical. Carl Sandburg, Edgar Lee Masters, Sherwood Anderson, and Willa Cather worked with the Midwest; Cather grounded her later work in the Southwest; Black Elk's Lakota autobiography recalled the high plains of South Dakota and Wyoming; John Steinbeck and Carlos Bulosan wrote about California; Edwin Arlington Robinson and Robert Frost identified their work with New England. An especially strong center of regional literary activity emerged in the South, which had a weak literary tradition up to the Civil War. Thomas Wolfe's was an Appalachian South of hardy mountain people; Katherine Anne Porter wrote about her native Texas as a heterogeneous combination of frontier, plantation, and Latin cultures. Zora Neale Hurston drew on her childhood memories of the all-black town of Eatonville, Florida, for much of her best-known fiction, including her novel *Their Eyes Were Watching God*. William Faulkner depicted a South at once specific to his native state of Mississippi and expanded into a mythic region anguished by racial and historical conflict.

As the pairing of Hurston and Faulkner suggests, the history of race in the United States was central to the specifically national subject matter to which many American modernists remained committed. Although race as a subject potentially implicated all American writers, it was African Americans whose contributions most signally differentiated American modernism from that of Europe. The numerous writers associated with the Harlem Renaissance made it impossible ever to think of a national literature without the work of black Americans. Countee Cullen, Langston Hughes, and Zora Neale Hurston attained particular prominence at the time; but others, including Claude McKay and Nella Larsen, were also well known. All were influenced by the values of modernism: both Hughes, for example, with his incorporation of blues rhythms into poetry, and Hurston, with her poetic depictions of folk culture, applied modernist techniques to represent twentieth-century African American lives. From time to time, writers associated with the Renaissance expressed protest and anger—Hughes, in particular, wrote a number of powerful antilynching and anticapitalist poems; but in general the movement was deliberately upbeat, taking the line that racial justice was about to become reality in the United States or, like Hurston, focusing more on the vitality of black culture than on the burdens of racism. At least part of this approach was strategic—the bulk of the readership for Harlem authors was white. The note of pure anger was not expressed until Richard Wright, who had come to literary maturity in Chicago, published *Native Son* in 1940. Contributions to the Harlem Renaissance came from artists in many media; an influence equal to or greater than that of the writers came from musicians. Jazz and blues, African American in origin, are felt by many to be the most authentically American art forms the nation has ever produced. African American singers and musicians in this period achieved worldwide reputations and were often much more highly regarded abroad than in the United States.

American literary women had been active on the national scene from Anne Bradstreet forward. Their increasing prominence in the nineteenth century generated a backlash from some male modernists, who asserted their own artistic seriousness by identifying women writers with the didactic, popular writing against which they rebelled. But women refused to stay on the sidelines and associated themselves with all the important literary trends of the era: H. D. and Amy Lowell with imagism, Marianne Moore and Mina Loy with high modernism; Willa Cather with mythic regionalism, Zora Neale Hurston and Nella Larsen with the Harlem Renaissance, Katherine Anne Porter with psychological fiction; Edna St. Vincent Millay and Kay Boyle with social and sexual liberation. Many of these writers concentrated on depictions of women characters or women's thoughts and experiences. Yet few labeled themselves feminists. The passage of the suffrage amendment in 1920 had taken some of the energy out of feminism that would not return until the 1960s. Some women writers found social causes like labor and racism more important than women's rights; others focused their energies on struggles less amenable to public, legal remedies, as when Mina Loy sought to link motherhood to an energetic vision of female sexuality. Nevertheless, these literary women were clearly pushing back the boundaries of the permissible, demanding new cultural freedom for women. Equally important, they were operating as public figures and taking positions on public causes.

DRAMA

Drama in America was slow to develop as a self-conscious literary form. It was not until 1920 (the year of Eugene O'Neill's *Beyond the Horizon*) that the United States produced a world-class playwright. This is not to say that *theater*—productions and performances—was new to American life. After the American Revolution theaters—at first with itinerant English actors and companies, then with American—opened throughout the East; among early centers were Boston and Philadelphia as well as New York City. As the country expanded westward, so did its theater, together with other kinds of performance: burlesques, showboats on the Mississippi, minstrel shows, pantomimes. As the nineteenth century went on, the activity became centered more and more in New York—indeed, within a few blocks, known as "Broadway." Managers originated plays there and then sent them out to tour through the rest of the country, as Eugene O'Neill's father did with his *Count of Monte Cristo*.

Changes in American theater are often in reaction against Broadway, a pattern observable as early as 1915 with the formation of the Washington Square Players and the Provincetown Players (organized by Susan Glaspell and others), both located in New York's Greenwich Village and both dedicated to the production of plays that more conservative managers refused. The Province-town Players would shortly be producing the first works of Glaspell and Eugene O'Neill. These fledgling companies, and others like them, often knew better what they opposed than what they wanted. European influence was strong. By 1915, Henrik Ibsen in Europe and George Bernard Shaw in England had shown that the theater could be an arena for serious ideas; while the psychological dramas of August Strindberg, the symbolic work of Maurice Maeterlinck, and the sophisticated criticism of Arthur Schnitzler provided other models. The American tours of European companies, in particular the Moscow Art Theatre in 1923, further exposed Americans to the theatrical avant-garde. American playwrights in the 1920s and 1930s were united not so much by a common cause of ideas, European or American, as by the new assumption that drama should be a branch of contemporary literature.

Just as his contemporaries in poetry and fiction were changing and questioning their forms, so Eugene O'Neill sought to refine his. He experimented less in language than in dramatic structure and in new production methods available through technology (e.g., lighting) or borrowed from the stylized realism of German expressionism. Almost as famous at the time was Maxwell Anderson, whose best plays—the tragic *Winterset* (1935) and the romantic comedy *High Tor* (1937)—embody a stylized blank verse, a language attempted by few modern dramatists. Playwrights such as Sidney Howard, Lillian Hellman, and Robert Sherwood wrote serious realistic plays. George Kaufman and his many collaborators, especially Moss Hart, invented a distinctively American form, the wisecracking domestic and social comedy, while S. N. Behrman and Philip Barry wrote higher comedies of ideas. The musical comedy was another distinctively American invention: beginning as an amalgam of jokes, songs, and dances, it progressed steadily toward an integration of its various elements, reaching new heights with the work of George and Ira Gershwin in the 1920s and 1930s and of Oscar Hammerstein in collaboration with Jerome Kern or Richard Rodgers from the 1920s on into the 1950s.

Social commentary and satire had been a thread in the bright weave of American drama since the early 1920s, beginning, perhaps, with Elmer Rice's fiercely expressionistic play about a rebellious nonentity, *The Adding Machine* (1923). During the Depression social criticism became a much more important dramatic theme, with political plays performed by many radical groups. Perhaps the most significant was Clifford Odets's *Waiting for Lefty* (1935), which dramatized a taxidrivers' strike meeting and turned the stage into a platform for argument. Many poets and fiction writers of the interwar period wrote plays—among them Ernest Hemingway, E. E. Cummings, William Carlos Williams, William Faulkner, Edna St. Vincent Millay, Langston Hughes, T. S. Eliot, John Steinbeck, and Robert Lowell. It was in this period that drama moved decisively into the American literary mainstream.

TEXTS	CONTEXTS
1910 Edward Arlington Robinson, **"Miniver Cheevy"**	
1914 Robert Frost, **"Home Burial"** • Carl Sandburg, **"Chicago"**	1914–18 World War I
1915 Edgar Lee Masters, *Spoon River Anthology* • Ezra Pound begins *Cantos*	1915 Great Migration of African Americans from the rural South to northern industrial cities
1916 Susan Glaspell, *Trifles*	
	1917 United States declares war on Germany • revolution in Russia brings Communist party to power
1918 Willa Cather, *My Ántonia*	1918 Daylight Savings Time instituted to allow more daylight for war production
1919 Sherwood Anderson, *Winesburg, Ohio* • Amy Lowell, **"Madonna of the Evening Flowers"**	1919 Senate limits U.S. participation in League of Nations; does not ratify Versailles Treaty to end World War I
1920 Pound, **"Hugh Selwyn Mauberley"** • Edwin Arlington Robinson, **"Mr. Flood's Party"**	1920 18th Amendment prohibits the manufacture, sale, and transportation of alcoholic beverages • 19th Amendment gives women the vote
	1920–27 Sacco-Vanzetti trial
1921 T. S. Eliot, *The Waste Land* • Claude McKay, **"Africa, America"** • Marianne Moore, **"Poetry"** • Langston Hughes, **"The Negro Speaks of Rivers"**	
1922 Mina Loy, **"Brancusi's Golden Bird"**	1922 Fascism rises in Europe; Mussolini becomes dictator of Italy
1923 Wallace Stevens, **"Sunday Morning"**	
1924 H. D. (Hilda Doolittle), **"Helen"**	1924 Exclusionary immigration act bars Asians
1925 Countee Cullen, **"Heritage"** • Gertrude Stein, *The Making of Americans* • Alain Locke publishes *The New Negro*, leading anthology of the Harlem Renaissance	
1926 Hart Crane, *The Bridge*	
1927 Zora Neale Hurston, **"The Eatonville Anthology"**	1927 *The Jazz Singer*, first full-length "talkie," is released
1928 Nella Larsen, *Quicksand*	
	1929 Stock market crashes; Great Depression begins
1930 Katherine Anne Porter, **"Flowering Judas"**	1930 Sinclair Lewis is first American to win Nobel Prize for literature

Boldface titles indicate works in the anthology.

TEXTS	CONTEXTS
1931 E. E. Cummings, **"i sing of Olaf glad and big"** • F. Scott Fitzgerald, **"Babylon Revisited"**	**1931** Scottsboro trial
1932 Black Elk and John G. Neihardt, *Black Elk Speaks* • Sterling A. Brown, **"He Was a Man"**	**1932** Franklin Delano Roosevelt's "New Deal" introduces social security, welfare, and unemployment insurance
	1933 Adolf Hitler's Nationalist Socialist (Nazi) party comes to power in Germany • 18th Amendment repealed
1934 William Carlos Williams, **"This Is Just to Say"**	**1934** Wheeler-Howard (Indian Reorganization) Act passed, ending Dawes era
1935 Kay Boyle, **"The White Horses of Vienna"**	
1936 Ernest Hemingway, **"The Snows of Kilimanjaro"**	**1936** Hitler begins armed occupation of Europe
	1936–39 Spanish Civil War: U.S. volunteers among those fighting against General Franco, who becomes dictator of Spain
1937 Thomas Wolfe, **"The Lost Boy"**	**1937** Stalin's purges
1938 John Dos Passos, *U.S.A.* • William Faulkner, **"Barn Burning"** • Raymond Chandler, **"Red Wind"**	
1939 Richard Wright, **"The Man Who Was Almost a Man"**	**1939–45** World War II • the Holocaust
1940 Eugene O'Neill, *Long Day's Journey into Night*	
	1941 Japan bombs Pearl Harbor, Hawaii • United States enters war against Japan and its allies, Germany and Italy
	1942 President Roosevelt orders internment of Japanese Americans in camps
	1944 D Day; Allied invasion of Normandy
	1945 German forces surrender in spring; Japan surrenders in August following explosion of two nuclear bombs over Japanese cities

BLACK ELK
1863–1950

JOHN G. NEIHARDT
1881–1973

Nicholas Black Elk, an Oglala Lakota, was born on the Little Powder River in Wyoming. Although every traditionally raised Lakota male engaged in a vision quest—*hanble ceyapi*, literally "crying for a vision"—a search for spiritual guidance in his life, Black Elk was granted a particularly powerful vision by the Thunder beings (*Wakinyan*), the powers of the west, at the early age of nine. He said nothing of this until he was seventeen, when he began to fear that continued silence might lead to his being struck by lightning—a particular danger for the Thunder Dreamer. It was most usual for the Thunder Dreamer to perform the *heyoka* ceremony and become a "sacred clown," one who, for a time, did things backward and foolishly. But Black Elk was advised to have the horse dance enacted instead. Once this had been done, Black Elk began to practice as a shamanic healer.

Some four years earlier, in 1876, although he was too young to fight, Black Elk had witnessed the defeat of General George A. Custer and his Seventh Cavalry on the Little Bighorn River by the Lakota and their Cheyenne allies, an event that did not, however, slow the encroachment of the whites onto Indian lands. Black Elk joined Buffalo Bill's Wild West Show in 1886, traveling to New York's Madison Square Garden and then to England where the show performed for the Golden Jubilee of Queen Victoria's reign. By that time, Black Elk had become an Episcopalian, fortunate in that the Wild West Show required all its Native American employees to be Christians.

Black Elk returned home in time to encounter the Ghost Dance movement at Pine Ridge. Skeptical at first, he eventually came to understand the Ghost Dance to be consistent both with his own great vision and with Christian teaching. The massacre of Big Foot's Minneconjou band at Wounded Knee Creek in December 1890 put a tragic end to the hopes of the Ghost Dancers and, as well, to any hopes Black Elk might have had that his vision could restore the sacred hoop of his people and help them to live in a manner consistent with traditional ways. Black Elk was baptized a Catholic at Holy Rosary Mission on December 6, 1904, the feast of St. Nicholas, at which time he took that saint's name. He never engaged in traditional healing practices again.

In August 1930, John G. Neihardt, poet laureate of Nebraska, on a trip to research material for the final volume of his epic poem, *A Cycle of the West*, drove up to Black Elk's cabin outside of Manderson, South Dakota. With Neihardt were his son, Sigurd, and a man named Emil Afraid of Hawk who had agreed to act as Neihardt's interpreter (Black Elk spoke little English). From all accounts, the two men responded strongly to each other. Neihardt told Black Elk that he was a writer of epic poetry, which, in Lakota, translated roughly to *hanbloglaka*, or "vision telling." As Raymond DeMallie has put it, "Neihardt perceived Black Elk's religion in terms of art; Black Elk perceived Neihardt's art in terms of religion." Although Black Elk was by then a Catholic catechist, he had not forgotten the promise of the great vision that had been granted to him. In Neihardt, he believed he had found one who could make that vision known to the world.

In May 1931, Neihardt again visited Black Elk; with him now were his two daughters, Hilda and Enid, the latter an accomplished stenographer. The two men began work at daybreak on May 10. Serving as interpreter this time was Black Elk's son, Ben, who had studied for a time at the Carlisle Indian School. As was the custom when any warrior gave his "kill talks"—"coup tales," accounts of brave deeds in war—contemporaries of Black Elk (the elders Fire Thunder, Standing Bear, Chase in the Morning, and Holy Black Tail Deer) were present to listen and to comment on his narration. Black Elk told the story of his life in Lakota; Ben translated roughly into English; Neihardt repeated Ben's words in standard English; and Enid wrote it all down as best she could.

It was on the basis of a number of such sessions that Neihardt produced the book known as *Black Elk Speaks* (1932). Black Elk said little about his Catholicism and Neihardt chose not to mention it at all. Neihardt also edited the great vision, minimizing its concern for the achievement of power in warfare—a central concern of Lakota males—in DeMallie's words once more, in order to "develop the universalistic message of the vision. . . . focusing on the powers to heal." "The beginning and ending" of the book, Neihardt himself acknowledged, "are mine; they are what [Black Elk] would have said if he had been able." The ending—an account of Neihardt and Black Elk's trip to Harney Peak, "the center of the world"; of Black Elk's admission of his failure to restore the sacred hoop and "make the tree bloom" again; and of Black Elk's uncanny power nonetheless to bring rain—has had widespread influence. It has appeared, in only slightly different form, as the ending to Thomas Berger's novel *Little Big Man* (1964), and in recognizable but very different form in Arthur Penn's film of the same name (1970). But, again, this ending is Neihardt's, not Black Elk's.

Although *Black Elk Speaks* was favorably reviewed at the time of its publication, it attracted little attention. This was not the case shortly after its reissue in 1961; from that point forward, as anthropologist William Powers has written, "When Black Elk Speaks everybody listens!" Although it is Powers's view (along with several others) that Neihardt's own strong mystical Christianity obscures Lakota religion rather than presenting it accurately, the eminent Lakota scholar Vine DeLoria Jr., to the contrary, thinks that is not the issue at all. Rather, for DeLoria, Neihardt has produced in *Black Elk Speaks* a "religious classic," a "North American bible of all tribes."

Neihardt interviewed Black Elk again in 1944, incorporating this new material into the novel *When the Tree Flowered* (1951). Black Elk also engaged in a series of interviews with Joseph Epes Brown in the late 1940s; Brown's book *The Sacred Pipe* appeared in 1953.

The selection reprinted here is the complete text of *The Great Vision*, Chapter 3 of *Black Elk Speaks*. In addition to explanatory information, the notes provide some supplementary material from Raymond DeMallie's *The Sixth Grandfather*, which presents "in full the notes of the interviews, the direct words of Black Elk as interpreted into English" by Neihardt's daughters, Enid and Hilda, who acted as stenographer and secretary, respectively. As DeMallie writes, these are "the most original records of Black Elk's teachings available, and they are the sources from which Neihardt wrote *Black Elk Speaks*." They should allow the reader some closer approach to Black Elk himself, as they should also allow some greater awareness of the nature of Neihardt's art.

From Black Elk Speaks

III. *The Great Vision*

What happened after that[1] until the summer I was nine years old is not a story. There were winters and summers, and they were good; for the Wasichus had made their iron road[2] along the Platte and traveled there. This had cut the bison herd in two, but those that stayed in our country with us were more than could be counted, and we wandered without trouble in our land.

Now and then the voices would come back when I was out alone, like someone calling me, but what they wanted me to do I did not know. This did not happen very often, and when it did not happen, I forgot about it; for I was growing taller and was riding horses now and could shoot prairie chickens

---

1. A brief vision experienced by Black Elk when he was five years old that was mentioned at the end of the preceding chapter.

2. "The Union Pacific Railway" [Neihardt's note]. "Wasichus": fat eaters (Lakota, literal trans.); i.e., white settlers, or those who take the best part.

and rabbits with my bow. The boys of my people began very young to learn the ways of men, and no one taught us; we just learned by doing what we saw, and we were warriors at a time when boys now are like girls.

It was the summer when I was nine years old, and our people were moving slowly towards the Rocky Mountains. We camped one evening in a valley beside a little creek just before it ran into the Greasy Grass,[3] and there was a man by the name of Man Hip who liked me and asked me to eat with him in his tepee.

While I was eating, a voice came and said: "It is time; now they are calling you." The voice was so loud and clear that I believed it, and I thought I would just go where it wanted me to go. So I got right up and started. As I came out of the tepee, both my thighs began to hurt me, and suddenly it was like waking from a dream, and there wasn't any voice. So I went back into the tepee, but I didn't want to eat. Man Hip looked at me in a strange way and asked me what was wrong. I told him that my legs were hurting me.

The next morning the camp moved again, and I was riding with some boys. We stopped to get a drink from a creek, and when I got off my horse, my legs crumpled under me and I could not walk. So the boys helped me up and put me on my horse; and when we camped again that evening, I was sick. The next day the camp moved on to where the different bands of our people were coming together, and I rode in a pony drag, for I was very sick. Both my legs and both my arms were swollen badly and my face was all puffed up.

When we had camped again, I was lying in our tepee and my mother and father were sitting beside me. I could see out through the opening, and there two men were coming from the clouds, head-first like arrows slanting down, and I knew they were the same that I had seen before.[4] Each now carried a long spear, and from the points of these a jagged lightning flashed. They came clear down to the ground this time and stood a little way off and looked at me and said: "Hurry! Come! Your Grandfathers are calling you!"[5]

Then they turned and left the ground like arrows slanting upward from the bow. When I got up to follow, my legs did not hurt me any more and I was very light. I went outside the tepee, and yonder where the men with flaming spears were going, a little cloud was coming very fast. It came and stooped and took me and turned back to where it came from, flying fast. And when I looked down I could see my mother and my father yonder, and I felt sorry to be leaving them.

Then there was nothing but the air and the swiftness of the little cloud that bore me and those two men still leading up to where white clouds were piled like mountains on a wide blue plain, and in them thunder beings lived and leaped and flashed.

Now suddenly there was nothing but a world of cloud, and we three were there alone in the middle of a great white plain with snowy hills and mountains staring at us; and it was very still; but there were whispers.

Then the two men spoke together and they said: "Behold him, the being with four legs!"

---

3. The Little Bighorn River [Neihardt's note].
4. In the vision Black Elk had four years earlier.
5. In DeMallie's transcription, Black Elk uses the singular, "Your Grandfather is calling you," refer-ring to the western Grandfather whose cloud tepee is the home of the Thunder beings. Neihardt deemphasizes the importance of the west and of the fearful Thunder beings in *Black Elk Speaks*.

I looked and saw a bay horse standing there, and he began to speak: "Behold me!" he said, "My life-history you shall see." Then he wheeled about to where the sun goes down, and said: "Behold them! Their history you shall know."

I looked, and there were twelve black[6] horses yonder all abreast with necklaces of bison hoofs, and they were beautiful, but I was frightened, because their manes were lightning and there was thunder in their nostrils.

Then the bay horse wheeled to where the great white giant lives (the north) and said: "Behold!" And yonder there were twelve white horses all abreast. Their manes were flowing like a blizzard wind and from their noses came a roaring, and all about them white geese soared and circled.

Then the bay wheeled round to where the sun shines continually (the east) and bade me look; and there twelve sorrel horses, with necklaces of elk's teeth,[7] stood abreast with eyes that glimmered like the daybreak star and manes of morning light.

Then the bay wheeled once again to look upon the place where you are always facing (the south), and yonder stood twelve buckskins all abreast with horns upon their heads and manes that lived and grew like trees and grasses.

And when I had seen all these, the bay horse said: "Your Grandfathers are having a council. These shall take you; so have courage."

Then all the horses went into formation, four abreast—the blacks, the whites, the sorrels, and the buckskins—and stood behind the bay, who turned now to the west and neighed; and yonder suddenly the sky was terrible with a storm of plunging horses in all colors that shook the world with thunder, neighing back.

Now turning to the north the bay horse whinnied, and yonder all the sky roared with a mighty wind of running horses in all colors, neighing back.

And when he whinnied to the east, there too the sky was filled with glowing clouds of manes and tails of horses in all colors singing back. Then to the south he called, and it was crowded with many colored, happy horses, nickering.[8]

Then the bay horse spoke to me again and said: "See how your horses all come dancing!" I looked, and there were horses, horses everywhere—a whole skyful of horses dancing round me.

"Make haste!" the bay horse said; and we walked together side by side, while the blacks, the whites, the sorrels, and the buckskins followed, marching four by four.

I looked about me once again, and suddenly the dancing horses without number changed into animals of every kind and into all the fowls that are, and these fled back to the four quarters of the world from whence the horses came, and vanished.

Then as we walked, there was a heaped up cloud ahead that changed into a tepee, and a rainbow[9] was the open door of it; and through the door I saw six old men sitting in a row.

The two men with the spears now stood beside me, one on either hand, and the horses took their places in their quarters, looking inward, four by four.

6. The color specifically associated with the Thunder beings and the color of difficulty but also of the courage to triumph over difficulty. Successful Lakota warriors, for example, would paint their faces black.

7. Symbols of durability and thus long life.
8. "Happy" and "nickering" are Neihardt's additions.
9. Symbol of the Thunder beings.

And the oldest of the Grandfathers spoke with a kind voice and said: "Come right in and do not fear." And as he spoke, all the horses of the four quarters neighed to cheer me. So I went in and stood before the six, and they looked older than men can ever be—old like hills, like stars.[1]

The oldest spoke again: "Your Grandfathers all over the world are having a council, and they have called you here to teach you." His voice was very kind, but I shook all over with fear now, for I knew that these were not old men, but the Powers of the World. And the first was the Power of the West; the second, of the North; the third, of the East; the fourth, of the South; the fifth, of the Sky; the sixth, of the Earth. I knew this, and was afraid, until the first Grandfather spoke again: "Behold them yonder where the sun goes down, the thunder beings! You shall see, and have from them my power;[2] and they shall take you to the high and lonely center of the earth that you may see; even to the place where the sun continually shines, they shall take you there to understand."

And as he spoke of understanding, I looked up and saw the rainbow leap with flames of many colors over me.

Now there was a wooden cup in his hand and it was full of water and in the water was the sky.

"Take this," he said. "It is the power to make live, and it is yours."

Now he had a bow in his hands. "Take this," he said. "It is the power to destroy, and it is yours."

Then he pointed to himself and said: "Look close at him who is your spirit now, for you are his body and his name is Eagle Wing Stretches."

And saying this, he got up very tall and started running toward where the sun goes down; and suddenly he was a black horse that stopped and turned and looked at me, and the horse was very poor and sick; his ribs stood out.

Then the second Grandfather, he of the North, arose with a herb of power in his hand, and said: "Take this and hurry." I took and held it toward the black horse yonder. He fattened and was happy and came prancing to his place again and was the first Grandfather sitting there.

The second Grandfather, he of the North, spoke again: "Take courage, younger brother," he said; "on earth a nation you shall make live, for yours shall be the power of the white giant's wing, the cleansing wind." Then he got up very tall and started running toward the north; and when he turned toward me, it was a white goose wheeling. I looked about me now, and the horses in the west were thunders and the horses of the north were geese.[3] And the second Grandfather sang two songs[4] that were like this:

> "They are appearing, may you behold!
> They are appearing, may you behold!
> The thunder nation is appearing, behold!
>
> They are appearing, may you behold!
> They are appearing, may you behold!
> The white geese nation is appearing, behold!"

1. "Older than men . . . like stars" is Neihardt's addition.
2. Literally, *tawacin,* "will power," which, for the Lakota, is the creative power of a mind made wise by means of a vision, a power that can be used on earth [adapted from DeMallie's note].
3. Neihardt has much condensed this section. In *The Sixth Grandfather,* Black Elk understands the second Grandfather to be saying that he will "create a nation," and "cure lots of sickness with this herb," thus causing the people to cry joyfully as geese do when returning to their northern home after the hard winter has passed [adapted from DeMallie's note].
4. Black Elk attributes the first song to the first Grandfather, of the west.

And now it was the third Grandfather who spoke, he of where the sun shines continually. "Take courage, younger brother," he said, "for across the earth they shall take you!" Then he pointed to where the daybreak star was shining, and beneath the star two men were flying. "From them you shall have power," he said, "from them who have awakened all the beings of the earth with roots and legs and wings." And as he said this, he held in his hand a peace pipe which had a spotted eagle outstretched upon the stem; and this eagle seemed alive, for it was poised there, fluttering, and its eyes were looking at me. "With this pipe," the Grandfather said, "you shall walk upon the earth, and whatever sickens there you shall make well." Then he pointed to a man who was bright red[5] all over, the color of good and of plenty, and as he pointed, the red man lay down and rolled and changed into a bison that got up and galloped toward the sorrel horses of the east, and they too turned to bison, fat and many.

And now the fourth Grandfather spoke, he of the place where you are always facing (the south), whence comes the power to grow. "Younger brother," he said, "with the powers of the four quarters you shall walk, a relative. Behold, the living center of a nation I shall give you, and with it many you shall save." And I saw that he was holding in his hand a bright red stick that was alive, and as I looked it sprouted at the top and sent forth branches, and on the branches many leaves came out and murmured and in the leaves the birds began to sing. And then for just a little while I thought I saw beneath it in the shade the circled villages of people and every living thing with roots or legs or wings, and all were happy. "It shall stand in the center of the nation's circle," said the Grandfather, "a cane to walk with and a people's heart; and by your powers you shall make it blossom."

Then when he had been still a little while to hear the birds sing, he spoke again: "Behold the earth!" So I looked down and saw it lying yonder like a hoop of peoples, and in the center bloomed the holy stick that was a tree, and where it stood there crossed two roads, a red one and a black. "From where the giant lives (the north) to where you always face (the south) the red road goes, the road of good," the Grandfather said, "and on it shall your nation walk. The black road goes from where the thunder beings live (the west) to where the sun continually shines (the east), a fearful road, a road of troubles and of war.[6] On this also you shall walk, and from it you shall have the power to destroy a people's foes. In four ascents you shall walk the earth with power."

I think he meant that I should see four generations, counting me, and now I am seeing the third.

Then he rose very tall and started running toward the south, and was an elk; and as he stood among the buckskins yonder, they too were elks.

Now the fifth Grandfather spoke, the oldest of them all, the Spirit of the Sky. "My boy," he said, "I have sent for you and you have come. My power you shall see!" He stretched his arms and turned into a spotted eagle hovering. "Behold," he said, "all the wings of the air shall come to you, and they and the winds and the stars shall be like relatives. You shall go across the earth with my power." Then the eagle soared above my head and fluttered there; and suddenly the sky was full of friendly wings all coming toward me.

5. Associated with the buffalo, with nourishment, and with health.
6. This is Neihardt's interpretation. Black Elk's own explanation seems fairly untroubled: he says, "From east to west I have power to destroy and from north to south power to do good."

Now I knew the sixth Grandfather was about to speak, he who was the Spirit of the Earth, and I saw that he was very old, but more as men are old. His hair was long and white, his face was all in wrinkles and his eyes were deep and dim.[7] I stared at him, for it seemed I knew him somehow; and as I stared, he slowly changed, for he was growing backwards into youth, and when he had become a boy, I knew that he was myself with all the years that would be mine at last.[8] When he was old again, he said: "My boy, have courage, for my power shall be yours, and you shall need it, for your nation on the earth will have great troubles. Come."[9]

He rose and tottered out through the rainbow door, and as I followed I was riding on the bay horse who had talked to me at first and led me to that place.

Then the bay horse stopped and faced the black horses of the west, and a voice said: "They have given you the cup of water to make live the greening day, and also the bow and arrow to destroy." The bay neighed, and the twelve black horses came and stood behind me, four abreast.

The bay faced the sorrels of the east, and I saw that they had morning stars upon their foreheads and they were very bright. And the voice said: "They have given you the sacred pipe and the power that is peace, and the good red day." The bay neighed, and the twelve sorrels stood behind me, four abreast.

My horse now faced the buckskins of the south, and a voice said: "They have given you the sacred stick and your nation's hoop, and the yellow day; and in the center of the hoop you shall set the stick and make it grow into a shielding tree, and bloom." The bay neighed, and the twelve buckskins came and stood behind me, four abreast.

Then I knew that there were riders on all the horses there behind me, and a voice said: "Now you shall walk the black road with these; and as you walk, all the nations that have roots or legs or wings shall fear you."

So I started, riding toward the east down the fearful road, and behind me came the horsebacks four abreast—the blacks, the whites, the sorrels, and the buckskins—and far away above the fearful road the daybreak star was rising very dim.

I looked below me where the earth was silent in a sick green light, and saw the hills look up afraid and the grasses on the hills and all the animals; and everywhere about me were the cries of frightened birds and sounds of fleeing wings. I was the chief of all the heavens riding there, and when I looked behind me, all the twelve black horses reared and plunged and thundered and their manes and tails were whirling hail and their nostrils snorted lightning. And when I looked below again, I saw the slant hail falling and the long, sharp rain, and where we passed, the trees bowed low and all the hills were dim.

Now the earth was bright again as we rode. I could see the hills and valleys and the creeks and rivers passing under. We came above a place where three streams made a big one—a source of mighty waters—and something terrible was there. Flames were rising from the waters and in the flames a blue man lived.[1] The dust was floating all about him in the air, the grass was short and withered, the trees were wilting, two-legged and four-legged beings lay there thin and panting, and wings too weak to fly.

---

7. "Wrinkles" and "deep and dim" are Neihardt's additions.
8. "With all the years . . . at last" is Neihardt's addition.
9. Black Elk also says, "This old man had in his hand a spear," which is omitted by Neihardt.
1. This section is much condensed. It is after several attacks on "a man" who is said to be "the enemy" that "a man painted blue" emerges from the splashing waters. Three songs are also omitted.

Then the black horse riders shouted "Hoka hey!" and charged down upon the blue man, but were driven back. And the white troop shouted, charging, and was beaten; then the red troop and the yellow.

And when each had failed, they all cried together: "Eagle Wing Stretches, hurry!" And all the world was filled with voices of all kinds that cheered me, so I charged. I had the cup of water in one hand and in the other was the bow that turned into a spear as the bay and I swooped down, and the spear's head was sharp lightning. It stabbed the blue man's heart, and as it struck I could hear the thunder rolling and many voices that cried "Un-hee!," meaning I had killed. The flames died. The trees and grasses were not withered any more and murmured happily together, and every living being cried in gladness with whatever voice it had. Then the four troops of horsemen charged down and struck the dead body of the blue man, counting coup; and suddenly it was only a harmless turtle.[2]

You see, I had been riding with the storm clouds, and had come to earth as rain, and it was drouth that I had killed with the power that the Six Grandfathers gave me. So we were riding on the earth now down along the river flowing full from the source of waters, and soon I saw ahead the circled village of a people in the valley. And a Voice said: "Behold a nation; it is yours. Make haste, Eagle Wing Stretches!"

I entered the village, riding, with the four horse troops behind me—the blacks, the whites, the sorrels, and the buckskins; and the place was filled with moaning and with mourning for the dead. The wind was blowing from the south like fever, and when I looked around I saw that in nearly every tepee the women and the children and the men lay dying with the dead.

So I rode around the circle of the village, looking in upon the sick and dead, and I felt like crying as I rode. But when I looked behind me, all the women and the children and the men were getting up and coming forth with happy faces.

And a Voice said: "Behold, they have given you the center of the nation's hoop to make it live."

So I rode to the center of the village, with the horse troops in their quarters round about me, and there the people gathered. And the Voice said: "Give them now the flowering stick that they may flourish, and the sacred pipe that they may know the power that is peace, and the wing of the white giant that they may have endurance and face all winds with courage."

So I took the bright red stick and at the center of the nation's hoop I thrust it in the earth. As it touched the earth it leaped mightily in my hand and was a waga chun, the rustling tree,[3] very tall and full of leafy branches and of all birds singing. And beneath it all the animals were mingling with the people like relatives and making happy cries. The women raised their tremolo of joy, and the men shouted all together: "Here we shall raise our children and be as little chickens under the mother sheo's[4] wing."

Then I heard the white wind blowing gently through the tree and singing there, and from the east the sacred pipe came flying on its eagle wings, and stopped before me there beneath the tree, spreading deep peace around it.

---

2. *Keya*, the turtle, is an ally of the Thunder beings and a benefactor of humankind, something more than "only a harmless turtle." Black Elk interprets his kill to mean that "sometime in the future [he] was going to kill an enemy."

3. "The cottonwood" [Neihardt's note]. A cottonwood is used as the center pole for the important Lakota ceremony the Sun Dance.
4. Prairie hen [Neihardt's note].

Then the daybreak star was rising, and a Voice said: "It shall be a relative to them; and who shall see it, shall see much more, for thence comes wisdom; and those who do not see it shall be dark." And all the people raised their faces to the east, and the star's light fell upon them, and all the dogs barked loudly and the horses whinnied.

Then when the many little voices ceased, the great Voice said: "Behold the circle of the nation's hoop, for it is holy, being endless, and thus all powers shall be one power in the people without end. Now they shall break camp and go forth upon the red road, and your Grandfathers shall walk with them." So the people broke camp and took the good road with the white wing on their faces, and the order of their going was like this:

First, the black horse riders with the cup of water; and the white horse riders with the white wing and the sacred herb; and the sorrel riders with the holy pipe; and the buckskins with the flowering stick. And after these the little children and the youths and maidens followed in a band.

Second, came the tribe's four chieftains, and their band was all young men and women.

Third, the nation's four advisers leading men and women neither young nor old.

Fourth, the old men hobbling with their canes and looking to the earth.

Fifth, old women hobbling with their canes and looking to the earth.

Sixth, myself all alone upon the bay with the bow and arrows that the First Grandfather gave me. But I was not the last; for when I looked behind me there were ghosts of people like a trailing fog as far as I could see—grandfathers of grandfathers and grandmothers of grandmothers without number. And over these a great Voice—the Voice that was the South—lived, and I could feel it silent.

And as we went the Voice behind me said: "Behold a good nation walking in a sacred manner in a good land!"

Then I looked up and saw that there were four ascents ahead, and these were generations I should know. Now we were on the first ascent, and all the land was green. And as the long line climbed, all the old men and women raised their hands, palms forward, to the far sky yonder and began to croon a song together, and the sky ahead was filled with clouds of baby faces.

When we came to the end of the first ascent we camped in the sacred circle as before, and in the center stood the holy tree, and still the land about us was all green.

Then we started on the second ascent, marching as before, and still the land was green, but it was getting steeper. And as I looked ahead, the people changed into elks and bison and all four-footed beings and even into fowls, all walking in a sacred manner on the good red road together. And I myself was a spotted eagle soaring over them. But just before we stopped to camp at the end of that ascent, all the marching animals grew restless and afraid that they were not what they had been, and began sending forth voices of trouble, calling to their chiefs. And when they camped at the end of that ascent, I looked down and saw that leaves were falling from the holy tree.

And the Voice said: "Behold your nation, and remember what your Six Grandfathers gave you, for thenceforth your people walk in difficulties."

Then the people broke camp again, and saw the black road before them towards where the sun goes down, and black clouds coming yonder; and they did not want to go but could not stay. And as they walked the third ascent, all the animals and fowls that were the people ran here and there, for each one seemed to have his own little vision that he followed and his own rules; and all over the universe I could hear the winds at war like wild beasts fighting.

And when we reached the summit of the third ascent and camped, the nation's hoop was broken like a ring of smoke that spreads and scatters and the holy tree seemed dying and all its birds were gone. And when I looked ahead I saw that the fourth ascent would be terrible.

Then when the people were getting ready to begin the fourth ascent, the Voice spoke like some one weeping, and it said: "Look there upon your nation." And when I looked down, the people were all changed back to human, and they were thin, their faces sharp, for they were starving. Their ponies were only hide and bones, and the holy tree was gone.

And as I looked and wept, I saw that there stood on the north side of the starving camp a sacred man who was painted red all over his body, and he held a spear as he walked into the center of the people, and there he lay down and rolled. And when he got up, it was a fat bison standing there, and where the bison stood a sacred[5] herb sprang up right where the tree had been in the center of the nation's hoop. The herb grew and bore four blossoms on a single stem while I was looking—a blue, a white, a scarlet, and a yellow—and the bright rays of these flashed to the heavens.

I know now what this meant, that the bison were the gift of a good spirit and were our strength, but we should lose them, and from the same good spirit we must find another strength. For the people all seemed better when the herb had grown and bloomed, and the horses raised their tails and neighed and pranced around, and I could see a light breeze going from the north among the people like a ghost; and suddenly the flowering tree was there again at the center of the nation's hoop where the four-rayed herb had blossomed.

I was still the spotted eagle floating, and I could see that I was already in the fourth ascent and the people were camping yonder at the top of the third long rise. It was dark and terrible about me, for all the winds of the world were fighting. It was like rapid gun-fire and like whirling smoke, and like women and children wailing and like horses screaming all over the world.

I could see my people yonder running about, setting the smoke-flap poles and fastening down their tepees against the wind, for the storm cloud was coming on them very fast and black, and there were frightened swallows without number fleeing before the cloud.

Then a song of power came to me and I sang it there in the midst of that terrible place where I was. It went like this:

> A good nation I will make live.
> This the nation above has said.
> They have given me the power to make over.

And when I had sung this, a Voice said: "To the four quarters you shall run for help, and nothing shall be strong before you. Behold him!"[6]

Now I was on my bay horse again, because the horse is of the earth, and it was there my power would be used. And as I obeyed the Voice and looked,

---

5. Neihardt's addition; he also added "sacred" to the description of the red-painted man above.
6. Neihardt omits passages concerned with

flames, lightning, and thunder and, in particular, Black Elk's killing a dog spirit that is white on one side and black on the other.

there was a horse all skin and bones yonder in the west, a faded brownish black. And a Voice there said: "Take this and make him over; and it was the four-rayed herb that I was holding in my hand. So I rode above the poor horse in a circle, and as I did this I could hear the people yonder calling for spirit power, "A-hey! a-hey! a-hey! a-hey!" Then the poor horse neighed and rolled and got up, and he was a big, shiny, black stallion with dapples all over him and his mane about him like a cloud. He was the chief of all the horses; and when he snorted, it was a flash of lightning and his eyes were like the sunset star. He dashed to the west and neighed, and the west was filled with a dust of hoofs, and horses without number, shiny black, came plunging from the dust. Then he dashed toward the north and neighed, and to the east and to the south, and the dust clouds answered, giving forth their plunging horses without number—whites and sorrels and buckskins, fat, shiny, rejoicing in their fleetness and their strength. It was beautiful, but it was also terrible.

Then they all stopped short, rearing, and were standing in a great hoop about their black chief at the center, and were still. And as they stood, four virgins, more beautiful than women of the earth can be, came through the circle, dressed in scarlet, one from each of the four quarters, and stood about the great black stallion in their places; and one held the wooden cup of water, and one the white wing, and one the pipe, and one the nation's hoop. All the universe was silent, listening; and then the great black stallion raised his voice and sang. The song he sang was this:

> "My horses, prancing they are coming.
> My horses, neighing they are coming;
> Prancing, they are coming.
> All over the universe they come.
> They will dance; may you behold them.
>
> (4 times)
> A horse nation, they will dance. May you behold them."
>
> (4 times)

His voice was not loud, but it went all over the universe and filled it.[7] There was nothing that did not hear, and it was more beautiful than anything can be. It was so beautiful that nothing anywhere could keep from dancing. The virgins danced, and all the circled horses. The leaves on the trees, the grasses on the hills and in the valleys, the waters in the creeks and in the rivers and the lakes, the four-legged and the two-legged and the wings of the air—all danced together to the music of the stallion's song.

And when I looked down upon my people yonder, the cloud passed over, blessing them with friendly rain, and stood in the east with a flaming rainbow over it.

Then all the horses went singing back to their places beyond the summit of the fourth ascent, and all things sang along with them as they walked.

And a Voice said: "All over the universe they have finished a day of happiness." And looking down I saw that the whole wide circle of the day was beautiful and green, with all fruits growing and all things kind and happy.

Then a Voice said: "Behold this day, for it is yours to make. Now you shall stand upon the center of the earth to see, for there they are taking you."

---

7. What Black Elk actually said was "The horse's voice went all over the universe *like a radio* and everyone heard it" (emphasis added).

I was still on my bay horse, and once more I felt the riders of the west, the north, the east, the south, behind me in formation, as before, and we were going east. I looked ahead and saw the mountains there with rocks and forests on them, and from the mountains flashed all colors upward to the heavens. Then I was standing on the highest mountain of them all, and round about beneath me was the whole hoop of the world. And while I stood there I saw more than I can tell and I understood more than I saw; for I was seeing in a sacred manner the shapes of all things in the spirit, and the shape of all shapes as they must live together like one being. And I saw that the sacred hoop of my people was one of many hoops that made one circle, wide as daylight and as starlight, and in the center grew one mighty flowering tree to shelter all the children of one mother and one father. And I saw that it was holy.

Then as I stood there, two men were coming from the east, head first like arrows flying, and between them rose the day-break star. They came and gave a herb to me and said: "With this on earth you shall undertake anything and do it." It was the day-break-star herb, the herb of understanding, and they told me to drop it on the earth. I saw it falling far, and when it struck the earth it rooted and grew and flowered, four blossoms on one stem, a blue, a white, a scarlet, and a yellow; and the rays from these streamed upward to the heavens so that all creatures saw it and in no place was there darkness.[8]

Then the Voice said: "Your Six Grandfathers—now you shall go back to them."[9]

I had not noticed how I was dressed until now, and I saw that I was painted red all over, and my joints were painted black, with white stripes between the joints. My bay had lightning stripes all over him, and his mane was cloud. And when I breathed, my breath was lightning.

Now two men were leading me, head first like arrows slanting upward— the two that brought me from the earth. And as I followed on the bay, they turned into four flocks of geese that flew in circles, one above each quarter, sending forth a sacred voice as they flew: Br-r-r-p, br-r-r-p, br-r-r-p, br-r-r-p!

Then I saw ahead the rainbow flaming above the tepee of the Six Grandfathers, built and roofed with cloud and sewed with thongs of lightning; and underneath it were all the wings of the air and under them the animals and men. All these were rejoicing, and thunder was like happy laughter.

As I rode in through the rainbow door, there were cheering voices from all over the universe, and I saw the Six Grandfathers sitting in a row, with their arms held toward me and their hands, palms out; and behind them in the cloud were faces thronging, without number, of the people yet to be.

"He has triumphed!" cried the six together, making thunder. And as I passed before them there, each gave again the gift that he had given me before—the cup of water and the bow and arrows, the power to make live and to destroy; the white wing of cleansing and the healing herb; the sacred pipe; the flowering stick. And each one spoke in turn from west to south, explain-

---

8. Neihardt adds the light streaming to the heavens, but omits a passage in which Black Elk sees a white cloud in the south and the west over people who are sick. He interprets this as "probably the white people coming."

9. Here Neihardt omits a lengthy section in which Black Elk receives the soldier weed of destruction. It is at the end of this section that Black Elk notices how he is painted.

ing what he gave as he had done before, and as each one spoke he melted down into the earth and rose again; and as each did this, I felt nearer to the earth.

Then the oldest of them all said: "Grandson, all over the universe you have seen. Now you shall go back with power to the place from whence you came, and it shall happen yonder that hundreds shall be sacred, hundreds shall be flames! Behold!"

I looked below and saw my people there, and all were well and happy except one, and he was lying like the dead—and that one was myself. Then the oldest Grandfather[1] sang, and his song was like this:

> "There is someone lying on earth in a sacred manner.
> There is someone—on earth he lies.
> In a sacred manner I have made him to walk."

Now the tepee, built and roofed with cloud, began to sway back and forth as in a wind, and the flaming rainbow door was growing dimmer. I could hear voices of all kinds crying from outside: "Eagle Wing Stretches is coming forth! Behold him!"

When I went through the door, the face of the day of earth was appearing with the daybreak star upon its forehead; and the sun leaped up and looked upon me, and I was going forth alone.

And as I walked alone, I heard the sun singing as it arose, and it sang like this:

> "With visible face I am appearing.
> In a sacred manner I appear.
> For the greening earth a pleasantness I make.
> The center of the nation's hoop I have made pleasant.
> With visible face, behold me!
> The four-leggeds and two-leggeds, I have made them to walk;
> The wings of the air, I have made them to fly.
> With visible face I appear.
> My day, I have made it holy."[2]

When the singing stopped, I was feeling lost and very lonely. Then a Voice above me said: "Look back!" It was a spotted eagle that was hovering over me and spoke. I looked, and where the flaming rainbow tepee, built and roofed with cloud, had been, I saw only the tall rock mountain at the center of the world.

I was all alone on a broad plain now with my feet upon the earth, alone but for the spotted eagle guarding me. I could see my people's village far ahead, and I walked very fast, for I was homesick now. Then I saw my own tepee, and inside I saw my mother and my father bending over a sick boy that was myself.

---

1. I.e., the fourth Grandfather; his song is one Black Elk himself later used in curing. Neihardt omits a passage in which Black Elk sees himself lying ill on earth and is told to drink a cup of water in which there is a blue man, who is both a fish and a spirit. Black Elk says that he "received strange power" from the cup and that he could "actually make this blue man come out and swim in the cup" when he used it for curing.
2. This song does not appear at this point in the transcript.

And as I entered the tepee, some one was saying: "The boy is coming to; you had better give him some water."[3]

Then I was sitting up; and I was sad because my mother and my father didn't seem to know I had been so far away.

1932

3. Here Black Elk says, "They were giving me some medicine but it was not that that cured me—it was my vision that cured me."

EDGAR LEE MASTERS
1868–1950

Few books of poetry published in the United States have had an immediate impact like that of *Spoon River Anthology*. Its lack of rhyme and verse, its rough, flat, unpoetic diction, its forthright presentation of private yet ordinary lives, its representation of sex as a basic human motive, and its deeply critical view of small-town values—these traits of the volume ran counter to public expectations of what poetry should be like. But controversy was good for sales; the book went through nineteen printings in its first edition, a record for poetry up until then.

Edgar Lee Masters was practicing law in Chicago at the time of its publication in 1915. He was born in Kansas and grew up in two small Illinois towns, Petersburg and Lewiston. His father was a lawyer and politician, his mother a lover of music and literature homesick for her native New England. Masters attended Knox College in Galesburg, Illinois, for a year and then studied law in his father's office. He passed his bar exams and entered the legal profession to please his father, but broke decisively with both parents when he moved to Chicago in 1891.

In Chicago, Masters met many of the writers and intellectuals involved in the Chicago Renaissance, a movement aiming to make the city a cultural center. He worked with Harriet Monroe, editor of *Poetry: A Magazine of Verse,* an important little magazine of the era, and began to publish poetry of his own. A friend, William Marion Reedy, publisher of the influential St. Louis weekly *Reedy's Mirror,* gave him a copy of J. W. Mackail's *Selected Epigrams from the Greek Anthology*. In this collection of some four thousand short poems written between 700 B.C.E. and 1000 C.E., Masters found interconnected autobiographical poems, where the speaker in one poem talked bluntly about speakers in other poems. This structure showed Masters how to give poetic shape to a naturalistic vision more commonly associated with fiction.

All the speakers in *Spoon River Anthology* are dead, buried in the cemetery on "the hill," which is the title of the first poem in the book: "All, all, are sleeping on the hill." These lifelong friends and neighbors continue their loves and quarrels beyond the grave. Their dissonant voices converge in a lament for suppressed and wasted lives, only rarely varied by joy or gusto. Sex has driven them, but given little pleasure. They long for the sympathy that they withhold from each other. Yet the poems as a group are compassionate, not judgmental.

Masters's dramatic sense, his ability to condense and convey a whole life through the narration of one incident, contributed to the craft of the short story as well as to a new sense of what poetry might consist of. His work was immediate inspiration for hostile depictions of small-town and small-minded America in the work of 1920s writers like Sherwood Anderson and Sinclair Lewis. None of Masters's many other books of verse, except the sequel *The New Spoon River* in 1924, attained the reputation of

Spoon River Anthology. He was, however, a prolific writer in other modes. He composed several novels; biographies of Abraham Lincoln, Vachel Lindsay (the Chicago poet), Walt Whitman, and Mark Twain; and his own autobiography, *Across Spoon River,* in 1936.

In all, he wrote more than fifty books, committing himself after the success of *Spoon River Anthology* to a full-time literary career. He married twice and had four children. He gave up the law, left Chicago, and settled in New York City in 1920, living in later life at the Chelsea Hotel, a favorite residence for writers.

The text of the poems included here is that of *Spoon River Anthology* (1915).

Trainor, the Druggist

Only the chemist can tell, and not always the chemist,
What will result from compounding
Fluids or solids.
And who can tell
How men and women will interact   5
On each other, or what children will result?
There were Benjamin Pantier and his wife,
Good in themselves, but evil toward each other:
He oxygen, she hydrogen,
Their son, a devastating fire.   10
I Trainor, the druggist, a mixer of chemicals,
Killed while making an experiment,
Lived unwedded.

1915

Doc Hill

I went up and down the streets
Here and there by day and night,
Through all hours of the night caring for the poor who were sick.
Do you know why?
My wife hated me, my son went to the dogs.   5
And I turned to the people and poured out my love to them.
Sweet it was to see the crowds about the lawns on the day of my
        funeral,
And hear them murmur their love and sorrow.
But oh, dear God, my soul trembled, scarcely able
To hold to the railing of the new life   10
When I saw Em Stanton behind the oak tree
At the grave,
Hiding herself, and her grief!

1915

Margaret Fuller[1] Slack

I would have been as great as George Eliot[2]
But for an untoward fate.
For look at the photograph of me made by Penniwit,
Chin resting on hand, and deep-set eyes—
Gray, too, and far-searching.   5
But there was the old, old problem:
Should it be celibacy, matrimony or unchastity?
Then John Slack, the rich druggist, wooed me,
Luring me with the promise of leisure for my novel,
And I married him, giving birth to eight children,   10
And had no time to write.
It was all over with me, anyway,
When I ran the needle in my hand
While washing the baby's things,
And died from lock-jaw, an ironical death.   15
Hear me, ambitious souls,
Sex is the curse of life!

                                                                                      1915

Abel Melveny

I bought every kind of machine that's known—
Grinders, shellers, planters, mowers,
Mills and rakes and ploughs and threshers—
And all of them stood in the rain and sun,
Getting rusted, warped and battered,   5
For I had no sheds to store them in,
And no use for most of them.
And toward the last, when I thought it over,
There by my window, growing clearer
About myself, as my pulse slowed down,   10
And looked at one of the mills I bought—
Which I didn't have the slightest need of,
As things turned out, and I never ran—
A fine machine, once brightly varnished,
And eager to do its work,   15
Now with its paint washed off—
I saw myself as a good machine
That Life had never used.

                                                                                      1915

1. New England feminist, writer, and journalist
(1810–1850); symbol of an emancipated and intellectual woman.
2. English novelist (1819–1880), whose real name
was Mary Ann Evans; author of such classics as
The Mill on the Floss (1860) and *Middlemarch*
(1871–72).

Lucinda Matlock

I went to the dances at Chandlerville,
And played snap-out[1] at Winchester.
One time we changed partners,
Driving home in the moonlight of middle June,
And then I found Davis.   5
We were married and lived together for seventy years,
Enjoying, working, raising the twelve children,
Eight of whom we lost
Ere I had reached the age of sixty.
I spun, I wove, I kept the house, I nursed the sick,   10
I made the garden, and for holiday
Rambled over the fields where sang the larks,
And by Spoon River gathering many a shell,
And many a flower and medicinal weed—
Shouting to the wooded hills, singing to the green valleys.   15
At ninety-six I had lived enough, that is all,
And passed to a sweet repose.
What is this I hear of sorrow and weariness,
Anger, discontent and drooping hopes?
Degenerate sons and daughters,   20
Life is too strong for you—
It takes life to love Life.

1915

1. A kissing game.

EDWIN ARLINGTON ROBINSON
1869–1935

Like his own Miniver Cheevy, Edwin Arlington Robinson felt himself born too late. He turned to poetry in search of an alternative world of elegance and beauty, but wrote his best poems about wasted, blighted, or impoverished lives. His brief story and portrait poems are in traditional form with metrically regular verse, rhymes, and elevated diction. Such techniques dignify the subject matter and also provide a contrast, where his subject is unpoetic according to traditional standards, that emphasizes its sadness and banality.

Robinson was raised in Gardiner, Maine, the Tilbury Town of such poems as "Miniver Cheevy" and "Mr. Flood's Party." His father's lumber business and land speculations failed during the Great Panic of 1893. One of his brothers, a physician, became a drug addict; the other, a businessman, became an alcoholic. Robinson, by nature a scholar and book lover, was able to afford just two years at Harvard. Returning to Gardiner and trying to become a professional poet, he had to depend for support on friends and patrons, until a Pulitzer Prize in 1922 brought him some financial security. By this time he was over fifty.

Robinson studied alone and with friends long after his formal schooling ended. He read classic works in many languages as well as such American writers as Hawthorne, Whitman, Emerson, and Henry James, whom he interpreted as individualistic idealists. He was also drawn to the bleak, tragic vision of the British novelist Thomas Hardy. These influences were distilled in the gloomy, austere, yet sonorous verse of his second book, *Children of the Night* (1897—*The Torrent and the Night Before* had been published the previous year, at his own expense). Celebrating the pain of isolated lives, Robinson worked through to a residue of affirmation, an occasional "light" or "word" that is glimpsed in the "night" of these poems.

Robinson moved to New York City around the turn of the century. *The Town Down the River* (1910) and *The Man against the Sky* (1916) won increasing numbers of readers and critics' awards. *Avon's Harvest* and *Collected Poems* (both 1922) were successful, as was a trilogy of long poems in imitation of medieval narratives, beginning with *Merlin* (1917). The last of these, *Tristram* (1927), brought a third Pulitzer Prize. To some of the tougher-minded critics of the 1920s, the escapism of the later work (precisely what may have made it attractive to a larger audience), uncorrected by the somber wit and sustained irony of the Tilbury poems, seemed overly sentimental. The prizes and honors represented, to a large extent, their belated recognition of his earlier poetry.

Although in that earlier work Robinson was a New England regional poet like Robert Frost and a chronicler of small-town life like Edgar Lee Masters and Sherwood Anderson, he thought of himself as estranged both from his time and from the practices of other poets. The difference between him and these others lay in his ever-present sense of a lost, glorious past.

The text of the poems included here is that of *Collected Poems of Edwin Arlington Robinson* (1921, 1937).

Luke Havergal

Go to the western gate,[1] Luke Havergal,—
There where the vines cling crimson on the wall,—
And in the twilight wait for what will come.
The wind will moan, the leaves will whisper some,—
Whisper of her, and strike you as they fall;   5
But go, and if you trust her she will call.
Go to the western gate, Luke Havergal—
Luke Havergal.

No, there is not a dawn in eastern skies
To rift the fiery night that's in your eyes;   10
But there, where western glooms are gathering,
The dark will end the dark, if anything:
God slays Himself with every leaf that flies,
And hell is more than half of paradise.
No, there is not a dawn in eastern skies—   15
In eastern skies.

Out of a grave I come to tell you this,—
Out of a grave I come to quench the kiss

---

1. The natural symbolism of nightfall and autumn associates "the western gate" with the end of life.

That flames upon your forehead with a glow
That blinds you to the way that you must go.   20
Yes, there is yet one way to where she is,—
Bitter, but one that faith may never miss.
Out of a grave I come to tell you this—
To tell you this.

There is the western gate, Luke Havergal,   25
There are the crimson leaves upon the wall.
Go,—for the winds are tearing them away,—
Nor think to riddle the dead words they say,
Nor any more to feel them as they fall;
But go! and if you trust her she will call.   30
There is the western gate, Luke Havergal—
Luke Havergal.

1896

Richard Cory

Whenever Richard Cory went down town,
We people on the pavement looked at him:
He was a gentleman from sole to crown,
Clean favored, and imperially slim.

And he was always quietly arrayed,   5
And he was always human when he talked;
But still he fluttered pulses when he said,
"Good-morning," and he glittered when he walked.

And he was rich—yes, richer than a king,—
And admirably schooled in every grace: 10
In fine, we thought that he was everything
To make us wish that we were in his place.

So on we worked, and waited for the light,
And went without the meat, and cursed the bread;
And Richard Cory, one calm summer night,   15
Went home and put a bullet through his head.

1896

Miniver Cheevy

Miniver Cheevy, child of scorn,
    Grew lean while he assailed the seasons;
He wept that he was ever born,
    And he had reasons.

Miniver loved the days of old   5
    When swords were bright and steeds were prancing;
The vision of a warrior bold
    Would set him dancing.

Miniver sighed for what was not,
    And dreamed, and rested from his labors;   10
He dreamed of Thebes and Camelot,
    And Priam's neighbors.[1]

Miniver mourned the ripe renown
    That made so many a name so fragrant;
He mourned Romance, now on the town,   15
    And Art, a vagrant.

Miniver loved the Medici,[2]
    Albeit he had never seen one;
He would have sinned incessantly
    Could he have been one.   20

Miniver cursed the commonplace
    And eyed a khaki suit with loathing;
He missed the mediæval grace
    Of iron clothing.

Miniver scorned the gold he sought,   25
    But sore annoyed was he without it;
Miniver thought, and thought, and thought,
    And thought about it.

Miniver Cheevy, born too late,
    Scratched his head and kept on thinking;   30
Miniver coughed, and called it fate,
    And kept on drinking.

                                                        1910

Mr. Flood's Party

Old Eben Flood, climbing alone one night
Over the hill between the town below
And the forsaken upland hermitage
That held as much as he should ever know
On earth again of home, paused warily.   5
The road was his with not a native near;

---

1. The neighbors of King Priam in Homer's *Iliad* are his heroic compatriots in the doomed city of Troy. Thebes was an ancient city in Boeotia, rival of Athens and Sparta for supremacy in Greece and the setting of Sophocles' tragedies about Oedipus.

Camelot is the legendary court of King Arthur and the knights of the Round Table.
2. Family of wealthy merchants, politicians, churchmen, and art patrons in 16th-century Florence.

And Eben, having leisure, said aloud,
For no man else in Tilbury Town[1] to hear:

"Well, Mr. Flood, we have the harvest moon
Again, and we may not have many more;   10
The bird is on the wing, the poet says,[2]
And you and I have said it here before.
Drink to the bird." He raised up to the light
The jug that he had gone so far to fill,
And answered huskily: "Well, Mr. Flood,   15
Since you propose it, I believe I will."

Alone, as if enduring to the end
A valiant armor of scarred hopes outworn,
He stood there in the middle of the road
Like Roland's ghost winding a silent horn.[3]   20
Below him, in the town among the trees,
Where friends of other days had honored him,
A phantom salutation of the dead
Rang thinly till old Eben's eyes were dim.

Then, as a mother lays her sleeping child   25
Down tenderly, fearing it may awake,
He set the jug down slowly at his feet
With trembling care, knowing that most things break;
And only when assured that on firm earth
It stood, as the uncertain lives of men   30
Assuredly did not, he paced away,
And with his hand extended paused again:

"Well, Mr. Flood, we have not met like this
In a long time; and many a change has come
To both of us, I fear, since last it was   35
We had a drop together. Welcome home!"
Convivially returning with himself,
Again he raised the jug up to the light;
And with an acquiescent quaver said:
"Well, Mr. Flood, if you insist, I might.   40

"Only a very little, Mr. Flood—
For auld lang syne.[4] No more, sir; that will do."
So, for the time, apparently it did,
And Eben evidently thought so too;
For soon amid the silver loneliness   45

1. The fictive town in a number of Robinson's
poems, modeled on Gardiner, Maine.
2. Flood paraphrases stanza 7 of the Persian poem
The Rubáiyát of Omar Khayyám in the 1859 translation by the English poet Edward FitzGerald
(1809–1883): "Come, fill the Cup, and in the Fire
of Spring / Your Winter-garment of Repentance
fling: / The Bird of Time has but a little way / To
flutter—and the Bird is on the Wing."

3. Roland was King Charlemagne's nephew, celebrated in the *Chanson de Roland* (Song of Roland,
c. 1000). Just before dying in the battle of Ronce-
valles (778 C.E.), he sounded his horn for help.
4. Old long since (Scottish, literal trans.); hence
"the days of long ago," the title and refrain of a
famous song by the Scottish poet Robert Burns
(1759–1796).

Of night he lifted up his voice and sang,
Secure, with only two moons listening,
Until the whole harmonious landscape rang—

"For auld lang syne." The weary throat gave out,
The last word wavered, and the song was done.   50
He raised again the jug regretfully
And shook his head, and was again alone.
There was not much that was ahead of him,
And there was nothing in the town below—
Where strangers would have shut the many doors   55
That many friends had opened long ago.

1921

WILLA CATHER
1873–1947

Willa Cather was born in Virginia, the oldest child of Charles and Virginia Cather, who moved with their family to the Nebraska Divide when she was ten years old. After a year of farming, they relocated to the town of Red Cloud, and her father went into the real estate business. At seventeen, Cather moved on her own to Lincoln, the state capital and seat of the University of Nebraska; she attended preparatory school for two years and graduated from the university in 1896. In college she studied the classics and participated in the lively contemporary cultural life of the city by reviewing books, plays, and musical performances. Following graduation, she moved to Pittsburgh, Pennsylvania, to work as an editor of a women's magazine, the *Home Monthly*, a position she left five years later to teach high-school English and Latin. During this time she also wrote poems and stories, gathering poems into *April Twilights*, in 1903, and stories into *The Troll Garden*, in 1905. Also in Pittsburgh, in 1899, she met Isabelle McClung, from a prominent, wealthy family. She lived in the McClung home from 1901 to 1906, when she moved to New York City to write for the journal *McClure's*. Throughout her life, Cather remained devoted to McClung, experiencing her marriage in 1916 as a severe personal loss being and devastated by her death in 1938.

Having long wished to write novels, Cather took a leave of absence from *McClure's* in 1911, and wrote *Alexander's Bridge* (1912). This novel was successful, but it was the next three that made her reputation. Each focused on a western heroine: Alexandra Bergson in *O Pioneers!* (1913), Thea Kronberg in *The Song of the Lark* (1915), and Ántonia Shimerda in *My Ántonia* (1918). While Alexandra is extraordinary as the most successful farmer—the only woman farmer—on the Nebraska Divide, and Thea is extraordinary as a gifted opera singer, Ántonia has no unusual gifts; for Cather and the novel's many readers she stands for the entire experience of European settlement of the Great Plains. These three novels also manifest Cather's lyrical yet understated prose writing; they contain a wealth of detail about the lives of Nebraska settlers— Bohemian Czech, German, Danish, Swedish, Norwegian, French, Russian, and "Americans" from the East—as they learned to farm on the prairie and built communities in which their various ethnicities met and mingled. Cather's is no melting pot ethos, however; rather she sees the frontier as a shifting kaleidoscope of overlapping social groups and individuals. Recognizing that even by the second decade of the twentieth century this period in U.S. history had disappeared, Cather approached her characters with deep respect for what they had endured and accomplished.

Whether these novels (or any of Cather's other work) encode a lesbian sensibility has been a matter of much critical debate. In life Cather showed no romantic interest in men; in 1908 she began to share an apartment with Edith Lewis, a Nebraskan whom she had met in 1903, and they lived together until Cather's death. (They lived mostly in New York City, but Cather also traveled a great deal: to Europe, to New England, to the Southwest, and back to Red Cloud to visit her family.) Estrangement from conventional sexuality and sex roles is typical of many of her main characters, male and female; but heterosexual romance and sexual behavior is equally present in her novels. It seems fair to say that close friendship, much more than romantic or sexual love, is the great ideal in her fiction.

Around 1922, according to Cather, her world broke in two; she suffered from the combined effects of poor health, dissatisfaction with the progress of her career, and alarm at the increasing mechanization and mass-produced quality of American life. She joined the Episcopal Church, and her novels took a new direction. Although her books had always celebrated alternative values to the material and conventional, this theme became much more urgent, while the motif of heroic womanhood—which had led many to call her a feminist, though Cather herself kept aloof from all movements—receded. Important books from her "middle period" include *A Lost Lady* (1923) and *The Professor's House* (1925), which deal with spiritual and cultural crises in the lives of the main characters.

Published in 1927, the novel *Death Comes for the Archbishop* initiated her third stage. Like many other writers and artists in the 1920s, Cather had become entranced with the American Southwest—especially New Mexico; her first trip to the region in 1912 figured in her depiction (in *The Song of the Lark*) of Thea Kronberg finding spiritual renewal in this landscape. *Death Comes for the Archbishop*, partly written at Mary Austin's home in Santa Fe, is based on the career of Jean Baptiste Lamy (1814–1888), archbishop of New Mexico, and the priest Joseph Marchebeuf, his close friend and collaborator. Another historical novel, *Shadows on the Rock* (1931) is set even further back in time, in seventeenth-century Quebec. In both books, a composite image of high French culture, ceremonial spirituality, and the American landscape contrasts with the material trivia and empty banality of contemporary life.

Inspired by the classical Latin works that she loved so much, Cather believed in the ideas of art and the artist and strove to attain an artistic height from which she might survey the entire human scene. She tried to imbue the particularities of her stories with what she thought of as universal significance. In *My Ántonia*, which continues to be the favorite novel for most Cather readers, Jim Burden reflects on the aspirations of the poet Virgil to bring the muse to his own country for the first time; by country, Virgil means "not a nation or even a province, but the little rural neighborhood" where he was born. This is clearly what is intended in *My Ántonia*; the idea of combining artistic transcendence with local, especially rural, specificity, speaks to Cather's own goals. It is a measure of her ambition that she thinks of her work in Virgilian terms, since Virgil was the greatest of the Latin poets.

Politically, culturally, and aesthetically, Cather was in many respects deeply conservative as well as conflicted—a sophisticated populist, an agrarian urbanite. She believed in high art and superior people, but also thought great human gifts were more often found among the obscure and ordinary than among those with great advantages. Her vision of the United States had little room for Native Americans and African Americans; yet she preferred immigrants from Europe to migrants from the East Coast. She appreciated popular legends and folktales, which appear along with classical myth and allusion in her work. She paid little attention to formal structure; her novels often read more like chronicles than stories, which makes them seem artless and real while concealing the sentence-by-sentence care that has gone into the work.

She once described her work as deliberately "unfurnished," meaning that it was cut down to only those details absolutely necessary; "suggestion rather than enumeration" was another way she described her goal (see "The Novel Démeuble," p. 1508). The resulting spareness and clarity of her fiction puts it in the modernist tradition, even though in her lifetime she had little interest in the modernist movement.

The text of *My Ántonia* is that of the first edition (1918).

My Ántonia

Optima dies . . . prima fugit
—VIRGIL[1]

Introduction

Last summer I happened to be crossing the plains of Iowa in a season of intense heat, and it was my good fortune to have for a traveling companion James Quayle Burden—Jim Burden, as we still call him in the West. He and I are old friends—we grew up together in the same Nebraska town—and we had much to say to each other. While the train flashed through never-ending miles of ripe wheat, by country towns and bright-flowered pastures and oak groves wilting in the sun, we sat in the observation car, where the woodwork was hot to the touch and red dust lay deep over everything. The dust and heat, the burning wind, reminded us of many things. We were talking about what it is like to spend one's childhood in little towns like these, buried in wheat and corn, under stimulating extremes of climate: burning summers when the world lies green and billowy beneath a brilliant sky, when one is fairly stifled in vegetation, in the color and smell of strong weeds and heavy harvests; blustery winters with little snow, when the whole country is stripped bare and gray as sheet-iron. We agreed that no one who had not grown up in a little prairie town could know anything about it. It was a kind of freemasonry,[2] we said.

Although Jim Burden and I both live in New York, and are old friends, I do not see much of him there. He is legal counsel for one of the great Western railways, and is sometimes away from his New York office for weeks together. That is one reason why we do not often meet. Another is that I do not like his wife.

When Jim was still an obscure young lawyer, struggling to make his way in New York, his career was suddenly advanced by a brilliant marriage.[3] Genevieve Whitney was the only daughter of a distinguished man. Her marriage with young Burden was the subject of sharp comment at the time. It was said she had been brutally jilted by her cousin, Rutland Whitney, and that she married this unknown man from the West out of bravado. She was a restless, headstrong girl, even then, who liked to astonish her friends. Later, when I knew her, she was always doing something unexpected. She gave one of her town houses for a Suffrage headquarters, produced one of her own plays at the Princess Theater, was arrested for picketing during a garment-makers'

---

1. Roman poet (70–19 B.C.). "The best days . . . are the first to flee" (Latin); from the *Georgics* (29 B.C.), a long didactic poem idealizing farm life.
2. A secret fraternal organization; here a reference to secret, shared knowledge.

3. In the 1926 edition, Cather revised and shortened the *Introduction*, omitting most of the characterization of Burden's wife and details of his career as an advocate of "mines and timber and oil."

strike, etc. I am never able to believe that she has much feeling for the causes to which she lends her name and her fleeting interest. She is handsome, energetic, executive, but to me she seems unimpressionable and temperamentally incapable of enthusiasm. Her husband's quiet tastes irritate her, I think, and she finds it worth while to play the patroness to a group of young poets and painters of advanced ideas and mediocre ability. She has her own fortune and lives her own life. For some reason, she wishes to remain Mrs. James Burden.

As for Jim, no disappointments have been severe enough to chill his naturally romantic and ardent disposition. This disposition, though it often made him seem very funny when he was a boy, has been one of the strongest elements in his success. He loves with a personal passion the great country through which his railway runs and branches. His faith in it and his knowledge of it have played an important part in its development. He is always able to raise capital for new enterprises in Wyoming or Montana, and has helped young men out there to do remarkable things in mines and timber and oil. If a young man with an idea can once get Jim Burden's attention, can manage to accompany him when he goes off into the wilds hunting for lost parks or exploring new canyons, then the money which means action is usually forthcoming. Jim is still able to lose himself in those big Western dreams. Though he is over forty now, he meets new people and new enterprises with the impulsiveness by which his boyhood friends remember him. He never seems to me to grow older. His fresh color and sandy hair and quick-changing blue eyes are those of a young man, and his sympathetic, solicitous interest in women is as youthful as it is Western and American.

During that burning day when we were crossing Iowa, our talk kept returning to a central figure, a Bohemian[4] girl whom we had known long ago and whom both of us admired. More than any other person we remembered, this girl seemed to mean to us the country, the conditions, the whole adventure of our childhood. To speak her name was to call up pictures of people and places, to set a quiet drama going in one's brain. I had lost sight of her altogether, but Jim had found her again after long years, had renewed a friendship that meant a great deal to him, and out of his busy life had set apart time enough to enjoy that friendship. His mind was full of her that day. He made me see her again, feel her presence, revived all my old affection for her.

"I can't see," he said impetuously, "why you have never written anything about Ántonia."

I told him I had always felt that other people—he himself, for one—knew her much better than I. I was ready, however, to make an agreement with him; I would set down on paper all that I remembered of Ántonia if he would do the same. We might, in this way, get a picture of her.

He rumpled his hair with a quick, excited gesture, which with him often announces a new determination, and I could see that my suggestion took hold of him. "Maybe I will, maybe I will!" he declared. He stared out of the window for a few moments, and when he turned to me again his eyes had the sudden clearness that comes from something the mind itself sees. "Of course," he said, "I should have to do it in a direct way, and say a great deal

4. From Bohemia, a region in the Czech Republic. Immigrants to the United States from this part of eastern Europe began to arrive in great numbers during the 1880s, which is when the novel begins.

about myself. It's through myself that I knew and felt her, and I've had no practice in any other form of presentation."

I told him that how he knew her and felt her was exactly what I most wanted to know about Ántonia. He had had opportunities that I, as a little girl who watched her come and go, had not.

Months afterward Jim Burden arrived at my apartment one stormy winter afternoon, with a bulging legal portfolio sheltered under his fur overcoat. He brought it into the sitting-room with him and tapped it with some pride as he stood warming his hands.

"I finished it last night—the thing about Ántonia," he said. "Now, what about yours?"

I had to confess that mine had not gone beyond a few straggling notes.

"Notes? I didn't make any." He drank his tea all at once and put down the cup. "I didn't arrange or rearrange. I simply wrote down what of herself and myself and other people Ántonia's name recalls to me. I suppose it hasn't any form. It hasn't any title, either." He went into the next room, sat down at my desk and wrote on the pinkish face of the portfolio the word, "Ántonia." He frowned at this a moment, then prefixed another word, making it "My Ántonia." That seemed to satisfy him.

"Read it as soon as you can," he said, rising, "but don't let it influence your own story."

My own story was never written, but the following narrative is Jim's manuscript, substantially as he brought it to me.

Book I. The Shimerdas

I

I first heard of Ántonia[5] on what seemed to me an interminable journey across the great midland plain of North America. I was ten years old then; I had lost both my father and mother within a year, and my Virginia relatives were sending me out to my grandparents, who lived in Nebraska. I traveled in the care of a mountain boy, Jake Marpole, one of the "hands" on my father's old farm under the Blue Ridge, who was now going West to work for my grandfather. Jake's experience of the world was not much wider than mine. He had never been in a railway train until the morning when we set out together to try our fortunes in a new world.

We went all the way in day-coaches,[6] becoming more sticky and grimy with each stage of the journey. Jake bought everything the newsboys offered him: candy, oranges, brass collar buttons, a watch-charm, and for me a "Life of Jesse James,"[7] which I remember as one of the most satisfactory books I have ever read. Beyond Chicago we were under the protection of a friendly passenger conductor, who knew all about the country to which we were going and gave us a great deal of advice in exchange for our confidence. He seemed to us an experienced and worldly man who had been almost everywhere; in

5. "The Bohemian name *Ántonia* is strongly accented on the first syllable, like the English name *Anthony,* and the *i* is, of course, given the sound of long *e.* The name is pronounced An'-ton-ee-ah" [Cather's note].

6. Railroad passenger cars with no sleeping compartments.
7. Notorious American bandit (1847–1882) whose gang robbed banks and trains.

his conversation he threw out lightly the names of distant States and cities. He wore the rings and pins and badges of different fraternal orders to which he belonged. Even his cuff-buttons were engraved with hieroglyphics, and he was more inscribed than an Egyptian obelisk. Once when he sat down to chat, he told us that in the immigrant car ahead there was a family from "across the water" whose destination was the same as ours.

"They can't any of them speak English, except one little girl, and all she can say is 'We go Black Hawk, Nebraska.' She's not much older than you, twelve or thirteen, maybe, and she's as bright as a new dollar. Don't you want to go ahead and see her, Jimmy? She's got the pretty brown eyes, too!"

This last remark made me bashful, and I shook my head and settled down to "Jesse James." Jake nodded at me approvingly and said you were likely to get diseases from foreigners.

I do not remember crossing the Missouri River, or anything about the long day's journey through Nebraska. Probably by that time I had crossed so many rivers that I was dull to them. The only thing very noticeable about Nebraska was that it was still, all day long, Nebraska.

I had been sleeping, curled up in a red plush seat, for a long while when we reached Black Hawk. Jake roused me and took me by the hand. We stumbled down from the train to a wooden siding, where men were running about with lanterns. I couldn't see any town, or even distant lights; we were surrounded by utter darkness. The engine was panting heavily after its long run. In the red glow from the fire-box, a group of people stood huddled together on the platform, encumbered by bundles and boxes. I knew this must be the immigrant family the conductor had told us about. The woman wore a fringed shawl tied over her head, and she carried a little tin trunk in her arms, hugging it as if it were a baby. There was an old man, tall and stooped. Two half-grown boys and a girl stood holding oil-cloth bundles, and a little girl clung to her mother's skirts. Presently a man with a lantern approached them and began to talk, shouting and exclaiming. I pricked up my ears, for it was positively the first time I had ever heard a foreign tongue.

Another lantern came along. A bantering voice called out: "Hello, are you Mr. Burden's folks? If you are, it's me you're looking for. I'm Otto Fuchs. I'm Mr. Burden's hired man, and I'm to drive you out. Hello, Jimmy, ain't you scared to come so far west?"

I looked up with interest at the new face in the lantern light. He might have stepped out of the pages of "Jesse James." He wore a sombrero hat, with a wide leather band and a bright buckle, and the ends of his mustache were twisted up stiffly, like little horns. He looked lively and ferocious, I thought, and as if he had a history. A long scar ran across one cheek and drew the corner of his mouth up in a sinister curl. The top of his left ear was gone, and his skin was brown as an Indian's. Surely this was the face of a desperado. As he walked about the platform in his high-heeled boots, looking for our trunks, I saw that he was a rather slight man, quick and wiry, and light on his feet. He told us we had a long night drive ahead of us, and had better be on the hike. He led us to a hitching-bar where two farm wagons were tied, and I saw the foreign family crowding into one of them. The other was for us. Jake got on the front seat with Otto Fuchs, and I rode on the straw in the bottom of the wagon-box, covered up with a buffalo hide. The immigrants rumbled off into the empty darkness, and we followed them.

I tried to go to sleep, but the jolting made me bite my tongue, and I soon began to ache all over. When the straw settled down I had a hard bed. Cautiously I slipped from under the buffalo hide, got up on my knees and peered over the side of the wagon. There seemed to be nothing to see; no fences, no creeks or trees, no hills or fields. If there was a road, I could not make it out in the faint starlight. There was nothing but land: not a country at all, but the material out of which countries are made. No, there was nothing but land—slightly undulating, I knew, because often our wheels ground against the brake as we went down into a hollow and lurched up again on the other side. I had the feeling that the world was left behind, that we had got over the edge of it, and were outside man's jurisdiction. I had never before looked up at the sky when there was not a familiar mountain ridge against it. But this was the complete dome of heaven, all there was of it. I did not believe that my dead father and mother were watching me from up there; they would still be looking for me at the sheep-fold down by the creek, or along the white road that led to the mountain pastures. I had left even their spirits behind me. The wagon jolted on, carrying me I knew not whither. I don't think I was homesick. If we never arrived anywhere, it did not matter. Between that earth and that sky I felt erased, blotted out. I did not say my prayers that night: here, I felt, what would be would be.

II

I do not remember our arrival at my grandfather's farm sometime before daybreak, after a drive of nearly twenty miles with heavy work-horses. When I awoke, it was afternoon. I was lying in a little room, scarcely larger than the bed that held me, and the window-shade at my head was flapping softly in a warm wind. A tall woman, with wrinkled brown skin and black hair, stood looking down at me; I knew that she must be my grandmother. She had been crying, I could see, but when I opened my eyes she smiled, peered at me anxiously, and sat down on the foot of my bed.

"Had a good sleep, Jimmy?" she asked briskly. Then in a very different tone she said, as if to herself, "My, how you do look like your father!" I remembered that my father had been her little boy; she must often have come to wake him like this when he overslept. "Here are your clean clothes," she went on, stroking my coverlid with her brown hand as she talked. "But first you come down to the kitchen with me, and have a nice warm bath behind the stove. Bring your things; there's nobody about."

"Down to the kitchen" struck me as curious; it was always "out in the kitchen" at home.[8] I picked up my shoes and stockings and followed her through the living-room and down a flight of stairs into a basement. This basement was divided into a dining-room at the right of the stairs and a kitchen at the left. Both rooms were plastered and whitewashed—the plaster laid directly upon the earth walls, as it used to be in dugouts. The floor was of hard cement. Up under the wooden ceiling there were little half-windows with white curtains, and pots of geraniums and wandering Jew[9] in the deep sills. As I entered the kitchen I sniffed a pleasant smell of gingerbread baking. The stove was very large, with bright nickel trimmings, and behind it

---

8. Farm kitchens in the South typically were detached from the main house.

9. A type of showy, trailing plant.

there was a long wooden bench against the wall, and a tin washtub, into which grandmother poured hot and cold water. When she brought the soap and towels, I told her that I was used to taking my bath without help.

"Can you do your ears, Jimmy? Are you sure? Well, now, I call you a right smart little boy."

It was pleasant there in the kitchen. The sun shone into my bath-water through the west half-window, and a big Maltese cat came up and rubbed himself against the tub, watching me curiously. While I scrubbed, my grandmother busied herself in the dining-room until I called anxiously, "Grandmother, I'm afraid the cakes are burning!" Then she came laughing, waving her apron before her as if she were shooing chickens.

She was a spare, tall woman, a little stooped, and she was apt to carry her head thrust forward in an attitude of attention, as if she were looking at something, or listening to something, far away. As I grew older, I came to believe that it was only because she was so often thinking of things that were far away. She was quick-footed and energetic in all her movements. Her voice was high and rather shrill, and she often spoke with an anxious inflection, for she was exceedingly desirous that everything should go with due order and decorum. Her laugh, too, was high, and perhaps a little strident, but there was a lively intelligence in it. She was then fifty-five years old, a strong woman, of unusual endurance.

After I was dressed I explored the long cellar next to the kitchen. It was dug out under the wing of the house, was plastered and cemented, with a stairway and an outside door by which the men came and went. Under one of the windows there was a place for them to wash when they came in from work.

While my grandmother was busy about supper I settled myself on the wooden bench behind the stove and got acquainted with the cat—he caught not only rats and mice, but gophers, I was told. The patch of yellow sunlight on the floor traveled back toward the stairway, and grandmother and I talked about my journey, and about the arrival of the new Bohemian family; she said they were to be our nearest neighbors. We did not talk about the farm in Virginia, which had been her home for so many years. But after the men came in from the fields, and we were all seated at the supper-table, then she asked Jake about the old place and about our friends and neighbors there.

My grandfather said little. When he first came in he kissed me and spoke kindly to me, but he was not demonstrative. I felt at once his deliberateness and personal dignity, and was a little in awe of him. The thing one immediately noticed about him was his beautiful, crinkly, snow-white beard. I once heard a missionary say it was like the beard of an Arabian sheik. His bald crown only made it more impressive.

Grandfather's eyes were not at all like those of an old man; they were bright blue, and had a fresh, frosty sparkle. His teeth were white and regular—so sound that he had never been to a dentist in his life. He had a delicate skin, easily roughened by sun and wind. When he was a young man his hair and beard were red; his eyebrows were still coppery.

As we sat at the table Otto Fuchs and I kept stealing covert glances at each other. Grandmother had told me while she was getting supper that he was an Austrian who came to this country a young boy and had led an adventurous life in the Far West among mining-camps and cow outfits. His iron constitution was somewhat broken by mountain pneumonia, and he had drifted back to live in a milder country for a while. He had relatives in Bismarck, a German settlement to the north of us, but for a year now he had been working for grandfather.

The minute supper was over, Otto took me into the kitchen to whisper to me about a pony down in the barn that had been bought for me at a sale; he had been riding him to find out whether he had any bad tricks, but he was a "perfect gentleman," and his name was Dude. Fuchs told me everything I wanted to know: how he had lost his ear in a Wyoming blizzard when he was a stage-driver, and how to throw a lasso. He promised to rope a steer for me before sundown next day. He got out his "chaps" and silver spurs to show them to Jake and me, and his best cowboy boots, with tops stitched in bold design—roses, and true-lover's knots, and undraped female figures. These, he solemnly explained, were angels.

Before we went to bed Jake and Otto were called up to the living-room for prayers. Grandfather put on silver-rimmed spectacles and read several Psalms. His voice was so sympathetic and he read so interestingly that I wished he had chosen one of my favorite chapters in the Book of Kings. I was awed by his intonation of the word "Selah." *"He shall choose our inheritance for us, the excellency of Jacob whom He loved. Selah."*[1] I had no idea what the word meant; perhaps he had not. But, as he uttered it, it became oracular, the most sacred of words.

Early the next morning I ran out of doors to look about me. I had been told that ours was the only wooden house west of Black Hawk—until you came to the Norwegian settlement, where there were several. Our neighbors lived in sod houses and dugouts—comfortable, but not very roomy. Our white frame house, with a story and half-story above the basement, stood at the east end of what I might call the farmyard, with the windmill close by the kitchen door. From the windmill the ground sloped westward, down to the barns and granaries and pig-yards. This slope was trampled hard and bare, and washed out in winding gullies by the rain. Beyond the corncribs, at the bottom of the shallow draw,[2] was a muddy little pond, with rusty willow bushes growing about it. The road from the post-office came directly by our door, crossed the farmyard, and curved round this little pond, beyond which it began to climb the gentle swell of unbroken prairie to the west. There, along the western sky-line, it skirted a great cornfield, much larger than any field I had ever seen. This cornfield, and the sorghum patch behind the barn, were the only broken[3] land in sight. Everywhere, as far as the eye could reach, there was nothing but rough, shaggy, red grass, most of it as tall as I.

North of the house, inside the ploughed fire-breaks, grew a thick-set strip of box-elder trees, low and bushy, their leaves already turning yellow. This hedge was nearly a quarter of a mile long, but I had to look very hard to see it at all. The little trees were insignificant against the grass. It seemed as if the grass were about to run over them, and over the plum-patch behind the sod chicken-house.

As I looked about me I felt that the grass was the country, as the water is the sea. The red of the grass made all the great prairie the color of wine-

---

1. Psalm 47.4. The meaning of *Selah* is still unknown.
2. A gully that draws runoff water from rain and thaws.
3. I.e., plowed. Plowing land for the first time is extremely difficult work.

stains, or of certain seaweeds when they are first washed up. And there was so much motion in it; the whole country seemed, somehow, to be running.

I had almost forgotten that I had a grandmother, when she came out, her sunbonnet on her head, a grain-sack in her hand, and asked me if I did not want to go to the garden with her to dig potatoes for dinner. The garden, curiously enough, was a quarter of a mile from the house, and the way to it led up a shallow draw past the cattle corral. Grandmother called my attention to a stout hickory cane, tipped with copper, which hung by a leather thong from her belt. This, she said, was her rattlesnake cane. I must never go to the garden without a heavy stick or a corn-knife; she had killed a good many rattlers on her way back and forth. A little girl who lived on the Black Hawk road was bitten on the ankle and had been sick all summer.

I can remember exactly how the country looked to me as I walked beside my grandmother along the faint wagon-tracks on that early September morning. Perhaps the glide of long railway travel was still with me, for more than anything else I felt motion in the landscape; in the fresh, easy-blowing morning wind, and in the earth itself, as if the shaggy grass were a sort of loose hide, and underneath it herds of wild buffalo were galloping, galloping . . .

Alone, I should never have found the garden—except, perhaps, for the big yellow pumpkins that lay about unprotected by their withering vines—and I felt very little interest in it when I got there. I wanted to walk straight on through the red grass and over the edge of the world, which could not be very far away. The light air about me told me that the world ended here: only the ground and sun and sky were left, and if one went a little farther there would be only sun and sky, and one would float off into them, like the tawny hawks which sailed over our heads making slow shadows on the grass. While grandmother took the pitchfork we found standing in one of the rows and dug potatoes, while I picked them up out of the soft brown earth and put them into the bag, I kept looking up at the hawks that were doing what I might so easily do.

When grandmother was ready to go, I said I would like to stay up there in the garden awhile.

She peered down at me from under her sunbonnet. "Aren't you afraid of snakes?"

"A little," I admitted, "but I'd like to stay anyhow."

"Well, if you see one, don't have anything to do with him. The big yellow and brown ones won't hurt you; they're bull-snakes and help to keep the gophers down. Don't be scared if you see anything look out of that hole in the bank over there. That's a badger hole. He's about as big as a big 'possum, and his face is striped, black and white. He takes a chicken once in a while, but I won't let the men harm him. In a new country a body feels friendly to the animals. I like to have him come out and watch me when I'm at work."

Grandmother swung the bag of potatoes over her shoulder and went down the path, leaning forward a little. The road followed the windings of the draw; when she came to the first bend she waved at me and disappeared. I was left alone with this new feeling of lightness and content.

I sat down in the middle of the garden, where snakes could scarcely approach unseen, and leaned my back against a warm yellow pumpkin. There were some ground-cherry bushes growing along the furrows, full of fruit. I turned back the papery triangular sheaths that protected the berries and ate a few. All about me giant grasshoppers, twice as big as any I had ever seen, were doing acrobatic feats among the dried vines. The gophers scurried up and down the ploughed ground. There in the sheltered draw-bottom the wind did not blow very hard, but I could hear it singing its humming tune up on the level, and I could see the tall grasses wave. The earth was warm under me, and warm as I crumbled it through my fingers. Queer little red bugs came out and moved in slow squadrons around me. Their backs were polished vermilion, with black spots. I kept as still as I could. Nothing happened. I did not expect anything to happen. I was something that lay under the sun and felt it, like the pumpkins, and I did not want to be anything more. I was entirely happy. Perhaps we feel like that when we die and become a part of something entire, whether it is sun and air, or goodness and knowledge. At any rate, that is happiness; to be dissolved into something complete and great. When it comes to one, it comes as naturally as sleep.

III

On Sunday morning Otto Fuchs was to drive us over to make the acquaintance of our new Bohemian neighbors. We were taking them some provisions, as they had come to live on a wild place where there was no garden or chicken-house, and very little broken land. Fuchs brought up a sack of potatoes and a piece of cured pork from the cellar, and grandmother packed some loaves of Saturday's bread, a jar of butter, and several pumpkin pies in the straw of the wagon-box. We clambered up to the front seat and jolted off past the little pond and along the road that climbed to the big cornfield.

I could hardly wait to see what lay beyond that cornfield; but there was only red grass like ours, and nothing else, though from the high wagon-seat one could look off a long way. The road ran about like a wild thing, avoiding the deep draws, crossing them where they were wide and shallow. And all along it, wherever it looped or ran, the sunflowers grew; some of them were as big as little trees, with great rough leaves and many branches which bore dozens of blossoms. They made a gold ribbon across the prairie. Occasionally one of the horses would tear off with his teeth a plant full of blossoms, and walk along munching it, the flowers nodding in time to his bites as he ate down toward them.

The Bohemian family, grandmother told me as we drove along, had bought the homestead of a fellow-countryman, Peter Krajiek, and had paid him more than it was worth. Their agreement with him was made before they left the old country, through a cousin of his, who was also a relative of Mrs. Shimerda. The Shimerdas were the first Bohemian family to come to this part of the county. Krajiek was their only interpreter, and could tell them anything he chose. They could not speak enough English to ask for advice, or even to make their most pressing wants known. One son, Fuchs said, was well-grown, and strong enough to work the land; but the father was old and frail and knew nothing about farming. He was a weaver by trade; had been a skilled workman on tapestries and upholstery materials. He had brought his fiddle with him, which wouldn't be of much use here, though he used to pick up money by it at home.

"If they're nice people, I hate to think of them spending the winter in that cave of Krajiek's," said grandmother. "It's no better than a badger hole; no proper dugout at all. And I hear he's made them pay twenty dollars for his old cookstove that ain't worth ten."

"Yes'm," said Otto; "and he's sold 'em his oxen and his two bony old horses for the price of good work-teams. I'd have interfered about the horses—the old man can understand some German—if I'd 'a' thought it would do any good. But Bohemians has a natural distrust of Austrians."[4]

Grandmother looked interested. "Now, why is that, Otto?"

Fuchs wrinkled his brow and nose. "Well, ma'm, it's politics. It would take me a long while to explain."

The land was growing rougher; I was told that we were approaching Squaw Creek, which cut up the west half of the Shimerdas' place and made the land of little value for farming. Soon we could see the broken, grassy clay cliffs which indicated the windings of the stream, and the glittering tops of the cottonwoods and ash trees that grew down in the ravine. Some of the cottonwoods had already turned, and the yellow leaves and shining white bark made them look like the gold and silver trees in fairy tales.

As we approached the Shimerdas' dwelling, I could still see nothing but rough red hillocks, and draws with shelving banks and long roots hanging out where the earth had crumbled away. Presently, against one of those banks, I saw a sort of shed, thatched with the same wine-colored grass that grew everywhere. Near it tilted a shattered windmill-frame, that had no wheel. We drove up to this skeleton to tie our horses, and then I saw a door and window sunk deep in the draw-bank. The door stood open, and a woman and a girl of fourteen ran out and looked up at us hopefully. A little girl trailed along behind them. The woman had on her head the same embroidered shawl with silk fringes that she wore when she had alighted from the train at Black Hawk. She was not old, but she was certainly not young. Her face was alert and lively, with a sharp chin and shrewd little eyes. She shook grandmother's hand energetically.

"Very glad, very glad!" she ejaculated. Immediately she pointed to the bank out of which she had emerged and said, "House no good, house no good!"

Grandmother nodded consolingly. "You'll get fixed up comfortable after while, Mrs. Shimerda; make good house."

My grandmother always spoke in a very loud tone to foreigners, as if they were deaf. She made Mrs. Shimerda understand the friendly intention of our visit, and the Bohemian woman handled the loaves of bread and even smelled them, and examined the pies with lively curiosity, exclaiming, "Much good, much thank!"—and again she wrung grandmother's hand.

The oldest son, Ambrož,—they called it Ambrosch,—came out of the cave and stood beside his mother. He was nineteen years old, short and broad-backed, with a close-cropped, flat head, and a wide, flat face. His hazel eyes were little and shrewd, like his mother's, but more sly and suspicious; they fairly snapped at the food. The family had been living on corncakes and sorghum molasses for three days.

The little girl was pretty, but Án-tonia—they accented the name thus, strongly, when they spoke to her—was still prettier. I remembered what the conductor had said about her eyes. They were big and warm and full of light,

4. Bohemia shared a border with Austria and for centuries had been involved in warfare with that nation. At the time in which *My Ántonia* is set, Bohemia was a dominion of the Austro-Hungarian Empire ruled by the Hapsburg monarchy.

like the sun shining on brown pools in the wood. Her skin was brown, too, and in her cheeks she had a glow of rich, dark color. Her brown hair was curly and wild-looking. The little sister, whom they called Yulka (Julka), was fair, and seemed mild and obedient. While I stood awkwardly confronting the two girls, Krajiek came up from the barn to see what was going on. With him was another Shimerda son. Even from a distance one could see that there was something strange about this boy. As he approached us, he began to make uncouth noises, and held up his hands to show us his fingers, which were webbed to the first knuckle, like a duck's foot. When he saw me draw back, he began to crow delightedly, "Hoo, hoo-hoo, hoo-hoo!" like a rooster. His mother scowled and said sternly, "Marek!" then spoke rapidly to Krajiek in Bohemian.

"She wants me to tell you he won't hurt nobody, Mrs. Burden. He was born like that. The others are smart. Ambrosch, he make good farmer." He struck Ambrosch on the back, and the boy smiled knowingly.

At that moment the father came out of the hole in the bank. He wore no hat, and his thick, iron-gray hair was brushed straight back from his forehead. It was so long that it bushed out behind his ears, and made him look like the old portraits I remembered in Virginia. He was tall and slender, and his thin shoulders stooped. He looked at us understandingly, then took grandmother's hand and bent over it. I noticed how white and well-shaped his own hands were. They looked calm, somehow, and skilled. His eyes were melancholy, and were set back deep under his brow. His face was ruggedly formed, but it looked like ashes—like something from which all the warmth and light had died out. Everything about this old man was in keeping with his dignified manner. He was neatly dressed. Under his coat he wore a knitted gray vest, and, instead of a collar, a silk scarf of a dark bronze-green, carefully crossed and held together by a red coral pin. While Krajiek was translating for Mr. Shimerda, Ántonia came up to me and held out her hand coaxingly. In a moment we were running up the steep drawside together, Yulka trotting after us.

When we reached the level and could see the gold tree-tops, I pointed toward them, and Ántonia laughed and squeezed my hand as if to tell me how glad she was I had come. We raced off toward Squaw Creek and did not stop until the ground itself stopped—fell away before us so abruptly that the next step would have been out into the tree-tops. We stood panting on the edge of the ravine, looking down at the trees and bushes that grew below us. The wind was so strong that I had to hold my hat on, and the girls' skirts were blown out before them. Ántonia seemed to like it; she held her little sister by the hand and chattered away in that language which seemed to me spoken so much more rapidly than mine. She looked at me, her eyes fairly blazing with things she could not say.

"Name? What name?" she asked, touching me on the shoulder. I told her my name, and she repeated it after me and made Yulka say it. She pointed into the gold cottonwood tree behind whose top we stood and said again, "What name?"

We sat down and made a nest in the long red grass. Yulka curled up like a baby rabbit and played with a grasshopper. Ántonia pointed up to the sky and questioned me with her glance. I gave her the word, but she was not satisfied and pointed to my eyes. I told her, and she repeated the word, making it sound like "ice." She pointed up to the sky, then to my eyes, then back to the sky, with movements so quick and impulsive that she distracted me, and I had no idea what she wanted. She got up on her knees and wrung her hands. She pointed to her own eyes and shook her head, then to mine and to the sky, nodding violently.

"Oh," I exclaimed, "blue; blue sky."

She clapped her hands and murmured, "Blue sky, blue eyes," as if it amused her. While we snuggled down there out of the wind she learned a score of words. She was quick, and very eager. We were so deep in the grass that we could see nothing but the blue sky over us and the gold tree in front of us. It was wonderfully pleasant. After Ántonia had said the new words over and over, she wanted to give me a little chased[5] silver ring she wore on her middle finger. When she coaxed and insisted, I repulsed her quite sternly. I didn't want her ring, and I felt there was something reckless and extravagant about her wishing to give it away to a boy she had never seen before. No wonder Krajiek got the better of these people, if this was how they behaved.

While we were disputing about the ring, I heard a mournful voice calling, "Án-tonia, Án-tonia!" She sprang up like a hare. *"Tatinek,[6] Tatinek!"* she shouted, and we ran to meet the old man who was coming toward us. Ántonia reached him first, took his hand and kissed it. When I came up, he touched my shoulder and looked searchingly down into my face for several seconds. I became somewhat embarrassed, for I was used to being taken for granted by my elders.

We went with Mr. Shimerda back to the dugout, where grandmother was waiting for me. Before I got into the wagon, he took a book out of his pocket, opened it, and showed me a page with two alphabets, one English and the other Bohemian. He placed this book in my grandmother's hands, looked at her entreatingly, and said with an earnestness which I shall never forget, "Te-e-ach, te-e-ach my Án-tonia!"

IV

On the afternoon of that same Sunday I took my first long ride on my pony, under Otto's direction. After that Dude and I went twice a week to the post-office, six miles east of us, and I saved the men a good deal of time by riding on errands to our neighbors. When we had to borrow anything, or to send about word that there would be preaching at the sod schoolhouse, I was always the messenger. Formerly Fuchs attended to such things after working hours.

All the years that have passed have not dimmed my memory of that first glorious autumn. The new country lay open before me: there were no fences in those days, and I could choose my own way over the grass uplands, trusting the pony to get me home again. Sometimes I followed the sunflower-bordered roads. Fuchs told me that the sunflowers were introduced into that country by the Mormons; that at the time of the persecution, when they left Missouri and struck out into the wilderness to find a place where they could worship God in their own way, the members of the first exploring party, crossing the plains to Utah, scattered sunflower seed as they went. The next summer,

5. Embossed.
6. Father (Bohemian); affectionate term equivalent to *daddy*.

when the long trains of wagons came through with all the women and children, they had the sunflower trail to follow. I believe that botanists do not confirm Jake's story, but insist that the sunflower was native to those plains. Nevertheless, that legend has stuck in my mind, and sunflower-bordered roads always seem to me the roads to freedom.

I used to love to drift along the pale yellow cornfields, looking for the damp spots one sometimes found at their edges, where the smartweed soon turned a rich copper color and the narrow brown leaves hung curled like cocoons about the swollen joints of the stem. Sometimes I went south to visit our German neighbors and to admire their catalpa grove, or to see the big elm tree that grew up out of a deep crack in the earth and had a hawk's nest in its branches. Trees were so rare in that country, and they had to make such a hard fight to grow, that we used to feel anxious about them, and visit them as if they were persons. It must have been the scarcity of detail in that tawny landscape that made detail so precious.

Sometimes I rode north to the big prairie-dog town to watch the brown, earth-owls fly home in the late afternoon and go down to their nests underground with the dogs. Ántonia Shimerda liked to go with me, and we used to wonder a great deal about these birds of subterranean habit. We had to be on our guard there, for rattlesnakes were always lurking about. They came to pick up an easy living among the dogs and owls, which were quite defenseless against them; took possession of their comfortable houses and ate the eggs and puppies. We felt sorry for the owls. It was always mournful to see them come flying home at sunset and disappear under the earth. But, after all, we felt, winged things who would live like that must be rather degraded creatures. The dog-town was a long way from any pond or creek. Otto Fuchs said he had seen populous dog-towns in the desert where there was no surface water for fifty miles; he insisted that some of the holes must go down to water—nearly two hundred feet, hereabouts. Ántonia said she didn't believe it; that the dogs probably lapped up the dew in the early morning, like the rabbits.

Ántonia had opinions about everything, and she was soon able to make them known. Almost every day she came running across the prairie to have her reading lesson with me. Mrs. Shimerda grumbled, but realized it was important that one member of the family should learn English. When the lesson was over, we used to go up to the watermelon patch behind the garden. I split the melons with an old corn-knife, and we lifted out the hearts and ate them with the juice trickling through our fingers. The white Christmas melons we did not touch, but we watched them with curiosity. They were to be picked late, when the hard frosts had set in, and put away for winter use. After weeks on the ocean, the Shimerdas were famished for fruit. The two girls would wander for miles along the edge of the cornfields, hunting for ground-cherries.

Ántonia loved to help grandmother in the kitchen and to learn about cooking and house-keeping. She would stand beside her, watching her every movement. We were willing to believe that Mrs. Shimerda was a good housewife in her own country, but she managed poorly under new conditions: the conditions were bad enough, certainly!

I remember how horrified we were at the sour, ashy-gray bread she gave her family to eat. She mixed her dough, we discovered, in an old tin peckmeasure[7] that Krajiek had used about the barn. When she took the paste out to bake it, she left smears of dough sticking to the sides of the measure, put the measure on the shelf behind the stove, and let this residue ferment. The next time she made bread, she scraped this sour stuff down into the fresh dough to serve as yeast.

During those first months the Shimerdas never went to town. Krajiek encouraged them in the belief that in Black Hawk they would somehow be mysteriously separated from their money. They hated Krajiek, but they clung to him because he was the only human being with whom they could talk or from whom they could get information. He slept with the old man and the two boys in the dugout barn, along with the oxen. They kept him in their hole and fed him for the same reason that the prairie dogs and the brown owls housed the rattlesnakes—because they did not know how to get rid of him.

V

We knew that things were hard for our Bohemian neighbors, but the two girls were light-hearted and never complained. They were always ready to forget their troubles at home, and to run away with me over the prairie, scaring rabbits or starting up flocks of quail.

I remember Ántonia's excitement when she came into our kitchen one afternoon and announced: "My papa find friends up north, with Russian mans. Last night he take me for see, and I can understand very much talk. Nice mans, Mrs. Burden. One is fat and all the time laugh. Everybody laugh. The first time I see my papa laugh in this kawn-tree. Oh, very nice!"

I asked her if she meant the two Russians who lived up by the big dog-town. I had often been tempted to go to see them when I was riding in that direction, but one of them was a wild-looking fellow and I was a little afraid of him. Russia seemed to me more remote than any other country—farther away than China, almost as far as the North Pole. Of all the strange, uprooted people among the first settlers, those two men were the strangest and the most aloof. Their last names were unpronounceable, so they were called Pavel and Peter. They went about making signs to people, and until the Shimerdas came they had no friends. Krajiek could understand them a little, but he had cheated them in a trade, so they avoided him. Pavel, the tall one, was said to be an anarchist; since he had no means of imparting his opinions, probably his wild gesticulations and his generally excited and rebellious manner gave rise to this supposition. He must once have been a very strong man, but now his great frame, with big, knotty joints, had a wasted look, and the skin was drawn tight over his high cheek-bones. His breathing was hoarse, and he always had a cough.

Peter, his companion, was a very different sort of fellow; short, bow-legged, and as fat as butter. He always seemed pleased when he met people on the road, smiled and took off his cap to every one, men as well as women. At a distance, on his wagon, he looked like an old man; his hair and beard were of such a pale flaxen color that they seemed white in the sun. They were as thick and curly as carded wool. His rosy face, with its snub nose, set in this fleece,

7. Equal to two gallons. The implication is that the container is an unsuitable size for bread making. The sourdough bread of the Shimerda family is also seen as an inferior product.

was like a melon among its leaves. He was usually called "Curly Peter," or "Rooshian Peter."

The two Russians made good farmhands, and in summer they worked out together. I had heard our neighbors laughing when they told how Peter always had to go home at night to milk his cow. Other bachelor homesteaders used canned milk, to save trouble. Sometimes Peter came to church at the sod schoolhouse. It was there I first saw him, sitting on a low bench by the door, his plush cap in his hands, his bare feet tucked apologetically under the seat.

After Mr. Shimerda discovered the Russians, he went to see them almost every evening, and sometimes took Ántonia with him. She said they came from a part of Russia where the language was not very different from Bohemian, and if I wanted to go to their place, she could talk to them for me. One afternoon, before the heavy frosts began, we rode up there together on my pony.

The Russians had a neat log house built on a grassy slope, with a windlass well beside the door. As we rode up the draw we skirted a big melon patch, and a garden where squashes and yellow cucumbers lay about on the sod. We found Peter out behind his kitchen, bending over a washtub. He was working so hard that he did not hear us coming. His whole body moved up and down as he rubbed, and he was a funny sight from the rear, with his shaggy head and bandy legs. When he straightened himself up to greet us, drops of perspiration were rolling from his thick nose down on to his curly beard. Peter dried his hands and seemed glad to leave his washing. He took us down to see his chickens, and his cow that was grazing on the hillside. He told Ántonia that in his country only rich people had cows, but here any man could have one who would take care of her. The milk was good for Pavel, who was often sick, and he could make butter by beating sour cream with a wooden spoon. Peter was very fond of his cow. He patted her flanks and talked to her in Russian while he pulled up her lariat pin and set it in a new place.

After he had shown us his garden, Peter trundled a load of watermelons up the hill in his wheelbarrow. Pavel was not at home. He was off somewhere helping to dig a well. The house I thought very comfortable for two men who were "batching." Besides the kitchen, there was a living-room, with a wide double bed built against the wall, properly made up with blue gingham sheets and pillows. There was a little storeroom, too, with a window, where they kept guns and saddles and tools, and old coats and boots. That day the floor was covered with garden things, drying for winter; corn and beans and fat yellow cucumbers. There were no screens or window-blinds in the house, and all the doors and windows stood wide open, letting in flies and sunshine alike.

Peter put the melons in a row on the oil-cloth-covered table and stood over them, brandishing a butcher knife. Before the blade got fairly into them, they split of their own ripeness, with a delicious sound. He gave us knives, but no plates, and the top of the table was soon swimming with juice and seeds. I had never seen any one eat so many melons as Peter ate. He assured us that they were good for one—better than medicine; in his country people lived on them at this time of year. He was very hospitable and jolly. Once, while he was looking at Ántonia, he sighed and told us that if he had stayed at home in Russia perhaps by this time he would have had a pretty daughter of his own to cook and keep house for him. He said he had left his country because of a "great trouble."

When we got up to go, Peter looked about in perplexity for something that would entertain us. He ran into the storeroom and brought out a gaudily painted harmonica, sat down on a bench, and spreading his fat legs apart began to play like a whole band. The tunes were either very lively or very doleful, and he sang words to some of them.

Before we left, Peter put ripe cucumbers into a sack for Mrs. Shimerda and gave us a lard-pail full of milk to cook them in. I had never heard of cooking cucumbers, but Ántonia assured me they were very good. We had to walk the pony all the way home to keep from spilling the milk.

VI

One afternoon we were having our reading lesson on the warm, grassy bank where the badger lived. It was a day of amber sunlight, but there was a shiver of coming winter in the air. I had seen ice on the little horse-pond that morning, and as we went through the garden we found the tall asparagus, with its red berries, lying on the ground, a mass of slimy green.

Tony was barefooted, and she shivered in her cotton dress and was comfortable only when we were tucked down on the baked earth, in the full blaze of the sun. She could talk to me about almost anything by this time. That afternoon she was telling me how highly esteemed our friend the badger was in her part of the world, and how men kept a special kind of dog, with very short legs, to hunt him. Those dogs, she said, went down into the hole after the badger and killed him there in a terrific struggle underground; you could hear the barks and yelps outside. Then the dog dragged himself back, covered with bites and scratches, to be rewarded and petted by his master. She knew a dog who had a star on his collar for every badger he had killed.

The rabbits were unusually spry that afternoon. They kept starting up all about us, and dashing off down the draw as if they were playing a game of some kind. But the little buzzing things that lived in the grass were all dead—all but one. While we were lying there against the warm bank, a little insect of the palest, frailest green hopped painfully out of the buffalo grass and tried to leap into a bunch of bluestem. He missed it, fell back, and sat with his head sunk between his long legs, his antennæ quivering, as if he were waiting for something to come and finish him. Tony made a warm nest for him in her hands; talked to him gayly and indulgently in Bohemian. Presently he began to sing for us—a thin, rusty little chirp. She held him close to her ear and laughed, but a moment afterward I saw there were tears in her eyes. She told me that in her village at home there was an old beggar woman who went about selling herbs and roots she had dug up in the forest. If you took her in and gave her a warm place by the fire, she sang old songs to the children in a cracked voice, like this. Old Hata, she was called, and the children loved to see her coming and saved their cakes and sweets for her.

When the bank on the other side of the draw began to throw a narrow shelf of shadow, we knew we ought to be starting homeward; the chill came on quickly when the sun got low, and Ántonia's dress was thin. What were we to do with the frail little creature we had lured back to life by false pretenses? I offered my pockets, but Tony shook her head and carefully put the green insect in her hair, tying her big handkerchief down loosely over her curls. I said I would go with her until we could see Squaw Creek, and then turn and run home. We drifted along lazily, very happy, through the magical light of the late afternoon.

All those fall afternoons were the same, but I never got used to them. As far as we could see, the miles of copper-red grass were drenched in sunlight that was stronger and fiercer than at any other time of the day. The blond cornfields were red gold, the haystacks turned rosy and threw long shadows. The whole prairie was like the bush that burned with fire and was not consumed.[8] That hour always had the exultation of victory, of triumphant ending, like a hero's death—heroes who died young and gloriously. It was a sudden transfiguration, a lifting-up of day.

How many an afternoon Ántonia and I have trailed along the prairie under that magnificence! And always two long black shadows flitted before us or followed after, dark spots on the ruddy grass.

We had been silent a long time, and the edge of the sun sank nearer and nearer the prairie floor, when we saw a figure moving on the edge of the upland, a gun over his shoulder. He was walking slowly, dragging his feet along as if he had no purpose. We broke into a run to overtake him.

"My papa sick all the time," Tony panted as we flew. "He not look good, Jim."

As we neared Mr. Shimerda she shouted, and he lifted his head and peered about. Tony ran up to him, caught his hand and pressed it against her cheek. She was the only one of his family who could rouse the old man from the torpor in which he seemed to live. He took the bag from his belt and showed us three rabbits he had shot, looked at Ántonia with a wintry flicker of a smile and began to tell her something. She turned to me.

"My *tatinek* make me little hat with the skins, little hat for win-ter!" she exclaimed joyfully. "Meat for eat, skin for hat,"—she told off these benefits on her fingers.

Her father put his hand on her hair, but she caught his wrist and lifted it carefully away, talking to him rapidly. I heard the name of old Hata. He untied the handkerchief, separated her hair with his fingers, and stood looking down at the green insect. When it began to chirp faintly, he listened as if it were a beautiful sound.

I picked up the gun he had dropped; a queer piece from the old country, short and heavy, with a stag's head on the cock. When he saw me examining it, he turned to me with his faraway look that always made me feel as if I were down at the bottom of a well. He spoke kindly and gravely, and Ántonia translated:—

"My *tatinek* say when you are big boy, he give you his gun. Very fine, from Bohemie. It was belong to a great man, very rich, like what you not got here; many fields, many forests, many big house. My papa play for his wedding, and he give my papa fine gun, and my papa give you."

I was glad that this project was one of futurity. There never were such people as the Shimerdas for wanting to give away everything they had. Even the mother was always offering me things, though I knew she expected substantial presents in return. We stood there in friendly silence, while the feeble minstrel sheltered in Ántonia's hair went on with its scratchy chirp. The old

---

8. In Exodus 3.2, God's angel appeared to Moses in the middle of a bush that burned, but "was not consumed."

man's smile, as he listened, was so full of sadness, of pity for things, that I never afterward forgot it. As the sun sank there came a sudden coolness and the strong smell of earth and drying grass. Ántonia and her father went off hand in hand, and I buttoned up my jacket and raced my shadow home.

VII

Much as I liked Ántonia, I hated a superior tone that she sometimes took with me. She was four years older than I, to be sure, and had seen more of the world; but I was a boy and she was a girl, and I resented her protecting manner. Before the autumn was over she began to treat me more like an equal and to defer to me in other things than reading lessons. This change came about from an adventure we had together.

One day when I rode over to the Shimerdas' I found Ántonia starting off on foot for Russian Peter's house, to borrow a spade Ambrosch needed. I offered to take her on the pony, and she got up behind me. There had been another black frost the night before, and the air was clear and heady as wine. Within a week all the blooming roads had been despoiled—hundreds of miles of yellow sunflowers had been transformed into brown, rattling, burry stalks.

We found Russian Peter digging his potatoes. We were glad to go in and get warm by his kitchen stove and to see his squashes and Christmas melons, heaped in the store-room for winter. As we rode away with the spade, Ántonia suggested that we stop at the prairie-dog town and dig into one of the holes. We could find out whether they ran straight down, or were horizontal, like mole-holes; whether they had underground connections; whether the owls had nests down there, lined with feathers. We might get some puppies, or owl eggs, or snake-skins.

The dog-town was spread out over perhaps ten acres. The grass had been nibbled short and even, so this stretch was not shaggy and red like the surrounding country, but gray and velvety. The holes were several yards apart, and were disposed with a good deal of regularity, almost as if the town had been laid out in streets and avenues. One always felt that an orderly and very sociable kind of life was going on there. I picketed Dude down in a draw, and we went wandering about, looking for a hole that would be easy to dig. The dogs were out, as usual, dozens of them, sitting up on their hind legs over the doors of their houses. As we approached, they barked, shook their tails at us, and scurried underground. Before the mouths of the holes were little patches of sand and gravel, scratched up, we supposed, from a long way below the surface. Here and there, in the town, we came on larger gravel patches, several yards away from any hole. If the dogs had scratched the sand up in excavating, how had they carried it so far? It was on one of these gravel beds that I met my adventure.

We were examining a big hole with two entrances. The burrow sloped into the ground at a gentle angle, so that we could see where the two corridors united, and the floor was dusty from use, like a little highway over which much travel went. I was walking backward, in a crouching position, when I heard Ántonia scream. She was standing opposite me, pointing behind me and shouting something in Bohemian. I whirled round, and there, on one of those dry gravel beds, was the biggest snake I had ever seen. He was sunning himself, after the cold night, and he must have been asleep when Ántonia screamed. When I turned he was lying in long loose waves, like a letter "W."

He twitched and began to coil slowly. He was not merely a big snake, I thought—he was a circus monstrosity. His abominable muscularity, his loathsome, fluid motion, somehow made me sick. He was as thick as my leg, and looked as if millstones couldn't crush the disgusting vitality out of him. He lifted his hideous little head, and rattled. I didn't run because I didn't think of it—if my back had been against a stone wall I couldn't have felt more cornered. I saw his coils tighten—now he would spring, spring his length, I remembered. I ran up and drove at his head with my spade, struck him fairly across the neck, and in a minute he was all about my feet in wavy loops. I struck now from hate. Ántonia, barefooted as she was, ran up behind me. Even after I had pounded his ugly head flat, his body kept on coiling and winding, doubling and falling back on itself. I walked away and turned my back. I felt seasick. Ántonia came after me, crying, "O Jimmy, he not bite you? You sure? Why you not run when I say?"

"What did you jabber Bohunk[9] for? You might have told me there was a snake behind me!" I said petulantly.

"I know I am just awful, Jim, I was so scared." She took my handkerchief from my pocket and tried to wipe my face with it, but I snatched it away from her. I suppose I looked as sick as I felt.

"I never know you was so brave, Jim," she went on comfortingly. "You is just like big mans; you wait for him lift his head and then you go for him. Ain't you feel scared a bit? Now we take that snake home and show everybody. Nobody ain't seen in this kawn-tree so big snake like you kill."

She went on in this strain until I began to think that I had longed for this opportunity, and had hailed it with joy. Cautiously we went back to the snake; he was still groping with his tail, turning up his ugly belly in the light. A faint, fetid smell came from him, and a thread of green liquid oozed from his crushed head.

"Look, Tony, that's his poison," I said.

I took a long piece of string from my pocket, and she lifted his head with the spade while I tied a noose around it. We pulled him out straight and measured him by my riding-quirt;[1] he was about five and a half feet long. He had twelve rattles, but they were broken off before they began to taper, so I insisted that he must once have had twenty-four. I explained to Ántonia how this meant that he was twenty-four years old, that he must have been there when white men first came, left on from buffalo and Indian times. As I turned him over I began to feel proud of him, to have a kind of respect for his age and size. He seemed like the ancient, eldest Evil. Certainly his kind have left horrible unconscious memories in all warm-blooded life. When we dragged him down into the draw, Dude sprang off to the end of his tether and shivered all over—wouldn't let us come near him.

We decided that Ántonia should ride Dude home, and I would walk. As she rode along slowly, her bare legs swinging against the pony's sides, she kept shouting back to me about how astonished everybody would be. I followed with the spade over my shoulder, dragging my snake. Her exultation was contagious. The great land had never looked to me so big and free. If the red grass were full of rattlers, I was equal to them all. Nevertheless, I stole furtive

---

9. Bohemian (slang).　　　　　　　　　1. A whip with a short handle and rawhide lash.

glances behind me now and then to see that no avenging mate, older and bigger than my quarry, was racing up from the rear.

The sun had set when we reached our garden and went down the draw toward the house. Otto Fuchs was the first one we met. He was sitting on the edge of the cattle-pond, having a quiet pipe before supper. Ántonia called him to come quick and look. He did not say anything for a minute, but scratched his head and turned the snake over with his boot.

"Where did you run onto that beauty, Jim?"

"Up at the dog-town," I answered laconically.

"Kill him yourself? How come you to have a weepon?"

"We'd been up to Russian Peter's, to borrow a spade for Ambrosch."

Otto shook the ashes out of his pipe and squatted down to count the rattles. "It was just luck you had a tool," he said cautiously. "Gosh! I wouldn't want to do any business with that fellow myself, unless I had a fence-post along. Your grandmother's snake-cane wouldn't more than tickle him. He could stand right up and talk to you, he could. Did he fight hard?"

Ántonia broke in: "He fight something awful! He is all over Jimmy's boots. I scream for him to run, but he just hit and hit that snake like he was crazy."

Otto winked at me. After Ántonia rode on he said: "Got him in the head first crack, didn't you? That was just as well."

We hung him up to the windmill, and when I went down to the kitchen I found Ántonia standing in the middle of the floor, telling the story with a great deal of color.

Subsequent experiences with rattlesnakes taught me that my first encounter was fortunate in circumstance. My big rattler was old, and had led too easy a life; there was not much fight in him. He had probably lived there for years, with a fat prairie dog for breakfast whenever he felt like it, a sheltered home, even an owl-feather bed, perhaps, and he had forgot that the world doesn't owe rattlers a living. A snake of his size, in fighting trim, would be more than any boy could handle. So in reality it was a mock adventure; the game was fixed for me by chance, as it probably was for many a dragon-slayer. I had been adequately armed by Russian Peter; the snake was old and lazy; and I had Ántonia beside me, to appreciate and admire.

That snake hung on our corral fence for several days; some of the neighbors came to see it and agreed that it was the biggest rattler ever killed in those parts. This was enough for Ántonia. She liked me better from that time on, and she never took a supercilious air with me again. I had killed a big snake—I was now a big fellow.

VIII

While the autumn color was growing pale on the grass and cornfields, things went badly with our friends the Russians. Peter told his troubles to Mr. Shimerda: he was unable to meet a note which fell due on the first of November; had to pay an exorbitant bonus on renewing it, and to give a mortgage on his pigs and horses and even his milk cow. His creditor was Wick Cutter, the merciless Black Hawk money-lender, a man of evil name throughout the county, of whom I shall have more to say later. Peter could give no very clear account of his transactions with Cutter. He only knew that he had first borrowed two hundred dollars, then another hundred, then fifty—that each time a bonus was added to the principal, and the debt grew faster than any crop he planted. Now everything was plastered with mortgages.

Soon after Peter renewed his note, Pavel strained himself lifting timbers for a new barn, and fell over among the shavings with such a gush of blood from the lungs that his fellow-workmen thought he would die on the spot. They hauled him home and put him into his bed, and there he lay, very ill indeed. Misfortune seemed to settle like an evil bird on the roof of the log house, and to flap its wings there, warning human beings away. The Russians had such bad luck that people were afraid of them and liked to put them out of mind.

One afternoon Ántonia and her father came over to our house to get buttermilk, and lingered, as they usually did, until the sun was low. Just as they were leaving, Russian Peter drove up. Pavel was very bad, he said, and wanted to talk to Mr. Shimerda and his daughter; he had come to fetch them. When Ántonia and her father got into the wagon, I entreated grandmother to let me go with them: I would gladly go without my supper, I would sleep in the Shimerdas' barn and run home in the morning. My plan must have seemed very foolish to her, but she was often large-minded about humoring the desires of other people. She asked Peter to wait a moment, and when she came back from the kitchen she brought a bag of sandwiches and doughnuts for us.

Mr. Shimerda and Peter were on the front seat; Ántonia and I sat in the straw behind and ate our lunch as we bumped along. After the sun sank, a cold wind sprang up and moaned over the prairie. If this turn in the weather had come sooner, I should not have got away. We burrowed down in the straw and curled up close together, watching the angry red die out of the west and the stars begin to shine in the clear, windy sky. Peter kept sighing and groaning. Tony whispered to me that he was afraid Pavel would never get well. We lay still and did not talk. Up there the stars grew magnificently bright. Though we had come from such different parts of the world, in both of us there was some dusky superstition that those shining groups have their influence upon what is and what is not to be. Perhaps Russian Peter, come from farther away than any of us, had brought from his land, too, some such belief.

The little house on the hillside was so much the color of the night that we could not see it as we came up the draw. The ruddy windows guided us—the light from the kitchen stove, for there was no lamp burning.

We entered softly. The man in the wide bed seemed to be asleep. Tony and I sat down on the bench by the wall and leaned our arms on the table in front of us. The firelight flickered on the hewn logs that supported the thatch overhead. Pavel made a rasping sound when he breathed, and he kept moaning. We waited. The wind shook the doors and windows impatiently, then swept on again, singing through the big spaces. Each gust, as it bore down, rattled the panes, and swelled off like the others. They made me think of defeated armies, retreating; or of ghosts who were trying desperately to get in for shelter, and then went moaning on. Presently, in one of those sobbing intervals between the blasts, the coyotes tuned up with their whining howl; one, two, three, then all together—to tell us that winter was coming. This sound brought an answer from the bed,—a long complaining cry,—as if Pavel were having bad dreams or were waking to some old misery. Peter listened, but did not stir. He was sitting on the floor by the kitchen stove. The coyotes broke out again; yap, yap, yap—then the high whine. Pavel called for something and struggled up on his elbow.

"He is scared of the wolves," Ántonia whispered to me. "In his country there are very many, and they eat men and women." We slid closer together along the bench.

I could not take my eyes off the man in the bed. His shirt was hanging open, and his emaciated chest, covered with yellow bristle, rose and fell horribly. He began to cough. Peter shuffled to his feet, caught up the tea-kettle and mixed him some hot water and whiskey. The sharp smell of spirits[2] went through the room.

Pavel snatched the cup and drank, then made Peter give him the bottle and slipped it under his pillow, grinning disagreeably, as if he had outwitted some one. His eyes followed Peter about the room with a contemptuous, unfriendly expression. It seemed to me that he despised him for being so simple and docile.

Presently Pavel began to talk to Mr. Shimerda, scarcely above a whisper. He was telling a long story, and as he went on, Ántonia took my hand under the table and held it tight. She leaned forward and strained her ears to hear him. He grew more and more excited, and kept pointing all around his bed, as if there were things there and he wanted Mr. Shimerda to see them.

"It's wolves, Jimmy," Ántonia whispered. "It's awful, what he says!"

The sick man raged and shook his fist. He seemed to be cursing people who had wronged him. Mr. Shimerda caught him by the shoulders, but could hardly hold him in bed. At last he was shut off by a coughing fit which fairly choked him. He pulled a cloth from under his pillow and held it to his mouth. Quickly it was covered with bright red spots—I thought I had never seen any blood so bright. When he lay down and turned his face to the wall, all the rage had gone out of him. He lay patiently fighting for breath, like a child with croup. Ántonia's father uncovered one of his long bony legs and rubbed it rhythmically. From our bench we could see what a hollow case his body was. His spine and shoulder-blades stood out like the bones under the hide of a dead steer left in the fields. The sharp backbone must have hurt him when he lay on it.

Gradually, relief came to all of us. Whatever it was, the worst was over. Mr. Shimerda signed to us that Pavel was asleep. Without a word Peter got up and lit his lantern. He was going out to get his team to drive us home. Mr. Shimerda went with him. We sat and watched the long bowed back under the blue sheet, scarcely daring to breathe.

On the way home, when we were lying in the straw, under the jolting and rattling Ántonia told me as much of the story as she could. What she did not tell me then, she told later; we talked of nothing else for days afterward.

When Pavel and Peter were young men, living at home in Russia, they were asked to be groomsmen for a friend who was to marry the belle of another village. It was in the dead of winter and the groom's party went over to the wed-

2. Alcohol.

ding in sledges. Peter and Pavel drove in the groom's sledge, and six sledges followed with all his relatives and friends.

After the ceremony at the church, the party went to a dinner given by the parents of the bride. The dinner lasted all afternoon; then it became a supper and continued far into the night. There was much dancing and drinking. At midnight the parents of the bride said good-bye to her and blessed her. The groom took her up in his arms and carried her out to his sledge and tucked her under the blankets. He sprang in beside her, and Pavel and Peter (our Pavel and Peter!) took the front seat. Pavel drove. The party set out with singing and the jingle of sleigh-bells, the groom's sledge going first. All the drivers were more or less the worse for merry-making, and the groom was absorbed in his bride.

The wolves were bad that winter, and every one knew it, yet when they heard the first wolf-cry, the drivers were not much alarmed. They had too much good food and drink inside them. The first howls were taken up and echoed and with quickening repetitions. The wolves were coming together. There was no moon, but the starlight was clear on the snow. A black drove came up over the hill behind the wedding party. The wolves ran like streaks of shadow; they looked no bigger than dogs, but there were hundreds of them.

Something happened to the hindmost sledge: the driver lost control,—he was probably very drunk,—the horses left the road, the sledge was caught in a clump of trees, and overturned. The occupants rolled out over the snow, and the fleetest of the wolves sprang upon them. The shrieks that followed made everybody sober. The drivers stood up and lashed their horses. The groom had the best team and his sledge was lightest—all the others carried from six to a dozen people.

Another driver lost control. The screams of the horses were more terrible to hear than the cries of the men and women. Nothing seemed to check the wolves. It was hard to tell what was happening in the rear; the people who were falling behind shrieked as piteously as those who were already lost. The little bride hid her face on the groom's shoulder and sobbed. Pavel sat still and watched his horses. The road was clear and white, and the groom's three blacks went like the wind. It was only necessary to be calm and to guide them carefully.

At length, as they breasted a long hill, Peter rose cautiously and looked back. "There are only three sledges left," he whispered.

"And the wolves?" Pavel asked.

"Enough! Enough for all of us."

Pavel reached the brow of the hill, but only two sledges followed him down the other side. In that moment on the hilltop, they saw behind them a whirling black group on the snow. Presently the groom screamed. He saw his father's sledge overturned, with his mother and sisters. He sprang up as if he meant to jump, but the girl shrieked and held him back. It was even then too late. The black ground-shadows were already crowding over the heap in the road, and one horse ran out across the fields, his harness hanging to him, wolves at his heels. But the groom's movement had given Pavel an idea.

They were within a few miles of their village now. The only sledge left out of six was not very far behind them, and Pavel's middle horse was failing. Beside a frozen pond something happened to the other sledge; Peter saw it plainly. Three big wolves got abreast of the horses, and the horses went crazy. They tried to jump over each other, got tangled up in the harness, and over-turned the sledge.

When the shrieking behind them died away, Pavel realized that he was alone upon the familiar road. "They still come?" he asked Peter.

"Yes."

"How many?"

"Twenty, thirty—enough."

Now his middle horse was being almost dragged by the other two. Pavel gave Peter the reins and stepped carefully into the back of the sledge. He called to the groom that they must lighten—and pointed to the bride. The young man cursed him and held her tighter. Pavel tried to drag her away. In the struggle, the groom rose. Pavel knocked him over the side of the sledge and threw the girl after him. He said he never remembered exactly how he did it, or what happened afterward. Peter, crouching in the front seat, saw nothing. The first thing either of them noticed was a new sound that broke into the clear air, louder than they had ever heard before—the bell of the monastery of their own village, ringing for early prayers.

Pavel and Peter drove into the village alone, and they had been alone ever since. They were run out of their village. Pavel's own mother would not look at him. They went away to strange towns, but when people learned where they came from, they were always asked if they knew the two men who had fed the bride to the wolves. Wherever they went, the story followed them. It took them five years to save money enough to come to America. They worked in Chicago, Des Moines, Fort Wayne, but they were always unfortunate. When Pavel's health grew so bad, they decided to try farming.

Pavel died a few days after he unburdened his mind to Mr. Shimerda, and was buried in the Norwegian graveyard. Peter sold off everything, and left the country—went to be cook in a railway construction camp where gangs of Russians were employed.

At his sale we bought Peter's wheelbarrow and some of his harness. During the auction he went about with his head down, and never lifted his eyes. He seemed not to care about anything. The Black Hawk money-lender who held mortgages on Peter's live-stock was there, and he bought in the sale notes at about fifty cents on the dollar. Every one said Peter kissed the cow before she was led away by her new owner. I did not see him do it, but this I know: after all his furniture and his cook-stove and pots and pans had been hauled off by the purchasers, when his house was stripped and bare, he sat down on the floor with his clasp-knife and ate all the melons that he had put away for winter. When Mr. Shimerda and Krajiek drove up in their wagon to take Peter to the train, they found him with a dripping beard, surrounded by heaps of melon rinds.

The loss of his two friends had a depressing effect upon old Mr. Shimerda. When he was out hunting, he used to go into the empty log house and sit there, brooding. This cabin was his hermitage until the winter snows penned him in his cave. For Ántonia and me, the story of the wedding party was never at an end. We did not tell Pavel's secret to any one, but guarded it jealously— as if the wolves of the Ukraine had gathered that night long ago, and the wedding party been sacrificed, to give us a painful and peculiar pleasure. At night, before I went to sleep, I often found myself in a sledge drawn by three horses, dashing through a country that looked something like Nebraska and something like Virginia.

IX

The first snowfall came early in December. I remember how the world looked from our sitting-room window as I dressed behind the stove that morning: the low sky was like a sheet of metal; the blond cornfields had faded out into ghostliness at last; the little pond was frozen under its stiff willow bushes. Big white flakes were whirling over everything and disappearing in the red grass.

Beyond the pond, on the slope that climbed to the cornfield, there was, faintly marked in the grass, a great circle where the Indians used to ride. Jake and Otto were sure that when they galloped round that ring the Indians tortured prisoners, bound to a stake in the center; but grandfather thought they merely ran races or trained horses there. Whenever one looked at this slope against the setting sun, the circle showed like a pattern in the grass; and this morning, when the first light spray of snow lay over it, it came out with wonderful distinctness, like strokes of Chinese white on canvas. The old figure stirred me as it had never done before and seemed a good omen for the winter.

As soon as the snow had packed hard I began to drive about the country in a clumsy sleigh that Otto Fuchs made for me by fastening a wooden goods-box on bobs.[3] Fuchs had been apprenticed to a cabinet-maker in the old country and was very handy with tools. He would have done a better job if I hadn't hurried him. My first trip was to the post-office, and the next day I went over to take Yulka and Ántonia for a sleigh-ride.

It was a bright, cold day. I piled straw and buffalo robes into the box, and took two hot bricks wrapped in old blankets. When I got to the Shimerdas' I did not go up to the house, but sat in my sleigh at the bottom of the draw and called. Ántonia and Yulka came running out, wearing little rabbit-skin hats their father had made for them. They had heard about my sledge from Ambrosch and knew why I had come. They tumbled in beside me and we set off toward the north, along a road that happened to be broken.

The sky was brilliantly blue, and the sunlight on the glittering white stretches of prairie was almost blinding. As Ántonia said, the whole world was changed by the snow; we kept looking in vain for familiar landmarks. The deep arroyo[4] through which Squaw Creek wound was now only a cleft between snowdrifts—very blue when one looked down into it. The tree-tops that had been gold all the autumn were dwarfed and twisted, as if they would never have any life in them again. The few little cedars, which were so dull and dingy before, now stood out a strong, dusky green. The wind had the burning taste of fresh snow; my throat and nostrils smarted as if some one had opened a hartshorn[5] bottle. The cold stung, and at the same time delighted one. My horse's breath rose like steam, and whenever we stopped he smoked all over. The cornfields got back a little of their color under the dazzling light, and stood the palest possible gold in the sun and snow. All

3. Short runners. The sleigh probably had two pairs, one front and one back.
4. A water-carved gully (Spanish).

5. Ammonia preparation used as a stimulant via nasal inhalation.

about us the snow was crusted in shallow terraces, with tracings like ripple-marks at the edges, curly waves that were the actual impression of the sting-ing lash in the wind.

The girls had on cotton dresses under their shawls; they kept shivering beneath the buffalo robes and hugging each other for warmth. But they were so glad to get away from their ugly cave and their mother's scolding that they begged me to go on and on, as far as Russian Peter's house. The great fresh open, after the stupefying warmth indoors, made them behave like wild things. They laughed and shouted, and said they never wanted to go home again. Couldn't we settle down and live in Russian Peter's house, Yulka asked, and couldn't I go to town and buy things for us to keep house with?

All the way to Russian Peter's we were extravagantly happy, but when we turned back,—it must have been about four o'clock,—the east wind grew stronger and began to howl; the sun lost its heartening power and the sky became gray and somber. I took off my long woolen comforter and wound it around Yulka's throat. She got so cold that we made her hide her head under the buffalo robe. Ántonia and I sat erect, but I held the reins clumsily, and my eyes were blinded by the wind a good deal of the time. It was growing dark when we got to their house, but I refused to go in with them and get warm. I knew my hands would ache terribly if I went near a fire. Yulka forgot to give me back my comforter, and I had to drive home directly against the wind. The next day I came down with an attack of quinsy,[6] which kept me in the house for nearly two weeks.

The basement kitchen seemed heavenly safe and warm in those days—like a tight little boat in a winter sea. The men were out in the fields all day, husk-ing corn, and when they came in at noon, with long caps pulled down over their ears and their feet in red-lined over-shoes, I used to think they were like Arctic explorers.

In the afternoons, when grandmother sat upstairs darning, or making husking-gloves, I read "The Swiss Family Robinson"[7] aloud to her, and I felt that the Swiss family had no advantages over us in the way of an adventur-ous life. I was convinced that man's strongest antagonist is the cold. I admired the cheerful zest with which grandmother went about keeping us warm and comfortable and well-fed. She often reminded me, when she was preparing for the return of the hungry men, that this country was not like Vir-ginia; and that here a cook had, as she said, "very little to do with."[8] On Sun-days she gave us as much chicken as we could eat, and on other days we had ham or bacon or sausage meat. She baked either pies or cake for us every day, unless, for a change, she made my favorite pudding, striped with currants and boiled in a bag.

Next to getting warm and keeping warm, dinner and supper were the most interesting things we had to think about. Our lives centered around warmth and food and the return of the men at nightfall. I used to wonder, when they came in tired from the fields, their feet numb and their hands cracked and sore, how they could do all the chores so conscientiously: feed and water and bed the horses, milk the cows, and look after the pigs. When supper was over,

6. Severe sore throat.
7. Popular children's novel (1813), by Swiss writer Johann Rudolph Wyss (1787–1813), showing how a family wrecked on a desert island manages to survive.
8. I.e., the range of foodstuffs available on the prairie is extremely limited.

it took them a long while to get the cold out of their bones. While grand-mother and I washed the dishes and grandfather read his paper upstairs, Jake and Otto sat on the long bench behind the stove, "easing"[9] their inside boots, or rubbing mutton tallow into their cracked hands.

Every Saturday night we popped corn or made taffy, and Otto Fuchs used to sing, "For I Am a Cowboy and Know I've Done Wrong," or, "Bury Me Not on the Lone Prairee." He had a good baritone voice and always led the singing when we went to church services at the sod schoolhouse.

I can still see those two men sitting on the bench; Otto's close-clipped head and Jake's shaggy hair slicked flat in front by a wet comb. I can see the sag of their tired shoulders against the whitewashed wall. What good fellows they were, how much they knew, and how many things they had kept faith with!

Fuchs had been a cowboy, a stage-driver, a bar-tender, a miner; had wan-dered all over that great Western country and done hard work everywhere, though, as grandmother said, he had nothing to show for it. Jake was duller than Otto. He could scarcely read, wrote even his name with difficulty, and he had a violent temper which sometimes made him behave like a crazy man—tore him all to pieces and actually made him ill. But he was so soft-hearted that any one could impose upon him. If he, as he said, "forgot him-self" and swore before grandmother, he went about depressed and shamefaced all day. They were both of them jovial about the cold in winter and the heat in summer, always ready to work overtime and to meet emer-gencies. It was a matter of pride with them not to spare themselves. Yet they were the sort of men who never get on, somehow, or do anything but work hard for a dollar or two a day.

On those bitter, starlit nights, as we sat around the old stove that fed us and warmed us and kept us cheerful, we could hear the coyotes howling down by the corrals, and their hungry, wintry cry used to remind the boys of wonder-ful animal stories; about gray wolves and bears in the Rockies, wildcats and panthers in the Virginia mountains. Sometimes Fuchs could be persuaded to talk about the outlaws and desperate characters he had known. I remember one funny story about himself that made grandmother, who was working her bread on the bread-board, laugh until she wiped her eyes with her bare arm, her hands being floury. It was like this:—

When Otto left Austria to come to America, he was asked by one of his rel-atives to look after a woman who was crossing on the same boat, to join her husband in Chicago. The woman started off with two children, but it was clear that her family might grow larger on the journey. Fuchs said he "got on fine with the kids," and liked the mother, though she played a sorry trick on him. In mid-ocean she proceeded to have not one baby, but three! This event made Fuchs the object of undeserved notoriety, since he was traveling with her. The steerage stewardess was indignant with him, the doctor regarded him with suspicion. The first-cabin passengers, who made up a purse for the woman, took an embarrassing interest in Otto, and often inquired of him about his charge. When the triplets were taken ashore at New York, he had, as he said, "to carry some of them." The trip to Chicago was even worse than the ocean voyage. On the train it was very difficult to get milk for the babies and to keep their bottles clean. The mother did her best, but no woman, out

9. Manipulating the inside of the boot to soften it.

of her natural resources, could feed three babies. The husband, in Chicago, was working in a furniture factory for modest wages, and when he met his family at the station he was rather crushed by the size of it. He, too, seemed to consider Fuchs in some fashion to blame. "I was sure glad," Otto concluded, "that he didn't take his hard feeling out on that poor woman; but he had a sullen eye for me, all right! Now, did you ever hear of a young feller's having such hard luck, Mrs. Burden?"

Grandmother told him she was sure the Lord had remembered these things to his credit, and had helped him out of many a scrape when he didn't realize that he was being protected by Providence.

X

For several weeks after my sleigh-ride, we heard nothing from the Shimerdas. My sore throat kept me indoors, and grandmother had a cold which made the housework heavy for her. When Sunday came she was glad to have a day of rest. One night at supper Fuchs told us he had seen Mr. Shimerda out hunting.

"He's made himself a rabbit-skin cap, Jim, and a rabbit-skin collar that he buttons on outside his coat. They ain't got but one overcoat among 'em over there, and they take turns wearing it. They seem awful scared of cold, and stick in that hole in the bank like badgers."

"All but the crazy boy," Jake put in. "He never wears the coat. Krajiek says he's turrible strong and can stand anything. I guess rabbits must be getting scarce in this locality. Ambrosch come along by the cornfield yesterday where I was at work and showed me three prairie dogs he'd shot. He asked me if they was good to eat. I spit and made a face and took on, to scare him, but he just looked like he was smarter'n me and put 'em back in his sack and walked off."

Grandmother looked up in alarm and spoke to grandfather. "Josiah, you don't suppose Krajiek would let them poor creatures eat prairie dogs, do you?"

"You had better go over and see our neighbors to-morrow, Emmaline," he replied gravely.

Fuchs put in a cheerful word and said prairie dogs were clean beasts and ought to be good for food, but their family connections were against them. I asked what he meant, and he grinned and said they belonged to the rat family.

When I went downstairs in the morning, I found grandmother and Jake packing a hamper basket in the kitchen.

"Now, Jake," grandmother was saying, "if you can find that old rooster that got his comb froze, just give his neck a twist, and we'll take him along. There's no good reason why Mrs. Shimerda couldn't have got hens from her neighbors last fall and had a henhouse going by now. I reckon she was confused and didn't know where to begin. I've come strange to a new country myself, but I never forgot hens are a good thing to have, no matter what you don't have."

"Just as you say, mam," said Jake, "but I hate to think of Krajiek getting a leg of that old rooster." He tramped out through the long cellar and dropped the heavy door behind him.

After breakfast grandmother and Jake and I bundled ourselves up and climbed into the cold front wagon-seat. As we approached the Shimerdas' we heard the frosty whine of the pump and saw Ántonia, her head tied up and her cotton dress blown about her, throwing all her weight on the pump-handle as it went up and down. She heard our wagon, looked back over her shoulder, and catching up her pail of water, started at a run for the hole in the bank.

Jake helped grandmother to the ground, saying he would bring the provisions after he had blanketed his horses. We went slowly up the icy path toward the door sunk in the drawside. Blue puffs of smoke came from the stovepipe that stuck out through the grass and snow, but the wind whisked them roughly away.

Mrs. Shimerda opened the door before we knocked and seized grandmother's hand. She did not say "How do!" as usual, but at once began to cry, talking very fast in her own language, pointing to her feet which were tied up in rags, and looking about accusingly at every one.

The old man was sitting on a stump behind the stove, crouching over as if he were trying to hide from us. Yulka was on the floor at his feet, her kitten in her lap. She peeped out at me and smiled, but, glancing up at her mother, hid again. Ántonia was washing pans and dishes in a dark corner. The crazy boy lay under the only window, stretched on a gunnysack[1] stuffed with straw. As soon as we entered he threw a grainsack over the crack at the bottom of the door. The air in the cave was stifling, and it was very dark, too. A lighted lantern, hung over the stove, threw out a feeble yellow glimmer.

Mrs. Shimerda snatched off the covers of two barrels behind the door, and made us look into them. In one there were some potatoes that had been frozen and were rotting, in the other was a little pile of flour. Grandmother murmured something in embarrassment, but the Bohemian woman laughed scornfully, a kind of whinny-laugh, and catching up an empty coffee-pot from the shelf, shook it at us with a look positively vindictive.

Grandmother went on talking in her polite Virginia way, not admitting their stark need or her own remissness, until Jake arrived with the hamper, as if in direct answer to Mrs. Shimerda's reproaches. Then the poor woman broke down. She dropped on the floor beside her crazy son, hid her face on her knees, and sat crying bitterly. Grandmother paid no heed to her, but called Ántonia to come and help empty the basket. Tony left her corner reluctantly. I had never seen her crushed like this before.

"You not mind my poor *mamenka*, Mrs. Burden. She is so sad," she whispered, as she wiped her wet hands on her skirt and took the things grandmother handed her.

The crazy boy, seeing the food, began to make soft, gurgling noises and stroked his stomach. Jake came in again, this time with a sack of potatoes. Grandmother looked about in perplexity.

"Haven't you got any sort of cave or cellar outside, Ántonia? This is no place to keep vegetables. How did your potatoes get frozen?"

"We get from Mr. Bushy, at the post-office,—what he throw out. We got no potatoes, Mrs. Burden," Tony admitted mournfully.

When Jake went out, Marek crawled along the floor and stuffed up the door-crack again. Then, quietly as a shadow, Mr. Shimerda came out from behind the stove. He stood brushing his hand over his smooth gray hair, as if

1. Large sack made from gunny, a coarse heavy fabric.

he were trying to clear away a fog about his head. He was clean and neat as usual, with his green neckcloth and his coral pin. He took grandmother's arm and led her behind the stove, to the back of the room. In the rear wall was another little cave; a round hole, not much bigger than an oil barrel, scooped out in the black earth. When I got up on one of the stools and peered into it, I saw some quilts and a pile of straw. The old man held the lantern. "Yulka," he said in a low, despairing voice, "Yulka; my Ántonia!"

Grandmother drew back. "You mean they sleep in there,—your girls?" He bowed his head.

Tony slipped under his arm. "It is very cold on the floor, and this is warm like the badger hole. I like for sleep there," she insisted eagerly. "My *mamenka* have nice bed, with pillows from our own geese in Bohemie. See, Jim?" She pointed to the narrow bunk which Krajiek had built against the wall for himself before the Shimerdas came.

Grandmother sighed. "Sure enough, where *would* you sleep, dear! I don't doubt you're warm there. You'll have a better house after while, Ántonia, and then you'll forget these hard times."

Mr. Shimerda made grandmother sit down on the only chair and pointed his wife to a stool beside her. Standing before them with his hand on Ántonia's shoulder, he talked in a low tone, and his daughter translated. He wanted us to know that they were not beggars in the old country; he made good wages, and his family were respected there. He left Bohemia with more than a thousand dollars in savings, after their passage money was paid. He had in some way lost on exchange in New York, and the railway fare to Nebraska was more than they had expected. By the time they paid Krajiek for the land, and bought his horses and oxen and some old farm machinery, they had very little money left. He wished grandmother to know, however, that he still had some money. If they could get through until spring came, they would buy a cow and chickens and plant a garden, and would then do very well. Ambrosch and Ántonia were both old enough to work in the fields, and they were willing to work. But the snow and the bitter weather had disheartened them all.

Ántonia explained that her father meant to build a new house for them in the spring; he and Ambrosch had already split the logs for it, but the logs were all buried in the snow, along the creek where they had been felled.

While grandmother encouraged and gave them advice, I sat down on the floor with Yulka and let her show me her kitten. Marek slid cautiously toward us and began to exhibit his webbed fingers. I knew he wanted to make his queer noises for me—to bark like a dog or whinny like a horse,—but he did not dare in the presence of his elders. Marek was always trying to be agreeable, poor fellow, as if he had it on his mind that he must make up for his deficiencies.

Mrs. Shimerda grew more calm and reasonable before our visit was over, and, while Ántonia translated, put in a word now and then on her own account. The woman had a quick ear, and caught up phrases whenever she heard English spoken. As we rose to go, she opened her wooden chest and brought out a bag made of bed-ticking, about as long as a flour sack and half as wide, stuffed full of something. At sight of it, the crazy boy began to smack his lips. When Mrs. Shimerda opened the bag and stirred the contents with her hand, it gave out a salty, earthy smell, very pungent, even among the other odors of that cave. She measured a teacup full, tied it up in a bit of sacking, and presented it ceremoniously to grandmother.

"For cook," she announced. "Little now; be very much when cook," spreading out her hands as if to indicate that the pint would swell to a gallon. "Very good. You no have in this country. All things for eat better in my country."

"Maybe so, Mrs. Shimerda," grandmother said drily. "I can't say but I prefer our bread to yours, myself."

Ántonia undertook to explain. "This very good, Mrs. Burden,"—she clasped her hands as if she could not express how good,—"it make very much when you cook, like what my mama say. Cook with rabbit, cook with chicken, in the gravy,—oh, so good!"

All the way home grandmother and Jake talked about how easily good Christian people could forget they were their brothers' keepers.

"I will say, Jake, some of our brothers and sisters are hard to keep: Where's a body to begin, with these people? They're wanting in everything, and most of all in horse-sense. Nobody can give 'em that, I guess. Jimmy, here, is about as able to take over a homestead as they are. Do you reckon that boy Ambrosch has any real push in him?"

"He's a worker, all right, mam, and he's got some ketch-on[2] about him; but he's a mean one. Folks can be mean enough to get on in this world; and then, ag'in, they can be too mean."

That night, while grandmother was getting supper, we opened the package Mrs. Shimerda had given her. It was full of little brown chips that looked like the shavings of some root. They were as light as feathers, and the most noticeable thing about them was their penetrating, earthy odor. We could not determine whether they were animal or vegetable.

"They might be dried meat from some queer beast, Jim. They ain't dried fish, and they never grew on stalk or vine. I'm afraid of 'em. Anyhow, I shouldn't want to eat anything that had been shut up for months with old clothes and goose pillows."

She threw the package into the stove, but I bit off a corner of one of the chips I held in my hand, and chewed it tentatively. I never forgot the strange taste; though it was many years before I knew that those little brown shavings, which the Shimerdas had brought so far and treasured so jealously, were dried mushrooms. They had been gathered, probably, in some deep Bohemian forest . . . .

XI

During the week before Christmas, Jake was the most important person of our household, for he was to go to town and do all our Christmas shopping. But on the 21st of December, the snow began to fall. The flakes came down so thickly that from the sitting-room windows I could not see beyond the windmill—its frame looked dim and gray, unsubstantial like a shadow. The snow did not stop falling all day, or during the night that followed. The cold was not severe, but the storm was quiet and resistless. The men could not go farther than the barns and corral. They sat about the house most of the day

2. Alertness (slang); literally, the ability to catch on.

as if it were Sunday; greasing their boots, mending their suspenders, plaiting whiplashes.

On the morning of the 22d, grandfather announced at breakfast that it would be impossible to go to Black Hawk for Christmas purchases. Jake was sure he could get through on horseback, and bring home our things in saddle-bags; but grandfather told him the roads would be obliterated, and a new-comer in the country would be lost ten times over. Anyway, he would never allow one of his horses to be put to such a strain.

We decided to have a country Christmas, without any help from town. I had wanted to get some picture-books for Yulka and Ántonia; even Yulka was able to read a little now. Grandmother took me into the ice-cold storeroom, where she had some bolts of gingham and sheeting. She cut squares of cotton cloth and we sewed them together into a book. We bound it between pasteboards, which I covered with brilliant calico, representing scenes from a circus. For two days I sat at the dining-room table, pasting this book full of pictures for Yulka. We had files of those good old family magazines which used to publish colored lithographs of popular paintings, and I was allowed to use some of these. I took "Napoleon Announcing the Divorce to Josephine"[3] for my frontispiece. On the white pages I grouped Sunday-School cards and advertising cards which I had brought from my "old country." Fuchs got out the old candle-moulds and made tallow candles. Grandmother hunted up her fancy cake-cutters and baked gingerbread men and roosters, which we decorated with burnt sugar and red cinnamon drops.

On the day before Christmas, Jake packed the things we were sending to the Shimerdas in his saddle-bags and set off on grandfather's gray gelding. When he mounted his horse at the door, I saw that he had a hatchet slung to his belt, and he gave grandmother a meaning look which told me he was planning a surprise for me. That afternoon I watched long and eagerly from the sitting-room window. At last I saw a dark spot moving on the west hill, beside the half-buried cornfield, where the sky was taking on a coppery flush from the sun that did not quite break through. I put on my cap and ran out to meet Jake. When I got to the pond I could see that he was bringing in a little cedar tree across his pommel. He used to help my father cut Christmas trees for me in Virginia, and he had not forgotten how much I liked them.

By the time we had placed the cold, fresh-smelling little tree in a corner of the sitting-room, it was already Christmas Eve. After supper we all gathered there, and even grandfather, reading his paper by the table, looked up with friendly interest now and then. The cedar was about five feet high and very shapely. We hung it with the gingerbread animals, strings of popcorn, and bits of candle which Fuchs had fitted into pasteboard sockets. Its real splendors, however, came from the most unlikely place in the world—from Otto's cowboy trunk. I had never seen anything in that trunk but old boots and spurs and pistols, and a fascinating mixture of yellow leather thongs, cartridges, and shoemaker's wax. From under the lining he now produced a collection of brilliantly colored paper figures, several inches high and stiff enough to stand alone. They had been sent to him year after year, by his old mother in Aus-

3. Josephine (1763–1814), empress of France and wife of Napoleon Bonaparte, who married her in 1796 and divorced her in 1809 to marry Marie Louise, daughter of the Austrian emperor. In American popular culture, she became a symbol of the deserted wife.

tria. There was a bleeding heart, in tufts of paper lace; there were the three kings, gorgeously appareled, and the ox and the ass and the shepherds; there was the Baby in the manger, and a group of angels, singing; there were camels and leopards, held by the black slaves of the three kings. Our tree became the talking tree of the fairy tale; legends and stories nestled like birds in its branches. Grandmother said it reminded her of the Tree of Knowledge. We put sheets of cotton wool under it for a snow-field, and Jake's pocket-mirror for a frozen lake.

XII

On Christmas morning, when I got down to the kitchen, the men were just coming in from their morning chores—the horses and pigs always had their breakfast before we did. Jake and Otto shouted "Merry Christmas"! to me, and winked at each other when they saw the waffle-irons on the stove. Grandfather came down, wearing a white shirt and his Sunday coat. Morning prayers were longer than usual. He read the chapters from St. Matthew about the birth of Christ, and as we listened it all seemed like something that had happened lately, and near at hand. In his prayer he thanked the Lord for the first Christmas, and for all that it had meant to the world ever since. He gave thanks for our food and comfort, and prayed for the poor and destitute in great cities, where the struggle for life was harder than it was here with us. Grandfather's prayers were often very interesting. He had the gift of simple and moving expression. Because he talked so little, his words had a peculiar force; they were not worn dull from constant use. His prayers reflected what he was thinking about at the time, and it was chiefly through them that we got to know his feelings and his views about things.

After we sat down to our waffles and sausage, Jake told us how pleased the Shimerdas had been with their presents; even Ambrosch was friendly and went to the creek with him to cut the Christmas tree. It was a soft gray day outside, with heavy clouds working across the sky, and occasional squalls of snow. There were always odd jobs to be done about the barn on holidays, and the men were busy until afternoon. Then Jake and I played dominoes, while Otto wrote a long letter home to his mother. He always wrote to her on Christmas Day, he said, no matter where he was, and no matter how long it had been since his last letter. All afternoon he sat in the dining-room. He would write for a while, then sit idle, his clenched fist lying on the table, his eyes following the pattern of the oilcloth. He spoke and wrote his own language so seldom that it came to him awkwardly. His effort to remember entirely absorbed him.

At about four o'clock a visitor appeared: Mr. Shimerda, wearing his rabbit-skin cap and collar, and new mittens his wife had knitted. He had come to thank us for the presents, and for all grandmother's kindness to his family. Jake and Otto joined us from the basement and we sat about the stove, enjoying the deepening gray of the winter afternoon and the atmosphere of comfort and security in my grandfather's house. This feeling seemed completely to take possession of Mr. Shimerda. I suppose, in the crowded clutter of their cave, the old man had come to believe that peace and order had vanished from the earth, or existed only in the old world he had left so far behind. He sat still and passive, his head resting against the back of the wooden rocking-chair, his hands relaxed upon the arms. His face had a look of weariness and pleasure, like that of sick people when they feel relief from pain. Grandmother insisted on his drinking a glass of Virginia apple-brandy after his long walk in the cold, and when a faint flush came up in his cheeks, his features might have been cut out of a shell, they were so transparent. He said almost nothing, and smiled rarely; but as he rested there we all had a sense of his utter content.

As it grew dark, I asked whether I might light the Christmas tree before the lamp was brought. When the candle ends sent up their conical yellow flames, all the colored figures from Austria stood out clear and full of meaning against the green boughs. Mr. Shimerda rose, crossed himself, and quietly knelt down before the tree, his head sunk forward. His long body formed a letter "S." I saw grandmother look apprehensively at grandfather. He was rather narrow in religious matters, and sometimes spoke out and hurt people's feelings. There had been nothing strange about the tree before, but now, with some one kneeling before it,—images, candles, . . . Grandfather merely put his fingertips to his brow and bowed his venerable head, thus Protestantizing the atmosphere.[4]

We persuaded our guest to stay for supper with us. He needed little urging. As we sat down to the table, it occurred to me that he liked to look at us, and that our faces were open books to him. When his deep-seeing eyes rested on me, I felt as if he were looking far ahead into the future for me, down the road I would have to travel.

At nine o'clock Mr. Shimerda lighted one of our lanterns and put on his overcoat and fur collar. He stood in the little entry hall, the lantern and his fur cap under his arm, shaking hands with us. When he took grandmother's hand, he bent over it as he always did, and said slowly, "Good wo-man!" He made the sign of the cross over me, put on his cap and went off in the dark. As we turned back to the sitting-room, grandfather looked at me searchingly. "The prayers of all good people are good," he said quietly.

XIII

The week following Christmas brought in a thaw, and by New Year's Day all the world about us was a broth of gray slush, and the guttered slope between the windmill and the barn was running black water. The soft black earth stood out in patches along the roadsides. I resumed all my chores, carried in the cobs and wood and water, and spent the afternoons at the barn, watching Jake shell corn with a hand-sheller.

One morning, during this interval of fine weather, Ántonia and her mother rode over on one of their shaggy old horses to pay us a visit. It was the first time Mrs. Shimerda had been to our house, and she ran about examining our carpets and curtains and furniture, all the while commenting upon them to her daughter in an envious, complaining tone. In the kitchen she caught up an iron pot that stood on the back of the stove and said: "You got many, Shimerdas no got." I thought it weak-minded of grandmother to give the pot to her.

4. Traditional forms of Protestantism (the Burdens are Baptists) strongly opposed modes of worship involving images, statues, and rituals, which were interpreted as superstitions. It is therefore notable when, at the end of the chapter, Grandfather justifies Mr. Shimerda's making the sign of the cross.

After dinner, when she was helping to wash the dishes, she said, tossing her head: "You got many things for cook. If I got all things like you, I make much better."

She was a conceited, boastful old thing, and even misfortune could not humble her. I was so annoyed that I felt coldly even toward Ántonia and listened unsympathetically when she told me her father was not well.

"My papa sad for the old country. He not look good. He never make music any more. At home he play violin all the time; for weddings and for dance. Here never. When I beg him for play, he shake his head no. Some days he take his violin out of his box and make with his fingers on the strings, like this, but never he make the music. He don't like this kawn-tree."

"People who don't like this country ought to stay at home," I said severely. "We don't make them come here."

"He not want to come, nev-er!" she burst out. "My *mamenka* make him come. All the time she say: 'America big country; much money, much land for my boys, much husband for my girls.' My papa, he cry for leave his old friends what make music with him. He love very much the man what play the long horn like this"—she indicated a slide trombone. "They go to school together and are friends from boys. But my mama, she want Ambrosch for be rich, with many cattle."

"Your mama," I said angrily, "wants other people's things."

"Your grandfather is rich," she retorted fiercely. "Why he not help my papa? Ambrosch be rich, too, after while, and he pay back. He is very smart boy. For Ambrosch my mama come here."

Ambrosch was considered the important person in the family. Mrs. Shimerda and Ántonia always deferred to him, though he was often surly with them and contemptuous toward his father. Ambrosch and his mother had everything their own way. Though Ántonia loved her father more than she did any one else, she stood in awe of her elder brother.

After I watched Ántonia and her mother go over the hill on their miserable horse, carrying our iron pot with them, I turned to grandmother, who had taken up her darning, and said I hoped that snooping old woman wouldn't come to see us any more.

Grandmother chuckled and drove her bright needle across a hole in Otto's sock. "She's not old, Jim, though I expect she seems old to you. No, I wouldn't mourn, if she never came again. But, you see, a body never knows what traits poverty might bring out in 'em. It makes a woman grasping to see her children want for things. Now read me a chapter in 'The Prince of the House of David.'[5] Let's forget the Bohemians."

We had three weeks of this mild, open weather. The cattle in the corral ate corn almost as fast as the men could shell it for them, and we hoped they would be ready for an early market. One morning the two big bulls, Gladstone and Brigham Young,[6] thought spring had come, and they began to tease and butt at each other across the barbed wire that separated them. Soon they got

5. Best-selling American novel of 1855, by Joseph Holt Ingraham (1809–1860); based on the life of Jesus Christ. A pious household like the Burdens' would oppose novel reading in general; biblical novels would be exceptions.

6. Mormon leader (1801–1877) who led the Mormons to Salt Lake City in 1846–47 and directed the settlement there. William Gladstone (1809–1898), English statesman who was prime minister four times. The two bulls are humorously named.

angry. They bellowed and pawed up the soft earth with their hoofs, rolling their eyes and tossing their heads. Each withdrew to a far corner of his own corral, and then they made for each other at a gallop. Thud, thud, we could hear the impact of their great heads, and their bellowing shook the pans on the kitchen shelves. Had they not been dehorned, they would have torn each other to pieces. Pretty soon the fat steers took it up and began butting and horning each other. Clearly, the affair had to be stopped. We all stood by and watched admiringly while Fuchs rode into the corral with a pitchfork and prodded the bulls again and again, finally driving them apart.

The big storm of the winter began on my eleventh birthday, the 20th of January. When I went down to breakfast that morning, Jake and Otto came in white as snow-men, beating their hands and stamping their feet. They began to laugh boisterously when they saw me, calling:—

"You've got a birthday present this time, Jim, and no mistake. They was a full-grown blizzard ordered for you."

All day the storm went on. The snow did not fall this time, it simply spilled out of heaven, like thousands of feather-beds being emptied. That afternoon the kitchen was a carpenter-shop; the men brought in their tools and made two great wooden shovels with long handles. Neither grandmother nor I could go out in the storm, so Jake fed the chickens and brought in a pitiful contribution of eggs.

Next day our men had to shovel until noon to reach the barn—and the snow was still falling! There had not been such a storm in the ten years my grandfather had lived in Nebraska. He said at dinner that we would not try to reach the cattle—they were fat enough to go without their corn for a day or two; but to-morrow we must feed them and thaw out their water-tap so that they could drink. We could not so much as see the corrals, but we knew the steers were over there, huddled together under the north bank. Our ferocious bulls, subdued enough by this time, were probably warming each other's backs. "This'll take the bile out of 'em!" Fuchs remarked gleefully.

At noon that day the hens had not been heard from. After dinner Jake and Otto, their damp clothes now dried on them, stretched their stiff arms and plunged again into the drifts. They made a tunnel under the snow to the hen-house, with walls so solid that grandmother and I could walk back and forth in it. We found the chickens asleep; perhaps they thought night had come to stay. One old rooster was stirring about, pecking at the solid lump of ice in their water-tin. When we flashed the lantern in their eyes, the hens set up a great cackling and flew about clumsily, scattering down-feathers. The mottled, pinheaded, guinea-hens, always resentful of captivity, ran screeching out into the tunnel and tried to poke their ugly, painted faces through the snow walls. By five o'clock the chores were done—just when it was time to begin them all over again! That was a strange, unnatural sort of day.

I can see them now, exactly as they looked, working about the table in the lamplight: Jake with his heavy features, so rudely moulded that his face seemed, somehow, unfinished; Otto with his half-ear and the savage scar that made his upper lip curl so ferociously under his twisted mustache. As I remember them, what unprotected faces they were; their very roughness and violence made them defenseless. These boys had no practiced manner behind which they could retreat and hold people at a distance. They had only their hard fists to batter at the world with. Otto was already one of those drifting, case-hardened laborers who never marry or have children of their own. Yet he was so fond of children!

XIV

On the morning of the 22d I wakened with a start. Before I opened my eyes, I seemed to know that something had happened. I heard excited voices in the kitchen—grandmother's was so shrill that I knew she must be almost beside herself. I looked forward to any new crisis with delight. What could it be, I wondered, as I hurried into my clothes. Perhaps the barn had burned; perhaps the cattle had frozen to death; perhaps a neighbor was lost in the storm.

Down in the kitchen grandfather was standing before the stove with his hands behind him. Jake and Otto had taken off their boots and were rubbing their woolen socks. Their clothes and boots were steaming, and they both looked exhausted. On the bench behind the stove lay a man, covered up with a blanket. Grandmother motioned me to the dining-room. I obeyed reluctantly. I watched her as she came and went, carrying dishes. Her lips were tightly compressed and she kept whispering to herself: "Oh, dear Saviour!" "Lord, Thou knowest!"

Presently grandfather came in and spoke to me: "Jimmy, we will not have prayers this morning, because we have a great deal to do. Old Mr. Shimerda is dead, and his family are in great distress. Ambrosch came over here in the middle of the night, and Jake and Otto went back with him. The boys have had a hard night, and you must not bother them with questions. That is Ambrosch, asleep on the bench. Come in to breakfast, boys."

After Jake and Otto had swallowed their first cup of coffee, they began to talk excitedly, disregarding grandmother's warning glances. I held my tongue, but I listened with all my ears.

"No, sir," Fuchs said in answer to a question from grandfather, "nobody heard the gun go off. Ambrosch was out with the ox team, trying to break a road, and the women folks was shut up tight in their cave. When Ambrosch come in it was dark and he didn't see nothing, but the oxen acted kind of queer. One of 'em ripped around and got away from him—bolted clean out of the stable. His hands is blistered where the rope run through. He got a lantern and went back and found the old man, just as we seen him."

"Poor soul, poor soul!" grandmother groaned. "I'd like to think he never done it. He was always considerate and un-wishful to give trouble. How could he forget himself and bring this on us!"

"I don't think he was out of his head for a minute, Mrs. Burden," Fuchs declared. "He done everything natural. You know he was always sort of fixy,[7] and fixy he was to the last. He shaved after dinner, and washed hisself all over after the girls was done the dishes. Ántonia heated the water for him. Then he put on a clean shirt and clean socks, and after he was dressed he kissed her and the little one and took his gun and said he was going out to hunt rabbits. He must have gone right down to the barn and done it then. He layed down on that bunk-bed, close to the ox stalls, where he always slept. When

---

7. Finicky, fastidious.

we found him, everything was decent except,"—Fuchs wrinkled his brow and hesitated,—"except what he couldn't nowise foresee. His coat was hung on a peg, and his boots was under the bed. He'd took off that silk neckcloth he always wore, and folded it smooth and stuck his pin through it. He turned back his shirt at the neck and rolled up his sleeves."

"I don't see how he could do it!" grandmother kept saying.

Otto misunderstood her. "Why, mam, it was simple enough; he pulled the trigger with his big toe. He layed over on his side and put the end of the barrel in his mouth, then he drew up one foot and felt for the trigger. He found it all right!"

"Maybe he did," said Jake grimly. "There's something mighty queer about it."

"Now what do you mean, Jake?" grandmother asked sharply.

"Well, mam, I found Krajiek's axe under the manger, and I picks it up and carries it over to the corpse, and I take my oath it just fit the gash in the front of the old man's face. That there Krajiek had been sneakin' round, pale and quiet, and when he seen me examinin' the axe, he begun whimperin', 'My God, man, don't do that!' 'I reckon I'm a-goin' to look into this,' says I. Then he begun to squeal like a rat and run about wringin' his hands. 'They'll hang me!' says he. 'My God, they'll hang me sure!' "

Fuchs spoke up impatiently. "Krajiek's gone silly, Jake, and so have you. The old man wouldn't have made all them preparations for Krajiek to murder him, would he? It don't hang together. The gun was right beside him when Ambrosch found him."

"Krajiek could 'a' put it there, couldn't he?" Jake demanded.

Grandmother broke in excitedly: "See here, Jake Marpole, don't you go trying to add murder to suicide. We're deep enough in trouble. Otto reads you too many of them detective stories."

"It will be easy to decide all that, Emmaline," said grandfather quietly. "If he shot himself in the way they think, the gash will be torn from the inside outward."

"Just so it is, Mr. Burden," Otto affirmed. "I seen bunches of hair and stuff sticking to the poles and straw along the roof. They was blown up there by gunshot, no question."

Grandmother told grandfather she meant to go over to the Shimerdas with him.

"There is nothing you can do," he said doubtfully. "The body can't be touched until we get the coroner here from Black Hawk, and that will be a matter of several days, this weather."

"Well, I can take them some victuals, anyway, and say a word of comfort to them poor little girls. The oldest one was his darling, and was like a right hand to him. He might have thought of her. He's left her alone in a hard world." She glanced distrustfully at Ambrosch, who was now eating his breakfast at the kitchen table.

Fuchs, although he had been up in the cold nearly all night, was going to make the long ride to Black Hawk to fetch the priest and the coroner. On the gray gelding, our best horse, he would try to pick his way across the country with no roads to guide him.

"Don't you worry about me, Mrs. Burden," he said cheerfully, as he put on a second pair of socks. "I've got a good nose for directions, and I never did need much sleep. It's the gray I'm worried about. I'll save him what I can, but it'll strain him, as sure as I'm telling you!"

"This is no time to be over-considerate of animals, Otto; do the best you can for yourself. Stop at the Widow Steavens's for dinner. She's a good woman, and she'll do well by you."

After Fuchs rode away, I was left with Ambrosch. I saw a side of him I had not seen before. He was deeply, even slavishly, devout. He did not say a word all morning, but sat with his rosary in his hands, praying, now silently, now aloud. He never looked away from his beads, nor lifted his hands except to cross himself. Several times the poor boy fell asleep where he sat, wakened with a start, and began to pray again.

No wagon could be got to the Shimerdas' until a road was broken, and that would be a day's job. Grandfather came from the barn on one of our big black horses, and Jake lifted grandmother up behind him. She wore her black hood and was bundled up in shawls. Grandfather tucked his bushy white beard inside his overcoat. They looked very Biblical as they set off, I thought. Jake and Ambrosch followed them, riding the other black and my pony, carrying bundles of clothes that we had got together for Mrs. Shimerda. I watched them go past the pond and over the hill by the drifted cornfield. Then, for the first time, I realized that I was alone in the house.

I felt a considerable extension of power and authority, and was anxious to acquit myself creditably. I carried in cobs[8] and wood from the long cellar, and filled both the stoves. I remembered that in the hurry and excitement of the morning nobody had thought of the chickens, and the eggs had not been gathered. Going out through the tunnel, I gave the hens their corn, emptied the ice from their drinking-pan, and filled it with water. After the cat had had his milk, I could think of nothing else to do, and I sat down to get warm. The quiet was delightful, and the ticking clock was the most pleasant of companions. I got "Robinson Crusoe"[9] and tried to read, but his life on the island seemed dull compared with ours. Presently, as I looked with satisfaction about our comfortable sitting-room, it flashed upon me that if Mr. Shimerda's soul were lingering about in this world at all, it would be here, in our house, which had been more to his liking than any other in the neighborhood. I remembered his contented face when he was with us on Christmas Day. If he could have lived with us, this terrible thing would never have happened.

I knew it was homesickness that had killed Mr. Shimerda, and I wondered whether his released spirit would not eventually find its way back to his own country. I thought of how far it was to Chicago, and then to Virginia, to Baltimore,—and then the great wintry ocean. No, he would not at once set out upon that long journey. Surely, his exhausted spirit, so tired of cold and crowding and the struggle with the ever-falling snow, was resting now in this quiet house.

I was not frightened, but I made no noise. I did not wish to disturb him. I went softly down to the kitchen which, tucked away so snugly underground, always seemed to me the heart and center of the house. There, on the bench behind the stove, I thought and thought about Mr. Shimerda. Outside I could

---

8. After the corn kernels have been scraped from them, the cobs can be used for fuel.
9. A 1719 novel by English writer Daniel Defoe (1660?–1731), based on the true adventures of

Alexander Selkirk in 1704. The story tells how Robinson Crusoe, shipwrecked on an uninhabited island, learns to survive.

hear the wind singing over hundreds of miles of snow. It was as if I had let the old man in out of the tormenting winter, and were sitting there with him. I went over all that Ántonia had ever told me about his life before he came to this country; how he used to play the fiddle at weddings and dances. I thought about the friends he had mourned to leave, the trombone-player, the great forest full of game,—belonging, as Ántonia said, to the "nobles,"—from which she and her mother used to steal wood on moonlight nights. There was a white hart that lived in that forest, and if any one killed it, he would be hanged, she said. Such vivid pictures came to me that they might have been Mr. Shimerda's memories, not yet faded out from the air in which they had haunted him.

It had begun to grow dark when my household returned, and grandmother was so tired that she went at once to bed. Jake and I got supper, and while we were washing the dishes he told me in loud whispers about the state of things over at the Shimerdas'. Nobody could touch the body until the coroner came. If any one did, something terrible would happen, apparently. The dead man was frozen through, "just as stiff as a dressed turkey you hang out to freeze," Jake said. The horses and oxen would not go into the barn until he was frozen so hard that there was no longer any smell of blood. They were stabled there now, with the dead man, because there was no other place to keep them. A lighted lantern was kept hanging over Mr. Shimerda's head. Ántonia and Ambrosch and the mother took turns going down to pray beside him. The crazy boy went with them, because he did not feel the cold. I believed he felt cold as much as any one else, but he liked to be thought insensible to it. He was always coveting distinction, poor Marek!

Ambrosch, Jake said, showed more human feeling than he would have supposed him capable of; but he was chiefly concerned about getting a priest, and about his father's soul, which he believed was in a place of torment and would remain there until his family and the priest had prayed a great deal for him.[1] "As I understand it," Jake concluded, "it will be a matter of years to pray his soul out of Purgatory, and right now he's in torment."

"I don't believe it," I said stoutly. "I almost know it isn't true." I did not, of course, say that I believed he had been in that very kitchen all afternoon, on his way back to his own country. Nevertheless, after I went to bed, this idea of punishment and Purgatory came back on me crushingly. I remembered the account of Dives[2] in torment, and shuddered. But Mr. Shimerda had not been rich and selfish; he had only been so unhappy that he could not live any longer.

XV

Otto Fuchs got back from Black Hawk at noon the next day. He reported that the coroner would reach the Shimerdas' sometime that afternoon, but the missionary priest was at the other end of his parish, a hundred miles away, and the trains were not running. Fuchs had got a few hours' sleep at the livery barn in town, but he was afraid the gray gelding had strained himself. Indeed, he was never the same horse afterward. That long trip through the deep snow had taken all the endurance out of him.

1. The Catholic Shimerdas believe that suicide is a mortal sin.
2. In Luke 16.19–31, Jesus recounts the story of Dives, a rich selfish man who suffers the torments of hell, and Lazarus, a beggar who goes to heaven.

Fuchs brought home with him a stranger, a young Bohemian who had taken a homestead near Black Hawk, and who came on his only horse to help his fellow-countrymen in their trouble. That was the first time I ever saw Anton Jelinek. He was a strapping young fellow in the early twenties then, handsome, warm-hearted, and full of life, and he came to us like a miracle in the midst of that grim business. I remember exactly how he strode into our kitchen in his felt boots and long wolf-skin coat, his eyes and cheeks bright with the cold. At sight of grandmother, he snatched off his fur cap, greeting her in a deep, rolling voice which seemed older than he.

"I want to thank you very much, Mrs. Burden, for that you are so kind to poor strangers from my kawn-tree."

He did not hesitate like a farmer boy, but looked one eagerly in the eye when he spoke. Everything about him was warm and spontaneous. He said he would have come to see the Shimerdas before, but he had hired out to husk corn all the fall, and since winter began he had been going to the school by the mill, to learn English, along with the little children. He told me he had a nice "lady-teacher" and that he liked to go to school.

At dinner grandfather talked to Jelinek more than he usually did to strangers.

"Will they be much disappointed because we cannot get a priest?" he asked.

Jelinek looked serious. "Yes, sir, that is very bad for them. Their father has done a great sin," he looked straight at grandfather. "Our Lord has said that."

Grandfather seemed to like his frankness. "We believe that, too, Jelinek. But we believe that Mr. Shimerda's soul will come to its Creator as well off without a priest. We believe that Christ is our only intercessor."

The young man shook his head. "I know how you think. My teacher at the school has explain. But I have seen too much. I believe in prayer for the dead. I have seen too much."

We asked him what he meant.

He glanced around the table. "You want I shall tell you? When I was a little boy like this one, I begin to help the priest at the altar. I make my first communion very young; what the Church teach seem plain to me. By 'n' by war-times come, when the Austrians fight us. We have very many soldiers in camp near my village, and the cholera[3] break out in that camp, and the men die like flies. All day long our priest go about there to give the Sacrament to dying men, and I go with him to carry the vessels with the Holy Sacrament. Everybody that go near that camp catch the sickness but me and the priest. But we have no sickness, we have no fear, because we carry that blood and that body of Christ, and it preserve us." He paused, looking at grandfather. "That I know, Mr. Burden, for it happened to myself. All the soldiers know, too. When we walk along the road, the old priest and me, we meet all the time soldiers marching and officers on horse. All those officers, when they see what I carry under the cloth, pull up their horses and kneel down on the ground in the road until we pass. So I feel very bad for my kawntree-man to die without the Sacrament, and to die in a bad way for his soul, and I feel sad for his family."

3. A highly contagious gastrointestinal disease that causes severe and often fatal dehydration.

We had listened attentively. It was impossible not to admire his frank, manly faith.

"I am always glad to meet a young man who thinks seriously about these things," said grandfather, "and I would never be the one to say you were not in God's care when you were among the soldiers."

After dinner it was decided that young Jelinek should hook our two strong black farmhorses to the scraper and break a road through to the Shimerdas', so that a wagon could go when it was necessary. Fuchs, who was the only cabinet-maker in the neighborhood, was set to work on a coffin.

Jelinek put on his long wolfskin coat, and when we admired it, he told us that he had shot and skinned the coyotes, and the young man who "batched" with him, Jan Bouska, who had been a fur-worker in Vienna, made the coat. From the windmill I watched Jelinek come out of the barn with the blacks, and work his way up the hillside toward the cornfield. Sometimes he was completely hidden by the clouds of snow that rose about him; then he and the horses would emerge black and shining.

Our heavy carpenter's bench had to be brought from the barn and carried down into the kitchen. Fuchs selected boards from a pile of planks grandfather had hauled out from town in the fall to make a new floor for the oats bin. When at last the lumber and tools were assembled, and the doors were closed again and the cold drafts shut out, grandfather rode away to meet the coroner at the Shimerdas', and Fuchs took off his coat and settled down to work. I sat on his work-table and watched him. He did not touch his tools at first, but figured for a long while on a piece of paper, and measured the planks and made marks on them. While he was thus engaged, he whistled softly to himself, or teasingly pulled at his half-ear. Grandmother moved about quietly, so as not to disturb him. At last he folded his ruler and turned a cheerful face to us.

"The hardest part of my job's done," he announced. "It's the head end of it that comes hard with me, especially when I'm out of practice. The last time I made one of these, Mrs. Burden," he continued, as he sorted and tried his chisels, "was for a fellow in the Black Tiger mine, up above Silverton, Colorado. The mouth of that mine goes right into the face of the cliff, and they used to put us in a bucket and run us over on a trolley and shoot us into the shaft. The bucket traveled across a box cañon three hundred feet deep, and about a third full of water. Two Swedes had fell out of that bucket once, and hit the water, feet down. If you'll believe it, they went to work the next day. You can't kill a Swede. But in my time a little Eyetalian tried the high dive, and it turned out different with him. We was snowed in then, like we are now, and I happened to be the only man in camp that could make a coffin for him. It's a handy thing to know, when you knock about like I've done."

"We'd be hard put to it now, if you didn't know, Otto," grandmother said.

"Yes,'m," Fuchs admitted with modest pride. "So few folks does know how to make a good tight box that'll turn water. I sometimes wonder if there'll be anybody about to do it for me. However, I'm not at all particular that way."

All afternoon, wherever one went in the house, one could hear the panting wheeze of the saw or the pleasant purring of the plane. They were such cheerful noises, seeming to promise new things for living people: it was a pity that those freshly planed pine boards were to be put underground so soon.

The lumber was hard to work because it was full of frost, and the boards gave off a sweet smell of pine woods, as the heap of yellow shavings grew higher and higher. I wondered why Fuchs had not stuck to cabinet-work, he settled down to it with such ease and content. He handled the tools as if he liked the feel of them; and when he planed, his hands went back and forth over the boards in an eager, beneficent way as if he were blessing them. He broke out now and then into German hymns, as if this occupation brought back old times to him.

At four o'clock Mr. Bushy, the postmaster, with another neighbor who lived east of us, stopped in to get warm. They were on their way to the Shimerdas'. The news of what had happened over there had somehow got abroad through the snow-blocked country. Grandmother gave the visitors sugar-cakes and hot coffee. Before these callers were gone, the brother of the Widow Steavens, who lived on the Black Hawk road, drew up at our door, and after him came the father of the German family, our nearest neighbors on the south. They dismounted and joined us in the dining-room. They were all eager for any details about the suicide, and they were greatly concerned as to where Mr. Shimerda would be buried. The nearest Catholic cemetery was at Black Hawk, and it might be weeks before a wagon could get so far. Besides, Mr. Bushy and grandmother were sure that a man who had killed himself could not be buried in a Catholic graveyard. There was a burying-ground over by the Norwegian church, west of Squaw Creek; perhaps the Norwegians would take Mr. Shimerda in.

After our visitors rode away in single file over the hill, we returned to the kitchen. Grandmother began to make the icing for a chocolate cake, and Otto again filled the house with the exciting, expectant song of the plane. One pleasant thing about this time was that everybody talked more than usual. I had never heard the postmaster say anything but "Only papers, to-day," or, "I've got a sackful of mail for ye," until this afternoon. Grandmother always talked, dear woman; to herself or to the Lord, if there was no one else to listen; but grandfather was naturally taciturn, and Jake and Otto were often so tired after supper that I used to feel as if I were surrounded by a wall of silence. Now every one seemed eager to talk. That afternoon Fuchs told me story after story; about the Black Tiger mine, and about violent deaths and casual buryings, and the queer fancies of dying men. You never really knew a man, he said, until you saw him die. Most men were game, and went without a grudge.

The postmaster, going home, stopped to say that grandfather would bring the coroner back with him to spend the night. The officers of the Norwegian church, he told us, had held a meeting and decided that the Norwegian graveyard could not extend its hospitality to Mr. Shimerda.

Grandmother was indignant. "If these foreigners are so clannish, Mr. Bushy, we'll have to have an American graveyard that will be more liberal-minded. I'll get right after Josiah to start one in the spring. If anything was to happen to me, I don't want the Norwegians holding inquisitions over me to see whether I'm good enough to be laid amongst 'em."

Soon grandfather returned, bringing with him Anton Jelinek, and that important person, the coroner. He was a mild, flurried old man, a Civil War veteran, with one sleeve hanging empty. He seemed to find this case very perplexing, and said if it had not been for grandfather he would have sworn out a warrant against Krajiek. "The way he acted, and the way his axe fit the wound, was enough to convict any man."

Although it was perfectly clear that Mr. Shimerda had killed himself, Jake and the coroner thought something ought to be done to Krajiek because he behaved like a guilty man. He was badly frightened, certainly, and perhaps he even felt some stirrings of remorse for his indifference to the old man's misery and loneliness.

At supper the men ate like vikings, and the chocolate cake, which I had hoped would linger on until to-morrow in a mutilated condition, disappeared on the second round. They talked excitedly about where they should bury Mr. Shimerda; I gathered that the neighbors were all disturbed and shocked about something. It developed that Mrs. Shimerda and Ambrosch wanted the old man buried on the southwest corner of their own land; indeed, under the very stake that marked the corner. Grandfather had explained to Ambrosch that some day, when the country was put under fence and the roads were confined to section lines, two roads would cross exactly on that corner. But Ambrosch only said, "It makes no matter."

Grandfather asked Jelinek whether in the old country there was some superstition to the effect that a suicide must be buried at the cross-roads.

Jelinek said he didn't know; he seemed to remember hearing there had once been such a custom in Bohemia. "Mrs. Shimerda is made up her mind," he added. "I try to persuade her, and say it looks bad for her to all the neighbors; but she say so it must be. 'There I will bury him, if I dig the grave myself,' she say. I have to promise her I help Ambrosch make the grave to-morrow."

Grandfather smoothed his beard and looked judicial. "I don't know whose wish should decide the matter, if not hers. But if she thinks she will live to see the people of this country ride over that old man's head, she is mistaken."

XVI

Mr. Shimerda lay dead in the barn four days, and on the fifth they buried him. All day Friday Jelinek was off with Ambrosch digging the grave, chopping out the frozen earth with old axes. On Saturday we breakfasted before daylight and got into the wagon with the coffin. Jake and Jelinek went ahead on horseback to cut the body loose from the pool of blood in which it was frozen fast to the ground.

When grandmother and I went into the Shimerdas' house, we found the women-folk alone; Ambrosch and Marek were at the barn. Mrs. Shimerda sat crouching by the stove, Ántonia was washing dishes. When she saw me she ran out of her dark corner and threw her arms around me. "Oh, Jimmy," she sobbed, "what you tink for my lovely papa!" It seemed to me that I could feel her heart breaking as she clung to me.

Mrs. Shimerda, sitting on the stump by the stove, kept looking over her shoulder toward the door while the neighbors were arriving. They came on horseback, all except the post-master, who brought his family in a wagon over the only broken wagon-trail. The Widow Steavens rode up from her farm eight miles down the Black Hawk road. The cold drove the women into the cave-house, and it was soon crowded. A fine, sleety snow was beginning to fall, and every one was afraid of another storm and anxious to have the burial over with.

Grandfather and Jelinek came to tell Mrs. Shimerda that it was time to start. After bundling her mother up in clothes the neighbors had brought, Ántonia put on an old cape from our house and the rabbit-skin hat her father had made for her. Four men carried Mr. Shimerda's box up the hill; Krajiek slunk along behind them. The coffin was too wide for the door, so it was put down on the slope outside. I slipped out from the cave and looked at Mr. Shimerda. He was lying on his side, with his knees drawn up. His body was draped in a black shawl, and his head was bandaged in white muslin, like a mummy's; one of his long, shapely hands lay out on the black cloth; that was all one could see of him.

Mrs. Shimerda came out and placed an open prayer-book against the body, making the sign of the cross on the bandaged head with her fingers. Ambrosch knelt down and made the same gesture, and after him Ántonia and Marek. Yulka hung back. Her mother pushed her forward, and kept saying something to her over and over. Yulka knelt down, shut her eyes, and put out her hand a little way, but she drew it back and began to cry wildly. She was afraid to touch the bandage. Mrs. Shimerda caught her by the shoulders and pushed her toward the coffin, but grandmother interfered.

"No, Mrs. Shimerda," she said firmly, "I won't stand by and see that child frightened into spasms. She is too little to understand what you want of her. Let her alone."

At a look from grandfather, Fuchs and Jelinek placed the lid on the box, and began to nail it down over Mr. Shimerda. I was afraid to look at Ántonia. She put her arms round Yulka and held the little girl close to her.

The coffin was put into the wagon. We drove slowly away, against the fine, icy snow which cut our faces like a sand-blast. When we reached the grave, it looked a very little spot in that snow-covered waste. The men took the coffin to the edge of the hole and lowered it with ropes. We stood about watching them, and the powdery snow lay without melting on the caps and shoulders of the men and the shawls of the women. Jelinek spoke in a persuasive tone to Mrs. Shimerda, and then turned to grandfather.

"She says, Mr. Burden, she is very glad if you can make some prayer for him here in English, for the neighbors to understand."

Grandmother looked anxiously at grandfather. He took off his hat, and the other men did likewise. I thought his prayer remarkable. I still remember it. He began, "Oh, great and just God, no man among us knows what the sleeper knows, nor is it for us to judge what lies between him and Thee." He prayed that if any man there had been remiss toward the stranger come to a far country, God would forgive him and soften his heart. He recalled the promises to the widow and the fatherless, and asked God to smooth the way before this widow and her children, and to "incline the hearts of men to deal justly with her." In closing, he said we were leaving Mr. Shimerda at "Thy judgment seat, which is also Thy mercy seat."

All the time he was praying, grandmother watched him through the black fingers of her glove, and when he said "Amen," I thought she looked satisfied with him. She turned to Otto and whispered, "Can't you start a hymn, Fuchs? It would seem less heathenish."

Fuchs glanced about to see if there was general approval of her suggestion, then began, "Jesus, Lover of my Soul," and all the men and women took it up after him. Whenever I have heard the hymn since, it has made me remember that white waste and the little group of people; and the bluish air, full of fine, eddying snow, like long veils flying:—

> "While the nearer waters roll,
> While the tempest still is high."

• • • • •

Years afterward, when the open-grazing days were over, and the red grass had been ploughed under and under until it had almost disappeared from the prairie; when all the fields were under fence, and the roads no longer ran about like wild things, but followed the surveyed section-lines, Mr. Shimerda's grave was still there, with a sagging wire fence around it, and an unpainted wooden cross. As grandfather had predicted, Mrs. Shimerda never saw the roads going over his head. The road from the north curved a little to the east just there, and the road from the west swung out a little to the south; so that the grave, with its tall red grass that was never mowed, was like a little island; and at twilight, under a new moon or the clear evening star, the dusty roads used to look like soft gray rivers flowing past it. I never came upon the place without emotion, and in all that country it was the spot most dear to me. I loved the dim superstition, the propitiatory intent, that had put the grave there; and still more I loved the spirit that could not carry out the sentence—the error from the surveyed lines, the clemency of the soft earth roads along which the home-coming wagons rattled after sunset. Never a tired driver passed the wooden cross, I am sure, without wishing well to the sleeper.

XVII

When spring came, after that hard winter, one could not get enough of the nimble air. Every morning I wakened with a fresh consciousness that winter was over. There were none of the signs of spring for which I used to watch in Virginia, no budding woods or blooming gardens. There was only—spring itself; the throb of it, the light restlessness, the vital essence of it everywhere; in the sky, in the swift clouds, in the pale sunshine, and in the warm, high wind—rising suddenly, sinking suddenly, impulsive and playful like a big puppy that pawed you and then lay down to be petted. If I had been tossed down blindfold on that red prairie, I should have known that it was spring.

Everywhere now there was the smell of burning grass. Our neighbors burned off their pasture before the new grass made a start, so that the fresh growth would not be mixed with the dead stand of last year. Those light, swift fires, running about the country, seemed a part of the same kindling that was in the air.

The Shimerdas were in their new log house by then. The neighbors had helped them to build it in March. It stood directly in front of their old cave, which they used as a cellar. The family were now fairly equipped to begin their struggle with the soil. They had four comfortable rooms to live in, a new windmill,—bought on credit,—a chicken-house and poultry. Mrs. Shimerda had paid grandfather ten dollars for a milk cow, and was to give him fifteen more as soon as they harvested their first crop.

When I rode up to the Shimerdas' one bright windy afternoon in April, Yulka ran out to meet me. It was to her, now, that I gave reading lessons; Ántonia was busy with other things. I tied my pony and went into the kitchen where Mrs. Shimerda was baking bread, chewing poppy seeds as she worked. By this time she could speak enough English to ask me a great many questions about what our men were doing in the fields. She seemed to think that my elders withheld helpful information, and that from me she might get valuable secrets. On this occasion she asked me very craftily when grandfather expected to begin planting corn. I told her, adding that he thought we should have a dry spring and that the corn would not be held back by too much rain, as it had been last year.

She gave me a shrewd glance. "He not Jesus," she blustered; "he not know about the wet and the dry."

I did not answer her; what was the use? As I sat waiting for the hour when Ambrosch and Ántonia would return from the fields, I watched Mrs. Shimerda at her work. She took from the oven a coffee-cake which she wanted to keep warm for supper, and wrapped it in a quilt stuffed with feathers. I have seen her put even a roast goose in this quilt to keep it hot. When the neighbors were there building the new house they saw her do this, and the story got abroad that the Shimerdas kept their food in their feather beds.

When the sun was dropping low, Ántonia came up the big south draw with her team. How much older she had grown in eight months! She had come to us a child, and now she was a tall, strong young girl, although her fifteenth birthday had just slipped by. I ran out and met her as she brought her horses up to the windmill to water them. She wore the boots her father had so thoughtfully taken off before he shot himself, and his old fur cap. Her outgrown cotton dress switched about her calves, over the boot-tops. She kept her sleeves rolled up all day, and her arms and throat were burned as brown as a sailor's. Her neck came up strongly out of her shoulders, like the bole of a tree out of the turf. One sees that draft-horse neck among the peasant women in all old countries.

She greeted me gayly, and began at once to tell me how much ploughing she had done that day. Ambrosch, she said, was on the north quarter, breaking sod with the oxen.

"Jim, you ask Jake how much he ploughed to-day. I don't want that Jake get more done in one day than me. I want we have very much corn this fall."

While the horses drew in the water, and nosed each other, and then drank again, Ántonia sat down on the windmill step and rested her head on her hand. "You see the big prairie fire from your place last night? I hope your grandpa ain't lose no stacks?"

"No, we didn't. I came to ask you something, Tony. Grandmother wants to know if you can't go to the term of school that begins next week over at the sod schoolhouse. She says there's a good teacher, and you'd learn a lot."

Ántonia stood up, lifting and dropping her shoulders as if they were stiff. "I ain't got time to learn. I can work like mans now. My mother can't say no more how Ambrosch do all and nobody to help him. I can work as much as him. School is all right for little boys. I help make this land one good farm."

She clucked to her team and started for the barn. I walked beside her, feeling vexed. Was she going to grow up boastful like her mother, I wondered? Before we reached the stable, I felt something tense in her silence, and glancing up I saw that she was crying. She turned her face from me and looked off at the red streak of dying light, over the dark prairie.

I climbed up into the loft and threw down the hay for her, while she unharnessed her team. We walked slowly back toward the house. Ambrosch had come in from the north quarter, and was watering his oxen at the tank.

Ántonia took my hand. "Sometime you will tell me all those nice things you learn at the school, won't you, Jimmy?" she asked with a sudden rush of feeling in her voice. "My father, he went much to school. He know a great deal; how to make the fine cloth like what you not got here. He play horn and violin, and he read so many books that the priests in Bohemie come to talk to him. You won't forget my father, Jim?"

"No," I said, "I will never forget him."

Mrs. Shimerda asked me to stay for supper. After Ambrosch and Ántonia had washed the field dust from their hands and faces at the wash-basin by the kitchen door, we sat down at the oilcloth-covered table. Mrs. Shimerda ladled meal mush out of an iron pot and poured milk on it. After the mush we had fresh bread and sorghum molasses, and coffee with the cake that had been kept warm in the feathers. Ántonia and Ambrosch were talking in Bohemian; disputing about which of them had done more ploughing that day. Mrs. Shimerda egged them on, chuckling while she gobbled her food.

Presently Ambrosch said sullenly in English: "You take them ox to-morrow and try the sod plough. Then you not be so smart."

His sister laughed. "Don't be mad. I know it's awful hard work for break sod. I milk the cow for you to-morrow, if you want."

Mrs. Shimerda turned quickly to me. "That cow not give so much milk like what your grandpa say. If he make talk about fifteen dollars, I send him back the cow."

"He doesn't talk about the fifteen dollars," I exclaimed indignantly. "He doesn't find fault with people."

"He say I break his saw when we build, and I never," grumbled Ambrosch.

I knew he had broken the saw, and then hid it and lied about it. I began to wish I had not stayed for supper. Everything was disagreeable to me. Ántonia ate so noisily now, like a man, and she yawned often at the table and kept stretching her arms over her head, as if they ached. Grandmother had said, "Heavy field work'll spoil that girl. She'll lose all her nice ways and get rough ones." She had lost them already.

After supper I rode home through the sad, soft spring twilight. Since winter I had seen very little of Ántonia. She was out in the fields from sun-up until sun-down. If I rode over to see her where she was ploughing, she stopped at the end of a row to chat for a moment, then gripped her ploughhandles, clucked to her team, and waded on down the furrow, making me feel that she was now grown up and had no time for me. On Sundays she helped her mother make garden or sewed all day. Grandfather was pleased with Ántonia. When we complained of her, he only smiled and said, "She will help some fellow get ahead in the world."

Nowadays Tony could talk of nothing but the prices of things, or how much she could lift and endure. She was too proud of her strength. I knew, too, that Ambrosch put upon her some chores a girl ought not to do, and that the farmhands around the country joked in a nasty way about it. Whenever I saw her come up the furrow, shouting to her beasts, sun-burned, sweaty, her dress open at the neck, and her throat and chest dust-plastered, I used to think of the tone in which poor Mr. Shimerda, who could say so little, yet managed to say so much when he exclaimed, "My Án-tonia!"

XVIII

After I began to go to the country school, I saw less of the Bohemians. We were sixteen pupils at the sod schoolhouse, and we all came on horseback and brought our dinner. My schoolmates were none of them very interesting, but I somehow felt that by making comrades of them I was getting even with Ántonia for her indifference. Since the father's death, Ambrosch was more than ever the head of the house and he seemed to direct the feelings as well as the fortunes of his women-folk. Ántonia often quoted his opinions to me, and she let me see that she admired him, while she thought of me only as a little boy. Before the spring was over, there was a distinct coldness between us and the Shimerdas. It came about in this way.

One Sunday I rode over there with Jake to get a horse-collar which Ambrosch had borrowed from him and had not returned. It was a beautiful blue morning. The buffalo-peas were blooming in pink and purple masses along the roadside, and the larks, perched on last year's dried sunflower stalks, were singing straight at the sun, their heads thrown back and their yellow breasts a-quiver. The wind blew about us in warm, sweet gusts. We rode slowly, with a pleasant sense of Sunday indolence.

We found the Shimerdas working just as if it were a week-day. Marek was cleaning out the stable, and Ántonia and her mother were making garden, off across the pond in the draw-head. Ambrosch was up on the wind-mill tower, oiling the wheel. He came down, not very cordially. When Jake asked for the collar, he grunted and scratched his head. The collar belonged to grandfather, of course, and Jake, feeling responsible for it, flared up.

"Now, don't you say you haven't got it, Ambrosch, because I know you have, and if you ain't a-going to look for it, I will."

Ambrosch shrugged his shoulders and sauntered down the hill toward the stable. I could see that it was one of his mean days. Presently he returned, carrying a collar that had been badly used—trampled in the dirt and gnawed by rats until the hair was sticking out of it.

"This what you want?" he asked surlily.

Jake jumped off his horse. I saw a wave of red come up under the rough stubble on his face. "That ain't the piece of harness I loaned you, Ambrosch; or if it is, you've used it shameful. I ain't a-going to carry such a looking thing back to Mr. Burden."

Ambrosch dropped the collar on the ground. "All right," he said coolly, took up his oil-can, and began to climb the mill. Jake caught him by the belt of his trousers and yanked him back. Ambrosch's feet had scarcely touched the ground when he lunged out with a vicious kick at Jake's stomach. Fortunately Jake was in such a position that he could dodge it. This was not the sort of thing country boys did when they played at fisticuffs, and Jake was furious. He landed Ambrosch a blow on the head—it sounded like the crack of an axe on a cow-pumpkin. Ambrosch dropped over, stunned.

We heard squeals, and looking up saw Ántonia and her mother coming on the run. They did not take the path around the pond, but plunged through the muddy water, without even lifting their skirts. They came on, screaming and clawing the air. By this time Ambrosch had come to his senses and was sputtering with nose-bleed. Jake sprang into his saddle. "Let's get out of this, Jim," he called.

Mrs. Shimerda threw her hands over her head and clutched as if she were going to pull down lightning. "Law, law!" she shrieked after us. "Law for knock my Ambrosch down!"

"I never like you no more, Jake and Jim Burden," Ántonia panted. "No friends any more!"

Jake stopped and turned his horse for a second. "Well, you're a damned ungrateful lot, the whole pack of you," he shouted back. "I guess the Burdens can get along without you. You've been a sight of trouble to them, anyhow!"

We rode away, feeling so outraged that the fine morning was spoiled for us. I hadn't a word to say, and poor Jake was white as paper and trembling all over. It made him sick to get so angry. "They ain't the same, Jimmy," he kept saying in a hurt tone. "These foreigners ain't the same. You can't trust 'em to be fair. It's dirty to kick a feller. You heard how the women turned on you—and after all we went through on account of 'em last winter! They ain't to be trusted. I don't want to see you get too thick with any of 'em."

"I'll never be friends with them again, Jake," I declared hotly. "I believe they are all like Krajiek and Ambrosch underneath."

Grandfather heard our story with a twinkle in his eye. He advised Jake to ride to town to-morrow, go to a justice of the peace, tell him he had knocked young Shimerda down, and pay his fine. Then if Mrs. Shimerda was inclined to make trouble—her son was still under age—she would be forestalled. Jake said he might as well take the wagon and haul to market the pig he had been fattening. On Monday, about an hour after Jake had started, we saw Mrs. Shimerda and her Ambrosch proudly driving by, looking neither to the right nor left. As they rattled out of sight down the Black Hawk road, grandfather chuckled, saying he had rather expected she would follow the matter up.

Jake paid his fine with a ten-dollar bill grandfather had given him for that purpose. But when the Shimerdas found that Jake sold his pig in town that day, Ambrosch worked it out in his shrewd head that Jake had to sell his pig to pay his fine. This theory afforded the Shimerdas great satisfaction, apparently. For weeks afterward, whenever Jake and I met Ántonia on her way to the post-office, or going along the road with her work-team, she would clap her hands and call to us in a spiteful, crowing voice:—

"Jake-y, Jake-y, sell the pig and pay the slap!"

Otto pretended not to be surprised at Ántonia's behavior. He only lifted his brows and said, "You can't tell me anything new about a Czech; I'm an Austrian."

Grandfather was never a party to what Jake called our feud with the Shimerdas. Ambrosch and Ántonia always greeted him respectfully, and he asked them about their affairs and gave them advice as usual. He thought the future looked hopeful for them. Ambrosch was a far-seeing fellow; he soon realized that his oxen were too heavy for any work except breaking sod, and he succeeded in selling them to a newly arrived German. With the money he bought another team of horses, which grandfather selected for him. Marek was strong, and Ambrosch worked him hard; but he could never teach him to cultivate corn, I remember. The one idea that had ever got through poor Marek's thick head was that all exertion was meritorious. He always bore down on the handles of the cultivator and drove the blades so deep into the earth that the horses were soon exhausted.

In June Ambrosch went to work at Mr. Bushy's for a week, and took Marek with him at full wages. Mrs. Shimerda then drove the second cultivator; she and Ántonia worked in the fields all day and did the chores at night. While the two women were running the place alone, one of the new horses got colic and gave them a terrible fright.

Ántonia had gone down to the barn one night to see that all was well before she went to bed, and she noticed that one of the roans was swollen about the middle and stood with its head hanging. She mounted another horse, without waiting to saddle him, and hammered on our door just as we were going to bed. Grandfather answered her knock. He did not send one of his men, but rode back with her himself, taking a syringe and an old piece of carpet he kept for hot applications when our horses were sick. He found Mrs. Shimerda sitting by the horse with her lantern, groaning and wringing her hands. It took but a few moments to release the gases pent up in the poor beast, and the two women heard the rush of wind and saw the roan visibly diminish in girth.

"If I lose that horse, Mr. Burden," Ántonia exclaimed, "I never stay here till Ambrosch come home! I go drown myself in the pond before morning."

When Ambrosch came back from Mr. Bushy's, we learned that he had given Marek's wages to the priest at Black Hawk, for masses for their father's soul. Grandmother thought Ántonia needed shoes more than Mr. Shimerda needed prayers, but grandfather said tolerantly, "If he can spare six dollars, pinched as he is, it shows he believes what he professes."

It was grandfather who brought about a reconciliation with the Shimerdas. One morning he told us that the small grain was coming on so well, he thought he would begin to cut his wheat on the first of July. He would need more men, and if it were agreeable to every one he would engage Ambrosch for the reaping and thrashing, as the Shimerdas had no small grain of their own.

"I think, Emmaline," he concluded, "I will ask Ántonia to come over and help you in the kitchen. She will be glad to earn something, and it will be a good time to end misunderstandings. I may as well ride over this morning and make arrangements. Do you want to go with me, Jim?" His tone told me that he had already decided for me.

After breakfast we set off together. When Mrs. Shimerda saw us coming, she ran from her door down into the draw behind the stable, as if she did not want to meet us. Grandfather smiled to himself while he tied his horse, and we followed her.

Behind the barn we came upon a funny sight. The cow had evidently been grazing somewhere in the draw. Mrs. Shimerda had run to the animal, pulled up the lariat pin, and, when we came upon her, she was trying to hide the cow in an old cave in the bank. As the hole was narrow and dark, the cow held back, and the old woman was slapping and pushing at her hind quarters, trying to spank her into the draw-side.

Grandfather ignored her singular occupation and greeted her politely. "Good-morning, Mrs. Shimerda. Can you tell me where I will find Ambrosch? Which field?"

"He with the sod corn." She pointed toward the north, still standing in front of the cow as if she hoped to conceal it.

"His sod corn will be good for fodder this winter," said grandfather encouragingly. "And where is Ántonia?"

"She go with." Mrs. Shimerda kept wiggling her bare feet about nervously in the dust.

"Very well. I will ride up there. I want them to come over and help me cut my oats and wheat next month. I will pay them wages. Good-morning. By the way, Mrs. Shimerda," he said as he turned up the path, "I think we may as well call it square about the cow."

She started and clutched the rope tighter. Seeing that she did not understand, grandfather turned back. "You need not pay me anything more; no more money. The cow is yours."

"Pay no more, keep cow?" she asked in a bewildered tone, her narrow eyes snapping at us in the sunlight.

"Exactly. Pay no more, keep cow." He nodded.

Mrs. Shimerda dropped the rope, ran after us, and crouching down beside grandfather, she took his hand and kissed it. I doubt if he had ever been so much embarrassed before. I was a little startled, too. Somehow, that seemed to bring the Old World very close.

We rode away laughing, and grandfather said: "I expect she thought we had come to take the cow away for certain, Jim. I wonder if she wouldn't have scratched a little if we'd laid hold of that lariat rope!"

Our neighbors seemed glad to make peace with us. The next Sunday Mrs. Shimerda came over and brought Jake a pair of socks she had knitted. She presented them with an air of great magnanimity, saying, "Now you not come any more for knock my Ambrosch down?"

Jake laughed sheepishly. "I don't want to have no trouble with Ambrosch. If he'll let me alone, I'll let him alone."

"If he slap you, we ain't got no pig for pay the fine," she said insinuatingly.

Jake was not at all disconcerted. "Have the last word, mam," he said cheerfully. "It's a lady's privilege."

XIX

July came on with that breathless, brilliant heat which makes the plains of Kansas and Nebraska the best corn country in the world. It seemed as if we could hear the corn growing in the night; under the stars one caught a faint crackling in the dewy, heavy-odored cornfields where the feathered stalks stood so juicy and green. If all the great plain from the Missouri to the Rocky Mountains had been under glass, and the heat regulated by a thermometer, it could not have been better for the yellow tassels that were ripening and fertilizing the silk day by day. The cornfields were far apart in those times, with miles of wild grazing land between. It took a clear, meditative eye like my grandfather's to foresee that they would enlarge and multiply until they would be, not the Shimerdas' cornfields, or Mr. Bushy's, but the world's cornfields; that their yield would be one of the great economic facts, like the wheat crop of Russia, which underlie all the activities of men, in peace or war.

The burning sun of those few weeks, with occasional rains at night, secured the corn. After the milky ears were once formed, we had little to fear from dry weather. The men were working so hard in the wheatfields that they did not notice the heat,—though I was kept busy carrying water for them,—

and grandmother and Ántonia had so much to do in the kitchen that they could not have told whether one day was hotter than another. Each morning, while the dew was still on the grass, Ántonia went with me up to the garden to get early vegetables for dinner. Grandmother made her wear a sunbonnet, but as soon as we reached the garden she threw it on the grass and let her hair fly in the breeze. I remember how, as we bent over the pea-vines, beads of perspiration used to gather on her upper lip like a little mustache.

"Oh, better I like to work out of doors than in a house!" she used to sing joyfully. "I not care that your grandmother say it makes me like a man. I like to be like a man." She would toss her head and ask me to feel the muscles swell in her brown arm.

We were glad to have her in the house. She was so gay and responsive that one did not mind her heavy, running step, or her clattery way with pans. Grandmother was in high spirits during the weeks that Ántonia worked for us.

All the nights were close[4] and hot during that harvest season. The harvesters slept in the hayloft because it was cooler there than in the house. I used to lie in my bed by the open window, watching the heat lightning play softly along the horizon, or looking up at the gaunt frame of the windmill against the blue night sky. One night there was a beautiful electric storm, though not enough rain fell to damage the cut grain. The men went down to the barn immediately after supper, and when the dishes were washed Ántonia and I climbed up on the slanting roof of the chicken-house to watch the clouds. The thunder was loud and metallic, like the rattle of sheet iron, and the lightning broke in great zigzags across the heavens, making everything stand out and come close to us for a moment. Half the sky was checkered with black thunderheads, but all the west was luminous and clear: in the lightning-flashes it looked like deep blue water, with the sheen of moonlight on it; and the mottled part of the sky was like marble pavement, like the quay of some splendid sea-coast city, doomed to destruction. Great warm splashes of rain fell on our upturned faces. One black cloud, no bigger than a little boat, drifted out into the clear space unattended, and kept moving westward. All about us we could hear the felty beat of the raindrops on the soft dust of the farmyard. Grandmother came to the door and said it was late, and we would get wet out there.

"In a minute we come," Ántonia called back to her. "I like your grandmother, and all things here," she sighed. "I wish my papa live to see this summer. I wish no winter ever come again."

"It will be summer a long while yet," I reassured her. "Why aren't you always nice like this, Tony?"

"How nice?"

"Why, just like this; like yourself. Why do you all the time try to be like Ambrosch?"

She put her arms under her head and lay back, looking up at the sky. "If I live here, like you, that is different. Things will be easy for you. But they will be hard for us."

4. Humid.

Book II. The Hired Girls

I

I had been living with my grandfather for nearly three years when he decided to move to Black Hawk. He and grandmother were getting old for the heavy work of a farm, and as I was now thirteen they thought I ought to be going to school. Accordingly our homestead was rented to "that good woman, the Widow Steavens," and her bachelor brother, and we bought Preacher White's house, at the north end of Black Hawk. This was the first town house one passed driving in from the farm, a landmark which told country people their long ride was over.

We were to move to Black Hawk in March, and as soon as grandfather had fixed the date he let Jake and Otto know of his intention. Otto said he would not be likely to find another place that suited him so well; that he was tired of farming and thought he would go back to what he called the "wild West." Jake Marpole, lured by Otto's stories of adventure, decided to go with him. We did our best to dissuade Jake. He was so handicapped by illiteracy and by his trusting disposition that he would be an easy prey to sharpers.[5] Grandmother begged him to stay among kindly, Christian people, where he was known; but there was no reasoning with him. He wanted to be a prospector. He thought a silver mine was waiting for him in Colorado.

Jake and Otto served us to the last. They moved us into town, put down the carpets in our new house, made shelves and cupboards for grandmother's kitchen, and seemed loath to leave us. But at last they went, without warning. Those two fellows had been faithful to us through sun and storm, had given us things that cannot be bought in any market in the world. With me they had been like older brothers; had restrained their speech and manners out of care for me, and given me so much good comradeship. Now they got on the west-bound train one morning, in their Sunday clothes, with their oil-cloth valises—and I never saw them again. Months afterward we got a card from Otto, saying that Jake had been down with mountain fever but now they were both working in the Yankee Girl mine, and were doing well. I wrote to them at that address, but my letter was returned to me, "unclaimed." After that we never heard from them.

Black Hawk, the new world in which we had come to live, was a clean, well-planted little prairie town, with white fences and good green yards about the dwellings, wide, dusty streets, and shapely little trees growing along the wooden sidewalks. In the center of the town there were two rows of new brick "store" buildings, a brick schoolhouse, the court-house, and four white churches. Our own house looked down over the town, and from our upstairs windows we could see the winding line of the river bluffs, two miles south of us. That river was to be my compensation for the lost freedom of the farming country.

We came to Black Hawk in March, and by the end of April we felt like town people. Grandfather was a deacon in the new Baptist Church, grandmother was busy with church suppers and missionary societies, and I was quite

5. Swindlers.

another boy, or thought I was. Suddenly put down among boys of my own age, I found I had a great deal to learn. Before the spring term of school was over I could fight, play "keeps," tease the little girls, and use forbidden words as well as any boy in my class. I was restrained from utter savagery only by the fact that Mrs. Harling, our nearest neighbor, kept an eye on me, and if my behavior went beyond certain bounds I was not permitted to come into her yard or to play with her jolly children.

We saw more of our country neighbors now than when we lived on the farm. Our house was a convenient stopping-place for them. We had a big barn where the farmers could put up their teams, and their women-folk more often accompanied them, now that they could stay with us for dinner, and rest and set their bonnets right before they went shopping. The more our house was like a country hotel, the better I liked it. I was glad, when I came home from school at noon, to see a farm wagon standing in the back yard, and I was always ready to run downtown to get beefsteak or baker's bread for unexpected company. All through that first spring and summer I kept hoping that Ambrosch would bring Ántonia and Yulka to see our new house. I wanted to show them our red plush furniture, and the trumpet-blowing cherubs the German paper-hanger[6] had put on our parlor ceiling.

When Ambrosch came to town, however, he came alone, and though he put his horses in our barn, he would never stay for dinner, or tell us anything about his mother and sisters. If we ran out and questioned him as he was slipping through the yard, he would merely work his shoulders about in his coat and say, "They all right, I guess."

Mrs. Steavens, who now lived on our farm, grew as fond of Ántonia as we had been, and always brought us news of her. All through the wheat season, she told us, Ambrosch hired his sister out like a man, and she went from farm to farm, binding sheaves or working with the thrashers. The farmers liked her and were kind to her; said they would rather have her for a hand than Ambrosch. When fall came she was to husk corn for the neighbors until Christmas, as she had done the year before; but grandmother saved her from this by getting her a place to work with our neighbors, the Harlings.

II

Grandmother often said that if she had to live in town, she thanked God she lived next the Harlings. They had been farming people, like ourselves, and their place was like a little farm, with a big barn and a garden, and an orchard and grazing lots,—even a windmill. The Harlings were Norwegians, and Mrs. Harling had lived in Christiania[7] until she was ten years old. Her husband was born in Minnesota. He was a grain merchant and cattle buyer, and was generally considered the most enterprising business man in our county.[8] He controlled a line of grain elevators in the little towns along the railroad to the west of us, and was away from home a great deal. In his absence his wife was the head of the household.

Mrs. Harling was short and square and sturdy-looking, like her house. Every inch of her was charged with an energy that made itself felt the moment she entered a room. Her face was rosy and solid, with bright, twin-

---

6. Specialist in decorating with wallpaper.
7. Now Oslo, capital of Norway.
8. Successful plains agriculture required middle-men to store and market the grain and livestock that large farms were producing.

kling eyes and a stubborn little chin. She was quick to anger, quick to laughter, and jolly from the depths of her soul. How well I remember her laugh; it had in it the same sudden recognition that flashed into her eyes, was a burst of humor, short and intelligent. Her rapid footsteps shook her own floors, and she routed lassitude and indifference wherever she came. She could not be negative or perfunctory about anything. Her enthusiasm, and her violent likes and dislikes, asserted themselves in all the every-day occupations of life. Wash-day was interesting, never dreary, at the Harlings'. Preserving-time was a prolonged festival, and house-cleaning was like a revolution. When Mrs. Harling made garden that spring, we could feel the stir of her undertaking through the willow hedge that separated our place from hers.

Three of the Harling children were near me in age. Charley, the only son,—they had lost an older boy,—was sixteen; Julia, who was known as the musical one, was fourteen when I was; and Sally, the tomboy with short hair, was a year younger. She was nearly as strong as I, and uncannily clever at all boys' sports. Sally was a wild thing, with sun-burned yellow hair, bobbed about her ears, and a brown skin, for she never wore a hat. She raced all over town on one roller skate, often cheated at "keeps," but was such a quick shot one couldn't catch her at it.

The grown-up daughter, Frances, was a very important person in our world. She was her father's chief clerk, and virtually managed his Black Hawk office during his frequent absences. Because of her unusual business ability, he was stern and exacting with her. He paid her a good salary, but she had few holidays and never got away from her responsibilities. Even on Sundays she went to the office to open the mail and read the markets. With Charley, who was not interested in business, but was already preparing for Annapolis,[9] Mr. Harling was very indulgent; bought him guns and tools and electric batteries, and never asked what he did with them.

Frances was dark, like her father, and quite as tall. In winter she wore a sealskin coat and cap, and she and Mr. Harling used to walk home together in the evening, talking about grain-cars and cattle, like two men. Sometimes she came over to see grandfather after supper, and her visits flattered him. More than once they put their wits together to rescue some unfortunate farmer from the clutches of Wick Cutter, the Black Hawk money-lender. Grandfather said Frances Harling was as good a judge of credits as any banker in the country. The two or three men who had tried to take advantage of her in a deal acquired celebrity by their defeat. She knew every farmer for miles about; how much land he had under cultivation, how many cattle he was feeding, what his liabilities were. Her interest in these people was more than a business interest. She carried them all in her mind as if they were characters in a book or a play.

When Frances drove out into the country on business, she would go miles out of her way to call on some of the old people, or to see the women who seldom got to town. She was quick at understanding the grandmothers who spoke no English, and the most reticent and distrustful of them would tell her their story without realizing they were doing so. She went to country funerals and weddings in all weathers. A farmer's daughter who was to be married could count on a wedding present from Frances Harling.

9. I.e., U.S. Naval Academy, in Annapolis, Maryland.

In August the Harlings' Danish cook had to leave them. Grandmother entreated them to try Ántonia. She cornered Ambrosch the next time he came to town, and pointed out to him that any connection with Christian Harling would strengthen his credit and be of advantage to him. One Sunday Mrs. Harling took the long ride out to the Shimerdas' with Frances. She said she wanted to see "what the girl came from" and to have a clear understanding with her mother. I was in our yard when they came driving home, just before sunset. They laughed and waved to me as they passed, and I could see they were in great good humor. After supper, when grandfather set off to church, grandmother and I took my short cut through the willow hedge and went over to hear about the visit to the Shimerdas.

We found Mrs. Harling with Charley and Sally on the front porch, resting after her hard drive. Julia was in the hammock—she was fond of repose—and Frances was at the piano, playing without a light and talking to her mother through the open window.

Mrs. Harling laughed when she saw us coming. "I expect you left your dishes on the table to-night, Mrs. Burden," she called. Frances shut the piano and came out to join us.

They had liked Ántonia from their first glimpse of her; felt they knew exactly what kind of girl she was. As for Mrs. Shimerda, they found her very amusing. Mrs. Harling chuckled whenever she spoke of her. "I expect I am more at home with that sort of bird than you are, Mrs. Burden. They're a pair, Ambrosch and that old woman!"

They had had a long argument with Ambrosch about Ántonia's allowance for clothes and pocket-money. It was his plan that every cent of his sister's wages should be paid over to him each month, and he would provide her with such clothing as he thought necessary. When Mrs. Harling told him firmly that she would keep fifty dollars a year for Ántonia's own use, he declared they wanted to take his sister to town and dress her up and make a fool of her. Mrs. Harling gave us a lively account of Ambrosch's behavior throughout the interview; how he kept jumping up and putting on his cap as if he were through with the whole business, and how his mother tweaked his coat-tail and prompted him in Bohemian. Mrs. Harling finally agreed to pay three dollars a week for Ántonia's services—good wages in those days—and to keep her in shoes. There had been hot dispute about the shoes, Mrs. Shimerda finally saying persuasively that she would send Mrs. Harling three fat geese every year to "make even." Ambrosch was to bring his sister to town next Saturday.

"She'll be awkward and rough at first, like enough," grandmother said anxiously, "but unless she's been spoiled by the hard life she's led, she has it in her to be a real helpful girl."

Mrs. Harling laughed her quick, decided laugh. "Oh, I'm not worrying, Mrs. Burden! I can bring something out of that girl. She's barely seventeen, not too old to learn new ways. She's good-looking, too!" she added warmly.

Frances turned to grandmother. "Oh, yes, Mrs. Burden, you didn't tell us that! She was working in the garden when we got there, barefoot and ragged. But she has such fine brown legs and arms, and splendid color in her cheeks—like those big dark red plums."

We were pleased at this praise. Grandmother spoke feelingly. "When she first came to this country, Frances, and had that genteel old man to watch over her, she was as pretty a girl as ever I saw. But, dear me, what a life she's led, out in the fields with those rough thrashers! Things would have been very different with poor Ántonia if her father had lived."

The Harlings begged us to tell them about Mr. Shimerda's death and the big snowstorm. By the time we saw grandfather coming home from church we had told them pretty much all we knew of the Shimerdas.

"The girl will be happy here, and she'll forget those things," said Mrs. Harling confidently, as we rose to take our leave.

III

On Saturday Ambrosch drove up to the back gate, and Ántonia jumped down from the wagon and ran into our kitchen just as she used to do. She was wearing shoes and stockings, and was breathless and excited. She gave me a playful shake by the shoulders. "You ain't forget about me, Jim?"

Grandmother kissed her. "God bless you, child! Now you've come, you must try to do right and be a credit to us."

Ántonia looked eagerly about the house and admired everything. "Maybe I be the kind of girl you like better, now I come to town," she suggested hopefully.

How good it was to have Ántonia near us again; to see her every day and almost every night! Her greatest fault, Mrs. Harling found, was that she so often stopped her work and fell to playing with the children. She would race about the orchard with us, or take sides in our hay-fights in the barn, or be the old bear that came down from the mountain and carried off Nina. Tony learned English so quickly that by the time school began she could speak as well as any of us.

I was jealous of Tony's admiration for Charley Harling. Because he was always first in his classes at school, and could mend the water-pipes or the door-bell and take the clock to pieces, she seemed to think him a sort of prince. Nothing that Charley wanted was too much trouble for her. She loved to put up lunches for him when he went hunting, to mend his ball-gloves and sew buttons on his shooting-coat, baked the kind of nut-cake he liked, and fed his setter dog when he was away on trips with his father. Ántonia had made herself cloth working-slippers out of Mr. Harling's old coats, and in these she went padding about after Charley, fairly panting with eagerness to please him.

Next to Charley, I think she loved Nina best. Nina was only six, and she was rather more complex than the other children. She was fanciful, had all sorts of unspoken preferences, and was easily offended. At the slightest disappointment or displeasure her velvety brown eyes filled with tears, and she would lift her chin and walk silently away. If we ran after her and tried to appease her, it did no good. She walked on unmollified. I used to think that no eyes in the world could grow so large or hold so many tears as Nina's. Mrs. Harling and Ántonia invariably took her part. We were never given a chance to explain. The charge was simply: "You have made Nina cry. Now, Jimmy can go home, and Sally must get her arithmetic." I liked Nina, too; she was so quaint and unexpected, and her eyes were lovely; but I often wanted to shake her.

We had jolly evenings at the Harlings when the father was away. If he was at home, the children had to go to bed early, or they came over to my house to play. Mr. Harling not only demanded a quiet house, he demanded all his wife's attention. He used to take her away to their room in the west ell, and talk over his business with her all evening. Though we did not realize it then, Mrs. Harling was our audience when we played, and we always looked to her for suggestions. Nothing flattered one like her quick laugh.

Mr. Harling had a desk in his bedroom, and his own easy-chair by the window, in which no one else ever sat. On the nights when he was at home, I could see his shadow on the blind, and it seemed to me an arrogant shadow. Mrs. Harling paid no heed to any one else if he was there. Before he went to bed she always got him a lunch of smoked salmon or anchovies and beer. He kept an alcohol lamp in his room, and a French coffee-pot, and his wife made coffee for him at any hour of the night he happened to want it.

Most Black Hawk fathers had no personal habits outside their domestic ones; they paid the bills, pushed the baby carriage after office hours, moved the sprinkler about over the lawn, and took the family driving on Sunday. Mr. Harling, therefore, seemed to me autocratic and imperial in his ways. He walked, talked, put on his gloves, shook hands, like a man who felt that he had power. He was not tall, but he carried his head so haughtily that he looked a commanding figure, and there was something daring and challenging in his eyes. I used to imagine that the "nobles" of whom Antonia was always talking probably looked very much like Christian Harling, wore caped overcoats like his, and just such a glittering diamond upon the little finger.

Except when the father was at home, the Harling house was never quiet. Mrs. Harling and Nina and Ántonia made as much noise as a houseful of children, and there was usually somebody at the piano. Julia was the only one who was held down to regular hours of practicing, but they all played. When Frances came home at noon, she played until dinner was ready. When Sally got back from school, she sat down in her hat and coat and drummed the plantation melodies that negro minstrel troupes brought to town. Even Nina played the Swedish Wedding March.

Mrs. Harling had studied the piano under a good teacher, and somehow she managed to practice every day. I soon learned that if I were sent over on an errand and found Mrs. Harling at the piano, I must sit down and wait quietly until she turned to me. I can see her at this moment; her short, square person planted firmly on the stool, her little fat hands moving quickly and neatly over the keys, her eyes fixed on the music with intelligent concentration.

IV

> "I won't have none of your weevily wheat, and I won't have none of your barley,
> But I'll take a measure of fine white flour, to make a cake for Charley."

We were singing rhymes to tease Ántonia while she was beating up one of Charley's favorite cakes in her big mixing-bowl. It was a crisp autumn evening, just cold enough to make one glad to quit playing tag in the yard, and retreat into the kitchen. We had begun to roll popcorn balls with syrup when we heard a knock at the back door, and Tony dropped her spoon and went to open it. A plump, fair-skinned girl was standing in the doorway. She looked demure and pretty, and made a graceful picture in her blue cashmere dress and little blue hat, with a plaid shawl drawn neatly about her shoulders and a clumsy pocketbook in her hand.

"Hello, Tony. Don't you know me?" she asked in a smooth, low voice, looking in at us archly.

Ántonia gasped and stepped back. "Why, it's Lena! Of course I didn't know you, so dressed up!"

Lena Lingard laughed, as if this pleased her. I had not recognized her for a moment, either. I had never seen her before with a hat on her head—or with shoes and stockings on her feet, for that matter. And here she was, brushed and smoothed and dressed like a town girl, smiling at us with perfect composure.

"Hello, Jim," she said carelessly as she walked into the kitchen and looked about her. "I've come to town to work, too, Tony."

"Have you, now? Well, ain't that funny!" Ántonia stood ill at ease, and didn't seem to know just what to do with her visitor.

The door was open into the dining-room, where Mrs. Harling sat crocheting and Frances was reading. Frances asked Lena to come in and join them.

"You are Lena Lingard, aren't you? I've been to see your mother, but you were off herding cattle that day. Mama, this is Chris Lingard's oldest girl."

Mrs. Harling dropped her worsted and examined the visitor with quick, keen eyes. Lena was not at all disconcerted. She sat down in the chair Frances pointed out, carefully arranging her pocketbook and gray cotton gloves on her lap. We followed with our popcorn, but Ántonia hung back— said she had to get her cake into the oven.

"So you have come to town," said Mrs. Harling, her eyes still fixed on Lena. "Where are you working?"

"For Mrs. Thomas, the dressmaker. She is going to teach me to sew. She says I have quite a knack. I'm through with the farm. There ain't any end to the work on a farm, and always so much trouble happens. I'm going to be a dressmaker."

"Well, there have to be dressmakers. It's a good trade. But I wouldn't run down the farm, if I were you," said Mrs. Harling rather severely. "How is your mother?"

"Oh, mother's never very well; she has too much to do. She'd get away from the farm, too, if she could. She was willing for me to come. After I learn to do sewing, I can make money and help her."

"See that you don't forget to," said Mrs. Harling skeptically, as she took up her crocheting again and sent the hook in and out with nimble fingers.

"No, 'm, I won't," said Lena blandly. She took a few grains of the popcorn we pressed upon her, eating them discreetly and taking care not to get her fingers sticky.

Frances drew her chair up nearer to the visitor. "I thought you were going to be married, Lena," she said teasingly. "Didn't I hear that Nick Svendsen was rushing you pretty hard?"

Lena looked up with her curiously innocent smile. "He did go with me quite a while. But his father made a fuss about it and said he wouldn't give Nick any land if he married me, so he's going to marry Annie Iverson. I wouldn't like to be her; Nick's awful sullen, and he'll take it out on her. He ain't spoke to his father since he promised."

Frances laughed. "And how do you feel about it?"

"I don't want to marry Nick, or any other man," Lena murmured. "I've seen a good deal of married life, and I don't care for it. I want to be so I can help my mother and the children at home, and not have to ask lief[1] of anybody."

"That's right," said Frances. "And Mrs. Thomas thinks you can learn dress-making?"

"Yes, 'm. I've always liked to sew, but I never had much to do with. Mrs. Thomas makes lovely things for all the town ladies. Did you know Mrs. Gardener is having a purple velvet made? The velvet came from Omaha. My, but it's lovely!" Lena sighed softly and stroked her cashmere folds. "Tony knows I never did like out-of-door work," she added.

Mrs. Harling glanced at her. "I expect you'll learn to sew all right, Lena, if you'll only keep your head and not go gadding about to dances all the time and neglect your work, the way some country girls do."

"Yes, 'm. Tiny Soderball is coming to town, too. She's going to work at the Boys' Home Hotel. She'll see lots of strangers," Lena added wistfully.

"Too many, like enough," said Mrs. Harling. "I don't think a hotel is a good place for a girl; though I guess Mrs. Gardener keeps an eye on her waitresses."

Lena's candid eyes, that always looked a little sleepy under their long lashes, kept straying about the cheerful rooms with naïve admiration. Presently she drew on her cotton gloves. "I guess I must be leaving," she said irresolutely.

Frances told her to come again, whenever she was lonesome or wanted advice about anything. Lena replied that she didn't believe she would ever get lonesome in Black Hawk.

She lingered at the kitchen door and begged Ántonia to come and see her often. "I've got a room of my own at Mrs. Thomas's, with a carpet."

Tony shuffled uneasily in her cloth slippers. "I'll come sometime, but Mrs. Harling don't like to have me run much," she said evasively.

"You can do what you please when you go out, can't you?" Lena asked in a guarded whisper. "Ain't you crazy about town, Tony? I don't care what anybody says, I'm done with the farm!" She glanced back over her shoulder toward the dining-room, where Mrs. Harling sat.

When Lena was gone, Frances asked Ántonia why she hadn't been a little more cordial to her.

"I didn't know if your mother would like her coming here," said Ántonia, looking troubled. "She was kind of talked about, out there."

"Yes, I know. But mother won't hold it against her if she behaves well here. You needn't say anything about that to the children. I guess Jim has heard all that gossip?"

When I nodded, she pulled my hair and told me I knew too much, anyhow. We were good friends, Frances and I.

I ran home to tell grandmother that Lena Lingard had come to town. We were glad of it, for she had a hard life on the farm.

Lena lived in the Norwegian settlement west of Squaw Creek, and she used to herd her father's cattle in the open country between his place and the Shimerdas'. Whenever we rode over in that direction we saw her out among

---

1. Leave, permission.

her cattle, bareheaded and barefooted, scantily dressed in tattered clothing, always knitting as she watched her herd. Before I knew Lena, I thought of her as something wild, that always lived on the prairie, because I had never seen her under a roof. Her yellow hair was burned to a ruddy thatch on her head; but her legs and arms, curiously enough, in spite of constant exposure to the sun, kept a miraculous whiteness which somehow made her seem more undressed than other girls who went scantily clad. The first time I stopped to talk to her, I was astonished at her soft voice and easy, gentle ways. The girls out there usually got rough and mannish after they went to herding. But Lena asked Jake and me to get off our horses and stay awhile, and behaved exactly as if she were in a house and were accustomed to having visitors. She was not embarrassed by her ragged clothes, and treated us as if we were old acquaintances. Even then I noticed the unusual color of her eyes—a shade of deep violet—and their soft, confiding expression.

Chris Lingard was not a very successful farmer, and he had a large family. Lena was always knitting stockings for little brothers and sisters, and even the Norwegian women, who disapproved of her, admitted that she was a good daughter to her mother. As Tony said, she had been talked about. She was accused of making Ole Benson lose the little sense he had—and that at an age when she should still have been in pinafores.

Ole lived in a leaky dugout somewhere at the edge of the settlement. He was fat and lazy and discouraged, and bad luck had become a habit with him. After he had had every other kind of misfortune, his wife, "Crazy Mary," tried to set a neighbor's barn on fire, and was sent to the asylum at Lincoln. She was kept there for a few months, then escaped and walked all the way home, nearly two hundred miles, traveling by night and hiding in barns and haystacks by day. When she got back to the Norwegian settlement, her poor feet were as hard as hoofs. She promised to be good, and was allowed to stay at home—though every one realized she was as crazy as ever, and she still ran about barefooted through the snow, telling her domestic troubles to her neighbors.

Not long after Mary came back from the asylum, I heard a young Dane, who was helping us to thrash, tell Jake and Otto that Chris Lingard's oldest girl had put Ole Benson out of his head, until he had no more sense than his crazy wife. When Ole was cultivating his corn that summer, he used to get discouraged in the field, tie up his team, and wander off to wherever Lena Lingard was herding. There he would sit down on the draw-side and help her watch her cattle. All the settlement was talking about it. The Norwegian preacher's wife went to Lena and told her she ought not to allow this; she begged Lena to come to church on Sundays. Lena said she hadn't a dress in the world any less ragged than the one on her back. Then the minister's wife went through her old trunks and found some things she had worn before her marriage.

The next Sunday Lena appeared at church, a little late, with her hair done up neatly on her head, like a young woman, wearing shoes and stockings, and the new dress, which she had made over for herself very becomingly. The congregation stared at her. Until that morning no one—unless it were Ole—had realized how pretty she was, or that she was growing up. The swelling lines of her figure had been hidden under the shapeless rags she wore in the fields. After the last hymn had been sung, and the congregation was dismissed, Ole slipped out to the hitch-bar and lifted Lena on her horse. That, in itself, was shocking; a married man was not expected to do such things. But it was nothing to the scene that followed. Crazy Mary darted out from the group of women at the church door, and ran down the road after Lena, shouting horrible threats.

"Look out, you Lena Lingard, look out! I'll come over with a corn-knife one day and trim some of that shape off you. Then you won't sail round so fine, making eyes at the men! . . ."

The Norwegian women didn't know where to look. They were formal housewives, most of them, with a severe sense of decorum. But Lena Lingard only laughed her lazy, good-natured laugh and rode on, gazing back over her shoulder at Ole's infuriated wife.

The time came, however, when Lena didn't laugh. More than once Crazy Mary chased her across the prairie and round and round the Shimerdas' cornfield. Lena never told her father; perhaps she was ashamed; perhaps she was more afraid of his anger than of the cornknife. I was at the Shimerdas' one afternoon when Lena came bounding through the red grass as fast as her white legs could carry her. She ran straight into the house and hid in Ántonia's feather-bed. Mary was not far behind; she came right up to the door and made us feel how sharp her blade was, showing us very graphically just what she meant to do to Lena. Mrs. Shimerda, leaning out of the window, enjoyed the situation keenly, and was sorry when Ántonia sent Mary away, mollified by an apronful of bottle-tomatoes. Lena came out from Tony's room behind the kitchen, very pink from the heat of the feathers, but otherwise calm. She begged Ántonia and me to go with her, and help get her cattle together; they were scattered and might be gorging themselves in somebody's cornfield.

"Maybe you lose a steer and learn not to make somethings with your eyes at married men," Mrs. Shimerda told her hectoringly.

Lena only smiled her sleepy smile. "I never made anything to him with my eyes. I can't help it if he hangs around, and I can't order him off. It ain't my prairie."

V

After Lena came to Black Hawk I often met her downtown, where she would be matching sewing silk or buying "findings" for Mrs. Thomas. If I happened to walk home with her, she told me all about the dresses she was helping to make, or about what she saw and heard when she was with Tiny Soderball at the hotel on Saturday nights.

The Boys' Home was the best hotel on our branch of the Burlington, and all the commercial travelers[2] in that territory tried to get into Black Hawk for Sunday. They used to assemble in the parlor after supper on Saturday nights. Marshall Field's[3] man, Anson Kirkpatrick, played the piano and sang all the latest sentimental songs. After Tiny had helped the cook wash the dishes, she and Lena sat on the other side of the double doors between the parlor and the dining-room, listening to the music and giggling at the jokes and stories. Lena often said she hoped I would be a traveling man when I grew up. They had a gay life of it; nothing to do but ride about on trains all day and go to

2. Traveling salesmen.
3. Prominent Chicago-based merchant (1834–1906) who pioneered many modern retailing prac-

tices; best known now for the department-store chain bearing his name.

theaters when they were in big cities. Behind the hotel there was an old store building, where the salesmen opened their big trunks and spread out their samples on the counters. The Black Hawk merchants went to look at these things and order goods, and Mrs. Thomas, though she was "retail trade," was permitted to see them and to "get ideas." They were all generous, these traveling men; they gave Tiny Soderball handkerchiefs and gloves and ribbons and striped stockings, and so many bottles of perfume and cakes of scented soap that she bestowed some of them on Lena.

One afternoon in the week before Christmas I came upon Lena and her funny, square-headed little brother Chris, standing before the drug-store, gazing in at the wax dolls and blocks and Noah's arks arranged in the frosty show window. The boy had come to town with a neighbor to do his Christmas shopping, for he had money of his own this year. He was only twelve, but that winter he had got the job of sweeping out the Norwegian church and making the fire in it every Sunday morning. A cold job it must have been, too!

We went into Duckford's dry-goods store, and Chris unwrapped all his presents and showed them to me—something for each of the six younger than himself, even a rubber pig for the baby. Lena had given him one of Tiny Soderball's bottles of perfume for his mother, and he thought he would get some handkerchiefs to go with it. They were cheap, and he hadn't much money left. We found a tableful of handkerchiefs spread out for view at Duckford's. Chris wanted those with initial letters in the corner, because he had never seen any before. He studied them seriously, while Lena looked over his shoulder, telling him she thought the red letters would hold their color best. He seemed so perplexed that I thought perhaps he hadn't enough money, after all. Presently he said gravely,—

"Sister, you know mother's name is Berthe. I don't know if I ought to get B for Berthe, or M for Mother."

Lena patted his bristly head. "I'd get the B, Chrissy. It will please her for you to think about her name. Nobody ever calls her by it now."

That satisfied him. His face cleared at once, and he took three reds and three blues. When the neighbor came in to say that it was time to start, Lena wound Chris's comforter about his neck and turned up his jacket collar—he had no overcoat—and we watched him climb into the wagon and start on his long, cold drive. As we walked together up the windy street, Lena wiped her eyes with the back of her woolen glove. "I get awful homesick for them, all the same," she murmured, as if she were answering some remembered reproach.

VI

Winter comes down savagely over a little town on the prairie. The wind that sweeps in from the open country strips away all the leafy screens that hide one yard from another in summer, and the houses seem to draw closer together. The roofs, that looked so far away across the green tree-tops, now stare you in the face, and they are so much uglier than when their angles were softened by vines and shrubs.

In the morning, when I was fighting my way to school against the wind, I couldn't see anything but the road in front of me; but in the late afternoon, when I was coming home, the town looked bleak and desolate to me. The pale, cold light of the winter sunset did not beautify—it was like the light of truth itself. When the smoky clouds hung low in the west and the red sun went down behind them, leaving a pink flush on the snowy roofs and the blue drifts, then the wind sprang up afresh, with a kind of bitter song, as if it said: "This is reality, whether you like it or not. All those frivolities of summer, the light and shadow, the living mask of green that trembled over everything, they were lies, and this is what was underneath. This is the truth." It was as if we were being punished for loving the loveliness of summer.

If I loitered on the playground after school, or went to the post-office for the mail and lingered to hear the gossip about the cigar-stand, it would be growing dark by the time I came home. The sun was gone; the frozen streets stretched long and blue before me; the lights were shining pale in kitchen windows, and I could smell the suppers cooking as I passed. Few people were abroad, and each one of them was hurrying toward a fire. The glowing stoves in the houses were like magnets. When one passed an old man, one could see nothing of his face but a red nose sticking out between a frosted beard and a long plush cap. The young men capered along with their hands in their pockets, and sometimes tried a slide on the icy sidewalk. The children, in their bright hoods and comforters, never walked, but always ran from the moment they left their door, beating their mittens against their sides. When I got as far as the Methodist Church, I was about halfway home. I can remember how glad I was when there happened to be a light in the church, and the painted glass window shone out at us as we came along the frozen street. In the winter bleakness a hunger for color came over people, like the Laplander's craving for fats and sugar. Without knowing why, we used to linger on the sidewalk outside the church when the lamps were lighted early for choir practice or prayer-meeting, shivering and talking until our feet were like lumps of ice. The crude reds and greens and blues of that colored glass held us there.

On winter nights, the lights in the Harlings' windows drew me like the painted glass. Inside that warm, roomy house there was color, too. After supper I used to catch up my cap, stick my hands in my pockets, and dive through the willow hedge as if witches were after me. Of course, if Mr. Harling was at home, if his shadow stood out on the blind of the west room, I did not go in, but turned and walked home by the long way, through the street, wondering what book I should read as I sat down with the two old people.

Such disappointments only gave greater zest to the nights when we acted charades, or had a costume ball in the back parlor, with Sally always dressed like a boy. Frances taught us to dance that winter, and she said, from the first lesson, that Ántonia would make the best dancer among us. On Saturday nights, Mrs. Harling used to play the old operas for us,—"Martha," "Norma," "Rigoletto,"[4]—telling us the story while she played. Every Saturday night was like a party. The parlor, the back parlor, and the dining-room were warm and brightly lighted, with comfortable chairs and sofas, and gay pictures on the walls. One always felt at ease there. Ántonia brought her sewing and sat with us—she was already beginning to make pretty clothes for herself. After the long winter evenings on the prairie, with Ambrosch's sullen silences and her mother's complaints, the Harlings' house seemed, as she said, "like Heaven" to her. She was never too tired to make taffy or chocolate cookies for us. If

4. Prominent 19th-century operas, which are still performed. *Martha,* by Friedrich von Flotow (1812–1883), first performed in 1847. *Norma,* by Vicenzo Bellini (1801–1835), first performed in 1831. *Rigoletto,* by Giuseppe Verdi (1813–1901), first performed in 1851.

Sally whispered in her ear, or Charley gave her three winks, Tony would rush into the kitchen and build a fire in the range on which she had already cooked three meals that day.

While we sat in the kitchen waiting for the cookies to bake or the taffy to cool, Nina used to coax Ántonia to tell her stories—about the calf that broke its leg, or how Yulka saved her little turkeys from drowning in the freshet, or about old Christmases and weddings in Bohemia. Nina interpreted the stories about the crèche fancifully, and in spite of our derision she cherished a belief that Christ was born in Bohemia a short time before the Shimerdas left that country. We all liked Tony's stories. Her voice had a peculiarly engaging quality; it was deep, a little husky, and one always heard the breath vibrating behind it. Everything she said seemed to come right out of her heart.

One evening when we were picking out kernels for walnut taffy, Tony told us a new story.

"Mrs. Harling, did you ever hear about what happened up in the Norwegian settlement last summer, when I was thrashing there? We were at Iversons', and I was driving one of the grain wagons."

Mrs. Harling came out and sat down among us. "Could you throw the wheat into the bin yourself, Tony?" She knew what heavy work it was.

"Yes, mam, I did. I could shovel just as fast as that fat Andern boy that drove the other wagon. One day it was just awful hot. When we got back to the field from dinner, we took things kind of easy. The men put in the horses and got the machine going, and Ole Iverson was up on the deck, cutting bands. I was sitting against a straw stack, trying to get some shade. My wagon wasn't going out first, and somehow I felt the heat awful that day. The sun was so hot like it was going to burn the world up. After a while I see a man coming across the stubble, and when he got close I see it was a tramp.[5] His toes stuck out of his shoes, and he hadn't shaved for a long while, and his eyes was awful red and wild, like he had some sickness. He comes right up and begins to talk like he knows me already. He says: 'The ponds in this country is done got so low a man couldn't drownd himself in one of 'em.'

"I told him nobody wanted to drownd themselves, but if we didn't have rain soon we'd have to pump water for the cattle.

" 'Oh, cattle,' he says, 'you'll all take care of your cattle! Ain't you got no beer here?' I told him he'd have to go to the Bohemians for beer; the Norwegians didn't have none when they thrashed. 'My God!' he says, 'so it's Norwegians now, is it? I thought this was Americy.'

"Then he goes up to the machine and yells out to Ole Iverson, 'Hello, partner, let me up there. I can cut bands, and I'm tired of trampin'. I won't go no farther.'

"I tried to make signs to Ole, 'cause I thought that man was crazy and might get the machine stopped up. But Ole, he was glad to get down out of the sun and chaff—it gets down your neck and sticks to you something awful when it's hot like that. So Ole jumped down and crawled under one of the wagons for shade, and the tramp got on the machine. He cut bands all right for a few minutes, and then, Mrs. Harling, he waved his hand to me and jumped head-first right into the thrashing machine after the wheat.

5. Vagabond.

"I begun to scream, and the men run to stop the horses, but the belt had sucked him down, and by the time they got her stopped he was all beat and cut to pieces. He was wedged in so tight it was a hard job to get him out, and the machine ain't never worked right since."

"Was he clear dead, Tony?" we cried.

"Was he dead? Well, I guess so! There, now, Nina's all upset. We won't talk about it. Don't you cry, Nina. No old tramp won't get you while Tony's here."

Mrs. Harling spoke up sternly. "Stop crying, Nina, or I'll always send you upstairs when Ántonia tells us about the country. Did they never find out where he came from, Ántonia?"

"Never, mam. He hadn't been seen nowhere except in a little town they call Conway. He tried to get beer there, but there wasn't any saloon. Maybe he came in on a freight, but the brakeman hadn't seen him. They couldn't find no letters nor nothing on him; nothing but an old penknife in his pocket and the wishbone of a chicken wrapped up in a piece of paper, and some poetry."

"Some poetry?" we exclaimed.

"I remember," said Frances. "It was 'The Old Oaken Bucket,'[6] cut out of a newspaper and nearly worn out. Ole Iverson brought it into the office and showed it to me."

"Now, wasn't that strange, Miss Frances?" Tony asked thoughtfully. "What would anybody want to kill themselves in summer for? In thrashing time, too! It's nice everywhere then."

"So it is, Ántonia," said Mrs. Harling heartily. "Maybe I'll go home and help you thrash next summer. Isn't that taffy nearly ready to eat? I've been smelling it a long while."

There was a basic harmony between Antonia and her mistress. They had strong, independent natures, both of them. They knew what they liked, and were not always trying to imitate other people. They loved children and animals and music, and rough play and digging in the earth. They liked to prepare rich, hearty food and and to see people eat it; to make up soft white beds and to see youngsters asleep in them. They ridiculed conceited people and were quick to help unfortunate ones. Deep down in each of them there was a kind of hearty joviality, a relish of life, not over-delicate, but very invigorating. I never tried to define it, but I was distinctly conscious of it. I could not imagine Ántonia's living for a week in any other house in Black Hawk than the Harlings'.

VII

Winter lies too long in country towns; hangs on until it is stale and shabby, old and sullen. On the farm the weather was the great fact, and men's affairs went on underneath it, as the streams creep under the ice. But in Black Hawk the scene of human life was spread out shrunken and pinched, frozen down to the bare stalk.

Through and choppy, and the snow on the river bluffs was gray and mournful-looking. I was tired of school, tired of winter clothes, of the rutted streets, of the dirty drifts and the piles of cinders that had lain in the yards so long. There was only one break in the dreary monotony of that month; when Blind d'Arnault, the negro pianist, came to town. He gave a concert at the

---

6. Popular poem by the American writer Samuel Woodworth (1785–1842), first published in 1826.

Opera House on Monday night, and he and his manager spent Saturday and Sunday at our comfortable hotel. Mrs. Harling had known d'Arnault for years. She told Ántonia she had better go to see Tiny that Saturday evening, as there would certainly be music at the Boys' Home.

Saturday night after supper I ran downtown to the hotel and slipped quietly into the parlor. The chairs and sofas were already occupied, and the air smelled pleasantly of cigar smoke. The parlor had once been two rooms, and the floor was sway-backed where the partition had been cut away. The wind from without made waves in the long carpet. A coal stove glowed at either end of the room, and the grand piano in the middle stood open.

There was an atmosphere of unusual freedom about the house that night, for Mrs. Gardener had gone to Omaha for a week. Johnnie had been having drinks with the guests until he was rather absent-minded. It was Mrs. Gardener who ran the business and looked after everything. Her husband stood at the desk and welcomed incoming travelers. He was a popular fellow, but no manager.

Mrs. Gardener was admittedly the best-dressed woman in Black Hawk, drove the best horse, and had a smart trap and a little white-and-gold sleigh. She seemed indifferent to her possessions, was not half so solicitous about them as her friends were. She was tall, dark, severe, with something Indian-like in the rigid immobility of her face. Her manner was cold, and she talked little. Guests felt that they were receiving, not conferring, a favor when they stayed at her house. Even the smartest traveling men were flattered when Mrs. Gardener stopped to chat with them for a moment. The patrons of the hotel were divided into two classes; those who had seen Mrs. Gardener's diamonds, and those who had not.

When I stole into the parlor Anson Kirkpatrick, Marshall Field's man, was at the piano, playing airs from a musical comedy then running in Chicago. He was a dapper little Irishman, very vain, homely as a monkey, with friends everywhere, and a sweetheart in every port, like a sailor. I did not know all the men who were sitting about, but I recognized a furniture salesman from Kansas City, a drug man, and Willy O'Reilly, who traveled for a jewelry house and sold musical instruments. The talk was all about good and bad hotels, actors and actresses and musical prodigies. I learned that Mrs. Gardener had gone to Omaha to hear Booth and Barrett, who were to play there next week, and that Mary Anderson was having a great success in "A Winter's Tale,"[7] in London.

The door from the office opened, and Johnnie Gardener came in, directing Blind d'Arnault,—he would never consent to be led. He was a heavy, bulky mulatto, on short legs, and he came tapping the floor in front of him with his gold-headed cane. His yellow face was lifted in the light, with a show of white teeth, all grinning, and his shrunken, papery eyelids lay motionless over his blind eyes.

"Good evening, gentlemen. No ladies here? Good-evening, gentlemen. We going to have a little music? Some of you gentlemen going to play for me this evening?" It was the soft, amiable negro voice, like those I remembered from early childhood, with the note of docile subservience in it. He had the negro

7. A play by William Shakespeare (1564–1616). Edwin Booth (1833–1893) and Lawrence Barrett (1838–1891), American actors who had a long partnership performing Shakespearean plays. The dates of these actors' lives allow for rather precise dating of the novel. Anderson, English actress.

head, too; almost no head at all; nothing behind the ears but folds of neck under close-clipped wool. He would have been repulsive if his face had not been so kindly and happy. It was the happiest face I had seen since I left Virginia.

He felt his way directly to the piano. The moment he sat down, I noticed the nervous infirmity of which Mrs. Harling had told me. When he was sitting, or standing still, he swayed back and forth incessantly, like a rocking toy. At the piano, he swayed in time to the music, and when he was not playing, his body kept up this motion, like an empty mill grinding on. He found the pedals and tried them, ran his yellow hands up and down the keys a few times, tinkling off scales, then turned to the company.

"She seems all right, gentlemen. Nothing happened to her since the last time I was here. Mrs. Gardener, she always has this piano tuned up before I come. Now, gentlemen, I expect you've all got grand voices. Seems like we might have some good old plantation songs to-night."

The men gathered round him, as he began to play "My Old Kentucky Home."[8] They sang one negro melody after another, while the mulatto sat rocking himself, his head thrown back, his yellow face lifted, its shriveled eyelids never fluttering.

He was born in the Far South, on the d'Arnault plantation, where the spirit if not the fact of slavery persisted. When he was three weeks old he had an illness which left him totally blind. As soon as he was old enough to sit up alone and toddle about, another affliction, the nervous motion of his body, became apparent. His mother, a buxom young negro wench who was laundress for the d'Arnaults, concluded that her blind baby was "not right" in his head, and she was ashamed of him. She loved him devotedly, but he was so ugly, with his sunken eyes and his "fidgets," that she hid him away from people. All the dainties she brought down from the "Big House" were for the blind child, and she beat and cuffed her other children whenever she found them teasing him or trying to get his chicken-bone away from him. He began to talk early, remembered everything he heard, and his mammy said he "wasn't all wrong." She named him Samson, because he was blind, but on the plantation he was known as "yellow Martha's simple child." He was docile and obedient, but when he was six years old he began to run away from home, always taking the same direction. He felt his way through the lilacs, along the boxwood hedge, up to the south wing of the "Big House," where Miss Nellie d'Arnault practiced the piano every morning. This angered his mother more than anything else he could have done; she was so ashamed of his ugliness that she couldn't bear to have white folks see him. Whenever she caught him slipping away from the cabin, she whipped him unmercifully, and told him what dreadful things old Mr. d'Arnault would do to him if he ever found him near the "Big House." But the next time Samson had a chance, he ran away again. If Miss d'Arnault stopped practicing for a moment and went toward the window, she saw this hideous little pickaninny, dressed in an old piece of sacking, standing in the open space between the hollyhock rows, his body rocking automatically, his blind face

8. Nostalgic, popular song about the South by Stephen Foster (1826–1864), who composed for minstrel shows, where white performers acted in blackface. Foster's songs were often mistaken for folk songs and, as Cather shows here, were performed by black musicians as well as white.

lifted to the sun and wearing an expression of idiotic rapture. Often she was tempted to tell Martha that the child must be kept at home, but somehow the memory of his foolish, happy face deterred her. She remembered that his sense of hearing was nearly all he had,—though it did not occur to her that he might have more of it than other children.

One day Samson was standing thus while Miss Nellie was playing her lesson to her music-master. The windows were open. He heard them get up from the piano, talk a little while, and then leave the room. He heard the door close after them. He crept up to the front windows and stuck his head in: there was no one there. He could always detect the presence of any one in a room. He put one foot over the window sill and straddled it. His mother had told him over and over how his master would give him to the big mastiff if he ever found him "meddling." Samson had got too near the mastiff's kennel once, and had felt his terrible breath in his face. He thought about that, but he pulled in his other foot.

Through the dark he found his way to the Thing, to its mouth. He touched it softly, and it answered softly, kindly. He shivered and stood still. Then he began to feel it all over, ran his finger tips along the slippery sides, embraced the carved legs, tried to get some conception of its shape and size, of the space it occupied in primeval night. It was cold and hard, and like nothing else in his black universe. He went back to its mouth, began at one end of the keyboard and felt his way down into the mellow thunder, as far as he could go. He seemed to know that it must be done with the fingers, not with the fists or the feet. He approached this highly artificial instrument through a mere instinct, and coupled himself to it, as if he knew it was to piece him out and make a whole creature of him. After he had tried over all the sounds, he began to finger out passages from things Miss Nellie had been practicing, passages that were already his, that lay under the bones of his pinched, conical little skull, definite as animal desires. The door opened; Miss Nellie and her music-master stood behind it, but blind Samson, who was so sensitive to presences, did not know they were there. He was feeling out the pattern that lay all ready-made on the big and little keys. When he paused for a moment, because the sound was wrong and he wanted another, Miss Nellie spoke softly. He whirled about in a spasm of terror, leaped forward in the dark, struck his head on the open window, and fell screaming and bleeding to the floor. He had what his mother called a fit. The doctor came and gave him opium.

When Samson was well again, his young mistress led him back to the piano. Several teachers experimented with him. They found he had absolute pitch, and a remarkable memory. As a very young child he could repeat, after a fashion, any composition that was played for him. No matter how many wrong notes he struck, he never lost the intention of a passage, he brought the substance of it across by irregular and astonishing means. He wore his teachers out. He could never learn like other people, never acquired any finish. He was always a negro prodigy who played barbarously and wonderfully. As piano playing, it was perhaps abominable, but as music it was something real, vitalized by a sense of rhythm that was stronger than his other physical senses,—that not only filled his dark mind, but worried his body incessantly. To hear him, to watch him, was to see a negro enjoying himself as only a negro can. It was as if all the agreeable sensations possible to creatures of flesh and blood were heaped up on those black and white keys, and he were gloating over them and trickling them through his yellow fingers.

In the middle of a crashing waltz d'Arnault suddenly began to play softly, and, turning to one of the men who stood behind him, whispered, "Somebody dancing in there." He jerked his bullet head toward the dining-room. "I hear little feet,—girls, I 'spect."

Anson Kirkpatrick mounted a chair and peeped over the transom. Springing down, he wrenched open the doors and ran out into the dining-room. Tiny and Lena, Ántonia and Mary Dusak, were waltzing in the middle of the floor. They separated and fled toward the kitchen, giggling.

Kirkpatrick caught Tiny by the elbows. "What's the matter with you girls? Dancing out here by yourselves, when there's a roomful of lonesome men on the other side of the partition! Introduce me to your friends, Tiny."

The girls, still laughing, were trying to escape. Tiny looked alarmed. "Mrs. Gardener wouldn't like it," she protested. "She'd be awful mad if you was to come out here and dance with us."

"Mrs. Gardener's in Omaha, girl. Now, you're Lena, are you?—and you're Tony and you're Mary. Have I got you all straight?"

O'Reilly and the others began to pile the chairs on the tables. Johnnie Gardener ran in from the office.

"Easy, boys, easy!" he entreated them. "You'll wake the cook, and there'll be the devil to pay for me. She won't hear the music, but she'll be down the minute anything's moved in the dining-room."

"Oh, what do you care, Johnnie? Fire the cook and wire Molly to bring another. Come along, nobody'll tell tales."

Johnnie shook his head. " 'S a fact, boys," he said confidentially. "If I take a drink in Black Hawk, Molly knows it in Omaha!"

His guests laughed and slapped him on the shoulder. "Oh, we'll make it all right with Molly. Get your back up, Johnnie."

Molly was Mrs. Gardener's name, of course. "Molly Bawn" was painted in large blue letters on the glossy white side of the hotel bus, and "Molly" was engraved inside Johnnie's ring and on his watch-case—doubtless on his heart, too. He was an affectionate little man, and he thought his wife a wonderful woman; he knew that without her he would hardly be more than a clerk in some other man's hotel.

At a word from Kirkpatrick, d'Arnault spread himself out over the piano, and began to draw the dance music out of it, while the perspiration shone on his short wool and on his uplifted face. He looked like some glistening African god of pleasure, full of strong, savage blood. Whenever the dancers paused to change partners or to catch breath, he would boom out softly, "Who's that goin' back on me? One of these city gentlemen, I bet! Now, you girls, you ain't goin' to let that floor get cold?"

Ántonia seemed frightened at first, and kept looking questioningly at Lena and Tiny over Willy O'Reilly's shoulder. Tiny Soderball was trim and slender, with lively little feet and pretty ankles—she wore her dresses very short. She was quicker in speech, lighter in movement and manner than the other girls. Mary Dusak was broad and brown of countenance, slightly marked by smallpox, but handsome for all that. She had beautiful chestnut hair, coils of it; her forehead was low and smooth, and her commanding dark eyes regarded the world indifferently and fearlessly. She looked bold and resourceful and unscrupulous, and she was all of these. They were handsome girls, had the fresh color of their country up-bringing, and in their eyes that brilliancy which is called,—by no metaphor, alas!—"the light of youth."

D'Arnault played until his manager came and shut the piano. Before he left us, he showed us his gold watch which struck the hours, and a topaz ring, given him by some Russian nobleman who delighted in negro melodies, and had heard d'Arnault play in New Orleans. At last he tapped his way upstairs, after bowing to everybody, docile and happy. I walked home with Ántonia. We were so excited that we dreaded to go to bed. We lingered a long while at the Harlings' gate, whispering in the cold until the restlessness was slowly chilled out of us.

VIII

The Harling children and I were never happier, never felt more contented and secure, than in the weeks of spring which broke that long winter. We were out all day in the thin sunshine, helping Mrs. Harling and Tony break the ground and plant the garden, dig around the orchard trees, tie up vines and clip the hedges. Every morning, before I was up, I could hear Tony singing in the garden rows. After the apple and cherry trees broke into bloom, we ran about under them, hunting for the new nests the birds were building, throwing clods at each other, and playing hide-and-seek with Nina. Yet the summer which was to change everything was coming nearer every day. When boys and girls are growing up, life can't stand still, not even in the quietest of country towns; and they have to grow up, whether they will or no. That is what their elders are always forgetting.

It must have been in June, for Mrs. Harling and Ántonia were preserving cherries, when I stopped one morning to tell them that a dancing pavilion had come to town. I had seen two drays hauling the canvas and painted poles up from the depot.

That afternoon three cheerful-looking Italians strolled about Black Hawk, looking at everything, and with them was a dark, stout woman who wore a long gold watch chain about her neck and carried a black lace parasol. They seemed especially interested in children and vacant lots. When I overtook them and stopped to say a word, I found them affable and confiding. They told me they worked in Kansas City in the winter, and in summer they went out among the farming towns with their tent and taught dancing. When business fell off in one place, they moved on to another.

The dancing pavilion was put up near the Danish laundry, on a vacant lot surrounded by tall, arched cottonwood trees. It was very much like a merry-go-round tent, with open sides and gay flags flying from the poles. Before the week was over, all the ambitious mothers were sending their children to the afternoon dancing class. At three o'clock one met little girls in white dresses and little boys in the round-collared shirts of the time, hurrying along the sidewalk on their way to the tent. Mrs. Vanni received them at the entrance, always dressed in lavender with a great deal of black lace, her important watch chain lying on her bosom. She wore her hair on the top of her head, built up in a black tower, with red coral combs. When she smiled, she showed two rows of strong, crooked yellow teeth. She taught the little children herself, and her husband, the harpist, taught the older ones.

Often the mothers brought their fancy-work[9] and sat on the shady side of the tent during the lesson. The popcorn man wheeled his glass wagon under the big cottonwood by the door, and lounged in the sun, sure of a good trade when the dancing was over. Mr. Jensen, the Danish laundryman, used to bring a chair from his porch and sit out in the grass plot. Some ragged little boys from the depot sold pop and iced lemonade under a white umbrella at the corner, and made faces at the spruce youngsters who came to dance. That vacant lot soon became the most cheerful place in town. Even on the hottest afternoons the cottonwoods made a rustling shade, and the air smelled of popcorn and melted butter, and Bouncing Bets wilting in the sun. Those hardy flowers had run away from the laundry-man's garden, and the grass in the middle of the lot was pink with them.

The Vannis kept exemplary order, and closed every evening at the hour suggested by the City Council. When Mrs. Vanni gave the signal, and the harp struck up "Home, Sweet Home,"[1] all Black Hawk knew it was ten o'clock. You could set your watch by that tune as confidently as by the Round House[2] whistle.

At last there was something to do in those long, empty summer evenings, when the married people sat like images on their front porches, and the boys and girls tramped and tramped the board sidewalks—northward to the edge of the open prairie, south to the depot, then back again to the post-office, the ice-cream parlor, the butcher shop. Now there was a place where the girls could wear their new dresses, and where one could laugh aloud without being reproved by the ensuing silence. That silence seemed to ooze out of the ground, to hang under the foliage of the black maple trees with the bats and shadows. Now it was broken by light-hearted sounds. First the deep purring of Mr. Vanni's harp came in silvery ripples through the blackness of the dusty-smelling night; then the violins fell in—one of them was almost like a flute. They called so archly, so seductively, that our feet hurried toward the tent of themselves. Why hadn't we had a tent before?

Dancing became popular now, just as roller skating had been the summer before. The Progressive Euchre[3] Club arranged with the Vannis for the exclusive use of the floor on Tuesday and Friday nights. At other times any one could dance who paid his money and was orderly; the railroad men, the Round House mechanics, the delivery boys, the ice-man, the farmhands who lived near enough to ride into town after their day's work was over.

I never missed a Saturday night dance. The tent was open until midnight then. The country boys came in from farms eight and ten miles away, and all the country girls were on the floor,—Ántonia and Lena and Tiny, and the Danish laundry girls and their friends. I was not the only boy who found these dances gayer than the others. The young men who belonged to the Progressive Euchre Club used to drop in late and risk a tiff with their sweet-hearts and general condemnation for a waltz with "the hired girls."

IX

There was a curious social situation in Black Hawk. All the young men felt the attraction of the fine, well-set-up country girls who had come to town to

9. Embroidery.
1. Extremely popular song featured in the play *Clari; or, The Maid of Milan* (first produced in 1823) by the American John Howard Payne

(1791–1823).
2. Circular building for housing and repairing locomotives.
3. Card game for four players.

earn a living, and, in nearly every case, to help the father struggle out of debt, or to make it possible for the younger children of the family to go to school.

Those girls had grown up in the first bitter-hard times, and had got little schooling themselves. But the younger brothers and sisters, for whom they made such sacrifices and who have had "advantages," never seem to me, when I meet them now, half as interesting or as well educated. The older girls, who helped to break up the wild sod, learned so much from life, from poverty, from their mothers and grandmothers; they had all, like Ántonia, been early awakened and made observant by coming at a tender age from an old country to a new. I can remember a score of these country girls who were in service in Black Hawk during the few years I lived there, and I can remember something unusual and engaging about each of them. Physically they were almost a race apart, and out-of-door work had given them a vigor which, when they got over their first shyness on coming to town, developed into a positive carriage and freedom of movement, and made them conspicuous among Black Hawk women.

That was before the day of High-School athletics. Girls who had to walk more than half a mile to school were pitied. There was not a tennis court in the town; physical exercise was thought rather inelegant for the daughters of well-to-do families. Some of the High-School girls were jolly and pretty, but they stayed indoors in winter because of the cold, and in summer because of the heat. When one danced with them their bodies never moved inside their clothes; their muscles seemed to ask but one thing—not to be disturbed. I remember those girls merely as faces in the schoolroom, gay and rosy, or listless and dull, cut off below the shoulders, like cherubs, by the ink-smeared tops of the high desks that were surely put there to make us round-shouldered and hollow-chested.

The daughters of Black Hawk merchants had a confident, uninquiring belief that they were "refined," and that the country girls, who "worked out," were not. The American[4] farmers in our country were quite as hard-pressed as their neighbors from other countries. All alike had come to Nebraska with little capital and no knowledge of the soil they must subdue. All had borrowed money on their land. But no matter in what straits the Pennsylvanian or Virginian found himself, he would not let his daughters go out into service. Unless his girls could teach a country school, they sat at home in poverty. The Bohemian and Scandinavian girls could not get positions as teachers, because they had had no opportunity to learn the language. Determined to help in the struggle to clear the homestead from debt, they had no alternative but to go into service. Some of them, after they came to town, remained as serious and as discreet in behavior as they had been when they ploughed and herded on their father's farm. Others, like the three Bohemian Marys, tried to make up for the years of youth they had lost. But every one of them did what she had set out to do, and sent home those hard-earned dollars. The girls I knew were always helping to pay for ploughs and reapers, brood-sows, or steers to fatten.

One result of this family solidarity was that the foreign farmers in our county were the first to become prosperous. After the fathers were out of debt, the daughters married the sons of neighbors,—usually of like nationality,—and the girls who once worked in Black Hawk kitchens are to-day man-

---

4. I.e., born in America, nonimmigrant.

aging big farms and fine families of their own; their children are better off than the children of the town women they used to serve.

I thought the attitude of the town people toward these girls very stupid. If I told my schoolmates that Lena Lingard's grandfather was a clergyman, and much respected in Norway, they looked at me blankly. What did it matter? All foreigners were ignorant people who couldn't speak English. There was not a man in Black Hawk who had the intelligence or cultivation, much less the personal distinction, of Ántonia's father. Yet people saw no difference between her and the three Marys; they were all Bohemians, all "hired girls."

I always knew I should live long enough to see my country girls come into their own, and I have. To-day the best that a harassed Black Hawk merchant can hope for is to sell provisions and farm machinery and automobiles to the rich farms where that first crop of stalwart Bohemian and Scandinavian girls are now the mistresses.

The Black Hawk boys looked forward to marrying Black Hawk girls, and living in a brand-new little house with best chairs that must not be sat upon, and hand-painted china that must not be used. But sometimes a young fellow would look up from his ledger, or out through the grating of his father's bank, and let his eyes follow Lena Lingard, as she passed the window with her slow, undulating walk, or Tiny Soderball, tripping by in her short skirt and striped stockings.

The country girls were considered a menace to the social order. Their beauty shone out too boldly against a conventional background. But anxious mothers need have felt no alarm. They mistook the mettle of their sons. The respect for respectability was stronger than any desire in Black Hawk youth.

Our young man of position was like the son of a royal house; the boy who swept out his office or drove his delivery wagon might frolic with the jolly country girls, but he himself must sit all evening in a plush parlor where conversation dragged so perceptibly that the father often came in and made blundering efforts to warm up the atmosphere. On his way home from his dull call, he would perhaps meet Tony and Lena, coming along the sidewalk whispering to each other, or the three Bohemian Marys in their long plush coats and caps, comporting themselves with a dignity that only made their eventful histories the more piquant. If he went to the hotel to see a traveling man on business, there was Tiny, arching her shoulders at him like a kitten. If he went into the laundry to get his collars, there were the four Danish girls, smiling up from their ironing-boards, with their white throats and their pink cheeks.

The three Marys were the heroines of a cycle of scandalous stories, which the old men were fond of relating as they sat about the cigar-stand in the drug-store. Mary Dusak had been housekeeper for a bachelor rancher from Boston, and after several years in his service she was forced to retire from the world for a short time. Later she came back to town to take the place of her friend, Mary Svoboda, who was similarly embarrassed.[5] The three Marys were considered as dangerous as high explosives to have about the kitchen, yet they were such good cooks and such admirable house-keepers that they never had to look for a place.

The Vannis' tent brought the town boys and the country girls together on neutral ground. Sylvester Lovett, who was cashier in his father's bank, always

---

5. Both women had out-of-wedlock babies.

found his way to the tent on Saturday night. He took all the dances Lena Lingard would give him, and even grew bold enough to walk home with her. If his sisters or their friends happened to be among the onlookers on "popular nights," Sylvester stood back in the shadow under the cottonwood trees, smoking and watching Lena with a harassed expression. Several times I stumbled upon him there in the dark, and I felt rather sorry for him. He reminded me of Ole Benson, who used to sit on the draw-side and watch Lena herd her cattle. Later in the summer, when Lena went home for a week to visit her mother, I heard from Ántonia that young Lovett drove all the way out there to see her, and took her buggy-riding. In my ingenuousness I hoped that Sylvester would marry Lena, and thus give all the country girls a better position in the town.

Sylvester dallied about Lena until he began to make mistakes in his work; had to stay at the bank until after dark to make his books balance. He was daft about her, and every one knew it. To escape from his predicament he ran away with a widow six years older than himself, who owned a half-section.[6] This remedy worked, apparently. He never looked at Lena again, nor lifted his eyes as he ceremoniously tipped his hat when he happened to meet her on the sidewalk.

So that was what they were like, I thought, these white-handed, high-collared clerks and bookkeepers! I used to glare at young Lovett from a distance and only wished I had some way of showing my contempt for him.

X

It was at the Vannis' tent that Ántonia was discovered. Hitherto she had been looked upon more as a ward of the Harlings than as one of the "hired girls." She had lived in their house and yard and garden; her thoughts never seemed to stray outside that little kingdom. But after the tent came to town she began to go about with Tiny and Lena and their friends. The Vannis often said that Ántonia was the best dancer of them all. I sometimes heard murmurs in the crowd outside the pavilion that Mrs. Harling would soon have her hands full with that girl. The young men began to joke with each other about "the Harlings' Tony" as they did about "the Marshalls' Anna" or "the Gardeners' Tiny."

Ántonia talked and thought of nothing but the tent. She hummed the dance tunes all day. When supper was late, she hurried with her dishes, dropped and smashed them in her excitement. At the first call of the music, she became irresponsible. If she hadn't time to dress, she merely flung off her apron and shot out of the kitchen door. Sometimes I went with her; the moment the lighted tent came into view she would break into a run, like a boy. There were always partners waiting for her; she began to dance before she got her breath.

Ántonia's success at the tent had its consequences. The iceman lingered too long now, when he came into the covered porch to fill the refrigerator. The delivery boys hung about the kitchen when they brought the groceries. Young farmers who were in town for Saturday came tramping through the yard to

6. One-half of a square mile, or 320 acres.

the back door to engage dances, or to invite Tony to parties and picnics. Lena and Norwegian Anna dropped in to help her with her work, so that she could get away early. The boys who brought her home after the dances sometimes laughed at the back gate and wakened Mr. Harling from his first sleep. A crisis was inevitable.

One Saturday night Mr. Harling had gone down to the cellar for beer. As he came up the stairs in the dark, he heard scuffling on the back porch, and then the sound of a vigorous slap. He looked out through the side door in time to see a pair of long legs vaulting over the picket fence. Ántonia was standing there, angry and excited. Young Harry Paine, who was to marry his employer's daughter on Monday, had come to the tent with a crowd of friends and danced all evening. Afterward, he begged Ántonia to let him walk home with her. She said she supposed he was a nice young man, as he was one of Miss Frances's friends, and she didn't mind. On the back porch he tried to kiss her, and when she protested,—because he was going to be married on Monday,—he caught her and kissed her until she got one hand free and slapped him.

Mr. Harling put his beer bottles down on the table. "This is what I've been expecting, Ántonia. You've been going with girls who have a reputation for being free and easy, and now you've got the same reputation. I won't have this and that fellow tramping about my back yard all the time. This is the end of it, to-night. It stops, short. You can quit going to these dances, or you can hunt another place. Think it over."

The next morning when Mrs. Harling and Frances tried to reason with Ántonia, they found her agitated but determined. "Stop going to the tent?" she panted. "I wouldn't think of it for a minute! My own father couldn't make me stop! Mr. Harling ain't my boss outside my work. I won't give up my friends, either. The boys I go with are nice fellows. I thought Mr. Paine was all right, too, because he used to come here. I guess I gave him a red face for his wedding, all right!" she blazed out indignantly.

"You'll have to do one thing or the other, Ántonia," Mrs. Harling told her decidedly. "I can't go back on what Mr. Harling has said. This is his house."

"Then I'll just leave, Mrs. Harling. Lena's been wanting me to get a place closer to her for a long while. Mary Svoboda's going away from the Cutters' to work at the hotel, and I can have her place."

Mrs. Harling rose from her chair. "Ántonia, if you go to the Cutters to work, you cannot come back to this house again. You know what that man is. It will be the ruin of you."

Tony snatched up the tea-kettle and began to pour boiling water over the glasses, laughing excitedly. "Oh, I can take care of myself! I'm a lot stronger than Cutter is. They pay four dollars there, and there's no children. The work's nothing; I can have every evening, and be out a lot in the afternoons."

"I thought you liked children. Tony, what's come over you?"

"I don't know, something has." Ántonia tossed her head and set her jaw. "A girl like me has got to take her good times when she can. Maybe there won't be any tent next year. I guess I want to have my fling, like the other girls."

Mrs. Harling gave a short, harsh laugh. "If you go to work for the Cutters, you're likely to have a fling that you won't get up from in a hurry."

Frances said, when she told grandmother and me about this scene, that every pan and plate and cup on the shelves trembled when her mother walked out of the kitchen. Mrs. Harling declared bitterly that she wished she had never let herself get fond of Ántonia.

XI

Wick Cutter was the money-lender who had fleeced poor Russian Peter. When a farmer once got into the habit of going to Cutter, it was like gambling or the lottery; in an hour of discouragement he went back.

Cutter's first name was Wycliffe,[7] and he liked to talk about his pious bringing-up. He contributed regularly to the Protestant churches, "for sentiment's sake," as he said with a flourish of the hand. He came from a town in Iowa where there were a great many Swedes, and could speak a little Swedish, which gave him a great advantage with the early Scandinavian settlers.

In every frontier settlement there are men who have come there to escape restraint. Cutter was one of the "fast set" of Black Hawk business men. He was an inveterate gambler, though a poor loser. When we saw a light burning in his office late at night, we knew that a game of poker was going on. Cutter boasted that he never drank anything stronger than sherry, and he said he got his start in life by saving the money that other young men spent for cigars. He was full of moral maxims for boys. When he came to our house on business, he quoted "Poor Richard's Almanack"[8] to me, and told me he was delighted to find a town boy who could milk a cow. He was particularly affable to grandmother, and whenever they met he would begin at once to talk about "the good old times" and simple living. I detested his pink, bald head, and his yellow whiskers, always soft and glistening. It was said he brushed them every night, as a woman does her hair. His white teeth looked factory-made. His skin was red and rough, as if from perpetual sunburn; he often went away to hot springs to take mud baths. He was notoriously dissolute with women. Two Swedish girls who had lived in his house were the worse for the experience. One of them he had taken to Omaha and established in the business for which he had fitted her.[9] He still visited her.

Cutter lived in a state of perpetual warfare with his wife, and yet, apparently, they never thought of separating. They dwelt in a fussy, scroll-work house, painted white and buried in thick evergreens, with a fussy white fence and barn. Cutter thought he knew a great deal about horses, and usually had a colt which he was training for the track. On Sunday mornings one could see him out at the fair grounds, speeding around the race-course in his trotting-buggy, wearing yellow gloves and a black-and-white-check traveling cap, his whiskers blowing back in the breeze. If there were any boys about, Cutter would offer one of them a quarter to hold the stop-watch, and then drive off, saying he had no change and would "fix it up next time." No one could cut his lawn or wash his buggy to suit him. He was so fastidious and prim about his place that a boy would go to a good deal of trouble to throw a dead cat into his back yard, or to dump a sackful of tin cans in his alley. It was a peculiar combination of old-maidishness and licentiousness that made Cutter seem so despicable.

7. After John Wycliffe (1328–1384), English Protestant reformer.
8. A farmer's almanac written and published in Philadelphia by Benjamin Franklin from 1733 to 1758 and famous for maxims and proverbs through which Franklin taught an ethic of hard work and prudence.
9. I.e., prostitution.

He had certainly met his match when he married Mrs. Cutter. She was a terrifying-looking person; almost a giantess in height, raw-boned, with iron-gray hair, a face always flushed, and prominent, hysterical eyes. When she meant to be entertaining and agreeable, she nodded her head incessantly and snapped her eyes at one. Her teeth were long and curved, like a horse's; people said babies always cried if she smiled at them. Her face had a kind of fascination for me; it was the very color and shape of anger. There was a gleam of something akin to insanity in her full, intense eyes. She was formal in manner, and made calls in rustling, steel-gray brocades and a tall bonnet with bristling aigrettes.[1]

Mrs. Cutter painted china so assiduously that even her washbowls and pitchers, and her husband's shaving-mug, were covered with violets and lilies. Once when Cutter was exhibiting some of his wife's china to a caller, he dropped a piece. Mrs. Cutter put her handkerchief to her lips as if she were going to faint and said grandly: "Mr. Cutter, you have broken all the Commandments—spare the finger-bowls!"

They quarreled from the moment Cutter came into the house until they went to bed at night, and their hired girls reported these scenes to the town at large. Mrs. Cutter had several times cut paragraphs about unfaithful husbands out of the newspapers and mailed them to Cutter in a disguised handwriting. Cutter would come home at noon, find the mutilated journal in the paper-rack, and triumphantly fit the clipping into the space from which it had been cut. Those two could quarrel all morning about whether he ought to put on his heavy or his light underwear, and all evening about whether he had taken cold or not.

The Cutters had major as well as minor subjects for dispute. The chief of these was the question of inheritance: Mrs. Cutter told her husband it was plainly his fault they had no children. He insisted that Mrs. Cutter had purposely remained childless, with the determination to outlive him and to share his property with her "people," whom he detested. To this she would reply that unless he changed his mode of life, she would certainly outlive him. After listening to her insinuations about his physical soundness, Cutter would resume his dumb-bell practice for a month, or rise daily at the hour when his wife most liked to sleep, dress noisily, and drive out to the track with his trotting-horse.

Once when they had quarreled about house-hold expenses, Mrs. Cutter put on her brocade and went among their friends soliciting orders for painted china, saying that Mr. Cutter had compelled her "to live by her brush." Cutter wasn't shamed as she had expected; he was delighted!

Cutter often threatened to chop down the cedar trees which half-buried the house. His wife declared she would leave him if she were stripped of the "privacy" which she felt these trees afforded her. That was his opportunity, surely; but he never cut down the trees. The Cutters seemed to find their relations to each other interesting and stimulating, and certainly the rest of us found them so. Wick Cutter was different from any other rascal I have ever known, but I have found Mrs. Cutters all over the world; sometimes found-

1. Sprays of feathers.

ing new religions, sometimes being forcibly fed—easily recognizable, even when superficially tamed.

XII

After Ántonia went to live with the Cutters, she seemed to care about nothing but picnics and parties and having a good time. When she was not going to a dance, she sewed until midnight. Her new clothes were the subject of caustic comment. Under Lena's direction she copied Mrs. Gardener's new party dress and Mrs. Smith's street costume so ingeniously in cheap materials that those ladies were greatly annoyed, and Mrs. Cutter, who was jealous of them, was secretly pleased.

Tony wore gloves now, and high-heeled shoes and feathered bonnets, and she went downtown nearly every afternoon with Tiny and Lena and the Marshalls' Norwegian Anna. We High-School boys used to linger on the playground at the afternoon recess to watch them as they came tripping down the hill along the board sidewalk, two and two. They were growing prettier every day, but as they passed us, I used to think with pride that Ántonia, like Snow-White in the fairy tale, was still "fairest of them all."

Being a Senior now, I got away from school early. Sometimes I overtook the girls down-town and coaxed them into the ice-cream parlor, where they would sit chattering and laughing, telling me all the news from the country. I remember how angry Tiny Soderball made me one afternoon. She declared she had heard grandmother was going to make a Baptist preacher of me. "I guess you'll have to stop dancing and wear a white necktie then. Won't he look funny, girls?"

Lena laughed. "You'll have to hurry up, Jim. If you're going to be a preacher, I want you to marry me. You must promise to marry us all, and then baptize the babies."

Norwegian Anna, always dignified, looked at her reprovingly.

"Baptists don't believe in christening babies, do they, Jim?"

I told her I didn't know what they believed, and didn't care, and that I certainly wasn't going to be a preacher.

"That's too bad," Tiny simpered. She was in a teasing mood. "You'd make such a good one. You're so studious. Maybe you'd like to be a professor. You used to teach Tony, didn't you?"

Ántonia broke in. "I've set my heart on Jim being a doctor. You'd be good with sick people, Jim. Your grandmother's trained you up so nice. My papa always said you were an awful smart boy."

I said I was going to be whatever I pleased. "Won't you be surprised, Miss Tiny, if I turn out to be a regular devil of a fellow?"

They laughed until a glance from Norwegian Anna checked them; the High-School Principal had just come into the front part of the shop to buy bread for supper. Anna knew the whisper was going about that I was a sly one. People said there must be something queer about a boy who showed no interest in girls of his own age, but who could be lively enough when he was with Tony and Lena or the three Marys.

The enthusiasm for the dance, which the Vannis had kindled, did not at once die out. After the tent left town, the Euchre Club became the Owl Club, and gave dances in the Masonic Hall once a week. I was invited to join, but declined. I was moody and restless that winter, and tired of the people I saw every day. Charley Harling was already at Annapolis, while I was still sitting in Black Hawk, answering to my name at roll-call every morning, rising from my desk at the sound of a bell and marching out like the grammar-school children. Mrs. Harling was a little cool toward me, because I continued to champion Ántonia. What was there for me to do after supper? Usually I had learned next day's lessons by the time I left the school building, and I couldn't sit still and read forever.

In the evening I used to prowl about, hunting for diversion. There lay the familiar streets, frozen with snow or liquid with mud. They led to the houses of good people who were putting the babies to bed, or simply sitting still before the parlor stove, digesting their supper. Black Hawk had two saloons. One of them was admitted, even by the church people, to be as respectable as a saloon could be. Handsome Anton Jelinek, who had rented his homestead and come to town, was the proprietor. In his saloon there were long tables where the Bohemian and German farmers could eat the lunches they brought from home while they drank their beer. Jelinek kept rye bread on hand, and smoked fish and strong imported cheeses to please the foreign palate. I liked to drop into his bar-room and listen to the talk. But one day he overtook me on the street and clapped me on the shoulder.

"Jim," he said, "I am good friends with you and I always like to see you. But you know how the church people think about saloons. Your grandpa has always treated me fine, and I don't like to have you come into my place, because I know he don't like it, and it puts me in bad with him."

So I was shut out of that.

One could hang about the drug-store, and listen to the old men who sat there every evening, talking politics and telling raw stories. One could go to the cigar factory and chat with the old German who raised canaries for sale, and look at his stuffed birds. But whatever you began with him, the talk went back to taxidermy. There was the depot, of course; I often went down to see the night train come in, and afterward sat awhile with the disconsolate telegrapher who was always hoping to be transferred to Omaha or Denver, "where there was some life." He was sure to bring out his pictures of actresses and dancers. He got them with cigarette coupons and nearly smoked himself to death to possess these desired forms and faces. For a change, one could talk to the station agent; but he was another malcontent; spent all his spare time writing letters to officials requesting a transfer. He wanted to get back to Wyoming where he could go trout-fishing on Sundays. He used to say "there was nothing in life for him but trout streams, ever since he'd lost his twins."

These were the distractions I had to choose from. There were no other lights burning downtown after nine o'clock. On starlight nights I used to pace up and down those long, cold streets, scowling at the little, sleeping houses on either side, with their storm-windows and covered back porches. They were flimsy shelters, most of them poorly built of light wood, with spindle porch-posts horribly mutilated by the turning-lathe. Yet for all their frailness, how much jealousy and envy and unhappiness some of them managed to contain! The life that went on in them seemed to me made up of evasions and negations; shifts to save cooking, to save washing and cleaning, devices to propitiate the tongue of gossip. This guarded mode of existence was like living under a tyranny. People's speech, their voices, their very glances, became furtive and repressed. Every individual taste, every natural appetite, was bridled by caution. The people asleep in those houses, I thought, tried to live like the mice in their own kitchens; to make no noise, to leave no trace, to slip over the surface of things in the dark. The growing piles of ashes and cinders in the back yards were the only evidence that the wasteful, consuming process of life went on at all. On Tuesday nights the Owl Club danced; then there was a little stir in the streets, and here and there one could see a lighted window until midnight. But the next night all was dark again.

After I refused to join "the Owls," as they were called, I made a bold resolve to go to the Saturday night dances at Firemen's Hall. I knew it would be useless to acquaint my elders with any such plan. Grandfather didn't approve of dancing anyway; he would only say that if I wanted to dance I could go to the Masonic Hall, among "the people we knew." It was just my point that I saw altogether too much of the people we knew.

My bedroom was on the ground floor, and as I studied there, I had a stove in it. I used to retire to my room early on Saturday night, change my shirt and collar and put on my Sunday coat. I waited until all was quiet and the old people were asleep, then raised my window, climbed out, and went softly through the yard. The first time I deceived my grandparents I felt rather shabby, perhaps even the second time, but I soon ceased to think about it.

The dance at the Firemen's Hall was the one thing I looked forward to all the week. There I met the same people I used to see at the Vannis' tent. Sometimes there were Bohemians from Wilber, or German boys who came down on the afternoon freight from Bismarck. Tony and Lena and Tiny were always there, and the three Bohemian Marys, and the Danish laundry girls.

The four Danish girls lived with the laundryman and his wife in their house behind the laundry, with a big garden where the clothes were hung out to dry. The laundryman was a kind, wise old fellow, who paid his girls well, looked out for them, and gave them a good home. He told me once that his own daughter died just as she was getting old enough to help her mother, and that he had been "trying to make up for it ever since." On summer afternoons he used to sit for hours on the sidewalk in front of his laundry, his newspaper lying on his knee, watching his girls through the big open window while they ironed and talked in Danish. The clouds of white dust that blew up the street, the gusts of hot wind that withered his vegetable garden, never disturbed his calm. His droll expression seemed to say that he had found the secret of contentment. Morning and evening he drove about in his spring wagon, distributing freshly ironed clothes, and collecting bags of linen that cried out for his suds and sunny drying-lines. His girls never looked so pretty at the dances as they did standing by the ironing-board, or over the tubs, washing the fine pieces, their white arms and throats bare, their cheeks bright as the brightest wild roses, their gold hair moist with the steam or the heat and curling in little damp spirals about their ears. They had not learned much English, and were not so ambitious as Tony or Lena; but they were kind, simple girls and they were always happy. When one danced with them, one smelled their clean, freshly ironed clothes that had been put away with rosemary leaves from Mr. Jensen's garden.

There were never girls enough to go round at those dances, but every one wanted a turn with Tony and Lena. Lena moved without exertion, rather indolently, and her hand often accented the rhythm softly on her partner's shoulder. She smiled if one spoke to her, but seldom answered. The music seemed to put her into a soft, waking dream, and her violet-colored eyes looked sleepily and confidingly at one from under her long lashes. When she sighed she exhaled a heavy perfume of sachet powder. To dance "Home, Sweet Home," with Lena was like coming in with the tide. She danced every dance like a waltz, and it was always the same waltz—the waltz of coming home to something, of inevitable, fated return. After a while one got restless under it, as one does under the heat of a soft, sultry summer day.

When you spun out into the floor with Tony, you didn't return to anything. You set out every time upon a new adventure. I liked to schottische[2] with her; she had so much spring and variety, and was always putting in new steps and slides. She taught me to dance against and around the hard-and-fast beat of the music. If, instead of going to the end of the railroad, old Mr. Shimerda had stayed in New York and picked up a living with his fiddle, how different Ántonia's life might have been!

Ántonia often went to the dances with Larry Donovan, a passenger conductor who was a kind of professional ladies' man, as we said. I remember how admiringly all the boys looked at her the night she first wore her velveteen dress, made like Mrs. Gardener's black velvet. She was lovely to see, with her eyes shining, and her lips always a little parted when she danced. That constant, dark color in her cheeks never changed.

One evening when Donovan was out on his run, Ántonia came to the hall with Norwegian Anna and her young man, and that night I took her home. When we were in the Cutter's yard, sheltered by the evergreens, I told her she must kiss me good-night.

"Why, sure Jim." A moment later she drew her face away and whispered indignantly, "Why, Jim! You know you ain't right to kiss me like that. I'll tell your grandmother on you!"

"Lena Lingard lets me kiss her," I retorted, "and I'm not half as fond of her as I am of you."

"Lena does?" Tony gasped. "If she's up to any of her nonsense with you, I'll scratch her eyes out!" She took my arm again and we walked out of the gate and up and down the sidewalk. "Now, don't you go and be a fool like some of these town boys. You're not going to sit around here and whittle store-boxes and tell stories all your life. You are going away to school and make something of yourself. I'm just awful proud of you. You won't go and get mixed up with the Swedes, will you?"

"I don't care anything about any of them but you," I said. "And you'll always treat me like a kid, I suppose."

She laughed and threw her arms around me. "I expect I will, but you're a kid I'm awful fond of, anyhow! You can like me all you want to, but if I see you hanging round with Lena much, I'll go to your grandmother, as sure as your name's Jim Burden! Lena's all right, only—well, you know yourself she's soft that way. She can't help it. It's natural to her."

If she was proud of me, I was so proud of her that I carried my head high as I emerged from the dark cedars and shut the Cutters' gate softly behind me. Her warm, sweet face, her kind arms, and the true heart in her; she was,

---

2. A group dance in the round, like a polka only somewhat slower.

oh, she was still my Ántonia! I looked with contempt at the dark, silent little houses about me as I walked home, and thought of the stupid young men who were asleep in some of them. I knew where the real women were, though I was only a boy; and I would not be afraid of them, either!

I hated to enter the still house when I went home from the dances, and it was long before I could get to sleep. Toward morning I used to have pleasant dreams: sometimes Tony and I were out in the country, sliding down straw-stacks as we used to do; climbing up the yellow mountains over and over, and slipping down the smooth sides into soft piles of chaff.

One dream I dreamed a great many times, and it was always the same. I was in a harvest-field full of shocks, and I was lying against one of them. Lena Lingard came across the stubble barefoot, in a short skirt, with a curved reaping-hook in her hand, and she was flushed like the dawn, with a kind of luminous rosiness all about her. She sat down beside me, turned to me with a soft sigh and said, "Now they are all gone, and I can kiss you as much as I like."

I used to wish I could have this flattering dream about Ántonia, but I never did.

XIII

I noticed one afternoon that grandmother had been crying. Her feet seemed to drag as she moved about the house, and I got up from the table where I was studying and went to her, asking if she didn't feel well, and if I couldn't help her with her work.

"No, thank you, Jim. I'm troubled, but I guess I'm well enough. Getting a little rusty in the bones, maybe," she added bitterly.

I stood hesitating. "What are you fretting about, grandmother? Has grandfather lost any money?"

"No, it ain't money. I wish it was. But I've heard things. You must 'a' known it would come back to me sometime." She dropped into a chair, and covering her face with her apron, began to cry. "Jim," she said, "I was never one that claimed old folks could bring up their grandchildren. But it came about so; there wasn't any other way for you, it seemed like."

I put my arms around her. I couldn't bear to see her cry.

"What is it, grandmother? Is it the Firemen's dances?"

She nodded.

"I'm sorry I sneaked off like that. But there's nothing wrong about the dances, and I haven't done anything wrong. I like all those country girls, and I like to dance with them. That's all there is to it."

"But it ain't right to deceive us, son, and it brings blame on us. People say you are growing up to be a bad boy, and that ain't just to us."

"I don't care what they say about me, but if it hurts you, that settles it. I won't go to the Firemen's Hall again."

I kept my promise, of course, but I found the spring months dull enough. I sat at home with the old people in the evenings now, reading Latin that was not in our High-School course. I had made up my mind to do a lot of college requirement work in the summer, and to enter the freshman class at the University without conditions in the fall. I wanted to get away as soon as possible.

Disapprobation hurt me, I found,—even that of people whom I did not admire. As the spring came on, I grew more and more lonely, and fell back on the telegrapher and the cigar-maker and his canaries for companionship. I remember I took a melancholy pleasure in hanging a May-basket for Nina Harling that spring. I bought the flowers from an old German woman who always had more window plants than any one else, and spent an afternoon trimming a little work-basket. When dusk came on, and the new moon hung in the sky, I went quietly to the Harlings' front door with my offering, rang the bell, and then ran away as was the custom. Through the willow hedge I could hear Nina's cries of delight, and I felt comforted.

On those warm, soft spring evenings I often lingered downtown to walk home with Frances, and talked to her about my plans and about the reading I was doing. One evening she said she thought Mrs. Harling was not seriously offended with me.

"Mama is as broad-minded as mothers ever are, I guess. But you know she was hurt about Ántonia, and she can't understand why you like to be with Tiny and Lena better than with the girls of your own set."

"Can you?" I asked bluntly.

Frances laughed. "Yes, I think I can. You knew them in the country, and you like to take sides. In some ways you're older than boys of your age. It will be all right with mama after you pass your college examinations and she sees you're in earnest."

"If you were a boy," I persisted, "you wouldn't belong to the Owl Club, either. You'd be just like me."

She shook her head. "I would and I wouldn't. I expect I know the country girls better than you do. You always put a kind of glamour over them. The trouble with you, Jim, is that you're romantic. Mama's going to your Commencement. She asked me the other day if I knew what your oration is to be about. She wants you to do well."

I thought my oration very good. It stated with fervor a great many things I had lately discovered. Mrs. Harling came to the Opera House to hear the Commencement exercises, and I looked at her most of the time while I made my speech. Her keen, intelligent eyes never left my face. Afterward she came back to the dressing-room where we stood, with our diplomas in our hands, walked up to me, and said heartily: "You surprised me, Jim. I didn't believe you could do as well as that. You didn't get that speech out of books." Among my graduation presents there was a silk umbrella from Mrs. Harling, with my name on the handle.

I walked home from the Opera House alone. As I passed the Methodist Church, I saw three white figures ahead of me, pacing up and down under the arching maple trees, where the moonlight filtered through the lush June foliage. They hurried toward me; they were waiting for me—Lena and Tony and Anna Hansen.

"Oh, Jim, it was splendid!" Tony was breathing hard, as she always did when her feelings outran her language. "There ain't a lawyer in Black Hawk could make a speech like that. I just stopped your grandpa and said so to him. He won't tell you, but he told us he was awful surprised himself, didn't he, girls?"

Lena sidled up to me and said teasingly: "What made you so solemn? I thought you were scared. I was sure you'd forget."

Anna spoke wistfully. "It must make you happy, Jim, to have fine thoughts like that in your mind all the time, and to have words to put them in. I always wanted to go to school, you know."

"Oh, I just sat there and wished my papa could hear you! Jim,"—Ántonia took hold of my coat lapels,—"there was something in your speech that made me think so about my papa!"

"I thought about your papa when I wrote my speech, Tony," I said. "I dedicated it to him."

She threw her arms around me, and her dear face was all wet with tears.

I stood watching their white dresses glimmer smaller and smaller down the sidewalk as they went away. I have had no other success that pulled at my heartstrings like that one.

XIV

The day after Commencement I moved my books and desk upstairs, to an empty room where I should be undisturbed, and I fell to studying in earnest. I worked off a year's trigonometry that summer, and began Virgil[3] alone. Morning after morning I used to pace up and down my sunny little room, looking off at the distant river bluffs and the roll of the blond pastures between, scanning the Æneid aloud and committing long passages to memory. Sometimes in the evening Mrs. Harling called to me as I passed her gate, and asked me to come in and let her play for me. She was lonely for Charley, she said, and liked to have a boy about. Whenever my grandparents had misgivings, and began to wonder whether I was not too young to go off to college alone, Mrs. Harling took up my cause vigorously. Grandfather had such respect for her judgment that I knew he would not go against her.

I had only one holiday that summer. It was in July. I met Ántonia downtown on Saturday afternoon, and learned that she and Tiny and Lena were going to the river next day with Anna Hansen—the elder[4] was all in bloom now, and Anna wanted to make elder-blow wine.

"Anna's to drive us down in the Marshalls' delivery wagon, and we'll take a nice lunch and have a picnic. Just us; nobody else. Couldn't you happen along, Jim? It would be like old times."

I considered a moment. "Maybe I can, if I won't be in the way."

On Sunday morning I rose early and got out of Black Hawk while the dew was still heavy on the long meadow grasses. It was the high season for summer flowers. The pink bee-bush stood tall along the sandy roadsides, and the cone-flowers and rose mallow grew everywhere. Across the wire fence, in the long grass, I saw a clump of flaming orange-colored milkweed, rare in that part of the State. I left the road and went around through a stretch of pasture that was always cropped short in summer, where the gaillardia came up year after year and matted over the ground with the deep, velvety red that is in Bokhara carpets. The country was empty and solitary except for the larks that Sunday morning, and it seemed to lift itself up to me and to come very close.

The river was running strong for midsummer; heavy rains to the west of us had kept it full. I crossed the bridge and went upstream along the wooded

3. Roman poet (70–19 B.C.E.), most famous for his epic, the *Aeneid,* about the founding of Rome by the Trojan hero Aeneas. The poem was part of a basic classical education in the United States, and Jim Burden would be studying it in its original Latin. See also p. 000, epigraph and n. 1.
4. A shrub that bears flowers used for a mild, sweet wine as well as edible berries.

shore to a pleasant dressing-room I knew among the dogwood bushes, all overgrown with wild grapevines. I began to undress for a swim. The girls would not be along yet. For the first time it occurred to me that I would be homesick for that river after I left it. The sandbars, with their clean white beaches and their little groves of willows and cottonwood seedlings, were a sort of No Man's Land, little newly-created worlds that belonged to the Black Hawk boys. Charley Harling and I had hunted through these woods, fished from the fallen logs, until I knew every inch of the river shores and had a friendly feeling for every bar and shallow.

After my swim, while I was playing about indolently in the water, I heard the sound of hoofs and wheels on the bridge. I struck downstream and shouted, as the open spring wagon came into view on the middle span. They stopped the horse, and the two girls in the bottom of the cart stood up, steadying themselves by the shoulders of the two in front, so that they could see me better. They were charming up there, huddled together in the cart and peering down at me like curious deer when they come out of the thicket to drink. I found bottom near the bridge and stood up, waving to them.

"How pretty you look!" I called.

"So do you!" they shouted altogether, and broke into peals of laughter. Anna Hansen shook the reins and they drove on, while I zigzagged back to my inlet and clambered up behind an overhanging elm. I dried myself in the sun, and dressed slowly, reluctant to leave that green enclosure where the sunlight flickered so bright through the grapevine leaves and the woodpecker hammered away in the crooked elm that trailed out over the water. As I went along the road back to the bridge I kept picking off little pieces of scaly chalk from the dried water gullies, and breaking them up in my hands.

When I came upon the Marshalls' delivery horse, tied in the shade, the girls had already taken their baskets and gone down the east road which wound through the sand and scrub. I could hear them calling to each other. The elder bushes did not grow back in the shady ravines between the bluffs, but in the hot, sandy bottoms along the stream, where their roots were always in moisture and their tops in the sun. The blossoms were unusually luxuriant and beautiful that summer.

I followed a cattle path through the thick underbrush until I came to a slope that fell away abruptly to the water's edge. A great chunk of the shore had been bitten out by some spring freshet, and the scar was masked by elder bushes, growing down to the water in flowery terraces. I did not touch them. I was overcome by content and drowsiness and by the warm silence about me. There was no sound but the high, sing-song buzz of wild bees and the sunny gurgle of the water underneath. I peeped over the edge of the bank to see the little stream that made the noise; it flowed along perfectly clear over the sand and gravel, cut off from the muddy main current by a long sandbar. Down there, on the lower shelf of the bank, I saw Ántonia, seated alone under the pagoda-like elders. She looked up when she heard me, and smiled, but I saw that she had been crying. I slid down into the soft sand beside her and asked her what was the matter.

"It makes me homesick, Jimmy, this flower, this smell," she said softly. "We have this flower very much at home, in the old country. It always grew in our yard and my papa had a green bench and a table under the bushes. In summer, when they were in bloom, he used to sit there with his friend that played the trombone. When I was little I used to go down there to hear them talk—beautiful talk, like what I never hear in this country."

"What did they talk about?" I asked her.

She sighed and shook her head. "Oh, I don't know! About music, and the woods, and about God, and when they were young." She turned to me suddenly and looked into my eyes. "You think, Jimmy, that maybe my father's spirit can go back to those old places?"

I told her about the feeling of her father's presence I had on that winter day when my grandparents had gone over to see his dead body and I was left alone in the house. I said I felt sure then that he was on his way back to his own country, and that even now, when I passed his grave, I always thought of him as being among the woods and fields that were so dear to him.

Ántonia had the most trusting, responsive eyes in the world; love and credulousness seemed to look out of them with open faces. "Why didn't you ever tell me that before? It makes me feel more sure for him." After a while she said: "You know, Jim, my father was different from my mother. He did not have to marry my mother, and all his brothers quarreled with him because he did. I used to hear the old people at home whisper about it. They said he could have paid my mother money, and not married her.[5] But he was older than she was, and he was too kind to treat her like that. He lived in his mother's house, and she was a poor girl come in to do the work. After my father married her, my grandmother never let my mother come into her house again. When I went to my grandmother's funeral was the only time I was ever in my grandmother's house. Don't that seem strange?"

While she talked, I lay back in the hot sand and looked up at the blue sky between the flat bouquets of elder. I could hear the bees humming and singing, but they stayed up in the sun above the flowers and did not come down into the shadow of the leaves. Ántonia seemed to me that day exactly like the little girl who used to come to our house with Mr. Shimerda.

"Some day, Tony, I am going over to your country, and I am going to the little town where you lived. Do you remember all about it?"

"Jim," she said earnestly, "if I was put down there in the middle of the night, I could find my way all over that little town; and along the river to the next town, where my grandmother lived. My feet remember all the little paths through the woods, and where the big roots stick out to trip you. I ain't never forgot my own country."

There was a crackling in the branches above us, and Lena Lingard peered down over the edge of the bank.

"You lazy things!" she cried. "All this elder, and you two lying there! Didn't you hear us calling you?" Almost as flushed as she had been in my dream, she leaned over the edge of the bank and began to demolish our flowery pagoda. I had never seen her so energetic; she was panting with zeal, and the perspiration stood in drops on her short, yielding upper lip. I sprang to my feet and ran up the bank.

It was noon now, and so hot that the dogwoods and scrub-oaks began to turn up the silvery under-side of their leaves, and all the foliage looked soft and wilted. I carried the lunch-basket to the top of one of the chalk bluffs, where even on the calmest days there was always a breeze. The flat-topped,

5. Implying that he had gotten her pregnant.

twisted little oaks threw light shadows on the grass. Below us we could see the windings of the river, and Black Hawk, grouped among its trees, and, beyond, the rolling country, swelling gently until it met the sky. We could recognize familiar farmhouses and windmills. Each of the girls pointed out to me the direction in which her father's farm lay, and told me how many acres were in wheat that year and how many in corn.

"My old folks," said Tiny Soderball, "have put in twenty acres of rye. They get it ground at the mill, and it makes nice bread. It seems like my mother ain't been so homesick, ever since father's raised rye flour for her."

"It must have been a trial for our mothers," said Lena, "coming out here and having to do everything different. My mother had always lived in town. She says she started behind in farm-work, and never has caught up."

"Yes, a new country's hard on the old ones, sometimes," said Anna thoughtfully. "My grandmother's getting feeble now, and her mind wanders. She's forgot about this country, and thinks she's at home in Norway. She keeps asking mother to take her down to the waterside and the fish market. She craves fish all the time. Whenever I go home I take her canned salmon and mackerel."

"Mercy, it's hot!" Lena yawned. She was supine under a little oak, resting after the fury of her elder-hunting, and had taken off the high-heeled slippers she had been silly enough to wear. "Come here, Jim. You never got the sand out of your hair." She began to draw her fingers slowly through my hair.

Ántonia pushed her away. "You'll never get it out like that," she said sharply. She gave my head a rough touzling and finished me off with something like a box on the ear. "Lena, you oughtn't to try to wear those slippers any more. They're too small for your feet. You'd better give them to me for Yulka."

"All right," said Lena good-naturedly, tucking her white stockings under her skirt. "You get all Yulka's things, don't you? I wish father didn't have such bad luck with his farm machinery; then I could buy more things for my sisters. I'm going to get Mary a new coat this fall, if the sulky plough's never paid for!"

Tiny asked her why she didn't wait until after Christmas, when coats would be cheaper. "What do you think of poor me?" she added; "with six at home, younger than I am? And they all think I'm rich, because when I go back to the country I'm dressed so fine!" She shrugged her shoulders. "But, you know, my weakness is playthings. I like to buy them playthings better than what they need."

"I know how that is," said Anna. "When we first came here, and I was little, we were too poor to buy toys. I never got over the loss of a doll somebody gave me before we left Norway. A boy on the boat broke her, and I still hate him for it."

"I guess after you got here you had plenty of live dolls to nurse, like me!" Lena remarked cynically.

"Yes, the babies came along pretty fast, to be sure. But I never minded. I was fond of them all. The youngest one, that we didn't any of us want, is the one we love best now."

Lena sighed. "Oh, the babies are all right; if only they don't come in winter. Ours nearly always did. I don't see how mother stood it. I tell you what girls," she sat up with sudden energy; "I'm going to get my mother out of that old sod house where she's lived so many years. The men will never do it. Johnnie, that's my oldest brother, he's wanting to get married now, and build a house for his girl instead of his mother. Mrs. Thomas says she thinks I can move to some other town pretty soon, and go into business for myself. If I don't get into business, I'll maybe marry a rich gambler."

"That would be a poor way to get on," said Anna sarcastically. "I wish I could teach school, like Selma Kronn. Just think! She'll be the first Scandinavian girl to get a position in the High School. We ought to be proud of her."

Selma was a studious girl, who had not much tolerance for giddy things like Tiny and Lena; but they always spoke of her with admiration.

Tiny moved about restlessly, fanning herself with her straw hat. "If I was smart like her, I'd be at my books day and night. But she was born smart— and look how her father's trained her! He was something high up in the old country."

"So was my mother's father," murmured Lena, "but that's all the good it does us! My father's father was smart, too, but he was wild. He married a Lapp.[6] I guess that's what's the matter with me; they say Lapp blood will out."

"A real Lapp, Lena?" I exclaimed. "The kind that wear skins?"

"I don't know if she wore skins, but she was a Lapp all right, and his folks felt dreadful about it. He was sent up north on some Government job he had, and fell in with her. He would marry her."

"But I thought Lapland women were fat and ugly, and had squint eyes, like Chinese?" I objected.

"I don't know, maybe. There must be something mighty taking about the Lapp girls, though; mother says the Norwegians up north are always afraid their boys will run after them."

In the afternoon, when the heat was less oppressive, we had a lively game of "Pussy Wants a Corner," on the flat bluff-top, with the little trees for bases. Lena was Pussy so often that she finally said she wouldn't play any more. We threw ourselves down on the grass, out of breath.

"Jim," Ántonia said dreamily, "I want you to tell the girls about how the Spanish first came here, like you and Charley Harling used to talk about. I've tried to tell them, but I leave out so much."

They sat under a little oak, Tony resting against the trunk and the other girls leaning against her and each other, and listened to the little I was able to tell them about Coronado[7] and his search for the Seven Golden Cities. At school we were taught that he had not got so far north as Nebraska, but had given up his quest and turned back somewhere in Kansas. But Charley Harling and I had a strong belief that he had been along this very river. A farmer in the county north of ours, when he was breaking sod, had turned up a metal stirrup of fine workmanship, and a sword with a Spanish inscription on the blade. He lent these relics to Mr. Harling, who brought them home with him. Charley and I scoured them, and they were on exhibition in the Harling office all summer. Father Kelly, the priest, had found the name of the Spanish maker on the sword, and an abbreviation that stood for the city of Cordova.[8]

"And that I saw with my own eyes," Ántonia put in triumphantly. "So Jim and Charley were right, and the teachers were wrong!"

The girls began to wonder among themselves. Why had the Spaniards come so far? What must this country have been like, then? Why had Coro-

6. Nomadic people of northern Scandinavia.
7. Francisco Vázquez de Coronado (ca. 1510–1554), Spanish governor of a Mexican province, who set out in 1840 in quest of the fabled Seven Cities and their immense wealth.
8. In Spain.

nado never gone back to Spain, to his riches and his castles and his king? I couldn't tell them. I only knew the school books said he "died in the wilderness, of a broken heart."

"More than him has done that," said Ántonia sadly, and the girls murmured assent.

We sat looking off across the country, watching the sun go down. The curly grass about us was on fire now. The bark of the oaks turned red as copper. There was a shimmer of gold on the brown river. Out in the stream the sandbars glittered like glass, and the light trembled in the willow thickets as if little flames were leaping among them. The breeze sank to stillness. In the ravine a ringdove mourned plaintively, and somewhere off in the bushes an owl hooted. The girls sat listless, leaning against each other. The long fingers of the sun touched their foreheads.

Presently we saw a curious thing: There were no clouds, the sun was going down in a limpid, gold-washed sky. Just as the lower edge of the red disc rested on the high fields against the horizon, a great black figure suddenly appeared on the face of the sun. We sprang to our feet, straining our eyes toward it. In a moment we realized what it was. On some upland farm, a plough had been left standing in the field. The sun was sinking just behind it. Magnified across the distance by the horizontal light, it stood out against the sun, was exactly contained within the circle of the disc; the handles, the tongue, the share—black against the molten red. There it was, heroic in size, a picture writing on the sun.[9]

Even while we whispered about it, our vision disappeared; the ball dropped and dropped until the red tip went beneath the earth. The fields below us were dark, the sky was growing pale, and that forgotten plough had sunk back to its own littleness somewhere on the prairie.

XV

Late in August the Cutters went to Omaha for a few days, leaving Ántonia in charge of the house. Since the scandal about the Swedish girl, Wick Cutter could never get his wife to stir out of Black Hawk without him.

The day after the Cutters left, Ántonia came over to see us. Grandmother noticed that she seemed troubled and distracted. "You've got something on your mind, Ántonia," she said anxiously.

"Yes, Mrs. Burden. I couldn't sleep much last night." She hesitated, and then told us how strangely Mr. Cutter had behaved before he went away. He put all the silver in a basket and placed it under her bed, and with it a box of papers which he told her were valuable. He made her promise that she would not sleep away from the house, or be out late in the evening, while he was gone. He strictly forbade her to ask any of the girls she knew to stay with her at night. She would be perfectly safe, he said, as he had just put a new Yale lock on the front door.

Cutter had been so insistent in regard to these details that now she felt uncomfortable about staying there alone. She hadn't liked the way he kept coming into the kitchen to instruct her, or the way he looked at her. "I feel as if he is up to some of his tricks again, and is going to try to scare me, somehow."

---

9. In Cather's agrarian mythology, the land is conquered or tamed by the plow, not the sword.

Grandmother was apprehensive at once. "I don't think it's right for you to stay there, feeling that way. I suppose it wouldn't be right for you to leave the place alone, either, after giving your word. Maybe Jim would be willing to go over there and sleep, and you could come here nights. I'd feel safer, knowing you were under my own roof. I guess Jim could take care of their silver and old usury notes as well as you could."

Ántonia turned to me eagerly. "Oh, would you, Jim? I'd make up my bed nice and fresh for you. It's a real cool room, and the bed's right next the window. I was afraid to leave the window open last night."

I liked my own room, and I didn't like the Cutters' house under any circumstances; but Tony looked so troubled that I consented to try this arrangement. I found that I slept there as well as anywhere, and when I got home in the morning, Tony had a good breakfast waiting for me. After prayers she sat down at the table with us, and it was like old times in the country.

The third night I spent at the Cutters', I awoke suddenly with the impression that I had heard a door open and shut. Everything was still, however, and I must have gone to sleep again immediately.

The next thing I knew, I felt some one sit down on the edge of the bed. I was only half awake, but I decided that he might take the Cutters' silver, whoever he was. Perhaps if I did not move, he would find it and get out without troubling me. I held my breath and lay absolutely still. A hand closed softly on my shoulder, and at the same moment I felt something hairy and cologne-scented brushing my face. If the room had suddenly been flooded with electric light, I couldn't have seen more clearly the detestable bearded countenance that I knew was bending over me. I caught a handful of whiskers and pulled, shouting something. The hand that held my shoulder was instantly at my throat. The man became insane; he stood over me, choking me with one fist and beating me in the face with the other, hissing and chuckling and letting out a flood of abuse.

"So this is what she's up to when I'm away, is it? Where is she, you nasty whelp, where is she? Under the bed, are you, hussy? I know your tricks! Wait till I get at you! I'll fix this rat you've got in here. He's caught, all right!"

So long as Cutter had me by the throat, there was no chance for me at all. I got hold of his thumb and bent it back, until he let go with a yell. In a bound, I was on my feet, and easily sent him sprawling to the floor. Then I made a dive for the open window, struck the wire screen, knocked it out, and tumbled after it into the yard.

Suddenly I found myself running across the north end of Black Hawk in my nightshirt, just as one sometimes finds one's self behaving in bad dreams. When I got home I climbed in at the kitchen window. I was covered with blood from my nose and lip, but I was too sick to do anything about it. I found a shawl and an overcoat on the hatrack, lay down on the parlor sofa, and in spite of my hurts, went to sleep.

Grandmother found me there in the morning. Her cry of fright awakened me. Truly, I was a battered object. As she helped me to my room, I caught a glimpse of myself in the mirror. My lip was cut and stood out like a snout. My nose looked like a big blue plum, and one eye was swollen shut and hideously discolored. Grandmother said we must have the doctor at once, but I implored her, as I had never begged for anything before, not to send for him. I could stand anything, I told her, so long as nobody saw me or knew what had happened to me. I entreated her not to let grandfather, even, come into my room. She seemed to understand, though I was too faint and miserable to go into explanations. When she took off my nightshirt, she found such bruises on my chest and shoulders that she began to cry. She spent the whole morning bathing and poulticing me, and rubbing me with arnica.[1] I heard Ántonia sobbing outside my door, but I asked grandmother to send her away. I felt that I never wanted to see her again. I hated her almost as much as I hated Cutter. She had let me in for all this disgustingness. Grandmother kept saying how thankful we ought to be that I had been there instead of Ántonia. But I lay with my disfigured face to the wall and felt no particular gratitude. My one concern was that grandmother should keep every one away from me. If the story once got abroad, I would never hear the last of it. I could well imagine what the old men down at the drug-store would do with such a theme.

While grandmother was trying to make me comfortable, grandfather went to the depot and learned that Wick Cutter had come home on the night express from the east, and had left again on the six o'clock train for Denver that morning. The agent said his face was striped with court-plaster, and he carried his left hand in a sling. He looked so used up, that the agent asked him what had happened to him since ten o'clock the night before; whereat Cutter began to swear at him and said he would have him discharged for incivility.

That afternoon, while I was asleep, Ántonia took grandmother with her, and went over to the Cutters' to pack her trunk. They found the place locked up, and they had to break the window to get into Ántonia's bedroom. There everything was in shocking disorder. Her clothes had been taken out of her closet, thrown into the middle of the room, and trampled and torn. My own garments had been treated so badly that I never saw them again; grandmother burned them in the Cutters' kitchen range.

While Ántonia was packing her trunk and putting her room in order, to leave it, the front-door bell rang violently. There stood Mrs. Cutter,—locked out, for she had no key to the new lock—her head trembling with rage. "I advised her to control herself, or she would have a stroke," grandmother said afterwards.

Grandmother would not let her see Ántonia at all, but made her sit down in the parlor while she related to her just what had occurred the night before. Ántonia was frightened, and was going home to stay for a while, she told Mrs. Cutter; it would be useless to interrogate the girl, for she knew nothing of what had happened.

Then Mrs. Cutter told her story. She and her husband had started home from Omaha together the morning before. They had to stop over several hours at Waymore Junction to catch the Black Hawk train. During the wait, Cutter left her at the depot and went to the Waymore bank to attend to some business. When he returned, he told her that he would have to stay overnight there, but she could go on home. He bought her ticket and put her on the train. She saw him slip a twenty-dollar bill into her handbag with her ticket. That bill, she said, should have aroused her suspicions at once—but did not.

1. A medicinal herb; here in the form of a soothing lotion.

The trains are never called at little junction towns; everybody knows when they come in. Mr. Cutter showed his wife's ticket to the conductor, and settled her in her seat before the train moved off. It was not until nearly nightfall that she discovered she was on the express bound for Kansas City, that her ticket was made out to that point, and that Cutter must have planned it so. The conductor told her the Black Hawk train was due at Waymore twelve minutes after the Kansas City train left. She saw at once that her husband had played this trick in order to get back to Black Hawk without her. She had no choice but to go on to Kansas City and take the first fast train for home.

Cutter could have got home a day earlier than his wife by any one of a dozen simpler devices; he could have left her in the Omaha hotel, and said he was going on to Chicago for a few days. But apparently it was part of his fun to outrage her feelings as much as possible.

"Mr. Cutter will pay for this, Mrs. Burden. He will pay!" Mrs. Cutter avouched, nodding her horselike head and rolling her eyes.

Grandmother said she hadn't a doubt of it.

Certainly Cutter liked to have his wife think him a devil. In some way he depended upon the excitement he could arouse in her hysterical nature. Perhaps he got the feeling of being a rake more from his wife's rage and amazement than from any experiences of his own. His zest in debauchery might wane, but never Mrs. Cutter's belief in it. The reckoning with his wife at the end of an escapade was something he counted on—like the last powerful liqueur after a long dinner. The one excitement he really couldn't do without was quarreling with Mrs. Cutter!

Book III. Lena Lingard

I

At the University I had the good fortune to come immediately under the influence of a brilliant and inspiring young scholar. Gaston Cleric had arrived in Lincoln only a few weeks earlier than I, to begin his work as head of the Latin Department. He came West at the suggestion of his physicians, his health having been enfeebled by a long illness in Italy. When I took my entrance examinations he was my examiner, and my course was arranged under his supervision.

I did not go home for my first summer vacation, but stayed in Lincoln, working off a year's Greek, which had been my only condition on entering the Freshman class. Cleric's doctor advised against his going back to New England, and except for a few weeks in Colorado, he, too, was in Lincoln all that summer. We played tennis, read, and took long walks together. I shall always look back on that time of mental awakening as one of the happiest in my life. Gaston Cleric introduced me to the world of ideas; when one first enters that world everything else fades for a time, and all that went before is as if it had not been. Yet I found curious survivals; some of the figures of my old life seemed to be waiting for me in the new.

In those days there were many serious young men among the students who had come up to the University from the farms and the little towns scattered over the thinly settled State. Some of those boys came straight from the cornfields with only a summer's wages in their pockets, hung on through the four years, shabby and underfed, and completed the course by really heroic self-sacrifice. Our instructors were oddly assorted; wandering pioneer school-teachers, stranded ministers of the Gospel, a few enthusiastic young men just out of graduate schools. There was an atmosphere of endeavor, of expectancy and bright hopefulness about the young college that had lifted its head from the prairie only a few years before.

Our personal life was as free as that of our instructors. There were no college dormitories; we lived where we could and as we could. I took rooms with an old couple, early settlers in Lincoln, who had married off their children and now lived quietly in their house at the edge of town, near the open country. The house was inconveniently situated for students, and on that account I got two rooms for the price of one. My bedroom, originally a linen closet, was unheated and was barely large enough to contain my cot bed, but it enabled me to call the other room my study. The dresser, and the great walnut wardrobe which held all my clothes, even my hats and shoes, I had pushed out of the way, and I considered them non-existent, as children eliminate incongruous objects when they are playing house. I worked at a commodious green-topped table placed directly in front of the west window which looked out over the prairie. In the corner at my right were all my books, in shelves I had made and painted myself. On the blank wall at my left the dark, old-fashioned wall-paper was covered by a large map of ancient Rome, the work of some German scholar. Cleric had ordered it for me when he was sending for books from abroad. Over the bookcase hung a photograph of the Tragic Theater at Pompeii,[2] which he had given me from his collection.

When I sat at work I half faced a deep, upholstered chair which stood at the end of my table, its high back against the wall. I had bought it with great care. My instructor sometimes looked in upon me when he was out for an evening tramp, and I noticed that he was more likely to linger and become talkative if I had a comfortable chair for him to sit in, and if he found a bottle of Bénédictine[3] and plenty of the kind of cigarettes he liked, at his elbow. He was, I had discovered, parsimonious about small expenditures—a trait absolutely inconsistent with his general character. Sometimes when he came he was silent and moody, and after a few sarcastic remarks went away again, to tramp the streets of Lincoln, which were almost as quiet and oppressively domestic as those of Black Hawk. Again, he would sit until nearly midnight, talking about Latin and English poetry, or telling me about his long stay in Italy.

I can give no idea of the peculiar charm and vividness of his talk. In a crowd he was nearly always silent. Even for his classroom he had no platitudes, no stock of professorial anecdotes. When he was tired his lectures were clouded, obscure, elliptical; but when he was interested they were wonderful. I believe that Gaston Cleric narrowly missed being a great poet, and I have sometimes thought that his bursts of imaginative talk were fatal to his poetic gift. He squandered too much in the heat of personal communication. How often I have seen him draw his dark brows together, fix his eyes upon some object on the wall or a figure in the carpet, and then flash into the lamplight the very

2. Ancient city in southwest Italy, which was buried by an eruption of Mt. Vesuvius in 79 C.E.; its buildings were preserved in superb condition.

3. After-dinner liqueur made in France by Benedictine monks.

image that was in his brain. He could bring the drama of antique life before one out of the shadows—white figures against blue backgrounds. I shall never forget his face as it looked one night when he told me about the solitary day he spent among the sea temples at Paestum:[4] the soft wind blowing through the roofless columns, the birds flying low over the flowering marsh grasses, the changing lights on the silver, cloud-hung mountains. He had willfully stayed the short summer night there, wrapped in his coat and rug, watching the constellations on their path down the sky until "the bride of old Tithonus"[5] rose out of the sea, and the mountains stood sharp in the dawn. It was there he caught the fever which held him back on the eve of his departure for Greece and of which he lay ill so long in Naples. He was still, indeed, doing penance for it.

I remember vividly another evening, when something led us to talk of Dante's[6] veneration for Virgil. Cleric went through canto after canto of the "Commedia," repeating the discourse between Dante and his "sweet teacher," while his cigarette burned itself out unheeded between his long fingers. I can hear him now, speaking the lines of the poet Statius,[7] who spoke for Dante: *"I was famous on earth with the name which endures longest and honors most. The seeds of my ardor were the sparks from that divine flame whereby more than a thousand have kindled; I speak of the Æneid, mother to me and nurse to me in poetry."*

Although I admired scholarship so much in Cleric, I was not deceived about myself; I knew that I should never be a scholar. I could never lose myself for long among impersonal things. Mental excitement was apt to send me with a rush back to my own naked land and the figures scattered upon it. While I was in the very act of yearning toward the new forms that Cleric brought up before me, my mind plunged away from me, and I suddenly found myself thinking of the places and people of my own infinitesimal past. They stood out strengthened and simplified now, like the image of the plough against the sun. They were all I had for an answer to the new appeal. I begrudged the room that Jake and Otto and Russian Peter took up in my memory, which I wanted to crowd with other things. But whenever my consciousness was quickened, all those early friends were quickened within it, and in some strange way they accompanied me through all my new experiences. They were so much alive in me that I scarcely stopped to wonder whether they were alive anywhere else, or how.

II

One March evening in my Sophomore year I was sitting alone in my room after supper. There had been a warm thaw all day, with mushy yards and little streams of dark water gurgling cheerfully into the streets out of old snowbanks. My window was open, and the earthy wind blowing through made me indolent. On the edge of the prairie, where the sun had gone down, the sky was turquoise blue, like a lake, with gold light throbbing in it. Higher up, in

4. Coastal town in southern Italy containing Roman temples from the 5th and 6th centuries B.C.E.
5. I.e., Eos, the goddess of the dawn. In Greek myth Tithonus was the son of the king of Troy.
6. Dante Alighieri (1265–1321), Italian poet, famous for the *Divine Comedy*, a long poem

recounting the poet's journey through Hell (*Inferno*), Purgatory (*Purgatorio*), and Heaven (*Paradiso*). Virgil is his guide in Hell and Purgatory.
7. Roman poet (ca. 45–96 C.E.) who, in Cantos 21 and 22 of the *Purgatorio*, meets Virgil and speaks the quoted lines.

the utter clarity of the western slope, the evening star hung like a lamp suspended by silver chains—like the lamp engraved upon the title-page of old
Latin texts, which is always appearing in new heavens, and waking new
desires in men. It reminded me, at any rate, to shut my window and light my
wick in answer. I did so regretfully, and the dim objects in the room emerged
from the shadows and took their place about me with the helpfulness which
custom breeds.

I propped my book open and stared listlessly at the page of the Georgics
where tomorrow's lesson began. It opened with the melancholy reflection
that, in the lives of mortals, the best days are the first to flee. *"Optima dies . . .
prima fugit."* I turned back to the beginning of the third book, which we had
read in class that morning. *"Primus ego in patriam mecum . . . deducam
Musas"*; "for I shall be the first, if I live, to bring the Muse into my country."
Cleric had explained to us that "patria" here meant, not a nation or even a
province, but the little rural neighborhood on the Mincio where the poet was
born. This was not a boast, but a hope, at once bold and devoutly humble,
that he might bring the Muse (but lately come to Italy from her cloudy Grecian mountains), not to the capital, the *palatia Romana,* but to his own little
"country"; to his father's fields, "sloping down to the river and to the old beech
trees with broken tops."

Cleric said he thought Virgil, when he was dying at Brindisi, must have
remembered that passage. After he had faced the bitter fact that he was to
leave the Æneid unfinished, and had decreed that the great canvas, crowded
with figures of gods and men, should be burned rather than survive him
unperfected, then his mind must have gone back to the perfect utterance of
the Georgics, where the pen was fitted to the matter as the plough is to the
furrow; and he must have said to himself with the thankfulness of a good
man, "I was the first to bring the Muse into my country."

We left the classroom quietly, conscious that we had been brushed by the
wing of a great feeling, though perhaps I alone knew Cleric intimately
enough to guess what that feeling was. In the evening, as I sat staring at my
book, the fervor of his voice stirred through the quantities on the page before
me. I was wondering whether that particular rocky strip of New England
coast about which he had so often told me was Cleric's *patria.* Before I had
got far with my reading I was disturbed by a knock. I hurried to the door and
when I opened it saw a woman standing in the dark hall.

"I expect you hardly know me, Jim."

The voice seemed familiar, but I did not recognize her until she stepped
into the light of my doorway and I beheld—Lena Lingard! She was so quietly
conventionalized by city clothes that I might have passed her on the street
without seeing her. Her black suit fitted her figure smoothly, and a black lace
hat, with pale-blue forget-me-nots, sat demurely on her yellow hair.

I led her toward Cleric's chair, the only comfortable one I had, questioning her confusedly.

She was not disconcerted by my embarrassment. She looked about her
with the naïve curiosity I remembered so well. "You are quite comfortable
here, aren't you? I live in Lincoln now, too, Jim. I'm in business for myself. I
have a dressmaking shop in the Raleigh Block, out on O Street. I've made a
real good start."

"But, Lena, when did you come?"

"Oh, I've been here all winter. Didn't your grandmother ever write you? I've thought about looking you up lots of times. But we've all heard what a studious young man you've got to be, and I felt bashful. I didn't know whether you'd be glad to see me." She laughed her mellow, easy laugh, that was either very artless or very comprehending, one never quite knew which. "You seem the same, though,—except you're a young man, now, of course. Do you think I've changed?"

"Maybe you're prettier—though you were always pretty enough. Perhaps it's your clothes that make a difference."

"You like my new suit? I have to dress pretty well in my business." She took off her jacket and sat more at ease in her blouse, of some soft, flimsy silk. She was already at home in my place, had slipped quietly into it, as she did into everything. She told me her business was going well, and she had saved a little money.

"This summer I'm going to build the house for mother I've talked about so long. I won't be able to pay up on it at first, but I want her to have it before she is too old to enjoy it. Next summer I'll take her down new furniture and carpets, so she'll have something to look forward to all winter."

I watched Lena sitting there so smooth and sunny and well cared-for, and thought of how she used to run barefoot over the prairie until after the snow began to fly, and how Crazy Mary chased her round and round the cornfields. It seemed to me wonderful that she should have got on so well in the world. Certainly she had no one but herself to thank for it.

"You must feel proud of yourself, Lena," I said heartily. "Look at me; I've never earned a dollar, and I don't know that I'll ever be able to."

"Tony says you're going to be richer than Mr. Harling some day. She's always bragging about you, you know."

"Tell me, how *is* Tony?"

"She's fine. She works for Mrs. Gardener at the hotel now. She's house-keeper. Mrs. Gardener's health isn't what it was, and she can't see after everything like she used to. She has great confidence in Tony. Tony's made it up with the Harlings, too. Little Nina is so fond of her that Mrs. Harling kind of overlooked things."

"Is she still going with Larry Donovan?"

"Oh, that's on, worse than ever! I guess they're engaged. Tony talks about him like he was president of the railroad. Everybody laughs about it, because she was never a girl to be soft. She won't hear a word against him. She's so sort of innocent."

I said I didn't like Larry, and never would.

Lena's face dimpled. "Some of us could tell her things, but it wouldn't do any good. She'd always believe him. That's Ántonia's failing, you know; if she once likes people, she won't hear anything against them."

"I think I'd better go home and look after Ántonia," I said.

"I think you had." Lena looked up at me in frank amusement. "It's a good thing the Harlings are friendly with her again. Larry's afraid of them. They ship so much grain, they have influence with the railroad people. What are you studying?" She leaned her elbows on the table and drew my book toward her. I caught a faint odor of violet sachet. "So that's Latin, is it? It looks hard. You do go to the theater sometimes, though, for I've seen you there. Don't you just love a good play, Jim? I can't stay at home in the evening if there's one in town. I'd be willing to work like a slave, it seems to me, to live in a place where there are theaters."

"Let's go to a show together sometime. You are going to let me come to see you, aren't you?"

"Would you like to? I'd be ever so pleased. I'm never busy after six o'clock, and I let my sewing girls go at half-past five. I board, to save time, but sometimes I cook a chop for myself, and I'd be glad to cook one for you. Well,"— she began to put on her white gloves,—"it's been awful good to see you, Jim."

"You needn't hurry, need you? You've hardly told me anything yet."

"We can talk when you come to see me. I expect you don't often have lady visitors. The old woman downstairs didn't want to let me come up very much. I told her I was from your home town, and had promised your grandmother to come and see you. How surprised Mrs. Burden would be!" Lena laughed softly as she rose.

When I caught up my hat she shook her head. "No, I don't want you to go with me. I'm to meet some Swedes at the drug-store. You wouldn't care for them. I wanted to see your room so I could write Tony all about it, but I must tell her how I left you right here with your books. She's always so afraid some one will run off with you!" Lena slipped her silk sleeves into the jacket I held for her, smoothed it over her person, and buttoned it slowly. I walked with her to the door. "Come and see me sometimes when you're lonesome. But maybe you have all the friends you want. Have you?" She turned her soft cheek to me. "Have you?" she whispered teasingly in my ear. In a moment I watched her fade down the dusky stairway.

When I turned back to my room the place seemed much pleasanter than before. Lena had left something warm and friendly in the lamplight. How I loved to hear her laugh again! It was so soft and unexcited and appreciative— gave a favorable interpretation to everything. When I closed my eyes I could hear them all laughing—the Danish laundry girls and the three Bohemian Marys. Lena had brought them all back to me. It came over me, as it had never done before, the relation between girls like those and the poetry of Virgil. If there were no girls like them in the world, there would be no poetry. I understood that clearly, for the first time. This revelation seemed to me inestimably precious. I clung to it as if it might suddenly vanish.

As I sat down to my book at last, my old dream about Lena coming across the harvest field in her short skirt seemed to me like the memory of an actual experience. It floated before me on the page like a picture, and underneath it stood the mournful line: *Optima dies . . . prima fugit.*

III

In Lincoln the best part of the theatrical season came late, when the good companies stopped off there for one-night stands, after their long runs in New York and Chicago. That spring Lena went with me to see Joseph Jefferson in "Rip Van Winkle," and to a war play called "Shenandoah."[8] She was inflexible about paying for her own seat; said she was in business now, and she wouldn't have a schoolboy spending his money on her. I liked to watch a

8. A four-act play (1889), by American playwright Bronson Howard (1842–1908), about lovers separated by the Civil War. Jefferson (1829–1905), a well-known American comedian who from 1865 on mainly played the role of Rip Van Winkle in a stage version of Washington Irving's 1819 story.

play with Lena; everything was wonderful to her, and everything was true. It was like going to revival meetings with some one who was always being converted. She handed her feelings over to the actors with a kind of fatalistic resignation. Accessories of costume and scene meant much more to her than to me. She sat entranced through "Robin Hood"[9] and hung upon the lips of the contralto who sang, "Oh, Promise Me!"

Toward the end of April, the billboards, which I watched anxiously in those days, bloomed out one morning with gleaming white posters on which two names were impressively printed in blue Gothic letters: the name of an actress of whom I had often heard, and the name "Camille."[1]

I called at the Raleigh Block for Lena on Saturday evening, and we walked down to the theater. The weather was warm and sultry and put us both in a holiday humor. We arrived early, because Lena liked to watch the people come in. There was a note on the programme, saying that the "incidental music" would be from the opera "Traviata,"[2] which was made from the same story as the play. We had neither of us read the play, and we did not know what it was about—though I seemed to remember having heard it was a piece in which great actresses shone. "The Count of Monte Cristo," which I had seen James O'Neill play that winter, was by the only Alexandre Dumas[3] I knew. This play, I saw, was by his son, and I expected a family resemblance. A couple of jack-rabbits, run in off the prairie, could not have been more innocent of what awaited them than were Lena and I.

Our excitement began with the rise of the curtain, when the moody Varville, seated before the fire, interrogated Nanine. Decidedly, there was a new tang about this dialogue. I had never heard in the theater lines that were alive, that presupposed and took for granted, like those which passed between Varville and Marguerite in the brief encounter before her friends entered.[4] This introduced the most brilliant, worldly, the most enchantingly gay scene I had ever looked upon. I had never seen champagne bottles opened on the stage before—indeed, I had never seen them opened anywhere. The memory of that supper makes me hungry now; the sight of it then, when I had only a students' boarding-house dinner behind me, was delicate torment. I seem to remember gilded chairs and tables (arranged hurriedly by footmen in white gloves and stockings), linen of dazzling whiteness, glittering glass, silver dishes, a great bowl of fruit, and the reddest of roses. The room was invaded by beautiful women and dashing young men, laughing and talking together. The men were dressed more or less after the period in which the play was written; the women were not. I saw no inconsistency. Their talk seemed to open to one the brilliant world in which they lived; every sentence made one older and wiser, every pleasantry enlarged one's horizon. One could experience excess and satiety without the inconvenience of learning what to do with

9. A three-act comic opera (1819), by American Reginald De Koven (1859–1920). "Oh, Promise Me!" was its most popular song.
1. A play based on the novel (1848) and play (1852) by the French writer Alexandre Dumas, *fils* (1825–1895), *La Dame aux Camélias* (The lady of the camellias), brought to the United States in an English version in 1853. The actress is probably Clara Morris (1848–1925).
2. Verdi's 1853 opera was also based on the Dumas novel.

3. French writer (*père*, 1802–1870) who published *The Count of Monte Cristo* in 1844–45. O'Neill (1847–1920), father of Eugene O'Neill, performed the leading role for more than a quarter century, starting in 1883.
4. The story is about the romance between Marguerite Gautier, a woman of the world, and the young Armand Duval. Armand's father persuades her to give Armand up. Other characters are Varville, her patron; Nanine, her maid; and Gaston, a friend.

one's hands in a drawing-room! When the characters all spoke at once and I missed some of the phrases they flashed at each other, I was in misery. I strained my ears and eyes to catch every exclamation.

The actress who played Marguerite was even then old-fashioned, though historic. She had been a member of Daly's[5] famous New York company, and afterward a "star" under his direction. She was a woman who could not be taught, it is said, though she had a crude natural force which carried with people whose feelings were accessible and whose taste was not squeamish. She was already old, with a ravaged countenance and a physique curiously hard and stiff. She moved with difficulty—I think she was lame—I seem to remember some story about a malady of the spine. Her Armand was dispro-portionately young and slight, a handsome youth, perplexed in the extreme. But what did it matter? I believed devoutly in her power to fascinate him, in her dazzling loveliness. I believed her young, ardent, reckless, disillusioned, under sentence, feverish, avid of pleasure. I wanted to cross the footlights and help the slim-waisted Armand in the frilled shirt to convince her that there was still loyalty and devotion in the world. Her sudden illness, when the gayety was at its height, her pallor, the handkerchief she crushed against her lips, the cough she smothered under the laughter while Gaston kept playing the piano lightly—it all wrung my heart. But not so much as her cynicism in the long dialogue with her lover which followed. How far was I from ques-tioning her unbelief! While the charmingly sincere young man pleaded with her—accompanied by the orchestra in the old "Traviata" duet, *"misterioso, misterioso!"*—she maintained her bitter skepticism, and the curtain fell on her dancing recklessly with the others, after Armand had been sent away with his flower.

Between the acts we had no time to forget. The orchestra kept sawing away at the "Traviata" music, so joyous and sad, so thin and far-away, so clap-trap and yet so heart-breaking. After the second act I left Lena in tearful contem-plation of the ceiling, and went out into the lobby to smoke. As I walked about there I congratulated myself that I had not brought some Lincoln girl who would talk during the waits about the Junior dances, or whether the cadets would camp at Plattsmouth. Lena was at least a woman, and I was a man.

Through the scene between Marguerite and the elder Duval, Lena wept unceasingly, and I sat helpless to prevent the closing of that chapter of idyl-lic love, dreading the return of the young man whose ineffable happiness was only to be the measure of his fall.

I suppose no woman could have been further in person, voice, and tem-perament from Dumas' appealing heroine than the veteran actress who first acquainted me with her. Her conception of the character was as heavy and uncompromising as her diction; she bore hard on the idea and on the conso-nants. At all times she was highly tragic, devoured by remorse. Lightness of stress or behavior was far from her. Her voice was heavy and deep: "Ar-r-r-mond!" she would begin, as if she were summoning him to the bar of Judg-ment. But the lines were enough. She had only to utter them. They created the character in spite of her.

The heartless world which Marguerite reentered with Varville had never been so glittering and reckless as on the night when it gathered in Olympe's

---

5. John Augustin Daly (1838–1899), playwright, producer, and director in the American theater.

salon for the fourth act. There were chandeliers hung from the ceiling, I remember, many servants in livery, gaming-tables where the men played with piles of gold, and a staircase down which the guests made their entrance. After all the others had gathered round the card tables, and young Duval had been warned by Prudence, Marguerite descended the staircase with Varville; such a cloak, such a fan, such jewels—and her face! One knew at a glance how it was with her. When Armand, with the terrible words, "Look, all of you, I owe this woman nothing!" flung the gold and bank-notes at the half-swooning Marguerite, Lena cowered beside me and covered her face with her hands.

The curtain rose on the bedroom scene. By this time there wasn't a nerve in me that hadn't been twisted. Nanine alone could have made me cry. I loved Nanine tenderly; and Gaston, how one clung to that good fellow! The New Year's presents were not too much; nothing could be too much now. I wept unrestrainedly. Even the handkerchief in my breast-pocket, worn for elegance and not at all for use, was wet through by the time that moribund woman sank for the last time into the arms of her lover.

When we reached the door of the theater, the streets were shining with rain. I had prudently brought along Mrs. Harling's useful Commencement present, and I took Lena home under its shelter. After leaving her, I walked slowly out into the country part of the town where I lived. The lilacs were all blooming in the yards, and the smell of them after the rain, of the new leaves and the blossoms together, blew into my face with a sort of bitter sweetness. I tramped through the puddles and under the showery trees, mourning for Marguerite Gauthier as if she had died only yesterday, sighing with the spirit of 1840, which had sighed so much, and which had reached me only that night, across long years and several languages, through the person of an infirm old actress. The idea is one that no circumstances can frustrate. Wherever and whenever that piece is put on, it is April.

IV

How well I remember the stiff little parlor where I used to wait for Lena: the hard horse-hair furniture, bought at some auction sale, the long mirror, the fashion-plates on the wall. If I sat down even for a moment I was sure to find threads and bits of colored silk clinging to my clothes after I went away. Lena's success puzzled me. She was so easy-going; had none of the push and self-assertiveness that get people ahead in business. She had come to Lincoln, a country girl, with no introductions except to some cousins of Mrs. Thomas who lived there, and she was already making clothes for the women of "the young married set." She evidently had great natural aptitude for her work. She knew, as she said, "what people looked well in." She never tired of poring over fashion books. Sometimes in the evening I would find her alone in her work-room, draping folds of satin on a wire figure, with a quite blissful expression of countenance. I couldn't help thinking that the years when Lena literally hadn't enough clothes to cover herself might have something to do with her untiring interest in dressing the human figure. Her clients said that Lena "had style," and overlooked her habitual inaccuracies. She never, I discovered, finished anything by the time she had promised, and she frequently spent more money on materials than her customer had authorized. Once, when I arrived at six o'clock, Lena was ushering out a fidgety mother and her awkward, overgrown daughter. The woman detained Lena at the door to say apologetically:—

"You'll try to keep it under fifty for me, won't you, Miss Lingard? You see, she's really too young to come to an expensive dressmaker, but I knew you could do more with her than anybody else."

"Oh, that will be all right, Mrs. Herron. I think we'll manage to get a good effect," Lena replied blandly.

I thought her manner with her customers very good, and wondered where she had learned such self-possession.

Sometimes after my morning classes were over, I used to encounter Lena downtown, in her velvet suit and a little black hat, with a veil tied smoothly over her face, looking as fresh as the spring morning. Maybe she would be carrying home a bunch of jonquils or a hyacinth plant. When we passed a candy store her footsteps would hesitate and linger. "Don't let me go in," she would murmur. "Get me by if you can." She was very fond of sweets, and was afraid of growing too plump.

We had delightful Sunday breakfasts together at Lena's. At the back of her long work-room was a bay-window, large enough to hold a box-couch and a reading-table. We breakfasted in this recess, after drawing the curtains that shut out the long room, with cutting-tables and wire women and sheet-draped garments on the walls. The sunlight poured in, making everything on the table shine and glitter and the flame of the alcohol lamp disappear altogether. Lena's curly black water-spaniel, Prince, breakfasted with us. He sat beside her on the couch and behaved very well until the Polish violin-teacher across the hall began to practice, when Prince would growl and sniff the air with disgust. Lena's landlord, old Colonel Raleigh, had given her the dog, and at first she was not at all pleased. She had spent too much of her life taking care of animals to have much sentiment about them. But Prince was a knowing little beast, and she grew fond of him. After breakfast I made him do his lessons; play dead dog, shake hands, stand up like a soldier. We used to put my cadet cap on his head—I had to take military drill at the University—and give him a yard-measure to hold with his front leg. His gravity made us laugh immoderately.

Lena's talk always amused me. Ántonia had never talked like the people about her. Even after she learned to speak English readily there was always something impulsive and foreign in her speech. But Lena had picked up all the conventional expressions she heard at Mrs. Thomas's dressmaking shop. Those formal phrases, the very flower of small-town proprieties, and the flat commonplaces, nearly all hypocritical in their origin, became very funny, very engaging, when they were uttered in Lena's soft voice, with her caressing intonation and arch naïveté. Nothing could be more diverting than to hear Lena, who was almost as candid as Nature, call a leg a "limb" or a house a "home."

We used to linger a long while over our coffee in that sunny corner. Lena was never so pretty as in the morning; she wakened fresh with the world every day, and her eyes had a deeper color then, like the blue flowers that are never so blue as when they first open. I could sit idle all through a Sunday morning and look at her. Ole Benson's behavior was now no mystery to me.

"There was never any harm in Ole," she said once. "People needn't have troubled themselves. He just liked to come over and sit on the draw-side and forget about his bad luck. I liked to have him. Any company's welcome when you're off with cattle all the time."

"But wasn't he always glum?" I asked. "People said he never talked at all."

"Sure he talked, in Norwegian. He'd been a sailor on an English boat and had seen lots of queer places. He had wonderful tattoos. We used to sit and look at them for hours; there wasn't much to look at out there. He was like a picture book. He had a ship and a strawberry girl on one arm, and on the other a girl standing before a little house, with a fence and gate and all, waiting for her sweetheart. Farther up his arm, her sailor had come back and was kissing her. 'The Sailor's Return,' he called it."

I admitted it was no wonder Ole liked to look at a pretty girl once in a while, with such a fright at home.

"You know," Lena said confidentially, "he married Mary because he thought she was strong-minded and would keep him straight. He never could keep straight on shore. The last time he landed in Liverpool he'd been out on a two years' voyage. He was paid off one morning, and by the next he hadn't a cent left, and his watch and compass were gone. He'd got with some women, and they'd taken everything. He worked his way to this country on a little passenger boat. Mary was a stewardess, and she tried to convert him on the way over. He thought she was just the one to keep him steady. Poor Ole! He used to bring me candy from town, hidden in his feed-bag. He couldn't refuse anything to a girl. He'd have given away his tattoos long ago, if he could. He's one of the people I'm sorriest for."

If I happened to spend an evening with Lena and stayed late, the Polish violin-teacher across the hall used to come out and watch me descend the stairs, muttering so threateningly that it would have been easy to fall into a quarrel with him. Lena had told him once that she liked to hear him practice, so he always left his door open, and watched who came and went.

There was a coolness between the Pole and Lena's landlord on her account. Old Colonel Raleigh had come to Lincoln from Kentucky and invested an inherited fortune in real estate, at the time of inflated prices. Now he sat day after day in his office in the Raleigh Block, trying to discover where his money had gone and how he could get some of it back. He was a widower, and found very little congenial companionship in this casual Western city. Lena's good looks and gentle manners appealed to him. He said her voice reminded him of Southern voices, and he found as many opportunities of hearing it as possible. He painted and papered her rooms for her that spring, and put in a porcelain bathtub in place of the tin one that had satisfied the former tenant. While these repairs were being made, the old gentleman often dropped in to consult Lena's preferences. She told me with amusement how Ordinsky, the Pole, had presented himself at her door one evening, and said that if the landlord was annoying her by his attentions, he would promptly put a stop to it.

"I don't exactly know what to do about him," she said, shaking her head, "he's so sort of wild all the time. I wouldn't like to have him say anything rough to that nice old man. The Colonel is long-winded, but then I expect he's lonesome. I don't think he cares much for Ordinsky, either. He said once that if I had any complaints to make of my neighbors, I mustn't hesitate."

One Saturday evening when I was having supper with Lena we heard a knock at her parlor door, and there stood the Pole, coatless, in a dress shirt and collar. Prince dropped on his paws and began to growl like a mastiff, while the visitor apologized, saying that he could not possibly come in thus attired, but he begged Lena to lend him some safety pins.

"Oh, you'll have to come in, Mr. Ordinsky, and let me see what's the matter." She closed the door behind him. "Jim, won't you make Prince behave?"

I rapped Prince on the nose, while Ordinsky explained that he had not had his dress clothes on for a long time, and to-night, when he was going to play for a concert, his waistcoat had split down the back. He thought he could pin it together until he got it to a tailor.

Lena took him by the elbow and turned him round. She laughed when she saw the long gap in the satin. "You could never pin that, Mr. Ordinsky. You've kept it folded too long, and the goods is all gone along the crease. Take it off. I can put a new piece of lining-silk in there for you in ten minutes." She disappeared into her work-room with the vest, leaving me to confront the Pole, who stood against the door like a wooden figure. He folded his arms and glared at me with his excitable, slanting brown eyes. His head was the shape of a chocolate drop, and was covered with dry, straw-colored hair that fuzzed up about his pointed crown. He had never done more than mutter at me as I passed him, and I was surprised when he now addressed me.

"Miss Lingard," he said haughtily, "is a young woman for whom I have the utmost, the utmost respect."

"So have I," I said coldly.

He paid no heed to my remark, but began to do rapid finger-exercises on his shirt-sleeves, as he stood with tightly folded arms.

"Kindness of heart," he went on, staring at the ceiling, "sentiment, are not understood in a place like this. The noblest qualities are ridiculed. Grinning college boys, ignorant and conceited, what do they know of delicacy!"

I controlled my features and tried to speak seriously.

"If you mean me, Mr. Ordinsky, I have known Miss Lingard a long time, and I think I appreciate her kindness. We come from the same town, and we grew up together."

His gaze traveled slowly down from the ceiling and rested on me. "Am I to understand that you have this young woman's interests at heart? That you do not wish to compromise her?"

"That's a word we don't use much here, Mr. Ordinsky. A girl who makes her own living can ask a college boy to supper without being talked about. We take some things for granted."

"Then I have misjudged you, and I ask your pardon,"—he bowed gravely. "Miss Lingard," he went on, "is an absolutely trustful heart. She has not learned the hard lessons of life. As for you and me, *noblesse oblige*,"[6]—he watched me narrowly.

Lena returned with the vest. "Come in and let us look at you as you go out, Mr. Ordinsky. I've never seen you in your dress suit," she said as she opened the door for him.

A few moments later he reappeared with his violin case—a heavy muffler about his neck and thick woolen gloves on his bony hands. Lena spoke encouragingly to him, and he went off with such an important, professional

6. Rank carries its obligations (French).

air, that we fell to laughing as soon as we had shut the door. "Poor fellow," Lena said indulgently, "he takes everything so hard."

After that Ordinsky was friendly to me, and behaved as if there were some deep understanding between us. He wrote a furious article, attacking the musical taste of the town, and asked me to do him a great service by taking it to the editor of the morning paper. If the editor refused to print it, I was to tell him that he would be answerable to Ordinsky "in person." He declared that he would never retract one word, and that he was quite prepared to lose all his pupils. In spite of the fact that nobody ever mentioned his article to him after it appeared—full of typographical errors which he thought intentional—he got a certain satisfaction from believing that the citizens of Lincoln had meekly accepted the epithet "coarse barbarians." "You see how it is," he said to me, "where there is no chivalry, there is no *amour propre*."[7] When I met him on his rounds now, I thought he carried his head more disdainfully than ever, and strode up the steps of front porches and rang doorbells with more assurance. He told Lena he would never forget how I had stood by him when he was "under fire."

All this time, of course, I was drifting. Lena had broken up my serious mood. I wasn't interested in my classes. I played with Lena and Prince, I played with the Pole, I went buggy-riding with the old Colonel, who had taken a fancy to me and used to talk to me about Lena and the "great beauties" he had known in his youth. We were all three in love with Lena.

Before the first of June, Gaston Cleric was offered an instructorship at Harvard College, and accepted it. He suggested that I should follow him in the fall, and complete my course at Harvard. He had found out about Lena—not from me—and he talked to me seriously.

"You won't do anything here now. You should either quit school and go to work, or change your college and begin again in earnest. You won't recover yourself while you are playing about with this handsome Norwegian. Yes, I've seen her with you at the theater. She's very pretty, and perfectly irresponsible, I should judge."

Cleric wrote my grandfather that he would like to take me East with him. To my astonishment, grandfather replied that I might go if I wished. I was both glad and sorry on the day when the letter came. I stayed in my room all evening and thought things over; I even tried to persuade myself that I was standing in Lena's way—it is so necessary to be a little noble!—and that if she had not me to play with, she would probably marry and secure her future.

The next evening I went to call on Lena. I found her propped up on the couch in her bay window, with her foot in a big slipper. An awkward little Russian girl whom she had taken into her work-room had dropped a flat-iron on Lena's toe. On the table beside her there was a basket of early summer flowers which the Pole had left after he heard of the accident. He always managed to know what went on in Lena's apartment.

Lena was telling me some amusing piece of gossip about one of her clients, when I interrupted her and picked up the flower basket.

"This old chap will be proposing to you some day, Lena."

"Oh, he has—often!" she murmured.

7. Self-respect (French).

"What! After you've refused him?"

"He doesn't mind that. It seems to cheer him to mention the subject. Old men are like that, you know. It makes them feel important to think they're in love with somebody."

"The Colonel would marry you in a minute. I hope you won't marry some old fellow; not even a rich one."

Lena shifted her pillows and looked up at me in surprise. "Why, I'm not going to marry anybody. Didn't you know that?"

"Nonsense, Lena. That's what girls say, but you know better. Every handsome girl like you marries, of course."

She shook her head. "Not me."

"But why not? What makes you say that?" I persisted.

Lena laughed. "Well, it's mainly because I don't want a husband. Men are all right for friends, but as soon as you marry them they turn into cranky old fathers, even the wild ones. They begin to tell you what's sensible and what's foolish, and want you to stick at home all the time. I prefer to be foolish when I feel like it, and be accountable to nobody."

"But you'll be lonesome. You'll get tired of this sort of life, and you'll want a family."

"Not me. I like to be lonesome. When I went to work for Mrs. Thomas I was nineteen years old, and I had never slept a night in my life when there weren't three in the bed. I never had a minute to myself except when I was off with the cattle."

Usually, when Lena referred to her life in the country at all, she dismissed it with a single remark, humorous or mildly cynical. But to-night her mind seemed to dwell on those early years. She told me she couldn't remember a time when she was so little that she wasn't lugging a heavy baby about, helping to wash for babies, trying to keep their little chapped hands and faces clean. She remembered home as a place where there were always too many children, a cross man, and work piling up around a sick woman.

"It wasn't mother's fault. She would have made us comfortable if she could. But that was no life for a girl! After I began to herd and milk I could never get the smell of the cattle off me. The few underclothes I had I kept in a cracker box. On Saturday nights, after everybody was in bed, then I could take a bath if I wasn't too tired. I could make two trips to the windmill to carry water, and heat it in the wash-boiler on the stove. While the water was heating, I could bring in a washtub out of the cave, and take my bath in the kitchen. Then I could put on a clean nightgown and get into bed with two others, who likely hadn't had a bath unless I'd given it to them. You can't tell me anything about family life. I've had plenty to last me."

"But it's not all like that," I objected.

"Near enough. It's all being under somebody's thumb. What's on your mind, Jim? Are you afraid I'll want you to marry me some day?"

Then I told her I was going away.

"What makes you want to go away, Jim? Haven't I been nice to you?"

"You've been just awfully good to me, Lena," I blurted. "I don't think about much else. I never shall think about much else while I'm with you. I'll never settle down and grind if I stay here. You know that." I dropped down beside her and sat looking at the floor. I seemed to have forgotten all my reasonable explanations.

Lena drew close to me, and the little hesitation in her voice that had hurt me was not there when she spoke again.

"I oughtn't to begun it, ought I?" she murmured. "I oughn't to have gone to see you that first time. But I did want to. I guess I've always been a little foolish about you. I don't know what first put it into my head, unless it was Ántonia, always telling me I mustn't be up to any of my nonsense with you. I let you alone for a long while, though, didn't I?"

She was a sweet creature to those she loved, that Lena Lingard!

At last she sent me away with her soft, slow, renunciatory kiss. "You aren't sorry I came to see you that time?" she whispered. "It seemed so natural. I used to think I'd like to be your first sweetheart. You were such a funny kid!" She always kissed one as if she were sadly and wisely sending one away forever.

We said many good-byes before I left Lincoln, but she never tried to hinder me or hold me back. "You are going, but you haven't gone yet, have you?" she used to say.

My Lincoln chapter closed abruptly. I went home to my grandparents for a few weeks, and afterward visited my relatives in Virginia until I joined Cleric in Boston. I was then nineteen years old.

Book IV. The Pioneer Woman's Story

I

Two years after I left Lincoln I completed my academic course at Harvard. Before I entered the Law School I went home for the summer vacation. On the night of my arrival Mrs. Harling and Frances and Sally came over to greet me. Everything seemed just as it used to be. My grandparents looked very little older. Frances Harling was married now, and she and her husband managed the Harling interests in Black Hawk. When we gathered in grandmother's parlor, I could hardly believe that I had been away at all. One subject, however, we avoided all evening.

When I was walking home with Frances, after we had left Mrs. Harling at her gate, she said simply, "You know, of course, about poor Ántonia."

Poor Ántonia! Every one would be saying that now, I thought bitterly. I replied that grandmother had written me how Ántonia went away to marry Larry Donovan at some place where he was working; that he had deserted her, and that there was now a baby. This was all I knew.

"He never married her," Frances said. "I haven't seen her since she came back. She lives at home, on the farm, and almost never comes to town. She brought the baby in to show it to mama once. I'm afraid she's settled down to be Ambrosch's drudge for good."

I tried to shut Ántonia out of my mind. I was bitterly disappointed in her. I could not forgive her for becoming an object of pity, while Lena Lingard, for whom people had always foretold trouble, was now the leading dressmaker of Lincoln, much respected in Black Hawk. Lena gave her heart away when she felt like it, but she kept her head for her business and had got on in the world.

Just then it was the fashion to speak indulgently of Lena and severely of Tiny Soderball, who had quietly gone West to try her fortune the year before.

A Black Hawk boy, just back from Seattle, brought the news that Tiny had not gone to the coast on a venture, as she had allowed people to think, but with very definite plans. One of the roving promoters that used to stop at Mrs. Gardener's hotel owned idle property along the waterfront in Seattle, and he had offered to set Tiny up in business in one of his empty buildings. She was now conducting a sailors' lodging-house. This, every one said, would be the end of Tiny. Even if she had begun by running a decent place, she couldn't keep it up; all sailors' boarding-houses were alike.

When I thought about it, I discovered that I had never known Tiny as well as I knew the other girls. I remembered her tripping briskly about the dining-room on her high heels, carrying a big tray full of dishes, glancing rather pertly at the spruce traveling men, and contemptuously at the scrubby ones—who were so afraid of her that they didn't dare to ask for two kinds of pie. Now it occurred to me that perhaps the sailors, too, might be afraid of Tiny. How astonished we would have been, as we sat talking about her on Frances Harling's front porch, if we could have known what her future was really to be! Of all the girls and boys who grew up together in Black Hawk, Tiny Soderball was to lead the most adventurous life and to achieve the most solid worldly success.

This is what actually happened to Tiny: While she was running her lodging-house in Seattle, gold was discovered in Alaska.[8] Miners and sailors came back from the North with wonderful stories and pouches of gold. Tiny saw it and weighed it in her hands. That daring which nobody had ever suspected in her, awoke. She sold her business and set out for Circle City, in company with a carpenter and his wife whom she had persuaded to go along with her. They reached Skaguay in a snowstorm, went in dog sledges over the Chilkoot Pass, and shot the Yukon in flatboats. They reached Circle City on the very day when some Siwash Indians came into the settlement with the report that there had been a rich gold strike farther up the river, on a certain Klondike Creek. Two days later Tiny and her friends, and nearly every one else in Circle City, started for the Klondike fields on the last steamer that went up the Yukon before it froze for the winter. That boatload of people founded Dawson City. Within a few weeks there were fifteen hundred homeless men in camp. Tiny and the carpenter's wife began to cook for them, in a tent. The miners gave her a lot, and the carpenter put up a log hotel for her. There she sometimes fed a hundred and fifty men a day. Miners came in on snowshoes from their placer claims twenty miles away to buy fresh bread from her, and paid for it in gold.

That winter Tiny kept in her hotel a Swede whose legs had been frozen one night in a storm when he was trying to find his way back to his cabin. The poor fellow thought it great good fortune to be cared for by a woman, and a woman who spoke his own tongue. When he was told that his feet must be amputated, he said he hoped he would not get well; what could a working-man do in this hard world without feet? He did, in fact, die from the operation, but not before he had deeded Tiny Soderball his claim on Hunker Creek. Tiny sold her hotel, invested half her money in Dawson building lots, and with the rest she developed her claim. She went off into the wilds and

8. In the winter of 1897–98.

lived on it. She bought other claims from discouraged miners, traded or sold them on percentages.

After nearly ten years in the Klondike, Tiny returned, with a considerable fortune, to live in San Francisco. I met her in Salt Lake City in 1908. She was a thin, hard-faced woman, very well-dressed, very reserved in manner. Curiously enough, she reminded me of Mrs. Gardener, for whom she had worked in Black Hawk so long ago. She told me about some of the desperate chances she had taken in the gold country, but the thrill of them was quite gone. She said frankly that nothing interested her much now but making money. The only two human beings of whom she spoke with any feeling were the Swede, Johnson, who had given her his claim, and Lena Lingard. She had persuaded Lena to come to San Francisco and go into business there.

"Lincoln was never any place for her," Tiny remarked. "In a town of that size Lena would always be gossiped about. Frisco's the right field for her. She has a fine class of trade. Oh, she's just the same as she always was! She's careless, but she's level-headed. She's the only person I know who never gets any older. It's fine for me to have her there; somebody who enjoys things like that. She keeps an eye on me and won't let me be shabby. When she thinks I need a new dress, she makes it and sends it home—with a bill that's long enough, I can tell you!"

Tiny limped slightly when she walked. The claim on Hunker Creek took toll from its possessors. Tiny had been caught in a sudden turn of weather, like poor Johnson. She lost three toes from one of those pretty little feet that used to trip about Black Hawk in pointed slippers and striped stockings. Tiny mentioned this mutilation quite casually—didn't seem sensitive about it. She was satisfied with her success, but not elated. She was like some one in whom the faculty of becoming interested is worn out.

II

Soon after I got home that summer I persuaded my grandparents to have their photographs taken, and one morning I went into the photographer's shop to arrange for sittings. While I was waiting for him to come out of his developing-room, I walked about trying to recognize the likenesses on his walls: girls in Commencement dresses, country brides and grooms holding hands, family groups of three generations. I noticed, in a heavy frame, one of those depressing "crayon enlargements" often seen in farmhouse parlors, the subject being a round-eyed baby in short dresses. The photographer came out and gave a constrained, apologetic laugh.

"That's Tony Shimerda's baby. You remember her; she used to be the Harling's Tony. Too bad! She seems proud of the baby, though; wouldn't hear to a cheap frame for the picture. I expect her brother will be in for it Saturday."

I went away feeling that I must see Ántonia again. Another girl would have kept her baby out of sight, but Tony, of course, must have its picture on exhibition at the town photographer's, in a great gilt frame. How like her! I could forgive her, I told myself, if she hadn't thrown herself away on such a cheap sort of fellow.

Larry Donovan was a passenger conductor, one of those train-crew aristocrats who are always afraid that some one may ask them to put up a car-window, and who, if requested to perform such a menial service, silently point to the button that calls the porter. Larry wore this air of official aloofness even on the street, where there were no car-windows to compromise his dignity. At the end of his run he stepped indifferently from the train along with the passengers, his street hat on his head and his conductor's cap in an alligator-skin bag, went directly into the station and changed his clothes. It was a matter of the utmost importance to him never to be seen in his blue trousers away from his train. He was usually cold and distant with men, but with all women he had a silent, grave familiarity, a special handshake, accompanied by a significant, deliberate look. He took women, married or single, into his confidence; walked them up and down in the moonlight, telling them what a mistake he had made by not entering the office branch of the service, and how much better fitted he was to fill the post of General Passenger Agent in Denver than the roughshod man who then bore that title. His unappreciated worth was the tender secret Larry shared with his sweethearts, and he was always able to make some foolish heart ache over it.

As I drew near home that morning, I saw Mrs. Harling out in her yard, digging round her mountain-ash tree. It was a dry summer, and she had now no boy to help her. Charley was off in his battleship, cruising somewhere on the Caribbean sea. I turned in at the gate—it was with a feeling of pleasure that I opened and shut that gate in those days; I liked the feel of it under my hand. I took the spade away from Mrs. Harling, and while I loosened the earth around the tree, she sat down on the steps and talked about the oriole family that had a nest in its branches.

"Mrs. Harling," I said presently, "I wish I could find out exactly how Ántonia's marriage fell through."

"Why don't you go out and see your grandfather's tenant, the Widow Steavens? She knows more about it than anybody else. She helped Ántonia get ready to be married, and she was there when Ántonia came back. She took care of her when the baby was born. She could tell you everything. Besides, the Widow Steavens is a good talker, and she has a remarkable memory."

III

On the first or second day of August I got a horse and cart and set out for the high country, to visit the Widow Steavens. The wheat harvest was over, and here and there along the horizon I could see black puffs of smoke from the steam thrashing-machines. The old pasture land was now being broken up into wheatfields and cornfields, the red grass was disappearing, and the whole face of the country was changing. There were wooden houses where the old sod dwellings used to be, and little orchards, and big red barns; all this meant happy children, contented women, and men who saw their lives coming to a fortunate issue. The windy springs and the blazing summers, one after another, had enriched and mellowed that flat tableland; all the human effort that had gone into it was coming back in long, sweeping lines of fertility. The changes seemed beautiful and harmonious to me; it was like watching the growth of a great man or of a great idea. I recognized every tree and sandbank and rugged draw. I found that I remembered the conformation of the land as one remembers the modeling of human faces.

When I drew up to our old windmill, the Widow Steavens came out to meet me. She was brown as an Indian woman, tall, and very strong. When I was little, her massive head had always seemed to me like a Roman senator's. I told her at once why I had come.

"You'll stay the night with us, Jimmy? I'll talk to you after supper. I can take more interest when my work is off my mind. You've no prejudice against hot biscuit for supper? Some have, these days."

While I was putting my horse away I heard a rooster squawking. I looked at my watch and sighed; it was three o'clock, and I knew that I must eat him at six.

After supper Mrs. Steavens and I went upstairs to the old sitting-room, while her grave, silent brother remained in the basement to read his farm papers. All the windows were open. The white summer moon was shining outside, the windmill was pumping lazily in the light breeze. My hostess put the lamp on a stand in the corner, and turned it low because of the heat. She sat down in her favorite rocking-chair and settled a little stool comfortably under her tired feet. "I'm troubled with callouses, Jim; getting old," she sighed cheerfully. She crossed her hands in her lap and sat as if she were at a meeting of some kind.

"Now, it's about that dear Ántonia you want to know? Well, you've come to the right person. I've watched her like she'd been my own daughter.

"When she came home to do her sewing that summer before she was to be married, she was over here about every day. They've never had a sewing machine at the Shimerdas', and she made all her things here. I taught her hemstitching, and I helped her to cut and fit. She used to sit there at that machine by the window, pedaling the life out of it—she was so strong—and always singing them queer Bohemian songs, like she was the happiest thing in the world.

"Ántonia," I used to say, 'don't run that machine so fast. You won't hasten the day none that way.'

"Then she'd laugh and slow down for a little, but she'd soon forget and begin to pedal and sing again. I never saw a girl work harder to go to house-keeping right and well-prepared. Lovely table linen the Harlings had given her, and Lena Lingard had sent her nice things from Lincoln. We hem-stitched all the tablecloths and pillow-cases, and some of the sheets. Old Mrs. Shimerda knit yards and yards of lace for her underclothes. Tony told me just how she meant to have everything in her house. She'd even bought silver spoons and forks, and kept them in her trunk. She was always coaxing brother to go to the post-office. Her young man did write her real often, from the different towns along his run.

"The first thing that troubled her was when he wrote that his run had been changed, and they would likely have to live in Denver. 'I'm a country girl,' she said, 'and I doubt if I'll be able to manage so well for him in a city. I was count-ing on keeping chickens, and maybe a cow.' She soon cheered up, though.

"At last she got the letter telling her when to come. She was shaken by it; she broke the seal and read it in this room. I suspected then that she'd begun to get faint-hearted, waiting; though she'd never let me see it.

"Then there was a great time of packing. It was in March, if I remember rightly, and a terrible muddy, raw spell, with the roads bad for hauling her things to town. And here let me say, Ambrosch did the right thing. He went to Black Hawk and bought her a set of plated silver in a purple velvet box, good enough for her station. He gave her three hundred dollars in money; I saw the check. He'd collected her wages all those first years she worked out, and it was but right. I shook him by the hand in this room. 'You're behaving like a man, Ambrosch,' I said, 'and I'm glad to see it, son.'

" 'Twas a cold, raw day he drove her and her three trunks into Black Hawk to take the night train for Denver—the boxes had been shipped before. He stopped the wagon here, and she ran in to tell me good-bye. She threw her arms around me and kissed me, and thanked me for all I'd done for her. She was so happy she was crying and laughing at the same time, and her red cheeks was all wet with rain.

" 'You're surely handsome enough for any man,' I said, looking her over.

"She laughed kind of flighty like, and whispered, 'Good-bye, dear house!' and then ran out to the wagon. I expect she meant that for you and your grandmother, as much as for me, so I'm particular to tell you. This house had always been a refuge to her.

"Well, in a few days we had a letter saying she got to Denver safe, and he was there to meet her. They were to be married in a few days. He was trying to get his promotion before he married, she said. I didn't like that, but I said nothing. The next week Yulka got a postal card, saying she was 'well and happy.' After that we heard nothing. A month went by, and old Mrs. Shimerda began to get fretful. Ambrosch was as sulky with me as if I'd picked out the man and arranged the match.

"One night brother William came in and said that on his way back from the fields he had passed a livery team from town, driving fast out the west road. There was a trunk on the front seat with the driver, and another behind. In the back seat there was a woman all bundled up; but for all her veils, he thought 't was Ántonia Shimerda, or Ántonia Donovan, as her name ought now to be.

"The next morning I got brother to drive me over. I can walk still, but my feet ain't what they used to be, and I try to save myself. The lines outside the Shimerdas' house was full of washing, though it was the middle of the week. As we got nearer I saw a sight that made my heart sink—all those underclothes we'd put so much work on, out there swinging in the wind. Yulka came bringing a dishpanful of wrung clothes, but she darted back into the house like she was loath to see us. When I went in, Ántonia was standing over the tubs, just finishing up a big washing. Mrs. Shimerda was going about her work, talking and scolding to herself. She didn't so much as raise her eyes. Tony wiped her hand on her apron and held it out to me, looking at me steady but mournful. When I took her in my arms she drew away. 'Don't, Mrs. Steavens,' she says, 'you'll make me cry, and I don't want to.'

"I whispered and asked her to come out of doors with me. I knew she couldn't talk free before her mother. She went out with me, bareheaded, and we walked up toward the garden.

" 'I'm not married, Mrs. Steavens,' she says to me very quiet and natural-like, 'and I ought to be.'

" 'Oh, my child,' says I, 'what's happened to you? Don't be afraid to tell me!'

"She sat down on the draw-side, out of sight of the house. 'He's run away from me,' she said. 'I don't know if he ever meant to marry me.'

" 'You mean he's thrown up his job and quit the country?' says I.

" 'He didn't have any job. He'd been fired; blacklisted for knocking down fares.[9] I didn't know. I thought he hadn't been treated right. He was sick when I got there. He'd just come out of the hospital. He lived with me till my money gave out, and afterwards I found he hadn't really been hunting work at all. Then he just didn't come back. One nice fellow at the station told me, when I kept going to look for him, to give it up. He said he was afraid Larry'd gone bad and wouldn't come back any more. I guess he's gone to Old Mexico. The conductors get rich down there, collecting half-fares off the natives and robbing the company. He was always talking about fellows who had got ahead that way.'

"I asked her, of course, why she didn't insist on a civil marriage at once—that would have given her some hold on him. She leaned her head on her hands, poor child, and said, 'I just don't know, Mrs. Steavens. I guess my patience was wore out, waiting so long. I thought if he saw how well I could do for him, he'd want to stay with me.'

"Jimmy, I sat right down on that bank beside her and made lament. I cried like a young thing. I couldn't help it. I was just about heart-broke. It was one of them lovely warm May days, and the wind was blowing and the colts jumping around in the pastures; but I felt bowed with despair. My Ántonia, that had so much good in her, had come home disgraced. And that Lena Lingard, that was always a bad one, say what you will, had turned out so well, and was coming home here every summer in her silks and her satins, and doing so much for her mother. I give credit where credit is due, but you know well enough, Jim Burden, there is a great difference in the principles of those two girls. And here it was the good one that had come to grief! I was poor comfort to her. I marveled at her calm. As we went back to the house, she stopped to feel of her clothes to see if they was drying well, and seemed to take pride in their whiteness—she said she'd been living in a brick block, where she didn't have proper conveniences to wash them.

"The next time I saw Ántonia, she was out in the fields ploughing corn. All that spring and summer she did the work of a man on the farm; it seemed to be an understood thing. Ambrosch didn't get any other hand to help him. Poor Marek had got violent and been sent away to an institution a good while back. We never even saw any of Tony's pretty dresses. She didn't take them out of her trunks. She was quiet and steady. Folks respected her industry and tried to treat her as if nothing had happened. They talked, to be sure; but not like they would if she'd put on airs. She was so crushed and quiet that nobody seemed to want to humble her. She never went anywhere. All that summer she never once came to see me. At first I was hurt, but I got to feel that it was because this house reminded her of too much. I went over there when I could, but the times when she was in from the fields were the times when I was busiest here. She talked about the grain and the weather as if she'd never had another interest, and if I went over at night she always looked dead weary. She was afflicted with toothache; one tooth after another ulcerated, and she went about with her face swollen half the time. She wouldn't go to Black Hawk to a dentist for fear of meeting people she knew. Ambrosch had got over his good spell long ago, and was always surly. Once I told him he ought not

9. Selling tickets at reduced prices and keeping the money for himself.

to let Ántonia work so hard and pull herself down. He said, 'If you put that in her head, you better stay home.' And after that I did.

"Ántonia worked on through harvest and thrashing, though she was too modest to go out thrashing for the neighbors, like when she was young and free. I didn't see much of her until late that fall when she begun to herd Ambrosch's cattle in the open ground north of here, up toward the big dog town. Sometimes she used to bring them over the west hill, there, and I would run to meet her and walk north a piece with her. She had thirty cattle in her bunch; it had been dry, and the pasture was short, or she wouldn't have brought them so far.

"It was a fine open fall, and she liked to be alone. While the steers grazed, she used to sit on them grassy banks along the draws and sun herself for hours. Sometimes I slipped up to visit with her, when she hadn't gone too far.

" 'It does seem like I ought to make lace, or knit like Lena used to,' she said one day, 'but if I start to work, I look around and forget to go on. It seems such a little while ago when Jim Burden and I was playing all over this country. Up here I can pick out the very places where my father used to stand. Sometimes I feel like I'm not going to live very long, so I'm just enjoying every day of this fall.'

"After the winter begun she wore a man's long overcoat and boots, and a man's felt hat with a wide brim. I used to watch her coming and going, and I could see that her steps were getting heavier. One day in December, the snow began to fall. Late in the afternoon I saw Ántonia driving her cattle homeward across the hill. The snow was flying round her and she bent to face it, looking more lonesome-like to me than usual. 'Deary me,' I says to myself, 'the girl's stayed out too late. It'll be dark before she gets them cattle put into the corral.' I seemed to sense she'd been feeling too miserable to get up and drive them.

"That very night, it happened. She got her cattle home, turned them into the corral, and went into the house, into her room behind the kitchen, and shut the door. There, without calling to anybody, without a groan, she lay down on the bed and bore her child.

"I was lifting supper when old Mrs. Shimerda came running down the basement stairs, out of breath and screeching:—

" 'Baby come, baby come!' she says. 'Ambrosch much like devil!'

"Brother William is surely a patient man. He was just ready to sit down to a hot supper after a long day in the fields. Without a word he rose and went down to the barn and hooked up his team. He got us over there as quick as it was humanly possible. I went right in, and began to do for Ántonia; but she laid there with her eyes shut and took no account of me. The old woman got a tubful of warm water to wash the baby. I overlooked what she was doing and I said out loud:—

" 'Mrs. Shimerda, don't you put that strong yellow soap near that baby. You'll blister its little skin.' I was indignant.

" 'Mrs. Steavens,' Ántonia said from the bed, 'if you'll look in the top tray of my trunk, you'll see some fine soap.' That was the first word she spoke.

"After I'd dressed the baby, I took it out to show it to Ambrosch. He was muttering behind the stove and wouldn't look at it.

" 'You'd better put it out in the rain barrel,' he says.

" 'Now, see here, Ambrosch,' says I, 'there's a law in this land, don't forget that. I stand here a witness that this baby has come into the world sound and strong, and I intend to keep an eye on what befalls it.' I pride myself I cowed him.

"Well, I expect you're not much interested in babies, but Ántonia's got on fine. She loved it from the first as dearly as if she'd had a ring on her finger, and was never ashamed of it. It's a year and eight months old now, and no baby was ever better cared-for. Ántonia is a natural-born mother. I wish she could marry and raise a family, but I don't know as there's much chance now."

I slept that night in the room I used to have when I was a little boy, with the summer wind blowing in at the windows, bringing the smell of the ripe fields. I lay awake and watched the moonlight shining over the barn and the stacks and the pond, and the windmill making its old dark shadow against the blue sky.

IV

The next afternoon I walked over to the Shimerdas'. Yulka showed me the baby and told me that Ántonia was shocking wheat on the southwest quarter. I went down across the fields, and Tony saw me from a long way off. She stood still by her shocks, leaning on her pitchfork, watching me as I came. We met like the people in the old song, in silence, if not in tears. Her warm hand clasped mine.

"I thought you'd come, Jim. I heard you were at Mrs. Steavens's last night. I've been looking for you all day."

She was thinner than I had ever seen her, and looked, as Mrs. Steavens said, "worked down," but there was a new kind of strength in the gravity of her face, and her color still gave her that look of deep-seated health and ardor. Still? Why, it flashed across me that though so much had happened in her life and in mine, she was barely twenty-four years old.

Ántonia stuck her fork in the ground, and instinctively we walked toward that unploughed patch at the crossing of the roads as the fittest place to talk to each other. We sat down outside the sagging wire fence that shut Mr. Shimerda's plot off from the rest of the world. The tall red grass had never been cut there. It had died down in winter and come up again in the spring until it was as thick and shrubby as some tropical gardengrass. I found myself telling her everything: why I had decided to study law and to go into the law office of one of my mother's relatives in New York City; about Gaston Cleric's death from pneumonia last winter, and the difference it had made in my life. She wanted to know about my friends and my way of living, and my dearest hopes.

"Of course it means you are going away from us for good," she said with a sigh. "But that don't mean I'll lose you. Look at my papa here; he's been dead all these years, and yet he is more real to me than almost anybody else. He never goes out of my life. I talk to him and consult him all the time. The older I grow, the better I know him and the more I understand him."

She asked me whether I had learned to like big cities. "I'd always be miserable in a city. I'd die of lonesomeness. I like to be where I know every stack and tree, and where all the ground is friendly. I want to live and die here. Father Kelly says everybody's put into this world for something, and I know what I've got to do. I'm going to see that my little girl has a better chance than ever I had. I'm going to take care of that girl, Jim."

I told her I knew she would. "Do you know, Ántonia, since I've been away, I think of you more often than of any one else in this part of the world. I'd have liked to have you for a sweetheart, or a wife, or my mother or my sister—anything that a woman can be to a man. The idea of you is a part of my mind; you influence my likes and dislikes, all my tastes, hundreds of times when I don't realize it. You really are a part of me."

She turned her bright, believing eyes to me, and the tears came up in them slowly. "How can it be like that, when you know so many people, and when I've disappointed you so? Ain't it wonderful, Jim, how much people can mean to each other? I'm so glad we had each other when we were little. I can't wait till my little girl's old enough to tell her about all the things we used to do. You'll always remember me when you think about old times, won't you? And I guess everybody thinks about old times, even the happiest people."

As we walked homeward across the fields, the sun dropped and lay like a great golden globe in the low west. While it hung there, the moon rose in the east, as big as a cartwheel, pale silver and streaked with rose color, thin as a bubble or a ghost-moon. For five, perhaps ten minutes, the two luminaries confronted each other across the level land, resting on opposite edges of the world. In that singular light every little tree and shock of wheat, every sunflower stalk and clump of snow-on-the-mountain, drew itself up high and pointed; the very clods and furrows in the fields seemed to stand up sharply. I felt the old pull of the earth, the solemn magic that comes out of those fields at night-fall. I wished I could be a little boy again, and that my way could end there.

We reached the edge of the field, where our ways parted. I took her hands and held them against my breast, feeling once more how strong and warm and good they were, those brown hands, and remembering how many kind things they had done for me. I held them now a long while, over my heart. About us it was growing darker and darker, and I had to look hard to see her face, which I meant always to carry with me; the closest, realest face, under all the shadows of women's faces, at the very bottom of my memory.

"I'll come back," I said earnestly, through the soft, intrusive darkness.

"Perhaps you will"—I felt rather than saw her smile. "But even if you don't, you're here, like my father. So I won't be lonesome."

As I went back alone over that familiar road, I could almost believe that a boy and girl ran along beside me, as our shadows used to do, laughing and whispering to each other in the grass.

Book V. Cuzak's Boys

I

I told Ántonia I would come back, but life intervened, and it was twenty years before I kept my promise. I heard of her from time to time; that she married, very soon after I last saw her, a young Bohemian, a cousin of Anton Jelinek; that they were poor, and had a large family. Once when I was abroad

I went into Bohemia, and from Prague I sent Ántonia some photographs of her native village. Months afterward came a letter from her, telling me the names and ages of her many children, but little else; signed, "Your old friend, Ántonia Cuzak." When I met Tiny Soderball in Salt Lake, she told me that Ántonia had not "done very well"; that her husband was not a man of much force, and she had had a hard life. Perhaps it was cowardice that kept me away so long. My business took me West several times every year, and it was always in the back of my mind that I would stop in Nebraska some day and go to see Ántonia. But I kept putting it off until the next trip. I did not want to find her aged and broken; I really dreaded it. In the course of twenty crowded years one parts with many illusions. I did not wish to lose the early ones. Some memories are realities, and are better than anything that can ever happen to one again.

I owe it to Lena Lingard that I went to see Ántonia at last. I was in San Francisco two summers ago when both Lena and Tiny Soderball were in town. Tiny lives in a house of her own, and Lena's shop is in an apartment house just around the corner. It interested me, after so many years, to see the two women together. Tiny audits Lena's accounts occasionally, and invests her money for her; and Lena, apparently, takes care that Tiny doesn't grow too miserly. "If there's anything I can't stand," she said to me in Tiny's presence, "it's a shabby rich woman." Tiny smiled grimly and assured me that Lena would never be either shabby or rich. "And I don't want to be," the other agreed complacently.

Lena gave me a cheerful account of Ántonia and urged me to make her a visit.

"You really ought to go, Jim. It would be such a satisfaction to her. Never mind what Tiny says. There's nothing the matter with Cuzak. You'd like him. He isn't a hustler, but a rough man would never have suited Tony. Tony has nice children—ten or eleven of them by this time, I guess. I shouldn't care for a family of that size myself, but somehow it's just right for Tony. She'd love to show them to you."

On my way East I broke my journey at Hastings, in Nebraska, and set off with an open buggy and a fairly good livery team to find the Cuzak farm. At a little past midday, I knew I must be nearing my destination. Set back on a swell of land at my right, I saw a wide farmhouse, with a red barn and an ash grove, and cattle yards in front that sloped down to the high road. I drew up my horses and was wondering whether I should drive in here, when I heard low voices. Ahead of me, in a plum thicket beside the road, I saw two boys bending over a dead dog. The little one, not more than four or five, was on his knees, his hands folded, and his close-clipped, bare head drooping forward in deep dejection. The other stood beside him, a hand on his shoulder, and was comforting him in a language I had not heard for a long while. When I stopped my horses opposite them, the older boy took his brother by the hand and came toward me. He, too, looked grave. This was evidently a sad afternoon for them.

"Are you Mrs. Cuzak's boys?" I asked.

The younger one did not look up; he was submerged in his own feelings, but his brother met me with intelligent gray eyes. "Yes, sir."

"Does she live up there on the hill? I am going to see her. Get in and ride up with me."

He glanced at his reluctant little brother. "I guess we'd better walk. But we'll open the gate for you."

I drove along the side-road and they followed slowly behind. When I pulled up at the windmill, another boy, barefooted and curly-headed, ran out of the barn to tie my team for me. He was a handsome one, this chap, fair-skinned and freckled, with red cheeks and a ruddy pelt as thick as a lamb's wool, growing down on his neck in little tufts. He tied my team with two flourishes of his hands, and nodded when I asked him if his mother was at home. As he glanced at me, his face dimpled with a seizure of irrelevant merriment, and he shot up the windmill tower with a lightness that struck me as disdainful. I knew he was peering down at me as I walked toward the house.

Ducks and geese ran quacking across my path. White cats were sunning themselves among yellow pumpkins on the porch steps. I looked through the wire screen into a big, light kitchen with a white floor. I saw a long table, rows of wooden chairs against the wall; and a shining range in one corner. Two girls were washing dishes at the sink, laughing and chattering, and a little one, in a short pinafore, sat on a stool playing with a rag baby. When I asked for their mother, one of the girls dropped her towel, ran across the floor with noiseless bare feet, and disappeared. The older one, who wore shoes and stockings, came to the door to admit me. She was a buxom girl with dark hair and eyes, calm and self-possessed.

"Won't you come in? Mother will be here in a minute."

Before I could sit down in the chair she offered me, the miracle happened; one of those quiet moments that clutch the heart, and take more courage than the noisy, excited passages in life. Ántonia came in and stood before me; a stalwart, brown woman, flat-chested, her curly brown hair a little grizzled. It was a shock, of course. It always is, to meet people after long years, especially if they have lived as much and as hard as this woman had. We stood looking at each other. The eyes that peered anxiously at me were—simply Ántonia's eyes. I had seen no others like them since I looked into them last, though I had looked at so many thousands of human faces. As I confronted her, the changes grew less apparent to me, her identity stronger. She was there, in the full vigor of her personality, battered but not diminished, looking at me, speaking to me in the husky, breathy voice I remembered so well.

"My husband's not at home, sir. Can I do anything?"

"Don't you remember me, Ántonia? Have I changed so much?"

She frowned into the slanting sunlight that made her brown hair look redder than it was. Suddenly her eyes widened, her whole face seemed to grow broader. She caught her breath and put out two hard-worked hands.

"Why, it's Jim! Anna, Yulka, it's Jim Burden!" She had no sooner caught my hands than she looked alarmed. "What's happened? Is anybody dead?"

I patted her arm. "No. I didn't come to a funeral this time. I got off the train at Hastings and drove down to see you and your family."

She dropped my hand and began rushing about. "Anton, Yulka, Nina, where are you all? Run, Anna, and hunt for the boys. They're off looking for that dog, somewhere. And call Leo. Where is that Leo!" She pulled them out of corners and came bringing them like a mother cat bringing in her kittens. "You don't have to go right off, Jim? My oldest boy's not here. He's gone with papa to the street fair at Wilber. I won't let you go! You've got to stay and see Rudolph and our papa." She looked at me imploringly, panting with excitement.

While I reassured her and told her there would be plenty of time, the barefooted boys from outside were slipping into the kitchen and gathering about her.

"Now, tell me their names, and how old they are."

As she told them off in turn, she made several mistakes about ages, and they roared with laughter. When she came to my light-footed friend of the windmill, she said, "This is Leo, and he's old enough to be better than he is."

He ran up to her and butted her playfully with his curly head, like a little ram, but his voice was quite desperate. "You've forgot! You always forget mine. It's mean! Please tell him, mother!" He clenched his fists in vexation and looked up at her impetuously.

She wound her forefinger in his yellow fleece and pulled it, watching him. "Well, how old are you?"

"I'm twelve," he panted, looking not at me but at her; "I'm twelve years old, and I was born on Easter day!"

She nodded to me. "It's true. He was an Easter baby."

The children all looked at me, as if they expected me to exhibit astonishment or delight at this information. Clearly, they were proud of each other, and of being so many. When they had all been introduced, Anna, the eldest daughter, who had met me at the door, scattered them gently, and came bringing a white apron which she tied round her mother's waist.

"Now, mother, sit down and talk to Mr. Burden. We'll finish the dishes quietly and not disturb you."

Ántonia looked about, quite distracted. "Yes, child, but why don't we take him into the parlor, now that we've got a nice parlor for company?"

The daughter laughed indulgently, and took my hat from me. "Well, you're here, now, mother, and if you talk here, Yulka and I can listen, too. You can show him the parlor after while." She smiled at me, and went back to the dishes, with her sister. The little girl with the rag doll found a place on the bottom step of an enclosed back stairway, and sat with her toes curled up, looking out at us expectantly.

"She's Nina, after Nina Harling," Ántonia explained. "Ain't her eyes like Nina's? I declare, Jim, I loved you children almost as much as I love my own. These children know all about you and Charley and Sally, like as if they'd grown up with you. I can't think of what I want to say, you've got me so stirred up. And then, I've forgot my English so. I don't often talk it any more. I tell the children I used to speak real well." She said they always spoke Bohemian at home. The little ones could not speak English at all—didn't learn it until they went to school.

"I can't believe it's you, sitting here, in my own kitchen. You wouldn't have known me, would you, Jim? You've kept so young, yourself. But it's easier for a man. I can't see how my Anton looks any older than the day I married him. His teeth have kept so nice. I haven't got many left. But I feel just as young as I used to, and I can do as much work. Oh, we don't have to work so hard now! We've got plenty to help us, papa and me. And how many have you got, Jim?"

When I told her I had no children she seemed embarrassed. "Oh, ain't that too bad! Maybe you could take one of my bad ones, now? That Leo; he's the worst of all." She leaned toward me with a smile. "And I love him the best," she whispered.

"Mother!" the two girls murmured reproachfully from the dishes.

Ántonia threw up her head and laughed. "I can't help it. You know I do. Maybe it's because he came on Easter day, I don't know. And he's never out of mischief one minute!"

I was thinking, as I watched her, how little it mattered—about her teeth, for instance. I know so many women who have kept all the things that she had lost, but whose inner glow has faded. Whatever else was gone, Ántonia had not lost the fire of life. Her skin, so brown and hardened, had not that look of flabbiness, as if the sap beneath it had been secretly drawn away.

While we were talking, the little boy whom they called Jan came in and sat down on the step beside Nina, under the hood of the stairway. He wore a funny long gingham apron, like a smock, over his trousers, and his hair was clipped so short that his head looked white and naked. He watched us out of his big, sorrowful gray eyes.

"He wants to tell you about the dog, mother. They found it dead," Anna said, as she passed us on her way to the cupboard.

Ántonia beckoned the boy to her. He stood by her chair, leaning his elbows on her knees and twisting her apron strings in his slender fingers, while he told her his story softly in Bohemian, and the tears brimmed over and hung on his long lashes. His mother listened, spoke soothingly to him, and in a whisper promised him something that made him give her a quick, teary smile. He slipped away and whispered his secret to Nina, sitting close to her and talking behind his hand.

When Anna finished her work and had washed her hands, she came and stood behind her mother's chair. "Why don't we show Mr. Burden our new fruit cave?" she asked.

We started off across the yard with the children at our heels. The boys were standing by the windmill, talking about the dog; some of them ran ahead to open the cellar door. When we descended, they all came down after us, and seemed quite as proud of the cave as the girls were. Ambrosch, the thoughtful-looking one who had directed me down by the plum bushes, called my attention to the stout brick walls and the cement floor. "Yes, it is a good way from the house," he admitted. "But, you see, in winter there are nearly always some of us around to come out and get things."

Anna and Yulka showed me three small barrels; one full of dill pickles, one full of chopped pickles, and one full of pickled watermelon rinds.

"You wouldn't believe, Jim, what it takes to feed them all!" their mother exclaimed. "You ought to see the bread we bake on Wednesdays and Saturdays! It's no wonder their poor papa can't get rich, he has to buy so much sugar for us to preserve with. We have our own wheat ground for flour,—but then there's that much less to sell."

Nina and Jan, and a little girl named Lucie, kept shyly pointing out to me the shelves of glass jars. They said nothing, but glancing at me, traced on the glass with their finger-tips the outline of the cherries and strawberries and crab-apples within, trying by a blissful expression of countenance to give me some idea of their deliciousness.

"Show him the spiced plums, mother. Americans don't have those," said one of the older boys. "Mother uses them to make *kolaches*,"[1] he added.

Leo, in a low voice, tossed off some scornful remark in Bohemian.

---

1. Fruit-filled sweet rolls.

I turned to him. "You think I don't know what *kolaches* are, eh? You're mistaken, young man. I've eaten your mother's *kolaches* long before that Easter day when you were born."

"Always too fresh, Leo," Ambrosch remarked with a shrug.

Leo dived behind his mother and grinned out at me.

We turned to leave the cave; Ántonia and I went up the stairs first, and the children waited. We were standing outside talking, when they all came running up the steps together, big and little, tow heads and gold heads and brown, and flashing little naked legs; a veritable explosion of life out of the dark cave into the sunlight. It made me dizzy for a moment.

The boys escorted us to the front of the house, which I hadn't yet seen; in farmhouses, somehow, life comes and goes by the back door. The roof was so steep that the eaves were not much above the forest of tall hollyhocks, now brown and in seed. Through July, Ántonia said, the house was buried in them; the Bohemians, I remembered, always planted hollyhocks. The front yard was enclosed by a thorny locust hedge, and at the gate grew two silvery, moth-like trees of the mimosa family. From here one looked down over the cattle yards, with their two long ponds, and over a wide stretch of stubble which they told me was a rye-field in summer.

At some distance behind the house were an ash grove and two orchards; a cherry orchard, with gooseberry and currant bushes between the rows, and an apple orchard, sheltered by a high hedge from the hot winds. The older children turned back when we reached the hedge, but Jan and Nina and Lucie crept through it by a hole known only to themselves and hid under the low-branching mulberry bushes.

As we walked through the apple orchard, grown up in tall bluegrass, Ántonia kept stopping to tell me about one tree and another. "I love them as if they were people," she said, rubbing her hand over the bark. "There wasn't a tree here when we first came. We planted every one, and used to carry water for them, too—after we'd been working in the fields all day. Anton, he was a city man, and he used to get discouraged. But I couldn't feel so tired that I wouldn't fret about these trees when there was a dry time. They were on my mind like children. Many a night after he was asleep I've got up and come out and carried water to the poor things. And now, you see, we have the good of them. My man worked in the orange groves in Florida, and he knows all about grafting. There ain't one of our neighbors has an orchard that bears like ours."

In the middle of the orchard we came upon a grape-arbor, with seats built along the sides and a warped plank table. The three children were waiting for us there. They looked up at me bashfully and made some request of their mother.

"They want me to tell you how the teacher has the school picnic here every year. These don't go to school yet, so they think it's all like the picnic."

After I had admired the arbor sufficiently, the youngsters ran away to an open place where there was a rough jungle of French pinks, and squatted down among them, crawling about and measuring with a string. "Jan wants to bury his dog there," Ántonia explained. "I had to tell him he could. He's kind of like Nina Harling; you remember how hard she used to take little things? He has funny notions, like her."

We sat down and watched them. Ántonia leaned her elbows on the table. There was the deepest peace in that orchard. It was surrounded by a triple enclosure; the wire fence, then the hedge of thorny locusts, then the mulberry hedge which kept out the hot winds of summer and held fast to the protecting snows of winter. The hedges were so tall that we could see nothing but the blue sky above them, neither the barn roof nor the windmill. The afternoon sun poured down on us through the drying grape leaves. The orchard seemed full of sun, like a cup, and we could smell the ripe apples on the trees. The crabs hung on the branches as thick as beads on a string, purple-red, with a thin silvery glaze over them. Some hens and ducks had crept through the hedge and were pecking at the fallen apples. The drakes were handsome fellows, with pinkish gray bodies, their heads and necks covered with iridescent green feathers which grew close and full, changing to blue like a peacock's neck. Ántonia said they always reminded her of soldiers—some uniform she had seen in the old country, when she was a child.

"Are there any quail left now?" I asked. I reminded her how she used to go hunting with me the last summer before we moved to town. "You weren't a bad shot, Tony. Do you remember how you used to want to run away and go for ducks with Charley Harling and me?"

"I know, but I'm afraid to look at a gun now." She picked up one of the drakes and ruffled his green capote with her fingers. "Ever since I've had children, I don't like to kill anything. It makes me kind of faint to wring an old goose's neck. Ain't that strange, Jim?"

"I don't know. The young Queen of Italy said the same thing once, to a friend of mine. She used to be a great huntswoman, but now she feels as you do, and only shoots clay pigeons."

"Then I'm sure she's a good mother," Ántonia said warmly.

She told me how she and her husband had come out to this new country when the farm land was cheap and could be had on easy payments. The first ten years were a hard struggle. Her husband knew very little about farming and often grew discouraged. "We'd never have got through if I hadn't been so strong. I've always had good health, thank God, and I was able to help him in the fields until right up to the time before my babies came. Our children were good about taking care of each other. Martha, the one you saw when she was a baby, was such a help to me, and she trained Anna to be just like her. My Martha's married now, and has a baby of her own. Think of that, Jim!

"No, I never got down-hearted. Anton's a good man, and I loved my children and always believed they would turn out well. I belong on a farm. I'm never lonesome here like I used to be in town. You remember what sad spells I used to have, when I didn't know what was the matter with me? I've never had them out here. And I don't mind work a bit, if I don't have to put up with sadness." She leaned her chin on her hand and looked down through the orchard, where the sunlight was growing more and more golden.

"You ought never to have gone to town, Tony," I said, wondering at her.

She turned to me eagerly. "Oh, I'm glad I went! I'd never have known anything about cooking or housekeeping if I hadn't. I learned nice ways at the Harlings', and I've been able to bring my children up so much better. Don't you think they are pretty well-behaved for country children? If it hadn't been for what Mrs. Harling taught me, I expect I'd have brought them up like wild rabbits. No, I'm glad I had a chance to learn; but I'm thankful none of my daughters will ever have to work out. The trouble with me was, Jim, I never could believe harm of anybody I loved."

While we were talking, Ántonia assured me that she could keep me for the night. "We've plenty of room. Two of the boys sleep in the haymow till cold weather comes, but there's no need for it. Leo always begs to sleep there, and Ambrosch goes along to look after him."

I told her I would like to sleep in the haymow, with the boys.

"You can do just as you want to. The chest is full of clean blankets, put away for winter. Now I must go, or my girls will be doing all the work, and I want to cook your supper myself."

As we went toward the house, we met Ambrosch and Anton, starting off with their milking-pails to hunt the cows. I joined them, and Leo accompanied us at some distance, running ahead and starting up at us out of clumps of ironweed, calling, "I'm a jack rabbit," or, "I'm a big bull-snake."

I walked between the two older boys—straight, well-made fellows, with good heads and clear eyes. They talked about their school and the new teacher, told me about the crops and the harvest, and how many steers they would feed that winter. They were easy and confidential with me, as if I were an old friend of the family—and not too old. I felt like a boy in their company, and all manner of forgotten interests revived in me. It seemed, after all, so natural to be walking along a barbed-wire fence beside the sunset, toward a red pond, and to see my shadow moving along at my right, over the close-cropped grass.

"Has mother shown you the pictures you sent her from the old country?" Ambrosch asked. "We've had them framed and they're hung up in the parlor. She was so glad to get them. I don't believe I ever saw her so pleased about anything." There was a note of simple gratitude in his voice that made me wish I had given more occasion for it.

I put my hand on his shoulder. "Your mother, you know, was very much loved by all of us. She was a beautiful girl."

"Oh, we know!" They both spoke together; seemed a little surprised that I should think it necessary to mention this. "Everybody liked her, didn't they? The Harlings and your grandmother, and all the town people."

"Sometimes," I ventured, "it doesn't occur to boys that their mother was ever young and pretty."

"Oh, we know!" they said again, warmly. "She's not very old now," Ambrosch added. "Not much older than you."

"Well," I said, "if you weren't nice to her, I think I'd take a club and go for the whole lot of you. I couldn't stand it if you boys were inconsiderate, or thought of her as if she were just somebody who looked after you. You see I was very much in love with your mother once, and I know there's nobody like her."

The boys laughed and seemed pleased and embarrassed. "She never told us that," said Anton. "But she's always talked lots about you, and about what good times you used to have. She has a picture of you that she cut out of the Chicago paper once, and Leo says he recognized you when you drove up to the windmill. You can't tell about Leo, though; sometimes he likes to be smart."

We brought the cows home to the corner nearest the barn, and the boys milked them while night came on. Everything was as it should be: the strong smell of sunflowers and ironweed in the dew, the clear blue and gold of the sky, the evening star, the purr of the milk into the pails, the grunts and squeals of the pigs fighting over their supper. I began to feel the loneliness of the farm-boy at evening, when the chores seem everlastingly the same, and the world so far away.

What a tableful we were at supper; two long rows of restless heads in the lamplight, and so many eyes fastened excitedly upon Ántonia as she sat at the head of the table, filling the plates and starting the dishes on their way. The children were seated according to a system; a little one next an older one, who was to watch over his behavior and to see that he got his food. Anna and Yulka left their chairs from time to time to bring fresh plates of *kolaches* and pitchers of milk.

After supper we went into the parlor, so that Yulka and Leo could play for me. Ántonia went first, carrying the lamp. There were not nearly chairs enough to go round, so the younger children sat down on the bare floor. Little Lucie whispered to me that they were going to have a parlor carpet if they got ninety cents for their wheat. Leo, with a good deal of fussing, got out his violin. It was old Mr. Shimerda's instrument, which Ántonia had always kept, and it was too big for him. But he played very well for a self-taught boy. Poor Yulka's efforts were not so successful. While they were playing, little Nina got up from her corner, came out into the middle of the floor, and began to do a pretty little dance on the boards with her bare feet. No one paid the least attention to her, and when she was through she stole back and sat down by her brother.

Ántonia spoke to Leo in Bohemian. He frowned and wrinkled up his face. He seemed to be trying to pout, but his attempt only brought out dimples in unusual places. After twisting and screwing the keys, he played some Bohemian airs, without the organ to hold him back, and that went better. The boy was so restless that I had not had a chance to look at his face before. My first impression was right; he really was faun-like. He hadn't much head behind his ears, and his tawny fleece grew down thick to the back of his neck. His eyes were not frank and wide apart like those of the other boys, but were deep-set, gold-green in color, and seemed sensitive to the light. His mother said he got hurt oftener than all the others put together. He was always trying to ride the colts before they were broken, teasing the turkey gobbler, seeing just how much red the bull would stand for, or how sharp the new axe was.

After the concert was over Ántonia brought out a big boxful of photographs; she and Anton in their wedding clothes, holding hands; her brother Ambrosch and his very fat wife, who had a farm of her own, and who bossed her husband, I was delighted to hear; the three Bohemian Marys and their large families.

"You wouldn't believe how steady those girls have turned out," Ántonia remarked. "Mary Svoboda's the best butter-maker in all this country, and a fine manager. Her children will have a grand chance."

As Ántonia turned over the pictures the young Cuzaks stood behind her chair, looking over her shoulder with interested faces. Nina and Jan, after trying to see round the taller ones, quietly brought a chair, climbed up on it, and stood close together, looking. The little boy forgot his shyness and grinned delightedly when familiar faces came into view. In the group about Ántonia I was conscious of a kind of physical harmony. They leaned this way and that, and were not afraid to touch each other. They contemplated the photographs with pleased recognition; looked at some admiringly, as if these characters in their mother's girlhood had been remarkable people. The little children, who could not speak English, murmured comments to each other in their rich old language.

Ántonia held out a photograph of Lena that had come from San Francisco last Christmas. "Does she still look like that? She hasn't been home for six years now." Yes, it was exactly like Lena, I told her; a comely woman, a trifle too plump, in a hat a trifle too large, but with the old lazy eyes, and the old dimpled ingenuousness still lurking at the corners of her mouth.

There was a picture of Frances Harling in a be-frogged[2] riding costume that I remembered well. "Isn't she fine!" the girls murmured. They all assented. One could see that Frances had come down as a heroine in the family legend. Only Leo was unmoved.

"And there's Mr. Harling, in his grand fur coat. He was awfully rich, wasn't he, mother?"

"He wasn't any Rockefeller," put in Master Leo, in a very low tone, which reminded me of the way in which Mrs. Shimerda had once said that my grandfather "wasn't Jesus." His habitual skepticism was like a direct inheritance from that old woman.

"None of your smart speeches," said Ambrosch severely.

Leo poked out a supple red tongue at him, but a moment later broke into a giggle at a tintype of two men, uncomfortably seated, with an awkward-looking boy in baggy clothes standing between them; Jake and Otto and I! We had it taken, I remembered, when we went to Black Hawk on the first Fourth of July I spent in Nebraska. I was glad to see Jake's grin again, and Otto's ferocious mustaches. The young Cuzaks knew all about them.

"He made grandfather's coffin, didn't he?" Anton asked.

"Wasn't they good fellows, Jim?" Ántonia eyes filled. "To this day I'm ashamed because I quarreled with Jake that way. I was saucy and impertinent to him, Leo, like you are with people sometimes, and I wish somebody had made me behave."

"We aren't through with you, yet," they warned me. They produced a photograph taken just before I went away to college; a tall youth in striped trousers and a straw hat, trying to look easy and jaunty.

"Tell us, Mr. Burden," said Charley, "about the rattler you killed at the dog town. How long was he? Sometimes mother says six feet and sometimes she says five."

These children seemed to be upon very much the same terms with Ántonia as the Harling children had been so many years before. They seemed to feel the same pride in her, and to look to her for stories and entertainment as we used to do.

It was eleven o'clock when I at last took my bag and some blankets and started for the barn with the boys. Their mother came to the door with us, and we tarried for a moment to look out at the white slope of the corral and the two ponds asleep in the moonlight, and the long sweep of the pasture under the star-sprinkled sky.

The boys told me to choose my own place in the haymow, and I lay down before a big window, left open in warm weather, that looked out into the stars. Ambrosch and Leo cuddled up in a hay-cave, back under the eaves, and lay

---

2. Decorated with ornamental braiding.

giggling and whispering. They tickled each other and tossed and tumbled in the hay; and then, all at once, as if they had been shot, they were still. There was hardly a minute between giggles and bland slumber.

I lay awake for a long while, until the slow-moving moon passed my window on its way up the heavens. I was thinking about Ántonia and her children; about Anna's solicitude for her, Ambrosch's grave affection, Leo's jealous, animal little love. That moment, when they all came tumbling out of the cave into the light, was a sight any man might have come far to see. Ántonia had always been one to leave images in the mind that did not fade—that grew stronger with time. In my memory there was a succession of such pictures, fixed there like the old woodcuts of one's first primer: Ántonia kicking her bare legs against the sides of my pony when we came home in triumph with our snake; Ántonia in her black shawl and fur cap, as she stood by her father's grave in the snowstorm; Ántonia coming in with her work-team along the evening sky-line. She lent herself to immemorial human attitudes which we recognize by instinct as universal and true. I had not been mistaken. She was a battered woman now, not a lovely girl; but she still had that something which fires the imagination, could still stop one's breath for a moment by a look or gesture that somehow revealed the meaning in common things. She had only to stand in the orchard, to put her hand on a little crab tree and look up at the apples, to make you feel the goodness of planting and tending and harvesting at last. All the strong things of her heart came out in her body, that had been so tireless in serving generous emotions.

It was no wonder that her sons stood tall and straight. She was a rich mine of life, like the founders of early races.

II

When I awoke in the morning long bands of sunshine were coming in at the window and reaching back under the eaves where the two boys lay. Leo was wide awake and was tickling his brother's leg with a dried cone-flower he had pulled out of the hay. Ambrosch kicked at him and turned over. I closed my eyes and pretended to be asleep. Leo lay on his back, elevated one foot, and began exercising his toes. He picked up dried flowers with his toes and brandished them in the belt of sunlight. After he had amused himself thus for some time, he rose on one elbow and began to look at me, cautiously, then critically, blinking his eyes in the light. His expression was droll; it dismissed me lightly. "This old fellow is no different from other people. He doesn't know my secret." He seemed conscious of possessing a keener power of enjoyment than other people; his quick recognitions made him frantically impatient of deliberate judgments. He always knew what he wanted without thinking.

After dressing in the hay, I washed my face in cold water at the windmill. Breakfast was ready when I entered the kitchen, and Yulka was baking griddle-cakes. The three older boys set off for the fields early. Leo and Yulka were to drive to town to meet their father, who would return from Wilber on the noon train.

"We'll only have a lunch at noon," Ántonia said, "and cook the geese for supper, when our papa will be here. I wish my Martha could come down to see you. They have a Ford car now, and she don't seem so far away from me as she used to. But her husband's crazy about his farm and about having everything just right, and they almost never get away except on Sundays. He's a handsome boy, and he'll be rich some day. Everything he takes hold of turns out well. When they bring that baby in here, and unwrap him, he looks like a little prince; Martha takes care of him so beautiful. I'm reconciled to her being away from me now, but at first I cried like I was putting her into her coffin."

We were alone in the kitchen, except for Anna, who was pouring cream into the churn. She looked up at me. "Yes, she did. We were just ashamed of mother. She went round crying, when Martha was so happy, and the rest of us were all glad. Joe certainly was patient with you, mother."

Ántonia nodded and smiled at herself. "I know it was silly, but I couldn't help it. I wanted her right here. She'd never been away from me a night since she was born. If Anton had made trouble about her when she was a baby, or wanted me to leave her with my mother, I wouldn't have married him. I couldn't. But he always loved her like she was his own."

"I didn't even know Martha wasn't my full sister until after she was engaged to Joe," Anna told me.

Toward the middle of the afternoon the wagon drove in, with the father and the eldest son. I was smoking in the orchard, and as I went out to meet them, Ántonia came running down from the house and hugged the two men as if they had been away for months.

"Papa" interested me, from my first glimpse of him. He was shorter than his older sons; a crumpled little man, with run-over boot heels, and he carried one shoulder higher than the other. But he moved very quickly, and there was an air of jaunty liveliness about him. He had a strong, ruddy color, thick black hair, a little grizzled, a curly mustache, and red lips. His smile showed the strong teeth of which his wife was so proud, and as he saw me his lively, quizzical eyes told me that he knew all about me. He looked like a humorous philosopher who had hitched up one shoulder under the burdens of life, and gone on his way having a good time when he could. He advanced to meet me and gave me a hard hand, burned red on the back and heavily coated with hair. He wore his Sunday clothes, very thick and hot for the weather, an unstarched white shirt, and a blue necktie with big white dots, like a little boy's, tied in a flowing bow. Cuzak began at once to talk about his holiday— from politeness he spoke in English.

"Mama, I wish you had see the lady dance on the slack-wire in the street at night. They throw a bright light on her and she float through the air something beautiful, like a bird! They have a dancing bear, like in the old country, and two three merry-go-around, and people in balloons, and what you call the big wheel, Rudolph?"

"A Ferris wheel," Rudolph entered the conversation in a deep baritone voice. He was six foot two, and had a chest like a young black-smith. "We went to the big dance in the hall behind the saloon last night, mother, and I danced with all the girls, and so did father. I never saw so many pretty girls. It was a Bohunk crowd, for sure. We didn't hear a word of English on the street, except from the show people, did we, papa?"

Cuzak nodded. "And very many send word to you, Ántonia. You will excuse"—turning to me—"if I tell her." While we walked toward the house he related incidents and delivered messages in the tongue he spoke fluently, and I dropped a little behind, curious to know what their relations had become—or remained. The two seemed to be on terms of easy friendliness, touched with humor. Clearly, she was the impulse, and he the corrective. As they went up the hill he kept glancing at her sidewise, to see whether she got his point, or how she received it. I noticed later that he always looked at people sidewise, as a work-horse does at its yoke-mate. Even when he sat opposite me in the kitchen, talking, he would turn his head a little toward the clock or the stove and look at me from the side, but with frankness and good-nature. This trick did not suggest duplicity or secretiveness, but merely long habit, as with the horse.

He had brought a tintype of himself and Rudolph for Ántonia's collection, and several paper bags of candy for the children. He looked a little disappointed when his wife showed him a big box of candy I had got in Denver—she hadn't let the children touch it the night before. He put his candy away in the cupboard, "for when she rains," and glanced at the box, chuckling. "I guess you must have hear about how my family ain't so small," he said.

Cuzak sat down behind the stove and watched his women-folk and the little children with equal amusement. He thought they were nice, and he thought they were funny, evidently. He had been off dancing with the girls and forgetting that he was an old fellow, and now his family rather surprised him; he seemed to think it a joke that all these children should belong to him. As the younger ones slipped up to him in his retreat, he kept taking things out of his pockets; penny dolls, a wooden clown, a balloon pig that was inflated by a whistle. He beckoned to the little boy they called Jan, whispered to him, and presented him with a paper snake, gently, so as not to startle him. Looking over the boy's head he said to me, "This one is bashful. He gets left."

Cuzak had brought home with him a roll of illustrated Bohemian papers. He opened them and began to tell his wife the news, much of which seemed to relate to one person. I heard the name Vasakova, Vasakova, repeated several times with lively interest, and presently I asked him whether he were talking about the singer, Maria Vasak.

"You know? You have heard, maybe?" he asked incredulously. When I assured him that I had heard her, he pointed out her picture and told me that Vasak had broken her leg, climbing in the Austrian Alps, and would not be able to fill her engagements. He seemed delighted to find that I had heard her sing in London and in Vienna; got out his pipe and lit it to enjoy our talk the better. She came from his part of Prague. His father used to mend her shoes for her when she was a student. Cuzak questioned me about her looks, her popularity, her voice; but he particularly wanted to know whether I had noticed her tiny feet, and whether I thought she had saved much money. She was extravagant, of course but he hoped she wouldn't squander everything, and have nothing left when she was old. As a young man, working in Wienn, he had seen a good many artists who were old and poor, making one glass of beer last all evening, and "it was not very nice, that."

When the boys came in from milking and feeding, the long table was laid, and two brown geese, stuffed with apples, were put down sizzling before Ántonia. She began to carve, and Rudolph, who sat next his mother, started the plates on their way. When everybody was served, he looked across the table at me.

"Have you been to Black Hawk lately, Mr. Burden? Then I wonder if you've heard about the Cutters?"

No, I had heard nothing at all about them.

"Then you must tell him, son, though it's a terrible thing to talk about at supper. Now, all you children be quiet, Rudolph is going to tell about the murder."

"Hurrah! The murder!" the children murmured, looking pleased and interested.

Rudolph told his story in great detail, with occasional promptings from his mother or father.

Wick Cutter and his wife had gone on living in the house that Ántonia and I knew so well, and in the way we knew so well. They grew to be very old people. He shriveled up, Ántonia said, until he looked like a little old yellow monkey, for his beard and his fringe of hair never changed color. Mrs. Cutter remained flushed and wild-eyed as we had known her, but as the years passed she became afflicted with a shaking palsy which made her nervous nod continuous instead of occasional. Her hands were so uncertain that she could no longer disfigure china, poor woman! As the couple grew older, they quarreled more and more about the ultimate disposition of their "property." A new law was passed in the State, securing the surviving wife a third of her husband's estate under all conditions. Cutter was tormented by the fear that Mrs. Cutter would live longer than he, and that eventually her "people," whom he had always hated so violently, would inherit. Their quarrels on this subject passed the boundary of the close-growing cedars, and were heard in the street by whoever wished to loiter and listen.

One morning, two years ago, Cutter went into the hardware store and bought a pistol, saying he was going to shoot a dog, and adding that he "thought he would take a shot at an old cat while he was about it." (Here the children interrupted Rudolph's narrative by smothered giggles.)

Cutter went out behind the hardware store, put up a target, practiced for an hour or so, and then went home. At six o'clock that evening, when several men were passing the Cutter house on their way home to supper, they heard a pistol shot. They paused and were looking doubtfully at one another, when another shot came crashing through an upstairs window. They ran into the house and found Wick Cutter lying on a sofa in his upstairs bedroom, with his throat torn open, bleeding on a roll of sheets he had placed beside his head.

"Walk in, gentlemen," he said weakly. "I am alive, you see, and competent. You are witnesses that I have survived my wife. You will find her in her own room. Please make your examination at once, so that there will be no mistake."

One of the neighbors telephoned for a doctor, while the others went into Mrs. Cutter's room. She was lying on her bed, in her nightgown and wrapper, shot through the heart. Her husband must have come in while she was taking her afternoon nap and shot her, holding the revolver near her breast. Her nightgown was burned from the powder.

The horrified neighbors rushed back to Cutter. He opened his eyes and said distinctly, "Mrs. Cutter is quite dead, gentlemen, and I am conscious. My affairs are in order." Then, Rudolph said, "he let go and died."

On his desk the coroner found a letter, dated at five o'clock that afternoon. It stated that he had just shot his wife; that any will she might secretly have made would be invalid, as he survived her. He meant to shoot himself at six o'clock and would, if he had strength, fire a shot through the window in the hope that passers-by might come in and see him "before life was extinct," as he wrote.

"Now, would you have thought that man had such a cruel heart?" Ántonia turned to me after the story was told. "To go and do that poor woman out of any comfort she might have from his money after he was gone!"

"Did you ever hear of anybody else that killed himself for spite, Mr. Burden?" asked Rudolph.

I admitted that I hadn't. Every lawyer learns over and over how strong a motive hate can be, but in my collection of legal anecdotes I had nothing to match this one. When I asked how much the estate amounted to, Rudolph said it was a little over a hundred thousand dollars.

Cuzak gave me a twinkling, sidelong glance. "The lawyers, they got a good deal of it, sure," he said merrily.

A hundred thousand dollars; so that was the fortune that had been scraped together by such hard dealing, and that Cutter himself had died for in the end!

After supper Cuzak and I took a stroll in the orchard and sat down by the windmill to smoke. He told me his story as if it were my business to know it.

His father was a shoemaker, his uncle a furrier, and he, being a younger son, was apprenticed to the latter's trade. You never got anywhere working for your relatives, he said, so when he was a journeyman he went to Vienna and worked in a big fur shop, earning good money. But a young fellow who liked a good time didn't save anything in Vienna; there were too many pleasant ways of spending every night what he'd made in the day. After three years there, he came to New York. He was badly advised and went to work on furs during a strike, when the factories were offering big wages. The strikers won, and Cuzak was blacklisted. As he had a few hundred dollars ahead, he decided to go to Florida and raise oranges. He had always thought he would like to raise oranges! The second year a hard frost killed his young grove, and he fell ill with malaria. He came to Nebraska to visit his cousin, Anton Jelinek, and to look about. When he began to look about, he saw Ántonia, and she was exactly the kind of girl he had always been hunting for. They were married at once, though he had to borrow money from his cousin to buy the wedding-ring.

"It was a pretty hard job, breaking up this place and making the first crops grow," he said, pushing back his hat and scratching his grizzled hair. "Sometimes I git awful sore on this place and want to quit, but my wife she always say we better stick it out. The babies come along pretty fast, so it look like it be hard to move, anyhow. I guess she was right, all right. We got this place clear now. We pay only twenty dollars an acre then, and I been offered a hundred. We bought another quarter[3] ten years ago, and we got it most paid for. We got plenty boys; we can work a lot of land. Yes, she is a good wife for a poor man. She ain't always so strict with me, neither. Sometimes maybe I drink a little too much beer in town, and when I come home she don't say nothing. She don't ask me no questions. We always get along fine, her and

---

3. I.e., a quarter section, equal to one-quarter of a square mile, or 160 acres.

me, like at first. The children don't make trouble between us, like sometimes happens." He lit another pipe and pulled on it contentedly.

I found Cuzak a most companionable fellow. He asked me a great many questions about my trip through Bohemia, about Vienna and the Ringstrasse and the theaters.

"Gee! I like to go back there once, when the boys is big enough to farm the place. Sometimes when I read the papers from the old country, I pretty near run away," he confessed with a little laugh. "I never did think how I would be a settled man like this."

He was still, as Ántonia said, a city man. He liked theaters and lighted streets and music and a game of dominoes after the day's work was over. His sociability was stronger than his acquisitive instinct. He liked to live day by day and night by night, sharing in the excitement of the crowd.—Yet his wife had managed to hold him here on a farm, in one of the loneliest countries in the world.

I could see the little chap, sitting here every evening by the windmill, nursing his pipe and listening to the silence; the wheeze of the pump, the grunting of the pigs, an occasional squawking when the hens were disturbed by a rat. It did rather seem to me that Cuzak had been made the instrument of Ántonia's special mission. This was a fine life, certainly, but it wasn't the kind of life he had wanted to live. I wondered whether the life that was right for one was ever right for two!

I asked Cuzak if he didn't find it hard to do without the gay company he had always been used to. He knocked out his pipe against an upright, sighed, and dropped it into his pocket.

"At first I near go crazy with lonesomeness," he said frankly, "but my woman is got such a warm heart. She always make it as good for me as she could. Now it ain't so bad; I can begin to have some fun with my boys, already!"

As we walked toward the house, Cuzak cocked his hat jauntily over one ear and looked up at the moon. "Gee!" he said in a hushed voice, as if he had just wakened up, "it don't seem like I am away from there twenty-six year!"

III

After dinner the next day I said good-bye and drove back to Hastings to take the train for Black Hawk. Ántonia and her children gathered round my buggy before I started, and even the little ones looked up at me with friendly faces. Leo and Ambrosch ran ahead to open the lane gate. When I reached the bottom of the hill, I glanced back. The group was still there by the windmill. Ántonia was waving her apron.

At the gate Ambrosch lingered beside my buggy, resting his arm on the wheel-rim. Leo slipped through the fence and ran off into the pasture.

"That's like him," his brother said with a shrug. "He's a crazy kid. Maybe he's sorry to have you go, and maybe he's jealous. He's jealous of anybody mother makes a fuss over, even the priest."

I found I hated to leave this boy, with his pleasant voice and his fine head and eyes. He looked very manly as he stood there without a hat, the wind rippling his shirt about his brown neck and shoulders.

"Don't forget that you and Rudolph are going hunting with me up on the Niobrara[4] next summer," I said. "Your father's agreed to let you off after harvest."

He smiled. "I won't likely forget. I've never had such a nice thing offered to me before. I don't know what makes you so nice to us boys," he added, blushing.

"Oh, yes you do!" I said, gathering up my reins.

He made no answer to this, except to smile at me with unabashed pleasure and affection as I drove away.

My day in Black Hawk was disappointing. Most of my old friends were dead or had moved away. Strange children, who meant nothing to me, were playing in the Harlings' big yard when I passed; the mountain ash had been cut down, and only a sprouting stump was left of the tall Lombardy poplar that used to guard the gate. I hurried on. The rest of the morning I spent with Anton Jelinek, under a shady cottonwood tree in the yard behind his saloon. While I was having my mid-day dinner at the hotel, I met one of the old lawyers who was still in practice, and he took me up to his office and talked over the Cutter case with me. After that, I scarcely knew how to put in the time until the night express was due.

I took a long walk north of the town, out into the pastures where the land was so rough that it had never been ploughed up, and the long red grass of early times still grew shaggy over the draws and hillocks. Out there I felt at home again. Overhead the sky was that indescribable blue of autumn; bright and shadowless, hard as enamel. To the south I could see the dun-shaded river bluffs that used to look so big to me, and all about stretched drying corn-fields, of the pale-gold color I remembered so well. Russian thistles were blowing across the uplands and piling against the wire fences like barricades. Along the cattle paths the plumes of golden-rod were already fading into sun-warmed velvet, gray with gold threads in it. I had escaped from the curious depression that hangs over little towns, and my mind was full of pleasant things; trips I meant to take with the Cuzak boys, in the Bad Lands and up on the Stinking Water. There were enough Cuzaks to play with for a long while yet. Even after the boys grew up, there would always be Cuzak himself! I meant to tramp along a few miles of lighted streets with Cuzak.

As I wandered over those rough pastures, I had the good luck to stumble upon a bit of the first road that went from Black Hawk out to the north country; to my grandfather's farm, then on to the Shimerdas' and to the Norwegian settlement. Everywhere else it had been ploughed under when the highways were surveyed; this half-mile or so within the pasture fence was all that was left of that old road which used to run like a wild thing across the open prairie, clinging to the high places and circling and doubling like a rabbit before the hounds. On the level land the tracks had almost disappeared—were mere shadings in the grass, and a stranger would not have noticed them. But wherever the road had crossed a draw, it was easy to find. The rains had made channels of the wheel-ruts and washed them so deep that the sod had never healed over them. They looked like gashes torn by a grizzly's claws, on the slopes where the farm wagons used to lurch up out of the hollows with a

---

4. River flowing east from Wyoming across Nebraska.

pull that brought curling muscles on the smooth hips of the horses. I sat down and watched the haystacks turn rosy in the slanting sunlight.

This was the road over which Ántonia and I came on that night when we got off the train at Black Hawk and were bedded down in the straw, wondering children, being taken we knew not whither. I had only to close my eyes to hear the rumbling of the wagons in the dark, and to be again overcome by that obliterating strangeness. The feelings of that night were so near that I could reach out and touch them with my hand. I had the sense of coming home to myself, and of having found out what a little circle man's experience is. For Ántonia and for me, this had been the road of Destiny; had taken us to those early accidents of fortune which predetermined for us all that we can ever be. Now I understood that the same road was to bring us together again. Whatever we had missed, we possessed together the precious, the incommunicable past.

1918

AMY LOWELL
1874–1925

Born in Brookline, Massachusetts, the fifth and last child, twelve years younger than her nearest sibling, Amy Lowell hailed from one of Boston's wealthiest and most prestigious and powerful families. The first Lowell arrived at Massachusetts Bay Colony in 1639; from the revolutionary years on, when a Lowell was made a judge by George Washington, no era was without one or more Lowells prominent in the intellectual, religious, political, philanthropic, and commercial life of New England. In the early nineteenth century her paternal grandfather and his brothers established the Lowell textile mills in Lowell, Massachusetts—the town itself had been founded by the Lowells in 1653. The success of these mills changed the economy of New England. Profits were invested in utilities, highways, railroads, and banks. In the same generation her maternal grandfather, Abbot Lawrence, established a second New England textile dynasty. All the Lowell men went to Harvard. Traditionally, those who were not in business became Unitarian ministers or scholars—the poet James Russell Lowell was her great-uncle; her father, Augustus, was important to the founding of the Massachusetts Institute of Technology; her brother Percival was a pioneering scholar of Japanese and Korean civilization and an astronomer (he founded the Lowell Observatory and discovered the planet Pluto); her brother Abbot Lawrence was president of Harvard from 1909 to 1933.

But none of the millionaires, manufacturers, philanthropists, statesmen, ambassadors, judges, and scholars in Amy Lowell's background could give this energetic and unusually intelligent young woman a model to follow. They were all men, and the rules for Lowell women were different. Women in the family were expected to marry well, imbue their children with a strong sense of family pride, oversee the running of several homes, and participate in upper-class Boston's busy social world. None of this interested Lowell in the least. Yet she believed in the importance of her heritage and shared the self-confidence and drive to contribute notably to public life characteristic of Lowell men.

Resisting the kind of formal education available to women of her class at the time, she attended school only between the ages of ten and seventeen. She educated herself through the use of her family's extensive private library as well as the resources of the Boston Athenaeum, a dues-paying library club founded by one of her ancestors early in the nineteenth century. She had enjoyed writing from childhood on, but did not venture into professional authorship until 1912, at the age of thirty-eight. In that year, her first book of poems—*A Dome of Many-Coloured Glass*—achieved both popular and critical success.

The year 1912 was the year that Harriet Monroe launched her influential little magazine, *Poetry,* and when in January 1913 Lowell read H. D.'s imagistic poetry she was converted to this new style. She decided to devote her popularity and social prominence to popularizing imagism and with characteristic energy and self-confidence journeyed to England to meet H. D., Ezra Pound, D. H. Lawrence, Richard Aldington, and other participants in the informal movement. When Pound abandoned imagism for vorticism, Lowell became the chief spokesperson for the movement, editing several imagist anthologies. Two volumes of original criticism by Lowell—*Six French Poets* (1915) and *Tendencies in Modern American Poetry* (1917)—also forwarded the cause. Pound, upstaged as a publicist, enviously renamed the movement "Amygism." Lowell retorted that "it was not until I entered the arena and Ezra dropped out that Imagism had to be considered seriously."

Lowell's own poetry—published in *Sword Blades and Poppy Seed* (1914), *Men, Women, and Ghosts* (1916), *Can Grande's Castle* (1918), *Pictures of the Floating World* (1919), and *Legends* (1921)—was never exclusively imagistic but included long historical narrative poems and journalistic prose poems and used standard verse patterns, blank verse, and a Whitmanesque free verse resembling the open line developed by Carl Sandburg. Her best poems tend to enclose sharp imagistic representation within this relatively fluid line, thereby achieving an effect of simultaneous compactness and flexibility. Like many women poets, she worked with a symbolic vocabulary of flowers and color.

Lowell enjoyed her success and cheerfully went on the lecture circuit as a celebrity, making innumerable close friendships as a result of her warmth and generosity. Despite health problems that plagued her for most of her life, she remained full of energy and zest. She depended for support on the companionship of Ada Dwyer Russell, a former actress, for whom she wrote many of her most moving appreciations of female beauty. Although she traveled widely in Europe, she was ultimately committed to New England and the Lowell heritage, both of which fused in an attachment to her home, Sevenels, in Brookline. A devotee of Romantic poetry and especially of Keats, she had begun to collect Keats manuscripts in 1905; these now form the basis of the great collection at Harvard University. In addition to all her other activities in the 1920s, she worked on a two-volume biography of Keats that greatly extended the published information about the poet when it appeared in 1925, although its psychological approach offended many traditional critics.

Lowell was just fifty-one when she died. Despite continued sniping from the high modernist poets who thought her work was too accessible, her poetry continued to be both popular and critically esteemed until the 1950s, when scholars focused the canon on a very small number of writers. The efforts of feminists to rediscover and republicize the work of neglected women authors as well as the researches of literary historians into the whole picture of American literary achievement have together brought her work back into the spotlight that it occupied during her lifetime.

The texts printed here are from Lowell's *Complete Poems* (1955).

The Captured Goddess

> Over the housetops,
> Above the rotating chimney-pots,
> I have seen a shiver of amethyst,

And blue and cinnamon have flickered
A moment,   5
At the far end of a dusty street.

Through sheeted rain
Has come a lustre of crimson,
And I have watched moonbeams
Hushed by a film of palest green.   10

It was her wings,
Goddess!
Who stepped over the clouds,
And laid her rainbow feathers
Aslant on the currents of the air.   15

I followed her for long,
With gazing eyes and stumbling feet.
I cared not where she led me,
My eyes were full of colors:
Saffrons, rubies, the yellows of beryls,   20
And the indigo-blue of quartz;
Flights of rose, layers of chrysoprase,
Points of orange, spirals of vermilion,
The spotted gold of tiger-lily petals,
The loud pink of bursting hydrangeas.   25
I followed,
And watched for the flashing of her wings.

In the city I found her,
The narrow-streeted city.
In the market-place I came upon her,   30
Bound and trembling.
Her fluted wings were fastened to her sides with cords,
She was naked and cold,
For that day the wind blew
Without sunshine.   35

Men chaffered for her,
They bargained in silver and gold,
In copper, in wheat,
And called their bids across the market-place.

The Goddess wept.   40

Hiding my face I fled,
And the grey wind hissed behind me,
Along the narrow streets.

1914

Venus Transiens

Tell me,
Was Venus more beautiful
Than you are,
When she topped
The crinkled waves,   5
Drifting shoreward
On her plaited shell?
Was Botticelli's[1] vision
Fairer than mine;
And were the painted rosebuds   10
He tossed his lady,
Of better worth
Than the words I blow about you
To cover your too great loveliness
As with a gauze   15
Of misted silver?

For me,
You stand poised
In the blue and buoyant air,
Cinctured by bright winds,   20
Treading the sunlight.
And the waves which precede you
Ripple and stir
The sands at my feet.

1919

Madonna of the Evening Flowers

All day long I have been working,
Now I am tired.
I call: "Where are you?"
But there is only the oak tree rustling in the wind.
The house is very quiet,   5
The sun shines in on your books,
On your scissors and thimble just put down,
But you are not there.
Suddenly I am lonely:
Where are you?   10
I go about searching.

Then I see you,
Standing under a spire of pale blue larkspur,

1. Sandro Botticelli (ca. 1440–1510), Italian Renaissance painter among whose paintings is the famous *Birth of Venus*, depicting the Greek goddess of love and beauty rising from the ocean on a seashell.

With a basket of roses on your arm.
You are cool, like silver,   15
And you smile.
I think the Canterbury bells[1] are playing little tunes.

You tell me that the peonies need spraying,
That the columbines have overrun all bounds,
That the pyrus japonica should be cut back and rounded.   20
You tell me these things.
But I look at you, heart of silver,
White heart-flame of polished silver,
Burning beneath the blue steeples of the larkspur,
And I long to kneel instantly at your feet,   25
While all about us peal the loud, sweet *Te Deums* of the
    Canterbury bells.

                                                            1919

September, 1918

This afternoon was the colour of water falling through sunlight;
The trees glittered with the tumbling of leaves;
The sidewalks shone like alleys of dropped maple leaves;
And the houses ran along them laughing out of square, open
    windows.
Under a tree in the park,   5
Two little boys, lying flat on their faces,
Were carefully gathering red berries
To put in a pasteboard box.

Some day there will be no war.
Then I shall take out this afternoon   10
And turn it in my fingers,
And remark the sweet taste of it upon my palate,
And note the crisp variety of its flights of leaves.
To-day I can only gather it
And put it into my lunch-box,   15
For I have time for nothing
But the endeavour to balance myself
Upon a broken world.

                                                            1919

1. Little bell-shaped blue flowers. Lowell puns on the bells of Canterbury Cathedral in England pealing out
religious music.

Meeting-House Hill

I must be mad, or very tired,
When the curve of a blue bay beyond a railroad track
Is shrill and sweet to me like the sudden springing of a tune,
And the sight of a white church above thin trees in a city square
Amazes my eyes as though it were the Parthenon.   5
Clear, reticent, superbly final,
With the pillars of its portico refined to a cautious elegance,
It dominates the weak trees,
And the shot of its spire
Is cool and candid,   10
Rising into an unresisting sky.
Strange meeting-house
Pausing a moment upon a squalid hill-top.
I watch the spire sweeping the sky,
I am dizzy with the movement of the sky,   15
I might be watching a mast
With its royals set full
Straining before a two-reef breeze.
I might be sighting a tea-clipper,
Tacking into the blue bay,   20
Just back from Canton
With her hold full of green and blue porcelain
And a Chinese coolie leaning over the rail
Gazing at the white spire
With dull, sea-spent eyes.   25

                                                          1925

Summer Night Piece

The garden is steeped in moonlight,
Full to its high edges with brimming silver,
And the fish-ponds brim and darken
And run in little serpent lights soon extinguished.
Lily-pads lie upon the surface, beautiful as the tarnishings on frail
     old silver,   5
And the Harvest moon droops heavily out of the sky,
A ripe, white melon, intensely, magnificently, shining.
Your window is orange in the moonlight,
It glows like a lamp behind the branches of the old wisteria,
It burns like a lamp before a shrine,   10
The small, intimate, familiar shrine,
Placed reverently among the bricks,
Of a much-loved garden wall.

                                                          1925

St. Louis

June

Flat,
Flat,
Long as sight
Either way,
An immense country,   5
With a great river
Steaming it full of moist, unbearable heat.
The orchards are little quincunxes of Noah's Ark trees,
The plows and horses are children's toys tracing amusingly shallow lines
    upon an illimitable surface.
Great chunks of life to match the country,   10
Great lungs to breathe this hot, wet air.

But it is not mine.
Mine is a land of hills
Lying couchant in the angles of heraldic beasts
About white villages.   15
A land of singing elms and pine-trees.
A restless up and down land
Always mounting, dipping, slipping into a different contour,
Where the roads turn every hundred yards or so,
Where brooks rattle forgotten Indian names to tired farm-houses,   20
And faint spires of old meeting-houses
Flaunt their golden weather-cocks in a brave show of challenge at a sunset
    sky.

Here the heat stuffs down with the thickness of boiled feathers,
The river runs in steam.
There, lilacs are in bloom,   25
Cool blue-purples, wine-reds, whites,
Flying colour to quiet dooryards.
Grown year on year to a suddenness of old perfection,
Saying "Before! Before!" to each new Spring.
Here is "Now,"   30
But "Before" is mine with the lilacs,
With the white sea of everywhither,
With the heraldic, story-telling hills.

1927

New Heavens for Old

I am useless,
What I do is nothing.
What I think has no savour.
There is an almanac between the windows:
It is of the year when I was born.   5

My fellows call to me to join them,
They shout for me,
Passing the house in a great wind of vermillion banners.
They are fresh and fulminant,
They are indecent and strut with the thought of it.   10
They laugh, and curse, and brawl,
And cheer a holocaust of "Who comes Firsts!" at the iron fronts of the
    houses at the two edges of the street.
Young men with naked hearts jeering between iron house-fronts,
Young men with naked bodies beneath their clothes
Passionately conscious of them,   15
Ready to strip off their clothes,
Ready to strip off their customs, their usual routine,
Clamouring for the rawness of life,
In love with appetite,
Proclaiming it as a creed,   20
Worshipping youth,
Worshipping themselves.
They call for the women and the women come,
They bare the whiteness of their lusts to the dead gaze of the old house-
    fronts,
They roar down the street like flame,   25
They explode upon the dead houses like new, sharp fire.

But I—
I arrange three roses in a Chinese vase:
A pink one,
A red one,   30
A yellow one.
I fuss over their arrangement.
Then I sit in a South window
And sip pale wine with a touch of hemlock in it,
And think of Winter nights,   35
And field-mice crossing and re-crossing
The spot which will be my grave.

                                                                    1927

GERTRUDE STEIN
1874–1946

Among modernists active between the wars, Gertrude Stein was more radically experimental than most. She pushed language to its limits—and kept on pushing. Her work
was sometimes literal nonsense, often funny, and always exciting to those who
thought of writing as a craft and language as a medium. As Sherwood Anderson wrote,
"she is laying word against word, relating sound to sound, feeling for the taste, the
smell, the rhythm of the individual word. She is attempting to do something for the
writers of our English speech that may be better understood after a time, and she is
not in a hurry."

Stein's grandparents were well-off German Jewish immigrants who, at the time of
her birth, were established in business in Baltimore. Born in Allegheny, Pennsylvania,
she was the youngest of seven children; the family lived abroad from 1875 to 1879

and then settled in northern California. Her parents died when she was an adolescent, leaving their five surviving children well provided for. Stein made a family with her favorite brother, Leo, for many years. When he went to Harvard in 1892 she followed and was admitted to Harvard's "annex for women"—now Radcliffe College. She studied there with the great psychologist William James; some of her early writings—for example, *Three Lives* (1909) and *The Making of Americans*, which she completed in 1908 but did not publish until 1925—are probably trying to apply his theories of consciousness: consciousness as unique to each individual, as an ongoing stream, a perpetual present. In *Three Lives*, also, Stein set herself the difficult task of representing the consciousnesses of three ordinary, working-class women whose lives and minds were not the conventional material of serious literature.

When Leo moved on to Johns Hopkins to study biology, Stein followed, enrolling in the medical school. At the end of her fourth year, she failed intentionally, for several reasons: Leo had become interested in art and decided to go to Europe, she had begun to write, and she had become erotically involved with two women (the story of this triangle formed the basis of her novel *Q.E.D.*, published posthumously in 1950). In early 1903 Leo settled in Paris; Stein joined him that fall. They began to collect modern art and became good friends with many of the brilliant aspiring painters of the day, including Pablo Picasso, Georges Braque, and Henri Matisse. Stein's friendship with the painters was extremely important for her development, for she reproduced some of their experiments in the very different medium of words. Because of them, she came to think of words as tangible entities in themselves as well as vehicles conveying meaning or representing reality. The cubist movement in painting also affected her. Painters like Picasso and Braque believed that so-called representational paintings conveyed not what people actually saw but rather what they had learned to *think* they saw. The cubists wanted to reproduce a pure visual experience unmediated by cultural ideas. To see a "person" is to see a cultural construct. So they painted a human form reduced to various geometrical shapes as they might be seen from different angles when the form moved or the observer changed position. The degree to which their paintings shocked an audience measured, to Picasso and Braque, the degree to which that audience had lost its original perceiving power.

In 1909 the long companionship of Stein and her brother was complicated when Alice B. Toklas joined the household as Gertrude Stein's lover; she became her secretary, housekeeper, typist, editor, and lifelong companion. Leo moved out in 1913, and the art collection was divided, but the apartment at 27 rue de Fleurus continued to serve as a gathering place for French artists and intellectuals, American expatriates, and American visitors. Without much expectation that her work would achieve any wide audience, Stein continued to write and to advise younger writers like Ernest Hemingway and F. Scott Fitzgerald. "A great deal of description," she said about a draft of Hemingway's first novel, "and not particularly good description. Begin over again and concentrate." The need to concentrate and distill—the idea that description was too often an indulgence—was a lesson the younger writer took to heart.

In the 1920s Stein and Toklas began spending summers in the south of France, where they bought a small house in 1929. They lived there during the war, when they could not return to Paris. Devoted to their adopted country, Stein and Toklas did what they could for France during both world wars. They visited and entertained American soldiers, many of whom continued to write to the couple for years after they had returned to the United States and some of whom visited when they had occasion to return to France. Even though Stein returned to the United States only once, in 1934, on what turned into a very successful lecture tour, she and Toklas always thought of themselves as Americans.

Stein's work may be considered as falling into three overlapping chronological phases. In all three phases she wrote lesbian love poems that developed a complex private symbolism for socially unacceptable feelings and events—a symbolism so obscure that their eroticism is by no means apparent, even in a much more permissive age, and needs decoding if the poems are to be understood. At first she was interested in representing present time, which is the way she believed life was subjectively experienced. Experience goes on and yet changes minutely from instant to instant. In *The Making of Americans*, Stein explained, "there was a groping for using everything and there was a groping for a continuous present and there was an inevitable beginning of beginning again and again and again." And, she added humorously, "I went on to a thousand pages of it."

Stein's 1914 *Tender Buttons*, a cubist prose-poem collage of domestic objects, looked forward to her still more innovative work of the 1920s, where she treated words as things, carefully ignoring or defying the connection between words and meanings, continually undercutting expectations about order, coherence, and associations. Naturally, the effect of such writing is often absurd, because expected patterns do not appear but are continually disrupted and frustrated. There is a great deal of joking in this work, which she openly characterized as defiance of what she called, in one long essay-poem, "patriarchal poetry"—that is, orderly, hierarchical, rule-based poetry. Much of her experimental work remained unpublished in her lifetime.

The third phase of her work, in the 1930s, represents a campaign of self-promotion. Her autobiography, written as *The Autobiography of Alice B. Toklas* (1933), her *Everybody's Autobiography* (1937), and *Wars I Have Seen* (1945) are narratives that present some of her techniques in simplified form and also project her strong independent personality. Because they were easier to read, they were popular, as was her opera libretto *Four Saints in Three Acts* put to music by Virgil Thomson. By the time of her death she had become a public personality. In recent years, the extent of her influence on other writers and the intentions behind experiments that had previously seemed "meaningless" have become much more apparent. The women's movement, with its interest in women's lives, has also produced a new appreciation of her radical individualism.

The text of *The Making of Americans* is from the first edition (1925).

From The Making of Americans[1]

[INTRODUCTION]

Once an angry man dragged his father along the ground through his own orchard. "Stop!" cried the groaning old man at last, "Stop! I did not drag my father beyond this tree."

It is hard living down the tempers we are born with. We all begin well, for in our youth there is nothing we are more intolerant of than our own sins writ large in others and we fight them fiercely in ourselves; but we grow old and we see that these our sins are of all sins the really harmless ones to own, nay that they give a charm to any character, and so our struggle with them dies away.

I am writing for myself and strangers. This is the only way that I can do it. Everybody is a real one to me, everybody is like some one else too to me. No one of them that I know can want to know it and so I write for myself and strangers.

Every one is always busy with it, no one of them then ever want to know it that every one looks like some one else and they see it. Mostly every one dislikes to hear it. It is very important to me to always know it, to always see it which one looks like others and to tell it. I write for myself and strangers. I

---

1. This long book—over nine hundred pages—tells the story of Martha Hersland, who represents Stein herself, and her family. "Making" refers both to family history and to making the book.

do this for my own sake and for the sake of those who know I know it that they look like other ones, that they are separate and yet always repeated.[2] There are some who like it that I know they are like many others and repeat it, there are many who never can really like it.

There are many that I know and they know it. They are all of them repeating and I hear it. I love it and I tell it, I love it and now I will write it. This is now the history of the way some of them are it.

I write for myself and strangers. No one who knows me can like it. At least they mostly do not like it that every one is of a kind of men and women and I see it. I love it and I write it.

I want readers so strangers must do it. Mostly no one knowing me can like it that I love it that every one is a kind of men and women, that always I am looking and comparing and classifying of them, always I am seeing their repeating. Always more and more I love repeating, it may be irritating to hear from them but always more and more I love it of them. More and more I love it of them, the being in them, the mixing in them, the repeating in them, the deciding the kinds of them every one is who has human being.

This is now a little of what I love and how I write it. Later there will be much more of it.

There are many ways of making kinds of men and women. Now there will be descriptions of every kind of way every one can be a kind of men and women.

This is now a history of Martha Hersland. This is now a history of Martha and of every one who came to be of her living.

There will then be soon much description of every way one can think of men and women, in their beginning, in their middle living, and their ending.[3]

Every one then is an individual being. Every one then is like many others always living, there are many ways of thinking of every one, this is now a description of all of them. There must then be a whole history of each one of them. There must then now be a description of all repeating. Now I will tell all the meaning to me in repeating, the loving there is in me for repeating.

Every one is one inside them, every one reminds some one of some other one who is or was or will be living. Every one has it to say of each one he is like such a one I see it in him, every one has it to say of each one she is like some one else I can tell by remembering. So it goes on always in living, every one is always remembering some one who is resembling to the one at whom they are then looking. So they go on repeating, every one is themselves inside them and every one is resembling to others, and that is always interesting. There are many ways of making kinds of men and women. In each way of making kinds of them there is a different system of finding them resembling. Sometime there will be here every way there can be of seeing kinds of men and women. Sometime there will be then a complete history of each one. Every one always is repeating the whole of them and so sometime some one who sees them will have a complete history of every one. Sometime some one will know all the ways there are for people to be resembling, some one sometime then will have a completed history of every one.

---

2. Differences within basic similarities among people correspond to the differences within similar sentences employed as the chief experimental technique of *The Making of Americans*.

3. Here Stein expands her intention to encompass every variation of human life. The repetition of present participles (*-ing*) emphasizes current action, present time.

Soon now there will be a history of the way repeating comes out of them comes out of men and women when they are young, when they are children, they have then their own system of being resembling; this will soon be a description of the men and women in beginning, the being young in them, the being children.

There is then now and here the loving repetition, this is then, now and here, a description of the loving of repetition and then there will be a description of all the kinds of ways there can be seen to be kinds of men and women. Then there will be realised the complete history of every one, the fundamental character of every one, the bottom nature in them, the mixtures in them, the strength and weakness of everything they have inside them, the flavor of them, the meaning in them, the being in them, and then you have a whole history then of each one. Everything then they do in living is clear to the completed understanding, their living, loving, eating, pleasing, smoking, thinking, scolding, drinking, working, dancing, walking, talking, laughing, sleeping, everything in them. There are whole beings then, they are themselves inside them, repeating coming out of them makes a history of each one of them.

Always from the beginning there was to me all living as repeating. This is now a description of my feeling. As I was saying listening to repeating is often irritating,[4] always repeating is all of living, everything in a being[f]jis always repeating, more and more listening to repeating gives to me completed understanding. Each one slowly comes to be a whole one to me. Each one slowly comes to be a whole one in me. Soon then it commences to sound through my ears and eyes and feelings the repeating that is always coming out from each one, that is them, that makes then slowly of each one of them a whole one. Repeating then comes slowly then to be to one who has it to have loving repeating as natural being comes to be a full sound telling all the being in each one such a one is ever knowing. Sometimes it takes many years of knowing some one before the repeating that is that one gets to be a steady sounding to the hearing of one who has it as a natural being to love repeating that slowly comes out from every one. Sometimes it takes many years of knowing some one before the repeating in that one comes to be a clear history of such a one. Natures sometimes are so mixed up in some one that steady repeating in them is mixed up with changing. Soon then there will be a completed history of each one. Sometimes it is difficult to know it in some, for what these are saying is repeating in them is not the real repeating of them, is not the complete repeating for them. Sometimes many years of knowing some one pass before repeating of all being in them comes out clearly from them. As I was saying it is often irritating to listen to the repeating they are doing, always then that one that has it as being to love repeating that is the whole history of each one, such a one has it then that this irritation passes over into patient completed understanding. Loving repeating is one way of being. This is now a description of such feeling.

There are many that I know and they know it. They are all of them repeating and I hear it. I love it and I tell it. I love it and now I will write it. This is now a history of my love of it. I hear it and I love it and I write it. They repeat

---

4. Stein is aware that her techniques may irritate readers, just as human sameness may cause people to be irritated with each other.

it. They live it and I see it and I hear it. They live it and I hear it and I see it and I love it and now and always I will write it. There are many kinds of men and women and I know it. They repeat it and I hear it and I love it. This is now a history of the way they do it. This is now a history of the way I love it.[5]

Now I will tell of the meaning to me in repeating, of the loving there is in me for repeating.

Sometimes every one becomes a whole one to me. Sometimes every one has a completed history for me. Slowly each one is a whole one to me, with some, all their living is passing before they are a whole one to me. There is a completed history of them to me then when there is of them a completed understanding of the bottom nature in them of the nature or natures mixed up in them with the bottom nature of them or separated in them. There is then a history of the things they say and do and feel, and happen to them. There is then a history of the living in them. Repeating is always in all of them. Repeating in them comes out of them, slowly making clear to any one that looks closely at them the nature and the natures mixed up in them. This sometime comes to be clear in every one.

Often as I was saying repeating is very irritating to listen to from them and then slowly it settles into a completed history of them. Repeating is a wonderful thing in living being. Sometime then the nature of every one comes to be clear to some one listening to the repeating coming out of each one.

This is then now to be a little description of the loving feeling for understanding of the completed history of each one that comes to one who listens always steadily to all repeating. This is the history then of the loving feeling in me of repeating, the loving feeling in me for completed understanding of the completed history of every one as it slowly comes out in every one as patiently and steadily I hear it and see it as repeating in them. This is now a little a description of this loving feeling. This is now a little a history of it from the beginning.

Always then I listen and come back again and again to listen to every one. Always then I am thinking and feeling the repeating in every one. Sometime then there will be for me a completed history of every one. Every one is separate then and a kind of men and women.

Sometime it takes many years of knowing some one before the repeating in that one comes to be a clear history of such a one. Sometimes many years of knowing some one pass before repeating of all being in such a one comes out clearly from them, makes a completed understanding of them by some one listening, watching, hearing all the repeating coming out from such a one.

As I was saying loving listening, hearing always all repeating, coming to completed understanding of each one is to some a natural way of being. This is now more description of the feeling such a one has in them, this is now more description of the way listening to repeating comes to make complete understanding. This is now more description of the way repeating slowly comes to make in each one a completed history of them.

There are many that I know and always more and more I know it. They are all of them repeating and I hear it. More and more I understand it. Always

---

5. In telling about others with such care, Stein shows her love for them; hence the tale is about her love as well as their lives.

more and more I hear it, always more and more it has completed history in it.

Every one has their own being in them. Every one is of a kind of men and women. Many have mixed up in them some kind of many kinds of men and women. Slowly this comes clearly out from them in the repeating that is always in all living. Slowly it comes out from them to the most delicate gradation, to the gentlest flavor of them.[6] Always it comes out as repeating from them. Always it comes out as repeating, out of them. Then to the complete understanding they keep on repeating this, the whole of them and any one seeing them then can understand them. This is a joy to any one loving repeating when in any one repeating steadily tells over and over again the history of the complete being in them. This is a solid happy satisfaction to any one who has it in them to love repeating and completed understanding.

As I was saying often for many years some one is baffling. The repeated hearing of them does not make the completed being they have in them to any one. Sometimes many years pass in listening to repeating in such a one and the being of them is not a completed history to any one then listening to them. Sometimes then it comes out of them a louder repeating that before was not clear to anybody's hearing and then it is a completed being to some one listening to the repeating coming out of such a one.

This is then now a description of loving repeating being in some. This is then now a description of loving repeating being in one.

There are many that I know and they know it. They are all of them repeating and I hear it. More and more I understand it. I love it and I tell it. I love it and always I will tell it. They live it and I see it and I hear it. They repeat it and I hear it and I see it, sometimes then always I understand it, sometime then always there is a completed history of each one by it, sometime then I will tell the completed history of each one as by repeating I come to know it.

Every one always is repeating the whole of them. Every one is repeating the whole of them, such repeating is then always in them and so sometime some one who sees them will have a complete understanding of the whole of each one of them, will have a completed history of every man and every woman they ever come to know in their living, every man and every woman who were or are or will be living whom such a one can come to know in living.

This then is a history of many men and women, sometime there will be a history of every one.

As I was saying every one always is repeating the whole of them. As I was saying sometimes it takes many years of hearing the repeating in one before the whole being is clear to the understanding of one who has it as a being to love repeating, to know that always every one is repeating the whole of them.

This is then the way such a one, one who has it as a being to love repeating, to know that always every one is repeating the whole of them comes to a completed understanding of any one. This is now a description of such a way of hearing repeating.

Every one always is repeating the whole of them. Many always listen to all repeating that comes to them in their living. Some have it as being to love the repeating that is always in every one coming out from them as a whole of

6. Attentive awareness of tiny variations in repeated behavior enables one to find the unique identity of each individual.

them. This is now a description of such a one and the completed under-standing of each one who is repeating in such a one's living.

Every one always is repeating the whole of them. Always, one having lov-ing repeating to getting completed understanding must have in them an open feeling, a sense for all the slightest variations in repeating, must never lose themselves so in the solid steadiness of all repeating that they do not hear the slightest variation. If they get deadened by the steady pounding of repeating[7] they will not learn from each one even though each one always is repeating the whole of them they will not learn the completed history of them, they will not know the being really in them.

As I was saying every one always is repeating the whole of them. As I was saying sometimes it takes many years of listening, seeing, living, feeling, lov-ing the repeating there is in some before one comes to a completed under-standing. This is now a description, of such a way of hearing, seeing, feeling, living, loving, repetition.

Mostly every one loves some one's repeating. Mostly every one then, comes to know then the being of some one by loving the repeating in them, the repeating coming out of them. There are some who love everybody's repeating, this is now a description of such loving in one.

Mostly every one loves some one's repeating. Every one always is repeating the whole of them. This is now a history of getting completed understanding by loving repeating in every one the repeating that always is coming out of them as a history of them. This is now a description of learning to listen to all repeating that every one always is making of the whole of them.

Now I will tell of the meaning to me in repeating, of the loving there is in me for repeating.

Always from the beginning there was to me all living as repeating. This is now a description of loving repeating as a being. This is now a history of learn-ing to listen to repeating to come to a completed understanding.

To go on now giving all of the description of how repeating comes to have meaning, how it forms itself, how one must distinguish the different mean-ings in repeating. Sometimes it is very hard to understand the meaning of repeating. Sometime there will be a complete history of some one having lov-ing repeating as being, to a completed understanding. Now there will be a lit-tle description of such a one.

Sometime then there will be a complete history of all repeating to com-pleted understanding. Sometime then there will be a complete history of every one who ever was or is or will be living.

Sometimes there will be a complete history of some one having loving repeating to a completed understanding as being. Sometime then there will be a complete history of many women and many men.

Now there is to be some description of some one having loving repeating to a completed understanding as being. Then there will be a complete history of some.

More and more then there will be a history of many men and many women from their beginning to their ending, as being babies and children and grow-ing young men and growing young women and young grown men and young

7. The literary technique Stein uses has problems, as she recognizes: as with human relations, there may be boredom, lapses of attention, and estrangement.

grown women and men and women in their middle living and growing old men and growing old women and old men and old women.

More and more then there will be histories of all the kinds there are of men and women.

This is now a little description of having loving repeating as being. This is now a little description of one having loving repeating as being.

Loving repeating is one way of being. This is now a description of such being. Loving repeating is always in children. Loving repeating is in a way earth feeling. Some children have loving repeating for little things and story-telling, some have it as a more bottom being. Slowly this comes out in them in all their children being, in their eating, playing, crying, and laughing. Loving repeating is then in a way earth feeling. This is very strong in some. This is very strong in many, in children and in old age being. This is very strong in many in all ways of humorous being, this is very strong in some from their beginning to their ending. This is now some description of such being in one.

As I was saying loving repeating being is in a way earthy being. In some it is repeating that gives to them always a solid feeling of being. In some children there is more feeling in repeating eating and playing, in some in story-telling and their feeling. More and more in living as growing young men and women and grown young men and women and men and women in their middle living, more and more there comes to be in them differences in loving repeating in different kinds of men and women, there comes to be in some more and in some less loving repeating. Loving repeating in some is a going on always in them of earthy being, in some it is the way to completed understanding. Loving repeating then in some is their natural way of complete being.[8] This is now some description of one.

There is then always repeating in all living. There is then in each one always repeating their whole being, the whole nature in them. Much loving repeating has to be in a being so that that one can listen to all the repeating in every one. Almost every one loves all repeating in some one. This is now some description of loving repeating, all repeating, in every one.

To begin again with the children. To begin again with the repeating being in them. To begin again with the loving repeating being in them. As I was saying some children have it in them to love repeating in them of eating, of angry feeling in them, many of them have loving repeating for story-telling in them, many of them have loving repeating being in them for any kind of being funny, in making jokes or teasing, many of them having loving repeating being in them in all kinds of playing. Mostly every one when they are children, mostly every one has then loving repeating being strongly in them, some have it more some have it less in them and this comes out more and more in them as they come to be young adolescents in their being and then grown young men and grown young women.

To begin again then with children in their having loving repeating being. Mostly all children have loving repeating as being in them but some have it much more and some have it much less in them. Loving repeating being is more of that kind of being that has resisting as its natural way of fighting than of that kind of being that has attacking as its natural way of winning. But this

---

8. One difference between people is that some love repetition more and some love it less. To love repetition is to love life and people.

is a very complicated question. I know very much about these ways of being in men and women. I know it and can say it, it is a very complex question and I do not know yet the whole of it, so I can not yet say all I know of it.

As I was saying all little children have in them mostly very much loving repeating being. As they grow into bigger children some have it more some have it less in them. Some have it in them more and more as a conscious feeling. Many of them do not have it in them more and more as a conscious feeling. Mostly when they are growing to be young men and women they have not it in them to have loving repeating being in them as a conscious feeling.

Mostly every one has not it in them as a conscious feeling as a young grown man or young grown woman. Some have it in them, loving repeating feeling as steadily developing, this is now a history of one.

Many men and many women never have it in them the conscious feeling of loving repeating. Many men and many women never have it in them until old age weakening is in them, a consciousness of repeating. Many have it in them all their living as a conscious feeling as a humorous way of being in them. Some have it in them, the consciousness of always repeating the whole of them as a serious obligation. There are many many ways then of having repeating as conscious feeling, of having loving repeating as a bottom being, of having loving repeating being as a conscious feeling.

As I was saying mostly all children have in them loving repeating being as important in them to them and to every one around them. Mostly growing young men and growing young women have to themselves very little loving repeating being, they do not have it to each other then most of them, they have it to older ones then as older ones have it to them loving repeating being, not loving repeating being but repeating as the way of being in them, repeating of the whole of them as coming every minute from them.

In the middle living of men and women there are very different ways of feeling to repeating, some have more and more in them loving repeating as a conscious feeling, some have less and less liking in them for the repeating in, to them, of mostly every one. Mostly every one has a loving feeling for repeating in some way. Some have not any such loving even in the repeating going on inside themselves then, not even for any one they are loving.

Some then have always growing in them more and more loving feeling for the repeating in every one. Many have not any loving for repeating in many of those around them.

There are then many ways of feeling in one about repeating. There are many ways of knowing repeating when one sees and hears and feels it in every one.

Loving repeating then is important being in some. This is now some description of the importance of loving repeating being in one.

Some find it interesting to find inside them repeating in them of some one they have known or some relation to them coming out in them, some never have any such feeling in them, some have not any liking for such being in them. Some like to see such being in others around them but not in themselves inside them. There are many ways of feeling in one about all these kinds of repeating. Sometime there will be written the history of all of them.

To begin again then with some description of the meaning of loving repeating being when it is strongly in a man or in a woman, when it is in them their way of understanding everything in living and there are very many always living of such being. This is now again a beginning of a little description of it in one.

Repeating of the whole of them is then always in every one. There are different stages in being, there is being babies and children and then growing young men or women and grown young men or women and men or women in middle living and in growing old and in ending. There are many kinds of men and women and soon now there will be a beginning of a history of all of them who ever were or are or will be living. There will be then here written a history of some of them. To begin again then with loving repeating being as a bottom nature in some. To begin again with the developing of it in one.

As I was saying children have it in them to have strongly loving repeating being as a conscious feeling in so far as they can be said to have such a thing in them. It gives to them a solid feeling of knowing they are safe in living. With growing it comes to be more in some, it comes to be less in others of them. Mostly there is very little conscious loving repeating feeling in growing young men and women.

In the beginning then, in remembering, repeating was strongly in the feeling of one, in the feeling of many, in the feeling of most of them who have it to have strongly in them their earthy feeling of being part of the solid dirt around them. This is one kind of being. This is mostly of one kind of being, of slow-minded resisting fighting being. This is now a little a description of one.

Slowly then some go on living, they may be fairly quick in learning, some of such of them seem very quick and impetuous in learning and in acting but such learning has for such of them very little meaning, it is the slow repeating resisting inside them that has meaning for them. Now there will be a little a description of loving repeating being in one of such of them.

The kinds and ways of repeating, of attacking and resisting in different kinds of men and women, the practical, the emotional, the sensitive, the every kind of being in every one who ever was or is or will be living, I know so much about all of them, many of them are very clear in kinds of men and women, in individual men and women, I know them so well inside them, repeating in them has so much meaning to knowing, more and more I know all there is of all being, more and more I know it in all the ways it is in them and comes out of them, sometime there will be a history of every one, sometime all history of all men and women will be inside some one.

Now there will be a little description of the coming to be history of all men and women, in some one. This is then to be a little history of such a one. This is then now to be a little description of loving repeating being in one.

Almost every one has it in them in their beginning to have loving repeating being strongly in them. Some of them have attacking being as the bottom nature in them, some of them have resisting being as the bottom nature in them. Some of both these kinds of them have more or less in all their living loving repeating being in them, it works differently in them to come out of them in these two kinds of them. Later there will be much description of the way it comes out from them and is in them in the different kinds of them. Now there is to be a little description of it in one having resisting as the way of winning fighting. This is now some description of such a one having loving repeating being developing into completed understanding. Now to slowly begin.

The relation of learning to being, of thinking to feeling, of realisation to emotion, all these and many others are very complicated questions. Sometimes there will be much description of them with the kinds of men and women with being in them, with mixtures in them, that complicates them. There will sometime be a history of every one. This is a sure thing.

Now again to begin. The relation of learning and thinking to being, of feeling to realising is a complicated question. There will now be very little talking of such way of being. As I was saying some have it in them to have slowly resisting as their natural way of being can have learning and thinking come quickly enough in them. This is then not bottom being in them. It is bottom being in some of such of them. This is very clear now in my knowing. Now to begin again with it as telling.

Some then who are of that kind of being who have slow resisting being as their way to wisdom have it in them to be quick in learning and in thinking and in acting. As I was saying in some this is not of the bottom nature in them, in some it is bottom nature in them for the slow resisting winning bottom to them was not put in in the making of them, in some it is in them but dull and not mixing in their living, in some it is not sensitive to action in their living, it is there in them going on inside them not connecting on with the rest of them. This is not just talking, this all has real meaning. These are all then of a kind of men and women who have resisting being as the real wisdom in them. In some of such of them they seem to be winning by acting by attacking they live so very successfully in living but nevertheless they are of the kind of them that have resisting winning as their real way of fighting although never in their living does this act in them. Careful listening to the whole of them always repeating shows this in them, what kind they are of men and women.

To begin again. This is now some description of one having loving repeating as a way to wisdom, having slowly resisting winning as the bottom being. As I was saying learning in such a one and thinking about everything can be quick enough in the beginning.

The important thing then in knowing the bottom nature in any one is the way their real being slowly comes to be them, the whole of them comes to be repeating in them.

As I was saying some can have quick learning and nervous attacking or one or the other in them with slow resisting being in them as their natural way of winning. There is every kind of mixing. There is every degree of intensification. There is every degree of hastening the resisting into more rapid realisation. There is every degree of hurrying. In short there are all degrees of intensification and rapidity in motion and mixing and disguising and yet the kind he is each one, the kind she is each one, comes to be clear in the repeating that more and more steadily makes them clear to any one looking hard at them. These kinds then are existing, the independent dependent, the dependent independent, the one with attacking as the way of winning, the other with resisting as the way of wisdom for them. I know then this is true of every one that each one is of one or the other kind of these two kinds of them. I know it is in them, I know many more things about these two kinds of them. Slowly they come to be clearer in every one, sometime perhaps it will be clear to every one. Sometime perhaps some one will have completely in them the history of every one of everything in every one and the degree and kind and way of being of everything in each one in them from their beginning to their ending and coming out of them.

This is then a beginning of the way of knowing everything in every one, of knowing the complete history of each one who ever is or was or will be living. This is then a little description of the winning of so much wisdom.

As I was saying the important thing is having loving repeating being, that is the beginning of learning the complete history of every one. That being must always be in such a one, one who has it in them sometime to have in them the completed history of every one they ever can hear of as having being.

There are so many ways of beginning this description, and now once more to make a beginning.

Always repeating is all of living, everything that is being is always repeating, more and more listening to repeating gives to me completed understanding. Each one then slowly comes to be a whole one to me, each one slowly comes to be a whole one in me, slowly it sounds louder and louder and louder inside me through my ears and eyes and feelings and the talking there is always in me the repeating that is the whole of each one I come to know around, and each one of them then comes to be a whole one to me, comes to be a whole one in me. Loving repeating is one way of being. This is now a description of such being.

Always from the beginning there was to me all living as repeating. This was not in me then a conscious being. Always more and more this is in me developing to a completed being. This is now again a beginning of a little description of such being.

In their beginning as children every one has in them loving repeating being. This is for them then their natural being. Later in conscious being some have much in them of loving repeating being, some have in them almost nothing of such feeling. There are then these two kinds of them. This is then one way of thinking of them.

There are two kinds of men and women, those who have in them resisting as their way of winning those who have in them attacking as their way of winning fighting, there are many kinds, many very many kinds of each of these two kinds of men and women, sometime there will be written a description of all the kinds of them. Now this division is accepted by me and I will now give a little more description of loving repeating being and then go on to describing how it comes to slowly give to me completed understanding, loving repeating being always in me acting, of this one and that one, and then there will be some description of resembling coming to be clear by looking at the repeating in men and women and then there will be more history of Martha Hersland and the best coming out of her all her living and the being in every one she came to know in living.

Always then from the beginning there was in me always increasing as a conscious feeling loving repeating being, learning to know repeating in every one, hearing the whole being of any one always repeating in that one every minute of their living. There was then always in me as a bottom nature to me an earthy, resisting slow understanding, loving repeating being. As I was saying this has nothing to do with ordinary learning, in a way with ordinary living. This will be clearer later in this description.

Many have loving repeating being in them, many never come to know it of them, many never have it as a conscious feeling, many have in it a restful satisfaction. Some have in it always more and more understanding, many have in it very little enlarging understanding. There is every kind of way of having loving repeating being as a bottom. It is very clear to me and to my feeling, it is very slow in developing, it is very important to make it clear now in writing, it must be done now with a slow description. To begin again then with it in my feeling, to begin again then to tell of the meaning to me in all repeating, of the loving there is in me for repeating.

Sometime every one becomes a whole one to me. For many years this was just forming in me. Now sometimes it takes many years for some one to be a whole one to me. For many years loving repeating was a bottom to me, I was never thinking then of the meaning of it in me, it had nothing then much to do with the learning, the talking, the thinking, nor the living then in me. There was for many years a learning and talking and questioning in me and not listening to repeating in every one around me. Then slowly loving repeating being came to be a conscious feeling in me. Slowly then every one sometime became a whole one to me.

Now I will tell of the meaning in me of repeating, of the loving repeating being there is now always in me.

In loving repeating being then to completed understanding there must always be a feeling for all changing, a feeling for living being that is always in repeating. This is now again a beginning of a description of my feeling.

Always then I am thinking and feeling the repeating in each one as I know them. Always then slowly each one comes to be a whole one to me. As I was saying loving repeating in every one, hearing always all repeating, coming to completed understanding of each one is to me a natural way of being.

There are many that I know and always more and more I know it. They are all of them repeating and I hear it. They are all of them living and I know it. More and more I understand it, always more and more it has completed history in it.

Every one has their own being in them. Every one is of a kind of men and women. Always more and more I know the whole history of each one. This is now a little a description of such knowing me. This is now a little a description of beginning of hearing repeating all around me.

As I was saying learning, thinking, living in the beginning of being men and women often has in it very little of real being. Real being, the bottom nature, often does not then in the beginning do very loud repeating. Learning, thinking, talking, living, often then is not of the real bottom being. Some are this way all their living. Some slowly come to be repeating louder and more clearly the bottom being that makes them. Listening to repeating, knowing being in every one who ever was or is or will be living slowly came to be in me a louder and louder pounding. Now I have it to my feeling to feel all living, to be always listening to the slightest changing, to have each one come to be a whole one to me from the repeating in each one that sometime I come to be understanding. Listening to repeating is often irritating, listening to repeating can be dulling, always repeating is all of living, everything in a being is always repeating, always more and more listening to repeating gives to me completed understanding. Each one slowly comes to be a whole one to me. Each one slowly comes to be a whole one in me.

In the beginning then learning and thinking and talking and feeling and loving and working in me mostly was not bottom being in me. Slowly it came out in me the feeling for living in repeating that now by listening and watching and feeling everything coming out of each one and always repeating the whole one gives to me completed understanding.

There was a time when I was questioning, always asking, when I was talking, wondering, there was a time when I was feeling, thinking and all the time then I did not know repeating, I did not see or hear or feel repeating. There was a long time then when there was nothing in me using the bottom loving repeating being that now leads me to knowing. Then I was attacking, questioning, wondering, thinking, always at the bottom was loving repeating being, that was not then there to my conscious being. Sometime there will be written a long history of such a beginning.

Always then there was there a recognition of the thing always repeating, the being in each one, and always then thinking, feeling, talking, living, was not of this real being. Slowly I came to hear repeating. More and more then I came to listen, now always and always I listen and always now each one comes to be a whole one in me.

1906–8   1925

World War I and Its Aftermath

By some measures, World War I was a relatively contained event for citizens of the United States. The official American combat presence in the war lasted only seventeen months, from the declaration of war by the U.S. Congress on April 6, 1917, to the armistice declared in western Europe on November 11, 1918. The arrival of the first waves of United States forces in the summer and fall of 1917 helped break what had become an immensely bloody and costly stalemate between the Central Powers (Germany, Austria-Hungary, and Turkey) and the Allies (Great Britain, France, Russia, Italy, and Japan) along the line of trenches extending across western Europe. With the full weight of American industrial, financial, and agricultural power now fortifying the Allies, and with American president Woodrow Wilson having proposed a relatively merciful set of conditions for their surrender, the Central Powers began negotiating in earnest for peace. By the war's end, some 365,000 American soldiers had been killed or wounded in carrying out President Wilson's famous call to "make the world safe for democracy." American casualty rates were high, but the war had not devastated either the landscape or the economy of the United States. The American Civil War, by contrast, had raged over American soil for four years, from 1861 to 1865, costing the armies on both sides a total of more than 1.1 million killed and wounded (and many civilian casualties as well), and wrecked the Southern economy for decades.

The impact of World War I on the United States and its literature, however, was deep and broad. From the moment war broke out, Americans plunged into debate over the responsibilities of the United States in relation to the rest of the world. Some Americans, including writers and artists who had lived abroad or who felt specially connected to Great Britain and France, vociferously argued for an early U.S. entry into the war on the Allied side: during her American tour of 1916, for example, the pioneering modern dancer Isadora Duncan concluded her recitals with an impassioned solo on the French national anthem, the *Marseillaise,* coupled with a speech urging Americans to join the fight for the Allies. Some, like the poet Alan Seeger, acted on their loyalties by joining the French Foreign Legion or the ambulance corps of the Red Cross as volunteers early in the war. Still other Americans, however, felt that the United States ought to keep its distance from the war: why should Americans go to the rescue of a European continent entangled in ancient alliances and dynastic rivalries, decaying empires and stifling class hierarchies? In the conflict's early stages, antiwar Americans included committed left-wing activists and writers like John Reed, who saw revolutionary possibilities in the prospect of Europe's advanced capitalist societies destroying one another; Americans who had emigrated from Germany and other of the Central Powers; and religious pacifists and humanitarian liberals who believed that human progress could and should make war obsolete.

As the conflict went on, though, the German strategy of attacking merchant ships at sea—including ships carrying U.S. citizens as passengers—hardened American public opinion against the Central Powers and enabled President Wilson to obtain an overwhelming congressional majority in favor of American entry into the war. With war declared, the U.S. government acted quickly, on a wide front, to mobilize American society. For the first time since the Civil War, the U.S. Congress enacted a law to conscript men into the armed forces. A host of new government agencies sprang up to coordinate the American economy in the war effort: the Council of National Defense, the War Industries Board, the War Trade Board, the Food Administration. Other government agencies, like the Committee on Public Information, set out to sell the war to the American public with the aid of new twentieth-century media like films and newsreels. When some newspapers and magazines refused the government's invitation to self-censor their views on the war, Congress responded with the Espionage Act of June 1917, which outlawed statements intended "to interfere with the operation or success of the military or naval forces."

Writers and artists on the left protested these restrictions on freedom of speech, but they were not the only Americans to experience the contradiction between the war's declared aim of making the world safe for democracy abroad and their daily lives. Antiimmigrant feeling rose, especially against German-Americans; Woodrow Wilson declared to Congress in 1918 that "Any man who carries a hyphen about him carries a dagger that he is ready to plunge into the vitals of this Republic." Militant suffragists denounced the hypocrisy of crusading for democracy abroad while denying the vote to women at home. While some leaders of organized labor allied themselves with management and government in the war effort, others dissented. The draft and the growth of war-related industries opened up jobs that drew black Americans from the rural South to the cities of the North, where their growing urban communities came under white attack in a series of race riots both before and after the war. African Americans who volunteered for or were drafted into the segregated armed forces also registered the contradiction between American ideals of democracy and their treatment as second-class citizens. Many men and women caught up in it found that the fundamental conditions of modern warfare undermined clean-cut, idealistic notions of the war's aims. In E. E. Cummings's *The Enormous Room*, the French military bureaucracy oppresses the common soldiers of its own army no less than those of the enemy; in Ernest Hemingway's experience of the Italian front as recorded in his letters, the sheer firepower of modern artillery far exceeds his commanders' ability to make sense of either their immediate tactical situation or the war's ultimate purpose.

The waste and futility that marked so much of the military effort expended in World War I not only eroded popular deference to the wisdom of generals and politicians, but also licensed rebellion against literary traditions. Cummings's multilingual, colloquial literary style in *The Enormous Room* defies the routines of bureaucratic language even as his autobiographical narrator refuses to defer to his jailors. Gertrude Stein's matter-of-fact, concrete, at times gossipy tone in *The Autobiography of Alice B. Toklas* declines to moralize the end of the war as a high drama of ideals achieved. Whether they witnessed World War I at first hand or from a distance, Americans saw the home of nineteenth-century European high culture at once exploded into bits and, in another way, bound together by a shared nightmare. Both Europe's fragmentation and the grip of the war's shared experiences found their way into high modernist works of postwar American writing like T. S. Eliot's *The Waste Land* and Ezra Pound's "Hugh Selwyn Mauberley."

ALAN SEEGER

Born in New York City, Alan Seeger (1888–1916) was educated at private schools before entering Harvard in 1906, where he became one of the editors of the *Harvard Monthly* and a contributor of poetry to its pages; among his Harvard classmates was T. S. Eliot. Looking for literary circles, Seeger returned to New York after graduating from Harvard, and in 1912 moved on to Paris. Although Paris by that time was a hub of artistic experimentation and the home of radical American modernists like Gertrude Stein, Seeger's own artistic tastes were less adventurous, and he seems to have made little contact with Paris's innovators before the outbreak of World War I inspired him to join the French Foreign Legion. Seeger's wartime letters to newspapers in the United States acknowledged some of the miseries of trench combat for the soldier "[e]xposed to all the dangers of war, but with none of its enthusiasm or splendid *élan*"; his poetry, however, romanticized the sacrifices of military service. Published after Seeger's death in combat, "I Have a Rendezvous with Death . . ." became one of the most widely anthologized American poems of the war. Reviewing Seeger's poems after his death, his former classmate T. S. Eliot declared them "high-flown, heavily decorated and solemn"—and "so out of date as to be almost a positive quality."

I Have a Rendezvous with Death . . .

I have a rendezvous with Death
At some disputed barricade,
When Spring comes back with rustling shade
And apple-blossoms fill the air—
I have a rendezvous with Death   5
When Spring brings back blue days and fair.

It may be he shall take my hand
And lead me into his dark land
And close my eyes and quench my breath—
It may be I shall pass him still.   10
I have a rendezvous with Death
On some scarred slope of battered hill,
When Spring comes round again this year
And the first meadow-flowers appear.

God knows 'twere better to be deep   15
Pillowed in silk and scented down,
Where Love throbs out in blissful sleep,
Pulse nigh to pulse, and breath to breath,
Where hushed awakenings are dear . . .
But I've a rendezvous with Death   20
At midnight in some flaming town,
When Spring trips north again this year,
And I to my pledged word am true,
I shall not fail that rendezvous.

1917

JOHN REED

One of the most important left-leaning journalists of World War I, John Reed (1887–1920) was born to a well-off family in Portland, Oregon. Like Alan Seeger, he attended Harvard, became an editor and poetry contributor for the *Harvard Monthly*, and moved to New York City after graduating. In New York, however, Reed moved into increasingly radical political circles, and in 1913 he joined the staff of *The Masses*, a socialist journal. *The Masses* sent Reed to cover the Mexican revolution in 1914 and he made two extended trips to Europe during World War I; his foreign reporting during these years was collected into two books, *Insurgent Mexico* (1914) and *The War in Eastern Europe* (1916). Along with his wife, the journalist Louise Bryant (1885–1936), Reed made a trip to Russia in 1917; in Petrograd, then Russia's capital, they witnessed the revolution of October 1917 in which Vladimir Lenin's Bolshevik party seized power. Reed authored two enthusiastic books about the Russian Revolution, *Red Russia* and *Ten Days That Shook the World*; both became international sensations on their publication in 1919. Back in the United States, his articles opposing American involvement in the war contributed to charges of sedition being brought against *The Masses*, and after his return from Russia Reed himself was indicted for sedition. He fled to Europe on a forged passport and eventually made his way back to Russia, where he continued to report on the events of the Russian Revolution until his death from typhus—one of many such deaths in the crowded, impoverished cities of postwar eastern Europe—in 1920. "One Solid Month of Liberty," published in *The Masses* in September 1917, denounces wartime repressions of civil liberties in the United States and questions wartime propaganda that assigned all the brutalities of the war to the German side.

One Solid Month of Liberty

In America the month just past has been the blackest month for freemen our generation has known. With a sort of hideous apathy the country has acquiesced in a regime of judicial tyranny, bureaucratic suppression and industrial barbarism, which followed inevitably the first fine careless rapture of militarism.

Who that heard it will ever forget the feeling of despair he experienced when Judge Mayer charged the jury in the Berkman-Goldman trial.[1]

"This is not a question of free speech," he said, "for *free speech is guaranteed under the Constitution*. No American worthy of the name believes in anything else than free speech, *but free speech does not mean license* . . . . . . [sic] Free speech means that frank, free, clear and orderly expression in which every man and woman in the land, citizen or alien, may engage in *lawful and orderly fashion* . . . . . . [sic]"

The italics are ours. The definition is the new American definition of freedom—the freedom for which countless millions have died in the long uphill pull of civilization—which is, in effect, "freedom is the right to do what nobody in power can possibly object to."

* * *

1. Anarchists Alexander Berkman (1870–1936) and Emma Goldman (1869–1940) were convicted of conspiracy to defeat the military conscription laws and sentenced July 9, 1917, by Judge Julius M. Mayer to two years in prison; in 1919, following their prison terms, both were deported to the Soviet Union.

Next in order is the wholesale suppression of the radical press by the Post Office, some eighteen periodicals, among them THE MASSES, being denounced as "unmailable" under the Espionage Act, without any specific grounds being specified.[2]

"Because," Solicitor Lamar[3] is reported to have said to the representative of one paper, "if I told you what we objected to, you'd manage to get around the law some way."

Now I happen to have been one of those who lost a good many pounds fighting the original censorship provision of the Espionage Bill in Washington. And we licked it, finally, in the face of the whole Administration. But what did the Administration care? It does what it pleases, and finds a law to back it up. If the entire Espionage Act had been defeated, some obscure statute passed in 1796 would have been exhumed, and the radical press suppressed just the same.

All of which goes to prove that in America law is merely the instrument for good or evil of the most powerful interest, and there are no Constitutional safeguards worth the powder to blow them to hell.

The attack of soldiers and sailors in Boston upon the July first parade and the Socialist headquarters, which sent a thrill of rage through the heart of every lover of liberty in this country, was followed by two horrors more sinisterly suggestive.[4]

The first was the race riot in East Saint Louis, where the large negro town was sacked and burned, and more than thirty black people, men and women, were butchered. Eye-witnesses tell how innocent negro passers-by were pursued by white men with smoking guns, who shot them down in the streets and then kicked their dead faces to jelly; how white women with streaming hair and foaming lips dragged negresses from street cars and cut them mortally in the breasts with knives.[5]

All this of course outdoes the feeble German atrocities. It rivals the abominations of Putumayo and the Congo.[6] The "war of civilization" begins to lose its drawing power. And the spirit of our own American soldiers in battle is beginning to appall those who know it. Read Arthur Guy Empey's "Over the Top" if you want to know how barbarians revel in sheer butchery.[7] I met a friend who had served in the British army. "I have killed eight Huns with my own hands," he boasted, "and I want to kill ten more. Greatest sport in the world." Killing niggers is, of course, also great sport.

✳　✳　✳

2. Passed by the U.S. Congress on June 15, 1917, the Espionage Act imposed fines of $10,000 and up to 20 years of imprisonment for persons convicted of disclosing defense-related information or interfering with military recruiting; antiwar journalists and periodicals were prosecuted or denied access to the U.S. mail under the act on the grounds that they interfered with recruiting.
3. William H. Lamar (1859–1928), U.S. solicitor responsible for prosecuting cases under the Espionage Act.
4. On July 1, 1917, an antiwar march in Boston was broken up by gangs of sailors and soldiers, who also ransacked and burned the Socialist party headquarters.
5. On July 2, 1917, the black community of East

St. Louis, Illinois, was attacked by working-class whites angry that black workers had been given jobs at a local factory under a wartime government contract. Some forty African Americans and eight whites were killed in the riot.
6. The "Putumayo Scandal" of 1907–14 focused world attention on the systemic enslavement, mutilation, and killing of native workers exploited in the rubber trade in Colombia and the northern Amazon region of South America; similar conditions had been exposed in Belgium's African colony, the Belgian Congo, in 1903.
7. Arthur Guy Empey (1883–1963), American volunteer in the British Army, wrote a popular account of his war service, Over the Top (1917).

The second mile-stone in the history of the New Freedom was the whole-sale deportation, at the point of a gun, of some hundreds of striking work-ingmen from the mines in Bisbee, Arizona, into the American desert. These strikers were loudly heralded as "I. W. W.'s"[8] in an attempt to bemuse the truth; but it is slowly leaking out that the mining company deported from Bisbee all the men who were striking in an orderly fashion for decent living wages and conditions, whether I. W. W.'s or not. And not only that, but all sympathizers with the strikers, and *even the strikers' attorney*! Many of these men lived in Bisbee, owned property there; some of them were torn from the arms of their wives and children. They were loaded on cattle-cars and sent to Columbus, N. M., whose outraged citizens promptly shipped them back north, until they halted in the middle of the desert—foodless, waterless, homeless.

At the present writing the United States Army is feeding these dangerous characters, and there is talk of interning them for the balance of the war on the ground that they have been subsidized by German gold. And in the mean-while, the Phelps-Dodge corporation, which owns the mines—and Bisbee—is not allowing any one to enter the town without a passport!

Samuel Gompers protested to the German trades-unions against the deportation of Belgian workingmen. But even the Germans didn't deport Belgians into the middle of a desert, without food or water, as Bisbee did—and yet Gompers hasn't uttered a single peep about Bisbee.[9]

* * *

This country-wide movement to wipe out organized labor, which was launched a year ago in Wall Street with such a flourish of trumpets, [. . .] is developing quietly but powerfully. An investigation recently made in Omaha, Nebraska, by Carl Sandburg, shows the businessmen of that community organizing along the lines of San Francisco, sending out invitations to scabs everywhere, and evidently framing up something on which a union man can be railroaded to the electric chair, as they railroaded Tom Mooney on the coast.[1]

* * * The suffrage pickets in front of the White House, set upon by mobs of government clerks, then by the police, arrested time and time again upon no charge, and finally committed to the workhouse for sixty days, were, as the world knows, hurriedly pardoned by the President as soon as it was evident how prominent they and their husbands were.[2] But at the same time that he

---

8. On July 12, 1917, nearly 2,000 striking copper mineworkers in Bisbee were forced onto cattle cars by vigilante groups, deported into New Mexico, and ultimately left stranded. The International Workers of the World (I.W.W.) had presented the mine owners with demands, including better safety conditions and an end to discrimination against union members and immigrant and minority workers; mine owners retaliated with rumors that the I.W.W. was a front for German war interests.
9. Samuel Gompers (1850–1924), American labor leader and first president of the American Federation of Labor; he supported the United States' entry into World War I.
1. Carl Sandburg in June 1917 attended the American Federation of Labor meeting in Omaha, Nebraska. Thomas J. Mooney (1892–1942), Cali-

fornia labor leader imprisoned for murder in 1916 following the explosion of a bomb that killed ten people at a pro-war parade. Mooney's death sentence was commuted to life in prison by President Woodrow Wilson; after evidence accumulated that his conviction had been engineered by false testimony, he was formally pardoned and released in 1939.
2. Members of the Woman's Party picketed the White House in June and July 1917, linking their demands for women's suffrage at home to the war effort abroad. Some of those arrested were prominent society women, including the daughter of a former U.S. Secretary of State; Wilson not only pardoned them but eventually reversed his stand against women's suffrage, citing women's volunteer work during the war as justification.

pardoned them for their "crime," he intimated that he was too busy over his "War for Democracy" to give any attention to their petition—which was a petition for the fundamental rights of citizens.

It is the blackest month for freemen our generation has known.

1917

ERNEST HEMINGWAY

Denied entry into the U.S. armed forces because of poor eyesight, Ernest Hemingway (1899–1961) volunteered for the ambulance corps of the Red Cross and was sent to Italy in June 1918. On July 8, 1918, he was seriously wounded: hit by shrapnel from a mortar shell, he was awarded the Italian Silver Medal for Valor and spent several months recovering before returning home to Oak Park, Illinois, in January 1919. Hemingway's parents published some of his letters from the hospital in local newspapers; whether or not he knew this as he was writing, the letters seem to aim at a public tone of ironic, disillusioned courage and objective description. Hemingway drew on his experiences on the Italian front and in the military hospital for the character Frederic Henry, a wounded American officer, in his novel A Farewell to Arms (1929).

Letter of August 18, 1918, to His Parents

✷   ✷   ✷

You know they say there isn't anything funny about this war. And there isn't. I wouldn't say it was hell, because that's been a bit overworked since Gen. Sherman's time,[1] but there have been about 8 times when I would have welcomed Hell. Just on a chance that it couldn't come up to the phase of war I was experiencing. F'r example. In the trenches during an attack when a shell makes a direct hit in a group where you're standing. Shells aren't bad except direct hits. You must take chances on the fragments of the bursts. But when there is a direct hit your pals get spattered all over you. Spattered is literal. During the six days I was up in the Front line trenches, only 50 yds from the Austrians, I got the rep. of having a charmed life. The rep of having one doesn't mean much but having one does! I hope I have one. That knocking sound is my knuckles striking the wooden bed tray.

It's too hard to write on two sides of the paper so I'll skip.

Well I can now hold up my hand and say I've been shelled by high explosive, shrapnel and gas. Shot at by trench mortars, snipers and machine guns, and as an added attraction an aeroplane machine gunning the lines. I've never had a hand grenade thrown at me, but a rifle grenade struck rather close. Maybe I'll get a hand grenade later. Now out of all that mess to only be

---

1. William Tecumseh Sherman (1820–1891), a general in the Union Army during the Civil War noted for the destructiveness of his campaign in Georgia, said that "war is . . . hell" in an 1880 speech.

struck by a trench mortar and a machine gun bullet while advancing toward the rear, as the Irish say, was fairly lucky. What, Family?

The 227 wounds I got from the trench mortar didn't hurt a bit at the time, only my feet felt like I had rubber boots full of water on. Hot water. And my knee cap was acting queer. The machine gun bullet just felt like a sharp smack on my leg with an icy snow ball. However it spilled me. But I got up again and got my wounded into the dug out. I kind of collapsed at the dug out. The Italian I had with me had bled all over my coat and my pants looked like somebody had made current jelly in them and then punched holes to let the pulp out. Well the Captain who was a great pal of mine, It was his dug out said "Poor Hem he'll be R.I.P. soon." Rest In Peace, that is. You see they thought I was shot through the chest on account of my bloody coat. But I made them take my coat and shirt off. I wasn't wearing any undershirt, and the old torso was intact. Then they said I'd probably live. That cheered me up any amount. I told him in Italian that I wanted to see my legs, though I was afraid to look at them. So we took off my trousers and the old limbs were still there but gee they were a mess. They couldn't figure out how I had walked 150 yards with a load with both knees shot through and my right shoe punctured two big places. Also over 200 flesh wounds. "Oh," says I, "My Captain, it is of nothing. In America they all do it! It is thought well not to allow the enemy to perceive that they have captured our goats!"[2]

The goat speech required some masterful lingual ability but I got it across and then went to sleep for a couple of minutes. After I came to they carried me on a stretcher three kilometers to a dressing station. The stretcher bearers had to go over lots because the road was having the "entrails" shelled out of it. Whenever a big one would come, Whee - whoosh - Boom - they'd lay me down and get flat. My wounds were now hurting like 227 little devils were driving nails into the raw. The dressing station had been evacuated during the attack so I lay for two hours in a stable, with the roof shot off, waiting for an ambulance. When it came I ordered it down the road to get the soldiers that had been wounded first. It came back with a load and then they lifted me in. The shelling was still pretty thick and our batteries were going off all the time way back of us and the big 250's and 350's[3] going over head for Austria with a noise like a railway train. Then we'd hear the bursts back of the lines. Then there would come a big Austrian shell and then the crash of the burst. But we were giving them more and bigger stuff than they sent. Then a battery of field guns would go off, just back of the shed—boom, boom, boom, boom, and the Seventy-Fives or 149's[4] would go whipping over to the Austrian lines, and the star shells going up all the time and the machines going like rivetters, tat-a-tat, tat-a-tat.

✳ ✳ ✳

I sent you that cable so you wouldn't worry. I've been in the Hospital a month and 12 days and hope to be out in another month. The Italian Surgeon did a peach of a job on my right knee joint and right foot. Took 28 stitches and assures me that I will be able to walk as well as ever. The wounds

---

2. Hemingway plays with his Italian commander's ignorance of the American idiom "to get someone's goat"—i.e., to make someone betray anger or irritation.

3. Large artillery shells of 250 and 350 millimeters

in diameter (about 10 and 14 inches respectively).

4. Medium-caliber artillery guns designed to move with military units in the field and firing ammunition of 75 and 149 millimeters (about 3 and 6 inches respectively).

all healed up clean and there was no infection. He has my right leg in a plaster splint now so that the joint will be all right. I have some snappy souvenirs that he took out at the last operation.

I wouldn't really be comfortable now unless I had some pain. The Surgeon is going to cut the plaster off in a week now and will allow me on crutches in 10 days.

I'll have to learn to walk again.

✳   ✳   ✳

E. E. CUMMINGS

Following the U.S. entry into World War I, E. E. Cummings (1894–1962) volunteered for the Ambulance Corps of the American Red Cross in France. In Paris he befriended another American volunteer, William Slater Brown, who like Cummings was fluent in French. Brown and Cummings socialized with French soldiers, imbibing some of their cynicism about the war and about France's military bureaucracy; French wartime censors, reading Brown's letters, imprisoned both men. *The Enormous Room* records Cummings's ensuing three months in French jails and prison camps. The novelist John Dos Passos, reviewing *The Enormous Room* for *The Dial*, praised its "reckless," colloquial, and vividly personal style in rendering Cummings's encounter with "a bit of the underside of History." In this excerpt from an early chapter, Cummings is held in a detainment cell previously inhabited by both German and French prisoners.

From The Enormous Room

Chapter Two

EN ROUTE

I put the bed-roll down. I stood up.

I was myself.

An uncontrollable joy gutted me after three months of humiliation, of being bossed and herded and bullied and insulted. I was myself and my own master.

In this delirium of relief (hardly noticing what I did) I inspected the pile of straw, decided against it, set up my bed, disposed the roll on it, and began to examine my cell.

I have mentioned the length and breadth. The cell was ridiculously high; perhaps ten feet. The end with the door in it was peculiar. The door was not placed in the middle of this end, but at one side, allowing for a huge iron can waist-high which stood in the other corner. Over the door and across the end, a grating extended. A slit of sky was always visible.

Whistling joyously to myself, I took three steps which brought me to the door end. The door was massively made, all of iron or steel I should think. It delighted me. The can excited my curiosity. I looked over the edge of it. At the bottom reposefully lay a new human turd.

* * *

It was then that I noticed the walls. Arm-high they were covered with designs, mottos, pictures. The drawing had all been done in pencil. I resolved to ask for a pencil at the first opportunity.

There had been Germans and Frenchmen imprisoned in this cell. On the right wall, near the door-end, was a long selection from Goethe, laboriously copied. Near the other end of this wall a satiric landscape took place. The technique of this landscape frightened me. There were houses, men, children. And there were trees. I began to wonder what a tree looks like, and laughed copiously.

The back wall had a large and exquisite portrait of a German officer.

The left wall was adorned with a yacht, flying a number—13. "My beloved boat" was inscribed in German underneath. Then came a bust of a German soldier, very idealized, full of unfear. After this, a masterful crudity—a doughnut-bodied rider, sliding with fearful rapidity down the acute backbone of a totally transparent sausage-shaped horse who was moving simultaneously in five directions. The rider had a bored expression as he supported the stiff reins in one fist. His further leg assisted in his flight. He wore a German soldier's cap and was smoking. I made up my mind to copy the horse and rider at once, so soon that is as I should have obtained a pencil.

Last, I found a drawing surrounded by a scrolled motto. The drawing was a potted plant with four blossoms. The four blossoms were elaborately dead. Their death was drawn with a fearful care. An obscure deliberation was exposed in the depiction of their drooping petals. The pot tottered very crookedly on a sort of table, as near as I could see. All around ran a funereal scroll. I read: "Mes derniers adieux à ma femme aimée, Gaby."[1] A fierce hand, totally distinct from the former, wrote in proud letters above: "Tombé pour désert. Six ans de prison—dégradation militaire."[2]

It must have been five o'clock. Steps. A vast cluttering of the exterior of the door—by whom? Whang opens the door. Turnkey-creature extending a piece of chocolat with extreme and surly caution. I say "Merci"[3] and seize chocolat, Klang shuts the door.

I am lying on my back, the twilight does mistily bluish miracles thru the slit over the whang-klang. I can just see leaves, meaning trees.

Then from the left and way off, faintly, broke a smooth whistle, cool like a peeled willow-branch, and I found myself listening to an air from Pétrouchka, Pétrouchka, which we saw in Paris at the Châtelet, mon ami et moi . . .[4]

The voice stopped in the middle—and I finished the air. This code continued for a half-hour.

It was dark.

I had laid a piece of my piece of chocolat on the window-sill. As I lay on my back, a little silhouette came along the sill and ate that piece of a piece,

---

1. My last farewell to my beloved wife, Gaby (French).
2. Condemned for desertion. Six years in prison. Military degradation (French): loss of rank.
3. Thanks (French).

4. My friend and I (French). "Pétrouchka": modernist ballet set to music by Igor Stravinsky and choreographed by Mikhail Fokine (1911). "Châtelet": Théâtre de Châtelet, the Musical Theater of Paris.

taking something like four minutes to do so. He then looked at me, I then smiled at him, and we parted, each happier than before.

My cellule[5] was cool, and I fell asleep easily.

* * *

I contemplate the bowl which contemplates me. A glaze of greenish grease seals the mystery of its content. I induce two fingers to penetrate the seal. They bring me up a flat sliver of choux and a large, hard, thoughtful, solemn, uncooked bean. To pour the water off (it is warmish and sticky) without committing a nuisance is to lift the cover off Ça Pue.[6] I did.

Thus leaving beans and cabbage-slivers. Which I ate hurryingly, fearing a ventral misgiving.

I pass a lot of time cursing myself about the pencil, looking at my walls, my unique interior.

Suddenly I realize the indisputable grip of nature's humorous hand. One evidently stands on Ça Pue in such cases. Having finished, panting with stink, I tumble on the bed and consider my next move.

The straw will do. Ouch, but it's Dirty.—Several hours elapse . . .

Stepsandfumble. Klang. Repetition of promise to Monsieur Savy, etc.

Turnkeyish and turnkeyish. Identical expression. One body collapses sufficiently to deposit a hunk of bread and a piece of water.

Give your bowl.

I gave it, smiled and said: "Well, how about that pencil?"

"Pencil?" T-c looked at t-c.[7]

They recited then the following word: "Tomorrow." Klangandfootsteps.

So I took matches, burnt, and with just 60 of them wrote the first stanza of a ballade. Tomorrow I will write the second. Day after tomorrow the third. Next day the refrain. After—oh, well.

My whistling of Pétrouchka brought no response this evening.

So I climbed on Ça Pue, whom I now regarded with complete friendliness; the new moon was unclosing sticky wings in dusk, a far noise from near things.

I sang a song the "dirty Frenchmen" taught us, mon ami et moi. The song says Bon soir, Madame la Lune. . . . [8] I did not sing out loud, simply because the moon was like a mademoiselle, and I did not want to offend the moon. My friends: the silhouette and la lune, not counting Ça Pue, whom I regarded almost as a part of me.

Then I lay down, and heard (but could not see) the silhouette eat something or somebody . . . and saw, but could not hear, the incense of Ça Pue mount gingerly upon the taking air of twilight.

The next day.—Promise to M. Savy. Whang. "My pencil?"—"You don't need any pencil, you're going away."—"When?"—"Directly."—"How directly?"—"In an hour or two: your friend has already gone before. Get ready."

Klangandsteps.

Everyone very sore about me. Je m'en fous pas mal,[9] however.

5. Cell (French).
6. It Stinks (French); Cummings's nickname for the iron can that serves as his lavatory. "Choux": cabbage (French). Cummings is looking at a bowl of soup brought to him by his jailors.

7. Cummings's abbreviation of "Turnkey-creature," his contemptuous term for his jailors.
8. Good evening, Madame Moon (French); title of a popular prewar French cabaret tune.
9. I don't give a damn (French).

One hour I guess.
Steps. Sudden throwing of door open. Pause.
"Come out, American."

*　　*　　*

1922

JESSIE REDMON FAUSET

One of the central writers of the Harlem Renaissance, Jessie Redmon Fauset (1882?–1961) was the first black woman to attend Cornell University. She taught Latin and French in high schools in Washington D.C. and New York City before becoming literary editor at *The Crisis* magazine, the journal of the National Association for the Advancement of Colored People (NAACP). Her career as a novelist began with *There Is Confusion* (1924), a group portrait of young African Americans in the black communities of New York and Washington D.C. Like her other novels—including *Plum Bun* (1928), *The Chinaberry Tree* (1931), and *Comedy: American Style* (1933)—*There Is Confusion* concerns itself primarily with the dilemmas of a literate, ambitious black middle class. Although some critics, both in her own time and afterward, lamented Fauset's focus on genteel characters, she represents her urban middle-class communities as buzzing with debate over the standing of African Americans nationwide. In *There Is Confusion*, her characters monitor reports of lynching from the South, argue over whether blacks should enlist in World War I to fight on behalf of a segregated country, and trade reports of postwar repression aimed at African Americans. In this excerpt, Peter Bye, the well-educated but drifting son of a proud Philadelphia family, has enlisted in a black regiment sent to France, where he finds the Allied armies painfully divided by race. For African American soldiers in Fauset's novel, the willingness of French women to associate openly with black men comes as a revelation; white American soldiers retaliate violently to enforce the racial segregation they are accustomed to at home.

From There Is Confusion

*　　*　　*

This town, the end of Brittany and the furthest western outpost of France, always remained in Peter's memory as a horrible prelude to a most horrible war. Brest[1] up to the time that Europe had gone so completely and so suddenly insane, had been the typical, stupid, monotonous French town with picturesquely irregular pavements, narrow tortuous streets, dark, nestling little shops and the inevitable public square. Around and about the city to all sides stretched well ordered farms.

Then came the march of two million American soldiers across the town and the surrounding country. Under their careless feet the farms became mud, so that the name Brest recalls to the minds of thousands nothing if not a pic-

---

1. Major port city in northwestern France.

ture of the deepest, slimiest, stickiest mud that the world has known. All about were people, people, too many people, French and Americans. And finally the relations between the two nations, allies though they were, developed from misunderstandings into hot irritations, from irritations into clashes. First white Americans and Frenchmen clashed; separate restaurants and accommodations had to be arranged. Then came the inevitable clash between white and colored Americans; petty jealousies and meannesses arose over the courtesies of Frenchwomen and the lack of discrimination in the French cafés. The Americans found a new and inexplicable irritation in the French colored colonials.[2] Food was bad, prices were exorbitant; officers became tyrants. Everyone was at once in Brest and constantly about to leave it; real understanding and acquaintanceship were impossible.

Peter thought Dante might well have included this place in the description of his Inferno.[3] Here were Disease and Death, Mutilation and Murder. Stevedores and even soldiers became cattle and beasts of burden. Many black men were slaves. The thing from which France was to be defended could hardly be worse than this welter of human misunderstandings, the clashing of unknown tongues, the cynical investigations of the government, the immanence of war and the awful, persistent wretchedness of the weather.

The long wait turned into sudden activity and Peter's outfit was ordered to Lathus, thence to La Courtine,[4] one of the large training centers.

* * *

At Lathus, Harley Alexander met him in the little *place*.[5] "Seems to me you're got up regardless," Peter had commented. Alexander, one of the trimmest men in the regiment, was looking unusually shipshape, almost dapper.

The other struck him familiarly across the shoulder. "And that ain't all. Say, fellow, there's a band concert to-night right here in this little old square. I'm goin' and I'm goin' to take a lady."

"Lady! Where'd you get her?"

"Right here. These girls are all right. Not afraid of a dark skin. 'How should we have fear, m'soo,' one of them says to me, 'when you fight for our *patrie*[6] and when you are so *beau*? 'Beau' that's handsome, ain't it? Say this is some country to fight for; got some sense of appreciation. Better come along, old scout. There's a pile of loots[7] getting ready to come, each with a French dame in tow."

"I'll be there," Peter told him, laughing. "But count me out with the ladies. I can't get along with the domestic brand and I know I'll be out of luck with the foreign ones."

Some passing thought wiped the joy of anticipation from Harley's face. "My experience is that these foreign ones are a damn sight less foolish than some domestic ones I've met. Well, me for the concert."

---

2. Africans and other people of color from France's overseas colonies; some white American troops resented their relative social freedom in wartime France.
3. Dante Alighieri (1265–1321), Italian poet. The *Inferno*, the first part of Dante's epic *The Divine Comedy* (1310–14), tells of Dante's journey through hell.
4. Towns in central France.
5. Town square (French).
6. The fatherland (French).
7. Shortened, Americanized version of *poilus*, nickname for French infantrymen.

But that band concert never came off. At sunset a company of white American Southerners marched into Lathus down the main street, past the little *place*. There was a sudden uproar.

"Look! Darkies and white women! Come on, fellows, kill the damned niggers!"

There was a hasty onslaught in which the colored soldiers even taken by surprise gave as good as they took. Between these two groups from the same soil there was grimmer, more determined fighting than was seen at Verdun.[8] The French civil population stood on the church-steps opposite the square and watched with amazement.

"*Nom de dieu!*[9] Are they crazy, then, these Americans, that they kill each other!"

The next day saw Peter's company on its way to La Courtine, a training center, where there were no women. Thence they moved presently to the front in the Metz[1] sector.

*   *   *

1924

---

8. The battle of Verdun, one of the longest and bloodiest of World War I.
9. Name of God! (French).

1. City in northeastern France, near the German border.

JOHN ALLAN WYETH, JR.

Like Alan Seeger, John Allan Wyeth, Jr. (1894–1981) was born in New York City and attended an Ivy League college where he wrote poetry and had a more famous literary classmate: for Wyeth, the school was Princeton and his classmate the great modernist critic and journalist Edmund Wilson (1805–1972), who remembered Wyeth as the "aesthete" of his year. Unlike Seeger, Wyeth turned his combat experience in World War I—he enlisted in 1917, was sent to France in 1918, and saw the bloody battles on the Somme and at Verdun—into innovative rather than dated poetry. His only published book of poems, *This Man's Army: A War in Fifty-Odd Sonnets* (1928), transformed a literary form traditionally associated with love into a vehicle for colloquial dialogue and biting observation of men at war.

Fromereville[1]

War in Heaven[2]

A reek of steam—the bath-house rang with cries.
"Come across with the soap."
                    "Like hell, what makes you think it's yours?"
          "Don't turn *off the water*, that ain't fair

---

1. Village in the Alsatian region of France, near the German border; site of a large American station in World War I.
2. In John Milton's epic poem *Paradise Lost*

(1667), the angel Raphael tells Adam and Eve the story of the war in Heaven between the armies of God and those of Satan and the fallen angels.

I'm all *covered* with soap."
                                    "Hurry up, get out of the way."
"Thank God you're takin' a bath."
                                    "He wants to surprise us."
        "Oh is that so, well anyway I don't stink like you."

        "Air raid!"

                                    We ran out into the square,
naked and cold like souls on Judgment Day.
Over us, white clouds blazoned on blue skies,
and a green balloon on fire[3]—we watched it shrink
into flame and a fall of smoke. Around us, brute
guns belching puffs of shrapnel in the air,
where one plane swooping like a bird of prey
spat fire into a dangling parachute.

                                                            1928

3. Manned observation balloons were widely used in World War I to spy on the enemy's trench deployments. Under attack, their crews could attempt to escape by parachute.

GERTRUDE STEIN

One of the most accessible of Gertrude Stein's major works, *The Autobiography of Alice B. Toklas* is written in the voice of Stein's lover of several decades. Some of its most memorable recollections are of Toklas and Stein's time in France during World War I. Stein (1874–1946) and Toklas were traveling in England when the war broke out; as soon as the initial German advance on Paris was halted they returned to France, where they helped transport supplies for war relief efforts and provided warm hospitality to American soldiers after the U.S. entry into the war. When the Armistice was declared, they visited the frontline villages and the blasted landscapes left behind by trench warfare and bombardment. Back in Paris, they witnessed the parades celebrating victory and the influx of diplomats struggling to forge a lasting peace. *The Autobiography of Alice B. Toklas* appeared in 1933, as Hitler and the Nazi party were coming to power in Germany.

From The Autobiography of Alice B. Toklas

Time went on, we were very busy and then came the armistice.[1] We were the first to bring the news to many small villages. The french soldiers in the hospitals were relieved rather than glad. They seemed not to feel that it was going to be such a lasting peace. I remember one of them saying to Gertrude Stein when she said to him, well here is peace, at least for twenty years, he said.

        The next morning we had a telegram from Mrs. Lathrop.[2] Come at once want you to go with the french armies to Alsace.[3] We did not stop on the way. We made it in a day. Very shortly after we left for Alsace.

1. The November 11, 1918, armistice ending combat in World War I.
2. Isabel Stevens Lathrop (1868–1964), chair of the Paris depot of the American Fund for French

Wounded, was one of many socially well-connected American women involved in war relief.
3. Region of eastern France, on the German border.

* * *

Soon we came to the battle-fields and the lines of trenches of both sides. To any one who did not see it as it was then it is impossible to imagine it. It was not terrifying it was strange. We were used to ruined houses and even ruined towns but this was different. It was a landscape. And it belonged to no country.

I remember hearing a french nurse once say and the only thing she did say of the front was, c'est un paysage passionant, an absorbing landscape. And that was what it was as we saw it. It was strange. Camouflage, huts, everything was there. It was wet and dark and there were a few people, one did not know whether they were chinamen or europeans. Our fan-belt had stopped working. A staff car stopped and fixed it with a hairpin, we still wore hairpins.

Another thing that interested us enormously was how different the camouflage of the french looked from the camouflage of the germans, and then once we came across some very very neat camouflage and it was american.[4] The idea was the same but as after all it was different nationalities who did it the difference was inevitable. The colour schemes were different, the designs were different, the way of placing them was different, it made plain the whole theory of art and its inevitability.

* * *

Our business in Alsace was not hospitals but refugees. The inhabitants were returning to their ruined homes all over the devastated country and it was the aim of the A.F.F.W.[5] to give a pair of blankets, underclothing and children's and babies' woollen stockings and babies' booties to every family. There was a legend that the quantity of babies' booties sent to us came from the gifts sent to Mrs. Wilson who was supposed at that time to be about to produce a little Wilson.[6] There were a great many babies' booties but not too many for Alsace.

* * *

We once more returned to a changed Paris. We were restless. Gertrude Stein began to work very hard, it was at this time that she wrote her Accents in Alsace and other political plays, the last plays in Geography and Plays.[7] We were still in the shadow of war work and we went on doing some of it, visiting hospitals and seeing the soldiers left in them, now pretty well neglected by everybody. We had spent a great deal of our money during the war and we were economising, servants were difficult to get if not impossible, prices were high. We settled down for the moment with a femme de ménage[8] for only a few hours a day. I used to say Gertrude Stein was the chauffeur and I was the cook. We used to go over early in the morning to the public markets and get in our provisions. It was a confused world.

Jessie Whitehead[9] had come over with the peace commission as secretary to one of the delegations and of course we were very interested in knowing all about the peace. It was then that Gertrude Stein described one of the young men of the peace commission who was holding forth, as one who knew

---

4. Camouflage was invented in response to another innovation of World War I, attacks from airplanes on ground positions.
5. American Fund for French Wounded.
6. Edith Bolling Galt Wilson (1872–1961), second wife of U.S. president Woodrow Wilson.

7. *Geography and Plays*, published in 1922.
8. Cleaning woman (French).
9. Jessie Marie Whitehead, daughter of the mathematician and philosopher Alfred North Whitehead and Evelyn Whitehead, friends of Stein and Toklas in England.

all about the war, he had been here ever since the peace. Gertrude Stein's cousins came over, everybody came over, everybody was dissatisfied and every one was restless. It was a restless and disturbed world.

*　*　*

As I say we were restless and we were economical and all day and all evening we were seeing people and at last there was the defile, the procession under the Arc de Triomphe,[1] of the allies.

The members of the American Fund for French Wounded were to have seats on the benches that were put up the length of the Champs Elysées[2] but quite rightly the people of Paris objected as these seats would make it impossible for them to see the parade and so Clemenceau promptly had them taken down. Luckily for us Jessie Whitehead's room in her hotel looked right over the Arc de Triomphe and she asked us to come to it to see the parade. We accepted gladly. It was a wonderful day.

We got up at sunrise, as later it would have been impossible to cross Paris in a car. This was one of the last trips Auntie made.[3] By this time the red cross was painted off it but it was still a truck. Very shortly after it went its honourable way and was succeeded by Godiva, a two-seated runabout,[4] also a little ford. She was called Godiva because she had come naked into the world and each of our friends gave us something with which to bedeck her.

Auntie then was making practically her last trip. We left her near the river and walked up to the hotel. Everybody was on the streets, men, women, children, soldiers, priests, nuns, we saw two nuns being helped into a tree from which they would be able to see. And we ourselves were admirably placed and we saw perfectly.

We saw it all, we saw first the few wounded from the Invalides[5] in their wheeling chairs wheeling themselves. It is an old french custom that a military procession should always be preceded by the veterans from the Invalides. They all marched past through the Arc de Triomphe. Gertrude Stein remembered that when as a child she used to swing on the chains that were around the Arc de Triomphe her governess had told her that no one must walk underneath since the german armies had marched under it after 1870.[6] And now everybody except the germans were passing through.

All the nations marched differently, some slowly, some quickly, the french carry their flags the best of all, Pershing and his officer carrying the flag behind him were perhaps the most perfectly spaced. It was this scene that Gertrude Stein described in the movie she wrote about this time that I have published in Operas and Plays in the Plain Edition.[7]

However it all finally came to an end. We wandered up and we wandered down the Champs Elysées and the war was over and the piles of captured cannon that had made two pyramids were being taken away and peace was upon us.

1933

1. Triumphal Arch (French), monument in central Paris originally dedicated to Napoleon's military victories.
2. Elysian Fields (French), major avenue in central Paris.
3. Stein and Toklas had used "Auntie," their Ford truck, for Red Cross relief transport in the war.
4. Small, lightweight automobile. "Godiva": after Lady Godiva, who according to medieval legend rode naked through the streets of Coventry, England, to persuade her husband to forgive his tenants' debts.
5. Hôtel des Invalides, home for disabled war veterans built by Louis XIV in 1670.
6. Paris surrendered to German forces during the Franco-Prussian War of 1870–71.
7. Operas and Plays, published in 1932.

ROBERT FROST
1874–1963

Although he identified himself with New England, Robert Frost was born in California and lived there until his father died, when Frost was eleven. The family then moved to New England where his mother supported them by teaching school. Frost graduated from high school in 1891 in Lawrence, Massachusetts, sharing the post of valedictorian with Elinor White, whom he married three years later. Occasional attendance at Dartmouth College and Harvard, and a variety of different jobs including an attempt to run a farm in Derry, New Hampshire, marked the next twenty years. Frost made a new start in 1912, taking his family, which included four children, to England. There he worked on his poetry and found a publisher for his first book, *A Boy's Will* (1913). Ezra Pound reviewed it favorably, excited (as he put it in a letter) by this "VURRY Amur'k'n talent." Pound recommended Frost's poems to American editors and helped get his second book, *North of Boston*, published in 1914. *North of Boston* was widely praised by critics in America and England when it appeared; the favorable reception persuaded Frost to return home. He bought another farm in New Hampshire and prospered financially through sales of his books and papers, along with teaching and lecturing at various colleges. The success he enjoyed for the rest of his life, however, came too late to cancel the bitterness left by his earlier struggles. Moreover, he endured personal tragedy: a son committed suicide, and a daughter had a complete mental collapse.

The clarity of Frost's diction, the colloquial rhythms, the simplicity of his images, and above all the folksy speaker—these are intended to make the poems look natural, unplanned. In the context of the modernist movement, however, they can be seen as a thoughtful reply to high modernism's fondness for obscurity and difficulty. Although Frost's ruralism affirmed the modernist distaste for cities, he was writing the kind of traditional, accessible poetry that modernists argued could no longer be written. In addition, by investing in the New England terrain, he rejected modernist internationalism and revitalized the tradition of New England regionalism. Readers who accepted Frost's persona and his setting as typically American accepted the powerful myth that rural New England was the heart of America.

Frost achieved an internal dynamic in his poems by playing the rhythms of ordinary speech against formal patterns of line and verse and containing them within traditional forms. The interaction of colloquial diction with blank verse is especially central to his dramatic monologues. To Frost traditional forms were the essence of poetry, material with which poets responded to flux and disorder (what, adopting scientific terminology, he called "decay") by forging something permanent. Poetry, he wrote, was "one step backward taken," resisting time—a "momentary stay against confusion."

Throughout the 1920s Frost's poetic practice changed very little; later books—including *Mountain Interval* (1916), *New Hampshire* (1923), and *West-Running Brook* (1928)—confirmed the impression he had created in *North of Boston*. Most of his poems fall into a few types. Nature lyrics describing and commenting on a scene or event—like "Stopping by Woods on a Snowy Evening," "Birches," and "After Apple-Picking"—are probably the best known and the most popular. There are also dramatic narratives in blank verse about the griefs of country people, like "The Death of the Hired Man," and poems of commentary or generalization, like "The Gift Outright," which he read at John F. Kennedy's presidential inauguration in 1961. He could also be humorous or sardonic, as in "Fire and Ice." In the nature lyrics, a comparison often emerges between the outer scene and the psyche, a comparison of what Frost in one poem called "outer and inner weather."

Because he worked so much with outdoor scenery, and because he presented himself as a New Englander, Frost is often interpreted as an ideological descendant of the nineteenth-century American Transcendentalists. But he is far less affirmative about the universe than they; for where they, looking at nature, discerned a benign creator, he saw "no expression, nothing to express." Frost did share with Emerson and Thoreau, however, the belief that everybody was a separate individuality and that collective enterprises could do nothing but weaken the self. Politically conservative, therefore, he avoided movements of the left and the right precisely because they were movements, group undertakings. In the 1930s when writers tended to be political activists, he was seen as one whose old-fashioned values were inappropriate, even dangerous, in modern times. Frost deeply resented this criticism, and responded to it with a newly hortatory, didactic kind of poetry. In the last twenty years of his life, Frost increased his activities as a teacher and lecturer—at Amherst, at Dartmouth, at Harvard, at the Bread Loaf School of English at Middlebury College in Vermont, and in poetry readings and talks around the country.

The text of the poems included here is that of *The Poetry of Robert Frost* (1969).

The Pasture

I'm going out to clean the pasture spring;
I'll only stop to rake the leaves away
(And wait to watch the water clear, I may):
I shan't be gone long.—You come too.
I'm going out to fetch the little calf   5
That's standing by the mother. It's so young
It totters when she licks it with her tongue.
I shan't be gone long.—You come too.

1913

Mowing

There was never a sound beside the wood but one,
And that was my long scythe whispering to the ground.
What was it it whispered? I knew not well myself;
Perhaps it was something about the heat of the sun,
Something, perhaps, about the lack of sound—   5
And that was why it whispered and did not speak.
It was no dream of the gift of idle hours,
Or easy gold at the hand of fay or elf:
Anything more than the truth would have seemed too weak
To the earnest love that laid the swale[1] in rows,   10
Not without feeble-pointed spikes of flowers
(Pale orchises), and scared a bright green snake.
The fact is the sweetest dream that labor knows.
My long scythe whispered and left the hay to make.

1913

---

1. Grasses in a marshy meadow.

Mending Wall

Something there is that doesn't love a wall,
That sends the frozen-ground-swell under it,
And spills the upper boulders in the sun,
And makes gaps even two can pass abreast.
The work of hunters is another thing: 5
I have come after them and made repair
Where they have left not one stone on a stone,
But they would have the rabbit out of hiding,
To please the yelping dogs. The gaps I mean,
No one has seen them made or heard them made,   10
But at spring mending-time we find them there.
I let my neighbor know beyond the hill;
And on a day we meet to walk the line
And set the wall between us once again.
We keep the wall between us as we go.   15
To each the boulders that have fallen to each.
And some are loaves and some so nearly balls
We have to use a spell to make them balance:
"Stay where you are until our backs are turned!"
We wear our fingers rough with handling them.   20
Oh, just another kind of outdoor game,
One on a side. It comes to little more:
There where it is we do not need the wall:
He is all pine and I am apple orchard.
My apple trees will never get across   25
And eat the cones under his pines, I tell him.
He only says, "Good fences make good neighbors."
Spring is the mischief in me, and I wonder
If I could put a notion in his head:
"*Why* do they make good neighbors? Isn't it   30
Where there are cows? But here there are no cows.
Before I built a wall I'd ask to know
What I was walling in or walling out,
And to whom I was like to give offense.
Something there is that doesn't love a wall,   35
That wants it down." I could say "Elves" to him,
But it's not elves exactly, and I'd rather
He said it for himself. I see him there
Bringing a stone grasped firmly by the top
In each hand, like an old-stone savage armed.   40
He moves in darkness as it seems to me,
Not of woods only and the shade of trees.
He will not go behind his father's saying,
And he likes having thought of it so well
He says again, "Good fences make good neighbors."   45

                                                        1914

The Death of the Hired Man

Mary sat musing on the lamp-flame at the table
Waiting for Warren. When she heard his step,
She ran on tip-toe down the darkened passage
To meet him in the doorway with the news
And put him on his guard. "Silas is back."   5
She pushed him outward with her through the door
And shut it after her. "Be kind," she said.
She took the market things from Warren's arms
And set them on the porch, then drew him down
To sit beside her on the wooden steps.   10

"When was I ever anything but kind to him?
But I'll not have the fellow back," he said.
"I told him so last haying, didn't I?
If he left then, I said, that ended it.
What good is he? Who else will harbor him   15
At his age for the little he can do?
What help he is there's no depending on.
Off he goes always when I need him most.
He thinks he ought to earn a little pay,
Enough at least to buy tobacco with,   20
So he won't have to beg and be beholden.
'All right,' I say, 'I can't afford to pay
Any fixed wages, though I wish I could.'
'Someone else can.' 'Then someone else will have to.'
I shouldn't mind his bettering himself   25
If that was what it was. You can be certain,
When he begins like that, there's someone at him
Trying to coax him off with pocket-money,—
In haying time, when any help is scarce.
In winter he comes back to us. I'm done."   30

"Sh! not so loud: he'll hear you," Mary said.

"I want him to: he'll have to soon or late."

"He's worn out. He's asleep beside the stove.
When I came up from Rowe's I found him here,
Huddled against the barn-door fast asleep,   35
A miserable sight, and frightening, too—
You needn't smile—I didn't recognize him—
I wasn't looking for him—and he's changed.
Wait till you see."

        "Where did you say he'd been?"   40

"He didn't say. I dragged him to the house,
And gave him tea and tried to make him smoke.

I tried to make him talk about his travels.
Nothing would do: he just kept nodding off."

"What did he say? Did he say anything?"   45

"But little."

        "Anything? Mary, confess
He said he'd come to ditch the meadow for me."

"Warren!"

        "But did he? I just want to know."   50

"Of course he did. What would you have him say?
Surely you wouldn't grudge the poor old man
Some humble way to save his self-respect.
He added, if you really care to know,
He meant to clear the upper pasture, too.   55
That sounds like something you have heard before?
Warren, I wish you could have heard the way
He jumbled everything. I stopped to look
Two or three times—he made me feel so queer—
To see if he was talking in his sleep.   60
He ran on Harold Wilson—you remember—
The boy you had in haying four years since.
He's finished school, and teaching in his college.
Silas declares you'll have to get him back.
He says they two will make a team for work: 65
Between them they will lay this farm as smooth!
The way he mixed that in with other things.
He thinks young Wilson a likely lad, though daft
On education—you know how they fought
All through July under the blazing sun,   70
Silas up on the cart to build the load,
Harold along beside to pitch it on."

"Yes, I took care to keep well out of earshot."

"Well, those days trouble Silas like a dream.
You wouldn't think they would. How some things linger!   75
Harold's young college-boy's assurance piqued him.
After so many years he still keeps finding
Good arguments he sees he might have used.
I sympathize. I know just how it feels
To think of the right thing to say too late.   80
Harold's associated in his mind with Latin.
He asked me what I thought of Harold's saying
He studied Latin, like the violin,
Because he liked it—that an argument!
He said he couldn't make the boy believe   85
He could find water with a hazel prong—

Which showed how much good school had ever done him.
He wanted to go over that. But most of all
He thinks if he could have another chance
To teach him how to build a load of hay—"   90

"I know, that's Silas' one accomplishment.
He bundles every forkful in its place,
And tags and numbers it for future reference,
So he can find and easily dislodge it
In the unloading. Silas does that well.   95
He takes it out in bunches like big birds' nests.
You never see him standing on the hay
He's trying to lift, straining to lift himself."

"He thinks if he could teach him that, he'd be
Some good perhaps to someone in the world.   100
He hates to see a boy the fool of books.
Poor Silas, so concerned for other folk,
And nothing to look backward to with pride,
And nothing to look forward to with hope,
So now and never any different."   105

Part of a moon was falling down the west,
Dragging the whole sky with it to the hills.
Its light poured softly in her lap. She saw it
And spread her apron to it. She put out her hand
Among the harplike morning-glory strings,   110
Taut with the dew from garden bed to eaves,
As if she played unheard some tenderness
That wrought on him beside her in the night.
"Warren," she said, "he has come home to die:
You needn't be afraid he'll leave you this time."   115

"Home," he mocked gently.

                              "Yes, what else but home?
It all depends on what you mean by home.
Of course he's nothing to us, any more
Than was the hound that came a stranger to us   120
Out of the woods, worn out upon the trail."

"Home is the place where, when you have to go there,
They have to take you in."

                              "I should have called it
Something you somehow haven't to deserve."   125

Warren leaned out and took a step or two,
Picked up a little stick, and brought it back
And broke it in his hand and tossed it by.
"Silas has better claim on us you think
Than on his brother? Thirteen little miles   130

As the road winds would bring him to his door.
Silas has walked that far no doubt today.
Why doesn't he go there? His brother's rich,
A somebody—director in the bank."

"He never told us that."   135

                    "We know it though."

"I think his brother ought to help, of course.
I'll see to that if there is need. He ought of right
To take him in, and might be willing to—
He may be better than appearances.   140
But have some pity on Silas. Do you think
If he had any pride in claiming kin
Or anything he looked for from his brother,
He'd keep so still about him all this time?"

"I wonder what's between them."   145

                              "I can tell you.
Silas is what he is—we wouldn't mind him—
But just the kind that kinsfolk can't abide.
He never did a thing so very bad.
He don't know why he isn't quite as good   150
As anybody. Worthless though he is,
He won't be made ashamed to please his brother."

"I can't think Si ever hurt anyone."

"No, but he hurt my heart the way he lay
And rolled his old head on that sharp-edged chair-back.   155
He wouldn't let me put him on the lounge.
You must go in and see what you can do.
I made the bed up for him there tonight.
You'll be surprised at him—how much he's broken.
His working days are done; I'm sure of it."   160

"I'd not be in a hurry to say that."

"I haven't been. Go, look, see for yourself.
But, Warren, please remember how it is:
He's come to help you ditch the meadow.
He has a plan. You mustn't laugh at him.   165
He may not speak of it, and then he may.
I'll sit and see if that small sailing cloud
Will hit or miss the moon."

                    It hit the moon.
Then there were three there, making a dim row,   170
The moon, the little silver cloud, and she.

Warren returned—too soon, it seemed to her,
Slipped to her side, caught up her hand and waited.

"Warren?" she questioned.

     "Dead," was all he answered.   175

         1914

Home Burial[1]

He saw her from the bottom of the stairs
Before she saw him. She was starting down,
Looking back over her shoulder at some fear.
She took a doubtful step and then undid it
To raise herself and look again. He spoke   5
Advancing toward her: "What is it you see
From up there always—for I want to know."
She turned and sank upon her skirts at that,
And her face changed from terrified to dull.
He said to gain time: "What is it you see,"   10
Mounting until she cowered under him.
"I will find out now—you must tell me, dear."
She, in her place, refused him any help
With the least stiffening of her neck and silence.
She let him look, sure that he wouldn't see,   15
Blind creature; and awhile he didn't see.
But at last he murmured, "Oh," and again, "Oh."

"What is it—what?" she said.

       "Just that I see."

"You don't," she challenged. "Tell me what it is."   20

"The wonder is I didn't see at once.
I never noticed it from here before.
I must be wonted to it—that's the reason.
The little graveyard where my people are!
So small the window frames the whole of it.   25
Not so much larger than a bedroom, is it?
There are three stones of slate and one of marble,
Broad-shouldered little slabs there in the sunlight
On the sidehill. We haven't to mind *those*.

---

1. The title refers to the rural custom of burying members of the family on the home property.

But I understand: it is not the stones,
But the child's mound——"   30

                    "Don't, don't, don't, don't," she cried.

She withdrew shrinking from beneath his arm
That rested on the banister, and slid downstairs;
And turned on him with such a daunting look,   35
He said twice over before he knew himself:
"Can't a man speak of his own child he's lost?"

"Not you!—Oh, where's my hat? Oh, I don't need it!
I must get out of here. I must get air.—
I don't know rightly whether any man can."   40

"Amy! Don't go to someone else this time.
Listen to me. I won't come down the stairs."
He sat and fixed his chin between his fists.
"There's something I should like to ask you, dear."

"You don't know how to ask it."   45

                              "Help me, then."

Her fingers moved the latch for all reply.

"My words are nearly always an offense.
I don't know how to speak of anything
So as to please you. But I might be taught   50
I should suppose. I can't say I see how.
A man must partly give up being a man
With womenfolk. We could have some arrangement
By which I'd bind myself to keep hands off
Anything special you're a-mind to name.   55
Though I don't like such things 'twixt those that love.
Two that don't love can't live together without them.
But two that do can't live together with them."
She moved the latch a little. "Don't—don't go.
Don't carry it to someone else this time.   60
Tell me about it if it's something human.
Let me into your grief. I'm not so much
Unlike other folks as your standing there
Apart would make me out. Give me my chance.
I do think, though, you overdo it a little.   65
What was it brought you up to think it the thing
To take your mother-loss of a first child
So inconsolably—in the face of love.
You'd think his memory might be satisfied——"

"There you go sneering now!"   70
                         "I'm not, I'm not!

You make me angry. I'll come down to you.
God, what a woman! And it's come to this,
A man can't speak of his own child that's dead."

"You can't because you don't know how to speak.   75
If you had any feelings, you that dug
With your own hand—how could you?—his little grave;
I saw you from that very window there,
Making the gravel leap and leap in air,
Leap up, like that, like that, and land so lightly   80
And roll back down the mound beside the hole.
I thought, Who is that man? I didn't know you.
And I crept down the stairs and up the stairs
To look again, and still your spade kept lifting.
Then you came in. I heard your rumbling voice   85
Out in the kitchen, and I don't know why,
But I went near to see with my own eyes.
You could sit there with the stains on your shoes
Of the fresh earth from your own baby's grave
And talk about your everyday concerns.   90
You had stood the spade up against the wall
Outside there in the entry, for I saw it."

"I shall laugh the worst laugh I ever laughed.
I'm cursed. God, if I don't believe I'm cursed."

"I can repeat the very words you were saying: 95
'Three foggy mornings and one rainy day
Will rot the best birch fence a man can build.'
Think of it, talk like that at such a time!
What had how long it takes a birch to rot
To do with what was in the darkened parlor?   100
You *couldn't* care! The nearest friends can go
With anyone to death, comes so far short
They might as well not try to go at all.
No, from the time when one is sick to death,
One is alone, and he dies more alone.   105
Friends make pretense of following to the grave,
But before one is in it, their minds are turned
And making the best of their way back to life
And living people, and things they understand.
But the world's evil. I won't have grief so   110
If I can change it. Oh, I won't, I won't!"

"There, you have said it all and you feel better.
You won't go now. You're crying. Close the door.
The heart's gone out of it: why keep it up?
Amy! There's someone coming down the road!"   115

"*You*—oh, you think the talk is all. I must go—
Somewhere out of this house. How can I make you——"

"If—you—do!" She was opening the door wider.
"Where do you mean to go? First tell me that.
I'll follow and bring you back by force. I *will!*——" 120

1914

After Apple-Picking

My long two-pointed ladder's sticking through a tree
Toward heaven still,
And there's a barrel that I didn't fill
Beside it, and there may be two or three
Apples I didn't pick upon some bough. 5
But I am done with apple-picking now.
Essence of winter sleep is on the night,
The scent of apples: I am drowsing off.
I cannot rub the strangeness from my sight
I got from looking through a pane of glass 10
I skimmed this morning from the drinking trough
And held against the world of hoary grass.
It melted, and I let it fall and break.
But I was well
Upon my way to sleep before it fell, 15
And I could tell
What form my dreaming was about to take.
Magnified apples appear and disappear,
Stem end and blossom end,
And every fleck of russet showing clear. 20
My instep arch not only keeps the ache,
It keeps the pressure of a ladder-round.
I feel the ladder sway as the boughs bend.
And I keep hearing from the cellar bin
The rumbling sound 25
Of load on load of apples coming in.
For I have had too much
Of apple-picking: I am overtired
Of the great harvest I myself desired.
There were ten thousand thousand fruit to touch, 30
Cherish in hand, lift down, and not let fall.
For all
That struck the earth,
No matter if not bruised or spiked with stubble,
Went surely to the cider-apple heap 35
As of no worth.
One can see what will trouble
This sleep of mine, whatever sleep it is.
Were he not gone,
The woodchuck could say whether it's like his 40
Long sleep, as I describe its coming on,
Or just some human sleep.

1914

The Wood-Pile

Out walking in the frozen swamp one gray day,
I paused and said, "I will turn back from here.
No, I will go on farther—and we shall see."
The hard snow held me, save where now and then
One foot went through. The view was all in lines   5
Straight up and down of tall slim trees
Too much alike to mark or name a place by
So as to say for certain I was here
Or somewhere else: I was just far from home.
A small bird flew before me. He was careful   10
To put a tree between us when he lighted,
And say no word to tell me who he was
Who was so foolish as to think what *he* thought.
He thought that I was after him for a feather—
The white one in his tail; like one who takes   15
Everything said as personal to himself.
One flight out sideways would have undeceived him.
And then there was a pile of wood for which
I forgot him and let his little fear
Carry him off the way I might have gone,   20
Without so much as wishing him good-night.
He went behind it to make his last stand.
It was a cord of maple, cut and split
And piled—and measured, four by four by eight.
And not another like it could I see.   25
No runner tracks in this year's snow looped near it.
And it was older sure than this year's cutting,
Or even last year's or the year's before.
The wood was gray and the bark warping off it
And the pile somewhat sunken. Clematis   30
Had wound strings round and round it like a bundle.
What held it, though, on one side was a tree
Still growing, and on one a stake and prop,
These latter about to fall. I thought that only
Someone who lived in turning to fresh tasks   35
Could so forget his handiwork on which
He spent himself, the labor of his ax,
And leave it there far from a useful fireplace
To warm the frozen swamp as best it could
With the slow smokeless burning of decay.   40

1914

The Road Not Taken

Two roads diverged in a yellow wood,
And sorry I could not travel both
And be one traveler, long I stood

And looked down one as far as I could
To where it bent in the undergrowth;   5

Then took the other, as just as fair,
And having perhaps the better claim,
Because it was grassy and wanted wear;
Though as for that, the passing there
Had worn them really about the same,   10

And both that morning equally lay
In leaves no step had trodden black.
Oh, I kept the first for another day!
Yet knowing how way leads on to way,
I doubted if I should ever come back.   15

I shall be telling this with a sigh
Somewhere ages and ages hence:
Two roads diverged in a wood, and I—
I took the one less traveled by,
And that has made all the difference.   20

1916

The Oven Bird

There is a singer everyone has heard,
Loud, a mid-summer and a mid-wood bird,
Who makes the solid tree trunks sound again.
He says that leaves are old and that for flowers
Mid-summer is to spring as one to ten.   5
He says the early petal-fall is past,
When pear and cherry bloom went down in showers
On sunny days a moment overcast;
And comes that other fall we name the fall.
He says the highway dust is over all.   10
The bird would cease and be as other birds
But that he knows in singing not to sing.
The question that he frames in all but words
Is what to make of a diminished thing.

1916

Birches

When I see birches bend to left and right
Across the lines of straighter darker trees,
I like to think some boy's been swinging them.
But swinging doesn't bend them down to stay
As ice storms do. Often you must have seen them   5

Loaded with ice a sunny winter morning
After a rain. They click upon themselves
As the breeze rises, and turn many-colored
As the stir cracks and crazes their enamel.
Soon the sun's warmth makes them shed crystal shells   10
Shattering and avalanching on the snow crust—
Such heaps of broken glass to sweep away
You'd think the inner dome of heaven had fallen.
They are dragged to the withered bracken by the load,
And they seem not to break; though once they are bowed   15
So low for long, they never right themselves:
You may see their trunks arching in the woods
Years afterwards, trailing their leaves on the ground
Like girls on hands and knees that throw their hair
Before them over their heads to dry in the sun.   20
But I was going to say when Truth broke in
With all her matter of fact about the ice storm,
I should prefer to have some boy bend them
As he went out and in to fetch the cows—
Some boy too far from town to learn baseball,   25
Whose only play was what he found himself,
Summer or winter, and could play alone.
One by one he subdued his father's trees
By riding them down over and over again
Until he took the stiffness out of them,   30
And not one but hung limp, not one was left
For him to conquer. He learned all there was
To learn about not launching out too soon
And so not carrying the tree away
Clear to the ground. He always kept his poise   35
To the top branches, climbing carefully
With the same pains you use to fill a cup
Up to the brim, and even above the brim.
Then he flung outward, feet first, with a swish,
Kicking his way down through the air to the ground.   40
So was I once myself a swinger of birches.
And so I dream of going back to be.
It's when I'm weary of considerations,
And life is too much like a pathless wood
Where your face burns and tickles with the cobwebs   45
Broken across it, and one eye is weeping
From a twig's having lashed across it open.
I'd like to get away from earth awhile
And then come back to it and begin over.
May no fate willfully misunderstand me   50
And half grant what I wish and snatch me away
Not to return. Earth's the right place for love:
I don't know where it's likely to go better.
I'd like to go by climbing a birch tree,
And climb black branches up a snow-white trunk   55
Toward heaven, till the tree could bear no more,
But dipped its top and set me down again.

That would be good both going and coming back.
One could do worse than be a swinger of birches.

1916

"Out, Out—"[1]

The buzz saw snarled and rattled in the yard
And made dust and dropped stove-length sticks of wood,
Sweet-scented stuff when the breeze drew across it.
And from there those that lifted eyes could count
Five mountain ranges one behind the other   5
Under the sunset far into Vermont.
And the saw snarled and rattled, snarled and rattled,
As it ran light, or had to bear a load.
And nothing happened: day was all but done.
Call it a day, I wish they might have said   10
To please the boy by giving him the half hour
That a boy counts so much when saved from work.
His sister stood beside them in her apron
To tell them "Supper." At the word, the saw,
As if to prove saws knew what supper meant,   15
Leaped out at the boy's hand, or seemed to leap—
He must have given the hand. However it was,
Neither refused the meeting. But the hand!
The boy's first outcry was a rueful laugh,
As he swung toward them holding up the hand,   20
Half in appeal, but half as if to keep
The life from spilling. Then the boy saw all—
Since he was old enough to know, big boy
Doing a man's work, though a child at heart—
He saw all spoiled. "Don't let him cut my hand off—   25
The doctor, when he comes. Don't let him, sister!"
So. But the hand was gone already.
The doctor put him in the dark of ether.
He lay and puffed his lips out with his breath.
And then—the watcher at his pulse took fright.   30
No one believed. They listened at his heart.
Little—less—nothing!—and that ended it.
No more to build on there. And they, since they
Were not the one dead, turned to their affairs.

1916

---

1. From Shakespeare's *Macbeth* (5.5.23–24): "Out, out, brief candle! / Life's but a walking shadow."

Fire and Ice

Some say the world will end in fire,
Some say in ice.
From what I've tasted of desire
I hold with those who favor fire.
But if it had to perish twice,   5
I think I know enough of hate
To say that for destruction ice
Is also great
And would suffice.

1923

Nothing Gold Can Stay

Nature's first green is gold,
Her hardest hue to hold.
Her early leaf's a flower;
But only so an hour.
Then leaf subsides to leaf.   5
So Eden sank to grief,
So dawn goes down to day.
Nothing gold can stay.

1923

Stopping by Woods on a Snowy Evening

Whose woods these are I think I know.
His house is in the village, though;
He will not see me stopping here
To watch his woods fill up with snow.

My little horse must think it queer   5
To stop without a farmhouse near
Between the woods and frozen lake
The darkest evening of the year.

He gives his harness bells a shake
To ask if there is some mistake.   10
The only other sound's the sweep
Of easy wind and downy flake.

The woods are lovely, dark, and deep,
But I have promises to keep,
And miles to go before I sleep.   15
And miles to go before I sleep.

1923

Departmental

An ant on the tablecloth
Ran into a dormant moth
Of many times his size.
He showed not the least surprise.
His business wasn't with such.   5
He gave it scarcely a touch,
And was off on his duty run.
Yet if he encountered one
Of the hive's enquiry squad
Whose work is to find out God   10
And the nature of time and space,
He would put him onto the case.
Ants are a curious race;
One crossing with hurried tread
The body of one of their dead   15
Isn't given a moment's arrest—
Seems not even impressed.
But he no doubt reports to any
With whom he crosses antennae,
And they no doubt report   20
To the higher-up at court.
Then word goes forth in Formic:[1]
"Death's come to Jerry McCormic,
Our selfless forager Jerry.
Will the special Janizary[2]   25
Whose office it is to bury
The dead of the commissary
Go bring him home to his people.
Lay him in state on a sepal.
Wrap him for shroud in a petal.   30
Embalm him with ichor of nettle.
This is the word of your Queen."
And presently on the scene
Appears a solemn mortician;
And taking formal position   35
With feelers calmly atwiddle,
Seizes the dead by the middle,
And heaving him high in air,
Carries him out of there.
No one stands round to stare.   40
It is nobody else's affair.

It couldn't be called ungentle.
But how thoroughly departmental.

                                                              1936

---

1. Acid emitted by ants.   2. Troop of Turkish infantry soldiers.

Desert Places *the movement*

Snow falling and night falling fast, oh, fast
In a field I looked into going past,
And the ground almost covered smooth in snow,
But a few weeds and stubble showing last.

The woods around it have it—it is theirs.   5
All animals are smothered in their lairs.
I am too absent-spirited to count;
The loneliness includes me unawares.

And lonely as it is, that loneliness
Will be more lonely ere it will be less—   10
A blanker whiteness of benighted snow
With no expression, nothing to express.

They cannot scare me with their empty spaces
Between stars—on stars where no human race is.
I have it in me so much nearer home   15
To scare myself with my own desert places.

1936

Design

I found a dimpled spider, fat and white,
On a white heal-all,[1] holding up a moth
Like a white piece of rigid satin cloth—
Assorted characters of death and blight
Mixed ready to begin the morning right,   5
Like the ingredients of a witches' broth—
A snow-drop spider, a flower like a froth,
And dead wings carried like a paper kite.

What had that flower to do with being white,
The wayside blue and innocent heal-all?   10
What brought the kindred spider to that height,
Then steered the white moth thither in the night?
What but design of darkness to appall?—
If design govern in a thing so small.

1922, 1936

1. Common wildflower whose blossom is normally violet or blue.

Neither Out Far Nor In Deep

The people along the sand
All turn and look one way.
They turn their back on the land.
They look at the sea all day.

As long as it takes to pass   5
A ship keeps raising its hull;
The wetter ground like glass
Reflects a standing gull.

The land may vary more;
But wherever the truth may be—   10
The water comes ashore,
And the people look at the sea.

They cannot look out far.
They cannot look in deep.
But when was that ever a bar   15
To any watch they keep?

                                    1936

Provide, Provide

The witch that came (the withered hag)
To wash the steps with pail and rag
Was once the beauty Abishag,[1]

The picture pride of Hollywood.
Too many fall from great and good   5
For you to doubt the likelihood.

Die early and avoid the fate.
Or if predestined to die late,
Make up your mind to die in state.

Make the whole stock exchange your own!   10
If need be occupy a throne,
Where nobody can call *you* crone.

Some have relied on what they knew,
Others on being simply true.
What worked for them might work for you.   15

No memory of having starred
Atones for later disregard
Or keeps the end from being hard.

1. A beautiful maiden brought to comfort King David in his old age (1 Kings 1.2–4).

Better to go down dignified
With boughten friendship at your side   20
Than none at all. Provide, provide!

1934, 1936

The Gift Outright

The land was ours before we were the land's.
She was our land more than a hundred years
Before we were her people. She was ours
In Massachusetts, in Virginia,
But we were England's, still colonials,   5
Possessing what we still were unpossessed by,
Possessed by what we now no more possessed.
Something we were withholding made us weak
Until we found out that it was ourselves
We were withholding from our land of living,   10
And forthwith found salvation in surrender.
Such as we were we gave ourselves outright
(The deed of gift was many deeds of war)
To the land vaguely realizing westward,
But still unstoried, artless, unenhanced,   15
Such as she was, such as she would become.

1942

Directive

Back out of all this now too much for us,
Back in a time made simple by the loss
Of detail, burned, dissolved, and broken off
Like graveyard marble sculpture in the weather,
There is a house that is no more a house   5
Upon a farm that is no more a farm
And in a town that is no more a town.
The road there, if you'll let a guide direct you
Who only has at heart your getting lost,
May seem as if it should have been a quarry—   10
Great monolithic knees the former town
Long since gave up pretense of keeping covered.
And there's a story in a book about it:
Besides the wear of iron wagon wheels
The ledges show lines ruled southeast-northwest,   15
The chisel work of an enormous Glacier
That braced his feet against the Arctic Pole.
You must not mind a certain coolness from him
Still said to haunt this side of Panther Mountain.
Nor need you mind the serial ordeal   20
Of being watched from forty cellar holes

As if by eye pairs out of forty firkins.[1]
As for the woods' excitement over you
That sends light rustle rushes to their leaves,
Charge that to upstart inexperience. 25
Where were they all not twenty years ago?
They think too much of having shaded out
A few old pecker-fretted[2] apple trees.
Make yourself up a cheering song of how
Someone's road home from work this once was, 30
Who may be just ahead of you on foot
Or creaking with a buggy load of grain.
The height of the adventure is the height
Of country where two village cultures faded
Into each other. Both of them are lost. 35
And if you're lost enough to find yourself
By now, pull in your ladder road behind you
And put a sign up CLOSED to all but me.
Then make yourself at home. The only field
Now left's no bigger than a harness gall.[3] 40
First there's the children's house of make-believe,
Some shattered dishes underneath a pine,
The playthings in the playhouse of the children.
Weep for what little things could make them glad.
Then for the house that is no more a house, 45
But only a belilaced cellar hole,
Now slowly closing like a dent in dough.
This was no playhouse but a house in earnest.
Your destination and your destiny's
A brook that was the water of the house, 50
Cold as a spring as yet so near its source,
Too lofty and original to rage.
(We know the valley streams that when aroused
Will leave their tatters hung on barb and thorn.)
I have kept hidden in the instep arch 55
Of an old cedar at the waterside
A broken drinking goblet like the Grail[4]
Under a spell so the wrong ones can't find it,
So can't get saved, as Saint Mark[5] says they mustn't.
(I stole the goblet from the children's playhouse.) 60
Here are your waters and your watering place.
Drink and be whole again beyond confusion.

1947

1. Small wooden tubs for butter or lard.
2. Marked up with small holes by woodpeckers.
3. Sore on a horse's skin caused by the rubbing of the harness.
4. The cup used by Jesus at the Last Supper. According to legend, the Grail later disappeared from its keepers because of their moral impurity,
and various knights, including those of King Arthur's Round Table, went in quest of it. From this, the quest for the Grail has come to symbolize any spiritual search.
5. A reference to the Gospel of Mark, 4.11–12; see also Mark 16.16.

The Figure a Poem Makes[1]

Abstraction is an old story with the philosophers, but it has been like a new toy in the hands of the artists of our day. Why can't we have any one quality of poetry we choose by itself? We can have in thought. Then it will go hard if we can't in practice. Our lives for it.

Granted no one but a humanist much cares how sound a poem is if it is only *a* sound. The sound is the gold in the ore. Then we will have the sound out alone and dispense with the inessential. We do till we make the discovery that the object in writing poetry is to make all poems sound as different as possible from each other, and the resources for that of vowels, consonants, punctuation, syntax, words, sentences, meter are not enough. We need the help of context—meaning—subject matter. That is the greatest help towards variety. All that can be done with words is soon told. So also with meters— particularly in our language where there are virtually but two, strict iambic and loose iambic. The ancients with many were still poor if they depended on meters for all tune. It is painful to watch our sprung-rhythmists[2] straining at the point of omitting one short from a foot for relief from monotony. The possibilities for tune from the dramatic tones of meaning struck across the rigidity of a limited meter are endless. And we are back in poetry as merely one more art of having something to say, sound or unsound. Probably better if sound, because deeper and from wider experience.

Then there is this wildness whereof it is spoken. Granted again that it has an equal claim with sound to being a poem's better half. If it is a wild tune, it is a poem. Our problem then is, as modern abstractionists, to have the wildness pure; to be wild with nothing to be wild about. We bring up as aberrationists, giving way to undirected associations and kicking ourselves from one chance suggestion to another in all directions as of a hot afternoon in the life of a grasshopper. Theme alone can steady us down. Just as the first mystery was how a poem could have a tune in such a straightness as meter, so the second mystery is how a poem can have wildness and at the same time a subject that shall be fulfilled.

It should be of the pleasure of a poem itself to tell how it can. The figure a poem makes. It begins in delight and ends in wisdom. The figure is the same as for love. No one can really hold that the ecstasy should be static and stand still in one place. It begins in delight, it inclines to the impulse, it assumes direction with the first line laid down, it runs a course of lucky events, and ends in a clarification of life—not necessarily a great clarification, such as sects and cults are founded on, but in a momentary stay against confusion. It has denouement. It has an outcome that though unforeseen was predestined from the first image of the original mood—and indeed from the very mood. It is but a trick poem and no poem at all if the best of it was thought of first and saved for the last. It finds its own name as it goes and discovers the best waiting for it in some final phrase at once wise and sad—the happy-sad blend of the drinking song.

No tears in the writer, no tears in the reader. No surprise for the writer, no

---

1. This essay was published as an introduction to *The Collected Poems of Robert Frost* (1939).
2. "Sprung rhythm" was a term invented by the English poet Gerard Manley Hopkins (1844–1889) for meters depending not on repeated units of syllables and accents, as in traditional verse, but on irregularities.

surprise for the reader. For me the initial delight is in the surprise of remembering something I didn't know I knew. I am in a place, in a situation, as if I had materialized from cloud or risen out of the ground. There is a glad recognition of the long lost and the rest follows. Step by step the wonder of unexpected supply keeps growing. The impressions most useful to my purpose seem always those I was unaware of and so made no note of at the time when taken, and the conclusion is come to that like giants we are always hurling experience ahead of us to pave the future with against the day when we may want to strike a line of purpose across it for somewhere. The line will have the more charm for not being mechanically straight. We enjoy the straight crookedness of a good walking stick. Modern instruments of precision are being used to make things crooked as if by eye and hand in the old days.

I tell how there may be a better wildness of logic than of inconsequence. But the logic is backward, in retrospect, after the act. It must be more felt than seen ahead like prophecy. It must be a revelation, or a series of revelations, as much for the poet as for the reader. For it to be that there must have been the greatest freedom of the material to move about in it and to establish relations in it regardless of time and space, previous relation, and everything but affinity. We prate of freedom. We call our schools free because we are not free to stay away from them till we are sixteen years of age. I have given up my democratic prejudices and now willingly set the lower classes free to be completely taken care of by the upper classes. Political freedom is nothing to me. I bestow it right and left. All I would keep for myself is the freedom of my material—the condition of body and mind now and then to summon aptly from the vast chaos of all I have lived through.

Scholars and artists thrown together are often annoyed at the puzzle of where they differ. Both work from knowledge; but I suspect they differ most importantly in the way their knowledge is come by. Scholars get theirs with conscientious thoroughness along projected lines of logic; poets theirs cavalierly and as it happens in and out of books. They stick to nothing deliberately, but let what will stick to them like burrs where they walk in the fields. No acquirement is on assignment, or even self-assignment. Knowledge of the second kind is much more available in the wild free ways of wit and art. A school boy may be defined as one who can tell you what he knows in the order in which he learned it. The artist must value himself as he snatches a thing from some previous order in time and space into a new order with not so much as a ligature clinging to it of the old place where it was organic.

More than once I should have lost my soul to radicalism if it had been the originality it was mistaken for by its young converts. Originality and initiative are what I ask for my country. For myself the originality need be no more than the freshness of a poem run in the way I have described: from delight to wisdom. The figure is the same as for love. Like a piece of ice on a hot stove the poem must ride on its own melting. A poem may be worked over once it is in being, but may not be worried into being. Its most precious quality will remain its having run itself and carried away the poet with it. Read it a hundred times: it will forever keep its freshness as a petal keeps its fragrance. It can never lose its sense of a meaning that once unfolded by surprise as it went.

1939

SUSAN GLASPELL
1876–1948

Susan Glaspell—journalist, novelist, short-story writer, playwright, theatrical producer and director, actor—was a multitalented professional who eventually published more than fifty short stories, nine novels, and fourteen plays. Feminist rediscovery of *Trifles*, her first play—written and produced in 1916 and turned into a prize-winning short story, "A Jury of Her Peers," in 1917—has made this her best-known work today.

Born and raised in Davenport, Iowa, Glaspell worked for a year on the Davenport *Morning Republican* after high school graduation, then attended Drake University in Des Moines from 1895 to 1899. In college she wrote for the campus newspaper as well as various Des Moines papers; after graduation she worked for two years on the Des Moines *Daily News*. In 1901 she abandoned journalism, returning to Davenport with a plan to earn her living as a fiction writer. Her early stories, combining regional midwestern settings with romantic plots, found favor with the editors of such popular magazines as *Harper's*, the *Ladies' Home Journal*, the *American Magazine*, and the *Woman's Home Companion*. In 1909 she published her first novel, *The Glory of the Conquered*.

In 1913 she married the recently divorced George Cram Cook, a Harvard-educated native of Davenport, who was a writer and theatrical director much interested in modernist experimentation. The two moved to the East Coast, traveled widely, and collaborated on many projects. They helped found both the Washington Square Players in 1914 and the group that came to be known as the Provincetown Players in 1916.

The Provincetown Players, named for the New England seaport town where many of the members spent their summers, aimed to foster an American theater by producing plays by American playwrights only. Eugene O'Neill became the best-known dramatist of the group; Glaspell was a close second. She not only wrote plays but also acted in them, directed them, and helped produce them. From 1916 to 1922 she wrote nine plays, including *Trifles*, for the Provincetown Players; in 1922 Cook and Glaspell withdrew from the group, finding that it had become too commercially successful to suit their experimental aims.

Cook died in 1924; a later close relationship, with the novelist and playwright Norman Matson, ended in 1932. Throughout the 1930s and 1940s, Glaspell, now a year-round resident of Provincetown, continued to write and publish. Her novel *Judd Rankin's Wife* (1928) was made into a movie. She won the 1930 Pulitzer Prize for drama for *Alison's Room*, a play loosely based on the life of Emily Dickinson. Her last novel, *Judd Rankin's Daughter*, appeared in 1945, three years before she died at the age of seventy-two.

For Glaspell, the influence of such European playwrights as Henrik Ibsen and August Strindberg opened the door to much grimmer writing in a play like *Trifles* than in her popular short stories, with their formulaic happy endings. Her realism—her unsparing depiction of women's narrow, thwarted, isolated, and subjugated lives in rural, regional settings—produces effects quite unlike the nostalgic celebrations of woman-centered societies often associated with women regionalists. The efficiently plotted *Trifles* also features a formal device found in other Glaspell works, including *Alison's Room*: the main character at its center never appears.

The text is from *Plays by Susan Glaspell* (1987).

Trifles

Characters

GEORGE HENDERSON, *County Attorney*
HENRY PETERS, *Sheriff*
LEWIS HALE, *a Neighboring Farmer*
MRS PETERS
MRS HALE

SCENE: *The kitchen in the now abandoned farmhouse of* John Wright, *a gloomy kitchen, and left without having been put in order—unwashed pans under the sink, a loaf of bread outside the bread-box, a dish-towel on the table—other signs of incompleted work. At the rear the outer door opens and the* SHERIFF *comes in followed by the* COUNTY ATTORNEY *and* HALE. *The* SHERIFF *and* HALE *are men in middle life, the* COUNTY ATTORNEY *is a young man; all are much bundled up and go at once to the stove. They are followed by the two women—the* SHERIFF's *wife first; she is a slight wiry woman, a thin nervous face.* MRS HALE *is larger and would ordinarily be called more comfortable looking, but she is disturbed now and looks fearfully about as she enters. The women have come in slowly, and stand close together near the door.*

COUNTY ATTORNEY [*rubbing his hands*]   This feels good. Come up to the fire, ladies.

MRS PETERS [*after taking a step forward*]   I'm not—cold.

SHERIFF [*unbuttoning his overcoat and stepping away from the stove as if to mark the beginning of official business*]   Now, Mr Hale, before we move things about, you explain to Mr Henderson just what you saw when you came here yesterday morning.

COUNTY ATTORNEY   By the way, has anything been moved? Are things just as you left them yesterday?

SHERIFF [*looking about*]   It's just the same. When it dropped below zero last night I thought I'd better send Frank out this morning to make a fire for us—no use getting pneumonia with a big case on, but I told him not to touch anything except the stove—and you know Frank.

COUNTY ATTORNEY   Somebody should have been left here yesterday.

SHERIFF   Oh—yesterday. When I had to send Frank to Morris Center for that man who went crazy—I want you to know I had my hands full yesterday. I knew you could get back from Omaha by today and as long as I went over everything here myself—

COUNTY ATTORNEY   Well, Mr Hale, tell just what happened when you came here yesterday morning.

HALE   Harry and I had started to town with a load of potatoes. We came along the road from my place and as I got here I said, 'I'm going to see if I can't get John Wright to go in with me on a party telephone.'[1] I spoke to Wright about it once before and he put me off, saying folks talked too much anyway, and all he asked was peace and quiet—I guess you know about how much he talked himself; but I thought maybe if I went to the house and talked about it before his wife, though I said to Harry that I didn't know as what his wife wanted made much difference to John—

---

1. A single telephone line shared by several households.

COUNTY ATTORNEY   Let's talk about that later, Mr Hale. I do want to talk about that, but tell now just what happened when you got to the house.

HALE   I didn't hear or see anything; I knocked at the door, and still it was all quiet inside. I knew they must be up, it was past eight o'clock. So I knocked again, and I thought I heard somebody say, 'Come in.' I wasn't sure. I'm not sure yet, but I opened the door—this door [*indicating the door by which the two women are still standing*] and there in that rocker—[*pointing to it*] sat Mrs Wright.
    [*They all look at the rocker.*]

COUNTY ATTORNEY   What—was she doing?

HALE   She was rockin' back and forth. She had her apron in her hand and was kind of—pleating it.

COUNTY ATTORNEY   And how did she—look?

HALE   Well, she looked queer.

COUNTY ATTORNEY   How do you mean—queer?

HALE   Well, as if she didn't know what she was going to do next. And kind of done up.

COUNTY ATTORNEY   How did she seem to feel about your coming?

HALE   Why, I don't think she minded—one way or other. She didn't pay much attention. I said, 'How do. Mrs Wright it's cold, ain't it?' And she said, 'Is it?'—and went on kind of pleating at her apron. Well, I was surprised: she didn't ask me to come up to the stove, or to set down, but just sat there, not even looking at me, so I said, 'I want to see John.' And then she—laughed. I guess you would call it a laugh. I thought of Harry and the team outside, so I said a little sharp: 'Can't I see John?' 'No,' she says, kind o' dull like. 'Ain't he home?' says I. 'Yes,' says she, 'he's home.' 'Then why can't I see him?' I asked her, out of patience. ' 'Cause he's dead,' says she. '*Dead?*' says I. She just nodded her head, not getting a bit excited, but rockin' back and forth. 'Why—where is he?' says I, not knowing what to say. She just pointed upstairs—like that [*himself pointing to the room above*] I got up, with the idea of going up there. I walked from there to here—then I says, 'Why, what did he die of?' 'He died of a rope round his neck,' says she, and just went on pleatin' at her apron. Well, I went out and called Harry. I thought I might—need help. We went upstairs and there he was lyin'—

COUNTY ATTORNEY   I think I'd rather have you go into that upstairs, where you can point it all out. Just go on now with the rest of the story.

HALE   Well, my first thought was to get that rope off. It looked . . . [*stops, his face twitches*] . . . but Harry, he went up to him, and he said, 'No, he's dead all right, and we'd better not touch anything.' So we went back downstairs. She was still sitting that same way. 'Has anybody been notified?' I asked. 'No,' says she unconcerned. 'Who did this, Mrs Wright?' said Harry. He said it business-like—and she stopped pleatin' of her apron. 'I don't know,' she says. 'You don't *know*?' says Harry. 'No,' says she. 'Weren't you sleepin' in the bed with him?' says Harry. 'Yes,' says she, 'but I was on the inside.' 'Somebody slipped a rope round his neck and strangled him and you didn't wake up?' says Harry. 'I didn't wake up,' she said after him. We must 'a looked as if we didn't see how that could be, for after a minute she said, 'I sleep sound.' Harry was going to ask her more questions but I said maybe we ought to let her tell her story first to the coroner, or the sheriff, so Harry went fast as he could to Rivers' place, where there's a telephone.

COUNTY ATTORNEY   And what did Mrs Wright do when she knew that you had gone for the coroner?

HALE   She moved from that chair to this one over here [*pointing to a small chair in the corner*] and just sat there with her hands held together and looking down. I got a feeling that I ought to make some conversation, so I said I had come in to see if John wanted to put in a telephone, and at that she started to laugh, and then she stopped and looked at me—scared. [*the* COUNTY ATTORNEY, *who has had his notebook out, makes a note*] I dunno, maybe it wasn't scared. I wouldn't like to say it was. Soon Harry got back, and then Dr Lloyd came, and you, Mr Peters, and so I guess that's all I know that you don't.

COUNTY ATTORNEY   [*looking around*]   I guess we'll go upstairs first—and then out to the barn and around there. [*to the* SHERIFF] You're convinced that there was nothing important here—nothing that would point to any motive.

SHERIFF   Nothing here but kitchen things.

  [*The* COUNTY ATTORNEY, *after again looking around the kitchen, opens the door of a cupboard closet. He gets up on a chair and looks on a shelf. Pulls his hand away, sticky.*]

COUNTY ATTORNEY   Here's a nice mess.

  [*The women draw nearer.*]

MRS PETERS   [*to the other woman*]   Oh, her fruit: it did freeze. [*to the* LAWYER] She worried about that when it turned so cold. She said the fire'd go out and her jars would break.

SHERIFF   Well, can you beat the women! Held for murder and worryin' about her preserves.

COUNTY ATTORNEY   I guess before we're through she may have something more serious than preserves to worry about.

HALE   Well, women are used to worrying over trifles.

  [*The two women move a little closer together.*]

COUNTY ATTORNEY   [*with the gallantry of a young politician*]   And yet, for all their worries, what would we do without the ladies? [*the women do not unbend. He goes to the sink, takes a dipperful of water from the pail and pouring it into a basin, washes his hands. Starts to wipe them on the roller-towel, turns it for a cleaner place*] Dirty towels! [*kicks his foot against the pans under the sink*] Not much of a housekeeper, would you say, ladies?

MRS HALE   [*stiffly*]   There's a great deal of work to be done on a farm.

COUNTY ATTORNEY   To be sure. And yet [*with a little bow to her*] I know there are some Dickson county farmhouses which do not have such roller towels.

  [*He gives it a pull to expose its length again.*]

MRS HALE   Those towels get dirty awful quick. Men's hands aren't always as clean as they might be.

COUNTY ATTORNEY   Ah, loyal to your sex. I see. But you and Mrs Wright were neighbors. I suppose you were friends, too.

MRS HALE   [*shaking her head*]   I've not seen much of her of late years. I've not been in this house—it's more than a year.

COUNTY ATTORNEY   And why was that? You didn't like her?

MRS HALE   I liked her all well enough. Farmers' wives have their hands full, Mr Henderson. And then—

COUNTY ATTORNEY   Yes—?

MRS HALE [*looking about*]   It never seemed a very cheerful place.

COUNTY ATTORNEY   No—it's not cheerful. I shouldn't say she had the homemaking instinct.

MRS HALE   Well, I don't know as Wright had, either.

COUNTY ATTORNEY   You mean that they didn't get on very well?

MRS HALE   No. I don't mean anything. But I don't think a place'd be any cheerfuller for John Wright's being in it.

COUNTY ATTORNEY   I'd like to talk more of that a little later. I want to get the lay of things upstairs now.

[*He goes to the left, where three steps lead to a stair door.*]

SHERIFF   I suppose anything Mrs Peters does'll be all right. She was to take in some clothes for her, you know, and a few little things. We left in such a hurry yesterday.

COUNTY ATTORNEY   Yes, but I would like to see what you take, Mrs Peters, and keep an eye out for anything that might be of use to us.

MRS PETERS   Yes, Mr Henderson.

[*The women listen to the men's steps on the stairs, then look about the kitchen.*]

MRS HALE   I'd hate to have men coming into my kitchen, snooping around and criticising.

[*She arranges the pans under sink which the* LAWYER *had shoved out of place.*]

MRS PETERS   Of course it's no more than their duty.

MRS HALE   Duty's all right, but I guess that deputy sheriff that came out to make the fire might have got a little of this on. [*gives the roller towel a pull*] Wish I'd thought of that sooner. Seems mean to talk about her for not having things slicked up when she had to come away in such a hurry.

MRS PETERS [*who has gone to a small table in the left rear corner of the room, and lifted one end of a towel that covers a pan*]   She had bread set.

[*Stands still.*]

MRS HALE [*eyes fixed on a loaf of bread beside the bread-box, which is on a low shelf at the other side of the room. Moves slowly toward it*]   She was going to put this in there. [*picks up loaf, then abruptly drops it. In a manner of returning to familiar things*] It's a shame about her fruit. I wonder if it's all gone. [*gets up on the chair and looks*] I think there's some here that's all right, Mrs Peters. Yes—here; [*holding it toward the window*] this is cherries, too. [*looking again*] I declare I believe that's the only one. [*gets down, bottle in her hand. Goes to the sink and wipes it off on the outside*] She'll feel awful bad after all her hard work in the hot weather. I remember the afternoon I put up my cherries last summer.

[*She puts the bottle on the big kitchen table, center of the room. With a sigh, is about to sit down in the rocking-chair. Before she is seated realizes what chair it is; with a slow look at it, steps back. The chair which she has touched rocks back and forth.*]

MRS PETERS   Well, I must get those things from the front room closet. [*she goes to the door at the right, but after looking into the other room, steps back*] You coming with me, Mrs Hale? You could help me carry them.

[*They go in the other room; reappear,* MRS PETERS *carrying a dress and skirt,* MRS HALE *following with a pair of shoes.*]

MRS PETERS   My, it's cold in there.

[*She puts the clothes on the big table and hurries to the stove.*]

MRS HALE [*examining the skirt*]   Wright was close.[2] I think maybe that's why she kept so much to herself. She didn't even belong to the Ladies Aid. I suppose she felt she couldn't do her part, and then you don't enjoy things when you feel shabby. She used to wear pretty clothes and be lively, when she was Minnie Foster, one of the town girls singing in the choir. But that—oh, that was thirty years ago. This all you was to take in?

MRS PETERS   She said she wanted an apron. Funny thing to want, for there isn't much to get you dirty in jail, goodness knows. But I suppose just to make her feel more natural. She said they was in the top drawer in this cupboard. Yes, here. And then her little shawl that always hung behind the door. [*opens stair door and looks*] Yes, here it is.
       [*Quickly shuts door leading upstairs.*]
MRS HALE [*abruptly moving toward her*]   Mrs Peters?
MRS PETERS   Yes, Mrs Hale?
MRS HALE   Do you think she did it?
MRS PETERS [*in a frightened voice*]   Oh, I don't know.
MRS HALE   Well, I don't think she did. Asking for an apron and her little shawl. Worrying about her fruit.
MRS PETERS [*starts to speak, glances up, where footsteps are heard in the room above. In a low voice*]   Mr Peters says it looks bad for her. Mr Henderson is awful sarcastic in a speech and he'll make fun of her sayin' she didn't wake up.
MRS HALE   Well, I guess John Wright didn't wake when they was slipping that rope under his neck.
MRS PETERS   No, it's strange. It must have been done awful crafty and still. They say it was such a—funny way to kill a man, rigging it all up like that.
MRS HALE   That's just what Mr Hale said. There was a gun in the house. He says that's what he can't understand.
MRS PETERS   Mr Henderson said coming out that what was needed for the case was a motive; something to show anger, or—sudden feeling.
MRS HALE [*who is standing by the table*]   Well, I don't see any signs of anger around here. [*she puts her hand on the dish-towel which lies on the table, stands looking down at table, one half of which is clean, the other half messy*] It's wiped to here. [*makes a move as if to finish work, then turns and looks at loaf of bread outside the bread-box. Drops towel. In that voice of coming back to familiar things.*] Wonder how they are finding things upstairs. I hope she had it a little more red-up[3] up there. You know, it seems kind of *sneaking*. Locking her up in town and then coming out here and trying to get her own house to turn against her!
MRS PETERS   But Mrs Hale, the law is the law.
MRS HALE   I s'pose 'tis. [*unbuttoning her coat*] Better loosen up your things, Mrs Peters. You won't feel them when you go out.
       [MRS PETERS *takes off her fur tippet,[4] goes to hang it on hook at back of room, stands looking at the under part of the small corner table.*]
MRS PETERS   She was piecing a quilt.
       [*She brings the large sewing basket and they look at the bright pieces.*]
MRS HALE   It's log cabin pattern. Pretty, isn't it? I wonder if she was goin' to quilt it or just knot it?

2. Miserly.
3. Tidy.

4. Short cape, falling just below the shoulders.

[*Footsteps have been heard coming down the stairs. The* SHERIFF *enters followed by* HALE *and the* COUNTY ATTORNEY.]

SHERIFF   They wonder if she was going to quilt it or just knot it!

[*The men laugh, the women look abashed.*]

COUNTY ATTORNEY [*rubbing his hands over the stove*]   Frank's fire didn't do much up there, did it? Well, let's go out to the barn and get that cleared up.

[*The men go outside.*]

MRS HALE [*resentfully*]   I don't know as there's anything so strange, our takin' up our time with little things while we're waiting for them to get the evidence. [*she sits down at the big table smoothing out a block with decision*] I don't see as it's anything to laugh about.

MRS PETERS [*apologetically*]   Of course they've got awful important things on their minds.

[*Pulls up a chair and joins* MRS HALE *at the table.*]

MRS HALE [*examining another block*]   Mrs Peters, look at this one. Here, this is the one she was working on, and look at the sewing! All the rest of it has been so nice and even. And look at this! It's all over the place! Why, it looks as if she didn't know what she was about!

[*After she has said this they look at each other, then start to glance back at the door. After an instant* MRS HALE *has pulled at a knot and ripped the sewing.*]

MRS PETERS   Oh, what are you doing, Mrs Hale?

MRS HALE [*mildly*]   Just pulling out a stitch or two that's not sewed very good. [*threading a needle*] Bad sewing always made me fidgety.

MRS PETERS [*nervously*]   I don't think we ought to touch things.

MRS HALE   I'll just finish up this end. [*suddenly stopping and leaning forward*] Mrs Peters?

MRS PETERS   Yes, Mrs Hale?

MRS HALE   What do you suppose she was so nervous about?

MRS PETERS   Oh—I don't know. I don't know as she was nervous. I sometimes sew awful queer when I'm just tired. [MRS HALE *starts to say something, looks at* MRS PETERS, *then goes on sewing*] Well I must get these things wrapped up. They may be through sooner than we think. [*putting apron and other things together*] I wonder where I can find a piece of paper, and string.

MRS HALE   In that cupboard, maybe.

MRS PETERS [*looking in cupboard*]   Why, here's a bird-cage. [*holds it up*] Did she have a bird, Mrs Hale?

MRS HALE   Why, I don't know whether she did or not—I've not been here for so long. There was a man around last year selling canaries cheap, but I don't know as she took one; maybe she did. She used to sing real pretty herself.

MRS PETERS [*glancing around*]   Seems funny to think of a bird here. But she must have had one, or why would she have a cage? I wonder what happened to it.

MRS HALE   I s'pose maybe the cat got it.

MRS PETERS   No, she didn't have a cat. She's got that feeling some people have about cats—being afraid of them. My cat got in her room and she was real upset and asked me to take it out.

MRS HALE   My sister Bessie was like that. Queer, ain't it?

MRS PETERS [*examining the cage*]   Why, look at this door. It's broke. One hinge is pulled apart.

MRS HALE [*looking too*]   Looks as if someone must have been rough with it.

MRS PETERS   Why, yes.

[*She brings the cage forward and puts it on the table.*]

MRS HALE   I wish if they're going to find any evidence they'd be about it. I don't like this place.

MRS PETERS   But I'm awful glad you came with me, Mrs Hale. It would be lonesome for me sitting here alone.

MRS HALE   It would, wouldn't it? [*dropping her sewing*] But I tell you what I do wish, Mrs Peters. I wish I had come over sometimes when *she* was here. I—[*looking around the room*]—wish I had.

MRS PETERS   But of course you were awful busy. Mrs Hale—your house and your children.

MRS HALE   I could've come. I stayed away because it weren't cheerful—and that's why I ought to have come. I—I've never liked this place. Maybe because it's down in a hollow and you don't see the road. I dunno what it is, but it's a lonesome place and always was. I wish I had come over to see Minnie Foster sometimes. I can see now—[*shakes her head*]

MRS PETERS   Well, you mustn't reproach yourself, Mrs Hale. Somehow we just don't see how it is with other folks until—something comes up.

MRS HALE   Not having children makes less work—but it makes a quiet house, and Wright out to work all day, and no company when he did come in. Did you know John Wright, Mrs Peters?

MRS PETERS   Not to know him; I've seen him in town. They say he was a good man.

MRS HALE   Yes—good; he didn't drink, and kept his word as well as most, I guess, and paid his debts. But he was a hard man, Mrs Peters. Just to pass the time of day with him—[*shivers*] Like a raw wind that gets to the bone. [*pauses, her eye falling on the cage*] I should think she would a wanted a bird. But what do you suppose went with it?

MRS PETERS   I don't know, unless it got sick and died.

[*She reaches over and swings the broken door, swings it again, both women watch it.*]

MRS HALE   You weren't raised round here, were you? [MRS PETERS *shakes her head*] You didn't know—her?

MRS PETERS   Not till they brought her yesterday.

MRS HALE   She—come to think of it, she was kind of like a bird herself—real sweet and pretty, but kind of timid and—fluttery. How—she—did—change. [*silence: then as if struck by a happy thought and relieved to get back to everyday things*] Tell you what, Mrs Peters, why don't you take the quilt in with you? It might take up her mind.

MRS PETERS   Why, I think that's a real nice idea, Mrs Hale. There couldn't possibly be any objection to it, could there? Now, just what would I take? I wonder if her patches are in here—and her things.

[*They look in the sewing basket.*]

MRS HALE   Here's some red. I expect this has got sewing things in it. [*brings out a fancy box*] What a pretty box. Looks like something somebody would give you. Maybe her scissors are in here. [*Opens box. Suddenly puts her hand to her nose*] Why—[MRS PETERS *bends nearer, then turns her face away*] There's something wrapped up in this piece of silk.

MRS PETERS   Why, this isn't her scissors.

MRS HALE [*lifting the silk*]   Oh, Mrs Peters—it's—

    [MRS PETERS *bends closer.*]

MRS PETERS   It's the bird.

MRS HALE [*jumping up*]   But, Mrs Peters—look at it! It's neck! Look at its neck! It's all—other side *to*.

MRS PETERS   Somebody—wrung—its—neck.

    [*Their eyes meet. A look of growing comprehension, of horror. Steps are heard outside.* MRS HALE *slips box under quilt pieces, and sinks into her chair. Enter* SHERIFF *and* COUNTY ATTORNEY. MRS PETERS *rises.*]

COUNTY ATTORNEY [*as one turning from serious things to little pleasantries*]   Well ladies, have you decided whether she was going to quilt it or knot it?

MRS PETERS   We think she was going to—knot it.

COUNTY ATTORNEY   Well, that's interesting, I'm sure. [*seeing the bird-cage*] Has the bird flown?

MRS HALE [*putting more quilt pieces over the box*]   We think the—cat got it.

COUNTY ATTORNEY [*preoccupied*]   Is there a cat?

    [MRS HALE *glances in a quick covert way at* MRS PETERS.]

MRS PETERS   Well, not *now*. They're superstitious, you know. They leave.

COUNTY ATTORNEY [*to* SHERIFF PETERS, *continuing an interrupted conversation*]   No sign at all of anyone having come from the outside. Their own rope. Now let's go up again and go over it piece by piece. [*they start upstairs*] It would have to have been someone who knew just the—

    [MRS PETERS *sits down. The two women sit there not looking at one another, but as if peering into something and at the same time holding back. When they talk now it is in the manner of feeling their way over strange ground, as if afraid of what they are saying, but as if they can not help saying it.*]

MRS HALE   She liked the bird. She was going to bury it in that pretty box.

MRS PETERS [*in a whisper*]   When I was a girl—my kitten—there was a boy took a hatchet, and before my eyes—and before I could get there—[*covers her face an instant*] If they hadn't held me back I would have—[*catches herself, looks upstairs where steps are heard, falters weakly*]—hurt him.

MRS HALE [*with a slow look around her*]   I wonder how it would seem never to have had any children around. [*pause*] No, Wright wouldn't like the bird—a thing that sang. She used to sing. He killed that, too.

MRS PETERS [*moving uneasily*]   We don't know who killed the bird.

MRS HALE   I knew John Wright.

MRS PETERS   It was an awful thing was done in this house that night, Mrs Hale. Killing a man while he slept, slipping a rope around his neck that choked the life out of him.

MRS HALE   His neck. Choked the life out of him.

    [*Her hand goes out and rests on the bird-cage.*]

MRS PETERS [*with rising voice*]   We don't know who killed him. We don't *know*.

MRS HALE [*her own feeling not interrupted*]   If there'd been years and years of nothing, then a bird to sing to you, it would be awful—still, after the bird was still.

MRS PETERS [*something within her speaking*]   I know what stillness is. When we homesteaded in Dakota, and my first baby died—after he was two years old, and me with no other then—

MRS HALE [*moving*] How soon do you suppose they'll be through, looking for the evidence?

MRS PETERS I know what stillness is. [*pulling herself back*] The law has got to punish crime, Mrs Hale.

MRS HALE [*not as if answering that*] I wish you'd seen Minnie Foster when she wore a white dress with blue ribbons and stood up there in the choir and sang. [*a look around the room*] Oh, I *wish* I'd come over here once in a while! That was a crime! That was a crime! Who's going to punish that?

MRS PETERS [*looking upstairs*] We mustn't—take on.

MRS HALE I might have known she needed help! I know how things can be—for women. I tell you, it's queer. Mrs Peters. We live close together and we live far apart. We all go through the same things—it's all just a different kind of the same thing. [*brushes her eyes, noticing the bottle of fruit, reaches out for it*] If I was you, I wouldn't tell her her fruit was gone. Tell her it *ain't*. Tell her it's all right. Take this in to prove it to her. She—she may never know whether it was broke or not.

MRS PETERS [*takes the bottle, looks about for something to wrap it in; takes petticoat from the clothes brought from the other room, very nervously begins winding this around the bottle. In a false voice*] My, it's a good thing the men couldn't hear us. Wouldn't they just laugh! Getting all stirred up over a little thing like a—dead canary. As if that could have anything to do with—with—wouldn't they *laugh*!

[*The men are heard coming down stairs.*]

MRS HALE [*under her breath*] Maybe they would—maybe they wouldn't.

COUNTY ATTORNEY No, Peters, it's all perfectly clear except a reason for doing it. But you know juries when it comes to women. If there was some definite thing. Something to show—something to make a story about—a thing that would connect up with this strange way of doing it—

[*The women's eyes meet for an instant. Enter* HALE *from outer door.*]

HALE Well. I've got the team around. Pretty cold out there.

COUNTY ATTORNEY I'm going to stay here a while by myself. [*to the* SHERIFF] You can send Frank out for me, can't you? I want to go over everything. I'm not satisfied that we can't do better.

SHERIFF Do you want to see what Mrs Peters is going to take in?

[*The* LAWYER *goes to the table, picks up the apron, laughs.*]

COUNTY ATTORNEY Oh, I guess they're not very dangerous things the ladies have picked out. [*Moves a few things about, disturbing the quilt pieces which cover the box. Steps back*] No, Mrs Peters doesn't need supervising. For that matter, a sheriff's wife is married to the law. Ever think of it that way, Mrs Peters?

MRS PETERS Not—just that way.

SHERIFF [*chuckling*] Married to the law. [*moves toward the other room*] I just want you to come in here a minute, George. We ought to take a look at these windows.

COUNTY ATTORNEY [*scoffingly*] Oh, windows!

SHERIFF We'll be right out, Mr Hale.

[HALE *goes outside. The* SHERIFF *follows the* COUNTY ATTORNEY *into the other room. Then* MRS HALE *rises, hands tight together, looking intensely at* MRS PETERS, *whose eyes make a slow turn, finally meeting* MRS HALE'S. *A moment* MRS HALE *holds her, then her own eyes point the way to where the box is concealed. Suddenly* MRS PETERS *throws back quilt pieces and tries to put the box in the bag she is wearing. It is too big. She opens box, starts to take bird out, cannot touch it, goes to pieces, stands there help-less. Sound of a knob turning in the other room.* MRS HALE *snatches the box and puts it in the pocket of her big coat. Enter* COUNTY ATTORNEY *and* SHERIFF.]

COUNTY ATTORNEY [*facetiously*]   Well, Henry, at least we found out that she was not going to quilt it. She was going to—what is it you call it, ladies?

MRS HALE [*her hand against her pocket*]   We call it—knot it, Mr Hender-son.

CURTAIN

1916

SHERWOOD ANDERSON
1876–1941

Sherwood Anderson was approaching middle age when he abandoned a successful business career to become a writer. Living in Chicago, New Orleans, and Paris, meet-ing literary people, he worked furiously to make up for his late start, producing nov-els, short stories, essays, and an autobiography. His short fiction provided a model for younger writers, whose careers he encouraged by literary advice and by practical help in getting published as well. *Winesburg, Ohio*, which appeared in 1919 when he was forty-three years old, remains a major work of experimental fiction and was in its time a bold treatment of small-town life in the American Midwest in the tradition of Edgar Lee Masters's *Spoon River Anthology*.

Anderson was born in southern Ohio, the third of seven children in a family headed by a father whose training and skill as a harness maker were becoming useless in the new world of the automobile. Anderson's father kept his family on the move in search of work; the stamina and tenderness of his mother supplied coherence and security in this nomadic life. Not until 1894, when Anderson was sixteen, did they settle down in the town of Clyde, Ohio, which became the model for Winesburg. Anderson never finished high school. He held a variety of jobs, living in Chicago with an older brother in 1896 and again in 1900 when he worked as an advertising copywriter.

His first wife came from a successful Ohio business family; the couple settled in Ohio where Anderson managed a mail-order house as well as two paint firms. But he found increasingly that the need to write conflicted with his career. In 1912 he left his business and his marriage, returning to Chicago, where he met the writers and artists whose activities were creating the Chicago Renaissance. These included the novelists Floyd Dell and Theodore Dreiser; the poets Edgar Lee Masters, Vachel Lind-say, and Carl Sandburg; and the editors Harriet Monroe of *Poetry* and Margaret C. Anderson of the *Little Review*. His first major publication was *Windy McPherson's Son* (1916), the story of a man who runs away from a small Iowa town in futile search for life's meaning; his second was *Marching Men* (1917), about a charismatic lawyer who tries—unsuccessfully—to reorganize the factory system in a small town. These books reveal three of Anderson's preoccupations: the individual quest for self and social bet-terment, the small-town environment, and the distrust of modern industrial society.

Missing, however, is the interest in human psychology and the sense of conflict between inner and outer worlds that appear in *Winesburg* and later works.

In 1916 Anderson began writing and publishing the tales that were brought together in *Winesburg, Ohio*. The formal achievement of the book lay in its articulation of individual tales to a loose but coherent structure. The lives of a number of people living in the town of Winesburg are observed by the naïve adolescent George Willard, a reporter for the local newspaper. Their stories contribute to his understanding of life and to his preparation for a career as a writer. The book ends when his mother dies and he leaves Winesburg. With the help of the narrator, whose vision is larger than George's, the reader can see how the lives of the characters have been profoundly distorted by the frustration and suppression of so many of their desires. Anderson calls these characters "grotesques," but the intention of *Winesburg, Ohio* is to show that life in all American small towns is grotesque in the same way. Anderson's attitude toward the characters mixes compassion for the individual with dismay at a social order that can do so much damage. His criticism is not specifically political, however; he is measuring society by a utopian standard of free emotional and sensual expression.

Stylistically Anderson strove for the simplest possible prose, using brief or at least uncomplex sentences and an unsophisticated vocabulary appropriate to the muffled awareness and limited resources of his typical characters. Structurally, his stories build toward a moment when the character breaks out in some frenzied gesture of release that is revelatory of a hidden inner life. In both style and structure Anderson's works were important influences on other writers: he encouraged simplicity and directness of style, made attractive the use of the point of view of outsider characters as a way of criticizing conventional society, and gave the craft of the short story a decided push toward stories presenting a slice of life or a significant moment as opposed to panorama and summary.

Winesburg, Ohio appeared near the beginning of Anderson's literary career, and although he continued writing for two decades, he never repeated its success. His best later work was in short stories, published in three volumes: *The Triumph of the Egg* (1921), *Horses and Men* (1923), and *Death in the Woods and Other Stories* (1933). He also wrote a number of novels, including *Poor White* (1920), *Many Marriages* (1923), *Beyond Desire* (1932), and *Kit Brandon* (1936), as well as free verse, prose poems, plays, and essays. A series of autobiographical volumes advertised his career, attempted to define the writer's vocation in America, and discussed his impact on other writers. The more he claimed, however, the less other writers were willing to allow him; both Hemingway and Faulkner, for example, whom he had met in Paris and New Orleans, respectively, satirized his cult of the simple and thereby disavowed his influence. (In fact, he *had* stimulated and helped both of them—stimulated Hemingway in his quest for stylistic simplicity, Faulkner in his search for the proper subject matter.) During the 1930s Anderson, along with many other writers, was active in liberal causes, and he died at sea on the way to South America while on a goodwill mission for the State Department.

The text is that of *Winesburg, Ohio* (1919).

FROM WINESBURG, OHIO

Hands

Upon the half decayed veranda of a small frame house that stood near the edge of a ravine near the town of Winesburg, Ohio, a fat little old man walked nervously up and down. Across a long field that has been seeded for clover but that had produced only a dense crop of yellow mustard weeds, he could see the public highway along which went a wagon filled with berry pickers returning from the fields. The berry pickers, youths and maidens, laughed and shouted boisterously. A boy clad in a blue shirt leaped from the wagon and attempted to drag after him one of the maidens who screamed and protested shrilly. The feet of the boy in the road kicked up a cloud of dust that floated across the face of the departing sun. Over the long field came a thin girlish voice. "Oh, you Wing Biddlebaum, comb your hair, it's falling into your eyes," commanded the voice to the man, who was bald and whose nervous little hands fiddled about the bare white forehead as though arranging a mass of tangled locks.

Wing Biddlebaum, forever frightened and beset by a ghostly band of doubts, did not think of himself as in any way a part of the life of the town where he had lived for twenty years. Among all the people of Winesburg but one had come close to him. With George Willard, son of Tom Willard, the proprietor of the new Willard House, he had formed something like a friendship. George Willard was the reporter on the *Winesburg Eagle* and sometimes in the evenings he walked out along the highway to Wing Biddlebaum's house. Now as the old man walked up and down on the veranda, his hands moving nervously about, he was hoping that George Willard would come and spend the evening with him. After the wagon containing the berry pickers had passed, he went across the field through the tall mustard weeds and climbing a rail fence peered anxiously along the road to the town. For a moment he stood thus, rubbing his hands together and looking up and down the road, and then, fear overcoming him, ran back to walk again upon the porch on his own house.

In the presence of George Willard, Wing Biddlebaum, who for twenty years had been the town mystery, lost something of his timidity, and his shadowy personality, submerged in a sea of doubts, came forth to look at the world. With the young reporter at his side, he ventured in the light of day into Main Street or strode up and down on the rickety front porch of his own house, talking excitedly. The voice that had been low and trembling became shrill and loud. The bent figure straightened. With a kind of wriggle, like a fish returned to the brook by the fisherman, Biddlebaum the silent began to talk, striving to put into words the ideas that had been accumulated by his mind during long years of silence.

Wing Biddlebaum talked much with his hands. The slender expressive fingers, forever active, forever striving to conceal themselves in his pockets or behind his back, came forth and became the piston rods of his machinery of expression.

The story of Wing Biddlebaum is a story of hands. Their restless activity, like unto the beating of the wings of an imprisoned bird, had given him his name. Some obscure poet of the town had thought of it. The hands alarmed their owner. He wanted to keep them hidden away and looked with amazement at the quiet inexpressive hands of other men who worked beside him in the fields, or passed, driving sleepy teams on country roads.

When he talked to George Willard, Wing Biddlebaum closed his fists and beat with them upon a table or on the walls of his house. The action made him more comfortable. If the desire to talk came to him when the two were walking in the fields, he sought out a stump or the top board of a fence and with his hands pounding busily talked with renewed ease.

The story of Wing Biddlebaum's hands is worth a book in itself. Sympathetically set forth it would tap many strange, beautiful qualities in obscure men. It is a job for a poet. In Winesburg the hands had attracted attention merely because of their activity. With them Wing Biddlebaum had picked as high as a hundred and forty quarts of strawberries in a day. They became his distinguishing feature, the source of his fame. Also they made more grotesque an already grotesque and elusive individuality. Winesburg was proud of the hands of Wing Biddlebaum in the same spirit in which it was proud of Banker White's new stone house and Wesley Moyer's bay stallion, Tony Tip, that had won the two-fifteen trot at the fall races in Cleveland.

As for George Willard, he had many times wanted to ask about the hands. At times an almost overwhelming curiosity had taken hold of him. He felt that there must be a reason for their strange activity and their inclination to keep hidden away and only a growing respect for Wing Biddlebaum kept him from blurting out the questions that were often in his mind.

Once he had been on the point of asking. The two were walking in the fields on a summer afternoon and had stopped to sit upon a grassy bank. All afternoon Wing Biddlebaum had talked as one inspired. By a fence he had stopped and beating like a giant woodpecker upon the top board had shouted at George Willard, condemning his tendency to be too much influenced by the people about him. "You are destroying yourself," he cried. "You have the inclination to be alone and to dream and you are afraid of dreams. You want to be like others in town here. You hear them talk and you try to imitate them."

On the grassy bank Wing Biddlebaum had tried again to drive his point home. His voice became soft and reminiscent, and with a sigh of contentment he launched into a long rambling talk, speaking as one lost in a dream.

Out of the dream Wing Biddlebaum made a picture for George Willard. In the picture men lived again in a kind of pastoral golden age. Across a green open country came clean-limbed young men, some afoot, some mounted upon horses. In crowds the young men came to gather about the feet of an old man who sat beneath a tree in a tiny garden and who talked to them.[1]

Wing Biddlebaum became wholly inspired. For once he forgot the hands. Slowly they stole forth and lay upon George Willard's shoulders. Something new and bold came into the voice that talked. "You must try to forget all you have learned," said the old man. "You must begin to dream. From this time on you must shut your ears to the roaring of the voices."

Pausing in his speech, Wing Biddlebaum looked long and earnestly at George Willard. His eyes glowed. Again he raised the hands to caress the boy and then a look of horror swept over his face.

With a convulsive movement of his body, Wing Biddlebaum sprang to his feet and thrust his hands deep into his trousers pockets. Tears came to his eyes. "I must be getting along home. I can talk no more with you," he said nervously.

---

1. Biddlebaum's picture invokes ideals of the Greek Golden Age generally, and more particularly the image of the Athenian philosopher Socrates (469–399 B.C.E) teaching young Greek aristocrats.

Without looking back, the old man had hurried down the hillside and across a meadow, leaving George Willard perplexed and frightened upon the grassy slope. With a shiver of dread the boy arose and went along the road toward town. "I'll not ask him about his hands," he thought, touched by the memory of the terror he had seen in the man's eyes. "There's something wrong, but I don't want to know what it is. His hands have something to do with his fear of me and of everyone."

And George Willard was right. Let us look briefly into the story of the hands. Perhaps our talking of them will arouse the poet who will tell the hidden wonder story of the influence for which the hands were but fluttering pennants of promise.

In his youth Wing Biddlebaum had been a school teacher in a town in Pennsylvania. He was not then known as Wing Biddlebaum, but went by the less euphonic name of Adolph Myers.[2] As Adolph Myers he was much loved by the boys of his school.

Adolph Myers was meant by nature to be a teacher of youth. He was one of those rare, little-understood men who rule by a power so gentle that it passes as a lovable weakness. In their feeling for the boys under their charge such men are not unlike the finer sort of women in their love of men.

And yet that is but crudely stated. It needs the poet there. With the boys of his school, Adolph Myers had walked in the evening or had sat talking until dusk upon the schoolhouse steps lost in a kind of dream. Here and there went his hands, caressing the shoulders of the boys, playing about the tousled heads. As he talked his voice became soft and musical. There was a caress in that also. In a way the voice and the hands, the stroking of the shoulders and the touching of the hair was a part of the schoolmaster's effort to carry a dream into the young minds. By the caress that was in his fingers he expressed himself. He was one of those men in whom the force that creates life is diffused, not centralized. Under the caress of his hands doubt and disbelief went out of the minds of the boy and they began also to dream.

And then the tragedy. A half-witted boy of the school became enamored of the young master. In his bed at night he imagined unspeakable things and in the morning went forth to tell his dreams as facts. Strange, hideous accusations fell from his loose-hung lips. Through the Pennsylvania town went a shiver. Hidden, shadowy doubts that had been in men's minds concerning Adolph Myers were galvanized into beliefs.

The tragedy did not linger. Trembling lads were jerked out of bed and questioned. "He put his arms about me," said one. "His fingers were always playing in my hair," said another.

One afternoon a man of the town, Henry Bradford, who kept a saloon, came to the schoolhouse door. Calling Adolph Myers into the school yard he began to beat him with his fists. As his hard knuckles beat down into the frightened face of the schoolmaster, his wrath became more and more terrible. Screaming with dismay, the children ran here and there like disturbed insects "I'll teach you to put your hands on my boy, you beast," roared the saloon keeper, who, tired of beating the master, had begun to kick him about the yard.

2. Both his adopted surname and his original one underline Biddlebaum's foreignness by labeling him as German and, probably, Jewish.

Adolph Myers was driven from the Pennsylvania town in the night. With lanterns in their hands a dozen men came to the door of the house where he lived alone and commanded that he dress and come forth. It was raining and one of the men had a rope in his hands. They had intended to hang the schoolmaster, but something in his figure, so small, white, and pitiful, touched their hearts and they let him escape. As he ran away into the darkness they repented of their weakness and ran after him, swearing and throwing sticks and great balls of soft mud at the figure that screamed and ran faster and faster into the darkness.

For twenty years Adolph Myers had lived alone in Winesburg. He was but forty but looked sixty-five. The name of Biddlebaum he got from a box of goods seen at a freight station as he hurried through an eastern Ohio town. He had an aunt in Winesburg, a black-toothed old woman who raised chickens, and with her he lived until she died. He had been ill for a year after the experience in Pennsylvania, and after his recovery worked as a day laborer in the fields, going timidly about and striving to conceal his hands. Although he did not understand what had happened he felt that the hands must be to blame. Again and again the fathers of the boys had talked of the hands. "Keep your hands to yourself," the saloon keeper had roared, dancing with fury in the schoolhouse yard.

Upon the veranda of his house by the ravine, Wing Biddlebaum continued to walk up and down until the sun had disappeared and the road beyond the field was lost in the grey shadows. Going into his house he cut slices of bread and spread honey upon them. When the rumble of the evening train that took away the express cars loaded with the day's harvest of berries had passed and restored the silence of the summer night, he went again to walk upon the veranda. In the darkness he could not see the hands and they became quiet. Although he still hungered for the presence of the boy, who was the medium through which he expressed his love of man, the hunger became again a part of his loneliness and his waiting. Lighting a lamp, Wing Biddlebaum washed the few dishes soiled by his simple meal and, setting up a folding cot by the screen door that led to the porch, prepared to undress for the night. A few stray white bread crumbs lay on the cleanly washed floor by the table; putting the lamp upon a low stool he began to pick up the crumbs, carrying them to his mouth one by one with unbelievable rapidity. In the dense blotch of light beneath the table, the kneeling figure looked like a priest engaged in some service of his church. The nervous expressive fingers, flashing in and out of the light, might well have been mistaken for the fingers of the devotee going swiftly through decade after decade of his rosary.[3]

Mother

Elizabeth Willard, the mother of George Willard, was tall and gaunt and her face was marked with smallpox scars. Although she was but forty-five, some obscure disease had taken the fire out of her figure. Listlessly she went about the disorderly old hotel looking at the faded wall-paper and the ragged car-

3. String of beads used by Roman Catholics to keep track of prayers, divided into sections or "decades" of ten beads.

pets and, when she was able to be about, doing the work of a chambermaid among beds soiled by the slumbers of fat traveling men. Her husband, Tom Willard, a slender, graceful man with square shoulders, a quick military step, and a black mustache, trained to turn sharply up at the ends, tried to put the wife out of his mind. The presence of the tall ghostly figure, moving slowly through the halls, he took as a reproach to himself. When he thought of her he grew angry and swore. The hotel was unprofitable and forever on the edge of failure and he wished himself out of it. He thought of the old house and the woman who lived there with him as things defeated and done for. The hotel in which he had begun life so hopefully was now a mere ghost of what a hotel should be. As he went spruce and businesslike through the streets of Winesburg, he sometimes stopped and turned quickly about as though fearing that the spirit of the hotel and of the woman would follow him even into the streets. "Damn such a life, damn it!" he sputtered aimlessly.

Tom Willard had a passion for village politics and for years had been the leading Democrat in a strongly Republican community. Some day, he told himself, the tide of things political will turn in my favor and the years of ineffectual service count big in the bestowal of rewards. He dreamed of going to Congress and even of becoming governor. Once when a younger member of the party arose at a political conference and began to boast of his faithful service, Tom Willard grew white with fury. "Shut up, you," he roared, glaring about. "What do you know of service? What are you but a boy? Look at what I've done here! I was a Democrat here in Winesburg when it was a crime to be a Democrat. In the old days they fairly hunted us with guns."

Between Elizabeth and her one son George there was a deep unexpressed bond of sympathy, based on a girlhood dream that had long ago died. In the son's presence she was timid and reserved, but sometimes while he hurried about town intent upon his duties as a reporter, she went into his room and closing the door knelt by a little desk, made of a kitchen table, that sat near a window. In the room by the desk she went through a ceremony that was half a prayer, half a demand, addressed to the skies. In the boyish figure she yearned to see something half forgotten that had once been a part of herself recreated. The prayer concerned that. "Even though I die, I will in some way keep defeat from you," she cried, and so deep was her determination that her whole body shook. Her eyes glowed and she clenched her fists. "If I am dead and see him becoming a meaningless drab figure like myself, I will come back," she declared. "I ask God now to give me that privilege. I demand it. I will pay for it. God may beat me with his fists. I will take any blow that may befall if but this my boy be allowed to express something for us both." Pausing uncertainly, the woman stared about the boy's room. "And do not let him become smart and successful either," she added vaguely.

The communion between George Willard and his mother was outwardly a formal thing without meaning. When she was ill and sat by the window in her room he sometimes went in the evening to make her a visit. They sat by a window that looked over the roof of a small frame building into Main Street. By turning their heads they could see, through another window, along an alleyway that ran behind the Main Street stores and into the back door of Abner Groff's bakery. Sometimes as they sat thus a picture of village life presented itself to them. At the back door of his shop appeared Abner Groff with a stick or an empty milk bottle in his hand. For a long time there was a feud between the baker and a grey cat that belonged to Sylvester West, the druggist. The boy and his mother saw the cat creep into the door of the bakery and presently emerge followed by the baker who swore and waved his arms about. The baker's eyes were small and red and his black hair and beard were filled with flour dust. Sometimes he was so angry that, although the cat had disappeared, he hurled sticks, bits of broken glass, and even some of the tools of his trade about. Once he broke a window at the back of Sinning's Hardware Store. In the alley the grey cat crouched behind barrels filled with torn paper and broken bottles above which flew a black swarm of flies. Once when she was alone, and after watching a prolonged and ineffectual outburst on the part of the baker, Elizabeth Willard put her head down on her long white hands and wept. After that she did not look along the alleyway any more, but tried to forget the contest between the bearded man and the cat. It seemed like a rehearsal of her own life, terrible in its vividness.

In the evening when the son sat in the room with his mother, the silence made them both feel awkward. Darkness came on and the evening train came in at the station. In the street below feet tramped up and down upon a board sidewalk. In the station yard, after the evening train had gone, there was a heavy silence. Perhaps Skinner Leason, the express agent, moved a truck the length of the station platform. Over on Main Street sounded a man's voice, laughing. The door of the express office banged. George Willard arose and crossing the room fumbled for the doorknob. Sometimes he knocked against a chair, making it scrape along the floor. By the window sat the sick woman, perfectly still, listless. Her long hands, white and bloodless, could be seen drooping over the ends of the arms of the chair. "I think you had better be out among the boys. You are too much indoors," she said, striving to relieve the embarrassment of the departure. "I thought I would take a walk," replied George Willard, who felt awkward and confused.

One evening in July, when the transient guests who made the New Willard House their temporary homes had become scarce, and the hallways, lighted only by kerosene lamps turned low, were plunged in gloom, Elizabeth Willard had an adventure. She had been ill in bed for several days and her son had not come to visit her. She was alarmed. The feeble blaze of life that remained in her body was blown into a flame by her anxiety and she crept out of bed, dressed and hurried along the hallway toward her son's room, shaking with exaggerated fears. As she went along she steadied herself with her hand, slipped along the papered walls of the hall and breathed with difficulty. The air whistled through her teeth. As she hurried forward she thought how foolish she was. "He is concerned with boyish affairs," she told herself. "Perhaps he has now begun to walk about in the evening with girls."

Elizabeth Willard had a dread of being seen by guests in the hotel that had once belonged to her father and the ownership of which still stood recorded in her name in the county courthouse. The hotel was continually losing patronage because of its shabbiness and she thought of herself as also shabby. Her own room was in an obscure corner and when she felt able to work she voluntarily worked among the beds, preferring the labor that could be done when the guests were abroad seeking trade among the merchants of Winesburg.

By the door of her son's room the mother knelt upon the floor and listened for some sound from within. When she heard the boy moving about and talking in low tones a smile came to her lips. George Willard had a habit of talking aloud to himself and to hear him doing so had always given his mother a peculiar pleasure. The habit in him, she felt, strengthened the secret bond that existed between them. A thousand times she had whispered to herself of the matter. "He is groping about, trying to find himself," she thought. "He is not a dull clod, all words and smartness. Within him there is a secret something that is striving to grow. It is the thing I let be killed in myself."

In the darkness in the hallway by the door the sick woman arose and started again toward her own room. She was afraid that the door would open and the boy come upon her. When she had reached a safe distance and was about to turn a corner into a second hallway she stopped and bracing herself with her hands waited, thinking to shake off a trembling fit of weakness that had come upon her. The presence of the boy in the room had made her happy. In her bed, during the long hours alone, the little fears that had visited her had become giants. Now they were all gone. "When I get back to my room I shall sleep," she murmured gratefully.

But Elizabeth Willard was not to return to her bed and to sleep. As she stood trembling in the darkness the door of her son's room opened and the boy's father, Tom Willard, stepped out. In the light that streamed out at the door he stood with the knob in his hand and talked. What he said infuriated the woman.

Tom Willard was ambitious for his son. He had always thought of himself as a successful man, although nothing he had ever done had turned out successfully. However, when he was out of sight of the New Willard House and had no fear of coming upon his wife, he swaggered and began to dramatize himself as one of the chief men of the town. He wanted his son to succeed. He it was who had secured for the boy the position on the *Winesburg Eagle*. Now, with a ring of earnestness in his voice, he was advising concerning some course of conduct. "I tell you what, George, you've got to wake up," he said sharply. "Will Henderson has spoken to me three times concerning the matter. He says you go along for hours not hearing when you are spoken to and acting like a gawky girl. What ails you?" Tom Willard laughed good-naturedly. "Well, I guess you'll get over it," he said. "I told Will that. You're not a fool and you're not a woman. You're Tom Willard's son and you'll wake up. I'm not afraid. What you say clears things up. If being a newspaper man had put the notion of becoming a writer into your mind that's all right. Only I guess you'll have to wake up to do that too, eh?"

Tom Willard went briskly along the hallway and down a flight of stairs to the office. The woman in the darkness could hear him laughing and talking with a guest who was striving to wear away a dull evening by dozing in a chair by the office door. She returned to the door of her son's room. The weakness had passed from her body as by a miracle and she stepped boldly along. A thousand ideas raced through her head. When she heard the scraping of a chair and the sound of a pen scratching upon paper, she again turned and went back along the hallway to her own room.

A definite determination had come into the mind of the defeated wife of the Winesburg Hotel keeper. The determination was the result of long years of quiet and rather ineffectual thinking. "Now," she told herself, "I will act. There is something threatening my boy and I will ward it off." The fact that the conversation between Tom Willard and his son had been rather quiet and natural, as though an understanding existed between them, maddened her. Although for years she had hated her husband, her hatred had always before been a quite impersonal thing. He had been merely a part of something else that she hated. Now, and by the few words at the door, he had become the thing personified. In the darkness of her own room she clenched her fists and glared about. Going to a cloth bag that hung on a nail by the wall she took out a long pair of sewing scissors and held them in her hand like a dagger. "I will stab him," she said aloud. "He has chosen to be the voice of evil and I will kill him. When I have killed him something will snap within myself and I will die also. It will be a release for all of us."

In her girlhood and before her marriage with Tom Willard, Elizabeth had borne a somewhat shaky reputation in Winesburg. For years she had been what is called "stage-struck" and had paraded through the streets with traveling men guests at her father's hotel, wearing loud clothes and urging them to tell her of life in the cities out of which they had come. Once she startled the town by putting on men's clothes and riding a bicycle down Main Street.

In her own mind the tall girl had been in those days much confused. A great restlessness was in her and it expressed itself in two ways. First there was an uneasy desire for change, for some big definite movement to her life. It was this feeling that had turned her mind to the stage. She dreamed of joining some company and wandering over the world, seeing always new faces and giving something out of herself to all people. Sometimes at night she was quite beside herself with the thought, but when she tried to talk of the matter to the members of the theatrical companies that came to Winesburg and stopped at her father's hotel, she got nowhere. They did not seem to know what she meant, or if she did get something of her passion expressed, they only laughed. "It's not like that," they said. "It's as dull and uninteresting as this here. Nothing comes of it."

With the traveling men when she walked about with them, and later with Tom Willard, it was quite different. Always they seemed to understand and sympathize with her. On the side streets of the village, in the darkness under the trees, they took hold of her hand and she thought that something unexpressed in herself came forth and became a part of an unexpressed something in them.

And then there was the second expression of her restlessness. When that came she felt for a time released and happy. She did not blame the men who walked with her and later she did not blame Tom Willard. It was always the same, beginning with kisses and ending, after strange wild emotions, with peace and then sobbing repentance. When she sobbed she put her hand upon the face of the man and had always the same thought. Even though he were large and bearded she thought he had become suddenly a little boy. She wondered why he did not sob also.

In her room, tucked away in a corner of the old Willard House, Elizabeth Willard lighted a lamp and put it on a dressing table that stood by the door. A thought had come into her mind and she went to a closet and brought out a small square box and set it on the table. The box contained material for make-up and had been left with other things by a theatrical company that had once been stranded in Winesburg. Elizabeth Willard had decided that she would be beautiful. Her hair was still black and there was a great mass of it braided and coiled about her head. The scene that was to take place in the office below began to grow in her mind. No ghostly worn-out figure should confront Tom Willard, but something quite unexpected and startling. Tall and with dusky cheeks and hair that fell in a mass from her shoulders, a figure should come striding down the stairway before the startled loungers in the hotel office. The figure would be silent—it would be swift and terrible. As a tigress whose cub had been threatened would she appear, coming out of the shadows, stealing noiselessly along and holding the long wicked scissors in her hand.

With a little broken sob in her throat Elizabeth Willard blew out the light that stood upon the table and stood weak and trembling in the darkness. The strength that had been a miracle in her body left and she half reeled across the floor, clutching at the back of the chair in which she had spent so many long days staring out over the tin roofs into the main street of Winesburg. In the hallway there was the sound of footsteps and George Willard came in at the door. Sitting in a chair beside his mother he began to talk. "I'm going to get out of here," he said. "I don't know where I shall go or what I shall do but I am going away."

The woman in the chair waited and trembled. An impulse came to her. "I suppose you had better wake up," she said. "You think that? You will go to the city and make money, eh? It will be better for you, you think, to be a business man, to be brisk and smart and alive?" She waited and trembled.

The son shook his head. "I suppose I can't make you understand, but oh, I wish I could," he said earnestly. "I can't even talk to father about it. I don't try. There isn't any use. I don't know what I shall do. I just want to go away and look at people and think."

Silence fell upon the room where the boy and woman sat together. Again, as on the other evenings, they were embarrassed. After a time the boy tried again to talk. "I suppose it won't be for a year or two but I've been thinking about it," he said, rising and going toward the door. "Something father said makes it sure that I shall have to go away." He fumbled with the door knob. In the room the silence became unbearable to the woman. She wanted to cry out with joy because of the words that had come from the lips of her son, but the expression of joy had become impossible to her. "I think you had better go out among the boys. You are too much indoors," she said. "I thought I would go for a little walk," replied the son stepping awkwardly out of the room and closing the door.

Adventure

Alice Hindman, a woman of twenty-seven when George Willard was a mere boy, had lived in Winesburg all her life. She clerked in Winney's Dry Goods Store and lived with her mother, who had married a second husband.

Alice's step-father was a carriage painter, and given to drink. His story is an odd one. It will be worth telling some day.

At twenty-seven Alice was tall and somewhat slight. Her head was large and overshadowed her body. Her shoulders were a little stooped and her hair and eyes brown. She was very quiet but beneath a placid exterior a continual ferment went on.

When she was a girl of sixteen and before she began to work in the store, Alice had an affair with a young man. The young man, named Ned Currie, was older than Alice. He, like George Willard, was employed on the *Winesburg Eagle* and for a long time he went to see Alice almost every evening. Together the two walked under the trees through the streets of the town and talked of what they would do with their lives. Alice was then a very pretty girl and Ned Currie took her into his arms and kissed her. He became excited and said things he did not intend to say and Alice, betrayed by her desire to have something beautiful come into her rather narrow life, also grew excited. She also talked. The outer crust of her life, all of her natural diffidence and reserve, was torn away and she gave herself over to the emotions of love. When, late in the fall of her sixteenth year, Ned Currie went away to Cleveland where he hoped to get a place on a city newspaper and rise in the world, she wanted to go with him. With a trembling voice she told him what was in her mind. "I will work and you can work," she said. "I do not want to harness you to a needless expense that will prevent your making progress. Don't marry me now. We will get along without that and we can be together. Even though we live in the same house no one will say anything. In the city we will be unknown and people will pay no attention to us."

Ned Currie was puzzled by the determination and abandon of his sweetheart and was also deeply touched. He had wanted the girl to become his mistress but changed his mind. He wanted to protect and care for her. "You don't know what you're talking about," he said sharply; "you may be sure I'll let you do no such thing. As soon as I get a good job I'll come back. For the present you'll have to stay here. It's the only thing we can do."

On the evening before he left Winesburg to take up his new life in the city, Ned Currie went to call on Alice. They walked about through the streets for an hour and then got a rig from Wesley Moyer's livery and went for a drive in the country. The moon came up and they found themselves unable to talk. In his sadness the young man forgot the resolutions he had made regarding his conduct with the girl.

They got out of the buggy at a place where a long meadow ran down to the bank of Wine Creek and there in the dim light became lovers. When at midnight they returned to town they were both glad. It did not seem to them that anything that could happen in the future could blot out the wonder and beauty of the thing that had happened. "Now we will have to stick to each other, whatever happens we will have to do that," Ned Currie said as he left the girl at her father's door.

The young newspaper man did not succeed in getting a place on a Cleveland paper and went west to Chicago. For a time he was lonely and wrote to Alice almost every day. Then he was caught up by the life of the city; he began to make friends and found new interests in life. In Chicago he boarded at a house where there were several women. One of them attracted his attention and he forgot Alice in Winesburg. At the end of a year he had stopped writing letters, and only once in a long time, when he was lonely or when he went into one of the city parks and saw the moon shining on the grass as it had shone that night on the meadow by Wine Creek, did he think of her at all.

In Winesburg the girl who had been loved grew to be a woman. When she was twenty-two years old her father, who owned a harness repair shop, died suddenly. The harness maker was an old soldier, and after a few months his wife received a widow's pension. She used the first money she got to buy a loom and became a weaver of carpets, and Alice got a place in Winney's store. For a number of years nothing could have induced her to believe that Ned Currie would not in the end return to her.

She was glad to be employed because the daily round of toil in the store made the time of waiting seem less long and uninteresting. She began to save money, thinking that when she had saved two or three hundred dollars she would follow her lover to the city and try if her presence would not win back his affections.

Alice did not blame Ned Currie for what had happened in the moonlight in the field, but felt that she could never marry another man. To her the thought of giving to another what she still felt could belong only to Ned seemed monstrous. When other young men tried to attract her attention she would have nothing to do with them. "I am his wife and shall remain his wife whether he comes back or not," she whispered to herself, and for all of her willingness to support herself could not have understood the growing modern idea of a woman's owning herself and giving and taking for her own ends in life.

Alice worked in the dry goods store from eight in the morning until six at night and on three evenings a week went back to the store to stay from seven until nine. As time passed and she became more and more lonely she began to practice the devices common to lonely people. When at night she went upstairs into her own room she knelt on the floor to pray and in her prayers whispered things she wanted to say to her lover. She became attached to inanimate objects, and because it was her own, could not bear to have anyone touch the furniture of her room. The trick of saving money, begun for a purpose, was carried on after the scheme of going to the city to find Ned Currie had been given up. It became a fixed habit, and when she needed new clothes she did not get them. Sometimes on rainy afternoons in the store she got out her bank book and, letting it lie open before her, spent hours dreaming impossible dreams of saving money enough so that the interest would support both herself and her future husband.

"Ned always liked to travel about," she thought. "I'll give him the chance. Some day when we are married and I can save both his money and my own, we will be rich. Then we can travel together all over the world."

In the dry goods store weeks ran into months and months into years as Alice waited and dreamed of her lover's return. Her employer, a grey old man with false teeth and a thin grey mustache that drooped down over his mouth, was not given to conversation, and sometimes, on rainy days and in the winter when a storm raged in Main Street, long hours passed when no customers came in. Alice arranged and rearranged the stock. She stood near the front window where she could look down the deserted street and thought of the evenings when she had walked with Ned Currie and of what he had said. "We will have to stick to each other now." The words echoed and re-echoed through the mind of the maturing woman. Tears came into her eyes. Sometimes when her employer had gone out and she was alone in the store she put her head on the counter and wept. "Oh, Ned, I am waiting," she whispered over and over, and all the time the creeping fear that he would never come back grew stronger within her.

In the spring when the rains have passed and before the long hot days of summer have come, the country about Winesburg is delightful. The town lies in the midst of open fields, but beyond the fields are pleasant patches of woodlands. In the wooded places are many little cloistered nooks, quiet places where lovers go to sit on Sunday afternoons. Through the trees they look out across the fields and see farmers at work about the barns or people driving up and down on the roads. In the town bells ring and occasionally a train passes, looking like a toy thing in the distance.

For several years after Ned Currie went away Alice did not go into the wood with other young people on Sunday, but one day after he had been gone for two or three years and when her loneliness seemed unbearable, she put on her best dress and set out. Finding a little sheltered place from which she could see the town and a long stretch of the fields, she sat down. Fear of age and ineffectuality took possession of her. She could not sit still, and arose. As she stood looking out over the land something, perhaps the thought of never ceasing life as it expresses itself in the flow of the season, fixed her mind on the passing years. With a shiver of dread, she realized that for her the beauty and freshness of youth had passed. For the first time she felt that she had been cheated. She did not blame Ned Currie and did not know what to blame. Sadness swept over her. Dropping to her knees, she tried to pray, but instead of prayers words of protest came to her lips. "It is not going to come to me. I will never find happiness. Why do I tell myself lies?" she cried, and an odd sense of relief came with this, her first bold attempt to face the fear that had become a part of her everyday life.

In the year when Alice Hindman became twenty-five two things happened to disturb the dull uneventfulness of her days. Her mother married Bush Milton, the carriage painter of Winesburg, and she herself became a member of the Winesburg Methodist Church. Alice joined the church because she had become frightened by the loneliness of her position in life. Her mother's second marriage had emphasized her isolation. "I am becoming old and queer. If Ned comes he will not want me. In the city where he is living men are perpetually young. There is so much going on that they do not have time to grow old," she told herself with a grim little smile, and went resolutely about the business of becoming acquainted with people. Every Thursday evening when the store had closed she went to a prayer meeting in the basement of the church and on Sunday evening attended a meeting of an organization called The Epworth League.

When Will Hurley, a middle-aged man who clerked in a drug store and who also belonged to the church, offered to walk home with her she did not protest. "Of course I will not let him make a practice of being with me, but if he comes to see me once in a long time there can be no harm in that," she told herself, still determined in her loyalty to Ned Currie.

Without realizing what was happening, Alice was trying feebly at first, but with growing determination, to get a new hold upon life. Beside the drug clerk she walked in silence, but sometimes in the darkness as they went stolidly along she put out her hand and touched softly the folds of his coat. When he left her at the gate before her mother's house she did not go indoors, but stood for a moment by the door. She wanted to call to the drug clerk, to ask him to sit with her in the darkness on the porch before the house, but was afraid he would not understand. "It is not him that I want," she told herself; "I want to avoid being so much alone. If I am not careful I will grow unaccustomed to being with people."

During the early fall of her twenty-seventh year a passionate restlessness took possession of Alice. She could not bear to be in the company of the drug clerk, and when, in the evening, he came to walk with her she sent him away. Her mind became intensely active and when, weary from the long hours of standing behind the counter in the store, she went home and crawled into bed, she could not sleep. With staring eyes she looked into the darkness. Her imagination, like a child awakened from long sleep, played about the room. Deep within her there was something that would not be cheated by phantasies and that demanded some definite answer from life.

Alice took a pillow into her arms and held it tightly against her breasts. Getting out of bed, she arranged a blanket so that in the darkness it looked like a form lying between the sheets and, kneeling beside the bed, she caressed it, whispering words over and over, like a refrain. "Why doesn't something happen? Why am I left here alone?" she muttered. Although she sometimes thought of Ned Currie, she no longer depended on him. Her desire had grown vague. She did not want Ned Currie or any other man. She wanted to be loved, to have something answer the call that was growing louder and louder within her.

And then one night when it rained Alice had an adventure. It frightened and confused her. She had come home from the store at nine and found the house empty. Bush Milton had gone off to town and her mother to the house of a neighbor. Alice went upstairs to her room and undressed in the darkness. For a moment she stood by the window hearing the rain beat against the glass and then a strange desire took possession of her. Without stopping to think of what she intended to do, she ran downstairs through the dark house and out into the rain. As she stood on the little grass plot before the house and felt the cold rain on her body a mad desire to run naked through the streets took possession of her.

She thought that the rain would have some creative and wonderful effect on her body. Not for years had she felt so full of youth and courage. She wanted to leap and run, to cry out, to find some other lonely human and embrace him. On the brick sidewalk before the house a man stumbled homeward. Alice started to run. A wild, desperate mood took possession of her. "What do I care who it is. He is alone, and I will go to him," she thought; and then without stopping to consider the possible result of her madness, called softly. "Wait!" she cried. "Don't go away. Whoever you are, you must wait."

The man on the sidewalk stopped and stood listening. He was an old man and somewhat deaf. Putting his hand to his mouth, he shouted, "What? What say?" he called.

Alice dropped to the ground and lay trembling. She was so frightened at the thought of what she had done that when the man had gone on his way she did not dare get to her feet, but crawled on hands and knees through the grass to the house. When she got to her own room she bolted the door and drew her dressing table across the doorway. Her body shook as with a chill and her hands trembled so that she had difficulty getting into her nightdress.

When she got into bed she buried her face in the pillow and wept broken-heartedly. "What is the matter with me? I will do something dreadful if I am not careful," she thought, and turning her face to the wall, began trying to force herself to face bravely the fact that many people must live and die alone, even in Winesburg.

1919

CARL SANDBURG
1878–1967

Son of an immigrant Swedish blacksmith who had settled in Galesburg, Illinois, Carl Sandburg was an active populist and socialist, a journalist, and an important figure in the Chicago Renaissance of arts and letters. During the 1920s and 1930s he was one of the most widely read poets in the nation. His poetic aim was to celebrate the working people of America in poems that they could understand. He wrote sympathetically and affirmatively of the masses, using a long verse line unfettered by rhyme or regular meter, a line deriving from Whitman but with cadences closer to the rhythms of ordinary speech. "Simple poems for simple people," he said.

Sandburg's irregular schooling included brief attendance at Lombard College, but he was too restless to work through to a degree. He held a variety of jobs before moving to Chicago in 1913; he was in the army during the Spanish-American War, served as a war correspondent for the Galesburg *Evening Mail,* worked for the Social Democratic Party in Wisconsin, was secretary to the Socialist mayor of Milwaukee, and wrote editorials for the Milwaukee *Leader.* He had long been writing poetry but achieved success with the 1914 publication of his poem "Chicago" in *Poetry* magazine.

Poetry was one element in a surge of artistic activity in Chicago following the 1893 World's Fair. Such midwesterners as the architect Frank Lloyd Wright; the novelists Theodore Dreiser, Henry Blake Fuller, and Floyd Dell; and the poets Edgar Lee Masters and Vachel Lindsay believed not only that Chicago was a great city but that since the Midwest was America's heartland, it was in this region that the cultural life of the nation ought to center. Two literary magazines—*Poetry,* founded in 1912 by Harriet Monroe, and the *Little Review,* founded by Margaret C. Anderson in 1914—helped bring this informal movement to international attention. Nothing could be more apt to local interests than a celebratory poem called "Chicago."

Four volumes of poetry by Sandburg appeared in the next ten years: *Chicago Poems* (1914), *Cornhuskers* (1918), *Smoke and Steel* (1920), and *Slabs of the Sunburnt West* (1922). These present a panorama of America, concentrating on the prairies and cities of the Midwest. Like Whitman, Sandburg was aware that American life was increasingly urban, and he had little interest in the small town and its conventional middle class. The cities of the Midwest seemed to display both the vitality of the masses and their exploitation in an inequitable class system. Unlike many radicals whose politics were formed after the turn of the twentieth century, Sandburg believed that the people themselves, rather than a cadre of intellectuals acting on behalf of the people, would ultimately shape their own destiny. His political poems express appreciation for the people's energy and outrage at the injustices they suffer. They also balance strong declarative statements with passages of precise description. Other poems show Sandburg working in more lyrical or purely imagistic modes.

If the early "Chicago" is his best-known poem, his most ambitious is the book-length *The People, Yes* (1936), a collage of prose vignettes, anecdotes, and poetry, making use of his researches into American folk song. Sandburg had published these researches in *The American Songbag* in 1927, and he also composed a multivolume biography of Abraham Lincoln between 1926 and 1939. The purpose of this painstaking work was to present Lincoln as an authentic folk hero, a great man who had risen from among the people of the American heartland and represented its best values. He wrote features, editorials, and columns for the *Chicago Daily News* between 1922 and 1930, and pursued other literary projects as well. After World War II, when it became common for poets to read their works at campuses around the country, he enjoyed bringing his old-style populist radicalism to college students.

The text of the poems here is that of *The Complete Poems of Carl Sandburg* (1970).

Chicago

Hog Butcher for the World,
Tool Maker, Stacker of Wheat,
Player with Railroads and the Nation's Freight Handler;
Stormy, husky, brawling,
City of the Big Shoulders: 5

They tell me you are wicked and I believe them, for I have seen
    your painted women under the gas lamps luring the farm
    boys.
And they tell me you are crooked and I answer: Yes, it is true I
    have seen the gunman kill and go free to kill again.
And they tell me you are brutal and my reply is: On the faces of
    women and children I have seen the marks of wanton hunger.
And having answered so I turn once more to those who sneer at
    this my city, and I give them back the sneer and say to them:
Come and show me another city with lifted head singing so
    proud to be alive and coarse and strong and cunning.   10
Flinging magnetic curses amid the toil of piling job on job, here
    is a tall bold slugger set vivid against the little soft cities;
Fierce as a dog with tongue lapping for action, cunning as a
    savage pitted against the wilderness,
        Bareheaded,
        Shoveling,
        Wrecking,   15
        Planning,
        Building, breaking, rebuilding,
Under the smoke, dust all over his mouth, laughing with white
    teeth,
Under the terrible burden of destiny laughing as a young man
    laughs,
Laughing even as an ignorant fighter laughs who has never lost
    a battle,   20
Bragging and laughing that under his wrist is the pulse, and
    under his ribs the heart of the people,
        Laughing!

Laughing the stormy, husky, brawling laughter of Youth, half-
naked, sweating, proud to be Hog Butcher, Tool Maker,
Stacker of Wheat, Player with Railroads and Freight
Handler to the Nation.

1914, 1916

Fog

The fog comes
on little cat feet.

It sits looking
over harbor and city
on silent haunches   5
and then moves on.

1916

Cool Tombs

When Abraham Lincoln was shoveled into the tombs, he forgot the
copperheads and the assassin[1] . . . in the dust, in the cool tombs.

And Ulysses Grant lost all thought of con men and Wall Street, cash and
collateral turned ashes][2] . . . in the dust, in the cool tombs.

Pocahontas' body, lovely as a poplar, sweet as a red haw in November or a
pawpaw[3] in May, did she wonder? does she remember? . . . in the dust,
in the cool tombs?

Take any streetful of people buying clothes and groceries, cheering a hero or
throwing confetti and blowing tin horns . . . tell me if the lovers are
losers . . . tell me if any get more than the lovers . . . in the dust . . . in
the cool tombs.

1918

1. President Lincoln (1809–1865) was opposed
by southern sympathizers in the North, called Copperheads, and assassinated by John Wilkes Booth.
The copperhead is a poisonous snake.
2. The second administration of President Grant
(1822–1885) was riddled with bribery and political
corruption. After leaving office, Grant was

exploited in business and declared bankruptcy.
3. Colloquial for the fruit of the papaya tree. Pocahontas (1595?–1617), daughter of the Native
American chief Powhatan, intervened to save the
life of Captain John Smith. "Red haw": a type of
American hawthorn tree.

Grass[1]

Pile the bodies high at Austerlitz and Waterloo.
Shovel them under and let me work—
              I am the grass; I cover all.

And pile them high at Gettysburg
And pile them high at Ypres and Verdun.   5
Shovel them under and let me work.
Two years, ten years, and passengers ask the conductor:
              What place is this?
              Where are we now?

              I am the grass.   10
              Let me work.

                        1918

1. The proper names in this poem are all famous battlefields in the Napoleonic Wars, the American Civil War, and World War I.

WALLACE STEVENS
1879–1955

Wallace Stevens was raised in Reading, Pennsylvania, and went to Harvard for three years before leaving school in 1897 to pursue a literary career. Determined, however, that he would never "make a petty struggle for existence," he also looked for a well-paying job. After briefly trying journalism, he went to law school. In 1916 he began to work for the Hartford Accident and Indemnity Company and moved with his wife to Hartford, Connecticut. They made Hartford their lifelong home, Stevens writing his poetry at night and during summers. Visiting Florida frequently on business, he found the contrast between the South's lush vegetation and tropical climate and the chilly austerity of New England a useful metaphor for opposing ways of imagining the world, as poems like "The Snow Man" and "Sunday Morning" show.

    Stevens began to publish in little magazines around 1914. In the early years of his career, he frequented literary gatherings in New York City, becoming friends with William Carlos Williams and Marianne Moore, among others. Because his concern was with the private interaction of the observed and the observer, however, he had little interest in artistic causes—less still in politics—and after moving to Hartford, he dropped out of literary circles, although he maintained an active correspondence with his friends. A good businessman, by the mid-1930s Stevens was prosperous. He continued to work for the same company until his death, eventually becoming a vice president.

    His first volume of poetry, *Harmonium*, appeared in 1923. The poems in that book, mostly brief lyrics, are dazzling in their wit, imagery, and color; they established Stevens as one of the most accomplished poets of his era, although some critics found in them so much display as to make their "seriousness" questionable. But Stevens's purpose in part was to show that display was a valid poetic exercise—that poetry existed to illuminate the world's surfaces as well as its depths. He brought a newly perceived but real world before the reader, authenticating both the beauty of reality and the dependence of that beauty—indeed the dependence of reality itself—on the human observer. Two repeated activities are looking at things—the self as active observer of reality—and playing musical instruments or singing—the self as creator of reality (as in "The Idea of Order at Key West"). In this concern with the role of the perceiver in the creation of what is nevertheless real—the sense of an inescapable subjectivity in everything we know—Stevens clearly shared a modernist ideology. His search for belief in an era when, he thought, Christianity has lost its power; the idea, increasingly expressed in later poems, that with the fading of traditional religion poetry might become the forger of new faiths also coincides with the convictions of such poets as T. S. Eliot (in his earlier phase) and Ezra Pound. He has an almost postmodern sense, however, that any religious explanation of the world would have to be a fiction.

His poems feature the continually unexpected in diction and imagery. They abound in allusions to music and painting; are packed with sense images, especially of sound and color; and are elegant and funny. Consider the surprise and humor in the titles of the selections printed here as well as these: "Floral Decorations for Bananas," "Anatomy of Monotony," "The Bird with the Coppery, Keen Claws," "Frogs Eat Butterflies, Snakes Eat Frogs, Hogs Eat Snakes, Men Eat Hogs." Stevens's line is simple—either blank verse or brief stanzas, usually unrhymed—so that the reader's attention is directed to vocabulary and imagery rather than prosody. Invented words are frequent, some employed simply for sound effects. Multilayered puns that ingeniously convey many important meanings serve to thicken and lighten the poetic texture.

Among the poems in *Harmonium* at least three have become touchstones for critics: "The Comedian as the Letter C," "Peter Quince at the Clavier," and "Sunday Morning." "The Comedian as the Letter C" establishes a contrast between an idealistic would-be poet with his empty imaginings and the same poet enmeshed in the rich reality of the senses and human affections. "Peter Quince at the Clavier," again, opposes an idea of beauty in the mind with the reality of beauty in the flesh—paradoxically, it is beauty in the flesh that is immortal. "Sunday Morning" opens with a woman taking her ease at home on the day traditionally reserved for churchgoing, and mentally contrasting a fearful, death-obsessed Christianity with her own celebration of earthly pleasure. She would like to think that her behavior is a religion—a celebration—of life, yet death too is real and to some extent she knows that her behavior is as partial as the Christianity she cannot accept. She wonders whether there might ever be a religion that would take the real world rather than another world as its ground, accepting death and change as inevitable and beautiful. The poem, in the form of a meditation deriving from this opening situation, attempts to sketch out the resolution that the woman desires.

In the six years following the appearance of *Harmonium* Stevens published little new work. With the 1930s came a surge of creativity, beginning with the republication of *Harmonium* in an expanded version in 1931. New volumes and major works appeared regularly thereafter: *Ideas of Order* in 1935, *Owl's Clover* in 1936, *The Man with a Blue Guitar* in 1937, *Parts of a World* in 1942, *Transport to Summer* in 1947, and *The Auroras of Autumn* in 1950. A book collecting his occasional lectures appeared as *The Necessary Angel* in 1951; its gist was that poetry was "the supreme fiction" that enabled human beings to apprehend reality as a whole instead of in fragmentary flashes of insight. Stevens's poetry can be usefully thought of as reconceiving and expressing the ideas of the nineteenth-century American Transcendentalists in modernist terms, for they too located the individual at the center of the world while defining that individual chiefly as a perceiver rather than a doer or defining perceiving as the most important human activity. The difference is that the Transcendentalists confidently assumed that their perceptions were guaranteed by God. Stevens was more skeptical.

In his poetry of the 1930s and after, Stevens became increasingly abstract and theoretical; the dazzling effects diminished, the diction became plainer. Major, long poems from these years were *Notes toward a Supreme Fiction* (from *Transport to Summer*) and *An Ordinary Evening in New Haven* (from *The Auroras of Autumn*). In these later poems Stevens was more concerned about what active role poetry might play in the world than he had been in earlier work. These expository and discursive poems should have been easier to follow than the earlier compressed and elliptical poetry, but critics generally agree that the difficulty and abstractness of their ideas make them much more difficult. And to some readers the absence of the earlier specificity and sparkle also makes the later work less rewarding. But those who enjoyed a taxing poetry of ideas saw the late work as an advance. Stevens's complete *Collected Poems* (1954) has been celebrated as one of the most important books of American poetry in the twentieth century.

The text of the poems included here is that of *The Collected Poems of Wallace Stevens* (1954).

The Snow Man

One must have a mind of winter
To regard the frost and the boughs
Of the pine-trees crusted with snow;

And have been cold a long time
To behold the junipers shagged with ice,   5
The spruces rough in the distant glitter

Of the January sun; and not to think
Of any misery in the sound of the wind,
In the sound of a few leaves,

Which is the sound of the land   10
Full of the same wind
That is blowing in the same bare place

For the listener, who listens in the snow,
And, nothing himself, beholds
Nothing that is not there and the nothing that is.   15

                                                          1931

A High-Toned Old Christian Woman

Poetry is the supreme fiction, madame.
Take the moral law and make a nave[1] of it
And from the nave build haunted heaven. Thus,
The conscience is converted into palms,

---

1. Main body of a church building, especially the vaulted central portion of a Christian Gothic church.

Like windy citherns[2] hankering for hymns.   5
We agree in principle. That's clear. But take
The opposing law and make a peristyle,[3]
And from the peristyle project a masque[4]
Beyond the planets. Thus, our bawdiness,
Unpurged by epitaph, indulged at last,   10
Is equally converted into palms,
Squiggling like saxophones. And palm for palm,
Madame, we are where we began. Allow,
Therefore, that in the planetary scene
Your disaffected flagellants, well-stuffed,   15
Smacking their muzzy[5] bellies in parade,
Proud of such novelties of the sublime,
Such tink and tank and tunk-a-tunk-tunk,
May, merely may, madame, whip from themselves
A jovial hullabaloo among the spheres.   20
This will make widows wince. But fictive things
Wink as they will. Wink most when widows wince.

1923

The Emperor of Ice-Cream

Call the roller of big cigars,
The muscular one, and bid him whip
In kitchen cups concupiscent curds.
Let the wenches dawdle in such dress
As they are used to wear, and let the boys   5
Bring flowers in last month's newspapers.
Let be be finale of seem.
The only emperor is the emperor of ice-cream.

Take from the dresser of deal,[1]
Lacking the three glass knobs, that sheet   10
On which she embroidered fantails[2] once
And spread it so as to cover her face.
If her horny feet protrude, they come
To show how cold she is, and dumb.
Let the lamp affix its beam.   15
The only emperor is the emperor of ice-cream.

1923

---

2. I.e., citterns; pear-shaped guitars.
3. Colonnade surrounding a building, especially the cells or main chamber of an ancient Greek temple—an "opposing law" to a Christian church.
4. Spectacle or entertainment consisting of music, dancing, mime, and often poetry.
5. Sodden with drunkenness.
1. Plain, unfinished wood.
2. Stevens explained that "the word fantails does not mean fan, but fantail pigeons."

Disillusionment of Ten O'Clock

The houses are haunted
By white night-gowns.
None are green,
Or purple with green rings,
Or green with yellow rings,   5
Or yellow with blue rings.
None of them are strange,
With socks of lace
And beaded ceintures.
People are not going   10
To dream of baboons and periwinkles.
Only, here and there, an old sailor,
Drunk and asleep in his boots,
Catches tigers
In red weather.   15

1931

Sunday Morning[1]

I

Complacencies of the peignoir, and late
Coffee and oranges in a sunny chair,
And the green freedom of a cockatoo
Upon a rug mingle to dissipate
The holy hush of ancient sacrifice.   5
She dreams a little, and she feels the dark
Encroachment of that old catastrophe,
As a calm darkens among water-lights.
The pungent oranges and bright, green wings
Seem things in some procession of the dead,   10
Winding across wide water, without sound.
The day is like wide water, without sound,
Stilled for the passing of her dreaming feet
Over the seas, to silent Palestine,
Dominion of the blood and sepulchre.   15

II

Why should she give her bounty to the dead?
What is divinity if it can come
Only in silent shadows and in dreams?
Shall she not find in comforts of the sun,

1. This poem was first published in *Poetry* maga-zine in 1915; the editor, Harriet Monroe, printed only five of its eight stanzas but arranged them in the order Stevens suggested when consenting to the deletions (I, VIII, IV, V, and VII); he restored the deleted stanzas and the original sequence in subsequent printings.

In pungent fruit and bright, green wings, or else   20
In any balm or beauty of the earth,
Things to be cherished like the thought of heaven?
Divinity must live within herself:
Passions of rain, or moods in falling snow;
Grievings in loneliness, or unsubdued   25
Elations when the forest blooms; gusty
Emotions on wet roads on autumn nights;
All pleasures and all pains, remembering
The bough of summer and the winter branch.
These are the measures destined for her soul.   30

III

Jove[2] in the clouds had his inhuman birth.
No mother suckled him, no sweet land gave
Large-mannered motions to his mythy mind.
He moved among us, as a muttering king,
Magnificent, would move among his hinds,   35
Until our blood, commingling, virginal,
With heaven, brought such requital to desire
The very hinds[3] discerned it, in a star.
Shall our blood fail? Or shall it come to be
The blood of paradise? And shall the earth   40
Seem all of paradise that we shall know?
The sky will be much friendlier then than now,
A part of labor and a part of pain,
And next in glory to enduring love,
Not this dividing and indifferent blue.   45

IV

She says, "I am content when wakened birds,
Before they fly, test the reality
Of misty fields, by their sweet questionings;
But when the birds are gone, and their warm fields
Return no more, where, then, is paradise?"   50
There is not any haunt of prophecy,
Nor any old chimera[4] of the grave,
Neither the golden underground, nor isle
Melodious, where spirits gat them home,
Nor visionary south, nor cloudy palm   55
Remote on heaven's hill,[5] that has endured
As April's green endures; or will endure
Like her remembrance of awakened birds,
Or her desire for June and evening, tipped
By the consummation of the swallow's wings.   60

---

2. Supreme god in Roman mythology.
3. Farmhands; an allusion to the shepherds who saw the star of Bethlehem that signaled the birth of Jesus.

4. In Greek mythology, a monster with a lion's head, goat's body, and serpent's tail.
5. Versions of Paradise in diverse world religions.

V

She says, "But in contentment I still feel
The need of some imperishable bliss."
Death is the mother of beauty; hence from her,
Alone, shall come fulfillment to our dreams
And our desires. Although she strews the leaves   65
Of sure obliteration on our paths,
The path sick sorrow took, the many paths
Where triumph rang its brassy phrase, or love
Whispered a little out of tenderness,
She makes the willow shiver in the sun   70
For maidens who were wont to sit and gaze
Upon the grass, relinquished to their feet.
She causes boys to pile new plums and pears
On disregarded plate. The maidens taste
And stray impassioned in the littering leaves.   75

VI

Is there no change of death in paradise?
Does ripe fruit never fall? Or do the boughs
Hang always heavy in that perfect sky,
Unchanging, yet so like our perishing earth,
With rivers like our own that seek for seas   80
They never find, the same receding shores
That never touch with inarticulate pang?
Why set the pear upon those river-banks
Or spice the shores with odors of the plum?
Alas, that they should wear our colors there,   85
The silken weavings of our afternoons,
And pick the strings of our insipid lutes!
Death is the mother of beauty, mystical,
Within whose burning bosom we devise
Our earthly mothers waiting, sleeplessly.   90

VII

Supple and turbulent, a ring of men
Shall chant in orgy on a summer morn
Their boisterous devotion to the sun,
Not as a god, but as a god might be,
Naked among them, like a savage source.   95
Their chant shall be a chant of paradise,
Out of their blood, returning to the sky;
And in their chant shall enter, voice by voice,
The windy lake wherein their lord delights,
The trees, like serafin,[6] and echoing hills,   100
That choir among themselves long afterward.
They shall know well the heavenly fellowship
Of men that perish and of summer morn.

---

6. I.e., seraphim; angels.

And whence they came and whither they shall go
The dew upon their feet shall manifest.   105

VIII

She hears, upon that water without sound,
A voice that cries, "The tomb in Palestine
Is not the porch of spirits lingering.
It is the grave of Jesus, where he lay."
We live in an old chaos of the sun,   110
Or old dependency of day and night,
Or island solitude, unsponsored, free,
Of that wide water, inescapable.
Deer walk upon our mountains, and the quail
Whistle about us their spontaneous cries;   115
Sweet berries ripen in the wilderness;
And, in the isolation of the sky,
At evening, casual flocks of pigeons make
Ambiguous undulations as they sink,
Downward to darkness, on extended wings.   120

                                                        1915, 1923

Anecdote of the Jar

I placed a jar in Tennessee,
And round it was, upon a hill.
It made the slovenly wilderness
Surround that hill.

The wilderness rose up to it,   5
And sprawled around, no longer wild.
The jar was round upon the ground
And tall and of a port in air.

It took dominion everywhere.
The jar was gray and bare.   10
It did not give of bird or bush,
Like nothing else in Tennessee.

                                                        1923

Peter Quince¹ at the Clavier

I

Just as my fingers on these keys
Make music, so the selfsame sounds
On my spirit make a music, too.

---

1. Stage manager of the rustic actors in *A Mid-summer Night's Dream* by William Shakespeare; the name also echoes the poem "Quince to Lilac: to G. H." from the once-popular *More Songs from Vagabondia* by Bliss Carman and Richard Hovey (1895). Stevens was very fond of this book and its

Music is feeling, then, not sound;
And thus it is that what I feel,   5
Here in this room, desiring you,

Thinking of your blue-shadowed silk,
Is music. It is like the strain
Waked in the elders by Susanna.[2]

Of a green evening, clear and warm,   10
She bathed in her still garden, while
The red-eyed elders watching, felt

The basses of their beings throb
In witching chords, and their thin blood
Pulse pizzicati of Hosanna.[3]   15

II

In the green water, clear and warm,
Susanna lay.
She searched
The touch of springs,
And found   20
Concealed imaginings.
She sighed,
For so much melody.

Upon the bank, she stood
In the cool   25
Of spent emotions.
She felt, among the leaves,
The dew
Of old devotions.

She walked upon the grass,   30
Still quavering.
The winds were like her maids,
On timid feet,
Fetching her woven scarves,
Yet wavering.   35

A breath upon her hand
Muted the night.
She turned—
A cymbal crashed,
And roaring horns.   40

---

predecessor, *Songs from Vagabondia*, which
appeared in the same year.
2. Central character in chapter 13 of the Book of
Daniel in the Apocrypha. She rejects two elders
who attempt to seduce her; they retaliate by falsely

accusing her of sexual immorality. She is saved
from punishment by Daniel, who exposes discrepancies in the elders' testimony.
3. Expression of great praise. "Pizzicati": notes or
passages played by plucking strings.

III

Soon, with a noise like tambourines,
Came her attendant Byzantines.

They wondered why Susanna cried
Against the elders by her side;

And as they whispered, the refrain   45
Was like a willow swept by rain.

Anon, their lamps' uplifted flame
Revealed Susanna and her shame.

And then, the simpering Byzantines
Fled, with a noise like tambourines.   50

IV

Beauty is momentary in the mind—
The fitful tracing of a portal;
But in the flesh it is immortal.
The body dies; the body's beauty lives.
So evenings die, in their green going,   55
A wave, interminably flowing.
So gardens die, their meek breath scenting
The cowl of winter, done repenting.
So maidens die, to the auroral
Celebration of a maiden's choral.   60
Susanna's music touched the bawdy strings
Of those white elders; but, escaping,
Left only Death's ironic scraping.
Now, in its immortality, it plays
On the clear viol of her memory,   65
And makes a constant sacrament of praise.

                                        1923, 1931

Thirteen Ways of Looking at a Blackbird

I

Among twenty snowy mountains,
The only moving thing
Was the eye of the blackbird.

II

I was of three minds,
Like a tree   5
In which there are three blackbirds.

III

The blackbird whirled in the autumn winds.
It was a small part of the pantomime.

IV

A man and a woman
Are one.   10
A man and a woman and a blackbird
Are one.

V

I do not know which to prefer,
The beauty of inflections
Or the beauty of innuendoes,   15
The blackbird whistling
Or just after.

VI

Icicles filled the long window
With barbaric glass.
The shadow of the blackbird   20
Crossed it, to and fro.
The mood
Traced in the shadow
An indecipherable cause.

VII

O thin men of Haddam,[1]   25
Why do you imagine golden birds?
Do you not see how the blackbird
Walks around the feet
Of the women about you?

VIII

I know noble accents   30
And lucid, inescapable rhythms;
But I know, too,
That the blackbird is involved
In what I know.

IX

When the blackbird flew out of sight,   35
It marked the edge
Of one of many circles.

X

At the sight of blackbirds
Flying in a green light,

1. A city in Connecticut.

Even the bawds of euphony   40
Would cry out sharply.

XI

He rode over Connecticut
In a glass coach.
Once, a fear pierced him,
In that he mistook   45
The shadow of his equipage
For blackbirds.

XII

The river is moving.
The blackbird must be flying.

XIII

It was evening all afternoon.   50
It was snowing
And it was going to snow.
The blackbird sat
In the cedar-limbs.

                                                            1931

The Death of a Soldier

Life contracts and death is expected,
As in a season of autumn.
The soldier falls.

He does not become a three-days personage,
Imposing his separation,
Calling for pomp.   5

Death is absolute and without memorial,
As in a season of autumn,
When the wind stops,

When the wind stops and, over the heavens,   10
The clouds go, nevertheless,
In their direction.

                                                            1931

The Idea of Order at Key West[1]

She sang beyond the genius of the sea.
The water never formed to mind or voice,
Like a body wholly body, fluttering
Its empty sleeves; and yet its mimic motion
Made constant cry, caused constantly a cry,   5
That was not ours although we understood,
Inhuman, of the veritable ocean.

The sea was not a mask. No more was she.
The song and water were not medleyed sound
Even if what she sang was what she heard,   10
Since what she sang was uttered word by word.
It may be that in all her phrases stirred
The grinding water and the gasping wind;
But it was she and not the sea we heard.

For she was the maker of the song she sang.   15
The ever-hooded, tragic-gestured sea
Was merely a place by which she walked to sing.
Whose spirit is this? we said, because we knew
It was the spirit that we sought and knew
That we should ask this often as she sang.   20

If it was only the dark voice of the sea
That rose, or even colored by many waves;
If it was only the outer voice of sky
And cloud, of the sunken coral water-walled,
However clear, it would have been deep air,   25
The heaving speech of air, a summer sound
Repeated in a summer without end
And sound alone. But it was more than that,
More even than her voice, and ours, among
The meaningless plungings of water and the wind,   30
Theatrical distances, bronze shadows heaped
On high horizons, mountainous atmospheres
Of sky and sea.
                    It was her voice that made
The sky acutest at its vanishing.   35
She measured to the hour its solitude.
She was the single artificer of the world
In which she sang. And when she sang, the sea,
Whatever self it had, became the self
That was her song, for she was the maker. Then we,   40
As we beheld her striding there alone,
Knew that there never was a world for her
Except the one she sang and, singing, made.

---

1. One of the islands off the southern coast of Florida, where Stevens vacationed. The poem begins with
the scene of a woman walking by the sea and singing.

Ramon Fernandez,[2] tell me, if you know,
Why, when the singing ended and we turned   45
Toward the town, tell why the glassy lights,
The lights in the fishing boats at anchor there,
As the night descended, tilting in the air,
Mastered the night and portioned out the sea,
Fixing emblazoned zones and fiery poles,   50
Arranging, deepening, enchanting night.

Oh! Blessed rage for order, pale Ramon,
The maker's rage to order words of the sea,
Words of the fragrant portals, dimly-starred,
And of ourselves and of our origins,   55
In ghostlier demarcations, keener sounds.

                                                                  1936

A Postcard from the Volcano

Children picking up our bones
Will never know that these were once
As quick as foxes on the hill;

And that in autumn, when the grapes
Made sharp air sharper by their smell   5
These had a being, breathing frost;

And least will guess that with our bones
We left much more, left what still is
The look of things, left what we felt

At what we saw. The spring clouds blow   10
Above the shuttered mansion-house,
Beyond our gate and the windy sky

Cries out a literate despair.
We knew for long the mansion's look
And what we said of it became   15

A part of what it is . . . Children,
Still weaving budded aureoles,[1]
Will speak our speech and never know,

Will say of the mansion that it seems
As if he that lived there left behind   20
A spirit storming in blank walls,

A dirty house in a gutted world,
A tatter of shadows peaked to white,
Smeared with the gold of the opulent sun.

                                                                  1936

2. A French literary critic and essayist (1894–   accidental.
1944). Stevens said that he had invented the name   1. Haloes, radiances.
and that its coincidence with a real person was

Study of Two Pears

I

Opusculum paedagogum.[1]
The pears are not viols,
Nudes or bottles.
They resemble nothing else.

II

They are yellow forms   5
Composed of curves
Bulging toward the base.
They are touched red.

III

They are not flat surfaces
Having curved outlines.   10
They are round
Tapering toward the top.

IV

In the way they are modelled
There are bits of blue.
A hard dry leaf hangs   15
From the stem.

V

The yellow glistens.
It glistens with various yellows,
Citrons, oranges and greens
Flowering over the skin.   20

VI

The shadows of the pears
Are blobs on the green cloth.
The pears are not seen
As the observer wills.

                                                         1942

Of Modern Poetry

The poem of the mind in the act of finding
What will suffice. It has not always had
To find: the scene was set; it repeated what
Was in the script.

---

1. A small, didactic work (Latin).

          Then the theatre was changed   5
To something else. Its past was a souvenir.
It has to be living, to learn the speech of the place.
It has to face the men of the time and to meet
The women of the time. It has to think about war
And it has to find what will suffice. It has   10
To construct a new stage. It has to be on that stage
And, like an insatiable actor, slowly and
With meditation, speak words that in the ear,
In the delicatest ear of the mind, repeat,
Exactly, that which it wants to hear, at the sound   15
Of which, an invisible audience listens,
Not to the play, but to itself, expressed
In an emotion as of two people, as of two
Emotions becoming one. The actor is
A metaphysician in the dark, twanging   20
An instrument, twanging a wiry string that gives
Sounds passing through sudden rightnesses, wholly
Containing the mind, below which it cannot descend,
Beyond which it has no will to rise.
                         It must   25
Be the finding of a satisfaction, and may
Be of a man skating, a woman dancing, a woman
Combing. The poem of the act of the mind.

                                      1942

Asides on the Oboe

The prologues are over. It is a question, now,
Of final belief. So, say that final belief
Must be in a fiction. It is time to choose.

I

That obsolete fiction of the wide river[1] in
An empty land; the gods that Boucher[2] killed;   5
And the metal heroes that time granulates—
The philosophers' man alone still walks in dew,
Still by the sea-side mutters milky lines
Concerning an immaculate imagery.
If you say on the hautboy[3] man is not enough,   10
Can never stand as god, is ever wrong
In the end, however naked, tall, there is still
The impossible possible philosophers' man,
The man who has had the time to think enough,
The central man, the human globe, responsive   15

---

1. In Greek mythology, the Styx, the river that the souls of the dead had to cross on their journey from the realm of the living.
2. Jacques Boucher de Crèvecoeur de Perthes (1788–1868), French writer and archaeologist who discovered evidence that humans had existed in prebiblical times, thus suggesting that the biblical account of Creation was a myth.
3. An old French word for "oboe," but *haut* means "high" or "tall."

As a mirror with a voice, the man of glass,
Who in a million diamonds sums us up.

II

He is the transparence of the place in which
He is and in his poems we find peace.
He sets this peddler's pie and cries in summer,   20
The glass man, cold and numbered, dewily cries,
"Thou art not August unless I make thee so."
Clandestine steps upon imagined stairs
Climb through the night, because his cuckoos call.

III

One year, death and war prevented the jasmine scent   25
And the jasmine islands were bloody martyrdoms.
How was it then with the central man? Did we
Find peace? We found the sum of men. We found,
If we found the central evil, the central good.
We buried the fallen without jasmine crowns.   30
There was nothing he did not suffer, no; nor we.

It was not as if the jasmine ever returned.
But we and the diamond globe at last were one.
We had always been partly one. It was as we came
To see him, that we were wholly one, as we heard   35
Him chanting for those buried in their blood,
In the jasmine haunted forests, that we knew
The glass man, without external reference.

                                                                1942

The Plain Sense of Things

After the leaves have fallen, we return
To a plain sense of things. It is as if
We had come to an end of the imagination,
Inanimate in an inert savoir.[1]

It is difficult even to choose the adjective   5
For this blank cold, this sadness without cause.
The great structure has become a minor house.
No turban walks across the lessened floors.

The greenhouse never so badly needed paint.
The chimney is fifty years old and slants to one side.   10

---

1. Knowledge (French).

A fantastic effort has failed, a repetition
In a repetitiousness of men and flies.

Yet the absence of the imagination had
Itself to be imagined. The great pond,
The plain sense of it, without reflections, leaves,   15
Mud, water like dirty glass, expressing silence

Of a sort, silence of a rat come out to see,
The great pond and its waste of the lilies, all this
Had to be imagined as an inevitable knowledge,
Required, as a necessity requires.   20

1954

MINA LOY
1882–1966

Increasingly known today as one of the most freewheeling experimental poets of high
international modernism, Mina Loy led an expatriate life in most of the major artistic
centers of Europe and the United States before embracing American citizenship permanently in 1946. She was born in Hampstead, a suburb of London, and left home
in 1897 to attend art school, first in London, then in Munich and Paris, where she
also married and bore a daughter. She moved to Italy in 1907; there Loy met Americans like Gertrude Stein, and encountered F. T. Marinetti's Futurist movement—
which she admired for its dynamism but distrusted for its alignment of the heroic male
artist with "beautiful ideas which kill, and contempt for woman" (as Marinetti wrote
in his "Futurist Manifesto"; see p. 1500). Loy made her literary debut with "Aphorisms
on Futurism" (published in the little magazine *Camera Work* in 1914), which publicly
embraced Futurism's aggressive aesthetic of destruction and renovation even as her
"Feminist Manifesto" (circulated to friends, but not printed, in 1914; see p. 1502)
replied to Futurism's misogyny in its own experimental artistic idiom. She claimed the
female body as her own modernist subject in poems like "Parturition" and scandalized
readers with her surreal and erotically frank "Love Songs" (1915).

Loy sailed for New York in 1916, where she was already awaited as a minor celebrity,
and immediately made her way into high modernist circles that included the artist
Marcel Duchamp and writers like William Carlos Williams and Susan Glaspell. She
returned to Europe in 1921. A collection of her poems, *Lunar Baedecker*, was published in Paris in 1923. Named after the popular series of tourist guidebooks, the title
poem of the volume presents itself as a kind of guidebook to the hypercharged spectacle of the modern city, mapped through the poem's eye both as an underworld of
ancient mythologies and as a futurist metropolis on the moon. With Hitler's rise to
power making Europe dangerous for Jews, Loy returned to the United States in 1937.
An expanded collection of her poems (with the spelling of the title corrected) came
out as *Lunar Baedeker & Time-Tables* in 1958, reviving her reputation both among
older modernists and younger poets.

The text of the poems included here is that of *The Lost Lunar Baedeker* (1996).

Parturition

I am the centre
Of a circle of pain
Exceeding its boundaries in every direction

The business of the bland sun
Has no affair with me   5
In my congested cosmos of agony
From which there is no escape
On infinitely prolonged nerve-vibrations
Or in contraction
To the pin-point nucleus of being   10

Locate an irritation   without
It is   within
                               Within
It is without
The sensitized area   15
Is identical   with the extensity
Of intension

I am the false quantity
In the harmony of physiological potentiality
To which   20
Gaining self-control
I should be consonant
In time

Pain is no stronger than the resisting force
Pain calls up in me   25
The struggle is equal
The open window is full of a voice
A fashionable portrait-painter
Running up-stairs to a woman's apartment
Sings   30
     "All the girls are tid'ly did'ly
     All the girls are nice
     Whether they wear their hair in curls
     Or—"
At the back of the thoughts to which I permit crystallization   35
The conception   Brute
Why?
     The irresponsibility of the male
Leaves woman her superior Inferiority
He is running up-stairs   40

I am climbing a distorted mountain of agony
Incidentally with the exhaustion of control
I reach the summit

And gradually subside into anticipation of
Repose   45
Which never comes
For another mountain is growing up
Which   goaded by the unavoidable
I must traverse
Traversing myself   50

Something in the delirium of night-hours
Confuses while intensifying sensibility
Blurring spatial contours
So aiding elusion of the circumscribed
That the gurgling of a crucified wild beast   55
Comes from so far away
And the foam on the stretched muscles of a mouth
Is no part of myself
There is a climax in sensibility
When pain surpassing itself   60
Becomes Exotic
And the ego succeeds in unifying the positive and negative
          poles of sensation
Uniting the opposing and resisting forces
In lascivious revelation

Relaxation   65
Negation of myself as a unit
          Vacuum interlude
I should have been emptied of life
Giving life
For consciousness in crises   races   70
Through the subliminal deposits of evolutionary processes
Have I not
Somewhere
Scrutinized
A dead white feathered moth   75
Laying eggs?
A moment
Being realization
Can
Vitalized by cosmic initiation   80
Furnish an adequate apology
For the objective
Agglomeration of activities
Of a life.
LIFE   85
A leap with nature
Into the essence
Of unpredicted Maternity
Against my thigh
Touch of infinitesimal motion   90
Scarcely perceptible

Undulation
Warmth   moisture
Stir of incipient life
Precipitating into me   95
The contents of the universe
Mother I am
Identical
With infinite Maternity
       Indivisible   100
       Acutely
       I am absorbed
       Into
The was—is—ever—shall—be
Of cosmic reproductivity   105

Rises from the subconscious
Impression of a cat
With blind kittens
Among her legs
Same undulating life-stir   110
I am that cat

Rises from the sub-conscious
Impression of small animal carcass
Covered with blue-bottles[1]
—Epicurean—[2]   115
And through the insects
Waves that same undulation of living
Death
Life
I am knowing   120
All about
       Unfolding

The next morning
Each woman-of-the-people
Tip-toeing the red pile of the carpet   125
Doing hushed service
Each woman-of-the-people
Wearing a halo
A ludicrous little halo
Of which she is sublimely   unaware   130
I once heard in a church
—Man and woman God made them—[3]
                    Thank God.

                                                                        1914

1. Species of fly.   as the goal of life.
2. Devoted to pleasure; after Epicurus (341–270   3. "So God created man in his own image, . . .
B.C.E.), Greek philosopher who advocated pleasure   male and female created he them" (Genesis 2.27).

Brancusi's Golden Bird[1]

The toy
become the aesthetic archetype

As if
        some patient peasant God
        had rubbed and rubbed   5
        the Alpha and Omega[2]
        of Form
        into a lump of metal

A naked orientation
unwinged   unplumbed   10
  —the ultimate rhythm
has lopped the extremities
of crest and claw
from
the nucleus of flight   15

The absolute act
of art
conformed
to continent sculpture
—bare as the brow of Osiris—[3]   20
this breast of revelation

an incandescent curve
licked by chromatic flames
in labyrinths of reflections

This gong   25
of polished hyperaesthesia[4]
shrills with brass
as the aggressive light
strikes
its significance   30

The immaculate
conception[5]
of the inaudible bird
occurs
in gorgeous reticence . . .   35

1922

1. One of a series of bronze sculptures by Constantin Brancusi (1876–1957) depicting a stylized bird's wing. A photograph of "The Golden Bird" was published opposite Loy's poem in *The Dial*, Nov. 1922 (see the color insert to this volume).
2. First and last letters of the Greek alphabet; figuratively, the beginning and end.
3. Ancient Egyptian god, ruler of the underworld and of the rebirth of life from death.
4. Excessive sensitiveness; here suggesting the heightening of specifically artistic sensation.
5. In Roman Catholic doctrine proclaimed in 1854, the belief that Mary, mother of Jesus, was conceived without original sin (the burden of sin inherited from Adam and Eve's original disobedience).

Lunar Baedeker

A silver Lucifer
serves
cocaine in cornucopia

To some somnambulists
of adolescent thighs   5
draped
in satirical draperies

Peris[1] in livery
prepare
Lethe[2]   10
for posthumous parvenues[3]

Delirious Avenues
lit
with the chandelier souls
of infusoria[4]   15
from Pharoah's tombstones

lead
to mercurial doormsdays
Odious oasis
in furrowed phosphorous— — —   20

the eye-white sky-light
white-light district
of lunar lusts

— — —Stellectric signs
"Wing shows on Starway"   25
"Zodiac carrousel"

Cyclones
of ecstatic dust
and ashes whirl
crusaders   30
from hallucinatory citadels
of shattered glass
into evacuate craters

A flock of dreams
browse on Necropolis[5]   35

1. In Persian mythology, a fairy or angel.
2. In Greek mythology, the river in which the dead washed away their memories.
3. Literally, newly arrived persons (French); in English usage, social climbers.
4. One-celled waterborne microorganisms; in high concentrations, they may turn lake or river water reddish. Famous 19th-century zoological expeditions found their fossilized remains in Egyptian stone, leading to speculation that the biblical account of Moses turning the Nile into blood to punish Pharoah (Exodus 7.17–21) was based on an epidemic of infusoria.
5. City of the dead (Greek).

From the shores
of oval oceans
in the oxidized Orient

Onyx-eyed Odalisques[6]
and ornithologists   40
observe
the flight
of Eros obsolete

And "Immortality"
mildews . . .   45
in the museums of the moon

"Nocturnal cyclops"[7]
"Crystal concubine"
— — — — — —

Pocked with personification
the fossil virgin of the skies   50
waxes and wanes— — — —

1923

6. Female slaves or concubines.
7. In Greek mythology, member of a race of one-eyed giants.

WILLIAM CARLOS WILLIAMS
1883–1963

A modernist known for his disagreements with all the other modernists, William Carlos Williams thought of himself as the most underrated poet of his generation. His reputation has risen dramatically since World War II as a younger generation of poets testified to the influence of his work on their idea of what poetry should be. The simplicity of his verse forms, the matter-of-factness of both his subject matter and his means of describing it, seemed to bring poetry into natural relation with everyday life. He is now judged to be among the most important poets writing between the wars. His career continued into the 1960s, taking new directions as he produced, along with shorter lyrics, his epic five-part poem *Paterson*.

He was born in 1883 in Rutherford, New Jersey, a town near the city of Paterson. His maternal grandmother, an Englishwoman deserted by her husband, had come to America with her son, married again, and moved to Puerto Rico. Her son—Williams's father—married a woman descended on one side from French Basque people, on the other from Dutch Jews. This mix of origins always fascinated Williams and made him feel that he was different from what he thought of as mainstream Americans, i.e., northeasterners or midwesterners of English descent. After the family moved to New Jersey, Williams's father worked as a salesman for a perfume company; in childhood his father was often away from home, and the two women—mother and grandmother—were the most important adults to him. Throughout Williams's poetry the figure of woman as an earth mother, whom men require for completion and whose reason for being is to supply that completeness, appears, perhaps reflecting that early experience.

Except for a year in Europe, Williams attended local schools. He entered the School of Dentistry at the University of Pennsylvania directly after graduating from high school but soon switched to medicine. In college he met and became friends with Ezra Pound; Hilda Doolittle, later to become known as the poet H. D.; and the painter Charles Demuth. These friendships did much to steer him toward poetry, and even as he completed his medical work, interned in New York City, and did postgraduate study in Leipzig, Germany, he was reconceiving his commitment to medicine as a means of self-support in the more important enterprise of becoming a poet. Although he never lost his sense that he was a doctor in order to be a poet, his patients knew him as a dedicated old-fashioned physician, who made house calls, listened to people's problems, and helped them through life's crises. Pediatrics was his specialty; and in the course of his career, he delivered more than two thousand babies.

In 1912, after internship and study abroad, Williams married his fiancée of several years, Florence Herman. Despite strains in their relationship caused by Williams's continuing interest in other women, the marriage lasted and became, toward the end of Williams's life, the subject of some beautiful love poetry, including "Asphodel, that Greeny Flower." In the meantime women and the mixed belittlement–adoration accorded them by men (including the poet) were persistent themes. The couple settled in Rutherford, where Williams opened his practice. Except for a trip to Europe in 1924, when he saw Pound and met James Joyce, among others, and trips for lectures and poetry readings later in his career, Williams remained in Rutherford all his life, continuing his medical practice until poor health forced him to retire. He wrote at night, and spent weekends in New York City with friends who were writers and artists—the avant-garde painters Marcel Duchamp and Francis Picabia, the poets Marianne Moore and Wallace Stevens, and others. At their gatherings he acquired a reputation for outspoken hostility to most of the "-isms" of the day.

The characteristic Williams style emerged clearly in the landmark volume of mixed prose and poetry *Spring and All* (1923). One can see in this book that the gesture of staying at home was more for him than a practical assessment of his chances of self-support. Interested, like his friend Ezra Pound, in making a new kind of poetry, Williams also wanted always to speak as an American within an American context. One can observe this bias in the title of one of his books of essays, *In the American Grain* (1925), and in his choice of his own region as the setting and subject of *Paterson*, a long poem about his native city incorporating a great variety of textual fragments—letters, newspaper accounts, poetry—in a modernist collage.

Williams detested Eliot's *The Waste Land*, describing its popularity as a "catastrophe," deploring not only its internationalism but also its pessimism and deliberate obscurity. To him these characteristics were un-American. Yet Williams was not a sentimental celebrant of American life. He objected to Robert Frost's homespun poetry—which might be thought of as similar to his own work—for nostalgically evoking a bygone rural America rather than engaging with what he saw as the real American present. His America was made up of small cities like Paterson, with immigrants, factories, and poor working-class people struggling to get by. The sickness and suffering he saw as a physician entered into his poetry, as did his personal life; but the overall impact of his poetry is social rather than autobiographical.

The social aspect of Williams's poetry rises from its accumulation of detail; he opposed the use of poetry for general statements and abstract critique. "No ideas but in things," he wrote. Wallace Stevens had also written, "not ideas about the thing but the thing itself"; yet there is a world of difference between Williams's plainspoken and often opinionated writing and Stevens's cool elegance. Williams drew his vocabulary from up-to-date local speech and searched for a poetic line derived from the cadences of street talk. But he rejected "free verse" as an absurdity; rhythm within the line, and linking one line to another, was the heart of poetic craft to him. While working on *Paterson*, he invented the "triadic" or "stepped line," a long line broken into three segments, which he used in many poems, including several of the selections printed here.

Williams published fiction and essays as well as poetry, especially during the 1930s. Books of short stories (*The Edge of the Knife*, 1932, and *Life along the Passaic River*,

1938) and novels (*White Mule*, 1937, and *In the Money*, 1940) appeared in these years. He was also involved with others in the establishment of several little maga-zines, each designed to promulgate counterstatements to the powerful influences of Pound, Eliot, and the New Critics. All the time he remained active in his community and in political events; in the 1930s and 1940s he aligned himself with liberal Demo-cratic and, on occasion, leftist issues but always from the vantage point of an unre-constructed individualism. Some of his affiliations were held against him in the McCarthy era and to his great distress he was deprived in 1948 of the post of con-sultant in poetry at the Library of Congress.

It was also in 1948 that he had a heart attack, and in 1951 the first of a series of strokes required him to turn over his medical practice to one of his two sons and made writing increasingly difficult. Nevertheless, he persevered in his work on *Paterson*, whose five books were published in 1946, 1948, 1949, 1951, and 1958. *The Desert Music* (1954) and *Pictures from Brueghel* (1962), containing new poetry, also appeared; but by 1961 Williams had to stop writing. By the time of his death a host of younger poets, including Allen Ginsberg, Denise Levertov, Charles Olson, and Robert Creeley, had been inspired by his example. He won the National Book Award in 1950, the Bollingen Prize in 1953, and the Pulitzer Prize in 1962.

The texts of the poems included here are those of *The Collected Poems of William Carlos Williams*, Volume 1: *1909–1939* (1986), edited by A. Walton Litz and Christo-pher MacGowan, and *The Collected Poems of William Carlos Williams*, Volume 2: *1939–1962* (1988), edited by Christopher MacGowan.

The Young Housewife

At ten A.M. the young housewife
moves about in negligee behind
the wooden walls of her husband's house.
I pass solitary in my car.

Then again she comes to the curb   5
to call the ice-man, fish-man, and stands
shy, uncorseted, tucking in
stray ends of hair, and I compare her
to a fallen leaf.

The noiseless wheels of my car   10
rush with a crackling sound over
dried leaves as I bow and pass smiling.

                                                              1916, 1917

Portrait of a Lady

Your thighs are appletrees
whose blossoms touch the sky.
Which sky? The sky
where Watteau[1] hung a lady's

---

1. Jean Antoine Watteau (1684–1721), French artist who painted landscapes of elegantly dressed lovers in idealized rustic settings.

slipper. Your knees   5
are a southern breeze—or
a gust of snow. Agh! what
sort of man was Fragonard?[2]
—as if that answered
anything. Ah, yes—below   10
the knees, since the tune
drops that way, it is
one of those white summer days,
the tall grass of your ankles
flickers upon the shore—   15
Which shore?—
the sand clings to my lips—
Which shore?
Agh, petals maybe. How
should I know?   20
Which shore? Which shore?
I said petals from an appletree.

                                        1920, 1934

Queen-Anne's-Lace[1]

Her body is not so white as
anemone petals nor so smooth—nor
so remote a thing. It is a field
of the wild carrot taking
the field by force; the grass   5
does not raise above it.
Here is no question of whiteness,
white as can be, with a purple mole
at the center of each flower.
Each flower is a hand's span   10
of her whiteness. Wherever
his hand has lain there is
a tiny purple blemish. Each part
is a blossom under his touch
to which the fibres of her being   15
stem one by one, each to its end,
until the whole field is a
white desire, empty, a single stem,
a cluster, flower by flower,
a pious wish to whiteness gone over—   20
or nothing.

                                        1921

2. Jean Honoré Fragonard (1732–1806), French painter who depicted fashionable lovers in paintings more wittily and openly erotic than Watteau's. Fragonard's *The Swing* depicts a girl who has kicked her slipper into the air.

1. A common wildflower whose white bloom is composed of numerous tiny blossoms, each with a dark spot at the center, joined to the stalk by fibrous stems.

The Widow's Lament in Springtime

Sorrow is my own yard
where the new grass
flames as it has flamed
often before but not
with the cold fire   5
that closes round me this year.
Thirtyfive years
I lived with my husband.
The plumtree is white today
with masses of flowers.   10
Masses of flowers
load the cherry branches
and color some bushes
yellow and some red
but the grief in my heart   15
is stronger than they
for though they were my joy
formerly, today I notice them
and turn away forgetting.
Today my son told me   20
that in the meadows,
at the edge of the heavy woods
in the distance, he saw
trees of white flowers.
I feel that I would like   25
to go there
and fall into those flowers
and sink into the marsh near them.

1921

Spring and All[1]

By the road to the contagious hospital[2]
under the surge of the blue
mottled clouds driven from the
northeast—a cold wind. Beyond, the
waste of broad, muddy fields   5
brown with dried weeds, standing and fallen

patches of standing water
the scattering of tall trees

---

1. In the volume *Spring and All* (as originally published, 1923), prose statements were interspersed through the poems, which were identified by roman numerals. Williams added titles later and used the volume's title for the opening poem. For examples of the prose sections of *Spring and All*, see "Modernist Manifestos," p. xxxx.
2. I.e., a hospital for treating contagious diseases.

All along the road the reddish
purplish, forked, upstanding, twiggy   10
stuff of bushes and small trees
with dead, brown leaves under them
leafless vines—

Lifeless in appearance, sluggish
dazed spring approaches—   15

They enter the new world naked,
cold, uncertain of all
save that they enter. All about them
the cold, familiar wind—

Now the grass, tomorrow   20
the stiff curl of wildcarrot leaf

One by one objects are defined—
It quickens: clarity, outline of leaf

But now the stark dignity of
entrance—Still, the profound change   25
has come upon them: rooted, they
grip down and begin to awaken

                                        1923

To Elsie[1]

The pure products of America
go crazy—
mountain folk from Kentucky

or the ribbed north end of
Jersey   5
with its isolate lakes and

valleys, its deaf-mutes, thieves
old names
and promiscuity between

devil-may-care men who have taken   10
to railroading
out of sheer lust of adventure—

---

1. In *Spring and All*, this poem was originally numbered XVIII. Elsie, from the State Orphanage, worked for the Williams family as a nursemaid.

and young slatterns, bathed
in filth
from Monday to Saturday   15

to be tricked out that night
with gauds
from imaginations which have no

peasant traditions to give them
character   20
but flutter and flaunt

sheer rags—succumbing without
emotion
save numbed terror

under some hedge of choke-cherry   25
or viburnum—
which they cannot express—

Unless it be that marriage
perhaps
with a dash of Indian blood   30

will throw up a girl so desolate
so hemmed round
with disease or murder

that she'll be rescued by an
agent—   35
reared by the state and

sent out at fifteen to work in
some hard-pressed
house in the suburbs—

some doctor's family, some Elsie—   40
voluptuous water
expressing with broken

brain the truth about us—
her great
ungainly hips and flopping breasts   45

addressed to cheap
jewelry
and rich young men with fine eyes

as if the earth under our feet
were   50
an excrement of some sky

and we degraded prisoners
destined
to hunger until we eat filth

while the imagination strains   55
after deer
going by fields of goldenrod in

the stifling heat of September
Somehow
it seems to destroy us   60

It is only in isolate flecks that
something
is given off

No one
to witness   65
and adjust, no one to drive the car

                                          1923

The Red Wheelbarrow[1]

so much depends
upon

a red wheel
barrow

glazed with rain   5
water

beside the white
chickens

                                          1923

The Dead Baby

Sweep the house
    under the feet of the curious
    holiday seekers—
sweep under the table and the bed
    the baby is dead—   5

---

1. Numbered XXII in *Spring and All*.

The mother's eyes where she sits
   by the window, unconsoled—
have purple bags under them
   the father—
tall, wellspoken, pitiful   10
   is the abler of these two—

Sweep the house clean
   here is one who has gone up
   (though problematically)
to heaven, blindly   15
   by force of the facts—
a clean sweep
   is one way of expressing it—

Hurry up! any minute
   they will be bringing it
   from the hospital—   20
a white model of our lives
   a curiosity—
surrounded by fresh flowers

                                1927, 1935

The Wind Increases

The harried
earth is swept
               The trees
the tulip's bright
      tips   5
            sidle and
toss—

      Loose your love
to flow

Blow!   10

Good Christ what is
a poet—if any
         exists?

a man
whose words will   15
      bite
           their way
home—being actual

having the form
          of motion   20

At each twigtip

new

upon the tortured
body of thought
        gripping   25

the ground

a way
     to the last leaftip

                         1930, 1934

Death

He's dead

the dog won't have to
sleep on his potatoes
any more to keep them
from freezing   5

he's dead
the old bastard—
He's a bastard because

there's nothing
legitimate in him any   10
more
      he's dead

He's sick-dead

        he's
a godforsaken curio   15
without
any breath in it

He's nothing at all
      he's dead

Shrunken up to skin   20

      Put his head on
one chair and his

feet on another and
he'll lie there
like an acrobat—   25

Love's beaten. He
beat it. That's why
he's insufferable—

     because
he's here needing a   30
shave and making love
an inside howl
of anguish and defeat—

He's come out of the man
and he's let   35
the man go—
       the liar

Dead
    his eyes
rolled up out of   40
the light—a mockery

         which
love cannot touch—

just bury it
and hide its face—   45
for shame.

           1930, 1934

This Is Just to Say

I have eaten
the plums
that were in
the icebox

and which   5
you were probably
saving
for breakfast

Forgive me
they were delicious   10
so sweet
and so cold

           1934

A Sort of a Song

Let the snake wait under
his weed
and the writing
be of words, slow and quick, sharp
to strike, quiet to wait,   5
sleepless.

—through metaphor to reconcile
the people and the stones.
Compose. (No ideas
but in things) Invent!   10
Saxifrage is my flower that splits
the rocks.

1944

The Dance

In Brueghel's great picture, The Kermess,[1]
the dancers go round, they go round and
around, the squeal and the blare and the
tweedle of bagpipes, a bugle and fiddles
tipping their bellies (round as the thick-   5
sided glasses whose wash they impound)
their hips and their bellies off balance
to turn them. Kicking and rolling about
the Fair Grounds, swinging their butts, those
shanks must be sound to bear up under such   10
rollicking measures, prance as they dance
in Brueghel's great picture, The Kermess.

1944

Burning the Christmas Greens

Their time past, pulled down
cracked and flung to the fire
—go up in a roar
All recognition lost, burnt clean
clean in the flame, the green   5
dispersed, a living red,
flame red, red as blood wakes
on the ash—

---

1. *The Wedding Dance* by the Flemish painter Pieter Brueghel (or Breughel) the Elder (c. 1525–1569).

and ebbs to a steady burning
the rekindled bed become   10
a landscape of flame

At the winter's midnight
we went to the trees, the coarse
holly, the balsam and
the hemlock for their green   15

At the thick of the dark
the moment of the cold's
deepest plunge we brought branches
cut from the green trees

to fill our need, and over   20
doorways, about paper Christmas
bells covered with tinfoil
and fastened by red ribbons

we stuck the green prongs
in the windows hung   25
woven wreaths and above pictures
the living green. On the

mantle we built a green forest
and among those hemlock
sprays put a herd of small   30
white deer as if they

were walking there. All this!
and it seemed gentle and good
to us. Their time past,
relief! The room bare. We   35

stuffed the dead grate
with them upon the half burnt out
log's smoldering eye, opening
red and closing under them

and we stood there looking down.   40
Green is a solace
a promise of peace, a fort
against the cold (though we

did not say so) a challenge
above the snow's   45
hard shell. Green (we might
have said) that, where

small birds hide and dodge
and lift their plaintive
rallying cries, blocks for them   50
and knocks down

the unseeing bullets of
the storm. Green spruce boughs
pulled down by a weight of
snow—Transformed!   55

Violence leaped and appeared.
Recreant! roared to life
as the flame rose through and
our eyes recoiled from it.

In the jagged flames green   60
to red, instant and alive. Green!
those sure abutments . . . Gone!
lost to mind

and quick in the contracting
tunnel of the grate   65
appeared a world! Black
mountains, black and red—as

yet uncolored—and ash white,
an infant landscape of shimmering
ash and flame and we, in   70
that instant, lost,

breathless to be witnesses,
as if we stood
ourselves refreshed among
the shining fauna of that fire.   75

1944

Landscape with the Fall of Icarus[1]

According to Brueghel[2]
when Icarus fell
it was spring

a farmer was ploughing
his field   5
the whole pageantry

of the year was
awake tingling
near

1. In Greek mythology, a young man whose father made wings for him with feathers held together by wax. Icarus flew too close to the sun, the wax melted, and he fell into the sea and drowned.

2. A landscape by Flemish painter Pieter Brueghel the Elder (c. 1525–1569) in which Icarus is depicted by a tiny leg sticking out of the sea in one corner of the picture.

        the edge of the sea   10
        concerned
        with itself

        sweating in the sun
        that melted
        the wings' wax   15

        unsignificantly
        off the coast
        there was

        a splash quite unnoticed
        this was   20
        Icarus drowning

                                              1962

The Dance

When the snow falls the flakes
spin upon the long axis
that concerns them most intimately
two and two to make a dance

the mind dances with itself,   5
taking you by the hand,
your lover follows
there are always two,

yourself and the other,
the point of your shoe setting the pace,   10
if you break away and run
the dance is over

Breathlessly you will take
another partner
better or worse who will keep   15
at your side, at your stops ,

whirls and glides until he too
leaves off
on his way down as if
there were another direction   20

gayer, more carefree
spinning face to face but always down
with each other secure
only in each other's arms

But only the dance is sure!   25
make it your own.

Who can tell
what is to come of it?

in the woods of your
own nature whatever   30
twig interposes, and bare twigs
have an actuality of their own

this flurry of the storm
that holds us,
plays with us and discards us   35
dancing, dancing as may be credible.

1962

EZRA POUND
1885–1972

Ezra Loomis Pound was born in Hailey, Idaho. When he was still an infant his parents settled in a comfortable suburb near Philadelphia where his father was an assayer at the regional branch of the U.S. Mint. "I knew at fifteen pretty much what I wanted to do," he wrote in 1913; what he wanted was to become a poet. He had this goal in mind as an undergraduate at the University of Pennsylvania (where he met and became lifelong friends with William Carlos Williams and had a romance with Hilda Doolittle, who was later to become the poet H. D.) and at Hamilton College; it also motivated his graduate studies in languages—French, Italian, Old English, and Latin—at the University of Pennsylvania, where he received an M.A. in 1906. He planned to support himself as a college teacher while writing.

The poetry that he had in mind in these early years was in vogue at the turn of the twentieth century—melodious in versification and diction, romantic in themes, world-weary in tone—poetry for which the term *decadent* was used. A particular image of the poet went with such poetry: the poet committed to art for its own sake, careless of convention, and continually shocking the respectable middle class. A rebellious and colorful personality, Pound delighted in this role but quickly found that it was not compatible with the sober behavior expected from professors of language. He lost his first teaching job, at Wabash College in Indiana, in fewer than six months.

Convinced that his country had no place for him—and that a country with no place for him had no place for art—he went to Europe in 1908. He settled in London and quickly became involved in its literary life, and especially prominent in movements to revolutionize poetry and identify good new poets. He supported himself by teaching and reviewing for several journals. For a while he acted as secretary to the great Irish poet William Butler Yeats. He married Dorothy Shakespear, daughter of a close friend of Yeats, in 1914. Ten years later he became involved with the American expatriate Olga Rudge and maintained relationships with both women thereafter.

As an advocate of the new, he found himself propagandizing against the very poetry that had made him want to be a poet at the start; and this contradiction remained throughout his life: on the one hand, a desire to "make it new"; on the other, a deep attachment to the old. Many of his critical essays were later collected and published in books such as *Make It New* (1934), *The ABC of Reading* (1934), *Polite Essays* (1937), and *Literary Essays* (1954). He was generous in his efforts to assist other writers in their work and in their attempts to get published; he was helpful to H. D.,

T. S. Eliot, James Joyce, William Carlos Williams, Robert Frost, Ernest Hemingway, and Marianne Moore, to name just a few.

Pound first campaigned for "imagism," his name for a new kind of poetry. Rather than describing something—an object or situation—and then generalizing about it, imagist poets attempted to present the object directly, avoiding the ornate diction and complex but predictable verse forms of traditional poetry. Any significance to be derived from the image had to appear inherent in its spare, clean presentation. "Go in fear of abstraction," Pound wrote. Even the rules of grammar seemed artificial; hence this new poetry tended to work in disconnected fragments. Although imagism lasted only briefly as a formal movement, most subsequent twentieth-century poetry showed its influence. Pound soon moved on to "vorticism," which, although still espousing direct and bare presentation, sought for some principle of dynamism and energy in the image. In his imagist phase Pound was connected with H. D. and Richard Aldington, a British poet who became H. D.'s husband; as a vorticist he was allied with the icon-oclastic writer and artist Wyndham Lewis.

Pound thought of the United States as a culturally backward nation and longed to produce a sophisticated, worldly poetry on behalf of his country. Walt Whitman was his symbol of American poetic narrowness. His major works during his London years consisted of free translations of languages unknown to most Westerners: Provençal, Chinese, Japanese. He also experimented with the dramatic monologue form devel-oped by the English Victorian poet Robert Browning. Poems from these years appeared in his volumes *A Lume Spento* (By the spent light; Italian), which appeared in 1908, *A Quinzaine for This Yule* (1908), and *Personae* (1910). *Persona* means "mask," and the poems in this last volume developed the dramatic monologue as a means for the poet to assume various identities and to engage in acts of historical reconstruction and empathy.

Although his view of poetry would seem to exclude the long poem as a workable form, Pound could not overcome the traditional belief that a really great poem had to be long. He hoped to write such a poem himself, a poem for his time, which would unite biography and history by representing the total content of his mind and mem-ory. To this end he began working on his *Cantos* in 1915. The cantos were separate poems of varying lengths, combining reminiscence, meditation, description, and transcriptions from books Pound was reading, all of which were to be forged into unity by the heat of the poet's imagination. Ultimately, he produced 116 cantos, whose intri-cate obscurities continue to fascinate and challenge critics. The London period came to a close with two poems of disillusionment, "Hugh Selwyn Mauberley (Life and Contacts")" and "Mauberley," which described the decay of Western civilization in the aftermath of the Great War.

Looking for an explanation of what had gone wrong, Pound came upon the "social credit" theories of Major Clifford Hugh Douglas, a social economist who attributed all the ills of civilization to the interposition of money between human exchanges of goods. At this point, poetry and politics fused in Pound's work, and he began to search for a society in which art was protected from money and to record this search in poems and essays. This became a dominant theme in the *Cantos*. Leaving England for good in 1920, he lived on the Mediterranean Sea, in Paris for a time, and then settled in the small Italian town of Rapallo in 1925. His survey of history having persuaded him that the ideal society was a hierarchy with a strong leader and an agricultural econ-omy, he greeted the Italian fascist dictator Benito Mussolini as a deliverer. His inter-national perspective gave way to an intense localism. During World War II he voluntarily served the Italian government by making numerous English-language radio broadcasts beamed at England and the United States in which he vilified Jews, Pres-ident Franklin D. Roosevelt, and American society in general. When the U.S. Army occupied Italy, Pound was arrested, held for weeks in an open-air cage at the prison camp near Pisa, and finally brought to the United States to be tried for treason. The trial did not take place, however, because the court accepted a psychiatric report to the effect that Pound was "insane and mentally unfit to be tried." From 1946 to 1958 he was a patient and a prisoner in St. Elizabeth's Hospital for the criminally insane in Washington, D.C. During those years he received visits, wrote letters, composed cantos, and continued his polemic against American society.

In 1948 the *Pisan Cantos* (LXXIV–LXXXIV) won the Library of Congress's newly established Bollingen Prize for poetry, an event that provoked tremendous debate about Pound's stature as a poet as well as a citizen. Ten years later the efforts of a committee of writers succeeded in winning Pound's release; he returned to Italy, where he died at the age of eighty-seven. He remains one of the most controversial poets of the era.

The texts of the poems included here are those of *Personae: The Collected Poems* (rev., 1949) and *The Cantos* (1976).

To Whistler, American[1]

On the loan exhibit of his paintings at the Tate Gallery.

You also, our first great
Had tried all ways;
Tested and pried and worked in many fashions,
And this much gives me heart to play the game.

Here is a part that's slight, and part gone wrong,   5
And much of little moment, and some few
Perfect as Dürer![2]
"In the Studio" and these two portraits,[3] if I had my choice!
And then these sketches in the mood of Greece?

You had your searches, your uncertainties,   10
And this is good to know—for us, I mean,
Who bear the brunt of our America
And try to wrench her impulse into art.

You were not always sure, not always set
To hiding night or tuning "symphonies";[4]   15
Had not one style from birth, but tried and pried
And stretched and tampered with the media.

You and Abe Lincoln from that mass of dolts
Show us there's chance at least of winning through.

                                        1912, 1949

Portrait d'une Femme[1]

Your mind and you are our Sargasso Sea,[2]
London has swept about you this score years

---

1. James Abbott McNeill Whistler (1834–1903), expatriate American painter.
2. Albrecht Dürer (1471–1528), German painter and engraver.
3. " 'Brown and Gold—de Race,' 'Grenat et Or— Le Petit Cardinal' ('Garnet and Gold—The Little Cardinal')" [Pound's note]. Titles and subjects of

the portraits.
4. Whistler painted many night scenes and titled many paintings "symphonies."
1. Portrait of a lady (French).
2. Sea in the North Atlantic where boats were becalmed; named for its large masses of floating seaweed.

And bright ships left you this or that in fee:
Ideas, old gossip, oddments of all things,
Strange spars of knowledge and dimmed wares of price.   5
Great minds have sought you—lacking someone else.
You have been second always. Tragical?
No. You preferred it to the usual thing:
One dull man, dulling and uxorious,
One average mind—with one thought less, each year.   10
Oh, you are patient, I have seen you sit
Hours, where something might have floated up.
And now you pay one. Yes, you richly pay.
You are a person of some interest, one comes to you
And takes strange gain away: 15
Trophies fished up; some curious suggestion;
Fact that leads nowhere; and a tale or two,
Pregnant with mandrakes,[3] or with something else
That might prove useful and yet never proves,
That never fits a corner or shows use,   20
Or finds its hour upon the loom of days:
The tarnished, gaudy, wonderful old work;
Idols and ambergris and rare inlays,
These are your riches, your great store; and yet
For all this sea-hoard of deciduous things,   25
Strange woods half sodden, and new brighter stuff:
In the slow float of differing light and deep,
No! there is nothing! In the whole and all,
Nothing that's quite your own.
                    Yet this is you.   30

                                        1912

A Virginal[1]

No, no! Go from me. I have left her lately.
I will not spoil my sheath with lesser brightness,
For my surrounding air hath a new lightness;
Slight are her arms, yet they have bound me straitly
And left me cloaked as with a gauze of æther;   5
As with sweet leaves; as with subtle clearness.
Oh, I have picked up magic in her nearness
To sheathe me half in half the things that sheathe her.
No, no! Go from me. I have still the flavour,
Soft as spring wind that's come from birchen bowers.   10
Green come the shoots, aye April in the branches,
As winter's wound with her sleight hand she staunches,

---

3. Herb used as a cathartic; believed in legend to
have human properties, to shriek when pulled from
the ground, and to promote pregnancy.

1. A small pianolike instrument popular in the
16th and 17th centuries.

Hath of the trees a likeness of the savour:
As white their bark, so white this lady's hours.

1912

A Pact

I make a pact with you, Walt Whitman—
I have detested you long enough.
I come to you as a grown child
Who has had a pig-headed father;
I am old enough now to make friends.   5
It was you that broke the new wood,
Now is a time for carving.
We have one sap and one root—
Let there be commerce between us.

1913, 1916

The Rest

O helpless few in my country,
O remnant enslaved!

Artists broken against her,
A-stray, lost in the villages,
Mistrusted, spoken-against,   5

Lovers of beauty, starved,
Thwarted with systems,
Helpless against the control;

You who can not wear yourselves out
By persisting to successes,   10
You who can only speak,
Who can not steel yourselves into reiteration;

You of the finer sense,
Broken against false knowledge,
You who can know at first hand,   15
Hated, shut in, mistrusted:

Take thought:
I have weathered the storm,
I have beaten out my exile.

1913, 1916

In a Station of the Metro[1]

The apparition of these faces in the crowd;
Petals on a wet, black bough.

1913, 1916

The River-Merchant's Wife: A Letter[1]

While my hair was still cut straight across my forehead
I played about the front gate, pulling flowers.
You came by on bamboo stilts, playing horse,
You walked about my seat, playing with blue plums.
And we went on living in the village of Chōkan: 5
Two small people, without dislike or suspicion.

At fourteen I married My Lord you.
I never laughed, being bashful.
Lowering my head, I looked at the wall.
Called to, a thousand times, I never looked back.   10

At fifteen I stopped scowling,
I desired my dust to be mingled with yours
Forever and forever and forever.
Why should I climb the look out?

At sixteen you departed,   15
You went into far Ku-tō-en, by the river of swirling eddies,
And you have been gone five months.
The monkeys make sorrowful noise overhead.

You dragged your feet when you went out.
By the gate now, the moss is grown, the different mosses,   20
Too deep to clear them away!
The leaves fall early this autumn, in wind.
The paired butterflies are already yellow with August
Over the grass in the West garden;
They hurt me. I grow older.   25
If you are coming down through the narrows of the river Kiang,
Please let me know beforehand,
And I will come out to meet you
          As far as Chō-fū-Sa.

By Rihaku

1915

1. Paris subway.
1. Adaptation from the Chinese of Li Po (701–762), named Rihaku in Japanese, from the papers of Ernest Fenollosa, an American scholar whose widow gave his papers on Japan and China to Pound.

Villanelle: The Psychological Hour[1]

I

I had over-prepared the event,
        that much was ominous.
With middle-ageing care
        I had laid out just the right books.
I had almost turned down the pages.   5

      Beauty is so rare a thing.
      So few drink of my fountain.

So much barren regret,
So many hours wasted!
And now I watch, from the window,   10
        the rain, the wandering busses.
"Their little cosmos is shaken"—
        the air is alive with that fact.
In their parts of the city
        they are played on by diverse forces.   15
How do I know?
        Oh, I know well enough.
For them there is something afoot.
        As for me;
I had over-prepared the event—   20

      Beauty is so rare a thing.
      So few drink of my fountain.

Two friends: a breath of the forest . . .
Friends? Are people less friends
        because one has just, at last, found them?   25
Twice they promised to come.

      "Between the night and morning?"[2]

      Beauty would drink of my mind.
      Youth would awhile forget
         my youth is gone from me.   30

II

("Speak up! You have danced so stiffly?
        Someone admired your works,
        And said so frankly.

---

1. The poem is not in the traditional villanelle stanza pattern.
2. In "The People," an uncollected poem published in 1916, William Butler Yeats complained of an "unmannerly town" that can ruin one's reputation "Between the night and the morning."

"Did you talk like a fool,
   The first night?   35
   The second evening?"

"But they promised again:
        'To-morrow at tea-time.' ")

III

Now the third day is here—
      no word from either;   40
No word from her nor him,
Only another man's note:
    "Dear Pound, I am leaving England."

                                1916

Hugh Selwyn Mauberley[1]
(Life and Contacts)[2]

"Vocat æstus in umbram"
             —Nemesianus,[3] *Ec. IV*

E. P. Ode pour l'election de Son Sepulchre[4]

For three years, out of key with his time,
He strove to resuscitate the dead art
Of poetry; to maintain "the sublime"
In the old sense. Wrong from the start—

No, hardly, but seeing he had been born   5
In a half savage country, out of date;
Bent resolutely on wringing lilies from the acorn;
Capaneus,[5] trout for factitious bait;

Ἴδμεν γάρ τοι πάνθ', ὅσ ἐνὶ Τροίῃ[6]
Caught in the unstopped ear;   10

---

1. This poem was published in 1920 when Pound was on the verge of leaving London. He declared that the poem was modeled partly on the technique of Henry James's prose fiction: it presents its subject through the medium of a character's mind or voice, a "center of consciousness" whose mind and standards are also part of the subject being treated and are exposed themselves to scrutiny and assessment. In "Hugh Selwyn Mauberley" the first thirteen lyrics are presented through "E. P." In the next section, titled "Mauberley" (I through "Medallion"), the persona of "E. P." is absorbed in the fictitious poet Mauberley, a second persona.
2. Echo of a conventional subtitle of literary biographies, "Life and Letters." In the 1957 edition, Pound reversed the sequence, claiming that "Contacts and Life" followed the "order of the subject matter." To the American edition of *Personae* in 1926 Pound added the following note: "The sequence is so distinctly a farewell to London that the reader who chooses to regard this as an exclusively American edition may as well omit it."
3. Carthaginian poet (third century). The Latin, from his *Eclogues* (4.38), reads "The heat calls us into the shade."
4. Adaptation of the title of an ode by Pierre de Ronsard (1524–1585), "On the Selection of His Tomb" (*Odes* 4.5).
5. One of the seven champions who attack Thebes in Aeschylus's tragedy *The Seven Against Thebes* (476 B.C.E.) and who is struck down by Zeus.
6. For we know all the toils [endured] in wide Troy (Greek). In Homer's *Odyssey* (12.189) part of the sirens' song to detain Odysseus. Odysseus stopped his comrades' ears with wax to prevent their succumbing to the lure.

Giving the rocks small lee-way
The chopped seas held him, therefore, that year.

His true Penelope was Flaubert,[7]
He fished by obstinate isles;
Observed the elegance of Circe's[8] hair   15
Rather than the mottoes on sun-dials.

Unaffected by "the march of events,"
He passed from men's memory in *l'an trentuniesme*
De son eage,[9] the case presents
No adjunct to the Muses' diadem.   20

II

The age demanded an image
Of its accelerated grimace,
Something for the modern stage,
Not, at any rate, an Attic grace;

Not, not certainly, the obscure reveries   25
Of the inward gaze;
Better mendacities
Than the classics in paraphrase!

The "age demanded" chiefly a mould in plaster,
Made with no loss of time,   30
A prose kinema,[1] not, not assuredly, alabaster
Or the "sculpture" of rhyme.

III

The tea-rose tea-gown, etc.
Supplants the mousseline of Cos,[2]
The pianola "replaces"   35
Sappho's barbitos.[3]

Christ follows Dionysus,[4]
Phallic and ambrosial
Made way for macerations[5]
Caliban casts out Ariel.[6]   40

---

7. Gustave Flaubert (1821–1880), French novelist who cultivated form and stylistic precision.
Penelope was Odysseus's wife; she remained faithful during his long absence, despite appeals from
many suitors.
8. Sorceress with whom Odysseus lived for a year
before returning home.
9. The thirty-first year of his age (Old French);
adapted from *The Testament* by the 15th-century
French poet François Villon.
1. Movement (Greek) and early spelling of *cin-
ema,* "motion pictures."

2. Gauzelike fabric for which the Aegean island
Cos was famous.
3. Lyrelike instrument used by the Greek poet
Sappho (fl. 600 B.C.E.).
4. Greek god of fertility, regenerative suffering,
wine, and poetic inspiration; his rites were characterized by frenzies and ecstasies.
5. Wasting, fasting. Pound contrasts Christian
asceticism to Dionysian rites.
6. Characters in Shakespeare's *Tempest*; Caliban
is earthbound and Ariel is a spirit of air.

All things are a flowing,
Sage Heracleitus[7] says;
But a tawdry cheapness
Shall outlast our days.

Even the Christian beauty   45
Defects—after Samothrace;[8]
We see τὸ καλὸν[9]
Decreed in the market place.

Faun's flesh is not to us,
Nor the saint's vision.   50
We have the press for wafer;
Franchise for circumcision.

All men, in law, are equals.
Free of Pisistratus,[1]
We choose a knave or an eunuch   55
To rule over us.

O bright Apollo,
τίν' ἄνδρα, τίν' ἥρωα, τινα θεόν,[2]
What god, man, or hero
Shall I place a tin wreath upon!   60

IV

These fought in any case,
and some believing,
            pro domo,[3] in any case . . .

Some quick to arm,
some for adventure,   65
some from fear of weakness,
some from fear of censure,
some for love of slaughter, in imagination,
learning later . . .
some in fear, learning love of slaughter;   70

Died some, pro patria,
            non "dulce" non "et decor"[4] . . .
walked eye-deep in hell
believing in old men's lies, then unbelieving
came home, home to a lie,   75
home to many deceits,

---

7. Greek philosopher (fl. 500 B.C.E.) who taught that all reality is flux or "a flowing."
8. North Aegean island, center of religious mystery cults.
9. The beautiful (Greek).
1. Athenian tyrant and art patron (fl. 6th century B.C.E.).
2. What man, what hero, what god (Greek).

Pound's version of Pindar's "What god, what hero, what man shall we loudly praise" (*Olympian Odes* 2.2).
3. For the home (Latin).
4. For one's native land, not sweetly, not gloriously (Latin). Adapted from Horace, "it is sweet and glorious to die for one's fatherland" (*Odes* 3.2.13).

home to old lies and new infamy;
usury age-old and age-thick
and liars in public places.

Daring as never before, wastage as never before.   80
Young blood and high blood,
fair cheeks, and fine bodies;

fortitude as never before

frankness as never before,
disillusions as never told in the old days,   85
hysterias, trench confessions,
laughter out of dead bellies.

V

There died a myriad,
And of the best, among them,
For an old bitch gone in the teeth,   90
For a botched civilization,

Charm, smiling at the good mouth,
Quick eyes gone under earth's lid,

For two gross of broken statues,
For a few thousand battered books.   95

Yeux Glauques⁵

Gladstone was still respected,
When John Ruskin produced
"King's Treasuries"; Swinburne
And Rossetti still abused.

Fœtid Buchanan lifted up his voice   100
When that faun's head of hers
Became a pastime for
Painters and adulterers.

The Burne-Jones cartoons⁶
Have preserved her eyes;   105
Still, at the Tate, they teach
Cophetua to rhapsodize;

5. The brilliant yellow-green eyes of Elizabeth Siddal, the favorite model of the Pre-Raphaelite painters and later the wife of the painter and poet Dante Gabriel Rossetti (1828–1882). She was the model for the beggar maid in *Cophetua and the Beggar Maid* (now hanging in the Tate Gallery, London), by Sir Edward Burne-Jones (1833–1898).
6. Drawings. The Pre-Raphaelites, including the poet Algernon Swinburne (1837–1909), were attacked as "The Fleshly School of Poetry" by Robert W. Buchanan (1841–1901) in 1871 and were defended by the critic John Ruskin (1819–1900), whose *Sesame and Lilies* (1865) contains a chapter titled "Kings' Treasuries," calling for the diffusion of literature and the improvement of English tastes in the arts. William E. Gladstone (1809–1898) was four times prime minister of Britain.

Thin like brook-water,
With a vacant gaze.
The English Rubaiyat was still-born[7]　　　　　　　　　110
In those days.

The thin, clear gaze, the same
Still darts out faun-like from the half-ruin'd face,
Questing and passive . . .
"Ah, poor Jenny's[8] case" . . .　　　　　　　　　　　115

Bewildered that a world
Shows no surprise
At her last maquero's[9]
Adulteries.

"Siena mi fe'; Disfecemi Maremma"[1]

Among the pickled foetuses and bottled bones,　　　120
Engaged in perfecting the catalogue,
I found the last scion of the
Senatorial families of Strasbourg, Monsieur Verog.[2]

For two hours he talked of Gallifet;[3]
Of Dowson; of the Rhymers' Club;　　　　　　　　125
Told me how Johnson (Lionel)[4] died
By falling from a high stool in a pub . . .

But showed no trace of alcohol
At the autopsy, privately performed—
Tissue preserved—the pure mind　　　　　　　　　130
Arose toward Newman[5] as the whiskey warmed.

Dowson found harlots cheaper than hotels;
Headlam for uplift; Image[6] impartially imbued
With raptures for Bacchus, Terpsichore[7] and the Church
So spoke the author of "The Dorian Mood,"　　　　135

M. Verog, out of step with the decade,
Detached from his contemporaries,

7. Edward FitzGerald (1809–1883) translated *The Rubáiyát of Omar Khayyám* in 1859, but it was not read ("still-born") until discovered later by the Pre-Raphaelites.
8. Prostitute, heroine of a poem by Rossetti.
9. Pimp.
1. Siena made me, Maremma unmade me (Medieval Italian); spoken by a Sienese woman, condemned by her husband to die in Maremma marshes for her infidelity, in Dante's *Purgatory* (5.134).
2. Victor Plarr (1863–1929), French poet ("In the Dorian Mood," 1896) and raconteur from Strasbourg, later librarian of the Royal College of Surgeons and member of the Rhymer's Club.
3. Marquis de Galliffet (1830–1909), French general at the battle of Sedan, which the French lost,

in the Franco-Prussian War.
4. Two members of the Rhymer's Club were Roman Catholic poets and heavy drinkers. Ernest Dowson (1867–1900), of whom Plarr published a memoir. Lionel Johnson (1867–1902), whose *Poetical Works* Pound edited in 1915.
5. John Henry Newman (1801–1890), editor and Roman Catholic convert and intellectual, later cardinal.
6. Two more members of the Rhymer's Club. The Reverend Stewart D. Headlam (1847–1924), forced to resign his curacy for lecturing on the dance to workers' clubs. Selwyn Image (1849–1930), founder with Headlam of the Church and Stage Guild.
7. Greek Muse of the dance.

Neglected by the young,
Because of these reveries.

Brennbaum

The sky-like limpid eyes,   140
The circular infant's face,
The stiffness from spats to collar
Never relaxing into grace;

The heavy memories of Horeb, Sinai and the forty years,[8]
Showed only when the daylight fell   145
Level across the face
Of Brennbaum "The Impeccable."

Mr. Nixon

In the cream gilded cabin of his steam yacht
Mr. Nixon advised me kindly, to advance with fewer
Dangers of delay. "Consider   150
     "Carefully the reviewer.

"I was as poor as you are;
"When I began I got, of course,
"Advance on royalties, fifty at first," said Mr. Nixon,
"Follow me, and take a column,   155
"Even if you have to work free.

"Butter reviewers. From fifty to three hundred
"I rose in eighteen months;
"The hardest nut I had to crack
"Was Dr. Dundas.   160

"I never mentioned a man but with the view
"Of selling my own works.
"The tip's a good one, as for literature
"It gives no man a sinecure.

"And no one knows, at sight, a masterpiece.   165
"And give up verse, my boy,
"There's nothing in it."

  . . . .

Likewise a friend of Blougram's once advised me:[9]
Don't kick against the pricks,
Accept opinion. The "Nineties"[1] tried your game   170
And died, there's nothing in it.

---

8. The Israelites wandered in the wilderness for forty years. Moses saw the burning bush at Horeb (Exodus 3.2); he received the Ten Commandments at Sinai (Exodus 19.20ff.).

9. In Browning's "Bishop Blougram's Apology," the bishop rationalized doctrinal laxity.
1. The 1890s.

X

Beneath the sagging roof
The stylist has taken shelter,
Unpaid, uncelebrated,
At last from the world's welter   175

Nature receives him;
With a placid and uneducated mistress
He exercises his talents
And the soil meets his distress.

The haven from sophistications and contentions   180
Leaks through its thatch;
He offers succulent cooking;
The door has a creaking latch.

XI

"Conservatrix of Milésien"[2]
Habits of mind and feeling,   185
Possibly. But in Ealing[3]
With the most bank-clerky of Englishmen?

No, "Milésian" is an exaggeration.
No instinct has survived in her
Older than those her grandmother   190
Told her would fit her station.

XII

"Daphne with her thighs in bark
Stretches toward me her leafy hands,"[4]
Subjectively. In the stuffed-satin drawing-room
I await The Lady Valentine's commands,   195

Knowing my coat has never been
Of precisely the fashion
To stimulate, in her,
A durable passion;

Doubtful, somewhat, of the value   200
Of well-gowned approbation
Of literary effort,
But never of The Lady Valentine's vocation:

Poetry, her border of ideas,
The edge, uncertain, but a means of blending   205

---

2. I.e., conservator of the erotic, for which the
Ionian city of Miletus and Aristides' *Milesian Tales*
(2nd century B.C.E.) were known.
3. London suburb.

4. In Greek mythology, the nymph Daphne
changed into a laurel tree to escape Apollo. Pound's
lines are a translation of Théophile Gautier's version of Ovid's story in *Le Château de Souvenir*.

With other strata
Where the lower and higher have ending;

A hook to catch the Lady Jane's attention,
A modulation toward the theatre,
Also, in the case of revolution,   210
A possible friend and comforter.

.   .   .   .

Conduct, on the other hand, the soul
"Which the highest cultures have nourished"[5]
To Fleet St. where
Dr. Johnson[6] flourished;   215

Beside this thoroughfare
The sale of half-hose has
Long since superseded the cultivation
Of Pierian roses.[7]

Envoi (1919)[8]

Go, dumb-born book,   220
Tell her that sang me once that song of Lawes:
Hadst thou but song
As thou hast subjects known,
Then were there cause in thee that should condone
Even my faults that heavy upon me lie,   225
And build her glories their longevity.

Tell her that sheds
Such treasure in the air,
Recking naught else but that her graces give
Life to the moment,   230
I would bid them live
As roses might, in magic amber laid,
Red overwrought with orange and all made
One substance and one colour
Braving time.   235

Tell her that goes
With song upon her lips
But sings not out the song, nor knows
The maker of it, some other mouth,
May be as fair as hers,   240
Might, in new ages, gain her worshippers,
When our two dusts with Waller's shall be laid,

---

5. A translation of two lines from "Complainte de
Pianos" by French poet Jules Laforgue (1860–
1887).
6. Samuel Johnson (1709–1784), man of letters
in mid-18th-century London. "Fleet St.": newspaper publishing center in London.

7. Roses of Pieria, place near Mount Olympus in
Greece, where the Muses were worshiped.
8. This section of the poem is modeled on "Go,
Lovely Rose" by Edmund Waller (1606–1687),
whose poems were set to music by Henry Lawes
(1596–1662).

Siftings on siftings in oblivion,
Till change hath broken down
All things save Beauty alone.   245

1920

FROM THE CANTOS

I[1]

And then went down to the ship,
Set keel to breakers, forth on the godly sea, and
We set up mast and sail on that swart ship,
Bore sheep aboard her, and our bodies also
Heavy with weeping, and winds from sternward   5
Bore us out onward with bellying canvas,
Circe's[2] this craft, the trim-coifed goddess.
Then sat we amidships, wind jamming the tiller,
Thus with stretched sail, we went over sea till day's end.
Sun to his slumber, shadows o'er all the ocean,   10
Came we then to the bounds of deepest water,
To the Kimmerian[3] lands, and peopled cities
Covered with close-webbed mist, unpierced ever
With glitter of sun-rays
Nor with stars stretched, nor looking back from heaven   15
Swartest night stretched over wretched men there
The ocean flowing backward, came we then to the place
Aforesaid by Circe.
Here did they rites, Perimedes and Eurylochus,[4]
And drawing sword from my hip   20
I dug the ell-square pitkin;[5]
Poured we libations unto each the dead,
First mead then sweet wine, water mixed with white flour.
Then prayed I many a prayer to the sickly death's-heads;
As set in Ithaca, sterile bulls of the best   25
For sacrifice, heaping the pyre with goods,
A sheep to Tiresias only, black and a bell-sheep.[6]
Dark blood flowed in the fosse,[7]
Souls out of Erebus,[8] cadaverous dead, of brides
Of youths and of the old who had borne much;   30
Souls stained with recent tears, girls tender,
Men many, mauled with bronze lance heads,
Battle spoil, bearing yet dreory[9] arms,

1. Lines 1–68 are an adaptation of book 11 of Homer's *Odyssey*, which recounts Odysseus's voyage to Hades, the underworld of the dead. Odysseus was a native of Ithaca, in Greece.
2. Odysseus lived for a year with Circe before he determined to return to Ithaca. She instructed him to get directions for his trip home by visiting the Theban prophet Tiresias in the underworld.
3. Mythical people living in a foggy region at the edge of the earth.
4. Two of Odysseus's companions.
5. Small pit, one ell (forty-five inches) on each side.
6. The prophet Tiresias is likened to a sheep that leads the herd.
7. Ditch, trench.
8. Land of the dead, Hades.
9. Bloody.

These many crowded about me; with shouting,
Pallor upon me, cried to my men for more beasts;   35
Slaughtered the herds, sheep slain of bronze;
Poured ointment, cried to the gods,
To Pluto the strong, and praised Proserpine;[1]
Unsheathed the narrow sword,
I sat to keep off the impetuous impotent dead,   40
Till I should hear Tiresias.
But first Elpenor[2] came, our friend Elpenor,
Unburied, cast on the wide earth,
Limbs that we left in the house of Circe,
Unwept, unwrapped in sepulchre, since toils urged other.   45
Pitiful spirit. And I cried in hurried speech:
"Elpenor, how art thou come to this dark coast?
"Cam'st thou afoot, outstripping seamen?"
            And he in heavy speech:
"Ill fate and abundant wine. I slept in Circe's ingle.[3]   50
"Going down the long ladder unguarded,
"I fell against the buttress,
"Shattered the nape-nerve, the soul sought Avernus.[4]
"But thou, O King, I bid remember me, unwept, unburied,
"Heap up mine arms, be tomb by sea-bord, and inscribed: 55
"*A man of no fortune, and with a name to come.*
"And set my oar up, that I swung mid fellows."

And Anticlea[5] came, whom I beat off, and then Tiresias Theban,
Holding his golden wand, knew me, and spoke first:
"A second time?[6] why? man of ill star,   60
"Facing the sunless dead and this joyless region?
"Stand from the fosse, leave me my bloody bever[7]
"For soothsay."
            And I stepped back,
And he strong with the blood, said then: "Odysseus   65
"Shalt return through spiteful Neptune,[8] over dark seas,
"Lose all companions." And then Anticlea came.
Lie quiet Divus. I mean, that is Andreas Divus,
In officina Wecheli, 1538, out of Homer.[9]
And he sailed, by Sirens and thence outward and away   70
And unto Circe.
            Venerandam,[1]
In the Cretan's phrase, with the golden crown, Aphrodite,

---

1. Goddess of regeneration and wife of Pluto, god of the underworld.
2. Odysseus's companion who fell to his death from the roof of Circe's house and was left unburied by his friends.
3. Corner, house.
4. Lake near Naples, the entrance to Hades.
5. Odysseus's mother. In the *Odyssey*, Odysseus weeps at the sight of her but obeys Circe's instructions to speak to no one until Tiresias has first drunk the libation of blood that will enable him to speak.

6. They met once before on earth.
7. Libation.
8. God of the sea, who was to delay Odysseus's return by a storm at sea.
9. Pound acknowledges using the Renaissance Latin translation of Homer, produced in the workshop ("officina") of Wechel in Paris in 1538, by Andreas Divus.
1. Commanding reverence; a phrase describing Aphrodite, the goddess of love, in the Latin translation of the second Homeric Hymn by Georgius Dartona Cretensis (the "Cretan" in line 73).

Cypri munimenta sortita est,[2] mirthful, orichalchi,[3] with golden
Girdles and breast bands, thou with dark eyelids   75
Bearing the golden bough of Argicida.[4] So that:

                                                          1925

XVII[1]

So that the vines burst from my fingers
And the bees weighted with pollen
More heavily in the vine-shoots:
chirr—chirr—chir-rikk—a purring sound,
And the birds sleepily in the branches.   5
         ZAGREUS! IO ZAGREUS.[2]
With the first pale-clear of the heaven
And the cities set in their hills,
And the goddess of the fair knees[3]
Moving there, with the oak-woods behind her,   10
The green slope, with white hounds
              leaping about her;
And thence down to the creek's mouth, until evening,
Flat water before me,
              and the trees growing in water,   15
Marble trunks out of stillness,[4]
On past the palazzi,
              in the stillness,
The light now, not of the sun.
              Chrysophrase,[5]   20
And the water green clear, and blue clear;
On, to the great cliffs of amber.
                   Between them,
Cave of Nerea,[6]
         she like a great shell curved,   25

2. The fortresses of Cyprus were her appointed realm (Latin).
3. Of copper (Latin); a reference to gifts presented to Aphrodite in the second Homeric Hymn.
4. Aeneas offered the Golden Bough to Proserpina before descending to the underworld. Pound associates Persephone with Aphrodite, goddess of love and slayer of the Greeks (Argi) during the Trojan War, and associates the Golden Bough, sacred to the goddess Diana, with the magic wand of the god Hermes, slayer of the many-eyed Argus ("Argicida") and liberator of Io.
1. This canto represents Pound's treatment of ancient myth and Renaissance history. Three sequences figure in this canto: Ulysses' (Odysseus's) voyage through the Mediterranean in search of home in Ithaca, Jason's voyage to the islands of Colchis in search of the Golden Fleece, and a ship's entrance into Venice. Among the personae that Pound assumes, besides Ulysses and Jason, are Dionysus (Zagreus), the Greek god of wine, rebirth, and ecstasy; Actaeon, who saw the goddess Diana bathing and was punished by being turned into a stag that was torn apart by his hounds; and Hades (Pluto), god of the underworld, who loved Koré (Persephone, goddess of regeneration) and who kidnaped her from a meadow but was later forced to allow her to return to earth for several months each year.
2. Zagreus! I am Zagreus. (Greek). A sacrificial god often identified in a Greek myth with Dionysus, Zagreus was the offspring of Persephone (Koré) and Zeus; Zeus raped her before she was kidnaped by Hades.
3. Diana, goddess of the hunt.
4. The first glimpse of Venice. The marble façades and columns of its *palazzi* (palaces) are presented in accordance with the theories of the landscape painter and art critic Adrian Stokes (1854–1935), a friend of Pound. Stokes (*The Stones of Rimini*, 1934) stressed the affinity of Venetian arts with the salt sea and the origin of marble from sunken forests and watery limestone: "Amid the sea Venice is built from the essence of the sea."
5. Green semiprecious stone.
6. Possibly the nymph Calypso, the temptress and death goddess who detained Ulysses for seven years in her island cave.

And the boat drawn without sound,
Without odour of ship-work,
Nor bird-cry, nor any noise of wave moving,
Nor splash of porpoise, nor any noise of wave moving,
Within her cave, Nerea,   30
            she like a great shell curved
In the suavity of the rock,
            cliff green-gray in the far,
In the near, the gate-cliffs of amber,
And the wave   35
            green clear, and blue clear,
And the cave salt-white, and glare-purple,
         cool, porphyry smooth,
         the rock sea-worn.
No gull-cry, no sound of porpoise,   40
Sand as of malachite,[7] and no cold there,
         the light not of the sun.

Zagreus, feeding his panthers,
         the turf clear as on hills under light.
And under the almond-trees, gods,   45
         with them, *choros nympharum.*[8] Gods,
Hermes and Athene,[9]
           As shaft of compass,
Between them, trembled—
To the left is the place of fauns,   50
         sylva nympharum;[1]
The low wood, moor-scrub,
         the doe, the young spotted deer,
         leap up through the broom-plants,
           as dry leaf amid yellow.   55
And by one cut of the hills,
         the great alley of Memnons.[2]
Beyond, sea, crests seen over dune
Night sea churning shingle,
To the left, the alley of cypress.   60
           A boat came,
One man holding her sail,
Guiding her with oar caught over gunwale, saying:
"   There, in the forest of marble,
"   the stone trees—out of water—   65
"   the arbours of stone—
"   marble leaf, over leaf,
"   silver, steel over steel,
"   silver beaks rising and crossing,
"   prow set against prow,   70

7. Green mineral.
8. Chorus of nymphs (Greek).
9. Ulysses' protectors. Hermes (messenger of the gods, patron of merchants and thieves) freed Ulysses from the bonds of Calypso. Athene (goddess of wisdom) calmed the waves for his final voyage home to Ithaca (*Odyssey* 5).
1. Forest of the nymphs (Greek).
2. Commander of Ethiopian troops in the defense of Troy, he was called "son of dawn." His statue near Thebes, here likened to a row of cypress trees, reputedly issued a musical sound at daybreak.

"   stone, ply over ply,
"   the gilt beams flare of an evening"
Borso, Carmagnola, the men of craft, *i vitrei*,[3]
Thither, at one time, time after time,
And the waters richer than glass,   75
Bronze gold, the blaze over the silver,
Dye-pots in the torch-light,
The flash of wave under prows,
And the silver beaks rising and crossing.
          Stone trees, white and rose-white in the darkness,   80
Cypress there by the towers,
          Drift under hulls in the night.

"In the gloom the gold
Gathers the light about it."[4] . . .

Now supine in burrow, half over-arched bramble,   85
One eye for the sea, through that peek-hole,
Gray light, with Athene.
Zothar and her elephants, the gold loin-cloth,
The sistrum,[5] shaken, shaken,
          the cohorts of her dancers.   90
And Aletha,[6] by bend of the shore,
          with her eyes seaward,
          and in her hands sea-wrack
Salt-bright with the foam.
Koré through the break meadow,   95
          with green-gray dust in the grass:
"For this hour, brother of Circe."[7]
Arm laid over my shoulder,
Saw the sun for three days, the sun fulvid,
As a lion lift over sand-plain;   100
          and that day,
And for three days, and none after,
Splendour, as the splendour of Hermes,
And shipped thence
          to the stone place,   105
Pale white, over water,
          known water,
And the white forest of marble, bent bough over bough,
The pleached arbour of stone,
Thither Borso, when they shot the barbed arrow at him,   110
And Carmagnola, between the two columns,

3. Glassmakers, for whom Venice is famous. Borse
d'Este (1431–1471) of Ferrara, patron of learning
whose assassination was attempted in Venice.
Francesco Bussone da Carmagnola (1390?–1432),
mercenary soldier, tried and executed for treason in
Venice.
4. Quoted from an earlier canto (XI) where
"about" reads "against."
5. An Egyptian metal rattle.
6. Zothar (line 88) and Aletha are probably

invented names.
7. I.e., Aetes, king of Colchis, who maintained a
cult of the sun (his father) on his island, and held
possession of the Golden Fleece sought by Jason.
Circe was the enchantress who detained Ulysses
for a year, then instructed him to consult Tiresias
in the underworld to learn his route home and told
him how to enter the world of the dead through the
Grove of Persephone.

Sigismundo,[8] after that wreck in Dalmatia.
  Sunset like the grasshopper flying.

1933

XLV

With *Usura*[1]

With usura hath no man a house of good stone
each block cut smooth and well fitting
that design might cover their face,
with usura   5
hath no man a painted paradise on his church wall
harpes et luz[2]
or where virgin receiveth message
and halo projects from incision,[3]
with usura   10
seeth no man Gonzaga[4] his heirs and his concubines
no picture is made to endure nor to live with
but it is made to sell and sell quickly
with usura, sin against nature,
is thy bread ever more of stale rags   15
is thy bread dry as paper,
with no mountain wheat, no strong flour
with usura the line grows thick
with usura is no clear demarcation
and no man can find site for his dwelling.   20
Stonecutter is kept from his stone
weaver is kept from his loom
WITH USURA
wool comes not to market
sheep bringeth no gain with usura   25
Usura is a murrain,[5] usura
blunteth the needle in the maid's hand
and stoppeth the spinner's cunning. Pietro Lombardo[6]
came not by usura
Duccio came not by usura   30
nor Pier della Francesca; Zuan Bellin'[7] not by usura

8. Sigismondo Malatesta (1417–1468), Renaissance ruler of Rimini whom Pound admired. An art patron, antipapist, and builder of the Tempio Malatestiana in Rimini, he fought for Venice and other cities and in 1464 reached the Dalmatian coast in an unsuccessful crusade.

1. Usury, or lending money at interest (Latin). Pound interpreted this practice as the root of all corruption in the modern world, the cause of the separation of the worker—whether farmer, laborer, or artist—from the work.

2. Harps and lutes (Latin). In medieval and Renaissance depictions of Paradise, the angels are shown playing on such instruments.

3. Description of scenes in religious paintings, especially the Annunciation, in which the Virgin Mary is informed that she is to be the mother of Christ.

4. Luigi Gonzaga (1267–1360), prince of Mantua and founder of a dynasty that ruled that Italian city until the eighteenth century.

5. A plague (archaic).

6. Italian sculptor (1435–1515).

7. Duccio di Buoninsegna (1260?–1318?), Piero della Francesca (1420?–1492), and Giovanni Bellini (1430?–1516) were Italian painters from Florence and nearby towns.

nor was 'La Calumnia'[8] painted.
Came not by usura Angelico; came not Ambrogio Praedis,[9]
Came no church of cut stone signed: *Adamo me fecit*.[1]
Not by usura St Trophime   35
Not by usura Saint Hilaire,[2]
Usura rusteth the chisel
It rusteth the craft and the craftsman
It gnaweth the thread in the loom
None learneth to weave gold in her pattern;   40
Azure hath a canker by usura; cramoisi[3] is unbroidered
Emerald findeth no Memling[4]
Usura slayeth the child in the womb
It stayeth the young man's courting
It hath brought palsey to bed, lyeth   45
between the young bride and her bridegroom
                 CONTRA NATURAM[5]
They have brought whores for Eleusis[6]
Corpses are set to banquet
at behest of usura.   50

N.B. Usury: A charge for the use of purchasing power, levied without regard to production; often without regard to the possibilities of production. (Hence the failure of the Medici bank.[7])

                                                          1937

---

8. Rumor (Italian); allegorical painting by Sandro Botticelli (1445–1510), one of the greatest of the Italian Renaissance painters.
9. Fra Angelico (1387?–1455) and Praedis (1455?–1506) were Italian painters.
1. Adam made me (Latin); words carved into the church of San Zeno Maggiore in Verona, Italy. To Pound, a symbol of the architect's pride in and feeling of connection with his work.
2. Medieval churches in the French cities of Arles and Poitiers, respectively.
3. Heavy crimson cloth (French).

4. Hans Memling (1430?–1495), Flemish painter.
5. Against nature (Latin).
6. City in ancient Greece, northwest of Athens, where secret religious rites in honor of Demeter and Persephone, the goddess of fertility and her daughter, were celebrated by priestesses every spring. The substitution of whores for priestesses represents the degradation of ancient rituals.
7. A bank operated from 1397 to 1494 by the Medici family of Florence; it anticipated modern banking techniques.

Modernist Manifestos

As an artistic movement, or set of movements, given to asserting its breaks with past traditions, modernism in the early twentieth century often proclaimed itself in the writing of manifestoes. The modernist manifesto is a public declaration of artistic convictions, relatively brief, often highly stylized or epigrammatic in the mode of other forms of modernist writing, and almost always an aggressively self-conscious declaration of artistic independence.

The word *manifesto*, derived from Latin and meaning "to make public," first entered English usage in the seventeenth century to describe printed declarations of belief and advocacy. Early manifestoes tended to be weapons forged by dissenting groups in religious and political struggles, a tradition that continued into the nineteenth century with perhaps the most famous political manifesto of the era, Karl Marx's *Communist Manifesto* (1848). In the nineteenth century, artistic groups also began to issue manifestos. The preface to the second edition of *Lyrical Ballads* (1800) by the poets William Wordsworth and Samuel Taylor Coleridge, for example, defended their "experiment" with a new kind of poetry; in the United States, Ralph Waldo Emerson's *Nature* (1836), the founding document of American transcendentalism, called for spiritual and artistic renewal; inspired partly by Emerson's example, Margaret Fuller's "The Great Lawsuit: MAN *versus* MEN. WOMAN *versus* WOMEN" (1843) linked women's pursuit of political rights to their pursuit of artistic expression and intellectual independence. In late nineteenth-century Paris, the "Symbolist Manifesto" (1886), by the poet Jean Moréas, turned the genre of the manifesto in some of its characteristically high modernist directions. Attacking not so much oppressive social conditions as oppressive conceptions of literature, the Symbolists declared their hostility to realism's "plain meanings, declamations, false sentimentality and matter-of-fact description" in order to claim for poetry a freer, less moralizing play of verbal imagination.

The writers of manifestos did not have one particular audience in mind; it was enough for them to get their positions into the public realm. But manifestos also worked to bring like-minded people together; a poet might publish a manifesto in a journal of poetry, a political radical in a radical journal, and so on. In the modernist period, manifestos increasingly reached an international community of self-consciously avant-garde, cosmopolitan artists. The Italian writer F. T. Marinetti published his "Manifesto of Futurism" in French; Ezra Pound's "A Retrospect" ranged freely over his contemporaries in British and American modernist poetry as well as over Pound's admired writers of the past in several languages—Dante, Goethe, Shakespeare; Willa Cather similarly juxtaposed American fiction with French, Russian, and British works in "The Novel Démeublé."

Hostility is often a rhetorical tool of the manifesto, and it was especially so in the modernist period. Modernist manifestoes often tried to grab their audiences by the lapels, to separate not only the new from the old but also a creative *us* from a "vulgar" or hidebound *them*. The us/them divide was intended to offend traditionalists as well as to unite the believers in new artistic movements, and it often succeeded in both aims. Marinetti's "Manifesto of Futurism" set the tone in 1909 by declaring that "No work without an aggressive character can be a masterpiece" and exalting "scorn for women" along with modern technology. By 1918, Ezra Pound in "A Retrospect" could manage to insult in one sentence both traditional poetic forms and would-be imitators of his own free verse: "The actual language and phrasing" of the new poetry, Pound complained, "is often as bad as that of our elders without even the excuse that the words are shoveled in to fill a metric pattern or to complete the noise of a rhyme-sound." The modernist boundary between *us* and *them*, Pound's "Retrospect" implies, will always be in motion, always pushing forward and leaving someone behind.

At the same time, however, the very aggression of some high modernist manifestoes encouraged some members of their audience to talk back with equal vigor. Marinetti denounced advocates of women's suffrage but recognized a counterpart to his own aggressive tactics in London's most radical suffragettes, to the point of joining them on a march that was broken up by mounted police. Mina Loy wrote and privately circulated her "Feminist Manifesto" as an enthusiastic member of Marinetti's circle; his take-no-prisoners example licensed her rhetoric of destruction and demolition, which she aimed not only at the institutions of sexism but also at less confrontational versions of feminism.

Other influential modernist manifestoes were more measured in their language or more subtle in their explorations of the relationship between modernist destruction and cultural production. William Carlos Williams's exuberant prose interludes in *Spring and All* asserted, with the aid of language borrowed from evolutionary biology, that modernism's sudden "SPRING" into the new was the explosive culmination of many small, repeated movements in the past. The title metaphor of Willa Cather's "The Novel Démeublé"—the novel "unfurnished"—suggested that modernism might prune the decorative excesses of nineteenth-century realism without abandoning its basic structure. And Langston Hughes, although he railed against "the mountain standing in the way of any true Negro art in America," ultimately envisioned the mountain—the internal and external struggles of black Americans to cast off white denigrations of African American culture—as the foundation of a higher and broader modernist art: "We build our temples for tomorrow, strong as we know how, and we stand on top of the mountain, free within ourselves."

F. T. MARINETTI

F. T. Marinetti (1876–1944) published two obscure volumes of poetry in his native Italian before "The Founding and Manifesto of Futurism" appeared in *Le Figaro*, an influential Parisian journal, in February 1909. The futurist manifesto attracted an international circle of artists and writers into Marinetti's orbit, including painters, architects, poets, sculptors, playwrights, and film directors. Across all the arts, futurism scorned traditional standards of artistic beauty, celebrated modern technologies of speed, and aimed to shock audiences: futurist painters adopted the mixed perspectives of cubism to celebrate speeding trains, and futurist theater drew on cabaret, variety shows, and circuses in staging free-form events that violated traditional theater's boundary between actors and audience. Futurism's aesthetic of aggression had unsettling political implications as well: true to his manifesto's declaration that war is "the only hygiene" of the world, Marinetti welcomed the technologically enhanced slaughter of World War I and supported the rise of Mussolini's Italian fascism.

From Manifesto of Futurism

1. We intend to sing the love of danger, the habit of energy and fearlessness.

2. Courage, audacity, and revolt will be essential elements of our poetry.

3. Up to now literature has exalted a pensive immobility, ecstasy, and sleep. We intend to exalt aggressive action, a feverish insomnia, the racer's stride, the mortal leap, the punch and the slap.

4. We say that the world's magnificence has been enriched by a new beauty; the beauty of speed. A racing car whose hood is adorned with great pipes, like serpents of explosive breath—a roaring car that seems to ride on grapeshot—is more beautiful than the *Victory of Samothrace*.[1]

5. We want to hymn the man at the wheel, who hurls the lance of his spirit across the Earth, along the circle of its orbit.

6. The poet must spend himself with ardor, splendor, and generosity, to swell the enthusiastic fervor of the primordial elements.

7. Except in struggle, there is no more beauty. No work without an aggressive character can be a masterpiece. Poetry must be conceived as a violent attack on unknown forces, to reduce and prostrate them before man.

8. We stand on the last promontory of the centuries! . . . Why should we look back, when what we want is to break down the mysterious doors of the Impossible? Time and Space died yesterday. We already live in the absolute, because we have created eternal, omnipresent speed.

9. We will glorify war—the world's only hygiene—militarism, patriotism, the destructive gesture of freedom-bringers, beautiful ideas worth dying for, and scorn for woman.

10. We will destroy the museums, libraries, academies of every kind, will fight moralism, feminism, every opportunistic or utilitarian cowardice.

11. We will sing of great crowds excited by work, by pleasure, and by riot; we will sing of the multicolored, polyphonic tides of revolution in the modern capitals; we will sing of the vibrant nightly fervor of arsenals and shipyards blazing with violent electric moons; greedy railway stations that devour smoke-plumed serpents; factories hung on clouds by the crooked lines of their smoke; bridges that stride the rivers like giant gymnasts, flashing in the sun with a glitter of knives; adventurous steamers that sniff the horizon; deep-chested locomotives whose wheels paw the tracks like the hooves of enormous steel horses bridled by tubing; and the sleek flight of planes whose propellers chatter in the wind like banners and seem to cheer like an enthusiastic crowd.

* * *

1909

---

1. Famous Greek statue of Nike, the winged goddess of victory, from the 2nd or 3rd century B.C.E.; discovered on the island of Samothrace in 1863, it became an icon of 19th-century high artistic taste.

MINA LOY

"Feminist Manifesto" was written during Loy's association with F. T. Marinetti but never published during her lifetime (1882–1966); it survives in a copy sent to a friend, the writer Mabel Dodge Luhan, in 1914. Loy's central demand is sexual freedom, the end of the divide between "the mistress" and "the mother," and the destruction of women's attachment to ideals of their own purity. Loy's modernist call for women's free sexual expression appeals to elite women's sense of race and class privilege: echoing nineteenth-century alarms that granting women life choices beyond marriage and childbearing would lead to white "race suicide," Loy urges "superior" women to embrace maternity as both a responsibility and an aspect of their own sexual development.

Feminist Manifesto

The feminist movement as at present instituted is

Inadequate

Women if you want to realise yourselves—you are on the eve of a devastating psychological upheaval—all your pet illusions must be unmasked—the lies of centuries have got to go— are you prepared for the **Wrench**—? There is no half-measure—NO scratching on the surface of the rubbish heap of tradition, will bring about **Reform**, the only method is

Absolute Demolition

Cease to place your confidence in economic legislation, vice-crusades & uniform education[1]—you are glossing over

Reality.

Professional & commercial careers are opening up for you—

Is that all you want ?

---

1. Securing women's legal right to own property, gaining access to education for women (especially higher education) on the same terms as men, and suppressing prostitution were all conspicuous goals of 19th- and early-20th-century feminist movements.

And if you honestly desire to find your level without prejudice—be Brave & deny at the outset—that pathetic clap-trap war cry Woman is the
equal of man—

She is NOT! for

The man who lives a life in which his activities conform to a
social code which is a protectorate of the feminine element—
——is no longer masculine
The women who adapt themselves to a theoretical valuation of
their sex as a relative impersonality, are not yet
Feminine
Leave off looking to men to find out what you are not —seek
within yourselves to find out what you are
As conditions are at present constituted—you have the choice
between Parasitism, & Prostitu-
tion —or Negation

Men & women are enemies, with the enmity of the exploited
for the parasite, the parasite for the exploited—at present they
are at the mercy of the advantage that each can take of the
others sexual dependence—. The only point at which the
interests of the sexes merge—is the sexual embrace.

The first illusion it is to your interest to demolish is the
division of women into two classes the mistress,
& the mother every well-balanced & developed woman
knows that is not true, Nature has endowed the complete
woman with a faculty for expressing herself through all her
functions—there are no restrictions the woman who is
so incompletely evolved as to be un-self-conscious in sex, will
prove a restrictive influence on the temperamental expansion
of the next generation; the woman who is a poor mistress will
be an incompetent mother—an inferior mentality—& will
enjoy an inadequate apprehension of Life .

To obtain results you must make sacrifices & the first & greatest sacrifice you have to make is of your "virtue"
The fictitious value of woman as identified with her physical purity—is too easy a stand-by——rendering her lethargic in the acquisition of intrinsic merits of character by which she could obtain a concrete value— therefore, the first self-enforced law for the female sex, as a protection against the man made bogey of virtue—which is the principle instrument of her subjection, would be the unconditional surgical destruction of virginity through-out the female population at puberty—.

The value of man is assessed entirely according to his use or interest to the community, the value of woman, depends entirely on chance, her success or insuccess in manoeuvering a man into taking the life-long responsibility of her—
The advantages of marriage of too ridiculously ample— compared to all other trades—for under modern conditions a woman can accept preposterously luxurious support from a man (with-out return of any sort—even offspring)—as a thank offering for her virginity
The woman who has not succeeded in striking that advantageous bargain—is prohibited from any but surreptitious re-action to Life-stimuli—& entirely debarred maternity.
Every woman has a right to maternity—
Every woman of superior intelligence should realize her race-responsibility, in producing children in adequate proportion to the unfit or degenerate members of her sex—

Each child of a superior woman should be the result of a definite period of psychic development in her life—& not necessarily of a possibly irksome & outworn continuance of an alliance—spontaneously adapted for vital creation in the beginning but not necessarily harmoniously balanced as the parties to it—follow their individual lines of personal evolution—

For the harmony of the race, each individual should be the
expression of an easy & ample interpenetration of the male &
female temperaments—free of stress
Woman must become more responsible for the child than
man—
Women must destroy in themselves, the desire to be loved—

The feeling that it is a personal insult when a man transfers
his attentions from her to another woman
The desire for comfortable protection instead of an intelligent
curiosity & courage in meeting & resisting the pressure of life
sex or so called love must be reduced to its initial element,
honour, grief, sentimentality, pride & consequently jealousy
must be detached from it.
Woman for her happiness must retain her deceptive fragility of
appearance, combined with indomitable will, irreducible
courage, & abundant health the outcome of sound nerves—
Another great illusion that woman must use all her
introspective clear-sightedness & unbiassed bravery to
destroy—for the sake of her self respect is the impurity of sex
the realisation in defiance of superstition that there is nothing
impure in sex—except in the mental attitude to it—will
constitute an incalculable & wider social regeneration than it
is possible for our generation to imagine.

1914   1982

EZRA POUND

"A Retrospect" summarizes Pound's early declarations of the principles of Imagism.
His famous list of "Don'ts," originally published in 1913, cautioned poets against
superfluous words, rigid metrical rhythms, and the use of abstract rhetoric rather than
"direct treatment" of poetic subjects. Pound's own poetry by 1918 was taking a turn
away from Imagism's characteristic emphasis on representing "an intellectual and
emotional complex in an instant of time" and toward longer poems, more engaged with
history and the inherited materials of art.

From A Retrospect

There has been so much scribbling about a new fashion in poetry, that I may perhaps be pardoned this brief recapitulation and retrospect.

In the spring or early summer of 1912, 'H. D.', Richard Aldington and myself decided[1] that we were agreed upon the three principles following:

1. Direct treatment of the 'thing' whether subjective or objective.
2. To use absolutely no word that does not contribute to the presentation.
3. As regarding rhythm: to compose in the sequence of the musical phrase, not in sequence of a metronome.

Upon many points of taste and of predilection we differed, but agreeing upon these three positions we thought we had as much right to a group name, at least as much right, as a number of French 'schools' proclaimed by Mr Flint in the August number of Harold Monro's magazine for 1911.[2]

This school has since been 'joined' or 'followed' by numerous people who, whatever their merits, do not show any signs of agreeing with the second specification. Indeed *vers libre*[3] has become as prolix and as verbose as any of the flaccid varieties that preceded it. It has brought faults of its own. The actual language and phrasing is often as bad as that of our elders without even the excuse that the words are shovelled in to fill a metric pattern or to complete the noise of a rhyme-sound. Whether or no the phrases followed by the followers are musical must be left to the reader's decision. At times I can find a marked metre in 'vers libres', as stale and hackneyed as any pseudo-Swinburnian,[4] at times the writers seem to follow no musical structure whatever. But it is, on the whole, good that the field should be ploughed. Perhaps a few good poems have come from the new method, and if so it is justified.

Criticism is not a circumscription or a set of prohibitions. It provides fixed points of departure. It may startle a dull reader into alertness. That little of it which is good is mostly in stray phrases; or if it be an older artist helping a younger it is in great measure but rules of thumb, cautions gained by experience.

I set together a few phrases on practical working about the time the first remarks on imagisme were published. The first use of the word 'Imagiste' was in my note to T. E. Hulme's[5] five poems, printed at the end of my 'Ripostes' in the autumn of 1912. I reprint my cautions from *Poetry* for March, 1913.

A FEW DON'TS

An 'Image' is that which presents an intellectual and emotional complex in an instant of time. I use the term 'complex' rather in the technical sense

---

1. H. D. and the British poet Richard Aldington (1892–1962), who married H. D. in 1913, were among the first poets designated "Imagistes" by Pound.
2. The British poet and translator Frank Stuart Flint (1885–1960) was a friend of Pound and another Imagist; the Scottish poet and critic Harold Munro founded the *Poetry Review* in 1911.
3. Free verse (French); poetry without a fixed pattern of rhyme or meter.
4. The British Victorian poet Algernon Swinburne (1837–1909) was famous for using elaborate poetic forms.
5. Thomas Ernest Hulme (1883–1917), British poet and critic who, with Pound, formulated early statements of Imagism.

employed by the newer psychologists, such as Hart,[6] though we might not agree absolutely in our application.

It is the presentation of such a 'complex' instantaneously which gives that sense of sudden liberation; that sense of freedom from time limits and space limits; that sense of sudden growth, which we experience in the presence of the greatest works of art.

It is better to present one Image in a lifetime than to produce voluminous works.

All this, however, some may consider open to debate. The immediate necessity is to tabulate A LIST OF DON'TS for those beginning to write verses. I can not put all of them into Mosaic[7] negative.

To begin with, consider the three propositions (demanding direct treatment, economy of words, and the sequence of the musical phrase), not as dogma—never consider anything as dogma—but as the result of long contemplation, which, even if it is some one else's contemplation, may be worth consideration.

Pay no attention to the criticism of men who have never themselves written a notable work. Consider the discrepancies between the actual writing of the Greek poets and dramatists, and the theories of the Graeco-Roman grammarians, concocted to explain their metres.

LANGUAGE

Use no superfluous word, no adjective which does not reveal something.

Don't use such an expression as 'dim lands *of peace.*' It dulls the image. It mixes an abstraction with the concrete. It comes from the writer's not realizing that the natural object is always the *adequate* symbol.

Go in fear of abstractions. Do not retell in mediocre verse what has already been done in good prose. Don't think any intelligent person is going to be deceived when you try to shirk all the difficulties of the unspeakably difficult art of good prose by chopping your composition into line lengths.

What the expert is tired of today the public will be tired of tomorrow.

Don't imagine that the art of poetry is any simpler than the art of music, or that you can please the expert before you have spent at least as much effort on the art of verse as the average piano teacher spends on the art of music.

Be influenced by as many great artists as you can, but have the decency either to acknowledge the debt outright, or to try to conceal it.

Don't allow 'influence' to mean merely that you mop up the particular decorative vocabulary of some one or two poets whom you happen to admire. A Turkish war correspondent was recently caught red-handed babbling in his despatches of 'dove-grey' hills, or else it was 'pearl-pale', I can not remember.

Use either no ornament or good ornament.

1918

---

6. British psychologist Bernard Hart (1879–1960), influenced by the theories of Sigmund Freud, popularized the idea of the "complex" as an "emotional system of ideas."

7. Referring to the "Thou shalt not . . ." formula of the Ten Commandments of Moses (Exodus 20.1–17).

WILLA CATHER

"The Novel Démeublé" strikes many familiar high modernist themes: distrust of mass production, the importance of distinguishing popular entertainment from serious art, and disdain for nineteenth-century realism with its consumerist catalogs of material objects. In this essay, however, Cather (1873–1947) sifts through the nineteenth-century heritage rather than rejecting it wholesale; she finds a precursor for her own ideal of the "unfurnished" modernist novel in Hawthorne's *The Scarlet Letter.*

From The Novel Démeublé

The novel, for a long while, has been over-furnished. The property-man has been so busy on its pages, the importance of material objects and their vivid presentation have been so stressed, that we take it for granted whoever can observe, and can write the English language, can write a novel. Often the latter qualification is considered unnecessary.

In any discussion of the novel, one must make it clear whether one is talking about the novel as a form of amusement, or as a form of art; since they serve very different purposes and in very different ways. One does not wish the egg one eats for breakfast, or the morning paper, to be made of the stuff of immortality. The novel manufactured to entertain great multitudes of people must be considered exactly like a cheap soap or a cheap perfume, or cheap furniture. Fine quality is a distinct disadvantage in articles made for great numbers of people who do not want quality but quantity, who do not want a thing that "wears," but who want change,—a succession of new things that are quickly thread-bare and can be lightly thrown away. Does anyone pretend that if the Woolworth store windows were piled high with Tanagra figurines at ten cents, they could for a moment compete with Kewpie brides[1] in the popular esteem? Amusement is one thing; enjoyment of art is another.

* * *

There is a popular superstition that "realism" asserts itself in the cataloguing of a great number of material objects, in explaining mechanical processes, the methods of operating manufactories and trades, and in minutely and unsparingly describing physical sensations. But is not realism, more than it is anything else, an attitude of mind on the part of the writer toward his material, a vague indication of the sympathy and candour with which he accepts, rather than chooses, his theme? Is the story of a banker who is unfaithful to his wife and who ruins himself by speculation in trying to gratify the caprices of his mistresses, at all reinforced by a masterly exposition of banking, our whole system of credits, the methods of the Stock Exchange? Of course, if the story is thin, these things do reinforce it in a sense,—any amount of red meat thrown into the scale to make the beam dip.

---

1. Kewpie dolls, enormously popular from their introduction in the 1910s, were manufactured in ceramic and, later, plastic. Named for their resemblance to images of Cupid, they were often distributed in bride and groom sets. "Woolworth's": American chain store founded in the late 19th century and noted for inexpensive merchandise. "Tanagra figurines": miniature terracotta statues, usually of fashionably dressed women, mass produced in Greece at the end of the 4th century B.C.E.

But are the banking system and the Stock Exchange worth being written about at all? Have such things any proper place in imaginative art?

* * *

If the novel is a form of imaginative art, it cannot be at the same time a vivid and brilliant form of journalism. Out of the teeming, gleaming stream of the present it must select the eternal material of art. There are hopeful signs that some of the younger writers are trying to break away from mere verisimilitude, and, following the development of modern painting, to interpret imaginatively the material and social investiture of their characters; to present their scene by suggestion rather than by enumeration. The higher processes of art are all processes of simplification. The novelist must learn to write, and then he must unlearn it; just as the modern painter learns to draw, and then learns when utterly to disregard his accomplishment, when to subordinate it to a higher and truer effect. In this direction only, it seems to me, can the novel develop into anything more varied and perfect than all the many novels that have gone before.

One of the very earliest American romances might well serve as a suggestion to later writers. In *The Scarlet Letter* how truly in the spirit of art is the mise-en-scène presented.[2] That drudge, the theme-writing high-school student, could scarcely be sent there for information regarding the manners and dress and interiors of Puritan society. The material investiture of the story is presented as if unconsciously; by the reserved, fastidious hand of an artist, not by the gaudy fingers of a showman or the mechanical industry of a department-store window-dresser. As I remember it, in the twilight melancholy of that book, in its consistent mood, one can scarcely ever see the actual surroundings of the people; one feels them, rather, in the dusk.

Whatever is felt upon the page without being specifically named there— that, one might say, is created. It is the inexplicable presence of the thing not named, of the overtone divined by the ear but not heard by it, the verbal mood, the emotional aura of the fact or the thing or the deed, that gives high quality to the novel or the drama, as well as to poetry itself.

* * *

How wonderful it would be if we could throw all the furniture out of the window; and along with it, all the meaningless reiterations concerning physical sensations, all the tiresome old patterns, and leave the room as bare as the stage of a Greek theatre, or as that house into which the glory of Pentacost[3] descended; leave the scene bare for the play of emotions, great and little—for the nursery tale, no less than the tragedy, is killed by tasteless amplitude. The elder Dumas[4] enunciated a great principle when he said that to make a drama, a man needed one passion, and four walls.

1922

---

2. *The Scarlet Letter* (1850), by American novelist Nathaniel Hawthorne (1804–1864).
3. Christian festival marking the descent of the Holy Spirit to Christ's disciples after his death and resurrection (Acts 2.1–4); often painted as

described in the Bible, with the disciples at a table in a closed room.
4. Alexandre Dumas (1802–1870), popular French novelist, author of *The Three Musketeers* (1844).

WILLIAM CARLOS WILLIAMS

Williams's 1923 *Spring and All* interspersed untitled short poems (many of them, like "Spring and All" and "The Red Wheelbarrow," now familiar to readers as free-standing lyrics) with sections of manifesto-style prose. *Spring and All* dramatizes repeatedly what Williams (1883–1963) calls "the leap from prose to the process of imagination," charting the rhythmic ebb and flow of imagination's force. Although the poems in *Spring and All* are numbered consecutively, the headings of the prose interludes frequently, as here, play with typographical conventions of numbering.

From Spring and All

CHAPTER VI

Now, in the imagination, all flesh, all human flesh has been dead upon the earth for ten million, billion years. The bird has turned into a stone within whose heart an egg, unlaid, remained hidden.

It is spring! but miracle of miracles a miraculous miracle has gradually taken place during these seemingly wasted eons. Through the orderly sequences of unmentionable time EVOLUTION HAS REPEATED ITSELF FROM THE BEGINNING.

Good God!

Every step once taken in the first advance of the human race, from the amoeba to the highest type of intelligence, has been duplicated, every step exactly paralleling the one that preceded in the dead ages gone by. A perfect plagiarism results. Everything is and is new. Only the imagination is undeceived.

At this point the entire complicated and laborious process begins to near a new day. (More of this in Chapter XIX) But for the moment everything is fresh, perfect, recreated.

In fact now, for the first time, everything IS new. Now at last the perfect effect is being witlessly discovered. The terms "veracity" "actuality" "real" "natural" "sincere" are being discussed at length, every word in the discussion being evolved from an identical discussion which took place the day before yesterday.

Yes, the imagination, drunk with prohibitions, has destroyed and recreated everything afresh in the likeness of that which it was. Now indeed men look about in amazement at each other with a full realization of the meaning of "art."

CHAPTER 2

It is spring: life again begins to assume its normal appearance as of "today." Only the imagination is undeceived. The volcanos are extinct. Coal is beginning to be dug again where the fern forests stood last night. (If an error is noted here, pay no attention to it.)

CHAPTER XIX

I realize that the chapters are rather quick in their sequence and that nothing much is contained in any one of them but no one should be surprised at this today.

THE TRADITIONALISTS OF PLAGIARISM

It is spring. That is to say, it is approaching THE BEGINNING.

In that huge and microscopic career of time, as it were a wild horse racing in an illimitable pampa[1] under the stars, describing immense and microscopic circles with his hoofs on the solid turf, running without a stop for the millionth part of a second until he is aged and worn to a heap of skin, bones and ragged hoofs—In that majestic progress of life, that gives the exact impression of Phidias' frieze,[2] the men and beasts of which, though they seem of the rigidity of marble are not so but move, with blinding rapidity, though we do not have the time to notice it, their legs advancing a millionth part of an inch every fifty thousand years—In that progress of life which seems stillness itself in the mass of its movements—at last SPRING is approaching.

In that colossal surge toward the finite and the capable life has now arrived for the second time at that exact moment when in the ages past the destruction of the species *Homo sapiens* occurred.

Now at last that process of miraculous verisimilitude, that great copying which evolution has followed, repeating move for move every move that it made in the past—is approaching the end.

Suddenly it is at an end. THE WORLD IS NEW.[3]

1923

1. Extensive grassy plains of central Argentina (Spanish, *la pampa*).
2. The most important sculptor of classical Athens, Phidias (c.500–c.432 B.C.E.) or his students executed the frieze (a long band of relief sculpture surmounting columns) decorating the Parthenon in Athens; the frieze depicts a festival procession of men and horses.
3. In the original publication, the poem "Spring and All" ("By the road to the contagious hospital"; see p. 1466) directly followed this section.

LANGSTON HUGHES

Where Willa Cather, along with many other modernists, sought to divide high art from popular entertainment, Langston Hughes (1902–1967) urged African American artists to embrace black popular culture, epitomized for Hughes and many other observers of the 1920s by the innovations of jazz. "The Negro Artist and the Racial Mountain," published at the height of the Harlem Renaissance, takes aim at white audiences who looked to black artists for easy, stereotypical entertainment. Hughes's essay reserves most of its anger, however, for black elites who—he charged—preferred their artists to imitate white standards.

From The Negro Artist and the Racial Mountain

One of the most promising of the young Negro poets said to me once, "I want to be a poet—not a Negro poet," meaning, I believe, "I want to write like a white poet"; meaning subconsciously, "I would like to be a white poet"; meaning behind that, "I would like to be white." And I was sorry the young man said that, for no great poet has ever been afraid of being himself. And I doubted then that, with his desire to run away spiritually from his race, this boy would ever be a great poet. But this is the mountain standing in the way of any true Negro art in America—this urge within the race toward whiteness, the desire to pour racial individuality into the mold of American standardization, and to be as little Negro and as much American as possible.

* * *

The Negro artist works against an undertow of sharp criticism and misunderstanding from his own group and unintentional bribes from the whites. "O, be respectable, write about nice people, show how good we are," say the Negroes. "Be stereotyped, don't go too far, don't shatter our illusions about you, don't amuse us too seriously. We will pay you," say the whites. Both would have told Jean Toomer not to write "Cane."[1] The colored people did not praise it. The white people did not buy it. Most of the colored people who did read "Cane" hate it. They are afraid of it. Although the critics gave it good reviews the public remained indifferent. Yet (excepting the work of Du Bois[2]) "Cane" contains the finest prose written by a Negro in America. And like the singing of Robeson,[3] it is truly racial.

* * *

Most of my own poems are racial in theme and treatment, derived from the life I know. In many of them I try to grasp and hold some of the meanings and rhythms of jazz. I am sincere as I know how to be in these poems and yet after every reading I answer questions like these from my own people: Do you think Negroes should always write about Negroes? I wish you wouldn't read some of your poems to white folks. How do you find anything interesting in a place like a cabaret? Why do you write about black people? You aren't black. What makes you do so many jazz poems?

But jazz to me is one of the inherent expressions of Negro life in America: the eternal tom-tom beating in the Negro soul—the tom-tom of revolt against weariness in a white world, a world of subway trains, and work, work, work; the tom-tom of joy and laughter, and pain swallowed in a smile. Yet the

---

1. Jean Toomer's *Cane* combines prose and poems in a modernist dual portrait of rural Georgia and the urban black community of Washington, D.C.; see p. 1816.
2. W. E. B. Du Bois (1868–1963), author of *The Souls of Black Folk* (1903) and other works on

African American life and history.
3. Paul Robeson (1898–1976), African American actor and singer; in 1925 he made his concert debut in New York City with a program of black spirituals.

Philadelphia clubwoman is ashamed to say that her face created it and she does not like me to write about it. The old subconscious "white is best" runs through her mind. Years of study under white teachers, a lifetime of white books, pictures, and papers, and white manners, morals, and Puritan standards made her dislike the spirituals. And now she turns up her nose at jazz and all its manifestations—likewise almost everything else distinctly racial. She doesn't care for the Winold Reiss[4] portraits of Negroes because they are "too Negro." She does not want a true picture of herself from anybody. She wants the artist to flatter her, to make the white world believe that all Negroes are as smug and as near white in soul as she wants to be. But, to my mind, it is the duty of the younger Negro artist, if he accepts any duties at all from outsiders, to change through the force of his art that old whispering "I want to be white," hidden in the aspirations of his people, to "Why should I want to be white? I am a Negro—and beautiful!"

So I am ashamed for the black poet who says, "I want to be a poet, not a Negro poet," as though his own racial world were not as interesting as any other world. I am ashamed, too, for the colored artist who runs from the painting of Negro faces to the painting of sunsets after the manner of the academicians because he fears the strange un-whiteness of his own features. An artist must be free to choose what he does, certainly, but he must also never be afraid to do what he might choose.

Let the blare of Negro Jazz bands and the bellowing voice of Bessie Smith singing Blues penetrate the closed ears of the colored near-intellectuals until they listen and perhaps understand. Let Paul Robeson singing Water Boy, and Rudolph Fisher writing about the streets of Harlem, and Jean Toomer holding the heart of Georgia in his hands, and Aaron Douglas[5] drawing strange black fantasies cause the smug Negro middle class to turn from their white, respectable, ordinary books and papers to catch a glimmer of their own beauty. We younger Negro artists who create now intend to express our individual dark-skinned selves without fear or shame. If white people are pleased we are glad. If they are not, it doesn't matter. We know we are beautiful. And ugly too. The tom-tom cries and the tom-tom laughs. If colored people are pleased we are glad. If they are not, their displeasure doesn't matter either. We build our temples for tomorrow, strong as we know how, and we stand on top of the mountain, free within ourselves.

1926

---

4. Winold Reiss (1886–1953), German-born artist known for his portraits of figures from the Harlem Renaissance.
5. Aaron Douglas (1899–1979), painter and muralist who studied with Winold Reiss and who became the first head of the Harlem Artists' Guild;

Bessie Smith (1894?–1937), noted blues singer at the height of her fame in the 1920s; Rudolph Fisher (1897–1934), Harlem Renaissance author and musician who arranged songs for Paul Robeson's 1925 New York concert debut.

H. D. (HILDA DOOLITTLE)
1886–1961

In January 1913, Harriet Monroe's influential little magazine, *Poetry*, printed three vivid poems by an unknown "H. D., Imagiste." These spare, elegant lyrics were among the first important products of the "imagist movement": poems devoid of explanation and declamation, unrhymed and lacking regular beat, depending on the power of an image to arrest attention and convey emotion. The poet's pen name, the movement's name, and the submission to the magazine were all the work of Ezra Pound, poet and tireless publicist for anything new in the world of poetry. The poems themselves had been written by his friend Hilda Doolittle. In later years, H. D. would look back at these events as epitomizing her dilemma: how to be a woman poet speaking in a world where women were spoken for and about by men. It is, perhaps, a symbol of her sense of difficulty that, though she strove for a voice that could be recognized as clearly feminine, she continued to publish under the name that Pound had devised for her.

She was born in Bethlehem, Pennsylvania, one girl in a family of five boys. Her mother was a musician and music teacher, active in the Moravian church to which many in Bethlehem belonged. The symbols and rituals of this group, along with its tradition of secrecy created in response to centuries of oppression, had much to do with H. D.'s interest in images and her attraction in later life to occult and other symbol systems: the cabala, numerology, the tarot, and psychoanalysis.

When her father, an astronomer and mathematician, was appointed director of the observatory at the University of Pennsylvania, the family moved to a suburb of Philadelphia. There, when she was fifteen years old, H. D. met Ezra Pound, a student at the university, already dedicated to poetry and acting the poet's role with dramatic intensity. The two were engaged for a while, but Pound's influence continued long after each had gone on to other partners. H. D. attended college at Bryn Mawr for two years; in 1911 she made a bold move to London, where Pound had gone some years earlier. She married a member of his circle, the English poet Richard Aldington, in 1913. With Aldington she studied Greek and read the classics, but the marriage was not a success and was destroyed by their separation during World War I when Aldington went into the army and served in France.

The year 1919 was terrible for H. D.: her brother Gilbert was killed in the fighting in France, her father died soon thereafter, her marriage broke up, close friendships with Pound and with D. H. Lawrence came to an end, she had a nearly fatal case of flu, and amid all this gave birth to a daughter who Aldington said was not his child. But she was rescued from the worst of her emotional and financial troubles by Winifred Ellerman, whose father, a shipping magnate, was one of the wealthiest men in England. Ellerman, a writer who had adopted the pen name Bryher, had initially been attracted by H. D.'s poetry; their relationship developed first as a love affair and then into a lifelong friendship.

In 1923, H. D. settled in Switzerland. With Bryher's financial help she raised her daughter and cared for her ailing mother, who had joined her household. During 1933 and 1934 she spent time in Vienna, where she underwent analysis by Sigmund Freud, hoping to understand both her writer's block and what she called her "two loves" of women and men. Freud's theory of the unconscious and the disguised ways in which it reaches expression accorded well with H. D.'s understanding of how the unexplained images in a poem could be significant; the images were coded personal meanings. H. D.'s religious mysticism clashed with Freud's materialism, however, and she had mixed reactions to Freud's developing theory that women's unhappiness was determined by their sense of biological inferiority to men. But H. D. was instrumental (with Bryher's help) in getting Freud, who was Jewish, safely to London when the Nazi regime took over in Austria. When World War II broke out H. D. went back to London to share England's fate in crisis.

During the 1930s she worked mostly in prose forms and composed several autobiographical pieces (some of which remain unpublished). Like many major poets of the era, H. D. came in time to feel the need to write longer works; the bombardment of London inspired three long related poems about World War II, *The Walls Do Not Fall* (1944), *Tribute to the Angels* (1945), and *The Flowering of the Rod* (1946), which appeared together as *Trilogy*. In them she combined layers of historical and personal experience; wars going back to the Trojan War all fused in one image of humankind forever imposing and enduring violence.

The personal and the historical had always been one to her, and she became increasingly attracted to the image of Helen, the so-called cause of the Trojan War, as an image of herself. According to Homer's *Iliad*, Helen's beauty led Paris, a Trojan prince, to steal her from her Greek husband, Menelaus; and all the Greek warriors made common cause to get her back. After ten years' encamped before the walls of Troy, they found a devious way to enter the city and destroy it. H. D. was struck by the fact that the legend was related entirely from the male point of view; Helen never had a chance to speak. The object of man's acts and the subject of their poems, she was herself always silent. If Helen tried to speak, would she even have a voice or a point of view? Out of these broodings, and helped by her study of symbols, H. D. wrote her meditative epic of more than fourteen hundred lines, *Helen in Egypt*. The poem, composed between 1951 and 1955, consists of three books of interspersed verse and prose commentary, which follow Helen's quest. "She herself is the writing" that she seeks to understand, the poet observes.

H. D.'s imagist poetry, for which she was known during her lifetime, represents the imagist credo with its vivid phrasing, compelling imagery, free verse, short poetic line, and avoidance of abstraction and generalization. She followed Pound's example in producing many translations of poetry from older literature, especially from her favorite Greek poets. Her natural images are influenced by her early immersion in astronomy as well as by Greek poetry's Mediterranean settings. Austere landscapes of sea, wind, stars, and sand are contrasted with sensual figures of jewels, honey, and shells. Traditional metaphorical resources of earlier women's poetry, such flowers and birds, are absorbed into modernism's aesthetic of "fiery tempered steel." As when her "Oread" calls upon the sea to "splash your great pines / on our rocks," H. D.'s best-known poems embody high modernism's goal of condensing forces at once lush and shattering, violent and creative, into a single arresting image.

The texts of the poems included here are those of *Collected Poems 1912–1944*, edited by Louis L. Martz (1983).

Mid-day

The light beats upon me.
I am startled—
a split leaf crackles on the paved floor—
I am anguished—defeated.

A slight wind shakes the seed-pods—   5
my thoughts are spent
as the black seeds.
My thoughts tear me,
I dread their fever.
I am scattered in its whirl.   10
I am scattered like
the hot shrivelled seeds.

The shrivelled seeds
are split on the path—
the grass bends with dust,   15
the grape slips
under its crackled leaf:
yet far beyond the spent seed-pods,
and the blackened stalks of mint,
the poplar is bright on the hill,   20
the poplar spreads out,
deep-rooted among trees.

O poplar, you are great
among the hill-stones,
while I perish on the path   25
among the crevices of the rocks.

                                                              1916

Oread[1]

Whirl up, sea—
whirl your pointed pines,
splash your great pines
on our rocks,
hurl your green over us,   5
cover us with your pools of fir.

                                                          1914, 1924

Leda[1]

Where the slow river
meets the tide,
a red swan lifts red wings
and darker beak,
and underneath the purple down   5
of his soft breast
uncurls his coral feet.

Through the deep purple
of the dying heat
of sun and mist,   10
the level ray of sun-beam
has caressed
the lily with dark breast,

1. A nymph of mountains and hills.
1. In Greek mythology, Leda is the mortal raped by Zeus, in the guise of a swan. Helen of Troy was her daughter.

and flecked with richer gold
its golden crest.   15

Where the slow lifting
of the tide,
floats into the river
and slowly drifts
among the reeds,   20
and lifts the yellow flags,
he floats
where tide and river meet.

Ah kingly kiss—
no more regret   25
nor old deep memories
to mar the bliss;
where the low sedge is thick,
the gold day-lily
outspreads and rests   30
beneath soft fluttering
of red swan wings
and the warm quivering
of the red swan's breast.

                                              1919, 1921

Fragment 113

"Neither honey nor bee for me."
                    —Sappho.[1]

Not honey,
not the plunder of the bee
from meadow or sand-flower
or mountain bush;
from winter-flower or shoot   5
born of the later heat:
not honey, not the sweet
stain on the lips and teeth:
not honey, not the deep
plunge of soft belly   10
and the clinging of the gold-edged
pollen-dusted feet;

not so—
though rapture blind my eyes,
and hunger crisp   15
dark and inert my mouth,

1. Greek woman lyric poet of Lesbos in the 7th century B.C.E.

not honey, not the south,
not the tall stalk
of red twin-lilies,
nor light branch of fruit tree   20
caught in flexible light branch;

not honey, not the south;
ah flower of purple iris,
flower of white,
or of the iris, withering the grass—   25
for fleck of the sun's fire,
gathers such heat and power,
that shadow-print is light,
cast through the petals
of the yellow iris flower;   30

not iris—old desire—old passion—
old forgetfulness—old pain—
not this, nor any flower,
but if you turn again,
seek strength of arm and throat,   35
touch as the god;
neglect the lyre-note;
knowing that you shall feel,
about the frame,
no trembling of the string   40
but heat, more passionate
of bone and the white shell
and fiery tempered steel.

                                        1922

Helen[1]

All Greece hates
the still eyes in the white face,
the lustre as of olives
where she stands,
and the white hands.   5

All Greece reviles
the wan face when she smiles,
hating it deeper still
when it grows wan and white,
remembering past enchantments   10
and past ills.

1. In Greek legend, the wife of Menelaus; her kid-naping by the Trojan prince Paris started the Trojan War. She was the daughter of the god Zeus, the product of his rape, when disguised as a swan, of the mortal Leda.

Greece sees unmoved,
God's daughter, born of love,
the beauty of cool feet
and slenderest knees,   15
could love indeed the maid,
only if she were laid,
white ash amid funereal cypresses.

                                                    1924

From The Walls Do Not Fall

To Bryher
FOR KARNAK 1923
FROM LONDON 1942

1

An incident here and there,
and rails gone (for guns)
from your (and my) old town square:

mist and mist-grey, no colour,
still the Luxor bee, chick and hare[1]   5
pursue unalterable purpose

in green, rose-red, lapis;
they continue to prophesy
from the stone papyrus:

there, as here, ruin opens   10
the tomb, the temple; enter,
there as here, there are no doors:

the shrine lies open to the sky,
the rain falls, here, there
sand drifts; eternity endures: 15

ruin everywhere, yet as the fallen roof
leaves the sealed room
open to the air,

so, through our desolation,
thoughts stir, inspiration stalks us   20
through gloom:

1. Luxor is a town on the Nile River in Egypt, close to the ruins of the ancient city of Thebes, where the Temple of Karnak is located. The bee, chick, and hare are carved symbols that appear on the temple.

unaware, Spirit announces the Presence;
shivering overtakes us,
as of old, Samuel:[2]

trembling at a known street-corner,   25
we know not nor are known;
the Pythian[3] pronounces—we pass on

to another cellar, to another sliced wall
where poor utensils show
like rare objects in a museum;   30

Pompeii[4] has nothing to teach us,
we know crack of volcanic fissure,
slow flow of terrible lava,

pressure on heart, lungs, the brain
about to burst its brittle case   35
(what the skull can endure!):

over us, Apocryphal[5] fire,
under us, the earth sway, dip of a floor,
slope of a pavement

where men roll, drunk   40
with a new bewilderment,
sorcery, bedevilment:

the bone-frame was made for
no such shock knit within terror,
yet the skeleton stood up to it: 45

the flesh? it was melted away,
the heart burnt out, dead ember,
tendons, muscles shattered, outer husk dismembered,

yet the frame held:
we passed the flame: we wonder   50
what saved us? what for?

2

Evil was active in the land,
Good was impoverished and sad;

Ill promised adventure,
Good was smug and fat;   55

---

2. A biblical seer and prophet.
3. Pythia is another name for Delphi, Greek town famous because the Oracle of Apollo was located there. The Pythian is the high priestess of that oracle, who was possessed by the Delphic spirit and prophesied.

4. Ancient Italian city near Naples, burned and buried in a few hours by the eruption of Mount Vesuvius in 79 C.E.
5. The Apocrypha are books rejected from the Bible because of doubtful authenticity.

Dev-ill was after us,
tricked up like Jehovah;

Good was the tasteless pod,
stripped from the manna-beans, pulse, lentils:

they were angry when we were so hungry   60
for the nourishment, God;

they snatched off our amulets,
charms are not, they said, grace;

but gods always face two-ways,
so let us search the old highways   65

for the true-rune, the right-spell,
recover old values;

nor listen if they shout out,
your beauty, Isis, Aset or Astarte,[6]

is a harlot; you are retrogressive,   70
zealot, hankering after old flesh-pots;

your heart, moreover,
is a dead canker,

they continue, and
your rhythm is the devil's hymn,   75

your stylus is dipped in corrosive sublimate,
how can you scratch out

indelible ink of the palimpsest[7]
of past misadventure?

3

Let us, however, recover the Sceptre,   80
the rod of power:

it is crowned with the lily-head
or the lily-bud:

it is Caduceus;[8] among the dying
it bears healing: 85

---

6. Three goddesses of fertility from Egyptian and
Phoenician mythologies.
7. A parchment or tablet that has been written on
more than once, with the underlying texts only
partly erased and hence still visible.
8. Name of the winged staff with two serpents
twined around it carried by Mercury (Hermes),
Greco-Roman messenger god and god of healing.

or evoking the dead,
it brings life to the living.

4

There is a spell, for instance,
in every sea-shell:

continuous, the sea-thrust   90
is powerless against coral,

bone, stone, marble
hewn from within by that craftsman,

the shell-fish:
oyster, clam, mollusc   95

is master-mason planning
the stone marvel:

yet that flabby, amorphous hermit
within, like the planet

senses the finite,   100
it limits its orbit

of being, its house,
temple, fane, shrine:

it unlocks the portals
at stated intervals: 105

prompted by hunger,
it opens to the tide-flow:

but infinity? no,
of nothing-too-much:

I sense my own limit,   110
my shell-jaws snap shut

at invasion of the limitless,
ocean-weight; infinite water

can not crack me, egg in egg-shell;
closed in, complete, immortal   115

full-circle, I know the pull
of the tide, the lull

as well as the moon;
the octopus-darkness

is powerless against   120
her cold immortality;

so I in my own way know
that the whale

can not digest me:[9]
be firm in your own small, static, limited   125

orbit and the shark-jaws
of outer circumstance

will spit you forth:
be indigestible, hard, ungiving.

so that, living within,   130
yet beget, self-out-of-self,

selfless,
that pearl-of-great-price.

                            5

When in the company of the gods,
I loved and was loved,   135

never was my mind stirred
to such rapture,

my heart moved
to such pleasure,

as now, to discover   140
over Love, a new Master:

His, the track in the sand
from a plum-tree in flower

to a half-open hut-door,
(or track would have been   145

but wind blows sand-prints from the sand,
whether seen or unseen):

His, the Genius in the jar
which the Fisherman finds,[1]

---

9. Allusion to the biblical story of Jonah, who was swallowed by a whale when he disobeyed God's orders; he was preserved in the whale's belly until he repented and then cast onto land.

1. In the folktale, a poor fisherman finds washed up on shore a bottle containing a genie, who carries out his orders and brings him prosperity and happiness.

He is Mage,[2]   150
bringing myrrh.

6

In me (the worm) clearly
is no righteousness, but this—

persistence; I escaped spider-snare,
bird-claw, scavenger bird-beak,   155

clung to grass-blade,
the back of a leaf

when storm-wind
tore it from its stem;

I escaped, I explored   160
rose-thorn forest,

was rain-swept
down the valley of a leaf;

was deposited on grass,
where mast by jewelled mast   165

bore separate ravellings
of encrusted gem-stuff

of the mist
from each banner-staff:

unintimidated by multiplicity   170
of magnified beauty,

such as your gorgon[3]-great
dull eye can not focus

nor compass, I profit
by every calamity;   175

I eat my way out of it;
gorged on vine-leaf and mulberry,

parasite, I find nourishment:
when you cry in disgust,

2. Wise man, especially referring to any of the three kings who followed the star of Bethlehem to Christ's cradle, bringing gifts.
3. In Greek mythology, any of three sisters with snakes in her hair, so ugly that anyone who looked at her was turned to stone. The most famous of the three was Medusa.

a worm on the leaf,   180
a worm in the dust,

a worm on the ear-of-wheat,
I am yet unrepentant,

for I know how the Lord God
is about to manifest, when I,   185

the industrious worm,
spin my own shroud.

*   *   *

20

Now it appears very clear
that the Holy Ghost,

childhood's mysterious enigma,
is the Dream;

that way of inspiration   430
is always open,

and open to everyone;
it acts as go-between, interpreter,

it explains symbols of the past
in to-day's imagery,   435

it merges the distant future
with most distant antiquity,

states economically
in a simple dream-equation

the most profound philosophy,   440
discloses the alchemist's secret

and follows the Mage
in the desert.

21

Splintered the crystal of identity,
shattered the vessel of integrity,   445

till the Lord *Amen*,
paw-er of the ground,

bearer of the curled horns,
bellows from the horizon:

here am I, Amen-Ra, 450
Amen, Aries,[4] the Ram;

time, time for you to begin a new spiral,
see—I toss you into the star-whirlpool;

till pitying, pitying,
snuffing the ground, 455

here am I, Amen-Ra whispers,
Amen, Aries, the Ram,

be cocoon, smothered in wool,
be Lamb,[5] mothered again.

22

Now my right hand, 460
now my left hand

clutch your curled fleece;
take me home, take me home,

my voice wails from the ground;
take me home, Father: 465

pale as the worm in the grass,
yet I am a spark

struck by your hoof from a rock:
Amen, you are so warm,

hide me in your fleece, 470
crop me up with the new-grass;

let your teeth devour me,
let me be warm in your belly,

the sun-disk,
the re-born Sun. 475

23

Take me home
where canals

---

4. Latin name for a constellation, one of the signs of the zodiac. Amen-Ra was the Egyptian god of life and reproduction. "*Amen*": may it be so, certainly, truly (Hebrew); said at the end of a prayer.
5. Traditional reference to Christ.

flow
between iris-banks:

where the heron   480
has her nest:

where the mantis
prays on the river-reed:

where the grasshopper says
Amen, Amen, Amen.   485

24

Or anywhere
where stars blaze through clear air,

where we may greet individually,
Sirius, Vega, Arcturus,[6]

where these separate entities   490
are intimately concerned with us,

where each, with its particular attribute,
may be invoked

with accurate charm, spell, prayer,
which will reveal unquestionably,   495

whatever healing or inspirational essence
is necessary for whatever particular ill

the inquiring soul is heir to:
O stars, little jars of that indisputable

and absolute Healer, Apothecary,   500
wrought, faceted, jewelled

boxes, very precious, to hold further
unguent, myrrh, incense:

jasper, beryl, sapphire
that, as we draw them nearer   505

by prayer, spell,
litany, incantation,

6. Three bright stars.

will reveal their individual fragrance,
personal magnetic influence,

become, as they once were,   510
personified messengers,

healers, helpers
of the One, *Amen,* All-father.

*   *   *

39

We have had too much consecration,
too little affirmation,

too much: but this, this, this
has been proved heretical,

too little: I know, I feel   790
the meaning that words hide;

they are anagrams, cryptograms,
little boxes, conditioned

to hatch butterflies . . .

40

For example: 795
Osiris equates O-sir-is or O-Sire-is;

Osiris,
the star Sirius,[7]

relates resurrection myth
and resurrection reality   800

through the ages;
plasterer, crude mason,

not too well equipped, my thought
would cover deplorable gaps

in time, reveal the regrettable chasm,   805
bridge that before-and-after schism,

---

7. The brightest star in the sky. Osiris was the Egyptian god of the underworld and the dead, brother and husband of Isis. "O-sir-is" and "O-sire-is" are wordplays on this name.

(*before Abraham was I am*)[8]
uncover cankerous growths

in present-day philosophy,
in an endeavour to make ready,   810

as it were, the patient for the Healer;
correlate faith with faith,

recover the secret of Isis,
which is: there was One

in the beginning, Creator,   815
Fosterer, Begetter, the Same-forever

in the papyrus-swamp
in the Judean meadow.

41

Sirius:
what mystery is this?   820

you are seed,
corn near the sand,
enclosed in black-lead,
ploughed land.

Sirius:
what mystery is this?   825

you are drowned
in the river;
the spring freshets
push open the water-gates.   830

Sirius:
what mystery is this?

where heat breaks and cracks
the sand-waste,
you are a mist   835
of snow: white, little flowers.

42

O, Sire, is this the path?
over sedge, over dune-grass,

---

8. Christ's words to the Jews, when asked about his connection to Abraham, first patriarch and ancestor of the Hebrews (John 8.58).

silently
sledge-runners pass. 840

O, Sire, is this the waste?
unbelievably,

sand glistens like ice,
cold, cold;

drawn to the temple gate, O, Sire, 845
is this union at last?

43

Still the walls do not fall,
I do not know why;

there is zrr-hiss,
lightning in a not-known, 850

unregistered dimension;
we are powerless,

dust and powder fill our lungs
our bodies blunder

through doors twisted on hinges, 855
and the lintels slant

cross-wise;
we walk continually

on thin air
that thickens to a blind fog, 860

then step swiftly aside,
for even the air

is independable,
thick where it should be fine

and tenuous 865
where wings separate and open,

and the ether
is heavier than the floor,

and the floor sags
like a ship floundering; 870

we know no rule
of procedure,

we are voyagers, discoverers
of the not-known,

the unrecorded;   875
we have no map;

possibly we will reach haven,
heaven.

                                                                              1944

MARIANNE MOORE
1887–1972

Marianne Moore was a radically inventive modernist, greatly admired by other poets of her generation, and a powerful influence on such later writers as Robert Lowell, Randall Jarrell, and Richard Wilbur. Like her forerunner Emily Dickinson, she made of the traditional and constraining "woman's place" a protected space to do her own work, but unlike Emily Dickinson, she was a deliberate professional, publishing her poems regularly, in touch with the movements and artists of her time. She was famous for the statement that poetry, though departing from the real world, re-created that world within its forms: poems were "imaginary gardens with real toads in them." Her earlier work is distinguished by great precision of observation and language, ornate diction, and complex stanza and prosodic patterns. Her later work is much less ornate; and in revising her poetry, she tended to simplify and shorten.

She was born in Kirkwood, Missouri, a suburb of St. Louis. In her childhood, the family was abandoned by her father; they moved to Carlisle, Pennsylvania, where—in a pattern common among both men and women writers of this period—her mother supported them by teaching school. She went to Bryn Mawr College, graduating in 1909; traveled with her mother in England and France in 1911; and returned to Carlisle to teach at the U.S. Indian School between 1911 and 1915. Having begun to write poetry in college, she was first published in 1915 and 1916 in such little magazines as the *Egoist* (an English magazine with which Ezra Pound was associated), *Poetry*, and *Others* (a journal for experimental writing with which William Carlos Williams was associated, founded by Alfred Kreymbourg, a New York poet and playwright). Through these magazines she entered the avant-garde and modernist world. She never married; in 1916 she and her mother merged their household with that of Moore's brother, a Presbyterian minister, and they moved with him to a parish in Brooklyn, New York. There Moore was close to literary circles and Ebbets Field, where the Dodgers, then a Brooklyn baseball team, had their home stadium. Moore was a lifelong fan.

While holding jobs in schools and libraries, Moore worked at her poetry. A volume called simply *Poems* was brought out in London in 1921 without her knowledge through the efforts of two women friends who were writers, H. D. (whom she had met at Bryn Mawr) and Bryher. Another book, *Observations,* appeared in 1924 and won the Dial Award. In 1925 she began to work as editor of the *Dial,* continuing in this influential position until the magazine was disbanded in 1929. Her reviews and editorial judgments were greatly respected, although her preference for elegance and decorum over sexual frankness was not shared by some of the writers—Hart Crane and James Joyce among them—whose work she rejected or published only after they revised it.

As a critic of poetry Moore wrote numerous essays—her collected prose makes a larger book than her collected poetry. She believed that poets usually undervalued prose; "precision, economy of statement, logic" were features of good prose that could "liberate" the imagination, she wrote. In writing about animals she was able to take advantage of two different prose modes that attracted her—scientific and historical description. Her poems were an amalgam of her own observation and her readings, which she acknowledged by quotation marks and often by footnotes as well. In Moore's writings, the reader almost never finds the conventional poetic allusions that invoke a great tradition and assert the present poet's place in it. Moore's poems typically juxtapose disparate areas of human knowledge and combine the elevated with the ordinary. Her notebooks suggest, for example, that the image of the kiwi bird in "The Mind is an Enchanting Thing" emerged from a sketch Moore made of a shoe-polish tin; she praises the human mind both for its capacity to be mesmerized by the small facets of its ordinary environment and for its changeful, self-undoing freedom.

Against the exactitude and "unbearable accuracy" (as she put it) of her language, Moore counterpointed a complex texture of stanza form and versification. Pound worked with the clause, Williams with the line, H. D. with the image, Stevens and Stein with the word; Moore, unlike these modernist contemporaries, used the entire stanza as the unit of her poetry. Her stanza is composed of regular lines counted by syllables, instead of by stress, which are connected in an elaborate verse pattern, and in which rhymes often occur at unaccented syllables and even in the middle of a word. The effects she achieves are complex and subtle; she was often called the "poet's poet" of her day because the reader needed expert technical understanding to recognize what she was doing.

Nevertheless, her poetry also had a thematic, declarative edge which the outbreak of World War II led her to expand. In "The Paper Nautilus," she drew on her characteristic vein of natural observation in order to will that a threatened civilization be protected by love. At the same time, Moore was keenly aware of her distance, as a civilian and a woman, from direct experience of combat; "In Distrust of Merits," her most famous poem of the war, reflects Moore's struggle to adopt an ethically responsible relationship toward the fighting she could only know through newsreels and photographs.

Moore received the Bollingen, National Book, and Pulitzer awards for *Collected Poems* in 1951. Throughout her lifetime she continued to revise, expand, cut, and select, so that from volume to volume a poem with the same name may be a very different work. Her *Complete Poems* of 1967 represented her poetry as she wanted it remembered, but a full understanding of Moore calls for reading all of the versions of her changing work.

Poetry[1]

I, too, dislike it: there are things that are important beyond all
    this fiddle.
  Reading it, however, with a perfect contempt for it, one
    discovers in
  it after all, a place for the genuine.
    Hands that can grasp, eyes
      that can dilate, hair that can rise
        if it must, these things are important not because a   5

1. The version printed here follows the text and format of *Selected Poems* (1935).

high-sounding interpretation can be put upon them but because
    they are
useful. When they become so derivative as to become
    unintelligible,
the same thing may be said for all of us, that we
    do not admire what   10
        we cannot understand: the bat
           holding on upside down or in quest of something to

eat, elephants pushing, a wild horse taking a roll, a tireless wolf
    under
a tree, the immovable critic twitching his skin like a horse
        that feels a flea, the base-
ball fan, the statistician—   15
    nor is it valid
        to discriminate against "business documents and

school-books";[2] all these phenomena are important. One must
    make a distinction
however: when dragged into prominence by half poets, the
    result is not poetry,
nor till the poets among us can be   20
    "literalists of
the imagination"[3]—above
    insolence and triviality and can present

for inspection, "imaginary gardens with real toads in them," shall
    we have
it. In the meantime, if you demand on the one hand,   25
the raw material of poetry in
    all its rawness and
    that which is on the other hand
genuine, then you are interested in poetry.

1921, 1935

A Grave[1]

Man looking into the sea,
taking the view from those who have as much right to it as you have to it
    yourself,

---

2. Diary of Tolstoy (Dutton), p. 84. "Where the boundary between prose and poetry lies, I shall never be able to understand. The question is raised in manuals of style, yet the answer to it lies beyond me. Poetry is verse; prose is not verse. Or else poetry is everything with the exception of business documents and school books" [Moore's note].
3. Yeats's *Ideas of Good and Evil* (A. H. Bullen), p. 182. "The limitation of his view was from the very intensity of his vision; he was a too literal realist of imagination, as others are of nature; and because he believed that the figures seen by the mind's eye, when exalted by inspiration, were 'eternal existences,' symbols of divine essences, he hated every grace of style that might obscure their lineaments" [Moore's note].
1. Text and format are those of *Selected Poems* (1935).

it is human nature to stand in the middle of a thing,
but you cannot stand in the middle of this;
the sea has nothing to give but a well excavated grave.   5
The firs stand in a procession, each with an emerald turkey-foot at the top,
reserved as their contours, saying nothing;
repression, however, is not the most obvious characteristic of the sea;
the sea is a collector, quick to return a rapacious look.
There are others besides you who have worn that look—   10
whose expression is no longer a protest; the fish no longer investigate them
for their bones have not lasted:
men lower nets, unconscious of the fact that they are desecrating a grave,
and row quickly away—the blades of the oars
moving together like the feet of water-spiders as if there were
    no such thing as death.   15
The wrinkles progress among themselves in a phalanx—beautiful
    under networks of foam,
and fade breathlessly while the sea rustles in and out of the seaweed;
the birds swim through the air at top speed, emitting cat-calls
    as heretofore—
the tortoise-shell scourges about the feet of the cliffs, in motion
    beneath them;
and the ocean, under the pulsation of lighthouses and noise of
    bell-buoys,   20
advances as usual, looking as if it were not that ocean in which
    dropped things are bound to sink—
in which if they turn and twist, it is neither with volition nor
    consciousness.

1924

To a Snail[1]

If "compression is the first grace of style,"[2]
you have it. Contractility is a virtue
as modesty is a virtue.
It is not the acquisition of any one thing
that is able to adorn,   5
or the incidental quality that occurs
as a concomitant of something well said,
that we value in style,
but the principle that is hid:
in the absence of feet, "a method of conclusions";   10
"a knowledge of principles,"
in the curious phenomenon of your occipital horn.

1924

1. The text is from *Complete Poems* (1967).
2. "The very first grace of style is that which comes
from compression." *Demetrius on Style* translated
by W. Hamilton Fyfe. Heinemann, 1932 [Moore's
note].

What Are Years?[1]

What is our innocence,
what is our guilt? All are
    naked, none is safe. And whence
is courage: the unanswered question,
the resolute doubt,—   5
dumbly calling, deafly listening—that
in misfortune, even death,
        encourages others
        and in its defeat, stirs

    the soul to be strong? He   10
sees deep and is glad, who
    accedes to mortality
and in his imprisonment rises
upon himself as
the sea in a chasm, struggling to be   15
free and unable to be,
        in its surrendering
        finds its continuing.

    So he who strongly feels,
behaves. The very bird,   20
    grown taller as he sings, steels
his form straight up. Though he is captive,
his mighty singing
says, satisfaction is a lowly
thing, how pure a thing is joy.   25
        This is mortality,
        this is eternity.

                                        1941, 1967

The Paper Nautilus[1]

    For authorities whose hopes
are shaped by mercenaries?
    Writers entrapped by
    teatime fame and by
commuters' comforts? Not for these   5
    the paper nautilus
    constructs her thin glass shell.

    Giving her perishable
souvenir of hope, a dull

10

white outside and smooth-
    edged inner surface
glossy as the sea, the watchful
    maker of it guards it
    day and night; she scarcely

    eats until the eggs are hatched.   15
Buried eight-fold in her eight
    arms, for she is in
    a sense a devil-
fish, her glass ram'shorn-cradled freight
    is hid but is not crushed;   20
    as Hercules,[2] bitten

    by a crab loyal to the hydra,
was hindered to succeed,
    the intensively
    watched eggs coming from   25
the shell free it when they are freed,—
    leaving its wasp-nest flaws
    of white on white, and close-

laid Ionic[3] chiton-folds
like the lines in the mane of   30
    a Parthenon[4] horse,
    round which the arms had
wound themselves as if they knew love
    is the only fortress
    strong enough to trust to.   35

1941, 1967

The Mind Is an Enchanting Thing[1]

is an enchanted thing
    like the glaze on a
katydid-wing
        subdivided by sun
        till the nettings are legion.   5
Like Gieseking playing Scarlatti;[2]

like the apteryx[3]-awl
    as a beak, or the
kiwi's rain-shawl

---

2. Hero of Greek myth, who performed numerous exploits including battle with the hydra, a many-headed monster.
3. Classical Greek, specifically Athenian.
4. Temple in Athens decorated by a carved marble band of sculptures, including processions of horses.

1. The text is from *Complete Poems* (1967).
2. Walter Wilhelm Gieseking (1895–1956), French-born German pianist, known for his renditions of compositions by the Italian composer Domenico Scarlatti (1685–1757).
3. A flightless New Zealand bird, related to the kiwi, with a beak shaped like an awl.

of haired feathers, the mind   10
feeling its way as though blind,
walks along with its eyes on the ground.

It has memory's ear
that can hear without
having to hear.   15
Like the gyroscope's fall,
truly unequivocal
because trued by regnant certainty,

it is a power of
strong enchantment. It   20
is like the dove-
neck animated by
sun; it is memory's eye;
it's conscientious inconsistency.

It tears off the veil; tears   25
the temptation, the
mist the heart wears,
from its eye—if the heart
has a face; it takes apart
dejection. It's fire in the dove-neck's   30

iridescence; in the
inconsistencies
of Scarlatti.
Unconfusion submits
its confusion to proof; it's   35
not a Herod's oath that cannot change.[4]

1944

In Distrust of Merits[1]

Strengthened to live, strengthened to die for
medals and positioned victories?
They're fighting, fighting, fighting the blind
man who thinks he sees,—
who cannot see that the enslaver is   5
enslaved; the hater, harmed. O shining O
film star, O tumultuous
ocean lashed till small things go
as they will, the mountainous
wave makes us who look, know   10

4. Herod Antipas (d. 39 c.e.), ruler of Judea
under the Romans. He had John the Baptist
beheaded to fulfill a promise to Salome (Mark

6.22–27).
1. The text is from *Complete Poems* (1967).

depth. Lost at sea before they fought! O
  star of David, star of Bethlehem,
O black imperial lion[2]
  of the Lord—emblem
of a risen world—be joined at last, be   15
joined. There is hate's crown beneath which all is
    death; there's love's without which none
        is king; the blessed deeds bless
    the halo. As contagion
        of sickness makes sickness,   20

contagion of trust can make trust. They're
  fighting in deserts and caves, one by
one, in battalions and squadrons;
  they're fighting that I
may yet recover from the disease, My   25
Self; some have it lightly; some will die. "Man's
    wolf to man" and we devour
        ourselves. The enemy could not
    have made a greater breach in our
        defenses. One pilot-   30

ing a blind man can escape him, but
  Job disheartened by false comfort[3] knew
that nothing can be so defeating
  as a blind man who
can see. O alive who are dead, who are   35
proud not to see, O small dust of the earth
    that walks so arrogantly
        trust begets power and faith is
    an affectionate thing. We
        vow, we make this promise   40

to the fighting—it's a promise—"We'll
  never hate black, white, red, yellow, Jew,
Gentile, Untouchable."[4] We are
  not competent to
make our vows. With set jaw they are fighting,   45
fighting, fighting,—some we love whom we know,
    some we love but know not—that
        hearts may feel and not be numb.
    It cures me; or am I what
        I can't believe in? Some   50

in snow, some on crags, some in quicksands,
  little by little, much by much, they

2. Emperor Haile Selassie of Ethiopia, leader of
his country's resistance against Italian occupation
during World War II; after Mussolini's fall in 1943,
Selassie declared Ethiopia "less interested in
vengeance for the past than in justice for the
future." "Star of David": a symbol of Judaism, "star
of Bethlehem": of Christianity.
3. When undergoing Jehovah's test of his fidelity,
Job rejected the attempts of friends to comfort
him.
4. The lowest hereditary caste in India.

are fighting fighting fighting that where
    there was death there may
be life. "When a man is prey to anger,   55
he is moved by outside things; when he holds
      his ground in patience patience
        patience, that is action or
beauty," the soldier's defense
      and hardest armor for   60

the fight. The world's an orphans' home. Shall
    we never have peace without sorrow?
without pleas of the dying for
    help that won't come? O
quiet form upon the dust, I cannot   65
look and yet I must. If these great patient
    dyings—all these agonies
      and wound bearings and bloodshed—
can teach us how to live, these
    dyings were not wasted.   70

Hate-hardened heart, O heart of iron,
    iron is iron till it is rust.
There never was a war that was
    not inward; I must
fight till I have conquered in myself what   75
causes war, but I would not believe it.
    I inwardly did nothing.
      O Iscariot[5]-like crime!
    Beauty is everlasting
      and dust is for a time.   80

              1944

5. Judas Iscariot was the apostle who betrayed Jesus Christ.

RAYMOND CHANDLER
1888–1959

Raymond Chandler traveled a long and indirect route to his current status as one of the undisputed fathers—along with Dashiell Hammett and James M. Cain—of hard-boiled detective fiction. Born in Chicago, Chandler moved to England with his mother after his parents divorced and his father, always erratic and often drunk, disappeared from his life. His mother's family offered them a home in a London suburb; their financial support was reliable enough to ensure Chandler a rigorous secondary education at nearby Dulwich College. At Dulwich, Chandler was a prize-winning student, with a special dedication to foreign languages—not only the French, German, and Spanish that his family thought good preparation for a career in international business, but also the Latin and Greek classics that still, in the opening years of the century, lay at the heart of a British gentlemanly education.

His brilliant performance on the civil service examination qualified Chandler for an administrative position with the Admiralty of the British Navy; he remained there for a mere six months before resigning. After spending two years as a journalist and free-lance essayist and poet, Chandler returned to the United States in 1912 and worked his way out to Los Angeles, where he found a job as an accountant. Still restless, he went to Victoria, British Columbia, in 1917 to enlist in the Canadian Army. After seeing action in France, he returned to southern California, where he started working for a California oil company—a newly booming business in the automobile-crazy 1920s. Starting as a bookkeeper, in 1924 he was named vice president in charge of the Dabney Oil Syndicate's Los Angeles office. In the same year, Chandler married his long-time love, an older divorcée, Pearl "Cissy" Pascal. Neither marriage nor professional success settled him into a permanent home or reconciled him to his job, and in 1932 he was fired for drinking and failing to show up at work. Middle-aged and unemployed in the grimmest years of the Great Depression, Chandler returned to his earlier ambitions to be a writer.

Chandler quickly found his genre and favored publication venue: the detective story as published in popular pulp magazines (named for the cheap wood-based paper on which they were printed). In 1933 he sold his first story, "Blackmailers Don't Shoot," to *Black Mask* for $180; "Red Wind" appeared in *Dime Detective* in 1938. With a string of successful pulp stories behind him, Chandler embarked on the novel, *The Big Sleep* (1939), that introduced his most famous character: Philip Marlowe, the detective who is lonely, jaded, cynical, but upright in a corrupt world. "Down these mean streets a man must go who is not himself mean, who is neither tarnished nor afraid," Chandler later wrote of his hardboiled hero. Beginning in the late 1930s, Chandler found in the film industry another outlet for his writing. The Great Depression had sparked popular appetite for films focused on gangsters and crime, which modulated into *film noir*—literally, "dark film," a term imported from post–World War II France—in the 1940s. (Movie studios shot these low-budget films in minimal lighting, a production economy that amplified their characteristic atmosphere of danger and moral ambiguity.) Chandler both sold the film rights to his own novels (*The Big Sleep*, starring Humphrey Bogart as Marlowe, was made in 1946) and successfully adapted other writers' crime fiction, like James M. Cain's *Double Indemnity*, for the screen.

As his career prospered, Chandler sometimes disclaimed the plot formulas of detective fiction as incidental rather than central to his literary aims: "All I'm looking for" in the genre, he once told the editor of *Harper's*, "is an excuse for certain experiments in dramatic dialogue." Chandler did perfect a new mode of fictional dialogue: clipped, tense, provocative, sarcastic, a hair removed from violence. His popular style has affinities with the stripped-down dialogue of high modernists like Ernest Hemingway; like Hemingway's, Chandler's heroes honor a masculine code of understatement, competence, and self-containment. Chandler also honed a new kind of urban writing about far-flung, automobile-centered, multilingual, multicultural Los Angeles. In his work, Los Angeles begins to take its literary place alongside the great cities—Boston, Philadelphia, New York City, Chicago—of nineteenth- and early-twentieth-century American literary realism and naturalism.

For all the enduring popularity of hardboiled detective fiction, Chandler's writing has often been accused of trading in sexist and racist stereotypes: his incorruptible white detective frequently finds himself used by an attractive, untrustworthy woman, and his vernacular language is peppered with racial and ethnic slurs. Chandler's work has also been defended for its biting representation of official corruption, police brutality, and the networks of urban power. In the contemporary United States, women and African American writers have stepped forward to revise Chandler's legacy: Sara Paretsky's V. I. Warshawski and Walter Mosley's Easy Rawlins are among the most popular of many literary detectives descended from Philip Marlowe.

The text of the story included here is from *Red Wind: A Collection of Short Stories* (1946).

Red Wind

I

There was a desert wind blowing that night. It was one of those hot dry Santa Anas[1] that come down through the mountain passes and curl your hair and make your nerves jump and your skin itch. On nights like that every booze party ends in a fight. Meek little wives feel the edge of the carving knife and study their husbands' necks. Anything can happen. You can even get a full glass of beer at a cocktail lounge.

I was getting one in a flossy[2] new place across the street from the apartment house where I lived. It had been open about a week and it wasn't doing any business. The kid behind the bar was in his early twenties and looked as if he had never had a drink in his life.

There was only one other customer, a souse on a bar stool with his back to the door. He had a pile of dimes stacked neatly in front of him, about two dollars' worth. He was drinking straight rye in small glasses and he was all by himself in a world of his own.

I sat farther along the bar and got my glass of beer and said: "You sure cut the clouds off them, buddy. I will say that for you."

"We just opened up," the kid said. "We got to build up trade. Been in before, haven't you, mister?"

"Uh-huh."

"Live around here?"

"In the Berglund Apartments across the street," I said. "And the name is John Dalmas."

"Thanks, mister. Mine's Lew Petrolle." He leaned close to me across the polished dark bar. "Know that guy?"

"No."

"He ought to go home, kind of. I ought to call a taxi and send him home. He's doing his next week's drinking too soon."

"A night like this," I said. "Let him alone."

"It's not good for him," the kid said, scowling at me.

"Rye!" the drunk croaked, without looking up. He snapped his fingers so as not to disturb his piles of dimes by banging on the bar.

The kid looked at me and shrugged. "Should I?"

"Whose stomach is it? Not mine."

The kid poured him another straight rye and I think he doctored it with water down behind the bar because when he came up with it he looked as guilty as if he'd kicked his grandmother. The drunk paid no attention. He lifted two dimes off his pile with the exact care of a crack surgeon operating on a brain tumor.

The kid came back and put more beer in my glass. Outside the wind howled. Every once in a while it blew the stained-glass swing-door open a few inches. It was a heavy door.

The kid said: "I don't like drunks in the first place and in the second place I don't like them getting drunk in here, and in the third place I don't like them in the first place."

---

1. Hot, dry winds out of the mountains surrounding Los Angeles.   2. Stylish, fancy.

"Warner Brothers could use that," I said.

"They did."

Just then we had another customer. A car squeaked to a stop outside and the swinging door came open. A fellow came in who looked a little in a hurry. He held the door and ranged the place quickly with flat, shiny, dark eyes. He was well set up, dark, good-looking in a narrow-faced, tight-lipped way. His clothes were dark and a white handkerchief peeped coyly from his pocket and he looked cool as well as under a tension of some sort. I guessed it was the hot wind. I felt a bit the same myself only not cool.

He looked at the drunk's back. The drunk was playing checkers with his empty glasses. The new customer looked at me, then he looked along the line of half-booths at the other side of the place. They were all empty. He came on in—down past where the drunk sat swaying and muttering to himself— and spoke to the bar kid.

"Seen a lady in here, buddy? Tall, pretty, brown hair, in a print bolero jacket over a blue crepe silk dress. Wearing a wide-brimmed straw hat with a velvet band." He had a tight voice I didn't like.

"No, sir. Nobody like that's been in," the bar kid said.

"Thanks. Straight Scotch. Make it fast, will you?"

The kid gave it to him and the fellow paid and put the drink down in a gulp and started to go out. He took three or four steps and stopped, facing the drunk. The drunk was grinning. He swept a gun from somewhere so fast that it was just a blur coming out. He held it steady and he didn't look any drunker than I was. The tall dark guy stood quite still and then his head jerked back a little and then he was still again.

A car tore by outside. The drunk's gun was a .22 target automatic, with a large front sight. It made a couple of hard snaps and a little smoke curled— very little.

"So long, Waldo," the drunk said.

Then he put the gun on the barman and me.

The dark guy took a week to fall down. He stumbled, caught himself, waved one arm, stumbled again. His hat fell off, and then he hit the floor with his face. After he hit it he might have been poured concrete for all the fuss he made.

The drunk slid down off the stool and scooped his dimes into a pocket and slid towards the door. He turned sideways, holding the gun across his body. I didn't have a gun. I hadn't thought I needed one to buy a glass of beer. The kid behind the bar didn't move or make the slightest sound.

The drunk felt the door lightly with his shoulder, keeping his eyes on us, then pushed through it backwards. When it was wide a hard gust of air slammed in and lifted the hair of the man on the floor. The drunk said: "Poor Waldo. I bet I made his nose bleed."

The door swung shut. I started to rush it—from long practice in doing the wrong thing. In this case it didn't matter. The car outside let out a roar and when I got onto the sidewalk it was flicking a red smear of tail-light around the nearby corner. I got its license number the way I got my first million.

There were people and cars up and down the block as usual. Nobody acted as if a gun had gone off. The wind was making enough noise to make the hard quick rap of .22 ammunition sound like a slammed door, even if anyone heard it. I went back into the cocktail bar.

The kid hadn't moved, even yet. He just stood with his hands flat on the bar, leaning over a little and looking down at the dark guy's back. The dark guy hadn't moved either. I bent down and felt his neck artery. He wouldn't move—ever.

The kid's face had as much expression as a cut of round steak and was about the same color. His eyes were more angry than shocked.

I lit a cigarette and blew smoke at the ceiling and said shortly: "Get on the phone."

"Maybe he's not dead," the kid said.

"When they use a .22 that means they don't make mistakes.[3] Where's the phone?"

"I don't have one. I got enough expenses without that. Boy, can I kick eight hundred bucks in the face!"

"You own this place?"

"I did till this happened."

He pulled his white coat off and his apron and came around the inner end of the bar. "I'm locking the door," he said, taking keys out.

He went out, swung the door to and jiggled the lock from the outside until the bolt clicked into place. I bent down and rolled Waldo over. At first I couldn't even see where the shots went in. Then I could. A couple of tiny holes in his coat, over his heart. There was a little blood on his shirt.

The drunk was everything you could ask—as a killer.

The prowl-car boys came in about eight minutes. The kid, Lew Petrolle, was back behind the bar by then. He had his white coat on again and he was counting the money in the register and putting it in his pocket and making notes in a little book.

I sat at the edge of one of the half-booths and smoked cigarettes and watched Waldo's face get deader and deader. I wondered who the girl in the print coat was, why Waldo had left the engine of his car running outside, why he was in a hurry, whether the drunk had been waiting for him or just happened to be there.

The prowl-car boys came in perspiring. They were the usual large size and one of them had a flower stuck under his cap and his cap on a bit crooked. When he saw the dead man he got rid of the flower and leaned down to feel Waldo's pulse.

"Seems to be dead," he said, and rolled him around a little more. "Oh yeah, I see where they went in. Nice clean work. You two see him get it?"

I said yes. The kid behind the bar said nothing. I told them about it, that the killer seemed to have left in Waldo's car.

The cop yanked Waldo's wallet out, went through it rapidly and whistled. "Plenty jack and no driver's license." He put the wallet away. "O.K., we didn't touch him, see? Just a chance we could find did he have a car and put it on the air."

"The hell you didn't touch him," Lew Petrolle said.

The cop gave him one of these looks. "O.K., pal," he said softly. "We touched him."

The kid picked up a clean highball glass and began to polish it. He polished it all the rest of the time we were there.

---

3. A .22 caliber gun fires a small bullet.

In another minute a homicide fast-wagon sirened up and screeched to a stop outside the door and four men came in, two dicks, a photographer and a laboratory man. I didn't know either of the dicks. You can be in the detecting business a long time and not know all the men on a big city force.

One of them was a short, smooth, dark, quiet, smiling man, with curly black hair and soft intelligent eyes. The other was big, rawboned, long-jawed, with a veined nose and glassy eyes. He looked like a heavy drinker. He looked tough, but he looked as if he thought he was a little tougher than he was. He shooed me into the last booth against the wall and his partner got the kid up front and the bluecoats went out. The fingerprint man and photographer set about their work.

A medical examiner came, stayed just long enough to get sore because there was no phone for him to call the morgue wagon.

The short dick emptied Waldo's pockets and then emptied his wallet and dumped everything into a large handkerchief on a booth table. I saw a lot of currency, keys, cigarettes, another handkerchief, very little else.

The big dick pushed me back into the end of the half-booth. "Give," he said. "I'm Copernik, Detective-Lieutenant."

I put my wallet in front of him. He looked at it, went through it, tossed it back, made a note in a book.

"John Dalmas, huh? A shamus.[4] You here on business?"

"Drinking business," I said. "I live just across the street in the Berglund."

"Know this kid up front?"

"I've been in here once since he opened up."

"See anything funny about him now?"

"No."

"Takes it too light for a young fellow, don't he? Never mind answering. Just tell the story."

I told it—three times. Once for him to get the outline, once for him to get the details and once for him to see if I had it too pat. At the end he said: "This dame interests me. And the killer called the guy Waldo, yet didn't seem to be anyways sure he would be in. I mean, if Waldo wasn't sure the dame would be here, nobody could be sure Waldo would be here."

"That's pretty deep," I said.

He studied me. I wasn't smiling. "Sounds like a grudge job, don't it? Don't sound planned. No getaway except by accident. A guy don't leave his car unlocked much in this town. And the killer works in front of two good witnesses. I don't like that."

"I don't like being a witness," I said. "The pay's too low."

He grinned. His teeth had a freckled look. "Was the killer drunk really?"

"With that shooting? No."

"Me too. Well, it's a simple job. The guy will have a record and he's left plenty prints. Even if we don't have his mug here we'll make him in hours. He had something on Waldo, but he wasn't meeting Waldo tonight. Waldo just dropped in to ask about a dame he had a date with and had missed connections on. It's a hot night and this wind would kill a girl's face. She'd be apt to drop in somewhere to wait. So the killer feeds Waldo two in the right place and scrams and don't worry about you boys at all. It's that simple."

---

4. A detective.

"Yeah," I said.

"It's so simple it stinks," Copernik said.

He took his felt hat off and tousled up his ratty blond hair and leaned his head on his hands. He had a long mean horse face. He got a handkerchief out and mopped it, and the back of his neck and the back of his hands. He got a comb out and combed his hair—he looked worse with it combed—and put his hat back on.

"I was just thinking," I said.

"Yeah? What?"

"This Waldo knew just how the girl was dressed. So he must already have been with her tonight."

"So what? Maybe he had to go to the can. And when he came back she's gone. Maybe she changed her mind about him."

"That's right," I said.

But that wasn't what I was thinking at all. I was thinking that Waldo had described the girl's clothes in a way the ordinary man wouldn't know how to describe them. Printed bolero jacket over blue crepe silk dress. I didn't even know what a bolero jacket was. And I might have said blue dress or even blue silk dress, but never blue crepe silk dress.

After a while two men came with a basket. Lew Petrolle was still polishing his glass and talking to the short dark dick.

We all went down to headquarters.

Lew Petrolle was all right when they checked on him. His father had a grape ranch near Antioch in Contra Costa County. He had given Lew a thousand dollars to go into business and Lew had opened the cocktail bar, neon sign and all, on eight hundred flat.

They let him go and told him to keep the bar closed until they were sure they didn't want to do any more printing. He shook hands all around and grinned and said he guessed the killing would be good for business after all, because nobody believed a newspaper account of anything and people would come to him for the story and buy drinks while he was telling it.

"There's a guy won't ever do any worrying," Copernik said, when he was gone. "Over anybody else."

"Poor Waldo," I said. "The prints any good?"

"Kind of smudged," Copernik said sourly. "But we'll get a classification and teletype it to Washington sometime tonight. If it don't click, you'll be in for a day on the steel picture-racks downstairs."

I shook hands with him and his partner, whose name was Ybarra, and left. They didn't know who Waldo was yet either. Nothing in his pockets told.

II

I got back to my street about 9 P.M. I looked up and down the block before I went into the Berglund. The cocktail bar was farther down on the other side, dark, with a nose or two against the glass, but no real crowd. People had seen the law and the morgue wagon, but they didn't know what had happened. Except the boys playing pinball games in the drugstore on the corner. They know everything, except how to hold a job.

The wind was still blowing, oven-hot, swirling dust and torn paper up against the walls.

I went into the lobby of the apartment house and rode the automatic elevator up to the fourth floor. I unwound the doors and stepped out and there was a tall girl standing there waiting for the car.

She had brown wavy hair under a wide-brimmed straw hat with a velvet band and loose bow. She had wide blue eyes and eyelashes that didn't quite reach her chin. She wore a blue dress that might have been crepe silk, simple in lines but not missing any curves. Over it she wore what might have been a print bolero jacket.

I said: "Is that a bolero jacket?"

She gave me a distant glance and made a motion as if to brush a cobweb out of the way.

"Yes. Would you mind—I'm rather in a hurry. I'd like——"

I didn't move. I blocked her off from the elevator. We stared at each other and she flushed very slowly.

"Better not go out on the street in those clothes," I said.

"Why, how dare you——"

The elevator clanked and started down again. I didn't know what she was going to say. Her voice lacked the edgy twang of a beer-parlor frill. It had a soft light sound, like spring rain.

"It's not a make," I said. "You're in trouble. If they come to this floor in the elevator, you have just that much time to get off the hall. First take off the hat and jacket—and snap it up!"

She didn't move. Her face seemed to whiten a little behind the not-too-heavy make-up.

"Cops," I said, "are looking for you. In those clothes. Give me the chance and I'll tell you why."

She turned her head swiftly and looked back along the corridor. With her looks I didn't blame her for trying one more bluff.

"You're impertinent, whoever you are. I'm Mrs. Leroy in Apartment Thirty-one. I can assure you——"

"That you're on the wrong floor," I said. "This is the fourth." The elevator had stopped down below. The sound of doors being wrenched open came up the shaft.

"Off!" I rapped. "Now!"

She switched her hat off and slipped out of the bolero jacket, fast. I grabbed them and wadded them into a mess under my arm. I took her elbow and turned her and we were going down the hall.

"I live in Forty-two. The front one across from yours, just a floor up. Take your choice. Once again—I'm not on the make."

She smoothed her hair with that quick gesture, like a bird preening itself. Ten thousand years of practice behind it.

"Mine," she said, and tucked her bag under her arm and strode down the hall fast. The elevator stopped at the floor below. She stopped when it stopped. She turned and faced me.

"The stairs are back by the elevator shaft," I said gently.

"I don't have an apartment," she said.

"I didn't think you had."

"Are they searching for me?"

"Yes, but they won't start gouging the block stone by stone before tomorrow. And then only if they don't make Waldo."

She stared at me. "Waldo?"

"Oh, you don't know Waldo," I said.

She shook her head slowly. The elevator started down in the shaft again. Panic flicked in her blue eyes like a ripple on water.

"No," she said breathlessly, "but take me out of this hall."

We were almost at my door. I jammed the key in and shook the lock around and heaved the door inward. I reached in far enough to switch lights on. She went in past me like a wave. Sandalwood floated on the air, very faint.

I shut the door, threw my hat into a chair and watched her stroll over to a card table on which I had a chess problem set out that I couldn't solve. Once inside, with the door locked, her panic had left her.

"So you're a chess-player," she said, in that guarded tone, as if she had come to look at my etchings. I wished she had.

We both stood still then and listened to the distant clang of elevator doors and then steps—going the other way.

I grinned, but with strain, not pleasure, went out into the kitchenette and started to fumble with a couple of glasses and then realized I still had her hat and bolero jacket under my arm. I went into the dressing-room behind the wall bed and stuffed them into a drawer, went back out to the kitchenette, dug out some extra fine Scotch and made a couple of highballs.

When I went in with the drinks she had a gun in her hand. It was a small automatic with a pearl grip. It jumped up at me and her eyes were full of horror.

I stopped, with a glass in each hand, and said: "Maybe this hot wind has got you crazy too. I'm a private detective. I'll prove it if you let me."

She nodded slightly and her face was white. I went over slowly and put a glass down beside her, and went back and set mine down and got a card out that had no bent corners. She was sitting down, smoothing one blue knee with her left hand, and holding the gun on the other. I put the card down beside her drink and sat with mine.

"Never let a guy get that close to you," I said. "Not if you mean business. And your safety catch is on."

She flashed her eyes down, shivered, and put the gun back in her bag. She drank half the drink without stopping, put the glass down hard and picked the card up.

"I don't give many people that liquor," I said. "I can't afford to."

Her lips curled. "I supposed you would want money."

"Huh?"

She didn't say anything. Her hand was close to her bag again.

"Don't forget the safety catch," I said. Her hand stopped. I went on: "This fellow I called Waldo is quite tall, say five-eleven, slim, dark, brown eyes with a lot of glitter. Nose and mouth too thin. Dark suit, white handkerchief showing, and in a hurry to find you. Am I getting anywhere?"

She took her glass again. "So that's Waldo," she said. "Well, what about him?" Her voice seemed to have a slight liquor edge now.

"Well, a funny thing. There's a cocktail bar across the street . . . Say, where have you been all evening?"

"Sitting in my car," she said coldly, "most of the time."

"Didn't you see a fuss across the street up the block?"

Her eyes tried to say no and missed. Her lips said: "I knew there was some kind of disturbance. I saw policemen and red searchlights. I supposed someone had been hurt."

"Someone was. And this Waldo was looking for you before that. In the cocktail bar. He described you and your clothes."

Her eyes were set like rivets now and had the same amount of expression. Her mouth began to tremble and kept on trembling.

"I was in there," I said, "talking to the kid that runs it. There was nobody in there but a drunk on a stool and the kid and myself. The drunk wasn't paying any attention to anything. Then Waldo came in and asked about you and we said no, we hadn't seen you and he started to leave."

I sipped my drink. I like an effect as well as the next fellow. Her eyes ate me.

"Just started to leave. Then this drunk that wasn't paying any attention to anyone called him Waldo and took a gun out. He shot him twice——" I snapped my fingers twice—"like that. Dead."

She fooled me. She laughed in my face. "So my husband hired you to spy on me," she said. "I might have known the whole thing was an act. You and your Waldo."

I gawked at her.

"I never thought of him as jealous," she snapped. "Not of a man who had been our chauffeur anyhow. A little about Stan, of course—that's natural. But Joseph Choate——"

I made motions in the air. "Lady, one of us has this book open at the wrong page," I grunted. "I don't know anybody named Stan or Joseph Choate. So help me, I didn't even know you had a chauffeur. People around here don't run to them. As for husbands—yeah, we do have a husband once in a while. Not often enough."

She shook her head slowly and her hand stayed near her bag and her blue eyes had glitters in them.

"Not good enough, Mr. Dalmas. No, not nearly good enough. I know you private detectives. You're all rotten. You tricked me into your apartment, if it is your apartment. More likely it's the apartment of some horrible man who will swear anything for a few dollars. Now you're trying to scare me. So you can blackmail me—as well as get money from my husband. All right," she said breathlessly, "how much do I have to pay?"

I put my empty glass aside and leaned back. "Pardon me if I light a cigarette," I said. "My nerves are frayed."

I lit it while she watched me grimly, no fear—or not enough fear for any real guilt to be under it. "So Joseph Choate is his name," I said. "The guy that killed him in the cocktail bar called him Waldo."

She smiled a bit disgustedly, but almost tolerantly. "Don't stall. How much?"

"Why were you trying to meet this Joseph Choate?"

"I was going to buy something he stole from me, of course. Something that's valuable in the ordinary way too. Almost fifteen thousand dollars. The man I loved gave it to me. He's dead. There! He's dead! He died in a burning plane. Now, go back and tell my husband that, you slimy little rat!"

"Hey, I weigh a hundred and ninety stripped," I yelled.

"You're still slimy," she yelled back. "And don't bother about telling my husband. I'll tell him myself. He probably knows anyway."

I grinned. "That's smart. Just what was I supposed to find out?"

She grabbed her glass and finished what was left of her drink. "So he thinks I'm meeting Joseph," she sneered. "Well, I was. But not to make love. Not with a chauffeur. Not with a bum I picked off the front step and gave a job to. I don't have to dig down that far, if I want to play around."

"Lady," I said, "you don't indeed."

"Now I'm going," she said. "You just try and stop me." She snatched the pearl-handled gun out of her bag.

I grinned and kept on grinning. I didn't move.

"Why you nasty little string of nothing," she stormed. "How do I know you're a private detective at all? You might be a crook. This card you gave me doesn't mean anything. Anybody can have cards printed."

"Sure," I said. "And I suppose I'm smart enough to live here two years because you were going to move in today so I could blackmail you for not meeting a man named Joseph Choate who was bumped off across the street under the name of Waldo. Have you got the money to buy this something that cost fifteen grand?"

"Oh! You think you'll hold me up, I suppose!"

"Oh!" I mimicked her, "I'm a stick-up artist now, am I? Lady, will you please either put that gun away or take the safety catch off? It hurts my professional feelings to see a nice gun made a monkey of that way."

"You're a full portion of what I don't like," she said. "Get out of my way."

I didn't move. She didn't move. We were both sitting down—and not even close to each other.

"Let me in on one secret before you go," I pleaded. "What in hell did you take the apartment down on the floor below for? Just to meet a guy down on the street?"

"Stop being silly," she snapped. "I didn't. I lied. It's his apartment."

"Joseph Choate's?"

She nodded sharply.

"Does my description of Waldo sound like Joseph Choate?"

She nodded sharply again.

"All right. That's one fact learned at last. Don't you realize Waldo described your clothes before he was shot—when he was looking for you—that the description was passed on to the police—that the police don't know who Waldo is—and are looking for somebody in those clothes to help tell them? Don't you get that much?"

The gun suddenly started to shake in her hand. She looked down at it, sort of vacantly, slowly put it back in her bag.

"I'm a fool," she whispered, "to be even talking to you." She stared at me for a long time, then pulled in a deep breath. "He told me where he was staying. He didn't seem afraid. I guess blackmailers are like that. He was to meet me on the street, but I was late. It was full of police when I got here. So I went back and sat in my car for a while. Then I came up to Joseph's apartment and knocked. Then I went back to my car and waited again. I came up here three times in all. The last time I walked up a flight to take the elevator. I had already been seen twice on the third floor. I met you. That's all."

"You said something about a husband," I grunted. "Where is he?"

"He's at a meeting."

"Oh, a meeting," I said nastily.

"My husband's a very important man. He has lots of meetings. He's a hydro-electric engineer. He's been all over the world. I'd have you know——"

"Skip it," I said. "I'll take him to lunch some day and have him tell me himself. Whatever Joseph had on you is dead stock now. Like Joseph."

She believed it at last. I hadn't thought she ever would somehow. "He's really dead?" she whispered. "Really?"

"He's dead," I said. "Dead, dead, dead. Lady, he's dead."

Her face fell apart like a bride's piecrust. Her mouth wasn't large, but I could have got my fist into it at that moment. In the silence the elevator stopped at my floor.

"Scream," I rapped, "and I'll give you two black eyes."

It didn't sound nice, but it worked. It jarred her out of it. Her mouth shut like a trap.

I heard steps coming down the hall. We all have hunches. I put my finger to my lips. She didn't move now. Her face had a frozen look. Her big blue eyes were as black as the shadows below them. The hot wind boomed against the shut windows. Windows have to be shut when a Santa Ana blows, heat or no heat.

The steps that came down the hall were the casual ordinary steps of one man. But they stopped outside my door, and somebody knocked.

I pointed to the dressing-room behind the wall bed. She stood up without a sound, her bag clenched against her side. I pointed again, to her glass. She lifted it swiftly, slid across the carpet, through the door, drew the door quietly shut after her.

I didn't know just what I was going to all this trouble for.

The knocking sounded again. The backs of my hands were wet. I creaked my chair and stood up and made a loud yawning sound. Then I went over and opened the door—without a gun. That was a mistake.

III

I didn't know him at first. Perhaps for the opposite reason Waldo hadn't seemed to know him. He'd had a hat on all the time over at the cocktail bar and he didn't have one on now. His hair ended completely and exactly where his hat would start. Above that line was hard white sweatless skin almost as glaring as scar tissue. He wasn't just twenty years older. He was a different man.

But I knew the gun he was holding, the .22 target automatic with the big front sight. And I knew his eyes. Bright, brittle, shallow eyes like the eyes of a lizard.

He was alone. He put the gun against my face very lightly and said between his teeth: "Yeah, me. Let's go on in."

I backed in just far enough and stopped. Just the way he would want me to, so he could shut the door without moving much. I knew from his eyes that he would want me to do just that.

I wasn't scared. I was paralyzed.

When he had the door shut he backed me some more, slowly, until there was something against the back of my legs. His eyes looked into mine.

"That's a card table," he said. "Some goon here plays chess. You?"

I swallowed. "I don't exactly play it. I just fool around."

"That means two," he said with a kind of hoarse softness, as if some cop had hit him across the windpipe with a blackjack once, in a third-degree session.

"It's a problem," I said. "Not a game. Look at the pieces."

"I wouldn't know."

"Well, I'm alone," I said, and my voice shook just enough.

"It don't make any difference," he said. "I'm washed up anyway. Some nose puts the but on me tomorrow, next week, what the hell? I just didn't like your map, pal. And that smug-faced pansy in the barcoat that played left tackle for Fordham or something. To hell with guys like you guys."

I didn't speak or move. The big front sight raked my cheek lightly, almost caressingly. The man smiled.

"It's kind of good business too," he said. "Just in case. An old con like me don't make good prints—not even when he's lit. And if I don't make good prints all I got against me is two witnesses. The hell with it. You're slammin' off, pal. I guess you know that."

"What did Waldo do to you?" I tried to make it sound as if I wanted to know, instead of just not wanting to shake too hard.

"Stooled on a bank job in Michigan and got me four years. Got himself a nolle prosse.[5] Four years in Michigan ain't no summer cruise. They make you be good in them lifer states."

"How'd you know he'd come in there?" I croaked.

"I didn't. Oh yeah, I was lookin' for him. I was wanting to see him all right. I got a flash of him on the street night before last but I lost him. Up to then I wasn't lookin' for him. Then I was. A cute guy, Waldo. How is he?"

"Dead," I said.

"I'm still good," he chuckled. "Drunk or sober. Well, that don't make no doughnuts for me now. They make me downtown yet?"

I didn't answer him quick enough. He jabbed the gun into my throat and I choked and almost grabbed for it by instinct.

"Naw," he cautioned me softly. "Naw. You ain't that dumb."

I put my hands back, down at my sides, open, the palms towards him. He would want them that way. He hadn't touched me, except with the gun. He didn't seem to care whether I might have one too. He wouldn't—if he just meant the one thing.

He didn't seem to care very much about anything, coming back on that block. Perhaps the hot wind did something to him. It was booming against my shut windows like the surf under a pier.

"They got prints," I said. "I don't know how good."

"They'll be good enough—but not for teletype work. Take 'em airmail time to Washington and back to check 'em right. Tell me why I come here, pal."

"You heard the kid and me talking in the bar. I told him my name, where I lived."

"That's how, pal. I said why." He smiled at me. It was a lousy smile to be the last one you might see.

"Skip it," I said. "The hangman won't ask you to guess why he's there."

"Say, you're tough at that. After you, I visit that kid. I tailed him home from headquarters, but I figure you're the guy to put the bee on first. I tail him home from the city hall, in the rent car Waldo had. From headquarters, pal. Them funny dicks. You can sit in their laps and they don't know you. Start runnin' for a street car and they open up with machine guns and bump two

---

5. Had criminal charges against him dropped; from *nolle prosequi* (Latin), "we will not prosecute."

pedestrians, a hacker asleep in his cab, and an old scrubwoman on the second floor workin' a mop. And they miss the guy they're after. Them funny lousy dicks."

He twisted the gun muzzle in my neck. His eyes looked madder than before.

"I got time," he said. "Waldo's rent car don't get a report right away. And they don't make Waldo very soon. I know Waldo. Smart he was. A smooth boy, Waldo."

"I'm going to vomit," I said, "if you don't take that gun out of my throat."

He smiled and moved the gun down to my heart. "This about right? Say when."

I must have spoken louder than I meant to. The door of the dressing-room by the wall bed showed a crack of darkness. Then an inch. Then four inches. I saw eyes, but I didn't look at them. I stared hard into the baldheaded man's eyes. Very hard. I didn't want him to take his eyes off mine.

"Scared?" he asked softly.

I leaned against his gun and began to shake. I thought he would enjoy seeing me shake. The girl came out through the door. She had her gun in her hand again. I was sorry as hell for her. She'd try to make the door—or scream. Either way it would be curtains—for both of us.

"Well, don't take all night about it," I bleated. My voice sounded far away, like a voice on a radio on the other side of a street.

"I like this, pal," he smiled. "I'm like that."

The girl floated in the air, somewhere behind him. Nothing was ever more soundless than the way she moved. It wouldn't do any good, though. He wouldn't fool around with her at all. I had known him all my life but I had been looking into his eyes for only five minutes.

"Suppose, I yell," I said.

"Yeah. Suppose you yell. Go ahead and yell," he said, with his killer's smile.

She didn't go near the door. She was right behind him.

"Well—here's where I yell," I said.

As if that was the cue she jabbed the little gun hard into his short ribs, without a single sound.

He had to react. It was like a knee reflex. His mouth snapped open and both his arms jumped out from his sides and he arched his back just a little. The gun was pointing at my right eye.

I sank and kneed him with all my strength, in the groin.

His chin came down and I hit it. I hit it as if I was driving the last spike on the first transcontinental railroad. I can still feel it when I flex my knuckles.

His gun raked the side of my face but it didn't go off. He was already limp. He writhed down gasping, his left side against the floor. I kicked his right shoulder—hard. The gun jumped away from him, skidded on the carpet, under a chair. I heard the chessmen tinkling on the floor behind me somewhere.

The girl stood over him, looking down. Then her wide dark horrified eyes came up and fastened on mine.

"That buys me," I said. "Anything I have is yours—now and forever."

She didn't hear me. Her eyes were strained open so hard that the whites showed under the vivid blue iris. She backed quickly to the door with her little gun up, felt behind her for the knob and twisted it. She pulled the door open and slipped out.

The door shut.

She was bareheaded and without her bolero jacket.

She had only the gun, and the safety catch on that was still set so that she couldn't fire it.

It was silent in the room then, in spite of the wind. Then I heard him gasping on the floor. His face had a greenish pallor. I moved behind him and pawed him for more guns, and didn't find any. I got a pair of store cuffs out of my desk and pulled his arms in front of him and snapped them on his wrists. They would hold if he didn't shake them too hard.

His eyes measured me for a coffin, in spite of their suffering. He lay in the middle of the floor, still on his left side, a twisted, wizened, bald-headed little guy with drawn-back lips and teeth spotted with cheap silver fillings. His mouth looked like a black pit and his breath came in little waves, choked, stopped, came on again, limping.

"I'm sorry, guy," I grunted. "What could I do?"

That—to this sort of killer.

I went into the dressing-room and opened the drawer of the chest. Her hat and jacket lay there on my shirts. I put them underneath, at the back, and smoothed the shirts over them. Then I went out to the kitchenette and poured a stiff jolt of whiskey and put it down and stood a moment listening to the hot wind howl against the window glass. A garage door banged, and a power-line wire with too much play between the insulators thumped the side of the building with a sound like somebody beating a carpet.

The drink worked on me. I went back into the living-room and opened a window. The guy on the floor hadn't smelled her sandalwood, but somebody else might.

I shut the window again, wiped the palms of my hands and used the phone to dial headquarters.

Copernik was still there. His smart-aleck voice said: "Yeah? Dalmas? Don't tell me. I bet you got an idea."

"Make that killer yet?"

"We're not saying, Dalmas. Sorry as all hell and so on. You know how it is."

"O.K. I don't care who he is. Just come and get him off the floor of my apartment."

"Holy—" Then his voice hushed and went down low. "Wait a minute, now. Wait a minute." A long way off I seemed to hear a door shut. Then his voice again. "Shoot," he said softly.

"Handcuffed," I said. "All yours. I had to knee him, but he'll be all right. He came here to eliminate a witness."

Another pause. The voice was full of honey. "Now listen, boy, who else is in this with you?"

"Who else? Nobody. Just me."

"Keep it that way, boy. All quiet. O.K.?"

"Think I want all the bums in the neighborhood in here sightseeing?"

"Take it easy, boy. Easy. Just sit tight and sit still. I'm practically there. No touch nothing. Get me?"

"Yeah." I gave him the address and apartment number again to save him time.

I could see his big bony face glisten. I got his .22 target gun from under the chair and sat holding it until feet hit the hallway outside my door and knuckles did a quiet tattoo on the door panel.

Copernik was alone. He filled the doorway quickly, pushed me back into the room with a tight grin and shut the door. He stood with his back to it, his hand under the left side of his coat. A big hard bony man with flat cruel eyes.

He lowered them slowly and looked at the man on the floor. The lad's neck was twitching a little. His eyes moved in short stabs—sick eyes.

"Sure it's the guy?" Copernik's voice was hoarse.

"Positive. Where's Ybarra?"

"Oh, he was busy." He didn't look at me when he said that. "Those your cuffs?"

"Yeah."

"Key."

I tossed it to him. He went down swiftly on one knee beside the killer and took my cuffs off his wrists, tossed them to one side. He got his own off his hip, twisted the bald man's hands behind him and snapped the cuffs on.

"All right, you—" the killer said tonelessly.

Copernik grinned and balled his fist and hit the handcuffed man in the mouth a terrific blow. His head snapped back almost enough to break his neck. Blood dribbled from the lower corner of his mouth.

"Get a towel," Copernik ordered.

I got a hand towel and gave it to him. He stuffed it between the handcuffed man's teeth, viciously, stood up and rubbed his bony fingers through his ratty blond hair.

"All right. Tell it."

I told it—leaving the girl out completely. It sounded a little funny. Copernik watched me, said nothing. He rubbed the side of his veined nose. Then he got his comb out and worked on his hair just as he had done earlier in the evening, in the cocktail bar.

I went over and gave him the gun. He looked at it casually, dropped it into his side pocket. His eyes had something in them and his face moved in a hard bright grin.

I bent down and began picking up my chessmen and dropping them into the box. I put the box on the mantel, straightened out a leg of the card table, played around for a while. All the time Copernik watched me. I wanted him to think something out.

At last he came out with it. "This guy uses a twenty-two," he said. "He uses it because he's good enough to get by with that much gun. That means he's good. He knocks at your door, pokes that gat in your belly, walks you back into the room, says he's here to close your mouth for keeps—and yet you take him. You not having any gun. You take him alone. You're kind of good yourself, pal."

"Listen," I said, and looked at the floor. I picked up another chessman and twisted it between my fingers. "I was doing a chess problem," I said. "Trying to forget things."

"You got something on your mind, pal," Copernik said softly. "You wouldn't try to fool an old copper, would you, boy?"

"It's a swell pinch and I'm giving it to you," I said. "What the hell more do you want?"

The man on the floor made a vague sound behind the towel. His bald head glistened with sweat.

"What's the matter, pal? You been up to something?" Copernik almost whispered.

I looked at him quickly, looked away again. "All right," I said. "You know damn well I couldn't take him alone. He had the gun on me and he shoots where he looks."

Copernik closed one eye and squinted at me amiably with the other. "Go on, pal. I kind of thought of that too."

I shuffled around a little more, to make it look good. I said slowly: "There was a kid here who pulled a job over in Boyle Heights, a heist job, and didn't take. A two-bit service station stickup. I know his family. He's not really bad. He was here trying to beg train money off me. When the knock came he sneaked in—there."

I pointed at the wall bed and the door beside. Copernik's head swiveled slowly, swiveled back. His eyes winked again. "And this kid had a gun," he said.

I nodded. "And he got behind him. That takes guts, Copernik. You've got to give the kid a break. You've got to let him stay out of it."

"Tag out for this kid?" Copernik asked softly.

"Not yet, he says. He's scared there will be."

Copernik smiled. "I'm a homicide man," he said. "What you have done, pal?"

I pointed down at the gagged and handcuffed man on the floor. "You took him, didn't you?" I said gently.

Copernik kept on smiling. A big whitish tongue came out and massaged his thick lower lip. "How'd I do it?" he whispered.

"Get the slugs out of Waldo?"

"Sure. Long twenty-twos. One smashed on a rib, one good."

"You're a careful guy. You don't miss any angles. You know anything about me. You dropped in on me to see what guns I had."

Copernik got up and went down on one knee again beside the killer. "Can you hear me, guy?" he asked with his face close to the face of the man on the floor.

The man made some vague sound. Copernik stood up and yawned. "Who the hell cares what he says? Go on, pal."

"You wouldn't expect to find I had anything, but you wanted to look around my place. And while you were mousing around in there"—I pointed to the dressing-room—"and me not saying anything, being a little sore, maybe, a knock came on the door. So he came in. So after a while you sneaked out and took him."

"Ah." Copernik grinned widely, with as many teeth as a horse. "You're on, pal. I socked him and I kneed him and I took him. You didn't have no gun and the guy swiveled on me pretty sharp and I left-hooked him down the back-stairs. O.K.?"

"O.K.," I said.

"You'll tell it like that downtown?"

"Yeah," I said.

"I'll protect you, pal. Treat me right and I'll always play ball. Forget about that kid. Let me know if he needs a break."

He came over and held out his hand. I shook it. It was as clammy as a dead fish. Clammy hands and the people who own them make me sick.

"There's just one thing," I said. "This partner of yours—Ybarra. Won't he be a bit sore you didn't bring him along on this?"

Copernik tousled his hair and wiped his hatband with a large yellowish silk handkerchief.

"That guinea?"[6] he sneered. "To hell with him!" He came close to me and breathed in my face. "No mistakes, pal—about that story of ours."

His breath was bad. It would be.

IV

There were just five of us in the chief-of-detectives' office when Copernik laid it before them. A stenographer, the chief, Copernik, myself, Ybarra. Ybarra sat on a chair tilted against the side wall. His hat was down over his eyes but their softness loomed underneath, and the small still smile hung at the corners of the cleancut Latin lips. He didn't look directly at Copernik. Copernik didn't look at him at all.

Outside in the corridor there had been photos of Copernik shaking hands with me, Copernik with his hat on straight and his gun in his hand and a stern, purposeful look on his face.

They said they knew who Waldo was, but they wouldn't tell me. I didn't believe they knew, because the chief-of-detectives had a morgue photo of Waldo on his desk. A beautiful job, his hair combed, his tie straight, the light hitting his eyes just right to make them glisten. Nobody would have known it was a photo of a dead man with two bullet holes in his heart. He looked like a dance-hall sheik making up his mind whether to take the blonde or the red-head.

It was about midnight when I got home. The apartment-door was locked and while I was fumbling for my keys a low voice spoke to me out of the darkness.

All it said was: "Please!" but I knew it. I turned and looked at a dark Cadillac coupe parked just off the loading zone. It had no lights. Light from the street touched the brightness of a woman's eyes.

I went over there. "You're a darn fool," I said.

She said: "Get in."

I climbed in and she started the car and drove it a block and a half along Franklin and turned down Kingsley Drive. The hot wind still burned and blustered. A radio lilted from an open, sheltered, side window of an apartment house. There were a lot of parked cars but she found a vacant space behind a small brand-new Packard cabriolet[7] that had the dealer's sticker on the windshield glass. After she'd jockeyed us up to the curb she leaned back in the corner with her gloved hands on the wheel.

She was all in black now, or dark brown, with a small foolish hat. I smelled the sandalwood in her perfume.

"I wasn't very nice to you, was I?" she said.

"All you did was save my life."

"What happened?"

"I called the law and fed a few lies to a cop I don't like and gave him all the credit for the pinch and that was that. That guy you took away from me was the man who killed Waldo."

---

6. Derogatory slang term for immigrants of Italian (usually) or, here, Spanish origin.   7. Convertible sportscar.

"You mean—you didn't tell them about me?"

"Lady," I said again, "all you did was save my life. What else do you want done? I'm ready, willing, and I'll try to be able."

She didn't say anything, or move.

"Nobody learned who you are from me," I said. "Incidentally, I don't know myself."

"I'm Mrs. Frank C. Barsaly, Two-twelve Fremont Place, Olympia Two-four-five-nine-six. Is that what you wanted?"

"Thanks," I mumbled, and rolled a dry unlit cigarette around in my fingers. "Why did you come back?" Then I snapped the fingers of my left hand. "The hat and jacket," I said. "I'll go up and get them."

"It's more than that," she said. "I want my pearls."

I might have jumped a little. It seemed as if there had been enough without pearls.

A car tore by down the street going twice as fast as it should. A thin bitter cloud of dust lifted in the street lights and whirled and vanished. The girl ran the window up quickly against it.

"All right," I said. "Tell me about the pearls. We have had a murder and a mystery woman and a mad killer and a heroic rescue and a police detective framed into making a false report. Now we will have pearls. All right—feed it to me."

"I was to buy them for five thousand dollars. From the man you call Waldo and I call Joseph Choate. He should have had them."

"No pearls," I said. "I saw what came out of his pockets. A lot of money but no pearls."

"Could they be hidden in his apartment?"

"Yes," I said. "So far as I know he could have had them hidden anywhere in California except in his pockets. How's Mr. Barsaly this hot night?"

"He's still downtown at his meeting. Otherwise I couldn't have come."

"Well, you could have brought him," I said. "He could have sat in the rumble seat."

"Oh, I don't know," she said. "Frank weighs two hundred pounds and he's pretty solid. I don't think he would like to sit in the rumble seat, Mr. Dalmas."

"What the hell are we talking about, anyway?"

She didn't answer. Her gloved hands tapped lightly, provokingly on the rim of the slender wheel. I threw the unlit cigarette out the window, turned a little and took hold of her.

I was shaking when I let go of her. She pulled as far away from me as she could against the side of the car and rubbed the back of her glove against her mouth. I sat quite still.

We didn't speak for some time. Then she said very slowly: "I meant you to do that. But I wasn't always that way. It's only been since Stan Phillips was killed in his plane. If it hadn't been for that, I'd be Mrs. Phillips now. Stan gave me the pearls. They cost fifteen thousand dollars, he said once. White pearls, forty-one of them, the largest about a third of an inch across. I don't know how many grains. I never had them appraised or showed them to a jeweler, so I don't know those things. But I loved them on Stan's account. I loved Stan. The way you do just the one time. Can you understand?"

"What's your first name?" I asked.

"Lola."

"Go on talking, Lola." I got another dry cigarette out of my pocket and fumbled it between my fingers just to give them something to do.

"They had a simple silver clasp in the shape of a two-bladed propeller. There was one small diamond where the boss[8] would be. That was because I told Frank they were store pearls I had bought myself. He didn't know the difference. It's not so easy to tell, I dare say. You see—Frank is pretty jealous."

In the darkness she came closer to me and her side touched my side. But I didn't move this time. The wind howled and the trees shook. I kept on rolling the cigarette around in my fingers.

"I suppose you've read that story," she said. "About the wife and the real pearls and her telling her husband—"

"I've read it," I said.

"I hired Joseph. My husband was in Argentina at the time. I was pretty lonely."

"*You* should be lonely," I said.

"Joseph and I went driving a good deal. Sometimes we had a drink or two together. But that's all. I don't go around—"

"You told him about the pearls," I snarled. "And when your two hundred pounds of beef came back from Argentina and kicked him out—he took the pearls, because he knew they were real. And then offered them back to you for five grand."

"Yes," she said simply. "Of course I didn't want to go to the police. And of course in the circumstance Joseph wasn't afraid of my knowing where he lived."

"Poor Waldo," I said. "I feel kind of sorry for him. It was a hell of a time to run into an old friend that had a down on you."

I struck a match on my shoe sole and lit the cigarette. The tobacco was so dry from the hot wind that it burned like grass. The girl sat quietly beside me, her hands on the wheel again.

"Hell with women—these fliers," I said. "And you're still in love with him, or think you are. Where did you keep the pearls?"

"In a Russian malachite jewelry box on my dressing-table. With some other costume jewelry. I had to, if I ever wanted to wear them."

"And they were worth fifteen grand. And you think Joseph might have hidden them in his apartment. Thirty-one, wasn't it?"

"Yes," she said. "I guess it's a lot to ask."

I opened the door and got out of the car. "I've been paid," I said. "I'll go look. The doors in my apartment house are not very obstinate. The cops will find out where Waldo lived when they publish his photo, but not tonight, I guess."

"It's awfully sweet of you," she said. "Shall I wait here?"

I stood with a foot on the running-board, leaning in, looking at her. I didn't answer her question. I just stood there looking in at the shine of her eyes. Then I shut the car door and walked up the street towards Franklin.

Even with the wind shriveling my face I could still smell the sandalwood in her hair. And feel her lips.

8. Hub of a propeller.

I unlocked the Berglund door, walked through the silent lobby to the elevator, and rode up to 3. Then I soft-footed along the silent corridor and peered down at the sill of Apartment 31. No light. I rapped—the old light, confidential tattoo of the bootlegger with the big smile and the extra-deep hip pockets. No answer. I took the piece of thick hard celluloid that pretended to be a window over the driver's license in my wallet, and eased it between the lock and the jamb, leaning hard on the knob, pushing it toward the hinges. The edge of the celluloid caught the slope of the spring lock and snapped it back with a small brittle sound, like an icicle breaking. The door yielded and I went into near darkness. Street light filtered in and touched a high spot here and there.

I shut the door and snapped the light on and just stood. There was a queer smell in the air. I made it in a moment—the smell of dark-cured tobacco. I prowled over to a smoking-stand by the window and looked down at four brown butts—Mexican or South American cigarettes.

Upstairs, on my floor, feet hit the carpet and somebody went into a bathroom. I heard the toilet flush. I went into the bathroom of Apartment 31. A little rubbish, nothing, no place to hide anything. The kitchenette was a longer job, but I only half searched. I knew there were no pearls in that apartment. I knew Waldo had been on his way out and that he was in a hurry and that something was riding him when he turned and took two bullets from an old friend.

I went back to the living-room and swung the wall bed and looked past its mirror side into the dressing-room for signs of still current occupancy. Swinging the bed farther I was no longer looking for pearls. I was looking at a man.

He was small, middle-aged, iron-gray at the temples, with a very dark skin, dressed in a fawn-colored suit with a wine-colored tie. His neat little brown hands hung limply by his sides. His small feet, in pointed polished shoes, pointed almost at the floor.

He was hanging by a belt around his neck from the metal top of the bed. His tongue stuck out farther than I thought it possible for a tongue to stick out.

He swung a little and I didn't like that, so I pulled the bed down and he nestled quietly between the two clamped pillows. I didn't touch him yet. I didn't have to touch him to know that he would be cold as ice.

I went around him into the dressing-room and used my handkerchief on drawer-knobs. The place was stripped clean except for the light litter of a man living alone.

I came out of there and began on the man. No wallet. Waldo would have taken that and ditched it. A flat box of cigarettes, half full, stamped in gold: "Louis Tapia y Cia, Calle de Paysand, 19, Montevideo."[9] Matches from the Spezzia Club. An under-arm holster of dark grained leather and in it a 9 millimeter Mauser.

The Mauser made him a professional, so I didn't feel so badly. But not a very good professional, or bare hands would not have finished him, with the Mauser—a gun you can blast through a wall with—undrawn in his shoulder holster.

---

9. Capital city of Uruguay. "Louis Tapia y Cia": Louis Tapia and Company (Spanish).

I made a little sense of it, not much. Four of the brown cigarettes had been smoked, so there had been either waiting or discussion. Somewhere along the line Waldo had got the little man by the throat and held him in just the right way to make him pass out in a matter of seconds. The Mauser had been less useful to him than a toothpick. Then Waldo had hung him up by the strap, probably dead already. That would account for haste, for cleaning out the apartment, for Waldo's anxiety about the girl. It would account for the car left unlocked outside the cocktail bar.

That is, it would account for these things if Waldo had killed him, if this was really Waldo's apartment—if I wasn't just being kidded.

I examined some more pockets. In the left trouser one I found a gold penknife, some silver. In the left hip pocket a handkerchief, folded, scented. On the right hip another, unfolded but clean. In the right leg pocket four or five tissue handkerchiefs. A clean little guy. He didn't like to blow his nose on his handkerchief. Under these there was a small new keytainer holding four new keys—car keys. Stamped in gold on the keytainer was: Compliments of R. K. Vogelsang, Inc. "The Packard House."

I put everything as I had found it, swung the bed back, used my handkerchief on knobs and other projections, and flat surfaces, killed the light and poked my nose out the door. The hall was empty. I went down to the street and around the corner to Kingsley Drive. The Cadillac hadn't moved.

I opened the car door and leaned on it. She didn't seem to have moved, either. It was hard to see any expression on her face. Hard to see anything but her eyes and chin, but not hard to smell the sandalwood.

"That perfume," I said, "would drive a deacon nuts . . . no pearls."

"Well—thanks for trying," she said in a low, soft, vibrant voice. "I guess I can stand it. Shall I . . . Do we . . . Or . . . ?"

"You go on home now," I said. "And whatever happens you never saw me before. Whatever happens. Just as you may never see me again."

"I'd hate—"

"Good luck, Lola." I shut the car door and stepped back.

The lights blazed on, the motor turned over. Against the wind at the corner the big coupe made a slow contemptuous turn and was gone. I stood there by the vacant space at the curb where it had been.

It was quite dark there now. Windows had become blanks in the apartment where the radio sounded. I stood looking at the back of a Packard cabriolet which seemed to be brand new. I had seen it before—before I went upstairs, in the same place, in front of Lola's car. Parked, dark, silent, with a blue sticker pasted to the right-hand corner of the shiny windshield.

And in my mind I was looking at something else, a set of brand-new car keys in a keytainer stamped, "The Packard House," upstairs, in a dead man's pocket.

I went up to the front of the cabriolet and put a small pocket flash on the blue slip. It was the same dealer all right. Written in ink below his name and slogan was a name and address—Eugenie Kolchenko, 5315 Arvieda Street, West Los Angeles.

It was crazy. I went back up to Apartment 31, jimmied the door as I had done before, stepped in behind the wall bed and took the keytainer from the trousers pocket of the neat brown dangling corpse. I was back down on the street beside the cabriolet in five minutes. The keys fitted.

V

It was a small house, near a canyon rim out beyond Sawtelle,[1] with a circle of writhing eucalyptus trees in front of it. Beyond that, on the other side of the street, one of those parties was going on where they come out and smash bottles on the sidewalk with a whoop like Yale making a touchdown against Princeton.

There was a wire fence at my number and some rose-trees and a flagged walk and a garage that was wide open and had no car in it. There was no car in front of the house either. I rang the bell. There was a long wait, then the door opened rather suddenly.

I wasn't the man she had been expecting. I could see it in her glittering kohl-rimmed eyes. Then I couldn't see anything in them. She just stood and looked at me, a long, lean, hungry brunette, with rouged cheekbones, thick black hair parted in the middle, a mouth made for three-decker sandwiches, coral-and-gold pajamas, sandals—and gilded toenails. Under her ear lobes a couple of miniature temple bells gonged lightly in the breeze. She made a slow disdainful motion with a cigarette in a holder as long as a baseball bat.

"We-el, what ees it, little man? You want sometheeng? You are lost from the bee-ootiful party across the street hein?"

"Ha, ha," I said. "Quite a party, isn't it? No. I just brought your car home. Lost it, didn't you?"

Across the street somebody had delirium tremens in the front yard and a mixed quartet tore what was left of the night into small strips and did what they could to make the strips miserable. While this was going on the exotic brunette didn't move more than one eyelash.

She wasn't beautiful, she wasn't even pretty, but she looked as if things would happen where she was.

"You have said what?" she got out, at last, in a voice as silky as a burnt crust of toast.

"Your car." I pointed over my shoulder and kept my eyes on her. She was the type that uses a knife.

The long cigarette holder dropped very slowly to her side and the cigarette fell out of it. I stamped it out, and that put me in the hall. She backed away from me and I shut the door.

The hall was like the long hall of a railroad flat. Lamps glowed pinkly in iron brackets. There was a bead curtain at the end, a tiger skin on the floor. The place went with her.

"You're Miss Kolchenko?" I asked, not getting any more action.

"Ye-es. I am Mees Kolchenko. What thee 'ell you want?"

She was looking at me now as if I had come to wash the windows, but at an inconvenient time.

I got a card out with my left hand, held it out to her. She read it in my hand, moving her head just enough. "A detective?" she breathed.

"Yeah."

She said something in a spitting language. Then in English: "Come in! Thees damn wind dry up my skeen like so much teessue paper."

---

1. Tough Los Angeles neighborhood south of Brentwood.

"We're in," I said. "I just shut the door. Snap out of it, Nazimova.[2] Who was he? The little guy?"

Beyond the bead curtain a man coughed. She jumped as if she had been stuck with an oyster fork. Then she tried to smile. It wasn't very successful.

"A reward," she said softly. "You weel wait 'ere? Ten dollars it is fair to pay, no?"

"No," I said.

I reached a finger towards her slowly and added: "He's dead."

She jumped about three feet and let out a yell.

A chair creaked harshly. Feet pounded beyond the bead curtain, a large hand plunged into view and snatched it aside, and a big hard-looking blond man was with us. He had a purple robe over his pajamas. His right hand held something in his robe pocket. He stood quite still as soon as he was through the curtain, his feet planted solidly, his jaw out, his colorless eyes like gray ice. He looked like a man who would be hard to take out on an off-tackle play.

"What's the matter, honey?" He had a solid, burring voice, with just the right sappy tone to belong to a guy who would go for a woman with gilded toenails.

"I came about Miss Kolchenko's car," I said.

"Well, you could take your hat off," he said. "Just for a light workout."

I took it off and apologized.

"O.K.," he said, and kept his right hand shoved down hard in the purple pocket. "So you came about Miss Kolchenko's car. Take it from there."

I pushed past the woman and went closer to him. She shrank back against the wall and flattened her palms against it. Camille[3] in a high-school play. The long holder lay empty at her toes.

When I was six feet from the big man he said easily: "I can hear you from there. Just take it easy. I've got a gun in this pocket and I've had to learn to use one. Now about the car?"

"The man who borrowed it couldn't bring it," I said, and pushed the card I was still holding towards his face. He barely glanced at it. He looked back at me.

"So what?" he said.

"Are you always this tough?" I asked, "or only when you have your pajamas on?"

"So why couldn't he bring it himself?" he asked. "And skip the mushy talk."

The dark woman made a stuffed sound at my elbow.

"It's all right, honeybunch," the man said. "I'll handle this. Go on in."

She slid past both of us and flicked through the bead curtain.

I waited a little while. The big man didn't move a muscle. He didn't look any more bothered than a toad in the sun.

"He couldn't bring it because somebody bumped him off," I said. "Let's see you handle that."

"Yeah?" he said. "Did you bring him with you to prove it?"

"No," I said. "But if you put your tie and crush hat on, I'll take you down and show you."

2. Allusion to Alla Nazimova (1879–1945), Russian-born actress known for exotic roles.

3. Courtesan heroine of *Camille* (1852), a popular play by Alexandre Dumas (1824–1895).

"Who the hell did you say you were, now?"

"I didn't say. I thought maybe you could read." I held the card at him some more.

"Oh, that's right," he said. "John Dalmas, Private Investigator. Well, well. So I should go with you to look at who, why?"

"Maybe he stole the car," I said.

The big man nodded. "That's a thought. Maybe he did. Who?"

"The little brown guy who had the keys to it in his pocket, and had it parked around the corner from the Berglund Apartments."

He thought that over, without any apparent embarrassment. "You've got something there," he said. "Not much. But a little. I guess this must be the night of the Police Smoker. So you're doing all their work for them."

"Huh?"

"The card says private detective to me," he said. "Have you got some cops outside that were too shy to come in?"

"No, I'm alone."

He grinned. The grin showed white ridges in his tanned skin. "So you find somebody dead and take some keys and find a car and come riding out here—all alone. No cops. Am I right?"

"Correct."

He sighed. "Let's go inside," he said. He yanked the bead curtain aside and made an opening for me to go through. "It might be you have an idea I ought to hear."

I went past him and he turned, keeping his heavy pocket towards me. I hadn't noticed until I got quite close that there were beads of sweat on his face. It might have been the hot wind, but I didn't think so.

We were in the living-room of the house.

We sat down and looked at each other across a dark floor, on which a few Navajo rugs and a few dark Turkish rugs made a decorating combination with some well-used over-stuffed furniture. There was a fireplace, a small baby grand, a Chinese screen, a tall Chinese lantern on a teakwood pedestal, and gold net curtains against lattice windows. The windows to the south were open. A fruit tree with a white washed trunk whipped about outside the screen, adding its bit to the noise from across the street.

The big man eased back into a brocaded chair and put his slippered feet on a footstool. He kept his right hand where it had been since I met him—on his gun.

The brunette hung around in the shadows and a bottle gurgled and her temple bells gonged in her ears.

"It's all right, honeybunch," the man said. "It's all under control. Somebody bumped somebody off and this lad thinks we're interested. Just sit down and relax."

The girl tilted her head and poured half a tumbler of whisky down her throat. She sighed, said, "Goddam," in a casual voice, and curled up on a davenport. It took all of the davenport. She had plenty of legs. Her gilded toenails winked at me from the shadowy corner where she kept herself quiet from then on.

I got a cigarette out without being shot at, lit it and went into my story. It wasn't all true, but some of it was. I told them about the Berglund Apartments and that I had lived there and that Waldo was living there in Apartment 31 on the floor below mine and that I had been keeping an eye on him for business reasons.

"Waldo what?" the blond man put in. "And what business reasons?"

"Mister," I said, "have you no secrets?" He reddened slightly.

I told him about the cocktail lounge across the street from the Berglund and what had happened there. I didn't tell him about the printed bolero jacket or the girl who had worn it. I left her out of the story altogether.

"It was an undercover job—from my angle," I said. "If you know what I mean." He reddened again, bit his teeth. I went on: "I got back from the city hall without telling anybody I knew Waldo. In due time, when I decided they couldn't find out where he lived that night, I took the liberty of examining his apartment."

"Looking for what?" the big man said thickly.

"For some letters. I might mention in passing there was nothing there at all—except a dead man. Strangled and hanging by a belt to the top of the wall bed—well out of sight. A small man, about forty-five, Mexican or South American, well-dressed in a fawn-colored—"

"That's enough," the big man said. "I'll bite, Dalmas. Was it a blackmail job you were on?"

"Yeah. The funny part was this little brown man had plenty of gun under his arm."

"He wouldn't have five hundred bucks in twenties in his pocket, of course? Or are you saying?"

"He wouldn't. But Waldo had over seven hundred in currency when he was killed in the cocktail bar."

"Looks like I underrated this Waldo," the big man said calmly. "He took my guy and his payoff money, gun and all. Waldo have a gun?"

"Not on him."

"Get us a drink, honeybunch," the big man said. "Yes, I certainly did sell this Waldo person shorter than a bargain-counter shirt."

The brunette unwound her legs and made two drinks with soda and ice. She took herself another gill without trimmings, wound herself back on the davenport. Her big glittering black eyes watched me solemnly.

"Well, here's how," the big man said, lifting his glass in salute. "I haven't murdered anybody, but I've got a divorce suit on my hands from now on. You haven't murdered anybody, the way you tell it, but you laid an egg down at police headquarters. What the hell! Life's a lot of trouble, anyway you look at it. I've still got honeybunch, here. She's a white Russian[4] I met in Shanghai. She's safe as a vault and she looks as if she would cut your throat for a nickel. That's what I like about her. You get the glamor without the risk."

"You talk damn foolish," the girl spat at him.

"You look O.K. to me," the big man went on ignoring her. "That is, for a keyhole peeper. Is there an out?"

"Yeah. But it will cost a little money."

"I expected that. How much?"

"Say another five hundred."

---

4. One of the supporters of the Russian tsar; many of them fled the country after the Communist victory in the revolution of 1917.

"Goddamn, thees hot wind make me dry like the ashes of love," the Russian girl said bitterly.

"Five hundred might do," the blond man said. "What do I get for it?"

"If I swing it—you get left out of the story. If I don't—you don't pay."

He thought it over. His face looked lined and tired now. The small beads of sweat twinkled in his short blond hair.

"This murder will make you talk," he grumbled. "The second one, I mean. And I don't have what I was going to buy. And if it's a hush, I'd rather buy it direct."

"Who was the little brown man?" I asked.

"Name's Leon Valesanos, a Uruguayan. Another of my importations. I'm in a business that takes me a lot of places. He was working in the Spezzia Club in Chiseltown—you know, the strip of Sunset next to Beverly Hills. Working on roulette, I think. I gave him the five hundred to go down to this—this Waldo—and buy back some bills for stuff Miss Kolchenko had charged to my account and delivered here. That wasn't bright, was it? I had them in my brief case and this Waldo got a chance to steal them. What's your hunch about what happened?"

I sipped my drink and looked at him down my nose. "Your Uruguayan pal probably talked cut and Waldo didn't listen good. Then the little guy thought maybe that Mauser might help his argument—and Waldo was too quick for him. I wouldn't say Waldo was a killer—not by intention. A blackmailer seldom is. Maybe he lost his temper and maybe he just held on to the little guy's neck too long. Then he had to take it on the lam. But he had another date, with more money coming up. And he worked the neighborhood looking for the party. And accidentally he ran into a pal who was hostile enough and drunk enough to blow him down."

"There's a hell of a lot of coincidence in all this business," the big man said.

"It's the hot wind," I grinned. "Everybody's screwy tonight."

"For the five hundred you guarantee nothing? If I don't get my cover-up, you don't get your dough. Is that it?"

"That's it," I said, smiling at him.

"Screwy is right," he said, and drained his highball. "I'm taking you up on it."

"There are just two things," I said softly, leaning forward in my chair. "Waldo had a getaway car parked outside the cocktail bar where he was killed, unlocked with the motor running. The killer took it. There's always the chance of a kickback from that direction. You see, all Waldo's stuff must have been in that car."

"Including my bills and your letters."

"Yeah. But the police are reasonable about things like that—unless you're good for a lot of publicity. If you're not, I think I can eat some stale dog downtown and get by. If you are—that's the second thing. What did you say your name was?"

The answer was a long time coming. When it came I didn't get as much kick out of it as I thought I would. All at once it was too logical.

"Frank C. Barsaly," he said.

After a while the Russian girl called me a taxi. When I left the party across the street was still doing all that a party could do. I noticed the walls of the house were still standing. That seemed a pity.

VI

When I unlocked the glass entrance door of the Berglund I smelled policeman. I looked at my wrist watch. It was nearly 3 A.M. In the dark corner of
the lobby a man dozed in a chair with a newspaper over his face. Large feet
stretched out before him. A corner of the paper lifted an inch, dropped again.
The man made no other movement.

I went on along the hall to the elevator and rode up to my floor. I soft-
footed along the hallway, unlocked my door, pushed it wide and reached in
for the light-switch.

A chain-switch tinkled and light glared from a standing-lamp by the easy
chair, beyond the card table on which my chessmen were still scattered.

Copernik sat there with a stiff unpleasant grin on his face. The short dark
man, Ybarra, sat across the room from him, on my left, silent, half-smiling as
usual.

Copernik showed more of his big yellow horse teeth and said: "Hi. Long
time no see. Been out with the girls?"

I shut the door and took my hat off and wiped the back of my neck slowly,
over and over again. Copernik went on grinning. Ybarra looked at nothing
with his soft dark eyes.

"Take a seat, pal," Copernik drawled. "Make yourself to home. We got pow-
wow to make. Boy, do I hate this night sleuthing. Did you know you were all
out of hooch?"[5]

"I could have guessed it," I said. I leaned against the wall.

Copernik kept on grinning. "I always did hate private dicks," he said, "but
I never had a chance to twist one like I got tonight."

He reached down lazily beside his chair and picked up a printed bolero
jacket, tossed it on the card table. He reached down again and put a wide-
brimmed hat beside it.

"I bet you look cuter than all hell with these on," he said.

I took hold of a straight chair, twisted it around and straddled it, leaned my
folded arms on the chair and looked at Copernik.

He got up very slowly—with an elaborate slowness, walked across the room
and stood in front of me smoothing his coat down. Then he lifted his open
right hand and hit me across the face with it—hard. It stung but I didn't
move.

Ybarra looked at the wall, looked at the floor, looked at nothing.

"Shame on you, pal," Copernik said lazily. "The way you was taking care of
this nice exclusive merchandise. Wadded down behind your old shirts. You
punk peepers always did make me sick."

He stood there over me for a moment. I didn't move or speak. I looked into
his glazed drinker's eyes. He doubled a fist at his side, then shrugged and
turned and went back to the chair.

"O.K.," he said. "The rest will keep. Where did you get these things?"

"They belong to a lady."

"Do tell. They belong to a lady. Ain't you the light-hearted—! I'll tell you
what lady they belong to. They belong to the lady a guy named Waldo asked

5. Liquor.

about in a bar across the street—about two minutes before he got shot kind of dead. Or would that have slipped your mind?"

I didn't say anything.

"You was curious about her yourself," Copernik sneered on. "But you were smart, pal. You fooled me."

"That wouldn't make me smart," I said.

His face twisted suddenly and he started to get up. Ybarra laughed, suddenly and softly, almost under his breath. Copernik's eyes swung on him, hung there. Then he faced me again, blank-eyed.

"The guinea likes you," he said. "He thinks you're good."

The smile left Ybarra's face, but no expression took its place. No expression at all.

Copernik said: "You knew who the dame was all the time. You knew who Waldo was and where he lived. Right across the hall a floor below you. You knew this Waldo person had bumped a guy off and started to lam, only this broad came into his plans somewhere and he was anxious to meet up with her before he went away. Only he never got the chance. A heist guy from back East named Al Tessilore took care of that by taking care of Waldo. So you met the gal and hid her clothes and sent her on her way and kept your trap glued. That's the way guys like you make your beans. Am I right?"

"Yeah," I said. "Except that I only knew these things very recently. Who was Waldo?"

Copernik bared his teeth at me. Red spots burned high on his sallow cheeks. Ybarra, looking down at the floor, said very softly: "Waldo Ratigan. We got him from Washington by teletype. He was a two-bit porch-climber[6] with a few small terms on him. He drove a car in a bank stickup job in Detroit. He turned the gang in later and got a nolle prosse. One of the gang was this Al Tessilore. He hasn't talked a word, but we think the meeting across the street was purely accidental."

Ybarra spoke in the soft quiet modulated voice of a man for whom sounds have a meaning. I said: "Thanks, Ybarra. Can I smoke—or would Copernik kick it out of my mouth?"

Ybarra smiled suddenly. "You may smoke, sure," he said.

"The guinea likes you all right," Copernik jeered. "You never know what a guinea will like, do you?"

I lit a cigarette. Ybarra looked at Copernik and said very softly: "The word guinea—you overwork it. I don't like it so well applied to me."

"The hell with what you like, guinea."

Ybarra smiled a little more. "You are making a mistake," he said. He took a pocket nailfile out and began to use it, looking down.

Copernik blared: "I smelled something rotten on you from the start, Dalmas. So when we make these two mugs, Ybarra and me think we'll drift over and dabble a few more words with you. I bring one of Waldo's morgue photos—nice work, the light just right in his eyes, his tie all straight and a white handkerchief showing just right in his pocket. Nice work. So on the way up, just as a matter of routine, we rout out the manager here and let him lamp it. And he knows the guy. He's here as A. B. Hummel, Apartment Thirty-one. So

6. Burglar.

we go in there and find a stiff. Then we go round and round with that. Nobody knows him yet, but he's got some swell finger bruises under that strap and I hear they fit Waldo's fingers very nicely."

"That's something," I said. "I thought maybe I murdered him."

Copernik stared at me for a long time. His face had stopped grinning and was just a hard brutal face now. "Yeah. We got something else even," he said. "We got Waldo's getaway car—and what Waldo had in it to take with him."

I blew cigarette smoke jerkily. The wind pounded the shut windows. The air in the room was foul.

"Oh we're bright boys," Copernik sneered. "We never figured you with that much guts. Take a look at this."

He plunged his bony hand into his coat pocket and drew something up slowly over the edge of the card table, drew it along the green top and left it there stretched out, gleaming. A string of white pearls with a clasp like a two-bladed propeller. They shimmered softly in the thick smoky air.

Lola Barsaly's pearls. The pearls the flier had given her. The guy who was dead, the guy she still loved.

I stared at them, but I didn't move. After a long moment Copernik said almost gravely: "Nice, ain't they? Would you feel like telling us a story about now, Mis-ter Dalmas?"

I stood up and pushed the chair from under me, walked slowly across the room and stood looking down at the pearls. The largest was perhaps a third of an inch across. They were pure white, iridescent, with a mellow softness. I lifted them slowly off the card table from beside her clothes. They felt heavy, smooth, fine.

"Nice," I said. "A lot of the trouble was about these. Yeah, I'll talk now. They must be worth a lot of money."

Ybarra laughed behind me. It was a very gentle laugh. "About a hundred dollars," he said. "They're good phonies—but they're phony."

I lifted the pearls again. Copernik's glassy eyes gloated at me. "How do you tell?" I asked.

"I know pearls," Ybarra said. "These are good stuff, the kind women very often have made on purpose, as a kind of insurance. But they are slick like glass. Real pearls are gritty between the edges of the teeth. Try."

I put two or three of them between my teeth and moved my teeth back and forth, then sideways. Not quite biting them. The beads were hard and slick.

"Yes. They are very good," Ybarra said. "Several even have little waves and flat spots, as real pearls might have."

"Would they cost fifteen grand—if they were real?" I asked.

"Si. Probably. That's hard to say. It depends on a lot of things."

"This Waldo wasn't so bad," I said.

Copernik stood up quickly, but I didn't see him swing. I was still looking down at the pearls. His fist caught me on the side of the face, against the molars. I tasted blood at once. I staggered back and made it look like a worse blow than it was.

"Sit down and talk, you—!" Copernik almost whispered.

I sat down and used a handkerchief to pat my cheek. I licked at the cut inside my mouth. Then I got up again and went over and picked up the cigarette he had knocked out of my mouth. I crushed it out in a tray and sat down again.

Ybarra filed at his nails and held one up against the lamp. There were beads of sweat on Copernik's eyebrows, at the inner ends.

"You found the beads in Waldo's car," I said, looking at Ybarra. "Find any papers?"

He shook his head without looking up.

"I'd believe *you*," I said. "Here it is. I never saw Waldo until he stepped into the cocktail bar tonight and asked about the girl. I knew nothing I didn't tell. When I got home and stepped out of the elevator this girl, in the printed bolero jacket and the wide hat and the blue silk crepe dress—all as he had described them—was waiting for the elevator, here, on my floor. And she looked like a nice girl."

Copernik laughed jeeringly. It didn't make any difference to me. I had him cold. All he had to do was know that. He was going to know it now, very soon.

"I knew what she was up against as a police witness," I said. "And I suspected there was something else to it. But I didn't suspect for a minute that there was anything wrong with her. She was just a nice girl in a jam—and she didn't even know she was in a jam. I got her in here. She pulled a gun on me. But she didn't mean to use it."

Copernik sat up very suddenly and he began to lick his lips. His face had a stony look now. A look like wet gray stone. He didn't make a sound.

"Waldo had been her chauffeur," I went on. "His name then was Joseph Choate. Her name is Mrs. Frank C. Barsaly. Her husband is a big hydro-electric engineer. Some guy gave her the pearls once and she told her husband they were just store pearls. Waldo got wise somehow there was a romance behind them and when Barsaly come home from South America and fired him, because he was too good-looking, he lifted the pearls."

Ybarra lifted his head suddenly and his teeth flashed. "You mean he didn't know they were phony?"

"I thought he fenced the real ones and had imitations fixed up," I said.

Ybarra nodded. "It's possible."

"He lifted something else," I said. "Some stuff from Barsaly's briefcase that showed he was keeping a woman—out in Brentwood.[7] He was blackmailing wife and husband both, without either knowing about the other. Get it so far?"

"I get it," Copernik said harshly, between his tight lips. His face was still wet gray stone. "Get the hell on with it."

"Waldo wasn't afraid of them," I said. "He didn't conceal where he lived. That was foolish, but it saved a lot of finagling, if he was willing to risk it. The girl came down here tonight with five grand to buy back her pearls. She never met Waldo. She came up here to look for him and walked up a floor before she went back down. A woman's idea of being cagey. So I met her. So I brought her in here. So she was in that dressing-room when Al Tessilore visited me to rub out a witness." I pointed to the dressing-room door. "So she came out with her little gun and stuck it in his back and saved my life," I said.

Copernik didn't move. There was something horrible in his face now. Ybarra slipped his nailfile into a small leather case and slowly tucked it into his pocket.

"Is that all?" he asked gently.

7. Upper-middle-class neighborhood in western Los Angeles.

I nodded. "Except that she told me where Waldo's apartment was and I went in there and looked for the pearls. I found the dead man. In his pocket I found new car keys in a case from a Packard agency. And down on the street I found the Packard and took it to where it came from. Barsaly's kept woman. Barsaly had sent a friend from the Spezzia Club down to buy something and he had tried to buy it with his gun instead of the money Barsaly gave him. And Waldo beat him to the punch."

"Is that all?" Ybarra asked softly.

"That's all," I said, licking the torn place on the inside of my cheek.

Ybarra said slowly: "What do you want?"

Copernik's face convulsed and he slapped his long hard thigh. "This guy is good," he jeered. "He falls for a stray broad and breaks every law in the book and you ask him what does he want? I'll give him what he wants, guinea!"

Ybarra turned his head slowly and looked at him. "I don't think you will," he said. "I think you'll give him a clean bill of health and anything else he wants. He's giving you a lesson in police work."

Copernik didn't move or make a sound for a long minute. None of us moved. Then Copernik leaned forward and his coat fell open. The butt of his service gun looked out of its underarm holster.

"So what do you want?" he asked me.

"What's on the card table there. The jacket and hat and the phony pearls. And some names kept away from the papers. Is that too much?"

"Yeah—it's too much," Copernik said almost gently. He swayed sideways and his gun jumped neatly into his hand. He rested his forearm on his thigh and pointed the gun at my stomach.

"I like better that you get a slug in the guts resisting arrest," he said. "I like that better, because of a report I made out on Al Tessilore's arrest and how I made the pinch. Because of some photos of me that are in the morning sheets going out about now. I like it better that you don't live long enough to laugh about that, baby."

My mouth felt suddenly hot and dry. Far off I heard the wind booming. It seemed like the sound of guns.

Ybarra moved his feet on the floor and said coldly: "You've got a couple of cases all solved, policeman. All you do for it is leave some junk here and keep some names from the papers. Which means from the D.A. If he gets them anyway, too bad for you."

Copernik said: "I like the other way." The blue gun in his hand was like a rock. "And God help you, if you don't back me up on it."

Ybarra said: "If the woman is brought out into the open, you'll be a liar on a police report and a chiseler on your own partner. In a week they won't even speak your name at headquarters. The taste of it would make them sick."

The hammer clicked back on Copernik's gun and I watched his big bony finger slide in farther around the trigger. The back of my neck was as wet as a dog's nose.

Ybarra stood up. The gun jumped at him. He said: "We'll see how yellow a guinea is. I'm telling you to put that gun up, Sam."

He started to move. He moved four even steps. Copernik was a man without a breath of movement, a stone man.

Ybarra took one more step and quite suddenly the gun began to shake.

Ybarra said evenly: "Put it up, Sam. If you keep your head everything lies the way it is. If you don't—you're gone."

He took one more step. Copernik's mouth opened wide and made a gasping sound and then he sagged in the chair as if he had been hit on the head. His eyelids drooped.

Ybarra jerked the gun out of his hand with a movement so quick it was no movement at all. He stepped back quickly, held the gun low at his side.

"It's the hot wind, Sam. Let's forget it," he said in the same even, almost dainty voice.

Copernik's shoulders sagged lower and he put his face in his hands. "O.K.," he said between his fingers.

Ybarra went softly across the room and opened the door. He looked at me with lazy, half-closed eyes. "I'd do a lot for a woman who saved my life, too," he said. "I'm eating this dish, but as a cop you can't expect me to like it."

I said: "The little man in the bed is called Leon Valesanos. He was a croupier at the Spezzia Club."

"Thanks," Ybarra said. "Let's go, Sam."

Copernik got up heavily and walked across the room and out of the open door and out of my sight. Ybarra stepped through the door after him and started to close it.

I said: "Wait a minute."

He turned his head slowly, his left hand on the door, the blue gun hanging down close to his right side.

"I'm not in this for money," I said. "The Barsalys live at Two-twelve Fremont Place. You can take the pearls to her. If Barsaly's name stays out of the paper. I get five C's. It goes to the Police Fund. I'm not so damn smart as you think. It just happened that way—and you had a heel for a partner."

Ybarra looked across the room at the pearls on the card table. His eyes glistened. "You take them," he said. "The five hundred's O.K. I think the fund has it coming."

He shut the door quietly and in a moment I heard the elevator doors clang.

VII

I opened a window and stuck my head out into the wind and watched the squad car tool off down the block. The wind blew in hard and I let it blow. A picture fell off the wall and two chessmen rolled off the card table. The material of Lola Barsaly's bolero jacket lifted and shook.

I went out to the kitchenette and drank some Scotch and went back into the living-room and called her—late as it was.

She answered the phone herself, very quickly, with no sleep in her voice.

"Dalmas," I said. "O.K. your end?"

"Yes . . . yes," she said. "I'm alone."

"I found something," I said. "Or rather the police did. But your dark boy gypped you. I have a string of pearls. They're not real. He sold the real ones, I guess, and made you up a string of ringers, with your clasp."

She was silent for a long time. Then, a little faintly: "The police found them?"

"In Waldo's car. But they're not telling. We have a deal. Look at the papers in the morning and you'll be able to figure out why."

"There doesn't seem to be anything more to say," she said. "Can I have the clasp?"

"Yes. Can you meet me tomorrow at four in the Club Esquire bar?"

"You're rather sweet," she said in a dragged-out voice. "I can. Frank is still at his meeting."

"Those meetings—they take it out of a guy," I said. We said goodbye.

I called a West Los Angeles number. He was still there, with the Russian girl.

"You can send me a check for five hundred in the morning," I told him. "Made out to the Police Fund, if you want to. Because that's where it's going."

Copernik made the third page of the morning papers with two photos and a nice half-column. The little brown man in Apartment 31 didn't make the paper at all. The Apartment House Association has a good lobby too.

I went out after breakfast and the wind was all gone. It was soft, cool, a little foggy. The sky was close and comfortable and gray. I rode down to the boulevard and picked out the best jewelry store on it and laid a string of pearls on a black velvet mat under a daylight-blue lamp. A man in a wing collar and striped trousers looked down at them languidly.

"How good?" I asked.

"I'm sorry, sir. We don't make appraisals. I can give you the name of an appraiser."

"Don't kid me," I said. "They're Dutch."

He focused the light a little and leaned down and toyed with a few inches of the string.

"I want a string just like them, fitted to that clasp, and in a hurry," I added.

"How, like them?" He didn't look up. "And they're not Dutch. They're Bohemian."

"O.K., can you duplicate them?"

He shook his head and pushed the velvet pad away as if it soiled him. "In three months, perhaps. We don't blow glass like that in this country. If you wanted them matched—three months at least. And this house would not do that sort of thing at all."

"It must be swell to be that snooty," I said. I put a card under his black sleeve. "Give me a name that will—and not in three months—and maybe not exactly like them."

He shrugged, went away with the card, came back in five minutes and handed it back to me. There was something written on the back.

The old Levantine had a shop on Melrose, a junk shop with everything in the window from a folding baby carriage to a French horn, from a mother-of-pearl lorgnette in a faded plush case to one of those .44 Special Single Action Six-shooters they still make for Western peace officers whose grandfathers were tough.

The old Levantine wore a skull cap and two pairs of glasses and a full beard. He studied my pearls, shook his head sadly, and said: "For twenty dollars, almost so good. Not so good, you understand. Not so good glass."

"How like will they look?"

He spread his firm strong hands. "I am telling you the truth," he said. "They would not fool a baby."

"Make them up," I said. "With this clasp. And I want the others back too, of course."

"Yah. Two o'clock," he said.

Leon Valesanos, the little brown man from Uruguay, made the afternoon papers. He had been found hanging in an unnamed apartment. The police were investigating.

At four o'clock I walked into the long cool bar of the Club Esquire and prowled along the row of booths until I found one where a woman sat alone. She wore a hat like a shallow soup plate with a very wide edge, a brown tailor-made suit with a severe mannish shirt and tie.

I sat down beside her and slipped a parcel along the seat. "You don't open that," I said. "In fact you can slip it into the incinerator as is, if you want to."

She looked at me with dark tired eyes. Her fingers twisted a thin glass that smelled of peppermint. "Thanks." Her face was very pale.

I ordered a highball and the waiter went away. "Read the papers?"

"Yes."

"You understand now about this fellow Copernik who stole your act? That's why they won't change the story or bring you into it."

"It doesn't matter now," she said. "Thank you, all the same. Please—please, show them to me."

I pulled a string of pearls out of the loosely wrapped tissue paper in my pocket and slid them across to her. The silver propeller clasp winked in the light of the wall bracket. The little diamond winked. The pearls were as dull as white soap. They didn't even match in size.

"You were right," she said tonelessly. "They are not my pearls."

The waiter came with my drink and she put her bag on them deftly. When he was gone she fingered them slowly once more, dropped them into the bag and gave me a dry mirthless smile.

"As you said—I'll keep the clasp."

I said slowly: "You don't know anything about me. You saved my life last night and we had a moment, but it was just a moment. You still don't know anything about me. There's a detective downtown named Ybarra, a Mexican of the nice sort, who was on the job when the pearls were found in Waldo's suitcase. That's in case you would like to make sure—"

She said: "Don't be silly. It's all finished. It was a memory. I'm too young to nurse memories. It may be all for the best. I loved Stan Phillips—but he's gone—long gone."

I stared at her, didn't say anything."

She added quietly: "This morning my husband told me something I hadn't known. We are to separate. So I have very little to laugh about today."

"I'm sorry," I said lamely. "There's nothing to say. I may see you sometime. Maybe not. I don't move much in your circle. Good luck."

I stood up. We looked at each other for a moment. "You haven't touched your drink," she said.

"You drink it. That peppermint stuff will just make you sick."

I stood there a moment with a hand hard on the table.

"If anybody ever bothers you," I said, "let me know."

I went out of the bar without looking back at her, got into my car and drove west on Sunset and down all the way to the Coast Highway. Everywhere along the way gardens were full of withered and blackened leaves and flowers which the hot wind had burned.

But the ocean looked cool and languid and just the same as ever. I drove on almost to Malibu and then parked and went and sat on a big rock that was inside somebody's wire fence. It was about half-tide and coming in. The air smelled of kelp. I watched the water for a while and then I pulled a string of Bohemian glass imitation pearls out of my pocket and cut the knot at one end and slipped the pearls off one by one.

When I had them all loose in my left hand I held them like that for a while and thought. There wasn't really anything to think about. I was sure.

"To the memory of Mr. Stan Phillips," I said loud. "Just another four-flusher."[8]

I flipped her pearls out into the water one by one, at the floating seagulls.

They made little splashes and the seagulls rose off the water and swooped at the splashes.

1938

8. Bluffer or loser; from poker, in which a hand with four cards of the same suit falls short of a true flush, five cards of the same suit.

T. S. ELIOT
1888–1965

The publication in 1922 of *The Waste Land* in the British little magazine *Criterion* and the American *Dial* was a cultural and literary event. The poem's title and the view it incorporated of modern civilization seemed, to many, to catch precisely the state of culture and society after World War I. The war, supposedly fought to save European civilization, had been the most brutal and destructive in Western history: what kind of civilization, after all, could have allowed it to take place? The long, fragmented structure of *The Waste Land,* too, contained so many technical innovations that ideas of what poetry was and how it worked seemed fundamentally changed. A generation of poets either imitated or resisted it.

The author of this poem was an American living in London, T. S. Eliot. He had a comfortable upbringing in St. Louis: his mother was involved in cultural and charitable activities and wrote poetry; his father was a successful businessman. His grandfather Eliot had been a New England Unitarian minister who, moving to St. Louis, had founded Washington University. Eliot was thus a product of that New England–based "genteel tradition" that shaped the nation's cultural life after the Civil War. He attended Harvard for both undergraduate and graduate work (1906–10, 1911–14). He studied at the Sorbonne in Paris from 1910 to 1911 and at Oxford from 1915 to 1916, writing a dissertation on the idealistic philosophy of the English logician and metaphysician F. H. Bradley (1846–1924). The war prevented Eliot from returning to Harvard for the oral defense for his doctoral degree, and this delay became the occasion of his turning to a life in poetry and letters rather than in academics.

Eliot had begun writing traditional poetry as a college student. In 1908, however, he read Arthur Symons's *The Symbolist Movement in Literature* and learned about Jules LaForgue and other French Symbolist poets. Symons's book altered Eliot's view of poetry, as "The Love Song of J. Alfred Prufrock" (published in *Poetry* in 1915) and "Preludes" (published in *Blast* in the same year) clearly showed. Ezra Pound, reading this work, began enthusiastically introducing Eliot in literary circles as a young American who had "trained himself *and* modernized himself *on his own.*" Pound helped Eliot over several years to get financially established. In addition, he was a perceptive reader and critic of Eliot's draft poems.

Eliot settled in England, marrying Vivian Haigh-Wood in 1915. Separated in 1932, they never divorced; Haigh-Wood died in a mental institution in 1947. After marrying, Eliot worked in London, first as a teacher and then from 1917 to 1925 in the foreign department of Lloyd's Bank, hoping to find time to write poetry and literary essays. His criticism was published in the *Egoist* and then in the little magazine that he founded, *Criterion*, which was published from 1922 to 1939. His persuasive style, a mixture of advocacy and judiciousness, effectively counterpointed Pound's aggressive, confrontational approach; the two together had a tremendous effect on how poetry of the day was written and how poetry of the past was evaluated. More than any other Americans they defined what is now thought of as "high" modernism.

Eliot began working on *The Waste Land* in 1921 and finished it in a Swiss sanatorium while recovering from a mental collapse brought on by overwork, marital problems, and general depression. He accepted some alterations suggested by his wife and cut huge chunks out of the poem on Pound's advice. Indeed, although Pound's work on the poem was all excision, study of the manuscript before and after Pound's suggestions were incorporated has led some critics to suggest that we should think of *The Waste Land* as jointly authored. The poem as published in *Criterion* and the *Dial* had no footnotes; these were added for its publication in book form and added yet another layer (possibly self-mocking) to the complex texture of the poem.

The Waste Land consists of five discontinuous segments, each composed of fragments incorporating multiple voices and characters, literary and historical allusions, vignettes of contemporary life, surrealistic images, myths and legends. "These fragments I have shored against my ruins," the poet writes, asking whether he can form any coherent structure from the splinters of civilization. Lacking narrative and expository shape, the poem is organized by recurrent allusions to the myth of seasonal death and rebirth that, according to much anthropological thinking of the time, underlay all religions. In Sir James Frazer's multivolume *The Golden Bough* (1890–1915) and Jessie Weston's *From Ritual to Romance* (1920) Eliot found a repertory of myths through which he could invoke, without specifically naming any religion, the story of a desert land brought to life by a king's sacrifice. Although it gestured toward religious belief, *The Waste Land* was not affirmative; the quest for regeneration in a cacophonous, desolate landscape remains unfulfilled.

Many readers saw *The Waste Land* as the definitive cultural statement of its time, but it was not definitive for Eliot. In fact, for Eliot himself the poem may have been much less broadly conceived and, above all, an indirect confession of personal discord. Whatever the fate of culture, the individual needed to work for personal certainty. In a preface to the collection of essays *For Lancelot Andrewes* (1928) he declared himself a "classicist in literature, royalist in politics, and anglo-catholic in religion." After "The Hollow Men" and the "Sweeney" poems, which continue *The Waste Land*'s critique of modern civilization, he turned increasingly to poems of religious doubt and reconciliation. "The Journey of the Magi" and "Ash Wednesday" are poems about the search for a faith that is desperately needed, yet difficult to sustain. The *Four Quartets*, begun with "Burnt Norton" in 1934 and completed in 1943, are poems written after his conversion to Anglicanism; they are not so much reports of secure faith as dramatizations of the difficult process of arriving at belief. In this process Eliot found a center for his own life as well as for his later poetry. The *Four Quartets* incorporate a good deal of the discursive and expository, elements that he had objected to in his earlier essays and dropped from his earlier poems.

An emphasis on order, hierarchy, and racial homogeneity emerged in Eliot's social essays of the later 1920s and 1930s; a strain of crude anti-Semitism had appeared in the earlier Sweeney poems. As European politics became increasingly turbulent, the initial cosmopolitan, international sensibility of modernists like Eliot and Pound tended to be replaced by a belief in localism. In addition, the stability promised by totalitarian regimes was often appealing, and the Communist rejection of all religion tended to drive the more theistic modernists into the opposing camp of fascism. Pound's and Eliot's fascist sympathies in the 1930s, together with their immense influence on poetry, had the result of linking the modernist movement with reactionary politics in the public's perception. Modernists, however, did not form a unified group; their politics ranged from the extreme right to the far left; many were centrists or liberals; and many despised politics completely.

When World War II began, Eliot, unlike Pound, abandoned politics. He had also put forth a poetics according to which poetry existed in a realm of its own, in which poems were to be considered only in terms of their own structures and in connection with other poetry. This was the thesis of his influential "Tradition and the Individual Talent," which defined the Western poetic tradition as an organic whole, an elastic equilibrium that constantly reformed itself to accommodate new poets who, therefore, became part of this whole. This antipolitical approach had a major influence on the practices of the close-reading critics whose work is known collectively as the "New Criticism." In other essays, Eliot denigrated didactic, expository, or narrative poets like Milton and the Victorians while applauding the verbally complex, ironic, indirect, symbolic work of seventeenth-century Metaphysical poets like Donne and Herbert.

For the New Criticism, which analyzed poems for imagery, allusion, ambiguity, and the like, Eliot's essays provided theory, his poetry opportunities for practical criticism. But when critics used Eliot's standards of difficult indirection to judge literary quality and made interpretation the main task of readers, they often overlooked the simple lyricism, obvious didacticism, and straightforward humor of Eliot's own poetry. And they failed to see the poems' specific cultural and autobiographical content.

However elitist his pronouncements, however hostile to modernity he claimed to be, Eliot actually drew heavily on popular forms and longed to have wide cultural influence. There are vaudeville turns throughout The Waste Land. He admired Charlie Chaplin and wanted "as large and miscellaneous an audience as possible." He pursued this ambition by writing verse plays. Murder in the Cathedral (1935) was a church pageant; The Family Reunion (1939), The Cocktail Party (1949), The Confidential Clerk (1953), and The Elder Statesman (1959), all religious in theme (though their symbolism was often hidden), were successfully produced in London and on Broadway. He never became a popular poet, however, despite his tremendous impact on the teaching and writing of poetry. Although Eliot remained a resident of England, he returned to the United States frequently to lecture and to give readings of his poems. He married his assistant, Valerie Fletcher, in 1957. By the time of his death he had become a social and cultural institution.

The text of the poems is that of The Complete Poems and Plays of T. S. Eliot (1969).

The Love Song of J. Alfred Prufrock

S'io credessi che mia risposta fosse
a persona che mai tornasse al mondo,
questa fiamma staria senza più scosse.
Ma per ciò che giammai di questo fondo
non tornò vivo alcun, s'i'odo il vero,
senza tema d'infamia ti rispondo.[1]

Let us go then, you and I,
When the evening is spread out against the sky
Like a patient etherised upon a table;
Let us go, through certain half-deserted streets,
The muttering retreats   5
Of restless nights in one-night cheap hotels
And sawdust restaurants with oyster-shells:
Streets that follow like a tedious argument
Of insidious intent
To lead you to an overwhelming question . . .   10
Oh, do not ask, 'What is it?'
Let us go and make our visit.

In the room the women come and go
Talking of Michelangelo.

The yellow fog that rubs its back upon the window-panes,   15
The yellow smoke that rubs its muzzle on the window-panes,
Licked its tongue into the corners of the evening,

Lingered upon the pools that stand in drains,
Let fall upon its back the soot that falls from chimneys,
Slipped by the terrace, made a sudden leap,   20
And seeing that it was a soft October night,
Curled once about the house, and fell asleep.

And indeed there will be time[2]
For the yellow smoke that slides along the street
Rubbing its back upon the window-panes;   25
There will be time, there will be time
To prepare a face to meet the faces that you meet;
There will be time to murder and create,
And time for all the works and days[3] of hands
That lift and drop a question on your plate;   30
Time for you and time for me,
And time yet for a hundred indecisions,

---

1. If I thought that my reply would be to one who would ever return to the world, this flame would stay without further movement; but since none has ever returned alive from this depth, if what I hear is true, I answer you without fear of infamy (Italian; Dante's *Inferno* 27.61–66). The speaker, Guido da Montefeltro, consumed in flame as punishment for giving false counsel, confesses his shame without fear of its being reported since he believes Dante cannot return to earth.
2. An echo of Andrew Marvell, "To His Coy Mistress" (1681): "Had we but world enough and time."
3. *Works and Days* is a didactic poem about farming by the Greek poet Hesiod (8th century B.C.E.).

And for a hundred visions and revisions,
Before the taking of a toast and tea.

In the room the women come and go   35
Talking of Michelangelo.

And indeed there will be time
To wonder, 'Do I dare?' and, 'Do I dare?'
Time to turn back and descend the stair,
With a bald spot in the middle of my hair—   40
(They will say: 'How his hair is growing thin!')
My morning coat, my collar mounting firmly to the chin,
My necktie rich and modest, but asserted by a simple pin—
(They will say: 'But how his arms and legs are thin!')
Do I dare   45
Disturb the universe?
In a minute there is time
For decisions and revisions which a minute will reverse.

For I have known them all already, known them all—
Have known the evenings, mornings, afternoons,   50
I have measured out my life with coffee spoons;
I know the voices dying with a dying fall[4]
Beneath the music from a farther room.
      So how should I presume?

And I have known the eyes already, known them all—   55
The eyes that fix you in a formulated phrase,
And when I am formulated, sprawling on a pin,
When I am pinned and wriggling on the wall,
Then how should I begin
To spit out all the butt-ends of my days and ways?   60
      And how should I presume?
And I have known the arms already, known them all—
Arms that are braceleted and white and bare
(But in the lamplight, downed with light brown hair!)
Is it perfume from a dress   65
That makes me so digress?
Arms that lie along a table, or wrap about a shawl.
      And should I then presume?
      And how should I begin?
      .   .   .   .   .   .

Shall I say, I have gone at dusk through narrow streets   70
And watched the smoke that rises from the pipes
Of lonely men in shirt-sleeves, leaning out of windows? . . .

---

4. Echo of Duke Orsino's invocation of music in Shakespeare's *Twelfth Night* 1.1.4: "If music be the food of love, play on. . . . That strain again! It had a dying fall."

I should have been a pair of ragged claws
Scuttling across the floors of silent seas.
  . . . . . .

And the afternoon, the evening, sleeps so peacefully!   75
Smoothed by long fingers,
Asleep . . . tired . . . or it malingers,
Stretched on the floor, here beside you and me.
Should I, after tea and cakes and ices,
Have the strength to force the moment to its crisis?   80
But though I have wept and fasted, wept and prayed,
Though I have seen my head (grown slightly bald) brought in
    upon a platter,[5]
I am no prophet—and here's no great matter;
I have seen the moment of my greatness flicker,
And I have seen the eternal Footman hold my coat, and snicker, 85
And in short, I was afraid.

And would it have been worth it, after all,
After the cups, the marmalade, the tea,
Among the porcelain, among some talk of you and me,
Would it have been worth while,   90
To have bitten off the matter with a smile,
To have squeezed the universe into a ball
To roll it towards some overwhelming question,
To say: 'I am Lazarus,[6] come from the dead,
Come back to tell you all, I shall tell you all'—   95
If one, settling a pillow by her head,
    Should say: 'That is not what I meant at all.
    That is not it, at all.'

And would it have been worth it, after all,
Would it have been worth while,   100
After the sunsets and the dooryards and the sprinkled streets,
After the novels, after the teacups, after the skirts that trail
    along the floor—
And this, and so much more?—
It is impossible to say just what I mean!
But as if a magic lantern threw the nerves in patterns on a screen: 105
Would it have been worth while
If one, settling a pillow or throwing off a shawl,
And turning toward the window, should say:
    'That is not it at all,
    That is not what I meant, at all.'   110
  . . . . . .

No! I am not Prince Hamlet, nor was meant to be;
Am an attendant lord, one that will do
To swell a progress,[7] start a scene or two,

---

5. The head of the prophet John the Baptist, who was killed at the behest of Princess Salome, was brought to her on a platter (see Mark 6.17–20, Matthew 14.3–11).

6. The resurrection of Lazarus is recounted in John 11.1–44.
7. A journey or procession made by royal courts and often portrayed on Elizabethan stages.

Advise the prince; no doubt, an easy tool,
Deferential, glad to be of use,   115
Politic, cautious, and meticulous;
Full of high sentence,[8] but a bit obtuse;
At times, indeed, almost ridiculous—
Almost, at times, the Fool.

I grow old . . . I grow old . . .   120
I shall wear the bottoms of my trousers rolled.

Shall I part my hair behind? Do I dare to eat a peach?
I shall wear white flannel trousers, and walk upon the beach.
I have heard the mermaids singing, each to each.

I do not think that they will sing to me.   125

I have seen them riding seaward on the waves
Combing the white hair of the waves blown back
When the wind blows the water white and black.

We have lingered in the chambers of the sea
By sea-girls wreathed with seaweed red and brown   130
Till human voices wake us, and we drown.

1915, 1917

Sweeney among the Nightingales[1]

ὤμοι, πέπληγμαι καιρίαν πληγὴν ἔσω.[2]

Apeneck Sweeney spreads his knees
Letting his arms hang down to laugh,
The zebra stripes along his jaw
Swelling to maculate giraffe.

The circles of the stormy moon   5
Slide westward toward the River Plate,[3]
Death and the Raven drift above
And Sweeney guards the hornèd gate.[4]

Gloomy Orion and the Dog[5]
Are veiled; and hushed the shrunken seas;   10

---

8. Opinions, sententiousness.
1. The poem juxtaposes the imminent death of Sweeney in a nonheroic present, the ritual sacrifice of Christ enacted in a convent, the murder (by his wife and her lover) of Agamemnon in Aeschylus's tragedy, and the tragedy of Philomela in Greek mythology. Raped by her sister's husband, who then cut out her tongue, Philomela was transformed into a nightingale whose song springs from the violation she has suffered but cannot report.

2. Alas, I am struck a mortal blow within (Greek; Aeschylus's *Agamemnon*); this is Agamemnon's cry when he is murdered.
3. Estuary between Argentina and Uruguay.
4. The Gates of Horn, in the Greek underworld; dreams pass through them to the upper world.
5. Sirius, also called the Dog Star: the brightest star in the sky. "Orion": a constellation representing the mythical hunter; Sirius is said to be his dog.

The person in the Spanish cape
Tries to sit on Sweeney's knees

Slips and pulls the table cloth
Overturns a coffee-cup,
Reorganised upon the floor   15
She yawns and draws a stocking up;

The silent man in mocha brown
Sprawls at the window-sill and gapes;
The waiter brings in oranges
Bananas figs and hothouse grapes;   20

The silent vertebrate in brown
Contracts and concentrates, withdraws;
Rachel *née* Rabinovitch
Tears at the grapes with murderous paws;

She and the lady in the cape   25
Are suspect, thought to be in league;
Therefore the man with heavy eyes
Declines the gambit, shows fatigue,

Leaves the room and reappears
Outside the window, leaning in,   30
Branches of wistaria
Circumscribe a golden grin;

The host with someone indistinct
Converses at the door apart,
The nightingales are singing near   35
The Convent of the Sacred Heart,

And sang within the bloody wood
When Agamemnon cried aloud
And let their liquid siftings fall
To stain the stiff dishonoured shroud.   40

1918, 1919

From Tradition and the Individual Talent[1]

In English writing we seldom speak of tradition, though we occasionally apply
its name in deploring its absence. We cannot refer to "the tradition" or to "a
tradition"; at most, we employ the adjective in saying that the poetry of So-and-
so is "traditional" or even "too traditional." Seldom, perhaps, does the word
appear except in a phrase of censure. If otherwise, it is vaguely approbative,
with the implication, as to the work approved, of some pleasing archaeologi-
cal reconstruction. You can hardly make the word agreeable to English ears
without this comfortable reference to the reassuring science of archaeology.

---

1. From *The Sacred Wood* (1920), first published in the *Egoist* (1919). The text is that of *Selected Essays*
(1951).

Certainly the word is not likely to appear in our appreciations of living or dead writers. Every nation, every race, has not only its own creative, but its own critical turn of mind; and is even more oblivious of the shortcomings and limitations of its critical habits than of those of its creative genius. We know, or think we know, from the enormous mass of critical writing that has appeared in the French language the critical method or habit of the French; we only conclude (we are such unconscious people) that the French are "more critical" than we, and sometimes even plume ourselves a little with the fact, as if the French were the less spontaneous. Perhaps they are; but we might remind ourselves that criticism is as inevitable as breathing, and that we should be none the worse for articulating what passes in our minds when we read a book and feel an emotion about it, for criticizing our own minds in their work of criticism. One of the facts that might come to light in this process is our tendency to insist, when we praise a poet, upon those aspects of his work in which he least resembles anyone else. In these aspects or parts of his work we pretend to find what is individual, what is the peculiar essence of the man. We dwell with satisfaction upon the poet's difference from his predecessors, especially his immediate predecessors; we endeavour to find something that can be isolated in order to be enjoyed. Whereas if we approach a poet without this prejudice we shall often find that not only the best, but the most individual parts of his work may be those in which the dead poets, his ancestors, assert their immortality most vigorously. And I do not mean the impressionable period of adolescence, but the period of full maturity.

Yet if the only form of tradition, of handing down, consisted in following the ways of the immediate generation before us in a blind or timid adherence to its successes, "tradition" should positively be discouraged. We have seen many such simple currents soon lost in the sand; and novelty is better than repetition. Tradition is a matter of much wider significance. It cannot be inherited, and if you want it you must obtain it by great labor. It involves, in the first place, the historical sense, which we may call nearly indispensable to anyone who would continue to be a poet beyond his twenty-fifth year; and the historical sense involves a perception, not only of the pastness of the past, but of its presence; the historical sense compels a man to write not merely with his own generation in his bones, but with a feeling that the whole of the literature of Europe from Homer and within it the whole of the literature of his own country has a simultaneous existence and composes a simultaneous order. This historical sense, which is a sense of the timeless as well as of the temporal and of the timeless and of the temporal together, is what makes a writer traditional. And it is at the same time what makes a writer most acutely conscious of his place in time, of his own contemporaneity.

No poet, no artist of any art, has his complete meaning alone. His significance, his appreciation is the appreciation of his relation to the dead poets and artists. You cannot value him alone; you must set him, for contrast and comparison, among the dead. I mean this as a principle of aesthetic, not merely historical, criticism. The necessity that he shall conform, that he shall cohere, is not onesided; what happens when a new work of art is created is something that happens simultaneously to all the works of art which preceded it. The existing monuments form an ideal order among themselves, which is modified by the introduction of the new (the really new) work of art among them. The existing order is complete before the new work arrives; for order to persist after the supervention of novelty, the *whole* existing order must be, if ever so slightly, altered; and so the relations, proportions, values of each work of art toward the whole are readjusted; and this is conformity between the old and the new. Whoever has approved this idea of order, of the form of European, of English literature will not find it preposterous that the past should be altered by the present as much as the present is directed by the past. And the poet who is aware of this will be aware of great difficulties and responsibilities.

* * *

II

Honest criticism and sensitive appreciation are directed not upon the poet but upon the poetry. If we attend to the confused cries of the newspaper critics and the susurrus of popular repetition that follows, we shall hear the names of poets in great numbers; if we seek not Blue-book[2] knowledge but the enjoyment of poetry, and ask for a poem, we shall seldom find it. I have tried to point out the importance of the relation of the poem to other poems by other authors, and suggested the conception of poetry as a living whole of all the poetry that has ever been written. The other aspect of this Impersonal theory of poetry is the relation of the poem to its author. And I hinted, by an analogy, that the mind of the mature poet differs from that of the immature one not precisely in any valuation of "personality," not being necessarily more interesting, or having "more to say," but rather by being a more finely perfected medium in which special, or very varied, feelings are at liberty to enter into new combinations.

The analogy was that of the catalyst. When the two gases previously mentioned are mixed in the presence of a filament of platinum, they form sulfurous acid. This combination takes place only if the platinum is present; nevertheless the newly formed acid contains no trace of platinum, and the platinum itself is apparently unaffected: has remained inert, neutral, and unchanged. The mind of the poet is the shred of platinum. It may partly or exclusively operate upon the experience of the man himself; but, the more perfect the artist, the more completely separate in him will be the man who suffers and the mind which creates; the more perfectly will the mind digest and transmute the passions which are its material.

* * *

It is not in his personal emotions, the emotions provoked by particular events in his life, that the poet is in any way remarkable or interesting. His particular emotions may be simple, or crude, or flat. The emotion in his poetry will be a very complex thing, but not with the complexity of the emotions of people who have very complex or unusual emotions in life. One error, in fact, of eccentricity in poetry is to seek for new human emotions to express, and in this search for novelty in the wrong place it discovers the perverse. The business of the poet is not to find new emotions, but to use the ordinary ones and, in working them up into poetry, to express feelings which are not in

---

2. Official guidebooks. "Susurrus": murmuring, buzzing (Latin).

actual emotions at all. And emotions which he has never experienced will serve his turn as well as those familiar to him. Consequently, we must believe that "emotion recollected in tranquillity"[3] is an inexact formula. For it is neither emotion, nor recollection, nor, without distortion of meaning, tranquillity. It is a concentration, and a new thing resulting from the concentration, of a very great number of experiences which to the practical and active person would not seem to be experiences at all; it is a concentration which does not happen consciously or of deliberation. These experiences are not "recollected," and they finally unite in an atmosphere which is "tranquil" only in that it is a passive attending upon the event. Of course this is not quite the whole story. There is a great deal, in the writing of poetry, which must be conscious and deliberate. In fact, the bad poet is usually unconscious where he ought to be conscious, and conscious where he ought to be unconscious. Both errors tend to make him "personal." Poetry is not a turning loose of emotion, but an escape from emotion; it is not the expression of personality, but an escape from personality. But, of course, only those who have personality and emotions know what it means to want to escape from these things.

III

ὁ δὲ νοῦς ἴσως θειότερόν τι χαὶ ἀπαθές ἐστιν.[4]

This essay proposes to halt at the frontiers of metaphysics or mysticism, and confine itself to such practical conclusions as can be applied by the responsible person interested in poetry. To divert interest from the poet to the poetry is a laudable aim: for it would conduce to a juster estimation of actual poetry, good and bad. There are many people who appreciate the expression of sincere emotion in verse, and there is a smaller number of people who can appreciate technical excellence. But very few know when there is an expression of *significant* emotion, emotion which has its life in the poem and not in the history of the poet. The emotion of art is impersonal. And the poet cannot reach this impersonality without surrendering himself wholly to the work to be done. And he is not likely to know what is to be done unless he lives in what is not merely the present, but the present moment of the past, unless he is conscious, not of what is dead, but of what is already living.

1919, 1920

---

3. From Wordsworth's "Preface" to *Lyrical Ballads* (2nd ed., 1800): "poetry takes its origin from emotion recollected in tranquility."

4. No doubt the mind is something divine and not subject to external impressions (Greek; Aristotle's *De Anima* [On the soul] 1.4).

Gerontion[1]

Thou hast nor youth nor age
But as it were an after dinner sleep
Dreaming of both.[2]

Here I am, an old man in a dry month,
Being read to by a boy, waiting for rain.
I was neither at the hot gates[3]
Nor fought in the warm rain
Nor knee deep in the salt-marsh, heaving a cutlass,   5
Bitten by flies, fought.
My house is a decayed house,
And the Jew squats on the window sill, the owner,
Spawned in some estaminet[4] of Antwerp,
Blistered in Brussels, patched and peeled in London.[5]   10
The goat coughs at night in the field overhead;
Rocks, moss, stonecrop, iron, merds.[6]
The woman keeps the kitchen, makes tea,
Sneezes at evening, poking the peevish gutter.
                              I an old man,   15
A dull head among windy spaces.

Signs are taken for wonders. 'We would see a sign!'[7]
The word within a word, unable to speak a word,
Swaddled with darkness. In the juvescence of the year
Came Christ the tiger   20

In depraved May,[8] dogwood and chestnut, flowering judas,
To be eaten, to be divided, to be drunk
Among whispers;[9] by Mr. Silvero
With caressing hands, at Limoges
Who walked all night in the next room;   25
By Hakagawa, bowing among the Titians;
By Madame de Tornquist, in the dark room
Shifting the candles; Fräulein von Kulp
Who turned in the hall, one hand on the door.
                    Vacant shuttles   30
Weave the wind. I have no ghosts,
An old man in a draughty house
Under a windy knob.

1. Eliot intended to reprint this dramatic monologue as a prelude to *The Waste Land* until persuaded not to by Ezra Pound. The title is derived from the Greek word meaning "an old man."
2. Lines spoken by the duke of Vienna to describe death in Shakespeare's *Measure for Measure* 3.1.32–34.
3. An allusion to Thermopylae, the mountain pass where the Spartans heroically resisted the Persians (480 B.C.E.).
4. Café. The anti-Semitic passage identifies the landlord with urban decay.
5. Allusions to symptoms of and cures for venereal disease.

6. Dung.
7. Echoes of the "signs and wonders" expected as testimony to Christ's divinity in John 4.48 and the demand "Master, we would see a sign from thee" in Matthew 12.38.
8. Cf. *The Education of Henry Adams* (1918), chapter 18: the "passionate depravity that marked the Maryland May."
9. In lines 18–22, Gerontion imagines Christ as a powerful beast, like "the Lion of the tribe of Juda" (Revelation 5.5). Line 22 alludes to dividing and eating the bread, and drinking the wine, in Christian Communion.

After such knowledge, what forgiveness? Think now
History has many cunning passages, contrived corridors   35
And issues, deceives with whispering ambitions,
Guides us by vanities. Think now
She gives when our attention is distracted
And what she gives, gives with such supple confusions
That the giving famishes the craving. Gives too late   40
What's not believed in, or is still believed,
In memory only, reconsidered passion. Gives too soon
Into weak hands, what's thought can be dispensed with
Till the refusal propagates a fear. Think
Neither fear nor courage saves us. Unnatural vices   45
Are fathered by our heroism. Virtues
Are forced upon us by our impudent crimes.
These tears are shaken from the wrath-bearing tree.

The tiger springs in the new year. Us he devours. Think at last
We have not reached conclusion, when I   50
Stiffen in a rented house. Think at last
I have not made this show purposelessly
And it is not by any concitation
Of the backward devils.
I would meet you upon this honestly.   55
I that was near your heart was removed therefrom
To lose beauty in terror, terror in inquisition.
I have lost my passion: why should I need to keep it
Since what is kept must be adulterated?
I have lost my sight, smell, hearing, taste and touch: 60
How should I use them for your closer contact?

These with a thousand small deliberations
Protract the profit of their chilled delirium,
Excite the membrane, when the sense has cooled,
With pungent sauces, multiply variety   65
In a wilderness of mirrors. What will the spider do,
Suspend its operations, will the weevil
Delay? De Bailhache, Fresca, Mrs. Cammel, whirled
Beyond the circuit of the shuddering Bear[1]
In fractured atoms. Gull against the wind, in the windy straits   70
Of Belle Isle, or running on the Horn.
White feathers in the snow, the Gulf claims,
And an old man driven by the Trades[2]
To a sleepy corner.

                          Tenants of the house,   75
Thoughts of a dry brain in a dry season.

                                                          1920

---

1. The polestar in the constellation the Bear.   2. Trade winds.

The Waste Land[1]

'Nam Sibyllam quidem Cumis ego ipse oculis meis vidi in ampulla
pendere, et cum illi pueri dicerent: Σίβυλλα τί θέλεις: respondebat
illa: ἀποθανεῖν θέλω.'[2]

FOR EZRA POUND
IL MIGLIOR FABBRO.[3]

I. The Burial of the Dead[4]

April is the cruellest month, breeding
Lilacs out of the dead land, mixing
Memory and desire, stirring
Dull roots with spring rain.
Winter kept us warm, covering   5
Earth in forgetful snow, feeding
A little life with dried tubers.
Summer surprised us, coming over the Starnbergersee[5]
With a shower of rain; we stopped in the colonnade,
And went on in sunlight, into the Hofgarten,[6]   10
And drank coffee, and talked for an hour.
Bin gar keine Russin, stamm' aus Litauen, echt deutsch.[7]
And when we were children, staying at the arch-duke's,
My cousin's, he took me out on a sled,
And I was frightened. He said, Marie,   15
Marie, hold on tight. And down we went.
In the mountains, there you feel free.
I read, much of the night, and go south in the winter.

What are the roots that clutch, what branches grow
Out of this stony rubbish? Son of man,[8]   20
You cannot say, or guess, for you know only
A heap of broken images, where the sun beats,
And the dead tree gives no shelter, the cricket no relief,[9]
And the dry stone no sound of water. Only
There is shadow under this red rock,[1]   25
(Come in under the shadow of this red rock),

1. Eliot's notes for the first hardcover edition of
The Waste Land opened with his acknowledgment
that "not only the title, but the plan and a good deal
of the incidental symbolism of the poem" were suggested by Jessie L. Weston's book on the Grail Legend, *From Ritual to Romance* (1920), and that he
was indebted also to James G. Frazer's *The Golden
Bough* (1890–1915), "especially the two volumes
Adonis, Attis, Osiris," which deal with vegetation
myths and fertility rites. Eliot's notes are incorporated in the footnotes to this text. Many critics
believe that the notes were added in a spirit of par-
ody. The numerous and extensive literary quotations add to the multivocal effect of the poem.
2. A quotation from Petronius's *Satyricon* (1st century C.E.) about the Sibyl (prophetess) of Cumae,
blessed with eternal life by Apollo but doomed to
perpetual old age, who guided Aeneas through
Hades in Virgil's *Aeneid:* "For once I myself saw
with my own eyes the Sibyl at Cumae hanging in a
cage, and when the boys said to her 'Sibyl, what do
you want?' she replied, 'I want to die.' "
3. "The better maker," the tribute in Dante's *Pur-*

gatorio 26.117 to the Provençal poet Arnaut
Daniel.
4. The title of the Anglican burial service.
5. A lake near Munich. Lines 8–16 were suggested by the Countess Marie Larisch's memoir,
My Past (1913).
6. A public park in Munich, with cafés; former
grounds of a Bavarian palace.
7. I am certainly not Russian; I come from Lithua-
nia, a true German (German).
8. "Cf. Ezekiel II, i" [Eliot's note]. There God
addresses the prophet Ezekiel as "Son of man" and
declares: "stand upon thy feet, and I will speak
unto thee."
9. "Cf. Ecclesiastes XII, v" [Eliot's note]. There
the preacher describes the bleakness of old age
when "the grasshopper shall be a burden, and
desire shall fail."
1. Cf. Isaiah 32.1–2 and the prophecy that the
reign of the Messiah "shall be . . . as rivers of water
in a dry place, as the shadow of a great rock in a
weary land."

And I will show you something different from either
Your shadow at morning striding behind you
Or your shadow at evening rising to meet you;
I will show you fear in a handful of dust.   30
              Frisch weht der Wind
              Der Heimat zu
              Mein Irisch Kind,
              Wo weilest du?[2]
'You gave me hyacinths first a year ago;   35
'They called me the hyacinth girl.'
—Yet when we came back, late, from the hyacinth[3] garden,
Your arms full, and your hair wet, I could not
Speak, and my eyes failed, I was neither
Living nor dead, and I knew nothing,   40
Looking into the heart of light, the silence.
Oed' und leer das Meer.[4]

Madame Sosostris,[5] famous clairvoyante,
Had a bad cold, nevertheless
Is known to be the wisest woman in Europe,   45
With a wicked pack of cards.[6] Here, said she,
Is your card, the drowned Phoenician Sailor,[7]
(Those are pearls that were in his eyes.[8] Look!)
Here is Belladonna, the Lady of the Rocks,[9]
The lady of situations.   50
Here is the man with three staves, and here the Wheel,
And here is the one-eyed merchant,[1] and this card,
Which is blank, is something he carries on his back,
Which I am forbidden to see. I do not find
The Hanged Man. Fear death by water.   55
I see crowds of people, walking round in a ring.
Thank you. If you see dear Mrs. Equitone,
Tell her I bring the horoscope myself:
One must be so careful these days.

---

2. "V. [see] *Tristan und Isolde*, I, verses 5–8" [Eliot's note]. In Wagner's opera, a sailor aboard Tristan's ship recalls his love back in Ireland: "Fresh blows the wind to the homeland; my Irish child, where are you waiting?"

3. The boy Hyacinth, in Ovid's *Metamorphoses* 10, was beloved by Apollo but slain by a jealous rival. The Greeks celebrated his festival in May.

4. "III, verse 24" [Eliot's note]. In *Tristan* III, verse 24, the dying Tristan, awaiting the ship that carries his beloved Isolde, is told that "Empty and barren is the sea."

5. Eliot derived the name from "Sesostris, the Sorceress of Ectabana," the pseudo-Egyptian name assumed by a woman who tells fortunes in Aldous Huxley's novel *Chrome Yellow* (1921). Sesostris was a 12th-dynasty Egyptian king.

6. The tarot deck of cards. Eliot's note to this passage reads: "I am not familiar with the exact constitution of the Tarot pack of cards, from which I have obviously departed to suit my own convenience. The Hanged Man, a member of the traditional pack, fits my purpose in two ways: because he is associated in my mind with the Hanged God

of Frazer, and because I associate him with the hooded figure in the passage of the disciples to Emmaus in Part V. The Phoenician Sailor and the Merchant appear later; also the 'crowds of people,' and Death by Water is executed in Part IV. The Man with Three Staves (an authentic member of the Tarot pack) I associate, quite arbitrarily, with the Fisher King himself."

7. A symbolic figure that includes "Mr. Eugenides, the Smyrna merchant" in Part III and "Phlebas the Phoenician" in Part IV. The ancient Phoenicians were seagoing merchants who spread Egyptian fertility cults throughout the Mediterranean.

8. The line is a quotation from Ariel's song in Shakespeare's *Tempest* 1.2.398. Prince Ferdinand, disconsolate because he thinks his father has drowned in the storm, is consoled when Ariel sings of a miraculous sea change that has transformed death into "something rich and strange."

9. Belladonna, literally "beautiful lady," is the name of both the poisonous plant deadly nightshade and a cosmetic.

1. These three figures are from the Tarot deck.

Unreal City,[2]   60
Under the brown fog of a winter dawn,
A crowd flowed over London Bridge, so many,
I had not thought death had undone so many.[3]
Sighs, short and infrequent, were exhaled,[4]
And each man fixed his eyes before his feet.   65
Flowed up the hill and down King William Street,
To where Saint Mary Woolnoth kept the hours
With a dead sound on the final stroke of nine.[5]
There I saw one I knew, and stopped him, crying: 'Stetson!
'You who were with me in the ships at Mylae![6]   70
'That corpse you planted last year in your garden,
'Has it begun to sprout? Will it bloom this year?
'Or has the sudden frost disturbed its bed?
'O keep the Dog far hence, that's friend to men,
'Or with his nails he'll dig it up again![7]   75
'You! hypocrite lecteur!—mon semblable,—mon frère!'[8]

II. A Game of Chess[9]

The Chair she sat in, like a burnished throne,[1]
Glowed on the marble, where the glass
Held up by standards wrought with fruited vines
From which a golden Cupidon peeped out   80
(Another hid his eyes behind his wing)
Doubled the flames of sevenbranched candelabra
Reflecting light upon the table as
The glitter of her jewels rose to meet it,
From satin cases poured in rich profusion.   85
In vials of ivory and coloured glass
Unstoppered, lurked her strange synthetic perfumes,
Unguent, powdered, or liquid—troubled, confused
And drowned the sense in odours; stirred by the air

2. "Cf. Baudelaire: 'Fourmillante cité, cité pleine de rêves, / Où le spectre en plein jour raccroche le passant' " [Eliot's note]. The lines are quoted from "Les Sept Vieillards" (The Seven Old Men), poem 93 of Les Fleurs du Mal (The Flowers of Evil, 1857) by the French Symbolist Charles Baudelaire (1821–1867), and may be translated from the French: "Swarming city, city full of dreams, / Where the specter in broad daylight accosts the passerby."
3. "Cf. Inferno III, 55–57" [Eliot's note]. The note continues to quote Dante's lines, which may be translated: "So long a train of people, / That I should never have believed / That death had undone so many."
4. "Cf. Inferno IV, 25–27" [Eliot's note]. Dante describes, in Limbo, the virtuous pagan dead, who, living before Christ, could not hope for salvation. The lines read: "Here, so far as I could tell by listening, / There was no lamentation except sighs, / which caused the eternal air to tremble."
5. "A phenomenon which I have often noticed" [Eliot's note]. The church named is in the financial district of London.
6. The battle of Mylae (260 B.C.E.) was a victory for Rome against Carthage. "Stetson": a hat manufacturer.
7. "Cf. the dirge in Webster's White Devil" [Eliot's

note]. In the play by John Webster (d. 1625), a crazed woman fears that the corpses of her decadent and murdered relatives might be disinterred: "But keep the wolf far thence, that's foe to men, / For with his nails he'll dig them up again." In echoing the lines Eliot altered "foe" to "friend" and the "wolf" to "Dog," invoking the brilliant Dog Star Sirius, whose rise in the heavens accompanied the flooding of the Nile and promised the return of fertility to Egypt.
8. "V. Baudelaire, Preface to Fleurs du Mal" [Eliot's note]. The last line of the introductory poem to Les Fleurs du Mal. "Au Lecteur" (To the Reader) may be translated from the French: "Hypocrite reader!—my likeness—my brother!"
9. The title suggests two plays by Thomas Middleton: A Game of Chess (1627), about a marriage of political expediency, and Women Beware Women (1657), containing a scene in which a mother-in-law is engrossed in a chess game while her daughter-in-law is seduced nearby. Eliot's note to line 118 refers readers to this play. It is now believed that much of this section reflects Eliot's disintegrating marriage.
1. "Cf. Antony and Cleopatra, II, ii. 190" [Eliot's note]. In Shakespeare's play, Enobarbus's description of Cleopatra begins: "The barge she sat in, like a burnish'd throne, / Burn'd on the water."

That freshened from the window, these ascended   90
In fattening the prolonged candle-flames,
Flung their smoke into the laquearia,[2]
Stirring the pattern on the coffered ceiling.
Huge sea-wood fed with copper
Burned green and orange, framed by the coloured stone,   95
In which sad light a carvèd dolphin swam.
Above the antique mantel was displayed
As though a window gave upon the sylvan scene[3]
The change of Philomel, by the barbarous king
So rudely forced; yet there the nightingale   100
Filled all the desert with inviolable voice
And still she cried, and still the world pursues,
'Jug Jug'[4] to dirty ears.
And other withered stumps of time
Were told upon the walls; staring forms   105
Leaned out, leaning, hushing the room enclosed.
Footsteps shuffled on the stair.
Under the firelight, under the brush, her hair
Spread out in fiery points
Glowed into words, then would be savagely still.   110

'My nerves are bad to-night. Yes, bad. Stay with me.
'Speak to me. Why do you never speak. Speak.
     'What are you thinking of? What thinking? What?
'I never know what you are thinking. Think.'

I think we are in rats' alley[5]   115
Where the dead men lost their bones.

'What is that noise?'
                    The wind under the door.[6]
'What is that noise now? What is the wind doing?'
                    Nothing again nothing.   120
                                        'Do
'You know nothing? Do you see nothing? Do you remember
'Nothing?'

          I remember
Those are pearls that were his eyes.   125
'Are you alive, or not? Is there nothing in your head?'
                    But

O O O O that Shakespeherian Rag—
It's so elegant

---

2. "Laquearia, V. *Aeneid*, I, 726" [Eliot's note]. Eliot quotes the passage containing the term *laquearia* ("paneled ceiling") and describing the banquet hall where Queen Dido welcomed Aeneas to Carthage. It reads: "Blazing torches hang from the gilded paneled ceiling, and torches conquer the night with flames." Aeneas became Dido's lover but abandoned her to continue his journey to found Rome, and she committed suicide.

3. Eliot's notes for lines 98–99 refer the reader to "Milton, *Paradise Lost*, IV, 140" for the phrase "sylvan scene" and to "Ovid, *Metamorphoses*, VI, Philomela." The lines splice the setting of Eve's temptation in the Garden of Eden, first described

through Satan's eyes, with the rape of Philomela by her sister's husband, King Tereus, and her transformation into the nightingale. Eliot's note for line 100 refers the reader ahead to the nightingale's song in Part III, line 204, of his own poem.

4. The conventional rendering of the nightingale's song in Elizabethan poetry.

5. Eliot's note refers readers to "Part III, l. 195."

6. "Cf. Webster: 'Is the wind in that door still?'" [Eliot's note]. In John Webster's *The Devil's Law Case* (1623) 3.2.162, a duke is cured of an infection by a wound intended to kill him; a surprised surgeon asks the quoted question, meaning, "Is he still alive?"

So intelligent   130
'What shall I do now? What shall I do?'
'I shall rush out as I am, and walk the street
'With my hair down, so. What shall we do tomorrow?
'What shall we ever do?'
               The hot water at ten.   135
And if it rains, a closed car at four.
And we shall play a game of chess,
Pressing lidless eyes and waiting for a knock upon the door.

When Lil's husband got demobbed,[7] I said—
I didn't mince my words, I said to her myself,   140
HURRY UP PLEASE ITS TIME[8]
Now Albert's coming back, make yourself a bit smart.
He'll want to know what you done with that money he gave you
To get yourself some teeth. He did, I was there.
You have them all out, Lil, and get a nice set,   145
He said, I swear, I can't bear to look at you.
And no more can't I, I said, and think of poor Albert,
He's been in the army four years, he wants a good time,
And if you don't give it him, there's others will, I said.
Oh is there, she said. Something o' that, I said.   150
Then I'll know who to thank, she said, and give me a straight look.
HURRY UP PLEASE ITS TIME
If you don't like it you can get on with it, I said.
Others can pick and choose if you can't.
But if Albert makes off, it won't be for lack of telling.   155
You ought to be ashamed, I said, to look so antique.
(And her only thirty-one.)
I can't help it, she said, pulling a long face,
It's them pills I took, to bring it off, she said.
(She's had five already, and nearly died of young George.)   160
The chemist[9] said it would be all right, but I've never been the same.
You *are* a proper fool, I said.
Well, if Albert won't leave you alone, there it is, I said,
What you get married for if you don't want children?
HURRY UP PLEASE ITS TIME   165
Well, that Sunday Albert was home, they had a hot gammon,[1]
And they asked me in to dinner, to get the beauty of it hot—
HURRY UP PLEASE ITS TIME
HURRY UP PLEASE ITS TIME
Goonight Bill, Goonight Lou. Goonight May. Goonight.   170
Ta ta. Goonight. Goonight.
Good night, ladies, good night, sweet ladies, good night, good night.[2]

III. The Fire Sermon[3]

The river's tent is broken; the last fingers of leaf
    Clutch and sink into the wet bank. The wind

---

7. Slang for "demobilized," discharged from the army.
8. Routine call of British bartenders to clear the pub at closing time.
9. Pharmacist.
1. Ham or bacon.

2. A double echo of the popular song "Good night ladies, we're going to leave you now" and mad Ophelia's farewell before drowning, in Shakespeare, *Hamlet* 4.5.72.
3. I.e., Buddha's Fire Sermon. See n. 7, p. 1595.

Crosses the brown land, unheard. The nymphs are departed. 175
Sweet Thames, run softly, till I end my song.[4]
The river bears no empty bottles, sandwich papers,
Silk handkerchiefs, cardboard boxes, cigarette ends
Or other testimony of summer nights. The nymphs are departed.
And their friends, the loitering heirs of City directors; 180
Departed, have left no addresses.
By the waters of Leman I sat down and wept[5] . . .
Sweet Thames, run softly till I end my song,
Sweet Thames, run softly, for I speak not loud or long.
But at my back in a cold blast I hear[6] 185
The rattle of the bones, and chuckle spread from ear to ear.

A rat crept softly through the vegetation
Dragging its slimy belly on the bank
While I was fishing in the dull canal
On a winter evening round behind the gashouse 190
Musing upon the king my brother's wreck[7]
And on the king my father's death before him.
White bodies naked on the low damp ground
And bones cast in a little low dry garret,
Rattled by the rat's foot only, year to year. 195
But at my back from time to time I hear
The sound of horns and motors, which shall bring
Sweeney to Mrs. Porter in the spring.[8]
O the moon shone bright on Mrs. Porter
And on her daughter 200
They wash their feet in soda water[9]
Et, O ces voix d'enfants, chantant dans la coupole!;[1]

Twit twit twit
Jug jug jug jug jug jug

So rudely forc'd. 205
Tereu[2]

Unreal City
Under the brown fog of a winter noon

4. "V. Spenser, *Prothalamion*" [Eliot's note]. The line is the refrain of the marriage song by Edmund Spenser (1552–1599), a pastoral celebration of marriage set along the Thames River near London.
5. The phrasing recalls Psalm 137.1, in which the exiled Jews mourn for their homeland: "By the rivers of Babylon, there we sat down, yea, we wept, when we remembered Zion." Lake Leman is another name for Lake Geneva, location of the sanatorium where Eliot wrote the bulk of *The Waste Land*. The archaic term *leman*, for "illicit mistress," led to the phrase "waters of leman" signifying lusts.
6. This line and line 196 echo Andrew Marvell (1621–1678), *To His Coy Mistress*, lines 21–24: "But at my back I always hear / Time's wingèd chariot hurrying near; / And yonder all before us lie / Deserts of vast eternity."
7. "Cf. *The Tempest*, I, ii" [Eliot's note]. Another allusion to Shakespeare's play, 1.2.389–90, where Prince Ferdinand, thinking his father dead, describes himself as "Sitting on a bank, / Weeping again the King my father's wrack."

8. "Cf. Day, *Parliament of Bees*: 'When of the sudden, listening, you shall hear, / A noise of horns and hunting, which shall bring / Actaeon to Diana in the spring, / Where all shall see her naked skin' " [Eliot's note]. Actaeon was changed into a stag and hunted to death as punishment for seeing Diana, goddess of chastity, bathing. John Day (1574–c. 1640), English poet.
9. "I do not know the origin of the ballad from which these lines are taken: it was reported to me from Sydney, Australia" [Eliot's note]. The bawdy song was popular among World War I troops.
1. "V. Verlaine, *Parsifal*" [Eliot's note]. The last line of the sonnet "Parsifal" by the French Symbolist Paul Verlaine (1844–1896) reads: "And O those children's voices singing in the cupola." In Wagner's opera, the feet of Parsifal, the questing knight, are washed before he enters the sanctuary of the Grail.
2. Alludes to Tereus, who raped Philomela, and like *jug* is a conventional Elizabethan term for the nightingale's song; also a slang pronunciation of *true*.

Mr. Eugenides, the Smyrna merchant
Unshaven, with a pocket full of currants   210
C.i.f.[3] London: documents at sight,
Asked me in demotic French
To luncheon at the Cannon Street Hotel
Followed by a weekend at the Metropole.

At the violet hour, when the eyes and back   215
Turn upward from the desk, when the human engine waits
Like a taxi throbbing waiting,
I Tiresias,[4] though blind, throbbing between two lives,
Old man with wrinkled female breasts, can see
At the violet hour, the evening hour that strives   220
Homeward, and brings the sailor home from sea,[5]
The typist home at teatime, clears her breakfast, lights
Her stove, and lays out food in tins.
Out of the window perilously spread
Her drying combinations touched by the sun's last rays,   225
On the divan are piled (at night her bed)
Stockings, slippers, camisoles, and stays.
I Tiresias, old man with wrinkled dugs
Perceived the scene, and foretold the rest—
I too awaited the expected guest.   230
He, the young man carbuncular, arrives,
A small house agent's clerk, with one bold stare,
One of the low on whom assurance sits
As a silk hat on a Bradford[6] millionaire.
The time is now propitious, as he guesses,   235
The meal is ended, she is bored and tired,
Endeavours to engage her in caresses
Which still are unreproved, if undesired.
Flushed and decided, he assaults at once;
Exploring hands encounter no defence;   240
His vanity requires no response,
And makes a welcome of indifference.

3. "The currants were quoted at a price 'carriage and insurance free to London'; and the Bill of Lading, etc. were to be handed to the buyer upon payment of the sight draft" [Eliot's note]. Some have suggested another possibility for the phrase "carriage and insurance free": "cost, insurance and freight."
4. Eliot's note reads: "Tiresias, although a mere spectator and not indeed a 'character,' is yet the most important personage in the poem, uniting all the rest. Just as the one-eyed merchant, seller of currants, melts into the Phoenician Sailor, and the latter is not wholly distinct from Ferdinand Prince of Naples, so all the women are one woman, and the two sexes meet in Tiresias. What Tiresias *sees*, in fact, is the substance of the poem. The whole passage from Ovid is of great anthropological interest." The note quotes the Latin passage from Ovid, *Metamorphoses* 2.421–43, which may be translated: "Jove [very drunk] said jokingly to Juno: 'You women have greater pleasure in love than that enjoyed by men.' She denied it. So they decided to refer the question to wise Tiresias who knew love from both points of view. For once, with a blow of his staff, he had separated two huge snakes who were copulating in the forest, and miraculously was changed instantly from a man into a woman and remained so for seven years. In the eighth year he saw the snakes again and said: 'If a blow against you is so powerful that it changes the sex of the author of it, now I shall strike you again.' With these words he struck them, and his former shape and masculinity were restored. As referee in the sportive quarrel, he supported Jove's claim. Juno, overly upset by the decision, condemned the arbitrator to eternal blindness. But the all-powerful father (inasmuch as no god can undo what has been done by another god) gave him the power of prophecy, with this honor compensating him for the loss of sight."
5. "This may not appear as exact as Sappho's lines, but I had in mind the 'longshore' or 'dory' fisherman, who returns at nightfall" [Eliot's note]. Fragment 149, by the female Greek poet Sappho (fl. 600 B.C.E.), celebrates the Evening Star who "brings homeward all those / Scattered by the dawn, / The sheep to fold . . . / The children to their mother's side." A more familiar echo is "Home is the sailor, home from sea" in "Requiem" by Robert Louis Stevenson (1850–1894).
6. A Yorkshire, England, manufacturing town where fortunes were made during World War I.

(And I Tiresias have foresuffered all
Enacted on this same divan or bed;
I who have sat by Thebes below the wall[7]
And walked among the lowest of the dead.)
Bestows one final patronising kiss,
And gropes his way, finding the stairs unlit . . .

She turns and looks a moment in the glass,
Hardly aware of her departed lover;
Her brain allows one half-formed thought to pass:
'Well now that's done: and I'm glad it's over.'
When lovely woman stoops to folly and
Paces about her room again, alone,
She smoothes her hair with automatic hand,
And puts a record on the gramophone.[8]

'This music crept by me upon the waters'[9]
And along the Strand, up Queen Victoria Street.
O City city, I can sometimes hear
Beside a public bar in Lower Thames Street,
The pleasant whining of a mandoline
And a clatter and a chatter from within
Where fishmen lounge at noon: where the walls
Of Magnus Martyr[1] hold
Inexplicable splendour of Ionian white and gold.

        The river sweats[2]
        Oil and tar
        The barges drift
        With the turning tide
        Red sails
        Wide
        To leeward, swing on the heavy spar.
        The barges wash
        Drifting logs
        Down Greenwich reach
        Past the Isle of Dogs.[3]
              Weialala leia
              Wallala leialala

245

250

255

260

265

270

275

---

7. Tiresias prophesied in the marketplace below the wall of Thebes, witnessed the tragedies of Oedipus and Creon in that city, and retained his prophetic powers in the underworld.
8. Eliot's note refers to the novel *The Vicar of Wakefield* (1766) by Oliver Goldsmith (1728–1774) and the song sung by Olivia when she revisits the scene of her seduction: "When lovely woman stoops to folly / And finds too late that men betray / What charm can soothe her melancholy, / What art can wash her guilt away? / The only art her guilt to cover, / To hide her shame from every eye, / To give repentance to her lover / And wring his bosom—is to die."
9. Eliot's note refers to Shakespeare's *The Tempest*, the scene where Ferdinand listens to Ariel's song telling of his father's miraculous sea change: "This music crept by me on the waters, / Allaying

both their fury and my passion / With its sweet air" (1.2.391–93).
1. "The interior of St. Magnus Martyr is to my mind one of the finest among [Christopher] Wren's interiors" [Eliot's note].
2. "The Song of the (three) Thames-daughters begins here. From line 292 to 306 inclusive they speak in turn. V. *Götterdämmerung*, III, i: the Rhine-daughters" [Eliot's note]. Lines 277–78 and 290–91 are from the lament of the Rhine maidens for the lost beauty of the Rhine River in the opera by Richard Wagner (1813–1883), *Die Götterdämmerung* (The Twilight of the Gods, 1876).
3. A peninsula in the Thames opposite Greenwich, a borough of London and the birthplace of Queen Elizabeth. Throughout this section Eliot has named places along the Thames River.

Elizabeth and Leicester[4]
Beating oars   280
The stern was formed
A gilded shell
Red and gold
The brisk swell
Rippled both shores   285
Southwest wind
Carried down stream
The peal of bells
White towers
    Weialala leia   290
    Wallala leialala

Trams and dusty trees.
Highbury bore me. Richmond and Kew
Undid me.[5] By Richmond I raised my knees
Supine on the floor of a narrow canoe.'   295
'My feet are at Moorgate, and my heart
Under my feet. After the event
He wept. He promised "a new start."
I made no comment. What should I resent?'

'On Margate Sands,   300
I can connect
Nothing with nothing.
The broken fingernails of dirty hands.
My people humble people who expect
Nothing.'   305
    la la

To Carthage then I came[6]

Burning burning burning burning[7]
O Lord Thou pluckest me out[8]
O Lord Thou pluckest   310

burning

IV. Death by Water

Phlebas the Phoenician, a fortnight dead,
Forgot the cry of gulls, and the deep sea swell

---

4. Reference to the romance between Queen Elizabeth and the earl of Leicester. Eliot's note refers to the historian James A. Froude, "*Elizabeth*, Vol. I. ch. iv, letter of [bishop] De Quadra [the ambassador] to Philip of Spain: 'In the afternoon we were in a barge, watching the games on the river. (The queen) was alone with Lord Robert and myself on the poop, when they began to talk nonsense, and went so far that Lord Robert at last said, as I was on the spot there was no reason why they should not be married if the queen pleased.' "
5. "Cf. *Purgatorio*, V, 133" [Eliot's note]. Eliot parodies Dante's lines, which may be translated: "Remember me, who am La Pia. / Siena made me, Maremma undid me."

6. "V. St. Augustine's *Confessions:* 'to Carthage then I came, where a cauldron of unholy loves sang all about mine ears' " [Eliot's note]. Augustine here recounts his licentious youth.
7. Eliot's note to lines 307–09 refers to "Buddha's Fire Sermon (which corresponds in importance to the Sermon on the Mount)" and "St. Augustine's Confessions." The "collocation of these two representatives of eastern and western asceticism, as the culmination of this part of the poem, is not an accident."
8. The line is from Augustine's *Confessions* and echoes also Zechariah 3.2, where Jehovah, rebuking Satan, calls the high priest Joshua "a brand plucked out of the fire."

And the profit and loss.

                    A current under sea   315
Picked his bones in whispers. As he rose and fell
He passed the stages of his age and youth
Entering the whirlpool.

                    Gentile or Jew
O you who turn the wheel and look to windward,   320
Consider Phlebas, who was once handsome and tall as you.

V. What the Thunder Said[9]

After the torchlight red on sweaty faces
After the frosty silence in the gardens
After the agony in stony places
The shouting and the crying   325
Prison and palace and reverberation
Of thunder of spring over distant mountains
He who was living is now dead
We who were living are now dying
With a little patience[1]   330

Here is no water but only rock
Rock and no water and the sandy road
The road winding above among the mountains
Which are mountains of rock without water
If there were water we should stop and drink   335
Amongst the rock one cannot stop or think
Sweat is dry and feet are in the sand
If there were only water amongst the rock
Dead mountain mouth of carious teeth that cannot spit
Here one can neither stand nor lie nor sit   340
There is not even silence in the mountains
But dry sterile thunder without rain
There is not even solitude in the mountains
But red sullen faces sneer and snarl
From doors of mudcracked houses   345
                    If there were water

    And no rock
    If there were rock
    And also water
    And water   350
    A spring
    A pool among the rock
    If there were the sound of water only
    Not the cicada[2]

9. "In the first part of Part V three themes are employed: the journey to Emmaus, the approach to the Chapel Perilous (see Miss Weston's book) and the present decay of eastern Europe" [Eliot's note]. During his disciples' journey to Emmaus, after his Crucifixion and Resurrection, Jesus walked alongside and conversed with them, but they did not rec-

ognize him (Luke 24.13–34).
1. The opening nine lines allude to Christ's imprisonment and trial, to his agony in the garden of Gethsemane, and to his Crucifixion on Golgotha (Calvary) and burial.
2. Grasshopper. Cf. line 23 and see n. 9, p. 1587.

And dry grass singing 355
But sound of water over a rock
Where the hermit-thrush[3] sings in the pine trees
Drip drop drip drop drop drop drop
But there is no water

Who is the third who walks always beside you?[4] 360
When I count, there are only you and I together
But when I look ahead up the white road
There is always another one walking beside you
Gliding wrapt in a brown mantle, hooded
I do not know whether a man or a woman 365
—But who is that on the other side of you?

What is that sound high in the air[5]
Murmur of maternal lamentation
Who are those hooded hordes swarming
Over endless plains, stumbling in cracked earth 370
Ringed by the flat horizon only
What is the city over the mountains
Cracks and reforms and bursts in the violet air
Falling towers
Jerusalem Athens Alexandria 375
Vienna London
Unreal

A woman drew her long black hair out tight
And fiddled whisper music on those strings
And bats with baby faces in the violet light 380
Whistled, and beat their wings
And crawled head downward down a blackened wall
And upside down in air were towers
Tolling reminiscent bells, that kept the hours
And voices singing out of empty cisterns and exhausted wells. 385

In this decayed hole among the mountains
In the faint moonlight, the grass is singing
Over the tumbled graves, about the chapel
There is the empty chapel, only the wind's home.
It has no windows, and the door swings, 390
Dry bones can harm no one.
Only a cock stood on the rooftree
Co co rico co co rico[6]

3. "This is . . . the hermit-thrush which I have heard in Quebec Province. Chapman says (*Handbook of Birds of Eastern North America*) 'it is most at home in secluded woodland and thickety retreats.' . . . Its 'water dripping song' is justly celebrated" [Eliot's note].

4. "The following lines were stimulated by the account of one of the Antarctic expeditions (I forget which, but I think one of Shackleton's): it was related that the party of explorers, at the extremity of their strength, had the constant delusion that there was *one more member* than could actually be counted" [Eliot's note].

5. Eliot's note quotes a passage in German from *Blick ins Chaos* (1920) by Hermann Hesse (1877–1962), which may be translated: "Already half of Europe, already at least half of Eastern Europe, on the way to Chaos, drives drunk in sacred infatuation along the edge of the precipice, since drunkenly, as though hymn-singing, as Dimitri Karamazov sang in [the novel] *The Brothers Karamazov* [1882] by Feodor Dostoevsky [1821–1881]. The offended bourgeois laughs at the songs; the saint and the seer hear them with tears."

6. A cock's crow in folklore signaled the departure of ghosts (as in Shakespeare's *Hamlet* 1.1.157ff.);

In a flash of lightning. Then a damp gust
Bringing rain   395

Ganga[7] was sunken, and the limp leaves
Waited for rain, while the black clouds
Gathered far distant, over Himavant.[8]
The jungle crouched, humped in silence.
Then spoke the thunder   400
Da[9]
Datta: what have we given?
My friend, blood shaking my heart
The awful daring of a moment's surrender
Which an age of prudence can never retract   405
By this, and this only, we have existed
Which is not to be found in our obituaries
Or in memories draped by the beneficient spider[1]
Or under seals broken by the lean solicitor
In our empty rooms   410
Da
Dayadhvam: I have heard the key[2]
Turn in the door once and turn once only
We think of the key, each in his prison
Thinking of the key, each confirms a prison   415
Only at nightfall, aethereal rumours
Revive for a moment a broken Coriolanus[3]
Da
Damyata: The boat responded
Gaily, to the hand expert with sail and oar   420
The sea was calm, your heart would have responded
Gaily, when invited, beating obedient
To controlling hands

                              I sat upon the shore
Fishing,[4] with the arid plain behind me   425
Shall I at least set my lands in order?[5]

---

in Matthew 26.34 and 74, a cock crowed, as Christ predicted, when Peter denied him three times.

7. The Indian river Ganges.

8. A mountain in the Himalayas.

9. " 'Datta, dayadhvam, damyata' (Give, sympathise, control). The fable of the meaning of the Thunder is found in the *Brihadaranyaka—Upanishad*, 5, 1" [Eliot's note]. In the Hindu legend, the injunction of Prajapati (supreme deity) is *Da*, which is interpreted in three different ways by gods, men, and demons, to mean "control ourselves," "give alms," and "have compassion." Prajapati assures them that when "the divine voice, The Thunder," repeats the syllable it means all three things and that therefore "one should practice . . . Self-Control, Alms-giving, and Compassion."

1. Eliot's note refers to Webster's *The White Devil* 5.6: "they'll remarry / Ere the worm pierce your winding-sheet, ere the spider / Make a thin curtain for your epitaphs."

2. "Cf. *Inferno*, XXXIII, 46" [Eliot's note]. At this point Ugolino recalls his imprisonment with his children, where they starved to death: "And I heard below the door of the horrible tower being locked up." Eliot's note continues: "Also F. H. Bradley, *Appearance and Reality*, p. 346. 'My external sensations are no less private to myself than are my thoughts or my feelings. In either case my experience falls within my own circle, a circle closed on the outside; and, with all its elements alike, every sphere is opaque to the others which surround it. . . . In brief, regarded as an existence which appears in a soul, the whole world for each is peculiar and private to that soul.' "

3. Roman patrician who defiantly chose self-exile when threatened with banishment by the leaders of the populace. He is the tragic protagonist in Shakespeare's *Coriolanus* (1608).

4. "V. Weston: *From Ritual to Romance*; chapter on the Fisher King" [Eliot's note].

5. Cf. Isaiah 38.1: "Thus saith the Lord, Set thine house in order: for thou shalt die, and not live."

London Bridge is falling down falling down falling down
Poi s'ascose nel foco che gli affina[6]
Quando fiam uti chelidon[7]—O swallow swallow
Le Prince d'Aquitaine à la tour abolie[8]   430
These fragments I have shored against my ruins
Why then Ile fit you. Hieronymo's mad againe.[9]
Datta. Dayadhvam. Damyata.
                    Shantih   shantih   shantih[1]

1921   1922

The Hollow Men

Mistah Kurtz—he dead.[1]
                    A penny for the Old Guy[2]

I

We are the hollow men
We are the stuffed men
Leaning together
Headpiece filled with straw. Alas!
Our dried voices, when   5
We whisper together
Are quiet and meaningless
As wind in dry grass
Or rats' feet over broken glass
In our dry cellar   10

Shape without form, shade without colour,
Paralysed force, gesture without motion;

Those who have crossed
With direct eyes, to death's other Kingdom

6. Eliot's note to *Purgatorio* 26 quotes in Italian the passage (lines 145–48) where the Provençal poet Arnaut Daniel, recalling his lusts, addresses Dante: "I pray you now, by the Goodness that guides you to the summit of this staircase, reflect in due season on my suffering." Then, in the line quoted in *The Waste Land*, "he hid himself in the fire that refines them."
7. Eliot's note refers to the *Pervigilium Veneris* (The Vigil of Venus), an anonymous Latin poem, and suggests a comparison with "Philomela in Parts II and III" of *The Waste Land*. The last stanzas of the *Pervigilium* recreate the myth of the nightingale in the image of a swallow, and the poet listening to the bird speaks the quoted line, "When shall I be as the swallow," and adds: "that I may cease to be silent." "O Swallow, Swallow" are the opening words of one of the songs interspersed in Tennyson's narrative poem *The Princess* (1847).
8. "V. Gerard de Nerval, Sonnet *El Desdichado*" [Eliot's note]. The line reads: "The Prince of Aquitaine in the ruined tower."
9. Eliot's note refers to Thomas Kyd's revenge play,

The Spanish Tragedy, subtitled *Hieronymo's Mad Againe* (1594). In it Hieronymo is asked to write a court play and he answers, "I'll fit you," in the double sense of "oblige" and "get even." He manages, although mad, to kill the murderers of his son by acting in the play and assigning parts appropriately, then commits suicide.
1. "Shantih. Repeated as here, a formal ending to an Upanishad. 'The peace which passeth understanding' is our equivalent to this word" [Eliot's note]. The Upanishad is a Vedic treatise, a sacred Hindu text.
1. Quotation from *Heart of Darkness*, by Joseph Conrad (1857–1924). Kurtz went into the African jungle as an official of a trading company and degenerated into an evil, tyrannical man. His dying words were "the horror!"
2. Guy Fawkes led a group of conspirators who planned to blow up the English House of Commons in 1605; he was caught and executed before the plan was carried out. On the day of his execution (November 5) children make straw effigies of the "guy" and beg for pennies for fireworks.

Remember us—if at all—not as lost   15
Violent souls, but only
As the hollow men
The stuffed men.

II

Eyes I dare not meet in dreams
In death's dream kingdom   20
These do not appear:
There, the eyes are
Sunlight on a broken column
There, is a tree swinging
And voices are   25
In the wind's singing
More distant and more solemn
Than a fading star.

Let me be no nearer
In death's dream kingdom   30
Let me also wear
Such deliberate disguises
Rat's coat, crowskin, crossed staves
In a field
Behaving as the wind behaves   35
No nearer—

Not that final meeting
In the twilight kingdom

III

This is the dead land
This is cactus land   40
Here the stone images
Are raised, here they receive
The supplication of a dead man's hand
Under the twinkle of a fading star.

Is it like this   45
In death's other kingdom
Waking alone
At the hour when we are
Trembling with tenderness
Lips that would kiss   50
Form prayers to broken stone.

IV

The eyes are not here
There are no eyes here
In this valley of dying stars

In this hollow valley   55
This broken jaw of our lost kingdoms

In this last of meeting places
We grope together
And avoid speech
Gathered on this beach of the tumid river   60

Sightless, unless
The eyes reappear
As the perpetual star
Multifoliate rose[3]
Of death's twilight kingdom   65
The hope only
Of empty men.

V

Here we go round the prickly pear
Prickly pear prickly pear
Here we go round the prickly pear   70
At five o'clock in the morning.[4]

Between the idea
And the reality
Between the motion
And the act   75
Falls the Shadow

                                            For Thine is the Kingdom[5]

Between the conception
And the creation
Between the emotion   80
And the response
Falls the Shadow

                                                    Life is very long

Between the desire
And the spasm   85
Between the potency
And the existence
Between the essence
And the descent
Falls the Shadow   90

3. Part 3 of *The Divine Comedy,* by Dante Alighieri (1265–1321), is a vision of Paradise. The souls of the saved in heaven range themselves around the deity in the figure of a "multifoliate rose" (*Paradiso* 28.30).

4. Allusion to a children's rhyming game, "Here we go round the mulberry bush," substituting a prickly pear cactus for the mulberry bush.
5. Part of a line from the Lord's Prayer.

For Thine is the Kingdom

For Thine is
Life is
For Thine is the

This is the way the world ends   95
This is the way the world ends
This is the way the world ends
Not with a bang but a whimper.

1925

Journey of the Magi[1]

'A cold coming we had of it,
Just the worst time of the year
For a journey, and such a long journey:
The ways deep and the weather sharp,
The very dead of winter.'[2]   5
And the camels galled, sore-footed, refractory,
Lying down in the melting snow.
There were times we regretted
The summer palaces on slopes, the terraces,
And the silken girls bringing sherbet.   10
Then the camel men cursing and grumbling
And running away, and wanting their liquor and women,
And the night-fires going out, and the lack of shelters,
And the cities hostile and the towns unfriendly
And the villages dirty and charging high prices: 15
A hard time we had of it.
At the end we preferred to travel all night,
Sleeping in snatches,
With the voices singing in our ears, saying
That this was all folly.   20

Then at dawn we came down to a temperate valley,
Wet, below the snow line, smelling of vegetation,
With a running stream and a water-mill beating the darkness,
And three trees on the low sky.
And an old white horse galloped away in the meadow.   25
Then we came to a tavern with vine-leaves over the lintel,
Six hands at an open door dicing for pieces of silver,
And feet kicking the empty wine-skins.
But there was no information, and so we continued
And arrived at evening, not a moment too soon   30
Finding the place; it was (you may say) satisfactory.

---

1. The three wise men, or kings, who followed the star of Bethlehem, bringing gifts to the newly born Christ.

2. These lines are adapted from the sermon preached at Christmas, in 1622, by Bishop Lancelot Andrewes.

All this was a long time ago, I remember,
And I would do it again, but set down
This set down
This: were we led all that way for   35
Birth or Death? There was a Birth, certainly,
We had evidence and no doubt. I had seen birth and death,
But had thought they were different; this Birth was
Hard and bitter agony for us, like Death, our death.
We returned to our places, these Kingdoms,   40
But no longer at ease here, in the old dispensation,
With an alien people clutching their gods.
I should be glad of another death.

1935

FROM FOUR QUARTETS

Burnt Norton[1]

τοῦ λόγον δ'εόντος ξυνοῦ ζώουσιν οἱ πολλοί
ὡς ἰδίαν ἔχοντες φρόνησιν.
                              I. p. 77. Fr. 2.
ὁδὸς ἄνω κάτω μία καὶ ὠυτή.
                              I. p. 89. Fr. 60.[2]
                —Diels: *Die Fragmente der Vorsokratiker*
                                        (Herakleitos)

I[3]

Time present and time past
Are both perhaps present in time future,
And time future contained in time past.
If all time is eternally present
All time is unredeemable.   5
What might have been is an abstraction
Remaining a perpetual possibility
Only in a world of speculation.
What might have been and what has been
Point to one end, which is always present.   10
Footfalls echo in the memory
Down the passage which we did not take

---

1. Eliot made "Burnt Norton," published originally as a separate poem, the basis and formal
model for "East Coker" (1940), "The Dry Salvages"
(1941), and "Little Gidding" (1942). Together they
make up *Four Quartets* (1943). The *Quartets* seeks
to capture those rare moments when eternity
"intersects" the temporal continuum, while treating also the relations between those moments and
the flux of time. Central to "Burnt Norton" is the
idea of the Spanish mystic St. John of the Cross
(1542–1591) that the ascent of a soul to union
with God is facilitated by memory and disciplined
meditation but that meditation is superseded by a
"dark night of the soul" that deepens paradoxically

the nearer one approaches the light of God. Burnt
Norton is a manor house in Gloucestershire, England.
2. The Greek epigraphs are from the pre-Socratic
philosopher Heraclitus (540?–475 B.C.E.) and may
be translated: "But although the Word is common
to all, the majority of people live as though they
had each an understanding peculiarly his own"
and "The way up and the way down are one and the
same."
3. The opening lines echo Ecclesiastes 3.15: "That
which hath been is now; and that which is to be
hath already been."

Towards the door we never opened
Into the rose-garden.[4] My words echo
Thus, in your mind.   15
                                   But to what purpose
Disturbing the dust on a bowl of rose-leaves
I do not know.
                           Other echoes
Inhabit the garden. Shall we follow?   20
Quick, said the bird, find them, find them,
Round the corner. Through the first gate,
Into our first world, shall we follow
The deception of the thrush? Into our first world.
There they were, dignified, invisible,   25
Moving without pressure, over the dead leaves,
In the autumn heat, through the vibrant air,
And the bird called, in response to
The unheard music hidden in the shrubbery,
And the unseen eyebeam crossed, for the roses   30
Had the look of flowers that are looked at.
There they were as our guests, accepted and accepting.
So we moved, and they, in a formal pattern,
Along the empty alley, into the box circle,[5]
To look down into the drained pool.   35
Dry the pool, dry concrete, brown edged,
And the pool was filled with water out of sunlight,
And the lotos rose, quietly, quietly,
The surface glittered out of heart of light,[6]
And they were behind us, reflected in the pool.   40
Then a cloud passed, and the pool was empty.
Go, said the bird, for the leaves were full of children,
Hidden excitedly, containing laughter.
Go, go, go, said the bird: human kind
Cannot bear very much reality.   45
Time past and time future
What might have been and what has been.
Point to one end, which is always present.

II

Garlic and sapphires in the mud
Clot the bedded axle-tree.   50
The trilling wire in the blood
Sings below inveterate scars
Appeasing long forgotten wars.
The dance along the artery
The circulation of the lymph   55
Are figured in the drift of stars
Ascend to summer in the tree

4. The rose is a symbol of sexual and spiritual love; in Christian traditions it is associated with the harmony of religious truth and with the Virgin Mary. The memory may be personal as well.

5. Evergreen boxwood shrubs, planted in a circle.
6. An echo of Dante, *Paradiso* 12.28–29: "From out of the heart of one of the new lights there moved a voice."

We move above the moving tree
In light upon the figured leaf[7]
And hear upon the sodden floor
Below, the boarhound and the boar
Pursue their pattern as before
But reconciled among the stars.

At the still point of the turning world. Neither flesh nor fleshless;
Neither from nor towards; at the still point, there the dance is,
But neither arrest nor movement. And do not call it fixity,
Where past and future are gathered. Neither movement from
        nor towards,
Neither ascent nor decline. Except for the point, the still point,
There would be no dance and there is only the dance.
I can only say, *there* we have been: but I cannot say where.
And I cannot say, how long, for that is to place it in time.
The inner freedom from the practical desire,
The release from action and suffering, release from the inner
And the outer compulsion, yet surrounded
By a grace of sense, a white light still and moving,
Erhebung[8] without motion, concentration
Without elimination, both a new world
And the old made explicit, understood
In the completion of its partial ecstasy,
The resolution of its partial horror.
Yet the enchainment of past and future
Woven in the weakness of the changing body,
Protects mankind from heaven and damnation
Which flesh cannot endure.
                    Time past and time future
Allow but a little consciousness.
To be conscious is not to be in time
But only in time can the moment in the rose-garden,
The moment in the arbour where the rain beat,
The moment in the draughty church at smokefall
Be remembered; involved with past and future.
Only through time time is conquered.

III

Here is a place of disaffection
Time before and time after
In a dim light: neither daylight
Investing form with lucid stillness
Turning shadow into transient beauty
With slow rotation suggesting permanence
Nor darkness to purify the soul
Emptying the sensual with deprivation
Cleansing affection from the temporal.
Neither plenitude nor vacancy. Only a flicker

7. An echo of the description of death in Tennyson, *In Memoriam* (1850) 43.10–12: "So that
still garden of the souls / In many a figured leaf
enrolls / The total world since life began."
8. Exaltation (German).

Over the strained time-ridden faces
Distracted from distraction by distraction
Filled with fancies and empty of meaning   105
Tumid apathy with no concentration
Men and bits of paper, whirled by the cold wind
That blows before and after time,
Wind in and out of unwholesome lungs
Time before and time after.   110
Eructation of unhealthy souls
Into the faded air, the torpid
Driven on the wind that sweeps the gloomy hills of London,
Hampstead and Clerkenwell, Campden and Putney,
Highgate, Primrose and Ludgate.⁹ Not here   115
Not here the darkness, in this twittering world.

Descend lower, descend only
Into the world of perpetual solitude,
World not world, but that which is not world,
Internal darkness, deprivation   120
And destitution of all property,
Desiccation of the world of sense,
Evacuation of the world of fancy,
Inoperancy of the world of spirit;
This is the one way, and the other   125
Is the same, not in movement
But abstention from movement; while the world moves
In appetency, on its metalled ways
Of time past and time future.

IV

Time and the bell have buried the day,   130
The black cloud carries the sun away.
Will the sunflower turn to us, will the clematis
Stray down, bend to us; tendril and spray
Clutch and cling?
Chill   135
Fingers of yew be curled
Down on us? After the kingfisher's wing
Has answered light to light, and is silent, the light is still
At the still point of the turning world.

V

Words move, music moves   140
Only in time; but that which is only living
Can only die. Words, after speech, reach
Into the silence. Only by the form, the pattern,
Can words or music reach
The stillness, as a Chinese jar still   145

9. Districts and neighborhoods in London.

Moves perpetually in its stillness.
Not the stillness of the violin, while the note lasts,
Not that only, but the co-existence,
Or say that the end precedes the beginning,
And the end and the beginning were always there   150
Before the beginning and after the end.
And all is always now. Words strain,
Crack and sometimes break, under the burden,
Under the tension, slip, slide, perish,
Decay with imprecision, will not stay in place,   155
Will not stay still. Shrieking voices
Scolding, mocking, or merely chattering,
Always assail them. The Word in the desert[1]
Is most attacked by voices of temptation,
The crying shadow in the funeral dance,   160
The loud lament of the disconsolate chimera.[2]
The detail of the pattern is movement,
As in the figure of the ten stairs.[3]
Desire itself is movement
Not in itself desirable;   165
Love is itself unmoving,
Only the cause and end of movement,
Timeless, and undesiring
Except in the aspect of time
Caught in the form of limitation   170
Between un-being and being.
Sudden in a shaft of sunlight
Even while the dust moves
There rises the hidden laughter
Of children in the foliage   175
Quick, now, here, now always—
Ridiculous the waste sad time
Stretching before and after.

                                                1936, 1943

1. An allusion to Christ's temptation in the wilderness (Luke 4.1–4).
2. A monster in Greek mythology and a symbol of fantasies and delusions.
3. An allusion to St. John of the Cross's figure for the soul's ascent to God: "The Ten Degrees of the Mystical Ladder of Divine Love."

EUGENE O'NEILL
1888–1953

Eugene O'Neill, the nation's first major playwright, the first to explore serious themes in the theater and to experiment with theatrical conventions, was born on October 16, 1888. His father was James O'Neill, an actor who made a fortune playing the lead role in a dramatization of Alexander Dumas's swashbuckling novel *The Count of Monte Cristo,* which he performed on tour more than five thousand times. O'Neill's mother, Ella Quinlan, the daughter of a successful Irish immigrant businessman in Cincinnati, hated backstage life and became addicted to morphine. An older brother, James Jr., was born in 1878 and during most of Eugene's childhood was away at various boarding schools. Later "Jamie," his brother's idol, became an actor and an alcoholic.

During O'Neill's childhood, his parents toured for part of every year, lived in New York City hotels for another part, and spent summers at their home in New London, Connecticut. O'Neill went to good preparatory schools and started college at Princeton in 1906. He quit after a year. For the next five years he drank and drifted—he eloped, but the marriage was quickly terminated, he shipped out to sea for a year, and he searched for gold in South America. Most of the time he spent in Greenwich Village—an area of lower Manhattan that was becoming home to artists and political radicals. After tuberculosis nearly killed him in 1912, O'Neill decided to stay sober and write plays. His Greenwich Village friends helped him: he joined a new experimental theater group called the Provincetown Players, because in the summer its members staged plays on a wharf in Provincetown, Massachusetts. For the rest of the year they used a small theater in the Village. They did O'Neill's one-act play *Thirst* in the summer of 1917.

The Provincetown group gave O'Neill his forum, and—working closely with Susan Glaspell—he gave them a place in American theater history. Play followed play in these early years; in 1913–14, he wrote nine plays; in 1916–17, six; in 1918, four. The works with likely appeal for general audiences were moved uptown from the Village to Broadway, where their stagings made O'Neill both famous and financially successful. Many of O'Neill's first plays were grim one-acters based on his experiences at sea. In these, the dialogue was a striking departure from stage rhetoric of the day: crude, natural, and slangy. Instead of the elegant witticisms of drawing-room comedy or the flowery eloquence of historical drama, audiences were faced with ships' holds and sailors' bars. An exaggerated realism, veering toward expressionism, was the mode of these earliest works.

Around 1920, his plays became longer and his aims more ambitious. He began to experiment with techniques to convey inner emotions that usually were not openly expressed in dramatizable action—the world of the mind, of memories and fears. He ignored standard play divisions of scenes and acts; paid no attention to the expected length of plays (the *Mourning Becomes Electra* sequence ran for nine hours); made his characters wear masks; split one character between two actors; and reintroduced ghosts, choruses, and Shakespearean-style monologue and direct addresses to the audience. He employed sets, lighting, and sounds to enhance emotion rather than to represent a real place. Important works from this period include *The Emperor Jones* (1920), in which, under stress, civilized veneer gives way to primitive fear; *The Hairy Ape* (1922), in which a sailor, becoming aware of how he is viewed by the upper class, degenerates into what he is perceived to be; *Desire under the Elms* (1924), about family conflict and desire; *The Great God Brown* (1926), exposing the inner life of a business magnate; and *Strange Interlude* (1928), similarly uncovering the hidden life of a beautiful woman. In different forms, all these plays subject their leading characters to experiences so intense that their "characters" disintegrate, exposing the chaotic or primitive interior self.

O'Neill's father had died in 1920, his mother in 1921, his brother in 1923. During the mid-1920s O'Neill became interested in dramatizing the complicated pattern of his family's life. He was influenced by the popularization of certain ideas of the Viennese psychoanalyst Sigmund Freud: the power of irrational drives; the existence of a subconscious; the roles of repression, suppression, and inhibition in the formation of personality and in adult suffering; the importance of sex; and above all the lifelong influence of parents. But where Freud posited a universal dynamic in the relation between children and parents and rooted development in biology, O'Neill saw each child's experiences as uniquely determined by particular parents. His strongly felt individualism came to focus on the family, rather than the person, as the fundamental human unit. He found inspiration and confirmation for this approach in classical

Greek drama, which had always centered on families. His 1931 *Mourning Becomes Electra*, based on the *Oresteia* cycle of the classical Greek playwright Aeschylus, situated the ancient story of family murder and divine retribution in Civil War America with great success.

Twice-married after the annulment of his early elopement, O'Neill began to suffer from a rare disease of the nervous system in the 1930s and lived in relative seclusion for the last twenty years of his life. Following the production of *Mourning Becomes Electra*, his output slowed noticeably. Much of his work of the 1930s and 1940s remained in manuscript until after his death, and there was a twelve-year gap in the staging of his plays—between *Days without End* (1934), which failed on Broadway, and *The Iceman Cometh*, in 1946, which also did poorly. As a young man, he had been attracted to socialists, communists, and anarchists, more on account of their rebelliousness and energetic nonconformity than their political doctrines. When his play about an interracial marriage appeared (*All God's Chillun Got Wings*, 1924), he insisted that it was not about race but about "the special lives of individual human beings. It is primarily a study of the two principal characters and their tragic struggle for happiness." Although, as the Edmund character who stands for O'Neill in *Long Day's Journey* shows, he did experience his Irishness partly in class terms, his radicalism was based on a sense that individual merit should be the human measure, not on a belief in class solidarity.

Three years after O'Neill's death, *Iceman* was successfully revived, and O'Neill's work reattained prominence. His widow released other plays, which were widely acclaimed in posthumous productions. Among such stagings were parts of a projected nine- or eleven-play sequence (critics differ in their interpretation of the surviving manuscript material) about an Irish family in America named the Melody family and some obviously autobiographical dramas about a family named the Tyrones. The Melody plays produced after O'Neill's death include *A Touch of the Poet*, produced in 1957, and *More Stately Mansions*, which was staged in 1967; the Tyrone plays include *Long Day's Journey into Night*, produced in 1956, and *A Moon for the Misbegotten* produced in 1957.

In inscribing the manuscript of *Long Day's Journey* to his wife, O'Neill wrote that he had faced his dead in this play, writing "with deep pity and understanding and forgiveness for *all* the four haunted Tyrones." By this he seemed to mean that his treatment made it impossible to blame any of the characters for the suffering they inflicted on the others; each Tyrone was both a victim and an oppressor, and none of them could escape. O'Neill's word *haunted* catches his sense that the Tyrones are at the mercy of the past—their psyches are the dwelling places of ghosts, and the word *ghosts* recurs throughout the play: ghosts of those they remember, those who influenced them, their younger selves, their dreams and ambitions, and their disappointments. A spectator or a first-time reader of the play may experience *Long Day's Journey* simply as unabating raw emotion, but study shows that O'Neill designed the play as a series of encounters—each character is placed with one, two, or three of the others, until every combination is worked through. At the same time that these various configurations are staged, the family is followed through one day, from the simulacrum of conventional family life in the morning to the tragic truth of their night. It is thus a literal day in the lives of the Tyrones, and also the Tyrones' journey through life toward death, that we witness.

Romantic, realistic, naturalistic, melodramatic, sentimental, cynical, poetic—the family dramas, indeed O'Neill's work in general, are all of these. Even while he made his characters espouse philosophical positions, O'Neill was not trying to write philosophical drama. Nor was he designing plays to fit into a familiar dramatic type: tragedy, comedy, and the like. He wanted to make plays conveying emotions of such intensity and complexity that the theater would become a vital force in American life. In all his works, the spectacle of emotional intensity was meant to produce emotional response in an audience—what Aristotle, in his *Poetics*, had called "catharsis." As one critic wrote, "The meaning and unity of his work lies not in any controlling intellectual idea and certainly not in a 'message,' but merely in the fact that each play is an experience of extraordinary intensity." O'Neill's plays have been translated and staged all over the world; he won the Pulitzer Prize four times and the Nobel Prize in 1936, the first and so far only American dramatist to do so.

The text is that of the Yale University Press Edition (1956).

Long Day's Journey into Night

CHARACTERS

JAMES TYRONE
MARY CAVAN TYRONE, *his wife*
JAMES TYRONE, JR., *their elder son*
EDMUND TYRONE, *their younger son*
CATHLEEN, *second girl*[1]

SCENES

ACT 1 *Living room of the Tyrones' summer home* 8:30 A.M. *of a day in August, 1912*
ACT 2 SCENE 1 *The same, around* 12:45
       SCENE 2 *The same, about a half hour later*
ACT 3 *The same, around* 6:30 *that evening*
ACT 4 *The same, around midnight*

Act 1

SCENE—*Living room of* JAMES TYRONE's *summer home on a morning in August, 1912.*

At rear are two double doorways with portieres. The one at right leads into a front parlor with the formally arranged, set appearance of a room rarely occupied. The other opens on a dark, windowless back parlor, never used except as a passage from living room to dining room. Against the wall between the doorways is a small bookcase, with a picture of Shakespeare above it, containing novels by Balzac, Zola, Stendhal, philosophical and sociological works by Schopenhauer, Nietzsche, Marx, Engels, Kropotkin, Max Sterner, plays by Ibsen, Shaw, Strindberg, poetry by Swinburne, Rossetti, Wilde, Ernest Dowson, Kipling, etc.[2]

In the right wall, rear, is a screen door leading out on the porch which extends halfway around the house. Farther forward, a series of three windows looks over the front lawn to the harbor and the avenue that runs along the water front. A small wicker table and an ordinary oak desk are against the wall, flanking the windows.

In the left wall, a similar series of windows looks out on the grounds in back of the house. Beneath them is a wicker couch with cushions, its head toward rear. Farther back is a large, glassed-in bookcase with sets of Dumas, Victor Hugo, Charles Lever, three sets of Shakespeare, The World's Best Literature in fifty large volumes, Hume's History of England, Thiers' History of the Consulate and Empire,

---

1. A servant.
2. A variety of 19th-century (especially late-19th-century) authors are cited. Nobody in the audience would be able to read the titles and authors on these books—an example of O'Neill's novelistic approach to theatrical detail, also seen in the minute physical descriptions he provides of the characters' appearance and behavior throughout.

Smollett's History of England, Gibbon's Roman Empire and miscellaneous volumes of old plays, poetry, and several histories of Ireland. The astonishing thing about these sets is that all the volumes have the look of having been read and reread.

The hardwood floor is nearly covered by a rug, inoffensive in design and color. At center is a round table with a green shaded reading lamp, the cord plugged in one of the four sockets in the chandelier above. Around the table within reading-light range are four chairs, three of them wicker armchairs, the fourth (at right front of table) a varnished oak rocker with leather bottom.

It is around 8:30. Sunshine comes through the windows at right.

As the curtain rises, the family have just finished breakfast. MARY TYRONE *and her husband enter together from the back parlor, coming from the dining room.*

MARY *is fifty-four, about medium height. She still has a young, graceful figure, a trifle plump, but showing little evidence of middle-aged waist and hips, although she is not tightly corseted. Her face is distinctly Irish in type. It must once have been extremely pretty, and is still striking. It does not match her healthy figure but is thin and pale with the bone structure prominent. Her nose is long and straight, her mouth wide with full, sensitive lips. She uses no rouge or any sort of make-up. Her high forehead is framed by thick, pure white hair. Accentuated by her pallor and white hair, her dark brown eyes appear black. They are unusually large and beautiful, with black brows and long curling lashes.*

What strikes one immediately is her extreme nervousness. Her hands are never still. They were once beautiful hands, with long, tapering fingers, but rheumatism has knotted the joints and warped the fingers, so that now they have an ugly crippled look. One avoids looking at them, the more so because one is conscious she is sensitive about their appearance and humiliated by her inability to control the nervousness which draws attention to them.

She is dressed simply but with a sure sense of what becomes her. Her hair is arranged with fastidious care. Her voice is soft and attractive. When she is merry, there is a touch of Irish lilt in it.

Her most appealing quality is the simple, unaffected charm of a shy convent-girl youthfulness she has never lost—an innate unworldly innocence.

JAMES TYRONE *is sixty-five but looks ten years younger. About five feet eight, broad-shouldered and deep-chested, he seems taller and slenderer because of his bearing, which has a soldierly quality of head up, chest out, stomach in, shoulders squared. His face has begun to break down but he is still remarkably good looking—a big, finely shaped head, a handsome profile, deep-set light-brown eyes. His grey hair is thin with a bald spot like a monk's tonsure.*

The stamp of his profession is unmistakably on him. Not that he indulges in any of the deliberate temperamental posturings of the stage star. He is by nature and preference a simple, unpretentious man, whose inclinations are still close to his humble beginnings and his Irish farmer forebears. But the actor shows in all his unconscious habits of speech, movement and gesture. These have the quality of belonging to a studied technique. His voice is remarkably fine, resonant and flexible, and he takes great pride in it.

His clothes, assuredly, do not costume any romantic part. He wears a thread-bare, ready-made, grey sack suit and shineless black shoes, a collar-less shirt with a thick white handkerchief knotted loosely around his throat. There is nothing picturesquely careless about this get-up. It is commonplace shabby. He believes in wearing his clothes to the limit of usefulness, is dressed now for gardening, and doesn't give a damn how he looks.

He has never been really sick a day in his life. He has no nerves. There is a lot of stolid, earthy peasant in him, mixed with streaks of sentimental melancholy and rare flashes of intuitive sensibility.

TYRONE's *arm is around his wife's waist as they appear from the back parlor. Entering the living room he gives her a playful hug.*

TYRONE   You're a fine armful now, Mary, with those twenty pounds you've gained.

MARY [*smiles affectionately*]   I've gotten too fat, you mean, dear. I really ought to reduce.

TYRONE   None of that, my lady! You're just right. We'll have no talk of reducing. Is that why you ate so little breakfast?

MARY   So little? I thought I ate a lot.

TYRONE   You didn't. Not as much as I'd like to see, anyway.

MARY [*teasingly*]   Oh you! You expect everyone to eat the enormous breakfast you do. No one else in the world could without dying of indigestion. [*She comes forward to stand by the right of table.*]

TYRONE [*following her*]   I hope I'm not as big a glutton as that sounds. [*with hearty satisfaction*] But thank God, I've kept my appetite and I've the digestion of a young man of twenty, if I am sixty-five.

MARY   You surely have, James. No one could deny that.
        [*She laughs and sits in the wicker armchair at right rear of table. He comes around in back of her and selects a cigar from a box on the table and cuts off the end with a little clipper. From the dining room* JAMIE's *and* EDMUND's *voices are heard. Mary turns her head that way.*]
Why did the boys stay in the dining room, I wonder? Cathleen must be waiting to clear the table.

TYRONE [*jokingly but with an undercurrent of resentment*]   It's a secret confab they don't want me to hear, I suppose. I'll bet they're cooking up some new scheme to touch the Old Man.
        [*She is silent on this, keeping her head turned toward their voices. Her hands appear on the table top, moving restlessly. He lights his cigar and sits down in the rocker at right of table, which is his chair, and puffs contentedly.*]
There's nothing like the first after-breakfast cigar, if it's a good one, and this new lot have the right mellow flavor. They're a great bargain, too. I got them dead cheap. It was McGuire put me on to them.

MARY [*a trifle acidly*]   I hope he didn't put you on to any new piece of property at the same time. His real estate bargains don't work out so well.

TYRONE [*defensively*]   I wouldn't say that, Mary. After all, he was the one who advised me to buy that place on Chestnut Street and I made a quick turnover on it for a fine profit.

MARY [*smiles now with teasing affection*]   I know. The famous one stroke of good luck. I'm sure McGuire never dreamed—[*Then she pats his hand.*] Never mind, James. I know it's a waste of breath trying to convince you you're not a cunning real estate speculator.

TYRONE [*huffily*]   I've no such idea. But land is land, and it's safer than the stocks and bonds of Wall Street swindlers. [*then placatingly*] But let's not argue about business this early in the morning.
        [*A pause. The boys' voices are again heard and one of them has a fit of coughing.* MARY *listens worriedly. Her fingers play nervously on the table top.*]

MARY   James, it's Edmund you ought to scold for not eating enough. He hardly touched anything except coffee. He needs to eat to keep up his strength. I keep telling him that but he says he simply has no appetite. Of course, there's nothing takes away your appetite like a bad summer cold.

TYRONE   Yes, it's only natural. So don't let yourself get worried—

MARY [*quickly*]   Oh, I'm not. I know he'll be all right in a few days if he takes care of himself. [*as if she wanted to dismiss the subject but can't*] But it does seem a shame he should have to be sick right now.

TYRONE   Yes, it is bad luck. [*He gives her a quick, worried look.*] But you mustn't let it upset you, Mary. Remember, you've got to take care of yourself, too.

MARY [*quickly*]   I'm not upset. There's nothing to be upset about. What makes you think I'm upset?

TYRONE   Why, nothing, except you've seemed a bit high-strung the past few days.

MARY [*forcing a smile*]   I have? Nonsense, dear. It's your imagination. [*with sudden tenseness*] You really must not watch me all the time, James. I mean, it makes me self-conscious.

TYRONE [*putting a hand over one of her nervously playing ones*]   Now, now, Mary. That's your imagination. If I've watched you it was to admire how fat and beautiful you looked. [*His voice is suddenly moved by deep feeling.*] I can't tell you the deep happiness it gives me, darling, to see you as you've been since you came back to us, your dear old self again. [*He leans over and kisses her cheek impulsively—then turning back adds with a constrained air*] So keep up the good work, Mary.

MARY [*has turned her head away*]   I will, dear. [*She gets up restlessly and goes to the windows at right.*] Thank heavens, the fog is gone. [*She turns back.*] I do feel out of sorts this morning. I wasn't able to get much sleep with that awful foghorn going all night long.

TYRONE   Yes, it's like having a sick whale in the back yard. It kept me awake, too.

MARY [*affectionately amused*]   Did it? You had a strange way of showing your restlessness. You were snoring so hard I couldn't tell which was the foghorn! [*She comes to him, laughing, and pats his cheek playfully.*] Ten foghorns couldn't disturb you. You haven't a nerve in you. You've never had.

TYRONE [*his vanity piqued—testily*]   Nonsense. You always exaggerate about my snoring.

MARY   I couldn't. If you could only hear yourself once—
  [*A burst of laughter comes from the dining room. She turns her head, smiling.*]
What's the joke, I wonder?

TYRONE [*grumpily*]   It's on me. I'll bet that much. It's always on the Old Man.

MARY [*teasingly*]   Yes, it's terrible the way we all pick on you, isn't it? You're so abused! [*She laughs—then with a pleased, relieved air*] Well, no matter what the joke is about, it's a relief to hear Edmund laugh. He's been so down in the mouth lately.

TYRONE [*ignoring this—resentfully*]   Some joke of Jamie's, I'll wager. He's forever making sneering fun of somebody, that one.

MARY   Now don't start in on poor Jamie, dear. [*without conviction*] He'll turn out all right in the end, you wait and see.

TYRONE   He'd better start soon, then. He's nearly thirty-four.

MARY [*ignoring this*]   Good heavens, are they going to stay in the dining room all day? [*She goes to the back parlor doorway and calls*] Jamie! Edmund! Come in the living room and give Cathleen a chance to clear the table.

[EDMUND *calls back, "We're coming, Mama." She goes back to the table.*]

TYRONE [*grumbling*]   You'd find excuses for him no matter what he did.

MARY [*sitting down beside him, pats his hand*]   Shush.

Their sons JAMES, JR., *and* EDMUND *enter together from the back parlor. They are both grinning, still chuckling over what had caused their laughter, and as they come forward they glance at their father and their grins grow broader.*

JAMIE, *the elder, is thirty-three. He has his father's broad-shouldered, deep-chested physique, is an inch taller and weighs less, but appears shorter and stouter because he lacks* TYRONE'*s bearing and graceful carriage. He also lacks his father's vitality. The signs of premature disintegration are on him. His face is still good looking, despite marks of dissipation, but it has never been handsome like* TYRONE'*s, although* JAMIE *resembles him rather than his mother. He has fine brown eyes, their color midway between his father's lighter and his mother's darker ones. His hair is thinning and already there is indication of a bald spot like* TYRONE'*s. His nose is unlike that of any other member of the family, pronouncedly aquiline. Combined with his habitual expression of cynicism it gives his countenance a Mephistophelian cast. But on the rare occasions when he smiles without sneering, his personality possesses the remnant of a humorous, romantic, irresponsible Irish charm—that of the beguiling ne'er-do-well, with a strain of the sentimentally poetic, attractive to women and popular with men.*

He is dressed in an old sack suit, not as shabby as TYRONE'*s, and wears a collar and tie. His fair skin is sunburned a reddish, freckled tan.*

EDMUND *is ten years younger than his brother, a couple of inches taller, thin and wiry. Where* JAMIE *takes after his father, with little resemblance to his mother,* EDMUND *looks like both his parents, but is more like his mother. Her big, dark eyes are the dominant feature in his long, narrow Irish face. His mouth has the same quality of hypersensitiveness hers possesses. His high fore-head is hers accentuated, with dark brown hair, sunbleached to red at the ends, brushed straight back from it. But his nose is his father's and his face in profile recalls* TYRONE'*s.* EDMUND'*s hands are noticeably like his mother's, with the same exceptionally long fingers. They even have to a minor degree the same nervousness. It is in the quality of extreme nervous sensibility that the likeness of* EDMUND *to his mother is most marked.*

He is plainly in bad health. Much thinner than he should be, his eyes appear feverish and his cheeks are sunken. His skin, in spite of being sunburned a deep brown, has a parched sallowness. He wears a shirt, collar and tie, no coat, old flannel trousers, brown sneakers.

MARY [*turns smilingly to them, in a merry tone that is a bit forced*]   I've been teasing your father about his snoring. [*to* TYRONE] I'll leave it to the boys, James. They must have heard you. No, not you, Jamie. I could hear you down the hall almost as bad as your father. You're like him. As soon as your head touches the pillow you're off and ten foghorns couldn't wake you. [*She stops abruptly, catching* JAMIE'*s eyes regarding her with an uneasy, probing look. Her smile vanishes and her manner becomes self-conscious.*] Why are you staring, Jamie? [*Her hands flutter up to her hair.*] Is my hair coming down? It's hard for me to do it up properly now. My eyes are getting so bad and I never can find my glasses.

JAMIE [*looks away guiltily*]   Your hair's all right, Mama. I was only thinking how well you look.

TYRONE [*heartily*]   Just what I've been telling her, Jamie. She's so fat and sassy, there'll soon be no holding her.

EDMUND   Yes, you certainly look grand, Mama. [*She is reassured and smiles at him lovingly. He winks with a kidding grin.*] I'll back you up about Papa's snoring. Gosh, what a racket!

JAMIE   I heard him, too. [*He quotes, putting on a ham-actor manner*] "The Moor, I know his trumpet."[3]
    [*His mother and brother laugh.*]

TYRONE [*scathingly*]   If it takes my snoring to make you remember Shakespeare instead of the dope sheet on the ponies, I hope I'll keep on with it.

MARY   Now, James! You mustn't be so touchy.
    [JAMIE *shrugs his shoulders and sits down in the chair on her right.*]

EDMUND [*irritably*]   Yes, for Pete's sake, Papa! The first thing after breakfast! Give it a rest, can't you? [*He slumps down in the chair at left of table next to his brother. His father ignores him.*]

MARY [*reprovingly*]   Your father wasn't finding fault with you. You don't have to always take Jamie's part. You'd think you were the one ten years older.

JAMIE [*boredly*]   What's all the fuss about? Let's forget it.

TYRONE [*contemptuously*]   Yes, forget! Forget everything and face nothing! It's a convenient philosophy if you've no ambition in life except to—

MARY   James, do be quiet. [*She puts an arm around his shoulder—coaxingly*] You must have gotten out of the wrong side of the bed this morning. [*to the boys, changing the subject*] What were you two grinning about like Cheshire cats when you came in? What was the joke?

TYRONE [*with a painful effort to be a good sport*]   Yes, let us in on it, lads. I told your mother I knew damned well it would be one on me, but never mind that, I'm used to it.

JAMIE [*dryly*]   Don't look at me. This is the Kid's story.

EDMUND [*grins*]   I meant to tell you last night, Papa, and forgot it. Yesterday when I went for a walk I dropped in at the Inn—

MARY [*worriedly*]   You shouldn't drink now, Edmund.

EDMUND [*ignoring this*]   And who do you think I met there, with a beautiful bun on,[4] but Shaughnessy, the tenant on that farm of yours.

MARY [*smiling*]   That dreadful man! But he is funny.

TYRONE [*scowling*]   He's not so funny when you're his landlord. He's a wily Shanty Mick, that one. He could hide behind a corkscrew. What's he complaining about now, Edmund—for I'm damned sure he's complaining. I suppose he wants his rent lowered. I let him have the place for almost nothing, just to keep someone on it, and he never pays that till I threaten to evict him.

EDMUND   No, he didn't beef about anything. He was so pleased with life he even bought a drink, and that's practically unheard of. He was delighted because he'd had a fight with your friend, Harker, the Standard Oil millionaire, and won a glorious victory.

---

3. Shakespeare's *Othello* 2.1.180.   4. I.e., drunk.

MARY [*with amused dismay*]   Oh, Lord! James, you'll really have to do something—

TYRONE   Bad luck to Shaughnessy, anyway!

JAMIE [*maliciously*]   I'll bet the next time you see Harker at the Club and give him the old respectful bow, he won't see you.

EDMUND   Yes. Harker will think you're no gentleman for harboring a tenant who isn't humble in the presence of a king of America.

TYRONE   Never mind the Socialist gabble. I don't care to listen—

MARY [*tactfully*]   Go on with your story, Edmund.

EDMUND [*grins at his father provocatively*]   Well, you remember, Papa, the ice pond on Harker's estate is right next to the farm, and you remember Shaughnessy keeps pigs. Well, it seems there's a break in the fence and the pigs have been bathing in the millionaire's ice pond, and Harker's foreman told him he was sure Shaughnessy had broken the fence on purpose to give his pigs a free wallow.

MARY [*shocked and amused*]   Good heavens!

TYRONE [*sourly, but with a trace of admiration*]   I'm sure he did, too, the dirty scallywag. It's like him.

EDMUND   So Harker came in person to rebuke Shaughnessy. [*He chuckles.*] A very bonehead play! If I needed any further proof that our ruling plutocrats, especially the ones who inherited their boodle, are not mental giants, that would clinch it.

TYRONE [*with appreciation, before he thinks*]   Yes, he'd be no match for Shaughnessy. [*then he growls*] Keep your damned anarchist remarks to yourself. I won't have them in my house. [*But he is full of eager anticipation.*] What happened?

EDMUND   Harker had as much chance as I would with Jack Johnson.[5] Shaughnessy got a few drinks under his belt and was waiting at the gate to welcome him. He told me he never gave Harker a chance to open his mouth. He began by shouting that he was no slave Standard Oil could trample on. He was a King of Ireland, if he had his rights, and scum was scum to him, no matter how much money it had stolen from the poor.

MARY   Oh, Lord! [*But she can't help laughing.*]

EDMUND   Then he accused Harker of making his foreman break down the fence to entice the pigs into the ice pond in order to destroy them. The poor pigs, Shaughnessy yelled, had caught their death of cold. Many of them were dying of pneumonia, and several others had been taken down with cholera from drinking the poisoned water. He told Harker he was hiring a lawyer to sue him for damages. And he wound up by saying that he had to put up with poison ivy, ticks, potato bugs, snakes and skunks on his farm, but he was an honest man who drew the line somewhere, and he'd be damned if he'd stand for a Standard Oil thief trespassing. So would Harker kindly remove his dirty feet from the premises before he sicked the dog on him. And Harker did! [*He and JAMIE laugh.*]

MARY [*shocked but giggling*]   Heavens, what a terrible tongue that man has!

TYRONE [*admiringly before he thinks*]   The damned old scoundrel! By God, you can't beat him! [*He laughs—then stops abruptly and scowls.*] The dirty blackguard! He'll get me in serious trouble yet. I hope you told him I'd be mad as hell—

5. Famous prizefighter, the first African American heavyweight boxing champion of the world.

EDMUND   I told him you'd be tickled to death over the great Irish victory, and so you are. Stop faking, Papa.

TYRONE   Well, I'm not tickled to death.

MARY [*teasingly*]   You are, too, James. You're simply delighted!

TYRONE   No, Mary, a joke is a joke, but—

EDMUND   I told Shaughnessy he should have reminded Harker that a Standard Oil millionaire ought to welcome the flavor of hog in his ice water as an appropriate touch.

TYRONE   The devil you did! [*frowning*] Keep your damned Socialist anarchist sentiments out of my affairs!

EDMUND   Shaughnessy almost wept because he hadn't thought of that one, but he said he'd include it in a letter he's writing to Harker, along with a few other insults he'd overlooked. [*He and* JAMIE *laugh.*]

TYRONE   What are you laughing at? There's nothing funny—A fine son you are to help that blackguard get me into a lawsuit!

MARY   Now, James, don't lose your temper.

TYRONE [*turns on* JAMIE]   And you're worse than he is, encouraging him. I suppose you're regretting you weren't there to prompt Shaughnessy with a few nastier insults. You've a fine talent for that, if for nothing else.

MARY   James! There's no reason to scold Jamie.
    [JAMIE *is about to make some sneering remark to his father, but he shrugs his shoulders.*]

EDMUND [*with sudden nervous exasperation*]   Oh, for God's sake, Papa! If you're starting that stuff again, I'll beat it. [*He jumps up.*] I left my book upstairs, anyway. [*He goes to the front parlor, saying disgustedly*] God, Papa, I should think you'd get sick of hearing yourself—
    [*He disappears.* TYRONE *looks after him angrily.*]

MARY   You musn't mind Edmund, James. Remember he isn't well.
    [EDMUND *can be heard coughing as he goes upstairs. She adds nervously*] A summer cold makes anyone irritable.

JAMIE [*genuinely concerned*]   It's not just a cold he's got. The Kid is damned sick.
    [*His father gives him a sharp warning look but he doesn't see it.*]

MARY [*turns on him resentfully*]   Why do you say that? It *is* just a cold! Anyone can tell that! You always imagine things!

TYRONE [*with another warning glance at* JAMIE—*easily*]   All Jamie meant was Edmund might have a touch of something else, too, which makes his cold worse.

JAMIE   Sure, Mama. That's all I meant.

TYRONE   Doctor Hardy thinks it might be a bit of malarial fever he caught when he was in the tropics. If it is, quinine will soon cure it.

MARY [*a look of contemptuous hostility flashes across her face*]   Doctor Hardy! I wouldn't believe a thing he said, if he swore on a stack of Bibles! I know what doctors are. They're all alike. Anything, they don't care what, to keep you coming to them. [*She stops short, overcome by a fit of acute self-consciousness as she catches their eyes fixed on her. Her hands jerk nervously to her hair. She forces a smile.*] What is it? What are you looking at? Is my hair—?

TYRONE [*puts his arm around her—with guilty heartiness, giving her a playful hug*]   There's nothing wrong with your hair. The healthier and fatter you get, the vainer you become. You'll soon spend half the day primping before the mirror.

MARY [*half reassured*]   I really should have new glasses. My eyes are so bad now.

TYRONE [*with Irish blarney*]   Your eyes are beautiful, and well you know it. [*He gives her a kiss. Her face lights up with a charming, shy embarrassment. Suddenly and startlingly one sees in her face the girl she had once been, not a ghost of the dead, but still a living part of her.*]

MARY   You mustn't be so silly, James. Right in front of Jamie!

TYRONE   Oh, he's on to you, too. He knows this fuss about eyes and hair is only fishing for compliments. Eh, Jamie?

JAMIE [*his face has cleared, too, and there is an old boyish charm in his loving smile at his mother*]   Yes, You can't kid us, Mama.

MARY [*laughs and an Irish lilt comes into her voice*]   Go along with both of you! [*then she speaks with a girlish gravity*] But I did truly have beautiful hair once, didn't I, James?

TYRONE   The most beautiful in the world!

MARY   It was a rare shade of reddish brown and so long it came down below my knees. You ought to remember it, too, Jamie. It wasn't until after Edmund was born that I had a single grey hair. Then it began to turn white. [*The girlishness fades from her face.*]

TYRONE [*quickly*]   And that made it prettier than ever.

MARY [*again embarrassed and pleased*]   Will you listen to your father, Jamie—after thirty-five years of marriage! He isn't a great actor for nothing, is he? What's come over you, James? Are you pouring coals of fire on my head for teasing you about snoring? Well, then, I take it all back. It must have been only the foghorn I heard. [*She laughs, and they laugh with her. Then she changes to a brisk businesslike air.*] But I can't stay with you any longer, even to hear compliments. I must see the cook about dinner and the day's marketing. [*She gets up and sighs with humorous exaggeration.*] Bridget is so lazy. And so sly. She begins telling me about her relatives so I can't get a word in edgeways and scold her. Well, I might as well get it over. [*She goes to the back-parlor doorway, then turns, her face worried again.*] You mustn't make Edmund work on the grounds with you, James, remember. [*again with the strange obstinate set to her face*] Not that he isn't strong enough, but he'd perspire and he might catch more cold.

[*She disappears through the back parlor.* TYRONE *turns on* JAMIE *condemningly.*]

TYRONE   You're a fine lunkhead! Haven't you any sense? The one thing to avoid is saying anything that would get her more upset over Edmund.

JAMIE [*shrugging his shoulders*]   All right. Have it your way. I think it's the wrong idea to let Mama go on kidding yourself. It will only make the shock worse when she has to face it. Anyway, you can see she's deliberately fooling herself with that summer cold talk. She knows better.

TYRONE   Knows? Nobody knows yet.

JAMIE   Well, I do. I was with Edmund when he went to Doc Hardy on Monday. I heard him pull that touch of malaria stuff. He was stalling. That isn't what he thinks any more. You know it as well as I do. You talked to him when you went uptown yesterday, didn't you?

TYRONE   He couldn't say anything for sure yet. He's to phone me today before Edmund goes to him.

JAMIE [*slowly*]   He thinks it's consumption,[6] doesn't he, Papa?

TYRONE [*reluctantly*]   He said it might be.

JAMIE [*moved, his love for his brother coming out*]   Poor kid! God damn it! [*He turns on his father accusingly.*] It might never have happened if you'd sent him to a real doctor when he first got sick.

TYRONE   What's the matter with Hardy? He's always been our doctor up here.

JAMIE   Everything's the matter with him! Even in this hick burg he's rated third class! He's a cheap old quack!

TYRONE   That's right! Run him down! Run down everybody! Everyone is a fake to you!

JAMIE [*contemptuously*]   Hardy only charges a dollar. That's what makes you think he's a fine doctor!

TYRONE [*stung*]   That's enough! You're not drunk now! There's no excuse— [*He controls himself—a bit defensively*] If you mean I can't afford one of the fine society doctors who prey on the rich summer people—

JAMIE   Can't afford? You're one of the biggest property owners around here.

TYRONE   That doesn't mean I'm rich. It's all mortgaged—

JAMIE   Because you always buy more instead of paying off mortgages. If Edmund was a lousy acre of land you wanted, the sky would be the limit!

TYRONE   That's a lie! And your sneers against Doctor Hardy are lies! He doesn't put on frills, or have an office in a fashionable location, or drive around in an expensive automobile. That's what you pay for with those other five-dollars-to-look-at-your-tongue fellows, not their skill.

JAMIE [*with a scornful shrug of his shoulders*]   Oh, all right. I'm a fool to argue. You can't change the leopard's spots.

TYRONE [*with rising anger*]   No, you can't. You've taught me that lesson only too well. I've lost all hope you will ever change yours. You dare tell me what I can afford? You've never known the value of a dollar and never will! You've never saved a dollar in your life! At the end of each season you're penniless! You've thrown your salary away every week on whores and whiskey!

JAMIE   My salary! Christ!

TYRONE   It's more than you're worth, and you couldn't get that if it wasn't for me. If you weren't my son, there isn't a manager in the business who would give you a part, your reputation stinks so. As it is, I have to humble my pride and beg for you, saying you've turned over a new leaf, although I know it's a lie!

JAMIE   I never wanted to be an actor. You forced me on the stage.

TYRONE   That's a lie! You made no effort to find anything else to do. You left it to me to get you a job and I have no influence except in the theater. Forced you! You never wanted to do anything except loaf in barrooms! You'd have been content to sit back like a lazy lunk and sponge on me for the rest of your life! After all the money I'd wasted on your education, and all you did was get fired in disgrace from every college you went to!

JAMIE   Oh, for God's sake, don't drag up that ancient history!

6. Tuberculosis.

TYRONE It's not ancient history that you have to come home every summer to live on me.

JAMIE I earn my board and lodging working on the grounds. It saves you hiring a man.

TYRONE Bah! You have to be driven to do even that much! [*His anger ebbs into a weary complaint.*] I wouldn't give a damn if you ever displayed the slightest sign of gratitude. The only thanks is to have you sneer at me for a dirty miser, sneer at my profession, sneer at every damned thing in the world—except yourself.

JAMIE [*wryly*] That's not true, Papa. You can't hear me talking to myself, that's all.

TYRONE [*stares at him puzzledly, then quotes mechanically*] "Ingratitude, the vilest weed that grows"![7]

JAMIE I could see that line coming! God, how many thousand times—! [*He stops, bored with their quarrel, and shrugs his shoulders.*] All right, Papa. I'm a bum. Anything you like, so long as it stops the argument.

TYRONE [*with indignant appeal now*] If you'd get ambition in your head instead of folly! You're young yet. You could still make your mark. You had the talent to become a fine actor! You have it still. You're my son—!

JAMIE [*boredly*] Let's forget me. I'm not interested in the subject. Neither are you. [TYRONE *gives up.* JAMIE *goes on casually.*] What started us on this? Oh, Doc Hardy. When is he going to call you up about Edmund?

TYRONE Around lunch time. [*He pauses—then defensively*] I couldn't have sent Edmund to a better doctor. Hardy's treated him whenever he was sick up here, since he was knee high. He knows his constitution as no other doctor could. It's not a question of my being miserly, as you'd like to make out. [*bitterly*] And what could the finest specialist in America do for Edmund, after he's deliberately ruined his health by the mad life he's led ever since he was fired from college? Even before that when he was in prep school, he began dissipating and playing the Broadway sport to imitate you, when he's never had your constitution to stand it. You're a healthy hulk like me—or you were at his age—but he's always been a bundle of nerves like his mother. I've warned him for years his body couldn't stand it, but he wouldn't heed me, and now it's too late.

JAMIE [*sharply*] What do you mean, too late? You talk as if you thought—

TYRONE [*guiltily explosive*] Don't be a damned fool! I meant nothing but what's plain to anyone! His health has broken down and he may be an invalid for a long time.

JAMIE [*stares at his father, ignoring his explanation*] I know it's an Irish peasant idea consumption is fatal. It probably is when you live in a hovel on a bog, but over here, with modern treatment—

TYRONE Don't I know that! What are you gabbing about, anyway? And keep your dirty tongue off Ireland, with your sneers about peasants and bogs and hovels! [*accusingly*] The less you say about Edmund's sickness, the better for your conscience! You're more responsible than anyone!

JAMIE [*stung*] That's a lie! I won't stand for that, Papa!

TYRONE It's the truth! You've been the worst influence for him. He grew up admiring you as a hero! A fine example you set him! If you ever gave him advice except in the ways of rottenness, I've never heard of it! You

7. Shakespeare's *King Lear* 1.4.

made him old before his time, pumping him full of what you consider worldly wisdom, when he was too young to see that your mind was so poisoned by your own failure in life, you wanted to believe every man was a knave with his soul for sale, and every woman who wasn't a whore was a fool!

JAMIE [*with a defensive air of weary indifference again*]   All right. I did put Edmund wise to things, but not until I saw he'd started to raise hell, and knew he'd laugh at me if I tried the good advice, older brother stuff. All I did was make a pal of him and be absolutely frank so he'd learn from my mistakes that—[*He shrugs his shoulders—cynically*] Well, that if you can't be good you can at least be careful.

    [*His father snorts contemptuously. Suddenly* JAMIE *becomes really moved.*]

That's a rotten accusation, Papa. You know how much the Kid means to me, and how close we've always been—not like the usual brothers! I'd do anything for him.

TYRONE [*impressed—mollifyingly*]   I know you may have thought it was for the best, Jamie. I didn't say you did it deliberately to harm him.

JAMIE   Besides it's damned rot! I'd like to see anyone influence Edmund more than he wants to be. His quietness fools people into thinking they can do what they like with him. But he's stubborn as hell inside and what he does is what he wants to do, and to hell with anyone else! What had I to do with all the crazy stunts he's pulled in the last few years—working his way all over the map as a sailor and all that stuff. I thought that was a damned fool idea, and I told him so. You can't imagine me getting fun out of being on the beach in South America, or living in filthy dives, drinking rotgut, can you? No, thanks! I'll stick to Broadway, and a room with a bath, and bars that serve bonded Bourbon.

TYRONE   You and Broadway! It's made you what you are! [*with a touch of pride*] Whatever Edmund's done, he's had the guts to go off on his own, where he couldn't come whining to me the minute he was broke.

JAMIE [*stung into sneering jealousy*]   He's always come home broke finally, hasn't he? And what did his going away get him? Look at him now! [*He is suddenly shamefaced.*] Christ! That's a lousy thing to say. I don't mean that.

TYRONE [*decides to ignore this*]   He's been doing well on the paper. I was hoping he'd found the work he wants to do at last.

JAMIE [*sneering jealously again*]   A hick town rag! Whatever bull they hand you, they tell me he's a pretty bum reporter. If he weren't your son— [*ashamed again*] No, that's not true! They're glad to have him, but it's the special stuff that gets him by. Some of the poems and parodies he's written are damned good. [*grudgingly again*] Not that they'd ever get him anywhere on the big time. [*hastily*] But he's certainly made a damned good start.

TYRONE   Yes. He's made a start. You used to talk about wanting to become a newspaper man but you were never willing to start at the bottom. You expected—

JAMIE   Oh, for Christ's sake, Papa! Can't you lay off me!

TYRONE [*stares at him—then looks away—after a pause*]   It's damnable luck Edmund should be sick right now. It couldn't have come at a worse time for him. [*He adds, unable to conceal an almost furtive uneasiness*] Or for your mother. It's damnable she should have this to upset her, just when she needs peace and freedom from worry. She's been so well in the two months since she came home. [*His voice grows husky and trembles a little.*] It's been heaven to me. This home has been a home again. But I needn't tell you, Jamie.

[*His son looks at him, for the first time with an understanding sympathy. It is as if suddenly a deep bond of common feeling existed between them in which their antagonisms could be forgotten.*]

JAMIE [*almost gently*]   I've felt the same way, Papa.

TYRONE   Yes, this time you can see how strong and sure of herself she is. She's a different woman entirely from the other times. She has control of her nerves—or she had until Edmund got sick. Now you can feel her growing tense and frightened underneath. I wish to God we could keep the truth from her, but we can't if he has to be sent to a sanatorium. What makes it worse is her father died of consumption. She worshiped him and she's never forgotten. Yes, it will be hard for her. But she can do it! She has the will power now! We must help her, Jamie, in every way we can!

JAMIE [*moved*]   Of course, Papa. [*hesitantly*] Outside of nerves, she seems perfectly all right this morning.

TYRONE [*with hearty confidence now*]   Never better. She's full of fun and mischief. [*Suddenly he frowns at* JAMIE *suspiciously.*] Why do you say, seems? Why shouldn't she be all right? What the hell do you mean?

JAMIE   Don't start jumping down my throat! God, Papa, this ought to be one thing we can talk over frankly without a battle.

TYRONE   I'm sorry, Jamie. [*tensely*] But go on and tell me—

JAMIE   There's nothing to tell. I was all wrong. It's just that last night— Well, you know how it is, I can't forget the past. I can't help being suspicious. Any more than you can. [*bitterly*] That's the hell of it. And it makes it hell for Mama! She watches us watching her—

TYRONE [*sadly*]   I know. [*tensely*] Well, what was it! Can't you speak out!

JAMIE   Nothing, I tell you. Just my damned foolishness. Around three o'clock this morning, I woke up and heard her moving around in the spare room. Then she went to the bathroom. I pretended to be asleep. She stopped in the hall to listen, as if she wanted to make sure I was.

TYRONE [*with forced scorn*]   For God's sake, is that all? She told me herself the foghorn kept her awake all night, and every night since Edmund's been sick she's been up and down, going to his room to see how he was.

JAMIE [*eagerly*]   Yes, that's right, she did stop to listen outside his room. [*hesitantly again*] It was her being in the spare room that scared me. I couldn't help remembering that when she starts sleeping alone in there, it has always been a sign—

TYRONE   It isn't this time! It's easily explained. Where else could she go last night to get away from my snoring? [*He gives way to a burst of resentful anger.*] By God, how you can live with a mind that sees nothing but the worst motives behind everything is beyond me!

JAMIE [*stung*]   Don't pull that! I've just said I was all wrong. Don't you suppose I'm as glad of that as you are!

TYRONE [*mollifyingly*]   I'm sure you are, Jamie. [*A pause. His expression becomes somber. He speaks slowly with a superstitious dread.*] It would be like a curse she can't escape if worry over Edmund—It was her long sickness after bringing him into the world that she first—

JAMIE   She didn't have anything to do with it!

TYRONE   I'm not blaming her.

JAMIE [*bitingly*]   Then who are you blaming? Edmund, for being born?

TYRONE   You damned fool! No one was to blame.

JAMIE   The bastard of a doctor was! From what Mama's said, he was another cheap quack like Hardy! You wouldn't pay for a first-rate—

TYRONE   That's a lie! [*furiously*] So I'm to blame! That's what you're driving at, is it? You evil-minded loafer!

JAMIE [*warningly as he hears his mother in the dining room*]   Ssh!
    [*TYRONE gets hastily to his feet and goes to look out the windows at right. JAMIE speaks with a complete change of tone.*]
Well, if we're going to cut the front hedge today, we'd better go to work. [*MARY comes in from the back parlor. She gives a quick, suspicious glance from one to the other, her manner nervously self-conscious.*]

TYRONE [*turns from the window—with an actor's heartiness*]   Yes, it's too fine a morning to waste indoors arguing. Take a look out the window, Mary. There's no fog in the harbor. I'm sure the spell of it we've had is over now.

MARY [*going to him*]   I hope so, dear. [*to JAMIE, forcing a smile*] Did I actually hear you suggesting work on the front hedge, Jamie? Wonders will never cease! You must want pocket money badly.

JAMIE [*kiddingly*]   When don't I? [*He winks at her, with a derisive glance at his father.*] I expect a salary of at least one large iron man[8] at the end of the week—to carouse on!

MARY [*does not respond to his humor—her hands fluttering over the front of her dress*]   What were you two arguing about?

JAMIE [*shrugs his shoulders*]   The same old stuff.

MARY   I heard you say something about a doctor, and your father accusing you of being evil-minded.

JAMIE [*quickly*]   Oh, that. I was saying again Doc Hardy isn't my idea of the world's greatest physician.

MARY [*knows he is lying—vaguely*]   Oh. No, I wouldn't say he was either. [*changing the subject—forcing a smile*] That Bridget! I thought I'd never get away. She told me about her second cousin on the police force in St. Louis. [*then with nervous irritation*] Well, if you're going to work on the hedge why don't you go? [*hastily*] I mean, take advantage of the sunshine before the fog comes back. [*strangely, as if talking aloud to herself*] Because I know it will. [*Suddenly she is self-consciously aware that they are both staring fixedly at her—flurriedly, raising her hands*] Or I should say, the rheumatism in my hands knows. It's a better weather prophet than you are, James. [*She stares at her hands with fascinated repulsion.*] Ugh! How ugly they are! Who'd ever believe they were once beautiful?
    [*They stare at her with a growing dread.*]

TYRONE [*takes her hands and gently pushes them down*]   Now, now, Mary. None of that foolishness. They're the sweetest hands in the world.
    [*She smiles, her face lighting up, and kisses him gratefully. He turns to his son.*]
Come on Jamie. Your mother's right to scold us. The way to start work is to start work. The hot sun will sweat some of that booze fat off your middle.

8. Slang for "dollar."

[*He opens the screen door and goes out on the porch and disappears down a flight of steps leading to the ground.* JAMIE *rises from his chair and, taking off his coat, goes to the door. At the door he turns back but avoids looking at her, and she does not look at him.*]

JAMIE [*with an awkward, uneasy tenderness*]   We're all so proud of you, Mama, so darned happy.

[*She stiffens and stares at him with a frightened defiance. He flounders on.*]

But you've still got to be careful. You mustn't worry so much about Edmund. He'll be all right.

MARY [*with a stubborn, bitterly resentful look*]   Of course, he'll be all right. And I don't know what you mean, warning me to be careful.

JAMIE [*rebuffed and hurt, shrugs his shoulders*]   All right, Mama. I'm sorry I spoke.

[*He goes out on the porch. She waits rigidly until he disappears down the steps. Then she sinks down in the chair he had occupied, her face betraying a frightened, furtive desperation, her hands roving over the table top, aimlessly moving objects around. She hears* EDMUND *descending the stairs in the front hall. As he nears the bottom he has a fit of coughing. She springs to her feet, as if she wanted to run away from the sound, and goes quickly to the windows at right. She is looking out, apparently calm, as he enters from the front parlor, a book in one hand. She turns to him, her lips set in a welcoming, motherly smile.*]

MARY   Here you are. I was just going upstairs to look for you.

EDMUND   I waited until they went out. I don't want to mix up in any arguments. I feel too rotten.

MARY [*almost resentfully*]   Oh, I'm sure you don't feel half as badly as you make out. You're such a baby. You like to get us worried so we'll make a fuss over you. [*hastily*] I'm only teasing, dear. I know how miserably uncomfortable you must be. But you feel better today, don't you? [*worriedly, taking his arm*] All the same, you've grown much too thin. You need to rest all you can. Sit down and I'll make you comfortable.

[*He sits down in the rocking chair and she puts a pillow behind his back.*] There, How's that?

EDMUND   Grand. Thanks, Mama.

MARY [*kisses him—tenderly*]   All you need is your mother to nurse you. Big as you are, you're still the baby of the family to me, you know.

EDMUND [*takes her hand—with deep seriousness*]   Never mind me. You take care of yourself. That's all that counts.

MARY [*evading his eyes*]   But I am, dear. [*forcing a laugh*] Heavens, don't you see how fat I've grown! I'll have to have all my dresses let out. [*She turns away and goes to the windows at right. She attempts a light, amused tone.*] They've started clipping the hedge. Poor Jamie! How he hates working in front where everyone passing can see him. There go the Chatfields in their new Mercedes. It's a beautiful car, isn't it? Not like our second-hand Packard. Poor Jamie! He bent almost under the hedge so they wouldn't notice him. They bowed to your father and he bowed back as if he were taking a curtain call. In that filthy old suit I've tried to make him throw away. [*Her voice has grown bitter.*] Really, he ought to have more pride than to make such a show of himself.

EDMUND   He's right not to give a damn what anyone thinks. Jamie's a fool

to care about the Chatfields. For Pete's sake, who ever heard of them outside this hick burg?

MARY [*with satisfaction*]   No one. You're quite right, Edmund. Big frogs in
a small puddle. It is stupid of Jamie. [*She pauses, looking out the window—then with an undercurrent of lonely yearning*] Still, the Chatfields
and people like them stand for something. I mean they have decent, presentable homes they don't have to be ashamed of. They have friends who
entertain them and whom they entertain. They're not cut off from everyone. [*She turns back from the window.*] Not that I want anything to do
with them. I've always hated this town and everyone in it. You know that.
I never wanted to live here in the first place, but your father liked it and
insisted on building this house, and I've had to come here every summer.

EDMUND   Well, it's better than spending the summer in a New York hotel,
isn't it? And this town's not so bad. I like it well enough. I suppose because
it's the only home we've had.

MARY   I've never felt it was my home. It was wrong from the start. Everything was done in the cheapest way. Your father would never spend the
money to make it right. It's just as well we haven't any friends here. I'd be
ashamed to have them step in the door. But he's never wanted family
friends. He hates calling on people, or receiving them. All he likes is to
hobnob with men at the Club or in a barroom. Jamie and you are the
same way, but you're not to blame. You've never had a chance to meet
decent people here. I know you both would have been so different if you'd
been able to associate with nice girls instead of—You'd never have disgraced yourselves as you have, so that now no respectable parents will let
their daughters be seen with you.

EDMUND [*irritably*]   Oh, Mama, forget it! Who cares? Jamie and I would be
bored stiff. And about the Old Man, what's the use of talking? You can't
change him.

MARY [*mechanically rebuking*]   Don't call your father the Old Man. You
should have more respect. [*then dully*] I know it's useless to talk. But
sometimes I feel so lonely. [*Her lips quiver and she keeps her head turned
away.*]

EDMUND   Anyway, you've got to be fair, Mama. It may have been all his
fault in the beginning, but you know that later on, even if he'd wanted to,
we couldn't have had people here—[*He flounders guiltily.*] I mean, you
wouldn't have wanted them.

MARY [*wincing—her lips quivering pitifully*]   Don't. I can't bear having you
remind me.

EDMUND   Don't take it that way! Please, Mama! I'm trying to help. Because
it's bad for you to forget. The right way is to remember. So you'll always
be on your guard. You know what's happened before. [*miserably*] God,
Mama, you know I hate to remind you. I'm doing it because it's been so
wonderful having you home the way you've been, and it would be terrible—

MARY [*strickenly*]   Please, dear. I know you mean it for the best, but—[*A
defensive uneasiness comes into her voice again.*] I don't understand why you
should suddenly say such things. What put it in your mind this morning?

EDMUND [*evasively*]   Nothing. Just because I feel rotten and blue, I suppose.

MARY   Tell me the truth. Why are you so suspicious all of a sudden?

EDMUND   I'm not!

MARY   Oh, yes you are. I can feel it. Your father and Jamie, too—particularly Jamie.

EDMUND   Now don't start imagining things, Mama.

MARY [her hands fluttering]   It makes it so much harder, living in this atmosphere of constant suspicion, knowing everyone is spying on me, and none of you believe in me, or trust me.

EDMUND   That's crazy, Mama. We do trust you.

MARY   If there was only some place I could go to get away for a day, or even an afternoon, some woman friend I could talk to—not about anything serious, simply laugh and gossip and forget for a while—someone besides the servants—that stupid Cathleen!

EDMUND [gets up worriedly and puts his arm around her]   Stop it, Mama. You're getting yourself worked up over nothing.

MARY   Your father goes out. He meets his friends in barrooms or at the Club. You and Jamie have the boys you know. You go out. But I am alone. I've always been alone.

EDMUND [soothingly]   Come now! You know that's a fib. One of us always stays around to keep you company, or goes with you in the automobile when you take a drive.

MARY [bitterly]   Because you're afraid to trust me alone! [She turns on him—sharply.] I insist you tell me why you act so differently this morning—why you felt you had to remind me—

EDMUND [hesitates—then blurts out guiltily]   It's stupid. It's just that I wasn't asleep when you came in my room last night. You didn't go back to your and Papa's room. You went in the spare room for the rest of the night.

MARY   Because your father's snoring was driving me crazy! For heaven's sake, haven't I often used the spare room as my bedroom? [bitterly] But I see what you thought. That was when—

EDMUND [too vehemently]   I didn't think anything!

MARY   So you pretended to be asleep in order to spy on me!

EDMUND   No! I did it because I knew if you found out I was feverish and couldn't sleep, it would upset you.

MARY   Jamie was pretending to be asleep, too, I'm sure, and I suppose your father—

EDMUND   Stop it, Mama!

MARY   Oh, I can't bear it, Edmund, when even you—! [Her hands flutter up to pat her hair in their aimless, distracted way. Suddenly a strange undercurrent of revengefulness comes into her voice.] It would serve all of you right if it was true!

EDMUND   Mama! Don't say that! That's the way you talk when—

MARY   Stop suspecting me! Please, dear! You hurt me! I couldn't sleep because I was thinking about you. That's the real reason! I've been so worried ever since you've been sick. [She puts her arms around him and hugs him with a frightened, protective tenderness.]

EDMUND [soothingly]   That's foolishness. You know it's only a bad cold.

MARY   Yes, of course, I know that!

EDMUND   But listen, Mama. I want you to promise me that even if it should turn out to be something worse, you'll know I'll soon be all right again, anyway, and you won't worry yourself sick, and you'll keep on taking care of yourself—

MARY [*frightenedly*]   I won't listen when you're so silly! There's absolutely no reason to talk as if you expected something dreadful! Of course, I promise you. I give you my sacred word of honor! [*then with a sad bitterness*] But I suppose you're remembering I've promised before on my word of honor.

EDMUND   No!

MARY [*her bitterness receding into a resigned helplessness*]   I'm not blaming you, dear. How can you help it? How can any one of us forget? [*strangely*] That's what makes it so hard—for all of us. We can't forget.

EDMUND [*grabs her shoulder*]   Mama! Stop it!

MARY [*forcing a smile*]   All right, dear. I didn't mean to be so gloomy. Don't mind me. Here. Let me feel your head. Why, it's nice and cool. You certainly haven't any fever now.

EDMUND   Forget! It's you—

MARY   But I'm quite all right, dear. [*with a quick, strange, calculating, almost sly glance at him*] Except I naturally feel tired and nervous this morning, after such a bad night. I really ought to go upstairs and lie down until lunch time and take a nap.

[*He gives her an instinctive look of suspicion—then, ashamed of himself, looks quickly away. She hurries on nervously.*]

What are you going to do? Read here? It would be much better for you to go out in the fresh air and sunshine. But don't get overheated, remember. Be sure and wear a hat.

[*She stops, looking straight at him now. He avoids her eyes. There is a tense pause. Then she speaks jeeringly.*]

Or are you afraid to trust me alone?

EDMUND [*tormentedly*]   No! Can't you stop talking like that! I think you ought to take a nap. [*He goes to the screen door—forcing a joking tone*] I'll go down and help Jamie bear up. I love to lie in the shade and watch him work.

[*He forces a laugh in which she makes herself join. Then he goes out on the porch and disappears down the steps. Her first reaction is one of relief. She appears to relax. She sinks down in one of the wicker armchairs at rear of table and leans her head back, closing her eyes. But suddenly she grows terribly tense again. Her eyes open and she strains forward, seized by a fit of nervous panic. She begins a desperate battle with herself. Her long fingers, warped and knotted by rheumatism, drum on the arms of the chair, driven by an insistent life of their own, without her consent.*]

CURTAIN

Act 2

SCENE 1

SCENE—*The same. It is around quarter to one. No sunlight comes into the room now through the windows at right. Outside the day is still fine but increasingly sultry, with a faint haziness in the air which softens the glare of the sun.*

EDMUND *sits in the armchair at left of table, reading a book. Or rather he is trying to concentrate on it but cannot. He seems to be listening for some sound from upstairs. His manner is nervously apprehensive and he looks more sickly than in the previous act.*

The second girl, CATHLEEN, *enters from the back parlor. She carries a tray on which is a bottle of bonded Bourbon, several whiskey glasses and a pitcher of ice water. She is a buxom Irish peasant, in her early twenties, with a red-cheeked comely face, black hair and blue eyes—amiable, ignorant, clumsy, and possessed by a dense, well-meaning stupidity. She puts the tray on the table.* EDMUND *pretends to be so absorbed in his book he does not notice her, but she ignores this.*

CATHLEEN [*with garrulous familiarity*] Here's the whiskey. It'll be lunch time soon. Will I call your father and Mister Jamie, or will you?

EDMUND [*without looking up from his book*] You do it.

CATHLEEN It's a wonder your father wouldn't look at his watch once in a while. He's a divil for making the meals late, and then Bridget curses me as if I was to blame. But he's a grand handsome man, if he is old. You'll never see the day you're as good looking—nor Mister Jamie, either. [*She chuckles.*] I'll wager Mister Jamie wouldn't miss the time to stop work and have his drop of whiskey if he had a watch to his name!

EDMUND [*gives up trying to ignore her and grins*] You win that one.

CATHLEEN And here's another I'd win, that you're making me call them so you can sneak a drink before they come.

EDMUND Well, I hadn't thought of that—

CATHLEEN Oh no, not you! Butter wouldn't melt in your mouth, I suppose.

EDMUND But now you suggest it—

CATHLEEN [*suddenly primly virtuous*] I'd never suggest a man or a woman touch drink, Mister Edmund. Sure, didn't it kill an uncle of mine in the old country. [*relenting*] Still, a drop now and then is no harm when you're in low spirits, or have a bad cold.

EDMUND Thanks for handing me a good excuse. [*then with forced casualness*] You'd better call my mother, too.

CATHLEEN What for? She's always on time without any calling. God bless her, she has some consideration for the help.

EDMUND She's been taking a nap.

CATHLEEN She wasn't asleep when I finished my work upstairs a while back. She was lying down in the spare room with her eyes wide open. She'd a terrible headache, she said.

EDMUND [*his casualness more forced*] Oh well then, just call my father.

CATHLEEN [*goes to the screen door, grumbling good-naturedly*] No wonder my feet kill me each night. I won't walk out in this heat and get sunstroke. I'll call from the porch.

[*She goes out on the side porch, letting the screen door slam behind her, and disappears on her way to the front porch. A moment later she is heard shouting.*]

Mister Tyrone! Mister Jamie! It's time!

[EDMUND, *who has been staring frightenedly before him, forgetting his book, springs to his feet nervously.*]

EDMUND God, what a wench!

[*He grabs the bottle and pours a drink, adds ice water and drinks. As he does so, he hears someone coming in the front door. He puts the glass hastily on the tray and sits down again, opening his book.* JAMIE *comes in from the front parlor, his coat over his arm. He has taken off collar and tie and carries them in his hand. He is wiping sweat from his forehead*]

with a handkerchief. EDMUND *looks up as if his reading was interrupted.*
JAMIE *takes one look at the bottle and glasses and smiles cynically.*]

JAMIE   Sneaking one, eh? Cut out the bluff, Kid. You're a rottener actor
than I am.

EDMUND [*grins*]   Yes, I grabbed one while the going was good.

JAMIE [*puts a hand affectionately on his shoulder*]   That's better. Why kid
me? We're pals, aren't we?

EDMUND   I wasn't sure it was you coming.

JAMIE   I made the Old Man look at his watch. I was halfway up the walk
when Cathleen burst into song. Our wild Irish lark! She ought to be a
train announcer.

EDMUND   That's what drove me to drink. Why don't you sneak one while
you've got a chance?

JAMIE   I was thinking of that little thing. [*He goes quickly to the window at
right.*] The Old Man was talking to old Captain Turner. Yes, he's still at it.
[*He comes back and takes a drink.*] And now to cover up from his eagle eye.
[*He measures two drinks of water and pours them in the whiskey bottle and
shakes it up.*] There. That fixes it. [*He pours water in the glass and sets it on
the table by* EDMUND.] And here's the water you've been drinking.

EDMUND   Fine! You don't think it will fool him, do you?

JAMIE   Maybe not, but he can't prove it. [*Putting on his collar and tie.*] I
hope he doesn't forget lunch listening to himself talk. I'm hungry. [*He sits
across the table from* EDMUND—*irritably*] That's what I hate about working down in front. He puts on an act for every damned fool that comes
along.

EDMUND [*gloomily*]   You're in luck to be hungry. The way I feel I don't care
if I ever eat again.

JAMIE [*gives him a glance of concern*]   Listen, Kid. You know me. I've never
lectured you, but Doctor Hardy was right when he told you to cut out the
redeye.

EDMUND   Oh, I'm going to after he hands me the bad news this afternoon.
A few before then won't make any difference.

JAMIE [*hesitates—then slowly*]   I'm glad you've got your mind prepared for
bad news. It won't be such a jolt. [*He catches* EDMUND *staring at him.*] I
mean, it's a cinch you're really sick, and it would be wrong dope to kid
yourself.

EDMUND [*disturbed*]   I'm not. I know how rotten I feel, and the fever and
chills I get at night are no joke. I think Doctor Hardy's last guess was
right. It must be the damned malaria come back on me.

JAMIE   Maybe, but don't be too sure.

EDMUND   Why? What do you think it is?

JAMIE   Hell, how would I know? I'm no Doc. [*abruptly*] Where's Mama?

EDMUND   Upstairs.

JAMIE [*looks at him sharply*]   When did she go up?

EDMUND   Oh, about the time I came down to the hedge, I guess. She said
she was going to take a nap.

JAMIE   You didn't tell me—

EDMUND [*defensively*]   Why should I? What about it? She was tired out.
She didn't get much sleep last night.

JAMIE   I know she didn't.

[*A pause. The brothers avoid looking at each other.*]

EDMUND   That damned foghorn kept me awake, too.

    [*Another pause.*]

JAMIE   She's been upstairs alone all morning, eh? You haven't seen her?

EDMUND   No. I've been reading here. I wanted to give her a chance to sleep.

JAMIE   Is she coming down to lunch?

EDMUND   Of course.

JAMIE [*dryly*]   No of course about it. She might not want any lunch. Or she might start having most of her meals alone upstairs. That's happened, hasn't it?

EDMUND [*with frightened resentment*]   Cut it out, Jamie! Can't you think anything but—? [*persuasively*] You're all wrong to suspect anything. Cathleen saw her not long ago. Mama didn't tell her she wouldn't be down to lunch.

JAMIE   Then she wasn't taking a nap?

EDMUND   Not right then, but she was lying down, Cathleen said.

JAMIE   In the spare room?

EDMUND   Yes. For Pete's sake, what of it?

JAMIE [*bursts out*]   You damned fool! Why did you leave her alone so long? Why didn't you stick around?

EDMUND   Because she accused me—and you and Papa—of spying on her all the time and not trusting her. She made me feel ashamed. I know how rotten it must be for her. And she promised on her sacred word of honor—

JAMIE [*with a bitter weariness*]   You ought to know that doesn't mean anything.

EDMUND   It does this time!

JAMIE   That's what we thought the other times. [*He leans over the table to give his brother's arm an affectionate grasp.*] Listen, Kid, I know you think I'm a cynical bastard, but remember I've seen a lot more of this game than you have. You never knew what was really wrong until you were in prepschool. Papa and I kept it from you. But I was wise ten years or more before we had to tell you. I know the game backwards and I've been thinking all morning of the way she acted last night when she thought we were asleep. I haven't been able to think of anything else. And now you tell me she got you to leave her alone upstairs all morning.

EDMUND   She didn't! You're crazy!

JAMIE [*placatingly*]   All right, Kid. Don't start a battle with me. I hope as much as you do I'm crazy. I've been as happy as hell because I'd really begun to believe that this time—[*He stops—looking through the front parlor toward the hall—lowering his voice, hurriedly*] She's coming downstairs. You win on that. I guess I'm a damned suspicious louse.

    [*They grow tense with a hopeful, fearful expectancy.* JAMIE *mutters*] Damn! I wish I'd grabbed another drink.

EDMUND   Me, too.

    [*He coughs nervously and this brings on a real fit of coughing.* JAMIE *glances at him with worried pity.* MARY *enters from the front parlor. At first one notices no change except that she appears to be less nervous, to be more as she was when we first saw her after breakfast, but then one becomes aware that her eyes are brighter, and there is a peculiar detachment in her voice and manner, as if she were a little withdrawn from her words and actions.*]

1914–1945

Portrait of a German Officer, Marsden Hartley, 1914

Hartley's abstract "portrait" represents its wartime subject in fragments of ribbons and flags. Like T. S. Eliot's *The Waste Land,* this work registers a world blown to pieces. Completed while Hartley was living in Berlin and before the United States entered World War I, the painting memorializes Hartley's friend Karl von Freyburg, a German cavalry officer who had been killed in combat. Among the elements incorporated into the painting are Freyburg's initials (K v F) and the age at which he died (24). Hartley's *Portrait* is deliberately far from the kind of traditional memorial art that might have idealized an officer on his horse, but it is abstracted as well from the bloody mire of the war.

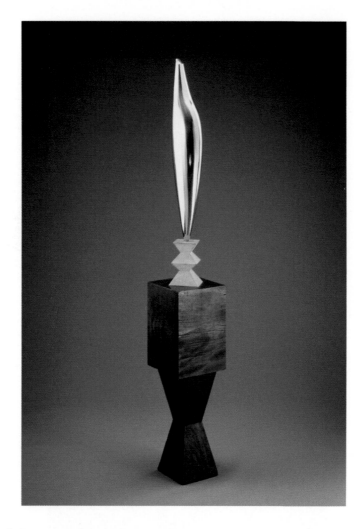

Golden Bird, Constantin Brancusi, 1919–20

Brancusi's famous series of bird sculptures (beginning in 1910 and running through the 1930s) began with more realistic bird forms and moved toward increasingly simple, abstract forms representing the pure idea of flight. The elaborately carved pedestal is Brancusi's own work and an integral part of the sculpture, which contrasts an earthy, primitivist ground with the smooth, soaring metal of modern flight—conjoining different aspects of the high modernist aesthetic in one object. *Golden Bird* was quickly embraced as a high modernist icon. In 1922 *The Dial*, an important modernist magazine, printed a photograph of the sculpture alongside Mina Loy's poem "Brancusi's Golden Bird."

Black Belt, Archibald J. Motley, 1934

Motley's painting captures the social breadth and vitality of Chicago's South Side and other emerging African American urban centers, using a stylized realism of vivid colors and flat perspective. His men and women include well-dressed couples, a matronly, homeward-bound woman, and the stoic, downcast worker in the foreground. In the middle background a man in a suit and hat glances warily over his shoulder toward the viewer; in his poem about the South Side, Langston Hughes explicitly challenged outsiders looking in on black life. Chicago's diverse African American community was an important setting for Nella Larsen's novel *Quicksand*.

River Rouge Plant, Charles Sheeler, 1932

This painting of a Ford Motor Company factory near Detroit grew out of a series of photographs that Sheeler took for an advertising agency. Along with other "precisionist" painters of the 1920s and 1930s, Sheeler was influenced by Futurism's celebration of the machine and by Cubism's breaking of traditional unified perspective into multiple flat planes. Sheeler's painterly style, however, remained realistic; he sought the broken planes and angles of Cubism in the objects themselves (here, the multiple white planes of the factory and its reflection) and avoided calling attention to the medium of paint—its texture and brushwork, the surface of the canvas—over what it represented. Like the poet Hart Crane, Sheeler found the materials for a modernist art in the American industrial landscape.

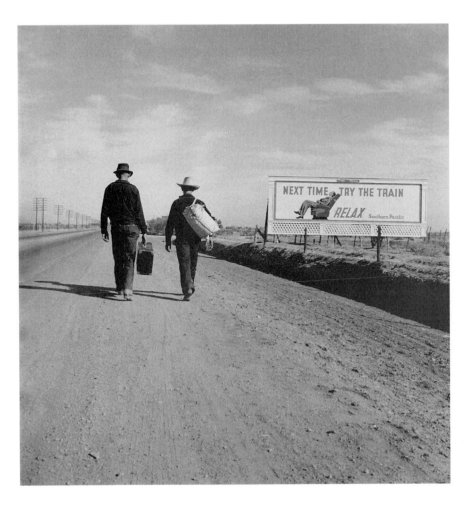

Towards Los Angeles, 1937, Dorothea Lange, 1937

During the Great Depression, the Farm Security Administration—one of the government agencies created by President Franklin D. Roosevelt in response to the economic emergency—employed a number of well-known documentary photographers. Lange's portraits of migrants displaced by the Dust Bowl are some of the most memorable images produced under FSA sponsorship. Like John Steinbeck in *The Grapes of Wrath,* Lange sought to create sympathy for the tenant farmers of the Southwest who had lost their homes and livelihoods. *Towards Los Angeles, 1937* contrasts the migrants' hard journey with an advertising billboard celebrating the speed and luxury of intercity rail travel.

From the Faraway, Nearby, Georgia O'Keeffe, 1937

O'Keeffe found inspiration in the landscapes of the American Southwest. Noted in the 1920s for her large, vivid paintings of flowers "with great sexy involutions" (as *Life* magazine observed), O'Keeffe in the 1930s began painting the bones she found scattered about the New Mexico desert. In this almost surrealist image, the sharp lines of the elk antlers floating in the foreground are echoed in softer form by the hills; the painting's perspective collapses the middle distance to put the faraway and the nearby on top of one another. O'Keeffe's paintings became modernist icons of the American landscape; the bones of the Southwest, she wrote, opened her work up to "the wideness and wonder of the world as I live in it."

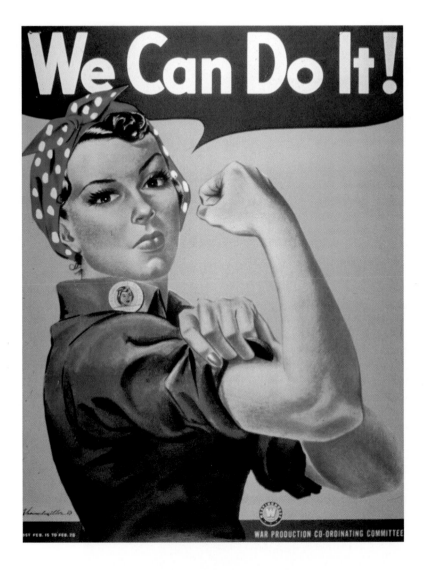

We Can Do It! ("Rosie the Riveter"), J. Howard Miller, c. 1942

World War II drew many women out of traditional roles in the home and into the industrial labor force and various forms of war-related work. Miller's poster *We Can Do It!*, produced by the defense contractor Westinghouse for the War Production Coordinating Committee, uses the bright colors and clean, simple lines of advertising to make the dislocations of traditional gender patterns familiar and acceptable, at least for the duration of the war. The worker's pert face and feminine grooming balance her assertively flexed bicep. A popular wartime song, "Rosie the Riveter," gave Miller's anonymous heroine her familiar nickname.

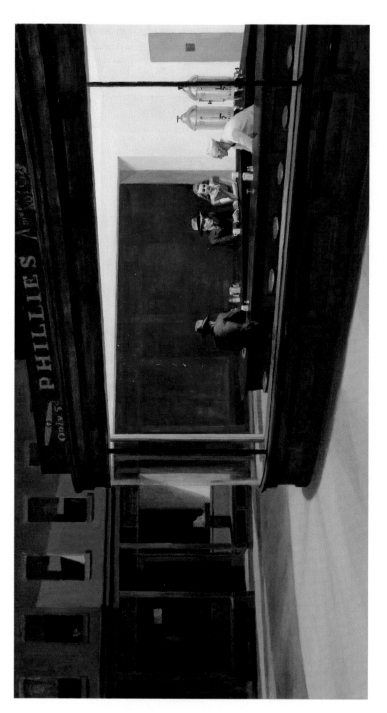

Night Hawks, Edward Hopper, 1942

Hopper's painting represents the night life of loners in the city. Its stylized realism preserves traditional perspective, accentuated by the deep view through the restaurant's large plate-glass window, but simplifies both realistic detail and painterly brushwork. *Night Hawks* depicts a clean, well-lighted restaurant against a dark urban background of uncertain danger or promise. A man and a woman sit at the counter, apparently a couple, but without intimate gestures their level of mutual trust or distrust remains unclear. The customer with his back to the viewer, like one of Chandler's detectives, keeps to himself but stands in for the viewer's anonymous perspective on the scene. In both style and subject this painting is often compared to the work of writers such as Ernest Hemingway and Raymond Chandler.

MARY [*goes worriedly to* EDMUND *and puts her arm around him*]   You mustn't cough like that. It's bad for your throat. You don't want to get a sore throat on top of your cold.

> [*She kisses him. He stops coughing and gives her a quick apprehensive glance, but if his suspicions are aroused her tenderness makes him renounce them and he believes what he wants to believe for the moment. On the other hand,* JAMIE *knows after one probing look at her that his suspicions are justified. His eyes fall to stare at the floor, his face sets in an expression of embittered, defensive cynicism.* MARY *goes on, half sitting on the arm of* EDMUND's *chair, her arm around him, so her face is above and behind his and he cannot look into her eyes.*]

But I seem to be always picking on you, telling you don't do this and don't do that. Forgive me, dear. It's just that I want to take care of you.

EDMUND   I know, Mama. How about you? Do you feel rested?

MARY   Yes, ever so much better. I've been lying down ever since you went out. It's what I needed after such a restless night. I don't feel nervous now.

EDMUND   That's fine.

> [*He pats her hand on his shoulder.* JAMIE *gives him a strange, almost contemptuous glance, wondering if his brother can really mean this.* EDMUND *does not notice but his mother does.*]

MARY [*in a forced teasing tone*]   Good heavens, how down in the mouth you look, Jamie. What's the matter now?

JAMIE [*without looking at her*]   Nothing.

MARY   Oh, I'd forgotten you've been working on the front hedge. That accounts for your sinking into the dumps, doesn't it?

JAMIE   If you want to think so, Mama.

MARY [*keeping her tone*]   Well, that's the effect it always has, isn't it? What a big baby you are! Isn't he, Edmund?

EDMUND   He's certainly a fool to care what anyone thinks.

MARY [*strangely*]   Yes, the only way is to make yourself not care.

> [*She catches* JAMIE *giving her a bitter glance and changes the subject.*]

Where is your father? I heard Cathleen call him.

EDMUND   Gabbing with old Captain Turner, Jamie says. He'll be late, as usual.

> [JAMIE *gets up and goes to the windows at right, glad of an excuse to turn his back.*]

MARY   I've told Cathleen time and again she must go wherever he is and tell him. The idea of screaming as if this were a cheap boardinghouse!

JAMIE [*looking out the window*]   She's down there now. [*sneeringly*] Interrupting the famous Beautiful Voice! She should have more respect.

MARY [*sharply—letting her resentment toward him come out*]   It's you who should have more respect. Stop sneering at your father! I won't have it! You ought to be proud you're his son! He may have his faults. Who hasn't? But he's worked hard all his life. He made his way up from ignorance and poverty to the top of his profession! Everyone else admires him and you should be the last one to sneer—you, who, thanks to him, have never had to work hard in your life!

> [*Stung,* JAMIE *has turned to stare at her with accusing antagonism. Her eyes waver guiltily and she adds in a tone which begins to placate*]

Remember your father is getting old, Jamie. You really ought to show more consideration.

JAMIE   *I* ought to?

EDMUND [*uneasily*]   Oh, dry up, Jamie!

[JAMIE *looks out the window again.*]

And, for Pete's sake, Mama, why jump on Jamie all of a sudden?

MARY [*bitterly*]   Because he's always sneering at someone else, always looking for the worst weakness in everyone. [*then with a strange, abrupt change to a detached, impersonal tone*] But I suppose life has made him like that, and he can't help it. None of us can help the things life has done to us. They're done before you realize it, and once they're done they make you do other things until at last everything comes between you and what you'd like to be, and you've lost your true self forever.

[EDMUND *is made apprehensive by her strangeness. He tries to look up in her eyes but she keeps them averted.* JAMIE *turns to her—then looks quickly out of the window again.*]

JAMIE [*dully*]   I'm hungry. I wish the Old Man would get a move on. It's a rotten trick the way he keeps meals waiting, and then beefs because they're spoiled.

MARY [*with a resentment that has a quality of being automatic and on the surface while inwardly she is indifferent*]   Yes, it's very trying, Jamie. You don't know how trying. You don't have to keep house with summer servants who don't care because they know it isn't a permanent position. The really good servants are all with people who have homes and not merely summer places. And your father won't even pay the wages the best summer help ask. So every year I have stupid, lazy greenhorns to deal with. But you've heard me say this a thousand times. So has he, but it goes in one ear and out the other. He thinks money spent on a home is money wasted. He's lived too much in hotels. Never the best hotels, of course. Second-rate hotels. He doesn't understand a home. He doesn't feel at home in it. And yet, he wants a home. He's even proud of having this shabby place. He loves it here. [*She laughs—a hopeless and yet amused laugh.*] It's really funny, when you come to think of it. He's a peculiar man.

EDMUND [*again attempting uneasily to look up in her eyes*]   What makes you ramble on like that, Mama?

MARY [*quickly casual—patting his cheek*]   Why, nothing in particular, dear. It *is* foolish.

[*As she speaks,* CATHLEEN *enters from the back parlor.*]

CATHLEEN [*volubly*]   Lunch is ready, Ma'am, I went down to Mister Tyrone, like you ordered, and he said he'd come right away, but he kept on talking to that man, telling him of the time when—

MARY [*indifferently*]   All right, Cathleen. Tell Bridget I'm sorry but she'll have to wait a few minutes until Mister Tyrone is here.

[CATHLEEN *mutters,* "Yes, Ma'am," *and goes off through the back parlor, grumbling to herself.*]

JAMIE   Damn it! Why don't you go ahead without him? He told us to.

MARY [*with a remote, amused smile*]   He doesn't mean it. Don't you know your father yet? He'd be so terribly hurt.

EDMUND [*jumps up—as if he was glad of an excuse to leave*]   I'll make him get a move on.

[*He goes out on the side porch. A moment later he is heard calling from the porch exasperatedly.*]

Hey! Papa! Come on! We can't wait all day!

[MARY *has risen from the arm of the chair. Her hands play restlessly over the table top. She does not look at* JAMIE *but she feels the cynically appraising glance he gives her face and hands.*]

MARY [*tensely*] Why do you stare like that?

JAMIE You know. [*He turns back to the window.*]

MARY I don't know.

JAMIE Oh, for God's sake, do you think you can fool me, Mama? I'm not blind.

MARY [*looks directly at him now, her face set again in an expression of blank, stubborn denial*] I don't know what you're talking about.

JAMIE No? Take a look at your eyes in the mirror!

EDMUND [*coming in from the porch*] I got Papa moving. He'll be here in a minute. [*with a glance from one to the other, which his mother avoids— uneasily*] What happened? What's the matter, Mama?

MARY [*disturbed by his coming, gives way to a flurry of guilty, nervous excite- ment*] Your brother ought to be ashamed of himself. He's been insinu- ating I don't know what.

EDMUND [*turns on* JAMIE] God damn you!

[*He takes a threatening step toward him.* JAMIE *turns his back with a shrug and looks out the window.*]

MARY [*more upset, grabs* EDMUND's *arm—excitedly*] Stop this at once, do you hear me? How dare you use such language before me! [*Abruptly her tone and manner change to the strange detachment she has shown before.*] It's wrong to blame your brother. He can't help being what the past has made him. Any more than your father can. Or you. Or I.

EDMUND [*frightenedly—with a desperate hoping against hope*] He's a liar! It's a lie, isn't it, Mama?

MARY [*keeping her eyes averted*] What is a lie? Now you're talking in rid- dles like Jamie. [*Then her eyes meet his stricken, accusing look. She stam- mers*] Edmund! Don't! [*She looks away and her manner instantly regains the quality of strange detachment—calmly*] There's your father coming up the steps now. I must tell Bridget.

[*She goes through the back parlor.* EDMUND *moves slowly to his chair. He looks sick and hopeless.*]

JAMIE [*from the window, without looking around*] Well?

EDMUND [*refusing to admit anything to his brother yet—weakly defiant*] Well, what? You're a liar.

[JAMIE *again shrugs his shoulders. The screen door on the front porch is heard closing.* EDMUND *says dully*]

Here's Papa. I hope he loosens up with the old bottle.

[TYRONE *comes in through the front parlor. He is putting on his coat.*]

TYRONE Sorry I'm late. Captain Turner stopped to talk and once he starts gabbing you can't get away from him.

JAMIE [*without turning—dryly*] You mean once he starts listening.

[*His father regards him with dislike. He comes to the table with a quick measuring look at the bottle of whiskey. Without turning,* JAMIE *senses this.*]

It's all right. The level in the bottle hasn't changed.

TYRONE I wasn't noticing that. [*He adds caustically*] As if it proved anything with you around. I'm on to your tricks.

EDMUND [*dully*]   Did I hear you say, let's all have a drink?

TYRONE [*frowns at him*]   Jamie is welcome after his hard morning's work, but I won't invite you. Doctor Hardy—

EDMUND   To hell with Doctor Hardy! One isn't going to kill me. I feel—all in, Papa.

TYRONE [*with a worried look at him—putting on a fake heartiness*]   Come along, then. It's before a meal and I've always found that good whiskey, taken in moderation as an appetizer, is the best of tonics.

[EDMUND *gets up as his father passes the bottle to him. He pours a big drink.* TYRONE *frowns admonishingly.*]

I said, in moderation.

[*He pours his own drink and passes the bottle to* JAMIE, *grumbling.*]

It'd be a waste of breath mentioning moderation to you.

[*Ignoring the hint,* JAMIE *pours a big drink. His father scowls—then, giving it up, resumes his hearty air, raising his glass.*]

Well, here's health and happiness!

[EDMUND *gives a bitter laugh.*]

EDMUND   That's a joke!

TYRONE   What is?

EDMUND   Nothing. Here's how. [*They drink.*]

TYRONE [*becoming aware of the atmosphere*]   What's the matter here? There's gloom in the air you could cut with a knife. [*turns on* JAMIE *resentfully*] You got the drink you were after, didn't you? Why are you wearing that gloomy look on your mug?

JAMIE [*shrugging his shoulders*]   You won't be singing a song yourself soon.

EDMUND   Shut up, Jamie.

TYRONE [*uneasy now—changing the subject*]   I thought lunch was ready. I'm hungry as a hunter. Where is your mother?

MARY [*returning through the back parlor, calls*]   Here I am.

[*She comes in. She is excited and self-conscious. As she talks, she glances everywhere except at any of their faces.*]

I've had to calm down Bridget. She's in a tantrum over your being late again, and I don't blame her. If your lunch is dried up from waiting in the oven, she said it served you right, you could like it or leave it for all she cared. [*with increasing excitement*] Oh, I'm so sick and tired of pretending this is a home! You won't help me! You won't put yourself out the least bit! You don't know how to act in a home! You don't really want one! You never have wanted one—never since the day we were married! You should have remained a bachelor and lived in second-rate hotels and entertained your friends in barrooms! [*She adds strangely, as if she were now talking aloud to herself rather than to* TYRONE] Then nothing would ever have happened.

[*They stare at her.* TYRONE *knows now. He suddenly looks a tired, bitterly sad old man.* EDMUND *glances at his father and sees that he knows, but he still cannot help trying to warn his mother.*]

EDMUND   Mama! Stop talking. Why don't we go in to lunch.

MARY [*Starts and at once the quality of unnatural detachment settles on her face again. She even smiles with an ironical amusement to herself.*]   Yes, it is inconsiderate of me to dig up the past, when I know your father and Jamie must be hungry. [*putting her arm around* EDMUND's *shoulder—with a fond solicitude which is at the same time remote*] I do hope you have an appetite, dear. You really must eat more [*Her eyes become fixed on the whiskey glass on the table beside him—sharply*] Why is that glass there? Did you take a drink? Oh, how can you be such a fool? Don't you know it's the worst thing? [*She turns on* TYRONE.] You're to blame, James. How could you let him? Do you want to kill him? Don't you remember my father? He wouldn't stop after he was stricken. He said doctors were fools! He thought, like you, that whiskey is a good tonic! [*A look of terror comes into her eyes and she stammers*] But, of course, there's no comparison at all. I don't know why I—Forgive me for scolding you, James. One small drink won't hurt Edmund. It might be good for him, if it gives him an appetite.

    [*She pats* EDMUND's *cheek playfully, the strange detachment again in her manner. He jerks his head away. She seems not to notice, but she moves instinctively away.*]

JAMIE [*roughly, to hide his tense nerves*]   For God's sake, let's eat. I've been working in the damned dirt under the hedge all morning. I've earned my grub.

    [*He comes around in back of his father, not looking at his mother, and grabs* EDMUND's *shoulder.*]

Come on, Kid. Let's put on the feed bag.

    [EDMUND *gets up, keeping his eyes averted from his mother. They pass her, heading for the back parlor.*]

TYRONE [*dully*]   Yes, you go in with your mother, lads. I'll join you in a second.

    [*But they keep on without waiting for her. She looks at their backs with a helpless hurt and, as they enter the back parlor, starts to follow them.* TYRONE's *eyes are on her, sad and condemning. She feels them and turns sharply without meeting his stare.*]

MARY   Why do you look at me like that? [*Her hands flutter up to pat her hair.*] Is it my hair coming down? I was so worn out from last night, I thought I'd better lie down this morning. I drowsed off and had a nice refreshing nap. But I'm sure I fixed my hair again when I woke up. [*forcing a laugh*] Although, as usual, I couldn't find my glasses. [*sharply*] Please stop staring! One would think you were accusing me—[*then pleadingly*] James! You don't understand!

TYRONE [*with dull anger*]   I understand that I've been a God-damned fool to believe in you!

    [*He walks away from her to pour himself a big drink.*]

MARY [*her face again sets in stubborn defiance*]   I don't know what you mean by "believing in me." All I've felt was distrust and spying and suspicion. [*then accusingly*] Why are you having another drink? You never have more than one before lunch. [*bitterly*] I know what to expect. You will be drunk tonight. Well, it won't be the first time, will it—or the thousandth? [*again she bursts out pleadingly*] Oh, James, please! You don't understand! I'm worried about Edmund! I'm so afraid he—

TYRONE   I don't want to listen to excuses, Mary.

MARY [*strickenly*]   Excuses? You mean—? Oh, you can't believe that of me! You mustn't believe that, James! [*then slipping away into her strange detachment—quite casually*] Shall we not go into lunch dear? I don't want anything but I know you're hungry.

    [*He walks slowly to where she stands in the doorway. He walks like an old man. As he reaches her she bursts out piteously.*]

James! I tried so hard! I tried so hard! Please believe—!

TYRONE [*moved in spite of himself—helplessly*]   I suppose you did, Mary. [*then grief-strickenly*] For the love of God, why couldn't you have the strength to keep on?

MARY [*her face setting into that stubborn denial again*]   I don't know what you're talking about. Have the strength to keep on what?

TYRONE [*hopelessly*]   Never mind. It's no use now.

[*He moves on and she keeps beside him as they disappear in the back parlor.*]

CURTAIN

Act 2

SCENE 2

SCENE—*The same, about a half hour later. The tray with the bottle of whiskey has been removed from the table. The family are returning from lunch as the curtain rises.* MARY *is the first to enter from the back parlor. Her husband follows. He is not with her as he was in the similar entrance after breakfast at the opening of Act One. He avoids touching her or looking at her. There is condemnation in his face, mingled now with the beginning of an old weary, helpless resignation.* JAMIE *and* EDMUND *follow their father.* JAMIE's *face is hard with defensive cynicism.* EDMUND *tries to copy this defense but without success. He plainly shows he is heartsick as well as physically ill.*

MARY *is terribly nervous again, as if the strain of sitting through lunch with them had been too much for her. Yet at the same time, in contrast to this, her expression shows more of that strange aloofness which seems to stand apart from her nerves and the anxieties which harry them.*

She is talking as she enters—a stream of words that issues casually, in a routine of family conversation, from her mouth. She appears indifferent to the fact that their thoughts are not on what she is saying any more than her own are. As she talks, she comes to the left of the table and stands, facing front, one hand fumbling with the bosom of her dress, the other playing over the table top. TYRONE *lights a cigar and goes to the screen door, staring out.* JAMIE *fills a pipe from a jar on top of the bookcase at rear. He lights it as he goes to look out the window at right.* EDMUND *sits in a chair by the table, turned half away from his mother so he does not have to watch her.*

MARY   It's no use finding fault with Bridget. She doesn't listen. I can't threaten her, or she'd threaten she'd leave. And she does do her best at times. It's too bad they seem to be just the times you're sure to be late, James. Well, there's this consolation: it's difficult to tell from her cooking whether she's doing her best or her worst. [*She gives a little laugh of detached amusement—indifferently*] Never mind. The summer will soon be over, thank goodness. Your season will open again and we can go back to second-rate hotels and trains. I hate them, too, but at least I don't expect them to be like a home, and there's no housekeeping to worry about. It's unreasonable to expect Bridget or Cathleen to act as if this was a home. They know it isn't as well as we know it. It never has been and it never will be.

TYRONE [*bitterly without turning around*]   No, it never can be now. But it was once, before you—

MARY [*her face instantly set in blank denial*]   Before I what? [*There is dead silence. She goes on with a return of her detached air.*] No, no. Whatever you mean, it isn't true, dear. It was never a home. You've always preferred the Club or barroom. And for me it's always been as lonely as a dirty room in a one-night stand hotel. In a real home one is never lonely. You forget I know from experience what a home is like. I gave up one to marry you— my father's home. [*At once, through an association of ideas she turns to* EDMUND. *Her manner becomes tenderly solicitous, but there is the strange quality of detachment in it.*] I'm worried about you, Edmund. You hardly touched a thing at lunch. That's no way to take care of yourself. It's all right for me not to have an appetite. I've been growing too fat. But you must eat. [*coaxingly maternal*] Promise me you will, dear, for my sake.

EDMUND [*dully*]   Yes, Mama.

MARY [*pats his cheek as he tries not to shrink away*]   That's a good boy.
  [*There is another pause of dead silence. Then the telephone in the front hall rings and all of them stiffen startledly.*]

TYRONE [*hastily*]   I'll answer. McGuire said he'd call me. [*He goes out through the front parlor.*]

MARY [*indifferently*]   McGuire. He must have another piece of property on his list that no one would think of buying except your father. It doesn't matter any more, but it's always seemed to me your father could afford to keep on buying property but never to give me a home.
  [*She stops to listen as* TYRONE's *voice is heard from the hall.*]

TYRONE   Hello. [*with forced heartiness*] Oh, how are you, Doctor?
  [JAMIE *turns from the window.* MARY's *fingers play more rapidly on the table top.* TYRONE's *voice, trying to conceal, reveals that he is hearing bad news.*]

I see—[*hurriedly*] Well, you'll explain all about it when you see him this afternoon. Yes, he'll be in without fail. Four o'clock. I'll drop in myself and have a talk with you before that. I have to go uptown on business, anyway. Goodbye, Doctor.

EDMUND [*dully*]   That didn't sound like glad tidings.
  [JAMIE *gives him a pitying glance—then looks out the window again.* MARY's *face is terrified and her hands flutter distractedly.* TYRONE *comes in. The strain is obvious in his casualness as he addresses* EDMUND.]

TYRONE   It was Doctor Hardy. He wants you to be sure and see him at four.

EDMUND [*dully*]   What did he say? Not that I give a damn now.

MARY [*bursts out excitedly*]   I wouldn't believe him if he swore on a stack of Bibles. You mustn't pay attention to a word he says, Edmund.

TYRONE [*sharply*]   Mary!

MARY [*more excitedly*]   Oh, we all realize why you like him, James! Because he's cheap! But please don't try to tell me! I know all about Doctor Hardy. Heaven knows I ought to after all these years. He's an ignorant fool! There should be a law to keep men like him from practicing. He hasn't the slightest idea—When you're in agony and half insane, he sits and holds your hand and delivers sermons on will power! [*Her face is drawn in an expression of intense suffering by the memory. For the moment, she loses all caution. With bitter hatred*] He deliberately humiliates you! He makes you beg and plead! He treats you like a criminal! He understands nothing! And yet it was exactly the same type of cheap quack who first gave you the medicine—and you never knew what it was until too late! [*passionately*] I hate doctors! They'll sell their souls! What's worse, they'll sell yours, and you never know it till one day you find yourself in hell!

EDMUND   Mama! For God's sake, stop talking.

TYRONE [*shakily*]   Yes, Mary, it's no time—

MARY [*suddenly is overcome by guilty confusion—stammers*]   I—Forgive me, dear. You're right. It's useless to be angry now. [*There is again a pause of dead silence. When she speaks again, her face has cleared and is calm, and the quality of uncanny detachment is in her voice and manner.*] I'm going upstairs for a moment, if you'll excuse me. I have to fix my hair. [*she adds smilingly*] That is if I can find my glasses. I'll be right down.

TYRONE [*as she starts through the doorway—pleading and rebuking*]   Mary!

MARY [*turns to stare at him calmly*]   Yes, dear? What is it?

TYRONE [*helplessly*]   Nothing.

MARY [*with a strange derisive smile*]   You're welcome to come up and watch me if you're so suspicious.

TYRONE   As if that could do any good! You'd only postpone it. And I'm not your jailor. This isn't a prison.

MARY   No. I know you can't help thinking it's a home. [*She adds quickly with a detached contrition*] I'm sorry, dear. I don't mean to be bitter. It's not your fault.

[*She turns and disappears through the back parlor. The three in the room remain silent. It is as if they were waiting until she got upstairs before speaking.*]

JAMIE [*cynically brutal*]   Another shot in the arm!

EDMUND [*angrily*]   Cut out that kind of talk!

TYRONE   Yes! Hold your foul tongue and your rotten Broadway loafer's lingo! Have you no pity or decency? [*losing his temper*] You ought to be kicked out in the gutter! But if I did it, you know damned well who'd weep and plead for you, and excuse you and complain till I let you come back.

JAMIE [*a spasm of pain crosses his face*]   Christ, don't I know that? No pity? I have all the pity in the world for her. I understand what a hard game to beat she's up against—which is more than you ever have! My lingo didn't mean I had no feeling. I was merely putting bluntly what we all know, and have to live with now, again. [*bitterly*] The cures are no damned good except for a while. The truth is there is no cure and we've been saps to hope—[*cynically*] They never come back!

EDMUND [*scornfully parodying his brother's cynicism*]   They never come back! Everything is in the bag! It's all a frame-up! We're all fall guys and suckers and we can't beat the game! [*disdainfully*] Christ, if I felt the way you do—!

JAMIE [*stung for a moment—then shrugging his shoulders, dryly*]   I thought you did. Your poetry isn't very cheery. Nor the stuff you read and claim to admire. [*He indicates the small bookcase at rear.*] Your pet with the unpronounceable name, for example.

EDMUND   Nietzsche. You don't know what you're talking about. You haven't read him.

JAMIE   Enough to know it's a lot of bunk!

TYRONE   Shut up, both of you! There's little choice between the philosophy you learned from Broadway loafers, and the one Edmund got from his books. They're both rotten to the core. You've both flouted the faith you were born and brought up in—the one true faith of the Catholic Church—and your denial has brought nothing but self-destruction!

[*His two sons stare at him contemptuously. They forget their quarrel and are as one against him on this issue.*]

EDMUND   That's the bunk, Papa!

JAMIE   We don't pretend, at any rate. [*caustically*] I don't notice you've worn any holes in the knees of your pants going to Mass.

TYRONE   It's true I'm a bad Catholic in the observance, God forgive me. But I believe! [*angrily*] And you're a liar! I may not go to church but every night and morning of my life I get on my knees and pray!

EDMUND [*bitingly*]   Did you pray for Mama?

TYRONE   I did. I've prayed to God these many years for her.

EDMUND   Then Nietzsche must be right. [*He quotes from* Thus Spake Zarathustra.] "God is dead: of His pity for man hath God died."

TYRONE [*ignores this*]   If your mother had prayed, too—She hasn't denied her faith, but she's forgotten it, until now there's no strength of the spirit left in her to fight against her curse. [*then dully resigned*] But what's the good of talk? We've lived with this before and now we must again. There's no help for it. [*bitterly*] Only I wish she hadn't led me to hope this time. By God, I never will again!

EDMUND   That's a rotten thing to say, Papa! [*defiantly*] Well, I'll hope! She's just started. It can't have got a hold on her yet. She can still stop. I'm going to talk to her.

JAMIE [*shrugs his shoulders*]   You can't talk to her now. She'll listen but she won't listen. She'll be here but she won't be here. You know the way she gets.

TYRONE   Yes, that's the way the poison acts on her always. Every day from now on, there'll be the same drifting away from us until by the end of each night—

EDMUND [*miserably*]   Cut it out, Papa! [*He jumps up from his chair.*] I'm going to get dressed. [*bitterly, as he goes*] I'll make so much noise she can't suspect I've come to spy on her.

[*He disappears through the front parlor and can be heard stamping noisily upstairs.*]

JAMIE [*after a pause*]   What did Doc Hardy say about the Kid?

TYRONE [*dully*]   It's what you thought. He's got consumption.

JAMIE   God damn it!

TYRONE   There is no possible doubt, he said.

JAMIE   He'll have to go to a sanatorium.

TYRONE   Yes, and the sooner the better, Hardy said, for him and everyone around him. He claims that in six months to a year Edmund will be cured, if he obeys orders. [*He sighs—gloomily and resentfully*] I never thought a child of mine—It doesn't come from my side of the family. There wasn't one of us that didn't have lungs as strong as an ox.

JAMIE   Who gives a damn about that part of it! Where does Hardy want to send him?

TYRONE   That's what I'm to see him about.

JAMIE   Well, for God's sake, pick out a good place and not some cheap dump!

TYRONE [*stung*] I'll send him wherever Hardy thinks best!

JAMIE Well, don't give Hardy your old over-the-hills-to-the-poorhouse song about taxes and mortgages.

TYRONE I'm no millionaire who can throw money away! Why shouldn't I tell Hardy the truth?

JAMIE Because he'll think you want him to pick a cheap dump, and because he'll know it isn't the truth—especially if he hears afterwards you've seen McGuire and let that flannel-mouth, gold-brick merchant sting you with another piece of bum property!

TYRONE Keep your nose out of my business!

JAMIE This is Edmund's business. What I'm afraid of is, with your Irish bog trotter idea that consumption is fatal, you'll figure it would be a waste of money to spend any more than you can help.

TYRONE You liar!

JAMIE All right. Prove I'm a liar. That's what I want. That's why I brought it up.

TYRONE [*his rage still smoldering*] I have every hope Edmund will be cured. And keep your dirty tongue off Ireland! You're a fine one to sneer, with the map of it on your face!

JAMIE Not after I wash my face. [*Then before his father can react to this insult to the Old Sod he adds dryly, shrugging his shoulders*] Well, I've said all I have to say. It's up to you. [*abruptly*] What do you want me to do this afternoon, now you're going uptown? I've done all I can do on the hedge until you cut more of it. You don't want me to go ahead with your clipping, I know that.

TYRONE No. You'd get it crooked, as you get everything else.

JAMIE Then I'd better go uptown with Edmund. The bad news coming on top of what's happened to Mama may hit him hard.

TYRONE [*forgetting his quarrel*] Yes, go with him, Jamie. Keep up his spirits, if you can. [*He adds caustically*] If you can without making it an excuse to get drunk!

JAMIE What would I use for money? The last I heard they were still selling booze, not giving it away. [*He starts for the front-parlor doorway.*] I'll get dressed.

[*He stops in the doorway as he sees his mother approaching from the hall, and moves aside to let her come in. Her eyes look brighter, and her manner is more detached. This change becomes more marked as the scene goes on.*]

MARY [*vaguely*] You haven't seen my glasses anywhere, have you, Jamie? [*She doesn't look at him. He glances away, ignoring her question but she doesn't seem to expect an answer. She comes forward, addressing her husband without looking at him.*]
You haven't seen them, have you, James?
[*Behind her* JAMIE *disappears through the front parlor.*]

TYRONE [*turns to look out the screen door*] No, Mary.

MARY What's the matter with Jamie? Have you been nagging at him again? You shouldn't treat him with such contempt all the time. He's not to blame. If he'd been brought up in a real home, I'm sure he would have been different. [*She comes to the windows at right—lightly*] You're not much of a weather prophet, dear. See how hazy it's getting. I can hardly see the other shore.

TYRONE [*trying to speak naturally*]   Yes, I spoke too soon. We're in for another night of fog, I'm afraid.

MARY   Oh, well, I won't mind it tonight.

TYRONE   No, I don't imagine you will, Mary.

MARY [*flashes a glance at him—after a pause*]   I don't see Jamie going down to the hedge. Where did he go?

TYRONE   He's going with Edmund to the Doctor's. He went up to change his clothes. [*then, glad of an excuse to leave her*] I'd better do the same or I'll be late for my appointment at the Club.
  [*He makes a move toward the front-parlor doorway, but with a swift impulsive movement she reaches out and clasps his arm.*]

MARY [*a note of pleading in her voice*]   Don't go yet, dear. I don't want to be alone. [*hastily*] I mean, you have plenty of time. You know you boast you can dress in one-tenth the time it takes the boys. [*vaguely*] There is something I wanted to say. What is it? I've forgotten. I'm glad Jamie is going uptown. You didn't give him any money, I hope.

TYRONE   I did not.

MARY   He'd only spend it on drink and you know what a vile, poisonous tongue he has when he's drunk. Not that I would mind anything he said tonight, but he always manages to drive you into a rage, especially if you're drunk, too, as you will be.

TYRONE [*resentfully*]   I won't. I never get drunk.

MARY [*teasing indifferently*]   Oh, I'm sure you'll hold it well. You always have. It's hard for a stranger to tell, but after thirty-five years of marriage—

TYRONE   I've never missed a performance in my life. That's the proof! [*then bitterly*] If I did get drunk it is not you who should blame me. No man has ever had a better reason.

MARY   Reason? What reason? You always drink too much when you go to the Club, don't you? Particularly when you meet McGuire. He sees to that. Don't think I'm finding fault, dear. You must do as you please. I won't mind.

TYRONE   I know you won't. [*He turns toward the front parlor, anxious to escape.*] I've got to get dressed.

MARY [*again she reaches out and grasps his arm—pleadingly*]   No, please wait a little while, dear. At least, until one of the boys comes down. You will all be leaving me so soon.

TYRONE [*with bitter sadness*]   It's you who are leaving us, Mary.

MARY   I? That's a silly thing to say, James. How could I leave? There is nowhere I could go. Who would I go to see? I have no friends.

TYRONE   It's your own fault—[*He stops and sighs helplessly—persuasively*] There's surely one thing you can do this afternoon that will be good for you, Mary. Take a drive in the automobile. Get away from the house. Get a little sun and fresh air. [*injuredly*] I bought the automobile for you. You know I don't like the damned things. I'd rather walk any day, or take a trolley. [*with growing resentment*] I had it here waiting for you when you came back from the sanatorium. I hoped it would give you pleasure and distract your mind. You used to ride in it every day, but you've hardly used it at all lately. I paid a lot of money I couldn't afford, and there's the chauffeur I have to board and lodge and pay high wages whether he drives you or not. [*bitterly*] Waste! The same old waste that will land me in the poorhouse in my old age! What good did it do you? I might as well have thrown the money out the window.

MARY [*with detached calm*] Yes, it was a waste of money, James. You shouldn't have bought a secondhand automobile. You were swindled again as you always are, because you insist on secondhand bargains in everything.

TYRONE It's one of the best makes! Everyone says it's better than any of the new ones!

MARY [*ignoring this*] It was another waste to hire Smythe, who was only a helper in a garage and had never been a chauffeur. Oh, I realize his wages are less than a real chauffeur's, but he more than makes up for that, I'm sure, by the graft he gets from the garage on repair bills. Something is always wrong. Smythe sees to that, I'm afraid.

TYRONE I don't believe it! He may not be a fancy millionaire's flunky but he's honest! You're as bad as Jamie, suspecting everyone!

MARY You mustn't be offended, dear. I wasn't offended when you gave me the automobile. I knew you didn't mean to humiliate me. I knew that was the way you had to do everything. I was grateful and touched. I knew buying the car was a hard thing for you to do, and it proved how much you loved me, in your way, especially when you couldn't really believe it would do me any good.

TYRONE Mary! [*He suddenly hugs her to him—brokenly*] Dear Mary! For the love of God, for my sake and the boys' sake and your own, won't you stop now?

MARY [*stammers in guilty confusion for a second*] I—James! Please! [*Her strange, stubborn defense comes back instantly.*] Stop what? What are you talking about?

[*He lets his arm fall to his side brokenly. She impulsively puts her arm around him.*]

James! We've loved each other! We always will! Let's remember only that, and not try to understand what we cannot understand, or help things that cannot be helped—the things life has done to us we cannot excuse or explain.

TYRONE [*as if he hadn't heard—bitterly*] You won't even try?

MARY [*her arms drop hopelessly and she turns away—with detachment*] Try to go for a drive this afternoon, you mean? Why, yes, if you wish me to, although it makes me feel lonelier than if I stayed here. There is no one I can invite to drive with me, and I never know where to tell Smythe to go. If there was a friend's house where I could drop in and laugh and gossip awhile. But, of course, there isn't. There never has been. [*her manner becoming more and more remote*] At the Convent I had so many friends. Girls whose families lived in lovely homes. I used to visit them and they'd visit me in my father's home. But, naturally, after I married an actor—you know how actors were considered in those days—a lot of them gave me the cold shoulder. And then, right after we were married, there was the scandal of that woman who had been your mistress, suing you. From then on, all my old friends either pitied me or cut me dead. I hated the ones who cut me much less than the pitiers.

TYRONE [*with guilty resentment*] For God's sake, don't dig up what's long forgotten. If you're that far gone in the past already, when it's only the beginning of the afternoon, what will you be tonight?

MARY [*stares at him defiantly now*]   Come to think of it, I do have to drive uptown. There's something I must get at the drugstore.

TYRONE [*bitterly scornful*]   Leave it to you to have some of the stuff hidden, and prescriptions for more! I hope you'll lay in a good stock ahead so we'll never have another night like the one when you screamed for it, and ran out of the house in your nightdress half crazy, to try and throw yourself off the dock!

MARY [*tries to ignore this*]   I have to get tooth powder and toilet soap and cold cream—[*She breaks down pitiably.*] James! You mustn't remember! You mustn't humiliate me so!

TYRONE [*ashamed*]   I'm sorry. Forgive me, Mary!

MARY [*defensively detached again*]   It doesn't matter. Nothing like that ever happened. You must have dreamed it.

> [*He stares at her hopelessly. Her voice seems to drift farther and farther away.*]

I was so healthy before Edmund was born. You remember, James. There wasn't a nerve in my body. Even traveling with you season after season, with week after week of one-night stands, in trains without Pullmans, in dirty rooms of filthy hotels, eating bad food, bearing children in hotel rooms, I still kept healthy. But bearing Edmund was the last straw. I was so sick afterwards, and that ignorant quack of a cheap hotel doctor—All he knew was I was in pain. It was easy for him to stop the pain.

TYRONE   Mary! For God's sake, forget the past!

MARY [*with strange objective calm*]   Why? How can I? The past is the present, isn't it? It's the future, too. We all try to lie out of that but life won't let us. [*going on*] I blame only myself. I swore after Eugene died I would never have another baby. I was to blame for his death. If I hadn't left him with my mother to join you on the road, because you wrote telling me you missed me and were so lonely, Jamie would never have been allowed, when he still had measles, to go in the baby's room. [*her face hardening*] I've always believed Jamie did it on purpose. He was jealous of the baby. He hated him. [*as* TYRONE *starts to protest*] Oh, I know Jamie was only seven, but he was never stupid. He'd been warned it might kill the baby. He knew. I've never been able to forgive him for that.

TYRONE [*with bitter sadness*]   Are you back with Eugene now? Can't you let our dead baby rest in peace?

MARY [*as if she hadn't heard him*]   It was my fault. I should have insisted on staying with Eugene and not have let you persuade me to join you, just because I loved you. Above all, I shouldn't have let you insist I have another baby to take Eugene's place, because you thought that would make me forget his death. I knew from experience by then that children should have homes to be born in, if they are to be good children, and women need homes, if they are to be good mothers. I was afraid all the time I carried Edmund. I knew something terrible would happen. I knew I'd proved by the way I'd left Eugene that I wasn't worthy to have another baby, and that God would punish me if I did. I never should have borne Edmund.

TYRONE [*with an uneasy glance through the front parlor*]   Mary! Be careful with your talk. If he heard you he might think you never wanted him. He's feeling bad enough already without—

MARY [*violently*]   It's a lie! I did want him! More than anything in the world! You don't understand! I meant, for his sake. He has never been happy. He never will be. Nor healthy. He was born nervous and too sensitive, and that's my fault. And now, ever since he's been so sick I've kept remembering Eugene and my father and I've been so frightened and guilty— [*then, catching herself, with an instant change to stubborn denial*] Oh, I know it's foolish to imagine dreadful things when there's no reason for it. After all, everyone has colds and gets over them.

> [TYRONE *stares at her and sighs helplessly. He turns away toward the front parlor and sees* EDMUND *coming down the stairs in the hall.*]

TYRONE [*sharply, in a low voice*]   Here's Edmund. For God's sake try and be yourself—at least until he goes! You can do that much for him!

> [*He waits, forcing his face into a pleasantly paternal expression. She waits frightenedly, seized again by a nervous panic, her hands fluttering over the bosom of her dress, up to her throat and hair, with a distracted aimlessness. Then, as* EDMUND *approaches the doorway, she cannot face him. She goes swiftly away to the windows at left and stares out with her back to the front parlor.* EDMUND *enters. He has changed to a ready-made blue serge suit, high stiff collar and tie, black shoes. With an actor's heartiness*]

Well! You look spic and span. I'm on my way up to change, too. [*He starts to pass him.*]

EDMUND [*dryly*]   Wait a minute, Papa. I hate to bring up disagreeable topics, but there's the matter of carfare. I'm broke.

TYRONE [*starts automatically on a customary lecture*]   You'll always be broke until you learn the value—[*checks himself guiltily, looking at his son's sick face with worried pity*] But you've been learning, lad. You worked hard before you took ill. You've done splendidly. I'm proud of you.

> [*He pulls out a small roll of bills from his pants pocket and carefully selects one.* EDMUND *takes it. He glances at it and his face expresses astonishment. His father again reacts customarily—sarcastically*]

Thank you. [*He quotes*] "How sharper than a serpent's tooth it is—"

EDMUND   "To have a thankless child."[9] I know. Give me a chance, Papa. I'm knocked speechless. This isn't a dollar. It's a ten spot.

TYRONE [*embarrassed by his generosity*]   Put it in your pocket. You'll probably meet some of your friends uptown and you can't hold your end up and be sociable with nothing in your jeans.

EDMUND   You meant it? Gosh, thank you, Papa. [*He is genuinely pleased and grateful for a moment—then he stares at his father's face with uneasy suspicion.*] But why all of a sudden—? [*cynically*] Did Doc Hardy tell you I was going to die? [*Then he sees his father is bitterly hurt.*] No! That's a rotten crack. I was only kidding, Papa. [*He puts an arm around his father impulsively and gives him an affectionate hug.*] I'm very grateful. Honest, Papa.

TYRONE [*touched, returns his hug*]   You're welcome, lad.

MARY [*suddenly turns to them in a confused panic of frightened anger*]   I won't have it! [*She stamps her foot.*] Do you hear, Edmund! Such morbid nonsense! Saying you're going to die! It's the books you read! Nothing but sadness and death! Your father shouldn't allow you to have them. And some of the poems you've written yourself are even worse! You'd think you

---

9. Shakespeare's *King Lear* 1.4.312.

didn't want to live! A boy of your age with everything before him! It's just a pose you get out of books! You're not really sick at all!

TYRONE   Mary! Hold your tongue!

MARY [*instantly changing to a detached tone*]   But, James, it's absurd of Edmund to be so gloomy and make such a great to-do about nothing. [*turning to* EDMUND *but avoiding his eyes—teasingly affectionate*] Never mind, dear. I'm on to you. [*She comes to him.*] You want to be petted and spoiled and made a fuss over, isn't that it? You're still such a baby. [*She puts her arm around him and hugs him. He remains rigid and unyielding. Her voice begins to tremble.*] But please don't carry it too far, dear. Don't say horrible things. I know it's foolish to take them seriously but I can't help it. You've got me—so frightened.

[*She breaks and hides her face on his shoulder, sobbing.* EDMUND *is moved in spite of himself. He pats her shoulder with an awkward tenderness.*]

EDMUND   Don't, mother. [*His eyes meet his father's.*]

TYRONE [*huskily—clutching at hopeless hope*]   Maybe if you asked your mother now what you said you were going to—[*He fumbles with his watch.*] By God, look at the time! I'll have to shake a leg.

[*He hurries away through the front parlor.* MARY *lifts her head. Her manner is again one of detached motherly solicitude. She seems to have forgotten the tears which are still in her eyes.*]

MARY   How do you feel, dear? [*She feels his forehead.*] Your head is a little hot, but that's just from going out in the sun. You look ever so much better than you did this morning. [*taking his hand*] Come and sit down. You mustn't stand on your feet so much. You must learn to husband your strength.

[*She gets him to sit and she sits sideways on the arm of his chair, an arm around his shoulder, so he cannot meet her eyes.*]

EDMUND [*starts to blurt out the appeal he now feels is quite hopeless*]   Listen, Mama—

MARY [*interrupting quickly*]   Now, now! Don't talk. Lean back and rest. [*persuasively*] You know, I think it would be much better for you if you stayed home this afternoon and let me take care of you. It's such a tiring trip uptown in the dirty old trolley on a hot day like this. I'm sure you'd be much better off here with me.

EDMUND [*dully*]   You forget I have an appointment with Hardy. [*trying again to get his appeal started*] Listen, Mama—

MARY [*quickly*]   You can telephone and say you don't feel well enough. [*excitedly*] It's simply a waste of time and money seeing him. He'll only tell you some lie. He'll pretend he's found something serious the matter because that's his bread and butter. [*She gives a hard sneering little laugh.*] The old idiot! All he knows about medicine is to look solemn and preach will power!

EDMUND [*trying to catch her eyes*]   Mama! Please listen! I want to ask you something! You—You're only just started. You can still stop. You've got the will power! We'll all help you. I'll do anything! Won't you, Mama?

MARY [*stammers pleadingly*]   Please don't—talk about things you don't understand!

EDMUND [*dully*]   All right, I give up. I knew it was no use.

MARY [*in blank denial now*]   Anyway, I don't know what you're referring to. But I do know you should be the last one—Right after I returned from the sanatorium, you began to be ill. The doctor there had warned me I must have peace at home with nothing to upset me, and all I've done is worry about you. [*then distractedly*] But that's no excuse! I'm only trying to explain. It's not an excuse! [*She hugs him to her—pleadingly*] Promise me, dear, you won't believe I made you an excuse.

EDMUND [*bitterly*]   What else can I believe?

MARY [*slowly takes her arm away—her manner remote and objective again*] Yes, I suppose you can't help suspecting that.

EDMUND [*ashamed but still bitter*]   What do you expect?

MARY   Nothing, I don't blame you. How could you believe me—when I can't believe myself? I've become such a liar. I never lied about anything once upon a time. Now I have to lie, especially to myself. But how can you understand, when I don't myself. I've never understood anything about it, except that one day long ago I found I could no longer call my soul my own. [*She pauses—then lowering her voice to a strange tone of whispered confidence*] But some day, dear, I will find it again—some day when you're all well, and I see you healthy and happy and successful, and I don't have to feel guilty any more—some day when the Blessed Virgin Mary forgives me and gives me back the faith in Her love and pity I used to have in my convent days, and I can pray to Her again—when She sees no one in the world can believe in me even for a moment any more, then She will believe in me, and with Her help it will be so easy. I will hear myself scream with agony, and at the same time I will laugh because I will be so sure of myself. [*then as* EDMUND *remains hopelessly silent, she adds sadly*] Of course, you can't believe that, either. [*She rises from the arm of his chair and goes to stare out the windows at right with her back to him— casually*] Now I think of it, you might as well go uptown. I forgot I'm taking a drive. I have to go to the drugstore. You would hardly want to go there with me. You'd be so ashamed.

EDMUND [*brokenly*]   Mama! Don't!

MARY   I suppose you'll divide that ten dollars your father gave you with Jamie. You always divide with each other, don't you? Like good sports. Well, I know what he'll do with his share. Get drunk someplace where he can be with the only kind of woman he understands or likes. [*She turns to him, pleading frightenedly*] Edmund! Promise me you won't drink! It's so dangerous! You know Doctor Hardy told you—

EDMUND [*bitterly*]   I thought he was an old idiot. Anyway, by tonight, what will you care?

MARY [*pitifully*]   Edmund!

[JAMIE's *voice is heard from the front hall,* "Come on, Kid, let's beat it."
MARY's *manner at once becomes detached again.*]

Go on, Edmund. Jamie's waiting. [*She goes to the front-parlor doorway.*] There comes your father downstairs, too.

[TYRONE's *voice calls,* "Come on, Edmund."]

EDMUND [*jumping up from his chair*]   I'm coming.

[*He stops beside her—without looking at her.*]

Goodbye, Mama.

MARY [*kisses him with detached affection*]   Goodbye, dear. If you're coming home for dinner, try not to be late. And tell your father. You know what Bridget is.

[*He turns and hurries away.* TYRONE *calls from the hall,* "Goodbye, Mary," *and then* JAMIE, "Goodbye, Mama." *She calls back*]

Goodbye. [*The front screen door is heard closing after them. She comes and stands by the table, one hand drumming on it, the other fluttering up to pat her hair. She stares about the room with frightened, forsaken eyes and whispers to herself.*] It's so lonely here. [*Then her face hardens into bitter self-contempt.*] You're lying to yourself again. You wanted to get rid of them. Their contempt and disgust aren't pleasant company. You're glad they're gone. [*She gives a little despairing laugh.*] Then Mother of God, why do I feel so lonely?

CURTAIN

Act 3

SCENE—*The same. It is around half past six in the evening. Dusk is gathering in the living room, an early dusk due to the fog which has rolled in from the Sound and is like a white curtain drawn down outside the windows. From a lighthouse beyond the harbor's mouth, a foghorn is heard at regular intervals, moaning like a mournful whale in labor, and from the harbor itself, intermittently, comes the warning ringing of bells on yachts at anchor.*

The tray with the bottle of whiskey, glasses, and pitcher of ice water is on the table, as it was in the pre-luncheon scene of the previous act. MARY *and the second girl,* CATHLEEN, *are discovered. The latter is standing at left of table. She holds an empty whiskey glass in her hand as if she'd forgotten she had it. She shows the effects of drink. Her stupid, good-humored face wears a pleased and flattered simper.*

MARY *is paler than before and her eyes shine with unnatural brilliance. The strange detachment in her manner has intensified. She has hidden deeper within herself and found refuge and release in a dream where present reality is but an appearance to be accepted and dismissed unfeelingly—even with a hard cynicism—or entirely ignored. There is at times an uncanny gay, free youthfulness in her manner, as if in spirit she were released to become again, simply and without self-consciousness, the naive, happy, chattering schoolgirl of her convent days. She wears the dress into which she had changed for her drive to town, a simple, fairly expensive affair, which would be extremely becoming if it were not for the careless, almost slovenly way she wears it. Her hair is no longer fastidiously in place. It has a slightly disheveled, lopsided look. She talks to* CATHLEEN *with a confiding familiarity, as if the second girl were an old, intimate friend. As the curtain rises, she is standing by the screen door looking out. A moan of the foghorn is heard.*

MARY [*amused—girlishly*] That foghorn! Isn't it awful, Cathleen?

CATHLEEN [*talks more familiarly than usual but never with intentional impertinence because she sincerely likes her mistress*] It is indeed, Ma'am. It's like a banshee.

MARY [*Goes on as if she hadn't heard. In nearly all the following dialogue there is the feeling that she has* CATHLEEN *with her merely as an excuse to keep talking.*] I don't mind it tonight. Last night it drove me crazy. I lay awake worrying until I couldn't stand it any more.

CATHLEEN Bad cess to it.[1] I was scared out of my wits riding back from town. I thought that ugly monkey, Smythe, would drive us in a ditch or

---

1. Bad luck to it (Irish).

against a tree. You couldn't see your hand in front of you. I'm glad you had me sit in back with you, Ma'am. If I'd been in front with that monkey— He can't keep his dirty hands to himself. Give him half a chance and he's pinching me on the leg or you-know-where—asking your pardon, Ma'am, but it's true.

MARY [*dreamily*]   It wasn't the fog I minded, Cathleen, I really love fog.

CATHLEEN   They say it's good for the complexion.

MARY   It hides you from the world and the world from you. You feel that everything has changed, and nothing is what it seemed to be. No one can find or touch you any more.

CATHLEEN   I wouldn't care so much if Smythe was a fine, handsome man like some chauffeurs I've seen—I mean, if it was all in fun, for I'm a decent girl. But for a shriveled runt like Smythe—! I've told him, you must think I'm hard up that I'd notice a monkey like you. I've warned him, one day I'll give a clout that'll knock him into next week. And so I will!

MARY   It's the foghorn I hate. It won't let you alone. It keeps reminding you, and warning you, and calling you back. [*She smiles strangely.*] But it can't tonight. It's just an ugly sound. It doesn't remind me of anything. [*She gives a teasing, girlish laugh.*] Except, perhaps, Mr. Tyrone's snores. I've always had such fun teasing him about it. He has snored ever since I can remember, especially when he's had too much to drink, and yet he's like a child, he hates to admit it. [*She laughs, coming to the table.*] Well, I suppose I snore at times, too, and I don't like to admit it. So I have no right to make fun of him, have I? [*She sits in the rocker at right of table.*]

CATHLEEN   Ah, sure, everybody healthy snores. It's a sign of sanity, they say. [*then, worriedly*] What time is it, Ma'am? I ought to go back in the kitchen. The damp is in Bridget's rheumatism and she's like a raging divil. She'll bite my head off.

> [*She puts her glass on the table and makes a movement toward the back parlor.*]

MARY [*with a flash of apprehension*]   No, don't go, Cathleen. I don't want to be alone, yet.

CATHLEEN   You won't be for long. The Master and the boys will be home soon.

MARY   I doubt if they'll come back for dinner. They have too good an excuse to remain in the barrooms where they feel at home.

> [*CATHLEEN stares at her, stupidly puzzled. MARY goes on smilingly*]

Don't worry about Bridget. I'll tell her I kept you with me, and you can take a big drink of whiskey to her when you go. She won't mind then.

CATHLEEN [*grins—at her ease again*]   No, Ma'am. That's the one thing can make her cheerful. She loves her drop.

MARY   Have another drink yourself, if you wish, Cathleen.

CATHLEEN   I don't know if I'd better, Ma'am. I can feel what I've had already. [*reaching for the bottle*] Well, maybe one more won't harm. [*She pours a drink.*] Here's your good health, Ma'am. [*She drinks without bothering about a chaser.*]

MARY [*dreamily*]   I really did have good health once, Cathleen. But that was long ago.

CATHLEEN [*worried again*]   The Master's sure to notice what's gone from the bottle. He has the eye of a hawk for that.

MARY [*amusedly*] Oh, we'll play Jamie's trick on him. Just measure a few drinks of water and pour them in.

CATHLEEN [*does this—with a silly giggle*] God save me, it'll be half water. He'll know by the taste.

MARY [*indifferently*] No, by the time he comes home he'll be too drunk to tell the difference. He has such a good excuse, he believes, to drown his sorrows.

CATHLEEN [*philosophically*] Well, it's a good man's failing. I wouldn't give a trauneen[2] for a teetotaler. They've no high spirits. [*then, stupidly puzzled*] Good excuse? You mean Master Edmund, Ma'am? I can tell the Master is worried about him.

MARY [*stiffens defensively—but in a strange way the reaction has a mechanical quality, as if it did not penetrate to real emotion*] Don't be silly, Cathleen. Why should he be? A touch of grippe is nothing. And Mr. Tyrone never is worried about anything, except money and property and the fear he'll end his days in poverty. I mean, deeply worried. Because he cannot really understand anything else. [*She gives a little laugh of detached, affectionate amusement.*] My husband is a very peculiar man, Cathleen.

CATHLEEN [*vaguely resentful*] Well, he's a fine, handsome, kind gentleman just the same, Ma'am. Never mind his weakness.

MARY Oh, I don't mind. I've loved him dearly for thirty-six years. That proves I know he's lovable at heart and can't help being what he is, doesn't it?

CATHLEEN [*hazily reassured*] That's right. Ma'am. Love him dearly, for any fool can see he worships the ground you walk on. [*fighting the effect of her last drink and trying to be soberly conversational*] Speaking of acting, Ma'am, how is it you never went on the stage?

MARY [*resentfully*] I? What put that absurd notion in your head? I was brought up in a respectable home and educated in the best convent in the Middle West. Before I met Mr. Tyrone I hardly knew there was such a thing as a theater. I was a very pious girl. I even dreamed of becoming a nun. I've never had the slightest desire to be an actress.

CATHLEEN [*bluntly*] Well, I can't imagine you a holy nun, Ma'am. Sure, you never darken the door of a church, God forgive you.

MARY [*ignores this*] I've never felt at home in the theater. Even though Mr. Tyrone has made me go with him on all his tours, I've had little to do with the people in his company, or with anyone on the stage. Not that I have anything against them. They have always been kind to me, and I to them. But I've never felt at home with them. Their life is not my life. It has always stood between me and—[*She gets up—abruptly*] But let's not talk of old things that couldn't be helped. [*She goes to the porch door and stares out.*] How thick the fog is. I can't see the road. All the people in the world could pass by and I would never know. I wish it was always that way. It's getting dark already. It will soon be night, thank goodness. [*She turns back—vaguely*] It was kind of you to keep me company this afternoon, Cathleen. I would have been lonely driving uptown alone.

CATHLEEN Sure, wouldn't I rather ride in a fine automobile than stay here and listen to Bridget's lies about her relations? It was like a vacation, Ma'am. [*She pauses—then stupidly*] There was only one thing I didn't like.

2. Coin of very low value (Irish).

MARY [*vaguely*]   What was that, Cathleen?

CATHLEEN   The way the man in the drugstore acted when I took in the prescription for you. [*indignantly*] The impidence[3] of him!

MARY [*with stubborn blankness*]   What are you talking about? What drug-
store? What prescription? [*then hastily, as* CATHLEEN *stares in stupid
amazement*] Oh, of course, I'd forgotten. The medicine for the rheumatism in my hands. What did the man say? [*then with indifference*] Not
that it matters, as long as he filled the prescription.

CATHLEEN   It mattered to me, then! I'm not used to being treated like a
thief. He gave me a long look and says insultingly, "Where did you get
hold of this?" and I says, "It's none of your damned business, but if you
must know, it's for the lady I work for, Mrs. Tyrone, who's sitting out in
the automobile." That shut him up quick. He gave a look out at you and
said, "Oh," and went to get the medicine.

MARY [*vaguely*]   Yes, he knows me. [*She sits in the armchair at right rear
of table. She adds in a calm, detached voice*] It's a special kind of medicine. I have to take it because there is no other that can stop the pain—
all the pain—I mean, in my hands. [*She raises her hands and regards
them with melancholy sympathy. There is no tremor in them now.*] Poor
hands! You'd never believe it, but they were once one of my good points,
along with my hair and eyes, and I had a fine figure, too. [*Her tone has
become more and more far-off and dreamy.*] They were a musician's
hands. I used to love the piano. I worked so hard at my music in the
Convent—if you can call it work when you do something you love.
Mother Elizabeth and my music teacher both said I had more talent
than any student they remembered. My father paid for special lessons.
He spoiled me. He would do anything I asked. He would have sent me
to Europe to study after I graduated from the Convent. I might have
gone—if I hadn't fallen in love with Mr. Tyrone. Or I might have
become a nun. I had two dreams. To be a nun, that was the more beautiful one. To become a concert pianist, that was the other. [*She pauses,
regarding her hands fixedly.* CATHLEEN *blinks her eyes to fight off drowsiness and a tipsy feeling.*] I haven't touched a piano in so many years. I
couldn't play with such crippled fingers, even if I wanted to. For a time
after my marriage I tried to keep up my music. But it was hopeless.
One-night stands, cheap hotels, dirty trains, leaving children, never
having a home—[*She stares at her hands with fascinated disgust.*] See,
Cathleen, how ugly they are! So maimed and crippled! You would think
they'd been through some horrible accident! [*She gives a strange little
laugh.*] So they have, come to think of it. [*She suddenly thrusts her hands
behind her back.*] I won't look at them. They're worse than the foghorn
for reminding me—[*then with defiant self-assurance*] But even they can't
touch me now. [*She brings her hands from behind her back and deliberately stares at them—calmly*] They're far away. I see them, but the pain
has gone.

CATHLEEN [*stupidly puzzled*]   You've taken some of the medicine? It made
you act funny, Ma'am. If I didn't know better, I'd think you'd a drop taken.

MARY [*dreamily*]   It kills the pain. You go back until at last you are beyond

3. Impudence.

its reach. Only the past when you were happy is real. [*She pauses—then as if her words had been an evocation which called back happiness she changes in her whole manner and facial expression. She looks younger. There is a quality of an innocent convent girl about her, and she smiles shyly.*] If you think Mr. Tyrone is handsome now, Cathleen, you should have seen him when I first met him. He had the reputation of being one of the best looking men in the country. The girls in the Convent who had seen him act, or seen his photographs, used to rave about him. He was a great matinee idol then, you know. Women used to wait at the stage door just to see him come out. You can imagine how excited I was when my father wrote me he and James Tyrone had become friends, and that I was to meet him when I came home for Easter vacation. I showed the letter to all the girls, and how envious they were! My father took me to see him act first. It was a play about the French Revolution and the leading part was a nobleman. I couldn't take my eyes off him. I wept when he was thrown in prison—and then was so mad at myself because I was afraid my eyes and nose would be red. My father had said we'd go backstage to his dressing room right after the play, and so we did. [*She gives a little excited, shy laugh.*] I was so bashful all I could do was stammer and blush like a little fool. But he didn't seem to think I was a fool. I know he liked me the first moment we were introduced. [*coquettishly*] I guess my eyes and nose couldn't have been red, after all. I was really very pretty then, Cathleen. And he was handsomer than my wildest dream, in his make-up and his nobleman's costume that was so becoming to him. He was different from all ordinary men, like someone from another world. At the same time he was simple, and kind, and unassuming, not a bit stuck-up or vain. I fell in love right then. So did he, he told me afterwards. I forgot all about becoming a nun or a concert pianist. All I wanted was to be his wife. [*She pauses, staring before her with unnaturally bright, dreamy eyes, and a rapt, tender, girlish smile.*] Thirty-six years ago, but I can see it as clearly as if it were tonight! We've loved each other ever since. And in all those thirty-six years, there has never been a breath of scandal about him. I mean, with any other woman. Never since he met me. That has made me very happy, Cathleen. It has made me forgive so many other things.

CATHLEEN [*fighting tipsy drowsiness—sentimentally*]   He's a fine gentleman and you're a lucky woman. [*then, fidgeting*] Can I take the drink to Bridget, Ma'am? It must be near dinnertime and I ought to be in the kitchen helping her. If she don't get something to quiet her temper, she'll be after me with the cleaver.

MARY [*with a vague exasperation at being brought back from her dream*]   Yes, yes, go. I don't need you now.

CATHLEEN [*with relief*]   Thank you, Ma'am. [*She pours out a big drink and starts for the back parlor with it.*] You won't be alone long. The Master and the boys—

MARY [*impatiently*]   No, no, they won't come. Tell Bridget I won't wait. You can serve dinner promptly at half past six. I'm not hungry but I'll sit at the table and we'll get it over with.

CATHLEEN   You ought to eat something, Ma'am. It's a queer medicine if it takes away your appetite.

MARY [*has begun to drift into dreams again—reacts mechanically*]   What medicine? I don't know what you mean. [*in dismissal*] You better take the drink to Bridget.

CATHLEEN   Yes, Ma'am.

[*She disappears through the back parlor.* MARY *waits until she hears the pantry door close behind her. Then she settles back in relaxed dreaminess, staring fixedly at nothing. Her arms rest limply along the arms of the chair, her hands with long, warped, swollen-knuckled, sensitive fingers drooping in complete calm. It is growing dark in the room. There is a pause of dead quiet. Then from the world outside comes the melancholy moan of the foghorn, followed by a chorus of bells, muffled by the fog, from the anchored craft in the harbor.* MARY's *face gives no sign she has heard, but her hands jerk and the fingers automatically play for a moment on the air. She frowns and shakes her head mechanically as if a fly had walked across her mind. She suddenly loses all the girlish quality and is an aging, cynically sad, embittered woman.*]

MARY [*bitterly*]   You're a sentimental fool. What is so wonderful about that first meeting between a silly romantic schoolgirl and a matinee idol? You were much happier before you knew he existed, in the Convent when you used to pray to the Blessed Virgin. [*longingly*] If I could only find the faith I lost, so I could pray again! [*She pauses—then begins to recite the Hail Mary in a flat, empty tone.*] "Hail, Mary, full of grace! The Lord is with Thee; blessed art Thou among women." [*sneeringly*] You expect the Blessed Virgin to be fooled by a lying dope fiend reciting words! You can't hide from her! [*She springs to her feet. Her hands fly up to pat her hair distractedly.*] I must go upstairs. I haven't taken enough. When you start again you never know exactly how much you need. [*She goes toward the front parlor—then stops in the doorway as she hears the sound of voices from the front path. She starts guiltily.*] That must be them—[*She hurries back to sit down. Her face sets in stubborn defensiveness—resentfully*] Why are they coming back? They don't want to. And I'd much rather be alone. [*Suddenly her whole manner changes. She becomes pathetically relieved and eager.*] Oh, I'm so glad they've come! I've been so horribly lonely!

[*The front door is heard closing and* TYRONE *calls uneasily from the hall.*]

TYRONE   Are you there, Mary?

[*The light in the hall is turned on and shines through the front parlor to fall on* MARY.]

MARY [*rises from her chair, her face lighting up lovingly—with excited eagerness*]   I'm here, dear. In the living room. I've been waiting for you.

[TYRONE *comes in through the front parlor.* EDMUND *is behind him.* TYRONE *has had a lot to drink but beyond a slightly glazed look in his eyes and a trace of blur in his speech, he does not show it.* EDMUND *has also had more than a few drinks without much apparent effect, except that his sunken cheeks are flushed and his eyes look bright and feverish. They stop in the doorway to stare appraisingly at her. What they see fulfills their worst expectations. But for the moment* MARY *is unconscious of their condemning eyes. She kisses her husband and then* EDMUND. *Her manner is unnaturally effusive. They submit shrinkingly. She talks excitedly.*]

I'm so happy you've come. I had given up hope. I was afraid you wouldn't come home. It's such a dismal, foggy evening. It must be much more cheerful in the barrooms uptown, where there are people you can talk and joke with. No, don't deny it. I know how you feel. I don't blame you a bit. I'm all the more grateful to you for coming home. I was sitting here so lonely and blue. Come and sit down.

[*She sits at left rear of table,* EDMUND *at left of table, and* TYRONE *in the rocker at right of it.*]

Dinner won't be ready for a minute. You're actually a little early. Will wonders never cease. Here's the whiskey, dear. Shall I pour a drink for you? [*Without waiting for a reply she does so.*] And you, Edmund? I don't want to encourage you, but one before dinner, as an appetizer, can't do any harm.

[*She pours a drink for him. They make no move to take the drinks. She talks on as if unaware of their silence.*]

Where's Jamie? But, of course, he'll never come home so long as he has the price of a drink left. [*She reaches out and clasps her husband's hand— sadly*] I'm afraid Jamie has been lost to us for a long time, dear. [*Her face hardens.*] But we mustn't allow him to drag Edmund down with him, as he'd like to do. He's jealous because Edmund has always been the baby— just as he used to be of Eugene. He'll never be content until he makes Edmund as hopeless a failure as he is.

EDMUND [*miserably*]   Stop talking, Mama.

TYRONE [*dully*]   Yes, Mary, the less you say now—[*then to Edmund, a bit tipsily*] All the same there's truth in your mother's warning. Beware of that brother of yours, or he'll poison life for you with his damned sneering serpent's tongue!

EDMUND [*as before*]   Oh, cut it out, Papa.

MARY [*goes on as if nothing had been said*]   It's hard to believe, seeing Jamie as he is now, that he was ever my baby. Do you remember what a healthy, happy baby he was, James? The one-night stands and filthy trains and cheap hotels and bad food never made him cross or sick. He was always smiling or laughing. He hardly ever cried. Eugene was the same, too, happy and healthy, during the two years he lived before I let him die through my neglect.

TYRONE   Oh, for the love of God! I'm a fool for coming home!

EDMUND   Papa! Shut up!

MARY [*smiles with detached tenderness at* EDMUND]   It was Edmund who was the crosspatch when he was little, always getting upset and frightened about nothing at all. [*She pats his hand—teasingly*] Everyone used to say, dear, you'd cry at the drop of a hat.

EDMUND [*cannot control his bitterness*]   Maybe I guessed there was a good reason not to laugh.

TYRONE [*reproving and pitying*]   Now, now, lad. You know better than to pay attention—

MARY [*as if she hadn't heard—sadly again*]   Who would have thought Jamie would grow up to disgrace us. You remember, James, for years after he went to boarding school, we received such glowing reports. Everyone liked him. All his teachers told us what a fine brain he had, and how easily he learned his lessons. Even after he began to drink and they had to expel him, they wrote us how sorry they were, because he was so likable and such a brilliant student. They predicted a wonderful future for him if he would only learn to take life seriously. [*She pauses—then adds with a strange, sad detachment*] It's such a pity. Poor Jamie! It's hard to understand—[*Abruptly a change comes over her. Her face hardens and she stares at her husband with accusing hostility.*] No, it isn't at all. You brought him up to be a boozer. Since he first opened his eyes, he's seen you drinking. Always a bottle on the bureau in the cheap hotel rooms! And if he had a nightmare when he was little, or a stomach-ache, your remedy was to give him a teaspoonful of whiskey to quiet him.

TYRONE [*stung*] So I'm to blame because that lazy hulk has made a drunken loafer of himself? Is that what I came home to listen to? I might have known! When you have the poison in you, you want to blame everyone but yourself!

EDMUND Papa! You told me not to pay attention. [*then, resentfully*] Anyway it's true. You did the same thing with me. I can remember that teaspoonful of booze every time I woke up with a nightmare.

MARY [*in a detached reminiscent tone*] Yes, you were continually having nightmares as a child. You were born afraid. Because I was so afraid to bring you into the world. [*She pauses—then goes on with the same detachment*] Please don't think I blame your father, Edmund. He didn't know any better. He never went to school after he was ten. His people were the most ignorant kind of poverty-stricken Irish. I'm sure they honestly believed whiskey is the healthiest medicine for a child who is sick or frightened.

[TYRONE *is about to burst out in angry defense of his family but* EDMUND *intervenes.*]

EDMUND [*sharply*] Papa! [*changing the subject*] Are we going to have this drink, or aren't we?

TYRONE [*controlling himself—dully*] You're right. I'm a fool to take notice. [*He picks up his glass listlessly.*] Drink hearty, lad.

[EDMUND *drinks but* TYRONE *remains staring at the glass in his hand.* EDMUND *at once realizes how much the whiskey has been watered. He frowns, glancing from the bottle to his mother—starts to say something but stops.*]

MARY [*in a changed tone—repentantly*] I'm sorry if I sounded bitter, James. I'm not. It's all so far away. But I did feel a little hurt when you wished you hadn't come home. I was so relieved and happy when you came, and grateful to you. It's very dreary and sad to be here alone in the fog with night falling.

TYRONE [*moved*] I'm glad I came, Mary, when you act like your real self.

MARY I was so lonesome I kept Cathleen with me just to have someone to talk to. [*Her manner and quality drift back to the shy convent girl again.*] Do you know what I was telling her, dear? About the night my father took me to your dressing room and I first fell in love with you. Do you remember?

TYRONE [*deeply moved—his voice husky*] Can you think I'd ever forget, Mary?

[EDMUND *looks away from them, sad and embarrassed.*]

MARY [*tenderly*] No. I know you still love me, James, in spite of everything.

TYRONE [*His face works and he blinks back tears—with quiet intensity*] Yes! As God is my judge! Always and forever, Mary!

MARY And I love you, dear, in spite of everything.

[*There is a pause in which* EDMUND *moves embarrassedly. The strange detachment comes over her manner again as if she were speaking impersonally of people seen from a distance.*]

But I must confess, James, although I couldn't help loving you, I would never have married you if I'd known you drank so much. I remember the first night your barroom friends had to help you up to the door of our hotel room, and knocked and then ran away before I came to the door. We were still on our honeymoon, do you remember?

TYRONE [*with guilty vehemence*]   I don't remember! It wasn't on our honeymoon! And I never in my life had to be helped to bed, or missed a performance!

MARY [*as though he hadn't spoken*]   I had waited in that ugly hotel room hour after hour. I kept making excuses for you. I told myself it must be some business connected with the theater. I knew so little about the theater. Then I became terrified. I imagined all sorts of horrible accidents. I got on my knees and prayed that nothing had happened to you—and then they brought you up and left you outside the door. [*She gives a little, sad sigh.*] I didn't know how often that was to happen in the years to come, how many times I was to wait in ugly hotel rooms. I became quite used to it.

EDMUND [*bursts out with a look of accusing hate at his father*]   Christ! No wonder—! [*He controls himself—gruffly*] When is dinner, Mama? It must be time.

TYRONE [*overwhelmed by shame which he tries to hide, fumbles with his watch*]   Yes. It must be. Let's see. [*He stares at his watch without seeing it—pleadingly*] Mary! Can't you forget—?

MARY [*with detached pity*]   No, dear. But I forgive. I always forgive you. So don't look so guilty. I'm sorry I remembered out loud. I don't want to be sad, or to make you sad. I want to remember only the happy part of the past. [*Her manner drifts back to the shy, gay convent girl.*] Do you remember our wedding, dear? I'm sure you've completely forgotten what my wedding gown looked like. Men don't notice such things. They don't think they're important. But it was important to me, I can tell you! How I fussed and worried! I was so excited and happy! My father told me to buy anything I wanted and never mind what it cost. The best is none too good, he said. I'm afraid he spoiled me dreadfully. My mother didn't. She was very pious and strict. I think she was a little jealous. She didn't approve of my marrying—especially an actor. I think she hoped I would become a nun. She used to scold my father. She'd grumble, "You never tell me, never mind what it costs, when I buy anything! You've spoiled that girl so, I pity her husband if she ever marries. She'll expect him to give her the moon. She'll never make a good wife." [*She laughs affectionately.*] Poor mother! [*She smiles at TYRONE with a strange, incongruous coquetry.*] But she was mistaken, wasn't she, James? I haven't been such a bad wife, have I?

TYRONE [*huskily, trying to force a smile*]   I'm not complaining, Mary.

MARY [*a shadow of vague guilt crosses her face*]   At least, I've loved you dearly, and done the best I could—under the circumstances. [*The shadow vanishes and her shy, girlish expression returns.*] That wedding gown was nearly the death of me and the dressmaker, too! [*She laughs.*] I was so particular. It was never quite good enough. At last she said she refused to touch it any more or she might spoil it, and I made her leave so I could be alone to examine myself in the mirror. I was so pleased and vain. I thought to myself, "Even if your nose and mouth and ears are a trifle too large, your eyes and hair and figure, and your hands, make up for it. You're just as pretty as any actress he's ever met, and you don't have to use paint." [*She pauses, wrinkling her brow in an effort of memory.*] Where is my wedding gown now, I wonder? I kept it wrapped up in tissue paper in my trunk. I used to hope I would have a daughter and when it came time for her to marry—She couldn't have bought a lovelier gown, and I knew, James, you'd never tell her, never mind the cost. You'd want her to pick up something at a bargain. It was made of soft, shimmering satin, trimmed with wonderful old duchesse lace, in tiny ruffles around the neck and sleeves, and worked in with the folds that were draped round in a bustle effect at the back. The basque[4] was boned and very tight. I remember I held my breath when it was fitted, so my waist would be as small as possible. My father even let me have duchesse lace on my white satin slippers, and lace with orange blossoms in my veil. Oh, how I loved that gown! It was so beautiful! Where is it now, I wonder? I used to take it out from time to time when I was lonely, but it always made me cry, so finally a long while ago—[*She wrinkles her forehead again.*] I wonder where I hid it? Probably in one of the old trunks in the attic. Some day I'll have to look.

[*She stops, staring before her.* TYRONE *sighs, shaking his head hopelessly, and attempts to catch his son's eye, looking for sympathy, but* EDMUND *is staring at the floor.*]

TYRONE [*forces a casual tone*]   Isn't it dinner time, dear? [*with a feeble attempt at teasing*] You're forever scolding me for being late, but now I'm on time for once, it's dinner that's late.

[*She doesn't appear to hear him. He adds, still pleasantly*]

Well, if I can't eat yet, I can drink. I'd forgotten I had this.

[*He drinks his drink.* EDMUND *watches him.* TYRONE *scowls and looks at his wife with sharp suspicion—roughly*]

Who's been tampering with my whiskey? The damned stuff is half water! Jamie's been away and he wouldn't overdo his trick like this, anyway. Any fool could tell—Mary, answer me! [*with angry disgust*] I hope to God you haven't taken to drink on top of—

EDMUND   Shut up, Papa! [*to his mother, without looking at her*] You treated Cathleen and Bridget, isn't that it, Mama?

MARY [*with indifferent casualness*]   Yes, of course. They work hard for poor wages. And I'm the housekeeper, I have to keep them from leaving. Besides, I wanted to treat Cathleen because I had her drive uptown with me, and sent her to get my prescription filled.

EDMUND   For God's sake, Mama! You can't trust her! Do you want everyone on earth to know?

MARY [*her face hardening stubbornly*]   Know what? That I suffer from rheumatism in my hands and have to take medicine to kill the pain? Why should I be ashamed of that? [*turns on* EDMUND *with a hard, accusing antagonism—almost a revengeful enmity*] I never knew what rheumatism was before you were born! Ask your father!

[EDMUND *looks away, shrinking into himself.*]

---

4. Tight-fitting bodice.

TYRONE   Don't mind her, lad. It doesn't mean anything. When she gets to the stage where she gives the old crazy excuse about her hands she's gone far away from us.

MARY [*turns on him—with a strangely triumphant, taunting smile*]   I'm glad you realize that, James! Now perhaps you'll give up trying to remind me, you and Edmund! [*abruptly, in a detached, matter-of-fact tone*] Why don't you light the light, James? It's getting dark. I know you hate to, but Edmund has proved to you that one bulb burning doesn't cost much. There's no sense letting your fear of the poorhouse make you too stingy.

TYRONE [*reacts mechanically*]   I never claimed one bulb cost much! It's having them on, one here and one there, that makes the Electric Light Company rich. [*He gets up and turns on the reading lamp—roughly*] But I'm a fool to talk reason to you. [*to EDMUND*] I'll get a fresh bottle of whiskey, lad, and we'll have a real drink. [*He goes through the back parlor.*]

MARY [*with detached amusement*]   He'll sneak around to the outside cellar door so the servants won't see him. He's really ashamed of keeping his whiskey padlocked in the cellar. Your father is a strange man, Edmund. It took many years before I understood him. You must try to understand and forgive him, too, and not feel contempt because he's close-fisted. His father deserted his mother and their six children a year or so after they came to America. He told them he had a premonition he would die soon, and he was homesick for Ireland, and wanted to go back there to die. So he went and he did die. He must have been a peculiar man, too. Your father had to go to work in a machine shop when he was only ten years old.

EDMUND [*protests dully*]   Oh, for Pete's sake, Mama. I've heard Papa tell that machine shop story ten thousand times.

MARY   Yes, dear, you've had to listen, but I don't think you've ever tried to understand.

EDMUND [*ignoring this—miserably*]   Listen, Mama! You're not so far gone yet you've forgotten everything. You haven't asked me what I found out this afternoon. Don't you care a damn?

MARY [*shakenly*]   Don't say that! You hurt me, dear!

EDMUND   What I've got is serious, Mama. Doc Hardy knows for sure now.

MARY [*stiffens into scornful, defensive stubbornness*]   That lying old quack! I warned you he'd invent—!

EDMUND [*miserably dogged*]   He called in a specialist to examine me, so he'd be absolutely sure.

MARY [*ignoring this*]   Don't tell me about Hardy! If you heard what the doctor at the sanatorium, who really knows something, said about how he'd treated me! He said he ought to be locked up! He said it was a wonder I hadn't gone mad! I told him I had once, that time I ran down in my nightdress to throw myself off the dock. You remember that, don't you? And yet you want me to pay attention to what Doctor Hardy says. Oh, no!

EDMUND [*bitterly*]   I remember, all right. It was right after that Papa and Jamie decided they couldn't hide it from me any more. Jamie told me. I called him a liar! I tried to punch him in the nose. But I knew he wasn't lying. [*His voice trembles, his eyes begin to fill with tears.*] God, it made everything in life seem rotten!

MARY [*pitiably*]   Oh, don't. My baby! You hurt me so dreadfully!

EDMUND [*dully*]   I'm sorry, Mama. It was you who brought it up. [*then with a bitter, stubborn persistence*] Listen, Mama. I'm going to tell you whether you want to hear or not. I've got to go to a sanatorium.

MARY [*dazedly, as if this was something that had never occurred to her*]   Go away? [*violently*] No! I won't have it! How dare Doctor Hardy advise such a thing without consulting me! How dare your father allow him! What right has he? You are my baby! Let him attend to Jamie! [*more and more excited and bitter*] I know why he wants you sent to a sanatorium. To take you from me! He's always tried to do that. He's been jealous of every one of my babies! He kept finding ways to make me leave them. That's what caused Eugene's death. He's been jealous of you most of all. He knew I loved you most because—

EDMUND [*miserably*]   Oh, stop talking crazy, can't you, Mama! Stop trying to blame him. And why are you so against my going away now? I've been away a lot, and I've never noticed it broke your heart!

MARY [*bitterly*]   I'm afraid you're not very sensitive, after all. [*sadly*] You might have guessed, dear, that after I knew you knew—about me—I had to be glad whenever you were where you couldn't see me.

EDMUND [*brokenly*]   Mama! Don't! [*He reaches out blindly and takes her hand—but he drops it immediately, overcome by bitterness again.*] All this talk about loving me—and you won't even listen when I try to tell you how sick—

MARY [*with an abrupt transformation into a detached bullying motherliness*]   Now, now. That's enough! I don't care to hear because I know it's nothing but Hardy's ignorant lies.

   [*He shrinks back into himself. She keeps on in a forced, teasing tone but with an increasing undercurrent of resentment.*]

You're so like your father, dear. You love to make a scene out of nothing so you can be dramatic and tragic. [*with a belittling laugh*] If I gave you the slightest encouragement, you'd tell me next you were going to die—

EDMUND   People do die of it. Your own father—

MARY [*sharply*]   Why do you mention him? There's no comparison at all with you. He had consumption. [*angrily*] I hate you when you become gloomy and morbid! I forbid you to remind me of my father's death, do you hear me?

EDMUND [*his face hard—grimly*]   Yes, I hear you, Mama. I wish to God I didn't! [*He gets up from his chair and stands staring condemningly at her— bitterly*] It's pretty hard to take at times, having a dope fiend for a mother!

   [*She winces—all life seeming to drain from her face, leaving it with the appearance of a plaster cast. Instantly EDMUND wishes he could take back what he has said. He stammers miserably.*]

Forgive me, Mama. I was angry. You hurt me.

   [*There is a pause in which the foghorn and the ships' bells are heard.*]

MARY [*goes slowly to the windows at right like an automaton—looking out, a blank, far-off quality in her voice*]   Just listen to that awful foghorn. And the bells. Why is it fog makes everything sound so sad and lost, I wonder?

EDMUND [*brokenly*]   I—I can't stay here. I don't want any dinner.

   [*He hurries away through the front parlor. She keeps staring out the window until she hears the front door close behind him. Then she comes back and sits in her chair, the same blank look on her face.*]

MARY [*vaguely*]   I must go upstairs. I haven't taken enough. [*She pauses—then longingly*] I hope, sometime, without meaning it, I will take an overdose. I never could do it deliberately. The Blessed Virgin would never forgive me, then.

> [*She hears* TYRONE *returning and turns as he comes in, through the back parlor, with a bottle of whiskey he has just uncorked. He is fuming.*]

TYRONE [*wrathfully*]   The padlock is all scratched. That drunken loafer has tried to pick the lock with a piece of wire, the way he's done before. [*with satisfaction, as if this was a perpetual battle of wits with his elder son*] But I've fooled him this time. It's a special padlock a professional burglar couldn't pick. [*He puts the bottle on the tray and suddenly is aware of* EDMUND's *absence.*] Where's Edmund?

MARY [*with a vague far-away air*]   He went out. Perhaps he's going uptown again to find Jamie. He still has some money left, I suppose, and it's burning a hole in his pocket. He said he didn't want any dinner. He doesn't seem to have any appetite these days. [*then stubbornly*] But it's just a summer cold.

> [TYRONE *stares at her and shakes his head helplessly and pours himself a big drink and drinks it. Suddenly it is too much for her and she breaks out and sobs.*]

Oh, James, I'm so frightened! [*She gets up and throws her arms around him and hides her face on his shoulder—sobbingly*] I know he's going to die!

TYRONE   Don't say that! It's not true! They promised me in six months he'd be cured.

MARY   You don't believe that! I can tell when you're acting! And it will be my fault. I should never have borne him. It would have been better for his sake. I could never hurt him then. He wouldn't have had to know his mother was a dope fiend—and hate her!

TYRONE [*his voice quivering*]   Hush, Mary, for the love of God! He loves you. He knows it was a curse put on you without your knowing or willing it. He's proud you're his mother! [*abruptly as he hears the pantry door opening*] Hush, now! Here comes Cathleen. You don't want her to see you crying.

> [*She turns quickly away from him to the windows at right, hastily wiping her eyes. A moment later* CATHLEEN *appears in the back-parlor doorway. She is uncertain in her walk and grinning woozily.*]

CATHLEEN [*starts guiltily when she sees* TYRONE—*with dignity*]   Dinner is served, Sir. [*raising her voice unnecessarily*] Dinner is served, Ma'am. [*She forgets her dignity and addresses* TYRONE *with good-natured familiarity*] So you're here, are you? Well, well. Won't Bridget be in a rage! I told her the Madame said you wouldn't be home. [*then reading accusation in his eye*] Don't be looking at me that way. If I've a drop taken, I didn't steal it. I was invited.

> [*She turns with huffy dignity and disappears through the back parlor.*]

TYRONE [*sighs—then summoning his actor's heartiness*]   Come along, dear. Let's have our dinner. I'm hungry as a hunter.

MARY [*comes to him—her face is composed in plaster again and her tone is remote*]   I'm afraid you'll have to excuse me, James. I couldn't possibly eat anything. My hands pain me dreadfully. I think the best thing for me is to go to bed and rest. Good night dear.

[*She kisses him mechanically and turns toward the front parlor.*]

TYRONE [*harshly*]   Up to take more of that God-damned poison, is that it? You'll be like a mad ghost before the night's over!

MARY [*starts to walk away—blankly*]   I don't know what you're talking about, James. You say such mean, bitter things when you've drunk too much. You're as bad as Jamie or Edmund.

> [*She moves off through the front parlor. He stands a second as if not knowing what to do. He is a sad, bewildered, broken old man. He walks wearily off through the back parlor toward the dining room.*]

CURTAIN

Act 4

SCENE—*The same. It is around midnight. The lamp in the front hall has been turned out, so that now no light shines through the front parlor. In the living room only the reading lamp on the table is lighted. Outside the windows the wall of fog appears denser than ever. As the curtain rises, the foghorn is heard, followed by the ships' bells from the harbor.*

TYRONE is seated at the table. He wears his pince-nez[5] and is playing solitaire. He has taken off his coat and has on an old brown dressing gown. The whiskey bottle on the tray is three-quarters empty. There is a fresh full bottle on the table, which he has brought from the cellar so there will be an ample reserve on hand. He is drunk and shows it by the owlish, deliberate manner in which he peers at each card to make certain of its identity, and then plays it as if he wasn't certain of his aim. His eyes have a misted, oily look and his mouth is slack. But despite all the whiskey in him, he has not escaped, and he looks as he appeared at the close of the preceding act, a sad, defeated old man, possessed by hopeless resignation.

As the curtain rises, he finishes a game and sweeps the cards together. He shuffles them clumsily, dropping a couple on the floor. He retrieves them with difficulty, and starts to shuffle again, when he hears someone entering the front door. He peers over his pince-nez through the front parlor.

TYRONE [*his voice thick*]   Who's that? Is it you, Edmund?

> [EDMUND's *voice answers curtly,* "Yes." *Then he evidently collides with something in the dark hall and can be heard cursing. A moment later the hall lamp is turned on.* TYRONE *frowns and calls.*]

Turn that light out before you come in.

> [*But* EDMUND *doesn't. He comes in through the front parlor. He is drunk now, too, but like his father he carries it well, and gives little physical sign of it except in his eyes and a chip-on-the-shoulder aggressiveness in his manner.* TYRONE *speaks, at first with a warm, relieved welcome.*]

I'm glad you've come, lad. I've been damned lonely. [*then resentfully*] You're a fine one to run away and leave me to sit alone here all night when you know—[*with sharp irritation*] I told you to turn out that light! We're not giving a ball. There's no reason to have the house ablaze with electricity at this time of night, burning up money!

EDMUND [*angrily*]   Ablaze with electricity! One bulb! Hell, everyone keeps

---

5. Eyeglasses clipped to the nose.

a light on in the front hall until they go to bed. [*He rubs his knee.*] I damned near busted my knee on the hat stand.

TYRONE   The light from here shows in the hall. You could see your way well enough if you were sober.

EDMUND   If *I* was sober? I like that!

TYRONE   I don't give a damn what other people do. If they want to be wasteful fools, for the sake of show, let them be!

EDMUND   One bulb! Christ, don't be such a cheap skate! I've proved by figures if you left the light bulb on all night it wouldn't be as much as one drink!

TYRONE   To hell with your figures! The proof is in the bills I have to pay!

EDMUND [*sits down opposite his father—contemptuously*]   Yes, facts don't mean a thing, do they? What you want to believe, that's the only truth! [*derisively*] Shakespeare was an Irish Catholic, for example.

TYRONE [*stubbornly*]   So he was. The proof is in his plays.

EDMUND   Well he wasn't, and there's no proof of it in his plays, except to you! [*jeeringly*] The Duke of Wellington, there was another good Irish Catholic!

TYRONE   I never said he was a good one. He was a renegade but a Catholic just the same.

EDMUND   Well, he wasn't. You just want to believe no one but an Irish Catholic general could beat Napoleon.

TYRONE   I'm not going to argue with you. I asked you to turn out that light in the hall.

EDMUND   I heard you, and as far as I'm concerned it stays on.

TYRONE   None of your damned insolence! Are you going to obey me or not?

EDMUND   Not! If you want to be a crazy miser put it out yourself!

TYRONE [*with threatening anger*]   Listen to me! I've put up with a lot from you because from the mad things you've done at times I've thought you weren't quite right in your head. I've excused you and never lifted my hand to you. But there's a straw that breaks the camel's back. You'll obey me and put out that light or, big as you are, I'll give you a thrashing that'll teach you—! [*Suddenly he remembers* EDMUND'S *illness and instantly becomes guilty and shamefaced.*] Forgive me, lad. I forgot—You shouldn't goad me into losing my temper.

EDMUND [*ashamed himself now*]   Forget it, Papa. I apologize, too. I had no right being nasty about nothing. I am a bit soused, I guess. I'll put out the damned light. [*He starts to get up.*]

TYRONE   No, stay where you are. Let it burn.

[*He stands up abruptly—and a bit drunkenly—and begins turning on the three bulbs in the chandelier, with a childish, bitterly dramatic self-pity.*] We'll have them all on! Let them burn! To hell with them! The poorhouse is the end of the road, and it might as well be sooner as later! [*He finishes turning on the lights.*]

EDMUND [*has watched this proceeding with an awakened sense of humor—now he grins, teasing affectionately*]   That's a grand curtain. [*He laughs.*] You're a wonder, Papa.

TYRONE [*sits down sheepishly—grumbles pathetically*]   That's right, laugh at the old fool! The poor old ham! But the final curtain will be in the poorhouse just the same, and that's not comedy! [*Then as* EDMUND *is still grin-*

ning, he changes the subject.] Well, well, let's not argue. You've got brains in that head of yours, though you do your best to deny them. You'll live to learn the value of a dollar. You're not like your damned tramp of a brother. I've given up hope he'll ever get sense. Where is he, by the way?

EDMUND   How would I know?

TYRONE   I thought you'd gone back uptown to meet him.

EDMUND   No. I walked out to the beach. I haven't seen him since this afternoon.

TYRONE   Well, if you split the money I gave you with him, like a fool—

EDMUND   Sure I did. He's always staked me when he had anything.

TYRONE   Then it doesn't take a soothsayer to tell he's probably in the whorehouse.

EDMUND   What of it if he is? Why not?

TYRONE [*contemptuously*]   Why not, indeed. It's the fit place for him. If he's ever had a loftier dream than whores and whiskey, he's never shown it.

EDMUND   Oh, for Pete's sake, Papa! If you're going to start that stuff, I'll beat it. [*He starts to get up.*]

TYRONE [*placatingly*]   All right, all right, I'll stop. God knows, I don't like the subject either. Will you join me in a drink?

EDMUND   Ah! Now you're talking!

TYRONE [*passes the bottle to him—mechanically*]   I'm wrong to treat you. You've had enough already.

EDMUND [*pouring a big drink—a bit drunkenly*]   Enough is *not* as good as a feast. [*He hands back the bottle.*]

TYRONE   It's too much in your condition.

EDMUND   Forget my condition! [*He raises his glass.*] Here's how.

TYRONE   Drink hearty. [*They drink.*] If you walked all the way to the beach you must be damp and chilled.

EDMUND   Oh, I dropped in at the Inn on the way out and back.

TYRONE   It's not a night I'd pick for a long walk.

EDMUND   I loved the fog. It was what I needed. [*He sounds more tipsy and looks it.*]

TYRONE   You should have more sense than to risk—

EDMUND   To hell with sense! We're all crazy. What do we want with sense? [*He quotes from Dowson[6] sardonically.*]

> "They are not long, the weeping and the laughter,
> Love and desire and hate:
> I think they have no portion in us after
> We pass the gate.
>
> They are not long, the days of wine and roses:
> Out of a misty dream
> Our path emerges for a while, then closes
> Within a dream."

[*staring before him*] The fog was where I wanted to be. Halfway down the path you can't see this house. You'd never know it was here. Or any of the other places down the avenue. I couldn't see but a few feet ahead. I didn't

---

6. Ernest Dowson (1867–1900), English poet.

meet a soul. Everything looked and sounded unreal. Nothing was what it is. That's what I wanted—to be alone with myself in another world where truth is untrue and life can hide from itself. Out beyond the harbor, where the road runs along the beach, I even lost the feeling of being on land. The fog and the sea seemed part of each other. It was like walking on the bottom of the sea. As if I had drowned long ago. As if I was a ghost belonging to the fog, and the fog was the ghost of the sea. It felt damned peaceful to be nothing more than a ghost within a ghost. [*He sees his father staring at him with mingled worry and irritated disapproval. He grins mockingly.*] Don't look at me as if I'd gone nutty. I'm talking sense. Who wants to see life as it is, if they can help it? It's the three Gorgons[7] in one. You look in their faces and turn to stone. Or it's Pan.[8] You see him and you die—that is, inside you—and have to go on living as a ghost.

TYRONE [*impressed and at the same time revolted*]   You have a poet in you but it's a damned morbid one! [*forcing a smile*] Devil take your pessimism. I feel low-spirited enough. [*He sighs.*] Why can't you remember your Shakespeare and forget the third-raters. You'll find what you're trying to say in him—as you'll find everything else worth saying. [*He quotes, using his fine voice*] "We are such stuff as dreams are made on, and our little life is rounded with a sleep."[9]

EDMUND [*ironically*]   Fine! That's beautiful. But I wasn't trying to say that. We are such stuff as manure is made on, so let's drink up and forget it. That's more my idea.

TYRONE [*disgustedly*]   Ach! Keep such sentiments to yourself. I shouldn't have given you that drink.

EDMUND It did pack a wallop, all right. On you, too. [*He grins with affectionate teasing.*] Even if you've never missed a performance! [*aggressively*] Well, what's wrong with being drunk? It's what we're after, isn't it? Let's not kid each other, Papa. Not tonight. We know what we're trying to forget. [*hurriedly*] But let's not talk about it. It's no use now.

TYRONE [*dully*]   No. All we can do is try to be resigned—again.

EDMUND   Or be so drunk you can forget. [*He recites, and recites well, with bitter, ironical passion, the Symons' translation of Baudelaire's[1] prose poem.*] "Be always drunken. Nothing else matters: that is the only question. If you would not feel the horrible burden of Time weighing on your shoulders and crushing you to the earth, be drunken continually.

Drunken with what? With wine, with poetry, or with virtue, as you will. But be drunken.

And if sometimes, on the stairs of a palace, or on the green side of a ditch, or in the dreary solitude of your own room, you should awaken and the drunkenness be half or wholly slipped away from you, ask of the wind, or of the wave, or of the star, or of the bird, or of the clock, of whatever flies, or sighs, or rocks, or sings, or speaks, ask what hour it is; and the wind, wave, star, bird, clock, will answer you: 'It is the hour to be

---

7. In Greek mythology, three monstrous sisters so ugly that the sight of them turned one to stone.
8. Greek god of woods, fields, and flocks, half man and half goat, associated with wildness.

9. Shakespeare's *The Tempest* 4.1.156–58.
1. Charles Baudelaire (1821–1867), French poet. Arthur Symons (1865–1945), English poet and literary critic.

drunken! Be drunken, if you would not be martyred slaves of Time; be drunken continually! With wine, with poetry, or with virtue, as you will.' "
[*He grins at his father provocatively.*]

TYRONE [*thickly humorous*]   I wouldn't worry about the virtue part of it, if I were you. [*then disgustedly*] Pah! It's morbid nonsense! What little truth is in it you'll find nobly said in Shakespeare. [*then appreciatively*] But you recited it well, lad. Who wrote it?

EDMUND   Baudelaire.

TYRONE   Never heard of him.

EDMUND [*grins provocatively*]   He also wrote a poem about Jamie and the Great White Way.

TYRONE   That loafer! I hope to God he misses the last car and has to stay uptown!

EDMUND [*goes on, ignoring this*]   Although he was French and never saw Broadway and died before Jamie was born. He knew him and Little Old New York just the same. [*He recites the Symons' translation of Baudelaire's "Epilogue."*]

> "With heart at rest I climbed the citadel's
> Steep height, and saw the city as from a tower,
> Hospital, brothel, prison, and such hells,
>
> Where evil comes up softly like a flower.
> Thou knowest, O Satan, patron of my pain,
> Not for vain tears I went up at that hour;
>
> But like an old sad faithful lecher, fain
> To drink delight of that enormous trull
> Whose hellish beauty makes me young again.
>
> Whether thou sleep, with heavy vapours full,
> Sodden with day, or, new apparelled, stand
> In gold-laced veils of evening beautiful,
>
> I love thee, infamous city! Harlots and
> Hunted have pleasures of their own to give,
> The vulgar herd can never understand."

TYRONE [*with irritable disgust*]   Morbid filth! Where the hell do you get your taste in literature? Filth and despair and pessimism! Another atheist, I suppose. When you deny God, you deny hope. That's the trouble with you. If you'd get down on your knees—

EDMUND [*as if he hadn't heard—sardonically*]   It's a good likeness of Jamie, don't you think, hunted by himself and whiskey, hiding in a Broadway hotel room with some fat tart—he likes them fat—reciting Dowson's Cynara to her. [*He recites derisively, but with deep feeling*]

> "All night upon mine heart I felt her warm heart beat,
> Night-long within mine arms in love and sleep she lay;
> Surely the kisses of her bought red mouth were sweet;
> But I was desolate and sick of an old passion,
> When I awoke and found the dawn was gray:
> I have been faithful to thee, Cynara! in my fashion."

[*jeeringly*] And the poor fat burlesque queen doesn't get a word of it, but suspects she's being insulted! And Jamie never loved any Cynara, and was never faithful to a woman in his life, even in his fashion! But he lies there, kidding himself he is superior and enjoys pleasures "the vulgar herd can never understand"! [*He laughs.*] It's nuts—completely nuts!

TYRONE [*vaguely—his voice thick*] It's madness, yes. If you'd get on your knees and pray. When you deny God, you deny sanity.

EDMUND [*ignoring this*] But who am I to feel superior? I've done the same damned thing. And it's no more crazy than Dowson himself, inspired by an absinthe hangover, writing it to a dumb barmaid, who thought he was a poor crazy souse, and gave him the gate to marry a waiter! [*He laughs— then soberly, with genuine sympathy*] Poor Dowson. Booze and consumption got him. [*He starts and for a second looks miserable and frightened. Then with defensive irony*] Perhaps it would be tactful of me to change the subject.

TYRONE [*thickly*] Where you get your taste in authors—That damned library of yours! [*He indicates the small bookcase at rear.*] Voltaire, Rousseau, Schopenhauer, Nietzsche, Ibsen! Atheists, fools, and madmen! And your poets! This Dowson, and this Baudelaire, and Swinburne and Oscar Wilde, and Whitman and Poe! Whore-mongers and degenerates! Pah! When I've three good sets of Shakespeare there [*he nods at the large bookcase*] you could read.

EDMUND [*provocatively*] They say he was a souse, too.

TYRONE They lie! I don't doubt he liked his glass—it's a good man's failing—but he knew how to drink so it didn't poison his brain with morbidness and filth. Don't compare him with the pack you've got in there. [*He indicates the small bookcase again.*] Your dirty Zola! And your Dante Gabriel Rossetti who was a dope fiend! [*He starts and looks guilty.*]

EDMUND [*with defensive dryness*] Perhaps it would be wise to change the subject. [*a pause*] You can't accuse me of not knowing Shakespeare. Didn't I win five dollars from you once when you bet me I couldn't learn a leading part of his in a week, as you used to do in stock in the old days. I learned Macbeth and recited it letter perfect, with you giving me the cues.

TYRONE [*approvingly*] That's true. So you did. [*He smiles teasingly and sighs.*] It was a terrible ordeal, I remember, hearing you murder the lines. I kept wishing I'd paid over the bet without making you prove it.

[*He chuckles and* EDMUND *grins. Then he starts as he hears a sound from upstairs—with dread*]

Did you hear? She's moving around. I was hoping she'd gone to sleep.

EDMUND Forget it! How about another drink?

[*He reaches out and gets the bottle, pours a drink and hands it back. Then with a strained casualness, as his father pours a drink*]

When did Mama go to bed?

TYRONE Right after you left. She wouldn't eat any dinner. What made you run away?

EDMUND Nothing. [*Abruptly raising his glass.*] Well, here's how.

TYRONE [*mechanically*] Drink hearty, lad. [*They drink.* TYRONE *again listens to sounds upstairs—with dread*] She's moving around a lot. I hope to God she doesn't come down.

EDMUND [*dully*]   Yes. She'll be nothing but a ghost haunting the past by this time. [*He pauses—then miserably*] Back before I was born—

TYRONE   Doesn't she do the same with me? Back before she ever knew me. You'd think the only happy days she's ever known were in her father's home, or at the Convent, praying and playing the piano. [*jealous resentment in his bitterness*] As I've told you before, you must take her memories with a grain of salt. Her wonderful home was ordinary enough. Her father wasn't the great, generous, noble Irish gentleman she makes out. He was a nice enough man, good company and a good talker. I liked him and he liked me. He was prosperous enough, too, in his wholesale grocery business, an able man. But he had his weakness. She condemns my drinking but she forgets his. It's true he never touched a drop till he was forty, but after that he made up for lost time. He became a steady champagne drinker, the worst kind. That was his grand pose, to drink only champagne. Well, it finished him quick—that and the consumption—[*He stops with a guilty glance at his son.*]

EDMUND [*sardonically*]   We don't seem able to avoid unpleasant topics, do we?

TYRONE [*sighs sadly*]   No. [*then with a pathetic attempt at heartiness*] What do you say to a game or two of Casino, lad?

EDMUND   All right.

TYRONE [*shuffling the cards clumsily*]   We can't lock up and go to bed till Jamie comes on the last trolley—which I hope he won't—and I don't want to go upstairs, anyway, till she's asleep.

EDMUND   Neither do I.

TYRONE [*keeps shuffling the cards fumblingly, forgetting to deal them*]   As I was saying, you must take her tales of the past with a grain of salt. The piano playing and her dream of becoming a concert pianist. That was put in her head by the nuns flattering her. She was their pet. They loved her for being so devout. They're innocent women, anyway, when it comes to the world. They don't know that not one in a million who shows promise ever rises to concert playing. Not that your mother didn't play well for a schoolgirl, but that's no reason to take it for granted she could have—

EDMUND [*sharply*]   Why don't you deal, if we're going to play.

TYRONE   Eh? I am. [*dealing with very uncertain judgment of distance*] And the idea she might have become a nun. That's the worst. Your mother was one of the most beautiful girls you could ever see. She knew it, too. She was a bit of a rogue and a coquette, God bless her, behind all her shyness and blushes. She was never made to renounce the world. She was bursting with health and high spirits and the love of loving.

EDMUND   For God's sake, Papa! Why don't you pick up your hand?

TYRONE [*picks it up—dully*]   Yes, let's see what I have here.
> [*They both stare at their cards unseeingly. Then they both start.* TYRONE *whispers*]
Listen!

EDMUND   She's coming downstairs.

TYRONE [*hurriedly*]   We'll play our game. Pretend not to notice and she'll soon go up again.

EDMUND [*staring through the front parlor—with relief*]   I don't see her. She must have started down and then turned back.

TYRONE   Thank God.

EDMUND   Yes. It's pretty horrible to see her the way she must be now. [*with bitter misery*] The hardest thing to take is the blank wall she builds around her. Or it's more like a bank of fog in which she hides and loses herself. Deliberately, that's the hell of it! You know something in her does it deliberately—to get beyond our reach, to be rid of us, to forget we're alive! It's as if, in spite of loving us, she hated us!

TYRONE [*remonstrates gently*]   Now, now, lad. It's not her. It's the damned poison.

EDMUND [*bitterly*]   She takes it to get that effect. At least, I know she did this time! [*abruptly*] My play, isn't it? Here. [*He plays a card.*]

TYRONE [*plays mechanically—gently reproachful*]   She's been terribly frightened about your illness, for all her pretending. Don't be too hard on her, lad. Remember she's not responsible. Once that cursed poison gets a hold on anyone—

EDMUND [*his face grows hard and he stares at his father with bitter accusation*]   It never should have gotten a hold on her! I know damned well she's not to blame! And I know who is! You are! Your damned stinginess! If you'd spent money for a decent doctor when she was so sick after I was born, she'd never have known morphine existed! Instead you put her in the hands of a hotel quack who wouldn't admit his ignorance and took the easiest way out, not giving a damn what happened to her afterwards! All because his fee was cheap! Another one of your bargains!

TYRONE [*stung—angrily*]   Be quiet! How dare you talk of something you know nothing about! [*trying to control his temper*] You must try to see my side of it, too, lad. How was I to know he was that kind of a doctor? He had a good reputation—

EDMUND   Among the souses in the hotel bar, I suppose!

TYRONE   That's a lie! I asked the hotel proprietor to recommend the best—

EDMUND   Yes! At the same time crying poorhouse and making it plain you wanted a cheap one! I know your system! By God, I ought to after this afternoon!

TYRONE [*guiltily defensive*]   What about this afternoon?

EDMUND   Never mind now. We're talking about Mama! I'm saying no matter how you excuse yourself you know damned well your stinginess is to blame—

TYRONE   And I say you're a liar! Shut your mouth right now, or—

EDMUND [*ignoring this*]   After you found out she'd been made a morphine addict, why didn't you send her to a cure then, at the start, while she still had a chance? No, that would have meant spending some money! I'll bet you told her all she had to do was use a little will power! That's what you still believe in your heart, in spite of what doctors, who really know something about it, have told you!

TYRONE   You lie again! I know better than that now! But how was I to know then? What did I know of morphine? It was years before I discovered what was wrong. I thought she'd never got over her sickness, that's all. Why didn't I send her to a cure, you say? [*bitterly*] Haven't I? I've spent thousands upon thousands in cures! A waste. What good have they done her? She always started again.

EDMUND   Because you've never given her anything that would help her want to stay off it! No home except this summer dump in a place she hates and you've refused even to spend money to make this look decent, while you keep buying more property, and playing sucker for every con man with a gold mine, or a silver mine, or any kind of get-rich-quick swindle! You've dragged her around on the road, season after season, on one-night stands, with no one she could talk to, waiting night after night in dirty hotel rooms for you to come back with a bun on after the bars closed! Christ, is it any wonder she didn't want to be cured. Jesus, when I think of it I hate your guts!

TYRONE [*strickenly*] Edmund! [*then in a rage*] How dare you talk to your father like that, you insolent young cub! After all I've done for you.

EDMUND We'll come to that, what you're doing for me!

TYRONE [*looking guilty again—ignores this*] Will you stop repeating your mother's crazy accusations, which she never makes unless it's the poison talking? I never dragged her on the road against her will. Naturally, I wanted her with me. I loved her. And she came because she loved me and wanted to be with me. That's the truth, no matter what she says when she's not herself. And she needn't have been lonely. There was always the members of my company to talk to, if she'd wanted. She had her children, too, and I insisted, in spite of the expense, on having a nurse to travel with her.

EDMUND [*bitterly*] Yes, your one generosity, and that because you were jealous of her paying too much attention to us, and wanted us out of your way! It was another mistake, too! If she'd had to take care of me all by herself, and had that to occupy her mind, maybe she'd have been able—

TYRONE [*goaded into vindictiveness*] Or for that matter, if you insist in judging things by what she says when she's not in her right mind, if you hadn't been born she'd never—[*He stops ashamed.*]

EDMUND [*suddenly spent and miserable*] Sure. I know that's what she feels, Papa.

TYRONE [*protests penitently*] She doesn't! She loves you as dearly as ever mother loved a son! I only said that because you put me in such a God-damned rage, raking up the past, and saying you hate me—

EDMUND [*dully*] I didn't mean it, Papa. [*He suddenly smiles—kidding a bit drunkenly*] I'm like Mama, I can't help liking you, in spite of everything.

TYRONE [*grins a bit drunkenly in return*] I might say the same of you. You're no great shakes as a son. It's a case of "A poor thing but mine own."[2] [*They both chuckle with real, if alcoholic, affection. TYRONE changes the subject.*] What's happened to our game? Whose play is it?

EDMUND Yours, I guess.

[*TYRONE plays a card which EDMUND takes and the game gets forgotten again.*]

TYRONE You mustn't let yourself be too downhearted, lad, by the bad news you had today. Both the doctors promised me, if you obey orders at this place you're going, you'll be cured in six months, or a year at most.

EDMUND [*his face hard again*] Don't kid me. You don't believe that.

TYRONE [*too vehemently*] Of course I believe it! Why shouldn't I believe it when both Hardy and the specialist—?

---

2. Shakespeare's *As You Like It* 5.4.60.

EDMUND   You think I'm going to die.

TYRONE   That's a lie! You're crazy!

EDMUND [*more bitterly*]   So why waste money? That's why you're sending me to a state farm—

TYRONE [*in guilty confusion*]   What state farm? It's the Hilltown Sanatorium, that's all I know, and both doctors said it was the best place for you.

EDMUND [*scathingly*]   For the money! That is, for nothing, or practically nothing. Don't lie, Papa! You know damned well Hilltown Sanatorium is a state institution! Jamie suspected you'd cry poorhouse to Hardy and he wormed the truth out of him.

TYRONE [*furiously*]   That drunken loafer! I'll kick him out in the gutter! He's poisoned your mind against me ever since you were old enough to listen!

EDMUND   You can't deny it's the truth about the state farm, can you?

TYRONE   It's not true the way you look at it! What if it is run by the state? That's nothing against it. The state has the money to make a better place than any private sanatorium. And why shouldn't I take advantage of it? It's my right—and yours. We're residents. I'm a property owner. I help to support it. I'm taxed to death—

EDMUND [*with bitter irony*]   Yes, on property valued at a quarter of a million.

TYRONE   Lies! It's all mortgaged!

EDMUND   Hardy and the specialist know what you're worth. I wonder what they thought of you when they heard you moaning poorhouse and showing you wanted to wish me on charity!

TYRONE   It's a lie! All I told them was I couldn't afford any millionaire's sanatorium because I was land poor. That's the truth!

EDMUND   And then you went to the Club to meet McGuire and let him stick you with another bum piece of property! [*as* TYRONE *starts to deny*] Don't lie about it! We met McGuire in the hotel bar after he left you. Jamie kidded him about hooking you, and he winked and laughed!

TYRONE [*lying feebly*]   He's a liar if he said—

EDMUND   Don't lie about it! [*with gathering intensity*] God, Papa, ever since I went to sea and was on my own, and found out what hard work for little pay was, and what it felt like to be broke, and starve, and camp on park benches because I had no place to sleep, I've tried to be fair to you because I knew what you'd been up against as a kid. I've tried to make allowances. Christ, you have to make allowances in this damned family or go nuts! I have tried to make allowances for myself when I remember all the rotten stuff I've pulled! I've tried to feel like Mama that you can't help being what you are where money is concerned. But God Almighty, this last stunt of yours is too much! It makes me want to puke! Not because of the rotten way you're treating me. To hell with that! I've treated you rottenly, in my way, more than once. But to think when it's a question of your son having consumption, you can show yourself up before the whole town as such a stinking old tightwad! Don't you know Hardy will talk and the whole damned town will know! Jesus, Papa, haven't you any pride or shame? [*bursting with rage*] And don't think I'll let you get away with it! I won't go to any damned state farm just to save you a few lousy dollars to buy more bum property with! You stinking old miser—! [*He chokes huskily, his voice trembling with rage, and then is shaken by a fit of coughing.*]

TYRONE [*has shrunk back in his chair under this attack, his guilty contrition greater than his anger—he stammers*]   Be quiet! Don't say that to me! You're drunk! I won't mind you. Stop coughing, lad. You've got yourself worked up over nothing. Who said you had to go to this Hilltown place? You can go anywhere you like. I don't give a damn what it costs. All I care about is to have you get well. Don't call me a stinking miser, just because I don't want doctors to think I'm a millionaire they can swindle.

> [EDMUND *has stopped coughing. He looks sick and weak. His father stares at him frightenedly.*]

You look weak, lad. You'd better take a bracer.

EDMUND [*grabs the bottle and pours his glass brimfull—weakly*]   Thanks. [*He gulps down the whiskey.*]

TYRONE [*pours himself a big drink, which empties the bottle, and drinks it; his head bows and he stares dully at the cards on the table—vaguely*]   Whose play is it? [*He goes on dully, without resentment.*] A stinking old miser. Well, maybe you're right. Maybe I can't help being, although all my life since I had anything I've thrown money over the bar to buy drinks for everyone in the house, or loaned money to sponges I knew would never pay it back—[*with a loose-mouthed sneer of self-contempt*] But, of course, that was in barrooms, when I was full of whiskey. I can't feel that way about it when I'm sober in my home. It was at home I first learned the value of a dollar and the fear of the poorhouse. I've never been able to believe in my luck since. I've always feared it would change and every-thing I had would be taken away. But still, the more property you own, the safer you think you are. That may not be logical, but it's the way I have to feel. Banks fail, and your money's gone, but you think you can keep land beneath your feet. [*Abruptly his tone becomes scornfully superior.*] You said you realized what I'd been up against as a boy. The hell you do! How could you? You've had everything—nurses, schools, college, though you didn't stay there. You've had food, clothing. Oh, I know you had a fling of hard work with your back and hands, a bit of being homeless and pen-niless in a foreign land, and I respect you for it. But it was a game of romance and adventure to you. It was play.

EDMUND [*dully sarcastic*]   Yes, particularly the time I tried to commit sui-cide at Jimmie the Priest's, and almost did.

TYRONE   You weren't in your right mind. No son of mine would ever—You were drunk.

EDMUND   I was stone cold sober. That was the trouble. I'd stopped to think too long.

TYRONE [*with drunken peevishness*]   Don't start your damned atheist mor-bidness again! I don't care to listen. I was trying to make plain to you—[*scornfully*] What do you know of the value of a dollar? When I was ten my father deserted my mother and went back to Ireland to die. Which he did soon enough, and deserved to, and I hope he's roasting in hell. He mistook rat poison for flour, or sugar, or something. There was gossip it wasn't by mistake but that's a lie. No one in my family ever—

EDMUND   My bet is, it wasn't by mistake.

TYRONE   More morbidness! Your brother put that in your head. The worst he can suspect is the only truth for him. But never mind. My mother was left, a stranger in a strange land, with four small children, me and a sister a little older and two younger than me. My two older brothers had moved to other parts. They couldn't help. They were hard put to it to keep themselves alive. There was no damned romance in our poverty. Twice we were evicted from the miserable hovel we called home, with my mother's few sticks of furniture thrown out in the street, and my mother and sisters crying. I cried, too, though I tried hard not to, because I was the man of the family. At ten years old! There was no more school for me. I worked twelve hours a day in a machine shop, learning to make files. A dirty barn of a place where rain dripped through the roof, where you roasted in summer, and there was no stove in winter, and your hands got numb with cold, where the only light came through two small filthy windows, so on grey days I'd have to sit bent over with my eyes almost touching the files in order to see! You talk of work! And what do you think I got for it? Fifty cents a week! It's the truth! Fifty cents a week! And my poor mother washed and scrubbed for the Yanks by the day, and my older sister sewed, and my two younger stayed at home to keep the house. We never had clothes enough to wear, nor enough food to eat. Well I remember one Thanksgiving, or maybe it was Christmas, when some Yank in whose house mother had been scrubbing gave her a dollar extra for a present, and on the way home she spent it all on food. I can remember her hugging and kissing us and saying with tears of joy running down her tired face: "Glory be to God, for once in our lives we'll have enough for each of us!" [*He wipes tears from his eyes.*] A fine, brave, sweet woman. There never was a braver or finer.

EDMUND [*moved*]   Yes, she must have been.

TYRONE   Her one fear was she'd get old and sick and have to die in the poorhouse. [*He pauses—then adds with grim humor*] It was in those days I learned to be a miser. A dollar was worth so much then. And once you've learned a lesson, it's hard to unlearn it. You have to look for bargains. If I took this state farm sanatorium for a good bargain, you'll have to forgive me. The doctors did tell me it's a good place. You must believe that, Edmund. And I swear I never meant you to go there if you didn't want to. [*vehemently*] You can choose any place you like! Never mind what it costs! Any place I can afford. Any place you like—within reason.

[*At this qualification, a grin twitches* EDMUND'*s lips. His resentment has gone. His father goes on with an elaborately offhand, casual air.*]

There was another sanatorium the specialist recommended. He said it had a record as good as any place in the country. It's endowed by a group of millionaire factory owners, for the benefit of their workers principally, but you're eligible to go there because you're a resident. There's such a pile of money behind it, they don't have to charge much. It's only seven dollars a week but you get ten times that value. [*hastily*] I don't want to persuade you to anything, understand. I'm simply repeating what I was told.

EDMUND [*concealing his smile—casually*]   Oh, I know that. It sounds like a good bargain to me. I'd like to go there. So that settles that. [*Abruptly he is miserably desperate again—dully*] It doesn't matter a damn now, anyway. Let's forget it! [*changing the subject*] How about our game? Whose play is it?

TYRONE [*mechanically*]   I don't know. Mine, I guess. No, it's yours.

[EDMUND *plays a card. His father takes it. Then about to play from his hand, he again forgets the game.*]

Yes, maybe life overdid the lesson for me, and made a dollar worth too much, and the time came when that mistake ruined my career as a fine actor. [*sadly*] I've never admitted this to anyone before, lad, but tonight I'm so heartsick I feel at the end of everything, and what's the use of fake pride and pretense. That God-damned play I bought for a song and made such a great success in—a great money success—it ruined me with its promise of an easy fortune. I didn't want to do anything else, and by the time I woke up to the fact I'd become a slave to the damned thing and did try other plays, it was too late. They had identified me with that one part, and didn't want me in anything else. They were right, too. I'd lost the great talent I once had through years of easy repetition, never learning a new part, never really working hard. Thirty-five to forty thousand dollars net profit a season like snapping your fingers! It was too great a temptation. Yet before I bought the damned thing I was considered one of the three or four young actors with the greatest artistic promise in America. I'd worked like hell. I'd left a good job as a machinist to take supers'[3] parts because I loved the theater. I was wild with ambition. I read all the plays ever written. I studied Shakespeare as you'd study the Bible. I educated myself. I got rid of an Irish brogue you could cut with a knife. I loved Shakespeare. I would have acted in any of his plays for nothing, for the joy of being alive in his great poetry. And I acted well in him. I felt inspired by him. I could have been a great Shakespearean actor, if I'd kept on. I know that! In 1874 when Edwin Booth[4] came to the theater in Chicago where I was leading man, I played Cassius to his Brutus one night, Brutus to his Cassius the next, Othello to his Iago, and so on. The first night I played Othello, he said to our manager. "That young man is playing Othello better than I ever did!" [*proudly*] That from Booth, the greatest actor of his day or any other! And it was true! And I was only twenty-seven years old! As I look back on it now, that night was the high spot in my career. I had life where I wanted it! And for a time after that I kept on upward with ambition high. Married your mother. Ask her what I was like in those days. Her love was an added incentive to ambition. But a few years later my good bad luck made me find the big money-maker. It wasn't that in my eyes at first. It was a great romantic part I knew I could play better than anyone. But it was a great box office success from the start—and then life had me where it wanted me—at from thirty-five to forty thousand net profit a season! A fortune in those days—or even in these. [*bitterly*] What the hell was it I wanted to buy, I wonder, that was worth—Well, no matter. It's a late day for regrets. [*He glances vaguely at his cards.*] My play, isn't it?

EDMUND [*moved, stares at his father with understanding—slowly*] I'm glad you've told me this, Papa. I know you a lot better now.

TYRONE [*with a loose, twisted smile*] Maybe I shouldn't have told you. Maybe you'll only feel more contempt for me. And it's a poor way to convince you of the value of a dollar. [*Then as if this phrase automatically aroused an habitual association in his mind, he glances up at the chande-*

---

3. Supernumeraries, extras.
4. Edwin Booth (1833–1893), American actor and theatrical manager.

lier disapprovingly.] The glare from those extra lights hurts my eyes. You don't mind if I turn them out, do you? We don't need them, and there's no use making the Electric Company rich.

EDMUND [*controlling a wild impulse to laugh—agreeably*]   No, sure not. Turn them out.

TYRONE [*gets heavily and a bit waveringly to his feet and gropes uncertainly for the lights—his mind going back to its line of thought*]   No, I don't know what the hell it was I wanted to buy. [*He clicks out one bulb.*] On my solemn oath, Edmund, I'd gladly face not having an acre of land to call my own, nor a penny in the bank—[*He clicks out another bulb.*] I'd be willing to have no home but the poorhouse in my old age if I could look back now on having been the fine artist I might have been.

> [*He turns out the third bulb, so only the reading lamp is on, and sits down again heavily.* EDMUND *suddenly cannot hold back a burst of strained, ironical laughter.* TYRONE *is hurt.*]

What the devil are you laughing at?

EDMUND   Not at you, Papa. At life. It's so damned crazy.

TYRONE [*growls*]   More of your morbidness! There's nothing wrong with life. It's we who—[*He quotes*] "The fault, dear Brutus, is not in our stars, but in ourselves that we are underlings."[5] [*He pauses—then sadly*] The praise Edwin Booth gave my Othello. I made the manager put down his exact words in writing. I kept it in my wallet for years. I used to read it every once in a while until finally it made me feel so bad I didn't want to face it any more. Where is it now, I wonder? Somewhere in this house. I remember I put it away carefully—

EDMUND [*with a wry ironical sadness*]   It might be in an old trunk in the attic, along with Mama's wedding dress. [*Then as his father stares at him, he adds quickly*] For Pete's sake, if we're going to play cards, let's play.

> [*He takes the card his father had played and leads. For a moment, they play the game, like mechanical chess players. Then* TYRONE *stops, listening to a sound upstairs.*]

TYRONE   She's still moving around. God knows when she'll go to sleep.

EDMUND [*pleads tensely*]   For Christ's sake, Papa, forget it!

> [*He reaches out and pours a drink.* TYRONE *starts to protest, then gives it up.* EDMUND *drinks. He puts down the glass. His expression changes. When he speaks it is as if he were deliberately giving way to drunkenness and seeking to hide behind a maudlin manner.*]

Yes, she moves above and beyond us, a ghost haunting the past, and here we sit pretending to forget, but straining our ears listening for the slightest sound, hearing the fog drip from the eaves like the uneven tick of a rundown, crazy clock—or like the dreary tears of a trollop spattering in a puddle of stale beer on a honky-tonk table top! [*He laughs with maudlin appreciation.*] Not so bad, that last, eh? Original, not Baudelaire. Give me credit! [*then with alcoholic talkativeness*] You've just told me some high spots in your memories. Want to hear mine? They're all connected with the sea. Here's one. When I was on the Squarehead square rigger, bound for Buenos Aires. Full moon in the Trades. The old hooker driving fourteen knots. I lay on the bowsprit, facing astern, with the water foaming into spume under me, the masts with every sail white in the moonlight, towering high above me. I became drunk with the beauty and singing

---

5. Shakespeare's *Julius Caesar* 1.2.134.

rhythm of it, and for a moment I lost myself—actually lost my life. I was set free! I dissolved in the sea, became white sails and flying spray, became beauty and rhythm, became moonlight and the ship and the high dim-starred sky! I belonged, without past or future, within peace and unity and a wild joy, within something greater than my own life, or the life of Man, to Life itself! To God, if you want to put it that way. Then another time, on the American Line, when I was lookout on the crow's nest in the dawn watch. A calm sea, that time. Only a lazy ground swell and a slow drowsy roll of the ship. The passengers asleep and none of the crew in sight. No sound of man. Black smoke pouring from the funnels behind and beneath me. Dreaming, not keeping lookout, feeling alone, and above, and apart, watching the dawn creep like a painted dream over the sky and sea which slept together. Then the moment of ecstatic freedom came. The peace, the end of the quest, the last harbor, the joy of belonging to a fulfillment beyond men's lousy, pitiful, greedy fears and hopes and dreams! And several other times in my life, when I was swimming far out, or lying alone on a beach, I have had the same experience. Became the sun, the hot sand, green seaweed anchored to a rock, swaying in the tide. Like a saint's vision of beatitude. Like the veil of things as they seem drawn back by an unseen hand. For a second you see—and seeing the secret, are the secret. For a second there is meaning! Then the hand lets the veil fall and you are alone, lost in the fog again, and you stumble on toward nowhere, for no good reason! [*He grins wryly.*] It was a great mistake, my being born a man, I would have been much more successful as a sea gull or a fish. As it is, I will always be a stranger who never feels at home, who does not really want and is not really wanted, who can never belong, who must always be a little in love with death!

TYRONE [*stares at him—impressed*]   Yes, there's the makings of a poet in you all right. [*then protesting uneasily*] But that's morbid craziness about not being wanted and loving death.

EDMUND [*sardonically*]   The *makings* of a poet. No, I'm afraid I'm like the guy who is always panhandling for a smoke. He hasn't even got the makings. He's got only the habit. I couldn't touch what I tried to tell you just now. I just stammered. That's the best I'll ever do. I mean, if I live. Well, it will be faithful realism, at least. Stammering is the native eloquence of us fog people.

[*A pause. Then they both jump startledly as there is a noise from outside the house, as if someone had stumbled and fallen on the front steps.* EDMUND *grins.*]

Well, that sounds like the absent brother. He must have a peach of a bun on.

TYRONE [*scowling*]   That loafer! He caught the last car, bad luck to it. [*He gets to his feet.*] Get him to bed, Edmund. I'll go out on the porch. He has a tongue like an adder when he's drunk. I'd only lose my temper.

[*He goes out the door to the side porch as the front door in the hall bangs shut behind* JAMIE. EDMUND *watches with amusement* JAMIE's *wavering progress through the front parlor.* JAMIE *comes in. He is very drunk and woozy on his legs. His eyes are glassy, his face bloated, his speech blurred, his mouth slack like his father's, a leer on his lips.*]

JAMIE [*swaying and blinking in the doorway—in a loud voice*]   What ho! What ho!

EDMUND [*sharply*]   Nix on the loud noise!

JAMIE [*blinks at him*]   Oh, hello, Kid. [*with great seriousness*] I'm as drunk as a fiddler's bitch.

EDMUND [*dryly*]   Thanks for telling me your great secret.

JAMIE [*grins foolishly*]   Yes. Unneshesary information Number One, eh? [*He bends and slaps at the knees of his trousers.*] Had serious accident. The front steps tried to trample on me. Took advantage of fog to waylay me. Ought to be a lighthouse out there. Dark in here, too. [*scowling*] What the hell is this, the morgue? Lesh have some light on subject. [*He sways forward to the table, reciting Kipling*[6]]

> "Ford, ford, ford o' Kabul river,
> Ford o' Kabul river in the dark!
> Keep the crossing-stakes beside you, an' they
>   will surely guide you
> 'Cross the ford o' Kabul river in the dark."

[*He fumbles at the chandelier and manages to turn on the three bulbs.*] Thash more like it. The hell with old Gaspard.[7] Where is the old tight-wad?

EDMUND   Out on the porch.

JAMIE   Can't expect us to live in the Black Hole of Calcutta.[8] [*His eyes fix on the full bottle of whiskey.*] Say! Have I got the d.t.'s?[9] [*He reaches out fumblingly and grabs it.*] By God, it's real. What's matter with the Old Man tonight? Must be ossified to forget he left this out. Grab opportunity by the forelock. Key to my success. [*He slops a big drink into a glass.*]

EDMUND   You're stinking now. That will knock you stiff.

JAMIE   Wisdom from the mouth of babes. Can the wise stuff, Kid. You're still wet behind the ears. [*He lowers himself into a chair, holding the drink carefully aloft.*]

EDMUND   All right. Pass out if you want to.

JAMIE   Can't, that's trouble. Had enough to sink a ship, but can't sink. Well, here's hoping. [*He drinks.*]

EDMUND   Shove over the bottle. I'll have one, too.

JAMIE [*with sudden, big-brotherly solicitude, grabbing the bottle*]   No, you don't. Not while I'm around. Remember doctor's orders. Maybe no one else gives a damn if you die, but I do. My kid brother. I love your guts, Kid. Everything else is gone. You're all I've got left. [*pulling bottle closer to him*] So no booze for you, if I can help it. [*Beneath his drunken sentimentality there is a genuine sincerity.*]

EDMUND [*irritably*]   Oh, lay off it.

JAMIE [*is hurt and his face hardens*]   You don't believe I care, eh? Just drunken bull. [*He shoves the bottle over.*] All right. Go ahead and kill yourself.

EDMUND [*seeing he is hurt—affectionately*]   Sure I know you care, Jamie, and I'm going on the wagon. But tonight doesn't count. Too many damned things have happened today. [*He pours a drink.*] Here's how. [*He drinks.*]

---

6. Rudyard Kipling (1865–1936), English author.
7. Jamie's contemptuous name for his father, drawn from a character in the popular drama *The Bells*.
8. Small dungeon in Calcutta, India, where, on June 20, 1756, 123 of 146 British prisoners died of suffocation. Hence, any small, cramped space.
9. Delirium tremens.

JAMIE [*sobers up momentarily and with a pitying look*]   I know, Kid. It's been a lousy day for you. [*then with sneering cynicism*] I'll bet old Gaspard hasn't tried to keep you off booze. Probably give you a case to take with you to the state farm for pauper patients. The sooner you kick the bucket, the less expense. [*with contemptuous hatred*] What a bastard to have for a father! Christ, if you put him in a book, no one would believe it!

EDMUND [*defensively*]   Oh, Papa's all right, if you try to understand him— and keep your sense of humor.

JAMIE [*cynically*]   He's been putting on the old sob act for you, eh? He can always kid you. But not me. Never again. [*then slowly*] Although, in a way, I do feel sorry for him about one thing. But he has even that coming to him. He's to blame. [*hurriedly*] But to hell with that. [*He grabs the bottle and pours another drink, appearing very drunk again.*] That lash drink's getting me. This one ought to put the lights out. Did you tell Gaspard I got it out of Doc Hardy this sanatorium is a charity dump?

EDMUND [*reluctantly*]   Yes. I told him I wouldn't go there. It's all settled now. He said I can go anywhere I want. [*He adds, smiling without resentment*] Within reason, of course.

JAMIE [*drunkenly imitating his father*]   Of course, lad. Anything within reason. [*sneering*] That means another cheap dump. Old Gaspard, the miser in "The Bells," that's a part he can play without make-up.

EDMUND [*irritably*]   Oh, shut up, will you. I've heard that Gaspard stuff a million times.

JAMIE [*shrugs his shoulders—thickly*]   Aw right, if you're shatisfied—let him get away with it. It's your funeral—I mean, I hope it won't be.

EDMUND [*changing the subject*]   What did you do uptown tonight? Go to Mamie Burns?

JAMIE [*very drunk, his head nodding*]   Sure thing. Where else could I find suitable feminine companionship? And love. Don't forget love. What is a man without a good woman's love? A God-damned hollow shell.

EDMUND [*chuckles tipsily, letting himself go now and be drunk*]   You're a nut.

JAMIE [*quotes with gusto from Oscar Wilde's[1] "The Harlot's House"*]

> "Then, turning to my love, I said,
> 'The dead are dancing with the dead,
> The dust is whirling with the dust.'
>
> But she—she heard the violin,
> And left my side and entered in:
> Love passed into the house of lust.
>
> Then suddenly the tune went false,
> The dancers wearied of the waltz . . ."

[*He breaks off, thickly*] Not strictly accurate. If my love was with me, I didn't notice it. She must have been a ghost. [*He pauses.*] Guess which one of Mamie's charmers I picked to bless me with her woman's love. It'll hand you a laugh, Kid. I picked Fat Violet.

EDMUND [*laughs drunkenly*]   No, honest? Some pick! God, she weighs a ton. What the hell for, a joke?

---

1. Irish author (1854–1900).

JAMIE   No joke. Very serious. By the time I hit Mamie's dump I felt very sad about myself and all the other poor bums in the world. Ready for a weep on any old womanly bosom. You know how you get when John Barleycorn turns on the soft music inside you. Then, soon as I got in the door, Mamie began telling me all her troubles. Beefed how rotten business was, and she was going to give Fat Violet the gate. Customers didn't fall for Vi. Only reason she'd kept her was she could play the piano. Lately Vi's gone on drunks and been too boiled to play, and was eating her out of house and home, and although Vi was a goodhearted dumbbell, and she felt sorry for her because she didn't know how the hell she'd make a living, still business was business, and she couldn't afford to run a house for fat tarts. Well, that made me feel sorry for Fat Violet, so I squandered two bucks of your dough to escort her upstairs. With no dishonorable intentions whatever. I like them fat, but not that fat. All I wanted was a little heart-to-heart talk concerning the infinite sorrow of life.

EDMUND [*chuckles drunkenly*]   Poor Vi! I'll bet you recited Kipling and Swinburne and Dowson and gave her "I have been faithful to thee, Cynara, in my fashion."

JAMIE [*grins loosely*]   Sure—with the Old Master, John Barleycorn, playing soft music. She stood it for a while. Then she got good and sore. Got the idea I took her upstairs for a joke. Gave me a grand bawling out. Said she was better than a drunken bum who recited poetry. Then she began to cry. So I had to say I loved her because she was fat, and she wanted to believe that, and I stayed with her to prove it, and that cheered her up, and she kissed me when I left, and said she'd fallen hard for me, and we both cried a little more in the hallway, and everything was fine, except Mamie Burns thought I'd gone bughouse.

EDMUND [*quotes derisively*]

> "Harlots and
> Hunted have pleasures of their own to give,
> The vulgar herd can never understand."

JAMIE [*nods his head drunkenly*]   Egzactly! Hell of a good time, at that. You should have stuck around with me, Kid. Mamie Burns inquired after you. Sorry to hear you were sick. She meant it, too. [*He pauses—then with maudlin humor, in a ham-actor tone*] This night has opened my eyes to a great career in store for me, my boy! I shall give the art of acting back to the performing seals, which are its most perfect expression. By applying my natural God-given talents in their proper sphere, I shall attain the pinnacle of success! I'll be the lover of the fat woman in Barnum and Bailey's circus! [EDMUND *laughs.* JAMIE's *mood changes to arrogant disdain.*] Pah! Imagine me sunk to the fat girl in a hick town hooker shop! Me! Who have made some of the best-lookers on Broadway sit up and beg! [*He quotes from Kipling's "Sestina of the Tramp-Royal"*]

> "Speakin' in general, I 'ave tried 'em all,
> The 'appy roads that take you o'er the world."

[*with sodden melancholy*] Not so apt. Happy roads is bunk. Weary roads is right. Get you nowhere fast. That's where I've got—nowhere. Where everyone lands in the end, even if most of the suckers won't admit it.

EDMUND [*derisively*]   Can it! You'll be crying in a minute.

JAMIE [*starts and stares at his brother for a second with bitter hostility—
thickly*]   Don't get—too damned fresh. [*then abruptly*] But you're
right. To hell with repining! Fat Violet's a good kid. Glad I stayed with
her. Christian act. Cured her blues. Hell of a good time. You should
have stuck with me, Kid. Taken your mind off your troubles. What's the
use coming home to get the blues over what can't be helped. All over—
finished now—not a hope! [*He stops, his head nodding drunkenly, his
eyes closing—then suddenly he looks up, his face hard, and quotes jeeringly.*]

> "If I were hanged on the highest hill,
> Mother o' mine, O mother o' mine!
> I know whose love would follow me still . . ."

EDMUND [*violently*]   Shut up!

JAMIE [*in a cruel, sneering tone with hatred in it*]   Where's the hophead?
Gone to sleep?

[*EDMUND jerks as if he'd been struck. There is a tense silence. EDMUND's
face looks stricken and sick. Then in a burst of rage he springs from his
chair.*]

EDMUND   You dirty bastard!

[*He punches his brother in the face, a blow that glances off the cheek-
bone. For a second JAMIE reacts pugnaciously and half rises from his chair
to do battle, but suddenly he seems to sober up to a shocked realization of
what he has said and he sinks back limply.*]

JAMIE [*miserably*]   Thanks, Kid. I certainly had that coming. Don't know
what made me—booze talking—You know me, Kid.

EDMUND [*his anger ebbing*]   I know you'd never say that unless—But God,
Jamie, no matter how drunk you are, it's no excuse! [*He pauses—miserably*] I'm sorry I hit you. You and I never scrap—that bad. [*He sinks back
on his chair.*]

JAMIE [*huskily*]   It's all right. Glad you did. My dirty tongue. Like to cut it
out. [*He hides his face in his hands—dully*] I suppose it's because I feel so
damned sunk. Because this time Mama had me fooled. I really believed
she had it licked. She thinks I always believe the worst, but this time I
believed the best. [*His voice flutters.*] I suppose I can't forgive her—yet.
It meant so much. I'd begun to hope, if she'd beaten the game, I could,
too. [*He begins to sob, and the horrible part of his weeping is that it appears
sober, not the maudlin tears of drunkenness.*]

EDMUND [*blinking back tears himself*]   God, don't I know how you feel!
Stop it, Jamie!

JAMIE [*trying to control his sobs*]   I've known about Mama so much longer
than you. Never forget the first time I got wise. Caught her in the act with
a hypo. Christ, I'd never dreamed before that any women but whores took
dope! [*He pauses.*] And then this stuff of you getting consumption. It's got
me licked. We've been more than brothers. You're the only pal I've ever
had. I love your guts. I'd do anything for you.

EDMUND [*reaches out and pats his arm*]   I know that, Jamie.

JAMIE [*his crying over—drops his hands from his face—with a strange bitterness*]   Yet I'll bet you've heard Mama and old Gaspard spill so much bunk
about my hoping for the worst, you suspect right now I'm thinking to

myself that Papa is old and can't last much longer, and if you were to die, Mama and I would get all he's got, and so I'm probably hoping—

EDMUND [*indignantly*] Shut up, you damned fool! What the hell put that in your nut? [*He stares at his brother accusingly.*] Yes, that's what I'd like to know. What put that in your mind?

JAMIE [*confusedly—appearing drunk again*] Don't be a dumbbell! What I said! Always suspected of hoping for the worst. I've got so I can't help— [*then drunkenly resentful*] What are you trying to do, accuse me? Don't play the wise guy with me! I've learned more of life than you'll ever know! Just because you've read a lot of highbrow junk, don't think you can fool me! You're only an overgrown kid! Mama's baby and Papa's pet! The family White Hope! You've been getting a swelled head lately. About nothing! About a few poems in a hick town newspaper! Hell, I used to write better stuff for the Lit magazine in college! You better wake up! You're setting no rivers on fire! You let hick town boobs flatter you with bunk about your future—

[*Abruptly his tone changes to disgusted contrition.* EDMUND *has looked away from him, trying to ignore this tirade.*]

Hell, Kid, forget it. That goes for Sweeny. You know I don't mean it. No one hopes more than I do you'll knock 'em all dead. No one is prouder you've started to make good. [*drunkenly assertive*] Why shouldn't I be proud? Hell, it's purely selfish. You reflect credit on me. I've had more to do with bringing you up than anyone. I wised you up about women, so you'd never be a fall guy, or make any mistakes you didn't want to make! And who steered you on to reading poetry first? Swinburne,[2] for example? I did! And because I once wanted to write, I planted it in your mind that someday you'd write! Hell, you're more than my brother. I made you! You're my Frankenstein![3]

[*He has risen to a note of drunken arrogance.* EDMUND *is grinning with amusement now.*]

EDMUND All right, I'm your Frankenstein. So let's have a drink. [*He laughs.*] You crazy nut!

JAMIE [*thickly*] I'll have a drink. Not you. Got to take care of you. [*He reaches out with a foolish grin of doting affection and grabs his brother's hand.*] Don't be scared of this sanatorium business. Hell, you can beat that standing on your head. Six months and you'll be in the pink. Probably haven't got consumption at all. Doctors lot of fakers. Told me years ago to cut out booze or I'd soon be dead—and here I am. They're all con men. Anything to grab your dough. I'll bet this state farm stuff is political graft game. Doctors get a cut for every patient they send.

EDMUND [*disgustedly amused*] You're the limit! At the Last Judgment, you'll be around telling everyone it's in the bag.

JAMIE And I'll be right. Slip a piece of change to the Judge and be saved, but if you're broke you can go to hell!

[*He grins at this blasphemy and* EDMUND *has to laugh.* JAMIE *goes on.*]

"Therefore put money in thy purse."[4] That's the only dope. [*mockingly*] The secret of my success! Look what it's got me!

---

2. Algernon Charles Swinburne (1837–1909), English poet and critic.
3. In the novel *Frankenstein* by the English author Mary Shelley (1797–1851), the scientist Dr.

Frankenstein creates a monster. Jamie confuses the scientist with his creation, although it is possible that the mistake is O'Neill's.
4. Shakespeare's *Othello* 1.3.354.

[*He lets* EDMUND's *hand go to pour a big drink, and gulps it down. He stares at his brother with bleary affection—takes his hand again and begins to talk thickly but with a strange, convincing sincerity.*]

Listen, Kid, you'll be going away. May not get another chance to talk. Or might not be drunk enough to tell you truth. So got to tell you now. Something I ought to have told you long ago—for your own good.

[*He pauses—struggling with himself.* EDMUND *stares, impressed and uneasy. Jamie blurts out*]

Not drunken bull, but "in vino veritas"[5] stuff. You better take it seriously. Want to warn you—against me. Mama and Papa are right. I've been rotten bad influence. And worst of it is, I did it on purpose.

EDMUND [*uneasily*]   Shut up! I don't want to hear—

JAMIE   Nix, Kid! You listen! Did it on purpose to make a bum of you. Or part of me did. A big part. That part that's been dead so long. That hates life. My putting you wise so you'd learn from my mistakes. Believed that myself at times, but it's a fake. Made my mistakes look good. Made getting drunk romantic. Made whores fascinating vampires instead of poor, stupid, diseased slobs they really are. Made fun of work as sucker's game. Never wanted you to succeed and make me look even worse by comparison. Wanted you to fail. Always jealous of you. Mama's baby, Papa's pet! [*He stares at* EDMUND *with increasing enmity.*] And it was your being born that started Mama on dope. I know that's not your fault, but all the same, God damn you, I can't help hating your guts—!

EDMUND [*almost frightenedly*]   Jamie! Cut it out! You're crazy!

JAMIE   But don't get wrong idea, Kid. I love you more than I hate you. My saying what I'm telling you now proves it. I run the risk you'll hate me—and you're all I've got left. But I didn't mean to tell you that last stuff—go that far back. Don't know what made me. What I wanted to say is, I'd like to see you become the greatest success in the world. But you'd better be on your guard. Because I'll do my damnedest to make you fail. Can't help it. I hate myself. Got to take revenge. On everyone else. Especially you. Oscar Wilde's "Reading Gaol" has the dope twisted. The man was dead and so he had to kill the thing he loved. That's what it ought to be. The dead part of me hopes you won't get well. Maybe he's even glad the game has got Mama again! He wants company, he doesn't want to be the only corpse around the house! [*He gives a hard, tortured laugh.*]

EDMUND   Jesus, Jamie! You really have gone crazy!

JAMIE   Think it over and you'll see I'm right. Think it over when you're away from me in the sanatorium. Make up your mind you've got to tie a can to me—get me out of your life—think of me as dead—tell people, "I had a brother, but he's dead." And when you come back, look out for me. I'll be waiting to welcome you with that "my old pal" stuff, and give you the glad hand, and at the first good chance I get stab you in the back.

EDMUND   Shut up! I'll be God-damned if I'll listen to you any more—

JAMIE [*as if he hadn't heard*]   Only don't forget me. Remember I warned you—for your sake. Give me credit. Greater love hath no man than this, that he saveth his brother from himself. [*very drunkenly, his head bob-*

---

5. In wine there is truth (Latin).

bing] That's all. Feel better now. Gone to confession. Know you absolve me, don't you, Kid? You understand. You're a damned fine kid. Ought to be. I made you. So go and get well. Don't die on me. You're all I've got left. God bless you, Kid. [*His eyes close. He mumbles*] That last drink— the old K. O.

> [*He falls into a drunken doze, not completely asleep.* EDMUND *buries his face in his hands miserably.* TYRONE *comes in quietly through the screen door from the porch, his dressing gown wet with fog, the collar turned up around his throat. His face is stern and disgusted but at the same time pitying.* EDMUND *does not notice his entrance.*]

TYRONE [*in a low voice*]   Thank God he's asleep.

> [EDMUND *looks up with a start.*]

I thought he'd never stop talking. [*He turns down the collar of his dressing gown.*] We'd better let him stay where he is and sleep it off.

> [EDMUND *remains silent.* TYRONE *regards him—then goes on*]

I heard the last part of his talk. It's what I've warned you. I hope you'll heed the warning, now it comes from his own mouth.

> [EDMUND *gives no sign of having heard.* TYRONE *adds pityingly*]

But don't take it too much to heart, lad. He loves to exaggerate the worst of himself when he's drunk. He's devoted to you. It's the one good thing left in him. [*He looks down on* JAMIE *with a bitter sadness.*] A sweet spectacle for me! My first-born, who I hoped would bear my name in honor and dignity, who showed such brilliant promise!

EDMUND [*miserably*]   Keep quiet, can't you, Papa?

TYRONE [*pours a drink*]   A waste! A wreck, a drunken hulk, done with and finished!

> [*He drinks.* JAMIE *has become restless, sensing his father's presence, struggling up from his stupor. Now he gets his eyes open to blink up at* TYRONE. *The latter moves back a step defensively, his face growing hard.*]

JAMIE [*suddenly points a finger at him and recites with dramatic emphasis*]

> "Clarence is come, false, fleeting, perjured Clarence,
> That stabbed me in the field by Tewksbury.
> Seize on him, Furies, take him into torment."[6]

[*then resentfully*] What the hell are you staring at? [*He recites sardonically from Rossetti[7]*]

> "Look in my face. My name is Might-Have-Been;
> I am also called No More, Too Late, Farewell."

TYRONE   I'm well aware of that, and God knows I don't want to look at it.

EDMUND   Papa! Quit it!

JAMIE [*derisively*]   Got a great idea for you, Papa. Put on revival of "The Bells" this season. Great part in it you can play without make-up. Old Gaspard, the miser!

> [TYRONE *turns away, trying to control his temper.*]

---

6. Shakespeare's *Richard III* 1.4.55–57.
7. Dante Gabriel Rossetti (1821–1882), English poet and painter.

EDMUND   Shut up, Jamie!

JAMIE [*jeeringly*]   I claim Edwin Booth never saw the day when he could give as good a performance as a trained seal. Seals are intelligent and honest. They don't put up any bluffs about the Art of Acting. They admit they're just hams earning their daily fish.

TYRONE [*stung, turns on him in a rage*]   You loafer!

EDMUND   Papa! Do you want to start a row that will bring Mama down? Jamie, go back to sleep! You've shot off your mouth too much already.

[TYRONE *turns away.*]

JAMIE [*thickly*]   All right, Kid. Not looking for argument. Too damned sleepy.

[*He closes his eyes, his head nodding.* TYRONE *comes to the table and sits down, turning his chair so he won't look at* JAMIE. *At once he becomes sleepy, too.*]

TYRONE [*heavily*]   I wish to God she'd go to bed so that I could, too. [*drowsily*] I'm dog tired. I can't stay up all night like I used to. Getting old—old and finished. [*with a bone-cracking yawn*] Can't keep my eyes open. I think I'll catch a few winks. Why don't you do the same, Edmund? It'll pass the time until she—

[*His voice trails off. His eyes close, his chin sags, and he begins to breathe heavily through his mouth.* EDMUND *sits tensely. He hears something and jerks nervously forward in his chair, staring through the front parlor into the hall. He jumps up with a hunted, distracted expression. It seems for a second he is going to hide in the back parlor. Then he sits down again and waits, his eyes averted, his hands gripping the arms of his chair. Suddenly all five bulbs of the chandelier in the front parlor are turned on from a wall switch, and a moment later someone starts playing the piano in there—the opening of one of Chopin's[8] simpler waltzes, done with a forgetful, stiff-fingered groping, as if an awkward schoolgirl were practicing it for the first time.* TYRONE *starts to wide-awakeness and sober dread, and* JAMIE's *head jerks back and his eyes open. For a moment they listen frozenly. The playing stops as abruptly as it began, and* MARY *appears in the doorway. She wears a sky-blue dressing gown over her nightdress, dainty slippers and pompons on her bare feet. Her face is paler than ever. Her eyes look enormous. They glisten like polished black jewels. The uncanny thing is that her face now appears so youthful. Experience seems ironed out of it. It is a marble mask of girlish innocence, the mouth caught in a shy smile. Her white hair is braided in two pigtails which hang over her breast. Over one arm, carried neglectfully, trailing on the floor, as if she had forgotten she held it, is an old-fashioned white satin wedding gown, trimmed with duchesse lace. She hesitates in the doorway, glancing round the room, her forehead puckered puzzledly, like someone who has come to a room to get something but has become absent-minded on the way and forgotten what it was. They stare at her. She seems aware of them merely as she is aware of other objects in the room, the furniture, the windows, familiar things she accepts automatically as naturally belonging there but which she is too preoccupied to notice.*]

JAMIE [*breaks the cracking silence—bitterly, self-defensively sardonic*]   The Mad Scene. Enter Ophelia![9]

---

8. Frederic Chopin (1810–1849), Polish composer famous for works for the piano.

9. An allusion to Shakespeare's *Hamlet.*

[*His father and brother both turn on him fiercely.* EDMUND *is quicker. He slaps* JAMIE *across the mouth with the back of his hand.*]

TYRONE [*his voice trembling with suppressed fury*]   Good boy, Edmund. The dirty blackguard! His own mother!

JAMIE [*mumbles guiltily, without resentment*]   All right, Kid. Had it coming. But I told you how much I'd hoped—[*He puts his hands over his face and begins to sob.*]

TYRONE   I'll kick you out in the gutter tomorrow, so help me God. [*But* JAMIE's *sobbing breaks his anger, and he turns and shakes his shoulder, pleading*] Jamie, for the love of God, stop it!

[*Then* MARY *speaks, and they freeze into silence again, staring at her. She has paid no attention whatever to the incident. It is simply a part of the familiar atmosphere of the room, a background which does not touch her preoccupation; and she speaks aloud to herself, not to them.*]

MARY   I play so badly now. I'm all out of practice. Sister Theresa will give me a dreadful scolding. She'll tell me it isn't fair to my father when he spends so much money for extra lessons. She's quite right, it isn't fair, when he's so good and generous, and so proud of me. I'll practice every day from now on. But something horrible has happened to my hands. The fingers have gotten so stiff—[*She lifts her hands to examine them with a frightened puzzlement.*] The knuckles are all swollen. They're so ugly. I'll have to go to the Infirmary and show Sister Martha. [*with a sweet smile of affectionate trust*] She's old and a little cranky, but I love her just the same, and she has things in her medicine chest that'll cure anything. She'll give me something to rub on my hands, and tell me to pray to the Blessed Virgin, and they'll be well again in no time. [*She forgets her hands and comes into the room, the wedding gown trailing on the floor. She glances around vaguely, her forehead puckered again.*] Let me see. What did I come here to find? It's terrible, how absent-minded I've become. I'm always dreaming and forgetting.

TYRONE [*in a stifled voice*]   What's that she's carrying, Edmund?

EDMUND [*dully*]   Her wedding gown, I suppose.

TYRONE   Christ! [*He gets to his feet and stands directly in her path—in anguish*] Mary! Isn't it bad enough—? [*controlling himself—gently persuasive*] Here, let me take it, dear. You'll only step on it and tear it and get it dirty dragging it on the floor. Then you'd be sorry afterwards.

[*She lets him take it, regarding him from somewhere far away within herself, without recognition, without either affection or animosity.*]

MARY [*with the shy politeness of a well-bred young girl toward an elderly gentleman who relieves her of a bundle*]   Thank you. You are very kind. [*She regards the wedding gown with a puzzled interest.*] It's a wedding gown. It's very lovely, isn't it? [*A shadow crosses her face and she looks vaguely uneasy.*] I remember now. I found it in the attic hidden in a trunk. But I don't know what I wanted it for. I'm going to be a nun—that is, if I can only find—[*She looks around the room, her forehead puckered again.*] What is it I'm looking for? I know it's something I lost. [*She moves back from* TYRONE, *aware of him now only as some obstacle in her path.*]

TYRONE [*in hopeless appeal*]   Mary!

[*But it cannot penetrate her preoccupation. She doesn't seem to hear him. He gives up helplessly, shrinking into himself, even his defensive drunkenness taken from him, leaving him sick and sober. He sinks back* on his chair, holding the wedding gown in his arms with an unconscious clumsy, protective gentleness.]

JAMIE [drops his hand from his face, his eyes on the table top. He has suddenly sobered up, too—dully]   It's no good, Papa. [He recites from Swinburne's "A Leave-taking" and does it well, simply but with a bitter sadness.]

"Let us rise up and part; she will not know.
Let us go seaward as the great winds go,
Full of blown sand and foam; what help is here?
There is no help, for all these things are so,
And all the world is bitter as a tear.
And how these things are, though ye strove to show,
She would not know."

MARY [looking around her]   Something I miss terribly. It can't be altogether lost. [She starts to move around in back of JAMIE's chair.]

JAMIE [turns to look up into her face—and cannot help appealing pleadingly in his turn]   Mama!
[She does not seem to hear. He looks away hopelessly.]
Hell! What's the use? It's no good. [He recites from "A Leave-taking" again with increased bitterness.]

"Let us go hence, my songs; she will not hear.
Let us go hence together without fear;
Keep silence now, for singing-time is over,
And over all old things and all things dear.
She loves not you nor me as all we love her.
Yea, though we sang as angels in her ear,
She would not hear."

MARY [looking around her]   Something I need terribly. I remember when I had it I was never lonely nor afraid. I can't have lost it forever, I would die if I thought that. Because then there would be no hope.
[She moves like a sleepwalker, around the back of JAMIE's chair, then forward toward left front, passing behind EDMUND.]

EDMUND [turns impulsively and grabs her arm. As he pleads he has the quality of a bewilderedly hurt little boy.]   Mama! It isn't a summer cold! I've got consumption!

MARY [For a second he seems to have broken through to her. She trembles and her expression becomes terrified. She calls distractedly, as if giving a command to herself.]   No! [And instantly she is far away again. She murmurs gently but impersonally]   You must not try to touch me. You must not try to hold me. It isn't right, when I am hoping to be a nun.
[He lets his hand drop from her arm. She moves left to the front end of the sofa beneath the windows and sits down, facing front, her hands folded in her lap, in a demure school-girlish pose.]

JAMIE [gives Edmund a strange look of mingled pity and jealous gloating]   You damned fool. It's no good. [He recites again from the Swinburne poem.]

"Let us go hence, go hence; she will not see.
Sing all once more together; surely she,
She too, remembering days and words that were,
Will turn a little toward us, sighing; but we,

We are hence, we are gone, as though we had not been there.
Nay, and though all men seeing had pity on me,
She would not see."

TYRONE [*trying to shake off his hopeless stupor*]   Oh, we're fools to pay any
attention. It's the damned poison. But I've never known her to drown herself in it as deep as this. [*gruffly*] Pass me that bottle, Jamie. And stop
reciting that damned morbid poetry. I won't have it in my house!
>   [JAMIE *pushes the bottle toward him. He pours a drink without disar-
>   ranging the wedding gown he holds carefully over his other arm and on
>   his lap, and shoves the bottle back.* JAMIE *pours his and passes the bottle
>   to* EDMUND, *who, in turn, pours one.* TYRONE *lifts his glass and his sons
>   follow suit mechanically, but before they can drink* MARY *speaks and they
>   slowly lower their drinks to the table, forgetting them.*]
MARY [*staring dreamily before her. Her face looks extraordinarily youthful and
innocent. The shyly eager, trusting smile is on her lips as she talks aloud to
herself.*] I had a talk with Mother Elizabeth. She is so sweet and good. A
saint on earth. I love her dearly. It may be sinful of me but I love her better than my own mother. Because she always understands, even before
you say a word. Her kind blue eyes look right into your heart. You can't
keep any secrets from her. You couldn't deceive her, even if you were
mean enough to want to. [*She gives a little rebellious toss of her head—
with girlish pique*] All the same, I don't think she was so understanding
this time. I told her I wanted to be a nun. I explained how sure I was of
my vocation, that I had prayed to the Blessed Virgin to make me sure, and
to find me worthy. I told Mother I had had a true vision when I was praying in the shrine of Our Lady of Lourdes, on the little island in the lake.
I said I knew, as surely as I knew I was kneeling there, that the Blessed
Virgin had smiled and blessed me with her consent. But Mother Elizabeth
told me I must be more sure than that, even, that I must prove it wasn't
simply my imagination. She said, if I was so sure, then I wouldn't mind
putting myself to a test by going home after I graduated, and living as
other girls lived, going out to parties and dances and enjoying myself; and
then if after a year or two I still felt sure, I could come back to see her
and we would talk it over again. [*She tosses her head—indignantly*] I never
dreamed Holy Mother would give me such advice! I was really shocked.
I said, of course, I would do anything she suggested, but I knew it was
simply a waste of time. After I left her, I felt all mixed up, so I went to the
shrine and prayed to the Blessed Virgin and found peace again because I
knew she heard my prayer and would always love me and see no harm
ever came to me so long as I never lost my faith in her. [*She pauses and a
look of growing uneasiness comes over her face. She passes a hand over her
forehead as if brushing cobwebs from her brain—vaguely*] That was in the
winter of senior year. Then in the spring something happened to me. Yes,
I remember. I fell in love with James Tyrone and was so happy for a time.
[*She stares before her in a sad dream.* TYRONE *stirs in his chair.* EDMUND *and*
JAMIE *remain motionless.*]

CURTAIN

1940

CLAUDE McKAY
1889–1948

One of his biographers aptly calls Claude McKay a lifelong wanderer, a "sojourner" in the Harlem Renaissance. A Jamaican by birth, he did not become an American citizen until 1940; he left Harlem just when the Renaissance was getting started; he criticized leading black intellectuals like W. E. B. Du Bois and Alain Locke (who, in turn, criticized him). Nevertheless, *Harlem Shadows*, his 1922 book of poetry, is generally considered the book that initiated the Harlem Renaissance; his *Home to Harlem* (1928) was the only best-selling African American novel of the decade. Whether the Harlem Renaissance was a unified movement or a resonant label encompassing artists with diverse aims, whether McKay was an American Harlemite or a man of the world, he was unquestionably one of the most important black writers of the 1920s. As well as influencing African American literature, he has had a major impact on writing by West Indians and Africans.

Claude McKay (Festus Claudius McKay) was born in Sunny Ville, a rural village in central Jamaica. This village, with its setting of spectacular natural beauty, became in later years his symbol of a lost golden age. McKay's grandfather, a West African Ashanti, had been brought to the island as a slave, and McKay's father passed on to his son what he remembered of Ashanti values and rituals. Economic necessity led the young McKay to Kingston (Jamaica's principal city) in 1909, where he was apprenticed to a cabinetmaker and wheelwright. Combining his emerging literary ambitions with an interest in Jamaican folkways, McKay published two ground-breaking books of dialect poetry—*Songs of Jamaica* and *Constab Ballads*—in 1912. Prize money from these books took him to the United States to study agriculture, but his literary ambitions drew him to New York City after two years in school (first at the Tuskegee Institute, then at Kansas State College). He married his Jamaican sweetheart, Eulalie Imelda Lewars, in 1914; the couple had a daughter, but the marriage did not last. Supporting himself in jobs like restaurant kitchen helper and Pullman railroad waiter, he began to publish in avant-garde journals; by 1917 he was appearing in *The Seven Arts, Pearson's,* and the prominent left-wing *Liberator,* edited by Max Eastman. *The Liberator* published his famous poem "If We Must Die" in 1919. His poetry, much of it written in strict sonnet form, braided racial subject matter, radical politics, and poetic technique into compelling statements that were also good poetry according to traditional standards.

McKay's radical politics, already formed in Jamaica, rose from his belief that racism was inseparable from capitalism, which he saw as a structure designed to perpetuate economic inequality. To him, attacking capitalism was attacking racial injustice. Before the publication of *Harlem Shadows,* McKay had spent 1919–21 in England; in 1923 he went to Moscow, where he was welcomed as a celebrity. His connections to the Communist regime in Russia made him a target for the FBI, which issued orders to keep him from returning to the United States. He stayed in Europe until 1934, living mainly in France but also in Spain and Morocco. *Home to Harlem* (1928), written mostly in France, was an episodic guide to Harlem's artistic, popular, and intellectual life. Later events turned it into one of the movement's last statements; retrenchment in the publishing industry after the stock market crash of 1929, the emergence of younger African American writers with different values, and dissension among Harlem artists themselves combined to bring an end to the Harlem Renaissance and altered the character of life in Harlem itself.

When McKay was finally able to return to the United States in 1934, the nation was deep in the Great Depression. With general unemployment at over 25 percent, paid literary work was extremely hard to come by. In 1935 he joined the New York City branch of the Federal Writers' Project, a New Deal organization giving work to unemployed writers. Except for his important autobiography, *A Long Way from Home* (1937), he did little creative work, and his health failed. Through his friendship with Ellen Tarry, a young African American writer who was a Catholic, he received medical care from Friendship House, a Catholic lay organization in Harlem. In the later years of his life, appalled by Stalin's purges, McKay repudiated his earlier Communist sympathies. He began to work at Friendship House and, after moving to Chicago, worked for the Catholic Youth Organization. He converted to Catholicism in 1944 and died in Chicago four years later.

The text of "Moscow" is from *Selected Poems* (1953); all other texts are from *Harlem Shadows* (1922).

The Harlem Dancer

Applauding youths laughed with young prostitutes
And watched her perfect, half-clothed body sway;
Her voice was like the sound of blended flutes
Blown by black players upon a picnic day.
She sang and danced on gracefully and calm,   5
The light gauze hanging loose about her form;
To me she seemed a proudly-swaying palm
Grown lovelier for passing through a storm.
Upon her swarthy neck black shiny curls
Luxuriant fell; and tossing coins in praise,   10
The wine-flushed, bold-eyed boys, and even the girls,
Devoured her shape with eager, passionate gaze;
But looking at her falsely-smiling face,
I knew her self was not in that strange place.

1917, 1922

Harlem Shadows

I hear the halting footsteps of a lass
   In Negro Harlem when the night lets fall
Its veil. I see the shapes of girls who pass
   To bend and barter at desire's call.
Ah, little dark girls who in slippered feet   5
Go prowling through the night from street to street!

Through the long night until the silver break
   Of day the little gray feet know no rest;
Through the lone night until the last snow-flake
   Has dropped from heaven upon the earth's white breast, 10
The dusky, half-clad girls of tired feet
Are trudging, thinly shod, from street to street.

Ah, stern harsh world, that in the wretched way
   Of poverty, dishonor and disgrace,
Has pushed the timid little feet of clay,   15

The sacred brown feet of my fallen race!
Ah, heart of me, the weary, weary feet
In Harlem wandering from street to street.

1918, 1922

The Lynching

His Spirit in smoke ascended to high heaven.
His father, by the cruelest way of pain,
Had bidden him to his bosom once again;
The awful sin remained still unforgiven.
All night a bright and solitary star   5
(Perchance the one that ever guided him,
Yet gave him up at last to Fate's wild whim)
Hung pitifully o'er the swinging char.
Day dawned, and soon the mixed crowds came to view
The ghastly body swaying in the sun   10
The women thronged to look, but never a one
Showed sorrow in her eyes of steely blue;
And little lads, lynchers that were to be,
Danced round the dreadful thing in fiendish glee.

1919, 1922

If We Must Die

If we must die, let it not be like hogs
Hunted and penned in an inglorious spot,
While round us bark the mad and hungry dogs,
Making their mock at our accursèd lot.
If we must die, O let us nobly die,   5
So that our precious blood may not be shed
In vain; then even the monsters we defy
Shall be constrained to honor us though dead!
O kinsmen! we must meet the common foe!
Though far outnumbered let us show us brave,   10
And for their thousand blows deal one deathblow!
What though before us lies the open grave?
Like men we'll face the murderous, cowardly pack,
Pressed to the wall, dying, but fighting back!

1919, 1922

Africa

The sun sought thy dim bed and brought forth light,
The sciences were sucklings at thy breast;
When all the world was young in pregnant night

Thy slaves toiled at thy monumental best.
Thou ancient treasure-land, thou modern prize,   5
New peoples marvel at thy pyramids!
The years roll on, thy sphinx of riddle eyes
Watches the mad world with immobile lids.
The Hebrews humbled them at Pharaoh's name.
Cradle of Power! Yet all things were in vain!   10
Honor and Glory, Arrogance and Fame!
They went. The darkness swallowed thee again.
Thou art the harlot, now thy time is done,
Of all the mighty nations of the sun.

                                                    1921, 1922

America

Although she feeds me bread of bitterness,
And sinks into my throat her tiger's tooth,
Stealing my breath of life, I will confess
I love this cultured hell that tests my youth!
Her vigor flows like tides into my blood,   5
Giving me strength erect against her hate.
Her bigness sweeps my being like a flood.
Yet as a rebel fronts a king in state,
I stand within her walls with not a shred
Of terror, malice, not a word of jeer.   10
Darkly I gaze into the days ahead,
And see her might and granite wonders there,
Beneath the touch of Time's unerring hand,
Like priceless treasures sinking in the sand.

                                                    1921, 1922

Outcast

For the dim regions whence my fathers came
My spirit, bondaged by the body, longs.
Words felt, but never heard, my lips would frame;
My soul would sing forgotten jungle songs.
I would go back to darkness and to peace,   5
But the great western world holds me in fee,
And I may never hope for full release
While to its alien gods I bend my knee.
Something in me is lost, forever lost,
Some vital thing has gone out of my heart,   10
And I must walk the way of life a ghost
Among the sons of earth, a thing apart;
For I was born, far from my native clime,
Under the white man's menace, out of time.

                                                    1922

Moscow

Moscow for many loving her was dead . . .
And yet I saw a bright Byzantine[1] fair,
Of jewelled buildings, pillars, domes and spires
Of hues prismatic dazzling to the sight;
A glory painted on the Eastern air,   5
Of amorous sounding tones like passionate lyres;
All colors laughing richly their delight
And reigning over all the color red.[2]

My memory bears engraved the high-walled Kremlin,[3]
Of halls symbolic of the tiger will,   10
Of Czarist[4] instruments of mindless law . . .
And often now my nerves throb with the thrill
When, in that gilded place, I felt and saw
The presence and the simple voice of Lenin.[5]

1953

---

1. Relating to the Byzantine Empire, centered in Constantinople (present-day Istanbul), a city built on the site of the ancient Byzantium. The empire dominated much of eastern Europe, including Russia, from the 3rd to the 15th century. Byzantine art and architecture are characterized by spires, domes, gilding, and mosaics.
2. A reference to the red flags of the Communist government.
3. Walled area containing government buildings, churches, and museums in central Moscow, capital of Russia.
4. A reference to the rulers of Russia overthrown in the revolution of 1917.
5. Vladimir Ilyich Lenin (1870–1924), a major force in the Russian Revolution of 1917 and the first leader of the Bolshevik (later Communist) government. McKay met Lenin on his trip to Moscow.

KATHERINE ANNE PORTER
1890–1980

Over a long writing life Katherine Anne Porter produced only four books of stories and one novel, *Ship of Fools*, which did not appear until she was over seventy. Her reputation as a prose writer did not depend on quantity; each story was technically skilled, emotionally powerful, combining traditional narration with new symbolic techniques and contemporary subject matter.

Callie Porter—she changed the name to Katherine Anne when she became a writer—was born in the small settlement of Indian Creek, Texas; her mother died soon after giving birth to her fourth child, when Porter was not quite two years old. Her father moved them all to his mother's home in Kyle, Texas, where the maternal grandmother raised the family in extreme poverty. The father gave up all attempts to support them either financially or emotionally; the security provided by the strong, loving, but pious and stern grandmother ended with her death when Porter was eleven. Porter married to leave home immediately after her sixteenth birthday, only to find that rooted domesticity was not for her. Long before her divorce in 1915, she had separated from her first husband and begun a life of travel, activity, and changes of jobs.

She started writing in 1916 as a reporter for a Dallas newspaper. In 1917 she moved to Denver, the next year to New York City's Greenwich Village. Between 1918 and 1924 she lived mainly in Mexico, freelancing, meeting artists and intellectuals, and becoming involved in revolutionary politics. In Mexico she found the resources of journalism inadequate to her ambitions; using an anecdote she had heard from an archaeologist as a kernel, she wrote her first story, "María Concepción," which was published in the prestigious *Century* magazine in 1922. Like all her stories, it dealt with powerful emotions and had a strong sense of locale. Critics praised her as a major talent.

Although she considered herself a serious writer from this time on, Porter was distracted from fiction by many crosscurrents. A self-supporting woman with expensive tastes, she hesitated to give up lucrative freelance offers. She enjoyed travel and gladly took on jobs that sent her abroad. She became involved in political causes, including the Sacco-Vanzetti case. She was married four times.

Porter planned each story meticulously—taking extensive notes, devising scenarios, roughing out dialogue, and revising many times, sometimes over a period of years. She did not write confessional or simple autobiographical fiction, but each story originated in an important real experience of her life and drew on deep feelings. Although not a feminist, Porter devoted much of her work to exploring the tensions in women's lives in the modern era. The story that made her famous for life, so that everything else she published thereafter was looked on as a literary event, was "Flowering Judas" (1929), set in Mexico and dealing with revolutionary politics, lust, and betrayal. The reality of mixed motives and the difference between pure idealism and egotistical opportunism as they are encountered in revolutionary politics are among the themes in this deceptively simple narrative. It appeared in the little magazine *Hound and Horn*. The collections *Flowering Judas* and *Noon Wine* came out in 1930 and 1937. In 1930 Porter went back to Mexico and the following year to Europe on a Guggenheim fellowship; she lived in Berlin, Paris, and Basel before returning to the United States in 1936. Two more collections of stories and novellas appeared in 1939 (*Pale Horse, Pale Rider*) and in 1944 (*The Leaning Tower*). In these later collections there are several stories about Miranda Gay, a character who is partly autobiographical and partly an idealized image of the southern belle as she faces the modern world. *Pale Horse, Pale Rider* narrates Miranda's wartime romance and strongly endorses the personal over the political.

Soon after arriving in Europe in 1931 Porter began working on a novel, but it was not until 1962 that *Ship of Fools*, which runs to almost five hundred pages, appeared. Set on an ocean liner crossing the Atlantic to Germany in August 1931, it explores the characters and developing relationships of a large number of passengers; the ship, as Porter wrote in a preface, stands for "this world on its voyage to eternity." As in "Flowering Judas" and *Pale Horse, Pale Rider* the personal and the political intersect in *Ship of Fools*, since the coming of Nazism in Germany frames the interlinked stories of the travelers. In its film version, *Ship of Fools* brought Porter a great deal of money. Capitalizing on the publicity, her publishers brought out the *Collected Stories* in 1965, from which followed the National Book Award, the Pulitzer Prize, the Gold Medal for fiction of the National Institute of Arts and Letters, and election to the American Academy of Letters, all in the next two years. The happiest occasions in her later years—she lived to be ninety—were connected with endowing and establishing the Katherine Anne Porter Room at the University of Maryland, not far from her last home near Washington, D.C.

The text of "Flowering Judas" is from the *Collected Stories* (1965).

Flowering Judas[1]

Braggioni sits heaped upon the edge of a straight-backed chair much too small for him, and sings to Laura in a furry, mournful voice. Laura has begun

---

1. One of a genus of trees and shrubs with purplish rosy flowers. According to legend, Judas Iscariot, betrayer of Jesus, hanged himself from such a tree.

to find reasons for avoiding her own house until the latest possible moment, for Braggioni is there almost every night. No matter how late she is, he will be sitting there with a surly, waiting expression, pulling at his kinky yellow hair, thumbing the strings of his guitar, snarling a tune under his breath. Lupe the Indian maid meets Laura at the door, and says with a flicker of a glance towards the upper room, "He waits."

Laura wishes to lie down, she is tired of her hairpins and the feel of her long tight sleeves, but she says to him, "Have you a new song for me this evening?" If he says yes, she asks him to sing it. If he says no, she remembers his favorite one, and asks him to sing it again. Lupe brings her a cup of choco-late and a plate of rice, and Laura eats at the small table under the lamp, first inviting Braggioni, whose answer is always the same: "I have eaten, and besides, chocolate thickens the voice."

Laura says, "Sing, then," and Braggioni heaves himself into song. He scratches the guitar familiarly as though it were a pet animal, and sings pas-sionately off key, taking the high notes in a prolonged painful squeal. Laura, who haunts the markets listening to the ballad singers, and stops every day to hear the blind boy playing his reed-flute in Sixteenth of September Street,[2] listens to Braggioni with pitiless courtesy, because she dares not smile at his miserable performance. Nobody dares to smile at him. Braggioni is cruel to everyone, with a kind of specialized insolence, but he is so vain of his talents, and so sensitive to slights, it would require a cruelty and vanity greater than his own to lay a finger on the vast cureless wound of his self-esteem. It would require courage, too, for it is dangerous to offend him, and nobody has this courage.

Braggioni loves himself with such tenderness and amplitude and eternal charity that his followers—for he is a leader of men, a skilled revolutionist, and his skin has been punctured in honorable warfare—warm themselves in the reflected glow, and say to each other: "He has a real nobility, a love of humanity raised above mere personal affections." The excess of this self-love has flowed out, inconveniently for her, over Laura, who, with so many oth-ers, owes her comfortable situation and her salary to him. When he is in a very good humor, he tells her, "I am tempted to forgive you for being a *gringa*. *Gringita!*"[3] and Laura, burning, imagines herself leaning forward suddenly, and with a sound back-handed slap wiping the suety smile from his face. If he notices her eyes at these moments he gives no sign.

She knows what Braggioni would offer her, and she must resist tenaciously without appearing to resist, and if she could avoid it she would not admit even to herself the slow drift of his intention. During these long evenings which have spoiled a long month for her, she sits in her deep chair with an open book on her knees, resting her eyes on the consoling rigidity of the printed page when the sight and sound of Braggioni singing threaten to identify themselves with all her remembered afflictions and to add their weight to her uneasy premonitions of the future. The gluttonous bulk of Braggioni has become a symbol of her many disillusions, for a revolutionist should be lean, animated by heroic faith, a vessel of abstract virtues. This is nonsense, she knows it now and is ashamed of it. Revolution must have leaders, and lead-

2. A street in Morelia, a city in western Mexico where the story is set.
3. A young female foreigner, non-Mexican girl; a patronizing term meaning "cute little foreign girl." Diminutive of *gringa*, which is used pejoratively, especially for an American.

ership is a career for energetic men. She is, her comrades tell her, full of romantic error, for what she defines as cynicism in them is merely "a developed sense of reality." She is almost too willing to say, "I am wrong, I suppose I don't really understand the principles," and afterward she makes a secret truce with herself, determined not to surrender her will to such expedient logic. But she cannot help feeling that she has been betrayed irreparably by the disunion between her way of living and her feeling of what life should be, and at times she is almost contented to rest in this sense of grievance as a private store of consolation. Sometimes she wishes to run away, but she stays. Now she longs to fly out of this room, down the narrow stairs, and into the street where the houses lean together like conspirators under a single mottled lamp, and leave Braggioni singing to himself.

Instead she looks at Braggioni, frankly and clearly, like a good child who understands the rules of behavior. Her knees cling together under sound blue serge, and her round white collar is not purposely nun-like. She wears the uniform of an idea, and has renounced vanities. She was born Roman Catholic, and in spite of her fear of being seen by someone who might make a scandal of it, she slips now and again into some crumbling little church, kneels on the chilly stone, and says a Hail Mary on the gold rosary she bought in Tehuantepec. It is no good and she ends by examining the altar with its tinsel flowers and ragged brocades, and feels tender about the battered dollshape of some male saint whose white, lace-trimmed drawers hang limply around his ankles below the hieratic dignity of his velvet robe. She has encased herself in a set of principles derived from her early training, leaving no detail of gesture or of personal taste untouched, and for this reason she will not wear lace made on machines. This is her private heresy, for in her special group the machine is sacred, and will be the salvation of the workers. She loves fine lace, and there is a tiny edge of fluted cobweb on this collar, which is one of twenty precisely alike, folded in blue tissue paper in the upper drawer of her clothes chest.

Braggioni catches her glance solidly as if he had been waiting for it, leans forward, balancing his paunch between his spread knees, and sings with tremendous emphasis, weighing his words. He has, the song relates, no father and no mother, nor even a friend to console him; lonely as a wave of the sea he comes and goes, lonely as a wave. His mouth opens round and yearns sideways, his balloon cheeks grow oily with the labor of song. He bulges marvelously in his expensive garments. Over his lavender collar, crushed upon a purple necktie, held by a diamond hoop: over his ammunition belt of tooled leather worked in silver, buckled cruelly around his gasping middle: over the tops of his glossy yellow shoes Braggioni swells with ominous ripeness, his mauve silk hose stretched taut, his ankles bound with the stout leather thongs of his shoes.

When he stretches his eyelids at Laura she notes again that his eyes are the true tawny yellow cat's eyes. He is rich, not in money, he tells her, but in power, and this power brings with it the blameless ownership of things, and the right to indulge his love of small luxuries. "I have a taste for the elegant refinements," he said once, flourishing a yellow silk handkerchief before her nose. "Smell that? It is Jockey Club, imported from New York." Nonetheless he is wounded by life. He will say so presently. "It is true everything turns to dust in the hand, to gall on the tongue." He sighs and his leather belt creaks

like a saddle girth. "I am disappointed in everything as it comes. Everything."
He shakes his head. "You, poor thing, you will be disappointed too. You are
born for it. We are more alike than you realize in some things. Wait and see.
Some day you will remember what I have told you, you will know that Braggioni was your friend."

Laura feels a slow chill, a purely physical sense of danger, a warning in her
blood that violence, mutilation, a shocking death, wait for her with lessening
patience. She has translated this fear into something homely, immediate, and
sometimes hesitates before crossing the street. "My personal fate is nothing,
except as the testimony of a mental attitude," she reminds herself, quoting
from some forgotten philosophic primer, and is sensible enough to add, "Anyhow, I shall not be killed by an automobile if I can help it."

"It may be true I am as corrupt, in another way, as Braggioni," she thinks
in spite of herself, "as callous, as incomplete," and if this is so, any kind of
death seems preferable. Still she sits quietly, she does not run. Where could
she go? Uninvited she has promised herself to this place; she can no longer
imagine herself as living in another country, and there is no pleasure in
remembering her life before she came here.

Precisely what is the nature of this devotion, its true motives, and what are
its obligations? Laura cannot say. She spends part of her days in Xochimilco,
near by, teaching Indian children to say in English, "The cat is on the mat."
When she appears in the classroom they crowd about her with smiles on their
wise, innocent, clay-colored faces, crying, "Good morning, my titcher!" in
immaculate voices, and they make of her desk a fresh garden of flowers every
day.

During her leisure she goes to union meetings and listens to busy important voices quarreling over tactics, methods, internal politics. She visits the
prisoners of her own political faith in their cells, where they entertain themselves with counting cockroaches, repenting of their indiscretions, compos-
ing their memoirs, writing out manifestoes and plans for their comrades who
are still walking about free, hands in pockets, sniffing fresh air. Laura brings
them food and cigarettes and a little money, and she brings messages disguised in equivocal phrases from the men outside who dare not set foot in the
prison for fear of disappearing into the cells kept empty for them. If the prisoners confuse night and day, and complain, "Dear little Laura, time doesn't
pass in this infernal hole, and I won't know when it is time to sleep unless I
have a reminder," she brings them their favorite narcotics, and says in a tone
that does not wound them with pity, "Tonight will really be night for you," and
though her Spanish amuses them, they find her comforting, useful. If they
lose patience and all faith, and curse the slowness of their friends in coming
to their rescue with money and influence, they trust her not to repeat everything, and if she inquires, "Where do you think we can find money, or influence?" they are certain to answer, "Well, there is Braggioni, why doesn't he
do something?"

She smuggles letters from headquarters to men hiding from firing squads
in back streets in mildewed houses, where they sit in tumbled beds and talk
bitterly as if all Mexico were at their heels, when Laura knows positively they
might appear at the band concert in the Alameda[4] on Sunday morning, and

4. Public promenade bordered with trees.

no one would notice them. But Braggioni says, "Let them sweat a little. The next time they may be careful. It is very restful to have them out of the way for a while." She is not afraid to knock on any door in any street after midnight, and enter in the darkness, and say to one of these men who is really in danger: "They will be looking for you—seriously—tomorrow morning after six. Here is some money from Vicente. Go to Vera Cruz and wait."

She borrows money from the Roumanian agitator to give to his bitter enemy the Polish agitator. The favor of Braggioni is their disputed territory, and Braggioni holds the balance nicely, for he can use them both. The Polish agitator talks love to her over café tables, hoping to exploit what he believes is her secret sentimental preference for him, and he gives her misinformation which he begs her to repeat as the solemn truth to certain persons. The Roumanian is more adroit. He is generous with his money in all good causes, and lies to her with an air of ingenuous candor, as if he were her good friend and confidant. She never repeats anything they may say. Braggioni never asks questions. He has other ways to discover all that he wishes to know about them.

Nobody touches her, but all praise her gray eyes, and the soft, round under lip which promises gayety, yet is always grave, nearly always firmly closed: and they cannot understand why she is in Mexico. She walks back and forth on her errands, with puzzled eyebrows, carrying her little folder of drawings and music and school papers. No dancer dances more beautifully than Laura walks, and she inspires some amusing, unexpected ardors, which cause little gossip, because nothing comes of them. A young captain who had been a soldier in Zapata's[5] army attempted, during a horseback ride near Cuernavaca, to express his desire for her with the noble simplicity befitting a rude folk-hero: but gently, because he was gentle. This gentleness was his defeat, for when he alighted, and removed her foot from the stirrup, and essayed to draw her down into his arms, her horse, ordinarily a tame one, shied fiercely, reared and plunged away. The young hero's horse careered blindly after his stablemate, and the hero did not return to the hotel until rather late that evening. At breakfast he came to her table in full charro dress,[6] gray buckskin jacket and trousers with strings of silver buttons down the leg, and he was in a humorous, careless mood. "May I sit with you?" and "You are a wonderful rider. I was terrified that you might be thrown and dragged. I should never have forgiven myself. But I cannot admire you enough for your riding!"

"I learned to ride in Arizona," said Laura.

"If you will ride with me again this morning, I promise you a horse that will not shy with you," he said. But Laura remembered that she must return to Mexico City at noon.

Next morning the children made a celebration and spent their playtime writing on the blackboard, "We lov ar ticher," and with tinted chalks they drew wreaths of flowers around the words. The young hero wrote her a letter: "I am a very foolish, wasteful, impulsive man. I should have first said I love you, and then you would not have run away. But you shall see me again." Laura thought, "I must send him a box of colored crayons," but she

5. Emiliano Zapata (c. 1879–1919), Mexican peasant revolutionary general whose movement, *zapatismo*, combined agrarian and Mexican Indian cultural aspirations; one of the most significant figures in Mexico from 1910 to 1919, when he was murdered.
6. Costume worn by a peasant horseman of special status.

was trying to forgive herself for having spurred her horse at the wrong moment.

A brown, shock-haired youth came and stood in her patio one night and sang like a lost soul for two hours, but Laura could think of nothing to do about it. The moonlight spread a wash of gauzy silver over the clear spaces of the garden, and the shadows were cobalt blue. The scarlet blossoms of the Judas tree were dull purple, and the names of the colors repeated themselves automatically in her mind, while she watched not the boy, but his shadow, fallen like a dark garment across the fountain rim, trailing in the water. Lupe came silently and whispered expert counsel in her ear: "If you will throw him one little flower, he will sing another song or two and go away." Laura threw the flower, and he sang a last song and went away with the flower tucked in the band of his hat. Lupe said, "He is one of the organizers of the Typographers Union, and before that he sold corridos[7] in the Merced market, and before that, he came from Guanajuato, where I was born. I would not trust any man, but I trust least those from Guanajuato."

She did not tell Laura that he would be back again the next night, and the next, nor that he would follow her at a certain fixed distance around the Merced market, through the Zócolo, up Francisco I. Madero Avenue, and so along the Paseo de la Reforma to Chapultepec Park, and into the Philosopher's Footpath, still with that flower withering in his hat, and an indivisible attention in his eyes.

Now Laura is accustomed to him, it means nothing except that he is nineteen years old and is observing a convention with all propriety, as though it were founded on a law of nature, which in the end it might well prove to be. He is beginning to write poems which he prints on a wooden press, and he leaves them stuck like handbills in her door. She is pleasantly disturbed by the abstract, unhurried watchfulness of his black eyes which will in time turn easily towards another object. She tells herself that throwing the flower was a mistake, for she is twenty-two years old and knows better; but she refuses to regret it, and persuades herself that her negation of all external events as they occur is a sign that she is gradually perfecting herself in the stoicism she strives to cultivate against that disaster she fears, though she cannot name it.

She is not at home in the world. Every day she teaches children who remain strangers to her, though she loves their tender round hands and their charming opportunist savagery. She knocks at unfamiliar doors not knowing whether a friend or a stranger shall answer, and even if a known face emerges from the sour gloom of that unknown interior, still it is the face of a stranger. No matter what this stranger says to her, nor what her message to him, the very cells of her flesh reject knowledge and kinship in one monotonous word. No. No. No. She draws her strength from this one holy talismanic word which does not suffer her to be led into evil. Denying everything, she may walk anywhere in safety, she looks at everything without amazement.

No, repeats this firm unchanging voice of her blood; and she looks at Braggioni without amazement. He is a great man, he wishes to impress this simple girl who covers her great round breasts with thick dark cloth, and who hides long, invaluably beautiful legs under a heavy skirt. She is almost thin except for the incomprehensible fullness of her breasts, like a nursing

---

7. Popular ballads.

mother's, and Braggioni, who considers himself a judge of women, speculates again on the puzzle of her notorious virginity, and takes the liberty of speech which she permits without a sign of modesty, indeed, without any sort of sign, which is disconcerting.

"You think you are so cold, *gringita!* Wait and see. You will surprise yourself some day! May I be there to advise you!" He stretches his eyelids at her, and his ill-humored cat's eyes waver in a separate glance for the two points of light marking the opposite ends of a smoothly drawn path between the swollen curve of her breasts. He is not put off by that blue serge, nor by her resolutely fixed gaze. There is all the time in the world. His cheeks are bellying with the wind of song. "O girl with the dark eyes," he sings, and reconsiders. "But yours are not dark. I can change all that. O girl with the green eyes, you have stolen my heart away!" then his mind wanders to the song, and Laura feels the weight of his attention being shifted elsewhere. Singing thus, he seems harmless, he is quite harmless, there is nothing to do but sit patiently and say "No," when the moment comes. She draws a full breath, and her mind wanders also, but not far. She dares not wander too far.

Not for nothing has Braggioni taken pains to be a good revolutionist and a professional lover of humanity. He will never die of it. He has the malice, the cleverness, the wickedness, the sharpness of wit, the hardness of heart, stipulated for loving the world profitably. *He will never die of it.* He will live to see himself kicked out from his feeding trough by other hungry world-saviors. Traditionally he must sing in spite of his life which drives him to bloodshed, he tells Laura, for his father was a Tuscany[8] peasant who drifted to Yucatan and married a Maya woman: a woman of race, an aristocrat. They gave him the love and knowledge of music, thus: and under the rip of his thumbnail, the strings of the instrument complain like exposed nerves.

Once he was called Delgadito by all the girls and married women who ran after him; he was so scrawny all his bones showed under his thin cotton clothing, and he could squeeze his emptiness to the very backbone with his two hands. He was a poet and the revolution was only a dream then; too many women loved him and sapped away his youth, and he could never find enough to eat anywhere, anywhere! Now he is a leader of men, crafty men who whisper in his ear, hungry men who wait for hours outside his office for a word with him, emaciated men with wild faces who waylay him at the street gate with a timid, "Comrade, let me tell you . . ." and they blow the foul breath from their empty stomachs in his face.

He is always sympathetic. He gives them handfuls of small coins from his own pocket, he promises them work, there will be demonstrations, they must join the unions and attend the meetings, above all they must be on the watch for spies. They are closer to him than his own brothers, without them he can do nothing—until tomorrow, comrade!

Until tomorrow. "They are stupid, they are lazy, they are treacherous, they would cut my throat for nothing," he says to Laura. He has good food and abundant drink, he hires an automobile and drives in the Paseo on Sunday morning, and enjoys plenty of sleep in a soft bed beside a wife who dares not disturb him; and he sits pampering his bones in easy billows of fat, singing to Laura, who knows and thinks these things about him. When he was fifteen,

8. A region in north-central Italy.

he tried to drown himself because he loved a girl, his first love, and she laughed at him. "A thousand women have paid for that," and his tight little mouth turns down at the corners. Now he perfumes his hair with Jockey Club, and confides to Laura: "One woman is really as good as another for me, in the dark. I prefer them all."

His wife organizes unions among the girls in the cigarette factories, and walks in picket lines, and even speaks at meetings in the evening. But she cannot be brought to acknowledge the benefits of true liberty. "I tell her I must have my freedom, net. She does not understand my point of view." Laura has heard this many times. Braggioni scratches the guitar and meditates. "She is an instinctively virtuous woman, pure gold, no doubt of that. If she were not, I should lock her up, and she knows it."

His wife, who works so hard for the good of the factory girls, employs part of her leisure lying on the floor weeping because there are so many women in the world, and only one husband for her, and she never knows where nor when to look for him. He told her: "Unless you can learn to cry when I am not here, I must go away for good." That day he went away and took a room at the Hotel Madrid.

It is this month of separation for the sake of higher principles that has been spoiled not only for Mrs. Braggioni, whose sense of reality is beyond criticism, but for Laura, who feels herself bogged in a nightmare. Tonight Laura envies Mrs. Braggioni, who is alone, and free to weep as much as she pleases about a concrete wrong. Laura has just come from a visit to the prison, and she is waiting for tomorrow with a bitter anxiety as if tomorrow may not come, but time may be caught immovably in this hour, with herself transfixed, Braggioni singing on forever, and Eugenio's body not yet discovered by the guard.

Braggioni says: "Are you going to sleep?" Almost before she can shake her head, he begins telling her about the May-day disturbances coming on in Morelia, for the Catholics hold a festival in honor of the Blessed Virgin, and the Socialists celebrate their martyrs on that day. "There will be two independent processions, starting from either end of town, and they will march until they meet, and the rest depends . . ." He asks her to oil and load his pistols. Standing up, he unbuckles his ammunition belt, and spreads it laden across her knees. Laura sits with the shells slipping through the cleaning cloth dipped in oil, and he says again he cannot understand why she works so hard for the revolutionary idea unless she loves some man who is in it. "Are you not in love with someone?" "No," says Laura. "And no one is in love with you?" "No." "Then it is your own fault. No woman need go begging. Why, what is the matter with you? The legless beggar woman in the Alameda has a perfectly faithful lover. Did you know that?"

Laura peers down the pistol barrel and says nothing, but a long, slow faintness rises and subsides in her; Braggioni curves his swollen fingers around the throat of the guitar and softly smothers the music out of it, and when she hears him again he seems to have forgotten her, and is speaking in the hypnotic voice he uses when talking in small rooms to a listening, close-gathered crowd. Some day this world, now seemingly so composed and eternal, to the edges of every sea shall be merely a tangle of gaping trenches, of crashing walls and broken bodies. Everything must be torn from its accustomed place where it has rotted for centuries, hurled skyward and distributed, cast down again clean as rain, without separate identity. Nothing shall survive that the stiffened hands of poverty have created for the rich and no one shall be left alive except the elect spirits destined to procreate a new world cleansed of cruelty and injustice, ruled by benevolent anarchy: "Pistols are good, I love them, cannon are even better, but in the end I pin my faith to good dynamite," he concludes, and strokes the pistol lying in her hands. "Once I dreamed of destroying this city, in case it offered resistance to General Ortíz, but it fell into his hands like an overripe pear."

He is made restless by his own words, rises and stands waiting. Laura holds up the belt to him: "Put that on, and go kill somebody in Morelia, and you will be happier," she says softly. The presence of death in the room makes her bold. "Today, I found Eugenio going into a stupor. He refused to allow me to call the prison doctor. He had taken all the tablets I brought him yesterday. He said he took them because he was bored."

"He is a fool, and his death is his own business," says Braggioni, fastening his belt carefully.

"I told him if he had waited only a little while longer, you would have got him set free," says Laura. "He said he did not want to wait."

"He is a fool and we are well rid of him," says Braggioni, reaching for his hat.

He goes away. Laura knows his mood has changed, she will not see him any more for a while. He will send word when he needs her to go on errands into strange streets, to speak to the strange faces that will appear, like clay masks with the power of human speech, to mutter their thanks to Braggioni for his help. Now she is free, and she thinks, I must run while there is time. But she does not go.

Braggioni enters his own house where for a month his wife has spent many hours every night weeping and tangling her hair upon her pillow. She is weeping now, and she weeps more at the sight of him, the cause of all her sorrows. He looks about the room. Nothing is changed, the smells are good and familiar, he is well acquainted with the woman who comes toward him with no reproach except grief on her face. He says to her tenderly: "You are so good, please don't cry any more, you dear good creature." She says, "Are you tired, my angel? Sit here and I will wash your feet." She brings a bowl of water, and kneeling, unlaces his shoes, and when from her knees she raises her sad eyes under her blackened lids, he is sorry for everything, and bursts into tears. "Ah, yes, I am hungry, I am tired, let us eat something together," he says, between sobs. His wife leans her head on his arm and says, "Forgive me!" and this time he is refreshed by the solemn, endless rain of her tears.

Laura takes off her serge dress and puts on a white linen nightgown and goes to bed. She turns her head a little to one side, and lying still, reminds herself that it is time to sleep. Numbers tick in her brain like little clocks, soundless doors close of themselves around her. If you would sleep, you must not remember anything, the children will say tomorrow, good morning, my teacher, the poor prisoners who come every day bringing flowers to their jailor. 1-2-3-4-5—it is monstrous to confuse love with revolution, night with day, life with death—ah, Eugenio!

The tolling of the midnight bell is a signal, but what does it mean? Get up, Laura, and follow me: come out of your sleep, out of your bed, out of this strange house. What are you doing in this house? Without a word, without fear she rose and reached for Eugenio's hand, but he eluded her with a sharp, sly smile and drifted away. This is not all, you shall see—Murderer, he said, follow me, I will show you a new country, but it is far away and we must hurry.

No, said Laura, not unless you take my hand, no; and she clung first to the stair rail, and then to the topmost branch of the Judas tree that bent down slowly and set her upon the earth, and then to the rocky ledge of a cliff, and then to the jagged wave of a sea that was not water but a desert of crumbling stone. Where are you taking me, she asked in wonder but without fear. To death, and it is a long way off, and we must hurry, said Eugenio. No, said Laura, not unless you take my hand. Then eat these flowers, poor prisoner, said Eugenio in a voice of pity, take and eat: and from the Judas tree he stripped the warm bleeding flowers, and held them to her lips. She saw that his hand was fleshless, a cluster of small white petrified branches, and his eye sockets were without light, but she ate the flowers greedily for they satisfied both hunger and thirst. Murderer! said Eugenio, and Cannibal! This is my body and my blood. Laura cried No! and at the sound of her own voice, she awoke trembling, and was afraid to sleep again.

1929, 1930

ZORA NEALE HURSTON
1891–1960

Zora Neale Hurston was born in 1891 in Notasulga, Alabama, and moved with her family in 1892 to Eatonville, Florida, an all-black town. Her father, a Baptist preacher of considerable eloquence, was not a family man and made life difficult for his wife and eight children. The tie between mother and daughter was strong; Lucy Hurston was a driving force and strong support for all her children. But her death when Zora Hurston was about eleven left the child with little home life. Hitherto, the town of Eatonville had been like an extended family to her, and her early childhood was protected from racism because she encountered no white people. With her mother's death, Hurston's wanderings and her initiation into American racism began. The early security had given her the core of self-confidence she needed to survive. She moved from one relative's home to another until she was old enough to support herself, and with her earnings she began slowly to pursue an education. Although she had never finished grade school in Eatonville she was able to enter and complete college. In the early 1920s at Howard University in Washington, D.C. (the nation's leading African American university at that time), she studied with the great black educator Alain Locke, who was to make history with his anthology *The New Negro* in 1925. After a short story, "Drenched in Light," appeared in the New York African American magazine *Opportunity*, she decided to move to Harlem and pursue a literary career there.

As her biographer, Robert Hemenway, writes, "Zora Hurston was an extraordinarily witty woman, and she acquired an instant reputation in New York for her high spirits and side-splitting tales of Eatonville life. She could walk into a room of strangers . . . and almost immediately gather people, charm, amuse, and impress them." The Eatonville vignettes printed here convey the flavor of this discourse. Generous, outspoken, high spirited, an interesting conversationalist, she worked as a personal secretary for the politically liberal novelist Fannie Hurst and entered Barnard College. Her career took two simultaneous directions: at Barnard she studied with the famous anthropologist Franz Boas and developed an interest in black folk traditions, and in Harlem she became well known as a storyteller, an informal performing artist. Thus she was doubly committed to the oral narrative, and her work excels in its representation of people talking.

When she graduated from Barnard in 1927 she received a fellowship to return to Florida and study the oral traditions of Eatonville. From then on, she strove to achieve a balance between focusing on the folk and her origins and focusing on herself as an individual. After the fellowship money ran out, Hurston was supported by Mrs. R. Osgood Mason, an elderly white patron of the arts. Mason had firm ideas about what she wanted her protégés to produce; she required them all to get her permission before publishing any of the work that she had subsidized. In this relationship, Hurston experienced a difficulty that all the black artists of the Harlem Renaissance had to face—the fact that well-off white people were the sponsors of, and often the chief audience for, their work.

Hurston's work was not entirely popular with the male intellectual leaders of the Harlem community. She quarreled especially with Langston Hughes; she rejected the idea that a black writer's chief concern should be how blacks were being portrayed to the white reader. She did not write to "uplift her race," either; because in her view it was already uplifted, she (like Claude McKay) was not embarrassed to present her characters as mixtures of good and bad, strong and weak. Some of the other Harlem writers thought her either naïve or egotistical, but Hurston argued that freedom could only mean freedom from all coercion, no matter what the source.

The Great Depression brought an end to the structure that had undergirded Hurston's fieldwork, and she turned fully to writing. Unfortunately her most important work appeared in the mid-1930s when there was little interest in it, or in African American writing in general. She published *Jonah's Gourd Vine* in 1934 (a novel whose main character is based on her father); *Mules and Men* in 1935 (based on material from her field trips in Florida—this was her best-selling book, but it earned a total of only $943.75); and *Their Eyes Were Watching God*, in 1937. This novel about an African American woman's quest for selfhood has become a popular and critical favorite, both a woman's story, and a descriptive critique of southern African American folk society, showing its divisions and diversity. Technically, it is a loosely organized, highly metaphorical novel, with passages of broad folk humor and of extreme artistic compression. Other books followed in 1938 and 1939, and she wrote an autobiography—*Dust Tracks on a Road*—which appeared in 1942, with its occasional expression of antiwhite sentiments removed by her editors. At this point, however, Hurston had no audience. For the last decade of her life she lived in Florida, working from time to time as a maid.

The Eatonville Anthology[1]

I. The Pleading Woman

Mrs. Tony Roberts is the pleading woman. She just loves to ask for things. Her husband gives her all he can take and scrape, which is considerably more than most wives get for their housekeeping, but she goes from door to door begging for things.

She starts at the store. "Mist' Clarke," she sing-songs in a high keening voice, "gimme lil' piece uh meat tuh boil a pot uh greens wid. Lawd knows me an' mah chillen is so hongry! Hits uh SHAME! Tony don't fee-ee-eee-ed me!"

Mr. Clarke knows that she has money and that her larder is well stocked, for Tony Roberts is the best provider on his list. But her keening annoys him

---

1. The text is that of *I Love Myself When I Am Laughing . . . and Then Again When I Am Looking Mean and Impressive* (1979), edited by Alice Walker. Eatonville was Hurston's hometown; here she brings together many of the stories about its residents that she told at parties in Harlem. The stories are cast in the forms of traditional African American tales.

and he rises heavily. The pleader at his elbow shows all the joy of a starving man being seated at a feast.

"Thass right Mist' Clarke. De Lawd loveth de cheerful giver. Gimme jes' a lil' piece 'bout dis big (indicating the width of her hand) an' de Lawd'll bless yuh."

She follows this angel-on-earth to his meat tub and superintends the cutting, crying out in pain when he refuses to move the knife over just a teeny bit mo'.

Finally, meat in hand, she departs, remarking on the meanness of some people who give a piece of salt meat only two-fingers wide when they were plainly asked for a hand-wide piece. Clarke puts it down to Tony's account and resumes his reading.

With the slab of salt pork as a foundation, she visits various homes until she has collected all she wants for the day. At the Piersons for instance: "Sister Pierson, plee-ee-ease gimme uh han'full uh collard greens fuh me an' mah po' chillen! 'Deed, me an' mah chillen is so hongry. Tony doan' fee-ee-eed me!"

Mrs. Pierson picks a bunch of greens for her, but she springs away from them as if they were poison. "Lawd a mussy, Mis' Pierson, you ain't gonna gimme dat lil' eye-full uh greens fuh me an' mah chillen, is you? Don't be so graspin'; Gawd won't bless yuh. Gimme uh han'full mo'. Lawd, some folks is got everything, an' theys jes' as gripin' an stingy!"

Mrs. Pierson raises the ante, and the pleading woman moves on to the next place, and on and on. The next day, it commences all over.

II. Turpentine Love

Jim Merchant is always in good humor—even with his wife. He says he fell in love with her at first sight. That was some years ago. She has had all her teeth pulled out, but they still get along splendidly.

He says the first time he called on her he found out that she was subject to fits. This didn't cool his love, however. She had several in his presence.

One Sunday, while he was there, she had one, and her mother tried to give her a dose of turpentine to stop it. Accidentally, she spilled it in her eye and it cured her. She never had another fit, so they got married and have kept each other in good humor ever since.

III.

Becky Moore has eleven children of assorted colors and sizes. She has never been married, but that is not her fault. She has never stopped any of the fathers of her children from proposing, so if she has no father for her children it's not her fault. The men round about are entirely to blame.

The other mothers of the town are afraid that it is catching. They won't let their children play with hers.

IV. Tippy

Sykes Jones' family all shoot craps. The most interesting member of the family—also fond of bones, but another kind—is Tippy, the Jones' dog.

He is so thin, that it amazes one that he lives at all. He sneaks into village kitchens if the housewives are careless about the doors and steals meats, even off the stoves. He also sucks eggs.

For these offenses he has been sentenced to death dozens of times, and the sentences executed upon him, only they didn't work. He has been fed blue-stone, strychnine, nux vomica, even an entire Peruna[2] bottle beaten up. It didn't fatten him, but it didn't kill him. So Eatonville has resigned itself to the plague of Tippy, reflecting that it has erred in certain matters and is being chastened.

In spite of all the attempts upon his life, Tippy is still willing to be friendly with anyone who will let him.

V. *The Way of a Man with a Train*

Old Man Anderson lived seven or eight miles out in the country from Eatonville. Over by Lake Apopka. He raised feed-corn and cassava and went to market with it two or three times a year. He bought all of his victuals wholesale so he wouldn't have to come to town for several months more.

He was different from citybred folks. He had never seen a train. Everybody laughed at him for even the smallest child in Eatonville had either been to Maitland or Orlando and watched a train go by. On Sunday afternoons all of the young people of the village would go over to Maitland, a mile away, to see Number 35 whizz southward on its way to Tampa and wave at the passengers. So we looked down on him a little. Even we children felt superior in the presence of a person so lacking in worldly knowledge.

The grown-ups kept telling him he ought to go see a train. He always said he didn't have time to wait so long. Only two trains a day passed through Maitland. But patronage and ridicule finally had its effect and Old Man Anderson drove in one morning early. Number 78 went north to Jacksonville at 10:20. He drove his light wagon over in the woods beside the railroad below Maitland, and sat down to wait. He began to fear that his horse would get frightened and run away with the wagon. So he took him out and led him deeper into the grove and tied him securely. Then he returned to his wagon and waited some more. Then he remembered that some of the train-wise villagers had said the engine belched fire and smoke. He had better move his wagon out of danger. It might catch fire. He climbed down from the seat and placed himself between the shafts to draw it away. Just then 78 came thundering over the trestle spouting smoke, and suddenly began blowing for Maitland. Old Man Anderson became so frightened he ran away with the wagon through the woods and tore it up worse then the horse ever could have done. He doesn't know yet what a train looks like, and says he doesn't care.

VI. *Coon Taylor*

Coon Taylor never did any real stealing. Of course, if he saw a chicken or a watermelon he'd take it. The people used to get mad but they never could catch him. He took so many melons from Joe Clarke that he set up in the

---

2. A patent medicine cure-all.

melon patch one night with his shotgun loaded with rock-salt. He was going to fix Coon. But he was tired. It is hard work being a mayor, postmaster, store-keeper and everything. He dropped asleep sitting on a stump in the middle of the patch. So he didn't see Coon when he came. Coon didn't see him either, that is, not at first. He knew the stump was there, however. He had opened many of Clarke's juicy Florida Favorite on it. He selected his fruit, walked over to the stump and burst the melon on it. This is, he thought it was the stump until it fell over with a yell. Then he knew it was no stump and departed hastily from those parts. He had cleared the fence when Clarke came to, as it were. So the charge of rock-salt was wasted on the desert air.

During the sugar-cane season, he found he couldn't resist Clarke's soft green cane, but Clarke did not go to sleep this time. So after he had cut six or eight stalks by the moonlight, Clarke rose up out of the cane strippings with his shotgun and made Coon sit right down and chew up the last one of them on the spot. And the next day he made Coon leave his town for three months.

VII. *Village Fiction*

Joe Lindsay is said by Lum Boger to be the largest manufacturer of pre-varications in Eatonville; Brazzle (late owner of the world's leanest and mean-est mule) contends that his business is the largest in the state and his wife holds that he is the biggest liar in the world.

Exhibit A—He claims that while he was in Orlando one day he saw a doc-tor cut open a woman, remove everything—liver, lights and heart included—clean each of them separately; the doctor then washed out the empty woman, dried her out neatly with a towel and replaced the organs so expertly that she was up and about her work in a couple of weeks.

VIII.

Sewell is a man who lives all to himself. He moves a great deal. So often, that 'Lige Moseley says his chickens are so used to moving that every time he comes out into his backyard the chickens lie down and cross their legs, ready to be tied up again.

He is baldheaded; but he says he doesn't mind that, because he wants as little as possible between him and God.

IX.

Mrs. Clarke is Joe Clarke's wife. She is a soft-looking, middle-aged woman, whose bust and stomach are always holding a get-together.

She waits on the store sometimes and cries every time he yells at her which he does every time she makes a mistake, which is quite often. She calls her husband "Jody." They say he used to beat her in the store when he was a young man, but he is not so impatient now. He can wait until he goes home.

She shouts in Church every Sunday and shakes the hand of fellowship with everybody in the Church with her eyes closed, but somehow always misses her husband.

X.

Mrs. McDuffy goes to Church every Sunday and always shouts and tells her "determination." Her husband always sits in the back row and beats her as soon as they get home. He says there's no sense in her shouting, as big a devil as she is. She just does it to slur him. Elijah Moseley asked her why she didn't stop shouting, seeing she always got a beating about it. She says she can't "squinch the sperrit." Then Elijah asked Mr. McDuffy to stop beating her, seeing that she was going to shout anyway. He answered that she just did it for spite and that his fist was just as hard as her head. He could last just as long as she. So the village let the matter rest.

XI. *Double-Shuffle*

Back in the good old days before the World War, things were very simple in Eatonville. People didn't fox-trot. When the town wanted to put on its Sunday clothes and wash behind the ears, it put on a "breakdown." The daring younger set would two-step and waltz, but the good church members and the elders stuck to the grand march. By rural canons dancing is wicked, but one is not held to have danced until the feet have been crossed. Feet don't get crossed when one grand marches.

At elaborate affairs the organ from the Methodist church was moved up to the hall and Lizzimore, the blind man, presided. When informal gatherings were held, he merely played his guitar assisted by any volunteer with mouth organs or accordions.

Among white people the march is as mild as if it had been passed on by Volstead.[3] But it still has a kick in Eatonville. Everybody happy, shining eyes, gleaming teeth. Feet dragged 'shhlap, shhlap! to beat out the time. No orchestra needed. Round and round! Back again, parse-me-la! shlap! shlap! Strut! Strut! Seaboard! Shlap! Shalp! Tiddy bumm! Mr. Clarke in the lead with Mrs. Moseley.

It's too much for some of the young folks. Double shuffling commences. Buck and wing. Lizzimore about to break his guitar. Accordion doing contortions. People fall back against the walls, and let the soloist have it, shouting as they clap the old, old double-shuffle songs.

> 'Me an' mah honey got two mo' days
> Two mo' days tuh do de buck'

Sweating bodies, laughing mouths, grotesque faces, feet drumming fiercely. Deacons clapping as hard as the rest.

> "Great big nigger, black as tar
> Trying tuh git tuh hebben on uh 'lectric car."

> "Some love cabbage, some love kale
> But I love a gal wid a short skirt tail."

---

3. Andrew J. Volstead (1860–1947), congressman who introduced the Prohibition Amendment.

Long tall angel—steppin' down,
Long white robe an' starry crown.

'Ah would not marry uh black gal (bumm bumm!)
Tell yuh de reason why
Every time she comb her hair
She make de goo-goo eye.

Would not marry a yaller gal (bumm bumm!)
Tell yuh de reason why
Her neck so long an' stringy
Ahm 'fraid she'd never die.

Would not marry uh preacher
Tell yuh de reason why
Every time he comes tuh town
He makes de chicken fly.

When the buck dance[4] was over, the boys would give the floor to the girls and they would parse-me-la with a sly eye out of the corner to see if anybody was looking who might "have them up in church" on conference night.[5] Then there would be more dancing. Then Mr. Clarke would call for everybody's best attention and announce that *'freshments was served! Every gent'man would please take his lady by the arm and scorch*[6] her right up to de table fur a treat!

Then the men would stick their arms out with a flourish and ask their ladies: "You lak chicken? Well, then, take a wing." And the ladies would take the proferred "wings" and parade up to the long table and be served. Of course most of them had brought baskets in which were heaps of jointed and fried chicken, two or three kinds of pies, cakes, potato pone and chicken purlo.[7] The hall would separate into happy groups about the baskets until time for more dancing.

But the boys and girls got scattered about during the war, and now they dance the fox-trot by a brand new piano. They do waltz and two-step still, but no one now considers it good form to lock his chin over his partner's shoulder and stick out behind. One night just for fun and to humor the old folks, they danced, that is, they grand marched, but everyone picked up their feet. *Bah!!*

XII. The Head of the Nail

Daisy Taylor was the town vamp. Not that she was pretty. But sirens were all but non-existent in the town. Perhaps she was forced to it by circumstances. She was quite dark, with little bushy patches of hair squatting over her head. These were held down by shingle-nails often. No one knows whether she did this for artistic effect or for lack of hairpins, but there they were shining in the little patches of hair when she got all dressed for the afternoon and came up to Clarke's store to see if there was any mail for her.

---

4. All-male dance.
5. A formal meeting of church officials. The girls are afraid they might be accused of loose behavior.
6. Escort (dialect).
7. I.e., pilaf; a stew of rice, vegetables, and chicken.

It was seldom that anyone wrote to Daisy, but she knew that the men of the town would be assembled there by five o'clock, and some one could usually be induced to buy her some soda water or peanuts.

Daisy flirted with married men. There were only two single men in town. Lum Boger, who was engaged to the assistant school-teacher, and Hiram Lester, who had been off to school at Tuskegee and wouldn't look at a person like Daisy. In addition to other drawbacks, she was pigeon-toed and her petticoat was always showing so perhaps he was justified. There was nothing else to do except flirt with married men.

This went on for a long time. First one wife and then another complained of her, or drove her from the preserves by threat.

But the affair with Crooms was the most prolonged and serious. He was even known to have bought her a pair of shoes.

Mrs. Laura Crooms was a meek little woman who took all of her troubles crying, and talked a great deal of leaving things in the hands of God.

The affair came to a head one night in orange picking time. Crooms was over at Oneido picking oranges. Many fruit pickers move from one town to the other during the season.

The *town* was collected at the store-postoffice as is customary on Saturday nights. The *town* has had its bath and with its week's pay in pocket fares forth to be merry. The men tell stories and treat the ladies to soda water, peanuts and peppermint candy.

Daisy was trying to get treats, but the porch was cold to her that night.

"Ah don't keer if you don't treat me. What's a dirty lil nickel?" She flung this at Walter Thomas. "The everloving Mister Crooms will gimme anything atall Ah wants."

"You better shet up yo' mouf talking 'bout Albert Crooms. Heah his wife comes right now."

Daisy went akimbo. "Who? Me! Ah don't keer whut Laura Crooms think. If she ain't a heavy hip-ted Mama enough to keep him, she don't need to come crying to me."

She stood making goo-goo eyes as Mrs. Crooms walked upon the porch. Daisy laughed loud, made several references to Albert Crooms, and when she saw the mail-bag come in from Maitland she said, "Ah better go in an' see if Ah ain't got a letter from Oneido."

The more Daisy played the game of getting Mrs. Crooms' goat, the better she liked it. She ran in and out of the store laughing until she could scarcely stand. Some of the people present began to talk to Mrs. Crooms—to egg her on to halt Daisy's boasting, but she was for leaving it all in the hands of God. Walter Thomas kept on after Mrs. Crooms until she stiffened and resolved to fight. Daisy was inside when she came to this resolve and never dreamed anything of the kind could happen. She had gotten hold of an envelope and came laughing and shouting, "Oh, Ah can't stand to see Oneido lose!"

There was a box of ax-handles on display on the porch, propped up against the door jamb. As Daisy stepped upon the porch, Mrs. Crooms leaned the heavy end of one of those handles heavily upon her head. She staggered from the porch to the ground and the timid Laura, fearful of a counter-attack, struck again and Daisy toppled into the town ditch. There was not enough water in there to do more than muss her up. Every time she tried to rise, down would come that ax-handle again. Laura was fighting a scared fight. With

Daisy thoroughly licked, she retired to the store porch and left her fallen enemy in the ditch. But Elijah Moseley, who was some distance down the street when the trouble began, arrived as the victor was withdrawing. He rushed up and picked Daisy out of the mud and began feeling her head.

"Is she hurt much?" Joe Clarke asked from the doorway.

"I don't know," Elijah answered. "I was just looking to see if Laura had been lucky enough to hit one of those nails on the head and drive it in."

Before a week was up, Daisy moved to Orlando. There in a wider sphere, perhaps, her talents as a vamp were appreciated.

XIII. Pants and Cal'line

Sister Cal'line Potts was a silent woman. Did all of her laughing down inside, but did the thing that kept the town in an uproar of laughter. It was the general opinion of the village that Cal'line would do anything she had a mind to. And she had a mind to do several things.

Mitchell Potts, her husband, had a weakness for women. No one ever believed that she was jealous. She did things to the women, surely. But most any townsman would have said that she did them because she liked the novel situation and the queer things she could bring out of it.

Once he took up with Delphine—called Mis' Pheeny by the town. She lived on the outskirts on the edge of the piney woods. The town winked and talked. People don't make secrets of such things in villages. Cal'line went about her business with her thin black lips pursed tight as ever, and her shiny black eyes unchanged.

"Dat devil of a Cal'line's got somethin' up her sleeve!" The town smiled in anticipation.

"Delphine is too big a cigar for her to smoke. She ain't crazy," said some as the weeks went on and nothing happened. Even Pheeny herself would give an extra flirt to her over-starched petticoats as she rustled into church past her of Sundays.

Mitch Potts said furthermore, that he was tired of Cal'line's foolishness. She had to stay where he put her. His African soup-bone (arm) was too strong to let a woman run over him. 'Nough was 'nough. And he did some fancy cussing, and he was the fanciest cusser in the county.

So the town waited and the longer it waited, the odds changed slowly from the wife to the husband.

One Saturday, Mitch knocked off work at two o'clock and went over to Maitland. He came back with a rectangular box under his arm and kept straight on out to the barn to put it away. He ducked around the corner of the house quickly, but even so, his wife glimpsed the package. Very much like a shoe box. So!

He put on the kettle and took a bath. She stood in her bare feet at the ironing board and kept on ironing. He dressed. It was about five o'clock but still very light. He fiddled around outside. She kept on with her ironing. As soon as the sun got red, he sauntered out to the barn, got the parcel and walked away down the road, past the store and out into the piney woods. As soon as he left the house, Cal'line slipped on her shoes without taking time to don stockings, put on one of her husband's old Stetsons, worn and floppy, slung the axe over her shoulder and followed in his wake. He was hailed cheerily as he passed the sitters on the store porch and answered smiling sheepishly and passed on. Two minutes later passed his wife, silently, unsmilingly, and set the porch to giggling and betting.

An hour passed perhaps. It was dark. Clarke had long ago lighted the swinging kerosene lamp inside.

XIV.

Once 'way back yonder before the stars fell all the animals used to talk just like people. In them days dogs and rabbits was the best of friends—even tho both of them was stuck on the same gal—which was Miss Nancy Coon. She had the sweetest smile and the prettiest striped and bushy tail to be found anywhere.

They both run their legs nigh off trying to win her for themselves—fetching nice ripe persimmons and such. But she never give one or the other no satisfaction.

Finally one night Mr. Dog popped the question right out. "Miss Coon," he says, "Ma'am, also Ma'am which would you ruther be—a lark flyin' or a dove a settin'?"

Course Miss Nancy she blushed and laughed a little and hid her face behind her bushy tail for a spell. Then she said sorter shy like, "I does love yo' sweet voice, brother dawg—but—I ain't jes' exactly set my mind yit."

Her and Mr. Dog set on a spell, when up comes hopping Mr. Rabbit wid his tail fresh washed and his whiskers shining. He got right down to business and asked Miss Coon to marry him, too.

"Oh, Miss Nancy," he says, "Ma'am, also Ma'am, if you'd see me settin' straddle of a mud-cat[8] leadin' a minnow, what would you think? Ma'am also Ma'am?" Which is a out and out proposal as everybody knows.

"Youse awful nice, Brother Rabbit and a beautiful dancer, but you cannot sing like Brother Dog. Both you uns come back next week to gimme time for to decide."

They both left arm-in-arm. Finally Mr. Rabbit says to Mr. Dog. "Taint no use in me going back—she ain't gwinter have me. So I mought as well give up. She loves singing, and I ain't got nothing but a squeak."

"Oh, don't talk that a way," says Mr. Dog, tho' he is glad Mr. Rabbit can't sing none.

"Thass all right, Brer Dog. But if I had a sweet voice like you got, I'd have it worked on and make it sweeter."

"How! How! How!" Mr. Dog cried, jumping up and down.

"Lemme fix it for you, like I do for Sister Lark and Sister Mockingbird."

"When? Where?" asked Mr. Dog, all excited. He was figuring that if he could sing just a little better Miss Coon would be bound to have him.

"Just you meet me t'morrer in de huckleberry patch," says the rabbit and off they both goes to bed.

The dog is there on time next day and after a while the rabbit comes loping up.

"Mawnin', Brer Dawg," he says kinder chippy like. "Ready to git yo' voice sweetened?"

8. Catfish.

"Sholy, sholy, Brer Rabbit. Let's we all hurry about it. I wants tuh serenade Miss Nancy from the piney woods tuh night."

"Well, den, open yo' mouf and poke out yo' tongue," says the rabbit.

No sooner did Mr. Dog poke out his tongue than Mr. Rabbit split it with a knife and ran for all he was worth to a hollow stump and hid hisself.

The dog has been mad at the rabbit ever since.

Anybody who don't believe it happened, just look at the dog's tongue and he can see for himself where the rabbit slit it right up the middle.

Stepped on a tin, mah story ends.

1927

How It Feels to Be Colored Me[1]

I am colored but I offer nothing in the way of extenuating circumstances except the fact that I am the only Negro in the United States whose grandfather on the mother's side was *not an Indian chief.*

I remember the very day that I became colored. Up to my thirteenth year I lived in the little Negro town of Eatonville, Florida. It is exclusively a colored town. The only white people I knew passed through the town going to or coming from Orlando. The native whites rode dusty horses, the Northern tourists chugged down the sandy village road in automobiles. The town knew the Southerners and never stopped cane chewing when they passed. But the Northerners were something else again. They were peered at cautiously from behind the curtains by the timid. The more venturesome would come out on the porch to watch them go past and got just as much pleasure out of the tourists as the tourists got out of the village.

The front porch might seem a daring place for the rest of the town, but it was a gallery seat for me. My favorite place was atop the gate-post. Proscenium box[2] for a born first-nighter. Not only did I enjoy the show, but I didn't mind the actors knowing that I liked it. I usually spoke to them in passing. I'd wave at them and when they returned my salute, I would say something like this: "Howdy-do-well-I-thank-you-where-you-goin'?" Usually automobile or the horse paused at this, and after a queer exchange of compliments, I would probably "go a piece of the way" with them, as we say in farthest Florida. If one of my family happened to come to the front in time to see me, of course negotiations would be rudely broken off. But even so, it is clear that I was the first "welcome-to-our-state" Floridian, and I hope the Miami Chamber of Commerce will please take notice.

During this period, white people differed from colored to me only in that they rode through town and never lived there. They liked to hear me "speak pieces" and sing and wanted to see me dance the parse-me-la, and gave me generously of their small silver for doing these things, which seemed strange to me for I wanted to do them so much that I needed bribing to stop. Only they didn't know it. The colored people gave no dimes. They deplored any joy-

---

1. The text is that of *I Love Myself When I Am Laughing . . . and Then Again When I Am Looking Mean and Impressive* (1979), edited by Alice Walker.
2. Box at the front of the auditorium, closest to the stage.

ful tendencies in me, but I was their Zora nevertheless. I belonged to them, to the nearby hotels, to the county—everybody's Zora.

But changes came in the family when I was thirteen, and I was sent to school in Jacksonville. I left Eatonville, the town of the oleanders, as Zora. When I disembarked from the river-boat at Jacksonville, she was no more. It seemed that I had suffered a sea change. I was not Zora of Orange County any more, I was now a little colored girl. I found it out in certain ways. In my heart as well as in the mirror, I became a fast brown—warranted not to rub nor run.

But I am not tragically colored. There is no great sorrow dammed up in my soul, nor lurking behind my eyes. I do not mind at all. I do not belong to the sobbing school of Negrohood who hold that nature somehow has given them a lowdown dirty deal and whose feelings are all hurt about it. Even in the helter-skelter skirmish that is my life, I have seen that the world is to the strong regardless of a little pigmentation more or less. No, I do not weep at the world—I am too busy sharpening my oyster knife.

Someone is always at my elbow reminding me that I am the granddaughter of slaves. It fails to register depression with me. Slavery is sixty years in the past. The operation was successful and the patient is doing well, thank you. The terrible struggle that made me an American out of a potential slave said "On the line!" The Reconstruction said "Get set!"; and the generation before said "Go!" I am off to a flying start and I must not halt in the stretch to look behind and weep. Slavery is the price I paid for civilization, and the choice was not with me. It is a bully adventure and worth all that I have paid through my ancestors for it. No one on earth ever had a greater chance for glory. The world to be won and nothing to be lost. It is thrilling to think—to know that for any act of mine, I shall get twice as much praise or twice as much blame. It is quite exciting to hold the center of the national stage, with the spectators not knowing whether to laugh or to weep.

The position of my white neighbor is much more difficult. No brown specter pulls up a chair beside me when I sit down to eat. No dark ghost thrusts its leg against mine in bed. The game of keeping what one has is never so exciting as the game of getting.

I do not always feel colored. Even now I often achieve the unconscious Zora of Eatonville before the Hegira.[3] I feel most colored when I am thrown against a sharp white background.

For instance at Barnard. "Besides the waters of the Hudson" I feel my race. Among the thousand white persons, I am a dark rock surged upon, and overswept, but through it all, I remain myself. When covered by the waters, I am; and the ebb but reveals me again.

Sometimes it is the other way around. A white person is set down in our midst, but the contrast is just as sharp for me. For instance, when I sit in the drafty basement that is The New World Cabaret[4] with a white person, my color comes. We enter chatting about any little nothing that we have in com-

3. Forced march of Muhammad from Mecca to Medina in 622 C.E.; hence any forced flight or jour- ney for safety.
4. Popular Harlem nightclub in the 1920s.

mon and are seated by the jazz waiters. In the abrupt way that jazz orchestras have, this one plunges into a number. It loses no time in circumlocutions, but gets right down to business. It constricts the thorax and splits the heart with its tempo and narcotic harmonies. This orchestra grows rambunctious, rears on its hind legs and attacks the tonal veil with primitive fury, rending it, clawing it until it breaks through to the jungle beyond. I follow those heathen— follow them exultingly. I dance wildly inside myself; I yell within, I whoop; I shake my assegai[5] above my head, I hurl it true to the mark *yeeeeooww!* I am in the jungle and living in the jungle way. My face is painted red and yellow and my body is painted blue. My pulse is throbbing like a war drum. I want to slaughter something—give pain, give death to what, I do not know. But the piece ends. The men of the orchestra wipe their lips and rest their fingers. I creep back slowly to the veneer we call civilization with the last tone and find the white friend sitting motionless in his seat smoking calmly.

"Good music they have here," he remarks, drumming the table with his fingertips.

Music. The great blobs of purple and red emotion have not touched him. He has only heard what I felt. He is far away and I see him but dimly across the ocean and the continent that have fallen between us. He is so pale with his whiteness then and I am *so* colored.

At certain times I have no race, I am *me*. When I set my hat at a certain angle and saunter down Seventh Avenue, Harlem City, feeling as snooty as the lions in front of the Forty-Second Street Library, for instance. So far as my feelings are concerned, Peggy Hopkins Joyce on the Boule Mich[6] with her gorgeous raiment, stately carriage, knees knocking together in a most aristocratic manner, has nothing on me. The cosmic Zora emerges. I belong to no race nor time. I am the eternal feminine with its string of beads.

I have no separate feeling about being an American citizen and colored. I am merely a fragment of the Great Soul that surges within the boundaries. My country, right or wrong.

Sometimes, I feel discriminated against, but it does not make me angry. It merely astonishes me. How *can* any deny themselves the pleasure of my company? It's beyond me.

But in the main, I feel like a brown bag of miscellany propped against a wall. Against a wall in company with other bags, white, red and yellow. Pour out the contents, and there is discovered a jumble of small things priceless and worthless. A first-water diamond, an empty spool, bits of broken glass, lengths of string, a key to a door long since crumbled away, a rusty knife-blade, old shoes saved for a road that never was and never will be, a nail bent under the weight of things too heavy for any nail, a dried flower or two still a little fragrant. In your hand is the brown bag. On the ground before you is the jumble it held—so much like the jumble in the bags, could they be emptied, that all might be dumped in a single heap and the bags refilled without altering the content of any greatly. A bit of colored glass more or less would

---

5. A slender spear used by some South African peoples.
6. Boulevard St. Michel, a street on the Left Bank of Paris running through the Latin Quarter. It is

lined with cafés that were—and still are—frequented by Americans. Joyce was a much-photographed socialite and heiress.

not matter. Perhaps that is how the Great Stuffer of Bags filled them in the first place—who knows?

1928

The Gilded Six-Bits[1]

It was a Negro yard around a Negro house in a Negro settlement that looked to the payroll of the G and G Fertilizer works for its support.

But there was something happy about the place. The front yard was parted in the middle by a sidewalk from gate to door-step, a sidewalk edged on either side by quart bottles driven neck down into the ground on a slant. A mess of homey flowers planted without a plan but blooming cheerily from their helter-skelter places. The fence and house were whitewashed. The porch and steps scrubbed white.

The front door stood open to the sunshine so that the floor of the front room could finish drying after its weekly scouring. It was Saturday. Everything clean from the front gate to the privy house. Yard raked so that the strokes of the rake would make a pattern. Fresh newspaper cut in fancy edge on the kitchen shelves.

Missie May was bathing herself in the galvanized washtub in the bedroom. Her dark-brown skin glistened under the soapsuds that skittered down from her wash rag. Her stiff young breasts thrust forward aggressively like broad-based cones with the tips lacquered in black.

She heard men's voices in the distance and glanced at the dollar clock on the dresser.

"Humph! Ah'm way behind time t'day! Joe gointer be heah 'fore Ah git mah clothes on if Ah don't make haste."

She grabbed the clean meal sack at hand and dried herself hurriedly and began to dress. But before she could tie her slippers, there came the ring of singing metal on wood. Nine times.

Missie May grinned with delight. She had not seen the big tall man come stealing in the gate and creep up the walk grinning happily at the joyful mischief he was about to commit. But she knew that it was her husband throwing silver dollars in the door for her to pick up and pile beside her plate at dinner. It was this way every Saturday afternoon. The nine dollars hurled into the open door, he scurried to a hiding place behind the cape jasmine bush and waited.

Missie May promptly appeared at the door in mock alarm.

"Who dat chunkin' money in mah do'way?" She demanded. No answer from the yard. She leaped off the porch and began to search the shrubbery. She peeped under the porch and hung over the gate to look up and down the road. While she did this, the man behind the jasmine darted to the chinaberry tree. She spied him and gave chase.

"Nobody ain't gointer be chuckin' money at me and Ah not do 'em nothin'," she shouted in mock anger. He ran around the house with Missie May at his

1. The text is from the printing in *Story* magazine (1933). "Gilded": lightly plated with thin gold or gold-colored foil. "Six-bits": seventy-five cents (two bits equals one quarter).

heels. She overtook him at the kitchen door. He ran inside but could not close it after him before she crowded in and locked with him in a rough and tumble. For several minutes the two were a furious mass of male and female energy. Shouting, laughing, twisting, turning, tussling, tickling each other in the ribs; Missie May clutching onto Joe and Joe trying, but not too hard, to get away.

"Missie May, take yo' hand out mah pocket!" Joe shouted out between laughs.

"Ah ain't, Joe, not lessen you gwine gimme whateve' it is good you got in yo' pocket. Turn it go, Joe, do Ah'll tear yo' clothes."

"Go on tear 'em. You de one dat pushes de needles round heah. Move yo' hand Missie May."

"Lemme git dat paper sack out yo' pocket. Ah bet its candy kisses."

"Tain't. Move yo' hand. Woman ain't go no business in a man's clothes nohow. Go way."

Missie May gouged way down and gave an upward jerk and triumphed.

"Unhhunh! Ah got it. It 'tis so candy kisses. Ah knowed you had somethin' for me in yo' clothes. Now Ah got to see whut's in every pocket you got."

Joe smiled indulgently and let his wife go through all of his pockets and take out the things that he had hidden there for her to find. She bore off the chewing gum, the cake of sweet soap, the pocket handkerchief as if she had wrested them from him, as if they had not been bought for the sake of this friendly battle.

"Whew! dat play-fight done got me all warmed up," Joe exclaimed. "Got me some water in de kittle?"

"Yo' water is on de fire and yo' clean things is cross de bed. Hurry up and wash yo'self and git changed so we kin eat. Ah'm hongry." As Missie said this, she bore the steaming kettle into the bedroom.

"You ain't hongry, sugar," Joe contradicted her. "Youse jes' a little empty. Ah'm de one whut's hongry. Ah could eat up camp meetin', back off 'ssociation, and drink Jurdan[2] dry. Have it on de table when Ah git out de tub."

"Don't you mess wid mah business, man. You git in yo' clothes. Ah'm a real wife, not no dress and breath.[3] Ah might not look lak one, but if you burn me, you won't git a thing but wife ashes."

Joe splashed in the bedroom and Missie May fanned around in the kitchen. A fresh red and white checked cloth on the table. Big pitcher of buttermilk beaded with pale drops of butter from the churn. Hot fried mullet, crackling bread, ham hock atop a mound of string beans and new potatoes, and perched on the window-sill a pone[4] of spicy potato pudding.

Very little talk during the meal but that little consisted of banter that pretended to deny affection but in reality flaunted it. Like when Missie May reached for a second helping of the tater pone. Joe snatched it out of her reach.

After Missie May had made two or three unsuccessful grabs at the pan, she begged, "Aw, Joe gimme some mo' dat tater pone."

"Nope, sweetenin' is for us men-folks. Y'all pritty lil frail eels don't need nothin' lak dis. You too sweet already."

---

2. The Jordan River in biblical Palestine (now Israel).

3. All show; i.e., not a real wife.

4. Loaf- or oval-shaped cake.

"Please, Joe."

"Naw, naw. Ah don't want you to git no sweeter than whut you is already. We goin' down de road a lil piece t'night so you go put on yo' Sunday-go-to-meetin' things."

Missie May looked at her husband to see if he was playing some prank. "Sho nuff, Joe?"

"Yeah. We goin' to de ice cream parlor."

"Where de ice cream parlor at, Joe?"

"A new man done come heah from Chicago and he done got a place and took and opened it up for a ice cream parlor, and bein' as it's real swell, Ah wants you to be one de first ladies to walk in dere and have some set down."

"Do Jesus, Ah ain't knowed nothin' 'bout it. Who de man done it?"

"Mister Otis D. Slemmons, of spots and places—Memphis, Chicago, Jacksonville, Philadelphia and so on."

"Dat heavy-set man wid his mouth full of gold teethes?"

"Yeah. Where did you see 'im at?"

"Ah went down to de sto' tuh git a box of lye and Ah seen 'im standing' on de corner talkin' to some of de mens, and Ah come on back and went to scrubbin' de floor, and he passed and tipped his hat whilst Ah was scourin' de steps. Ah thought Ah never seen *him* befo'."

Joe smiled pleasantly. "Yeah, he's up to date. He got de finest clothes Ah ever seen on a colored man's back."

"Aw, he don't look no better in his clothes than you do in yourn. He got a puzzlegut on 'im and he so chuckle-headed,[5] he got a pone behind his neck."

Joe looked down at his own abdomen and said wistfully, "Wisht Ah had a build on me lak he got. He ain't puzzle-gutted, honey. He jes' got a corperation. Dat make 'm look lak a rich white man. All rich mens is got some belly on 'em."

"Ah seen de pitchers of Henry Ford and he's a spare-built man and Rockefeller look lak he ain't got but one gut. But Ford and Rockefeller and dis Slemmons and all de rest kin be as many-gutted as dey please, Ah'm satisfied wid you jes' lak you is, baby. God took pattern after a pine tree and built you noble. Youse a pritty man, and if Ah knowed any way to make you mo' pritty still Ah'd take and do it."

Joe reached over gently and toyed with Missie May's ear. "You jes' say dat cause you love me, but Ah know Ah can't hold no light to Otis D. Slemmons. Ah ain't never been nowhere and Ah ain't got nothin' but you."

Missie May got on his lap and kissed him and he kissed back in kind. Then he went on. "All de womens is crazy 'bout 'im everywhere he go."

"How you know dat, Joe?"

"He tole us so hisself."

"Dat don't make it so. His mouf is cut cross-ways, ain't it? Well, he kin lie jes' lak anybody else."

"Good Lawd, Missie! You womens sho is hard to sense into things. He's got a five-dollar gold piece for a stick-pin and he got a ten-dollar gold piece on his watch chain and his mouf is jes' crammed full of gold teethes. Sho wisht it wuz mine. And whut make it so cool, he got money 'cumulated. And womens give it all to 'im."

---

5. Stupid, blockheaded. "Puzzlegut": fat belly.

"Ah don't see whut de womens see on 'im. Ah wouldn't give 'im a wink if de sheriff wuz after 'im."

"Well, he tole us how de white womens in Chicago give 'im all dat gold money. So he don't 'low nobody to touch it at all. Not even put dey finger on it. Dey tole 'im not to. You kin make 'miration at it, but don't tetch it."

"Whyn't he stay up dere where dey so crazy 'bout 'im?"

"Ah reckon dey done made 'im vast-rich and he wants to travel some. He say dey wouldn't leave 'im hit a lick of work. He got mo' lady people crazy 'bout him than he kin shake a stick at."

"Joe, Ah hates to see you so dumb. Dat stray nigger jes' tell y'all anything and y'all b'lieve it."

"Go 'head on now, honey and put on yo' clothes. He talkin' 'bout his pritty womens—Ah want 'im to see *mine*."

Missie May went off to dress and Joe spent the time trying to make his stomach punch out like Slemmons' middle. He tried the rolling swagger of the stranger, but found that his tall bone-and-muscle stride fitted ill with it. He just had time to drop back into his seat before Missie May came in dressed to go.

On the way home that night Joe was exultant. "Didn't Ah say ole Otis was swell? Can't he talk Chicago talk? Wuzn't dat funny whut he said when great big fat ole Ida Armstrong come in? He asted me, 'Who is dat broad wid de forte shake?' Dat's a new word. Us always thought forty was a set of figgers but he showed us where it means a whole heap of things. Sometimes he don't say forty, he jes' say thirty-eight and two and dat mean de same thing. Know whut he tole me when Ah wuz payin' for our ice cream? He say, 'Ah have to hand it to you, Joe. Dat wife of yours is jes' thirty-eight and two. Yessuh, she's forte!' Ain't he killin'?"

"He'll do in case of a rush. But he sho is got uh heap uh gold on 'im. Dat's de first time Ah ever seed gold money. It lookted good on him sho nuff, but it'd look a whole heap better on you."

"Who, me? Missie May youse crazy! Where would a po' man lak me git gold money from?"

Missie May was silent for a minute, then she said, "Us might find some goin' long de road some time. Us could."

"Who would be losin' gold money round heah? We ain't even seen none dese white folks wearin' no gold money on dey watch chain. You must be figgerin' Mister Packard or Mister Cadillac goin' pass through heah."

"You don't know whut been lost 'round heah. Maybe somebody way back in memorial times[6] lost they gold money and went on off and it ain't never been found. And then if we wuz to find it, you could wear some 'thout havin' no gang of womens lak dat Slemmons say he got."

Joe laughed and hugged her. "Don't be so wishful 'bout me. Ah'm satisfied de way Ah is. So long as Ah be yo' husband, Ah don't keer 'bout nothin' else. Ah'd ruther all de other womens in de world to be dead than for you to have de toothache. Less we go to bed and git our night rest."

It was Saturday night once more before Joe could parade his wife in Slemmons' ice cream parlor again. He worked the night shift and Saturday was his only night off. Every other evening around six o'clock he left home, and dying

---

6. Wordplay on "in time immemorial"; time so long ago as to be forgotten.

dawn saw him hustling home around the lake where the challenging sun flung a flaming sword from east to west across the trembling water.

That was the best part of life—going home to Missie May. Their white-washed house, the mock battle on Saturday, the dinner and ice cream parlor afterwards, church on Sunday nights when Missie outdressed any woman in town—all, everything was right.

One night around eleven the acid[7] ran out at the G. and G. The foreman knocked off the crew and let the steam die down. As Joe rounded the lake on his way home, a lean moon rode the lake in a silver boat. If anybody had asked Joe about the moon on the lake, he would have said he hadn't paid it any attention. But he saw it with his feelings. It made him yearn painfully for Missie. Creation obsessed him. He thought about children. They had been married for more than a year now. They had money put away. They ought to be making little feet for shoes. A little boy child would be about right.

He saw a dim light in the bedroom and decided to come in through the kitchen door. He could wash the fertilizer dust off himself before presenting himself to Missie May. It would be nice for her not to know that he was there until he slipped into his place in bed and hugged her back. She always liked that.

He eased the kitchen door open slowly and silently, but when he went to set his dinner bucket on the table he bumped it into a pile of dishes, and something crashed to the floor. He heard his wife gasp in fright and hurried to reassure her.

"Iss me, honey. Don't get skeered."

There was a quick, large movement in the bedroom. A rustle, a thud, and a stealthy silence. The light went out.

What? Robbers? Murderers? Some varmint attacking his helpless wife, per-haps. He struck a match, threw himself on guard and stepped over the door-sill into the bedroom.

The great belt on the wheel of Time slipped and eternity stood still. By the match light he could see the man's legs fighting with his breeches in his fran-tic desire to get them on. He had both chance and time to kill the intruder in his helpless condition—half in and half out of his pants—but he was too weak to take action. The shapeless enemies of humanity that live in the hours of Time had waylaid Joe. He was assaulted in his weakness. Like Samson awak-ening after his haircut.[8] So he just opened his mouth and laughed.

The match went out and he struck another and lit the lamp. A howling wind raced across his heart, but underneath its fury he heard his wife sob-bing and Slemmons pleading for his life. Offering to buy it with all that he had. "Please, suh, don't kill me. Sixty-two dollars at de sto'. Gold money."

Joe just stood. Slemmons looked at the window, but it was screened. Joe stood out like a rough-backed mountain between him and the door. Barring him from escape, from sunrise, from life.

He considered a surprise attack upon the big clown that stood there laugh-ing like a chessy cat.[9] But before his fist could travel an inch, Joe's own rushed out to crush him like a battering ram. Then Joe stood over him.

---

7. Used in making fertilizer.
8. In Judges 13–16, Samson's exceptional strength resides in his hair, which his treacherous lover, Delilah, cuts off while he sleeps.

9. I.e., Cheshire cat; an allusion to the grinning cat in *Alice's Adventures in Wonderland* (1865), by Lewis Carroll (1832–1889).

"Git into yo' damn rags, Slemmons, and dat quick."

Slemmons scrambled to his feet and into his vest and coat. As he grabbed his hat, Joe's fury overrode his intentions and he grabbed at Slemmons with his left hand and struck at him with his right. The right landed. The left grazed the front of his vest. Slemmons was knocked a somersault into the kitchen and fled through the open door. Joe found himself alone with Missie May, with the golden watch charm clutched in his left fist. A short bit of broken chain dangled between his fingers.

Missie May was sobbing. Wails of weeping without words. Joe stood, and after awhile he found out that he had something in his hand. And then he stood and felt without thinking and without seeing with his natural eyes. Missie May kept on crying and Joe kept on feeling so much and not knowing what to do with all his feelings, he put Slemmons' watch charm in his pants pocket and took a good laugh and went to bed.

"Missie May, whut you cryin' for?"

"Cause Ah love you so hard and Ah know you don't love *me* no mo'."

Joe sank his face into the pillow for a spell then he said huskily, "You don't know de feelings of dat yet, Missie May."

"Oh Joe, honey, he said he wuz gointer give me dat gold money and he jes' kept on after me—"

Joe was very still and silent for a long time. Then he said, "Well, don't cry no mo', Missie May. Ah got yo' gold piece for you."

The hours went past on their rusty ankles. Joe still and quiet on one bedrail and Missie May wrung dry of sobs on the other. Finally the sun's tide crept upon the shore of night and drowned all its hours. Missie May with her face stiff and streaked towards the window saw the dawn come into her yard. It was day. Nothing more. Joe wouldn't be coming home as usual. No need to fling open the front door and sweep off the porch, making it nice for Joe. Never no more breakfast to cook; no more washing and starching of Joe's jumper-jackets and pants. No more nothing. So why get up?

With this strange man in her bed, she felt embarrassed to get up and dress. She decided to wait till he had dressed and gone. Then she would get up, dress quickly and be gone forever beyond reach of Joe's looks and laughs. But he never moved. Red light turned to yellow, then white.

From beyond the no-man's land between them came a voice. A strange voice that yesterday had been Joe's.

"Missie May, ain't you gonna fix me no breakfus'?"

She sprang out of bed. "Yeah, Joe. Ah didn't reckon you wuz hongry."

No need to die today. Joe needed her for a few more minutes anyhow.

Soon there was a roaring fire in the cook stove. Water bucket full and two chickens killed. Joe loved fried chicken and rice. She didn't deserve a thing and good Joe was letting her cook him some breakfast. She rushed hot biscuits to the table as Joe took his seat.

He ate with his eyes on his plate. No laughter, no banter.

"Missie May, you ain't eatin' yo' breakfus'."

"Ah don't choose none, Ah thank yuh."

His coffee cup was empty. She sprang to refill it. When she turned from the stove and bent to set the cup beside Joe's plate, she saw the yellow coin on the table between them.

She slumped into her seat and wept into her arms.

Presently Joe said calmly, "Missie May, you cry too much. Don't look back lak Lot's wife and turn to salt."[1]

The sun, the hero of every day, the impersonal old man that beams as brightly on death as on birth, came up every morning and raced across the blue dome and dipped into the sea of fire every evening. Water ran down hill and birds nested.

Missie knew why she didn't leave Joe. She couldn't. She loved him too much, but she could not understand why Joe didn't leave her. He was polite, even kind at times, but aloof.

There were no more Saturday romps. No ringing silver dollars to stack beside her plate. No pockets to rifle. In fact the yellow coin in his trousers was like a monster hiding in the cave of his pockets to destroy her.

She often wondered if he still had it, but nothing could have induced her to ask nor yet to explore his pockets to see for herself. Its shadow was in the house whether or no.

One night Joe came home around midnight and complained of pains in the back. He asked Missie to rub him down with liniment. It had been three months since Missie had touched his body and it all seemed strange. But she rubbed him. Grateful for the chance. Before morning, youth triumphed and Missie exulted. But the next day, as she joyfully made up their bed, beneath her pillow she found the piece of money with the bit of chain attached.

Alone to herself, she looked at the thing with loathing, but look she must. She took it into her hands with trembling and saw first thing that it was no gold piece. It was a gilded half dollar. Then she knew why Slemmons had forbidden anyone to touch his gold. He trusted village eyes at a distance not to recognize his stick-pin as a gilded quarter, and his watch charm as a four-bit piece.

She was glad at first that Joe had left it there. Perhaps he was through with her punishment. They were man and wife again. Then another thought came clawing at her. He had come home to buy from her as if she were any woman in the long house.[2] Fifty cents for her love. As if to say that he could pay as well as Slemmons. She slid the coin into his Sunday pants pocket and dressed herself and left his house.

Halfway between her house and the quarters[3] she met her husband's mother, and after a short talk she turned and went back home. Never would she admit defeat to that woman who prayed for it nightly. If she had not the substance of marriage she had the outside show. Joe must leave *her*. She let him see she didn't want his old gold four-bits too.

She saw no more of the coin for some time though she knew that Joe could not help finding it in his pocket. But his health kept poor, and he came home at least every ten days to be rubbed.

The sun swept around the horizon, trailing its robes of weeks and days. One morning as Joe came in from work, he found Missie May chopping wood. Without a word he took the ax and chopped a huge pile before he stopped.

"You ain't got no business choppin' wood, and you know it."

"How come? Ah been choppin' it for de last longest."

1. According to Genesis 19.26, Lot's wife was turned into a pillar of salt for looking back at the destroyed city of Sodom when she and her husband were fleeing from it.
2. House of prostitution.
3. Workers' dwellings.

"Ah ain't blind. You makin' feet for shoes."[4]

"Won't you be glad to have a lil baby chile, Joe?"

"You know dat 'thout astin' me."

"Iss gointer be a boy chile and de very spit of you." "You reckon, Missie May?"

"Who else could it look lak?"

Joe said nothing, but he thrust his hand deep into his pocket and fingered something there.

It was almost six months later Missie May took to bed and Joe went and got his mother to come wait on the house.

Missie May delivered a fine boy. Her travail was over when Joe came in from work one morning. His mother and the old women were drinking great bowls of coffee around the fire in the kitchen.

The minute Joe came into the room his mother called him aside.

"How did Missie May make out?" he asked quickly.

"Who, dat gal? She strong as a ox. She gointer have plenty mo'. We done fixed her wid de sugar and lard to sweeten her for de nex' one."

Joe stood silent awhile.

"You ain't ast 'bout de baby, Joe. You oughter be mighty proud cause he sho is de spittin' image of yuh, son. Dat's yourn all right, if you never git another one, dat un is yourn. And you know Ah'm mighty proud too, son, cause Ah never thought well of you marryin' Missie May cause her ma used tuh fan her foot round right smart and Ah been mighty skeered dat Missie May was goin-ter git misput on her road."

Joe said nothing. He fooled around the house till late in the day then just before he went to work, he went and stood at the foot of the bed and asked his wife how she felt. He did this every day during the week.

On Saturday he went to Orlando to make his market.[5] It had been a long time since he had done that.

Meat and lard, meal and flour, soap and starch. Cans of corn and tomatoes. All the staples. He fooled around town for awhile and bought bananas and apples. Way after while he went around to the candy store.

"Hellow, Joe," the clerk greeted him. "Ain't seen you in a long time."

"Nope, Ah ain't been heah. Been round in spots and places."

"Want some of them molasses kisses you always buy?"

"Yessuh." He threw the gilded half dollar on the counter. "Will dat spend?"

"Whut is it, Joe? Well, I'll be doggone! A gold-plated four-bit piece. Where'd you git it, Joe?"

"Offen a stray nigger dat come through Eatonville. He had it on his watch chain for a charm—goin' round making out iss gold money. Ha ha! He had a quarter on his tie pin and it wuz all golded up too. Tryin' to fool people. Makin' out he so rich and everything. Ha! Ha! Tryin' to tole off folkses wives from home."

"How did you git it, Joe? Did he fool you, too?"

"Who, me? Naw suh! He ain't fooled me none. Know whut Ah done? He come round me wid his smart talk. Ah hauled off and knocked 'im down and took his old four-bits way from 'im. Gointer buy my wife some good ole lasses kisses wid it. Gimme fifty cents worth of dem candy kisses."

4. You're pregnant (folk expression).   5. A big shopping trip.

"Fifty cents buys a mighty lot of candy kisses, Joe. Why don't you split it up and take some chocolate bars, too. They eat good, too."

"Yessuh, dey do, but Ah wants all dat in kisses. Ah got a lil boy chile home now. Tain't a week old yet, but he kin suck a sugar tit and maybe eat one them kisses hisself."

Joe got his candy and left the store. The clerk turned to the next customer. "Wisht I could be like these darkies. Laughin' all the time. Nothin' worries 'em."

Back in Eatonville, Joe reached his own front door. There was the ring of singing metal on wood. Fifteen times. Missie May couldn't run to the door, but she crept there as quickly as she could.

"Joe Banks, Ah hear you chunkin' money in mah do'way. You wait till Ah got mah strength back and Ah'm gointer fix you for dat."

1933

NELLA LARSEN
1891–1964

Harlem Renaissance leaders proposed that African American artists and intellectuals should uplift their race. In the famous phrase of W. E. B. Du Bois, it was the duty of the "talented tenth" to educate the masses of black Americans while at the same time leading the struggle against white prejudice. This ideology inspired many writers but produced divisive arguments: should African American writing be anchored in authentic popular black culture—whether found in the folkways of the rural South or in the jazz scene of urban communities—or should it represent the deliberately cosmopolitan, educated cultural style of the "New Negroes"? Modernist writers' interest in the "primitive" accentuated these debates. Writers of the Harlem Renaissance were well aware of how African Americans had been stereotypically demeaned as primitive, uncultured, indeed barely human; given that history, was it possible to celebrate an African American identity authentically rooted in black folk culture?

Nella Larsen's writings showed how uplift's demand for racial allegiance could tear apart the inner lives of African Americans. Her own mixed-race background enabled her to see that already in the 1920s the majority of Americans socially categorized as "Negroes" were in fact people of mixed racial ancestry and led her to ask how there could be such a thing as racial authenticity if there was no such thing as "pure" race. Nevertheless, she saw that even if race was an artificial construct, it had powerfully real effects—effects that to her were always destructive of African American selfhood.

Larsen was born in Chicago, of a white mother—a Danish immigrant—and a black West Indian father. He died when she was two, and her mother then married a white man. Larsen, a visibly dark child, was viewed by her visibly light family as an embarrassment. At the age of sixteen she attended a high school connected to Fisk University in Nashville, Tennessee. This, her first experience in an all-black environment, lasted for only a year (1907–08). She moved to Copenhagen, Denmark, where she stayed from 1909 to 1912, visiting relatives and auditing classes at the university. Up to this point—but not beyond it—her life story resembles that of Helga Crane, protagonist of Quicksand.

Returning to the United States after three years abroad, Larsen studied and then practiced nursing for several years. In 1919 she married Elmer Samuel Imes, a black research physicist who later became chair of Fisk University's Physics Department. In 1922, now residing in Harlem, she left nursing and began to work for the New York

Public Library system. By 1926 she and her husband were involved in the Harlem Renaissance scene, and she decided to become a writer.

Carl Van Vechten, wealthy white patron of Harlem Renaissance writers, helped get *Quicksand* (1928) and *Passing* (1929)—her two completed novels—published by the prestigious house of Alfred A. Knopf. Both books sold well and were praised by reviewers across the critical spectrum. Larsen won a Guggenheim fellowship in 1930 for creative writing—the first "black" woman to receive such an award—and went to Spain to work on a third novel, which never materialized. In fact, except for one controversial short story (she was accused of having plagiarized it) and her subsequent published defense of her integrity (in the African American journal *Forum*, in 1930), she seems to have published only the two novels.

Her retreat from literature may have been caused by the painful plagiarism incident; by a lengthy divorce proceeding; or as the result of sharply falling book sales, which affected all Harlem Renaissance authors after the stock market crashed in 1929. Whatever the explanation, she stopped writing, returned to nursing for self-support, moved from Harlem to Brooklyn, and cut her ties with former literary friends and colleagues. At the time of her death, her work had been forgotten. After the 1986 reissue of the two novels in one volume, with an introduction by Deborah E. McDowell, she quickly became recognized as an important Harlem Renaissance figure, perhaps the movement's best novelist.

Passing looks at "black" characters who are able to pass as "white," and do so to enjoy privileges that white people take for granted. Like *Quicksand*, it also represents the erotic fascination that such mixed or passing characters—especially women—inspire in both black and white observers. *Quicksand* is a psychological and episodic novel whose style embodies modernist principles of brevity and impressionistic subjectivity. The narration follows the point of view of the mixed-race Helga Crane, tracking her impatience with uplift's imperative of racial solidarity and her restless alienation from every community, black and white, she passes through. Like Jean Toomer's *Cane*, *Quicksand* takes its protagonist into both urban and rural black communities; like the paintings of Archibald Motley (see the color insert to this volume), *Quicksand* shows the full class spectrum of black Chicago and Harlem. In all of these communities, however, Helga is thwarted by external and internal racial pressures—internal because she interprets her own desires in stereotypical terms of the primitive and the civilized, external because she is always perceived in racial terms and her life options are thoroughly constrained by racial prejudice.

The text of *Quicksand* is the first edition of 1928.

Quicksand

> My old man died in a fine big house.
> My ma died in a shack.
> I wonder where I'm gonna die,
> Being neither white nor black?
> —Langston Hughes[1]

1

Helga Crane sat alone in her room, which at that hour, eight in the evening, was in soft gloom. Only a single reading lamp, dimmed by a great black and red shade, made a pool of light on the blue Chinese carpet, on the bright cov-

---

1. From "Cross," by Hughes (1902–1967), a major writer of the Harlem Renaissance; the poem appeared in his collection *The Weary Blues* (1926).

ers of the books which she had taken down from their long shelves, on the white pages of the opened one selected, on the shining brass bowl crowded with many-colored nasturtiums beside her on the low table, and on the oriental silk which covered the stool at her slim feet. It was a comfortable room, furnished with rare and intensely personal taste, flooded with Southern sun in the day, but shadowy just then with the drawn curtains and single shaded light. Large, too. So large that the spot where Helga sat was a small oasis in a desert of darkness. And eerily quiet. But that was what she liked after her taxing day's work, after the hard classes, in which she gave willingly and unsparingly of herself with no apparent return. She loved this tranquillity, this quiet, following the fret and strain of the long hours spent among fellow members of a carelessly unkind and gossiping faculty, following the strenuous rigidity of conduct required in this huge educational community of which she was an insignificant part. This was her rest, this intentional isolation for a short while in the evening, this little time in her own attractive room with her own books. To the rapping of other teachers, bearing fresh scandals, or seeking information, or other more concrete favors, or merely talk, at that hour Helga Crane never opened her door.

An observer would have thought her well fitted to that framing of light and shade. A slight girl of twenty-two years, with narrow, sloping shoulders and delicate, but well-turned, arms and legs, she had, none the less, an air of radiant, careless health. In vivid green and gold negligee and glistening brocaded mules, deep sunk in the big high-backed chair, against whose dark tapestry her sharply cut face, with skin like yellow satin, was distinctly outlined, she was—to use a hackneyed word—attractive. Black, very broad brows over soft, yet penetrating, dark eyes, and a pretty mouth, whose sensitive and sensuous lips had a slight questioning petulance and a tiny dissatisfied droop, were the features on which the observer's attention would fasten; though her nose was good, her ears delicately chiseled, and her curly blue-black hair plentiful and always straying in a little wayward, delightful way. Just then it was tumbled, falling unrestrained about her face and on to her shoulders.

Helga Crane tried not to think of her work and the school as she sat there. Ever since her arrival in Naxos[2] she had striven to keep these ends of the days from the intrusion of irritating thoughts and worries. Usually she was successful. But not this evening. Of the books which she had taken from their places she had decided on Marmaduke Pickthall's *Saïd the Fisherman*.[3] She wanted forgetfulness, complete mental relaxation, rest from thought of any kind. For the day had been more than usually crowded with distasteful encounters and stupid perversities. The sultry hot Southern spring had left her strangely tired, and a little unnerved. And annoying beyond all other happenings had been that affair of the noon period, now again thrusting itself on her already irritated mind.

She had counted on a few spare minutes in which to indulge in the sweet pleasure of a bath and a fresh, cool change of clothing. And instead her luncheon time had been shortened, as had that of everyone else, and immediately after the hurried gulping down of a heavy hot meal the hundreds of

---

2. Greek island in the Aegean Sea. The name connects the college to the Western classical, humanistic tradition. Critic Deborah E. McDowell notes that it is also an anagram for "Saxon."

3. Novel published in 1903 by Marmaduke William Pickthall (1875–1936), English author of popular travel books, adventure novels, and interpretive studies all focused on Islamic culture.

students and teachers had been herded into the sun-baked chapel to listen to the banal, the patronizing, and even the insulting remarks of one of the renowned white preachers of the state.

Helga shuddered a little as she recalled some of the statements made by that holy white man of God to the black folk sitting so respectfully before him.

This was, he had told them with obvious sectional pride, the finest school for Negroes anywhere in the country, north or south; in fact, it was better even than a great many schools for white children. And he had dared any Northerner to come south and after looking upon this great institution to say that the Southerner mistreated the Negro. And he had said that if all Negroes would only take a leaf out of the book of Naxos and conduct themselves in the manner of the Naxos products, there would be no race problem, because Naxos Negroes knew what was expected of them. They had good sense and they had good taste. They knew enough to stay in their places, and that, said the preacher, showed good taste. He spoke of his great admiration for the Negro race, no other race in so short a time had made so much progress, but he had urgently besought them to know when and where to stop. He hoped, he sincerely hoped, that they wouldn't become avaricious and grasping, thinking only of adding to their earthly goods, for that would be a sin in the sight of Almighty God. And then he had spoken of contentment, embellishing his words with scriptural quotations and pointing out to them that it was their duty to be satisfied in the estate to which they had been called, hewers of wood and drawers of water. And then he had prayed.

Sitting there in her room, long hours after, Helga again felt a surge of hot anger and seething resentment. And again it subsided in amazement at the memory of the considerable applause which had greeted the speaker just before he had asked his God's blessing upon them.

The South. Naxos. Negro education. Suddenly she hated them all. Strange, too, for this was the thing which she had ardently desired to share in, to be a part of this monument to one man's genius and vision. She pinned a scrap of paper about the bulb under the lamp's shade, for, having discarded her book in the certainty that in such a mood even *Saïd* and his audacious villainy could not charm her, she wanted an even more soothing darkness. She wished it were vacation, so that she might get away for a time.

"No, forever!" she said aloud.

The minutes gathered into hours, but still she sat motionless, a disdainful smile or an angry frown passing now and then across her face. Somewhere in the room a little clock ticked time away. Somewhere outside, a whippoor-will wailed. Evening died. A sweet smell of early Southern flowers rushed in on a newly-risen breeze which suddenly parted the thin silk curtains at the opened windows. A slender, frail glass vase fell from the sill with a tingling crash, but Helga Crane did not shift her position. And the night grew cooler, and older.

At last she stirred, uncertainly, but with an overpowering desire for action of some sort. A second she hesitated, then rose abruptly and pressed the electric switch with determined firmness, flooding suddenly the shadowy room with a white glare of light. Next she made a quick nervous tour to the end of the long room, paused a moment before the old bow-legged secretary that held with almost articulate protest her school-teacher paraphernalia of drab books and papers. Frantically Helga Crane clutched at the lot and then flung them violently, scornfully toward the wastebasket. It received a part, allowing the rest to spill untidily over the floor. The girl smiled ironically, seeing in the mess a simile of her own earnest endeavor to inculcate knowledge into her indifferent classes.

Yes, it was like that; a few of the ideas which she tried to put into the minds behind those baffling ebony, bronze, and gold faces reached their destination. The others were left scattered about. And, like the gay, indifferent wastebasket, it wasn't their fault. No, it wasn't the fault of those minds back of the diverse colored faces. It was, rather, the fault of the method, the general idea behind the system. Like her own hurried shot at the basket, the aim was bad, the material drab and badly prepared for its purpose.

This great community, she thought, was no longer a school. It had grown into a machine. It was now a show place in the black belt, exemplification of the white man's magnanimity, refutation of the black man's inefficiency. Life had died out of it. It was, Helga decided, now only a big knife with cruelly sharp edges ruthlessly cutting all to a pattern, the white man's pattern. Teachers as well as students were subjected to the paring process, for it tolerated no innovations, no individualisms. Ideas it rejected, and looked with open hostility on one and all who had the temerity to offer a suggestion or ever so mildly express a disapproval. Enthusiasm, spontaneity, if not actually suppressed, were at least openly regretted as unladylike or ungentlemanly qualities. The place was smug and fat with self-satisfaction.

A peculiar characteristic trait, cold, slowly accumulated unreason in which all values were distorted or else ceased to exist, had with surprising ferociousness shaken the bulwarks of that self-restraint which was also, curiously, a part of her nature. And now that it had waned as quickly as it had risen, she smiled again, and this time the smile held a faint amusement, which wiped away the little hardness which had congealed her lovely face. Nevertheless she was soothed by the impetuous discharge of violence, and a sigh of relief came from her.

She said aloud, quietly, dispassionately: "Well, I'm through with that," and, shutting off the hard, bright blaze of the overhead lights, went back to her chair and settled down with an odd gesture of sudden soft collapse, like a person who had been for months fighting the devil and then unexpectedly had turned round and agreed to do his bidding.

Helga Crane had taught in Naxos for almost two years, at first with the keen joy and zest of those immature people who have dreamed dreams of doing good to their fellow men. But gradually this zest was blotted out, giving place to a deep hatred for the trivial hypocrisies and careless cruelties which were, unintentionally perhaps, a part of the Naxos policy of uplift.[4] Yet she had continued to try not only to teach, but to befriend those happy singing children, whose charm and distinctiveness the school was so surely ready to destroy. Instinctively Helga was aware that their smiling submissiveness covered many poignant heartaches and perhaps much secret contempt for their instructors. But she was powerless. In Naxos between teacher and student, between condescending authority and smoldering resentment, the gulf was too great, and too few had tried to cross it. It couldn't be spanned

4. Policy dedicated to improving the condition of poor African Americans by educating and motivating them.

by one sympathetic teacher. It was useless to offer her atom of friendship, which under the existing conditions was neither wanted nor understood.

Nor was the general atmosphere of Naxos, its air of self-rightness and intolerant dislike of difference, the best of mediums for a pretty, solitary girl with no family connections. Helga's essentially likable and charming personality was smudged out. She had felt this for a long time. Now she faced with determination that other truth which she had refused to formulate in her thoughts, the fact that she was utterly unfitted for teaching, even for mere existence, in Naxos. She was a failure here. She had, she conceded now, been silly, obstinate, to persist for so long. A failure. Therefore, no need, no use, to stay longer. Suddenly she longed for immediate departure. How good, she thought, to go now, tonight!—and frowned to remember how impossible that would be. "The dignitaries," she said, "are not in their offices, and there will be yards and yards of red tape to unwind, gigantic, impressive spools of it."

And there was James Vayle to be told, and much-needed money to be got. James, she decided, had better be told at once. She looked at the clock racing indifferently on. No, too late. It would have to be tomorrow.

She hated to admit that money was the most serious difficulty. Knowing full well that it was important, she nevertheless rebelled at the unalterable truth that it could influence her actions, block her desires. A sordid necessity to be grappled with. With Helga it was almost a superstition that to concede to money its importance magnified its power. Still, in spite of her reluctance and distaste, her financial situation would have to be faced, and plans made, if she were to get away from Naxos with anything like the haste which she now so ardently desired.

Most of her earnings had gone into clothes, into books, into the furnishings of the room which held her. All her life Helga Crane had loved and longed for nice things. Indeed, it was this craving, this urge for beauty which had helped to bring her into disfavor in Naxos—"pride" and "vanity" her detractors called it.

The sum owing to her by the school would just a little more than buy her ticket back to Chicago. It was too near the end of the school term to hope to get teaching-work anywhere. If she couldn't find something else, she would have to ask Uncle Peter for a loan. Uncle Peter was, she knew, the one relative who thought kindly, or even calmly, of her. Her step-father, her step-brothers and sisters, and the numerous cousins, aunts, and other uncles could not be even remotely considered. She laughed a little, scornfully, reflecting that the antagonism was mutual, or, perhaps, just a trifle keener on her side than on theirs. They feared and hated her. She pitied and despised them. Uncle Peter was different. In his contemptuous way he was fond of her. Her beautiful, unhappy mother had been his favorite sister. Even so, Helga Crane knew that he would be more likely to help her because her need would strengthen his oft-repeated conviction that because of her Negro blood she would never amount to anything, than from motives of affection or loving memory. This knowledge, in its present aspect of truth, irritated her to an astonishing degree. She regarded Uncle Peter almost vindictively, although always he had been extraordinarily generous with her and she fully intended to ask his assistance. "A beggar," she thought ruefully, "cannot expect to choose."

Returning to James Vayle, her thoughts took on the frigidity of complete determination. Her resolution to end her stay in Naxos would of course inevitably end her engagement to James. She had been engaged to him since her first semester there, when both had been new workers, and both were lonely. Together they had discussed their work and problems in adjustment, and had drifted into a closer relationship. Bitterly she reflected that James had speedily and with entire ease fitted into his niche. He was now completely "naturalized," as they used laughingly to call it. Helga, on the other hand, had never quite achieved the unmistakable Naxos mold, would never achieve it, in spite of much trying. She could neither conform, nor be happy in her unconformity. This she saw clearly now, and with cold anger at all the past futile effort. What a waste! How pathetically she had struggled in those first months and with what small success. A lack somewhere. Always she had considered it a lack of understanding on the part of the community, but in her present new revolt she realized that the fault had been partly hers. A lack of acquiescence. She hadn't really wanted to be made over. This thought bred a sense of shame, a feeling of ironical disillusion. Evidently there were parts of her she couldn't be proud of. The revealing picture of her past striving was too humiliating. It was as if she had deliberately planned to steal an ugly thing, for which she had no desire, and had been found out.

Ironically she visualized the discomfort of James Vayle. How her maladjustment had bothered him! She had a faint notion that it was behind his ready assent to her suggestion anent a longer engagement than, originally, they had planned. He was liked and approved of in Naxos and loathed the idea that the girl he was to marry couldn't manage to win liking and approval also. Instinctively Helga had known that secretly he had placed the blame upon her. How right he had been! Certainly his attitude had gradually changed, though he still gave her his attentions. Naxos pleased him and he had become content with life as it was lived there. No longer lonely, he was now one of the community and so beyond the need or the desire to discuss its affairs and its failings with an outsider. She was, she knew, in a queer indefinite way, a disturbing factor. She knew too that a something held him, a something against which he was powerless. The idea that she was in but one nameless way necessary to him filled her with a sensation amounting almost to shame. And yet his mute helplessness against that ancient appeal by which she held him pleased her and fed her vanity—gave her a feeling of power. At the same time she shrank away from it, subtly aware of possibilities she herself couldn't predict.

Helga's own feelings defeated inquiry, but honestly confronted, all pretense brushed aside, the dominant one, she suspected, was relief. At least, she felt no regret that tomorrow would mark the end of any claim she had upon him. The surety that the meeting would be a clash annoyed her, for she had no talent for quarreling—when possible she preferred to flee. That was all.

The family of James Vayle, in near-by Atlanta, would be glad. They had never liked the engagement, had never liked Helga Crane. Her own lack of family disconcerted them. No family. That was the crux of the whole matter. For Helga, it accounted for everything, her failure here in Naxos, her former loneliness in Nashville. It even accounted for her engagement to James. Negro society, she had learned, was as complicated, and as rigid in its ramifications as the highest strata of white society. If you couldn't prove your ancestry and connections, you were tolerated, but you didn't "belong." You could be queer, or even attractive, or bad, or brilliant, or even love beauty and such nonsense if you were a Rankin, or a Leslie, or a Scoville; in other words, if you had a family. But if you were just plain Helga Crane, of whom nobody had ever heard, it was presumptuous of you to be anything but inconspicuous and conformable.

To relinquish James Vayle would most certainly be social suicide, for the Vayles were people of consequence. The fact that they were a "first family" had been one of James's attractions for the obscure Helga. She had wanted social background, but—she had not imagined that it could be so stuffy.

She made a quick movement of impatience and stood up. As she did so, the room whirled about her in an impish, hateful way. Familiar objects seemed suddenly unhappily distant. Faintness closed about her like a vise. She swayed, her small, slender hands gripping the chair arms for support. In a moment the faintness receded, leaving in its wake a sharp resentment at the trick which her strained nerves had played upon her. And after a moment's rest she got hurriedly into bed, leaving her room disorderly for the first time.

Books and papers scattered about the floor, fragile stockings and underthings and the startling green and gold negligee dripping about on chairs and stool, met the encounter of the amazed eyes of the girl who came in the morning to awaken Helga Crane.

2

She woke in the morning unrefreshed and with that feeling of half-terrified apprehension peculiar to Christmas and birthday mornings. A long moment she lay puzzling under the sun streaming in a golden flow through the yellow curtains. Then her mind returned to the night before. She had decided to leave Naxos. That was it.

Sharply she began to probe her decision. Reviewing the situation carefully, frankly, she felt no wish to change her resolution. Except—that it would be inconvenient. Much as she wanted to shake the dust of the place from her feet forever, she realized that there would be difficulties. Red tape. James Vayle. Money, Other work. Regretfully she was forced to acknowledge that it would be vastly better to wait until June, the close of the school year. Not so long, really. Half of March, April, May, some of June. Surely she could endure for that much longer conditions which she had borne for nearly two years. By an effort of will, her will, it could be done.

But this reflection, sensible, expedient, though it was, did not reconcile her. To remain seemed too hard. Could she do it? Was it possible in the present rebellious state of her feelings? The uneasy sense of being engaged with some formidable antagonist, nameless and un-understood, startled her. It wasn't, she was suddenly aware, merely the school and its ways and its decorous stupid people that oppressed her. There was something else, some other more ruthless force, a quality within herself, which was frustrating her, had always frustrated her, kept her from getting the things she had wanted. Still wanted.

But just what did she want? Barring a desire for material security, gracious ways of living, a profusion of lovely clothes, and a goodly share of envious admiration, Helga Crane didn't know, couldn't tell. But there was, she knew, something else. Happiness, she supposed. Whatever that might be. What, exactly, she wondered, was happiness. Very positively she wanted it. Yet her conception of it had no tangibility. She couldn't define it, isolate it, and contemplate it as she could some other abstract things. Hatred, for instance. Or kindness.

The strident ringing of a bell somewhere in the building brought back the fierce resentment of the night. It crystallized her wavering determination.

From long habit her biscuit-coloured feet had slipped mechanically out from under the covers at the bell's first unkind jangle. Leisurely she drew them back and her cold anger vanished as she decided that, now, it didn't at all matter if she failed to appear at the monotonous distasteful breakfast which was provided for her by the school as part of her wages.

In the corridor beyond her door was a medley of noises incident to the rising and preparing for the day at the same hour of many schoolgirls—foolish giggling, indistinguishable snatches of merry conversation, distant gurgle of running water, patter of slippered feet, low-pitched singing, good-natured admonitions to hurry, slamming of doors, clatter of various unnamable articles, and—suddenly—calamitous silence.

Helga ducked her head under the covers in the vain attempt to shut out what she knew would fill the pregnant silence—the sharp sarcastic voice of the dormitory matron. It came.

"Well! Even if every last one of you did come from homes where you weren't taught any manners, you might at least try to pretend that you're capable of learning some here, now that you have the opportunity. Who slammed the shower-baths door?"

Silence.

"Well, you needn't trouble to answer. It's rude, as all of you know. But it's just as well, because none of you can tell the truth. Now hurry up. Don't let me hear of a single one of you being late for breakfast. If I do there'll be extra work for everybody on Saturday. And *please* at least try to act like ladies and not like savages from the backwoods."

On her side of the door, Helga was wondering if it had ever occurred to the lean and desiccated Miss MacGooden that most of her charges had actually come from the backwoods. Quite recently too. Miss MacGooden, humorless, prim, ugly, with a face like dried leather, prided herself on being a "lady" from one of the best families—an uncle had been a congressman in the period of the Reconstruction. She was therefore, Helga Crane reflected, perhaps unable to perceive that the inducement to act like a lady, her own acrimonious example, was slight, if not altogether negative. And thinking on Miss MacGooden's "ladyness," Helga grinned a little as she remembered that one's expressed reason for never having married, or intending to marry. There were, so she had been given to understand, things in the matrimonial state that were of necessity entirely too repulsive for a lady of delicate and sensitive nature to submit to.

Soon the forcibly shut-off noises began to be heard again, as the evidently vanishing image of Miss MacGooden evaporated from the short memories of the ladies-in-making. Preparations for the intake of the day's quota of learning went on again. Almost naturally.

"So much for that!" said Helga, getting herself out of bed.

She walked to the window and stood looking down into the great quad-rangle below, at the multitude of students streaming from the six big dormi-tories which, two each, flanked three of its sides, and assembling into neat phalanxes preparatory to marching in military order to the sorry breakfast in Jones Hall on the fourth side. Here and there a male member of the faculty, important and resplendent in the regalia of an army officer, would pause in his prancing or strutting, to jerk a negligent or offending student into the proper attitude or place. The massed phalanxes increased in size and num-ber, blotting out pavements, bare earth, and grass. And about it all was a depressing silence, a sullenness almost, until with a horrible abruptness the waiting band blared into "The Star Spangled Banner." The goose-step began. Left, right. Left, right. Forward! March! The automatons moved. The squares disintegrated into fours. Into twos. Disappeared into the gaping doors of Jones Hall. After the last pair of marchers had entered, the huge doors were closed. A few unlucky late-comers, apparently already discouraged, tugged half-heartedly at the knobs, and finding, as they had evidently expected, that they were indeed barred out, turned resignedly away.

Helga Crane turned away from the window, a shadow dimming the pale amber loveliness of her face. Seven o'clock it was now. At twelve those chil-dren who by some accident had been a little minute or two late would have their first meal after five hours of work and so-called education. Discipline, it was called.

There came a light knocking on her door.

"Come in," invited Helga unenthusiastically. The door opened to admit Margaret Creighton, another teacher in the English department and to Helga the most congenial member of the whole Naxos faculty. Margaret, she felt, appreciated her.

Seeing Helga still in night robe seated on the bedside in a mass of cush-ions, idly dangling a mule across bare toes like one with all the time in the world before her, she exclaimed in dismay: "Helga Crane, do you know what time it is? Why, it's long after half past seven. The students—"

"Yes, I know," said Helga defiantly, "the students are coming out from breakfast. Well, let them. I, for one, wish that there was some way that they could forever stay out from the poisonous stuff thrown at them, literally thrown at them, Margaret Creighton, for food. Poor things."

Margaret laughed. "That's just ridiculous sentiment, Helga, and you know it. But you haven't had any breakfast, yourself. Jim Vayle asked if you were sick. Of course nobody knew. You never tell anybody anything about yourself. I said I'd look in on you."

"Thanks awfully," Helga responded, indifferently. She was watching the sunlight dissolve from thick orange into pale yellow. Slowly it crept across the room, wiping out in its path the morning shadows. She wasn't interested in what the other was saying.

"If you don't hurry, you'll be late to your first class. Can I help you?" Mar-garet offered uncertainly. She was a little afraid of Helga. Nearly everyone was.

"No. Thanks all the same." Then quickly in another, warmer tone: "I do mean it. Thanks, a thousand times, Margaret. I'm really awfully grateful, but—you see, it's like this, I'm not going to be late to my class. I'm not going to be there at all."

The visiting girl, standing in relief, like old walnut against the buff-colored wall, darted a quick glance at Helga. Plainly she was curious. But she only said formally: "Oh, then you *are* sick." For something there was about Helga which discouraged questionings.

No, Helga wasn't sick. Not physically. She was merely disgusted. Fed up with Naxos. If that could be called sickness. The truth was that she had made up her mind to leave. That very day. She could no longer abide being connected with a place of shame, lies, hypocrisy, cruelty, servility, and snobbishness. "It ought," she concluded, "to be shut down by law."

"But, Helga, you can't go now. Not in the middle of the term." The kindly Margaret was distressed.

"But I can. And I am. Today."

"They'll never let you," prophesied Margaret.

"*They* can't stop me. Trains leave here for civilization every day. All that's needed is money," Helga pointed out.

"Yes, of course. Everybody knows that. What I mean is that you'll only hurt yourself in your profession. They won't give you a reference if you jump up and leave like this now. At this time of the year. You'll be put on the black list. And you'll find it hard to get another teaching-job. Naxos has enormous influence in the South. Better wait till school closes."

"Heaven forbid," answered Helga fervently, "that I should ever again want work anywhere in the South! I hate it." And fell silent, wondering for the hundredth time just what form of vanity it was that had induced an intelligent girl like Margaret Creighton to turn what was probably nice live crinkly hair, perfectly suited to her smooth dark skin and agreeable round features, into a dead straight, greasy, ugly mass.

Looking up from her watch, Margaret said: "Well, I've really got to run, or I'll be late myself. And since I'm staying— Better think it over, Helga. There's no place like Naxos, you know. Pretty good salaries, decent rooms, plenty of men, and all that. Ta-ta." The door slid to behind her.

But in another moment it opened. She was back. "I do wish you'd stay. It's nice having you here, Helga. We all think so. Even the dead ones. We need a few decorations to brighten our sad lives." And again she was gone.

Helga was unmoved. She was no longer concerned with what anyone in Naxos might think of her, for she was now in love with the piquancy of leaving. Automatically her fingers adjusted the Chinese-looking pillows on the low couch that served for her bed. Her mind was busy with plans for departure. Packing, money, trains, and—could she get a berth?

3

On one side of the long, white, hot sand road that split the flat green, there was a little shade, for it was bordered with trees. Helga Crane walked there so that the sun could not so easily get at her. As she went slowly across the empty campus she was conscious of a vague tenderness for the scene spread out before her. It was so incredibly lovely, so appealing, and so facile. The trees in their spring beauty sent through her restive mind a sharp thrill of pleasure. Seductive, charming, and beckoning as cities were, they had not this easy unhuman loveliness. The trees, she thought, on city avenues and boulevards, in city parks and gardens, were tamed, held prisoners in a surrounding maze of human beings. Here they were free. It was human beings who were prisoners. It was too bad. In the midst of all this radiant life. They weren't, she knew, even conscious of its presence. Perhaps there was too much of it, and therefore it was less than nothing.

In response to her insistent demand she had been told that Dr. Anderson could give her twenty minutes at eleven o'clock. Well, she supposed that she could say all that she had to say in twenty minutes, though she resented being limited. Twenty minutes. In Naxos, she was as unimportant as that.

He was a new man, this principal, for whom Helga remembered feeling unaccountably sorry, when last September he had first been appointed to Naxos as its head. For some reason she had liked him, although she had seen little of him; he was so frequently away on publicity and money-raising tours. And as yet he had made but few and slight changes in the running of the school. Now she was a little irritated at finding herself wondering just how she was going to tell him of her decision. What did it matter to him? Why should she mind if it did? But there returned to her that indistinct sense of sympathy for the remote silent man with the tired gray eyes, and she wondered again by what fluke of fate such a man, apparently a humane and understanding person, had chanced into the command of this cruel educational machine. Suddenly, her own resolve loomed as an almost direct unkindness. This increased her annoyance and discomfort. A sense of defeat, of being cheated of justification, closed down on her. Absurd!

She arrived at the administration building in a mild rage, as unreasonable as it was futile, but once inside she had a sudden attack of nerves at the prospect of traversing that great outer room which was the workplace of some twenty odd people. This was a disease from which Helga had suffered at intervals all her life, and it was a point of honor, almost, with her never to give way to it. So, instead of turning away, as she felt inclined, she walked on, outwardly indifferent. Half-way down the long aisle which divided the room, the principal's secretary, a huge black man, surged toward her.

"Good-morning, Miss Crane, Dr. Anderson will see you in a few moments. Sit down right here."

She felt the inquiry in the shuttered eyes. For some reason this dissipated her self-consciousness and restored her poise. Thanking him, she seated herself, really careless now of the glances of the stenographers, book-keepers, clerks. Their curiosity and slightly veiled hostility no longer touched her. Her coming departure had released her from the need for conciliation which had irked her for so long. It was pleasant to Helga Crane to be able to sit calmly looking out of the window on to the smooth lawn, where a few leaves quite prematurely fallen dotted the grass, for once uncaring whether the frock which she wore roused disapproval or envy.

Turning from the window, her gaze wandered contemptuously over the dull attire of the women workers. Drab colors, mostly navy blue, black, brown; unrelieved, save for a scrap of white or tan about the hands and necks. Fragments of a speech made by the dean of women floated through her thoughts—"Bright colors are vulgar"—"Black, gray, brown, and navy blue are the most becoming colors for colored people"—"Dark-complected people shouldn't wear yellow, or green or red."—The dean was a woman from one of the "first families"—a great "race" woman;[5] she, Helga Crane, a despised

5. Person dedicated to the policy of uplift.

mulatto, but something intuitive, some unanalyzed driving spirit of loyalty to the inherent racial need for gorgeousness told her that bright colours *were* fitting and that dark-complexioned people *should* wear yellow, green, and red. Black, brown, and gray were ruinous to them, actually destroyed the luminous tones lurking in their dusky skins. One of the loveliest sights Helga had ever seen had been a sooty black girl decked out in a flaming orange dress, which a horrified matron had next day consigned to the dyer. Why, she wondered, didn't someone write *A Plea for Color?*

These people yapped loudly of race, of race consciousness, of race pride, and yet suppressed its most delightful manifestations, love of color, joy of rhythmic motion, naïve, spontaneous laughter. Harmony, radiance, and simplicity, all the essentials of spiritual beauty in the race they had marked for destruction.

She came back to her own problems. Clothes had been one of her difficulties in Naxos. Helga Crane loved clothes, elaborate ones. Nevertheless, she had tried not to offend. But with small success, for, although she had affected the deceptively simple variety, the hawk eyes of dean and matrons had detected the subtle difference from their own irreproachably conventional garments. Too, they felt that the colors were queer; dark purples, royal blues, rich greens, deep reds, in soft, luxurious woolens, or heavy, clinging silks. And the trimmings—when Helga used them at all—seemed to them odd. Old laces, strange embroideries, dim brocades. Her faultless, slim shoes made them uncomfortable and her small plain hats seemed to them positively indecent. Helga smiled inwardly at the thought that whenever there was an evening affair for the faculty, the dear ladies probably held their breaths until she had made her appearance. They existed in constant fear that she might turn out in an evening dress. The proper evening wear in Naxos was afternoon attire. And one could, if one wished, garnish the hair with flowers.

Quick, muted footfalls sounded. The secretary had returned.

"Dr. Anderson will see you now, Miss Crane."

She rose, followed, and was ushered into the guarded sanctum, without having decided just what she was to say. For a moment she felt behind her the open doorway and then the gentle impact of its closing. Before her at a great desk her eyes picked out the figure of a man, at first blurred slightly in outline in that dimmer light. At his "Miss Crane?" her lips formed for speech, but no sound came. She was aware of inward confusion. For her the situation seemed charged, unaccountably, with strangeness and something very like hysteria. An almost overpowering desire to laugh seized her. Then, miraculously, a complete ease, such as she had never known in Naxos, possessed her. She smiled, nodded in answer to his questioning salutation, and with a gracious "Thank you" dropped into the chair which he indicated. She looked at him frankly now, this man still young, thirty-five perhaps, and found it easy to go on in the vein of a simple statement.

"Dr. Anderson, I'm sorry to have to confess that I've failed in my job here. I've made up my mind to leave. Today."

A short, almost imperceptible silence, then a deep voice of peculiarly pleasing resonance, asking gently: "You don't like Naxos, Miss Crane?"

She evaded. "Naxos, the place? Yes, I like it. Who wouldn't like it? It's so beautiful. But I—well—I don't seem to fit here."

The man smiled, just a little. "The school? You don't like the school?"

The words burst from her. "No, I don't like it. I hate it!"

"Why?" The question was detached, too detached.

In the girl blazed a desire to wound. There he sat, staring dreamily out of the window, blatantly unconcerned with her or her answer. Well, she'd tell him. She pronounced each word with deliberate slowness.

"Well, for one thing, I hate hypocrisy. I hate cruelty to students, and to teachers who can't fight back. I hate backbiting, and sneaking, and petty jealousy. Naxos? It's hardly a place at all. It's more like some loathsome, venomous disease. Ugh! Everybody spending his time in a malicious hunting for the weaknesses of others, spying, grudging, scratching."

"I see. And you don't think it might help to cure us, to have someone who doesn't approve of these things stay with us? Even just one person, Miss Crane?"

She wondered if this last was irony. She suspected it was humor and so ignored the half-pleading note in his voice.

"No, I don't! It doesn't do the disease any good. Only irritates it. And it makes me unhappy, dissatisfied. It isn't pleasant to be always made to appear in the wrong, even when I know I'm right."

His gaze was on her now, searching. "Queer," she thought, "how some brown people have gray eyes. Gives them a strange, unexpected appearance. A little frightening."

The man said, kindly: "Ah, you're unhappy. And for the reasons you've stated?"

"Yes, partly. Then, too, the people here don't like me. They don't think I'm in the spirit of the work. And I'm not, not if it means suppression of individuality and beauty."

"And does it?"

"Well, it seems to work out that way."

"How old are you, Miss Crane?"

She resented this, but she told him, speaking with what curtness she could command only the bare figure: "Twenty-three."

"Twenty-three. I see. Some day you'll learn that lies, injustice, and hypocrisy are a part of every ordinary community. Most people achieve a sort of protective immunity, a kind of callousness, toward them. If they didn't, they couldn't endure. I think there's less of these evils here than in most places, but because we're trying to do such a big thing, to aim so high, the ugly things show more, they irk some of us more. Service is like clean white linen, even the tiniest speck shows." He went on, explaining, amplifying, pleading.

Helga Crane was silent, feeling a mystifying yearning which sang and throbbed in her. She felt again that urge for service, not now for her people, but for this man who was talking so earnestly of his work, his plans, his hopes. An insistent need to be a part of them sprang in her. With compunction tweaking at her heart for even having entertained the notion of deserting him, she resolved not only to remain until June, but to return next year. She was shamed, yet stirred. It was not sacrifice she felt now, but actual desire to stay, and to come back next year.

He came, at last, to the end of the long speech, only part of which she had heard. "You see, you understand?" he urged.

"Yes, oh yes, I do."

"What we need is more people like you, people with a sense of values, and proportion, an appreciation of the rarer things of life. You have something to give which we badly need here in Naxos. You mustn't desert us, Miss Crane."

She nodded, silent. He had won her. She knew that she would stay. "It's an elusive something," he went on. "Perhaps I can best explain it by the use of that trite phrase, 'You're a lady.' You have dignity and breeding."

At these words turmoil rose again in Helga Crane. The intricate pattern of the rug which she had been studying escaped her. The shamed feeling which had been her penance evaporated. Only a lacerated pride remained. She took firm hold of the chair arms to still the trembling of her fingers.

"If you're speaking of family, Dr. Anderson, why, I haven't any. I was born in a Chicago slum."

The man chose his words, carefully he thought. "That doesn't at all matter, Miss Crane. Financial, economic circumstances can't destroy tendencies inherited from good stock. You yourself prove that!"

Concerned with her own angry thoughts, which scurried here and there like trapped rats, Helga missed the import of his words. Her own words, her answer, fell like drops of hail.

"The joke is on you, Dr. Anderson. My father was a gambler who deserted my mother, a white immigrant. It is even uncertain that they were married. As I said at first, I don't belong here. I shall be leaving at once. This afternoon. Good-morning."

4

Long, soft white clouds, clouds like shreds of incredibly fine cotton, streaked the blue of the early evening sky. Over the flying landscape hung a very faint mist, disturbed now and then by a languid breeze. But no coolness invaded the heat of the train rushing north. The open windows of the stuffy day coach, where Helga Crane sat with others of her race, seemed only to intensify her discomfort. Her head ached with a steady pounding pain. This, added to her wounds of the spirit, made traveling something little short of a medieval torture. Desperately she was trying to right the confusion in her mind. The temper of the morning's interview rose before her like an ugly mutilated creature crawling horribly over the flying landscape of her thoughts. It was no use. The ugly thing pressed down on her, held her. Leaning back, she tried to doze as others were doing. The futility of her effort exasperated her.

Just what had happened to her there in that cool dim room under the quizzical gaze of those piercing gray eyes? Whatever it was had been so powerful, so compelling, that but for a few chance words she would still be in Naxos. And why had she permitted herself to be jolted into a rage so fierce, so illogical, so disastrous, that now after it was spent she sat despondent, sunk in shameful contrition? As she reviewed the manner of her departure from his presence, it seemed increasingly rude.

She didn't, she told herself, after all, like this Dr. Anderson. He was too controlled, too sure of himself and others. She detested cool, perfectly controlled people. Well, it didn't matter. He didn't matter. But she could not put him from her mind. She set it down to annoyance because of the cold discourtesy of her abrupt action. She disliked rudeness in anyone.

She had outraged her own pride, and she had terribly wronged her mother by her insidious implication. Why? Her thoughts lingered with her mother, long dead. A fair Scandinavian girl in love with life, with love, with passion, dreaming, and risking all in one blind surrender. A cruel sacrifice. In forgetting all but love she had forgotten, or had perhaps never known, that some things the world never forgives. But as Helga knew, she had remembered, or had learned in suffering and longing all the rest of her life. Her daughter hoped she had been happy, happy beyond most human creatures, in the little time it had lasted, the little time before that gay suave scoundrel, Helga's father, had left her. But Helga Crane doubted it. How could she have been? A girl gently bred, fresh from an older, more polished civilization, flung into poverty, sordidness, and dissipation. She visualized her now, sad, cold, and— yes, remote. The tragic cruelties of the years had left her a little pathetic, a little hard, and a little unapproachable.

That second marriage, to a man of her own race, but not of her own kind—so passionately, so instinctively resented by Helga even at the trivial age of six—she now understood as a grievous necessity. Even foolish, despised women must have food and clothing; even unloved little Negro girls must be somehow provided for. Memory, flown back to those years following the marriage, dealt her torturing stabs. Before her rose the pictures of her mother's careful management to avoid those ugly scarifying quarrels which even at this far-off time caused an uncontrollable shudder, her own childish self-effacement, the savage unkindness of her stepbrothers and sisters, and the jealous, malicious hatred of her mother's husband. Summers, winters, years, passing in one long, changeless stretch of aching misery of soul. Her mother's death, when Helga was fifteen. Her rescue by Uncle Peter, who had sent her to school, a school for Negroes, where for the first time she could breathe freely, where she discovered that because one was dark, one was not necessarily loathsome, and could, therefore, consider oneself without repulsion.

Six years. She had been happy there, as happy as a child unused to happiness dared be. There had been always a feeling of strangeness, of outsideness, and one of holding her breath for fear that it wouldn't last. It hadn't. It had dwindled gradually into eclipse of painful isolation. As she grew older, she became gradually aware of a difference between herself and the girls about her. They had mothers, fathers, brothers, and sisters of whom they spoke frequently, and who sometimes visited them. They went home for the vacations which Helga spent in the city where the school was located. They visited each other and knew many of the same people. Discontent for which there was no remedy crept upon her, and she was glad almost when these most peaceful years which she had yet known came to their end. She had been happier, but still horribly lonely.

She had looked forward with pleasant expectancy to working in Naxos when the chance came. And now this! What was it that stood in her way? Helga Crane couldn't explain it, put a name to it. She had tried in the early afternoon in her gentle but staccato talk with James Vayle. Even to herself her explanation had sounded inane and insufficient; no wonder James had been impatient and unbelieving. During their brief and unsatisfactory conversation she had had an odd feeling that he felt somehow cheated. And more than once she had been aware of a suggestion of suspicion in his attitude, a feeling that he was being duped, that he suspected her of some hidden purpose which he was attempting to discover.

Well, that was over. She would never be married to James Vayle now. It flashed upon her that, even had she remained in Naxos, she would never have been married to him. She couldn't have married him. Gradually, too, there stole into her thoughts of him a curious sensation of repugnance, for which she was at a loss to account. It was new, something unfelt before. Certainly she had never loved him overwhelmingly, not, for example, as her mother must have loved her father, but she *had* liked him, and she had expected to love him, after their marriage. People generally did love then, she imagined. No, she had not loved James, but she had wanted to. Acute nausea rose in her as she recalled the slight quivering of his lips sometimes when her hands had unexpectedly touched his; the throbbing vein in his forehead on a gay day when they had wandered off alone across the low hills and she had allowed him frequent kisses under the shelter of some low-hanging willows. Now she shivered a little, even in the hot train, as if she had suddenly come out from a warm scented place into cool, clear air. She must have been mad, she thought; but she couldn't tell why she thought so. This, too, bothered her.

Laughing conversation buzzed about her. Across the aisle a bronze baby, with bright staring eyes, began a fretful whining, which its young mother essayed to silence by a low droning croon. In the seat just beyond, a black and tan young pair were absorbed in the eating of a cold fried chicken, audibly crunching the ends of the crisp, browned bones. A little distance away a tired laborer slept noisily. Near him two children dropped the peelings of oranges and bananas on the already soiled floor. The smell of stale food and ancient tobacco irritated Helga like a physical pain. A man, a white man, strode through the packed car and spat twice, once in the exact centre of the dingy door panel, and once into the receptacle which held the drinking-water. Instantly Helga became aware of stinging thirst. Her eyes sought the small watch at her wrist. Ten hours to Chicago. Would she be lucky enough to prevail upon the conductor to let her occupy a berth, or would she have to remain here all night, without sleep, without food, without drink, and with that disgusting door panel to which her purposely averted eyes were constantly, involuntarily straying?

Her first effort was unsuccessful. An ill-natured "No, you know you can't," was the answer to her inquiry. But farther on along the road, there was a change of men. Her rebuff had made her reluctant to try again, but the entry of a farmer carrying a basket containing live chickens, which he deposited on the seat (the only vacant one) beside her, strengthened her weakened courage. Timidly, she approached the new conductor, an elderly gray-mustached man of pleasant appearance, who subjected her to a keen, appraising look, and then promised to see what could be done. She thanked him, gratefully, and went back to her shared seat, to wait anxiously. After half an hour he returned, saying he could "fix her up," there was a section she could have, adding: "It'll cost you ten dollars." She murmured: "All right. Thank you." It was twice the price, and she needed every penny, but she knew she was fortunate to get it even at that, and so was very thankful, as she followed his tall, loping figure out of that car and through seemingly endless others, and at last into one where she could rest a little.

She undressed and lay down, her thoughts still busy with the morning's encounter. Why hadn't she grasped his meaning? Why, if she had said so much, hadn't she said more about herself and her mother? He would, she was sure, have understood, even sympathized. Why had she lost her temper and given way to angry half-truths?—Angry half-truths—Angry half—

5

Gray Chicago seethed, surged, and scurried about her. Helga shivered a little, drawing her light coat closer. She had forgotten how cold March could be under the pale skies of the North. But she liked it, this blustering wind. She would even have welcomed snow, for it would more clearly have marked the contrast between this freedom and the cage which Naxos had been to her. Not but what it was marked plainly enough by the noise, the dash, the crowds.

Helga Crane, who had been born in this dirty, mad, hurrying city, had no home here. She had not even any friends here. It would have to be, she decided, the Young Women's Christian Association. "Oh dear! The uplift. Poor, poor colored people. Well, no use stewing about it. I'll get a taxi to take me out, bag and baggage, then I'll have a hot bath and a really good meal, peep into the shops—mustn't buy anything—and then for Uncle Peter. Guess I won't phone. More effective if I surprise him."

It was late, very late, almost evening, when finally Helga turned her steps northward, in the direction of Uncle Peter's home. She had put it off as long as she could, for she detested her errand. The fact that that one day had shown her its acute necessity did not decrease her distaste. As she approached the North Side, the distaste grew. Arrived at last at the familiar door of the old stone house, her confidence in Uncle Peter's welcome deserted her. She gave the bell a timid push and then decided to turn away, to go back to her room and phone, or, better yet, to write. But before she could retreat, the door was opened by a strange red-faced maid, dressed primly in black and white. This increased Helga's mistrust. Where, she wondered, was the ancient Rose, who had, ever since she could remember, served her uncle.

The hostile "Well?" of this new servant forcibly recalled the reason for her presence there. She said firmly: "Mr. Nilssen, please."

"Mr. Nilssen's not in," was the pert retort. "Will you see Mrs. Nilssen?"

Helga was startled. "Mrs. Nilssen! I beg your pardon, did you say Mrs. Nilssen?"

"I did," answered the maid shortly, beginning to close the door.

"What is it, Ida?" A woman's soft voice sounded from within.

"Someone for Mr. Nilssen, m'am." The girl looked embarrassed.

In Helga's face the blood rose in a deep-red stain. She explained: "Helga Crane, his niece."

"She says she's his niece, m'am."

"Well, have her come in."

There was no escape. She stood in the large reception hall, and was annoyed to find herself actually trembling. A woman, tall, exquisitely gowned, with shining gray hair piled high, came forward murmuring in a puzzled voice: "His niece, did you say?"

"Yes, Helga Crane. My mother was his sister, Karen Nilssen. I've been away. I didn't know Uncle Peter had married." Sensitive to atmosphere, Helga had felt at once the latent antagonism in the woman's manner.

"Oh, yes! I remember about you now. I'd forgotten for a moment. *Well,* he isn't exactly your uncle, is he? Your mother wasn't married, was she? I mean, to your father?"

"I—I don't know," stammered the girl, feeling pushed down to the uttermost depths of ignominy.

"Of course she wasn't." The clear, low voice held a positive note. "Mr. Nilssen has been very kind to you, supported you, sent you to school. But you mustn't expect anything else. And you mustn't come here any more. It—well, frankly, it isn't convenient. I'm sure an intelligent girl like yourself can understand that."

"Of course," Helga agreed, coldly, freezingly, but her lips quivered. She wanted to get away as quickly as possible. She reached the door. There was a second of complete silence, then Mrs. Nilssen's voice, a little agitated: "And please remember that my husband is not your uncle. No indeed! Why, that, that would make me your aunt! He's not—"

But at last the knob had turned in Helga's fumbling hand. She gave a little unpremeditated laugh and slipped out. When she was in the street, she ran. Her only impulse was to get as far away from her uncle's house, and this woman, his wife, who so plainly wished to dissociate herself from the outrage of her very existence. She was torn with mad fright, an emotion against which she knew but two weapons: to kick and scream, or to flee.

The day had lengthened. It was evening and much colder, but Helga Crane was unconscious of any change, so shaken she was and burning. The wind cut her like a knife, but she did not feel it. She ceased her frantic running, aware at last of the curious glances of passers-by. At one spot, for a moment less frequented than others, she stopped to give heed to her disordered appearance. Here a man, well groomed and pleasant-spoken, accosted her. On such occasions she was wont to reply scathingly, but, tonight, his pale Caucasian face struck her breaking faculties as too droll. Laughing harshly, she threw at him the words: "You're not my uncle."

He retired in haste, probably thinking her drunk, or possibly a little mad.

Night fell, while Helga Crane in the rushing swiftness of a roaring elevated train sat numb. It was as if all the bogies and goblins that had beset her unloved, unloving, and unhappy childhood had come to life with tenfold power to hurt and frighten. For the wound was deeper in that her long freedom from their presence had rendered her the more vulnerable. Worst of all was the fact that under the stinging hurt she understood and sympathized with Mrs. Nilssen's point of view, as always she had been able to understand her mother's, her stepfather's, and his children's points of view. She saw herself for an obscene sore in all their lives, at all costs to be hidden. She understood, even while she resented. It would have been easier if she had not.

Later in the bare silence of her tiny room she remembered the unaccomplished object of her visit. Money. Characteristically, while admitting its necessity, and even its undeniable desirability, she dismissed its importance. Its elusive quality she had as yet never known. She would find work of some kind. Perhaps the library. The idea clung. Yes, certainly the library. She knew books and loved them.

She stood intently looking down into the glimmering street, far below, swarming with people, merging into little eddies and disengaging themselves to pursue their own individual ways. A few minutes later she stood in the doorway, drawn by an uncontrollable desire to mingle with the crowd. The purple sky showed tremulous clouds piled up, drifting here and there with a sort of endless lack of purpose. Very like the myriad human beings pressing hurriedly on. Looking at these, Helga caught herself wondering who they were, what they did, and of what they thought. What was passing behind those dark molds of flesh. Did they really think at all? Yet, as she stepped out into the moving multi-colored crowd, there came to her a queer feeling of enthusiasm, as if she were tasting some agreeable, exotic food—sweetbreads, smothered with truffles and mushrooms—perhaps. And, oddly enough, she felt, too, that she had come home. She, Helga Crane, who had no home.

6

Helga woke to the sound of rain. The day was leaden gray, and misty black, and dullish white. She was not surprised, the night had promised it. She made a little frown, remembering that it was today that she was to search for work.

She dressed herself carefully, in the plainest garments she possessed, a suit of fine blue twill faultlessly tailored, from whose left pocket peeped a gay kerchief, an unadorned, heavy silk blouse, a small, smart, fawn-colored hat, and slim, brown oxfords, and chose a brown umbrella. In a near-by street she sought out an appealing little restaurant, which she had noted in her last night's ramble through the neighborhood, for the thick cups and the queer dark silver of the Young Women's Christian Association distressed her.

After a slight breakfast she made her way to the library, that ugly gray building, where was housed much knowledge and a little wisdom, on interminable shelves. The friendly person at the desk in the hall bestowed on her a kindly smile when Helga stated her business and asked for directions.

"The corridor to your left, then the second door to your right," she was told.

Outside the indicated door, for half a second she hesitated, then braced herself and went in. In less than a quarter of an hour she came out, in surprised disappointment. "Library training"—"civil service"—"library school"—"classification"—"cataloguing"—"training class"—"examination"—"probation period"—flitted through her mind.

"How erudite they must be!" she remarked sarcastically to herself, and ignored the smiling curiosity of the desk person as she went through the hall to the street. For a long moment she stood on the high stone steps above the avenue, then shrugged her shoulders and stepped down. It *was* a disappointment, but of course there were other things. She would find something else. But what? Teaching, even substitute teaching, was hopeless now, in March. She had no business training, and the shops didn't employ colored clerks or sales-people, not even the smaller ones. She couldn't sew, she couldn't cook. Well, she *could* do housework, or wait on table, for a short time at least. Until she got a little money together. With this thought she remembered that the Young Women's Christian Association maintained an employment agency.

"Of course, the very thing!" She exclaimed, aloud. "I'll go straight back."

But, though the day was still drear, rain had ceased to fall, and Helga, instead of returning, spent hours in aimless strolling about the hustling streets of the Loop district. When at last she did retrace her steps, the business day had ended, and the employment office was closed. This frightened her a little, this and the fact that she had spent money, too much money, for a book and a tapestry purse, things which she wanted, but did not need and certainly could not afford. Regretful and dismayed, she resolved to go without her dinner, as a self-inflicted penance, as well as an economy—and she would be at the employment office the first thing tomorrow morning.

But it was not until three days more had passed that Helga Crane sought the Association, or any other employment office. And then it was sheer necessity that drove her there, for her money had dwindled to a ridiculous sum. She had put off the hated moment, had assured herself that she was tired, needed a bit of vacation, was due one. It had been pleasant, the leisure, the walks, the lake, the shops and streets with their gay colors, their movement, after the great quiet of Naxos. Now she was panicky.

In the office a few nondescript women sat scattered about on the long rows of chairs. Some were plainly uninterested, others wore an air of acute expectancy, which disturbed Helga. Behind a desk two alert young women, both wearing a superior air, were busy writing upon and filing countless white cards. Now and then one stopped to answer the telephone.

"Y.W.C.A. employment. . . . Yes. . . . Spell it, please. . . . Sleep in or out? Thirty dollars?. . . . Thank you, I'll send one right over."

Or, "I'm awfully sorry, we haven't anybody right now, but I'll send you the first one that comes in."

Their manners were obtrusively business-like, but they ignored the already embarrassed Helga. Diffidently she approached the desk. The darker of the two looked up and turned on a little smile.

"Yes?" she inquired.

"I wonder if you can help me? I want work," Helga stated simply.

"Maybe. What kind? Have you references?"

Helga explained. She was a teacher. A graduate of Devon. Had been teaching in Naxos.

The girl was not interested. "Our kind of work wouldn't do for you," she kept repeating at the end of each of Helga's statements. "Domestic mostly."

When Helga said that she was willing to accept work of any kind, a slight, almost imperceptible change crept into her manner and her perfunctory smile disappeared. She repeated her question about the reference. On learning that Helga had none, she said sharply, finally: "I'm sorry, but we never send out help without references."

With a feeling that she had been slapped, Helga Crane hurried out. After some lunch she sought out an employment agency on State Street. An hour passed in patient sitting. Then came her turn to be interviewed. She said, simply, that she wanted work, work of any kind. A competent young woman, whose eyes stared frog-like from great tortoise-shell-rimmed glasses, regarded her with an appraising look and asked for her history, past and present, not forgetting the "references." Helga told her that she was a graduate of Devon, had taught in Naxos. But even before she arrived at the explanation of the lack of references, the other's interest in her had faded.

"I'm sorry, but we have nothing that you would be interested in," she said and motioned to the next seeker, who immediately came forward, proffering several much worn papers.

"References," thought Helga, resentfully, bitterly, as she went out the door into the crowded garish street in search of another agency, where her visit was equally vain.

Days of this sort of thing. Weeks of it. And of the futile scanning and answering of newspaper advertisements. She traversed acres of streets, but it seemed that in that whole energetic place nobody wanted her services. At least not the kind that she offered. A few men, both white and black, offered her money, but the price of the money was too dear. Helga Crane did not feel inclined to pay it.

She began to feel terrified and lost. And she was a little hungry too, for her small money was dwindling and she felt the need to economize somehow. Food was the easiest.

In the midst of her search for work she felt horribly lonely too. This sense of loneliness increased, it grew to appalling proportions, encompassing her, shutting her off from all of life around her. Devastated she was, and always on the verge of weeping. It made her feel small and insignificant that in all the climbing massed city no one cared one whit about her.

Helga Crane was not religious. She took nothing on trust. Nevertheless on Sundays she attended the very fashionable, very high services in the Negro Episcopal church on Michigan Avenue. She hoped that some good Christian would speak to her, invite her to return, or inquire kindly if she was a stranger in the city. None did, and she became bitter, distrusting religion more than ever. She was herself unconscious of that faint hint of offishness which hung about her and repelled advances, an arrogance that stirred in people a peculiar irritation. They noticed her, admired her clothes, but that was all, for the self-sufficient uninterested manner adopted instinctively as a protective measure for her acute sensitiveness, in her child days, still clung to her.

An agitated feeling of disaster closed in on her, tightened. Then, one afternoon, coming in from the discouraging round of agencies and the vain answering of newspaper wants to the stark neatness of her room, she found between door and sill a small folded note. Spreading it open, she read:

> Miss Crane:
> Please come into the employment office as soon as you return.
>
> Ida Ross

Helga spent some time in the contemplation of this note. She was afraid to hope. Its possibilities made her feel a little hysterical. Finally, after removing the dirt of the dusty streets, she went down, down to that room where she had first felt the smallness of her commercial value. Subsequent failures had augmented her feeling of incompetence, but she resented the fact that these clerks were evidently aware of her unsuccess. It required all the pride and indifferent hauteur she could summon to support her in their presence. Her additional arrogance passed unnoticed by those for whom it was assumed. They were interested only in the business for which they had summoned her, that of procuring a traveling-companion for a lecturing female on her way to a convention.

"She wants," Miss Ross told Helga, "someone intelligent, someone who can help her get her speeches in order on the train. We thought of you right away. Of course, it isn't permanent. She'll pay your expenses and there'll be twenty-five dollars besides. She leaves tomorrow. Here's her address. You're to go to see her at five o'clock. It's after four now. I'll phone that you're on your way."

The presumptuousness of their certainty that she would snatch at the opportunity galled Helga. She became aware of a desire to be disagreeable. The inclination to fling the address of the lecturing female in their face stirred in her, but she remembered the lone five-dollar bill in the rare old tapestry purse swinging from her arm. She couldn't afford anger. So she thanked them very politely and set out for the home of Mrs. Hayes-Rore on Grand Boulevard, knowing full well that she intended to take the job, if the lecturing one would take her. Twenty-five dollars was not to be looked at with nose in air when one was the owner of but five. And meals—meals for four days at least.

Mrs. Hayes-Rore proved to be a plump lemon-colored woman with badly straightened hair and dirty finger-nails. Her direct, penetrating gaze was somewhat formidable. Notebook in hand, she gave Helga the impression of having risen early for consultation with other harassed authorities on the race problem, and having been in conference on the subject all day. Evidently, she had had little time or thought for the careful donning of the five-years-behind-the-mode garments which covered her, and which even in their youth could hardly have fitted or suited her. She had a tart personality, and prying. She approved of Helga, after asking her endless questions about her education and her opinions on the race problem, none of which she was permitted to answer, for Mrs. Hayes-Rore either went on to the next or answered the question herself by remarking: "Not that it matters, if you can only do what I want done, and the girls at the 'Y' said that you could. I'm on the Board of Managers, and I know they wouldn't send me anybody who wasn't all right." After this had been repeated twice in a booming, oratorical voice, Helga felt that the Association secretaries had taken an awful chance in sending a person about whom they knew as little as they did about her.

"Yes, I'm sure you'll do. I don't really need ideas, I've plenty of my own. It's just a matter of getting someone to help me get my speeches in order, correct and condense them, you know. I leave at eleven in the morning. Can you be ready by then? . . . That's good. Better be here at nine. Now, don't disappoint me. I'm depending on you."

As she stepped into the street and made her way skillfully through the impassioned human traffic, Helga reviewed the plan which she had formed, while in the lecturing one's presence, to remain in New York. There would be twenty-five dollars, and perhaps the amount of her return ticket. Enough for a start. Surely she could get work there. Everybody did. Anyway, she would have a reference.

With her decision she felt reborn. She began happily to paint the future in vivid colors. The world had changed to silver, and life ceased to be a struggle and became a gay adventure. Even the advertisements in the shop windows seemed to shine with radiance.

Curious about Mrs. Hayes-Rore, on her return to the "Y" she went into the employment office, ostensibly to thank the girls and to report that that important woman would take her. Was there, she inquired, anything that she needed to know? Mrs. Hayes-Rore had appeared to put such faith in their recommendation of her that she felt almost obliged to give satisfaction. And she added: "I didn't get much chance to ask questions. She seemed so—er—busy."

Both the girls laughed. Helga laughed with them, surprised that she hadn't perceived before how really likable they were.

"We'll be through here in ten minutes. If you're not busy, come in and have your supper with us and we'll tell you about her," promised Miss Ross.

7

Having finally turned her attention to Helga Crane, Fortune now seemed determined to smile, to make amends for her shameful neglect. One had, Helga decided, only to touch the right button, to press the right spring, in order to attract the jade's notice.

For Helga that spring had been Mrs. Hayes-Rore. Ever afterwards on recalling that day on which with wellnigh empty purse and apprehensive heart she had made her way from the Young Women's Christian Association to the Grand Boulevard home of Mrs. Hayes-Rore, always she wondered at her own lack of astuteness in not seeing in the woman someone who by a few words was to have a part in the shaping of her life.

The husband of Mrs. Hayes-Rore had at one time been a dark thread in the soiled fabric of Chicago's South Side politics, who, departing this life hurriedly and unexpectedly and a little mysteriously, and somewhat before the whole of his suddenly acquired wealth had had time to vanish, had left his widow comfortably established with money and some of that prestige which in Negro circles had been his. All this Helga had learned from the secretaries at the "Y." And from numerous remarks dropped by Mrs. Hayes-Rore herself she was able to fill in the details more or less adequately.

On the train that carried them to New York, Helga had made short work of correcting and condensing the speeches, which Mrs. Hayes-Rore as a prominent "race" woman and an authority on the problem was to deliver before several meetings of the annual convention of the Negro Women's League of Clubs,[6] convening the next week in New York. These speeches proved to be merely patchworks of others' speeches and opinions. Helga had heard other lecturers say the same things in Devon and again in Naxos. Ideas, phrases, and even whole sentences and paragraphs were lifted bodily from previous orations and published works of Wendell Phillips, Frederick Douglass, Booker T. Washington, and other doctors of the race's ills. For variety Mrs. Hayes-Rore had seasoned hers with a peppery dash of Du Bois[7] and a few vinegary statements of her own. Aside from these it was, Helga reflected, the same old thing.

But Mrs. Hayes-Rore was to her, after the first short, awkward period, interesting. Her dark eyes, bright and investigating, had, Helga noted, a humorous gleam, and something in the way she held her untidy head gave the impression of a cat watching its prey so that when she struck, if she so decided, the blow would be unerringly effective. Helga, looking up from a last reading of the speeches, was aware that she was being studied. Her employer sat leaning back, the tips of her fingers pressed together, her head a bit on one

6. Fictional association similar to the National Association of Colored Women, formed in 1896, and devoted to uplift policies.
7. W. E. B. Du Bois (1868–1963), African American scholar, opponent of Washington's approach. Wendell Phillips (1811–1884), prominent white abolitionist. Frederick Douglass (1817?–1895), 19th-century African American author, editor, and speaker. Booker T. Washington (1856–1915), African American founder of Tuskegee Institute, a college associated with vocational training for rural African Americans.

side, her small inquisitive eyes boring into the girl before her. And as the train hurled itself frantically toward smoke-infested Newark, she decided to strike.

"Now tell me," she commanded, "how is it that a nice girl like you can rush off on a wildgoose chase like this at a moment's notice. I should think your people'd object, or'd make inquiries, or something."

At that command Helga Crane could not help sliding down her eyes to hide the anger that had risen in them. Was she to be forever explaining her people—or lack of them? But she said courteously enough, even managing a hard little smile: "Well you see, Mrs. Hayes-Rore, I haven't any people. There's only me, so I can do as I please."

"Ha!" said Mrs. Hayes-Rore.

Terrific, thought Helga Crane, the power of that sound from the lips of this woman. How, she wondered, had she succeeded in investing it with so much incredulity.

"If you didn't have people, you wouldn't be living. Everybody has people, Miss Crane. Everybody."

"*I* haven't, Mrs. Hayes-Rore."

Mrs. Hayes-Rore screwed up her eyes. "Well, that's mighty mysterious, and I detest mysteries." She shrugged, and into those eyes there now came with alarming quickness an accusing criticism.

"It isn't," Helga said defensively, "a mystery. It's a fact and a mighty unpleasant one. Inconvenient too," and she laughed a little, not wishing to cry.

Her tormentor, in sudden embarrassment, turned her sharp eyes to the window. She seemed intent on the miles of red clay sliding past. After a moment, however, she asked gently: "You wouldn't like to tell me about it, would you? It seems to bother you. And I'm interested in girls."

Annoyed, but still hanging, for the sake of the twenty-five dollars, to her self-control, Helga gave her head a little toss and flung out her hands in a helpless, beaten way. Then she shrugged. What did it matter? "Oh, well, if you really want to know. I assure you, it's nothing interesting. Or nasty," she added maliciously. "It's just plain horrid. For me." And she began mockingly to relate her story.

But as she went on, again she had that sore sensation of revolt, and again the torment which she had gone through loomed before her as something brutal and undeserved. Passionately, tearfully, incoherently, the final words tumbled from her quivering petulant lips.

The other woman still looked out of the window, apparently so interested in the outer aspect of the drab sections of the Jersey manufacturing city through which they were passing that, the better to see, she had now so turned her head that only an ear and a small portion of cheek were visible.

During the little pause that followed Helga's recital, the faces of the two women, which had been bare, seemed to harden. It was almost as if they had slipped on masks. The girl wished to hide her turbulent feeling and to appear indifferent to Mrs. Hayes-Rore's opinion of her story. The woman felt that the story, dealing as it did with race intermingling and possibly adultery, was beyond definite discussion. For among black people, as among white people, it is tacitly understood that these things are not mentioned—and therefore they do not exist.

Sliding adroitly out from under the precarious subject to a safer, more decent one, Mrs. Hayes-Rore asked Helga what she was thinking of doing when she got back to Chicago. Had she anything in mind?

Helga, it appeared, hadn't. The truth was she had been thinking of staying in New York. Maybe she could find something there. Everybody seemed to. At least she could make the attempt.

Mrs. Hayes-Rore sighed, for no obvious reason. "Um, maybe I can help you. I know people in New York. Do you?"

"No."

"New York's the lonesomest place in the world if you don't know anybody."

"It couldn't possibly be worse than Chicago," said Helga savagely, giving the table support a violent kick.

They were running into the shadow of the tunnel. Mrs. Hayes-Rore murmured thoughtfully: "You'd better come uptown and stay with me a few days. I may need you. Something may turn up."

It was one of those vicious mornings, windy and bright. There seemed to Helga, as they emerged from the depths of the vast station, to be a whirling malice in the sharp air of this shining city. Mrs. Hayes-Rore's words about its terrible loneliness shot through her mind. She felt its aggressive unfriendliness. Even the great buildings, the flying cabs, and the swirling crowds seemed manifestations of purposed malevolence. And for the first short minute she was awed and frightened and inclined to turn back to that other city, which, though not kind, was yet not strange. This New York seemed somehow more appalling, more scornful, in some inexplicable way even more terrible and uncaring than Chicago. Threatening almost. Ugly. Yes, perhaps she'd better turn back.

The feeling passed, escaped in the surprise of what Mrs. Hayes-Rore was saying. Her oratorical voice boomed above the city's roar. "I suppose I ought really to have phoned Anne from the station. About you, I mean. Well, it doesn't matter. She's got plenty of room. Lives alone in a big house, which is something Negroes in New York don't do. They fill 'em up with lodgers usually. But Anne's funny. Nice, though. You'll like her, and it will be good for you to know her if you're going to stay in New York. She's a widow, my husband's sister's son's wife. The war, you know."

"Oh," protested Helga Crane, with a feeling of acute misgiving, "but won't she be annoyed and inconvenienced by having me brought in on her like this? I supposed we were going to the 'Y' or a hotel or something like that. Oughtn't we really to stop and phone?"

The woman at her side in the swaying cab smiled, a peculiar invincible, self-reliant smile, but gave Helga Crane's suggestion no other attention. Plainly she was a person accustomed to having things her way. She merely went on talking of other plans. "I think maybe I can get you some work. With a new Negro insurance company. They're after me to put quite a tidy sum into it. Well, I'll just tell them that they may as well take you with the money," and she laughed.

"Thanks awfully," Helga said, "but will they like it? I mean being made to take me because of the money."

"They're not being made," contradicted Mrs. Hayes-Rore. "I intended to let them have the money anyway, and I'll tell Mr. Darling so—after he takes you. They ought to be glad to get you. Colored organizations always need more brains as well as more money. Don't worry. And don't thank me again. You haven't got the job yet, you know."

There was a little silence, during which Helga gave herself up to the distraction of watching the strange city and the strange crowds, trying hard to put out of her mind the vision of an easier future which her companion's words had conjured up; for, as had been pointed out, it was, as yet, only a possibility.

Turning out of the park into the broad thoroughfare of Lenox Avenue,[8] Mrs. Hayes-Rore said in a too carefully casual manner: "And, by the way, I wouldn't mention that my people are white, if I were you. Colored people won't understand it, and after all it's your own business. When you've lived as long as I have, you'll know that what others don't know can't hurt you. I'll just tell Anne that you're a friend of mine whose mother's dead. That'll place you well enough and it's all true. I never tell lies. She can fill in the gaps to suit herself and anyone else curious enough to ask."

"Thanks," Helga said again. And so great was her gratitude that she reached out and took her new friend's slightly soiled hand in one of her own fastidious ones, and retained it until their cab turned into a pleasant tree-lined street and came to a halt before one of the dignified houses in the center of the block. Here they got out.

In after years Helga Crane had only to close her eyes to see herself standing apprehensively in the small cream-colored hall, the floor of which was covered with deep silver-hued carpet; to see Mrs. Hayes-Rore pecking the cheek of the tall slim creature beautifully dressed in a cool green tailored frock; to hear herself being introduced to "my niece, Mrs. Grey" as "Miss Crane, a little friend of mine whose mother's died, and I think perhaps a while in New York will be good for her"; to feel her hand grasped in quick sympathy, and to hear Anne Grey's pleasant voice, with its faint note of wistfulness, saying: "I'm so sorry, and I'm glad Aunt Jeanette brought you here. Did you have a good trip? I'm sure you must be worn out. I'll have Lillie take you right up." And to feel like a criminal.

8

A year thick with various adventures had sped by since that spring day on which Helga Crane had set out away from Chicago's indifferent unkindness for New York in the company of Mrs. Hayes-Rore. New York she had found not so unkind, not so unfriendly, not so indifferent. There she had been happy, and secured work, had made acquaintances and another friend. Again she had had that strange transforming experience, this time not so fleetingly, that magic sense of having come home. Harlem, teeming black Harlem, had welcomed her and lulled her into something that was, she was certain, peace and contentment.

The request and recommendation of Mrs. Hayes-Rore had been sufficient for her to obtain work with the insurance company in which that energetic woman was interested. And through Anne it had been possible for her to meet

8. Major avenue in Harlem.

and to know people with tastes and ideas similar to her own. Their sophisticated cynical talk, their elaborate parties, the unobtrusive correctness of their clothes and homes, all appealed to her craving for smartness, for enjoyment. Soon she was able to reflect with a flicker of amusement on that constant feeling of humiliation and inferiority which had encompassed her in Naxos. Her New York friends looked with contempt and scorn on Naxos and all its works. This gave Helga a pleasant sense of avengement. Any shreds of self-consciousness or apprehension which at first she may have felt vanished quickly, escaped in the keenness of her joy at seeing at last to belong somewhere. For she considered that she had, as she put it, "found herself."

Between Anne Grey and Helga Crane there had sprung one of those immediate and peculiarly sympathetic friendships. Uneasy at first, Helga had been relieved that Anne had never returned to the uncomfortable subject of her mother's death so intentionally mentioned on their first meeting by Mrs. Hayes-Rore, beyond a tremulous brief: "You won't talk to me about it, will you? I can't bear the thought of death. Nobody ever talks to me about it. My husband, you know." This Helga discovered to be true. Later, when she knew Anne better, she suspected that it was a bit of a pose assumed for the purpose of doing away with the necessity of speaking regretfully of a husband who had been perhaps not too greatly loved.

After the first pleasant weeks, feeling that her obligation to Anne was already too great, Helga began to look about for a permanent place to live. It was, she found, difficult. She eschewed the "Y" as too bare, impersonal, and restrictive. Nor did furnished rooms or the idea of a solitary or a shared apartment appeal to her. So she rejoiced when one day Anne, looking up from her book, said lightly: "Helga, since you're going to be in New York, why don't you stay here with me? I don't usually take people. It's too disrupting. Still, it *is* sort of pleasant having somebody in the house and I don't seem to mind you. You don't bore me, or bother me. If you'd like to stay—Think it over."

Helga didn't, of course, require to think it over, because lodgment in Anne's home was in complete accord with what she designated as her "aesthetic sense." Even Helga Crane approved of Anne's house and the furnishings which so admirably graced the big cream-colored rooms. Beds with long, tapering posts to which tremendous age lent dignity and interest, bonneted old highboys, tables that might be by Duncan Phyfe,[9] rare spindle-legged chairs, and others whose ladder backs gracefully climbed the delicate wall panels. These historic things mingled harmoniously and comfortably with brass-bound Chinese tea-chests, luxurious deep chairs and davenports, tiny tables of gay color, a lacquered jade-green settee with gleaming black satin cushions, lustrous Eastern rugs, ancient copper, Japanese prints, some fine etchings, a profusion of precious bric-a-brac, and endless shelves filled with books.

Anne Grey herself was, as Helga expressed it, "almost too good to be true." Thirty, maybe, brownly beautiful, she had the face of a golden Madonna, grave and calm and sweet, with shining black hair and eyes. She carried herself as queens are reputed to bear themselves, and probably do not. Her manners were as agreeably gentle as her own soft name. She possessed an

---

9. American furniture maker (1768?–1854) whose chairs, tables, sofas, and sideboards exemplified the highest standards of craftmanship and design and were prized collectors' items.

impeccably fastidious taste in clothes, knowing what suited her and wearing it with an air of unconscious assurance. The unusual thing, a native New Yorker, she was also a person of distinction, financially independent, well connected and much sought after. And she was interesting, an odd confusion of wit and intense earnestness; a vivid and remarkable person. Yes, undoubtedly, Anne was almost too good to be true. She was almost perfect.

Thus established, secure, comfortable, Helga soon became thoroughly absorbed in the distracting interests of life in New York. Her secretarial work with the Negro insurance company filled her day. Books, the theater, parties, used up the nights. Gradually in the charm of this new and delightful pattern of her life she lost that tantalizing oppression of loneliness and isolation which always, it seemed, had been a part of her existence.

But, while the continuously gorgeous panorama of Harlem fascinated her, thrilled her, the sober mad rush of white New York failed entirely to stir her. Like thousands of other Harlem dwellers, she patronized its shops, its theaters, its art galleries, and its restaurants, and read its papers, without considering herself a part of the monster. And she was satisfied, unenvious. For her this Harlem was enough. Of that white world, so distant, so near, she asked only indifference. No, not at all did she crave, from those pale and powerful people, awareness. Sinister folk, she considered them, who had stolen her birthright. Their past contribution to her life, which had been but shame and grief, she had hidden away from brown folk in a locked closet, "never," she told herself, "to be reopened."

Some day she intended to marry one of those alluring brown or yellow men who danced attendance on her. Already financially successful, any one of them could give to her the things which she had now come to desire, a home like Anne's, cars of expensive makes such as lined the avenue, clothes and furs from Bendel's and Revillon Frères',[1] servants, and leisure.

Always her forehead wrinkled in distaste whenever, involuntarily, which was somehow frequently, her mind turned on the speculative gray eyes and visionary uplifting plans of Dr. Anderson. That other, James Vayle, had slipped absolutely from her consciousness. Of him she never thought. Helga Crane meant, now, to have a home and perhaps laughing, appealing dark-eyed children in Harlem. Her existence was bounded by Central Park, Fifth Avenue, St. Nicholas Park, and One Hundred and Forty-fifth street.[2] Not at all a narrow life, as Negroes live it, as Helga Crane knew it. Everything was there, vice and goodness, sadness and gayety, ignorance and wisdom, ugliness and beauty, poverty and richness. And it seemed to her that somehow of goodness, gayety, wisdom, and beauty always there was a little more than of vice, sadness, ignorance, and ugliness. It was only riches that did not quite transcend poverty.

"But," said Helga Crane, "what of that? Money isn't everything. It isn't even the half of everything. And here we have so much else—and by ourselves. It's only outside of Harlem among those others that money really counts for everything."

In the actuality of the pleasant present and the delightful vision of an agreeable future she was contented, and happy. She did not analyze this con-

---

1. Neither Bendel's, an exclusive department store, nor Revillon Frères', an expensive furrier, is in Harlem.
2. Geographical limits of Harlem.

tentment, this happiness, but vaguely, without putting it into words or even so tangible a thing as a thought, she knew it sprang from a sense of freedom, a release from the feeling of smallness which had hedged her in, first during her sorry, unchildlike childhood among hostile white folk in Chicago, and later during her uncomfortable sojourn among snobbish black folk in Naxos.

9

But it didn't last, this happiness of Helga Crane's.

Little by little the signs of spring appeared, but strangely the enchantment of the season, so enthusiastically, so lavishly greeted by the gay dwellers of Harlem, filled her only with restlessness. Somewhere, within her, in a deep recess, crouched discontent. She began to lose confidence in the fullness of her life, the glow began to fade from her conception of it. As the days multiplied, her need of something, something vaguely familiar, but which she could not put a name to and hold for definite examination, became almost intolerable. She went through moments of overwhelming anguish. She felt shut in, trapped. "Perhaps I'm tired, need a tonic, or something," she reflected. So she consulted a physician, who, after a long, solemn examination, said that there was nothing wrong, nothing at all. "A change of scene, perhaps for a week or so, or a few days away from work," would put her straight most likely. Helga tried this, tried them both, but it was no good. All interest had gone out of living. Nothing seemed any good. She became a little frightened, and then shocked to discover that, for some unknown reason, it was of herself she was afraid.

Spring grew into summer, languidly at first, then flauntingly. Without awareness on her part, Helga Crane began to draw away from those contacts which had so delighted her. More and more she made lonely excursions to places outside of Harlem. A sensation of estrangement and isolation encompassed her. As the days became hotter and the streets more swarming, a kind of repulsion came upon her. She recoiled in aversion from the sight of the grinning faces and from the sound of the easy laughter of all these people who strolled, aimlessly now, it seemed, up and down the avenues. Not only did the crowds of nameless folk on the street annoy her, she began also actually to dislike her friends.

Even the gentle Anne distressed her. Perhaps because Anne was obsessed by the race problem and fed her obsession. She frequented all the meetings of protest, subscribed to all the complaining magazines, and read all the lurid newspapers spewed out by the Negro yellow press. She talked, wept, and ground her teeth dramatically about the wrongs and shames of her race. At times she lashed her fury to surprising heights for one by nature so placid and gentle. And, though she would not, even to herself, have admitted it, she reveled in this orgy of protest.

"Social equality," "Equal opportunity for all," were her slogans, often and emphatically repeated. Anne preached these things and honestly thought that she believed them, but she considered it an affront to the race, and to all the vari-colored peoples that made Lenox and Seventh Avenues the rich spectacles which they were, for any Negro to receive on terms of equality any white person.

"To me," asserted Anne Grey, "the most wretched Negro prostitute that walks One Hundred and Thirty-fifth Street is more than any president of these United States, not excepting Abraham Lincoln." But she turned up her finely carved nose at their lusty churches, their picturesque parades, their naïve clowning on the streets. She would not have desired or even have been willing to live in any section outside the black belt, and she would have refused scornfully, had they been tendered, any invitation from white folk. She hated white people with a deep and burning hatred, with the kind of hatred which, finding itself held in sufficiently numerous groups, was capable some day, on some great provocation, of bursting into dangerously malignant flames.

But she aped their clothes, their manners, and their gracious ways of living. While proclaiming loudly the undiluted good of all things Negro, she yet disliked the songs, the dances, and the softly blurred speech of the race. Toward these things she showed only a disdainful contempt, tinged sometimes with a faint amusement. Like the despised people of the white race, she preferred Pavlova to Florence Mills, John McCormack to Taylor Gordon, Walter Hampden to Paul Robeson.[3] Theoretically, however, she stood for the immediate advancement of all things Negroid, and was in revolt against social inequality.

Helga had been entertained by this racial ardor in one so little affected by racial prejudice as Anne, and by her inconsistencies. But suddenly these things irked her with a great irksomeness and she wanted to be free of this constant prattling of the incongruities, the injustices, the stupidities, the viciousness of white people. It stirred memories, probed hidden wounds, whose poignant ache bred in her surprising oppression and corroded the fabric of her quietism. Sometimes it took all her self-control to keep from tossing sarcastically at Anne Ibsen's remark about there being assuredly something very wrong with the drains, but after all there were other parts of the edifice.

It was at this period of restiveness that Helga met again Dr. Anderson. She was gone, unwillingly, to a meeting, a health meeting, held in a large church—as were most of Harlem's uplift activities—as a substitute for her employer, Mr. Darling. Making her tardy arrival during a tedious discourse by a pompous saffron-hued physician, she was led by the irritated usher, whom she had roused from a nap in which he had been pleasantly freed from the intricacies of Negro health statistics, to a very front seat. Complete silence ensued while she subsided into her chair. The offended doctor looked at the ceiling, at the floor, and accusingly at Helga, and finally continued his lengthy discourse. When at last he had ended and Helga had dared to remove her eyes from his sweating face and look about, she saw with a sudden thrill that Robert Anderson was among her nearest neighbors. A peculiar, not wholly disagreeable, quiver ran down her spine. She felt an odd little faintness. The blood rushed to her face. She tried to jeer at herself for being so moved by the encounter.

He, meanwhile, she observed, watched her gravely. And having caught her attention, he smiled a little and nodded.

3. African American actor and singer (1898–1976). Anna Pavlova (1881–1931), Russian ballerina. Mills (1895–1927), African American dancer in popular black musicals of the 1920s. McCor-mack (1884–1945), Irish tenor. Gordon (1893–1971), African American singer, actor, and author. Hampden (1879–1955), Shakespearean actor.

When all who so desired had spouted to their hearts' content—if to little purpose—and the meeting was finally over, Anderson detached himself from the circle of admiring friends and acquaintances that had gathered around him and caught up with Helga half-way down the long aisle leading out to fresher air.

"I wondered if you were really going to cut me. I see you were," he began, with that half-quizzical smile which she remembered so well.

She laughed. "Oh, I didn't think you'd remember me." Then she added: "Pleasantly, I mean."

The man laughed too. But they couldn't talk yet. People kept breaking in on them. At last, however, they were at the door, and then he suggested that they share a taxi "for the sake of a little breeze." Helga assented.

Constraint fell upon them when they emerged into the hot street, made seemingly hotter by a low-hanging golden moon and the hundreds of blazing electric lights. For a moment, before hailing a taxi, they stood together looking at the slow moving mass of perspiring human beings. Neither spoke, but Helga was conscious of the man's steady gaze. The prominent gray eyes were fixed upon her, studying her, appraising her. Many times since turning her back on Naxos she had in fancy rehearsed this scene, this re-encounter. Now she found that rehearsal helped not at all. It was so absolutely different from anything that she had imagined.

In the open taxi they talked of impersonal things, books, places, the fascination of New York, of Harlem. But underneath the exchange of small talk lay another conversation of which Helga Crane was sharply aware. She was aware, too, of a strange ill-defined emotion, a vague yearning rising within her. And she experienced a sensation of consternation and keen regret when with a lurching jerk the cab pulled up before the house in One Hundred and Thirty-ninth Street. So soon, she thought.

But she held out her hand calmly, coolly. Cordially she asked him to call some time. "It is," she said, "a pleasure to renew our acquaintance." Was it, she was wondering, merely an acquaintance?

He responded seriously that he too thought it a pleasure, and added: "You haven't changed. You're still seeking for something, I think."

At his speech there dropped from her that vague feeling of yearning, that longing for sympathy and understanding which his presence evoked. She felt a sharp stinging sensation and a recurrence of that anger and defiant desire to hurt which had so seared her on that past morning in Naxos. She searched for a biting remark, but, finding none venomous enough, she merely laughed a little rude and scornful laugh and, throwing up her small head, bade him an impatient good-night and ran quickly up the steps.

Afterwards she lay for long hours without undressing, thinking angry self-accusing thoughts, recalling and reconstructing that other explosive contact. That memory filled her with a sort of aching delirium. A thousand indefinite longings beset her. Eagerly she desired to see him again to right herself in his thoughts. Far into the night she lay planning speeches for their next meeting, so that it was long before drowsiness advanced upon her.

When he did call, Sunday, three days later, she put him off on Anne and went out, pleading an engagement, which until then she had not meant to keep. Until the very moment of his entrance she had had no intention of running away, but something, some imp of contumacy, drove her from his presence, though she longed to stay. Again abruptly had come the uncontrollable wish to wound. Later, with a sense of helplessness and inevitability, she realized that the weapon which she had chosen had been a boomerang, for she herself had felt the keen disappointment of the denial. Better to have stayed and hurled polite sarcasms at him. She might then at least have had the joy of seeing him wince.

In this spirit she made her way to the corner and turned into Seventh Avenue. The warmth of the sun, though gentle on that afternoon, had nevertheless kissed the street into marvelous light and color. Now and then, greeting an acquaintance, or stopping to chat with a friend, Helga was all the time seeing its soft shining brightness on the buildings along its sides or on the gleaming bronze, gold, and copper faces of its promenaders. And another vision, too, came haunting Helga Crane; level gray eyes set down in a brown face which stared out at her, coolly, quizzically, disturbingly. And she was not happy.

The tea to which she had so suddenly made up her mind to go she found boring beyond endurance, insipid drinks, dull conversation, stupid men. The aimless talk glanced from John Wellinger's lawsuit for discrimination because of race against a downtown restaurant and the advantages of living in Europe, especially in France, to the significance, if any, of the Garvey movement.[4] Then it sped to a favorite Negro dancer who had just then secured a foothold on the stage of a current white musical comedy, to other shows, to a new book touching on Negroes. Thence to costumes for a coming masquerade dance, to a new jazz song, to Yvette Dawson's engagement to a Boston lawyer who had seen her one night at a party and proposed to her the next day at noon. Then back again to racial discrimination.

Why, Helga wondered, with unreasoning exasperation, didn't they find something else to talk of? Why must the race problem always creep in? She refused to go on to another gathering. It would, she thought, be simply the same old thing.

On her arrival home she was more disappointed than she cared to admit to find the house in darkness and even Anne gone off somewhere. She would have liked that night to have talked with Anne. Get her opinion of Dr. Anderson.

Anne it was who the next day told her that he had given up his work in Naxos; or rather that Naxos had given him up. He had been too liberal, too lenient, for education as it was inflicted in Naxos. Now he was permanently in New York, employed as welfare worker by some big manufacturing concern, which gave employment to hundreds of Negro men.

"Uplift," sniffed Helga contemptuously, and fled before the onslaught of Anne's harangue on the needs and ills of the race.

10

With the waning summer the acute sensitiveness of Helga Crane's frayed nerves grew keener. There were days when the mere sight of the serene tan and brown faces about her stung her like a personal insult. The care-free

4. I.e., the "back to Africa" movement, led by Marcus Garvey (1887–1940), who was born in Jamaica, studied in London, and settled in Harlem in 1916.

quality of their laughter roused in her the desire to scream at them: "Fools, fools! Stupid fools!" This passionate and unreasoning protest gained in intensity, swallowing up all else like some dense fog. Life became for her only a hateful place where one lived in intimacy with people one would not have chosen had one been given choice. It was, too, an excruciating agony. She was continually out of temper. Anne, thank the gods! was away, but her nearing return filled Helga with dismay.

Arriving at work one sultry day, hot and dispirited, she found waiting a letter, a letter from Uncle Peter. It had originally been sent to Naxos, and from there it had made the journey back to Chicago to the Young Women's Christian Association, and then to Mrs. Hayes-Rore. That busy woman had at last found time between conventions and lectures to readdress it and had sent it on to New York. Four months, at least, it had been on its travels. Helga felt no curiosity as to its contents, only annoyance at the long delay, as she ripped open the thin edge of the envelope, and for a space sat staring at the peculiar foreign script of her uncle.

> 715 Sheridan Road
> Chicago, Ill.
>
> Dear Helga:
>
> It is now over a year since you made your unfortunate call here. It was unfortunate for us all, you, Mrs. Nilssen, and myself. But of course you couldn't know. I blame myself. I should have written you of my marriage.
>
> I have looked for a letter, or some word from you; evidently, with your usual penetration, you understood thoroughly that I must terminate my outward relation with you. You were always a keen one.
>
> Of course I am sorry, but it can't be helped. My wife must be considered, and she feels very strongly about this.
>
> You know, of course, that I wish you the best of luck. But take an old man's advice and don't do as your mother did. Why don't you run over and visit your Aunt Katrina? She always wanted you. Maria Kirkeplads, No. 2, will find her.
>
> I enclose what I intended to leave you at my death. It is better and more convenient that you get it now. I wish it were more, but even this little may come in handy for a rainy day.
>
> Best wishes for your luck.
>
> Peter Nilssen

Beside the brief, friendly, but none the less final, letter there was a check for five thousand dollars. Helga Crane's first feeling was one of unreality. This changed almost immediately into one of relief, of liberation. It was stronger than the mere security from present financial worry which the check promised. Money as money was still not very important to Helga. But later, while on an errand in the big general office of the society, her puzzled bewilderment fled. Here the inscrutability of the dozen or more brown faces, all cast from the same indefinite mold, and so like her own, seemed pressing forward against her. Abruptly it flashed upon her that the harrowing irritation of the past weeks was a smoldering hatred. Then, she was overcome by another, so actual, so sharp, so horribly painful, that forever afterwards she preferred to forget it. It was as if she were shut up, boxed up, with hundreds of her race, closed up with that something in the racial character which had always been, to her, inexplicable, alien. Why, she demanded in fierce rebellion, should she be yoked to these despised black folk?

Back in the privacy of her own cubicle, self-loathing came upon her. "They're my own people, my own people," she kept repeating over and over to herself. It was no good. The feeling would not be routed. "I can't go on like this," she said to herself. "I simply can't."

There were footsteps. Panic seized her. She'd have to get out. She terribly needed to. Snatching hat and purse, she hurried to the narrow door, saying in a forced, steady voice, as it opened to reveal her employer: "Mr. Darling, I'm sorry, but I've got to go out. Please, may I be excused?"

At his courteous "Certainly, certainly. And don't hurry. It's much too hot," Helga Crane had the grace to feel ashamed, but there was no softening of her determination. The necessity for being alone was too urgent. She hated him and all the others too much.

Outside, rain had begun to fall. She walked bare-headed, bitter with self-reproach. But she rejoiced too. She didn't, in spite of her racial markings, belong to these dark segregated people. She was different. She felt it. It wasn't merely a matter of color. It was something broader, deeper, that made folk kin.

And now she was free. She would take Uncle Peter's money and advice and revisit her aunt in Copenhagen. Fleeting pleasant memories of her childhood visit there flew through her excited mind. She had been only eight, yet she had enjoyed the interest and the admiration which her unfamiliar color and dark curly hair, strange to those pink, white, and gold people, had evoked. Quite clearly now she recalled that her Aunt Katrina had begged for her to be allowed to remain. Why, she wondered, hadn't her mother consented? To Helga it seemed that it would have been the solution to all their problems, her mother's, her stepfather's, her own.

At home in the cool dimness of the big chintz-hung living-room, clad only in a fluttering thing of green chiffon, she gave herself up to day-dreams of a happy future in Copenhagen, where there were no Negroes, no problems, no prejudice, until she remembered with perturbation that this was the day of Anne's return from her vacation at the sea-shore. Worse. There was a dinner-party in her honor that very night. Helga sighed. She'd have to go. She couldn't possibly get out of a dinner-party for Anne, even though she felt that such an event on a hot night was little short of an outrage. Nothing but a sense of obligation to Anne kept her from pleading a splitting headache as an excuse for remaining quietly at home.

Her mind trailed off to the highly important matter of clothes. What should she wear? White? No, everybody would, because it was hot. Green? She shook her head, Anne would be sure to. The blue thing. Reluctantly she decided against it; she loved it, but she had worn it too often. There was that cobwebby black net touched with orange, which she had bought last spring in a fit of extravagance and never worn, because on getting it home both she and Anne had considered it too *décolleté*, and too *outré*.[5] Anne's words: "There's not enough of it, and what there is gives you the air of something about to fly," came back to her, and she smiled as she decided that she would

---

5. Exaggerated, excessive (French). *"Décolleté"*: very low-cut neckline (French).

certainly wear the black net. For her it would be a symbol. She was about to fly.

She busied herself with some absurdly expensive roses which she had ordered sent in, spending an interminable time in their arrangement. At last she was satisfied with their appropriateness in some blue Chinese jars of great age. Anne *did* have such lovely things, she thought, as she began conscientiously to prepare for her return, although there was really little to do; Lillie seemed to have done everything. But Helga dusted the tops of the books, placed the magazines in ordered carelessness, redressed Anne's bed in fresh-smelling sheets of cool linen, and laid out her best pale-yellow pajamas of *crêpe de Chine*.[6] Finally she set out two tall green glasses and made a great pitcher of lemonade, leaving only the ginger-ale and claret to be added on Anne's arrival. She was a little conscience-stricken, so she wanted to be particularly nice to Anne, who had been so kind to her when first she came to New York, a forlorn friendless creature. Yes, she was grateful to Anne; but, just the same, she meant to go. At once.

Her preparations over, she went back to the carved chair from which the thought of Anne's home-coming had drawn her. Characteristically she writhed at the idea of telling Anne of her impending departure and shirked the problem of evolving a plausible and inoffensive excuse for its suddenness. "That," she decided lazily, "will have to look out for itself; I can't be bothered just now. It's too hot."

She began to make plans and to dream delightful dreams of change, of life somewhere else. Some place where at last she would be permanently satisfied. Her anticipatory thoughts waltzed and eddied about to the sweet silent music of change. With rapture almost, she let herself drop into the blissful sensation of visualizing herself in different, strange places, among approving and admiring people, where she would be appreciated, and understood.

11

It was night. The dinner-party was over, but no one wanted to go home. Half-past eleven was, it seemed, much too early to tumble into bed on a Saturday night. It was a sulky, humid night, a thick furry night, through which the electric torches shone like silver fuzz—an atrocious night for cabareting, Helga insisted, but the others wanted to go, so she went with them, though half unwillingly. After much consultation and chatter they decided upon a place and climbed into two patiently waiting taxis, rattling things which jerked, wiggled, and groaned, and threatened every minute to collide with others of their kind, or with inattentive pedestrians. Soon they pulled up before a tawdry doorway in a narrow crosstown street and stepped out. The night was far from quiet, the streets far from empty. Clanging trolley bells, quarreling cats, cackling phonographs, raucous laughter, complaining motor-horns, low singing, mingled in the familiar medley that is Harlem. Black figures, white figures, little forms, big forms, small groups, large groups, sauntered, or hurried by. It was gay, grotesque, and a little weird. Helga Crane felt singularly apart from it all. Entering the waiting doorway, they descended through a furtive, nar-

---

6. Light silk or silky fabric.

row passage, into a vast subterranean room. Helga smiled, thinking that this was one of those places characterized by the righteous as a hell.

A glare of light struck her eyes, a blare of jazz split her ears. For a moment everything seemed to be spinning round; even she felt that she was circling aimlessly, as she followed with the others the black giant who led them to a small table, where, when they were seated, their knees and elbows touched. Helga wondered that the waiter, indefinitely carved out of ebony, did not smile as he wrote their order—"four bottles of White Rock,[7] four bottles of ginger-ale." Bah! Anne giggled, the others smiled and openly exchanged knowing glances, and under the tables flat glass bottles were extracted from the women's evening scarfs and small silver flasks drawn from the men's hip pockets. In a little moment she grew accustomed to the smoke and din.

They danced, ambling lazily to a crooning melody, or violently twisting their bodies, like whirling leaves, to a sudden streaming rhythm, or shaking themselves ecstatically to a thumping of unseen tomtoms. For the while, Helga was oblivious of the reek of flesh, smoke, and alcohol, oblivious of the oblivion of other gyrating pairs, oblivious of the color, the noise, and the grand distorted childishness of it all. She was drugged, lifted, sustained, by the extraordinary music, blown out, ripped out, beaten out, by the joyous, wild, murky orchestra. The essence of life seemed bodily motion. And when suddenly the music died, she dragged herself back to the present with a conscious effort; and a shameful certainty that not only had she been in the jungle, but that she had enjoyed it, began to taunt her. She hardened her determination to get away. She wasn't, she told herself, a jungle creature. She cloaked herself in a faint disgust as she watched the entertainers throw themselves about to the bursts of syncopated jangle, and when the time came again for the patrons to dance, she declined. Her rejected partner excused himself and sought an acquaintance a few tables removed. Helga sat looking curiously about her as the buzz of conversation ceased, strangled by the savage strains of music, and the crowd became a swirling mass. For the hundredth time she marveled at the gradations within this oppressed race of hers. A dozen shades slid by. There was sooty black, shiny black, taupe, mahogany, bronze, copper, gold, orange, yellow, peach, ivory, pinky white, pastry white. There was yellow hair, brown hair, black hair; straight hair, straightened hair, curly hair, crinkly hair, woolly hair. She saw black eyes in white faces, brown eyes in yellow faces, gray eyes in brown faces, blue eyes in tan faces. Africa, Europe, perhaps with a pinch of Asia, in a fantastic motley of ugliness and beauty, semi-barbaric, sophisticated, exotic, were here. But she was blind to its charm, purposely aloof and a little contemptuous, and soon her interest in the moving mosaic waned.

She had discovered Dr. Anderson sitting at a table on the far side of the room, with a girl in a shivering apricot frock. Seriously he returned her tiny bow. She met his eyes, gravely smiling, then blushed, furiously, and averted her own. But they went back immediately to the girl beside him, who sat indifferently sipping a colorless liquid from a high glass, or puffing a precariously hanging cigarette. Across dozens of tables, littered with corks, with

7. Brand of club soda.

ashes, with shriveled sandwiches, through slits in the swaying mob, Helga Crane studied her.

She was pale, with a peculiar, almost deathlike pallor. The brilliantly red, softly curving mouth was somehow sorrowful. Her pitch-black eyes, a little aslant, were veiled by long, drooping lashes and surmounted by broad brows, which seemed like black smears. The short dark hair was brushed severely back from the wide forehead. The extreme *décolleté* of her simple apricot dress showed a skin of unusual color, a delicate, creamy hue, with golden tones. "Almost like an alabaster," thought Helga.

Bang! Again the music died. The moving mass broke, separated. The others returned. Anne had rage in her eyes. Her voice trembled as she took Helga aside to whisper: "There's your Dr. Anderson over there, with Audrey Denney."

"Yes, I saw him. She's lovely. Who is she?"

"She's Audrey Denney, as I said, and she lives downtown. West Twenty-second Street. Hasn't much use for Harlem any more. It's a wonder she hasn't some white man hanging about. The disgusting creature! I wonder how she inveigled Anderson? But that's Audrey! If there is any desirable man about, trust her to attach him. She ought to be ostracized."

"Why?" asked Helga curiously, noting at the same time that three of the men in their own party had deserted and were now congregated about the offending Miss Denney.

"Because she goes about with white people," came Anne's indignant answer, "and they know she's colored."

"I'm afraid I don't quite see, Anne. Would it be all right if they didn't know she was colored?"

"Now, don't be nasty, Helga. You know very well what I mean." Anne's voice was shaking. Helga didn't see, and she was greatly interested, but she decided to let it go. She didn't want to quarrel with Anne, not now, when she had that guilty feeling about leaving her. But Anne was off on her favorite subject, race. And it seemed, too, that Audrey Denney was to her particularly obnoxious.

"Why, she gives parties for white and colored people together. And she goes to white people's parties. It's worse than disgusting, it's positively obscene."

"Oh, come, Anne, you haven't been to any of the parties, I know, so how can you be so positive about the matter?"

"No, but I've heard about them. I know people who've been."

"Friends of yours, Anne?"

Anne admitted that they were, some of them.

"Well, then, they can't be so bad. I mean, if your friends sometimes go, can they? Just what goes on that's so terrible?"

"Why, they drink, for one thing. Quantities, they say."

"So do we, at the parties here in Harlem," Helga responded. An idiotic impulse seized her to leave the place, Anne's presence, then, forever. But of course she couldn't. It would be foolish, and so ugly.

"And the white men dance with the colored women. Now you know, Helga Crane, that can mean only one thing." Anne's voice was trembling with cold hatred. As she ended, she made a little clicking noise with her tongue, indicating an abhorrence too great for words.

"Don't the colored men dance with the white women, or do they sit about, impolitely, while the other men dance with their women?" inquired Helga very softly, and with a slowness approaching almost to insolence. Anne's insinuations were too revolting. She had a slightly sickish feeling, and a flash of anger touched her. She mastered it and ignored Anne's inadequate answer.

"It's the principle of the thing that I object to. You can't get round the fact that her behavior is outrageous, treacherous, in fact. That's what's the matter with the Negro race. They won't stick together. She certainly ought to be ostracized. I've nothing but contempt for her, as has every other self-respecting Negro."

The other women and the lone man left to them—Helga's own escort—all seemingly agreed with Anne. At any rate, they didn't protest. Helga gave it up. She felt that it would be useless to tell them that what she felt for the beautiful, calm, cool girl who had the assurance, the courage, so placidly to ignore racial barriers and give her attention to people, was not contempt, but envious admiration. So she remained silent, watching the girl.

At the next first sound of music Dr. Anderson rose. Languidly the girl followed his movement, a faint smile parting her sorrowful lips at some remark he made. Her long, slender body swayed with an eager pulsing motion. She danced with grace and abandon, gravely, yet with obvious pleasure, her legs, her hips, her back, all swaying gently, swung by that wild music from the heart of the jungle. Helga turned her glance to Dr. Anderson. Her disinterested curiosity passed. While she still felt for the girl envious admiration, that feeling was now augmented by another, a more primitive emotion. She forgot the garish crowded room. She forgot her friends. She saw only two figures, closely clinging. She felt her heart throbbing. She felt the room receding. She went out the door. She climbed endless stairs. At last, panting, confused, but thankful to have escaped, she found herself again out in the dark night alone, a small crumpled thing in a fragile, flying black and gold dress. A taxi drifted toward her, stopped. She stepped into it, feeling cold, unhappy, misunderstood, and forlorn.

12

Helga Crane felt no regret as the cliff-like towers faded. The sight thrilled her as beauty, grandeur, of any kind always did, but that was all.

The liner drew out from churning slate-colored waters of the river into the open sea. The small seething ripples on the water's surface became little waves. It was evening. In the western sky was a pink and mauve light, which faded gradually into a soft gray-blue obscurity. Leaning against the railing, Helga stared into the approaching night, glad to be at last alone, free of that great superfluity of human beings, yellow, brown, and black, which, as the torrid summer burnt to its close, had so oppressed her. No, she hadn't belonged there. Of her attempt to emerge from that inherent aloneness which was part of her very being, only dullness had come, dullness and a great aversion.

Almost at once it was time for dinner. Somewhere a bell sounded. She turned and with buoyant steps went down. Already she had begun to feel happier. Just for a moment, outside the dining-salon, she hesitated, assailed with a tiny uneasiness which passed as quickly as it had come. She entered softly, unobtrusively. And, after all, she had had her little fear for nothing. The purser, a man grown old in the service of the Scandinavian-American Line, remembered her as the little dark girl who had crossed with her mother years ago, and so she must sit at his table. Helga liked that. It put her at her ease and made her feel important.

Everyone was kind in the delightful days which followed, and her first shyness under the politely curious glances of turquoise eyes of her fellow travelers soon slid from her. The old forgotten Danish of her childhood began to come, awkwardly at first, from her lips, under their agreeable tutelage. Evidently they were interested, curious, and perhaps a little amused about this Negro girl on her way to Denmark alone.

Helga was a good sailor, and mostly the weather was lovely with the serene calm of the lingering September summer, under whose sky the sea was smooth, like a length of watered silk, unruffled by the stir of any wind. But even the two rough days found her on deck, reveling like a released bird in her returned feeling of happiness and freedom, that blessed sense of belonging to herself alone and not to a race. Again, she had put the past behind her with an ease which astonished even herself. Only the figure of Dr. Anderson obtruded itself with surprising vividness to irk her because she could get no meaning from that keen sensation of covetous exasperation that had so surprisingly risen within her on the night of the cabaret party. This question Helga Crane recognized as not entirely new; it was but a revival of the puzzlement experienced when she had fled so abruptly from Naxos more than a year before. With the recollection of that previous flight and subsequent half-questioning a dim disturbing notion came to her. She wasn't, she couldn't be, in love with the man. It was a thought too humiliating, and so quickly dismissed. Nonsense! Sheer nonsense! When one is in love, one strives to please. Never, she decided, had she made an effort to be pleasing to Dr. Anderson. On the contrary, she had always tried, deliberately, to irritate him. She was, she told herself, a sentimental fool.

Nevertheless, the thought of love stayed with her, not prominent, definite; but shadowy, incoherent. And in a remote corner of her consciousness lurked the memory of Dr. Anderson's serious smile and gravely musical voice.

On the last morning Helga rose at dawn, a dawn outside old Copenhagen. She lay lazily in her long chair watching the feeble sun creeping over the ship's great green funnels with sickly light; watching the purply gray sky change to opal, to gold, to pale blue. A few other passengers, also early risen, excited by the prospect of renewing old attachments, of glad home-comings after long years, paced nervously back and forth. Now, at the last moment, they were impatient, but apprehensive fear, too, had its place in their rushing emotions. Impatient Helga Crane was not. But she *was* apprehensive. Gradually, as the ship drew into the lazier waters of the dock, she became prey to sinister fears and memories. A deep pang of misgiving nauseated her at the thought of her aunt's husband, acquired since Helga's childhood visit. Painfully, vividly, she remembered the frightened anger of Uncle Peter's new wife, and looking back at her precipitate departure from America, she was amazed at her own stupidity. She had not even considered the remote possibility that her aunt's husband might be like Mrs. Nilssen. For the first time in nine days she wished herself back in New York, in America.

The little gulf of water between the ship and the wharf lessened. The engines had long ago ceased their whirring, and now the buzz of conversation, too, died down. There was a sort of silence. Soon the welcoming crowd on the wharf stood under the shadow of the great sea-monster, their faces turned up to the anxious ones of the passengers who hung over the railing. Hats were taken off, handkerchiefs were shaken out and frantically waved. Chatter. Deafening shouts. A little quiet weeping. Sailors and laborers were yelling and rushing about. Cables were thrown. The gangplank was laid.

Silent, unmoving, Helga Crane stood looking intently down into the gesticulating crowd. Was anyone waving to her? She couldn't tell. She didn't in the least remember her aunt, save as a hazy pretty lady. She smiled a little at the thought that her aunt, or anyone waiting there in the crowd below, would have no difficulty in singling her out. But—had she been met? When she descended the gangplank she was still uncertain and was trying to decide on a plan of procedure in the event that she had not. A telegram before she went through the customs? Telephone? A taxi?

But, again, she had all her fears and questionings for nothing. A smart woman in olive-green came toward her at once. And, even in the fervent gladness of her relief, Helga took in the carelessly trailing purple scarf and correct black hat that completed the perfection of her aunt's costume, and had time to feel herself a little shabbily dressed. For it was her aunt; Helga saw that at once, the resemblance to her own mother was unmistakable. There was the same long nose, the same beaming blue eyes, the same straying palebrown hair so like sparkling beer. And the tall man with the fierce mustache who followed carrying hat and stick must be Herr[8] Dahl, Aunt Katrina's husband. How gracious he was in his welcome, and how anxious to air his faulty English, now that her aunt had finished kissing her and exclaimed in Danish: "Little Helga! Little Helga! Goodness! But how you have grown!"

Laughter from all three.

"Welcome to Denmark, to Copenhagen, to our home," said the new uncle in queer, proud, oratorical English. And to Helga's smiling, grateful "Thank you," he returned: "Your trunks? Your checks?" also in English, and then lapsed into Danish.

"Where in the world are the Fishers? We must hurry the customs."

Almost immediately they were joined by a breathless couple, a young grayhaired man and a fair, tiny, doll-like woman. It developed that they had lived in England for some years and so spoke English, real English, well. They were both breathless, all apologies and explanations.

"So early!" sputtered the man, Herr Fisher, "We inquired last night and they said nine. It was only by accident that we called again this morning to be sure. Well, you can imagine the rush we were in when they said eight! And of course we had trouble in finding a cab. One always does if one is late." All this in Danish. Then to Helga in English: "You see, I was especially asked to come because Fru[9] Dahl didn't know if you remembered your Danish, and your uncle's English—well—"

8. I.e., Mr. (German; also Danish and other Scandinavian languages).

9. I.e., Mrs. (Danish and other Scandinavian languages).

More laughter.

At last, the customs having been hurried and a cab secured, they were off, with much chatter, through the toy-like streets, weaving perilously in and out among the swarms of bicycles.

It had begun, a new life for Helga Crane.

13

She liked it, this new life. For a time it blotted from her mind all else. She took to luxury as the proverbial duck to water. And she took to admiration and attention even more eagerly.

It was pleasant to wake on that first afternoon, after the insisted-upon nap, with that sensation of lavish contentment and well-being enjoyed only by impecunious sybarites waking in the houses of the rich. But there was something more than mere contentment and well-being. To Helga Crane it was the realization of a dream that she had dreamed persistently ever since she was old enough to remember such vague things as day-dreams and longings. Always she had wanted, not money, but the things which money could give, leisure, attention, beautiful surroundings. Things. Things. Things.

So it was more than pleasant, it was important, this awakening in the great high room which held the great high bed on which she lay, small but exalted. It was important because to Helga Crane it was the day, so she decided, to which all the sad forlorn past had led, and from which the whole future was to depend. This, then, was where she belonged. This was her proper setting. She felt consoled at last for the spiritual wounds of the past.

A discreet knocking on the tall paneled door sounded. In response to Helga's "Come in" a respectful rosy-faced maid entered and Helga lay for a long minute watching her adjust the shutters. She was conscious, too, of the girl's sly curious glances at her, although her general attitude was quite correct, willing and disinterested. In New York, America, Helga would have resented this sly watching. Now, here, she was only amused. Marie, she reflected, had probably never seen a Negro outside the pictured pages of her geography book.

Another knocking. Aunt Katrina entered, smiling at Helga's quick, lithe spring from the bed. They were going out to tea, she informed Helga. What, the girl inquired, did one wear to tea in Copenhagen, meanwhile glancing at her aunt's dark purple dress and bringing forth a severely plain blue *crêpe* frock. But no! It seemed that that wouldn't at all do.

"Too sober," pronounced Fru Dahl. "Haven't you something lively, something bright?" And, noting Helga's puzzled glance at her own subdued costume, she explained laughingly: "Oh, I'm an old married lady, and a Dane. But you, you're young. And you're a foreigner, and different. You must have bright things to set off the color of your lovely brown skin. Striking things, exotic things. You must make an impression."

"I've only these," said Helga Crane, timidly displaying her wardrobe on couch and chairs. "Of course I intend to buy here. I didn't want to bring over too much that might be useless."

"And you were quite right too. Umm. Let's see. That black there, the one with the cerise and purple trimmings. Wear that."

Helga was shocked. "But for tea, Aunt! Isn't it too gay? Too—too—*outré?*"

"Oh dear, no. Not at all, not for you. Just right." Then after a little pause she added: "And we're having people in to dinner tonight, quite a lot. Perhaps we'd better decide on our frocks now." For she was, in spite of all her gentle kindness, a woman who left nothing to chance. In her own mind she had determined the role that Helga was to play in advancing the social fortunes of the Dahls of Copenhagen, and she meant to begin at once.

At last, after much trying on and scrutinizing, it was decided that Marie should cut a favorite emerald-green velvet dress a little lower in the back and add some gold and mauve flowers, "to liven it up a bit," as Fru Dahl put it.

"Now that," she said, pointing to the Chinese red dressing-gown in which Helga had wrapped herself when at last the fitting was over, "suits you. Tomorrow we'll shop. Maybe we can get something that color. That black and orange thing there is good too, but too high. What a prim American maiden you are, Helga, to hide such a fine back and shoulders. Your feet are nice too, but you ought to have higher heels—and buckles."

Left alone, Helga began to wonder. She was dubious, too, and not a little resentful. Certainly she loved color with a passion that perhaps only Negroes and Gypsies know. But she had a deep faith in the perfection of her own taste, and no mind to be bedecked in flaunting flashy things. Still—she had to admit that Fru Dahl was right about the dressing-gown. It did suit her. Perhaps an evening dress. And she knew that she had lovely shoulders, and her feet *were* nice.

When she was dressed in the shining black taffeta with its bizarre trimmings of purple and cerise, Fru Dahl approved her and so did Herr Dahl. Everything in her responded to his "She's beautiful; beautiful!" Helga Crane knew she wasn't that, but it pleased her that he could think so, and say so. Aunt Katrina smiled in her quiet, assured way, taking to herself her husband's compliment to her niece. But a little frown appeared over the fierce mustache, as he said, in his precise, faintly feminine voice: "She ought to have earrings, long ones. Is it too late for Garborg's? We could call up."

And call up they did. And Garborg, the jeweler, in Fredericksgaarde[1] waited for them. Not only were ear-rings bought, long ones brightly enameled, but glittering shoe-buckles and two great bracelets. Helga's sleeves being long, she escaped the bracelets for the moment. They were wrapped to be worn that night. The ear-rings, however, and the buckles came into immediate use and Helga felt like a veritable savage as they made their leisurely way across the pavement from the shop to the waiting motor. This feeling was intensified by the many pedestrians who stopped to stare at the queer dark creature, strange to their city. Her cheeks reddened, but both Herr and Fru Dahl seemed oblivious of the stares or the audible whispers in which Helga made out the one frequently recurring word "*sorte,*" which she recognized as the Danish word for "black."

Her Aunt Katrina merely remarked: "A high color becomes you, Helga. Perhaps tonight a little rouge—" To which her husband nodded in agreement and stroked his mustache meditatively. Helga Crane said nothing.

---

1. *Gaarde* is Danish for "street."

They were pleased with the success she was at the tea, or rather the coffee—for no tea was served—and later at dinner. Helga herself felt like nothing so much as some new and strange species of pet dog being proudly exhibited. Everyone was very polite and very friendly, but she felt the massed curiosity and interest, so discreetly hidden under the polite greetings. The very atmosphere was tense with it. "As if I had horns, or three legs," she thought. She was really nervous and a little terrified, but managed to present an outward smiling composure. This was assisted by the fact that it was taken for granted that she knew nothing or very little of the language. So she had only to bow and look pleasant. Herr and Fru Dahl did the talking, answered the questions. She came away from the coffee feeling that she had acquitted herself well in the first skirmish. And, in spite of the mental strain, she had enjoyed her prominence.

If the afternoon had been a strain, the evening was something more. It was more exciting too. Marie had indeed "cut down" the prized green velvet, until, as Helga put it, it was "practically nothing but a skirt." She was thankful for the barbaric bracelets, for the dangling ear-rings, for the beads about her neck. She was even thankful for the rouge on her burning cheeks and for the very powder on her back. No other woman in the stately pale-blue room was so greatly exposed. But she liked the small murmur of wonder and admiration which rose when Uncle Poul brought her in. She liked the compliments in the men's eyes as they bent over her hand. She liked the subtle half-understood flattery of her dinner partners. The women too were kind, feeling no need for jealousy. To them this girl, this Helga Crane, this mysterious niece of the Dahls, was not to be reckoned seriously in their scheme of things. True, she was attractive, unusual, in an exotic, almost savage way, but she wasn't one of them. She didn't at all count.

Near the end of the evening, as Helga sat effectively posed on a red satin sofa, the center of an admiring group, replying to questions about America and her trip over, in halting, inadequate Danish, there came a shifting of the curious interest away from herself. Following the other's eyes, she saw that there had entered the room a tallish man with a flying mane of reddish blond hair. He was wearing a great black cape, which swung gracefully from his huge shoulders, and in his long, nervous hand he held a wide soft hat. An artist, Helga decided at once, taking in the broad streaming tie. But how affected! How theatrical!

With Fru Dahl he came forward and was presented. "Herr Olsen, Herr Axel Olsen." To Helga Crane that meant nothing. The man, however, interested her. For an imperceptible second he bent over her hand. After that he looked intently at her for what seemed to her an incredibly rude length of time from under his heavy drooping lids. At last, removing his stare of startled satisfaction, he wagged his leonine head approvingly.

"Yes, you're right. She's amazing. Marvelous," he muttered.

Everyone else in the room was deliberately not staring. About Helga there sputtered a little staccato murmur of manufactured conversation. Meanwhile she could think of no proper word of greeting to the outrageous man before her. She wanted, very badly, to laugh. But the man was as unaware of her omission as of her desire. His words flowed on and on, rising and rising. She tried to follow, but his rapid Danish eluded her. She caught only words, phrases, here and there. "Superb eyes . . . color . . . neck column . . . yellow . . . hair . . . alive . . . wonderful . . ." His speech was for Fru Dahl. For a bit longer he lingered before the silent girl, whose smile had become a fixed aching mask, still gazing appraisingly, but saying no word to her, and then moved away with Fru Dahl, talking rapidly and excitedly to her and her husband, who joined them for a moment at the far side of the room. Then he was gone as suddenly as he had come.

"Who is he?" Helga put the question timidly to a hovering young army officer, a very smart captain just back from Sweden. Plainly he was surprised.

"Herr Olsen, Herr Axel Olsen, the painter. Portraits, you know."

"Oh," said Helga, still mystified.

"I guess he's going to paint you. You're lucky. He's queer.[2] Won't do everybody."

"Oh, no. I mean, I'm sure you're mistaken. He didn't ask, didn't say anything about it."

The young man laughed. "Ha ha! That's good! He'll arrange that with Herr Dahl. He evidently came just to see you, and it was plain that he was pleased." He smiled, approvingly.

"Oh," said Helga again. Then at last she laughed. It was too funny. The great man hadn't addressed a word to her. Here she was, a curiosity, a stunt, at which people came and gazed. And was she to be treated like a secluded young miss, a Danish *frøkken*,[3] not to be consulted personally even on matters affecting her personally? She, Helga Crane, who almost all her life had looked after herself, was she now to be looked after by Aunt Katrina and her husband? It didn't seem real.

It was late, very late, when finally she climbed into the great bed after having received an auntly kiss. She lay long awake reviewing the events of the crowded day. She was happy again. Happiness covered her like the lovely quilts under which she rested. She was mystified too. Her aunt's words came back to her. "You're young and a foreigner and—and different." Just what did that mean, she wondered. Did it mean that the difference was to be stressed, accented? Helga wasn't so sure that she liked that. Hitherto all her efforts had been toward similarity to those about her.

"How odd," she thought sleepily, "and how different from America!"

14

The young officer had been right in his surmise. Axel Olsen was going to paint Helga Crane. Not only was he going to paint her, but he was to accompany her and her aunt on their shopping expedition. Aunt Katrina was frankly elated. Uncle Poul was also visibly pleased. Evidently they were not above kotowing to a lion. Helga's own feelings were mixed; she was amused, grateful, and vexed. It had all been decided and arranged without her, and, also, she was a little afraid of Olsen. His stupendous arrogance awed her.

The day was an exciting, not easily to be forgotten one. Definitely, too, it conveyed to Helga her exact status in her new environment. A decoration. A curio. A peacock. Their progress through the shops was an event; an event for

---

2. Eccentric. 3. Miss, unmarried woman (Danish).

Copenhagen as well as for Helga Crane. Her dark, alien appearance was to most people an astonishment. Some stared surreptitiously, some openly, and some stopped dead in front of her in order more fully to profit by their stares. "Den Sorte" dropped freely, audibly, from many lips.

The time came when she grew used to the stares of the population. And the time came when the population of Copenhagen grew used to her outlandish presence and ceased to stare. But at the end of that first day it was with thankfulness that she returned to the sheltering walls of the house on Maria Kirkplads.[4]

They were followed by numerous packages, whose contents all had been selected or suggested by Olsen and paid for by Aunt Katrina. Helga had only to wear them. When they were opened and the things spread out upon the sedate furnishings of her chamber, they made a rather startling array. It was almost in a mood of rebellion that Helga faced the fantastic collection of garments incongruously laid out in the quaint, stiff, pale old room. There were batik dresses in which mingled indigo, orange, green, vermilion, and black; dresses of velvet and chiffon in screaming colors, blood-red, sulphur-yellow, sea-green; and one black and white thing in striking combination. There was a black Manila shawl strewn with great scarlet and lemon flowers, a leopard-skin coat, a glittering opera-cape. There were turban-like hats of metallic silks, feathers and furs, strange jewelry, enameled or set with odd semi-precious stones, a nauseous Eastern perfume, shoes with dangerously high heels. Gradually Helga's perturbation subsided in the unusual pleasure of having so many new and expensive clothes at one time. She began to feel a little excited, incited.

Incited. That was it, the guiding principle of her life in Copenhagen. She was incited to make an impression, a voluptuous impression. She was incited to inflame attention and admiration. She was dressed for it, subtly schooled for it. And after a little while she gave herself up wholly to the fascinating business of being seen, gaped at, desired. Against the solid background of Herr Dahl's wealth and generosity she submitted to her aunt's arrangement of her life to one end, the amusing one of being noticed and flattered. Intentionally she kept to the slow, faltering Danish. It was, she decided, more attractive than a nearer perfection. She grew used to the extravagant things with which Aunt Katrina chose to dress her. She managed, too, to retain that air of remoteness which had been in America so disastrous to her friendships. Here in Copenhagen it was merely a little mysterious and added another clinging wisp of charm.

Helga Crane's new existence was intensely pleasant to her; it gratified her augmented sense of self-importance. And it suited her. She had to admit that the Danes had the right idea. To each his own milieu. Enhance what was already in one's possession. In America Negroes sometimes talked loudly of this, but in their hearts they repudiated it. In their lives too. They didn't want to be like themselves. What they wanted, asked for, begged for, was to be like their white overlords. They were ashamed to be Negroes, but not ashamed to beg to be something else. Something inferior. Not quite genuine. Too bad!

Helga Crane didn't, however, think often of America, excepting in unfa-

4. City square in Copenhagen named for a church.

vorable contrast to Denmark. For she had resolved never to return to the existence of ignominy which the New World of opportunity and promise forced upon Negroes. How stupid she had been ever to have thought that she could marry and perhaps have children in a land where every dark child was handicapped at the start by the shroud of color! She saw, suddenly, the giving birth to little, helpless, unprotesting Negro children as a sin, an unforgivable outrage. More black folk to suffer indignities. More dark bodies for mobs to lynch. No, Helga Crane didn't think often of America. It was too humiliating, too disturbing. And she wanted to be left to the peace which had come to her. Her mental difficulties and questionings had become simplified. She now believed sincerely that there was a law of compensation, and that sometimes it worked. For all those early desolate years she now felt recompensed. She recalled a line that had impressed her in her lonely school-days, "The far-off interest of tears."[5]

To her, Helga Crane, it had come at last, and she meant to cling to it. So she turned her back on painful America, resolutely shutting out the griefs, the humiliations, the frustrations, which she had endured there.

Her mind was occupied with other and nearer things.

The charm of the old city itself, with its odd architectural mixture of medievalism and modernity, and the general air of well-being which pervaded it, impressed her. Even in the so-called poor sections there was none of that untidiness and squalor which she remembered as the accompaniment of poverty in Chicago, New York, and the Southern cities of America. Here the door-steps were always white from constant scrubbings, the women neat, and the children washed and provided with whole clothing. Here were no tatters and rags, no beggars. But, then, begging, she learned, was an offense punishable by law. Indeed, it was unnecessary in a country where everyone considered it a duty somehow to support himself and his family by honest work; or, if misfortune and illness came upon one, everyone else, including the State, felt bound to give assistance, a lift on the road to the regaining of independence.

After the initial shyness and consternation at the sensation caused by her strange presence had worn off, Helga spent hours driving or walking about the city, at first in the protecting company of Uncle Poul or Aunt Katrina or both, or sometimes Axel Olsen. But later, when she had become a little familiar with the city, and its inhabitants a little used to her, and when she had learned to cross the streets in safety, dodging successfully the innumerable bicycles like a true Copenhagener, she went often alone, loitering on the long bridge which spanned the placid lakes, or watching the pageant of the blue-clad, sprucely tailored soldiers in the daily parade at Amielenborg Palace, or in the historic vicinity of the long, low-lying Exchange, a picturesque structure in picturesque surroundings, skirting as it did the great canal, which always was alive with many small boats, flying broad white sails and pressing close on the huge ruined pile of the Palace of Christiansborg. There was also the Gammelstrand,[6] the congregating-place of the venders of fish, where

---

5. From *In Memoriam* (1850), section I, by Alfred Tennyson (1809–1892).
6. Various streets and places in Copenhagen, including the Royal Residence, stock exchange, and fish-market street.

daily was enacted a spirited and interesting scene between sellers and buyers, and where Helga's appearance always roused lively and audible, but friendly, interest, long after she became in other parts of the city an accepted curiosity. Here it was that one day an old countrywoman asked her to what manner of mankind she belonged and at Helga's replying: "I'm a Negro," had become indignant, retorting angrily that, just because she was old and a countrywoman she could not be so easily fooled, for she knew as well as everyone else that Negroes were black and had woolly hair.

Against all this walking the Dahls had at first uttered mild protest. "But, Aunt dear, I have to walk, or I'll get fat," Helga asserted. "I've never, never in all my life, eaten so much." For the accepted style of entertainment in Copenhagen seemed to be a round of dinner-parties, at which it was customary for the hostess to tax the full capacity not only of her dining-room, but of her guests as well. Helga enjoyed these dinner-parties, as they were usually spirited affairs, the conversation brilliant and witty, often in several languages. And always she came in for a goodly measure of flattering attention and admiration.

There were, too, those popular afternoon gatherings for the express purpose of drinking coffee together, where between much talk, interesting talk, one sipped the strong and steaming beverage from exquisite cups fashioned of Royal Danish porcelain and partook of an infinite variety of rich cakes and smørrebrød. This smørrebrød, dainty sandwiches of an endless and tempting array, was distinctly a Danish institution. Often Helga wondered just how many of these delicious sandwiches she had consumed since setting foot on Denmark's soil. Always, wherever food was served, appeared the inevitable smørrebrød, in the home of the Dahls, in every other home that she visited, in hotels, in restaurants.

At first she had missed, a little, dancing, for, though excellent dancers, the Danes seemed not to care a great deal for that pastime, which so delightfully combines exercise and pleasure. But in the winter there was skating, solitary, or in gay groups. Helga liked this sport, though she was not very good at it. There were, however, always plenty of efficient and willing men to instruct and to guide her over the glittering ice. One could, too, wear such attractive skating-things.

But mostly it was with Axel Olsen that her thoughts were occupied. Brilliant, bored, elegant, urbane, cynical, worldly, he was a type entirely new to Helga Crane, familiar only, and that but little, with the restricted society of American Negroes. She was aware, too, that this amusing, if conceited, man was interested in her. They were, because he was painting her, much together. Helga spent long mornings in the eccentric studio opposite the Folkemuseum, and Olsen came often to the Dahl home, where, as Helga and the man himself knew, he was something more than welcome. But in spite of his expressed interest and even delight in her exotic appearance, in spite of his constant attendance upon her, he gave no sign of the more personal kind of concern which—encouraged by Aunt Katrina's mild insinuations and Uncle Poul's subtle questionings—she had tried to secure. Was it, she wondered, race that kept him silent, held him back. Helga Crane frowned on this thought, putting it furiously from her, because it disturbed her sense of security and permanence in her new life, pricked her self-assurance.

Nevertheless she was startled when on a pleasant afternoon while drinking coffee in the Hotel Vivili, Aunt Katrina mentioned, almost casually, the desirability of Helga's making a good marriage.

"Marriage, Aunt dear!"

"Marriage," firmly repeated her aunt, helping herself to another anchovy and olive sandwich. "You are," she pointed out, "twenty-five."

"Oh, Aunt, I couldn't! I mean, there's nobody here for me to marry." In spite of herself and her desire not to be, Helga was shocked.

"Nobody?" There was, Fru Dahl asserted, Captain Frederick Skaargaard—and very handsome he was too—and he would have money. And there was Herr Hans Tietgen, not so handsome, of course, but clever and a good business man; he too would be rich, very rich, some day. And there was Herr Karl Pedersen, who had a good berth with the Landmands-bank and considerable shares in a prosperous cement-factory at Aalborg. There was, too, Christian Lende, the young owner of the new Odin Theater. Any of these Helga might marry, was Aunt Katrina's opinion. "And," she added, "others." Or maybe Helga herself had some ideas.

Helga had. She didn't, she responded, believe in mixed marriages, "between races, you know." They brought only trouble—to the children—as she herself knew but too well from bitter experience.

Fru Dahl thoughtfully lit a cigarette. Eventually, after a satisfactory glow had manifested itself, she announced: "Because your mother was a fool. Yes, she was! If she'd come home after she married, or after you were born, or even after your father—er—went off like that, it would have been different. If even she'd left you when she was here. But why in the world she should have married again, and a person like that, I can't see. She wanted to keep you, she insisted on it, even over his protest, I think. She loved you so much, she said.—And so she made you unhappy. Mothers, I suppose, are like that. Selfish. And Karen was always stupid. If you've got any brains at all they came from your father."

Into this Helga would not enter. Because of its obvious partial truths she felt the need for disguising caution. With a detachment that amazed herself she asked if Aunt Katrina didn't think, really, that miscegenation was wrong, in fact as well as principle.

"Don't," was her aunt's reply, "be a fool too, Helga. We don't think of those things here. Not in connection with individuals, at least." And almost immediately she inquired: "Did you give Herr Olsen my message about dinner tonight?"

"Yes, Aunt." Helga was cross, and trying not to show it.

"He's coming?"

"Yes, Aunt," with precise politeness.

"What about him?"

"I don't know. *What* about him?"

"He likes you?"

"I don't know. How can I tell that?" Helga asked with irritating reserve, her concentrated attention on the selection of a sandwich. She had a feeling of nakedness. Outrage.

Now Fru Dahl was annoyed and showed it. "What nonsense! Of course you know. Any girl does," and her satin-covered foot tapped, a little impatiently, the old tiled floor.

"Really, I don't know, Aunt," Helga responded in a strange voice, a strange manner, coldly formal, levelly courteous. Then suddenly contrite, she added: "Honestly, I don't. I can't tell a thing about him," and fell into a little silence. "Not a thing," she repeated. But the phrase, though audible, was addressed to no one. To herself.

She looked out into the amazing orderliness of the street. Instinctively she wanted to combat this searching into the one thing which, here, surrounded by all other things which for so long she had so positively wanted, made her a little afraid. Started vague premonitions.

Fru Dahl regarded her intently. It would be, she remarked with a return of her outward casualness, by far the best of all possibilities. Particularly desirable. She touched Helga's hand with her fingers in a little affectionate gesture. Very lightly.

Helga Crane didn't immediately reply. There was, she knew, so much reason—from one viewpoint—in her aunt's statement. She could only acknowledge it. "I know that," she told her finally. Inwardly she was admiring the cool, easy way in which Aunt Katrina had brushed aside the momentary acid note of the conversation and resumed her customary pitch. It took, Helga thought, a great deal of security. Balance.

"Yes," she was saying, while leisurely lighting another of those long, thin, brown cigarettes which Helga knew from distressing experience to be incredibly nasty tasting, "it would be the ideal thing for you, Helga." She gazed penetratingly into the masked face of her niece and nodded, as though satisfied with what she saw there. "And you of course realize that you are a very charming and beautiful girl. Intelligent too. If you put your mind to it, there's no reason in the world why you shouldn't—" Abruptly she stopped, leaving her implication at once suspended and clear. Behind her there were footsteps. A small gloved hand appeared on her shoulder. In the short moment before turning to greet Fru Fischer she said quietly, meaningly: "Or else stop wasting your time, Helga."

Helga Crane said: "Ah, Fru Fischer. It's good to see you." She meant it. Her whole body was tense with suppressed indignation. Burning inside like the confined fire of a hot furnace. She was so harassed that she smiled in self-protection. And suddenly she was oddly cold. An intimation of things distant, but none the less disturbing, oppressed her with a faintly sick feeling. Like a heavy weight, a stone weight, just where, she knew, was her stomach.

Fru Fischer was late. As usual. She apologized profusely. Also as usual. And, yes, she would have some coffee. And some *smørrebrød*. Though she must say that the coffee here at the Vivili was atrocious. Simply atrocious. "I don't see how you stand it." And the place was getting so common, always so many Bolsheviks and Japs and things. And she didn't—"begging your pardon, Helga"— like that hideous American music they were forever playing, even if it was considered very smart. "Give me," she said, "the good old-fashioned Danish melodies of Gade and Heise.[7] Which reminds me, Herr Olsen says that Nielsen's[8] "Helios" is being performed with great success just now in England. But I suppose you know all about it, Helga. He's already told you. What?" This last was accompanied with an arch and insinuating smile.

7. Niels William Gade (1870–1890) and Peter Arnold Heise (1830–1879), 19th-century Danish composers.

8. Carl August Nielsen (1865–1931), Danish composer from the period in which the novel is set.

A shrug moved Helga Crane's shoulders. Strange she'd never before noticed what a positively disagreeable woman Fru Fischer was. Stupid, too.

15

Well into Helga's second year in Denmark, came an indefinite discontent. Not clear, but vague, like a storm gathering far on the horizon. It was long before she would admit that she was less happy than she had been during her first year in Copenhagen, but she knew that it was so. And this subconscious knowledge added to her growing restlessness and little mental insecurity. She desired ardently to combat this wearing down of her satisfaction with her life, with herself. But she didn't know how.

Frankly the question came to this: what was the matter with her? Was there, without her knowing it, some peculiar lack in her? Absurd. But she began to have a feeling of discouragement and hopelessness. Why couldn't she be happy, content, somewhere? Other people managed, somehow, to be. To put it plainly, didn't she know how? Was she incapable of it?

And then on a warm spring day came Anne's letter telling of her coming marriage to Anderson, who retained still his shadowy place in Helga Crane's memory. It added, somehow, to her discontent, and to her growing dissatisfaction with her peacock's life. This, too, annoyed her.

What, she asked herself, was there about that man which had the power always to upset her? She began to think back to her first encounter with him. Perhaps if she hadn't come away— She laughed. Derisively. "Yes, if I hadn't come away, I'd be stuck in Harlem. Working every day of my life. Chattering about the race problem."

Anne, it seemed, wanted her to come back for the wedding. This, Helga had no intention of doing. True, she had liked and admired Anne better than anyone she had ever known, but even for her she wouldn't cross the ocean.

Go back to America, where they hated Negroes! To America, where Negroes were not people. To America, where Negroes were allowed to be beggars only, of life, of happiness, of security. To America, where everything had been taken from those dark ones, liberty, respect, even the labor of their hands. To America, where if one had Negro blood, one mustn't expect money, education, or, sometimes, even work whereby one might earn bread. Perhaps she was wrong to bother about it now that she was so far away. Helga couldn't, however, help it. Never could she recall the shames and often the absolute horrors of the black man's existence in America without the quickening of her heart's beating and a sensation of disturbing nausea. It was too awful. The sense of dread of it was almost a tangible thing in her throat.

And certainly she wouldn't go back for any such idiotic reason as Anne's getting married to that offensive Robert Anderson. Anne was really too amusing. Just why, she wondered, and how had it come about that he was being married to Anne. And why did Anne, who had so much more than so many others—more than enough—want Anderson too? Why couldn't she— "I think," she told herself, "I'd better stop. It's none of my business. I don't care in the least. Besides," she added irrelevantly, "I hate such nonsensical soul-searching."

One night not long after the arrival of Anne's letter with its curious news, Helga went with Olsen and some other young folk to the great Circus, a vaudeville house, in search of amusement on a rare off night. After sitting through several numbers they reluctantly arrived at the conclusion that the whole entertainment was dull, unutterably dull, and apparently without alleviation, and so not to be borne. They were reaching for their wraps when out upon the stage pranced two black men, American Negroes undoubtedly, for as they danced and cavorted, they sang in the English of America an old ragtime song that Helga remembered hearing as a child, "Everybody Gives Me Good Advice." At its conclusion the audience applauded with delight. Only Helga Crane was silent, motionless.

More songs, old, all of them old, but new and strange to that audience. And how the singers danced, pounding their thighs, slapping their hands together, twisting their legs, waving their abnormally long arms, throwing their bodies about with a loose ease! And how the enchanted spectators clapped and howled and shouted for more!

Helga Crane was not amused. Instead she was filled with a fierce hatred for the cavorting Negroes on the stage. She felt shamed, betrayed, as if these pale pink and white people among whom she lived had suddenly been invited to look upon something in her which she had hidden away and wanted to forget. And she was shocked at the avidity at which Olsen beside her drank it in.

But later, when she was alone, it became quite clear to her that all along they had divined its presence, had known that in her was something, some characteristic, different from any that they themselves possessed. Else why had they decked her out as they had? Why subtly indicated that she was different? And they hadn't despised it. No, they had admired it, rated it as a precious thing, a thing to be enhanced, preserved. Why? She, Helga Crane, didn't admire it. She suspected that no Negroes, no Americans, did. Else why their constant slavish imitation of traits not their own? Why their constant begging to be considered as exact copies of other people? Even the enlightened, the intelligent ones demanded nothing more. They were all beggars like the motley crowd in the old nursery rhyme:

> Hark! Hark!
> The dogs do bark.
> The beggars are coming to town.
> Some in rags,
> Some in tags,
> And some in velvet gowns.

The incident left her profoundly disquieted. Her old unhappy questioning mood came again upon her, insidiously stealing away more of the contentment from her transformed existence.

But she returned again and again to the Circus, always alone, gazing intently and solemnly at the gesticulating black figures, an ironical and silently speculative spectator. For she knew that into her plan for her life had thrust itself a suspensive conflict in which were fused doubts, rebellion, expediency, and urgent longings.

It was at this time that Axel Olsen asked her to marry him. And now Helga Crane was surprised. It was a thing that at one time she had much wanted, had tried to bring about, and had at last relinquished as impossible of achievement. Not so much because of its apparent hopelessness as because of a feeling, intangible almost, that, excited and pleased as he was with her,

her origin a little repelled him, and that, prompted by some impulse of racial antagonism, he had retreated into the fastness of a protecting habit of self-ridicule. A mordantly personal pride and sensitiveness deterred Helga from further efforts at incitation.

True, he had made, one morning, while holding his brush poised for a last, a very last stroke on the portrait, one admirably draped suggestion, speaking seemingly to the pictured face. Had he insinuated marriage, or something less—and easier? Or had he paid her only a rather florid compliment, in somewhat dubious taste? Helga, who had not at the time been quite sure, had remained silent, striving to appear unhearing.

Later, having thought it over, she flayed herself for a fool. It wasn't, she should have known, in the manner of Axel Olsen to pay florid compliments in questionable taste. And had it been marriage that he had meant, he would, of course, have done the proper thing. He wouldn't have stopped—or, rather, have begun—by making his wishes known to her when there was Uncle Poul to be formally consulted. She had been, she told herself, insulted. And a goodly measure of contempt and wariness was added to her interest in the man. She was able, however, to feel a gratifying sense of elation in the remembrance that she had been silent, ostensibly unaware of his utterance, and therefore, as far as he knew, not affronted.

This simplified things. It did away with the quandary in which the confession to the Dahls of such a happening would have involved her, for she couldn't be sure that they, too, might not put it down to the difference of her ancestry. And she could still go attended by him, and envied by others, to openings in Konigen's Nytorv, to showings at the Royal Academy or Charlottenborg's Palace.[9] He could still call for her and Aunt Katrina of an afternoon or go with her to Magasin du Nord[1] to select a scarf or a length of silk, of which Uncle Poul could say casually in the presence of interested acquaintances: "Um, pretty scarf"—or "frock"—"you're wearing, Helga. Is that the new one Olsen helped you with?"

Her outward manner toward him changed not at all, save that gradually she became, perhaps, a little more detached and indifferent. But definitely Helga Crane had ceased, even remotely, to consider him other than as someone amusing, desirable, and convenient to have about—if one was careful. She intended, presently, to turn her attention to one of the others. The decorative Captain of the Hussars, perhaps. But in the ache of her growing nostalgia, which, try as she might, she could not curb, she no longer thought with any seriousness on either Olsen or Captain Skaargaard. She must, she felt, see America again first. When she returned—

Therefore, where before she would have been pleased and proud at Olsen's proposal, she was now truly surprised. Strangely, she was aware also of a curious feeling of repugnance, as her eyes slid over his face, as smiling, assured, with just the right note of fervor, he made his declaration and request. She was astonished. Was it possible? Was it really this man that she had thought, even wished, she could marry?

He was, it was plain, certain of being accepted, as he was always certain of acceptance, of adulation, in any and every place that he deigned to honor

9. Streets and public buildings in Copenhagen.   1. Copenhagen's largest department store.

with his presence. Well, Helga was thinking, that wasn't as much his fault as her own, her aunt's, everyone's. He was spoiled, childish almost.

To his words, once she had caught their content and recovered from her surprise, Helga paid not much attention. They would, she knew, be absolutely appropriate ones, and they didn't at all matter. They meant nothing to her—now. She was too amazed to discover suddenly how intensely she disliked him, disliked the shape of his head, the mop of his hair, the line of his nose, the tones of his voice, the nervous grace of his long fingers; disliked even the very look of his irreproachable clothes. And for some inexplicable reason, she was a little frightened and embarrassed, so that when he had finished speaking, for a short space there was only stillness in the small room, into which Aunt Katrina had tactfully had him shown. Even Thor, the enormous Persian, curled on the window ledge in the feeble late afternoon sun, had rested for the moment from his incessant purring under Helga's idly stroking fingers.

Helga, her slight agitation vanished, told him that she was surprised. His offer was, she said, unexpected. Quite.

A little sardonically, Olsen interrupted her. He smiled too. "But of course I expected surprise. It is, is it not, the proper thing? And always you are proper, Frøkken Helga, always."

Helga, who had a stripped, naked feeling under his direct glance, drew herself up stiffly. Herr Olsen needn't, she told him, be sarcastic. She *was* surprised. He must understand that she was being quite sincere, quite truthful about that. Really, she hadn't expected him to do her so great an honor.

He made a little impatient gesture. Why, then, had she refused, ignored, his other, earlier suggestion?

At that Helga Crane took a deep indignant breath and was again, this time for an almost imperceptible second, silent. She had, then, been correct in her deduction. Her sensuous, petulant mouth hardened. That he should so frankly—so insolently, it seemed to her—admit his outrageous meaning was too much. She said, coldly: "Because, Herr Olsen, in my country the men, of my race, at least, don't make such suggestions to decent girls. And thinking that you were a gentleman, introduced to me by my aunt, I chose to think myself mistaken, to give you the benefit of the doubt."

"Very commendable, my Helga—and wise. Now you have your reward. Now I offer you marriage."

"Thanks," she answered, "thanks, awfully."

"Yes," and he reached for her slim cream hand, now lying quiet on Thor's broad orange and black back. Helga let it lie in his large pink one, noting their contrast. "Yes, because I, poor artist that I am, cannot hold out against the deliberate lure of you. You disturb me. The longing for you does harm to my work. You creep into my brain and madden me," and he kissed the small ivory hand. Quite decorously, Helga thought, for one so maddened that he was driven, against his inclination, to offer her marriage. But immediately, in extenuation, her mind leapt to the admirable casualness of Aunt Katrina's expressed desire for this very thing, and recalled the unruffled calm of Uncle Poul under any and all circumstances. It was, as she had long ago decided, security. Balance.

"But," the man before her was saying, "for me it will be an experience. It may be that with you, Helga, for wife, I will become great. Immortal. Who knows? I didn't want to love you, but I had to. That is the truth. I make of myself a present to you. For love." His voice held a theatrical note. At the same time he moved forward putting out his arms. His hands touched air. For Helga had moved back. Instantly he dropped his arms and took a step away, repelled by something suddenly wild in her face and manner. Sitting down, he passed a hand over his face with a quick, graceful gesture.

Tameness returned to Helga Crane. Her ironic gaze rested on the face of Axel Olsen, his leonine head, his broad nose—"broader than my own"—his bushy eyebrows, surmounting thick, drooping lids, which hid, she knew, sullen blue eyes. He stirred sharply, shaking off his momentary disconcertion.

In his assured, despotic way he went on: "You know, Helga, you are a contradiction. You have been, I suspect, corrupted by the good Fru Dahl, which is perhaps as well. Who knows? You have the warm impulsive nature of the women of Africa, but, my lovely, you have, I fear, the soul of a prostitute. You sell yourself to the highest buyer. I should of course be happy that it is I. And I am." He stopped, contemplating her, lost apparently, for the second, in pleasant thoughts of the future.

To Helga he seemed to be the most distant, the most unreal figure in the world. She suppressed a ridiculous impulse to laugh. The effort sobered her. Abruptly she was aware that in the end, in some way, she would pay for this hour. A quick brief fear ran through her, leaving in its wake a sense of impending calamity. She wondered if for this she would pay all that she'd had.

And, suddenly, she didn't at all care. She said, lightly, but firmly: "But you see, Herr Olsen, I'm not for sale. Not to you. Not to any white man. I don't at all care to be owned. Even by you."

The drooping lids lifted. The look in the blue eyes was, Helga thought, like the surprised stare of a puzzled baby. He hadn't at all grasped her meaning.

She proceeded, deliberately: "I think you don't understand me. What I'm trying to say is this, I don't want you. I wouldn't under any circumstances marry you," and since she was, as she put it, being brutally frank, she added: "Now."

He turned a little away from her, his face white but composed, and looked down into the gathering shadows in the little park before the house. At last he spoke, in a queer frozen voice: "You refuse me?"

"Yes," Helga repeated with intentional carelessness. "I refuse you."

The man's full upper lip trembled. He wiped his forehead, where the gold hair was now lying flat and pale and lusterless. His eyes still avoided the girl in the high-backed chair before him. Helga felt a shiver of compunction. For an instant she regretted that she had not been a little kinder. But wasn't it after all the greatest kindness to be cruel? But more gently, less indifferently, she said: "You see, I couldn't marry a white man. I simply couldn't. It isn't just you, not just personal, you understand. It's deeper, broader than that. It's racial. Some day maybe you'll be glad. We can't tell, you know; if we were married, you might come to be ashamed of me, to hate me, to hate all dark people. My mother did that."

"I have offered you marriage, Helga Crane, and you answer me with some strange talk of race and shame. What nonsense is this?"

Helga let that pass because she couldn't, she felt, explain. It would be too difficult, too mortifying. She had no words which could adequately, and without laceration to her pride, convey to him the pitfalls into which very easily they might step. "I might," she said, "have considered it once—when I first came. But you, hoping for a more informal arrangement, waited too long. You missed the moment. I had time to think. Now I couldn't. Nothing is worth the risk. We might come to hate each other. I've been through it, or something like it. I know. I couldn't do it. And I'm glad."

Rising, she held out her hand, relieved that he was still silent. "Good afternoon," she said formally. "It has been a great honor—"

"A tragedy," he corrected, barely touching her hand with his moist fingertips.

"Why?" Helga countered, and for an instant felt as if something sinister and internecine flew back and forth between them like poison.

"I mean," he said, and quite solemnly, "that though I don't entirely understand you, yet in a way I do too. And—" He hesitated. Went on. "I think that my picture of you is, after all, the true Helga Crane. Therefore—a tragedy. For someone. For me? Perhaps."

"Oh, the picture!" Helga lifted her shoulders in a little impatient motion.

Ceremoniously Axel Olsen bowed himself out, leaving her grateful for the urbanity which permitted them to part without too much awkwardness. No other man, she thought, of her acquaintance could have managed it so well—except, perhaps, Robert Anderson.

"I'm glad," she declared to herself in another moment, "that I refused him. And," she added honestly, "I'm glad that I had the chance. He took it awfully well, though—for a tragedy." And she made a tiny frown.

The picture—she had never quite, in spite of her deep interest in him, and her desire for his admiration and approval, forgiven Olsen for that portrait. It wasn't, she contended, herself at all, but some disgusting sensual creature with her features. Herr and Fru Dahl had not exactly liked it either, although collectors, artists, and critics had been unanimous in their praise and it had been hung on the line at an annual exhibition, where it had attracted much flattering attention and many tempting offers.

Now Helga went in and stood for a long time before it, with its creator's parting words in mind: ". . . a tragedy . . . my picture is, after all, the true Helga Crane." Vehemently she shook her head. "It isn't, it isn't at all," she said aloud. Bosh! Pure artistic bosh and conceit. Nothing else. Anyone with half an eye could see that it wasn't, at all, like her.

"Marie," she called to the maid passing in the hall, "do you think this is a good picture of me?"

Marie blushed. Hesitated. "Of course, Frøkken, I know Herr Olsen is a great artist, but no, I don't like that picture. It looks bad, wicked. Begging your pardon, Frøkken."

"Thanks, Marie, I don't like it either."

Yes, anyone with half an eye could see that it wasn't she.

16

Glad though the Dahls may have been that their niece had had the chance of refusing the hand of Axel Olsen, they were anything but glad that she had taken that chance. Very plainly they said so, and quite firmly they pointed out to her the advisability of retrieving the opportunity, if, indeed, such a thing were possible. But it wasn't, even had Helga been so inclined, for, they were to learn from the columns of *Politikken*,[2] Axel Olsen had gone off suddenly to some queer place in the Balkans. To rest, the newspapers said. To get Frøkken Crane out of his mind, the gossips said.

Life in the Dahl ménage went on, smoothly as before, but not so pleasantly. The combined disappointment and sense of guilt of the Dahls and Helga colored everything. Though she had resolved not to think that they felt that she had, as it were, "let them down," Helga knew that they did. They had not so much expected as hoped that she would bring down Olsen, and so secure the link between the merely fashionable set to which they belonged and the artistic one after which they hankered. It was of course true that there were others, plenty of them. But there was only one Olsen. And Helga, for some idiotic reason connected with race, had refused him. Certainly there was no use in thinking, even, of the others. If she had refused him, she would refuse any and all for the same reason. It was, it seemed, all-embracing.

"It isn't," Uncle Poul had tried to point out to her, "as if there were hundreds of mulattoes here. That, I can understand, might make it a little different. But there's only you. You're unique here, don't you see? Besides, Olsen has money and enviable position. Nobody'd dare to say, or even to think anything odd or unkind of you or him. Come now, Helga, it isn't this foolishness about race. Not here in Denmark. You've never spoken of it before. It can't be just that. You're too sensible. It must be something else. I wish you'd try to explain. You don't perhaps like Olsen?"

Helga had been silent, thinking what a severe wrench to Herr Dahl's ideas of decency was this conversation. For he had an almost fanatic regard for reticence, and a peculiar shrinking from what he looked upon as indecent exposure of the emotions.

"Just what is it, Helga?" he asked again, because the pause had grown awkward, for him.

"I can't explain any better than I have," she had begun tremulously, "it's just something—something deep down inside of me," and had turned away to hide a face convulsed by threatening tears.

But that, Uncle Poul had remarked with a reasonableness that was wasted on the miserable girl before him, was nonsense, pure nonsense.

With a shaking sigh and a frantic dab at her eyes, in which had come a despairing look, she had agreed that perhaps it was foolish, but she couldn't help it. "Can't you, won't you understand, Uncle Poul?" she begged, with a pleading look at the kindly worldly man who at that moment had been thinking that this strange exotic niece of his wife's was indeed charming. He didn't blame Olsen for taking it rather hard.

The thought passed. She was weeping. With no effort at restraint. Charming, yes. But insufficiently civilized. Impulsive. Imprudent. Selfish.

"Try, Helga, to control yourself," he had urged gently. He detested tears. "If it distresses you so, we won't talk of it again. You, of course, must do as you yourself wish. Both your aunt and I want only that you should be happy." He had wanted to make an end of this fruitless wet conversation.

Helga had made another little dab at her face with the scrap of lace and raised shining eyes to his face. She had said, with sincere regret: "You've been

2. Politics (Danish, literal trans.); title of a Copenhagen newspaper.

marvelous to me, you and Aunt Katrina. Angelic. I don't want to seem ungrateful. I'd do anything for you, anything in the world but this."

Herr Dahl had shrugged. A little sardonically he had smiled. He had refrained from pointing out that this was the only thing she could do for them, the only thing that they had asked of her. He had been too glad to be through with the uncomfortable discussion.

So life went on. Dinners, coffees, theaters, pictures, music, clothes. More dinners, coffees, theaters, clothes, music. And that nagging aching for America increased. Augmented by the uncomfortableness of Aunt Katrina's and Uncle Poul's disappointment with her, that tormenting nostalgia grew to an unbearable weight. As spring came on with many gracious tokens of following summer, she found her thoughts straying with increasing frequency to Anne's letter and to Harlem, its dirty streets, swollen now, in the warmer weather, with dark, gay humanity.

Until recently she had had no faintest wish ever to see America again. Now she began to welcome the thought of a return. Only a visit, of course. Just to see, to prove to herself that there was nothing there for her. To demonstrate the absurdity of even thinking that there could be. And to relieve the slight tension here. Maybe when she came back—

Her definite decision to go was arrived at with almost bewildering suddenness. It was after a concert at which Dvořák's "New World Symphony"[3] had been wonderfully rendered. Those wailing undertones of "Swing Low, Sweet Chariot" were too poignantly familiar. They struck into her longing heart and cut away her weakening defenses. She knew at least what it was that had lurked formless and undesignated these many weeks in the back of her troubled mind. Incompleteness.

"I'm homesick, not for America, but for Negroes. That's the trouble."

For the first time Helga Crane felt sympathy rather than contempt and hatred for that father, who so often and so angrily she had blamed for his desertion of her mother. She understood, now, his rejection, his repudiation, of the formal calm her mother had represented. She understood his yearning, his intolerable need for the inexhaustible humor and the incessant hope of his own kind, his need for those things, not material, indigenous to all Negro environments. She understood and could sympathize with his facile surrender to the irresistible ties of race, now that they dragged at her own heart. And as she attended parties, the theater, the opera, and mingled with people on the streets, meeting only pale serious faces when she longed for brown laughing ones, she was able to forgive him. Also, it was as if in this understanding and forgiving she had come upon knowledge of almost sacred importance.

Without demur, opposition, or recrimination Herr and Fru Dahl accepted Helga's decision to go back to America. She had expected that they would be glad and relieved. It was agreeable to discover that she had done them less than justice. They were, in spite of their extreme worldliness, very fond of her, and would, as they declared, miss her greatly. And they did want her to come back to them, as they repeatedly insisted. Secretly they felt as she did, that perhaps when she returned— So it was agreed upon that it was only for a brief visit, "for your friend's wedding," and that she was to return in the early fall.

3. Antonín Dvořák (1841–1904), Czech composer whose *New World Symphony* (1893) incorporates themes from spirituals, including "Swing Low, Sweet Chariot."

The last day came. The last good-byes were said. Helga began to regret that she was leaving. Why couldn't she have two lives, or why couldn't she be satisfied in one place? Now that she was actually off, she felt heavy at heart. Already she looked back with infinite regret at the two years in the country which had given her so much, of pride, of happiness, of wealth, and of beauty.

Bells rang. The gangplank was hoisted. The dark strip of water widened. The running figures of friends suddenly grown very dear grew smaller, blurred into a whole, and vanished. Tears rose in Helga Crane's eyes, fear in her heart.

Good-bye Denmark! Good-bye. Good-bye!

17

A summer had ripened and fall begun. Anne and Dr. Anderson had returned from their short Canadian wedding journey. Helga Crane, lingering still in America, had tactfully removed herself from the house in One Hundred and Thirty-ninth Street to a hotel. It was, as she could point out to curious acquaintances, much better for the newly-married Andersons not to be bothered with a guest, not even with such a close friend as she, Helga, had been to Anne.

Actually, though she herself had truly wanted to get out of the house when they came back, she had been a little surprised and a great deal hurt that Anne had consented so readily to her going. She might at least, thought Helga indignantly, have acted a little bit as if she had wanted her to stay. After writing for her to come, too.

Pleasantly unaware was Helga that Anne, more silently wise than herself, more determined, more selfish, and less inclined to leave anything to chance, understood perfectly that in a large measure it was the voice of Robert Anderson's inexorable conscience that had been the chief factor in bringing about her second marriage—his ascetic protest against the sensuous, the physical. Anne had perceived that the decorous surface of her new husband's mind regarded Helga Crane with that intellectual and æsthetic appreciation which attractive and intelligent women would always draw from him, but that underneath that well-managed section, in a more lawless place where she herself never hoped or desired to enter, was another, a vagrant primitive groping toward something shocking and frightening to the cold asceticism of his reason. Anne knew also that though she herself was lovely—more beautiful than Helga—and interesting, with her he had not to struggle against that nameless and to him shameful impulse, that sheer delight, which ran through his nerves at mere proximity to Helga. And Anne intended that her marriage should be a success. She intended that her husband should be happy. She was sure that it could be managed by tact and a little cleverness on her own part. She was truly fond of Helga, but seeing how she had grown more charming, more aware of her power, Anne wasn't so sure that her sincere and urgent request to come over for her wedding hadn't been a mistake. She was, however, certain of herself. She could look out for her husband. She could carry out what she considered her obligation to him, keep him undisturbed, unhumiliated. It was impossible that she could fail. Unthinkable.

Helga, on her part, had been glad to get back to New York. How glad, or why, she did not truly realize. And though she sincerely meant to keep her promise to Aunt Katrina and Uncle Poul and return to Copenhagen, summer,

September, October, slid by and she made no move to go. Her uttermost intention had been a six or eight weeks' visit, but the feverish rush of New York, the comic tragedy of Harlem, still held her. As time went on, she became a little bored, a little restless, but she stayed on. Something of that wild surge of gladness that had swept her on the day when with Anne and Anderson she had again found herself surrounded by hundreds, thousands, of dark-eyed brown folk remained with her. *These* were her people. Nothing, she had come to understand now, could ever change that. Strange that she had never truly valued this kinship until distance had shown her its worth. How absurd she had been to think that another country, other people, could liberate her from the ties which bound her forever to these mysterious, these terrible, these fascinating, these lovable, dark hordes. Ties that were of the spirit. Ties not only superficially entangled with mere outline of features or color of skin. Deeper. Much deeper than either of these.

Thankful for the appeasement of that loneliness which had again tormented her like a fury, she gave herself up to the miraculous joyousness of Harlem. The easement which its heedless abandon brought to her was a real, a very definite thing. She liked the sharp contrast to her pretentious stately life in Copenhagen. It was as if she had passed from the heavy solemnity of a church service to a gorgeous care-free revel.

Not that she intended to remain. No. Helga Crane couldn't, she told herself and others, live in America. In spite of its glamour, existence in America, even in Harlem, was for Negroes too cramped, too uncertain, too cruel; something not to be endured for a lifetime if one could escape; something demanding a courage greater than was in her. No. She couldn't stay. Nor, she saw now, could she remain away. Leaving, she would have to come back.

This knowledge, this certainty of the division of her life into two parts in two lands, into physical freedom in Europe and spiritual freedom in America, was unfortunate, inconvenient, expensive. It was, too, as she was uncomfortably aware, even a trifle ridiculous, and mentally she caricatured herself moving shuttlelike from continent to continent. From the prejudiced restrictions of the New World to the easy formality of the Old, from the pale calm of Copenhagen to the colorful lure of Harlem.

Nevertheless she felt a slightly pitying superiority over those Negroes who were apparently so satisfied. And she had a fine contempt for the blatantly patriotic black Americans. Always when she encountered one of those picturesque parades in the Harlem streets, the Stars and Stripes streaming ironically, insolently, at the head of the procession tempered for her, a little, her amusement at the childish seriousness of the spectacle. It was too pathetic.

But when mental doors were deliberately shut on those skeletons that stalked lively and in full health through the consciousness of every person of Negro ancestry in America—conspicuous black, obvious brown, or indistinguishable white—life was intensely amusing, interesting, absorbing, and enjoyable; singularly lacking in that tone of anxiety which the insecurities of existence seemed to ferment in other peoples.

Yet Helga herself had an acute feeling of insecurity, for which she could not account. Sometimes it amounted to fright almost. "I must," she would say then, "get back to Copenhagen." But the resolution gave her not much pleasure. And for this she now blamed Axel Olsen. It was, she insisted, he who had driven her back, made her unhappy in Denmark. Though she knew well that it wasn't. Misgivings, too, rose in her. Why hadn't she married him? Anne was married—she would not say Anderson—Why not she? It would serve Anne right if she married a white man. But she knew in her soul that she wouldn't. "Because I'm a fool," she said bitterly.

18

One November evening, impregnated still with the kindly warmth of the dead Indian summer, Helga Crane was leisurely dressing in pleasant anticipation of the party to which she had been asked for that night. It was always amusing at the Tavenors'. Their house was large and comfortable, the food and music always of the best, and the type of entertainment always unexpected and brilliant. The drinks, too, were sure to be safe.

And Helga, since her return, was more than ever popular at parties. Her courageous clothes attracted attention, and her deliberate lure—as Olsen had called it—held it. Her life in Copenhagen had taught her to expect and accept admiration as her due. This attitude, she found, was as effective in New York as across the sea. It was, in fact, even more so. And it was more amusing too. Perhaps because it was somehow a bit more dangerous.

In the midst of curious speculation as to the possible identity of the other guests, with an indefinite sense of annoyance she wondered if Anne would be there. There was of late something about Anne that was to Helga distinctly disagreeable, a peculiar half-patronizing attitude, mixed faintly with distrust. Helga couldn't define it, couldn't account for it. She had tried. In the end she had decided to dismiss it, to ignore it.

"I suppose," she said aloud, "it's because she's married again. As if anybody couldn't get married. Anybody. That is, if mere marriage is all one wants."

Smoothing away the tiny frown from between the broad black brows, she got herself into a little shining, rose-colored slip of a frock knotted with a silver cord. The gratifying result soothed her ruffled feelings. It didn't really matter, this new manner of Anne's. Nor did the fact that Helga knew that Anne disapproved of her. Without words Anne had managed to make that evident. In her opinion, Helga had lived too long among the enemy, the detestable pale faces. She understood them too well, was too tolerant of their ignorant stupidities. If they had been Latins,[4] Anne might conceivably have forgiven the disloyalty. But Nordics![5] Lynchers! It was too traitorous. Helga smiled a little, understanding Anne's bitterness and hate, and a little of its cause. It was of a piece with that of those she so virulently hated. Fear. And then she sighed a little, for she regretted the waning of Anne's friendship. But, in view of diverging courses of their lives, she felt that even its complete extinction would leave her undevastated. Not that she wasn't still grateful to Anne for many things. It was only that she had other things now. And there would, forever, be Robert Anderson between them. A nuisance. Shutting them off from their previous confident companionship and understanding. "And anyway," she said again, aloud, "he's nobody much to have married. Anybody could have married him. Anybody. If a person wanted only to be married—If it had been somebody like Olsen— That would be different— something to crow over, perhaps."

---

4. People from southern European countries.   5. People from northern European countries.

The party was even more interesting than Helga had expected. Helen, Mrs. Tavenor, had given vent to a malicious glee, and had invited representatives of several opposing Harlem political and social factions, including the West Indian, and abandoned them helplessly to each other. Helga's observing eyes picked out several great and near-great sulking or obviously trying hard not to sulk in widely separated places in the big rooms. There were present, also, a few white people, to the open disapproval or discomfort of Anne and several others. There too, poised, serene, certain, surrounded by masculine black and white, was Audrey Denney.

"Do you know, Helen," Helga confided, "I've never met Miss Denney. I wish you'd introduce me. Not this minute. Later, when you can manage it. Not so—er—apparently by request, you know."

Helen Tavenor laughed. "No, you wouldn't have met her, living as you did with Anne Grey. Anderson, I mean. She's Anne's particular pet aversion. The mere sight of Audrey is enough to send her into a frenzy for a week. It's too bad, too, because Audrey's an awfully interesting person and Anne's said some pretty awful things about her. *You'll* like her, Helga."

Helga nodded. "Yes, I expect to. And I know about Anne. One night—" She stopped, for across the room she saw, with a stab of surprise, James Vayle. "Where, Helen did you get him?"

"Oh, that? That's something the cat brought in. Don't ask which one. He came with somebody, I don't remember who. I think he's shocked to death. Isn't he lovely? The dear baby. I was going to introduce him to Audrey and tell her to do a good job of vamping on him as soon as I could remember the darling's name, or when it got noisy enough so he wouldn't hear what I called him. But you'll do just as well. Don't tell me you know him!" Helga made a little nod. "Well! And I suppose you met him at some shockingly wicked place in Europe. That's always the way with those innocent-looking men."

"Not quite. I met him ages ago in Naxos. We were engaged to be married. Nice, isn't he? His name's Vayle. James Vayle."

"Nice," said Helen throwing out her hands in a characteristic dramatic gesture—she had beautiful hands and arms—"is exactly the word. Mind if I run off? I've got somebody here who's going to sing. *Not* spirituals. And I haven't the faintest notion where he's got to. The cellar, I'll bet."

James Vayle hadn't, Helga decided, changed at all. Someone claimed her for a dance and it was some time before she caught his eyes, half questioning, upon her. When she did, she smiled in a friendly way over her partner's shoulder and was rewarded by a dignified little bow. Inwardly she grinned, flattered. He hadn't forgotten. He was still hurt. The dance over, she deserted her partner and deliberately made her way across the room to James Vayle. He was for the moment embarrassed and uncertain. Helga Crane, however, took care of that, thinking meanwhile that Helen was right. Here he did seem frightfully young and delightfully unsophisticated. He must be, though, every bit of thirty-two or more.

"They say," was her bantering greeting, "that if one stands on the corner of One Hundred and Thirty-fifth Street and Seventh Avenue long enough, one will eventually see all the people one has ever known or met. It's pretty true, I guess. Not literally of course." He was, she saw, getting himself together. "It's only another way of saying that everybody, almost, some time sooner or later comes to Harlem, even you."

He laughed. "Yes, I guess that is true enough. I didn't come to stay, though." And then he was grave, his earnest eyes searchingly upon her.

"Well, anyway, you're here now, so let's find a quiet corner if that's possible, where we can talk. I want to hear all about you."

For a moment he hung back and a glint of mischief shone in Helga's eyes. "I see," she said, "you're just the same. However, you needn't be anxious. This isn't Naxos, you know. Nobody's watching us, or if they are, they don't care a bit what we do."

At that he flushed a little, protested a little, and followed her. And when at last they had found seats in another room, not so crowded, he said: "I didn't expect to see you here. I thought you were still abroad."

"Oh, I've been back some time, ever since Dr. Anderson's marriage. Anne, you know, is a great friend of mine. I used to live with her. I came for the wedding. But, of course, I'm not staying. I didn't think I'd be here this long."

"You don't mean that you're going to live over there? Do you really like it so much better?"

"Yes and no, to both questions. I was awfully glad to get back, but I wouldn't live here always. I couldn't. I don't think that any of us who've lived abroad for any length of time would ever live here altogether again if they could help it."

"Lot of them do, though," James Vayle pointed out.

"Oh, I don't mean tourists who rush over to Europe and rush all over the continent and rush back to America thinking they know Europe. I mean people who've actually lived there, actually lived among the people."

"I still maintain that they nearly all come back here eventually to live."

"That's because they can't help it," Helga Crane said firmly. "Money, you know."

"Perhaps, I'm not so sure. I was in the war. Of course, that's not really living over there, but I saw the country and the difference in treatment. But, I can tell you, I was pretty darn glad to get back. All the fellows were." He shook his head solemnly. "I don't think anything, money or lack of money, keeps us here. If it was only that, if we really wanted to leave, we'd go all right. No, it's something else, something deeper than that."

"And just what do you think it is?"

"I'm afraid it's hard to explain, but I suppose it's just that we like to be together. I simply can't imagine living forever away from colored people."

A suspicion of a frown drew Helga's brows. She threw out rather tartly: "I'm a Negro too, you know."

"Well, Helga, you were always a little different, a little dissatisfied, though I don't pretend to understand you at all. I never did," he said a little wistfully.

And Helga, who was beginning to feel that the conversation had taken an impersonal and disappointing tone, was reassured and gave him her most sympathetic smile and said almost gently: "And now let's talk about you. You're still at Naxos?"

"Yes I'm still there. I'm assistant principal now."

Plainly it was a cause for enthusiastic congratulation, but Helga could only manage a tepid "How nice!" Naxos was to her too remote, too unimportant. She did not even hate it now.

How long, she asked, would James be in New York?

He couldn't say. Business, important business for the school, had brought him. It was, he said, another tone creeping into his voice, another look stealing over his face, awfully good to see her. She was looking tremendously well. He hoped he would have the opportunity of seeing her again.

But of course. He must come to see her. Any time, she was always in, or would be for him. And how did he like New York, Harlem?

He didn't, it seemed, like it. It was nice to visit, but not to live in. Oh, there were so many things he didn't like about it, the rush, the lack of home life, the crowds, the noisy meaninglessness of it all.

On Helga's face there had come that pityingly sneering look peculiar to imported New Yorkers when the city of their adoption is attacked by alien Americans. With polite contempt she inquired: "And is that all you don't like?"

At her tone the man's bronze face went purple. He answered coldly, slowly, with a faint gesture in the direction of Helen Tavenor, who stood conversing gayly with one of her white guests: "And I don't like that sort of thing. In fact I detest it."

"Why?" Helga was striving hard to be casual in her manner.

James Vayle, it was evident, was beginning to be angry. It was also evident that Helga Crane's question had embarrassed him. But he seized the bull by the horns and said: "You know as well as I do, Helga, that it's the colored girls these men come up here to see. They wouldn't think of bringing their wives." And he blushed furiously at his own implication. The blush restored Helga's good temper. James was really too funny.

"That," she said softly, "is Hugh Wentworth, the novelist, you know." And she indicated a tall olive-skinned girl being whirled about to the streaming music in the arms of a towering black man. "And that is his wife. She isn't colored, as you've probably been thinking. And now let's change the subject again."

"All right! And this time let's talk about you. You say you don't intend to live here. Don't you ever intend to marry, Helga?"

"Some day, perhaps. I don't know. Marriage—that means children, to me. And why add more suffering to the world? Why add any more unwanted, tortured Negroes to America? Why *do* Negroes have children? Surely it must be sinful. Think of the awfulness of being responsible for the giving of life to creatures doomed to endure such wounds to the flesh, such wounds to the spirit, as Negroes have to endure."

James was aghast. He forgot to be embarrassed. "But Helga! Good heavens! Don't you see that if we—I mean people like us—don't have children, the others will still have. That's one of the things that's the matter with us. The race is sterile at the top. Few, very few Negroes of the better class have children, and each generation has to wrestle again with the obstacles of the preceding ones, lack of money, education, and background. I feel very strongly about this. We're the ones who must have the children if the race is to get anywhere."

"Well, I for one don't intend to contribute any to the cause. But how serious we are! And I'm afraid that I've really got to leave you. I've already cut two dances for your sake. Do come to see me."

"Oh, I'll come to see you all right. I've got several things that I want to talk to you about and one thing especially."

"Don't," Helga mocked, "tell me you're going to ask me again to marry you."

"That," he said, "is just what I intend to do."

Helga Crane was suddenly deeply ashamed and very sorry for James Vayle, so she told him laughingly that it was shameful of him to joke with her like that, and before he could answer, she had gone tripping off with a handsome coffee-colored youth whom she had beckoned from across the room with a little smile.

Later she had to go upstairs to pin up a place in the hem of her dress which had caught on a sharp chair corner. She finished the temporary repair and stepped out into the hall, and somehow, she never quite knew exactly just how, into the arms of Robert Anderson. She drew back and looked up smiling to offer an apology.

And then it happened. He stooped and kissed her, a long kiss, holding her close. She fought against him with all her might. Then, strangely, all power seemed to ebb away, and a long-hidden, half-understood desire welled up in her with the suddenness of a dream. Helga Crane's own arms went up about the man's neck. When she drew away, consciously confused and embarrassed, everything seemed to have changed in a space of time which she knew to have been only seconds. Sudden anger seized her. She pushed him indignantly aside and with a little pat for her hair and dress went slowly down to the others.

19

That night riotous and colorful dreams invaded Helga Crane's prim hotel bed. She woke in the morning weary and a bit shocked at the uncontrolled fancies which had visited her. Catching up a filmy scarf, she paced back and forth across the narrow room and tried to think. She recalled her flirtations and her mild engagement with James Vayle. She was used to kisses. But none had been like that of last night. She lived over those brief seconds, thinking not so much of the man whose arms had held her as of the ecstasy which had flooded her. Even recollection brought a little onrush of emotion that made her sway a little. She pulled herself together and began to fasten on the solid fact of Anne and experienced a pleasant sense of shock in the realization that Anne was to her exactly what she had been before the incomprehensible experience of last night. She still liked her in the same degree and in the same manner. She still felt slightly annoyed with her. She still did not envy her marriage with Anderson. By some mysterious process the emotional upheaval which had racked her had left all the rocks of her existence unmoved. Outwardly nothing had changed.

Days, weeks, passed; outwardly serene; inwardly tumultuous. Helga met Dr. Anderson at the social affairs to which often they were both asked. Sometimes she danced with him, always in perfect silence. She couldn't, she absolutely couldn't, speak a word to him when they were thus alone together, for at such times lassitude encompassed her; the emotion which had gripped her retreated, leaving a strange tranquillity, troubled only by a soft stir of desire. And shamed by his silence, his apparent forgetting, always after these dances she tried desperately to persuade herself to believe what she wanted to believe: that it had not happened, that she had never had that irrepressible longing. It was of no use.

As the weeks multiplied, she became aware that she must get herself out of the mental quagmire into which that kiss had thrown her. And she should be getting herself back to Copenhagen, but she had now no desire to go.

Abruptly one Sunday in a crowded room, in the midst of teacups and chatter, she knew that she couldn't go, that she hadn't since that kiss intended to go without exploring to the end that unfamiliar path into which she had strayed. Well, it was of no use lagging behind or pulling back. It was of no use trying to persuade herself that she didn't want to go on. A species of fatalism fastened on her. She felt that, ever since that last day in Naxos long ago, somehow she had known that this thing would happen. With this conviction came an odd sense of elation. While making a pleasant assent to some remark of a fellow guest she put down her cup and walked without haste, smiling and nodding to friends and acquaintances on her way to that part of the room where he stood looking at some examples of African carving. Helga Crane faced him squarely. As he took the hand which she held out with elaborate casualness, she noted that his trembled slightly. She was secretly congratulating herself on her own calm when it failed her. Physical weariness descended on her. Her knees wobbled. Gratefully she slid into the chair which he hastily placed for her. Timidity came over her. She was silent. He talked. She did not listen. He came at last to the end of his long dissertation on African sculpture, and Helga Crane felt the intentness of his gaze upon her.

"Well?" she questioned.

"I want very much to see you, Helga. Alone."

She held herself tensely on the edge of her chair, and suggested: "Tomorrow?"

He hesitated a second and then said quickly: "Why, yes, that's all right."

"Eight o'clock?"

"Eight o'clock," he agreed.

Eight o'clock tomorrow came. Helga Crane never forgot it. She had carried away from yesterday's meeting a feeling of increasing elation. It had seemed to her that she hadn't been so happy, so exalted, in years, if ever. All night, all day, she had mentally prepared herself for the coming consummation; physically too, spending hours before the mirror.

Eight o'clock had come at last and with it Dr. Anderson. Only then had uneasiness come upon her and a feeling of fear for possible exposure. For Helga Crane wasn't, after all, a rebel from society, Negro society. It did mean something to her. She had no wish to stand alone. But these late fears were overwhelmed by the hardiness of insistent desire; and she had got herself down to the hotel's small reception room.

It was, he had said, awfully good of her to see him. She instantly protested. No, she had wanted to see him. He looked at her surprised. "You know, Helga," he had begun with an air of desperation, "I can't forgive myself for acting such a swine at the Tavenors' party. I don't at all blame you for being angry and not speaking to me except when you had to."

But that, she exclaimed, was simply too ridiculous. "I wasn't angry a bit." And it had seemed to her that things were not exactly going forward as they should. It seemed that he had been very sincere, and very formal. Deliberately. She had looked down at her hands and inspected her bracelets, for she had felt that to look at him would be, under the circumstances, too exposing.

"I was afraid," he went on, "that you might have misunderstood; might have been unhappy about it. I could kick myself. It was, it must have been, Tavenor's rotten cocktails."

Helga Crane's sense of elation had abruptly left her. At the same time she had felt the need to answer carefully. No, she replied, she hadn't thought of it at all. It had meant nothing to her. She had been kissed before. It was really too silly of him to have been at all bothered about it. "For what," she had asked, "is one kiss more or less, these days, between friends?" She had even laughed a little.

Dr. Anderson was relieved. He had been, he told her, no end upset. Rising, he said: "I see you're going out. I won't keep you."

Helga Crane too had risen. Quickly. A sort of madness had swept over her. She felt that he had belittled and ridiculed her. And thinking this, she had suddenly savagely slapped Robert Anderson with all her might, in the face.

For a short moment they had both stood stunned, in the deep silence which had followed that resounding slap. Then, without a word of contrition or apology, Helga Crane had gone out of the room and upstairs.

She had, she told herself, been perfectly justified in slapping. Dr. Anderson, but she was not convinced. So she had tried hard to make herself very drunk in order that sleep might come to her, but had managed only to make herself very sick.

Not even the memory of how all living had left his face, which had gone a taupe gray hue, or the despairing way in which he had lifted his head and let it drop, or the trembling hands which he had pressed into his pockets, brought her any scrap of comfort. She had ruined everything. Ruined it because she had been so silly as to close her eyes to all indications that pointed to the fact that no matter what the intensity of his feelings or desires might be, he was not the sort of man who would for any reason give up one particle of his own good opinion of himself. Not even for her. Not even though he knew that she had wanted so terribly something special from him.

Something special. And now she had forfeited it forever. Forever. Helga had an instantaneous shocking perception of what forever meant. And then, like a flash, it was gone, leaving an endless stretch of dreary years before her appalled vision.

20

The day was a rainy one. Helga Crane, stretched out on her bed, felt herself so broken physically, mentally, that she had given up thinking. But back and forth in her staggered brain wavering, incoherent thoughts shot shuttle-like. Her pride would have shut out these humiliating thoughts and painful visions of herself. The effort was too great. She felt alone, isolated from all other human beings, separated even from her own anterior existence by the disaster of yesterday. Over and over, she repeated: "There's nothing left but to go now." Her anguish seemed unbearable.

For days, for weeks, voluptuous visions had haunted her. Desire had burned in her flesh with uncontrollable violence. The wish to give herself had been so intense that Dr. Anderson's surprising, trivial apology loomed as a direct refusal of the offering. Whatever outcome she had expected, it had been something else than this, this mortification, this feeling of ridicule and self-loathing, this knowledge that she had deluded herself. It was all, she told herself, as unpleasant as possible.

Almost she wished she could die. Not quite. It wasn't that she was afraid of death, which had, she thought, its picturesque aspects. It was rather that she knew she would not die. And death, after the debacle, would but intensify its absurdity. Also, it would reduce her, Helga Crane, to unimportance, to nothingness. Even in her unhappy present state, that did not appeal to her. Gradually, reluctantly, she began to know that the blow to her self-esteem, the certainty of having proved herself a silly fool, was perhaps the severest hurt which she had suffered. It was her self-assurance that had gone down in the crash. After all, what Dr. Anderson thought didn't matter. She could escape from the discomfort of his knowing gray eyes. But she couldn't escape from sure knowledge that she had made a fool of herself. This angered her further and she struck the wall with her hands and jumped up and began hastily to dress herself. She couldn't go on with the analysis. It was too hard. Why bother, when she could add nothing to the obvious fact that she had been a fool?

"I can't stay in this room any longer. I must get out or I'll choke." Her self-knowledge had increased her anguish. Distracted, agitated, incapable of containing herself, she tore open drawers and closets trying desperately to take some interest in the selection of her apparel.

It was evening and still raining. In the streets, unusually deserted, the electric lights cast dull glows. Helga Crane, walking rapidly, aimlessly, could decide on no definite destination. She had not thought to take umbrella or even rubbers. Rain and wind whipped cruelly about her, drenching her garments and chilling her body. Soon the foolish little satin shoes which she wore were sopping wet. Unheeding these physical discomforts, she went on, but at the open corner of One Hundred and Thirty-eighth Street a sudden more ruthless gust of wind ripped the small hat from her head. In the next minute the black clouds opened wider and spilled their water with unusual fury. The streets became swirling rivers. Helga Crane, forgetting her mental torment, looked about anxiously for a sheltering taxi. A few taxis sped by, but inhabited, so she began desperately to struggle through wind and rain toward one of the buildings, where she could take shelter in a store or a doorway. But another whirl of wind lashed her and, scornful of her slight strength, tossed her into the swollen gutter.

Now she knew beyond all doubt that she had no desire to die, and certainly not there nor then. Not in such a messy wet manner. Death had lost all of its picturesque aspects to the girl lying soaked and soiled in the flooded gutter. So, though she was very tired and very weak, she dragged herself up and succeeded finally in making her way to the store whose blurred light she had marked for her destination.

She had opened the door and had entered before she was aware that, inside, people were singing a song which she was conscious of having heard years ago—hundreds of years it seemed. Repeated over and over, she made out the words:

> . . . Showers of blessings,
> Showers of blessings . . .

She was conscious too of a hundred pairs of eyes upon her as she stood there, drenched and disheveled, at the door of this improvised meeting-house.

. . . Showers of blessings . . .

The appropriateness of the song, with its constant reference to showers, the ridiculousness of herself in such surroundings, was too much for Helga Crane's frayed nerves. She sat down on the floor, a dripping heap, and laughed and laughed and laughed.

It was into a shocked silence that she laughed. For at the first hysterical peal the words of the song had died in the singers' throats, and the wheezy organ had lapsed into stillness. But in a moment there were hushed solicitous voices; she was assisted to her feet and led haltingly to a chair near the low platform at the far end of the room. On one side of her a tall angular black woman under a queer hat sat down, on the other a fattish yellow man with huge outstanding ears and long, nervous hands.

The singing began again, this time a low wailing thing:

> Oh, bitter shame and sorrow
> That a time could ever be,
> When I let the Savior's pity
> Plead in vain, and proudly answered:
> "All of self and none of Thee,
> All of self and none of Thee."
>
> Yet He found me, I beheld Him,
> Bleeding on the cursed tree;
> Heard Him pray: "Forgive them, Father."
> And my wistful heart said faintly,
> "Some of self and some of Thee,
> Some of self and some of Thee."

There were, it appeared, endless moaning verses. Behind Helga a woman had begun to cry audibly, and soon, somewhere else, another. Outside, the wind still bellowed. The wailing singing went on:

> . . . Less of self and more of Thee,
> Less of self and more of Thee.

Helga too began to weep, at first silently, softly; then with great racking sobs. Her nerves were so torn, so aching, her body so wet, so cold! It was a relief to cry unrestrainedly, and she gave herself freely to soothing tears, not noticing that the groaning and sobbing of those about her had increased, unaware that the grotesque ebony figure at her side had begun gently to pat her arm to the rhythm of the singing and to croon softly: "Yes, chile, yes, chile." Nor did she notice the furtive glances that the man on her other side cast at her between his fervent shouts of "Amen!" and "Praise God for a sinner!"

She did notice, though, that the tempo, the atmosphere of the place, had changed, and gradually she ceased to weep and gave her attention to what was happening about her. Now they were singing:

> . . . Jesus knows all about my troubles . . .

Men and women were swaying and clapping their hands, shouting and stamping their feet to the frankly irreverent melody of the song. Without warning the woman at her side threw off her hat, leaped to her feet, waved her long arms, and shouted shrilly: "Glory! Hallelujah!" and then, in wild, ecstatic fury jumped up and down before Helga clutching at the girl's soaked coat, and screamed: "Come to Jesus, you pore los' sinner!" Alarmed for the fraction of a second, involuntarily Helga had shrunk from her grasp, wriggling out of the wet coat when she could not loosen the crazed creature's hold. At the sight of the bare arms and neck growing out of the clinging red dress, a shudder shook the swaying man at her right. On the face of the dancing woman before her a disapproving frown gathered. She shrieked: "A scarlet 'oman. Come to Jesus, you pore los' Jezebel!"[6]

At this the short brown man on the platform raised a placating hand and sanctimoniously delivered himself of the words: "Remembah de words of our Mastah: 'Let him that is without sin cast de first stone.' Let us pray for our errin' sistah."

Helga Crane was amused, angry, disdainful, as she sat there, listening to the preacher praying for her soul. But though she was contemptuous, she was being too well entertained to leave. And it was, at least, warm and dry. So she stayed, listening to the fervent exhortation to God to save her and to the zealous shoutings and groanings of the congregation. Particularly she was interested in the writhings and weepings of the feminine portion, which seemed to predominate. Little by little the performance took on an almost Bacchic[7] vehemence. Behind her, before her, beside her, frenzied women gesticulated, screamed, wept, and tottered to the praying of the preacher, which had gradually become a cadenced chant. When at last he ended, another took up the plea in the same moaning chant, and then another. It went on and on without pause with the persistence of some unconquerable faith exalted beyond time and reality.

Fascinated, Helga Crane watched until there crept upon her an indistinct horror of an unknown world. She felt herself in the presence of a nameless people, observing rites of a remote obscure origin. The faces of the men and women took on the aspect of a dim vision. "This," she whispered to herself, "is terrible. I must get out of here." But the horror held her. She remained motionless, watching, as if she lacked the strength to leave the place—foul, vile, and terrible, with its mixture of breaths, its contact of bodies, its concerted convulsions, all in wild appeal for a single soul. Her soul.

And as Helga watched and listened, gradually a curious influence penetrated her; she felt an echo of the weird orgy resound in her own heart; she felt herself possessed by the same madness; she too felt a brutal desire to shout and to sling herself about. Frightened at the strength of the obsession, she gathered herself for one last effort to escape, but vainly. In rising, weakness and nausea from last night's unsuccessful attempt to make herself drunk overcame her. She had eaten nothing since yesterday. She fell forward against the crude railing which enclosed the little platform. For a single moment she remained there in silent stillness, because she was afraid she was going to be

<hr />

6. In the Old Testament (1 Kings), an idol-worshiping queen of Israel whose name became an insulting term for a woman. Helga's red dress causes her to be mistaken for a "scarlet woman," a prostitute.

7. In classical Greece, the Bacchae were female priestesses whose ceremonies (bacchanalia) were associated with orgiastic excess.

sick. And in that moment she was lost—or saved. The yelling figures about her pressed forward, closing her in on all sides. Maddened, she grasped at the railing, and with no previous intention began to yell like one insane, drowning every other clamor, while torrents of tears streamed down her face. She was unconscious of the words she uttered, or their meaning: "Oh God, mercy, mercy. Have mercy on me!" but she repeated them over and over.

From those about her came a thunderclap of joy. Arms were stretched toward her with savage frenzy. The women dragged themselves upon their knees or crawled over the floor like reptiles, sobbing and pulling their hair and tearing off their clothing. Those who succeeded in getting near to her leaned forward to encourage the unfortunate sister, dropping hot tears and beads of sweat upon her bare arms and neck.

The thing became real. A miraculous calm came upon her. Life seemed to expand, and to become very easy. Helga Crane felt within her a supreme aspiration toward the regaining of simple happiness, a happiness unburdened by the complexities of the lives she had known. About her the tumult and the shouting continued, but in a lesser degree. Some of the more exuberant worshipers had fainted into inert masses, the voices of others were almost spent. Gradually the room grew quiet and almost solemn, and to the kneeling girl time seemed to sink back into the mysterious grandeur and holiness of far-off simpler centuries.

21

On leaving the mission Helga Crane had started straight back to her room at the hotel. With her had gone the fattish yellow man who had sat beside her. He had introduced himself as the Reverend Mr. Pleasant Green in proffering his escort for which Helga had been grateful because she had still felt a little dizzy and much exhausted. So great had been this physical weariness that as she had walked beside him, without attention to his verbose information about his own "field," as he called it, she had been seized with a hateful feeling of vertigo and obliged to lay firm hold on his arm to keep herself from falling. The weakness had passed as suddenly as it had come. Silently they had walked on. And gradually Helga had recalled that the man beside her had himself swayed slightly at their close encounter, and that frantically for a fleeting moment he had gripped at a protruding fence railing. That man! Was it possible? As easy as that?

Instantly across her still half-hypnotized consciousness little burning darts of fancy had shot themselves. No. She couldn't. It would be too awful. Just the same, what or who was there to hold her back? Nothing. Simply nothing. Nobody. Nobody at all.

Her searching mind had become in a moment quite clear. She cast at the man a speculative glance, aware that for a tiny space she had looked into his mind, a mind striving to be calm. A mind that was certain that it was secure because it was concerned only with things of the soul, spiritual things, which to him meant religious things. But actually a mind by habit at home amongst the mere material aspect of things, and at that moment consumed by some longing for the ecstasy that might lurk behind the gleam of her cheek, the flying wave of her hair, the pressure of her slim fingers on his heavy arm. An instant's flashing vision it had been and it was gone at once. Escaped in the aching of her own senses and the sudden disturbing fear that she herself had perhaps missed the supreme secret of life.

After all, there was nothing to hold her back. Nobody to care. She stopped sharply, shocked at what she was on the verge of considering. Appalled at where it might lead her.

The man—what was his name?—thinking that she was almost about to fall again, had reached out his arms to her. Helga Crane had deliberately stopped thinking. She had only smiled, a faint provocative smile, and pressed her fingers deep into his arms until a wild look had come into his slightly bloodshot eyes.

The next morning she lay for a long while, scarcely breathing, while she reviewed the happenings of the night before. Curious. She couldn't be sure that it wasn't religion that had made her feel so utterly different from dreadful yesterday. And gradually she became a little sad, because she realized that with every hour she would get a little farther away from this soothing haziness, this rest from her long trouble of body and of spirit; back into the clear bareness of her own small life and being, from which happiness and serenity always faded just as they had shaped themselves. And slowly bitterness crept into her soul. Because, she thought, all I've ever had in life has been things—except just this one time. At that she closed her eyes, for even remembrance caused her to shiver a little.

Things, she realized, hadn't been, weren't, enough for her. She'd have to have something else besides. It all came back to that old question of happiness. Surely this was it. Just for a fleeting moment Helga Crane, her eyes watching the wind scattering the gray-white clouds and so clearing a speck of blue sky, questioned her ability to retain, to bear, this happiness at such cost as she must pay for it. There was, she knew, no getting round that. The man's agitation and sincere conviction of sin had been too evident, too illuminating. The question returned in a slightly new form. Was it worth the risk? Could she take it? Was she able? Though what did it matter—now?

And all the while she knew in one small corner of her mind that such thinking was useless. She had made her decision. Her resolution. It was a chance at stability, at permanent happiness, that she meant to take. She had let so many other things, other chances, escape her. And anyway there was God, He would perhaps make it come out all right. Still confused and not so sure that it wasn't the fact that she was "saved" that had contributed to this after feeling of well-being, she clutched the hope, the desire to believe that now at last she had found some One, some Power, who was interested in her. Would help her.

She meant, however, for once in her life to be practical. So she would make sure of both things, God and man.

Her glance caught the calendar over the little white desk. The tenth of November. The steamer *Oscar II* sailed today. Yesterday she had half thought of sailing with it. Yesterday. How far away!

With the thought of yesterday came the thought of Robert Anderson and a feeling of elation, revenge. She had put herself beyond the need of help from him. She had made it impossible for herself ever again to appeal to him. Instinctively she had the knowledge that he would be shocked. Grieved. Horribly hurt even. Well, let him!

The need to hurry suddenly obsessed her. She must. The morning was almost gone. And she meant, if she could manage it, to be married today. Rising, she was seized with a fear so acute that she had to lie down again. For the thought came to her that she might fail. Might not be able to confront the situation. That would be too dreadful. But she became calm again. How could he, a naïve creature like that, hold out against her? If she pretended to distress? To fear? To remorse? He couldn't. It would be useless for him even to try. She screwed up her face into a little grin, remembering that even if protestations were to fail, there were other ways.

And, too, there was God.

22

And so in the confusion of seductive repentance Helga Crane was married to the grandiloquent Reverend Mr. Pleasant Green, that rattish yellow man, who had so kindly, so unctuously, proffered his escort to her hotel on the memorable night of her conversion. With him she willingly, even eagerly, left the sins and temptations of New York behind her to, as he put it, "labor in the vineyard of the Lord" in the tiny Alabama town where he was pastor to a scattered and primitive flock. And where, as the wife of the preacher, she was a person of relative importance. Only relative.

Helga did not hate him, the town, or the people. No. Not for a long time.

As always, at first the novelty of the thing, the change, fascinated her. There was a recurrence of the feeling that now, at last, she had found a place for herself, that she was really living. And she had her religion, which in her new status as a preacher's wife had of necessity become real to her. She believed in it. Because in its coming it had brought this other thing, this anæsthetic satisfaction for her senses. Hers was, she declared to herself, a truly spiritual union. This one time in her life, she was convinced, she had not clutched a shadow and missed the actuality. She felt compensated for all previous humiliations and disappointments and was glad. If she remembered that she had had something like this feeling before, she put the unwelcome memory from her with the thought: "This time I know I'm right. This time it will last."

Eagerly she accepted everything, even that bleak air of poverty which, in some curious way, regards itself as virtuous, for no other reason than that it is poor. And in her first hectic enthusiasm she intended and planned to do much good to her husband's parishioners. Her young joy and zest for the uplifting of her fellow men came back to her. She meant to subdue the cleanly scrubbed ugliness of her own surroundings to soft inoffensive beauty, and to help the other women to do likewise. Too, she would help them with their clothes, tactfully point out that sunbonnets, no matter how gay, and aprons, no matter how frilly, were not quite the proper things for Sunday church wear. There would be a sewing circle. She visualized herself instructing the children, who seemed most of the time to run wild, in ways of gentler deportment. She was anxious to be a true helpmate, for in her heart was a feeling of obligation, of humble gratitude.

In her ardor and sincerity Helga even made some small beginnings. True, she was not very successful in this matter of innovations. When she went about to try to interest the women in what she considered more appropriate clothing and in inexpensive ways of improving their homes according to her ideas of beauty, she was met, always, with smiling agreement and good-natured promises. "Yuh all is right, Mis' Green," and "Ah suttinly will, Mis' Green," fell courteously on her ear at each visit.

She was unaware that afterwards they would shake their heads sullenly over their wash-tubs and ironing-boards. And that among themselves they talked with amusement, or with anger, of "dat uppity, meddlin' No'the'n-ah," and "pore Reve'end," who in their opinion "would 'a done bettah to a ma'ied Clementine Richards." Knowing, as she did, nothing of this, Helga was unperturbed. But even had she known, she would not have been disheartened. The fact that it was difficult but increased her eagerness, and made the doing of it seem only the more worth while. Sometimes she would smile to think how changed she was.

And she was humble too. Even with Clementine Richards, a strapping black beauty of magnificent Amazon proportions and bold shining eyes of jet-like hardness. A person of awesome appearance. All chains, strings of beads, jingling bracelets, flying ribbons, feathery neck-pieces, and flowery hats. Clementine was inclined to treat Helga with an only partially concealed contemptuousness, considering her a poor thing without style, and without proper understanding of the worth and greatness of the man, Clementine's own adored pastor, whom Helga had somehow had the astounding good luck to marry. Clementine's admiration of the Reverend Mr. Pleasant Green was open. Helga was at first astonished. Until she learned that there was really no reason why it should be concealed. Everybody was aware of it. Besides, open adoration was the prerogative, the almost religious duty, of the female portion of the flock. If this unhidden and exaggerated approval contributed to his already oversized pomposity, so much the better. It was what they expected, liked, wanted. The greater his own sense of superiority became, the more flattered they were by his notice and small attentions, the more they cast at him killing glances, the more they hung enraptured on his words.

In the days before her conversion, with its subsequent blurring of her sense of humor, Helga might have amused herself by tracing the relation of this constant ogling and flattering on the proverbially large families of preachers; the often disastrous effect on their wives of this constant stirring of the senses by extraneous women. Now, however, she did not even think of it.

She was too busy. Every minute of the day was full. Necessarily. And to Helga this was a new experience. She was charmed by it. To be mistress in one's own house, to have a garden, and chickens, and a pig; to have a husband—and to be "right with God"—what pleasure did that other world which she had left contain that could surpass these? Here, she had found, she was sure, the intangible thing for which, indefinitely, always she had craved. It had received embodiment.

Everything contributed to her gladness in living. And so for a time she loved everything and everyone. Or thought she did. Even the weather. And it was truly lovely. By day a glittering gold sun was set in an unbelievably bright sky. In the evening silver buds sprouted in a Chinese blue sky, and the warm day was softly soothed by a slight, cool breeze. And night! Night, when a languid moon peeped through the wide-opened windows of her little house, a little mockingly, it may be. Always at night's approach Helga was bewildered by a disturbing medley of feelings. Challenge. Anticipation. And a small fear.

In the morning she was serene again. Peace had returned. And she could go happily, inexpertly, about the humble tasks of her household, cooking, dish-washing, sweeping, dusting, mending, and darning. And there was the garden. When she worked there, she felt that life was utterly filled with the glory and the marvel of God.

Helga did not reason about this feeling, as she did not at that time reason about anything. It was enough that it was there, coloring all her thoughts and acts. It endowed the four rooms of her ugly brown house with a kindly radiance, obliterating the stark bareness of its white plaster walls and the nakedness of its uncovered painted floors. It even softened the choppy lines of the shiny oak furniture and subdued the awesome horribleness of the religious pictures.

And all the other houses and cabins shared in this illumination. And the people. The dark undecorated women unceasingly concerned with the actual business of life, its rounds of births and christenings, of loves and marriages, of deaths and funerals, were to Helga miraculously beautiful. The smallest, dirtiest, brown child, barefooted in the fields or muddy roads, was to her an emblem of the wonder of life, of love, and of God's goodness.

For the preacher, her husband, she had a feeling of gratitude, amounting almost to sin. Beyond that, she thought of him not at all. But she was not conscious that she had shut him out from her mind. Besides, what need to think of him? He was there. She was at peace, and secure. Surely their two lives were one, and the companionship in the Lord's grace so perfect that to think about it would be tempting providence. She had done with soul-searching.

What did it matter that he consumed his food, even the softest varieties, audibly? What did it matter that, though he did no work with his hands, not even in the garden, his fingernails were always rimmed with black? What did it matter that he failed to wash his fat body, or to shift his clothing, as often as Helga herself did? There were things that more than outweighed these. In the certainty of his goodness, his righteousness, his holiness, Helga somehow overcame her first disgust at the odor of sweat and stale garments. She was even able to be unaware of it. Herself, Helga had come to look upon as a finicky, showy thing of unnecessary prejudices and fripperies. And when she sat in the dreary structure, which had once been a stable belonging to the estate of a wealthy horse-racing man and about which the odor of manure still clung, now the church and social center of the Negroes of the town, and heard him expound with verbal extravagance the gospel of blood and love, of hell and heaven, of fire and gold streets, pounding with clenched fists the frail table before him or shaking those fists in the faces of the congregation like direct personal threats, or pacing wildly back and forth and even sometimes shedding great tears as he besought them to repent, she was, she told herself, proud and gratified that he belonged to her. In some strange way she was able to ignore the atmosphere of self-satisfaction which poured from him like gas from a leaking pipe.

And night came at the end of every day. Emotional, palpitating, amorous, all that was living in her sprang like rank weeds at the tingling thought of night, with a vitality so strong that it devoured all shoots of reason.

23

After the first exciting months Helga was too driven, too occupied, and too sick to carry out any of the things for which she had made such enthusiastic plans, or even to care that she had made only slight progress toward their accomplishment. For she, who had never thought of her body save as something on which to hang lovely fabrics, had now constantly to think of it. It had persistently to be pampered to secure from it even a little service. Always she felt extraordinarily and annoyingly ill, having forever to be sinking into chairs. Or, if she was out, to be pausing by the roadside, clinging desperately to some convenient fence or tree, waiting for the horrible nausea and hateful faintness to pass. The light, care-free days of the past, when she had not felt heavy and reluctant or weak and spent, receded more and more and with increasing vagueness, like a dream passing from a faulty memory.

The children used her up. There were already three of them, all born within the short space of twenty months. Two great healthy twin boys, whose lovely bodies were to Helga like rare figures carved out of amber, and in whose sleepy and mysterious black eyes all that was puzzling, evasive, and aloof in life seemed to find expression. No matter how often or how long she looked at these two small sons of hers, never did she lose a certain delicious feeling in which were mingled pride, tenderness, and exaltation. And there was a girl, sweet, delicate, and flower-like. Not so healthy or so loved as the boys, but still miraculously her own proud and cherished possession.

So there was no time for the pursuit of beauty, or for the uplifting of other harassed and teeming women, or for the instruction of their neglected children.

Her husband was still, as he had always been, deferentially kind and incredulously proud of her—and verbally encouraging. Helga tried not to see that he had rather lost any personal interest in her, except for the short spaces between the times when she was preparing for or recovering from childbirth. She shut her eyes to the fact that his encouragement had become a little platitudinous, limited mostly to "The Lord will look out for you," "We must accept what God sends," or "My mother had nine children and was thankful for every one." If she was inclined to wonder a little just how they were to manage with another child on the way, he would point out to her that her doubt and uncertainty were a stupendous ingratitude. Had not the good God saved her soul from hell-fire and eternal damnation? Had He not in His great kindness given her three small lives to raise up for His glory? Had He not showered her with numerous other mercies (evidently too numerous to be named separately)?

"You must," the Reverend Mr. Pleasant Green would say unctuously, "trust the Lord more fully, Helga."

This pabulum[8] did not irritate her. Perhaps it was the fact that the preacher was, now, not so much at home that even lent to it a measure of real comfort. For the adoring women of his flock, noting how with increasing frequency their pastor's house went unswept and undusted, his children unwashed, and his wife untidy, took pleasant pity on him and invited him often to tasty orderly meals, specially prepared for him, in their own clean houses.

Helga, looking about in helpless dismay and sick disgust at the disorder around her, the permanent assembly of partly emptied medicine bottles on the clock-shelf, the perpetual array of drying baby-clothes on the chair-backs, the constant debris of broken toys on the floor, the unceasing litter of half-dead flowers on the table, dragged in by the toddling twins from the forlorn

---

8. Baby food.

garden, failed to blame him for the thoughtless selfishness of these absences. And, she was thankful, whenever possible, to be relieved from the ordeal of cooking. There were times when, having had to retreat from the kitchen in lumbering haste with her sensitive nose gripped between tightly squeezing fingers, she had been sure that the greatest kindness that God could ever show to her would be to free her forever from the sight and smell of food.

How, she wondered, did other women, other mothers, manage? Could it be possible that, while presenting such smiling and contented faces, they were all always on the edge of health? All always worn out and apprehensive? Or was it only she, a poor weak city-bred thing, who felt that the strain of what the Reverend Mr. Pleasant Green had so often gently and patiently reminded her was a natural thing, an act of God, was almost unendurable?

One day on her round of visiting—a church duty, to be done no matter how miserable one was—she summoned up sufficient boldness to ask several women how they felt, how they managed. The answers were a resigned shrug, or an amused snort, or an upward rolling of eyeballs with a mention of "de Lawd" looking after us all.

" 'Tain't nothin', nothin' at all, chile," said one, Sary Jones, who, as Helga knew, had had six children in about as many years. "Yuh all takes it too ha'd. Jes' remembah et's natu'al fo' a 'oman to hab chilluns an' don' fret so."

"But," protested Helga, "I'm always so tired and half sick. That can't be natural."

"Laws, chile, we's all ti'ed. An' Ah reckons we's all gwine a be ti'ed till kingdom come. Jes' make de bes' of et, honey. Jes' make de bes' yuh can."

Helga sighed, turning her nose away from the steaming coffee which her hostess had placed for her and against which her squeamish stomach was about to revolt. At the moment the compensations of immorality seemed very shadowy and very far away.

"Jes' remembah," Sary went on, staring sternly into Helga's thin face, "we all gits ouah res' by an' by. In de nex' worl' we's all recompense'. Jes' put yo' trus' in de Sabioah."[9]

Looking at the confident face of the little bronze figure on the opposite side of the immaculately spread table, Helga had a sensation of shame that she should be less than content. Why couldn't she be as trusting and as certain that her troubles would not overwhelm her as Sary Jones was? Sary, who in all likelihood had toiled every day of her life since early childhood except on those days, totalling perhaps sixty, following the birth of her six children. And who by dint of superhuman saving had somehow succeeded in feeding and clothing them and sending them all to school. Before her Helga felt humbled and oppressed by the sense of her own unworthiness and lack of sufficient faith.

"Thanks, Sary," she said, rising in retreat from the coffee, "you've done me a world of good. I'm really going to try to be more patient."

So, though with growing yearning she longed for the great ordinary things of life, hunger, sleep, freedom from pain, she resigned herself to the doing without them. The possibility of alleviating her burdens by a greater faith became lodged in her mind. She gave herself up to it. It *did* help. And the beauty of leaning on the wisdom of God, of trusting, gave to her a queer sort

9. Savior (dialect).

of satisfaction. Faith was really quite easy. One had only to yield. To ask no questions. The more weary, the more weak, she became, the easier it was. Her religion was to her a kind of protective coloring, shielding her from the cruel light of an unbearable reality.

This utter yielding in faith to what had been sent her found her favor, too, in the eyes of her neighbors. Her husband's flock began to approve and commend this submission and humility to a superior wisdom. The womenfolk spoke more kindly and more affectionately of the preacher's Northern wife. "Pore Mis' Green, wid all dem small chilluns at once. She suah do hab it ha'd. An' she don' nebah complains an' frets no mo'e. Jes' trus' in de Lawd lak de Good Book say. Mighty sweet lil' 'oman too."

Helga didn't bother much about the preparations for the coming child. Actually and metaphorically she bowed her head before God, trusting in Him to see her through. Secretly she was glad that she had not to worry about herself or anything. It was a relief to be able to put the entire responsibility on someone else.

24

It began, this next child-bearing, during the morning services of a breathless hot Sunday while the fervent choir soloist was singing: "Ah am freed of mah sorrow," and lasted far into the small hours of Tuesday morning. It seemed, for some reason, not to go off just right. And when, after that long frightfulness, the fourth little dab of amber humanity which Helga had contributed to a despised race was held before her for maternal approval, she failed entirely to respond properly to this sop of consolation for the suffering and horror through which she had passed. There was from her no pleased, proud smile, no loving, possessive gesture, no manifestation of interest in the important matters of sex and weight. Instead she deliberately closed her eyes, mutely shutting out the sickly infant, its smiling father, the soiled midwife, the curious neighbors, and the tousled room.

A week she lay so. Silent and listless. Ignoring food, the clamoring children, the comings and goings of solicitous, kind-hearted women, her hovering husband, and all of life about her. The neighbors were puzzled. The Reverend Mr. Pleasant Green was worried. The midwife was frightened.

On the floor, in and out among the furniture and under her bed, the twins played. Eager to help, the church-women crowded in and, meeting there others on the same laudable errand, stayed to gossip and to wonder. Anxiously the preacher sat, Bible in hand, beside his wife's bed, or in a nervous half-guilty manner invited the congregated parishioners to join him in prayer for the healing of their sister. Then, kneeling, they would beseech God to stretch out His all-powerful hand on behalf of the afflicted one, softly at first, but with rising vehemence, accompanied by moans and tears, until it seemed that the God to whom they prayed must in mercy to the sufferer grant relief. If only so that she might rise up and escape from the tumult, the heat, and the smell.

Helga, however, was unconcerned, undisturbed by the commotion about her. It was all part of the general unreality. Nothing reached her. Nothing penetrated the kind darkness into which her bruised spirit had retreated.

Even that red-letter event, the coming to see her of the old white physician from downtown, who had for a long time stayed talking gravely to her husband, drew from her no interest. Nor for days was she aware that a stranger, a nurse from Mobile, had been added to her household, a brusquely efficient woman who produced order out of chaos and quiet out of bedlam. Neither did the absence of the children, removed by good neighbors at Miss Hartley's insistence, impress her. While she had gone down into that appalling blackness of pain, the ballast of her brain had got loose and she hovered for a long time somewhere in that delightful borderland on the edge of unconsciousness, an enchanted and blissful place where peace and incredible quiet encompassed her.

After weeks she grew better, returned to earth, set her reluctant feet to the hard path of life again.

"Well, here you are!" announced Miss Hartley in her slightly harsh voice one afternoon just before the fall of evening. She had for some time been standing at the bedside gazing down at Helga with an intent speculative look.

"Yes," Helga agreed in a thin little voice, "I'm back." The truth was that she had been back for some hours. Purposely she had lain silent and still, wanting to linger forever in that serene haven, that effortless calm where nothing was expected of her. There she could watch the figures of the past drift by. There was her mother, whom she had loved from a distance and finally so scornfully blamed, who appeared as she had always remembered her, unbelievably beautiful, young, and remote. Robert Anderson, questioning, purposely detached, affecting, as she realized now, her life in a remarkably cruel degree; for at last she understood clearly how deeply, how passionately, she must have loved him. Anne, lovely, secure, wise, selfish. Axel Olsen, conceited, worldly, spoiled. Audrey Denney, placid, taking quietly and without fuss the things which she wanted. James Vayle, snobbish, smug, servile. Mrs. Hayes-Rore, important, kind, determined. The Dahls, rich, correct, climbing. Flashingly, fragmentarily, other long-forgotten figures, women in gay fashionable frocks and men in formal black and white, glided by in bright rooms to distant, vaguely familiar music.

It was refreshingly delicious, this immersion in the past. But it was finished now. It was over. The words of her husband, the Reverend Mr. Pleasant Green, who had been standing at the window looking mournfully out at the scorched melon-patch, ruined because Helga had been ill so long and unable to tend it, were confirmation of that.

"The Lord be praised," he said, and came forward. It was distinctly disagreeable. It was even more disagreeable to feel his moist hand on hers. A cold shiver brushed over her. She closed her eyes. Obstinately and with all her small strength she drew her hand away from him. Hid it far down under the bedcovering, and turned her face away to hide a grimace of unconquerable aversion. She cared nothing, at that moment, for his hurt surprise. She knew only that, in the hideous agony that for interminable hours—no, centuries— she had borne, the luster of religion had vanished; that revulsion had come upon her; that she hated this man. Between them the vastness of the universe had come.

Miss Hartley, all-seeing and instantly aware of a situation, as she had been quite aware that her patient had been conscious for some time before she herself had announced the fact, intervened, saying firmly: "I think it might be better if you didn't try to talk to her now. She's terribly sick and weak yet. She's still got some fever and we mustn't excite her or she's liable to slip back. And we don't want that, do we?"

No, the man, her husband, responded, they didn't want that. Reluctantly he went from the room with a last look at Helga, who was lying on her back with one frail, pale hand under her small head, her curly black hair scattered loose on the pillow. She regarded him from behind dropped lids. The day was hot, her breasts were covered only by a nightgown of filmy *crêpe*, a relic of prematrimonial days, which had slipped from one carved shoulder. He flinched. Helga's petulant lip curled, for she well knew that this fresh reminder of her desirability was like the flick of a whip.

Miss Hartley carefully closed the door after the retreating husband. "It's time," she said, "for your evening treatment, and then you've got to try to sleep for a while. No more visitors tonight."

Helga nodded and tried unsuccessfully to make a little smile. She was glad of Miss Hartley's presence. It would, she felt, protect her from so much. She mustn't, she thought to herself, get well too fast. Since it seemed she was going to get well. In bed she could think, could have a certain amount of quiet. Of aloneness.

In that period of racking pain and calamitous fright Helga had learned what passion and credulity could do to one. In her was born angry bitterness and an enormous disgust. The cruel, unrelieved suffering had beaten down her protective wall of artificial faith in the infinite wisdom, in the mercy, of God. For had she not called in her agony on Him? And He had not heard. Why? Because, she knew now, He wasn't there. Didn't exist. Into that yawning gap of unspeakable brutality had gone, too, her belief in the miracle and wonder of life. Only scorn, resentment, and hate remained—and ridicule. Life wasn't a miracle, a wonder. It was, for Negroes at least, only a great disappointment. Something to be got through with as best one could. No one was interested in them or helped them. God! Bah! And they were only a nuisance to other people.

Everything in her mind was hot and cold, beating and swirling about. Within her emaciated body raged disillusion. Chaotic turmoil. With the obscuring curtain of religion rent, she was able to look about her and see with shocked eyes this thing that she had done to herself. She couldn't, she thought ironically, even blame God for it, now that she knew that He didn't exist. No. No more than she could pray to Him for the death of her husband, the Reverend Mr. Pleasant Green. The white man's God. And His great love for all people regardless of race! What idiotic nonsense she had allowed herself to believe. How could she, how could anyone, have been so deluded? How could ten million black folk credit it when daily before their eyes was enacted its contradiction? Not that she at all cared about the ten million. But herself. Her sons. Her daughter. These would grow to manhood, to womanhood, in this vicious, this hypocritical land. The dark eyes filled with tears.

"I wouldn't," the nurse advised, "do that. You've been dreadfully sick, you know. I can't have you worrying. Time enough for that when you're well. Now you must sleep all you possibly can."

Helga did sleep. She found it surprisingly easy to sleep. Aided by Miss Hartley's rather masterful discernment, she took advantage of the ease with which this blessed enchantment stole over her. From her husband's praisings, prayers, and caresses she sought refuge in sleep, and from the neighbors' gifts, advice, and sympathy.

There was that day on which they told her that the last sickly infant, born of such futile torture and lingering torment, had died after a short week of slight living. Just closed his eyes and died. No vitality. On hearing it Helga too had just closed her eyes. Not to die. She was convinced that before her there were years of living. Perhaps of happiness even. For a new idea had come to her. She had closed her eyes to shut in any telltale gleam of the relief which she felt. One less. And she had gone off into sleep.

And there was that Sunday morning on which the Reverend Mr. Pleasant Green had informed her that they were that day to hold a special thanksgiving service for her recovery. There would, he said, be prayers, special testimonies, and songs. Was there anything particular she would like to have said, to have prayed for, to have sung? Helga had smiled from sheer amusement as she replied that there was nothing. Nothing at all. She only hoped that they would enjoy themselves. And, closing her eyes that he might be discouraged from longer tarrying, she had gone off into sleep.

Waking later to the sound of joyous religious abandon floating in through the opened windows, she had asked a little diffidently that she be allowed to read. Miss Hartley's sketchy brows contracted into a dubious frown. After a judicious pause she had answered: "No, I don't think so." Then, seeing the rebellious tears which had sprung into her patient's eyes, she added kindly: "But I'll read to you a little if you like."

That, Helga replied, would be nice. In the next room on a high-up shelf was a book. She'd forgotten the name, but its author was Anatole France.[1] There was a story, "The Procurator of Judea."[2] Would Miss Hartley read that? "Thanks. Thanks awfully."

" 'Lælius Lamia, born in Italy of illustrious parents,' " began the nurse in her slightly harsh voice.

Helga drank it in.

" ' . . . For to this day the women bring down doves to the altar as their victims. . . . ' "

Helga closed her eyes.

" ' . . . . Africa and Asia have already enriched us with a considerable number of gods. . . . ' "

Miss Hartley looked up. Helga had slipped into slumber while the superbly ironic ending which she had so desired to hear was yet a long way off. A dull tale, was Miss Hartley's opinion, as she curiously turned the pages to see how it turned out.

" 'Jesus? . . . Jesus—of Nazareth? I cannot call him to mind.' "

"Huh!" she muttered, puzzled. "Silly." And closed the book.

1. Pseudonym of Jacques-Anatole-François Thibault (1844–1924), French novelist, story writer, and critic, winner of the 1921 Nobel Prize for literature.

2. A cynical story (1892) in which the aged Pontius Pilate does not remember Jesus the Nazarine, whom he had condemned to death years before.

25

During the long process of getting well, between the dreamy intervals when she was beset by the insistent craving for sleep, Helga had had too much time to think. At first she had felt only an astonished anger at the quagmire in which she had engulfed herself. She had ruined her life. Made it impossible ever again to do the things that she wanted, have the things that she loved, mingle with the people she liked. She had, to put it as brutally as anyone could, been a fool. The damnedest kind of a fool. And she had paid for it. Enough. More than enough.

Her mind, swaying back to the protection that religion had afforded her, almost she wished that it had not failed her. An illusion. Yes. But better, far better, than this terrible reality. Religion had, after all, its uses. It blunted the perceptions. Robbed life of its crudest truths. Especially it had its uses for the poor—and the blacks.

For the blacks. The Negroes.

And this, Helga decided, was what ailed the whole Negro race in America, this fatuous belief in the white man's God, this childlike trust in full compensation for all woes and privations in "kingdom come." Sary Jones's absolute conviction, "In de nex' worl' we's all recompense'," came back to her. And ten million souls were as sure of it as was Sary. How the white man's God must laugh at the great joke he had played on them! Bound them to slavery, then to poverty and insult, and made them bear it unresistingly, uncomplainingly almost, by sweet promises of mansions in the sky by and by.

"Pie in the sky," Helga said aloud derisively, forgetting for the moment Miss Hartley's brisk presence, and so was a little startled at hearing her voice from the adjoining room saying severely: "My goodness! No! I should say you can't have pie. It's too indigestible. Maybe when you're better—"

"That," assented Helga, "is what I said. Pie—by and by. That's the trouble."

The nurse looked concerned. Was this an approaching relapse? Coming to the bedside, she felt at her patient's pulse while giving her a searching look. No. "You'd better," she admonished, a slight edge to her tone, "try to get a little nap. You haven't had any sleep today, and you can't get too much of it. You've got to get strong, you know."

With this Helga was in full agreement. It seemed hundreds of years since she had been strong. And she would need strength. For in some way she was determined to get herself out of this bog into which she had strayed. Or—she would have to die. She couldn't endure it. Her suffocation and shrinking loathing were too great. Not to be borne. Again. For she had to admit that it wasn't new, this feeling of dissatisfaction, of asphyxiation. Something like it she had experienced before. In Naxos. In New York. In Copenhagen. This differed only in degree. And it was of the present and therefore seemingly more reasonable. The other revulsions were of the past, and now less explainable.

The thought of her husband roused in her a deep and contemptuous hatred. At his every approach she had forcibly to subdue a furious inclination to scream out in protest. Shame, too, swept over her at every thought of her marriage. Marriage. This sacred thing of which parsons and other Christian folk ranted so sanctimoniously, how immoral—according to their own standards—it could be! But Helga felt also a modicum of pity for him, as for one already abandoned. She meant to leave him. And it was, she had to concede, all of her own doing, this marriage. Nevertheless, she hated him.

The neighbors and churchfolk came in for their share of her all-embracing hatred. She hated their raucous laughter, their stupid acceptance of all things, and their unfailing trust in "de Lawd." And more than all the rest she hated the jangling Clementine Richards, with her provocative smirkings, because she had not succeeded in marrying the preacher and thus saving her, Helga, from that crowning idiocy.

Of the children Helga tried not to think. She wanted not to leave them— if that were possible. The recollection of her own childhood, lonely, unloved, rose too poignantly before her for her to consider calmly such a solution. Though she forced herself to believe that this was different. There was not the element of race, of white and black. They were all black together. And they would have their father. But to leave them would be a tearing agony, a rending of deepest fibers. She felt that through all the rest of her lifetime she would be hearing their cry of "Mummy, Mummy, Mummy," through sleepless nights. No. She couldn't desert them.

How, then, was she to escape from the oppression, the degradation, that her life had become? It was so difficult. It was terribly difficult. It was almost hopeless. So for a while—for the immediate present, she told herself—she put aside the making of any plan for her going. "I'm still," she reasoned, "too weak, too sick. By and by, when I'm really strong—"

It was so easy and so pleasant to think about freedom and cities, about clothes and books, about the sweet mingled smell of Houbigant[3] and cigarettes in softly lighted rooms filled with inconsequential chatter and laughter and sophisticated tuneless music. It was so hard to think out a feasible way of retrieving all these agreeable, desired things. Just then. Later. When she got up. By and by. She must rest. Get strong. Sleep. Then, afterwards, she could work out some arrangement. So she dozed and dreamed in snatches of sleeping and waking, letting time run on. Away.

And hardly had she left her bed and become able to walk again without pain, hardly had the children returned from the homes of the neighbors, when she began to have her fifth child.

1928

---

3. A French perfume.

EDNA ST. VINCENT MILLAY
1892–1950

Edna St. Vincent Millay's output ranged from Elizabethan sonnets through plays and sketches to political speeches. In the 1920s she became a kind of national symbol of the modern woman—liberated from Victorian mores, independent, self-supporting, full of energy and talent. She was raised in a small town on the coast of Maine by her divorced mother, who supported herself and three daughters through work as a practical nurse. The mother provided her children with books and music lessons and encouraged ambition and independence. Millay began to write poetry in high school and published her first book of poetry, *Renascence and Other Poems,* in 1917, when she was twenty-five. She went to Vassar College from 1913 to 1917 through the generosity of a benefactor impressed by her writing. At Vassar she studied languages, wrote songs and verse plays, and became interested in acting. After graduation she went to New York City, settling in the Greenwich Village section of the city and becoming associated with the unconventional life of the literary and political rebels who lived there. A member of the Provincetown Players group, she acted and also wrote two plays for them. *The Ballad of the Harp-Weaver* (1923, later retitled *The Harp-Weaver and Other Poems*) was awarded a Pulitzer Prize.

Millay lived in Europe from 1921 to 1923 and, upon her return, married and moved with her businessman husband Eugene Boissevain to a farm in upstate New York. She participated in the protests against the executions of Sacco and Vanzetti in 1927 and during the 1930s wrote anti-fascist newspaper verse, radio plays, and speeches. She was an advocate of early U.S. entrance into World War II.

Although as a young woman Millay achieved notoriety mainly for love poetry that described free, guiltless sexuality, her poems are more founded in the failure of love than in the joy of sex. The tone of her earliest work was flippantly cynical; later work became more muted and lyrical. Her New England poems, about nature and the familiar, fit into a regional tradition. Working with closed stanza forms and regular metrical lines, she displayed a high degree of technical virtuosity within quite deliberately chosen limits. "I will put chaos into fourteen lines," she wrote in one sonnet, joining the traditionalists like Robert Frost in a devotion to poetry as permanence.

The text of the poems included here is that of *Collected Poems: Edna St. Vincent Millay* (1956).

Recuerdo[1]

We were very tired, we were very merry—
We had gone back and forth all night on the ferry.
It was bare and bright, and smelled like a stable—
But we looked into a fire, we leaned across a table,
We lay on a hill-top underneath the moon;   5
And the whistles kept blowing, and the dawn came soon.

We were very tired, we were very merry—
We had gone back and forth all night on the ferry;
And you ate an apple, and I ate a pear,
From a dozen of each we had bought somewhere;   10
And the sky went wan, and the wind came cold,
And the sun rose dripping, a bucketful of gold.

We were very tired, we were very merry,
We had gone back and forth all night on the ferry.
We hailed, "Good morrow, mother!" to a shawl-covered head,   15
And bought a morning paper, which neither of us read;
And she wept, "God bless you!" for the apples and pears,
And we gave her all our money but our subway fares.

                                                                        1922

1. Remembrance, souvenir.

I Think I Should Have Loved You Presently

I think I should have loved you presently,
And given in earnest words I flung in jest;
And lifted honest eyes for you to see,
And caught your hand against my cheek and breast;
And all my pretty follies flung aside   5
That won you to me, and beneath your gaze,
Naked of reticence and shorn of pride,
Spread like a chart my little wicked ways.
I, that had been to you, had you remained,
But one more waking from a recurrent dream,   10
Cherish no less the certain stakes I gained,
And walk your memory's halls, austere, supreme,
A ghost in marble of a girl you knew
Who would have loved you in a day or two.

1922

[I, being born a woman]

I, being born a woman and distressed
By all the needs and notions of my kind,
Am urged by your propinquity to find
Your person fair, and feel a certain zest
To bear your body's weight upon my breast: 5
So subtly is the fume of life designed,
To clarify the pulse and cloud the mind,
And leave me once again undone, possessed.
Think not for this, however, the poor treason
Of my stout blood against my staggering brain,   10
I shall remember you with love, or season
My scorn with pity,—let me make it plain:
I find this frenzy insufficient reason
For conversation when we meet again.

1923

Apostrophe to Man

(On reflecting that the world is ready to go to war again)

Detestable race, continue to expunge yourself, die out.
Breed faster, crowd, encroach, sing hymns, build bombing airplanes;
Make speeches, unveil statues, issue bonds, parade;
Convert again into explosives the bewildered ammonia and the distracted
     cellulose;
Convert again into putrescent matter drawing flies   5

The hopeful bodies of the young; exhort,
Pray, pull long faces, be earnest, be all but overcome, be photographed;
Confer, perfect your formulae, commercialize
Bacteria harmful to human tissue,
Put death on the market;   10
Breed, crowd, encroach, expand, expunge yourself, die out,
Homo called *sapiens*.

                                                                                    1934

I Too beneath Your Moon, Almighty Sex

I too beneath your moon, almighty Sex,
Go forth at nightfall crying like a cat,
Leaving the lofty tower I laboured at
For birds to foul and boys and girls to vex
With tittering chalk; and you, and the long necks   5
Of neighbours sitting where their mothers sat
Are well aware of shadowy this and that
In me, that's neither noble nor complex.
Such as I am, however, I have brought
To what it is, this tower; it is my own;   10
Though it was reared To Beauty, it was wrought
From what I had to build with: honest bone
Is there, and anguish; pride; and burning thought;
And lust is there, and nights not spent alone.

                                                                                    1939

The Snow Storm

No hawk hangs over in this air:
The urgent snow is everywhere.
The wing adroiter than a sail
Must lean away from such a gale,
Abandoning its straight intent,   5
Or else expose tough ligament
And tender flesh to what before
Meant dampened feathers, nothing more.

Forceless upon our backs there fall
Infrequent flakes hexagonal,   10
Devised in many a curious style
To charm our safety for a while,
Where close to earth like mice we go
Under the horizontal snow.

                                                                                    1939

I Forgot for a Moment

July 1940

I forgot for a moment France; I forgot England; I forgot my care:
I lived for a moment in a world where I was free to be
With the things and people that I love, and I was happy there.
I forgot for a moment Holland, I forgot my heavy care.

I lived for a moment in a world so lovely, so inept   5
At twisted words and crookèd deeds, it was as if I slept and dreamt.

It seemed that all was well with Holland—not a tank had crushed
The tulips there.
Mile after mile the level lowlands blossomed—yellow square,
      white square,
Scarlet strip and mauve strip bright beneath the brightly clouded sky,
      the round clouds and the gentle air.   10
Along the straight canals between striped fields of tulips in the
      morning sailed
Broad ships, their hulls by tulip-beds concealed, only the sails showing.

It seemed that all was well with England—the harsh foreign voice
      hysterically vowing,
Once more, to keep its word, at length was disbelieved, and hushed.

It seemed that all was well with France, with her straight roads   15
Lined with slender poplars, and the peasants on the skyline ploughing.

1940

E. E. CUMMINGS
1894–1962

Beginning in the 1920s and 1930s, Edward Estlin Cummings built a reputation as author of a particularly agreeable kind of modernist poetry, distinguished by clever formal innovation, a tender lyricism, and the thematic celebration of individuals against mass society. These qualities were evident in his first literary success, a zesty prose account of his experience in a French prison camp during World War I, *The Enormous Room* (1922; see p. 1379). He and a friend had joined the ambulance corps in France the day after the United States entered the war; their disdain for the bureaucracy, expressed in outspoken letters home, aroused antagonism among French officials and they were imprisoned. To be made a prisoner by one's own side struck Cummings as outrageous and yet funny; from the experience he produced an ironic, profane celebration of the ordinary soldier and an attack on bureaucracy. His poetry continued the attack on depersonalized, commercial, exploitative mass culture and celebrated loners, lovers, and nonconformists.

He was born in Cambridge, Massachusetts. His father was a Congregationalist minister and teacher at Harvard; the family was close knit and Cummings, a much-loved son. While a student at Harvard (he graduated in 1915 and took an M.A. in 1916) he began to write poetry based on the intricate stanza patterns of the pre-Raphaelite and Metaphysical writers he was reading in English literature classes. When he began to innovate—as he did after discovering the poetry of Ezra Pound—he was able to build (like Pound himself) from a firm apprenticeship in traditional techniques.

After the war, Cummings established a life that included a studio in Greenwich Village, travel and sojourns in France, and summers at the family home in New Hampshire. He was a painter as well as a poet; simple living and careful management of a small allowance from his mother, along with prizes, royalties, and commissions, enabled him to work full time as an artist. He published four volumes of well-received poetry in the 1920s and a book of collected poems toward the end of the 1930s. In the 1950s he visited and read at many college campuses, where students enjoyed his tricks of verse and vocabulary and appreciated his tender yet earthy poetry. He received a special citation by the National Book Award committee in 1955 and the Bollingen Prize in 1957.

Cummings was less ambitious in his attempts to reshape poetry than Stein, Eliot, Pound, Stevens, or Williams, partly because he was much more concerned to be widely accessible. Cummings's verse is characterized by common speech and attention to the visual form of the poem—that is, the poem as it appears on the page as distinguished from its sound when read aloud. Experiments with capitalization or lack of it, punctuation, line breaks, hyphenation, and verse shapes were all carried out for the reader's eyes rather than ears. To express his sense that life was always in process, he wrote untitled poems without beginnings and endings, consisting of fragmentary lines. There is always humor in his poetry, and his outrage at cruelty and exploitation is balanced with gusto and celebration of the body.

The text of the poems included here is that of *Complete Poems* (1991).

Thy fingers make early flowers of

Thy fingers make early flowers of
all things.
thy hair mostly the hours love:
a smoothness which
sings,saying   5
(though love be a day)
do not fear,we will go amaying.

thy whitest feet crisply are straying.
Always
thy moist eyes are at kisses playing,   10
whose strangeness much
says;singing
(though love be a day)
for which girl art thou flowers bringing?

To be thy lips is a sweet thing   15
and small.
Death,Thee i call rich beyond wishing
if this thou catch,
else missing.
(though love be a day   20
and life be nothing,it shall not stop kissing).

1923

in Just-

in Just-
spring   when the world is mud-
luscious the little
lame balloonman

whistles   far   and wee   5

and eddieandbill come
running from marbles and
piracies and it's
spring

when the world is puddle-wonderful   10

the queer
old balloonman whistles
far   and   wee
and bettyandisbel come dancing

from hop-scotch and jump-rope and   15

it's
spring
and
    the

        goat-footed   20

balloonMan   whistles
far
and
wee

                        1920, 1923

O sweet spontaneous

O sweet spontaneous
earth how often have
the
doting

    fingers of   5
prurient philosophers pinched
and
poked

thee
,has the naughty thumb   10
of science prodded
thy

    beauty   .how
often have religions taken
thee upon their scraggy knees   15
squeezing and

buffeting thee that thou mightest conceive
gods
    (but
true   20

to the incomparable
couch of death thy
rhythmic
lover

    thou answerest   25

them only with

    spring)

                1920, 1923

Buffalo Bill 's

Buffalo Bill 's[1]
defunct
    who used to
    ride a watersmooth-silver
            stallion   5
and break onetwothreefourfive pigeonsjustlikethat
                Jesus

he was a handsome man
         and what i want to know is
how do you like your blueeyed boy   10
Mister Death

                1920, 1923

---

1. William F. Cody (1846–1917), American scout and Wild West showman.

the Cambridge ladies who live in furnished souls

the Cambridge ladies who live in furnished souls
are unbeautiful and have comfortable minds
(also,with the church's protestant blessings
daughters,unscented shapeless spirited)
they believe in Christ and Longfellow, both dead,[1]   5
are invariably interested in so many things—
at the present writing one still finds
delighted fingers knitting for the is it Poles?
perhaps. While permanent faces coyly bandy
scandal of Mrs. N and Professor D   10
. . . . the Cambridge ladies do not care,above
Cambridge if sometimes in its box of
sky lavender and cornerless,the
moon rattles like a fragment of angry candy

1923

"next to of course god america i

"next to of course god america i
love you land of the pilgrims' and so forth oh
say can you see by the dawn's early my
country 'tis of centuries come and go
and are no more what of it we should worry   5
in every language even deafanddumb
thy sons acclaim your glorious name by gorry
by jingo by gee by gosh by gum
why talk of beauty what could be more beautiful than these heroic happy dead   10
who rushed like lions to the roaring slaughter
they did not stop to think they died instead
then shall the voice of liberty be mute?"

He spoke.   And drank rapidly a glass of water

1926

i sing of Olaf glad and big

i sing of Olaf glad and big
whose warmest heart recoiled at war:
a conscientious object-or

his wellbelovéd colonel(trig
westpointer[1] most succinctly bred)   5

1. Henry Wadsworth Longfellow (1807–1882), American poet often used as a symbol for traditionalist writing and values. He was a professor of romance languages at Harvard University in Cambridge, Massachusetts.
1. Graduate of the U.S. Military Academy at West Point, New York.

took erring Olaf soon in hand;
but—though an host of overjoyed
noncoms(first knocking on the head
him)do through icy waters roll
that helplessness which others stroke   10
with brushes recently employed
anent this muddy toiletbowl,
while kindred intellects evoke
allegiance per blunt instruments—
Olaf(being to all intents   15
a corpse and wanting any rag
upon what God unto him gave)
responds,without getting annoyed
"I will not kiss your fucking flag"

straightway the silver bird looked grave   20
(departing hurriedly to shave)

but—though all kinds of officers
(a yearning nation's blueeyed pride)
their passive prey did kick and curse
until for wear their clarion   25
voices and boots were much the worse,
and egged the firstclassprivates on
his rectum wickedly to tease
by means of skilfully applied
bayonets roasted hot with heat—   30
Olaf(upon what were once knees)
does almost ceaselessly repeat
"there is some shit I will not eat"

our president,being of which
assertions duly notified   35
threw the yellowsonofabitch
into a dungeon,where he died

Christ(of His mercy infinite)
i pray to see;and Olaf,too

preponderatingly because   40
unless statistics lie he was
more brave than me:more blond than you.

1931

somewhere i have never travelled,gladly beyond

somewhere i have never travelled,gladly beyond
any experience,your eyes have their silence:
in your most frail gesture are things which enclose me,
or which i cannot touch because they are too near

your slightest look easily will unclose me   5
though i have closed myself as fingers,
you open always petal by petal myself as Spring opens
(touching skilfully,mysteriously)her first rose

or if your wish be to close me,iand
my life will shut very beautifully,suddenly,   10
as when the heart of this flower imagines
the snow carefully everywhere descending;

nothing which we are to perceive in this world equals
the power of your intense fragility:whose texture
compels me with the colour of its countries,   15
rendering death and forever with each breathing

(i do not know what it is about you that closes
and opens;only something in me understands
the voice of your eyes is deeper than all roses)
nobody,not even the rain,has such small hands   20

1931

anyone lived in a pretty how town

anyone lived in a pretty how town
(with up so floating many bells down)
spring summer autumn winter
he sang his didn't he danced his did.

Women and men(both little and small)   5
cared for anyone not at all
they sowed their isn't they reaped their same
sun moon stars rain

children guessed(but only a few
and down they forgot as up they grew   10
autumn winter spring summer)
that noone loved him more by more

when by now and tree by leaf
she laughed his joy she cried his grief
bird by snow and stir by still   15
anyone's any was all to her

someones married their everyones
laughed their cryings and did their dance
(sleep wake hope and then)they
said their nevers they slept their dream   20

stars rain sun moon
(and only the snow can begin to explain
how children are apt to forget to remember
with up so floating many bells down)

one day anyone died i guess   25
(and noone stooped to kiss his face)
busy folk buried them side by side
little by little and was by was

all by all and deep by deep
and more by more they dream their sleep   30
noone and anyone earth by april
wish by spirit and if by yes.

Women and men(both dong and ding)
summer autumn winter spring
reaped their sowing and went their came   35
sun moon stars rain

1940

my father moved through dooms of love

my father moved through dooms of love
through sames of am through haves of give,
singing each morning out of each night
my father moved through depths of height

this motionless forgetful where   5
turned at his glance to shining here;
that if(so timid air is firm)
under his eyes would stir and squirm

newly as from unburied which
floats the first who,his april touch   10
drove sleeping selves to swarm their fates
woke dreamers to their ghostly roots

and should some why completely weep
my father's fingers brought her sleep:
vainly no smallest voice might cry   15
for he could feel the mountains grow.

Lifting the valleys of the sea
my father moved through griefs of joy;
praising a forehead called the moon
singing desire into begin   20

joy was his song and joy so pure
a heart of star by him could steer
and pure so now and now so yes
the wrists of twilight would rejoice

keen as midsummer's keen beyond   25
conceiving mind of sun will stand,
so strictly(over utmost him
so hugely)stood my father's dream

his flesh was flesh his blood was blood:
no hungry man but wished him food;   30
no cripple wouldn't creep one mile
uphill to only see him smile.

Scorning the pomp of must and shall
my father moved through dooms of feel;
his anger was as right as rain   35
his pity was as green as grain

septembering arms of year extend
less humbly wealth to foe and friend
than he to foolish and to wise
offered immeasurable is   40

proudly and(by octobering flame
beckoned)as earth will downward climb,
so naked for immortal work
his shoulders marched against the dark

his sorrow was as true as bread: 45
no liar looked him in the head;
if every friend became his foe
he'd laugh and build a world with snow.

My father moved through theys of we,
singing each new leaf out of each tree   50
(and every child was sure that spring
danced when she heard my father sing)

then let men kill which cannot share,
let blood and flesh be mud and mire,
scheming imagine,passion willed,   55
freedom a drug that's bought and sold

giving to steal and cruel kind,
a heart to fear,to doubt a mind,
to differ a disease of same,
conform the pinnacle of am   60

though dull were all we taste as bright,
bitter all utterly things sweet,
maggoty minus and dumb death
all we inherit,all bequeath

and nothing quite so least as truth   65
—i say though hate were why men breathe—
because my father lived his soul
love is the whole and more than all

                                                                                  1940

pity this busy monster,manunkind

pity this busy monster,manunkind,

not.   Progress is a comfortable disease:
your victim(death and life safely beyond)

plays with the bigness of his littleness
—electrons deify one razorblade   5
into a mountainrange;lenses extend

unwish through curving wherewhen till unwish
returns on its unself.
                     A world of made
is not a world of born—pity poor flesh   10

and trees,poor stars and stones,but never this
fine specimen of hypermagical

ultraomnipotence.   We doctors know

a hopeless case if—listen:there's a hell
of a good universe next door;let's go   15

                                                                                  1944

JEAN TOOMER
1894–1967

Jean Toomer's *Cane*, the author's contribution to Harlem Renaissance literature, received immediate acclaim when it appeared in 1923. Unlike African American artists who felt they had to choose either to publicize the nobility of rural black people or to represent a sophisticated black artistic sensibility, Toomer reconciled the two, describing rural people through the analytic filter of a modern, urban literary style.

Born in Washington, D.C., Toomer never knew his father. He grew up with his grandfather, who had been an important Louisiana politician during the Reconstruction era, and his mother. After high school graduation he attended several colleges—the University of Wisconsin, the Massachusetts College of Agriculture, the American

College of Physical Training in Chicago, the University of Chicago, and the City College of New York—without completing a degree. He held numerous short-term jobs in various parts of the country, including four months in 1921 as superintendent of a small black school in Sparta, Georgia. This, his only sustained encounter with a rural population, formed the basis of *Cane*.

He began writing when he was in his middle twenties, publishing poems and stories in several avant-garde little magazines, among them *Broom*, the *Little Review*, and *Prairie*. He also published in such African American publications as the *Liberator*, *Crisis*, and *Opportunity*. Although *Cane* is a long work, it is composed as an assemblage of short stories, sketches, poems, even a play. These are combined in a three-part structure held together, like many modernist narratives, by the narrator's quest for wholeness. *Cane* asks whether an alienated, sophisticated, contemporary African American can find himself by connecting to a black folk heritage that he has never known. The circumstances are specifically African American, but the theme of returning to, or finding, or even inventing, one's roots is typical of much modernist art.

Part I of *Cane*, set in rural Georgia, depicts the difficult lives of rural blacks while celebrating their strength and integrity. Part II shows black urban life in Washington, D.C., and Chicago as it has been corrupted by white materialism. The autobiographical third part describes an African American intellectual teaching in the South, trying to put down roots in an unfamiliar setting that is nevertheless supposed to be "his." The work is distinguished by its poetic, imagistic, evocative prose, its linguistic innovativeness, and its method of construction. All these aspects of *Cane* show Toomer's awareness of contemporary literary movements and register his ambition to be both a Harlem Renaissance author and a literary modernist.

Toomer spent much of the last forty years of his life looking for a spiritual community; he had difficulty finding publishers for the writing he produced during these decades. For a while he was a disciple of the Russian mystic George I. Gurdjieff. In the late 1940s he became a committed Quaker. At his death he left many unpublished short stories, as well as novels, plays, and an autobiography.

The text is that of the first edition (1923) as corrected in 1973.

From Cane[1]

Georgia Dusk

The sky, lazily disdaining to pursue
    The setting sun, too indolent to hold
    A lengthened tournament for flashing gold,
Passively darkens for night's barbecue,

A feast of moon and men and barking hounds,   5
    An orgy for some genius of the South
    With blood-hot eyes and cane-lipped scented mouth,
Surprised in making folk-songs from soul sounds.

The sawmill blows its whistle, buzz-saws stop,
    And silence breaks the bud of knoll and hill,   10
    Soft settling pollen where plowed lands fulfill
Their early promise of a bumper crop.

---

1. Of the book's three sections, the first and the last are Georgia scenes. "Fern" appears in the first section after the poem "Georgia Dusk." "Portrait in Georgia" appears in the first section before the story of the lynching of a black woman's black lover by her white lover and his white cohorts. "Seventh Street" is the first sketch in the second section, which is devoted to Washington, D.C., and Chicago.

Smoke from the pyramidal sawdust pile
   Curls up, blue ghosts of trees, tarrying low
   Where only chips and stumps are left to show   15
The solid proof of former domicile.

Meanwhile, the men, with vestiges of pomp,
   Race memories of king and caravan,
   High-priests, an ostrich, and a juju-man,[2]
Go singing through the footpaths of the swamp.   20

Their voices rise . . the pine trees are guitars,
   Strumming, pine-needles fall like sheets of rain . .
   Their voices rise . . the chorus of the cane
Is caroling a vesper to the stars . .

O singers, resinous and soft your songs   25
   Above the sacred whisper of the pines,
   Give virgin lips to cornfield concubines,
Bring dreams of Christ to dusky cane-lipped throngs.

Fern

Face flowed into her eyes. Flowed in soft cream foam and plaintive ripples, in such a way that wherever your glance may momentarily have rested, it immediately thereafter wavered in the direction of her eyes. The soft suggestion of down slightly darkened, like the shadow of a bird's wing might, the creamy brown color of her upper lip. Why, after noticing it, you sought her eyes, I cannot tell you. Her nose was aquiline, Semitic. If you have heard a Jewish cantor[3] sing, if he has touched you and made your own sorrow seem trivial when compared with his, you will know my feeling when I follow the curves of her profile, like mobile rivers, to their common delta. They were strange eyes. In this, that they sought nothing—that is, nothing that was obvious and tangible and that one could see, and they gave the impression that nothing was to be denied. When a woman seeks, you will have observed, her eyes deny. Fern's eyes desired nothing that you could give her; there was no reason why they should withhold. Men saw her eyes and fooled themselves. Fern's eyes said to them that she was easy. When she was young, a few men took her, but got no joy from it. And then, once done, they felt bound to her (quite unlike their hit and run with other girls), felt as though it would take them a lifetime to fulfill an obligation which they could find no name for. They became attached to her, and hungered after finding the barest trace of what she might desire. As she grew up, new men who came to town felt as almost everyone did who ever saw her: that they would not be denied. Men were everlastingly bringing her their bodies. Something inside of her got tired of them, I guess, for I am certain that for the life of her she could not tell why or how she began to turn them off. A man in fever is no trifling thing to send away. They began to leave her, baffled and ashamed, yet vowing to themselves that some day they would do some fine thing for her: send her candy every week and not let her know whom it came from, watch out for her wedding-day and give her a magnificent something with no name on it, buy a house and deed it to her, rescue

---

2. West African tribesman who controls the magical fetish or charm, or "juju."   3. Singer in religious services.

her from some unworthy fellow who had tricked her into marrying him. As you know, men are apt to idolize or fear that which they cannot understand, especially if it be a woman. She did not deny them, yet the fact was that they were denied. A sort of superstition crept into their consciousness of her being somehow above them. Being above them meant that she was not to be approached by anyone. She became a virgin. Now a virgin in a small southern town is by no means the usual thing, if you will believe me. That the sexes were made to mate is the practice of the South. Particularly, black folks were made to mate. And it is black folks whom I have been talking about thus far. What white men thought of Fern I can arrive at only by analogy. They let her alone.

Anyone, of course, could see her, could see her eyes. If you walked up the Dixie Pike most any time of day, you'd be most like to see her resting listless-like on the railing of her porch, back propped against a post, head tilted a little forward because there was a nail in the porch post just where her head came which for some reason or other she never took the trouble to pull out. Her eyes, if it were sunset, rested idly where the sun, molten and glorious, was pouring down between the fringe of pines. Or maybe they gazed at the gray cabin on the knoll from which an evening folk-song was coming. Perhaps they followed a cow that had been turned loose to roam and feed on cotton-stalks and corn leaves. Like as not they'd settle on some vague spot above the horizon, though hardly a trace of wistfulness would come to them. If it were dusk, then they'd wait for the search-light of the evening train which you could see miles up the track before it flared across the Dixie Pike, close to her home. Wherever they looked, you'd follow them and then waver back. Like her face, the whole countryside seemed to flow into her eyes. Flowed into them with the soft listless cadence of Georgia's South. A young Negro, once, was looking at her, spellbound, from the road. A white man passing in a buggy had to flick him with his whip if he was to get by without running him over. I first saw her on her porch. I was passing with a fellow whose crusty numbness (I was from the North and suspected of being prejudiced and stuck-up) was melting as he found me warm. I asked him who she was. "That's Fern," was all that I could get from him. Some folks already thought that I was given to nosing around; I let it go at that, so far as questions were concerned. But at first sight of her I felt as if I heard a Jewish cantor sing. As if his singing rose above the unheard chorus of a folk-song. And I felt bound to her. I too had my dreams: something I would do for her. I have knocked about from town to town too much not to know the futility of mere change of place. Besides, picture if you can, this cream-colored solitary girl sitting at a tenement window looking down on the indifferent throngs of Harlem. Better that she listen to folk-songs at dusk in Georgia, you would say, and so would I. Or, suppose she came up North and married. Even a doctor or a lawyer, say, one who would be sure to get along—that is, make money. You and I know, who have had experience in such things, that love is not a thing like prejudice which can be bettered by changes of town. Could men in Washington, Chicago, or New York, more than the men of Georgia, bring her something left vacant by the bestowal of their bodies? You and I who know men in these cities will have to say, they could not. See her out and out a prostitute along State Street in Chicago. See her move into a southern town where white men are more aggressive. See her become a white man's concubine . . . Something I must do for her. There was myself. What could I do for her? Talk, of course.

Push back the fringe of pines upon new horizons. To what purpose? and what for? Her? Myself? Men in her case seem to lose their selfishness. I lost mine before I touched her. I ask you, friend (it makes no difference if you sit in the Pullman or the Jim Crow[4] as the train crosses her road), what thoughts would come to you—that is, after you'd finished with the thoughts that leap into men's minds at the sight of a pretty woman who will not deny them; what thoughts would come to you, had you seen her in a quick flash, keen and intuitively, as she sat there on her porch when your train thundered by? Would you have got off at the next station and come back for her to take her where? Would you have completely forgotten her as soon as you reached Macon, Atlanta, Augusta, Pasadena, Madison, Chicago, Boston, or New Orleans? Would you tell your wife or sweetheart about a girl you saw? Your thoughts can help me, and I would like to know. Something I would do for her . . .

One evening I walked up the Pike on purpose, and stopped to say hello. Some of her family were about, but they moved away to make room for me. Damn if I knew how to begin. Would you? Mr. and Miss So-and-So, people, the weather, the crops, the new preacher, the frolic, the church benefit, rabbit and possum hunting, the new soft drink they had at old Pap's store, the schedule of the trains, what kind of town Macon was, Negro's migration north, bollweevils, syrup, the Bible—to all these things she gave a yassur or nassur, without further comment. I began to wonder if perhaps my own emotional sensibility had played one of its tricks on me. "Lets take a walk," I at last ventured. The suggestion, coming after so long an isolation, was novel enough, I guess, to surprise. But it wasnt that. Something told me that men before me had said just that as a prelude to the offering of their bodies. I tried to tell her with my eyes. I think she understood. The thing from her that made my throat catch, vanished. Its passing left her visible in a way I'd thought, but never seen. We walked down the Pike with people on all the porches gaping at us. "Doesnt it make you mad?" She meant the row of petty gossiping people. She meant the world. Through a canebrake that was ripe for cutting, the branch was reached. Under a sweet-gum tree, and where reddish leaves had dammed the creek a little, we sat down. Dusk, suggesting the almost imperceptible procession of giant trees, settled with a purple haze about the cane. I felt strange, as I always do in Georgia, particularly at dusk. I felt that things unseen to men were tangibly immediate. It would not have surprised me had I had vision. People have them in Georgia more often than you would suppose. A black woman once saw the mother of Christ and drew her in charcoal on the courthouse wall . . . When one is on the soil of one's ancestors, most anything can come to one . . . From force of habit, I suppose, I held Fern in my arms—that is, without at first noticing it. Then my mind came back to her. Her eyes, unusually weird and open, held me. Held God. He flowed in as I've seen the countryside flow in. Seen men. I must have done something—what, I don't know, in the confusion of my emotion. She sprang up. Rushed some distance from me. Fell to her knees, and began swaying, swaying. Her body was tortured with something it could not let out. Like boiling sap it flooded arms and fingers till she shook them as if they burned her. It found her throat, and spattered inarticulately in plaintive, convulsive

4. In the segregated South, black persons were required to sit in the "Jim Crow" section of railway cars and were not allowed as passengers in the first-class "Pullman" lounges, or sleeping cars.

sounds, mingled with calls to Christ Jesus. And then she sang, brokenly. A Jewish cantor singing with a broken voice. A child's voice, uncertain, or an old man's. Dusk hid her; I could hear only her song. It seemed to me as though she were pounding her head in anguish upon the ground. I rushed at her. She fainted in my arms.

There was talk about her fainting with me in the canefield. And I got one or two ugly looks from town men who'd set themselves up to protect her. In fact, there was talk of making me leave town. But they never did. They kept a watch-out for me, though. Shortly after, I came back North. From the train window I saw her as I crossed her road. Saw her on her porch, head tilted a little forward where the nail was, eyes vaguely focused on the sunset. Saw her face flow into them, the countryside and something that I call God, flowing into them . . . Nothing ever really happened. Nothing ever came to Fern, not even I. Something I would do for her. Some fine unnamed thing . . . And, friend, you? She is still living, I have reason to know. Her name, against the chance that you might happen down that way, is Fernie May Rosen.

* * *

Portrait in Georgia

Hair—braided chestnut,
    coiled like a lyncher's rope,
Eyes—fagots,
Lips—old scars, or the first red blisters,
Breath—the last sweet scent of cane,   5
And her slim body, white as the ash
    of black flesh after flame.

* * *

Seventh Street

Money burns the pocket, pocket hurts,
Bootleggers in silken shirts,
Ballooned, zooming Cadillacs,
Whizzing, whizzing down the street-car tracks.

Seventh Street is a bastard of Prohibition and the War.[5] A crude-boned, soft-skinned wedge of nigger life breathing its loafer air, jazz songs and love, thrusting unconscious rhythms, black reddish blood into the white and whitewashed wood of Washington. Stale soggy wood of Washington. Wedges rust in soggy wood . . . Split it! In two! Again! Shred it! . . the sun. Wedges are brilliant in the sun; ribbons of wet wood dry and blow away. Black reddish blood. Pouring for crude-boned soft-skinned life, who set you flowing? Blood suckers of the War would spin in a frenzy of dizziness if they drank your blood. Prohibition would put a stop to it. Who set you flowing? White and whitewash disappear in blood. Who set you flowing? Flowing down the smooth asphalt of Seventh Street, in shanties, brick office buildings, theaters, drug stores, restaurants, and cabarets? Eddying on the corners? Swirling like a blood-red smoke up where the buzzards fly in heaven? God would not dare to suck black red blood. A Nigger God! He would duck his head in shame and call for the Judgment Day. Who set you flowing?

5. World War I.

Money burns the pocket, pocket hurts,
Bootleggers in silken shirts,
Ballooned, zooming Cadillacs,
Whizzing, whizzing down the street-car tracks.

1923

F. SCOTT FITZGERALD
1896–1940

In the 1920s and 1930s F. Scott Fitzgerald was equally famous as a writer and as a celebrity author whose lifestyle seemed to symbolize the two decades; in the 1920s he stood for all-night partying, drinking, and the pursuit of pleasure while in the 1930s he stood for the gloomy aftermath of excess. "Babylon Revisited," written immediately after the stock market crash, is simultaneously a personal and a national story.

Fitzgerald was born in a middle-class neighborhood in St. Paul, Minnesota, descended on his father's side from southern colonial landowners and legislators, on his mother's from Irish immigrants. Much of his boyhood was spent in Buffalo and Syracuse, New York. The family was not prosperous and it took an aunt's support to send him to a Catholic boarding school in New Jersey in 1911. Two years later he entered Princeton University, where he participated in extracurricular literary and dramatic activities, forming friendships with campus intellectuals like the prominent critic Edmund Wilson who were to help him in later years. But he failed to make the football team and felt the disappointment for years. After three years of college Fitzgerald quit to join the army, but the war ended before he saw active service. Stationed in Montgomery, Alabama, he met and courted Zelda Sayre, a local belle who rejected him. In 1919 he went to New York City, determined to make a fortune and win Zelda. Amazingly, he succeeded. A novel he had begun in college, revised, and published in 1920 as *This Side of Paradise* became an immediate bestseller, making its author rich and famous at the age of twenty-four. As one of the earliest examples of a novel about college life, *This Side of Paradise* was accepted as the voice of the younger generation in a society increasingly oriented toward youth. He combined the traditional narrative and rhetorical gifts of a good fiction writer, it appeared, with a thoroughly modern sensibility. A week after the novel appeared, Scott and Zelda were married. Living extravagantly in New York City and St. Paul, and on Long Island, they more than spent the money Fitzgerald made from two collections of short stories—*Flappers and Philosophers* (1921) and *Tales of the Jazz Age* (1922)—and a second novel, *The Beautiful and Damned* (1922). Their only child, a daughter, was born in 1921.

In 1924, the Fitzgeralds moved to Europe to live more cheaply. They made friends with American expatriates, Hemingway, Stein, and Pound among others. During this time Fitzgerald published his best-known and most successful novel, *The Great Gatsby* (1925), and another book of short stories, *All the Sad Young Men* (1926). *The Great Gatsby* tells the story of a self-made young man whose dream of success, personified in a rich and beautiful young woman named Daisy, turns out to be a fantasy in every sense: Daisy belongs to a corrupt society, Gatsby corrupts himself in the quest for her, and above all, the rich have no intention of sharing their privileges. The novel is narrated from the point of view of Nick Carraway, an onlooker who is both moved and repelled by the tale he tells and whose responses form a sort of subplot: this experiment in narrative point of view was widely imitated. The structure of *The Great Gatsby* is compact; the style dazzling; and its images of automobiles, parties, and garbage heaps seem to capture the contradictions of a consumer society. The novel became an instant classic and remains so to this day.

Fitzgerald wrote dozens of short stories during the twenties; many were published in the mass-circulation weekly the *Saturday Evening Post,* which paid extremely well. Despite the pace at which he worked—in all he wrote 178 short stories—the Fitzgeralds could not get out of debt. Scott became alcoholic, and Zelda broke down in 1930 and spent most of the rest of her life in mental institutions. In 1931 Fitzgerald reestablished himself permanently in the United States, living at first near Baltimore, where his wife was hospitalized. A fourth novel, *Tender Is the Night,* appeared in 1934. The novel follows the emotional decline of a young American psychiatrist whose personal energies are sapped, his career corroded equally by his marriage to a beautiful and wealthy patient and his own weakness of character ("character" was one of Fitzgerald's favorite concepts). As in *The Great Gatsby,* the character begins as a disciple of the work ethic and turns into a pursuer of wealth, and the American Dream accordingly turns into a nightmare. Unlike *Gatsby,* whose characters never really connect with each other, *Tender Is the Night* shows a range of intimacies, none of them successful. The novel did not sell well. In 1937 Fitzgerald turned to Hollywood screenwriting; toward the end of the decade things were looking up for him, and he planned to revive his career as a fiction writer. But his health had been ruined by heavy drinking; he died of a heart attack in Hollywood at the age of forty-four, leaving an unfinished novel about a film mogul, *The Last Tycoon,* which was brought out by Edmund Wilson in 1941. Wilson also successfully promoted Fitzgerald's posthumous reputation by editing a collection of his writings, which he called *The Crack-Up,* in 1945.

The text of "Winter Dreams" is from *Metropolitan* magazine (1922); that of "Babylon Revisited" is from *Stories of F. Scott Fitzgerald* (1951).

Winter Dreams

Some of the caddies were poor as sin and lived in one-room houses with a neurasthenic cow in the front yard, but Dexter Green's father owned the second best grocery store in Dillard—the best one was "The Hub," patronized by the wealthy people from Lake Erminie—and Dexter caddied only for pocket-money.

In the fall when the days became crisp and grey and the long Minnesota winter shut down like the white lid of a box, Dexter's skis moved over the snow that hid the fairways of the golf course. At these times the country gave him a feeling of profound melancholy—it offended him that the links should lie in enforced fallowness, haunted by ragged sparrows for the long season. It was dreary, too, that on the tees where the gay colors fluttered in summer there were now only the desolate sand-boxes knee-deep in crusted ice. When he crossed the hills the wind blew cold as misery, and if the sun was out he tramped with his eyes squinted up against the hard dimensionless glare.

In April the winter ceased abruptly. The snow ran down into Lake Erminie scarcely tarrying for the early golfers to brave the season with red and black balls. Without elation, without an interval of moist glory the cold was gone.

Dexter knew that there was something dismal about this northern spring, just as he knew there was something gorgeous about the fall. Fall made him clench his hands and tremble and repeat idiotic sentences to himself and make brisk abrupt gestures of command to imaginary audiences and armies.

October filled him with hope which November raised to a sort of ecstatic triumph, and in this wood the fleeting brilliant impressions of the summer at Lake Erminie were ready grist to his will. He became a golf champion and defeated Mr. T. A. Hedrick in a marvelous match played over a hundred times in the fairways of his imagination, a match each detail of which he changed about untiringly—sometimes winning with almost laughable ease, sometimes coming up magnificently from behind. Again, stepping from a Pierce-Arrow automobile, like Mr. Mortimer Jones, he strolled frigidly into the lounge of the Erminie Golf Club—or perhaps, surrounded by an admiring crowd, he gave an exhibition of fancy diving from the springboard of the Erminie Club raft. . . . Among those most impressed was Mr. Mortimer Jones.

And one day it came to pass that Mr. Jones, himself and not his ghost, came up to Dexter, almost with tears in his eyes and said that Dexter was the ——— best caddy in the club and wouldn't he decide not to quit if Mr. Jones made it worth his while, because every other ——— caddy in the club lost one ball a hole for him—regularly—

"No, sir," said Dexter, decisively, "I don't want to caddy any more." Then, after a pause, "I'm too old."

"You're—why, you're not more than fourteen. Why did you decide just this morning that you wanted to quit? You promised that next week you'd go over to the state tournament with me."

"I decided I was too old."

Dexter handed in his "A Class" badge, collected what money was due him from the caddy master and caught the train for Dillard.

"The best ——— caddy I ever saw," shouted Mr. Mortimer Jones over a drink that afternoon. "Never lost a ball! Willing! Intelligent! Quiet! Honest! Grateful!—"

The little girl who had done this was eleven—beautifully ugly as little girls are apt to be who are destined after a few years to be inexpressably lovely and bring no end of misery to a great number of men. The spark, however, was perceptible. There was a general ungodliness in the way her lips twisted down at the corners when she smiled and in the—Heaven help us!—in the almost passionate quality of her eyes. Vitality is born early in such women. It was utterly in evidence now, shining through her thin frame in a sort of glow.

She had come eagerly out on to the course at nine o'clock with a white linen nurse and five small new golf clubs in a white canvas bag which the nurse was carrying. When Dexter first saw her she was standing by the caddy house, rather ill-at-ease and trying to conceal the fact by engaging her nurse in an obviously unnatural conversation illumined by startling and irrelevant smiles from herself.

"Well, it's certainly a nice day, Hilda," Dexter heard her say, then she drew down the corners of her mouth, smiled and glanced furtively around, her eyes in transit falling for an instant on Dexter.

Then to the nurse:

"Well, I guess there aren't very many people out here this morning, are there?"

The smile again radiant, blatantly artificial—convincing.

"I don't know what we're supposed to do now," said the nurse, looking nowhere in particular.

"Oh, that's all right"—the smile—"I'll fix it up."

Dexter stood perfectly still, his mouth faintly ajar. He knew that if he moved forward a step his stare would be in her line of vision—if he moved backward he would lose his full view of her face—For a moment he had not realized how young she was. Now he remembered having seen her several times the year before—in bloomers.

Suddenly, involuntarily, he laughed, a short abrupt laugh—then, startled by himself, he turned and began to walk quickly away.

"Boy!"

Dexter stopped.

"Boy—"

Beyond question he was addressed. Not only that, but he was treated to that absurd smile, that preposterous smile—the memory of which at least half a dozen men were to carry to the grave.

"Boy, do you know where the golf teacher is?"

"He's giving a lesson."

"Well, do you know where the caddy-master is?"

"He's not here yet this morning."

"Oh." For a moment this baffled her. She stood alternately on her right and left foot.

"We'd like to get a caddy," said the nurse. "Mrs. Mortimer Jones sent us out to play golf and we don't know how without we get a caddy."

Here she was stopped by an ominous glance from Miss Jones, followed immediately by the smile.

"There aren't any caddies here except me," said Dexter to the nurse. "And I got to stay here in charge until the caddy-master gets here."

"Oh."

Miss Jones and her retinue now withdrew and at a proper distance from Dexter became involved in a heated conversation. The conversation was concluded by Miss Jones taking one of the clubs and hitting it on the ground with violence. For further emphasis she raised it again and was about to bring it down smartly upon the nurse's bosom, when the nurse seized the club and twisted it from her hands.

"You darn *fool!*" cried Miss Jones wildly.

Another argument ensued. Realizing that the elements of the comedy were implied in the scene, Dexter several times began to smile but each time slew the smile before it reached maturity. He could not resist the monstrous conviction that the little girl was justified in beating the nurse.

The situation was resolved by the fortuitous appearance of the caddy-master who was appealed to immediately by the nurse.

"Miss Jones is to have a little caddy and this one says he can't go."

"Mr. McKenna said I was to wait here till you came," said Dexter quickly.

"Well, he's here now." Miss Jones smiled cheerfully at the caddy-master. Then she dropped her bag and set off at a haughty mince toward the first tee.

"Well?" The caddy-master turned to Dexter. "What you standing there like a dummy for? Go pick up the young lady's clubs."

"I don't think I'll go out today," said Dexter.

"You don't—"

"I think I'll quit."

The enormity of his decision frightened him. He was a favorite caddy and the thirty dollars a month he earned through the summer were not to be made elsewhere in Dillard. But he had received a strong emotional shock and his perturbation required a violent and immediate outlet.

It is not so simple as that, either. As so frequently would be the case in the future, Dexter was unconsciously dictated to by his winter dreams.

Now, of course, the quality and the seasonability of these winter dreams varied, but the stuff of them remained. They persuaded Dexter several years later to pass up a business course at the State University—his father, prospering now, would have paid his way—for the precarious advantage of attending an older and more famous university in the East, where he was bothered by his scanty funds. But do not get the impression, because his winter dreams happened to be concerned at first with musings on the rich, that there was anything shoddy in the boy. He wanted not association with glittering things and glittering people—he wanted the glittering things themselves. Often he reached out for the best without knowing why he wanted it—and sometimes he ran up against the mysterious denials and prohibitions in which life indulges. It is with one of those denials and not with his career as a whole that this story deals.

He made money. It was rather amazing. After college he went to the city from which Lake Erminie draws its wealthy patrons. When he was only twenty-three and had been there not quite two years, there were already people who liked to say, "Now *there's* a boy—" All about him rich men's sons were peddling bonds precariously, or investing patrimonies precariously, or plodding through the two dozen volumes of canned rubbish in the "George Washington Commercial Course," but Dexter borrowed a thousand dollars on his college degree and his steady eyes, and bought a partnership in a *laundry*.

It was a small laundry when he went into it. Dexter made a specialty of learning how the English washed fine woolen golf stockings without shrinking them. Inside of a year he was catering to the trade who wore knickerbockers. Men were insisting that their shetland hose and sweaters go to his laundry just as they had insisted on a caddy who could find golf balls. A little later he was doing their wives' lingerie as well—and running five branches in different parts of the city. Before he was twenty-seven he owned the largest string of laundries in his section of the country. It was then that he sold out and went to New York. But the part of his story that concerns us here goes back to when he was making his first big success.

When he was twenty-three Mr. W. L. Hart, one of the grey-haired men who like to say "Now there's a boy"—gave him a guest card to the Lake Erminie Club for over a week-end. So he signed his name one day on the register, and that afternoon played golf in a foursome with Mr. Hart and Mr. Sandwood and Mr. T. A. Hedrick. He did not consider it necessary to remark that he had once carried Mr. Hart's bag over this same links and that he knew every trap and gully with his eyes shut—but he found himself glancing at the four caddies who trailed them, trying to catch a gleam or gesture that would remind him of himself, that would lessen the gap which lay between his past and his future.

It was a curious day, slashed abruptly with fleeting, familiar impressions. One minute he had the sense of being a trespasser—in the next he was impressed by the tremendous superiority he felt toward Mr. T. A. Hedrick, who was a bore and not even a good golfer any more.

Then, because of a ball Mr. Hart lost near the fifteenth green an enormous thing happened. While they were searching the stiff grasses of the rough there was a clear call of "Fore!" from behind a hill in their rear. And as they all turned abruptly from their search a bright new ball sliced abruptly over the hill and caught Mr. T. A. Hedrick rather neatly in the stomach.

Mr. T. A. Hedrick grunted and cursed.

"By Gad!" cried Mr. Hedrick, "they ought to put some of these crazy women off the course. It's getting to be outrageous."

A head and a voice came up together over the hill:

"Do you mind if we go through?"

"You hit me in the stomach!" thundered Mr. Hedrick.

"Did I?" The girl approached the group of men. "I'm sorry. I yelled 'Fore!' "

Her glance fell casually on each of the men. She nodded to Sandwood and then scanned the fairway for her ball.

"Did I bounce off into the rough?"

It was impossible to determine whether this question was ingenuous or malicious. In a moment, however, she left no doubt, for as her partner came up over the hill she called cheerfully.

"Here I am! I'd have gone on the green except that I hit something."

As she took her stance for a short mashie shot, Dexter looked at her closely. She wore a blue gingham dress, rimmed at throat and shoulders with a white edging that accentuated her tan. The quality of exaggeration, of thinness that had made her passionate eyes and down turning mouth absurd at eleven was gone now. She was arrestingly beautiful. The color in her cheeks was centered like the color in a picture—it was not a "high" color, but a sort of fluctuating and feverish warmth, so shaded that it seemed at any moment it would recede and disappear. This color and the mobility of her mouth gave a continual impression of flux, of intense life, of passionate vitality—balanced only partially by the sad luxury of her eyes.

She swung her mashie impatiently and without interest, pitching the ball into a sandpit on the other side of the green. With a quick insincere smile and a careless "Thank you!" she went on after it.

"That Judy Jones!" remarked Mr. Hedrick on the next tee, as they waited— some moments—for her to play on ahead. "All she needs is to be turned up and spanked for six months and then to be married off to an old-fashioned cavalry captain."

"Gosh, she's good looking!" said Mr. Sandwood, who was just over thirty.

"Good-looking!" cried Mr. Hedrick contemptuously. "She always looks as if she wanted to be kissed! Turning those big cow-eyes on every young calf in town!"

It is doubtful if Mr. Hedrick intended a reference to the maternal instinct.

"She'd play pretty good golf if she'd try," said Mr. Sandwood.

"She has no form," said Mr. Hedrick solemnly.

"She has a nice figure," said Mr. Sandwood.

"Better thank the Lord she doesn't drive a swifter ball," said Mr. Hart, winking at Dexter. "Come on. Let's go."

Later in the afternoon the sun went down with a riotous swirl of gold and varying blues and scarlets, and left the dry rustling night of western summer. Dexter watched from the verandah of the Erminie Club, watched the even overlap of the waters in the little wind, silver molasses under the harvest moon. Then the moon held a finger to her lips and the lake became a clear pool, pale and quiet. Dexter put on his bathing suit and swam out to the farthest raft, where he stretched dripping on the wet canvas of the spring board.

There was a fish jumping and a star shining and the lights around the lake were gleaming. Over on a dark peninsula a piano was playing the songs of last summer and of summers before that—songs from "The Pink Lady" and "The Chocolate Soldier" and "Mlle. Modiste"—and because the sound of a piano over a stretch of water had always seemed beautiful to Dexter he lay perfectly quiet and listened.

The tune the piano was playing at that moment had been gay and new five years before when Dexter was a sophomore at college. They had played it at a prom once and because he could not afford the luxury of proms in those days he had stood outside the gymnasium and listened. The sound of the tune and the splash of the fish jumping precipitated in him a sort of ecstasy and it was with that ecstasy he viewed what happened to him now. The ecstasy was a gorgeous appreciation. It was his sense that, for once, he was magnificently atune to life and that everything about him was radiating a brightness and a glamor he might never know again.

A low pale oblong detached itself suddenly from the darkness of the peninsula, spitting forth the reverberate sound of a racing motorboat. Two white streamers of cleft water rolled themselves out behind it and almost immediately the boat was beside him, drowning out the hot tinkle of the piano in the drone of its spray. Dexter raising himself on his arms was aware of a figure standing at the wheel, of two dark eyes regarding him over the lengthening space of water—then the boat had gone by and was sweeping in an immense and purposeless circle of spray round and round in the middle of the lake. With equal eccentricity one of the circles flattened out and headed back toward the raft.

"Who's that?" she called, shutting off the motor. She was so near now that Dexter could see her bathing suit, which consisted apparently of pink rompers. "Oh—you're one of the men I hit in the stomach."

The nose of the boat bumped the raft. After an inexpert struggle, Dexter managed to twist the line around a two-by-four. Then the raft tilted rakishly as she sprung on.

"Well, kiddo," she said huskily, "do you"—she broke off. She had sat herself upon the springboard, found it damp and jumped up quickly,—"do you want to go surf-board riding?"

He indicated that he would be delighted.

"The name is Judy Jones. Ghastly reputation but enormously popular." She favored him with an absurd smirk—rather, what tried to be a smirk, for, twist her mouth as she might, it was not grotesque, it was merely beautiful. "See that house over on the peninsula?"

"No."

"Well, there's a house there that I live in only you can't see it because it's too dark. And in that house there is a fella waiting for me. When he drove up by the door I drove out by the dock because he has watery eyes and asks me if I have an ideal."

There was a fish jumping and a star shining and the lights around the lake were gleaming. Dexter sat beside Judy Jones and she explained how her boat was driven. Then she was in the water, swimming to the floating surf-board with exquisite crawl. Watching her was as without effort to the eye as watching a branch waving or a sea-gull flying. Her arms, burned to butternut, moved sinuously among the dull platinum ripples, elbow appearing first, casting the forearm back with a cadence of falling water, then reaching out and down stabbing a path ahead.

They moved out into the lake and, turning, Dexter saw that she was kneeling on the low rear of the now up-tilted surf-board.

"Go faster," she called, "fast as it'll go."

Obediently he jammed the lever forward and the white spray mounted at the bow. When he looked around again the girl was standing up on the rushing board, her arms spread ecstatically, her eyes lifted toward the moon.

"It's awful cold, kiddo," she shouted. "What's your name anyways?"

"The name is Dexter Green. Would it amuse you to know how good you look back there?"

"Yes," she shouted, "it would amuse me. Except that I'm too cold. Come to dinner tomorrow night."

He kept thinking how glad he was that he had never caddied for this girl. The damp gingham clinging made her like a statue and turned her intense mobility to immobility at last.

"—At seven o'clock," she shouted, "Judy Jones, Girl, who hit man in stomach. Better write it down,"—and then, "Faster—oh, faster!"

Had he been as calm inwardly as he was in appearance, Dexter would have had time to examine his surroundings in detail. He received, however, an enduring impression that the house was the most elaborate he had ever seen. He had known for a long time that it was the finest on Lake Erminie, with a Pompeiian swimming pool and twelve acres of lawn and garden. But what gave it an air of breathless intensity was the sense that it was inhabited by Judy Jones—that it was as casual a thing to her as the little house in the village had once been to Dexter. There was a feeling of mystery in it, of bedrooms upstairs more beautiful and strange than other bedrooms, of gay and radiant activities taking place through these deep corridors and of romances that were not musty and laid already in lavender, but were fresh and breathing and set forth in rich motor cars and in great dances whose flowers were scarcely withered. They were more real because he could feel them all about him, pervading the air with the shades and echoes of still vibrant emotion.

And so while he waited for her to appear he peopled the soft deep summer room and the sun porch that opened from it with the men who had already loved Judy Jones. He knew the sort of men they were—the men who when he first went to college had entered from the great prep-schools with graceful clothes and the deep tan of healthy summer, who did nothing or anything with the same debonaire ease.

Dexter had seen that, in one sense, he was better than these men. He was newer and stronger. Yet in acknowledging to himself that he wished his children to be like them he was admitting that he was but the rough, strong stuff from which this graceful aristocracy eternally sprang.

When, a year before, the time had come when he could wear good clothes, he had known who were the best tailors in America, and the best tailor in America had made him the suit he wore this evening. He had acquired that particular reserve peculiar to his university, that set it off from other universities. He recognized the value to him of such a mannerism and he had adopted it; he knew that to be careless in dress and manner required more confidence than to be careful. But carelessness was for his children. His mother's name had been Krimslich. She was a Bohemian[1] of the peasant class and she had talked broken English to the end of her days. Her son must keep to the set patterns.

He waited for Judy Jones in her house, and he saw these other young men around him. It excited him that many men had loved her. It increased her value in his eyes.

At a little after seven Judy Jones came downstairs. She wore a blue silk afternoon dress. He was disappointed at first that she had not put on something more elaborate, and this feeling was accentuated when, after a brief greeting, she went to the door of a butler's pantry and pushing it open called: "You can have dinner, Martha." He had rather expected that a butler would announce dinner, that there would be a cocktail perhaps. It even offended him that she should know the maid's name.

Then he put these thoughts behind him as they sat down together on a chintz-covered lounge.

"Father and mother won't be here," she said.

"Ought I to be sorry?"

"They're really quite nice," she confessed, as if it had just occurred to her. "I think my father's the best looking man of his age I've ever seen. And mother looks about thirty."

He remembered the last time he had seen her father, and found he was glad the parents were not to be here tonight. They would wonder who he was. He had been born in Keeble, a Minnesota village fifty miles farther north and he always gave Keeble as his home instead of Dillard. Country towns were well enough to come from if they weren't inconveniently in sight and used as footstools by fashionable lakes.

Before dinner he found the conversation unsatisfactory. The beautiful Judy seemed faintly irritable—as much so as it was possible to be with a comparative stranger. They discussed Lake Erminie and its golf course, the surfboard riding of the night before and the cold she had caught, which made her voice more husky and charming than ever. They talked of his university which she had visited frequently during the past two years, and of the nearby city which supplied Lake Erminie with its patrons and whither Dexter would return next day to his prospering laundries.

During dinner she slipped into a moody depression which gave Dexter a feeling of guilt. Whatever petulance she uttered in her throaty voice worried him. Whatever she smiled at—at him, at a silver fork, at nothing—, it disturbed him that her smile could have no root in mirth, or even in amusement. When the red corners of her lips curved down, it was less a smile than an invitation to a kiss.

Then, after dinner, she led him out on the dark sun-porch and deliberately changed the atmosphere.

---

1. Native of Bohemia, in the Czech Republic.

"Do I seem gloomy?" she demanded.

"No, but I'm afraid I'm boring you," he answered quickly.

"You're not. I like you. But I've just had rather an unpleasant afternoon. There was a—man I cared about. He told me out of a clear sky that he was poor as a church-mouse. He'd never even hinted it before. Does this sound horribly mundane?"

"Perhaps he was afraid to tell you."

"I suppose he was," she answered thoughtfully. "He didn't start right. You see, if I'd thought of him as poor—well, I've been mad about loads of poor men, and fully intended to marry them all. But in this case, I hadn't thought of him that way and my interest in him wasn't strong enough to survive the shock."

"I know. As if a girl calmly informed her fiancé that she was a widow. He might not object to widows, but——"

"Let's start right," she suggested suddenly. "Who are you, anyhow?"

For a moment Dexter hesitated. There were two versions of his life that he could tell. There was Dillard and his caddying and his struggle through college, or——

"I'm nobody," he announced. "My career is largely a matter of futures."

"Are you poor?"

"No," he said frankly, "I'm probably making more money than any man my age in the northwest. I know that's an obnoxious remark, but you advised me to start right."

There was a pause. She smiled, and with a touch of amusement.

"You sound like a man in a play."

"It's your fault. You tempted me into being assertive."

Suddenly she turned her dark eyes directly upon him and the corners of her mouth drooped until her face seemed to open like a flower. He dared scarcely to breathe, he had the sense that she was exerting some force upon him; making him overwhelmingly conscious of the youth and mystery that wealth imprisons and preserves, the freshness of many clothes, of cool rooms and gleaming things, safe and proud above the hot struggles of the poor.

The porch was bright with the bought luxury of starshine. The wicker of the settee squeaked fashionably when he put his arm around her, commanded by her eyes. He kissed her curious and lovely mouth and committed himself to the following of a grail.

It began like that—and continued, with varying shades of intensity, on such a note right up to the dénouement. Dexter surrendered a part of himself to the most direct and unprincipled personality with which he had ever come in contact. Whatever the beautiful Judy Jones desired, she went after with the full pressure of her charm. There was no divergence of method, no jockeying for position or premeditation of effects—there was very little mental quality in any of her affairs. She simply made men conscious to the highest degree of her physical loveliness.

Dexter had no desire to change her. Her deficiencies were knit up with a passionate energy that transcended and justified them.

When, as Judy's head lay against his shoulder that first night, she whispered:

"I don't know what's the matter with me. Last night I thought I was in love with a man and tonight I think I'm in love with you—"

—it seemed to him a beautiful and romantic thing to say. It was the exquisite excitability that for the moment he controlled and owned. But a week later he was compelled to view this same quality in a different light. She took him in her roadster to a picnic supper and after supper she disappeared, likewise in her roadster, with another man. Dexter became enormously upset and was scarcely able to be decently civil to the other people present. When she assured him that she had not kissed the other man he knew she was lying— yet he was glad that she had taken the trouble to lie to him.

He was, as he found before the summer ended, one of a dozen, a varying dozen, who circulated about her. Each of them had at one time been favored above all others—about half of them still basked in the solace of occasional sentimental revivals. Whenever one showed signs of dropping out through long neglect she granted him a brief honeyed hour which encouraged him to tag along for a year or so longer. Judy made these forays upon the helpless and defeated without malice, indeed half unconscious that there was anything mischievous in what she did.

When a new man came to town everyone dropped out—dates were automatically cancelled.

The helpless part of trying to do anything about it was that she did it all herself. She was not a girl who could be "won" in the kinetic sense—she was proof against cleverness, she was proof against charm, if any of these assailed her too strongly she would immediately resolve the affair to a physical basis and under the magic of her physical splendor the strong as well as the brilliant played her game and not their own. She was entertained only by the gratification of her desires and by the direct exercise of her own charm. Perhaps from so much youthful love, so many youthful lovers she had come, in self defense, to nourish herself wholly from within.

Succeeding Dexter's first exhilaration came restlessness and dissatisfaction. The helpless ecstasy of losing himself in her charm was a powerful opiate rather than a tonic. It was fortunate for his work during the winter that those moments of ecstasy came infrequently. Early in their acquaintance it had seemed for a while that there was a deep and spontaneous mutual attraction—that first August for example—three days of long evenings on her dusky verandah, of strange wan kisses through the late afternoon, in shadowy alcoves or behind the protecting trellises of the garden arbors, of mornings when she was fresh as a dream and almost shy at meeting him in the clarity of the rising day. There was all the ecstasy of an engagement about it, sharpened by his realization that there was no engagement. It was during those three days that, for the first time, he had asked her to marry him. She said "maybe some day," she said "kiss me," she said "I'd like to marry you," she said "I love you,"—she said—nothing.

The three days were interrupted by the arrival of a New York man who visited the Jones' for half September. To Dexter's agony, rumor engaged them. The man was the son of the president of a great trust company. But at the end of a month it was reported that Judy was yawning. At a dance one night she sat all evening in a motor boat with an old beau, while the New Yorker searched the club for her frantically. She told the old beau that she was bored with her visitor and two days later he left. She was seen with him at the station and it was reported that he looked very mournful indeed.

On this note the summer ended. Dexter was twenty-four and he found himself increasingly in a position to do as he wished. He joined two clubs in the city and lived at one of them. Though he was by no means an integral part of the stag-lines at these clubs he managed to be on hand at dances where Judy Jones was likely to appear. He could have gone out socially as much as he liked—he was an eligible young man, now, and popular with downtown fathers. His confessed devotion to Judy Jones had rather solidified his position. But he had no social aspirations and rather despised the dancing men who were always on tap for the Thursday or Saturday parties and who filled in at dinners with the younger married set. Already he was playing with the idea of going East to New York. He wanted to take Judy Jones with him. No disillusion as to the world in which she had grown up could cure his illusion as to her desirability.

Remember that—for only in the light of it can what he did for her be understood.

Eighteen months after he first met Judy Jones he became engaged to another girl. Her name was Irene Scheerer and her father was one of the men who had always believed in Dexter. Irene was light haired and sweet and honorable and a little stout and she had two beaus whom she pleasantly relinquished when Dexter formally asked her to marry him.

Summer, fall, winter, spring, another summer, another fall—so much he had given of his active life to the curved lips of Judy Jones. She had treated him with interest, with encouragement, with malice, with indifference, with contempt. She had inflicted on him the innumerable little slights and indignities possible in such a case—as if in revenge for having ever cared for him at all. She had beckoned him and yawned at him and beckoned him again and he had responded often with bitterness and narrowed eyes. She had brought him ecstatic happiness and intolerable agony of spirit. She had caused him untold inconvenience and not a little trouble. She had insulted him and she had ridden over him and she had played his interest in her against his interest in his work—for fun. She had done everything to him except to criticize him—this she had not done—it seemed to him only because it might have sullied the utter indifference she manifested and sincerely felt toward him.

When autumn had come and gone again it occurred to him that he could not have Judy Jones. He had to beat this into his mind but he convinced himself at last. He lay awake at night for a while and argued it over. He told himself the trouble and the pain she had caused him, he enumerated her glaring deficiencies as a wife. Then he said to himself that he loved her and after a while he fell asleep. For a week, lest he imagine her husky voice over the telephone or her eyes opposite him at lunch, he worked hard and late and at night he went to his office and plotted out his years.

At the end of a week he went to a dance and cut in on her once. For almost the first time since they had met he did not ask her to sit out with him or tell her that she was lovely. It hurt him that she did not miss these things—that was all. He was not jealous when he saw that there was a new man tonight. He had been hardened against jealousy long before.

He stayed late at the dance. He sat for an hour with Irene Scheerer and talked about books and about music. He knew very little about either. But he was beginning to be master of his own time now and he had a rather priggish notion that he—the young and already fabulously successful Dexter Green—should know more about such things.

That was in October when he was twenty-five. In January Dexter and Irene became engaged. It was to be announced in June and they were to be married three months later.

The Minnesota winter prolonged itself interminably and it was almost May when the winds came soft and the snow ran down into Lake Erminie at last. For the first time in over a year Dexter was enjoying a certain tranquility of spirit. Judy Jones had been in Florida and afterwards in Hot Springs and somewhere she had been engaged and somewhere she had broken it off. At first, when Dexter had definitely given her up, it had made him sad that people still linked them together and asked for news of her, but when he began to be placed at dinner next to Irene Scheerer people didn't ask him about her any more—they told him about her. He ceased to be an authority on her.

May at last. Dexter walked the streets at night when the darkness was damp as rain, wondering that so soon, with so little done, so much of ecstasy had gone from him. May one year back had been marked by Judy's poignant, unforgivable, yet forgiven turbulence—it had been one of those rare times when he fancied she had grown to care for him. That old penny's worth of happiness he had spent for this bushel of content. He knew that Irene would be no more than a curtain spread behind him, a hand moving among gleaming tea cups, a voice calling to children . . . fire and loveliness were gone, magic of night and the hushed wonder of the hours and seasons . . . slender lips, down turning, dropping to his lips like poppy petals, bearing him up into a heaven of eyes . . . a haunting gesture, light of a warm lamp on her hair. The thing was deep in him. He was too strong, too alive for it to die lightly.

In the middle of May when the weather balanced for a few days on the thin bridge that led to deep summer he turned in one night at Irene's house. Their engagement was to be announced in a week now—no one would be surprised at it. And tonight they would sit together on the lounge at the College Club and look on for an hour at the dancers. It gave him a sense of solidity to go with her—. She was so sturdily popular, so intensely a "good egg."

He mounted the steps of the brown stone house and stepped inside.

"Irene," he called.

Mrs. Scheerer came out of the living room to meet him.

"Dexter," she said. "Irene's gone upstairs with a splitting headache. She wanted to go with you but I made her go to bed."

"Nothing serious I—"

"Oh, no. She's going to play golf with you in the morning. You can spare her for just one night, can't you, Dexter?"

Her smile was kind. She and Dexter liked each other. In the living room he talked for a moment before he said goodnight.

Returning to the College Club, where he had rooms, he stood in the doorway for a moment and watched the dancers. He leaned against the door post, nodded at a man or two—yawned.

"Hello, kiddo."

The familiar voice at his elbow startled him. Judy Jones had left a man and crossed the room to him—Judy Jones, a slender enamelled doll in cloth of gold, gold in a band at her head, gold in two slipper points at her dress's hem. The fragile glow of her face seemed to blossom as she smiled at him. A breeze of warmth and light blew through the room. His hands in the pockets of his dinner jacket tightened spasmodically. He was filled with a sudden excitement.

"When did you get back?" he asked casually.

"Come here and I'll tell you about it."

She turned and he followed her. She had been away—he could have wept at the wonder of her return. She had passed through enchanted streets, doing young things that were like plaintive music. All mysterious happenings, all fresh and quickening hopes, had gone away with her, come back with her now.

She turned in the doorway.

"Have you a car here? If you haven't I have."

"I have a coupe."

In then, with a rustle of golden cloth. He slammed the door. Into so many cars she had stepped—like this—like that—her back against the leather, so— her elbow resting on the door—waiting. She would have been soiled long since had there been anything to soil her,—except herself—but these things were all her own outpouring.

With an effort he forced himself to start the car and avoiding her surprised glance backed into the street. This was nothing, he must remember. She had done this before and he had put her behind him, as he would have slashed a bad account from his books.

He drove slowly downtown and affecting a disinterested abstraction traversed the deserted streets of the business section, peopled here and there, where a movie was giving out its crowd or where consumptive or pugilistic youth lounged in front of pool halls. The clink of glasses and the slap of hands on the bars issued from saloons, cloisters of glazed glass and dirty yellow light.

She was watching him closely and the silence was embarrassing yet in this crisis he could find no casual word with which to profane the hour. At a convenient turning he began to zig-zag back toward the College Club.

"Have you missed me?" she asked suddenly.

"Everybody missed you."

He wondered if she knew of Irene Scheerer. She had been back only a day—her absence had been almost contemporaneous with his engagement.

"What a remark!" Judy laughed sadly—without sadness. She looked at him searchingly. He became absorbed for a moment in the dashboard.

"You're handsomer than you used to be," she said thoughtfully. "Dexter, you have the most rememberable eyes."

He could have laughed at this, but he did not laugh. It was the sort of thing that was said to sophomores. Yet it stabbed at him.

"I'm awfully tired of everything, kiddo." She called everyone kiddo, endowing the obsolete slang with careless, individual camaraderie. "I wish you'd marry me."

The directness of this confused him. He should have told her now that he was going to marry another girl but he could not tell her. He could as easily have sworn that he had never loved her.

"I think we'd get along," she continued, on the same note, "unless probably you've forgotten me and fallen in love with another girl."

Her confidence was obviously enormous. She had said, in effect, that she found such a thing impossible to believe, that if it were true he had merely committed a childish indiscretion—and probably to show off. She would forgive him, because it was not a matter of any moment but rather something to be brushed aside lightly.

"Of course you could never love anybody but me," she continued. "I like the way you love me. Oh, Dexter, have you forgotten last year?"

"No, I haven't forgotten."

"Neither have I!"

Was she sincerely moved—or was she carried along by the wave of her own acting?

"I wish we could be like that again," she said, and he forced himself to answer:

"I don't think we can."

"I suppose not. . . . I hear you're giving Irene Scheerer a violent rush."

There was not the faintest emphasis on the name, yet Dexter was suddenly ashamed.

"Oh, take me home," cried Judy suddenly. "I don't want to go back to that idiotic dance—with those children."

Then, as he turned up the street that led to the residence district, Judy began to cry quietly to herself. He had never seen her cry before.

The dark street lightened, the dwellings of the rich loomed up around them, he stopped his coupé in front of the great white bulk of the Mortimer Jones' house, somnolent, gorgeous, drenched with the splendor of the damp moonlight. Its solidity startled him. The strong walls, the fine steel of the girders, the breadth and beam and pomp of it were there only to bring out the contrast with the young beauty beside him. It was sturdy to accentuate her slightness—as if to show what a breeze could be generated by a butterfly's wing.

He sat perfectly quiet, his nerves in wild clamor, afraid that if he moved he would find her irresistibly in his arms. Two tears had rolled down her wet face and trembled on her upper lip.

"I'm more beautiful than anybody else," she said brokenly, "why can't I be happy?" Her moist eyes tore at his stability—mouth turned slowly downward with an exquisite sadness. "I'd like to marry you if you'll have me, Dexter. I suppose you think I'm not worth having but I'll be so beautiful for you, Dexter."

A million phrases of anger, of pride, of passion, of hatred, of tenderness fought on his lips. Then a perfect wave of emotion washed over him, carrying off with it a sediment of wisdom, of convention, of doubt, of honor. This was his girl who was speaking, his own, his beautiful, his pride.

"Won't you come in?" he heard her draw in her breath sharply.

Waiting.

"All right," his voice was trembling, "I'll come in."

It seems strange to say that neither when it was over nor a long time afterward did he regret that night. Looking at it from the perspective of ten years, the fact that Judy's flare for him endured just one month seemed of little importance. Nor did it matter that by his yielding he subjected himself to a deeper agony in the end and gave serious hurt to Irene Scheerer and to Irene's parents who had befriended him. There was nothing sufficiently pictorial about Irene's grief to stamp itself on his mind.

Dexter was at bottom hard-minded. The attitude of the city on his action was of no importance to him, not because he was going to leave the city, but because any outside attitude on the situation seemed superficial. He was completely indifferent to popular opinion. Nor, when he had seen that it was no use, that he did not possess in himself the power to move fundamentally or to hold Judy Jones, did he bear any malice toward her. He loved her and he would love her until the day he was too old for loving—but he could not have her. So he tasted the deep pain that is reserved only for the strong, just as he had tasted for a little while the deep happiness.

Even the ultimate falsity of the grounds upon which Judy terminated the engagement—that she did not want to "take him away" from Irene, that it— was on her conscience—did not revolt him. He was beyond any revulsion or any amusement.

He went east in February with the intention of selling out his laundries and settling in New York—but the war[2] came to America in March and changed his plans. He returned to the west, handed over the management of the business to his partner and went into the first officers' training camp in late April. He was one of those young thousands who greeted the war with a certain amount of relief, welcoming the liberation from webs of tangled emotion.

This story is not his biography, remember, although things creep into it which have nothing to do with those dreams he had when he was young. We are almost done with them and with him now. There is only one more incident to be related here and it happens seven years farther on.

It took place in New York, where he had done well—so well that there were no barriers too high for him now. He was thirty-two years old, and, except for one flying trip immediately after the war, he had not been west in seven years. A man named Devlin from Detroit came into his office to see him in a business way, and then and there this incident occurred, and closed out, so to speak, this particular side of his life.

"So you're from the middle west," said the man Devlin with careless curiosity. "That's funny—I thought men like you were probably born and raised on Wall Street. You know—wife of one of my best friends in Detroit came from your city. I was an usher at the wedding."

Dexter waited with no apprehension of what was coming. There was a magic that his city would never lose for him. Just as Judy's house had always seemed to him more mysterious and gay than other houses, so his dream of the city itself, now that he had gone from it, was pervaded with a melancholy beauty.

"Judy Simms," said Devlin with no particular interest, "Judy Jones she was once."

"Yes. I knew her." A dull impatience spread over him. He had heard, of course, that she was married,—perhaps deliberately he had heard no more.

"Awfully nice girl," brooded Devlin, meaninglessly, "I'm sort of sorry for her."

"Why?" Something in Dexter was alert, receptive, at once.

"Oh, Joe Simms has gone to pieces in a way. I don't mean he beats her, you understand, or anything like that. But he drinks and runs around—"

"Doesn't she run around?"

2. World War I, which the United States entered in 1917.

"No. Stays at home with her kids."

"Oh."

"She's a little too old for him," said Devlin.

"Too old!" cried Dexter, "why man, she's only twenty-seven."

He was possessed with a wild notion of rushing out into the streets and taking a train to Detroit. He rose to his feet, spasmodically, involuntarily.

"I guess you're busy," Devlin apologized quickly. "I didn't realize——"

"No, I'm not busy," said Dexter, steadying his voice. "I'm not busy at all. Not busy at all. Did you say she was—twenty-seven. No, I said she was twenty-seven."

"Yes, you did," agreed Devlin drily.

"Go on, then. Go on."

"What do you mean?"

"About Judy Jones."

Devlin looked at him helplessly.

"Well, that's—I told you all there is to it. He treats her like the devil. Oh, they're not going to get divorced or anything. When he's particularly outrageous she forgives him. In fact, I'm inclined to think she loves him. She was a pretty girl when she first came to Detroit."

A pretty girl! The phrase struck Dexter as ludicrous.

"Isn't she—a pretty girl any more?"

"Oh, she's all right."

"Look here," said Dexter, sitting down suddenly, "I don't understand. You say she was a 'pretty girl' and now you say she's 'all right.' I don't understand what you mean—Judy Jones wasn't a pretty girl, at all. She was a great beauty. Why, I knew her, I knew her. She was——"

Devlin laughed pleasantly.

"I'm not trying to start a row," he said. "I think Judy's a nice girl and I like her. I can't understand how a man like Joe Simms could fall madly in love with her, but he did." Then he added, "Most of the women like her."

Dexter looked closely at Devlin, thinking wildly that there must be a reason for this, some insensitivity in the man or some private malice.

"Lots of women fade just-like-*that*." Devlin snapped his fingers. "You must have seen it happen. Perhaps I've forgotten how pretty she was at her wedding. I've seen her so much since then, you see. She has nice eyes."

A sort of dullness settled down upon Dexter. For the first time in his life he felt like getting very drunk. He knew that he was laughing loudly at something Devlin had said but he did not know what it was or why it was funny. When Devlin went, in a few minutes, he lay down on his lounge and looked out the window at the New York skyline into which the sun was sinking in dully lovely shades of pink and gold.

He had thought that having nothing else to lose he was invulnerable at last—but he knew that he had just lost something more, as surely as if he had married Judy Jones and seen her fade away before his eyes.

The dream was gone. Something had been taken from him. In a sort of panic he pushed the palms of his hands into his eyes and tried to bring up a picture of the waters lapping at Lake Erminie and the moonlit verandah, and gingham on the golf links and the dry sun and the gold color of her neck's soft down. And her mouth damp to his kisses and her eyes plaintive with melancholy and her freshness like new fine linen in the morning. Why these things were no longer in the world. They had existed and they existed no more.

For the first time in years the tears were streaming down his face. But they were for himself now. He did not care about mouth and eyes and moving hands. He wanted to care and he could not care. For he had gone away and he could never go back any more. The gates were closed, the sun was gone down and there was no beauty but the grey beauty of steel that withstands all time. Even the grief he could have borne was left behind in the country of illusion, of youth, of the richness of life, where his winter dreams had flourished.

"Long ago," he said, "long ago, there was something in me, but now that thing is gone. Now that thing is gone, that thing is gone. I cannot cry. I cannot care. That thing will come back no more."

1922

Babylon Revisited[1]

"And where's Mr. Campbell?" Charlie asked.

"Gone to Switzerland. Mr. Campbell's a pretty sick man, Mr. Wales."

"I'm sorry to hear that. And George Hardt?" Charlie inquired.

"Back in America, gone to work."

"And where is the Snow Bird?"

"He was in here last week. Anyway, his friend, Mr. Schaeffer, is in Paris."

Two familiar names from the long list of a year and a half ago. Charlie scribbled an address in his notebook and tore out the page.

"If you see Mr. Schaeffer, give him this," he said. "It's my brother-in-law's address. I haven't settled on a hotel yet."

He was not really disappointed to find Paris was so empty. But the stillness in the Ritz bar was strange and portentous. It was not an American bar any more—he felt polite in it, and not as if he owned it. It had gone back into France. He felt the stillness from the moment he got out of the taxi and saw the doorman, usually in a frenzy of activity at this hour, gossiping with a *chasseur*[2] by the servants' entrance.

Passing through the corridor, he heard only a single, bored voice in the once-clamorous women's room. When he turned into the bar he traveled the twenty feet of green carpet with his eyes fixed straight ahead by old habit; and then, with his foot firmly on the rail, he turned and surveyed the room, encountering only a single pair of eyes that fluttered up from a newspaper in the corner. Charlie asked for the head barman, Paul, who in the latter days of the bull market had come to work in his own custom-built car—disembarking, however, with due nicety at the nearest corner. But Paul was at his country house today and Alix giving him information.

"No, no more," Charlie said, "I'm going slow these days."

Alix congratulated him: "You were going pretty strong a couple of years ago."

1. Babylon was an ancient, prosperous city in Mesopotamia, associated by the Hebrews and Greeks with materialism and sensual pleasure; here, the reference is to Paris, where the story is set in the aftermath of the stock market crash of 1929. 2. Messenger-boy, errand runner (French).

"I'll stick to it all right," Charlie assured him. "I've stuck to it for over a year and a half now."

"How do you find conditions in America?"

"I haven't been to America for months. I'm in business in Prague, representing a couple of concerns there. They don't know about me down there."

Alix smiled.

"Remember the night of George Hardt's bachelor dinner here?" said Charlie. "By the way, what's become of Claude Fessenden?"

Alix lowered his voice confidentially: "He's in Paris, but he doesn't come here any more. Paul doesn't allow it. He ran up a bill of thirty thousand francs, charging all his drinks and his lunches, and usually his dinner, for more than a year. And when Paul finally told him he had to pay, he gave him a bad check."

Alix shook his head sadly.

"I don't understand it, such a dandy fellow. Now he's all bloated up—" He made a plump apple of his hands.

Charlie watched a group of strident queens installing themselves in a corner.

"Nothing affects them," he thought. "Stocks rise and fall, people loaf or work, but they go on forever." The place oppressed him. He called for the dice and shook with Alix for the drink.

"Here for long, Mr. Wales?"

"I'm here for four or five days to see my little girl."

"Oh-h! You have a little girl?"

Outside, the fire-red, gas-blue, ghost-green signs shone smokily through the tranquil rain. It was late afternoon and the streets were in movement; the bistros[3] gleamed. At the corner of the Boulevard des Capucines he took a taxi. The Place de la Concorde moved by in pink majesty; they crossed the logical Seine, and Charlie felt the sudden provincial quality of the left bank.[4]

Charlie directed his taxi to the Avenue de l'Opera, which was out of his way. But he wanted to see the blue hour spread over the magnificent façade, and imagine that the cab horns, playing endlessly the first few bars of Le Plus que Lent,[5] were the trumpets of the Second Empire. They were closing the iron grill in front of Brentano's Book-store, and people were already at dinner behind the trim little bourgeois hedge of Duval's. He had never eaten at a really cheap restaurant in Paris. Five-course dinner, four francs fifty, eighteen cents, wine included. For some odd reason he wished that he had.

As they rolled on to the Left Bank and he felt its sudden provincialism, he thought, "I spoiled this city for myself. I didn't realize it, but the days came along one after another, and then two years were gone, and everything was gone, and I was gone."

He was thirty-five, and good to look at. The Irish mobility of his face was sobered by a deep wrinkle between his eyes. As he rang his brother-in-law's bell in the Rue Palatine, the wrinkle deepened till it pulled down his brows; he felt a cramping sensation in his belly. From behind the maid who opened

3. Small, informal restaurants.
4. Paris is divided by the Seine River; the grander buildings and broader streets are on the Right Bank. To Charlie, the Left Bank is more like a town than a city.
5. La plus que lente (More than slow), piano composition by French composer Claude Debussy (1862–1918).

the door darted a lovely little girl of nine who shrieked "Daddy!" and flew up, struggling like a fish, into his arms. She pulled his head around by one ear and set her cheek against his.

"My old pie," he said.

"Oh, daddy, daddy, daddy, daddy, dads, dads, dads!"

She drew him into the salon, where the family waited, a boy and a girl his daughter's age, his sister-in-law and her husband. He greeted Marion with his voice pitched carefully to avoid either feigned enthusiasm or dislike, but her response was more frankly tepid, though she minimized her expression of unalterable distrust by directing her regard toward his child. The two men clasped hands in a friendly way and Lincoln Peters rested his for a moment on Charlie's shoulder.

The room was warm and comfortably American. The three children moved intimately about, playing through the yellow oblongs that led to other rooms; the cheer of six o'clock spoke in the eager smacks of the fire and the sounds of French activity in the kitchen. But Charlie did not relax; his heart sat up rigidly in his body and he drew confidence from his daughter, who from time to time came close to him, holding in her arms the doll he had brought.

"Really extremely well," he declared in answer to Lincoln's question. "There's a lot of business there that isn't moving at all, but we're doing even better than ever. In fact, damn well. I'm bringing my sister over from America next month to keep house for me. My income last year was bigger than it was when I had money. You see, the Czechs—"

His boasting was for a specific purpose; but after a moment, seeing a faint restiveness in Lincoln's eye, he changed the subject:

"Those are fine children of yours, well brought up, good manners."

"We think Honoria's a great little girl too."

Marion Peters came back from the kitchen. She was a tall woman with worried eyes, who had once possessed a fresh American loveliness. Charlie had never been sensitive to it and was always surprised when people spoke of how pretty she had been. From the first there had been an instinctive antipathy between them.

"Well, how do you find Honoria?" she asked.

"Wonderful. I was astonished how much she's grown in ten months. All the children are looking well."

"We haven't had a doctor for a year. How do you like being back in Paris?"

"It seems very funny to see so few Americans around."

"I'm delighted," Marion said vehemently. "Now at least you can go into a store without their assuming you're a millionaire. We've suffered like everybody, but on the whole it's a good deal pleasanter."

"But it was nice while it lasted," Charlie said. "We were a sort of royalty, almost infallible, with a sort of magic around us. In the bar this afternoon"—he stumbled, seeing his mistake—"there wasn't a man I knew."

She looked at him keenly. "I should think you'd have had enough of bars."

"I only stayed a minute. I take one drink every afternoon, and no more."

"Don't you want a cocktail before dinner?" Lincoln asked.

"I take only one drink every afternoon, and I've had that."

"I hope you keep to it," said Marion.

Her dislike was evident in the coldness with which she spoke, but Charlie only smiled; he had larger plans. Her very aggressiveness gave him an advantage, and he knew enough to wait. He wanted them to initiate the discussion of what they knew had brought him to Paris.

At dinner he couldn't decide whether Honoria was most like him or her mother. Fortunate if she didn't combine the traits of both that had brought them to disaster. A great wave of protectiveness went over him. He thought he knew what to do for her. He believed in character; he wanted to jump back a whole generation and trust in character again as the eternally valuable element. Everything else wore out.

He left soon after dinner, but not to go home. He was curious to see Paris by night with clearer and more judicious eyes than those of other days. He bought a *strapontin* for the Casino and watched Josephine Baker[6] go through her chocolate arabesques.

After an hour he left and strolled toward Montmartre, up the Rue Pigalle into the Place Blanche. The rain had stopped and there were a few people in evening clothes disembarking from taxis in front of cabarets, and *cocottes*[7] prowling singly or in pairs, and many Negroes. He passed a lighted door from which issued music, and stopped with the sense of familiarity; it was Bricktop's, where he had parted with so many hours and so much money. A few doors farther on he found another ancient rendezvous and incautiously put his head inside. Immediately an eager orchestra burst into sound, a pair of professional dancers leaped to their feet and a maître d'hôtel swooped toward him, crying, "Crowd just arriving, sir!" But he withdrew quickly.

"You have to be damn drunk," he thought.

Zelli's was closed, the bleak and sinister cheap hotels surrounding it were dark; up in the Rue Blanche there was more light and a local, colloquial French crowd. The Poet's Cave had disappeared, but the two great mouths of the Café of Heaven and the Café of Hell still yawned—even devoured, as he watched, the meager contents of a tourist bus—a German, a Japanese, and an American couple who glanced at him with frightened eyes.

So much for the effort and ingenuity of Montmartre. All the catering to vice and waste was on an utterly childish scale, and he suddenly realized the meaning of the word "dissipate"—to dissipate into thin air; to make nothing out of something. In the little hours of the night every move from place to place was an enormous human jump, an increase of paying for the privilege of slower and slower motion.

He remembered thousand-franc notes given to an orchestra for playing a single number, hundred-franc notes tossed to a doorman for calling a cab.

But it hadn't been given for nothing.

It had been given, even the most wildly squandered sum, as an offering to destiny that he might not remember the things most worth remembering, the things that now he would always remember—his child taken from his control, his wife escaped to a grave in Vermont.

In the glare of a *brasserie*[8] a woman spoke to him. He bought her some eggs and coffee, and then, eluding her encouraging stare, gave her a twenty-franc note and took a taxi to his hotel.

---

6. African American jazz singer and dancer (1906–1975) who arrived in Paris with a vaudeville troupe in 1925 and remained as a star entertainer. "*Strapontin*": folding seat.

7. Coquettes (French, literal trans.); prostitutes.
8. Large, plain restaurant specializing in simple meals and beer.

II

He woke upon a fine fall day—football weather. The depression of yesterday was gone and he liked the people on the streets. At noon he sat opposite Honoria at Le Grand Vatel, the only restaurant he could think of not reminiscent of champagne dinners and long luncheons that began at two and ended in a blurred and vague twilight.

"Now, how about vegetables? Oughtn't you to have some vegetables?"

"Well, yes."

"Here's *épinards* and *chou-fleur* and carrots and *haricots*."[9]

"I'd like *chou-fleur*."

"Wouldn't you like to have two vegetables?"

"I usually only have one at lunch."

The waiter was pretending to be inordinately fond of children. *"Qu'elle est mignonne la petite! Elle parle exactement comme une Française."*[1]

"How about dessert? Shall we wait and see?"

The waiter disappeared. Honoria looked at her father expectantly.

"What are we going to do?"

"First, we're going to that toy store in the Rue Saint-Honoré and buy you anything you like. And then we're going to the vaudeville at the Empire."

She hesitated. "I like it about the vaudeville, but not the toy store."

"Why not?"

"Well, you brought me this doll." She had it with her. "And I've got lots of things. And we're not rich any more, are we?"

"We never were. But today you are to have anything you want."

"All right," she agreed resignedly.

When there had been her mother and a French nurse he had been inclined to be strict; now he extended himself, reached out for a new tolerance; he must be both parents to her and not shut any of her out of communication.

"I want to get to know you," he said gravely. "First let me introduce myself. My name is Charles J. Wales, of Prague."

"Oh, daddy!" her voice cracked with laughter.

"And who are you, please?" he persisted, and she accepted a rôle immediately: "Honoria Wales, Rue Palatine, Paris."

"Married or single?"

"No, not married. Single."

He indicated the doll. "But I see you have a child, madame."

Unwilling to disinherit it, she took it to her heart and thought quickly: "Yes, I've been married, but I'm not married now. My husband is dead."

He went on quickly, "And the child's name?"

"Simone. That's after my best friend at school."

"I'm very pleased that you're doing so well at school."

"I'm third this month," she boasted. "Elsie"—that was her cousin—"is only about eighteenth, and Richard is about at the bottom."

"You like Richard and Elsie, don't you?"

"Oh, yes. I like Richard quite well and I like her all right."

---

9. Green beans (French). *"Épinards"*: spinach. *"Chou-fleur"*: cauliflower.

1. How cute she is! She speaks exactly like a French girl (French).

Cautiously and casually he asked: "And Aunt Marion and Uncle Lincoln— which do you like best?"

"Oh, Uncle Lincoln, I guess."

He was increasingly aware of her presence. As they came in, a murmur of ". . . adorable" followed them, and now the people at the next table bent all their silences upon her, staring as if she were something no more conscious than a flower.

"Why don't I live with you?" she asked suddenly. "Because mamma's dead?"

"You must stay here and learn more French. It would have been hard for daddy to take care of you so well."

"I don't really need much taking care of any more. I do everything for myself."

Going out of the restaurant, a man and a woman unexpectedly hailed him.

"Well, the old Wales!"

"Hello there, Lorraine. . . . Dunc."

Sudden ghosts out of the past: Duncan Schaeffer, a friend from college. Lorraine Quarrles, a lovely, pale blonde of thirty; one of a crowd who had helped them make months into days in the lavish times of three years ago.

"My husband couldn't come this year," she said, in answer to his question. "We're poor as hell. So he gave me two hundred a month and told me I could do my worst on that. . . . This your little girl?"

"What about coming back and sitting down?" Duncan asked.

"Can't do it." He was glad for an excuse. As always, he felt Lorraine's passionate, provocative attraction, but his own rhythm was different now.

"Well, how about dinner?" she asked.

"I'm not free. Give me your address and let me call you."

"Charlie, I believe you're sober," she said judicially. "I honestly believe he's sober, Dunc. Pinch him and see if he's sober."

Charlie indicated Honoria with his head. They both laughed.

"What's your address?" said Duncan skeptically.

He hesitated, unwilling to give the name of his hotel.

"I'm not settled yet. I'd better call you. We're going to see the vaudeville at the Empire."

"There! That's what I want to do," Lorraine said. "I want to see some clowns and acrobats and jugglers. That's just what we'll do, Dunc."

"We've got to do an errand first," said Charlie. "Perhaps we'll see you there."

"All right, you snob. . . . Good-by, beautiful little girl."

"Good-by."

Honoria bobbed politely.

Somehow, an unwelcome encounter. They liked him because he was functioning, because he was serious; they wanted to see him, because he was stronger than they were now, because they wanted to draw a certain sustenance from his strength.

At the Empire, Honoria proudly refused to sit upon her father's folded coat. She was already an individual with a code of her own, and Charlie was more and more absorbed by the desire of putting a little of himself into her before she crystallized utterly. It was hopeless to try to know her in so short a time.

Between the acts they came upon Duncan and Lorraine in the lobby where the band was playing.

"Have a drink?"

"All right, but not up at the bar. We'll take a table."

"The perfect father."

Listening abstractedly to Lorraine, Charlie watched Honoria's eyes leave their table, and he followed them wistfully about the room, wondering what they saw. He met her glance and she smiled.

"I liked that lemonade," she said.

What had she said? What had he expected? Going home in a taxi afterward, he pulled her over until her head rested against his chest.

"Darling, do you ever think about your mother?"

"Yes, sometimes," she answered vaguely.

"I don't want you to forget her. Have you got a picture of her?"

"Yes, I think so. Anyhow, Aunt Marion has. Why don't you want me to forget her?"

"She loved you very much."

"I loved her too."

They were silent for a moment.

"Daddy, I want to come and live with you," she said suddenly.

His heart leaped; he had wanted it to come like this.

"Aren't you perfectly happy?"

"Yes, but I love you better than anybody. And you love me better than anybody, don't you, now that mummy's dead?"

"Of course I do. But you won't always like me best, honey. You'll grow up and meet somebody your own age and go marry him and forget you ever had a daddy."

"Yes, that's true," she agreed tranquilly.

He didn't go in. He was coming back at nine o'clock and he wanted to keep himself fresh and new for the thing he must say then.

"When you're safe inside, just show yourself in that window."

"All right. Good-by, dads, dads, dads, dads."

He waited in the dark street until she appeared, all warm and glowing, in the window above and kissed her fingers out into the night.

III

They were waiting. Marion sat behind the coffee service in a dignified black dinner dress that just faintly suggested mourning. Lincoln was walking up and down with the animation of one who had already been talking. They were as anxious as he was to get into the question. He opened it almost immediately:

"I suppose you know what I want to see you about—why I really came to Paris."

Marion played with the black stars on her necklace and frowned.

"I'm awfully anxious to have a home," he continued. "And I'm awfully anxious to have Honoria in it. I appreciate your taking in Honoria for her mother's sake, but things have changed now"—he hesitated and then continued more forcibly—"changed radically with me, and I want to ask you to reconsider the matter. It would be silly for me to deny that about three years ago I was acting badly—"

Marion looked up at him with hard eyes.

"—but all that's over. As I told you, I haven't had more than a drink a day for over a year, and I take that drink deliberately, so that the idea of alcohol won't get too big in my imagination. You see the idea?"

"No," said Marion succinctly.

"It's a sort of stunt I set myself. It keeps the matter in proportion."

"I get you," said Lincoln. "You don't want to admit it's got any attraction for you."

"Something like that. Sometimes I forget and don't take it. But I try to take it. Anyhow, I couldn't afford to drink in my position. The people I represent are more than satisfied with what I've done, and I'm bringing my sister over from Burlington to keep house for me, and I want awfully to have Honoria too. You know that even when her mother and I weren't getting along well we never let anything that happened touch Honoria. I know she's fond of me and I know I'm able to take care of her and—well, there you are. How do you feel about it?"

He knew that now he would have to take a beating. It would last an hour or two hours, and it would be difficult, but if he modulated his inevitable resentment to the chastened attitude of the reformed sinner, he might win his point in the end.

Keep your temper, he told himself. You don't want to be justified. You want Honoria.

Lincoln spoke first: "We've been talking it over ever since we got your letter last month. We're happy to have Honoria here. She's a dear little thing, and we're glad to be able to help her, but of course that isn't the question—"

Marion interrupted suddenly. "How long are you going to stay sober, Charlie?" she asked.

"Permanently, I hope."

"How can anybody count on that?"

"You know I never did drink heavily until I gave up business and came over here with nothing to do. Then Helen and I began to run around with—"

"Please leave Helen out of it. I can't bear to hear you talk about her like that."

He stared at her grimly; he had never been certain how fond of each other the sisters were in life.

"My drinking only lasted about a year and a half—from the time we came over until I—collapsed."

"It was time enough."

"It was time enough," he agreed.

"My duty is entirely to Helen," she said. "I try to think what she would have wanted me to do. Frankly, from the night you did that terrible thing you haven't really existed for me. I can't help that. She was my sister."

"Yes."

"When she was dying she asked me to look out for Honoria. If you hadn't been in a sanitarium then, it might have helped matters."

He had no answer.

"I'll never in my life be able to forget the morning when Helen knocked at my door, soaked to the skin and shivering and said you'd locked her out."

Charlie gripped the sides of the chair. This was more difficult than he expected; he wanted to launch out into a long expostulation and explanation, but he only said: "The night I locked her out—" and she interrupted, "I don't feel up to going over that again."

After a moment's silence Lincoln said: "We're getting off the subject. You want Marion to set aside her legal guardianship and give you Honoria. I think the main point for her is whether she has confidence in you or not."

"I don't blame Marion," Charlie said slowly, "but I think she can have entire confidence in me. I had a good record up to three years ago. Of course, it's within human possibilities I might go wrong any time. But if we wait much longer I'll lose Honoria's childhood and my chance for a home." He shook his head, "I'll simply lose her, don't you see?"

"Yes, I see," said Lincoln.

"Why didn't you think of all this before?" Marion asked.

"I suppose I did, from time to time, but Helen and I were getting along badly. When I consented to the guardianship, I was flat on my back in a sanitarium and the market had cleaned me out. I knew I'd acted badly, and I thought if it would bring any peace to Helen, I'd agree to anything. But now it's different. I'm functioning, I'm behaving damn well, so far as—"

"Please don't swear at me," Marion said.

He looked at her, startled. With each remark the force of her dislike became more and more apparent. She had built up all her fear of life into one wall and faced it toward him. This trivial reproof was possibly the result of some trouble with the cook several hours before. Charlie became increasingly alarmed at leaving Honoria in this atmosphere of hostility against himself; sooner or later it would come out, in a word here, a shake of the head there, and some of that distrust would be irrevocably implanted in Honoria. But he pulled his temper down out of his face and shut it up inside him; he had won a point, for Lincoln realized the absurdity of Marion's remark and asked her lightly since when she had objected to the word "damn."

"Another thing," Charlie said: "I'm able to give her certain advantages now. I'm going to take a French governess to Prague with me. I've got a lease on a new apartment—"

He stopped, realizing that he was blundering. They couldn't be expected to accept with equanimity the fact that his income was again twice as large as their own.

"I suppose you can give her more luxuries than we can," said Marion. "When you were throwing away money we were living along watching every ten francs. . . . I suppose you'll start doing it again."

"Oh, no," he said. "I've learned. I worked hard for ten years, you know—until I got lucky in the market, like so many people. Terribly lucky. It won't happen again."

There was a long silence. All of them felt their nerves straining, and for the first time in a year Charlie wanted a drink. He was sure now that Lincoln Peters wanted him to have his child.

Marion shuddered suddenly; part of her saw that Charlie's feet were planted on the earth now, and her own maternal feeling recognized the naturalness of his desire; but she had lived for a long time with a prejudice—a prejudice founded on a curious disbelief in her sister's happiness, and which, in the shock of one terrible night, had turned to hatred for him. It had all happened at a point in her life where the discouragement of ill health and adverse circumstances made it necessary for her to believe in tangible villainy and a tangible villain.

"I can't help what I think!" she cried out suddenly. "How much you were responsible for Helen's death, I don't know. It's something you'll have to square with your own conscience."

An electric current of agony surged through him; for a moment he was almost on his feet, an unuttered sound echoing in his throat. He hung on to himself for a moment, another moment.

"Hold on there," said Lincoln uncomfortably. "I never thought you were responsible for that."

"Helen died of heart trouble," Charlie said dully.

"Yes, heart trouble." Marion spoke as if the phrase had another meaning for her.

Then, in the flatness that followed her outburst, she saw him plainly and she knew he had somehow arrived at control over the situation. Glancing at her husband, she found no help from him, and as abruptly as if it were a matter of no importance, she threw up the sponge.

"Do what you like!" she cried, springing up from her chair. "She's your child. I'm not the person to stand in your way. I think if it were my child I'd rather see her—" She managed to check herself. "You two decide it. I can't stand this. I'm sick. I'm going to bed."

She hurried from the room; after a moment Lincoln said:

"This has been a hard day for her. You know how strongly she feels—" His voice was almost apologetic: "When a woman gets an idea in her head."

"Of course."

"It's going to be all right. I think she sees now that you—can provide for the child, and so we can't very well stand in your way or Honoria's way."

"Thank you, Lincoln."

"I'd better go along and see how she is."

"I'm going."

He was still trembling when he reached the street, but a walk down the Rue Bonaparte to the *quais*[2] set him up, and as he crossed the Seine, fresh and new by the *quai* lamps, he felt exultant. But back in his room he couldn't sleep. The image of Helen haunted him. Helen whom he had loved so until they had senselessly begun to abuse each other's love, tear it into shreds. On that terrible February night that Marion remembered so vividly, a slow quarrel had gone on for hours. There was a scene at the Florida, and then he attempted to take her home, and then she kissed young Webb at a table; after that there was what she had hysterically said. When he arrived home alone he turned the key in the lock in wild anger. How could he know she would arrive an hour later alone, that there would be a snowstorm in which she wandered about in slippers, too confused to find a taxi? Then the aftermath, her escaping pneumonia by a miracle, and all the attendant horror. They were "reconciled," but that was the beginning of the end, and Marion, who had seen with her own eyes and who imagined it to be one of many scenes from her sister's martyrdom, never forgot.

---

2. Quays (French); a section of the Left Bank is lined with quays, or walking places along the river.

Going over it again brought Helen nearer, and in the white, soft light that steals upon half sleep near morning he found himself talking to her again. She said that he was perfectly right about Honoria and that she wanted Honoria to be with him. She said she was glad he was being good and doing better. She said a lot of other things—very friendly things—but she was in a swing in a white dress, and swinging faster and faster all the time, so that at the end he could not hear clearly all that she said.

IV

He woke up feeling happy. The door of the world was open again. He made plans, vistas, futures for Honoria and himself, but suddenly he grew sad, remembering all the plans he and Helen had made. She had not planned to die. The present was the thing—work to do and someone to love. But not to love too much, for he knew the injury that a father can do to a daughter or a mother to a son by attaching them too closely: afterward, out in the world, the child would seek in the marriage partner the same blind tenderness and, failing probably to find it, turn against love and life.

It was another bright, crisp day. He called Lincoln Peters at the bank where he worked and asked if he could count on taking Honoria when he left for Prague. Lincoln agreed that there was no reason for delay. One thing—the legal guardianship. Marion wanted to retain that a while longer. She was upset by the whole matter, and it would oil things if she felt that the situation was still in her control for another year. Charlie agreed, wanting only the tangible, visible child.

Then the question of a governess. Charles sat in a gloomy agency and talked to a cross Béarnaise and to a buxom Breton peasant,[3] neither of whom he could have endured. There were others whom he would see tomorrow.

He lunched with Lincoln Peters at Griffons, trying to keep down his exultation.

"There's nothing quite like your own child," Lincoln said. "But you understand how Marion feels too."

"She's forgotten how hard I worked for seven years there," Charlie said. "She just remembers one night."

"There's another thing." Lincoln hesitated. "While you and Helen were tearing around Europe throwing money away, we were just getting along. I didn't touch any of the prosperity because I never got ahead enough to carry anything but my insurance. I think Marion felt there was some kind of injustice in it—you not even working toward the end, and getting richer and richer."

"It went just as quick as it came," said Charlie.

"Yes, a lot of it stayed in the hands of *chasseurs* and saxophone players and maîtres d'hôtel—well, the big party's over now. I just said that to explain Marion's feeling about those crazy years. If you drop in about six o'clock tonight before Marion's too tired, we'll settle the details on the spot."

Back at his hotel, Charlie found a *pneumatique* that had been redirected from the Ritz bar where Charlie had left his address for the purpose of finding a certain man.

---

3. Béarn and Breton are two French provincial regions. The implication is that Charlie wants a higher-class (preferably Parisian) governess.

"Dear Charlie: You were so strange when we saw you the other day that I wondered if I did something to offend you. If so, I'm not conscious of it. In fact, I have thought about you too much for the last year, and it's always been in the back of my mind that I might see you if I came over here. We *did* have such good times that crazy spring, like the night you and I stole the butcher's tricycle, and the time we tried to call on the president and you had the old derby rim and the wire cane. Everybody seems so old lately, but I don't feel old a bit. Couldn't we get together some time today for old time's sake? I've got a vile hang-over for the moment, but will be feeling better this afternoon and will look for you about five in the sweatshop at the Ritz.

"Always devotedly,
Lorraine."

His first feeling was one of awe that he had actually, in his mature years, stolen a tricycle and pedaled Lorraine all over the Étoile between the small hours and dawn. In retrospect it was a nightmare. Locking out Helen didn't fit in with any other act of his life, but the tricycle incident did—it was one of many. How many weeks or months of dissipation to arrive at that condition of utter irresponsibility?

He tried to picture how Lorraine had appeared to him then—very attractive; Helen was unhappy about it, though she said nothing. Yesterday, in the restaurant, Lorraine had seemed trite, blurred, worn away. He emphatically did not want to see her, and he was glad Alix had not given away his hotel address. It was a relief to think, instead, of Honoria, to think of Sundays spent with her and of saying good morning to her and of knowing she was there in his house at night, drawing her breath in the darkness.

At five he took a taxi and bought presents for all the Peters—a piquant cloth doll, a box of Roman soldiers, flowers for Marion, big linen handkerchiefs for Lincoln.

He saw, when he arrived in the apartment, that Marion had accepted the inevitable. She greeted him now as though he were a recalcitrant member of the family, rather than a menacing outsider. Honoria had been told she was going; Charlie was glad to see that her tact made her conceal her excessive happiness. Only on his lap did she whisper her delight and the question "When?" before she slipped away with the other children.

He and Marion were alone for a minute in the room, and on an impulse he spoke out boldly:

"Family quarrels are bitter things. They don't go according to any rules. They're not like aches or wounds; they're more like splits in the skin that won't heal because there's not enough material. I wish you and I could be on better terms."

"Some things are hard to forget," she answered. "It's a question of confidence." There was no answer to this and presently she asked, "When do you propose to take her?"

"As soon as I can get a governess. I hoped the day after tomorrow."

"That's impossible. I've got to get her things in shape. Not before Saturday."

He yielded. Coming back into the room, Lincoln offered him a drink.

"I'll take my daily whisky," he said.

It was warm here, it was a home, people together by a fire. The children felt very safe and important; the mother and father were serious, watchful. They had things to do for the children more important than his visit here. A spoonful of medicine was, after all, more important than the strained relations between Marion and himself. They were not dull people, but they were very much in the grip of life and circumstances. He wondered if he couldn't do something to get Lincoln out of his rut at the bank.

A long peal at the door-bell; the *bonne à tout faire*[4] passed through and went down the corridor. The door opened upon another long ring, and then voices, and the three in the salon looked up expectantly; Richard moved to bring the corridor within his range of vision, and Marion rose. Then the maid came back along the corridor, closely followed by the voices, which developed under the light into Duncan Schaeffer and Lorraine Quarrles.

They were gay, they were hilarious, they were roaring with laughter. For a moment Charlie was astounded; unable to understand how they ferreted out the Peters' address.

"Ah-h-h!" Duncan wagged his finger roguishly at Charlie. "Ah-h-h!"

They both slid down another cascade of laughter. Anxious and at a loss, Charlie shook hands with them quickly and presented them to Lincoln and Marion. Marion nodded, scarcely speaking. She had drawn back a step toward the fire; her little girl stood beside her, and Marion put an arm about her shoulder.

With growing annoyance at the intrusion, Charlie waited for them to explain themselves. After some concentration Duncan said:

"We came to invite you out to dinner. Lorraine and I insist that all this shishi, cagy business 'bout your address got to stop."

Charlie came closer to them, as if to force them backward down the corridor.

"Sorry, but I can't. Tell me where you'll be and I'll phone you in half an hour."

This made no impression. Lorraine sat down suddenly on the side of a chair, and focusing her eyes on Richard, cried, "Oh, what a nice little boy! Come here, little boy." Richard glanced at his mother, but did not move. With a perceptible shrug of her shoulders, Lorraine turned back to Charlie:

"Come and dine. Sure your cousins won' mine. See you so sel'om. Or solemn."

"I can't," said Charlie sharply. "You two have dinner and I'll phone you."

Her voice became suddenly unpleasant. "All right, we'll go. But I remember once when you hammered on my door at four A.M. I was enough of a good sport to give you a drink. Come on, Dunc."

Still in slow motion, with blurred, angry faces, with uncertain feet, they retired along the corridor.

"Good night," Charlie said.

"Good night!" responded Lorraine emphatically.

When he went back into the salon Marion had not moved, only now her son was standing in the circle of her other arm. Lincoln was still swinging Honoria back and forth like a pendulum from side to side.

"What an outrage!" Charlie broke out. "What an absolute outrage!"

Neither of them answered. Charlie dropped into an armchair, picked up his drink, set it down again and said:

4. Maid of all work (French). The Peters family cannot afford to hire several servants with specialized tasks.

"People I haven't seen for two years having the colossal nerve—"

He broke off. Marion had made the sound "Oh!" in one swift, furious breath, turned her body from him with a jerk and left the room.

Lincoln set down Honoria carefully.

"You children go in and start your soup," he said, and when they obeyed, he said to Charlie:

"Marion's not well and she can't stand shocks. That kind of people make her really physically sick."

"I didn't tell them to come here. They wormed your name out of somebody. They deliberately—"

"Well, it's too bad. It doesn't help matters. Excuse me a minute."

Left alone, Charlie sat tense in his chair. In the next room he could hear the children eating, talking in monosyllables, already oblivious to the scene between their elders. He heard a murmur of conversation from a farther room and then the ticking bell of a telephone receiver picked up, and in a panic he moved to the other side of the room and out of earshot.

In a minute Lincoln came back. "Look here, Charlie. I think we'd better call off dinner for tonight. Marion's in bad shape."

"Is she angry with me?"

"Sort of," he said, almost roughly. "She's not strong and—"

"You mean she's changed her mind about Honoria?"

"She's pretty bitter right now. I don't know. You phone me at the bank tomorrow."

"I wish you'd explain to her I never dreamed these people would come here. I'm just as sore as you are."

"I couldn't explain anything to her now."

Charlie got up. He took his coat and hat and started down the corridor. Then he opened the door of the dining room and said in a strange voice, "Good night, children."

Honoria rose and ran around the table to hug him.

"Good night, sweetheart," he said vaguely, and then trying to make his voice more tender, trying to conciliate something, "Good night, dear children."

V

Charlie went directly to the Ritz bar with the furious idea of finding Lorraine and Duncan, but they were not there, and he realized that in any case there was nothing he could do. He had not touched his drink at the Peters, and now he ordered a whisky-and-soda. Paul came over to say hello.

"It's a great change," he said sadly. "We do about half the business we did. So many fellows I hear about back in the States lost everything, maybe not in the first crash, but then in the second. Your friend George Hardt lost every cent, I hear. Are you back in the States?"

"No, I'm in business in Prague."

"I heard that you lost a lot in the crash."

"I did," and he added grimly, "but I lost everything I wanted in the boom."

"Selling short."

"Something like that."

Again the memory of those days swept over him like a nightmare—the people they had met travelling; then people who couldn't add a row of figures or speak a coherent sentence. The little man Helen had consented to dance with at the ship's party, who had insulted her ten feet from the table; the women and girls carried screaming with drink or drugs out of public places—

—The men who locked their wives out in the snow, because the snow of twenty-nine wasn't real snow. If you didn't want it to be snow, you just paid some money.

He went to the phone and called the Peters' apartment; Lincoln answered.

"I called up because this thing is on my mind. Has Marion said anything definite?"

"Marion's sick," Lincoln answered shortly. "I know this thing isn't altogether your fault, but I can't have her go to pieces about it. I'm afraid we'll have to let it slide for six months; I can't take the chance of working her up to this state again."

"I see."

"I'm sorry, Charlie."

He went back to his table. His whisky glass was empty, but he shook his head when Alix looked at it questioningly. There wasn't much he could do now except send Honoria some things; he would send her a lot of things tomorrow. He thought rather angrily that this was just money—he had given so many people money. . . .

"No, no more," he said to another waiter. "What do I owe you?"

He would come back some day; they couldn't make him pay forever. But he wanted his child, and nothing was much good now, beside that fact. He wasn't young any more, with a lot of nice thoughts and dreams to have by himself. He was absolutely sure Helen wouldn't have wanted him to be so alone.

1931

JOHN DOS PASSOS
1896–1970

John Dos Passos's trilogy U.S.A. (1938) ranks with John Steinbeck's The Grapes of Wrath (1939) as a major piece of post-Depression leftist fiction. Always politically committed to the rights of the individual, Dos Passos evolved from social radicalism in the 1930s to social conservatism in the 1950s. He was born in Chicago of well-to-do Portuguese-American parents who were unmarried, and lived with his mother. He went to the exclusive Choate School and then to Harvard, graduating in 1916. At first he followed his father's wishes and studied architecture in Spain, but in 1917, like many young men impatient at the United States' delay in entering World War I, he joined the famous Norton-Harjes volunteer ambulance corps. After the United States entered the war, he became a medical corpsman in the U.S. Army.

After the war he married and spent a decade as a freelance journalist, traveling in Spain and Europe, and writing poetry, travel essays, plays, and fiction on the side. His novel Three Soldiers (1921) showed three young men from different backgrounds—a factory worker from San Francisco, a Harvard-educated composer, and a farm youth from Indiana—destroyed by their own bureaucratic army. Another novel, Manhattan Transfer (1925), experimented with kaleidoscopic and cinematic techniques to present the depersonalization of contemporary urban life.

Like many of the liberal and radical writers of the day, Dos Passos supported the accused anarchists Sacco and Vanzetti. In 1926 he joined the executive board of the Communist journal *The New Masses*. For the next eight years he took part in Communist activities but never joined the party, for he rejected the Communist demand that all writers in the party express only the party line. In 1934 the Communists broke up a Socialist rally at New York City's Madison Square Garden; this event persuaded Dos Passos that the Communists were more interested in power than social justice. Soon after he severed his Communist ties.

The three novels making up *U.S.A.—The 42nd Parallel, 1919,* and *The Big Money*—appeared between 1930 and 1936. The subject is twentieth-century America from coast to coast and at every social level; its portrayal is savagely satirical. It has a cast of eleven major characters, followed separately, whose lives occasionally intersect. Even the idealistic left-wing characters have a moral flabbiness and superficiality that, Dos Passos believed, was the effect of American materialism and its encouragement of personal greed. At that point in his life, Dos Passos believed that capitalism led to a division between rich and poor that could be remedied only by social change. And yet, because change could be produced only by individuals, and individuals were corrupted by their society, the source of change seemed elusive.

Dos Passos's blending of fiction with nonfiction in *U.S.A.* and his adaptation of cinematic strategies to written work were early uses of techniques that became commonplace in post–World War II fiction. Fiction alternated with other kinds of material—notably the "Newsreel" sections, in which newspaper excerpts and headlines, snippets from popular songs, and quotations from speeches and documents are brought together in an imitation of the weekly feature one saw at the movie house before television took over visual newscasting; the "Camera Eye" sections, which are impressionistic, emotional, lyrical fragments; and biographies of American notables like the dancer Isadora Duncan, the film star Rudolph Valentino, the inventors Thomas Edison and the Wright brothers, the financier J. P. Morgan, the labor leader Eugene Debs, the architect Frank Lloyd Wright, and the sociologist Thorstein Veblen.

Beginning with Franklin D. Roosevelt's second term in 1936, Dos Passos supported the president. But after the war his concern for personal liberty and his fear of institutions and of concentrated power led him to reconceive the threat to America as coming from the left rather than the right. He wrote a number of novels from this vantage point, including a trilogy called *District of Columbia* (1952), and *Midcentury* (1961), which returned to the format of *U.S.A.*

The text is that of the first complete edition of *U.S.A.* (1938).

FROM U.S.A.

The Big Money[1]

Newsreel LXVIII

WALL STREET STUNNED

This is not Thirtyeight, but it's old Ninetyseven[2]
You must put her in Center on time

MARKET SURE TO RECOVER FROM SLUMP

DECLINE IN CONTRACTS

---

1. The following sections come at the end of *The Big Money*.
2. The 1903 wreck of the "old Ninetyseven" train

between Washington, D.C., and Atlanta, Georgia, gave rise to several popular railroad ballads. A 1924 recording of one of these sold over a million copies.

POLICE TURN MACHINE GUNS ON COLORADO
MINE STRIKERS KILL 5 WOUND 40

sympathizers appeared on the scene just as thousands of office workers were pouring out of the buildings at the lunch hour. As they raised their placard high and started an indefinite march from one side to the other, they were jeered and hooted not only by the office workers but also by workmen on a building under construction

NEW METHODS OF SELLING SEEN

RESCUE CREWS TRY TO UPEND ILL-FATED CRAFT

WHILE WAITING FOR PONTOONS

He looked 'round an' said to his black greasy fireman
Jus' shovel in a little more coal
And when we cross that White Oak Mountain
You can watch your Ninety-seven roll

I find your column interesting and need advice. I have saved four thousand dollars which I want to invest for a better income. Do you think I might buy stocks?

POLICE KILLER FLICKS CIGARETTE AS HE GOES
TREMBLING TO DOOM

PLAY AGENCIES IN RING OF SLAVE GIRL MARTS

MAKER OF LOVE DISBARRED AS LAWYER

Oh the right wing clothesmakers
And the Socialist fakers
They make by the workers . . .
Double cross

They preach Social-ism
But practice Fasc-ism
To keep capitalism
By the boss[3]

MOSCOW CONGRESS OUSTS OPPOSITION[4]

It's a mighty rough road from Lynchburg to Danville
An' a line on a three mile grade
It was on that grade he lost his average
An' you see what a jump he made

MILL THUGS IN MURDER RAID

here is the most dangerous example of how at the decisive moment the bourgeois ideology liquidates class solidarity and turns a friend of the workingclass of yesterday into a most miserable propagandist for imperialism today

RED PICKETS FINED FOR PROTEST HERE

We leave our home in the morning
We kiss our children goodbye

---

3. Excerpts from this Socialist labor-union protest song are also interspersed in this "newsreel."

4. Probably the Seventh Congress of the Third International held in Moscow in 1935.

OFFICIALS STILL HOPE FOR RESCUE OF MEN

He was goin' downgrade makin' ninety miles an hour
When his whistle broke into a scream
He was found in the wreck with his hand on the throttle
An' was scalded to death with the steam

RADICALS FIGHT WITH CHAIRS AT UNITY MEETING

PATROLMEN PROTECT REDS

U.S. CHAMBER OF COMMERCE URGES CONFIDENCE

REAL VALUES UNHARMED

While we slave for the bosses
Our children scream an' cry
But when we draw our money
Our grocery bills to pay

PRESIDENT SEES PROSPERITY NEAR

Not a cent to spend for clothing
Not a cent to lay away

STEAMROLLER IN ACTION AGAINST MILITANTS

MINERS BATTLE SCABS

But we cannot buy for our children
Our wages are too low
Now listen to me you workers
Both you women and men
Let us win for them the victory
I'm sure it ain't no sin

CARILLON PEALS IN SINGING TOWER[5]

the President[6] declared it was impossible to view the increased advantages for the many without smiling at those who a short time ago expressed so much fear lest our country might come under the control of a few individuals of great wealth.

HAPPY CROWDS THRONG CEREMONY

on a tiny island nestling like a green jewel in the lake that mirrors the singing tower, the President today participated in the dedication of a bird sanctuary and its pealing carillon, fulfilling the dream of an immigrant boy

The Camera Eye (51)

at the head of the valley in the dark of the hills on the broken floor of a lurchedover cabin a man halfsits halflies propped up by an old woman two wrinkled girls that might be young   chunks of coal flare in the hearth flicker in his face white and sagging as dough   blacken the cavedin mouth the taut throat the belly swelled enormous with the wound he got working on the minetipple[7]

---

5. The Singing Tower was erected in Florida through the efforts of Edward W. Bok (1863–1930), Dutch-born editor and philanthropist.
6. President Calvin Coolidge, who spoke at the tower's dedication in 1929.
7. The apparatus at a coal mine that tips cars to unload the coal.

the barefoot girl brings him a tincup of water   the woman wipes sweat off his streaming face with a dirty denim sleeve   the firelight flares in his eyes stretched big with fever in the women's scared eyes and in the blanched faces of the foreigners

without help in the valley hemmed by dark strike-silent hills the man will die (my father died we know what it is like to see a man die) the women will lay him out on the rickety cot the miners will bury him

in the jail it's light too hot the steamheat hisses we talk through the green-painted iron bars to a tall white mustachioed old man some smiling miners in shirtsleeves a boy   faces white from mining have already the tallowy look of jailfaces

foreigners what can we say to the dead?   foreigners what can we say to the jailed?   the representative of the political party talks fast through the bars join up with us and no other union we'll send you tobacco candy solidarity our lawyers will write briefs speakers will shout your names at meetings they'll carry your names on cardboard on picketlines   the men in jail shrug their shoulders smile thinly our eyes look in their eyes through the bars

what can I say?   (in another continent I have seen the faces looking out through the barred basement windows behind the ragged sentry's boots I have seen before day the straggling footsore prisoners herded through the streets limping between bayonets   heard the volley

I have seen the dead lying out in those distant deeper valleys)   what can we say to the jailed?

in the law's office we stand against the wall the law is a big man with eyes angry in a big pumpkinface   who sits and stares at us meddling foreigners through the door the deputies crane with their guns   they stand guard at the mines   they blockade the miners' soupkitchens they've cut off the road up the valley   the hiredmen with guns stand ready to shoot (they have made us foreigners in the land where we were born they are the conquering army that has filtered into the country unnoticed they have taken the hilltops by stealth they levy toll they stand at the minehead   they stand at the polls   they stand by when the bailiffs carry the furniture of the family evicted from the city tenement out on the sidewalk they are there when the bankers foreclose on a farm they are ambushed and ready to shoot down the strikers marching behind the flag up the switchback road to the mine   those that the guns spare they jail)

the law stares across the desk out of angry eyes his face reddens in splotches like a gobbler's neck with the strut of the power of submachineguns sawedoffshotguns teargas and vomitinggas the power that can feed you or leave you to starve

sits easy at his desk his back is covered he feels strong behind him he feels the prosecutingattorney the judge an owner himself the political boss the minesuperintendent the board of directors   the president of the utility the manipulator of the holdingcompany

he lifts his hand towards the telephone
the deputies crowd in the door
we have only words against

* * *

1936

WILLIAM FAULKNER
1897–1962

Between 1929 and 1936 William Faulkner published novels about childhood, families, sex, race, obsessions, time, the past, his native South, and the modern world. He invented voices for characters ranging from sages to children, criminals, the insane, even the dead—sometimes all within one book. He developed, beyond this ventriloquism, his own unmistakable narrative voice, urgent, intense, highly rhetorical. He experimented with narrative chronology and with techniques for representing mind and memory. He invented an entire southern county and wrote its history.

He was a native Mississippian, born near Oxford, where his parents moved when he was about five. His great-grandfather had been a local legend: a colonel in the Civil War, lawyer, railroad builder, financier, politician, writer, and public figure who was shot and killed by a business and political rival in 1889. Faulkner's grandfather carried on some of the family enterprises, and his father worked first for the railroad (the Gulf and Chicago) and later as business manager of the University of Mississippi. The father was a reclusive man who loved to hunt, drink, and swap stories with his hunting friends; the mother, ambitious, sensitive, and literary, was a more profound influence on Faulkner, her favorite of four sons. In Faulkner's childhood his mother's mother also lived with them; she was a high-spirited, independent, and imaginative old lady whose death in 1907 seems to have affected Faulkner deeply.

Faulkner dropped out of high school in 1915 and had no further formal education beyond a year (1919–20) as a special student at the University of Mississippi. Through family connections, various jobs were made for him, but he was unhappy in all of them. In 1918 Estelle Oldham, his high school love, married someone else; Faulkner briefly left Oxford. First he went to New Haven where his best friend and informal tutor, Phil Stone, was in the Yale law school; then he enlisted in the British Royal Flying Corps and was sent to Canada to train. World War I ended before he saw active service; nevertheless, when he returned to Oxford in 1919 he was limping from what he claimed was a war wound.

Back at home, Faulkner drifted from one job to another and wrote poetry that was a mélange of Shakespearean, pastoral, Victorian, and Edwardian modes, with an overlay of French Symbolism, which he published in *The Marble Faun*, in 1924. In 1925 he went to New Orleans where, for the first time, he met and mingled with literary people, including Sherwood Anderson, who encouraged Faulkner to develop his own style, to concentrate on prose, and to use his region for material.

Faulkner wrote his first novel, *Soldier's Pay*, in New Orleans, and Anderson recommended it to his own publisher, Liveright; it appeared in 1926. He also published in the New Orleans magazine *The Double Dealer* and the newspaper *The Times Picayune*. He learned about the experimental writing of James Joyce and the ideas of Sigmund Freud. After a trip to Europe at the end of the same year, he returned to Oxford. In 1929 he married Estelle Oldham, who had been divorced and had returned to Oxford with her two children. They bought a ruined mansion, Rowan Oak, in 1930 and began to restore it to its antebellum appearance. A daughter born in 1931 died in infancy; a second daughter, Jill, was born in 1933.

Faulkner's second novel was a satire on New Orleans intellectuals called *Mosquitos* (1927). His more typical subject matter emerged with his rejected novel *Flags in the Dust*, and the shortened version of it that appeared in 1929 as *Sartoris*. In this work Faulkner focused on the interconnections between a prominent southern family and the local community: the Sartoris family as well as many other characters appeared in later works, and the region, renamed Yoknapatawpha County, was to become the locale of Faulkner's imaginative world.

The social and historical emphasis in *Sartoris* was not directly followed up in the works Faulkner wrote next. *The Sound and the Fury* (1929)—Faulkner's favorite novel—and *As I Lay Dying* (1930) were dramatically experimental attempts to articulate the inexpressible aspects of individual psychology. *The Sound and the Fury* has four sections, each with a different narrator, each supplying a different piece of the plot. Three of the narrators are brothers: Benjy, the idiot; Quentin, the suicide; and Jason, the business failure. Each of them, for different reasons, mourns the loss of their sister Caddie. While the story moves out to the disintegration of the old southern family to which these brothers belong, its focus is on the private obsessions of the brothers, and it invents an entirely different style for each narrator. Only the last section, told from a traditionally omniscient point of view, provides a sequential narration; the other three jump freely in time and space. The structure of *As I Lay Dying*, printed here in its entirety, is even more complex. Like *The Sound and the Fury*, it is organized around the loss of a beloved woman. The precipitating event in the novel is the death of a mother. The story moves forward in chronological time as the "poor white" Bundren family takes her body to the town of Jefferson for burial. Its narration is divided into fifty-nine sections of interior monologue by fifteen characters, each with a different perception of the action and a different way of relating to reality. The family's adventures and misadventures on the road are comic, tragic, grotesque, absurd, and deeply moving.

Neither these books nor his early short stories were very popular. *Sanctuary*, a sensational work about sex, gangsters, official corruption, and urban violence, attracted considerable attention, however. It appeared in 1931, and took its place in the large amount of hard-boiled fiction that appeared in the decade, notably by such authors as Dashiell Hammett and Raymond Chandler. During four different intervals—1932–37, 1942–45, 1951, and 1954—Faulkner spent time in Hollywood or on contract as a scriptwriter. He worked well with the director Howard Hawks, and wrote the scripts for two famous movies, an adaptation of Ernest Hemingway's *To Have and Have Not* and an adaptation of Raymond Chandler's *The Big Sleep*, both starring Humphrey Bogart and Lauren Bacall.

He continued to produce brilliant and inventive novels during these years. *Light in August* (1932) counterpointed a comic pastoral about the pregnant earth-mother figure Lena Grove with a grim tragedy about the embittered outcast Joe Christmas, who may or may not be racially mixed; it interrelated individual psychology and cultural pathology. *Absalom, Absalom!*, which followed in 1936, is thought by many to be Faulkner's masterpiece. The story of Thomas Sutpen, the ruthless would-be founder of a southern dynasty after the Civil War, is related by four different speakers, each trying to find "the meaning" of the story. The reader, observing how the story changes in each telling, comes to see that making stories is the human way of making meaning. Like Faulkner's earlier novels, *Absalom* is thus simultaneously about an individual, about the South, and about itself as a work of fiction. But its emphasis shifts from the private psychology that dominated in earlier work to social psychology: to the collective mind of the South.

With World War II, Faulkner's work became more traditional and less difficult. He began to write about the rise, in Yoknapatawpha County, of the poor white family named Snopes—this family had appeared in earlier works (like "Barn Burning")—and the simultaneous decline of the region's "aristocratic" families. *The Hamlet* (1940) was the first of three novels devoted to the Snopeses. Because all his works had been set in Yoknapatawpha County and were interconnected, the region and its people began to take on an existence independent of any one book in which they appeared.

Faulkner's national reputation soared after the publication in 1946 of an anthology of his writings, *The Portable Faulkner*, edited by the critic Malcolm Cowley. He already had a major reputation abroad, especially in France, where his work in translation was a powerful influence on the French so-called new novel and its practitioners such as Michel Butor and Alain Robbe-Grillet. His antiracist *Intruder in the Dust* (1948) occasioned the award of the Nobel Prize in 1950. In the 1950s Faulkner visited many college campuses. His writing took on more of the air of an old-fashioned yarn; he dealt with more legendary and local color materials; he rounded out the Snopes saga with *The Town* (1957) and *The Mansion* (1959). At the age of sixty-five he died of a heart attack.

The text of *As I Lay Dying* is that established by Noel Polk (1985). The text of "Barn Burning" is that of *Collected Stories* (1950).

As I Lay Dying[1]

Darl

Jewel and I come up from the field, following the path in single file. Although I am fifteen feet ahead of him, anyone watching us from the cottonhouse can see Jewel's frayed and broken straw hat a full head above my own.

The path runs straight as a plumb-line, worn smooth by feet and baked brick-hard by July, between the green rows of laid-by cotton,[2] to the cottonhouse in the center of the field, where it turns and circles the cottonhouse at four soft right angles and goes on across the field again, worn so by feet in fading precision.

The cottonhouse is of rough logs, from between which the chinking has long fallen. Square, with a broken roof set at a single pitch, it leans in empty and shimmering <u>dilapidation</u> in the sunlight, a single broad window in two opposite walls giving onto the approaches of the path. When we reach it I turn and follow the path which circles the house. Jewel, fifteen feet behind me, looking straight ahead, steps in a single stride through the window. Still staring straight ahead, his pale eyes like wood set into his wooden face, he crosses the floor in four strides with the rigid gravity of a cigar store Indian dressed in patched overalls and endued with life from the hips down, and steps in a single stride through the opposite window and into the path again just as I come around the corner. In single file and five feet apart and Jewel now in front, we go on up the path toward the foot of the bluff.

Tull's wagon stands beside the spring, hitched to the rail, the reins wrapped about the seat stanchion. In the wagon bed are two chairs. Jewel stops at the spring and takes the gourd from the willow branch and drinks. I pass him and mount the path, beginning to hear Cash's saw.

When I reach the top he has quit sawing. Standing in a litter of chips, he is fitting two of the boards together. Between the shadow spaces they are yellow as gold, like soft gold, bearing on their flanks in smooth <u>undulations</u> the marks of the adze blade: a good carpenter, Cash is. He holds the two planks on the trestle, fitted along the edges in a quarter of the finished box. He kneels and squints along the edge of them, then he lowers them and takes up the adze. A good carpenter. Addie Bundren could not want a better one, a better box to lie in. It will give her confidence and comfort. I go on to the house, followed by the

Chuck. Chuck. Chuck.

of the adze.

1. For assistance with the footnotes, we are indebted to Joseph Blotner's notes in William Faulkner, *Novels 1930–1935* (1985).

2. Cultivated cotton crop, waiting to be picked.

Cora

So I saved out the eggs and baked yesterday. The cakes turned out right well. We depend a lot on our chickens. They are good layers, what few we have left after the possums and such. Snakes too, in the summer. A snake will break up a hen-house quicker than anything. So after they were going to cost so much more than Mr Tull thought, and after I promised that the difference in the number of eggs would make it up, I had to be more careful than ever because it was on my final say-so we took them. We could have stocked cheaper chickens, but I gave my promise as Miss Lawington said when she advised me to get a good breed, because Mr Tull himself admits that a good breed of cows or hogs pays in the long run. So when we lost so many of them we couldn't afford to use the eggs ourselves, because I could not have had Mr Tull chide me when it was on my say-so we took them. So when Miss Lawington told me about the cakes I thought that I could bake them and earn enough at one time to increase the net value of the flock the equivalent of two head. And that by saving the eggs out one at a time, even the eggs wouldn't be costing anything. And that week they laid so well that I not only saved out enough eggs above what we had engaged to sell, to bake the cakes with, I had saved enough so that the flour and the sugar and the stove wood would not be costing anything. So I baked yesterday, more careful than ever I baked in my life, and the cakes turned out right well. But when we got to town this morning Miss Lawington told me the lady had changed her mind and was not going to have the party after all.

"She ought to taken those cakes anyway," Kate says.

"Well," I say, "I reckon she never had no use for them now."

"She ought to taken them," Kate says. "But those rich town ladies can change their minds. Poor folks cant."

Riches is nothing in the face of the Lord, for He can see into the heart. "Maybe I can sell them at the bazaar Saturday," I say. They turned out real well.

"You cant get two dollars a piece for them," Kate says.

"Well, it isn't like they cost me anything," I say. I saved them out and swapped a dozen of them for the sugar and flour. It isn't like the cakes cost me anything, as Mr Tull himself realises that the eggs I saved were over and beyond what we had engaged to sell, so it was like we had found the eggs or they had been given to us.

"She ought to taken those cakes when she same as gave you her word," Kate says. The Lord can see into the heart. If it is His will that some folks has different ideas of honesty from other folks, it is not my place to question His decree.

"I reckon she never had any use for them," I say. They turned out real well, too.

The quilt is drawn up to her chin, hot as it is, with only her two hands and her face outside. She is propped on the pillow, with her head raised so she can see out the window, and we can hear him every time he takes up the adze or the saw. If we were deaf we could almost watch her face and hear him, see him. Her face is wasted away so that the bones draw just under the skin in white lines. Her eyes are like two candles when you watch them gutter down into the sockets of iron candle-sticks. But the eternal and the everlasting salvation and grace is not upon her.

"They turned out real nice," I say. "But not like the cakes Addie used to bake." You can see that girl's washing and ironing in the pillow-slip, if ironed it ever was. Maybe it will reveal her blindness to her, laying there at the mercy and the ministration of four men and a tom-boy girl. "There's not a woman in this section could ever bake with Addie Bundren," I say. "First thing we know she'll be up and baking again, and then we wont have any sale for ours at all." Under the quilt she makes no more of a hump than a rail would, and the only way you can tell she is breathing is by the sound of the mattress shucks. Even the hair at her cheek does not move, even with that girl standing right over her, fanning her with the fan. While we watch she swaps the fan to the other hand without stopping it.

"Is she sleeping?" Kate whispers.

"She's just watching Cash yonder," the girl says. We can hear the saw in the board. It sounds like snoring. Eula turns on the trunk and looks out the window. Her necklace looks real nice with her red hat. You wouldn't think it only cost twenty-five cents.

"She ought to taken those cakes," Kate says.

I could have used the money real well. But it's not like they cost me anything except the baking. I can tell him that anybody is likely to make a miscue, but it's not all of them that can get out of it without loss, I can tell him. It's not everybody can eat their mistakes, I can tell him.

Someone comes through the hall. It is Darl. He does not look in as he passes the door. Eula watches him as he goes on and passes from sight again toward the back. Her hand rises and touches her beads lightly, and then her hair. When she finds me watching her, her eyes go blank.

Darl

Pa and Vernon are sitting on the back porch. Pa is tilting snuff from the lid of his snuff-box into his lower lip, holding the lip outdrawn between thumb and finger. They look around as I cross the porch and dip the gourd into the water bucket and drink.

"Where's Jewel?" pa says. When I was a boy I first learned how much better water tastes when it has set a while in a cedar bucket. Warmish-cool, with a faint taste like the hot July wind in cedar trees smells. It has to set at least six hours, and be drunk from a gourd. Water should never be drunk from metal.

And at night it is better still. I used to lie on the pallet in the hall, waiting until I could hear them all asleep, so I could get up and go back to the bucket. It would be black, the shelf black, the still surface of the water a round orifice in nothingness, where before I stirred it awake with the dipper I could see maybe a star or two in the bucket, and maybe in the dipper a star or two before I drank. After that I was bigger, older. Then I would wait until they all went to sleep so I could lie with my shirt-tail up, hearing them asleep, feeling myself without touching myself, feeling the cool silence blowing upon my parts and wondering if Cash was yonder in the darkness doing it too, had been doing it perhaps for the last two years before I could have wanted to or could have.

Pa's feet are badly splayed, his toes cramped and bent and warped, with no toenail at all on his little toes, from working so hard in the wet in homemade shoes when he was a boy. Beside his chair his brogans sit. They look as though they had been hacked with a blunt axe out of pig-iron. Vernon has been to town. I have never seen him go to town in overalls. His wife, they say. She taught school too, once.

I fling the dipper dregs to the ground and wipe my mouth on my sleeve. It is going to rain before morning. Maybe before dark. "Down to the barn," I say. "Harnessing the team."

Down there fooling with that horse. He will go on through the barn, into the pasture. The horse will not be in sight: he is up there among the pine seedlings, in the cool. Jewel whistles, once and shrill. The horse snorts, then Jewel sees him, glinting for a gaudy instant among the blue shadows. Jewel whistles again; the horse comes dropping down the slope, stiff-legged, his ears cocking and flicking, his mis-matched eyes rolling, and fetches up twenty feet away, broadside on, watching Jewel over his shoulder in an attitude kittenish and alert.

"Come here, sir," Jewel says. He moves. Moving that quick his coat, bunching, tongues swirling like so many flames. With tossing mane and tail and rolling eye the horse makes another short curvetting rush and stops again, feet bunched, watching Jewel. Jewel walks steadily toward him, his hands at his sides. Save for Jewel's legs they are like two figures carved for a tableau savage in the sun.

When Jewel can almost touch him, the horse stands on his hind legs and slashes down at Jewel. Then Jewel is enclosed by a glittering maze of hooves as by an illusion of wings; among them, beneath the upreared chest, he moves with the flashing limberness of a snake. For an instant before the jerk comes onto his arms he sees his whole body earth-free, horizontal, whipping snake-limber, until he finds the horse's nostrils and touches earth again. Then they are rigid, motionless, terrific, the horse back-thrust on stiffened, quivering legs, with lowered head; Jewel with dug heels, shutting off the horse's wind with one hand, with the other patting the horse's neck in short strokes myriad and caressing, cursing the horse with obscene ferocity.

They stand in rigid terrific hiatus, the horse trembling and groaning. Then Jewel is on the horse's back. He flows upward in a stooping swirl like the lash of a whip, his body in midair shaped to the horse. For another moment the horse stands spraddled, with lowered head, before it bursts into motion. They descend the hill in a series of spine-jolting jumps, Jewel high, leech-like on the withers, to the fence where the horse bunches to a scuttering halt again.

"Well," Jewel says, "you can quit now, if you got a-plenty."

Inside the barn Jewel slides running to the ground before the horse stops. The horse enters the stall, Jewel following. Without looking back the horse kicks at him, slamming a single hoof into the wall with a pistol-like report. Jewel kicks him in the stomach; the horse arches his neck back, crop-toothed; Jewel strikes him across the face with his fist and slides on to the trough and mounts upon it. Clinging to the hay-rack he lowers his head and peers out across the stall tops and through the doorway. The path is empty; from here he cannot even hear Cash sawing. He reaches up and drags down hay in hurried armsful and crams it into the rack.

"Eat," he says. "Get the goddamn stuff out of sight while you got a chance, you pussel-gutted[3] bastard. You sweet son of a bitch," he says.

Jewel

It's because he stays out there, right under the window, hammering and sawing on that goddamn box. Where she's got to see him. Where every breath she draws is full of his knocking and sawing where she can see him saying See. See what a good one I am making for you. I told him to go somewhere else. I said Good God do you want to see her in it. It's like when he was a little boy and she says if she had some fertilizer she would try to raise some flowers and he taken the bread pan and brought it back from the barn full of dung.

And now them others sitting there, like buzzards. Waiting, fanning themselves. Because I said If you wouldn't keep on sawing and nailing at it until a man cant sleep even and her hands laying on the quilt like two of them roots dug up and tried to wash and you couldn't get them clean. I can see the fan and Dewey Dell's arm. I said if you'd just let her alone. Sawing and knocking, and keeping the air always moving so fast on her face that when you're tired you cant breathe it, and that goddamn adze going One lick less. One lick less. One lick less until everybody that passes in the road will have to stop and see it and say what a fine carpenter he is. If it had just been me when Cash fell off of that church and if it had just been me when pa laid sick with that load of wood fell on him, it would not be happening with every bastard in the county coming in to stare at her because if there is a God what the hell is He for. It would just be me and her on a high hill and me rolling the rocks down the hill at their faces, picking them up and throwing them down the hill faces and teeth and all by God until she was quiet and not that goddamn adze going One lick less. One lick less and we could be quiet.

Darl

We watch him come around the corner and mount the steps. He does not look at us. "You ready?" he says.

"If you're hitched up," I say. I say "Wait." He stops, looking at pa. Vernon spits, without moving. He spits with decorous and deliberate precision into the pocked dust below the porch. Pa rubs his hands slowly on his knees. He is gazing out beyond the crest of the bluff, out across the land. Jewel watches him a moment, then he goes on to the pail and drinks again.

"I mislike undecision as much as ere a man," pa says.

"It means three dollars," I say. The shirt across pa's hump is faded lighter than the rest of it. There is no sweat stain on his shirt. I have never seen a sweat stain on his shirt. He was sick once from working in the sun when he was twenty-two years old, and he tells people that if he ever sweats, he will die. I suppose he believes it.

"But if she dont last until you get back," he says. "She will be disappointed."

Vernon spits into the dust. But it will rain before morning.

3. Fat.

"She's counted on it," pa says. "She'll want to start right away. I know her. I promised her I'd keep the team here and ready, and she's counting on it."

"We'll need that three dollars then, sure," I say. He gazes out over the land, rubbing his hands on his knees. Since he lost his teeth his mouth collapses in slow repetition when he dips. The stubble gives his lower face that appearance that old dogs have. "You'd better make up your mind soon, so we can get there and get a load on before dark," I say.

"Ma aint that sick," Jewel says. "Shut up, Darl."

"That's right," Vernon says. "She seems more like herself today than she has in a week. Time you and Jewel get back, she'll be setting up."

"You ought to know," Jewel says. "You been here often enough looking at her. You or your folks." Vernon looks at him. Jewel's eyes look like pale wood in his high-blooded face. He is a head taller than any of the rest of us, always was. I told them that's why ma always whipped him and petted him more. Because he was peakling around the house more. That's why she named him Jewel I told them.

"Shut up, Jewel," pa says, but as though he is not listening much. He gazes out across the land, rubbing his knees.

"You could borrow the loan of Vernon's team and we could catch up with you," I say. "If she didn't wait for us."

"Ah, shut your goddamn mouth," Jewel says.

"She'll want to go in ourn," pa says. He rubs his knees. "Dont ere a man mislike it more."

"It's laying there, watching Cash whittle on that damn . . ." Jewel says. He says it harshly, savagely, but he does not say the word. Like a little boy in the dark to flail his courage and suddenly aghast into silence by his own noise.

"She wanted that like she wants to go in our own wagon," pa says. "She'll rest easier for knowing it's a good one, and private. She was ever a private woman. You know it well."

"Then let it be private," Jewel says. "But how the hell can you expect it to be—" he looks at the back of pa's head, his eyes like pale wooden eyes.

"Sho," Vernon says, "she'll hold on till it's finished. She'll hold on till everything's ready, till her own good time. And with the roads like they are now, it wont take you no time to get her to town."

"It's fixing up to rain," pa says. "I am a luckless man. I have ever been." He rubs his hands on his knees. "It's that durn doctor, liable to come at any time. I couldn't get word to him till so late. If he was to come tomorrow and tell her the time was nigh, she wouldn't wait. I know her. Wagon or no wagon, she wouldn't wait. Then she'd be upset, and I wouldn't upset her for the living world. With that family burying-ground in Jefferson and them of her blood waiting for her there, she'll be impatient. I promised my word me and the boys would get her there quick as mules could walk it, so she could rest quiet." He rubs his hands on his knees. "No man ever misliked it more."

"If everybody wasn't burning hell to get her there," Jewel says in that harsh, savage voice. "With Cash all day long right under the window, hammering and sawing at that—"

"It was her wish," pa says. "You got no affection nor gentleness for her. You never had. We would be beholden to no man," he says, "me and her. We have never yet been, and she will rest quieter for knowing it and that it was her own blood sawed out the boards and drove the nails. She was ever one to clean up after herself."

"It means three dollars," I say. "Do you want us to go, or not?" Pa rubs his knees. "We'll be back by tomorrow sundown."

"Well . . ." pa says. He looks out over the land, awry-haired, mouthing the snuff slowly against his gums.

"Come on," Jewel says. He goes down the steps. Vernon spits neatly into the dust.

"By sundown, now," pa says. "I would not keep her waiting."

Jewel glances back, then he goes on around the house. I enter the hall, hearing the voices before I reach the door. Tilting a little down the hill, as our house does, a breeze draws through the hall all the time, upslanting. A feather dropped near the front door will rise and brush along the ceiling, slanting backward, until it reaches the down-turning current at the back door: so with voices. As you enter the hall, they sound as though they were speaking out of the air about your head.

Cora

It was the sweetest thing I ever saw. It was like he knew he would never see her again, that Anse Bundren was driving him from his mother's death bed, never to see her in this world again. I always said Darl was different from those others. I always said he was the only one of them that had his mother's nature, had any natural affection. Not that Jewel, the one she labored so to bear and coddled and petted so and him flinging into tantrums or sulking spells, inventing devilment to devil her until I would have frailed[4] him time and time. Not him to come and tell her goodbye. Not him to miss a chance to make that extra three dollars at the price of his mother's goodbye kiss. A Bundren through and through, loving nobody, caring for nothing except how to get something with the least amount of work. Mr Tull says Darl asked them to wait. He said Darl almost begged them on his knees not to force him to leave her in her condition. But nothing would do but Anse and Jewel must make that three dollars. Nobody that knows Anse could have expected different, but to think of that boy, that Jewel, selling all those years of self-denial and down-right partiality— they couldn't fool me: Mr Tull says Mrs Bundren liked Jewel the least of all, but I knew better. I knew she was partial to him, to the same quality in him that let her put up with Anse Bundren when Mr Tull said she ought to poisoned him—for three dollars, denying his dying mother the goodbye kiss.

Why, for the last three weeks I have been coming over every time I could, coming sometimes when I shouldn't have, neglecting my own family and duties so that somebody would be with her in her last moments and she would not have to face the Great Unknown without one familiar face to give her courage. Not that I deserve credit for it: I will expect the same for myself. But thank God it will be the faces of my loved kin, my blood and flesh, for in

4. I.e., "flailed"; beaten.

my husband and children I have been more blessed than most, trials though they have been at times.

She lived, a lonely woman, lonely with her pride, trying to make folks believe different, hiding the fact that they just suffered her, because she was not cold in the coffin before they were carting her forty miles away to bury her, flouting the will of God to do it. Refusing to let her lie in the same earth with those Bundrens.

"But she wanted to go," Mr Tull said. "It was her own wish to lie among her own people."

"Then why didn't she go alive?" I said. "Not one of them would have stopped her, with even that little one almost old enough now to be selfish and stone-hearted like the rest of them."

"It was her own wish," Mr Tull said. "I heard Anse say it was."

"And you would believe Anse, of course," I said. "A man like you would. Dont tell me."

"I'd believe him about something he couldn't expect to make anything off of me by not telling," Mr Tull said.

"Dont tell me," I said. "A woman's place is with her husband and children, alive or dead. Would you expect me to want to go back to Alabama and leave you and the girls when my time comes, that I left of my own will to cast my lot with yours for better and worse, until death and after?"

"Well, folks are different," he said.

I should hope so. I have tried to live right in the sight of God and man, for the honor and comfort of my Christian husband and the love and respect of my Christian children. So that when I lay me down in the consciousness of my duty and reward I will be surrounded by loving faces, carrying the farewell kiss of each of my loved ones into my reward. Not like Addie Bundren dying alone, hiding her pride and her broken heart. Glad to go. Lying there with her head propped up so she could watch Cash building the coffin, having to watch him so he would not skimp on it, like as not, with those men not worrying about anything except if there was time to earn another three dollars before the rain come and the river got too high to get across it. Like as not, if they hadn't decided to make that last load, they would have loaded her into the wagon on a quilt and crossed the river first and then stopped and give her time to die what Christian death they would let her.

Except Darl. It was the sweetest thing I ever saw. Sometimes I lose faith in human nature for a time; I am assailed by doubt. But always the Lord restores my faith and reveals to me His bounteous love for His creatures. Not Jewel, the one she had always cherished, not him. He was after that three extra dollars. It was Darl, the one that folks say is queer, lazy, pottering about the place no better than Anse, with Cash a good carpenter and always more building than he can get around to, and Jewel always doing something that made him some money or got him talked about, and that near-naked girl always standing over Addie with a fan so that every time a body tried to talk to her and cheer her up, would answer for her right quick, like she was trying to keep anybody from coming near her at all.

It was Darl. He come to the door and stood there, looking at his dying mother. He just looked at her, and I felt the bounteous love of the Lord again and His mercy. I saw that with Jewel she had just been pretending, but that it was between her and Darl that the understanding and the true love was.

He just looked at her, not even coming in where she could see him and get upset, knowing that Anse was driving him away and he would never see her again. He said nothing, just looking at her.

"What you want, Darl?" Dewey Dell said, not stopping the fan, speaking up quick, keeping even him from her. He didn't answer. He just stood and looked at his dying mother, his heart too full for words.

Dewey Dell

The first time me and Lafe picked on down the row. Pa dassent[5] sweat because he will catch his death from the sickness so that everybody that comes to help us. And Jewel dont care about anything he is not kin to us in caring, not care-kin. And Cash like sawing the long hot sad yellow days up into planks and nailing them to something. And pa thinks because neighbors will always treat one another that way because he has always been too busy letting neighbors do for him to find out. And I did not think that Darl would, that sits at the supper table with his eyes gone further than the food and the lamp, full of the land dug out of his skull and the holes filled with distance beyond the land.

We picked on down the row, the woods getting closer and closer and the secret shade, picking on into the secret shade with my sack and Lafe's sack. Because I said will I or wont I when the sack was half full because I said if the sack is full when we get to the woods it wont be me. I said if it dont mean for me to do it the sack will not be full and I will turn up the next row but if the sack is full, I cannot help it. It will be that I had to do it all the time and I cannot help it. And we picked on toward the secret shade and our eyes would drown together touching on his hands and my hands and I didn't say anything. I said "What are you doing?" and he said "I am picking into your sack." And so it was full when we came to the end of the row and I could not help it.

And so it was because I could not help it. It was then, and then I saw Darl and he knew. He said he knew without the words like he told me that ma is going to die without words, and I knew he knew because if he had said he knew with the words I would not have believed that he had been there and saw us. But he said he did know and I said "Are you going to tell pa are you going to kill him?" without the words I said it and he said "Why?" without the words. And that's why I can talk to him with knowing with hating because he knows.

He stands in the door, looking at her.

"What you want, Darl?" I say.

"She is going to die," he says. And old turkey-buzzard Tull coming to watch her die but I can fool them.

"When is she going to die?" I say.

"Before we get back," he says.

"Then why are you taking Jewel?" I say.

"I want him to help me load," he says.

5. Dares not.

Tull

Anse keeps on rubbing his knees. His overalls are faded; on one knee a serge patch cut out of a pair of Sunday pants, wore iron-slick. "No man mislikes it more than me," he says.

"A fellow's got to guess ahead now and then," I say. "But, come long and short, it wont be no harm done neither way."

"She'll want to get started right off," he says. "It's far enough to Jefferson at best."

"But the roads is good now," I say. It's fixing to rain tonight, too. His folks buries at New Hope, too, not three miles away. But it's just like him to marry a woman born a day's hard ride away and have her die on him.

He looks out over the land, rubbing his knees. "No man so mislikes it," he says.

"They'll get back in plenty of time," I say. "I wouldn't worry none."

"It means three dollars," he says.

"Might be it wont be no need for them to rush back, noways," I say. "I hope it."

"She's a-going," he says. "Her mind is set on it."

It's a hard life on women, for a fact. Some women. I mind my mammy lived to be seventy and more. Worked every day, rain or shine; never a sick day since her last chap was born until one day she kind of looked around her and then she went and taken that lace-trimmed night gown she had had forty-five years and never wore out of the chest and put it on and laid down on the bed and pulled the covers up and shut her eyes. "You all will have to look out for pa the best you can," she said. "I'm tired."

Anse rubs his hands on his knees. "The Lord giveth," he says. We can hear Cash a-hammering and sawing beyond the corner.

It's true. Never a truer breath was ever breathed. "The Lord giveth," I say.

That boy comes up the hill. He is carrying a fish nigh long as he is. He slings it to the ground and grunts "Hah" and spits over his shoulder like a man. Durn nigh long as he is.

"What's that?" I say. "A hog? Where'd you get it?"

"Down to the bridge," he says. He turns it over, the under side caked over with dust where it is wet, the eye coated over, humped under the dirt.

"Are you aiming to leave it laying there?" Anse says.

"I aim to show it to ma," Vardaman says. He looks toward the door. We can hear the talking, coming out on the draft. Cash too, knocking and hammering at the boards. "There's company in there," he says.

"Just my folks," I say. "They'd enjoy to see it too."

He says nothing, watching the door. Then he looks down at the fish laying in the dust. He turns it over with his foot and prods at the eye-bump with his toe, gouging at it. Anse is looking out over the land. Vardaman looks at Anse's face, then at the door. He turns, going toward the corner of the house, when Anse calls him without looking around.

"You clean that fish," Anse says.

Vardaman stops. "Why cant Dewey Dell clean it?" he says.

"You clean that fish," Anse says.

"Aw, pa," Vardaman says.

"You clean it," Anse says. He dont look around. Vardaman comes back and picks up the fish. It slides out of his hands, smearing wet dirt onto him, and flops down, dirtying itself again, gapmouthed, goggle-eyed, hiding into the dust like it was ashamed of being dead, like it was in a hurry to get back hid again. Vardaman cusses it. He cusses it like a grown man, standing a-straddle of it. Anse dont look around. Vardaman picks it up again. He goes on around the house, toting it in both arms like a armful of wood, it overlapping him on both ends, head and tail. Durn nigh big as he is.

Anse's wrists dangle out of his sleeves: I never see him with a shirt on that looked like it was his in all my life. They all looked like Jewel might have give him his old ones. Not Jewel, though. He's long-armed, even if he is spindling. Except for the lack of sweat. You could tell they aint been nobody else's but Anse's that way without no mistake. His eyes look like pieces of burnt-out cinder fixed in his face, looking out over the land.

When the shadow touches the steps he says "It's five oclock."

Just as I get up Cora comes to the door and says it's time to get on. Anse reaches for his shoes. "Now, Mr Bundren," Cora says, "dont you get up now." He puts his shoes on, stomping into them, like he does everything, like he is hoping all the time he really cant do it and can quit trying to. When we go up the hall we can hear them clumping on the floor like they was iron shoes. He comes toward the door where she is, blinking his eyes, kind of looking ahead of hisself before he sees, like he is hoping to find her setting up, in a chair maybe or maybe sweeping, and looks into the door in that surprised way like he looks in and finds her still in bed every time and Dewey Dell still a-fanning her with the fan. He stands there, like he dont aim to move again nor nothing else.

"Well, I reckon we better get on," Cora says. "I got to feed the chickens." It's fixing to rain, too. Clouds like that dont lie, and the cotton making every day the Lord sends. That'll be something else for him. Cash is still trimming at the boards. "If there's ere a thing we can do," Cora says.

"Anse'll let us know," I say.

Anse dont look at us. He looks around, blinking, in that surprised way, like he had wore hisself down being surprised and was even surprised at that. If Cash just works that careful on my barn.

"I told Anse it likely wont be no need," I say. "I so hope it."

"Her mind is set on it," he says. "I reckon she's bound to go."

"It comes to all of us," Cora says. "Let the Lord comfort you."

"About that corn," I say. I tell him again I will help him out if he gets into a tight, with her sick and all. Like most folks around here, I done help him so much already I cant quit now.

"I aimed to get to it today," he says. "Seems like I cant get my mind on nothing."

"Maybe she'll hold out till you are laid-by," I say.

"If God wills it," he says.

"Let Him comfort you," Cora says.

If Cash just works that careful on my barn. He looks up when we pass. "Dont reckon I'll get to you this week," he says.

" 'Taint no rush," I say. "Whenever you get around to it."

We get into the wagon. Cora sets the cake box on her lap. It's fixing to rain, sho.

"I dont know what he'll do," Cora says. "I just dont know."

"Poor Anse," I say. "She kept him at work for thirty-odd years. I reckon she is tired."

"And I reckon she'll be behind him for thirty years more," Kate says. "Or if it aint her, he'll get another one before cotton-picking."

"I reckon Cash and Darl can get married now," Eula says.

"That poor boy," Cora says. "The poor little tyke."

"What about Jewel?" Kate says.

"He can, too," Eula says.

"Hmph," Kate says. "I reckon he will. I reckon so. I reckon there's more gals than one around here that dont want to see Jewel tied down. Well, they needn't to worry."

"Why, Kate!" Cora says. The wagon begins to rattle. "The poor little tyke," Cora says.

It's fixing to rain this night. Yes, sir. A rattling wagon is mighty dry weather, for a Birdsell. But that'll be cured. It will for a fact.

"She ought to taken them cakes after she said she would," Kate says.

Anse

Durn that road. And it fixing to rain, too. I can stand here and same as see it with second-sight, a-shutting down behind them like a wall, shutting down betwixt them and my given promise. I do the best I can, much as I can get my mind on anything, but durn them boys.

A-laying there, right up to my door, where every bad luck that comes and goes is bound to find it. I told Addie it want[6] any luck living on a road when it come by here, and she said, for the world like a woman, "Get up and move, then." But I told her it want no luck in it, because the Lord put roads for travelling: why He laid them down flat on the earth. When He aims for something to be always a-moving, He makes it longways, like a road or a horse or a wagon, but when He aims for something to stay put, He makes it up-and-down ways, like a tree or a man. And so He never aimed for folks to live on a road, because which gets there first, I says, the road or the house? Did you ever know Him to set a road down by a house? I says. No you never, I says, because it's always men cant rest till they gets the house set where everybody that passes in a wagon can spit in the doorway, keeping the folks restless and wanting to get up and go somewheres else when He aimed for them to stay put like a tree or a stand of corn. Because if He'd a aimed for man to be always a-moving and going somewheres else, wouldn't He a put him longways on his belly, like a snake? It stands to reason He would.

Putting it where every bad luck prowling can find it and come straight to my door, charging me taxes on top of it. Making me pay for Cash having to get them carpenter notions when if it hadn't been no road come there, he wouldn't a got them; falling off of churches and lifting no hand in six months and me and Addie slaving and a-slaving, when there's plenty of sawing on this place he could do if he's got to saw.

And Darl too. Talking me out of him, durn them. It aint that I am afraid of work; I always is fed me and mine and kept a roof above us: it's that they

6. Wasn't.

would short-hand me just because he tends to his own business, just because he's got his eyes full of the land all the time. I says to them, he was alright at first, with his eyes full of the land, because the land laid up-and-down ways then; it wasn't till that ere road come and switched the land around longways and his eyes still full of the land, they begun to threaten me out of him, trying to short-hand me with the law.

Making me pay for it. She was well and hale as ere a woman ever were, except for that road. Just laying down, resting herself in her own bed, asking naught of none. "Are you sick, Addie?" I said.

"I am not sick," she said.

"You lay you down and rest you," I said. "I knowed you are not sick. You're just tired. You lay you down and rest."

"I am not sick," she said. "I will get up."

"Lay still and rest," I said. "You are just tired. You can get up tomorrow." And she was laying there, well and hale as ere a woman ever were, except for that road.

"I never sent for you," I said. "I take you to witness I never sent for you."

"I know you didn't," Peabody said. "I bound that. Where is she?"

"She's a-laying down," I said. "She's just a little tired, but she'll—"

"Get outen here, Anse," he said. "Go set on the porch a while."

And now I got to pay for it, me without a tooth in my head, hoping to get ahead enough so I could get my mouth fixed where I could eat God's own victuals as a man should, and her hale and well as ere a woman in the land until that day. Got to pay for being put to the need of that three dollars. Got to pay for the way for them boys to have to go away to earn it. And now I can see same as second sight the rain shutting down betwixt us, a-coming up that road like a durn man, like it want ere a other house to rain on in all the living land.

I have heard men cuss their luck, and right, for they were sinful men. But I do not say it's a curse on me, because I have done no wrong to be cussed by. I am not religious, I reckon. But peace is my heart: I know it is. I have done things but neither better nor worse than them that pretend otherlike, and I know that Old Marster will care for me as for ere a sparrow that falls.[7] But it seems hard that a man in his need could be so flouted by a road.

Vardaman comes around the house, bloody as a hog to his knees, and that ere fish chopped up with the axe like as not, or maybe throwed away for him to lie about the dogs et it. Well, I reckon I aint no call to expect no more of him than of his man-growed brothers. He comes along, watching the house, quiet, and sits on the steps. "Whew," he says, "I'm pure tired."

"Go wash them hands," I say. But couldn't no woman strove harder than Addie to make them right, man and boy: I'll say that for her.

"It was full of blood and guts as a hog," he says. But I just cant seem to get no heart into anything, with this here weather sapping me, too. "Pa," he says, "is ma sick some more?"

"Go wash them hands," I say. But I just cant seem to get no heart into it.

---

7. "As for every sparrow that falls." Cf. Matthew 10.29: "Are not two sparrows sold for a farthing? and one of them shall not fall on the ground without your Father."

Darl

He has been to town this week: the back of his neck is trimmed close, with a white line between hair and sunburn like a joint of white bone. He has not once looked back.

"Jewel," I say. Back running, tunnelled between the two sets of bobbing mule ears, the road vanishes beneath the wagon as though it were a ribbon and the front axle were a spool. "Do you know she is going to die, Jewel?"

It takes two people to make you, and one people to die. That's how the world is going to end.

I said to Dewey Dell: "You want her to die so you can get to town: is that it?" She wouldn't say what we both knew. "The reason you will not say it is, when you say it, even to yourself, you will know it is true: is that it? But you know it is true now. I can almost tell you the day when you knew it is true. Why wont you say it, even to yourself?" She will not say it. She just keeps on saying Are you going to tell pa? Are you going to kill him? "You cannot believe it is true because you cannot believe that Dewey Dell, Dewey Dell Bundren, could have such bad luck: is that it?"

The sun, an hour above the horizon, is poised like a bloody egg upon a crest of thunderheads; the light has turned copper: in the eye portentous, in the nose sulphurous, smelling of lightning. When Peabody comes, they will have to use the rope. He has pussel-gutted himself eating cold greens. With the rope they will haul him up the path, balloon-like up the sulphurous air.

"Jewel," I say, "do you know that Addie Bundren is going to die? Addie Bundren is going to die?"

Peabody

When Anse finally sent for me of his own accord, I said "He has wore her out at last." And I said a damn good thing, and at first I would not go because there might be something I could do and I would have to haul her back, by God. I thought maybe they have the same sort of fool ethics in heaven they have in the Medical College and that it was maybe Vernon Tull sending for me again, getting me there in the nick of time, as Vernon always does things, getting the most for Anse's money like he does for his own. But when it got far enough into the day for me to read weather sign I knew it couldn't have been anybody but Anse that sent. I knew that nobody but a luckless man could ever need a doctor in the face of a cyclone. And I knew that if it had finally occurred to Anse himself that he needed one, it was already too late.

When I reach the spring and get down and hitch the team, the sun has gone down behind a bank of black cloud like a topheavy mountain range, like a load of cinders dumped over there, and there is no wind. I could hear Cash sawing for a mile before I got there. Anse is standing at the top of the bluff above the path.

"Where's the horse?" I say.

"Jewel's taken and gone," he says. "Cant nobody else ketch hit. You'll have to walk up, I reckon."

"Me, walk up, weighing two hundred and twenty-five pounds?" I say. "Walk up that durn wall?" He stands there beside a tree. Too bad the Lord made the mistake of giving trees roots and giving the Anse Bundrens He makes feet and legs. If He'd just swapped them, there wouldn't ever be a worry about this country being deforested someday. Or any other country. "What do you aim for me to do?" I say. "Stay here and get blowed clean out of the country when that cloud breaks?" Even with the horse it would take me fifteen minutes to ride up across the pasture to the top of the ridge and reach the house. The path looks like a crooked limb blown against the bluff. Anse has not been in town in twelve years. And how his mother ever got up there to bear him, he being his mother's son.

"Vardaman's gittin the rope," he says.

After a while Vardaman appears with the plowline. He gives the end of it to Anse and comes down the path, uncoiling it.

"You hold it tight," I say. "I done already wrote this visit onto my books, so I'm going to charge you just the same, whether I get there or not."

"I got hit," Anse says. "You kin come on up."

I'll be damned if I can see why I dont quit. A man seventy years old, weighing two hundred and odd pounds, being hauled up and down a damn mountain on a rope. I reckon it's because I must reach the fifty thousand dollar mark of dead accounts on my books before I can quit. "What the hell does your wife mean," I say, "taking sick on top of a durn mountain?"

"I'm right sorry," he says. He let the rope go, just dropped it, and he has turned toward the house. There is a little daylight up here still, of the color of sulphur matches. The boards look like strips of sulphur. Cash does not look back. Vernon Tull says he brings each board up to the window for her to see it and say it is all right. The boy overtakes us. Anse looks back at him. "Wher's the rope?" he says.

"It's where you left it," I say. "But never you mind that rope. I got to get back down that bluff. I dont aim for that storm to catch me up here. I'd blow too durn far once I got started."

The girl is standing by the bed, fanning her. When we enter she turns her head and looks at us. She has been dead these ten days. I suppose it's having been a part of Anse for so long that she cannot even make that change, if change it be. I can remember how when I was young I believed death to be a phenomenon of the body; now I know it to be merely a function of the mind—and that of the minds of the ones who suffer the bereavement. The nihilists say it is the end; the fundamentalists, the beginning; when in reality it is no more than a single tenant or family moving out of a tenement or a town.

She looks at us. Only her eyes seem to move. It's like they touch us, not with sight or sense, but like the stream from a hose touches you, the stream at the instant of impact as dissociated from the nozzle as though it had never been there. She does not look at Anse at all. She looks at me, then at the boy. Beneath the quilt she is no more than a bundle of rotten sticks.

"Well, Miss Addie," I say. The girl does not stop the fan. "How are you, sister?" I say. Her head lies gaunt on the pillow, looking at the boy. "You picked out a fine time to get me out here and bring up a storm." Then I send Anse and the boy out. She watches the boy as he leaves the room. She has not moved save her eyes.

He and Anse are on the porch when I come out, the boy sitting on the steps, Anse standing by a post, not even leaning against it, his arms dangling, the hair pushed and matted up on his head like a dipped rooster. He turns his head, blinking at me.

"Why didn't you send for me sooner?" I say.

"Hit was jest one thing and then another," he says. "That ere corn me and the boys was aimin to git up with, and Dewey Dell a-takin good keer of her, and folks comin in, a-offerin to help and sich, till I jest thought . . ."

"Damn the money," I say. "Did you ever hear of me worrying a fellow before he was ready to pay?"

"Hit aint begrudgin the money," he says. "I jest kept a-thinking . . . She's goin, is she?" The durn little tyke is sitting on the top step, looking smaller than ever in the sulphur-colored light. That's the one trouble with this country: everything, weather, all, hangs on too long. Like our rivers, our land: opaque, slow, violent; shaping and creating the life of man in its implacable and brooding image. "I knowed hit," Anse says. "All the while I made sho. Her mind is sot on hit."

"And a damn good thing, too," I say. "With a trifling—" He sits on the top step, small, motionless in faded overalls. When I came out he looked up at me, then at Anse. But now he has stopped looking at us. He just sits there.

"Have you told her yit?" Anse says.

"What for?" I say. "What the devil for?"

"She'll know hit. I knowed that when she see you she would know hit, same as writing. You wouldn't need to tell her. Her mind—"

Behind us the girl says, "Paw." I look at her, at her face.

"You better go quick," I say.

When we enter the room she is watching the door. She looks at me. Her eyes look like lamps blaring up just before the oil is gone. "She wants you to go out," the girl says.

"Now, Addie," Anse says, "when he come all the way from Jefferson to git you well?" She watches me: I can feel her eyes. It's like she was shoving at me with them. I have seen it before in women. Seen them drive from the room them coming with sympathy and pity, with actual help, and clinging to some trifling animal to whom they never were more than pack-horses. That's what they mean by the love that passeth understanding: that pride, that furious desire to hide that abject nakedness which we bring here with us, carry with us into operating rooms, carry stubbornly and furiously with us into the earth again. I leave the room. Beyond the porch Cash's saw snores steadily into the board. A minute later she calls his name, her voice harsh and strong.

"Cash," she says; "you, Cash!"

Darl

Pa stands beside the bed. From behind his leg Vardaman peers, with his round head and his eyes round and his mouth beginning to open. She looks at pa; all her failing life appears to drain into her eyes, urgent, irremediable.

"It's Jewel she wants," Dewey Dell says.

"Why, Addie," pa says, "him and Darl went to make one more load. They thought there was time. That you would wait for them, and that three dollars and all . . ." He stoops laying his hand on hers. For a while yet she looks at him, without reproach, without anything at all, as if her eyes alone are listening to the irrevocable cessation of his voice. Then she raises herself, who has not moved in ten days. Dewey Dell leans down, trying to press her back.

"Ma," she says; "ma."

She is looking out the window, at Cash stooping steadily at the board in the failing light, laboring on toward darkness and into it as though the stroking of the saw illumined its own motion, board and saw engendered.

"You, Cash," she shouts, her voice harsh, strong, and unimpaired. "You, Cash!"

He looks up at the gaunt face framed by the window in the twilight. It is a composite picture of all time since he was a child. He drops the saw and lifts the board for her to see, watching the window in which the face has not moved. He drags a second plank into position and slants the two of them into their final juxtaposition, gesturing toward the ones yet on the ground, shaping with his empty hand in pantomime the finished box. For a while still she looks down at him from the composite picture, neither with censure nor approbation. Then the face disappears.

She lies back and turns her head without so much as glancing at pa. She looks at Vardaman; her eyes, the life in them, rushing suddenly upon them; the two flames glare up for a steady instant. Then they go out as though someone had leaned down and blown upon them.

"Ma," Dewey Dell says; "ma!" Leaning above the bed, her hands lifted a little, the fan still moving like it has for ten days, she begins to keen. Her voice is strong, young, tremulous and clear, rapt with its own timbre and volume, the fan still moving steadily up and down, whispering the useless air. Then she flings herself across Addie Bundren's knees, clutching her, shaking her with the furious strength of the young before sprawling suddenly across the handful of rotten bones that Addie Bundren left, jarring the whole bed into a chattering sibilance of mattress shucks, her arms outflung and the fan in one hand still beating with expiring breath into the quilt.

From behind pa's leg Vardaman peers, his mouth full open all color draining from his face into his mouth, as though he has by some means fleshed his own teeth in himself, sucking. He begins to move slowly backward from the bed, his eyes round, his pale face fading into the dusk like a piece of paper pasted on a failing wall, and so out of the door.

Pa leans above the bed in the twilight, his humped silhouette partaking of that owl-like quality of awry-feathered, disgruntled outrage within which lurks a wisdom too profound or too inert for even thought.

"Durn them boys," he says.

Jewel, I say. Overhead the day drives level and gray, hiding the sun by a flight of gray spears. In the rain the mules smoke a little, splashed yellow with mud, the off[8] one clinging in sliding lunges to the side of the road above the ditch. The tilted lumber gleams dull yellow, water-soaked and heavy as lead, tilted at a steep angle into the ditch above the broken wheel; about the shattered spokes and about Jewel's ankles a runnel of yellow neither water nor earth swirls, curving with the yellow road neither of earth nor water, down the hill dissolving into a streaming mass of dark green neither of earth nor sky, Jewel, I say

Cash comes to the door, carrying the saw. Pa stands beside the bed, humped, his arms dangling. He turns his head, his shabby profile, his chin collapsing slowly as he works the snuff against his gums.

8. Right.

"She's gone," Cash says.

"She taken and left us," pa says. Cash does not look at him. "How nigh are you done?" pa says. Cash does not answer. He enters, carrying the saw. "I reckon you better get at it," pa says. "You'll have to do the best you can, with them boys gone off that-a-way." Cash looks down at her face. He is not listening to pa at all. He does not approach the bed. He stops in the middle of the floor, the saw against his leg, his sweating arms powdered lightly with sawdust, his face composed. "If you get in a tight, maybe some of them'll get here tomorrow and help you," pa says. "Vernon could." Cash is not listening. He is looking down at her peaceful, rigid face fading into the dusk as though darkness were a precursor of the ultimate earth, until at last the face seems to float detached upon it, lightly as the reflection of a dead leaf. "There is Christians enough to help you," pa says. Cash is not listening. After a while he turns without looking at pa and leaves the room. Then the saw begins to snore again. "They will help us in our sorrow," pa says.

The sound of the saw is steady, competent, unhurried, stirring the dying light so that at each stroke her face seems to wake a little into an expression of listening and of waiting, as though she were counting the strokes. Pa looks down at the face, at the black sprawl of Dewey Dell's hair, the outflung arms, the clutched fan now motionless on the fading quilt. "I reckon you better get supper on," he says.

Dewey Dell does not move.

"Git up, now, and put supper on," pa says. "We got to keep our strength up. I reckon Doctor Peabody's right hungry, coming all this way. And Cash'll need to eat quick and get back to work so he can finish it in time."

Dewey Dell rises, heaving to her feet. She looks down at the face. It is like a casting of fading bronze upon the pillow, the hands alone still with any semblance of life: a curled, gnarled inertness; a spent yet alert quality from which weariness, exhaustion, travail has not yet departed, as though they doubted even yet the actuality of rest, guarding with horned and penurious alertness the cessation which they know cannot last.

Dewey Dell stoops and slides the quilt from beneath them and draws it up over them to the chin, smoothing it down, drawing it smooth. Then without looking at pa she goes around the bed and leaves the room.

She will go out where Peabody is, where she can stand in the twilight and look at his back with such an expression that, feeling her eyes and turning, he will say: I would not let it grieve me, now. She was old, and sick too. Suffering more than we knew. She couldn't have got well. Vardaman's getting big now, and with you to take good care of them all. I would try not to let it grieve me. I expect you'd better go and get some supper ready. It dont have to be much. But they'll need to eat, and she looking at him, saying You could do so much for me if you just would. If you just knew. I am I and you are you and I know it and you dont know it and you could do so much for me if you just would and if you just would then I could tell you and then nobody would have to know it except you and me and Darl

Pa stands over the bed, dangle-armed, humped, motionless. He raises his hand to his head, scouring his hair, listening to the saw. He comes nearer and rubs his hand, palm and back, on his thigh and lays it on her face and then on the hump of quilt where her hands are. He touches the quilt as he saw Dewey Dell do, trying to smoothe it up to the chin, but disarranging it instead. He tries to smoothe it again, clumsily, his hand awkward as a claw, smoothing at the wrinkles which he made and which continue to emerge beneath his hand with perverse ubiquity, so that at last he desists, his hand falling to his side and stroking itself again, palm and back, on his thigh. The sound of the saw snores steadily into the room. Pa breathes with a quiet, rasping sound, mouthing the snuff against his gums. "God's will be done," he says. "Now I can get them teeth."

Jewel's hat droops limp about his neck, channelling water onto the soaked towsack tied about his shoulders as, ankle-deep in the running ditch, he pries with a slipping two-by-four, with a piece of rotting log for fulcrum, at the axle. Jewel, I say, she is dead, Jewel. Addie Bundren is dead

Vardaman

Then I begin to run. I run toward the back and come to the edge of the porch and stop. Then I begin to cry. I can feel where the fish was in the dust. It is cut up into pieces of not-fish now, not-blood on my hands and overalls. Then it wasn't so. It hadn't happened then. And now she is getting so far ahead I cannot catch her.

The trees look like chickens when they ruffle out into the cool dust on the hot days. If I jump off the porch I will be where the fish was, and it all cut up into not-fish now. I can hear the bed and her face and them and I can feel the floor shake when he walks on it that came and did it. That came and did it when she was all right but he came and did it.

"The fat son of a bitch."

I jump from the porch, running. The top of the barn comes swooping up out of the twilight. If I jump I can go through it like the pink lady in the circus, into the warm smelling, without having to wait. My hands grab at the bushes; beneath my feet the rocks and dirt go rubbling down.

Then I can breathe again, in the warm smelling. I enter the stall, trying to touch him, and then I can cry then I vomit the crying. As soon as he gets through kicking I can and then I can cry, the crying can.

"He kilt her. He kilt her."

The life in him runs under the skin, under my hand, running through the splotches, smelling up into my nose where the sickness is beginning to cry, vomiting the crying, and then I can breathe, vomiting it. It makes a lot of noise. I can smell the life running up from under my hands, up my arms, and then I can leave the stall.

I cannot find it. In the dark, along the dust, the walls I cannot find it. The crying makes a lot of noise. I wish it wouldn't make so much noise. Then I find it in the wagon shed, in the dust, and I run across the lot and into the road, the stick jouncing on my shoulder.

They watch me as I run up, beginning to jerk back, their eyes rolling, snorting, jerking back on the hitch-rein. I strike. I can hear the stick striking; I can see it hitting their heads, the breast-yoke, missing altogether sometimes as they rear and plunge, but I am glad.

"You kilt my maw!"

The stick breaks, they rearing and snorting, their feet popping loud on the ground; loud because it is going to rain and the air is empty for the rain. But it is still long enough. I run this way and that as they rear and jerk at the hitch-rein, striking.

"You kilt her!"

I strike at them, striking, they wheeling in a long lunge, the buggy wheeling onto two wheels and motionless like it is nailed to the ground and the horses motionless like they are nailed by the hind feet to the center of a whirling plate.

I run in the dust. I cannot see, running in the sucking dust where the buggy vanishes tilted on two wheels. I strike, the stick hitting into the ground, bouncing, striking into the dust and then into the air again and the dust sucking on down the road faster than if a car was in it. And then I can cry, looking at the stick. It is broken down to my hand, not longer than stove wood that was a long stick. I throw it away and I can cry. It does not make so much noise now.

The cow is standing in the barn door, chewing. When she sees me come into the lot she lows, her mouth full of flopping green, her tongue flopping.

"I aint a-goin to milk you. I aint a-goin to do nothing for them."

I hear her turn when I pass. When I turn she is just behind me with her sweet, hot, hard breath.

"Didn't I tell you I wouldn't?"

She nudges me, snuffing. She moans deep inside, her mouth closed. I jerk my hand, cursing her like Jewel does.

"Git, now."

I stoop my hand to the ground and run at her. She jumps back and whirls away and stops, watching me. She moans. She goes on to the path and stands there, looking up the path.

It is dark in the barn, warm, smelling, silent. I can cry quietly, watching the top of the hill.

Cash comes to the hill, limping where he fell off of the church. He looks down at the spring, then up the road and back toward the barn. He comes down the path stiffly and looks at the broken hitch-rein and at the dust in the road and then up the road, where the dust is gone.

"I hope they've got clean past Tull's by now. I so hope hit."

Cash turns and limps up the path.

"Durn him. I showed him. Durn him."

I am not crying now. I am not anything. Dewey Dell comes to the hill and calls me. Vardaman. I am not anything. I am quiet. You, Vardaman. I can cry quiet now, feeling and hearing my tears.

"Then hit want. Hit hadn't happened then. Hit was a-layin right there on the ground. And now she's gittin ready to cook hit."

It is dark. I can hear wood, silence: I know them. But not living sounds, not even him. It is as though the dark were resolving him out of his integrity, into an unrelated scattering of components—snuffings and stampings; smells of cooling flesh and ammoniac hair; an illusion of a co-ordinated whole of splotched hide and strong bones within which, detached and secret and familiar, an *is* different from my *is*. I see him dissolve—legs, a rolling eye, a gaudy splotching like cold flames—and float upon the dark in fading solution; all one yet neither; all either yet none. I can see hearing coil toward him, caressing, shaping his hard shape—fetlock, hip, shoulder and head; smell and sound. I am not afraid.

"Cooked and et. Cooked and et."

Dewey Dell

He could do so much for me if he just would. He could do everything for me. It's like everything in the world for me is inside a tub full of guts, so that you wonder how there can be any room in it for anything else very important. He is a big tub of guts and I am a little tub of guts and if there is not any room for anything else important in a big tub of guts, how can it be room in a little tub of guts. But I know it is there because God gave women a sign when something has happened bad.

It's because I am alone. If I could just feel it, it would be different, because I would not be alone. But if I were not alone, everybody would know it. And he could do so much for me, and then I would not be alone. Then I could be all right alone.

I would let him come in between me and Lafe, like Darl came in between me and Lafe, and so Lafe is alone too. He is Lafe and I am Dewey Dell, and when mother died I had to go beyond and outside of me and Lafe and Darl to grieve because he could do so much for me and he dont know it. He dont even know it.

From the back porch I cannot see the barn. Then the sound of Cash's sawing comes in from that way. It is like a dog outside the house, going back and forth around the house to whatever door you come to, waiting to come in. He said I worry more than you do and I said You dont know what worry is so I cant worry. I try to but I cant think long enough to worry.

I light the kitchen lamp. The fish, cut into jagged pieces, bleeds quietly in the pan. I put it into the cupboard quick, listening into the hall, hearing. It took her ten days to die; maybe she dont know it is yet. Maybe she wont go until Cash. Or maybe until Jewel. I take the dish of greens from the cupboard and the bread pan from the cold stove, and I stop, watching the door.

"Where's Vardaman?" Cash says. In the lamp his sawdusted arms look like sand.

"I dont know. I aint seen him."

"Peabody's team run away. See if you can find Vardaman. The horse will let him catch him."

"Well. Tell them to come to supper."

I cannot see the barn. I said, I dont know how to worry. I dont know how to cry. I tried, but I cant. After a while the sound of the saw comes around, coming dark along the ground in the dust-dark. Then I can see him, going up and down above the plank.

"You come in to supper," I say. "Tell him." He could do everything for me. And he dont know it. He is his guts and I am my guts. And I am Lafe's guts. That's it. I dont see why he didn't stay in town. We are country people, not as good as town people. I dont see why he didn't. Then I can see the top of the barn. The cow stands at the foot of the path, lowing. When I turn back, Cash is gone.

I carry the buttermilk in. Pa and Cash and he are at the table.

"Where's that big fish Bud caught, sister?" he says.

I set the milk on the table. "I never had no time to cook it."

"Plain turnip greens is mighty spindling eating for a man my size," he says. Cash is eating. About his head the print of his hat is sweated into his hair. His shirt is blotched with sweat. He has not washed his hands and arms.

"You ought to took time," pa says. "Where's Vardaman?"

I go toward the door. "I cant find him."

"Here, sister," he says; "never mind about the fish. It'll save, I reckon. Come on and sit down."

"I aint minding it," I say. "I'm going to milk before it sets in to rain."

Pa helps himself and pushes the dish on. But he does not begin to eat. His hands are halfclosed on either side of his plate, his head bowed a little, his awry hair standing into the lamplight. He looks like right after the maul hits the steer and it no longer alive and dont yet know that it is dead.

But Cash is eating, and he is too. "You better eat something," he says. He is looking at pa. "Like Cash and me. You'll need it."

"Ay," pa says. He rouses up, like a steer that's been kneeling in a pond and you run at it. "She would not begrudge me it."

When I am out of sight of the house, I go fast. The cow lows at the foot of the bluff. She nuzzles at me, snuffing, blowing her breath in a sweet, hot blast, through my dress, against my hot nakedness, moaning. "You got to wait a little while. Then I'll tend to you." She follows me into the barn where I set the bucket down. She breathes into the bucket, moaning. "I told you. You just got to wait, now. I got more to do than I can tend to." The barn is dark. When I pass, he kicks the wall a single blow. I go on. The broken plank is like a pale plank standing on end. Then I can see the slope, feel the air moving on my face again, slow, pale with lesser dark and with empty seeing, the pine clumps blotched up the tilted slope, secret and waiting.

The cow in _silhouette_ against the door nuzzles at the silhouette of the bucket, moaning.

Then I pass the stall. I have almost passed it. I listen to it saying for a long time before it can say the word and the listening part is afraid that there may not be time to say it. I feel my body, my bones and flesh beginning to part and open upon the alone, and the process of coming unalone is terrible. Lafe. Lafe. "Lafe" Lafe. Lafe. I lean a little forward, one foot advanced with dead walking. I feel the darkness rushing past my breast, past the cow; I begin to rush upon the darkness but the cow stops me and the darkness rushes on upon the sweet blast of her moaning breath, filled with wood and with silence.

"Vardaman. You, Vardaman."

He comes out of the stall. "You durn little sneak! You durn little sneak!"

He does not resist; the last of rushing darkness flees whistling away. "What? I aint done nothing."

"You durn little sneak!" My hands shake him, hard. Maybe I couldn't stop them. I didn't know they could shake so hard. They shake both of us, shaking.

"I never done it," he says. "I never touched them."

My hands stop shaking him, but I still hold him. "What are you doing here? Why didn't you answer when I called you?"

"I aint doing nothing."

"You go on to the house and get your supper."

He draws back. I hold him. "You quit now. You leave me be."

"What are you doing down here? You didn't come down here to sneak after me?"

"I never. I never. You quit, now. I didn't even know you was down here. You leave me be."

I hold him, leaning down to see his face, feel it with my eyes. He is about to cry. "Go on, now. I done put supper on and I'll be there soon as I milk. You better go on before he eats everything up. I hope that team runs clean back to Jefferson."

"He kilt her," he says. He begins to cry.

"Hush."

"She never hurt him and he come and kilt her."

"Hush." He struggles. I hold him. "Hush."

"He kilt her." The cow comes up behind us, moaning. I shake him again.

"You stop it, now. Right this minute. You're fixing to make yourself sick and then you cant go to town. You go on to the house and eat your supper."

"I dont want no supper. I dont want to go to town."

"We'll leave you here, then. Lessen you behave, we will leave you. Go on, now, before that old green-eating tub of guts eats everything up from you." He goes on, disappearing slowly into the hill. The crest, the trees, the roof of the house stand against the sky. The cow nuzzles at me, moaning. "You'll just have to wait. What you got in you aint nothing to what I got in me, even if you are a woman too." She follows me, moaning. Then the dead, hot, pale air breathes on my face again. He could fix it all right, if he just would. And he dont even know it. He could do everything for me if he just knowed it. The cow breathes upon my hips and back, her breath warm, sweet, stertorous, moaning. The sky lies flat down the slope, upon the secret clumps. Beyond the hill sheet-lightning stains upward and fades. The dead air shapes the dead earth in the dead darkness, further away than seeing shapes the dead earth. It lies dead and warm upon me, touching me naked through my clothes. I said You dont know what worry is. I dont know what it is. I dont know whether I am worrying or not. Whether I can or not. I dont know whether I can cry or not, I dont know whether I have tried to or not. I feel like a wet seed wild in the hot blind earth.

Vardaman

When they get it finished they are going to put her in it and then for a long time I couldn't say it. I saw the dark stand up and go whirling away and I said "Are you going to nail her up in it, Cash? Cash? Cash?" I got shut up in the crib the new door it was too heavy for me it went shut I couldn't breathe because the rat was breathing up all the air, I said "Are you going to nail it shut, Cash? Nail it? *Nail* it?"

Pa walks around. His shadow walks around, over Cash going up and down above the saw, at the bleeding plank.

Dewey Dell said we will get some bananas. The train is behind the glass, red on the track. When it runs the track shines on and off. Pa said flour and sugar and coffee costs so much. Because I am a country boy because boys in town. Bicycles. Why do flour and sugar and coffee cost so much when he is a country boy. "Wouldn't you ruther have some bananas instead?" Bananas are gone, eaten. Gone. When it runs on the track shines again. "Why aint I a town boy, pa?" I said. God made me. I did not said to God to made me in the country. If He can make the train, why cant He make them all in the town because flour and sugar and coffee. "Wouldn't you ruther have bananas?"

He walks around. His shadow walks around.

It was not her. I was there, looking. I saw. I thought it was her, but it was not. It was not my mother. She went away when the other one laid down in her bed and drew the quilt up. She went away. "Did she go as far as town?" "She went further than town." "Did all those rabbits and possums go further than town?" God made the rabbits and possums. He made the train. Why must He make a different place for them to go if she is just like the rabbit.

Pa walks around. His shadow does. The saw sounds like it is asleep.

And so if Cash nails the box up, she is not a rabbit. And so if she is not a rabbit I couldn't breathe in the crib and Cash is going to nail it up. And so if she lets him it is not her. I know. I was there. I saw when it did not be her. I saw. They think it is and Cash is going to nail it up.

It was not her because it was laying right yonder in the dirt. And now it's all chopped up. I chopped it up. It's laying in the kitchen in the bleeding pan, waiting to be cooked and et. Then it wasn't and she was, and now it is and she wasn't. And tomorrow it will be cooked and et and she will be him and pa and Cash and Dewey Dell and there wont be anything in the box and so she can breathe. It was laying right yonder on the ground. I can get Vernon. He was there and he seen it, and with both of us it will be and then it will not be.

Tull

It was nigh to midnight and it had set in to rain when he woke us. It had been a misdoubtful night, with the storm making; a night when a fellow looks for most anything to happen before he can get the stock fed and himself to the house and supper et and in bed with the rain starting, and when Peabody's team come up, lathered, with the broke harness dragging and the neck-yoke betwixt the off critter's legs, Cora says "It's Addie Bundren. She's gone at last."

"Peabody mought have been to ere a one of a dozen houses hereabouts," I says. "Besides, how do you know it's Peabody's team?"

"Well, aint it?" she says. "You hitch up, now."

"What for?" I says. "If she is gone, we cant do nothing till morning. And it fixing to storm, too."

"It's my duty," she says. "You put the team in."

But I wouldn't do it. "It stands to reason they'd send for us if they needed us. You dont even know she's gone yet."

"Why, dont you know that's Peabody's team? Do you claim it aint? Well, then." But I wouldn't go. When folks wants a fellow, it's best to wait till they sends for him, I've found. "It's my Christian duty," Cora says. "Will you stand between me and my Christian duty?"

"You can stay there all day tomorrow, if you want," I says.

So when Cora waked me it had set in to rain. Even while I was going to the door with the lamp and it shining on the glass so he could see I am coming, it kept on knocking. Not loud, but steady, like he might have gone to sleep thumping, but I never noticed how low down on the door the knocking was till I opened it and never seen nothing. I held the lamp up, with the rain sparkling across it and Cora back in the hall saying "Who is it, Vernon?" but I couldn't see nobody a-tall at first until I looked down and around the door, lowering the lamp.

He looked like a drownded puppy, in them overalls, without no hat, splashed up to his knees where he had walked them four miles in the mud. "Well, I'll be durned," I says.

"Who is it, Vernon?" Cora says.

He looked at me, his eyes round and black in the middle like when you throw a light in a owl's face. "You mind[9] that ere fish," he says.

"Come in the house," I says. "What is it? Is your maw—"

"Vernon," Cora says.

He stood kind of around behind the door, in the dark. The rain was blowing onto the lamp, hissing on it so I am scared every minute it'll break. "You was there," he says. "You seen it."

Then Cora come to the door. "You come right in outen the rain," she says, pulling him in and him watching me. He looked just like a drownded puppy. "I told you," Cora says. "I told you it was a-happening. You go and hitch."

"But he aint said—" I says.

He looked at me, dripping onto the floor. "He's a-ruining the rug," Cora says. "You go get the team while I take him to the kitchen."

But he hung back, dripping, watching me with them eyes. "You was there. You seen it laying there. Cash is fixing to nail her up, and it was a-laying right there on the ground. You seen it. You seen the mark in the dirt. The rain never come up till after I was a-coming here. So we can get back in time."

I be durn if it didn't give me the creeps, even when I didn't know yet. But Cora did. "You get that team quick as you can," she says. "He's outen his head with grief and worry."

I be durn if it didn't give me the creeps. Now and then a fellow gets to thinking. About all the sorrow and afflictions in this world; how it's liable to strike anywhere, like lightning. I reckon it does take a powerful trust in the Lord to guard a fellow, though sometimes I think that Cora's a mite over-cautious, like she was trying to crowd the other folks away and get in closer than anybody else. But then, when something like this happens, I reckon she is right and you got to keep after it and I reckon I am blessed in having a wife that ever strives for sanctity and well-doing like she says I am.

Now and then a fellow gets to thinking about it. Not often, though. Which is a good thing. For the Lord aimed for him to do and not to spend too much time thinking, because his brain it's like a piece of machinery: it wont stand a whole lot of racking. It's best when it all runs along the same, doing the day's work and not no one part used no more than needful. I have said and I say again, that's ever living thing the matter with Darl: he just thinks by himself too much. Cora's right when she says all he needs is a wife to straighten him out. And when I think about that, I think that if nothing but being married will help a man, he's durn nigh hopeless. But I reckon Cora's right when she says the reason the Lord had to create women is because man dont know his own good when he sees it.

When I come back to the house with the team, they was in the kitchen. She was dressed on top of her nightgown, with a shawl over her head and her umbrella and her bible wrapped up in the oilcloth, and him sitting on a up-turned bucket on the stove-zinc where she had put him, dripping onto the floor. "I cant get nothing outen him except about a fish," she says. "It's a judg-

9. Remember.

ment on them. I see the hand of the Lord upon this boy for Anse Bundren's judgment and warning."

"The rain never come up till after I left," he says. "I had done left. I was on the way. And so it was there in the dust. You seen it. Cash is fixing to nail her, but you seen it."

When we got there it was raining hard, and him sitting on the seat between us, wrapped up in Cora's shawl. He hadn't said nothing else, just sitting there with Cora holding the umbrella over him. Now and then Cora would stop singing long enough to say "It's a judgment on Anse Bundren. May it show him the path of sin he is a-trodding." Then she would sing again, and him sitting there between us, leaning forward a little like the mules couldn't go fast enough to suit him.

"It was laying right yonder," he says, "but the rain come up after I taken and left. So I can go and open the windows, because Cash aint nailed her yet."

It was long a-past midnight when we drove the last nail, and almost dust-dawn when I got back home and taken the team out and got back in bed, with Cora's nightcap laying on the other pillow. And be durned if even then it wasn't like I could still hear Cora singing and feel that boy leaning forward between us like he was ahead of the mules, and still see Cash going up and down with that saw, and Anse standing there like a scarecrow, like he was a steer standing knee-deep in a pond and somebody come by and set the pond up on edge and he aint missed it yet.

It was nigh toward daybreak when we drove the last nail and toted it into the house, where she was laying on the bed with the window open and the rain blowing on her again. Twice he did it, and him so dead for sleep that Cora says his face looked like one of these here Christmas masts[1] that had done been buried a while and then dug up, until at last they put her into it and nailed it down so he couldn't open the window on her no more. And the next morning they found him in his shirt tail, laying asleep on the floor like a felled steer, and the top of the box bored clean full of holes and Cash's new auger broke off in the last one. When they taken the lid off they found that two of them had bored on into her face.

If it's a judgment, it aint right. Because the Lord's got more to do than that. He's bound to have. Because the only burden Anse Bundren's ever had is himself. And when folks talks him low, I think to myself he aint that less of a man or he couldn't a bore himself this long.

It aint right. I be durn if it is. Because He said Suffer little children to come unto Me dont make it right, neither. Cora said, "I have bore you what the Lord God sent me. I faced it without fear nor terror because my faith was strong in the Lord, a-bolstering and sustaining me. If you have no son, it's because the Lord has decreed otherwise in His wisdom. And my life is and has ever been a open book to ere a man or woman among His creatures because I trust in my God and my reward."

I reckon she's right. I reckon if there's ere a man or woman anywhere that He could turn it all over to and go away with His mind at rest, it would be Cora. And I reckon she would make a few changes, no matter how He was running it. And I reckon they would be for man's good. Leastways, we would have to like them. Leastways, we might as well go on and make like we did.

1. Masks.

Darl

The lantern sits on a stump. Rusted, grease-fouled, its cracked chimney smeared on one side with a soaring smudge of soot, it sheds a feeble and sultry glare upon the trestles and the boards and the adjacent earth. Upon the dark ground the chips look like random smears of soft pale paint on a black canvas. The boards look like long smooth tatters torn from the flat darkness and turned backside out.

Cash labors about the trestles, moving back and forth, lifting and placing the planks with long clattering reverberations in the dead air as though he were lifting and dropping them at the bottom of an invisible well, the sounds ceasing without departing, as if any movement might dislodge them from the immediate air in reverberant repetition. He saws again, his elbow flashing slowly, a thin thread of fire running along the edge of the saw, lost and recovered at the top and bottom of each stroke in unbroken elongation, so that the saw appears to be six feet long, into and out of pa's shabby and aimless silhouette. "Give me that plank," Cash says. "No; the other one." He puts the saw down and comes and picks up the plank he wants, sweeping pa away with the long swinging gleam of the balanced board.

The air smells like sulphur. Upon the impalpable plane of it their shadows form as upon a wall, as though like sound they had not gone very far away in falling but had merely congealed for a moment, immediate and musing. Cash works on, half turned into the feeble light, one thigh and one pole-thin arm braced, his face sloped into the light with a rapt, dynamic immobility above his tireless elbow. Below the sky sheet-lightning slumbers lightly; against it the trees, motionless, are ruffled out to the last twig, swollen, increased as though quick with young.

It begins to rain. The first harsh, sparse, swift drops rush through the leaves and across the ground in a long sigh, as though of relief from intolerable suspense. They are big as buckshot, warm as though fired from a gun; they sweep across the lantern in a vicious hissing. Pa lifts his face, slack-mouthed, the wet black rim of snuff plastered close along the base of his gums; from behind his slack-faced astonishment he muses as though from beyond time, upon the ultimate outrage. Cash looks once at the sky, then at the lantern. The saw has not faltered, the running gleam of its pistoning edge unbroken. "Get something to cover the lantern," he says.

Pa goes to the house. The rain rushes suddenly down, without thunder, without warning of any sort; he is swept onto the porch upon the edge of it and in an instant Cash is wet to the skin. Yet the motion of the saw has not faltered, as though it and the arm functioned in a tranquil conviction that rain was an illusion of the mind. Then he puts down the saw and goes and crouches above the lantern, shielding it with his body, his back shaped lean and scrawny by his wet shirt as though he had been abruptly turned wrong-side out, shirt and all.

Pa returns. He is wearing Jewel's raincoat and carrying Dewey Dell's. Squatting over the lantern, Cash reaches back and picks up four sticks and drives them into the earth and takes Dewey Dell's raincoat from pa and spreads it over the sticks, forming a roof above the lantern. Pa watches him. "I dont know what you'll do," he says. "Darl taken his coat with him."

"Get wet," Cash says. He takes up the saw again; again it moves up and down, in and out of that unhurried imperviousness as a piston moves in the oil; soaked, scrawny, tireless, with the lean light body of a boy or an old man. Pa watches him, blinking, his face streaming; again he looks up at the sky with that expression of dumb and brooding outrage and yet of vindication, as though he had expected no less; now and then he stirs; moves, gaunt and streaming, picking up a board or a tool and then laying it down. Vernon Tull is there now, and Cash is wearing Mrs Tull's raincoat and he and Vernon are hunting the saw. After a while they find it in pa's hand.

"Why don't you go on to the house, out of the rain?" Cash says. Pa looks at him, his face streaming slowly. It is as though upon a face carved by a savage caricaturist a monstrous burlesque of all bereavement flowed. "You go on in," Cash says. "Me and Vernon can finish it."

Pa looks at them. The sleeves of Jewel's coat are too short for him. Upon his face the rain streams, slow as cold glycerin. "I dont begrudge her the wetting," he says. He moves again and falls to shifting the planks, picking them up, laying them down again carefully, as though they are glass. He goes to the lantern and pulls at the propped raincoat until he knocks it down and Cash comes and fixes it back.

"You get on to the house," Cash says. He leads pa to the house and returns with the raincoat and folds it and places it beneath the shelter where the lantern sits. Vernon has not stopped. He looks up, still sawing.

"You ought to done that at first," he says. "You knowed it was fixing to rain."

"It's his fever," Cash says. He looks at the board.

"Ay," Vernon says. "He'd a come, anyway."

Cash squints at the board. On the long flank of it the rain crashed steadily, myriad, fluctuant. "I'm going to bevel it," he says.

"It'll take more time," Vernon says. Cash sets the plank on edge; a moment longer Vernon watches him, then he hands him the plane.

Vernon holds the board steady while Cash bevels the edge of it with the tedious and minute care of a jeweler. Mrs Tull comes to the edge of the porch and calls Vernon. "How near are you done?" she says.

Vernon does not look up. "Not long, Some, yet."

She watches Cash stooping at the plank, the turgid savage gleam of the lantern slicking on the raincoat as he moves. "You go down and get some planks off the barn and finish it and come in out of the rain," she says. "You'll both catch your death." Vernon does not move. "Vernon," she says.

"We wont be long," he says. "We'll be done after a spell." Mrs Tull watches them a while. Then she reenters the house.

"If we git in a tight, we could take some of them planks," Vernon says. "I'll help you put them back."

Cash ceases the plane and squints along the plank, wiping it with his palm. "Give me the next one," he says.

Some time toward dawn the rain ceases. But it is not yet day when Cash drives the last nail and stands stiffly up and looks down at the finished coffin, the others watching him. In the lantern light his face is calm, musing; slowly he strokes his hands on his raincoated thighs in a gesture deliberate, final and composed. Then the four of them—Cash and pa and Vernon and Peabody—raise the coffin to their shoulders and turn toward the house. It is light, yet they move slowly; empty, yet they carry it carefully; lifeless, yet they move with hushed precautionary words to one another, speaking of it as though, complete, it now slumbered lightly alive, waiting to come awake. On the dark floor their feet clump awkwardly, as though for a long time they have not walked on floors.

They set it down by the bed. Peabody says quietly: "Let's eat a snack. It's almost daylight. Where's Cash?"

He has returned to the trestles, stooped again in the lantern's feeble glare as he gathers up his tools and wipes them on a cloth carefully and puts them into the box with its leather sling to go over the shoulder. Then he takes up box, lantern and raincoat and returns to the house, mounting the steps into faint silhouette against the paling east.

In a strange room you must empty yourself for sleep. And before you are emptied for sleep, what are you. And when you are emptied for sleep, you are not. And when you are filled with sleep, you never were. I dont know what I am. I dont know if I am or not. Jewel knows he is, because he does not know that he does not know whether he is or not. He cannot empty himself for sleep because he is not what he is and he is what he is not. Beyond the unlamped wall I can hear the rain shaping the wagon that is ours, the load that is no longer theirs that felled and sawed it nor yet theirs that bought it and which is not ours either, lie on our wagon though it does, since only the wind and the rain shape it only to Jewel and me, that are not asleep. And since sleep is is-not and rain and wind are *was*, it is not. Yet the wagon *is*, because when the wagon is *was*, Addie Bundren will not be. And Jewel *is*, so Addie Bundren must be. And then I must be, or I could not empty myself for sleep in a strange room. And so if I am not emptied yet, I am *is*.

How often have I lain beneath rain on a strange roof, thinking of home.

Cash

I made it on the bevel.

1. There is more surface for the nails to grip.
2. There is twice the gripping-surface to each seam.
3. The water will have to seep into it on a slant. Water moves easiest up and down or straight across.
4. In a house people are upright two thirds of the time. So the seams and joints are made up-and-down. Because the stress is up-and-down.
5. In a bed where people lie down all the time, the joints and seams are made sideways, because the stress is sideways.
6. Except.
7. A body is not square like a crosstie.
8. Animal magnetism.
9. The animal magnetism of a dead body makes the stress come slanting, so the seams and joints of a coffin are made on the bevel.
10. You can see by an old grave that the earth sinks down on the bevel.
11. While in a natural hole it sinks by the center, the stress being up-and-down.
12. So I made it on the bevel.
13. It makes a neater job.

Vardaman

My mother is a fish.

Tull

It was ten oclock when I got back, with Peabody's team hitched on to the back of the wagon. They had already dragged the buckboard back from where Quick found it upside down straddle of the ditch about a mile from the spring. It was pulled out of the road at the spring, and about a dozen wagons was already there. It was Quick found it. He said the river was up and still rising. He said it had already covered the highest water-mark on the bridge-piling he had ever seen. "That bridge wont stand a whole lot of water," I said. "Has somebody told Anse about it?"

"I told him," Quick said. "He says he reckons them boys has heard and unloaded and are on the way back by now. He says they can load up and get across."

"He better go on and bury her at New Hope," Armstid said. "That bridge is old. I wouldn't monkey with it."

"His mind is set on taking her to Jefferson," Quick said.

"Then he better get at it soon as he can," Armstid said.

Anse meets us at the door. He has shaved, but not good. There is a long cut on his jaw, and he is wearing his Sunday pants and a white shirt with the neckband buttoned. It is drawn smooth over his hump, making it look bigger than ever, like a white shirt will, and his face is different too. He looks folks in the eye now, dignified, his face tragic and composed, shaking us by the hand as we walk up onto the porch and scrape our shoes, a little stiff in our Sunday clothes, our Sunday clothes rustling, not looking full at him as he meets us.

"The Lord giveth," we say.

"The Lord giveth."

That boy is not there. Peabody told about how he come into the kitchen, hollering, swarming and clawing at Cora when he found her cooking that fish, and how Dewey Dell taken him down to the barn. "My team all right?" Peabody says.

"All right," I tell him. "I give them a bait this morning. Your buggy seems all right too. It aint hurt."

"And no fault of somebody's," he says. "I'd give a nickel to know where that boy was when that team broke away."

"If it's broke anywhere, I'll fix it," I say.

The women folks go on into the house. We can hear them, talking and fanning. The fans go whish. whish. whish and them talking, the talking sounding kind of like bees murmuring in a water bucket. The men stop on the porch, talking some, not looking at one another.

"Howdy, Vernon," they say. "Howdy, Tull."

"Looks like more rain."

"It does for a fact."

"Yes, sir. It will rain some more."

"It come up quick."

"And going away slow. It dont fail."

I go around to the back. Cash is filling up the holes he bored in the top of it. He is trimming out plugs for them, one at a time, the wood wet and hard to work. He could cut up a tin can and hide the holes and nobody wouldn't know the difference. Wouldn't mind, anyway. I have seen him spend a hour trimming out a wedge like it was glass he was working, when he could have reached around and picked up a dozen sticks and drove them into the joint and made it do.

When we finished I go back to the front. The men have gone a little piece from the house, sitting on the ends of the boards and on the sawhorses where we made it last night, some sitting and some squatting. Whitfield aint come yet.

They look up at me, their eyes asking.

"It's about," I say. "He's ready to nail."

While they are getting up Anse comes to the door and looks at us and we return to the porch. We scrape our shoes again, careful, waiting for one another to go in first, milling a little at the door. Anse stands inside the door, dignified, composed. He waves us in and leads the way into the room.

They had laid her in it reversed. Cash made it clock-shape, like this

 with every joint and seam bevelled and scrubbed with the plane,

tight as a drum and neat as a sewing basket, and they had laid her in it head to foot so it wouldn't crush her dress. It was her wedding dress and it had a flare-out bottom, and they had laid her head to foot in it so the dress could spread out, and they had made her a veil out of a mosquito bar so the auger holes in her face wouldn't show.

When we are going out, Whitfield comes. He is wet and muddy to the waist, coming in. "The Lord comfort this house," he says. "I was late because the bridge has gone. I went down to the old ford and swum my horse over, the Lord protecting me. His grace be upon this house."

We go back to the trestles and plank-ends and sit or squat.

"I knowed it would go," Armstid says.

"It's been there a long time, that ere bridge," Quick says.

"The Lord has kept it there, you mean," Uncle Billy says. "I dont know ere a man that's touched hammer to it in twenty-five years."

"How long has it been there, Uncle Billy?" Quick says.

"It was built in . . . let me see . . . It was in the year 1888," Uncle Billy says. "I mind it because the first man to cross it was Peabody coming to my house when Jody was born."

"If I'd a crossed it every time your wife littered since, it'd a been wore out long before this, Billy," Peabody says.

We laugh, suddenly loud, then suddenly quiet again. We look a little aside at one another.

"Lots of folks has crossed it that wont cross no more bridges," Houston says.

"It's a fact," Littlejohn says. "It's so."

"One more aint, no ways," Armstid says. "It'd taken them two-three days to get her to town in the wagon. They'd be gone a week, getting her to Jefferson and back."

"What's Anse so itching to take her to Jefferson for, anyway?" Houston says.

"He promised her," I say. "She wanted it. She come from there. Her mind was set on it."

"And Anse is set on it, too," Quick says.

"Ay," Uncle Billy says. "It's like a man that's let everything slide all his life to get set on something that will make the most trouble for everybody he knows."

"Well, it'll take the Lord to get her over that river now," Peabody says. "Anse cant do it."

"And I reckon He will," Quick says. "He's took care of Anse a long time, now."

"It's a fact," Littlejohn says.

"Too long to quit now," Armstid says.

"I reckon He's like everybody else around here," Uncle Billy says. "He's done it so long now He cant quit."

Cash comes out. He has put on a clean shirt; his hair, wet, is combed smooth down on his brow, smooth and black as if he had painted it onto his head. He squats stiffly among us, we watching him.

"You feeling this weather, aint you?" Armstid says.

Cash says nothing.

"A broke bone always feels it," Littlejohn says. "A fellow with a broke bone can tell it a-coming."

"Lucky Cash got off with just a broke leg," Armstid says. "He might have hurt himself bed-rid. How far'd you fall, Cash?"

"Twenty-eight foot, four and a half inches, about," Cash says. I move over beside him.

"A fellow can sho slip quick on wet planks," Quick says.

"It's too bad," I say. "But you couldn't a holp it."

"It's them durn women," he says. "I made it to balance with her. I made it to her measure and weight."

If it takes wet boards for folks to fall, it's fixing to be lots of falling before this spell is done.

"You couldn't have holp it," I say.

I dont mind the folks falling. It's the cotton and corn I mind.

Neither does Peabody mind the folks falling. How bout it, Doc?

It's a fact. Washed clean outen the ground it will be. Seems like something is always happening to it.

Course it does. That's why it's worth anything. If nothing didn't happen and everybody made a big crop, do you reckon it would be worth the raising?

Well, I be durn if I like to see my work washed outen the ground, work I sweat over.

It's a fact. A fellow wouldn't mind seeing it washed up if he could just turn on the rain himself.

Who is that man can do that? Where is the color of his eyes?

Ay. The Lord made it to grow. It's Hisn to wash up if He sees it fitten so.

"You couldn't have holp it," I say.

"It's them durn women," he says.

In the house the women begin to sing. We hear the first line commence, beginning to swell as they take hold, and we rise and move toward the door, taking off our hats and throwing our chews away. We do not go in. We stop at the steps, clumped, holding our hats between our lax hands in front or behind, standing with one foot advanced and our heads lowered, looking aside, down at our hats in our hands and at the earth or now and then at the sky and at one another's grave, composed face.

The song ends; the voices quaver away with a rich and dying fall. Whitfield begins. His voice is bigger than him. It's like they are not the same. It's like he is one, and his voice is one, swimming on two horses side by side across the ford and coming into the house, the mud-splashed one and the one that never even got wet, triumphant and sad. Somebody in the house begins to cry. It sounds like her eyes and her voice were turned back inside her, listening; we move, shifting to the other leg, meeting one another's eye and making like they hadn't touched.

Whitfield stops at last. The women sing again. In the thick air it's like their voices come out of the air, flowing together and on in the sad, comforting tunes. When they cease it's like they hadn't gone away. It's like they had just disappeared into the air and when we moved we would loose them again out of the air around us, sad and comforting. Then they finish and we put on our hats, our movements stiff, like we hadn't never wore hats before.

On the way home Cora is still singing. "I am bounding toward my God and my reward," she sings, sitting on the wagon, the shawl around her shoulders and the umbrella open over her, though it is not raining.

"She has hern," I say. "Wherever she went, she has her reward in being free of Anse Bundren." *She laid there three days in that box, waiting for Darl and Jewel to come clean back home and get a new wheel and go back to where the wagon was in the ditch. Take my team, Anse, I said.*

We'll wait for ourn, he said. She'll want it so. She was ever a particular woman.

On the third day they got back and they loaded her into the wagon and started and it already too late. You'll have to go all the way round by Samson's bridge. It'll take you a day to get there. Then you'll be forty miles from Jefferson. Take my team, Anse.

We'll wait for ourn. She'll want it so.

It was about a mile from the house we saw him, sitting on the edge of the slough. It hadn't had a fish in it never that I knowed. He looked around at us, his eyes round and calm, his face dirty, the pole across his knees. Cora was still singing.

"This aint no good day to fish," I said. "You come on home with us and me and you'll go down to the river first thing in the morning and catch some fish."

"It's one in here," he said. "Dewey Dell seen it."

"You come on with us. The river's the best place."

"It's in here," he said. "Dewey Dell seen it."

"I'm bounding toward my God and my reward," Cora sung.

Darl

"It's not your horse that's dead, Jewel," I say. He sits erect on the seat, leaning a little forward, wooden-backed. The brim of his hat has soaked free of the crown in two places, dropping across his wooden face so that, head lowered, he looks through it like through the visor of a helmet, looking long across the valley to where the barn leans against the bluff, shaping the invisible horse. "See them?" I say. High above the house, against the quick thick sky, they hang in narrowing circles. From here they are no more than specks, implacable, patient, portentous. "But it's not your horse that's dead."

"Goddamn you," he says. "Goddamn you."

I cannot love my mother because I have no mother. Jewel's mother is a horse.

Motionless, the tall buzzards hang in soaring circles, the clouds giving them an illusion of retrograde.

Motionless, wooden-backed, wooden-faced, he shapes the horse in a rigid stoop like a hawk, hook-winged. They are waiting for us, ready for the moving of it, waiting for him. He enters the stall and waits until it kicks at him so that he can slip past and mount onto the trough and pause, peering out across the intervening stall-tops toward the empty path, before he reaches into the loft.

"Goddamn him. Goddamn him."

Cash

"It wont balance. If you want it to tote and ride on a balance, we will have—"

"Pick up. Goddamn you, pick up."

"I'm telling you it wont tote and it wont ride on a balance unless—"

"Pick up! Pick up, goddamn your thick-nosed soul to hell, pick up!"

It wont balance. If they want it to tote and ride on a balance, they will have

Darl

He stoops among us above it, two of the eight hands. In his face the blood goes in waves. In between them his flesh is greenish looking, about that smooth, thick, pale green of cow's cud; his face suffocated, furious, his lip lifted upon his teeth. "Pick up!" he says. "Pick up, goddamn your thick-nosed soul!"

He heaves, lifting one whole side so suddenly that we all spring into the lift to catch and balance it before he hurls it completely over. For an instant it resists, as though volitional, as though within it her pole-thin body clings furiously, even though dead, to a sort of modesty, as she would have tried to conceal a soiled garment that she could not prevent her body soiling. Then it breaks free, rising suddenly as though the emaciation of her body had added buoyancy to the planks or as though, seeing that the garment was about to be torn from her, she rushes suddenly after it in a passionate reversal that flouts its own desire and need. Jewel's face goes completely green and I can hear teeth in his breath.

We carry it down the hall, our feet harsh and clumsy on the floor, moving with shuffling steps, and through the door.

"Steady it a minute, now," pa says, letting go. He turns back to shut and lock the door, but Jewel will not wait.

"Come on," he says in that suffocating voice. "Come on."

We lower it carefully down the steps. We move, balancing it as though it were something infinitely precious, our faces averted, breathing through our teeth to keep our nostrils closed. We go down the path, toward the slope.

"We better wait," Cash says. "I tell you it aint balanced now. We'll need another hand on the hill."

"Then turn loose," Jewel says. He will not stop. Cash begins to fall behind, hobbling to keep up, breathing harshly; then he is distanced and Jewel carries the entire front end alone, so that, tilting as the path begins to slant, it begins to rush away from one and slip down the air like a sled upon invisible snow, smoothly ~~evacuating at~~mosphere in which the sense of it is still shaped.

"Wait, Jewel," I say. But he will not wait. He is almost running now and Cash is left behind. It seems to me that the end which I now carry alone has no weight, as though it coasts like a rushing straw upon the furious tide of Jewel's despair. I am not even touching it when, turning, he lets it overshoot him, swinging, and stops it and sloughs it into the wagon bed in the same motion and looks back at me, his face suffused with fury and despair.

"Goddamn you. Goddamn you."

Vardaman

We are going to town. Dewey Dell says it wont be sold because it belongs to Santa Claus and he taken it back with him until next Christmas. Then it will be behind the glass again, shining with waiting.

Pa and Cash are coming down the hill, but Jewel is going to the barn. "Jewel," pa says. Jewel does not stop. "Where you going?" pa says. But Jewel does not stop. "You leave that horse here," pa says. Jewel stops and looks at pa. Jewel's eyes look like marbles. "You leave that horse here," pa says. "We'll all go in the wagon with ma, like she wanted."

But my mother is a fish. Vernon seen it. He was there.

"Jewel's mother is a horse," Darl said.

"Then mine can be a fish, cant it, Darl?" I said.

Jewel is my brother.

"Then mine will have to be a horse, too," I said.

"Why?" Darl said. "If pa is your pa, why does your ma have to be a horse just because Jewel's is?"

"Why does it?" I said. "Why does it, Darl?"

Darl is my brother.

"Then what is your ma, Darl?" I said.

"I haven't got ere one," Darl said. "Because if I had one, it is *was*. And if it is *was*, it cant be *is*. Can it?"

"No," I said.

"Then I am not," Darl said. "Am I?"

"No," I said.

I am. Darl is my brother.

"But you *are*, Darl," I said.

"I know it," Darl said. "That's why I am not *is*. *Are* is too many for one woman to foal."

Cash is carrying his tool box. Pa looks at him. "I'll stop at Tull's on the way back," Cash says. "Get on that barn roof."

"It aint respectful," pa says. "It's a deliberate flouting of her and of me."

"Do you want him to come all the way back here and carry them up to Tull's afoot?" Darl says. Pa looks at Darl, his mouth chewing. Pa shaves every day now because my mother is a fish.

"It aint right," pa says.

Dewey Dell has the package in her hand. She has the basket with our dinner too.

"What's that?" pa says.

"Mrs Tull's cakes," Dewey Dell says, getting into the wagon. "I'm taking them to town for her."

"It aint right," pa says. "It's a flouting of the dead."

It'll be there. It'll be there come Christmas, she says, shining on the track. She says he wont sell it to no town boys.

Darl

He goes on toward the barn, entering the lot, woodenbacked.

Dewey Dell carries the basket on one arm, in the other hand something wrapped square in a newspaper. Her face is calm and sullen, her eyes brooding and alert; within them I can see Peabody's back like two round peas in two thimbles: perhaps in Peabody's back two of those worms which work surreptitious and steady through you and out the other side and you waking suddenly from sleep or from waking, with on your face an expression sudden, intent, and concerned. She sets the basket into the wagon and climbs in, her leg coming long from beneath her tightening dress: that lever which moves the world; one of that caliper which measures the length and breadth of life. She sits on the seat beside Vardaman and sets the parcel on her lap.

Then he enters the barn. He has not looked back.

"It aint right," pa says. "It's little enough for him to do for her."

"Go on," Cash says. "Leave him stay if he wants. He'll be all right here. Maybe he'll go up to Tull's and stay."

"He'll catch us," I say. "He'll cut across and meet us at Tull's lane."

"He would have rid that horse, too," pa says, "if I hadn't a stopped him. A durn spotted critter wilder than a cattymount.[2] A deliberate flouting of her and of me."

The wagon moves; the mules' ears begin to bob. Behind us, above the house, motionless in tall and soaring circles, they diminish and disappear.

Anse

I told him not to bring that horse out of respect for his dead ma, because it wouldn't look right, him prancing along on a durn circus animal and her wanting us all to be in the wagon with her that sprung from her flesh and blood, but we hadn't no more than passed Tull's lane when Darl begun to laugh. Setting back there on the plank seat with Cash, with his dead ma laying in her coffin at his feet, laughing. How many times I told him it's doing such things as that that makes folks talk about him, I dont know. I says I got some regard for what folks says about my flesh and blood even if you haven't, even if I have raised such a durn passel of boys, and when you fixes it so folks can say such about you, it's a reflection on your ma, I says, not me: I am a man and I can stand it; it's on your womenfolks, your ma and sister that you should care for, and I turned and looked back at him and him setting there, laughing.

2. Mountain lion.

"I dont expect you to have no respect for me," I says. "But with your own ma not cold in her coffin yet."

"Yonder," Cash says, jerking his head toward the lane. The horse is still a right smart piece away, coming up at a good pace, but I dont have to be told who it is. I just looked back at Darl, setting there laughing.

"I done my best," I says. "I tried to do as she would wish it. The Lord will pardon me and excuse the conduct of them He sent me." And Darl setting on the plank seat right above her where she was laying, laughing.

Darl

He comes up the lane fast, yet we are three hundred yards beyond the mouth of it when he turns into the road, the mud flying beneath the flicking drive of the hooves. Then he slows a little, light and erect in the saddle, the horse mincing through the mud.

Tull is in his lot. He looks at us, lifts his hand. We go on, the wagon creaking, the mud whispering on the wheels. Vernon still stands there. He watches Jewel as he passes, the horse moving with a light, high-kneed driving gait, three hundred yards back. We go on, with a motion so soporific, so dreamlike as to be uninferant of progress, as though time and not space were decreasing between us and it.

It turns off at right angles, the wheel-marks of last Sunday healed away now: a smooth, red scoriation curving away into the pines; a white signboard with faded lettering: New Hope Church. 3 mi. It wheels up like a motionless hand lifted above the profound desolation of the ocean; beyond it the red road lies like a spoke of which Addie Bundren is the rim. It wheels past, empty, unscarred, the white signboard turns away its fading and tranquil assertion. Cash looks up the road quietly, his head turning as we pass it like an owl's head, his face composed. Pa looks straight ahead, humped. Dewey Dell looks at the road too, then she looks back at me, her eyes watchful and repudiant, not like that question which was in those of Cash, for a smoldering while. The signboard passes; the unscarred road wheels on. Then Dewey Dell turns her head. The wagon creaks on.

Cash spits over the wheel. "In a couple of days now it'll be smelling," he says.

"You might tell Jewel that," I say.

He is motionless now, sitting the horse at the junction, upright, watching us, no less still than the signboard that lifts its fading capitulation opposite him.

"It aint balanced right for no long ride," Cash says.

"Tell him that, too," I say. The wagon creaks on.

A mile further along he passes us, the horse, archnecked, reined back to a swift singlefoot. He sits lightly, poised, upright, wooden-faced in the saddle, the broken hat raked at a swaggering angle. He passes us swiftly, without looking at us, the horse driving, its hooves hissing in the mud. A gout of mud, backflung, plops onto the box. Cash leans forward and takes a tool from his box and removes it carefully. When the road crosses Whiteleaf, the willows leaning near enough, he breaks off a branch and scours at the stain with the wet leaves.

Anse

It's a hard country on man; it's hard. Eight miles of the sweat of his body washed up outen the Lord's earth, where the Lord Himself told him to put it.[3] Nowhere in this sinful world can a honest, hardworking man profit. It takes them that runs the stores in the towns, doing no sweating, living off of them that sweats. It ain't the hardworking man, the farmer. Sometimes I wonder why we keep at it. It's because there is a reward for us above, where they cant take their autos and such. Every man will be equal there and it will be taken from them that have and give to them that have not by the Lord.[4]

But it's a long wait, seems like. It's bad that a fellow must earn the reward of his right-doing by flouting hisself and his dead. We drove all the rest of the day and got to Samson's at dusk-dark and then that bridge was gone, too. They hadn't never see the river so high, and it not done raining yet. There was old men that hadn't never see nor hear of it being so in the memory of man. I am the chosen of the Lord, for who He loveth, so doeth He chastiseth.[5] But I be durn if He dont take some curious ways to show it, seems like.

But now I can get them teeth. That will be a comfort. It will.

Samson

It was just before sundown. We were sitting on the porch when the wagon came up the road with the five of them in it and the other one on the horse behind. One of them raised his hand, but they were going on past the store without stopping.

"Who's that?" MacCallum says: I cant think of his name: Rafe's twin; that one it was.

"It's Bundren, from down beyond New Hope," Quick says. "There's one of them Snopes horses Jewel's riding."

"I didn't know there was ere a one of them horses left," MacCallum says. "I thought you folks down there finally contrived to give them all away."

"Try and get that one," Quick says. The wagon went on.

"I bet old man Lon never gave it to him," I says.

"No," Quick says. "He bought it from pappy." The wagon went on. "They must not a heard about the bridge," he says.

"What're they doing up here, anyway?" MacCallum says.

"Taking a holiday since he got his wife buried, I reckon," Quick says. "Heading for town, I reckon, with Tull's bridge gone too. I wonder if they aint heard about the bridge."

"They'll have to fly, then," I says. "I dont reckon there's ere a bridge between here and Mouth of Ishatawa."

They had something in the wagon. But Quick had been to the funeral three days ago and we naturally never thought anything about it except that they were heading away from home mighty late and that they hadn't heard about

---

3. Cf. Genesis 3.19: "In the sweat of thy face shalt thou eat bread, till thou return unto the ground."
4. Cf. Matthew 13.12: "For whosoever hath, to him shall be given, and he shall have more abundance: but whosoever hath not, from him shall be taken away even that he hath."
5. Cf. Hebrews 12.6: "For whom the Lord loveth he chasteneth, and scourgeth every son whom he receiveth."

the bridge. "You better holler at them," MacCallum says. Durn it, the name is right on the tip of my tongue. So Quick hollered and they stopped and he went to the wagon and told them.

He come back with them. "They're going to Jefferson," he says. "The bridge at Tull's is gone, too." Like we didn't know it, and his face looked funny, around the nostrils, but they just sat there, Bundren and the girl and the chap on the seat, and Cash and the second one, the one folks talks about, on a plank across the tail-gate, and the other one on that spotted horse. But I reckon they was used to it by then, because when I said to Cash that they'd have to pass by New Hope again and what they'd better do, he just says,

"I reckon we can get there."

I aint much for meddling. Let every man run his own business to suit himself, I say. But after I talked to Rachel about them not having a regular man to fix her and it being July and all, I went back down to the barn and tried to talk to Bundren about it.

"I give her my promise," he says. "Her mind was set on it."

I notice how it takes a lazy man, a man that hates moving, to get set on moving once he does get started off, the same as he was set on staying still, like it aint the moving he hates so much as the starting and the stopping. And like he would be kind of proud of whatever come up to make the moving or the setting still look hard. He set there on the wagon, hunched up, blinking, listening to us tell about how quick the bridge went and how high the water was, and I be durn if he didn't act like he was proud of it, like he had made the river rise himself.

"You say it's higher than you ever see it before?" he says. "God's will be done," he says. "I reckon it wont go down much by morning, neither," he says.

"You better stay here tonight," I says, "and get a early start for New Hope tomorrow morning." I was just sorry for them bone-gaunted mules. I told Rachel, I says, "Well, would you have had me turn them away at dark, eight miles from home? What else could I do," I says. "It wont be but one night, and they'll keep it in the barn, and they'll sholy get started by daylight." And so I says, "You stay here tonight and early tomorrow you can go back to New Hope. I got tools enough, and the boys can go on right after supper and have it dug and ready if they want" and then I found that girl watching me. If her eyes had a been pistols, I wouldn't be talking now. I be dog[6] if they didn't blaze at me. And so when I went down to the barn I come on them, her talking so she never noticed when I come up.

"You promised her," she says. "She wouldn't go until you promised. She thought she could depend on you. If you dont do it, it will be a curse on you."

"Cant no man say I dont aim to keep my word," Bundren says. "My heart is open to ere a man."

"I dont care what your heart is," she says. She was whispering, kind of, talking fast. "You promised her. You've got to. You—" then she seen me and quit, standing there. If they'd been pistols, I wouldn't be talking now. So when I talked to him about it, he says,

"I give her my promise. Her mind is set on it."

"But seems to me she'd rather have her ma buried close by, so she could—"

"It's Addie I give the promise to," he says. "Her mind is set on it."

6. Doggone or darned.

So I told them to drive it into the barn, because it was threatening rain again, and that supper was about ready. Only they didn't want to come in.

"I thank you," Bundren says. "We wouldn't discommode you. We got a little something in the basket. We can make out."

"Well," I says, "since you are so particular about your womenfolks, I am too. And when folks stops with us at meal time and wont come to the table, my wife takes it as a insult."

So the girl went on to the kitchen to help Rachel. And then Jewel come to me.

"Sho," I says. "Help yourself outen the loft. Feed him when you bait the mules."

"I rather pay you for him," he says.

"What for?" I says. "I wouldn't begrudge no man a bait for his horse."

"I rather pay you," he says; I thought he said extra.

"Extra for what?" I says. "Wont he eat hay and corn?"

"Extra feed," he says. "I feed him a little extra and I dont want him beholden to no man."

"You cant buy no feed from me, boy," I says. "And if he can eat that loft clean, I'll help you load the barn onto the wagon in the morning."

"He aint never been beholden to no man," he says. "I rather pay you for it."

And if I had my rathers, you wouldn't be here a-tall, I wanted to say. But I just says, "Then it's high time he commenced. You cant buy no feed from me."

When Rachel put supper on, her and the girl went and fixed some beds. But wouldn't any of them come in. "She's been dead long enough to get over that sort of foolishness," I says. Because I got just as much respect for the dead as ere a man, but you've got to respect the dead themselves, and a woman that's been dead in a box four days, the best way to respect her is to get her into the ground as quick as you can. But they wouldn't do it.

"It wouldn't be right," Bundren says. "Course, if the boys wants to go to bed, I reckon I can set up with her. I dont begrudge her it."

So when I went back down there they were squatting on the ground around the wagon, all of them. "Let that chap come to the house and get some sleep, anyway," I says. "And you better come too," I says to the girl. I wasn't aiming to interfere with them. And I sholy hadn't done nothing to her that I knowed.

"He's done already asleep," Bundren says. They had done put him to bed in the trough in a empty stall.

"Well, you come on, then," I says to her. But still she never said nothing. They just squatted there. You couldn't hardly see them. "How about you boys?" I says. "You got a full day tomorrow." After a while Cash says,

"I thank you. We can make out."

"We wouldn't be beholden," Bundren says. "I thank you kindly."

So I left them squatting there. I reckon after four days they was used to it. But Rachel wasn't.

"It's a outrage," she says. "A outrage."

"What could he a done?" I says. "He give her his promised word."

"Who's talking about him?" she says. "Who cares about him?" she says, crying. "I just wish that you and him and all the men in the world that torture us alive and flout us dead, dragging us up and down the country—"

"Now, now," I says. "You're upset."

"Dont you touch me!" she says. "Dont you touch me!"

A man cant tell nothing about them. I lived with the same one fifteen years and I be durn if I can. And I imagined a lot of things coming up between us, but I be durn if I ever thought it would be a body four days dead and that a woman. But they make life hard on them, not taking it as it comes up, like a man does.

So I laid there, hearing it commence to rain, thinking about them down there, squatting around the wagon and the rain on the roof, and thinking about Rachel crying there until after a while it was like I could still hear her crying even after she was asleep, and smelling it even when I knowed I couldn't. I couldn't decide even then whether I could or not, or if it wasn't just knowing it was what it was.

So next morning I never went down there. I heard them hitching up and then when I knowed they must be about ready to take out, I went out the front and went down the road toward the bridge until I heard the wagon come out of the lot and go back toward New Hope. And then when I come back to the house, Rachel jumped on me because I wasn't there to make them come in to breakfast. You cant tell about them. Just about when you decide they mean one thing, I be durn if you not only haven't got to change your mind, like as not you got to take a rawhiding for thinking they meant it.

But it was still like I could smell it. And so I decided then that it wasn't smelling it, but it was just knowing it was there, like you will get fooled now and then. But when I went to the barn I knew different. When I walked into the hallway I saw something. It kind of hunkered up when I come in and I thought at first it was one of them got left, then I saw what it was. It was a buzzard. It looked around and saw me and went on down the hall, spraddle-legged, with its wings kind of hunkered out, watching me first over one shoulder and then over the other, like a old baldheaded man. When it got outdoors it begun to fly. It had to fly a long time before it ever got up into the air, with it thick and heavy and full of rain like it was.

If they was bent on going to Jefferson, I reckon they could have gone around up by Mount Vernon, like MacCallum did. He'll get home about day after tomorrow, horseback. Then they'd be just eighteen miles from town. But maybe this bridge being gone too has learned him the Lord's sense and judgment.

That MacCallum. He's been trading with me off and on for twelve years. I have known him from a boy up; know his name as well as I do my own. But be durn if I can say it.

Dewey Dell

The signboard comes in sight. It is looking out at the road now, because it can wait. New Hope. 3 mi. it will say. New Hope. 3 mi. New Hope. 3 mi. And then the road will begin, curving away into the trees, empty with waiting, saying New Hope three miles.

I heard that my mother is dead. I wish I had time to let her die. I wish I had time to wish I had. It is because in the wild and outraged earth too soon too soon too soon. It's not that I wouldn't and will not it's that it is too soon too soon too soon.

Now it begins to say it. New Hope three miles. New Hope three miles. *That's what they mean by the womb of time: the agony and the despair of spreading bones, the hard girdle in which lie the outraged entrails of events*

Cash's head turns slowly as we approach, his pale empty sad composed and questioning face following the red and empty curve; beside the back wheel Jewel sits the horse, gazing straight ahead.

The land runs out of Darl's eyes; they swim to pinpoints. They begin at my feet and rise along my body to my face, and then my dress is gone: I sit naked on the seat above the unhurrying mules, above the travail. *Suppose I tell him to turn. He will do what I say. Dont you know he will do what I say?* Once I waked with a black void rushing under me. I could not see. I saw Vardaman rise and go to the window and strike the knife into the fish, the blood gushing, hissing like steam but I could not see. *He'll do as I say. He always does. I can persuade him to anything. You know I can. Suppose I say Turn here.* That was when I died that time. *Suppose I do. We'll go to New Hope. We wont have to go to town.* I rose and took the knife from the streaming fish still hissing and I killed Darl.

When I used to sleep with Vardaman I had a nightmare once I thought I was awake but I couldn't see and couldn't feel I couldn't feel the bed under me and I couldn't think what I was I couldn't think of my name I couldn't even think I am a girl I couldn't even think I nor even think I want to wake up nor remember what was opposite to awake so I could do that I knew that something was passing but I couldn't even think of time then all of a sudden I knew that something was it was wind blowing over me it was like the wind came and blew me back from where it was I was not blowing the room and Vardaman asleep and all of them back under me again and going on like a piece of cool silk dragging across my naked legs

It blows cool out of the pines, a sad steady sound. New Hope. Was 3 mi. Was 3 mi. I believe in God I believe in God.

"Why didn't we go to New Hope, pa?" Vardaman says. "Mr Samson said we was, but we done passed the road."

Darl says, "Look, Jewel." But he is not looking at me. He is looking at the sky. The buzzard is as still as if he were nailed to it.

We turn into Tull's lane. We pass the barn and go on, the wheels whispering in the mud, passing the green rows of cotton in the wild earth, and Vernon little across the field behind the plow. He lifts his hand as we pass and stands there looking after us for a long while.

"Look, Jewel," Darl says. Jewel sits on his horse like they were both made out of wood, looking straight ahead.

I believe in God, God. God, I believe in God.

Tull

After they passed I taken the mule out and looped up the trace chains and followed. They was setting in the wagon at the end of the levee when I caught up with them. Anse was setting there, looking at the bridge where it was swagged down into the river with just the two ends in sight. He was looking at it like he had believed all the time that folks had been lying to him about it being gone, but like he was hoping all the time it really was. Kind of pleased astonishment he looked, setting on the wagon in his Sunday pants, mumbling his mouth. Looking like a uncurried horse dressed up: I dont know.

The boy was watching the bridge where it was mid-sunk and logs and such drifted up over it and it swagging and shivering like the whole thing would go any minute, big-eyed he was watching it, like he was to a circus. And the gal too. When I come up she looked around at me, her eyes kind of blaring up and going hard like I had made to touch her. Then she looked at Anse again and then back at the water again.

It was nigh up to the levee on both sides, the earth hid except for the tongue of it we was on going out to the bridge and then down into the water, and except for knowing how the road and the bridge used to look, a fellow couldn't tell where was the river and where the land. It was just a tangle of yellow and the levee not less wider than a knife-back kind of, with us setting in the wagon and on the horse and the mule.

Darl was looking at me, and then Cash turned and looked at me with that look in his eyes like when he was figuring on whether the planks would fit her that night, like he was measuring them inside of him and not asking you to say what you thought and not even letting on he was listening if you did say it, but listening all right. Jewel hadn't moved. He sat there on the horse, leaning a little forward, with that same look on his face when him and Darl passed the house yesterday, coming back to get her.

"If it was just up, we could drive across," Anse says. "We could drive right on across it."

Sometimes a log would get shoved over the jam and float on, rolling and turning, and we could watch it go on to where the ford used to be. It would slow up and whirl crossways and hang out of water for a minute, and you could tell by that that the ford used to be there.

"But that dont show nothing," I say. "It could be a bar of quicksand built up there." We watch the log. Then the gal is looking at me again.

"Mr Whitfield crossed it," she says.

"He was a-horseback," I say. "And three days ago. It's a riz five foot since."

"If the bridge was just up," Anse says.

The log bobs up and goes on again. There is a lot of trash and foam, and you can hear the water.

"But it's down," Anse says.

Cash says, "A careful fellow could walk across yonder on the planks and logs."

"But you couldn't tote nothing," I say. "Likely time you set foot on that mess, it'll all go, too. What you think, Darl?"

He is looking at me. He dont say nothing; just looks at me with them queer eyes of hisn that makes folks talk. I always say it aint never been what he done so much or said or anything so much as how he looks at you. It's like he had got into the inside of you, someway. Like somehow you was looking at yourself and your doings outen his eyes. Then I can feel that gal watching me like I had made to touch her. She says something to Anse. ". . . Mr Whitfield. . . ." she says.

"I give her my promised word in the presence of the Lord," Anse says. "I reckon it aint no need to worry."

But still he does not start the mules. We set there above the water. Another log bobs up over the jam and goes on; we watch it check up and swing slow for a minute where the ford used to be. Then it goes on.

"It might start falling tonight," I say. "You could lay over one more day."

Then Jewel turns sideways on the horse. He has not moved until then, and he turns and looks at me. His face is kind of green, then it would go red and then green again. "Get to hell on back to your damn plowing," he says. "Who the hell asked you to follow us here?"

"I never meant no harm," I say.

"Shut up, Jewel," Cash says. Jewel looks back at the water, his face gritted, going red and green and then red. "Well," Cash says after a while, "what you want to do?"

Anse dont say nothing. He sets humped up, mumbling his mouth. "If it was just up, we could drive across it," he says.

"Come on," Jewel says, moving the horse.

"Wait," Cash says. He looks at the bridge. We look at him, except Anse and the gal. They are looking at the water. "Dewey Dell and Vardaman and pa better walk across on the bridge," Cash says.

"Vernon can help them," Jewel says. "And we can hitch his mule ahead of ourn."

"You ain't going to take my mule into that water," I say.

Jewel looks at me. His eyes look like pieces of a broken plate. "I'll pay for your damn mule. I'll buy it from you right now."

"My mule aint going into that water," I say.

"Jewel's going to use his horse," Darl says. "Why wont you risk your mule, Vernon?"

"Shut up, Darl," Cash says. "You and Jewel both."

"My mule aint going into that water," I say.

Darl

He sits the horse, glaring at Vernon, his lean face suffused up to and beyond the pale rigidity of his eyes. The summer when he was fifteen, he took a spell of sleeping. One morning when I went to feed the mules the cows were still in the tie-up and then I heard pa go back to the house and call him. When we came on back to the house for breakfast he passed us, carrying the milk buckets, stumbling along like he was drunk, and he was milking when we put the mules in and went on to the field without him. We had been there an hour and still he never showed up. When Dewey Dell came with our lunch, pa sent her back to find Jewel. They found him in the tie-up, sitting on the stool, asleep.

After that, every morning pa would go in and wake him. He would go to sleep at the supper table and soon as supper was finished he would go to bed, and when I came in to bed he would be lying there like a dead man. Yet still pa would have to wake him in the morning. He would get up, but he wouldn't hardly have half sense: he would stand for pa's jawing and complaining without a word and take the milk buckets and go to the barn, and once I found him asleep at the cow, the bucket in place and half full and his hands up to the wrists in the milk and his head against the cow's flank.

After that Dewey Dell had to do the milking. He still got up when pa waked him, going about what we told him to do in that dazed way. It was like he was trying hard to do them; that he was as puzzled as anyone else.

"Are you sick?" ma said. "Dont you feel all right?"

"Yes," Jewel said. "I feel all right."

"He's just lazy, trying me," pa said, and Jewel standing there, asleep on his feet like as not. "Ain't you?" he said, waking Jewel up again to answer.

"No," Jewel said.

"You take off and stay in the house today," ma said.

"With that whole bottom piece to be busted out?"[7] pa said. "If you aint sick, what's the matter with you?"

"Nothing," Jewel said. "I'm all right."

"All right?" pa said. "You're asleep on your feet this minute."

"No," Jewel said. "I'm all right."

"I want him to stay at home today," ma said.

"I'll need him," pa said. "It's tight enough, with all of us to do it."

"You'll just have to do the best you can with Cash and Darl," ma said. "I want him to stay in today."

But he wouldn't do it. "I'm all right," he said, going on. But he wasn't all right. Anybody could see it. He was losing flesh, and I have seen him go to sleep chopping; watched the hoe going slower and slower up and down, with less and less of an arc, until it stopped and he leaning on it motionless in the hot shimmer of the sun.

Ma wanted to get the doctor, but pa didn't want to spend the money without it was needful, and Jewel did seem all right except for his thinness and his way of dropping off to sleep at any moment. He ate hearty enough, except for his way of going to sleep in his plate, with a piece of bread halfway to his mouth and his jaws still chewing. But he swore he was all right.

It was ma that got Dewey Dell to do his milking, paid her somehow, and the other jobs around the house that Jewel had been doing before supper she found some way for Dewey Dell and Vardaman to do them. And doing them herself when pa wasn't there. She would fix him special things to eat and hide them for him. And that may have been when I first found it out, that Addie Bundren should be hiding anything she did, who had tried to teach us that deceit was such that, in a world where it was, nothing else could be very bad or very important, not even poverty. And at times when I went in to go to bed she would be sitting in the dark by Jewel where he was asleep. And I knew that she was hating herself for that deceit and hating Jewel because she had to love him so that she had to act the deceit.

One night she was taken sick and when I went to the barn to put the team in and drive to Tull's, I couldn't find the lantern. I remembered noticing it on the nail the night before, but it wasn't there now at midnight. So I hitched in the dark and went on and came back with Mrs Tull just after daylight. And there the lantern was, hanging on the nail where I remembered it and couldn't find it before. And then one morning while Dewey Dell was milking just before the sunup, Jewel came into the barn from the back, through the hole in the back wall, with the lantern in his hand.

I told Cash, and Cash and I looked at one another.

"Rutting," Cash said.

"Yes," I said. "But why the lantern? And every night, too. No wonder he's losing flesh. Are you going to say anything to him?"

"Wont do any good," Cash said.

"What he's doing now wont do any good, either."

"I know. But he'll have to learn that himself. Give him time to realise that it'll save, that there'll be just as much more tomorrow, and he'll be all right. I wouldn't tell anybody, I reckon."

"No," I said. "I told Dewey Dell not to. Not ma, anyway."

7. Plowed.

"No. Not ma."

After that I thought it was right comical: he acting so bewildered and willing and dead for sleep and gaunt as a bean-pole, and thinking he was so smart with it. And I wondered who the girl was. I thought of all I knew that it might be, but I couldn't say for sure.

" 'Taint any girl," Cash said. "It's a married woman somewhere. Aint any young girl got that much daring and staying power. That's what I dont like about it."

"Why?" I said. "She'll be safer for him than a girl would. More judgment."

He looked at me, his eyes fumbling, the words fumbling at what he was trying to say. "It ain't always the safe things in this world that a fellow . . ."

"You mean, the safe things are not always the best things?"

"Ay; best," he said, fumbling again. "It aint the best things, the things that are good for him. . . . A young boy. A fellow kind of hates to see . . . wallowing in somebody else's mire . . ." That's what he was trying to say. When something is new and hard and bright, there ought to be something a little better for it than just being safe, since the safe things are just the things that folks have been doing so long they have worn the edges off and there's nothing to the doing of them that leaves a man to say, That was not done before and it cannot be done again.

So we didn't tell, not even when after a while he'd appear suddenly in the field beside us and go to work, without having had time to get home and make out he had been in bed all night. He would tell ma that he hadn't been hungry at breakfast or that he had eaten a piece of bread while he was hitching up the team. But Cash and I knew that he hadn't been home at all on those nights and he had come up out of the woods when we got to the field. But we didn't tell. Summer was almost over then; we knew that when the nights began to get cool, she would be done if he wasn't.

But when fall came and the nights began to get longer, the only difference was that he would always be in bed for pa to wake him, getting him up at last in that first state of semi-idiocy like when it first started, worse than when he had stayed out all night.

"She's sure a stayer," I told Cash. "I used to admire her, but I downright respect her now."

"It aint a woman," he said.

"You know," I said. But he was watching me. "What is it, then?"

"That's what I aim to find out," he said.

"You can trail him through the woods all night if you want to," I said. "I'm not."

"I aint trailing him," he said.

"What do you call it, then?"

"I aint trailing him," he said. "I dont mean it that way."

And so a few nights later I heard Jewel get up and climb out the window, and then I heard Cash get up and follow him. The next morning when I went to the barn, Cash was already there, the mules fed, and he was helping Dewey Dell milk. And when I saw him I knew that he knew what it was. Now and then I would catch him watching Jewel with a queer look, like having found out where Jewel went and what he was doing had given him something to really think about at last. But it was not a worried look; it was the kind of look I would see on him when I would find him doing some of Jewel's work around the house, work that pa still thought Jewel was doing and that ma thought Dewey Dell was doing. So I said nothing to him, believing that when he got done digesting it in his mind, he would tell me. But he never did.

One morning—it was November then, five months since it started—Jewel was not in bed and he didn't join us in the field. That was the first time ma learned anything about what had been going on. She sent Vardaman down to find where Jewel was, and after a while she came down too. It was as though, so long as the deceit ran along quiet and monotonous, all of us let ourselves be deceived, abetting it unawares or maybe through cowardice, since all people are cowards and naturally prefer any kind of treachery because it has a bland outside. But now it was like we had all—and by a kind of telepathic agreement of admitted fear—flung the whole thing back like covers on the bed and we all sitting bolt upright in our nakedness, staring at one another and saying "Now is the truth. He hasn't come home. Something has happened to him. We let something happen to him."

Then we saw him. He came up along the ditch and then turned straight across the field, riding the horse. Its mane and tail were going, as though in motion they were carrying out the splotchy pattern of its coat: he looked like he was riding on a big pinwheel, barebacked, with a rope bridle, and no hat on his head. It was a descendant of those Texas ponies Flem Snopes brought here twenty-five years ago and auctioned off for two dollars a head and nobody but old Lon Quick ever caught his and still owned some of the blood because he could never give it away.

He galloped up and stopped, his heels in the horse's ribs and it dancing and swirling like the shape of its mane and tail and the splotches of its coat had nothing whatever to do with the flesh-and-bone horse inside them, and he sat there, looking at us.

"Where did you get that horse?" pa said.

"Bought it," Jewel said. "From Mr. Quick."

"Bought it?" pa said. "With what? Did you buy that thing on my word?"

"It was my money," Jewel said. "I earned it. You wont need to worry about it."

"Jewel," ma said; "Jewel."

"It's all right," Cash said. "He earned the money. He cleaned up that forty acres of new ground Quick laid out last spring. He did it single handed, working at night by lantern. I saw him. So I dont reckon that horse cost anybody anything except Jewel. I dont reckon we need worry."

"Jewel," ma said. "Jewel . . ." Then she said: "You come right to the house and go to bed."

"Not yet," Jewel said. "I aint got time. I got to get me a saddle and bridle. Mr. Quick says he . . ."

"Jewel," ma said, looking at him. "I'll give—I'll give . . . give . . ." Then she began to cry. She cried hard, not hiding her face, standing there in her faded wrapper, looking at him and him on the horse, looking down at her, his face growing cold and a little sick looking, until he looked away quick and Cash came and touched her.

"You go on to the house," Cash said. "This here ground is too wet for you. You go on, now." She put her hands to her face then and after a while she went on, stumbling a little on the plow-marks. But pretty soon she straightened up and went on. She didn't look back. When she reached the ditch she stopped and called Vardaman. He was looking at the horse, kind of dancing up and down by it.

"Let me ride, Jewel," he said. "Let me ride, Jewel."

Jewel looked at him, then he looked away again, holding the horse reined back. Pa watched him, mumbling his lip.

"So you bought a horse," he said. "You went behind my back and bought a horse. You never consulted me; you know how tight it is for us to make by, yet you bought a horse for me to feed. Taken the work from your flesh and blood and bought a horse with it."

Jewel looked at pa, his eyes paler than ever. "He wont never eat a mouthful of yours," he said. "Not a mouthful. I'll kill him first. Dont you never think it. Dont you never."

"Let me ride, Jewel," Vardaman said. "Let me ride, Jewel." He sounded like a cricket in the grass, a little one. "Let me ride, Jewel."

That night I found ma sitting beside the bed where he was sleeping, in the dark. She cried hard, maybe because she had to cry so quiet; maybe because she felt the same way about tears she did about deceit, hating herself for doing it, hating him because she had to. And then I knew that I knew. I knew that as plain on that day as I knew about Dewey Dell on that day.

Tull

So they finally got Anse to say what he wanted to do, and him and the gal and the boy got out of the wagon. But even when we were on the bridge Anse kept on looking back, like he thought maybe, once he was outen the wagon, the whole thing would kind of blow up and he would find himself back yonder in the field again and her laying up there in the house, waiting to die and it to do all over again.

"You ought to let them taken your mule," he says, and the bridge shaking and swaying under us, going down into the moiling water like it went clean through to the other side of the earth, and the other end coming up outen the water like it wasn't the same bridge a-tall and that them that would walk up outen the water on that side must come from the bottom of the earth. But it was still whole; you could tell that by the way when this end swagged, it didn't look like the other end swagged at all: just like the other trees and the bank yonder were swinging back and forth slow like on a big clock. And them logs scraping and bumping at the sunk part and tilting end-up and shooting clean outen the water and tumbling on toward the ford and the waiting, slick, whirling, and foamy.

"What good would that a done?" I says. "If your team cant find the ford and haul it across, what good would three mules or even ten mules do?"

"I aint asking it of you," he says. "I can always do for me and mine. I aint asking you to risk your mule. It aint your dead; I am not blaming you."

"They ought to went back and laid over until tomorrow," I says. The water was cold. It was thick, like slush ice. Only it kind of lived. One part of you knowed it was just water, the same thing that had been running under this same bridge for a long time, yet when them logs would come spewing up outen it, you were not surprised, like they was a part of water, of the waiting and the threat.

It was like when we was across, up out of the water again and the hard earth under us, that I was surprised. It was like we hadn't expected the bridge to end on the other bank, on something tame like the hard earth again that we had tromped on before this time and knowed well. Like it couldn't be me here, because I'd have had better sense than to done what I just done. And when I looked back and saw the other bank and saw my mule standing there where I used to be and knew that I'd have to get back there someway, I knew it couldn't be, because I just couldn't think of anything that could make me cross that bridge ever even once. Yet here I was, and the fellow that could make himself cross it twice, couldn't be me, not even if Cora told him to.

It was that boy. I said "Here; you better take a holt of my hand" and he waited and held to me. I be durn if it wasn't like he come back and got me; like he was saying They wont nothing hurt you. Like he was saying about a fine place he knowed where Christmas come twice with Thanksgiving and lasts on through the winter and the spring and the summer, and if I just stayed with him I'd be all right too.

When I looked back at my mule it was like he was one of these here spyglasses and I could look at him standing there and see all the broad land and my house sweated outen it like it was the more the sweat, the broader the land; the more the sweat, the tighter the house because it would take a tight house for Cora, to hold Cora like a jar of milk in the spring: you've got to have a tight jar or you'll need a powerful spring, so if you have a big spring, why then you have the incentive to have tight, wellmade jars, because it is your milk, sour or not, because you would rather have milk that will sour than to have milk that wont, because you are a man.

And him holding to my hand, his hand that hot and confident, so that I was like to say: Look-a-here. Cant you see that mule yonder? He never had no business over here, so he never come, not being nothing but a mule. Because a fellow can see ever now and then that children have more sense than him. But he dont like to admit it to them until they have beards. After they have a beard, they are too busy because they dont know if they'll ever quite make it back to where they were in sense before they was haired, so you dont mind admitting then to folks that are worrying about the same thing that aint worth the worry that you are yourself.

Then we was over and we stood there, looking at Cash turning the wagon around. We watched them drive back down the road to where the trail turned off into the bottom. After a while the wagon was out of sight.

"We better get on down to the ford and git ready to help," I said.

"I give her my word," Anse says. "It is sacred on me. I know you begrudge it, but she will bless you in heaven."

"Well, they got to finish circumventing the land before they can dare the water," I said. "Come on."

"It's the turning back," he said. "It ain't no luck in turning back."

He was standing there, humped, mournful, looking at the empty road beyond the swagging and swaying bridge. And that gal, too, with the lunch basket on one arm and that package under the other. Just going to town. Bent on it. They would risk the fire and the earth and the water and all just to eat a sack of bananas. "You ought to laid over a day," I said. "It would a fell some by morning. It mought not a rained tonight. And it cant get no higher."

"I give my promise," he says. "She is counting on it."

Darl

Before us the thick dark current runs. It talks up to us in a murmur become ceaseless and myriad, the yellow surface dimpled monstrously into fading swirls travelling along the surface for an instant, silent, impermanent and profoundly significant, as though just beneath the surface something huge and alive waked for a moment of lazy alertness out of and into light slumber again.

It clucks and murmurs among the spokes and about the mules' knees, yellow, skummed with flotsam and with thick soiled gouts of foam as though it had sweat, lathering, like a driven horse. Through the undergrowth it goes with a plaintive sound, a musing sound; in it the unwinded cane and saplings lean as before a little gale, swaying without reflections as though suspended on invisible wires from the branches overhead. Above the ceaseless surface they stand—trees, cane, vines—rootless, severed from the earth, spectral above a scene of immense yet circumscribed desolation filled with the voice of the waste and mournful water.

Cash and I sit in the wagon; Jewel sits the horse at the off rear wheel. The horse is trembling, its eye rolling wild and baby-blue in its long pink face, its breathing stertorous like groaning. He sits erect, poised, looking quietly and steadily and quickly this way and that, his face calm, a little pale, alert. Cash's face is also gravely composed; he and I look at one another with long probing looks, looks that plunge unimpeded through one another's eyes and into the ultimate secret place where for an instant Cash and Darl crouch flagrant and unabashed in all the old terror and the old foreboding, alert and secret and without shame. When we speak our voices are quiet, detached.

"I reckon we're still in the road, all right."

"Tull taken and cut them two big whiteoaks. I heard tell how at high water in the old days they used to line up the ford by them trees."

"I reckon he did that two years ago when he was logging down here. I reckon he never thought that anybody would ever use this ford again."

"I reckon not. Yes, it must have been then. He cut a sight of timber outen here then. Payed off that mortgage with it, I hear tell."

"Yes. Yes, I reckon so. I reckon Vernon could have done that."

"That's a fact. Most folks that logs in this here country, they need a durn good farm to support the sawmill. Or maybe a store. But I reckon Vernon could."

"I reckon so. He's a sight."

"Ay. Vernon is. Yes, it must still be here. He never would have got that timber out of here if he hadn't cleaned out that old road. I reckon we are still on it." He looks about quietly, at the position of the trees, leaning this way and that, looking back along the floorless road shaped vaguely high in air by the position of the lopped and felled trees, as if the road too had been soaked free of earth and floated upward, to leave in its spectral tracing a monument to a still more profound desolation than this above which we now sit, talking quietly of old security and old trivial things. Jewel looks at him, then at me, then his face turns in in that quiet, constant, questing about the scene, the horse trembling quietly and steadily between his knees.

"He could go on ahead slow and sort of feel it out," I say.

"Yes," Cash says, not looking at me. His face is in profile as he looks forward where Jewel has moved on ahead.

"He cant miss the river," I say. "He couldn't miss seeing it fifty yards ahead."

Cash does not look at me, his face in profile. "If I'd just suspicioned it, I could a come down last week and taken a sight on it."

"The bridge was up then," I say. He does not look at me. "Whitfield crossed it a-horseback."

Jewel looks at us again, his expression sober and alert and subdued. His voice is quiet. "What you want me to do?"

"I ought to come down last week and taken a sight on it," Cash says.

"We couldn't have known," I say. "There wasn't any way for us to know."

"I'll ride on ahead," Jewel says. "You can follow where I am." He lifts the horse. It shrinks, bowed; he leans to it, speaking to it, lifting it forward almost bodily, it setting its feet down with gingerly splashings, trembling, breathing harshly. He speaks to it, murmurs to it. "Go on," he says. "I aint going to let nothing hurt you. Go on, now."

"Jewel," Cash says. Jewel does not look back. He lifts the horse on.

"He can swim," I say. "If he'll just give the horse time, anyhow . . ." When he was born, he had a bad time of it. Ma would sit in the lamp-light, holding him on a pillow on her lap. We would wake and find her so. There would be no sound from them.

"That pillow was longer than him," Cash says. He is leaning a little forward. "I ought to come down last week and sighted. I ought to done it."

"That's right," I say. "Neither his feet nor his head would reach the end of it. You couldn't have known," I say.

"I ought to done it," he says. He lifts the reins. The mules move, into the traces; the wheels murmur alive in the water. He looks back and down at Addie. "It aint on a balance," he says.

At last the trees open; against the open river Jewel sits the horse, half turned, it belly deep now. Across the river we can see Vernon and pa and Vardaman and Dewey Dell. Vernon is waving at us, waving us further downstream.

"We are too high up," Cash says. Vernon is shouting too, but we cannot make out what he says for the noise of the water. It runs steady and deep now, unbroken, without sense of motion until a log comes along, turning slowly. "Watch it," Cash says. We watch it and see it falter and hang for a moment, the current building up behind it in a thick wave, submerging it for an instant before it shoots up and tumbles on.

"There it is," I say.

"Ay," Cash says. "It's there." We look at Vernon again. He is now flapping his arms up and down. We move on downstream, slowly and carefully, watching Vernon. He drops his hands. "This is the place," Cash says.

"Well, goddamn it, let's get across, then," Jewel says. He moves the horse on.

"You wait," Cash says. Jewel stops again.

"Well, by God—" he says. Cash looks at the water, then he looks back at Addie. "It aint on a balance," he says.

"Then go on back to the goddamn bridge and walk across," Jewel says. "You and Darl both. Let me on that wagon."

Cash does not pay him any attention. "It aint on a balance," he says. "Yes, sir. We got to watch it."

"Watch it, hell," Jewel says. "You get out of that wagon and let me have it. By God, if you're afraid to drive it over . . ." His eyes are pale as two bleached chips in his face. Cash is looking at him.

"We'll get it over," he says. "I tell you what you do. You ride on back and walk across the bridge and come down the other bank and meet us with the rope. Vernon'll take your horse home with him and keep it till we get back."

"You go to hell," Jewel says.

"You take the rope and come down the bank and be ready with it," Cash says. "Three cant do no more than two can—one to drive and one to steady it."

"Goddamn you," Jewel says.

"Let Jewel take the end of the rope and cross upstream of us and brace it," I say. "Will you do that, Jewel?"

Jewel watches me, hard. He looks quick at Cash, then back at me, his eyes alert and hard. "I dont give a damn. Just so we do something. Setting here, not lifting a goddamn hand . . ."

"Let's do that, Cash," I say.

"I reckon we'll have to," Cash says.

The river itself is not a hundred yards across, and pa and Vernon and Vardaman and Dewey Dell are the only things in sight not of that single monotony of desolation leaning with that terrific quality a little from right to left, as though we had reached the place where the motion of the wasted world accelerates just before the final precipice. Yet they appear dwarfed. It is as though the space between us were time: an irrevocable quality. It is as though time, no longer running straight before us in a diminishing line, now runs parallel between us like a looping string, the distance between the doubling accretion of the thread and not the interval between. The mules stand, their fore quarters already sloped a little, their rumps high. They too are breathing now with a deep groaning sound; looking back once, their gaze sweeps across us with in their eyes a wild, sad, profound and despairing quality as though they had already seen in the thick water the shape of the disaster which they could not speak and we could not see.

Cash turns back into the wagon. He lays his hands flat on Addie, rocking her a little. His face is calm, down-sloped, calculant, concerned. He lifts his box of tools and wedges it forward under the seat; together we shove Addie forward, wedging her between the tools and the wagon bed. Then he looks at me.

"No," I say. "I reckon I'll stay. Might take both of us."

From the tool box he takes his coiled rope and carries the end twice around the seat stanchion and passes the end to me without tying it. The other end he pays out to Jewel, who takes a turn about his saddle horn.

He must force the horse down into the current. It moves, highkneed, arch-necked, boring and chafing. Jewel sits lightly forward, his knees lifted a little;

again his swift alert calm gaze sweeps upon us and on. He lowers the horse into the stream, speaking to it in a soothing murmur. The horse slips, goes under to the saddle, surges to its feet again, the current building up against Jewel's thighs.

"Watch yourself," Cash says.

"I'm on it now," Jewel says. "You can come ahead now."

Cash takes the reins and lowers the team carefully and skillfully into the stream.

I felt the current take us and I knew we were on the ford by that reason, since it was only by means of that slipping contact that we could tell that we were in motion at all. What had once been a flat surface was now a succession of troughs and hillocks lifting and falling about us, shoving at us, teasing at us with light lazy touches in the vain instants of solidity underfoot. Cash looked back at me, and then I knew that we were gone. But I did not realise the reason for the rope until I saw the log. It surged up out of the water and stood for an instant upright upon that surging and heaving desolation like Christ. Get out and let the current take you down to the bend, Cash said, You can make it all right. No, I said, I'd get just as wet that way as this

The log appears suddenly between two hills, as if it had rocketed suddenly from the bottom of the river. Upon the end of it a long gout of foam hangs like the beard of an old man or a goat. When Cash speaks to me I know that he has been watching it all the time, watching it and watching Jewel ten feet ahead of us. "Let the rope go," he says. With his other hand he reaches down and reeves the two turns from the stanchion. "Ride on, Jewel," he says; "see if you can pull us ahead of the log."

Jewel shouts at the horse; again he appears to lift it bodily between his knees. He is just above the top of the ford and the horse has a purchase of some sort for it surges forward, shining wetly half out of water, crashing on in a succession of lunges. It moves unbelievably fast; by that token Jewel realises at last that the rope is free, for I can see him sawing back on the reins, his head turned, as the log rears in a long sluggish lunge between us, bearing down upon the team. They see it too; for a moment they also shine black out of water. Then the downstream one vanishes, dragging the other with him; the wagon sheers crosswise, poised on the crest of the ford as the log strikes it, tilting it up and on. Cash is half turned, the reins running taut from his hand and disappearing into the water, the other hand reached back upon Addie, holding her jammed over against the high side of the wagon. "Jump clear," he says quietly. "Stay away from the team and dont try to fight it. It'll swing you into the bend all right."

"You come too," I say. Vernon and Vardaman are running along the bank, pa and Dewey Dell stand watching us, Dewey Dell with the basket and the package in her arms. Jewel is trying to fight the horse back. The head of one mule appears, its eyes wide; it looks back at us for an instant, making a sound almost human. The head vanishes again.

"Back, Jewel," Cash shouts. "Back, Jewel." For another instant I see him leaning to the tilting wagon, his arm braced back against Addie and his tools; I see the bearded head of the rearing log strike up again, and beyond it Jewel holding the horse upreared, its head wrenched around, hammering its head with his fist. I jump from the wagon on the downstream side. Between two hills I see the mules once more. They roll up out of the water in succession, turning completely over, their legs stiffly extended as when they had lost contact with the earth.

Vardaman

Cash tried but she fell off and Darl jumped going under he went under and Cash hollering to catch her and I hollering running and hollering and Dewey Dell hollering at me Vardaman you vardaman you vardaman and Vernon passed me because he was seeing her come up and she jumped into the water again and Darl hadn't caught her yet

He came up to see and I hollering catch her Darl catch her and he didn't come back because she was too heavy he had to go on catching at her and I hollering catch her darl catch her darl because in the water she could go faster than a man and Darl had to grabble for her so I knew he could catch her because he is the best grabber even with the mules in the way again they dived up rolling their feet stiff rolling down again and their backs up now and Darl had to again because in the water she could go faster than a man or a woman and I passed Vernon and he wouldn't get in the water and help Darl he wouldn't grabble for her with Darl he knew but he wouldn't help.

The mules dived up again diving their legs stiff their stiff legs rolling slow and then Darl again and I hollering catch her darl catch her head her into the bank darl and Vernon wouldn't help and then Darl dodged past the mules where he could he had her under the water coming in to the bank coming in slow because in the water she fought to stay under the water but Darl is strong and he was coming in slow and so I knew he had her because he came slow and I ran down into the water to help and I couldn't stop hollering because Darl was strong and steady holding her under the water even if she did fight he would not let her go he was seeing me and he would hold her and it was all right now it was all right now it was all right

Then he comes up out of the water. He comes a long way up slow before his hands do but he's got to have her got to so I can bear it. Then his hands come up and all of him above the water. I cant stop. I have not got time to try. I will try to when I can but his hands came empty out of the water emptying the water emptying away

"Where is ma, Darl?" I said. "You never got her. You knew she is a fish but you let her get away. You never got her. Darl. Darl. Darl." I began to run along the bank, watching the mules dive up slow again and then down again.

Tull

When I told Cora how Darl jumped out of the wagon and left Cash sitting there trying to save it and the wagon turning over, and Jewel that was almost to the bank fighting that horse back where it had more sense than to go, she says "And you're one of the folks that says Darl is the queer one, the one that aint bright, and him the only one of them that had sense enough to get off that wagon. I notice Anse was too smart to been on it a-tall."

"He couldn't a done no good, if he'd been there," I said. "They was going about it right and they would have made it if it hadn't a been for that log."

"Log, fiddlesticks," Cora said. "It was the hand of God."

"Then how can you say it was foolish?" I said. "Nobody cant guard against the hand of God. It would be sacrilege to try to."

"Then why dare it?" Cora says. "Tell me that."

"Anse didn't," I said. "That's just what you faulted him for."

"His place was there," Cora said. "If he had been a man, he would a been there instead of making his sons do what he dursn't."

"I dont know what you want, then," I said. "One breath you say they was daring the hand of God to try it, and the next breath you jump on Anse because he wasn't with them." Then she begun to sing again, working at the washtub, with that singing look in her face like she had done give up folks and all their foolishness and had done went on ahead of them, marching up the sky, singing.

The wagon hung for a long time while the current built up under it, shoving it off the ford, and Cash leaning more and more, trying to keep the coffin braced so it wouldn't slip down and finish tilting the wagon over. Soon as the wagon got tilted good, to where the current could finish it, the log went on. It headed around the wagon and went on good as a swimming man could have done. It was like it had been sent there to do a job and done it and went on.

When the mules finally kicked loose, it looked for a minute like maybe Cash would get the wagon back. It looked like him and the wagon wasn't moving at all, and just Jewel fighting that horse back to the wagon. Then that boy passed me, running and hollering at Darl and the gal trying to catch him, and then I see the mules come rolling slow up out of the water, their legs spraddled stiff like they had balked upside down, and roll on into the water again.

Then the wagon tilted over and then it and Jewel and the horse was all mixed up together. Cash went outen sight, still holding the coffin braced, and then I couldn't tell anything for the horse lunging and splashing. I thought that Cash had give up then and was swimming for it and I was yelling at Jewel to come on back and then all of a sudden him and the horse went under too and I thought they was all going. I knew that the horse had got dragged off the ford too, and with that wild drowning horse and that wagon and that loose box, it was going to be pretty bad, and there I was, standing knee-deep in the water, yelling at Anse behind me: "See what you done now? See what you done now?"

The horse come up again. It was headed for the bank now, throwing its head up, and then I saw one of them holding to the saddle on the downstream side, so I started running along the bank, trying to catch sight of Cash because he couldn't swim, yelling at Jewel where Cash was like a durn fool, bad as that boy that was on down the bank still hollering at Darl.

So I went down into the water so I could still keep some kind of a grip in the mud, when I saw Jewel. He was middle deep, so I knew he was on the ford, anyway, leaning hard upstream, and then I see the rope, and then I see the water building up where he was holding the wagon snubbed just below the ford.

So it was Cash holding to the horse when it come splashing and scrambling up the bank, moaning and groaning like a natural man. When I come to it it was just kicking Cash loose from his holt on the saddle. His face turned up a second when he was sliding back into the water. It was gray, with his eyes closed and a long swipe of mud across his face. Then he let go and turned over in the water. He looked just like a old bundle of clothes kind of washing up and down against the bank. He looked like he was laying there in the water on his face, rocking up and down a little, looking at something on the bottom.

We could watch the rope cutting down into the water, and we could feel the weight of the wagon kind of blump and lunge lazy like, like it just as soon as not, and that rope cutting down into the water hard as a iron bar. We could hear the water hissing on it like it was red hot. Like it was a straight iron bar stuck into the bottom and us holding the end of it, and the wagon lazing up and down, kind of pushing and prodding at us like it had come around and got behind us, lazy like, like it just as soon as not when it made up its mind. There was a shoat come by, blowed up like a balloon: one of them spotted shoats of Lon Quick's. It bumped against the rope like it was a iron bar and bumped off and went on, and us watching that rope slanting down into the water. We watched it.

Darl

Cash lies on his back on the earth, his head raised on a rolled garment. His eyes are closed, his face is gray, his hair plastered in a smooth smear across his forehead as though done with a paint brush. His face appears sunken a little, sagging from the bony ridges of eye sockets, nose, gums, as though the wetting had slacked the firmness which had held the skin full; his teeth, set in pale gums, are parted a little as if he had been laughing quietly. He lies pole-thin in his wet clothes, a little pool of vomit at his head and a thread of it running from the corner of his mouth and down his cheek where he couldn't turn his head quick or far enough, until Dewey Dell stoops and wipes it away with the hem of her dress.

Jewel approaches. He has the plane. "Vernon just found the square," he says. He looks down at Cash, dripping too. "Aint he talked none yet?"

"He had his saw and hammer and chalk-line and rule," I say. "I know that."

Jewel lays the square down. Pa watches him. "They cant be far away," pa says. "It all went together. Was there ere a such misfortunate man."

Jewel does not look at Pa. "You better call Vardaman back here," he says. He looks at Cash. Then he turns and goes away. "Get him to talk soon as he can," he says, "so he can tell us what else there was."

We return to the river. The wagon is hauled clear, the wheels chocked (carefully: we all helped; it is as though upon the shabby, familiar, inert shape of the wagon there lingered somehow, latent yet still immediate, that violence which had slain the mules that drew it not an hour since) above the edge of the flood. In the wagon bed it lies profoundly, the long pale planks hushed a little with wetting yet still yellow, like gold seen through water, save for two long muddy smears. We pass it and go on to the bank.

One end of the rope is made fast to a tree. At the edge of the stream, knee-deep, Vardaman stands, bent forward a little, watching Vernon with rapt absorption. He has stopped yelling and he is wet to the armpits. Vernon is at the other end of the rope, shoulder-deep in the river, looking back at Vardaman. "Further back than that," he says. "You git back by the tree and hold the rope for me, so it cant slip."

Vardaman backs along the rope, to the tree, moving blindly, watching Vernon. When we come up he looks at us once, his eyes round and a little dazed. Then he looks at Vernon again in that posture of rapt alertness.

"I got the hammer too," Vernon says. "Looks like we ought to done already got that chalk-line. It ought to floated."

"Floated clean away," Jewel says. "We wont get it. We ought to find the saw, though."

"I reckon so," Vernon says. He looks at the water. "That chalk-line, too. What else did he have?"

"He aint talked yet," Jewel says, entering the water. He looks back at me. "You go back and get him roused up to talk," he says.

"Pa's there," I say. I follow Jewel into the water, along the rope. It feels alive in my hand, bellied faintly in a prolonged and resonant arc. Vernon is watching me.

"You better go," he says. "You better be there."

"Let's see what else we can get before it washes on down," I say.

We hold to the rope, the current curling and dimpling about our shoulders. But beneath that false blandness the true force of it leans against us lazily. I had not thought that water in July could be so cold. It is like hands molding and prodding at the very bones. Vernon is still looking back toward the bank.

"Reckon it'll hold us all?" he says. We too look back, following the rigid bar of the rope as it rises from the water to the tree and Vardaman crouched a little beside it, watching us. "Wish my mule wouldn't strike out for home," Vernon says.

"Come on," Jewel says. "Let's get outen here."

We submerge in turn, holding to the rope, being clutched by one another while the cold wall of the water sucks the slanting mud backward and upstream from beneath our feet and we are suspended so, groping along the cold bottom. Even the mud there is not still. It has a chill, scouring quality, as though the earth under us were in motion too. We touch and fumble at one another's extended arms, letting ourselves go cautiously against the rope; or, erect in turn, watch the water suck and boil where one of the other two gropes beneath the surface. Pa has come down to the shore, watching us.

Vernon comes up, streaming, his face sloped down into his pursed blowing mouth. His mouth is bluish, like a circle of weathered rubber. He has the rule.

"He'll be glad of that," I say. "It's right new. He bought it just last month out of the catalogue."

"If we just knowed for sho what else," Vernon says, looking over his shoulder and then turning to face where Jewel had disappeared. "Didn't he go down fore me?" Vernon says.

"I dont know," I say. "I think so. Yes. Yes, he did."

We watch the thick curling surface, streaming away from us in slow whorls.

"Give him a pull on the rope," Vernon says.

"He's on your end of it," I say.

"Aint nobody on my end of it," he says.

"Pull it in," I say. But he has already done that, holding the end above the water; and then we see Jewel. He is ten yards away; he comes up, blowing, and looks at us, tossing his long hair back with a jerk of his head, then he looks toward the bank; we can see him filling his lungs.

"Jewel," Vernon says, not loud, but his voice going full and clear along the water, peremptory yet tactful. "It'll be back here. Better come back."

Jewel dives again. We stand there, leaning back against the current, watching the water where he disappeared, holding the dead rope between us like two men holding the nozzle of a fire hose, waiting for the water. Suddenly Dewey Dell is behind us in the water. "You make him come back," she says. "Jewel!" she says. He comes up again, tossing his hair back from his eyes. He is swimming now, toward the bank, the current sweeping him downstream quartering. "You, Jewel!" Dewey Dell says. We stand holding the rope and see him gain the bank and climb out. As he rises from the water, he stoops and picks up something. He comes back along the bank. He has found the chalk-line. He comes opposite us and stands there, looking about as if he were seeking something. Pa goes on down the bank. He is going back to look at the mules again where their round bodies float and rub quietly together in the slack water within the bend.

"What did you do with the hammer, Vernon?" Jewel says.

"I give it to him," Vernon says, jerking his head at Vardaman. Vardaman is looking after pa. Then he looks at Jewel. "With the square." Vernon is watching Jewel. He moves toward the bank, passing Dewey Dell and me.

"You get on out of here," I say. She says nothing, looking at Jewel and Vernon.

"Where's the hammer?" Jewel says. Vardaman scuttles up the bank and fetches it.

"It's heavier than the saw," Vernon says. Jewel is tying the end of the chalk-line about the hammer shaft.

"Hammer's got the most wood in it," Jewel says. He and Vernon face one another, watching Jewels's hands.

"And flatter, too," Vernon says, "It'd float three to one, almost. Try the plane."

Jewel looks at Vernon. Vernon is tall, too; long and lean, eye to eye they stand in their close wet clothes. Lon Quick could look even at a cloudy sky and tell the time to ten minutes. Big Lon I mean, not little Lon.

"Why dont you get out of the water?" I say.

"It wont float like a saw," Jewel says.

"It'll float nigher to a saw than a hammer will," Vernon says.

"Bet you," Jewel says.

"I wont bet," Vernon says.

They stand there, watching Jewel's still hands.

"Hell," Jewel says. "Get the plane, then."

So they get the plane and tie it to the chalk-line and enter the water again. Pa comes back along the bank. He stops for a while and looks at us, hunched, mournful, like a failing steer or an old tall bird.

Vernon and Jewel return, leaning against the current. "Get out of the way," Jewel says to Dewey Dell. "Get out of the water."

She crowds against me a little so they can pass, Jewel holding the plane high as though it were perishable, the blue string trailing back over his shoulder. They pass us and stop; they fall to arguing quietly about just where the wagon went over.

"Darl ought to know," Vernon says. They look at me.

"I dont know," I says. "I wasn't there that long."

"Hell," Jewel says. They move on, gingerly, leaning against the current, reading the ford with their feet.

"Have you got a holt of the rope?" Vernon says. Jewel does not answer. He glances back at the shore, calculant, then at the water. He flings the plane outward, letting the string run through his fingers, his fingers turning blue where it runs over them. When the line stops, he hands it back to Vernon.

"Better let me go this time," Vernon says. Again Jewel does not answer; we watch him duck beneath the surface.

"Jewel," Dewey Dell whimpers.

"It aint so deep there," Vernon says. He does not look back. He is watching the water where Jewel went under.

When Jewel comes up he has the saw.

When we pass the wagon pa is standing beside it, scrubbing at the two mud smears with a handful of leaves. Against the jungle Jewel's horse looks like a patchwork quilt hung on a line.

Cash has not moved. We stand above him, holding the plane, the saw, the hammer, the square, the rule, the chalk-line, while Dewey Dell squats and lifts Cash's head. "Cash," she says; "Cash."

He opens his eyes, staring profoundly up at our inverted faces.

"If ever was such a misfortunate man," pa says.

"Look, Cash," we say, holding the tools up so he can see; "what else did you have?"

He tries to speak, rolling his head, shutting his eyes.

"Cash," we say; "Cash."

It is to vomit he is turning his head. Dewey Dell wipes his mouth on the wet hem of her dress; then he can speak.

"It's his saw-set," Jewel says. "The new one he bought when he bought the rule. He moves, turning away. Vernon looks up after him, still squatting. Then he rises and follows Jewel down to the water.

"If ever was such a misfortunate man," pa says. He looms tall above us as we squat; he looks like a figure carved clumsily from tough wood by a drunken caricaturist. "It's a trial," he says. "But I dont begrudge her it. No man can say I begrudge her it." Dewey Dell has laid Cash's head back on the folded coat, twisting his head a little to avoid the vomit. Beside him his tools lie. "A fellow might call it lucky it was the same leg he broke when he fell offen that church," pa says. "But I dont begrudge her it."

Jewel and Vernon are in the river again. From here they do not appear to violate the surface at all; it is as though it had severed them both at a single blow, the two torsos moving with infinitesimal and ludicrous care upon the surface. It looks peaceful, like machinery does after you have watched it and listened to it for a long time. As though the clotting which is you had dissolved into the myriad original motion, and seeing and hearing in themselves blind and deaf; fury in itself quiet with stagnation. Squatting, Dewey Dell's wet dress shapes for the dead eyes of three blind men those mammalian ludicrosities which are the horizons and the valleys of the earth.

Cash

It wasn't on a balance. I told them that if they wanted it to tote and ride on a balance, they would have to

Cora

One day we were talking. She had never been pure religious, not even after
that summer at the camp meeting when Brother Whitfield wrestled with her
spirit, singled her out and strove with the vanity in her mortal heart, and I said
to her many a time, "God gave you children to comfort your hard human lot
and for a token of His own suffering and love, for in love you conceived and
bore them." I said that because she took God's love and her duty to Him too
much as a matter of course, and such conduct is not pleasing to Him. I said,
"He gave us the gift to raise our voices in His undying praise" because I said
there is more rejoicing in heaven over one sinner than over a hundred that
never sinned.[8] And she said "My daily life is an acknowledgment and expia-
tion of my sin" and I said "Who are you, to say what is sin and what is not
sin? It is the Lord's part to judge; ours to praise His mercy and His holy name
in the hearing of our fellow mortals" because He alone can see into the heart,
and just because a woman's life is right in the sight of man, she cant know if
there is no sin in her heart without she opens her heart to the Lord and
receives His grace. I said, "Just because you have been a faithful wife is no
sign that there is no sin in your heart, and just because your life is hard is no
sign that the Lord's grace is absolving you." And she said, "I know my own sin.
I know that I deserve my punishment. I do not begrudge it." And I said, "It is
out of your vanity that you would judge sin and salvation in the Lord's place.
It is our mortal lot to suffer and to raise our voices in praise of Him who
judges the sin and offers the salvation through our trials and tribulations time
out of mind amen. Not even after Brother Whitfield, a godly man if ever one
breathed God's breath, prayed for you and strove as never a man could except
him," I said.

Because it is not us that can judge our sins or know what is sin in the Lord's
eyes. She has had a hard life, but so does every woman. But you'd think from
the way she talked that she knew more about sin and salvation than the Lord
God Himself, than them who have strove and labored with the sin in this
human world. When the only sin she ever committed was being partial to
Jewel that never loved her and was its own punishment, in preference to Darl
that was touched by God Himself and considered queer by us mortals and
that did love her. I said, "There is your sin. And your punishment too. Jewel
is your punishment. But where is your salvation? And life is short enough," I
said, "to win eternal grace in. And God is a jealous God. It is His to judge and
to mete; not yours."

"I know," she said. "I—" Then she stopped, and I said,

"Know what?"

"Nothing," she said. "He is my cross and he will be my salvation. He will
save me from the water and from the fire. Even though I have laid down my
life, he will save me."

"How do you know, without you open your heart to Him and lift your voice
in His praise?" I said. Then I realised that she did not mean God. I realised
that out of the vanity of her heart she had spoken sacrilege. And I went down

8. Cf. Luke 15.7: "I say unto you, that likewise joy shall be in heaven over one sinner that repenteth, more
than over ninety and nine just persons, which need no repentance."

on my knees right there. I begged her to kneel and open her heart and cast from it the devil of vanity and cast herself upon the mercy of the Lord. But she wouldn't. She just sat there, lost in her vanity and her pride, that had closed her heart to God and set that selfish mortal boy in His place. Kneeling there I prayed for her. I prayed for that poor blind woman as I had never prayed for me and mine.

Addie

In the afternoon when school was out and the last one had left with his little dirty snuffling nose, instead of going home I would go down the hill to the spring where I could be quiet and hate them. It would be quiet there then, with the water bubbling up and away and the sun slanting quiet in the trees and the quiet smelling of damp and rotting leaves and new earth; especially in the early spring, for it was worst then.

I could just remember how my father used to say that the reason for living was to get ready to stay dead a long time. And when I would have to look at them day after day, each with his and her secret and selfish thought, and blood strange to each other blood and strange to mine, and think that this seemed to be the only way I could get ready to stay dead, I would hate my father for having ever planted me. I would look forward to the times when they faulted, so I could whip them. When the switch fell I could feel it upon my flesh; when it welted and ridged it was my blood that ran, and I would think with each blow of the switch: Now you are aware of me! Now I am something in your secret and selfish life, who have marked your blood with my own for ever and ever.

And so I took Anse. I saw him pass the school house three or four times before I learned that he was driving four miles out of his way to do it. I noticed then how he was beginning to hump—a tall man and young—so that he looked already like a tall bird hunched in the cold weather, on the wagon seat. He would pass the school house, the wagon creaking slow, his head turning slow to watch the door of the school house as the wagon passed, until he went on around the curve and out of sight. One day I went to the door and stood there when he passed. When he saw me he looked quickly away and did not look back again.

In the early spring it was worst. Sometimes I thought that I could not bear it, lying in bed at night, with the wild geese going north and their honking coming faint and high and wild out of the wild darkness, and during the day it would seem as though I couldn't wait for the last one to go so I could go down to the spring. And so when I looked up that day and saw Anse standing there in his Sunday clothes, turning his hat round and round in his hands, I said:

"If you've got any womenfolks, why in the world dont they make you get your hair cut?"

"I aint got none," he said. Then he said suddenly, driving his eyes at me like two hounds in a strange yard: "That's what I come to see you about."

"And make you hold your shoulders up," I said. "You haven't got any? But you've got a house. They tell me you've got a house and a good farm. And you live there alone, doing for yourself, do you?" He just looked at me, turning the hat in his hands. "A new house," I said. "Are you going to get married?"

And he said again, holding his eyes to mine: "That's what I come to see you about."

Later he told me, "I aint got no people. So that wont be no worry to you. I dont reckon you can say the same."

"No. I have people. In Jefferson."

His face fell a little. "Well, I got a little property. I'm forehanded; I got a good honest name. I know how town folks are, but maybe when they talk to me . . ."

"They might listen," I said. "But they'll be hard to talk to." He was watching my face. "They're in the cemetery."

"But your living kin," he said. "They'll be different."

"Will they?" I said. "I dont know. I never had any other kind."

So I took Anse. And when I knew that I had Cash, I knew that living was terrible and that this was the answer to it. That was when I learned that words are no good; that words dont ever fit even what they are trying to say at. When he was born I knew that motherhood was invented by someone who had to have a word for it because the ones that had the children didn't care whether there was a word for it or not. I knew that fear was invented by someone that had never had the fear; pride, who never had the pride. I knew that it had been, not that they had dirty noses, but that we had had to use one another by words like spiders dangling by their mouths from a beam, swinging and twisting and never touching, and that only through the blows of the switch could my blood and their blood flow as one stream. I knew that it had been, not that my aloneness had to be violated over and over each day, but that it had never been violated until Cash came. Not even by Anse in the nights.

He had a word, too. Love, he called it. But I had been used to words for a long time. I knew that that word was like the others: just a shape to fill a lack; that when the right time came, you wouldn't need a word for that anymore than for pride or fear. Cash did not need to say it to me nor I to him, and I would say, Let Anse use it, if he wants to. So that it was Anse or love; love or Anse: it didn't matter.

I would think that even while I lay with him in the dark and Cash asleep in the cradle within the swing of my hand. I would think that if he were to wake and cry, I would suckle him, too. Anse or love: it didn't matter. My aloneness had been violated and then made whole again by the violation: time, Anse, love, and what you will, outside the circle.

Then I found that I had Darl. At first I would not believe it. Then I believed that I would kill Anse. It was as though he had tricked me, hidden within a word like within a paper screen and struck me in the back through it. But then I realised that I had been tricked by words older than Anse or love, and that the same word had tricked Anse too, and that my revenge would be that he would never know I was taking revenge. And when Darl was born I asked Anse to promise to take me back to Jefferson when I died, because I knew that father had been right, even when he couldn't have known he was right anymore than I could have known I was wrong.

"Nonsense," Anse said; "you and me aint nigh done chapping yet, with just two."

He did not know that he was dead, then. Sometimes I would lie by him in the dark, hearing the land that was now of my blood and flesh, and I would think: Anse. Why Anse. Why are you Anse. I would think about his name until after a while I could see the word as a shape, a vessel, and I would watch him liquify and flow into it like cold molasses flowing out of the darkness into the vessel, until the jar stood full and motionless: a significant shape profoundly without life like an empty door frame; and then I would find that I had forgotten the name of the jar. I would think: The shape of my body where I used to be a virgin is in the shape of a   and I couldn't think *Anse,* couldn't remember *Anse.* It was not that I could think of myself as no longer unvirgin, because I was three now. And when I would think *Cash* and *Darl* that way until their names would die and solidify into a shape and then fade away, I would say, All right. It doesn't matter. It doesn't matter what they call them.

And so when Cora Tull would tell me I was not a true mother, I would think how words go straight up in a thin line, quick and harmless, and how terribly doing goes along the earth, clinging to it, so that after a while the two lines are too far apart for the same person to straddle from one to the other; and that sin and love and fear are just sounds that people who never sinned nor loved nor feared have for what they never had and cannot have until they forget the words. Like Cora, who could never even cook.

She would tell me what I owed to my children and to Anse and to God. I gave Anse the children. I did not ask for them. I did not even ask him for what he could have given me: not-Anse. That was my duty to him, to not ask that, and that duty I fulfilled. I would be I; I would let him be the shape and echo of his word. That was more than he asked, because he could not have asked for that and been Anse, using himself so with a word.

And then he died. He did not know he was dead. I would lie by him in the dark, hearing the dark land talking of God's love and His beauty and His sin; hearing the dark voicelessness in which the words are the deeds, and the other words that are not deeds, that are just the gaps in peoples' lacks, coming down like the cries of the geese out of the wild darkness in the old terrible nights, fumbling at the deeds like orphans to whom are pointed out in a crowd two faces and told, That is your father, your mother.

I believed that I had found it. I believed that the reason was the duty to the alive, to the terrible blood, the red bitter flood boiling through the land. I would think of sin as I would think of the clothes we both wore in the world's face, of the circumspection necessary because he was he and I was I; the sin the more utter and terrible since he was the instrument ordained by God who created the sin, to sanctify that sin He had created. While I waited for him in the woods, waiting for him before he saw me, I would think of him as dressed in sin. I would think of him as thinking of me as dressed also in sin, he the more beautiful since the garment which he had exchanged for sin was sanctified. I would think of the sin as garments which we would remove in order to shape and coerce the terrible blood to the forlorn echo of the dead word high in the air. Then I would lay with Anse again—I did not lie to him: I just refused, just as I refused my breast to Cash and Darl after their time was up—hearing the dark land talking the voiceless speech.

I hid nothing. I tried to deceive no one. I would not have cared. I merely took the precautions that he thought necessary for his sake, not for my safety, but just as I wore clothes in the world's face. And I would think then when Cora talked to me, of how the high dead words in time seemed to lose even the significance of their dead sound.

Then it was over. Over in the sense that he was gone and I knew that, see him again though I would, I would never again see him coming swift and secret to me in the woods dressed in sin like a gallant garment already blowing aside with the speed of his secret coming.

But for me it was not over. I mean, over in the sense of beginning and ending, because to me there was no beginning nor ending to anything then. I even held Anse refraining still, not that I was holding him recessional, but as though nothing else had ever been. My children were of me alone, of the wild blood boiling along the earth, of me and of all that lived; of none and of all. Then I found that I had Jewel. When I waked to remember to discover it, he was two months gone.

My father said that the reason for living is getting ready to stay dead. I knew at last what he meant and that he could not have known what he meant himself, because a man cannot know anything about cleaning up the house afterward. And so I have cleaned my house. With Jewel—I lay by the lamp, holding up my own head, watching him cap and suture it before he breathed—the wild blood boiled away and the sound of it ceased. Then there was only the milk, warm and calm, and I lying calm in the slow silence, getting ready to clean my house.

I gave Anse Dewey Dell to negative Jewel. Then I gave him Vardaman to replace the child I had robbed him of. And now he has three children that are his and not mine. And then I could get ready to die.

One day I was talking to Cora. She prayed for me because she believed I was blind to sin, wanting me to kneel and pray too, because people to whom sin is just a matter of words, to them salvation is just words too.

Whitfield

When they told me she was dying, all that night I wrestled with Satan, and I emerged victorious. I woke to the enormity of my sin; I saw the true light at last, and I fell on my knees and confessed to God and asked His guidance and received it. "Rise," He said; "repair to that home in which you have put a living lie, among those people with whom you have outraged My Word; confess your sin aloud. It is for them, for that deceived husband, to forgive you: not I."

So I went. I heard that Tull's bridge was gone; I said "Thanks, O Lord, O Mighty Ruler of all;" for by those dangers and difficulties which I should have to surmount I saw that He had not abandoned me; that my reception again into His holy peace and love would be the sweeter for it. "Just let me not perish before I have begged the forgiveness of the man whom I betrayed," I prayed; "let me not be too late; let not the tale of mine and her transgression come from her lips instead of mine. She had sworn then that she would never tell it, but eternity is a fearsome thing to face: have I not wrestled thigh to thigh with Satan myself? let me not have also the sin of her broken vow upon my soul. Let not the waters of Thy Mighty Wrath encompass me until I have cleansed my soul in the presence of them whom I injured."

It was His hand that bore me safely above the flood, that fended from me the dangers of the waters. My horse was frightened, and my own heart failed me as the logs and the uprooted trees bore down upon my littleness. But not my soul: time after time I saw them averted at destruction's final instant, and I lifted my voice above the noise of the flood: "Praise to Thee, O Mighty Lord and King. By this token shall I cleanse my soul and gain again into the fold of Thy undying love."

I knew then that forgiveness was mine. The flood, the danger, behind, and as I rode on across the firm earth again and the scene of my Gethsemane drew closer and closer, I framed the words which I should use. I would enter the house; I would stop her before she had spoken; I would say to her husband: "Anse, I have sinned. Do with me as you will."

It was already as though it were done. My soul felt freer, quieter than it had in years; already I seemed to dwell in abiding peace again as I rode on. To either side I saw His hand; in my heart I could hear His voice: "Courage. I am with thee."

Then I reached Tull's house. His youngest girl came out and called to me as I was passing. She told me that she was already dead.

I have sinned, O Lord. Thou knowest the extent of my remorse and the will of my spirit. But He is merciful; He will accept the will for the deed, Who knew that when I framed the words of my confession it was to Anse I spoke them, even though he was not there. It was He in His infinite wisdom that restrained the tale from her dying lips as she lay surrounded by those who loved and trusted her; mine the travail by water which I sustained by the strength of His hand. Praise to Thee in Thy bounteous and omnipotent love; O praise.

I entered the house of bereavement, the lowly dwelling where another erring mortal lay while her soul faced the awful and irrevocable judgment, peace to her ashes.

"God's grace upon this house," I said.

Darl

On the horse he rode up to Armstid's and *came back on the horse*, leading Armstid's team. We hitched up and laid Cash on top of Addie. When we laid him down he vomited again, but he got his head over the wagon bed in time.

"He taken a lick in the stomach, too," Vernon said.

"The horse may have kicked him in the stomach too," I said. "Did he kick you in the stomach, Cash?"

He tried to say something. Dewey Dell wiped his mouth again.

"What's he say?" Vernon said.

"What is it, Cash?" Dewey Dell said. She leaned down. "His tools," she said. Vernon got them and put them into the wagon. Dewey Dell lifted Cash's head so he could see. We drove on, Dewey Dell and I sitting beside Cash to steady him *and he riding on ahead on the horse.* Vernon stood watching us for a while. Then he turned and went back toward the bridge. He walked gingerly, beginning to flap the wet sleeves of his shirt as though he had just got wet.

He was sitting the horse before the gate. Armstid was waiting at the gate. We stopped *and he got down* and we lifted Cash down and carried him into the house, where Mrs Armstid had the bed ready. We left her and Dewey Dell undressing him.

We followed pa out to the wagon. He went back and got into the wagon and drove on, we following on foot, into the lot. The wetting had helped, because Armstid said, "You're welcome to the house. You can put it there." *He followed, leading the horse, and stood beside the wagon, the reins in his hand.*

"I thank you," pa said. "We'll use in the shed yonder. I know it's a imposition on you."

"You're welcome to the house," Armstid said. *He had that wooden look on his face again; that bold, surly, high-colored rigid look like his face and eyes were two colors of wood, the wrong one pale and the wrong one dark. His shirt was beginning to dry, but it still clung close upon him when he moved.*

"She would appreciate it," pa said.

We took the team out and rolled the wagon back under the shed. One side of the shed was open.

"It wont rain under," Armstid said. "But if you'd rather . . ."

Back of the barn was some rusted sheets of tin roofing. We took two of them and propped them against the open side.

"You're welcome to the house," Armstid said.

"I thank you," pa said. "I'd take it right kind if you'd give them a litttle snack."

"Sho," Armstid said. "Lula'll have supper ready soon as she gets Cash comfortable." *He had gone back to the horse and he was taking the saddle off, his damp shirt lapping flat to him when he moved.*

Pa wouldn't come in the house.

"Come in and eat," Armstid said. "It's nigh ready."

"I wouldn't crave nothing," pa said. "I thank you."

"You come in and dry and eat," Armstid said. "It'll be all right here."

"It's for her," pa said. "It's for her sake I am taking the food. I got no team, no nothing. But she will be grateful to ere a one of you."

"Sho," Armstid said. "You folks come in and dry."

But after Armstid gave pa a drink, he felt better, and when we went in to see about Cash *he hadn't come in with us. When I looked back he was leading the horse into the barn* he was already talking about getting another team, and by supper time he had good as bought it. *He is down there in the barn, sliding fluidly past the gaudy lunging swirl, into the stall with it. He climbs onto the manger and drags the hay down and leaves the stall and seeks and finds the curry-comb. Then he returns and slips quickly past the single crashing thump and up against the horse, where it cannot overreach. He applies the curry-comb, holding himself within the horse's striking radius with the agility of an acrobat, cursing the horse in a whisper of obscene caress. Its head flashes back, tooth-cropped; its eyes roll in the dusk like marbles on a gaudy velvet cloth as he strikes it upon the face with the back of the curry-comb.*

Armstid

But time I give him another sup of whiskey and supper was about ready, he had done already bought a team from somebody, on a credit. Picking and choosing he were by then, saying how he didn't like this span and wouldn't put his money in nothing so-and-so owned, not even a hen coop.

"You might try Snopes," I said. "He's got three-four span. Maybe one of them would suit you."

Then he begun to mumble his mouth, looking at me like it was me that owned the only span of mules in the county and wouldn't sell them to him, when I knew that like as not it would be my team that would ever get them out of the lot at all. Only I dont know what they would do with them, if they had a team. Littlejohn had told me that the levee through Haley bottom had done gone for two miles and that the only way to get to Jefferson would be to go around by Mottson. But that was Anse's business.

"He's a close man to trade with," he says, mumbling his mouth. But when I give him another sup after supper, he cheered up some. He was aiming to go back to the barn and set up with her. Maybe he thought that if he just stayed down there ready to take out, Santa Claus would maybe bring him a span of mules. "But I reckon I can talk him around," he says. "A man'll always help a fellow in a tight, if he's got ere a drop of Christian blood in him."

"Of course you're welcome to the use of mine," I said, me knowing how much he believed that was the reason.

"I thank you," he said. "She'll want to go in ourn," and him knowing how much I believed that was the reason.

After supper Jewel rode over to the Bend to get Peabody. I heard he was to be there today at Varner's. Jewel come back about midnight. Peabody had gone down below Inverness somewhere, but Uncle Billy come back with him, with his satchel of horse-physic. Like he says, a man aint so different from a horse or a mule, come long come short, except a mule or a horse has got a little more sense. "What you been into now, boy?" he says, looking at Cash. "Get me a mattress and a chair and a glass of whisky," he says.

He made Cash drink the whiskey, then he run Anse out of the room. "Lucky it was the same leg he broke last summer," Anse says, mournful, mumbling and blinking. "That's something."

We folded the mattress across Cash's legs and set the chair on the mattress and me and Jewel set on the chair and the gal held the lamp and Uncle Billy taken a chew of tobacco and went to work. Cash fought pretty hard for a while, until he fainted. Then he laid still, with big balls of sweat standing on his face like they had started to roll down and then stopped to wait for him.

When he waked up, Uncle Billy had done packed up and left. He kept on trying to say something until the gal leaned down and wiped his mouth. "It's his tools," she said.

"I brought them in," Darl said. "I got them."

He tried to talk again; she leaned down. "He wants to see them," she said. So Darl brought them in where he could see them. They shoved them under the side of the bed, where he could reach his hand and touch them when he felt better. Next morning Anse taken that horse and rode over to the Bend to see Snopes. Him and Jewel stood in the lot talking a while, then Anse got on the horse and rode off. I reckon that was the first time Jewel ever let anybody ride that horse, and until Anse come back he hung around in that swole-up way, watching the road like he was half a mind to take out after Anse and get the horse back.

Along toward nine oclock it begun to get hot. That was when I see the first buzzard. Because of the wetting, I reckon. Anyway it wasn't until well into the day that I see them. Lucky the breeze was setting away from the house, so it wasn't until well into the morning. But soon as I see them it was like I could smell it in the field a mile away from just watching them, and them circling and circling for everybody in the county to see what was in my barn.

I was still a good half a mile from the house when I heard that boy yelling. I thought maybe he might have fell into the well or something, so I whipped up and come into the lot on the lope.

There must have been a dozen of them setting along the ridge-pole of the barn, and that boy was chasing another one around the lot like it was a turkey and it just lifting enough to dodge him and go flopping back to the roof of the shed again where he had found it setting on the coffin. It had got hot then, right, and the breeze had dropped or changed or something, so I went and found Jewel, but Lulu come out.

"You got to do something," she said. "It's a outrage."

"That's what I aim to do," I said.

"It's a outrage," she said. "He should be lawed for treating her so."

"He's getting her into the ground the best he can," I said. So I found Jewel and asked him if he didn't want to take one of the mules and go over to the Bend and see about Anse. He didn't say nothing. He just looked at me with his jaws going bone-white and them bone-white eyes of hisn, then he went and begun to call Darl.

"What you fixing to do?" I said.

He didn't answer. Darl come out. "Come on," Jewel said.

"What you aim to do?" Darl said.

"Going to move the wagon," Jewel said over his shoulder.

"Dont be a fool," I said. "I never meant nothing. You couldn't help it." And Darl hung back too, but nothing wouldn't suit Jewel.

"Shut your goddamn mouth," he says.

"It's got to be somewhere," Darl said. "We'll take out soon as pa gets back."

"You wont help me?" Jewel says, them white eyes of hisn kind of blaring and his face shaking like he had a aguer.[9]

"No," Darl said. "I wont. Wait till pa gets back."

So I stood in the door and watched him push and haul at that wagon. It was on a downhill, and once I thought he was fixing to beat out the back end of the shed. Then the dinner bell rung. I called him, but he didn't look around. "Come on to dinner," I said. "Tell that boy." But he didn't answer, so I went on to dinner. The gal went down to get that boy, but she come back without him. About half through dinner we heard him yelling again, running that buzzard out.

"It's a outrage," Lula said; "a outrage."

"He's doing the best he can," I said. "A fellow dont trade with Snopes in thirty minutes. They'll set in the shade all afternoon to dicker."

"Do?" she says. "Do? He's done too much, already."

And I reckon he had. Trouble is, his quitting was just about to start our doing. He couldn't buy no team from nobody, let alone Snopes, withouten he had something to mortgage he didn't know would mortgage yet. And so when

---

9. Ague or fever.

I went back to the field I looked at my mules and same as told them goodbye for a spell. And when I come back that evening and the sun shining all day on that shed, I wasn't so sho I would regret it.

He come riding up just as I went out to the porch, where they all was. He looked kind of funny: kind of more hang-dog than common, and kind of proud too. Like he had done something he thought was cute but wasn't so sho now how other folks would take it.

"I got a team," he said.

"You bought a team from Snopes?" I said.

"I reckon Snopes aint the only man in this country that can drive a trade," he said.

"Sho," I said. He was looking at Jewel, with that funny look, but Jewel had done got down from the porch and was going toward the horse. To see what Anse had done to it, I reckon.

"Jewel," Anse says. Jewel looked back. "Come here," Anse says. Jewel come back a little and stopped again.

"What you want?" he said.

"So you got a team from Snopes," I said. "He'll send them over tonight, I reckon? You'll want a early start tomorrow, long as you'll have to go by Mottson."

Then he quit looking like he had been for a while. He got that badgered look like he used to have, mumbling his mouth.

"I do the best I can," he said. "Fore God, if there were ere a man in the living world suffered the trials and floutings I have suffered."

"A fellow that just beat Snopes in a trade ought to feel pretty good," I said. "What did you give him, Anse?"

He didn't look at me. "I give a chattel mortgage on my cultivator and seeder," he said.

"But they aint worth forty dollars. How far do you aim to get with a forty dollar team?"

They were all watching him now, quiet and steady. Jewel was stopped, halfway back, waiting to go on to the horse. "I give other things," Anse said. He begun to mumble his mouth again, standing there like he was waiting for somebody to hit him and him with his mind already made up not to do nothing about it.

"What other things?" Darl said.

"Hell," I said. "You take my team. You can bring them back. I'll get along someway."

"So that's what you were doing in Cash's clothes last night," Darl said. He said it just like he was reading it outen the paper. Like he never give a durn himself one way or the other. Jewel had come back now, standing there, looking at Anse with them marble eyes of hisn. "Cash aimed to buy that talking machine from Suratt with that money," Darl said.

Anse stood there, mumbling his mouth. Jewel watched him. He aint never blinked yet.

"But that's just eight dollars more," Darl said, in that voice like he was just listening and never give a durn himself. "That still wont buy a team."

Anse looked at Jewel, quick, kind of sliding his eyes that way, then he looked down again. "God knows, if there were ere a man," he says. Still they didn't say nothing. They just watched him, waiting, and him sliding his eyes toward their feet and up their legs but no higher. "And the horse," he says.

"What horse?" Jewel said. Anse just stood there. I be durn, if a man cant keep the upper hand of his sons, he ought to run them away from home, no matter how big they are. And if he cant do that, I be durn if he oughtn't to leave himself. I be durn if I wouldn't. "You mean, you tried to swap my horse?" Jewel says.

Anse stands there, dangle-armed. "For fifteen years I aint had a tooth in my head," he says. "God knows it. He knows in fifteen years I aint et the victuals He aimed for man to eat to keep his strength up, and me saving a nickel here and nickel there so my family wouldn't suffer it, to buy them teeth so I could eat God's appointed food. I give that money. I thought that if I could do without eating, my sons could do without riding. God knows I did."

Jewel stands with his hands on his hips, looking at Anse. Then he looks away. He looked out across the field, his face still as a rock. Like it was somebody else talking about somebody else's horse and him not even listening. Then he spit, slow, and said "Hell" and he turned and went on to the gate and unhitched the horse and got on it. It was moving when he come into the saddle and by the time he was on it they was tearing down the road like the Law might have been behind them. They went out of sight that way, the two of them looking like some kind of a spotted cyclone.

"Well," I says. "You take my team," I said. But he wouldn't do it. And they wouldn't even stay, and that boy chasing them buzzards all day in the hot sun until he was nigh as crazy as the rest of them. "Leave Cash here, anyway," I said. But they wouldn't do that. They made a pallet for him with quilts on top of the coffin and laid him on it and set his tools by him, and we put my team in and hauled the wagon about a mile down the road.

"If we'll bother you here," Anse says, "just say so."

"Sho," I said. "It'll be fine here. Safe, too. Now let's go back and eat supper."

"I thank you," Anse said. "We got a little something in the basket. We can make out."

"Where'd you get it?" I said.

"We brought it from home."

"But it'll be stale now," I said. "Come and get some hot victuals."

But they wouldn't come. "I reckon we can make out," Anse said. So I went home and et and taken a basket back to them and tried again to make them come back to the house.

"I thank you," he said. "I reckon we can make out." So I left them there, squatting around a little fire, waiting; God knows what for.

I come on home. I kept thinking about them there, and about that fellow tearing away on that horse. And that would be the last they would see of him. And I be durn if I could blame him. Not for wanting to not give up his horse, but for getting shut of such a durn fool as Anse.

Or that's what I thought then. Because be durn if there aint something about a durn fellow like Anse that seems to make a man have to help him, even when he knows he'll be wanting to kick himself next minute. Because about a hour after breakfast next morning Eustace Grimm that works Snopes' place come up with a span of mules, hunting Anse.

"I thought him and Anse never traded," I said.

"Sho," Eustace said. "All they liked was the horse. Like I said to Mr Snopes, he was letting this team go for fifty dollars, because if his uncle Flem had a just kept them Texas horses when he owned them, Anse wouldn't a never—"

"The horse?" I said. "Anse's boy taken that horse and cleared out last night, probably halfway to Texas by now, and Anse—"

"I didn't know who brung it," Eustace said. "I never see them. I just found the horse in the barn this morning when I went to feed, and I told Mr Snopes and he said to bring the team on over here."

Well, that'll be the last they'll ever see of him now, sho enough. Come Christmas time they'll maybe get a postal card from him in Texas, I reckon. And if it hadn't been Jewel, I reckon it'd a been me; I owe him that much, myself. I be durn if Anse dont conjure a man, some way. I be durn if he aint a sight.

Vardaman

Now there are seven of them, in little tall black circles.

"Look, Darl," I say; "see?"

He looks up. We watch them in little tall black circles of not-moving.

"Yesterday there were just four," I say.

There were more than four on the barn.

"Do you know what I would do if he tries to light on the wagon again?" I say.

"What would you do?" Darl says.

"I wouldn't let him light on her," I say. "I wouldn't let him light on Cash, either."

Cash is sick. He is sick on the box. But my mother is a fish.

"We got to get some medicine in Mottson," pa says. "I reckon we'll just have to."

"How do you feel, Cash?" Darl says.

"It dont bother none," Cash says.

"Do you want it propped a little higher?" Darl says.

Cash has a broken leg. He has had two broken legs. He lies on the box with a quilt rolled under his head and a piece of wood under his knee.

"I reckon we ought to left him at Armstid's," pa says.

I haven't got a broken leg and pa hasn't and Darl hasn't and "It's just the bumps," Cash says. "It kind of grinds together a little on a bump. It dont bother none." Jewel *has gone away. He and his horse went away one supper time*

"It's because she wouldn't have us beholden," pa says. "Fore God, I do the best that ere a man" *Is it because Jewel's mother is a horse Darl? I said.*

"Maybe I can draw the ropes a little tighter," Darl says. *That's why Jewel and I were both in the shed and she was in the wagon because the horse lives in the barn and I had to keep on running the buzzard away from*

"If you just would," Cash says. And Dewey Dell hasn't got a broken leg and I haven't. Cash is my brother.

We stop. When Darl loosens the rope Cash begins to sweat again. His teeth look out.

"Hurt?" Darl says.

"I reckon you better put it back," Cash says.

Darl puts the rope back, pulling hard. Cash's teeth look out.

"Hurt?" Darl says.

"It dont bother none," Cash says.

"Do you want pa to drive slower?" Darl says.

"No," Cash says. "Aint no time to hang back. It dont bother none."

"We'll have to get some medicine at Mottson," pa says. "I reckon we'll have to."

"Tell him to go on," Cash says. We go on. Dewey Dell leans back and wipes Cash's face. Cash is my brother. *But Jewel's mother is a horse. My mother is a fish. Darl says that when we come to the water again I might see her and Dewey Dell said, She's in the box; how could she have got out? She got out through the holes I bored, into the water I said, and when we come to the water again I am going to see her. My mother is not in the box. My mother does not smell like that. My mother is a fish*

"Those cakes will be in fine shape by the time we get to Jefferson," Darl says.

Dewey Dell does not look around.

"You better try to sell them in Mottson," Darl says.

"When will we get to Mottson, Darl?" I say.

"Tomorrow," Darl says. "If this team dont rack to pieces. Snopes must have fed them on sawdust."

"Why did he feed them on sawdust, Darl?" I say.

"Look," Darl says. "See?"

Now there are nine of them, tall in little tall black circles.

When we come to the foot of the hill pa stops and Darl and Dewey Dell and I get out. Cash cant walk because he has a broken leg. "Come up, mules," pa says. The mules walk hard; the wagon creaks. Darl and Dewey Dell and I walk behind the wagon, up the hill. When we come to the top of the hill pa stops and we get back into the wagon.

Now there are ten of them, tall in little tall black circles on the sky.

Moseley

I happened to look up, and saw her outside the window, looking in. Not close to the glass, and not looking at anything in particular; just standing there with her head turned this way and her eyes full on me and kind of blank too, like she was waiting for a sign. When I looked up again she was moving toward the door.

She kind of bumbled at the screen door a minute, like they do, and came in. She had on a stiff-brimmed straw hat setting on the top of her head and she was carrying a package wrapped in newspaper: I thought that she had a quarter or a dollar at the most, and that after she stood around a while she would maybe buy a cheap comb or a bottle of nigger toilet water, so I never disturbed her for a minute or so except to notice that she was pretty in a kind of sullen, awkward way, and that she looked a sight better in her gingham dress and her own complexion than she would after she bought whatever she would finally decide on. Or tell that she wanted. I knew that she had already decided before she came in. But you have to let them take their time. So I went on with what I was doing, figuring to let Albert wait on her when he caught up at the fountain, when he came back to me.

"That woman," he said. "You better see what she wants."

"What does she want?" I said.

"I dont know. I cant get anything out of her. You better wait on her."

So I went around the counter. I saw that she was barefooted, standing with her feet flat and easy on the floor, like she was used to it. She was looking at me, hard, holding the package; I saw she had about as black a pair of eyes as ever I saw, and she was a stranger. I never remembered seeing her in Mottson before. "What can I do for you?" I said.

Still she didn't say anything. She stared at me without winking. Then she looked back at the folks at the fountain. Then she looked past me, toward the back of the store.

"Do you want to look at some toilet things?" I said. "Or is it medicine you want?"

"That's it," she said. She looked quick back at the fountain again. So I thought maybe her ma or somebody had sent her in for some of this female dope and she was ashamed to ask for it. I knew she couldn't have a complexion like hers and use it herself, let alone not being much more than old enough to barely know what it was for. It's a shame, the way they poison themselves with it. But a man's got to stock it or go out of business in this country.

"Oh," I said. "What do you use? We have—" She looked at me again, almost like she had said hush, and looked toward the back of the store again.

"I'd liefer go back there," she said.

"All right," I said. You have to humor them. You save time by it. I followed her to the back. She put her hand on the gate. "There's nothing back there but the prescription case," I said. "What do you want?" She stopped and looked at me. It was like she had taken some kind of a lid off her face, her eyes. It was her eyes: kind of dumb and hopeful and sullenly willing to be disappointed all at the same time. But she was in trouble of some sort; I could see that. "What's your trouble?" I said. "Tell me what it is you want. I'm pretty busy." I wasn't meaning to hurry her, but a man just hasn't got the time they have out there.

"It's the female trouble," she said.

"Oh," I said. "Is that all?" I thought maybe she was younger than she looked, and her first one had scared her, or maybe one had been a little abnormal as it will in young women. "Where's your ma?" I said. "Haven't you got one?"

"She's out yonder in the wagon," she said.

"Why not talk to her about it before you take any medicine," I said. "Any woman would have told you about it." She looked at me, and I looked at her again and said, "How old are you?"

"Seventeen," she said.

"Oh," I said. "I thought maybe you were . . ." She was watching me. But then, in the eyes all of them look like they had no age and knew everything in the world, anyhow. "Are you too regular, or not regular enough?"

She quit looking at me but she didn't move. "Yes," she said. "I reckon so. Yes."

"Well, which?" I said. "Dont you know?" It's a crime and a shame; but after all, they'll buy it from somebody. She stood there, not looking at me. "You want something to stop it?" I said. "Is that it?"

"No," she said. "That's it. It's already stopped."

"Well, what—" Her face was lowered a little, still, like they do in all their dealings with a man so he dont ever know just where the lightning will strike next. "You are not married, are you?" I said.

"No."

"Oh," I said. "And how long has it been since it stopped? about five months maybe?"

"It aint been but two," she said.

"Well, I haven't got anything in my store you want to buy," I said, "unless it's a nipple. And I'd advise you to buy that and go back home and tell your pa, if you have one, and let him make somebody buy you a wedding license. Was that all you wanted?"

But she just stood there, not looking at me.

"I got the money to pay you," she said.

"Is it your own, or did he act enough of a man to give you the money?"

"He give it to me. Ten dollars. He said that would be enough."

"A thousand dollars wouldn't be enough in my store and ten cents wouldn't be enough," I said. "You take my advice and go home and tell your pa or your brothers if you have any or the first man you come to in the road."

But she didn't move. "Lafe said I could get it at the drugstore. He said to tell you me and him wouldn't never tell nobody you sold it to us."

"And I just wish your precious Lafe had come for it himself; that's what I wish. I dont know: I'd have had a little respect for him then. And you can go back and tell him I said so—if he aint halfway to Texas by now, which I dont doubt. Me, a respectable druggist, that's kept store and raised a family and been a church-member for fifty-six years in this town. I'm a good mind to tell your folks myself, if I can just find who they are."

She looked at me now, her eyes and face kind of blank again like when I first saw her through the window. "I didn't know," she said. "He told me I could get something at the drugstore. He said they might not want to sell it to me, but if I had ten dollars and told them I wouldn't never tell nobody . . ."

"He never said this drugstore," I said. "If he did or mentioned my name, I defy him to prove it. I defy him to repeat it or I'll prosecute him to the full extent of the law, and you can tell him so."

"But maybe another drugstore would," she said.

"Then I dont want to know it. Me, that's—" Then I looked at her. But it's a hard life they have; sometimes a man . . . if there can ever be any excuse for sin, which it cant be. And then, life wasn't made to be easy on folks: they wouldn't ever have any reason to be good and die. "Look here," I said. "You get that notion out of your head. The Lord gave you what you have, even if He did use the devil to do it; you let Him take it away from you if it's His will to do so. You go on back to Lafe and you and him take that ten dollars and get married with it."

"Lafe said I could get something at the drugstore," she said.

"Then go and get it," I said. "You wont get it here."

She went out, carrying the package, her feet making a little hissing on the floor. She bumbled again at the door and went out. I could see her through the glass going on down the street.

It was Albert told me about the rest of it. He said the wagon was stopped in front of Grummet's hardware store, with the ladies all scattering up and down the street with handkerchiefs to their noses, and a crowd of hard-nosed men and boys standing around the wagon, listening to the marshal arguing with the man. He was a kind of tall, gaunted man sitting on the wagon, saying it was a public street and he reckoned he had as much right there as anybody, and the marshal telling him he would have to move on; folks couldn't stand it. It had been dead eight days, Albert said. They came from some place out in Yoknapatawpha county, trying to get to Jefferson with it. It must have been like a piece of rotten cheese coming into an ant-hill, in that ramshackle wagon that Albert said folks were scared would fall all to pieces before they could get it out of town, with that home-made box and another fellow with a broken leg lying on a quilt on top of it, and the father and a little boy sitting in the seat and the marshal trying to make them get out of town.

"It's a public street," the man says. "I reckon we can stop to buy something same as airy other man. We got the money to pay for hit, and hit aint airy law that says a man cant spend his money where he wants."

They had stopped to buy some cement. The other son was in Grummet's, trying to make Grummet break a sack and let him have ten cents' worth, and finally Grummet broke the sack to get him out. They wanted the cement to fix the fellow's broken leg, someway.

"Why, you'll kill him," the marshal said. "You'll cause him to lose his leg. You take him on to the doctor, and you get this thing buried soon as you can. Dont you know you're liable to jail for endangering the public health?"

"We're doing the best we can," the father said. Then he told a long tale about how they had to wait for the wagon to come back and how the bridge was washed away and how they went eight miles to another bridge and it was gone too so they came back and swum the ford and the mules got drowned and how they got another team and found that the road was washed out and they had to come clean around by Mottson, and then the one with the cement came back and told him to shut up.

"We'll be gone in a minute," he told the marshal.

"We never aimed to bother nobody," the father said.

"You take that fellow to a doctor," the marshal told the one with the cement.

"I reckon he's all right," he said.

"It aint that we're hard-hearted," the marshal said. "But I reckon you can tell yourself how it is."

"Sho," the other said. "We'll take out soon as Dewey Dell comes back. She went to deliver a package."

So they stood there with the folks backed off with handkerchiefs to their faces, until in a minute the girl came up with that newspaper package.

"Come on," the one with the cement said, "we've lost too much time." So they got in the wagon and went on. And when I went to supper it still seemed like I could smell it. And the next day I met the marshal and I begun to sniff and said,

"Smell anything?"

"I reckon they're in Jefferson by now," he said.

"Or in jail. Well, thank the Lord it's not our jail."

"That's a fact," he said.

Darl

"Here's a place," pa says. He pulls the team up and sits looking at the house. "We could get some water over yonder."

"All right," I say. "You'll have to borrow a bucket from them, Dewey Dell."

"God knows," pa says. "I wouldn't be beholden, God knows."

"If you see a good-sized can, you might bring it," I say. Dewey Dell gets down from the wagon, carrying the package. "You had more trouble than you expected, selling those cakes in Mottson," I say. How do our lives ravel out into the no-wind, no-sound, the weary gestures wearily recapitulant: echoes of old compulsions with no-hand on no-strings: in sunset we fall into furious attitudes, dead gestures of dolls. Cash broke his leg and now the sawdust is running out. He is bleeding to death is Cash.

"I wouldn't be beholden," pa says. "God knows."

"Then make some water yourself," I say. "We can use Cash's hat."

When Dewey Dell comes back the man comes with her. Then he stops and she comes on and he stands there and after a while he goes back to the house and stands on the porch, watching us.

"We better not try to lift him down," pa says. "We can fix it here."

"Do you want to be lifted down, Cash?" I say.

"Wont we get to Jefferson tomorrow?" he says. He is watching us, his eyes interrogatory, intent, and sad. "I can last it out."

"It'll be easier on you," pa says. "It'll keep it from rubbing together."

"I can last it," Cash says. "We'll lose time stopping."

"We done bought the cement now," pa says.

"I could last it," Cash says. "It aint but one more day. It dont bother to speak of." He looks at us, his eyes wide in his thin gray face, questioning. "It sets up so," he says.

"We done bought it now," pa says.

I mix the cement in the can, stirring the slow water into the pale green thick coils. I bring the can to the wagon where Cash can see. He lies on his back, his thin profile in silhouette, ascetic and profound against the sky. "Does that look about right?" I say.

"You dont want too much water, or it wont work right," he says.

"Is this too much?"

"Maybe if you could get a little sand," he says. "It aint but one more day," he says. "It dont bother me none."

Vardaman goes back down the road to where we crossed the branch and returns with sand. He pours it slowly into the thick coiling in the can. I go to the wagon again.

"Does that look all right?"

"Yes," Cash says. "I could have lasted. It dont bother me none."

We loosen the splints and pour the cement over his leg, slow.

"Watch out for it," Cash says. "Dont get none on it if you can help."

"Yes," I say. Dewey Dell tears a piece of paper from the package and wipes the cement from the top of it as it drips from Cash's leg.

"How does that feel?"

"It feels fine," he says. "It's cold. It feels fine."

"If it'll just help you," pa says. "I asks your forgiveness. I never foreseen it no more than you."

"It feels fine," Cash says.

If you could just ravel out into time. That would be nice. It would be nice if you could just ravel out into time.

We replace the splints, the cords, drawing them tight, the cement in thick pale green slow surges among the cords, Cash watching us quietly with that profound questioning look.

"That'll steady it," I say.

"Ay," Cash says. "I'm obliged."

Then we all turn on the wagon and watch him. He is coming up the road behind us, wooden-backed, wooden-faced, moving only from his hips down. He comes up without a word, with his pale rigid eyes in his high sullen face, and gets into the wagon.

"Here's a hill," pa says. "I reckon you'll have to get out and walk."

Vardaman

Darl and Jewel and Dewey Dell and I are walking up the hill, behind the wagon. Jewel came back. He came up the road and got into the wagon. He was walking. Jewel hasn't got a horse anymore. Jewel is my brother. Cash is my brother. Cash has a broken leg. We fixed Cash's leg so it doesn't hurt. Cash is my brother. Jewel is my brother too, but he hasn't got a broken leg.

Now there are five of them, tall in little tall black circles.

"Where do they stay at night, Darl?" I say. "When we stop at night in the barn, where do they stay?"

The hill goes off into the sky. Then the sun comes up from behind the hill and the mules and the wagon and pa walk on the sun. You cannot watch them, walking slow on the sun. In Jefferson it is red on the track behind the glass. The track goes shining round and round. Dewey Dell says so.

Tonight I am going to see where they stay while we are in the barn.

Darl

"Jewel" I say, "whose son are you?"

The breeze was setting up from the barn, so we put her under the apple tree, where the moonlight can dapple the apple tree upon the long slumbering flanks within which now and then she talks in little trickling bursts of secret and murmurous bubbling. I took Vardaman to listen. When we came up the cat leaped down from it and flicked away with silver claw and silver eye into the shadow.

"Your mother was a horse, but who was your father, Jewel?"

"You goddamn lying son of a bitch."

"Dont call me that," I say.

"You goddamn lying son of a bitch."

"Dont you call me that, Jewel." In the tall moonlight his eyes look like spots of white paper pasted on a high small football.

After supper Cash began to sweat a little. "It's getting a little hot," he said. "It was the sun shining on it all day, I reckon."

"You want some water poured on it?" we say. "Maybe that will ease it some."

"I'd be obliged," Cash said. "It was the sun shining on it, I reckon. I ought to thought and kept it covered."

"We ought to thought," we said. "You couldn't have suspicioned."

"I never noticed it getting hot," Cash said. "I ought to minded it."

So we poured the water over it. His leg and foot below the cement looked like they had been boiled. "Does that feel better?" we said.

"I'm obliged," Cash said. "It feels fine."

Dewey Dell wipes her face with the hem of her dress.

"See if you can get some sleep," we say.

"Sho," Cash says. "I'm right obliged. It feels fine now."

Jewel, I say, Who was your father, Jewel?

Goddamn you. Goddamn you.

Vardaman

She was under the apple tree and Darl and I go across the moon and the cat jumps down and runs and we can hear her inside the wood.

"Hear?" Darl says. "Put your ear close."

I put my ear close and I can hear her. Only I cant tell what she is saying.

"What is she saying, Darl?" I say. "Who is she talking to?"

"She's talking to God," Darl says. "She is calling on Him to help her."

"What does she want Him to do?" I say.

"She wants Him to hide her away from the sight of man," Darl says.

"Why does she want to hide her away from the sight of man, Darl?"

"So she can lay down her life," Darl says.

"Why does she want to lay down her life, Darl?"

"Listen," Darl says. We hear her. We hear her turn over on her side. "Listen," Darl says.

"She's turned over," I say. "She's looking at me through the wood."

"Yes," Darl says.

"How can she see through the wood, Darl?"

"Come," Darl says. "We must let her be quiet. Come."

"She cant see out there, because the holes are in the top," I say. "How can she see, Darl?"

"Let's go see about Cash," Darl says.

And I saw something Dewey Dell told me not to tell nobody

Cash is sick in his leg. We fixed his leg this afternoon, but he is sick in it again, lying on the bed. We pour water on his leg and then he feels fine.

"I feel fine," Cash says. "I'm obliged to you."

"Try to get some sleep," we say.

"I feel fine," Cash says. "I'm obliged to you."

And I saw something Dewey Dell told me not to tell nobody. It is not about pa and it is not about Cash and it is not about Jewel and it is not about Dewey Dell and it is not about me

Dewey Dell and I are going to sleep on the pallet. It is on the back porch, where we can see the barn, and the moon shines on half of the pallet and we will lie half in the white and half in the black, with the moonlight on our legs. And then I am going to see where they stay at night while we are in the barn. We are not in the barn tonight but I can see the barn and so I am going to find where they stay at night.

We lie on the pallet, with our legs in the moon.

"Look," I say, "my legs look black. Your legs look black, too."

"Go to sleep," Dewey Dell says.

Jefferson is a far piece.

"Dewey Dell."

"What."

"If it's not Christmas now, how will it be there?"

It goes round and round on the shining track. Then the track goes shining round and round.

"Will what be there?"

"That train. In the window."

"You go to sleep. You can see tomorrow if it's there."

Maybe Santa Claus wont know they are town boys.

"Dewey Dell."

"You go to sleep. He aint going to let none of them town boys have it."

It was behind the window, red on the track, the track shining round and round. It made my heart hurt. And then it was pa and Jewel and Darl and Mr Gillespie's boy. Mr Gillespie's boy's legs come down under his nightshirt. When he goes into the moon, his legs fuzz. They go on around the house toward the apple tree.

"What are they going to do, Dewey Dell?"

They went around the house toward the apple tree.

"I can smell her," I say. "Can you smell her, too?"

"Hush," Dewey Dell says. "The wind's changed. Go to sleep."

And so I am going to know where they stay at night soon. They come around the house, going across the yard in the moon, carrying her on their shoulders. They carry her down to the barn, the moon shining flat and quiet on her. Then they come back and go into the house again. While they were in the moon, Mr Gillespie's boy's legs fuzzed. And then I waited and I said Dewey Dell? and then I waited and then I went to find where they stay at night and I saw something that Dewey Dell told me not to tell nobody.

Darl

Against the dark doorway he seems to materialise out of darkness, lean as a race horse in his underclothes in the beginning of the glare. He leaps to the ground with on his face an expression of furious unbelief. He has seen me without even turning his head or his eyes in which the glare swims like two small torches. "Come on," he says, leaping down the slope toward the barn.

For an instant longer he runs silver in the moonlight, then he springs out like a flat figure cut leanly from tin against an abrupt and soundless explosion as the whole loft of the barn takes fire at once, as though it had been stuffed with powder. The front, the conical façade with the square orifice of doorway broken only by the square squat shape of the coffin on the sawhorses like a cubistic bug, comes into relief. Behind me pa and Gillespie and Mack and Dewey Dell and Vardaman emerge from the house.

He pauses at the coffin, stooping, looking at me, his face furious. Overhead the flames sound like thunder; across us rushes a cool draft: there is no heat in it at all yet, and a handful of chaff lifts suddenly and sucks swiftly along the stalls where a horse is screaming. "Quick," I say; "the horses."

He glares a moment longer at me, then at the roof overhead, then he leaps toward the stall where the horse screams. It plunges and kicks, the sound of the crashing blows sucking up into the sound of the flames. They sound like an interminable train crossing an endless trestle. Gillespie and Mack pass me, in knee-length nightshirts, shouting, their voices thin and high and mean-ingless and at the same time profoundly wild and sad: ". . . cow . . . stall . . ." Gillespie's nightshirt rushes ahead of him on the draft, ballooning about his hairy thighs.

The stall door has swung shut. Jewel thrusts it back with his buttocks and he appears, his back arched, the muscles ridged through his garment as he drags the horse out by its head. In the glare its eyes roll with soft, fleet, wild opaline fire; its muscles bunch and run as it flings its head about, lifting Jewel clear of the ground. He drags it on, slowly, terrifically; again he gives me across his shoulder a single glare furious and brief. Even when they are clear of the barn the horse continues to fight and lash backward toward the door-way until Gillespie passes me, stark-naked, his nightshirt wrapped about the mule's head, and beats the maddened horse on out of the door.

Jewel returns, running; again he looks down at the coffin. But he comes on. "Where's cow?" he cries, passing me. I follow him. In the stall Mack is struggling with the other mule. When its head turns into the glare I can see the wild rolling of its eye too, but it makes no sound. It just stands there, watching Mack over its shoulder, swinging its hind quarters toward him whenever he approaches. He looks back at us, his eyes and mouth three round holes in his face on which the freckles look like English peas on a plate. His voice is thin, high, faraway.

"I cant do nothing . . ." It is as though the sound had been swept from his lips and up and away, speaking back to us from an immense distance of exhaustion. Jewel slides past us; the mule whirls and lashes out, but he has already gained its head. I lean to Mack's ear:

"Nightshirt. Around his head."

Mack stares at me. Then he rips the nightshirt off and flings it over the mule's head, and it becomes docile at once. Jewel is yelling at him: "Cow? Cow?"

"Back," Mack cries. "Last stall."

The cow watches us as we enter. She is backed into the corner, head low-ered, still chewing though rapidly. But she makes no move. Jewel has paused, looking up, and suddenly we watch the entire floor to the loft dissolve. It just turns to fire; a faint litter of sparks rains down. He glances about. Back under the trough is a three-legged milking stool. He catches it up and swings it into the planking of the rear wall. He splinters a plank, then another, a third; we tear the fragments away. While we are stooping at the opening something charges into us from behind. It is the cow; with a single whistling breath she rushes between us and through the gap and into the outer glare, her tail erect and rigid as a broom nailed upright to the end of her spine.

Jewel turns back into the barn. "Here," I say; "Jewel!" I grasp at him; he strikes my hand down. "You fool," I say, "dont you see you cant make it back yonder?" The hallway looks like a searchlight turned into rain. "Come on," I say, "around this way."

When we are through the gap he begins to run. "Jewel," I say, running. He darts around the corner. When I reach it he has almost reached the next one, running against the glare like that figure cut from tin. Pa and Gillespie and Mack are some distance away, watching the barn, pink against the darkness where for the time the moonlight has been vanquished. "Catch him!" I cry; "stop him!"

When I reach the front, he is struggling with Gillespie; the one lean in underclothes, the other stark naked. They are like two figures in a Greek frieze, isolated out of all reality by the red glare. Before I can reach them he has struck Gillespie to the ground and turned and run back into the barn.

The sound of it has become quite peaceful now, like the sound of the river did. We watch through the dissolving proscenium of the doorway as Jewel runs crouching to the far end of the coffin and stoops to it. For an instant he looks up and out at us through the rain of burning hay like a portiere of flaming beads, and I can see his mouth shape as he calls my name.

"Jewel!" Dewey Dell cries; "Jewel!" It seems to me that I now hear the accumulation of her voice through the last five minutes, and I hear her scuffling and struggling as pa and Mack hold her, screaming "Jewel! Jewel!" But he is no longer looking at us. We see his shoulders strain as he upends the coffin and slides it single-handed from the sawhorses. It looms unbelievably tall, hiding him: I would not have believed that Addie Bundren would have needed that much room to lie comfortable in; for another instant it stands upright while the sparks rain on it in scattering bursts as though they engendered other sparks from the contact. Then it topples forward, gaining momentum, revealing Jewel and the sparks raining on him too in engendering gusts, so that he appears to be enclosed in a thin nimbus of fire. Without stopping it overends and rears again, pauses, then crashes slowly forward and through the curtain. This time Jewel is riding upon it, clinging to it, until it crashes down and flings him forward and clear and Mack leaps forward into the thin smell of scorching meat and slaps at the widening crimson-edged holes that bloom like flowers in his undershirt.

Vardaman

When I went to find where they stay at night, I saw something They said, "Where is Darl? Where did Darl go?"

They carried her back under the apple tree.

The barn was still red, but it wasn't a barn now. It was sunk down, and the red went swirling up. The barn went swirling up in little red pieces, against the sky and the stars so that the stars moved backward.

And then Cash was still awake. He turned his head from side to side, with sweat on his face.

"Do you want some more water on it, Cash?" Dewey Dell said.

Cash's leg and foot turned black. We held the lamp and looked at Cash's foot and leg where it was black.

"Your foot looks like a nigger's foot, Cash," I said.

"I reckon we'll have to bust it off," pa said.

"What in the tarnation you put it on there for," Mr Gillespie said.

"I thought it would steady it some," pa said. "I just aimed to help him."

They got the flat iron and the hammer. Dewey Dell held the lamp. They had to hit it hard. And then Cash went to sleep.

"He's asleep now," I said. "It cant hurt him while he's asleep."

It just cracked. It wouldn't come off.

"It'll take the hide, too," Mr Gillespie said. "Why in the tarnation you put it on there. Didn't none of you think to grease his leg first?"

"I just aimed to help him," pa said. "It was Darl put it on."

"Where is Darl?" they said.

"Didn't none of you have more sense than that?" Mr Gillespie said. "I'd a thought he would, anyway."

Jewel was lying on his face. His back was red. Dewey Dell put the medicine on it. The medicine was made out of butter and soot, to draw out the fire. Then his back was black.

"Does it hurt, Jewel?" I said. "Your back looks like a nigger's, Jewel," I said. Cash's foot and leg looked like a nigger's. Then they broke it off. Cash's leg bled.

"You go on back and lay down," Dewey Dell said. "You ought to be asleep."

"Where is Darl?" they said.

He is out there under the apple tree with her, lying on her. He is there so the cat wont come back. I said, "Are you going to keep the cat away, Darl?"

The moonlight dappled on him too. On her it was still, but on Darl it dappled up and down.

"You needn't to cry," I said. "Jewel got her out. You needn't to cry, Darl."

The barn is still red. It used to be redder than this. Then it went swirling, making the stars run backward without falling. It hurt my heart like the train did.

When I went to find where they stay at night, I saw something that Dewey Dell says I mustn't never tell nobody

Darl

We have been passing the signs for some time now: the drug stores, the clothing stores, the patent medicine and the garages and cafes, and the mileboards diminishing, becoming more starkly reaccruent: 3 mi. 2 mi. From the crest of a hill, as we get into the wagon again, we can see the smoke low and flat, seemingly unmoving in the unwinded afternoon.

"Is that it, Darl?" Vardaman says. "Is that Jefferson?" He too has lost flesh; like ours, his face has an expression strained, dreamy, and gaunt.

"Yes," I say. He lifts his head and looks at the sky. High against it they hang in narrowing circles, like the smoke, with an outward semblance of form and purpose, but with no inference of motion, progress or retrograde. We mount the wagon again where Cash lies on the box, the jagged shards of cement cracked about his leg. The shabby mules droop rattling and clanking down the hill.

"We'll have to take him to the doctor," pa says. "I reckon it aint no way around it." The back of Jewel's shirt, where it touches him, stains slow and black with grease. Life was created in the valleys. It blew up onto the hills on the old terrors, the old lusts, the old despairs. That's why you must walk up the hills so you can ride down.

Dewey Dell sits on the seat, the newspaper package on her lap. When we reach the foot of the hill where the road flattens between close walls of trees, she begins to look about quietly from one side of the road to the other. At last she says,

"I got to stop."

Pa looks at her, his shabby profile that of anticipant and disgruntled annoyance. He does not check the team. "What for?"

"I got to go to the bushes," Dewey Dell says.

Pa does not check the team. "Cant you wait till we get to town? It aint over a mile now."

"Stop," Dewey Dell says. "I got to go to the bushes."

Pa stops in the middle of the road and we watch Dewey Dell descend, carrying the package. She does not look back.

"Why not leave your cakes here?" I say. "We'll watch them."

She descends steadily, not looking at us.

"How would she know where to go if she waited till we get to town?" Vardaman says. "Where would you go to do it in town, Dewey Dell?"

She lifts the package down and turns and disappears among the trees and undergrowth.

"Dont be no longer than you can help," pa says. "We aint got no time to waste." She does not answer. After a while we cannot hear her even. "We ought to done like Armstid and Gillespie said and sent word to town and had it dug and ready," he says.

"Why didn't you?" I say. "You could have telephoned."

"What for?" Jewel says. "Who the hell cant dig a hole in the ground?"

A car comes over the hill. It begins to sound the horn, slowing. It runs along the roadside in low gear, the outside wheels in the ditch, and passes us and goes on. Vardaman watches it until it is out of sight.

"How far is it now, Darl?" he says.

"Not far," I say.

"We ought to done it," pa says. "I just never wanted to be beholden to none except her flesh and blood."

"Who the hell cant dig a damn hole in the ground?" Jewel says.

"It aint respectful, talking that way about her grave," pa says. "You all dont know what it is. You never pure loved her, none of you." Jewel does not answer. He sits a little stiffly erect, his body arched away from his shirt. His high-colored jaw juts.

Dewey Dell returns. We watch her emerge from the bushes, carrying the package, and climb into the wagon. She now wears her Sunday dress, her beads, her shoes and stockings.

"I thought I told you to leave them clothes to home," pa says. She does not answer, does not look at us. She sets the package in the wagon and gets in. The wagon moves on.

"How many more hills now, Darl?" Vardaman says.

"Just one," I say. "The next one goes right up into town."

This hill is red sand, bordered on either hand by negro cabins; against the sky ahead the massed telephone lines run, and the clock on the courthouse lifts among the trees. In the sand the wheels whisper, as though the very earth would hush our entry. We descend as the hill commences to rise.

We follow the wagon, the whispering wheels, passing the cabins where faces come suddenly to the doors, white-eyed. We hear sudden voices, ejaculant. Jewel has been looking from side to side; now his head turns forward and I can see his ears taking on a still deeper tone of furious red. Three negroes walk beside the road ahead of us; ten feet ahead of them a white man walks. When we pass the negroes their heads turn suddenly with that expression of shock and instinctive outrage. "Great God," one says; "what they got in that wagon?"

Jewel whirls. "Son of a bitches," he says. As he does so he is abreast of the white man, who has paused. It is as though Jewel had gone blind for the moment, for it is the white man toward whom he whirls.

"Darl!" Cash says from the wagon. I grasp at Jewel. The white man has fallen back a pace, his face still slack-jawed; then his jaw tightens, claps to. Jewel leans above him, his jaw muscles gone white.

"What did you say?" he says.

"Here," I say. "He dont mean anything, mister. Jewel," I say. When I touch him he swings at the man. I grasp his arm; we struggle. Jewel has never looked at me. He is trying to free his arm. When I see the man again he has an open knife in his hand.

"Hold on, mister," I say; "I've got him. Jewel," I say.

"Thinks because he's a goddamn town fellow," Jewel says, panting, wrenching at me. "Son of a bitch," he says.

The man moves. He begins to edge around me, watching Jewel, the knife low against his flank. "Cant no man call me that," he says. Pa has got down, and Dewey Dell is holding Jewel, pushing at him. I release him and face the man.

"Wait," I say. "He dont mean nothing. He's sick; got burned in a fire last night, and he aint himself."

"Fire or no fire," the man says, "cant no man call me that."

"He thought you said something to him," I say.

"I never said nothing to him. I never see him before."

"Fore God," pa says; "fore God."

"I know," I say. "He never meant anything. He'll take it back."

"Let him take it back, then."

"Put up your knife, and he will."

The man looks at me. He looks at Jewel. Jewel is quiet now.

"Put up your knife," I say.

The man shuts the knife.

"Fore God," pa says. "Fore God."

"Tell him you didn't mean anything, Jewel," I say.

"I thought he said something," Jewel says. "Just because he's—"

"Hush," I say. "Tell him you didn't mean it."

"I didn't mean it," Jewel says.

"He better not," the man says. "Calling me a—"

"Do you think he's afraid to call you that?" I say.

The man looks at me. "I never said that," he said.

"Don't think it, neither," Jewel says.

"Shut up," I say. "Come on. Drive on, pa."

The wagon moves. The man stands watching us. Jewel does not look back. "Jewel would a whipped him," Vardaman says.

We approach the crest, where the street runs, where cars go back and forth; the mules haul the wagon up and onto the crest and the street. Pa stops them. The street runs on ahead, where the square opens and the monument stands before the courthouse. We mount again while the heads turn with that expression which we know; save Jewel. He does not get on, even though the wagon has started again. "Get in, Jewel," I say. "Come on. Let's get away from here." But he does not get in. Instead he sets his foot on the turning hub of the rear wheel, one hand grasping the stanchion, and with the hub turning smoothly under his sole he lifts the other foot and squats there, staring straight ahead, motionless, lean, wooden-backed, as though carved squatting out of the lean wood.

Cash

It wasn't nothing else to do. It was either send him to Jackson, or have Gillespie sue us, because he knowed some way that Darl set fire to it. I dont know how he knowed, but he did. Vardaman see him do it, but he swore he never told nobody but Dewey Dell and that she told him not to tell nobody. But Gillespie knowed it. But he would a suspicioned it sooner or later. He could have done it that night just watching the way Darl acted.

And so pa said, "I reckon there aint nothing else to do," and Jewel said, "You want to fix him now?"

"Fix him?" pa said.

"Catch him and tie him up," Jewel said. "Goddamn it, do you want to wait until he sets fire to the goddamn team and wagon?"

But there wasn't no use in that. "There aint no use in that," I said. "We can wait till she is underground." A fellow that's going to spend the rest of his life locked up, he ought to be let to have what pleasure he can have before he goes.

"I reckon he ought to be there," pa says. "God knows, it's a trial on me. Seems like it aint no end to bad luck when once it starts."

Sometimes I aint so sho who's got ere a right to say when a man is crazy and when he aint. Sometimes I think it aint none of us pure crazy and aint none of us pure sane until the balance of us talks him that-a-way. It's like it aint so much what a fellow does, but it's the way the majority of folks is looking at him when he does it.

Because Jewel is too hard on him. Of course it was Jewel's horse was traded to get her that nigh to town, and in a sense it was the value of his horse Darl tried to burn up. But I thought more than once before we crossed the river and after, how it would be God's blessing if He did take her outen our hands and get shut of her in some clean way, and it seemed to me that when Jewel worked so to get her outen the river, he was going against God in a way, and then when Darl seen that it looked like one of us would have to do something, I can almost believe he done right in a way. But I dont reckon nothing excuses setting fire to a man's barn and endangering his stock and destroying his property. That's how I reckon a man is crazy. That's how he cant see eye to eye with other folks. And I reckon they aint nothing else to do with him but what the most folks says is right.

But it's a shame, in a way. Folks seems to get away from the olden right teaching that says to drive the nails down and trim the edges well always like it was for your own use and comfort you were making it. It's like some folks has the smooth, pretty boards to build a courthouse with and others dont have no more than rough lumber fitten to build a chicken coop. But it's better to build a tight chicken coop than a shoddy courthouse, and when they both build shoddy or build well, neither because it's one or tother is going to make a man feel the better nor the worse.

So we went up the street, toward the square, and he said, "We better take Cash to the doctor first. We can leave him there and come back for him." That's it. It's because me and him was born close together, and it nigh ten years before Jewel and Dewey Dell and Vardaman begun to come along. I feel kin to them, all right, but I dont know. And me being the oldest, and thinking already the very thing that he done: I dont know.

Pa was looking at me, then at him, mumbling his mouth.

"Go on," I said. "We'll get it done first."

"She would want us all there," pa says.

"Let's take Cash to the doctor first," Darl said. "She'll wait. She's already waited nine days."

"You all dont know," pa says. "The somebody you was young with and you growed old in her and she growed old in you, seeing the old coming on and it was the one somebody you could hear say it dont matter and know it was the truth outen the hard world and all a man's grief and trials. You all dont know."

"We got the digging to do, too," I said.

"Armstid and Gillespie both told you to send word ahead," Darl said. "Dont you want to go to Peabody's now, Cash?"

"Go on," I said. "It feels right easy now. It's best to get things done in the right place."

"If it was just dug," pa says. "We forgot our spade, too."

"Yes," Darl said. "I'll go to the hardware store. We'll have to buy one."

"It'll cost money," pa says.

"Do you begrudge her it?" Darl says.

"Go on and get a spade," Jewel said. "Here. Give me the money."

But pa didn't stop. "I reckon we can get a spade," he said. "I reckon there are Christians here." So Darl set still and we went on, with Jewel squatting on the tail-gate, watching the back of Darl's head. He looked like one of these bull dogs, one of these dogs that dont bark none, squatting against the rope, watching the thing he was waiting to jump at.

He set that way all the time we was in front of Mrs Bundren's house, hearing the music, watching the back of Darl's head with them hard white eyes of hisn.

The music was playing in the house. It was one of them graphophones.[1] It was natural as a music-band.

"Do you want to go to Peabody's?" Darl said. "They can wait here and tell pa, and I'll drive you to Peabody's and come back for them."

1. Trademark of an early machine for playing recorded music using wax platters.

"No," I said. It was better to get her underground, now we was this close, just waiting until pa borrowed the shovel. He drove along the street until we could hear the music.

"Maybe they got one here," he said. He pulled up at Mrs Bundren's. It was like he knowed. Sometimes I think that if a working man could see work as far ahead as a lazy man can see laziness. So he stopped there like he knowed, before that little new house, where the music was. We waited there, hearing it. I believe I could have dickered Suratt down to five dollars on that one of his. It's a comfortable thing, music is. "Maybe they got one here," pa says.

"You want Jewel to go," Darl says, "or do you reckon I better?"

"I reckon I better," pa says. He got down and went up the path and around the house to the back. The music stopped, then it started again.

"He'll get it, too," Darl said.

"Ay," I said. It was just like he knowed, like he could see through the walls and into the next ten minutes.

Only it was more than ten minutes. The music stopped and never commenced again for a good spell, where her and pa was talking at the back. We waited in the wagon.

"You let me take you back to Peabody's," Darl said.

"No," I said. "We'll get her underground."

"If he ever gets back," Jewel said. He begun to cuss. He started to get down from the wagon. "I'm going," he said.

Then we saw pa coming back. He had two spades, coming around the house. He laid them in the wagon and got in and we went on. The music never started again. Pa was looking back at the house. He kind of lifted his hand a little and I saw the shade pulled back a little at the window and her face in it.

But the curiousest thing was Dewey Dell. It surprised me. I see all the while how folks could say he was queer, but that was the very reason couldn't nobody hold it personal. It was like he was outside of it too, same as you, and getting mad at it would be kind of like getting mad at a mud-puddle that splashed you when you stepped in it. And then I always kind of had a idea that him and Dewey Dell kind of knowed things betwixt them. If I'd a said it was ere a one of us she liked better than ere a other, I'd a said it was Darl. But when we got it filled and covered and drove out the gate and turned into the lane where them fellows was waiting, when they come out and come on him and he jerked back, it was Dewey Dell that was on him before even Jewel could get at him. And then I believed I knowed how Gillespie knowed about how his barn taken fire.

She hadn't said a word, hadn't even looked at him, but when them fellows told him what they wanted and that they had come to get him and he throwed back, she jumped on him like a wild cat so that one of the fellows had to quit and hold her and her scratching and clawing at him like a wild cat, while the other one and pa and Jewel throwed Darl down and held him lying on his back, looking up at me.

"I thought you would have told me," he said. "I never thought you wouldn't have."

"Darl," I said. But he fought again, him and Jewel and the fellow, and the other one holding Dewey Dell and Vardaman yelling and Jewel saying,

"Kill him. Kill the son of a bitch."

It was bad so. It was bad. A fellow cant get away from a shoddy job. He cant do it. I tried to tell him, but he just said, "I thought you'd a told me. It's not that I," he said, then he begun to laugh. The other fellow pulled Jewel off of him and he sat there on the ground, laughing.

I tried to tell him. If I could have just moved, even set up. But I tried to tell him and he quit laughing, looking up at me.

"Do you want me to go?" he said.

"It'll be better for you," I said. "Down there it'll be quiet, with none of the bothering and such. It'll be better for you, Darl," I said.

"Better," he said. He begun to laugh again. "Better," he said. He couldn't hardly say it for laughing. He sat on the ground and us watching him, laughing and laughing. It was bad. It was bad so. I be durn if I could see anything to laugh at. Because there just aint nothing justifies the deliberate destruction of what a man has built with his own sweat and stored the fruit of his sweat into.

But I aint so sho that ere a man has the right to say what is crazy and what aint. It's like there was a fellow in every man that's done a-past the sanity or the insanity, that watches the sane and the insane doings of that man with the same horror and the same astonishment.

Peabody

I said, "I reckon a man in a tight might let Bill Varner patch him up like a damn mule, but I be damned if the man that'd let Anse Bundren treat him with raw cement aint got more spare legs than I have."

"They just aimed to ease hit some," he said.

"Aimed, hell," I said. "What in hell did Armstid mean by even letting them put you on that wagon again?"

"Hit was gittin right noticeable," he said. "We never had time to wait." I just looked at him. "Hit never bothered me none," he said.

"Dont you lie there and try to tell me you rode six days on a wagon without springs, with a broken leg and it never bothered you."

"It never bothered me much," he said.

"You mean, it never bothered Anse much," I said. "No more than it bothered him to throw that poor devil down in the public street and handcuff him like a damn murderer. Dont tell me. And dont tell me it aint going to bother you to lose sixty-odd square inches of skin to get that concrete off. And dont tell me it aint going to bother you to have to limp around on one short leg for the balance of your life—if you walk at all again. Concrete," I said. "God Amighty, why didn't Anse carry you to the nearest sawmill and stick your leg in the saw? That would have cured it. Then you all could have stuck his head into the saw and cured a whole family . . . Where is Anse, anyway? What's he up to now?"

"He's takin back them spades he borrowed," he said.

"That's right," I said. "Of course he'd have to borrow a spade to bury his wife with. Unless he could borrow a hole in the ground. Too bad you all didn't put him in it too . . . Does that hurt?"

"Not to speak of," he said, and the sweat big as marbles running down his face and his face about the color of blotting paper.

"Course not," I said. "About next summer you can hobble around fine on this leg. Then it wont bother you, not to speak of . . . If you had anything you could call luck, you might say it was lucky this is the same leg you broke before," I said.

"Hit's what paw says," he said.

MacGowan

It happened I am back of the prescription case, pouring up some chocolate sauce, when Jody comes back and says, "Say, Skeet, there's a woman up front that wants to see the doctor and when I said What doctor you want to see, she said she wants to see the doctor that works here and when I said There aint any doctor works here, she just stood there, looking back this way."

"What kind of a woman is it?" I says. "Tell her to go upstairs to Alford's office."

"Country woman," he says.

"Send her to the courthouse," I says. "Tell her all the doctors have gone to Memphis to a Barbers' Convention."

"All right," he says, going away. "She looks pretty good for a country girl," he says.

"Wait," I says. He waited and I went and peeped through the crack. But I couldn't tell nothing except she had a good leg against the light. "Is she young, you say?" I says.

"She looks like a pretty hot mamma, for a country girl," he says.

"Take this," I says, giving him the chocolate. I took off my apron and went up there. She looked pretty good. One of them black eyed ones that look like she'd as soon put a knife in you as not if you two-timed her. She looked pretty good. There wasn't nobody else in the store; it was dinner time.

"What can I do for you?" I says.

"Are you the doctor?" she says.

"Sure," I says. She quit looking at me and was kind of looking around.

"Can we go back yonder?" she says.

It was just a quarter past twelve, but I went and told Jody to kind of watch out and whistle if the old man come in sight, because he never got back before one.

"You better lay off of that," Jody says. "He'll fire your stern out of here so quick you cant wink."

"He dont never get back before one," I says. "You can see him go into the postoffice. You keep your eye peeled, now, and give me a whistle."

"What you going to do?" he says.

"You keep your eye out. I'll tell you later."

"Aint you going to give me no seconds on it?" he says.

"What the hell do you think this is?" I says; "a stud-farm? You watch out for him. I'm going into conference."

So I go on to the back. I stopped at the glass and smoothed my hair, then I went behind the prescription case, where she was waiting. She is looking at the medicine cabinet, then she looks at me.

"Now madam," I says; "what is your trouble?"

"It's the female trouble," she says, watching me. "I got the money," she says.

"Ah," I says. "Have you got female troubles or do you want female troubles? If so, you come to the right doctor." Them country people. Half the time they dont know what they want, and the balance of the time they cant tell it to you. The clock said twenty past twelve.

"No," she says.

"No which?" I says.

"I aint had it," she says. "That's it." She looked at me. "I got the money," she says.

So I knew what she was talking about.

"Oh," I says. "You got something in your belly you wish you didn't have." She looks at me. "You wish you had a little more or a little less, huh?"

"I got the money," she says. "He said I could git something at the drugstore for hit."

"Who said so?" I says.

"He did," she says, looking at me.

"You dont want to call no names," I says. "The one that put the acorn in your belly? He the one that told you?" She dont say nothing. "You aint married, are you?" I says. I never saw no ring. But like as not, they aint heard yet out there that they use rings.

"I got the money," she says. She showed it to me, tied up in her handkerchief: a ten spot.

"I'll swear you have," I says. "He give it to you?"

"Yes," she says.

"Which one?" I says. She looks at me. "Which one of them give it to you?"

"It aint but one," she says. She looks at me.

"Go on," I says. She dont say nothing. The trouble about the cellar is, it aint but one way out and that's back up the inside stairs. The clock says twenty-five to one. "A pretty girl like you," I says.

She looks at me. She begins to tie the money back up in the handkerchief. "Excuse me a minute," I says. I go around the prescription case. "Did you hear about that fellow sprained his ear?" I says. "After that he couldn't even hear a belch."

"You better get her out from back there before the old man comes," Jody says.

"If you'll stay up there in front where he pays you to stay, he wont catch nobody but me," I says.

He goes on, slow, toward the front. "What you doing to her, Skeet?" he says.

"I cant tell you," I says. "It wouldn't be ethical. You go on up there and watch."

"Say, Skeet," he says.

"Ah, go on," I says. "I aint doing nothing but filling a prescription."

"He may not do nothing about that woman back there, but if he finds you monkeying with that prescription case, he'll kick your stern clean down them cellar stairs."

"My stern has been kicked by bigger bastards than him," I says. "Go back and watch out for him, now."

So I come back. The clock said fifteen to one. She is tying the money in the handkerchief. "You aint the doctor," she says.

"Sure I am," I says. She watches me. "Is it because I look too young, or am I too handsome?" I says. "We used to have a bunch of old water-jointed doctors here," I says; "Jefferson used to be a kind of Old Doctors' Home for them. But business started falling off and folks stayed so well until one day they found out that the women wouldn't never get sick at all. So they run all the old doctors out and got us young good-looking ones that the women would like and then the women begun to get sick again and so business picked up. They're doing that all over the country. Hadn't you heard about it? Maybe it's because you aint never needed a doctor."

"I need one now," she says.

"And you come to the right one," I says. "I already told you that."

"Have you got something for it?" she says. "I got the money."

"Well," I says, "of course a doctor has to learn all sorts of things while he's learning to roll calomel; he cant help himself. But I dont know about your trouble."

"He told me I could get something. He told me I could get it at the drugstore."

"Did he tell you the name of it?" I says. "You better go back and ask him."

She quit looking at me, kind of turning the handkerchief in her hands. "I got to do something," she says.

"How bad do you want to do something?" I says. She looks at me. "Of course, a doctor learns all sorts of things folks dont think he knows. But he aint supposed to tell all he knows. It's against the law."

Up front Jody says, "Skeet."

"Excuse me a minute," I says. I went up front. "Do you see him?" I says.

"Aint you done yet?" he says. "Maybe you better come up here and watch and let me do that consulting."

"Maybe you'll lay a egg," I says. I come back. She is looking at me. "Of course you realise that I could be put in the penitentiary for doing what you want," I says. "I would lose my license and then I'd have to go to work. You realise that?"

"I aint got but ten dollars," she says. "I could bring the rest next month, maybe."

"Pooh," I says, "ten dollars? You see, I cant put no price on my knowledge and skill. Certainly not for no little paltry sawbuck."

She looks at me. She dont even blink. "What you want, then?"

The clock said four to one. So I decided I better get her out. "You guess three times and then I'll show you," I says.

She dont even blink her eyes. "I got to do something," she says. She looks behind her and around, then she looks toward the front. "Gimme the medicine first," she says.

"You mean, you're ready to right now?" I says. "Here?"

"Gimme the medicine first," she says.

So I took a graduated glass and kind of turned my back to her and picked out a bottle that looked all right, because a man that would keep poison setting around in a unlabelled bottle ought to be in jail, anyway. It smelled like turpentine. I poured some into the glass and give it to her. She smelled it, looking at me across the glass.

"Hit smells like turpentine," she says.

"Sure," I says. "That's just the beginning of the treatment. You come back at ten oclock tonight and I'll give you the rest of it and perform the operation."

"Operation?" she says.

"It wont hurt you. You've had the same operation before. Ever hear about the hair of the dog?"

She looks at me. "Will it work?" she says.

"Sure it'll work. If you come back and get it."

So she drunk whatever it was without batting a eye, and went out. I went up front.

"Didn't you get it?" Jody says.

"Get what?" I says.

"Ah, come on," he says. "I aint going to try to beat your time."

"Oh, her," I says. "She just wanted a little medicine. She's got a bad case of dysentery and she's a little ashamed about mentioning it with a stranger there."

It was my night, anyway, so I helped the old bastard check up and I got his hat on him and got him out of the store by eight-thirty. I went as far as the corner with him and watched him until he passed under two street lamps and went on out of sight. Then I come back to the store and waited until nine-thirty and turned out the front lights and locked the door and left just one light burning at the back, and I went back and put some talcum powder into six capsules and kind of cleared up the cellar and then I was all ready.

She come in just at ten, before the clock had done striking. I let her in and she come in, walking fast. I looked out the door, but there wasn't nobody but a boy in overalls sitting on the curb. "You want something?" I says. He never said nothing, just looking at me. I locked the door and turned off the light and went on back. She was waiting. She didn't look at me now.

"Where is it?" she said.

I gave her the box of capsules. She held the box in her hand, looking at the capsules.

"Are you sure it'll work?" she says.

"Sure," I says. "When you take the rest of the treatment."

"Where do I take it?" she says.

"Down in the cellar," I says.

Vardaman

Now it is wider and lighter, but the stores are dark because they have all gone home. The stores are dark, but the lights pass on the windows when we pass. The lights are in the trees around the courthouse. They roost in the trees, but the courthouse is dark. The clock on it looks four ways, because it is not dark. The moon is not dark too. Not very dark. *Darl he went to Jackson is my brother Darl is my brother*   Only it was over that way, shining on the track.

"Let's go that way, Dewey Dell," I say.

"What for?" Dewey Dell says. The track went shining around the window, it red on the track. But she said he would not sell it to the town boys. "But it will be there Christmas," Dewey Dell says. "You'll have to wait till then, when he brings it back."

Darl went to Jackson. Lots of people didn't go to Jackson. Darl is my brother. My brother is going to Jackson

While we walk the lights go around, roosting in the trees. On all sides it is the same. They go around the courthouse and then you cannot see them. But you can see them in the black windows beyond. They have all gone home to bed except me and Dewey Dell.

Going on the train to Jackson. My brother

There is a light in the store, far back. In the window are two big glasses of soda water, red and green. Two men could not drink them. Two mules could not. Two cows could not. *Darl*

A man comes to the door. He looks at Dewey Dell.

"You wait out here," Dewey Dell says.

"Why cant I come in?" I say. "I want to come in, too."

"You wait out here," she says.

"All right," I say.

Dewey Dell goes in.

Darl is my brother. Darl went crazy

The walk is harder than sitting on the ground. He is in the open door. He looks at me. "You want something?" he says. His head is slick. Jewel's head is slick sometimes. Cash's head is not slick. *Darl he went to Jackson my brother Darl* In the street he ate a banana. *Wouldn't you rather have bananas? Dewey Dell said. You wait till Christmas. It'll be there then. Then you can see it. So we are going to have some bananas. We are going to have a bag full, me and Dewey Dell.* He locks the door. Dewey Dell is inside. Then the light winks out.

He went to Jackson. He went crazy and went to Jackson both. Lots of people didn't go crazy. Pa and Cash and Jewel and Dewey Dell and me didn't go crazy. We never did go crazy. We didn't go to Jackson either. Darl

I hear the cow a long time, clopping   on the street. Then she comes into the square. She goes across the square, her head down   clopping   . She lows. There was nothing in the square before she lowed, but it wasn't empty. Now it is empty after she lowed. She goes on,   clopping   . She lows. *My brother is Darl. He went to Jackson on the train. He didn't go on the train to go crazy. He went crazy in our wagon. Darl* She has been in there a long time. And the cow is gone too. A long time. She has been in there longer than the cow was. But not as long as empty. *Darl is my brother. My brother Darl*

Dewey Dell comes out. She looks at me.

"Let's go around that way now," I say.

She looks at me. "It aint going to work," she says. "That son of a bitch."

"What aint going to work, Dewey Dell?"

"I just know it wont," she says. She is not looking at anything. "I just know it."

"Let's go that way," I say.

"We got to go back to the hotel. It's late. We got to slip back in."

"Cant we go by and see, anyway?"

"Hadn't you rather have bananas? Hadn't you rather?"

"All right." *My brother he went crazy and he went to Jackson too. Jackson is further away than crazy*

"It wont work," Dewey Dell says. "I just know it wont."

"What wont work?" I say. *He had to get on the train to go to Jackson. I have not been on the train, but Darl has been on the train. Darl. Darl is my brother. Darl. Darl*

Darl

Darl has gone to Jackson. They put him on the train, laughing, down the long car laughing, the heads turning like the heads of owls when he passed. "What are you laughing at?" I said.

"Yes yes yes yes yes."

Two men put him on the train. They wore mismatched coats, bulging behind over their right hip pockets. Their necks were shaved to a hairline, as though the recent and simultaneous barbers had had a chalk-line like Cash's. "Is it the pistols you're laughing at?" I said. "Why do you laugh? I said. "Is it because you hate the sound of laughing?"

They pulled two seats together so Darl could sit by the window to laugh. One of them sat beside him, the other sat on the seat facing him, riding backward. One of them had to ride backward because the state's money has a face to each backside and a backside to each face, and they are riding on the state's money which is incest. A nickel has a woman on one side and a buffalo on the other; two faces and no back. I dont know what that is. Darl had a little spy-glass he got in France at the war. In it it had a woman and a pig with two backs and no face. I know what that is. "Is that why you are laughing, Darl?"

"Yes yes yes yes yes yes."

The wagon stands on the square, hitched, the mules motionless, the reins wrapped about the seat-spring, the back of the wagon toward the courthouse. It looks no different from a hundred other wagons there; Jewel standing beside it and looking up the street like any other man in town that day, yet there is something different, distinctive. There is about it that unmistakable air of definite and imminent departure that trains have, perhaps due to the fact that Dewey Dell and Vardaman on the seat and Cash on a pallet in the wagon bed are eating bananas from a paper bag. "Is that why you are laughing, Darl?"

Darl is our brother, our brother Darl. Our brother Darl in a cage in Jackson where, his grimed hands lying light in the quiet interstices, looking out he foams.

"Yes yes yes yes yes yes yes yes."

Dewey Dell

When he saw the money I said, "It's not my money, it doesn't belong to me."

"Whose is it, then?"

"It's Cora Tull's money. It's Mrs Tull's. I sold the cakes for it."

"Ten dollars for two cakes?"

"Dont you touch it. It's not mine."

"You never had them cakes. It's a lie. It was them Sunday clothes you had in that package."

"Dont you touch it! If you take it you are a thief."

"My own daughter accuses me of being a thief. My own daughter."

"Pa. Pa."

"I have fed you and sheltered you. I give you love and care, yet my own daughter, the daughter of my dead wife, calls me a thief over her mother's grave."

"Its not mine, I tell you. If it was, God knows you could have it."

"Where did you get ten dollars?"

"Pa. Pa."

"You wont tell me. Did you come by it so shameful you dare not?"

"It's not mine, I tell you. Cant you understand it's not mine?"

"It's not like I wouldn't pay it back. But she calls her own father a thief."

"I cant, I tell you. I tell you it's not my money. God knows you could have it."

"I wouldn't take it. My own born daughter that has et my food for seventeen years, begrudges me the loan of ten dollars."

"It's not mine. I cant."

"Whose is it, then?"

"It was give to me. To buy something with."

"To buy what with?"

"Pa. Pa."

"It's just a loan. God knows, I hate for my blooden children to reproach me. But I give them what was mine without stint. Cheerful I give them, without stint. And now they deny me. Addie. It was lucky for you you died, Addie."

"Pa. Pa."

"God knows it is."

He took the money and went out.

Cash

So when we stopped there to borrow the shovels we heard the graphophone playing in the house, and so when we got done with the shovels pa says, "I reckon I better take them back."

So we went back to the house. "We better take Cash on to Peabody's," Jewel said.

"It wont take but a minute," pa said. He got down from the wagon. The music was not playing now.

"Let Vardaman do it," Jewel said. "He can do it in half the time you can. Or here, you let me—"

"I reckon I better do it," pa says. "Long as it was me that borrowed them."

So we set in the wagon, but the music wasn't playing now. I reckon it's a good thing we aint got ere a one of them. I reckon I wouldn't never get no work done a-tall for listening to it. I dont know if a little music aint about the nicest thing a fellow can have. Seems like when he comes in tired of a night, it aint nothing could rest him like having a little music played and him resting. I have see them that shuts up like a hand-grip, with a handle and all, so a fellow can carry it with him wherever he wants.

"What you reckon he's doing?" Jewel says. "I could a toted them shovels back and forth ten times by now."

"Let him take his time," I said. "He aint as spry as you, remember."

"Why didn't he let me take them back, then? We got to get your leg fixed up so we can start home tomorrow."

"We got plenty of time," I said. "I wonder what them machines costs on the installment."

"Installment of what?" Jewel said. "What you got to buy it with?"

"A fellow cant tell," I said. "I could a bought that one from Suratt for five dollars, I believe."

And so pa come back and we went to Peabody's. While we was there pa said he was going to the barbershop and get a shave. And so that night he said he had some business to tend to, kind of looking away from us while he said it, with his hair combed wet and slick and smelling sweet with perfume, but I said leave him be; I wouldn't mind hearing a little more of that music myself.

And so next morning he was gone again, then he come back and told us to get hitched up and ready to take out and he would meet us and when they was gone he said,

"I dont reckon you got no more money."

"Peabody just give me enough to pay the hotel with," I said. "We dont need nothing else, do we?"

"No," pa said; "no. We dont need nothing." He stood there, not looking at me.

"If it is something we got to have, I reckon maybe Peabody," I said.

"No," he said; "it aint nothing else. You all wait for me at the corner."

So Jewel got the team and come for me and they fixed me a pallet in the wagon and we drove across the square to the corner where pa said, and we was waiting there in the wagon, with Dewey Dell and Vardaman eating bananas, when we see them coming up the street. Pa was coming along with that kind of daresome and hangdog look all at once like when he has been up to something he knows ma aint going to like, carrying a grip in his hand, and Jewel says,

"Who's that?"

Then we see it wasn't the grip that made him look different; it was his face, and Jewel says, "He got them teeth."

It was a fact. It made him look a foot taller, kind of holding his head up, hangdog and proud too, and then we see her behind him, carrying the other grip—a kind of duck-shaped woman all dressed up, with them kind of hard-looking pop eyes like she was daring ere a man to say nothing. And there we set watching them, with Dewey Dell's and Vardaman's mouth half open and half-et bananas in their hands and her coming around from behind pa, looking at us like she dared ere a man. And then I see that the grip she was carrying was one of them little graphophones. It was for a fact, all shut up as pretty as a picture, and everytime a new record would come from the mail order and us setting in the house in the winter, listening to it, I would think what a shame Darl couldn't be to enjoy it too. But it is better so for him. This world is not his world; this life his life.

"It's Cash and Jewel and Vardaman and Dewey Dell," pa says, kind of hangdog and proud too, with his teeth and all, even if he wouldn't look at us. "Meet Mrs Bundren," he says.

1930

Barn Burning

The store in which the Justice of the Peace's court was sitting smelled of cheese. The boy, crouched on his nail keg at the back of the crowded room, knew he smelled cheese, and more: from where he sat he could see the ranked shelves close-packed with the solid, squat, dynamic shapes of tin cans whose labels his stomach read, not from the lettering which meant nothing to his mind but from the scarlet devils and the silver curve of fish—this, the cheese which he knew he smelled and the hermetic meat which his intestines believed he smelled coming in intermittent gusts momentary and brief between the other constant one, the smell and sense just a little of fear because mostly of despair and grief, the old fierce pull of blood. He could not see the table where the Justice sat and before which his father and his father's enemy (*our enemy* he thought in that despair; *ourn! mine and hisn both! He's my father!*) stood, but he could hear them, the two of them that is, because his father had said no word yet:

"But what proof have you, Mr. Harris?"

"I told you. The hog got into my corn. I caught it up and sent it back to him. He had no fence that would hold it. I told him so, warned him. The next time I put the hog in my pen. When he came to get it I gave him enough wire to patch up his pen. The next time I put the hog up and kept it. I rode down to his house and saw the wire I gave him still rolled on to the spool in his yard. I told him he could have the hog when he paid me a dollar pound fee. That evening a nigger came with the dollar and got the hog. He was a strange nigger. He said, 'He say to tell you wood and hay kin burn.' I said, 'What?' 'That whut he say to tell you,' the nigger said. 'Wood and hay kin burn.' That night my barn burned. I got the stock out but I lost the barn."

"Where is the nigger? Have you got him?"

"He was a strange nigger, I tell you. I don't know what became of him."

"But that's not proof. Don't you see that's not proof?"

"Get that boy up here. He knows." For a moment the boy thought too that the man meant his older brother until Harris said, "Not him. The little one. The boy," and, crouching, small for his age, small and wiry like his father, in patched and faded jeans even too small for him, with straight, uncombed, brown hair and eyes gray and wild as storm scud, he saw the men between himself and the table part and become a lane of grim faces, at the end of which he saw the Justice, a shabby, collarless, graying man in spectacles, beckoning him. He felt no floor under his bare feet; he seemed to walk beneath the palpable weight of the grim turning faces. His father, stiff in his black Sunday coat donned not for the trial but for the moving, did not even look at him. *He aims for me to lie,* he thought, again with that frantic grief and despair. *And I will have to do hit.*

"What's your name, boy?" the Justice said.

"Colonel Sartoris Snopes,"[1] the boy whispered.

"Hey?" the Justice said. "Talk louder. Colonel Sartoris? I reckon anybody named for Colonel Sartoris in this country can't help but tell the truth, can they?" The boy said nothing. *Enemy! Enemy!* he thought; for a moment he could not even see, could not see that the Justice's face was kindly nor discern that his voice was troubled when he spoke to the man named Harris: "Do you want me to question this boy?" But he could hear, and during those subsequent long seconds while there was absolutely no sound in the crowded little room save that of quiet and intent breathing it was as if he had swung outward at the end of a grape vine, over a ravine, and at the top of the swing had been caught in a prolonged instant of mesmerized gravity, weightless in time.

"No!" Harris said violently, explosively. "Damnation! Send him out of here!" Now time, the fluid world, rushed beneath him again, the voices com-

---

1. The boy is named for Colonel Sartoris, a leading citizen of Jefferson (the fictional town that Faulkner based on his hometown of Oxford, Mississippi) and officer in the Confederate Army. The Snopeses are a poor white family from the same area. Both families appear in other works by Faulkner.

ing to him again through the smell of cheese and sealed meat, the fear and despair and the old grief of blood:

"This case is closed. I can't find against you, Snopes, but I can give you advice. Leave this country and don't come back to it."

His father spoke for the first time, his voice cold and harsh, level, without emphasis: "I aim to. I don't figure to stay in a country among people who . . ." he said something unprintable and vile, addressed to no one.

"That'll do," the Justice said. "Take your wagon and get out of this country before dark. Case dismissed."

His father turned, and he followed the stiff black coat, the wiry figure walking a little stiffly from where a Confederate provost's man's musket ball had taken him in the heel on a stolen horse thirty years ago, followed the two backs now, since his older brother had appeared from somewhere in the crowd, no taller than the father but thicker, chewing tobacco steadily, between the two lines of grim-faced men and out of the store and across the worn gallery and down the sagging steps and among the dogs and half-grown boys in the mild May dust, where as he passed a voice hissed:

"Barn burner!"

Again he could not see, whirling; there was a face in a red haze, moonlike, bigger than the full moon, the owner of it half again his size, he leaping in the red haze toward the face, feeling no blow, feeling no shock when his head struck the earth, scrabbling up and leaping again, feeling no blow this time either and tasting no blood, scrabbling up to see the other boy in full flight and himself already leaping into pursuit as his father's hand jerked him back, the harsh, cold voice speaking above him: "Go get in the wagon."

It stood in a grove of locusts and mulberries across the road. His two hulking sisters in their Sunday dresses and his mother and her sister in calico and sunbonnets were already in it, sitting on and among the sorry residue of the dozen and more movings which even the boy could remember—the battered stove, the broken beds and chairs, the clock inlaid with mother-of-pearl, which would not run, stopped at some fourteen minutes past two o'clock of a dead and forgotten day and time, which had been his mother's dowry. She was crying, though when she saw him she drew her sleeve across her face and began to descend from the wagon. "Get back," the father said.

"He's hurt. I got to get some water and wash his . . ."

"Get back in the wagon," his father said. He got in too, over the tail-gate. His father mounted to the seat where the older brother already sat and struck the gaunt mules two savage blows with the peeled willow, but without heat. It was not even sadistic; it was exactly that same quality which in later years would cause his descendants to over-run the engine before putting a motor car into motion, striking and reining back in the same movement. The wagon went on, the store with its quiet crowd of grimly watching men dropped behind; a curve in the road hid it. *Forever* he thought. *Maybe he's done satisfied now, now that he has . . .* stopping himself, not to say it aloud even to himself. His mother's hand touched his shoulder.

"Does hit hurt?" she said.

"Naw," he said. "Hit don't hurt. Lemme be."

"Can't you wipe some of the blood off before hit dries?"

"I'll wash to-night," he said. "Lemme be, I tell you."

The wagon went on. He did not know where they were going. None of them ever did or ever asked, because it was always somewhere, always a house of sorts waiting for them a day or two days or even three days away. Likely his father had already arranged to make a crop on another farm before he . . . Again he had to stop himself. He (the father) always did. There was something about his wolflike independence and even courage when the advantage was at least neutral which impressed strangers, as if they got from his latent ravening ferocity not so much a sense of dependability as a feeling that his ferocious conviction in the rightness of his own actions would be of advantage to all whose interest lay with his.

That night they camped, in a grove of oaks and beeches where a spring ran. The nights were still cool and they had a fire against it, of a rail lifted from a nearby fence and cut into lengths—a small fire, neat, niggard almost, a shrewd fire; such fires were his father's habit and custom always, even in freezing weather. Older, the boy might have remarked this and wondered why not a big one; why should not a man who had not only seen the waste and extravagance of war, but who had in his blood an inherent voracious prodigality with material not his own, have burned everything in sight? Then he might have gone a step farther and thought that that was the reason: that niggard blaze was the living fruit of nights passed during those four years in the woods hiding from all men, blue or gray, with his strings of horses (captured horses, he called them). And older still, he might have divined the true reason: that the element of fire spoke to some deep mainspring of his father's being, as the element of steel or of powder spoke to other men, as the one weapon for the preservation of integrity, else breath were not worth the breathing, and hence to be regarded with respect and used with discretion.

But he did not think this now and he had seen those same niggard blazes all his life. He merely ate his supper beside it and was already half asleep over his iron plate when his father called him, and once more he followed the stiff back, the stiff and ruthless limp, up the slope and on to the starlit road where, turning, he could see his father against the stars but without face or depth— a shape black, flat, and bloodless as though cut from tin in the iron folds of the frockcoat which had not been made for him, the voice harsh like tin and without heat like tin:

"You were fixing to tell them. You would have told him." He didn't answer. His father struck him with the flat of his hand on the side of the head, hard but without heat, exactly as he had struck the two mules at the store, exactly as he would strike either of them with any stick in order to kill a horse fly, his voice still without heat or anger: "You're getting to be a man. You got to learn. You got to learn to stick to your own blood or you ain't going to have any blood to stick to you. Do you think either of them, any man there this morning, would? Don't you know all they wanted was a chance to get at me because they knew I had them beat? Eh?" Later, twenty years later, he was to tell himself, "If I had said they wanted only truth, justice, he would have hit me again." But now he said nothing. He was not crying. He just stood there. "Answer me," his father said.

"Yes," he whispered. His father turned.

"Get on to bed. We'll be there to-morrow."

To-morrow they were there. In the early afternoon the wagon stopped before a paintless two-room house identical almost with the dozen others it had stopped before even in the boy's ten years, and again, as on the other dozen occasions, his mother and aunt got down and began to unload the wagon, although his two sisters and his father and brother had not moved.

"Likely hit ain't fitten for hawgs," one of the sisters said.

"Nevertheless, fit it will and you'll hog it and like it," his father said. "Get out of them chairs and help your Ma unload."

The two sisters got down, big, bovine, in a flutter of cheap ribbons; one of them drew from the jumbled wagon bed a battered lantern, the other a worn broom. His father handed the reins to the older son and began to climb stiffly over the wheel. "When they get unloaded, take the team to the barn and feed them." Then he said, and at first the boy thought he was still speaking to his brother: "Come with me."

"Me?" he said.

"Yes," his father said. "You."

"Abner," his mother said. His father paused and looked back—the harsh level stare beneath the shaggy, graying, irascible brows.

"I reckon I'll have a word with the man that aims to begin to-morrow owning me body and soul for the next eight months."

They went back up the road. A week ago—or before last night, that is—he would have asked where they were going, but not now. His father had struck him before last night but never before had he paused afterward to explain why; it was as if the blow and the following calm, outrageous voice still rang, repercussed, divulging nothing to him save the terrible handicap of being young, the light weight of his few years, just heavy enough to prevent his soaring free of the world as it seemed to be ordered but not heavy enough to keep him footed solid in it, to resist it and try to change the course of its events.

Presently he could see the grove of oaks and cedars and the other flowering trees and shrubs where the house would be, though not the house yet. They walked beside a fence massed with honeysuckle and Cherokee roses and came to a gate swinging open between two brick pillars, and now, beyond a sweep of drive, he saw the house for the first time and at that instant he forgot his father and the terror and despair both, and even when he remembered his father again (who had not stopped) the terror and despair did not return. Because, for all the twelve movings, they had sojourned until now in a poor country, a land of small farms and fields and houses, and he had never seen a house like this before. *Hit's big as a courthouse* he thought quietly, with a surge of peace and joy whose reason he could not have thought into words, being too young for that: *They are safe from him. People whose lives are a part of this peace and dignity are beyond his touch, he no more to them than a buzzing wasp: capable of stinging for a little moment but that's all; the spell of this peace and dignity rendering even the barns and stable and cribs which belong to it impervious to the puny flames he might contrive . . .* this, the peace and joy, ebbing for an instant as he looked again at the stiff black back, the stiff and implacable limp of the figure which was not dwarfed by the house, for the reason that it had never looked big anywhere and which now, against the serene columned backdrop, had more than ever that impervious quality of something cut ruthlessly from tin, depthless, as though, sidewise to the sun, it would cast no shadow. Watching him, the boy remarked the absolutely undeviating course which his father held and saw the stiff foot come squarely down in a pile of fresh droppings where a horse had stood in the drive and which his father could have avoided by a simple change of stride. But it ebbed only for a moment, though he could not have thought this into words either, walking on in the spell of the house, which he could even want but without envy, without sorrow, certainly never with that ravening and jealous rage which unknown to him walked in the ironlike black coat before him: *Maybe he will feel it too. Maybe it will even change him now from what maybe he couldn't help but be.*

They crossed the portico. Now he could hear his father's stiff foot as it came down on the boards with clocklike finality, a sound out of all proportion to the displacement of the body it bore and which was not dwarfed either by the white door before it, as though it had attained to a sort of vicious and ravening minimum not to be dwarfed by anything—the flat, wide, black hat, the formal coat of broadcloth which had once been black but which had now that friction-glazed greenish cast of the bodies of old house flies, the lifted sleeve which was too large, the lifted hand like a curled claw. The door opened so promptly that the boy knew the Negro must have been watching them all the time, an old man with neat grizzled hair, in a linen jacket, who stood barring the door with his body, saying, "Wipe yo foots, white man, fo you come in here. Major ain't home nohow."

"Get out of my way, nigger," his father said, without heat too, flinging the door back and the Negro also and entering, his hat still on his head. And now the boy saw the prints of the stiff foot on the doorjamb and saw them appear on the pale rug behind the machinelike deliberation of the foot which seemed to bear (or transmit) twice the weight which the body compassed. The Negro was shouting "Miss Lula! Miss Lula!" somewhere behind them, then the boy, deluged as though by a warm wave by a suave turn of carpeted stair and a pendant glitter of chandeliers and a mute gleam of gold frames, heard the swift feet and saw her too, a lady—perhaps he had never seen her like before either—in a gray, smooth gown with lace at the throat and an apron tied at the waist and the sleeves turned back, wiping cake or biscuit dough from her hands with a towel as she came up the hall, looking not at his father at all but at the tracks on the blond rug with an expression of incredulous amazement.

"I tried," the Negro cried. "I tole him to . . ."

"Will you please go away?" she said in a shaking voice. "Major de Spain is not at home. Will you please go away?"

His father had not spoken again. He did not speak again. He did not even look at her. He just stood stiff in the center of the rug, in his hat, the shaggy iron-gray brows twitching slightly above the pebble-colored eyes as he appeared to examine the house with brief deliberation. Then with the same deliberation he turned; the boy watched him pivot on the good leg and saw the stiff foot drag round the arc of the turning, leaving a final long and fading smear. His father never looked at it, he never once looked down at the rug. The Negro held the door. It closed behind them, upon the hysteric and indistinguishable woman-wail. His father stopped at the top of the steps and scraped his boot clean on the edge of it. At the gate he stopped again. He stood for a moment, planted stiffly on the stiff foot, looking back at the house. "Pretty and white, ain't it?" he said. "That's sweat. Nigger sweat. Maybe it ain't white enough yet to suit him. Maybe he wants to mix some white sweat with it."

Two hours later the boy was chopping wood behind the house within which his mother and aunt and the two sisters (the mother and aunt, not the two girls, he knew that; even at this distance and muffled by walls the flat loud voices of the two girls emanated an incorrigible idle inertia) were setting up the stove to prepare a meal, when he heard the hooves and saw the linen-clad man on a fine sorrel mare, whom he recognized even before he saw the rolled rug in front of the Negro youth following on a fat bay carriage horse—a suffused, angry face vanishing, still at full gallop, beyond the corner of the house where his father and brother were sitting in the two tilted chairs; and a moment later, almost before he could have put the axe down, he heard the hooves again and watched the sorrel mare go back out of the yard, already galloping again. Then his father began to shout one of the sisters' names, who presently emerged backward from the kitchen door dragging the rolled rug along the ground by one end while the other sister walked behind it.

"If you ain't going to tote, go on and set up the wash pot," the first said.

"You, Sarty!" the second shouted. "Set up the wash pot!" His father appeared at the door, framed against that shabbiness, as he had been against that other bland perfection, impervious to either, the mother's anxious face at his shoulder.

"Go on," the father said. "Pick it up." The two sisters stooped, broad, lethargic; stooping, they presented an incredible expanse of pale cloth and a flutter of tawdry ribbons.

"If I thought enough of a rug to have to git hit all the way from France I wouldn't keep hit where folks coming in would have to tromp on hit," the first said. They raised the rug.

"Abner," the mother said. "Let me do it."

"You go back and git dinner," his father said. "I'll tend to this."

From the woodpile through the rest of the afternoon the boy watched them, the rug spread flat in the dust beside the bubbling wash-pot, the two sisters stooping over it with that profound and lethargic reluctance, while the father stood over them in turn, implacable and grim, driving them though never raising his voice again. He could smell the harsh homemade lye they were using; he saw his mother come to the door once and look toward them with an expression not anxious now but very like despair; he saw his father turn, and he fell to with the axe and saw from the corner of his eye his father raise from the ground a flattish fragment of field stone and examine it and return to the pot, and this time his mother actually spoke: "Abner. Abner. Please don't. Please, Abner."

Then he was done too. It was dusk; the whippoorwills had already begun. He could smell coffee from the room where they would presently eat the cold food remaining from the mid-afternoon meal, though when he entered the house he realized they were having coffee again probably because there was a fire on the hearth, before which the rug now lay spread over the backs of the two chairs. The tracks of his father's foot were gone. Where they had been were now long, water-cloudy scoriations resembling the sporadic course of a lilliputian mowing machine.

It still hung there while they ate the cold food and then went to bed, scattered without order or claim up and down the two rooms, his mother in one bed, where his father would later lie, the older brother in the other, himself, the aunt, and the two sisters on pallets on the floor. But his father was not in bed yet. The last thing the boy remembered was the depthless, harsh silhouette of the hat and coat bending over the rug and it seemed to him that he had not even closed his eyes when the silhouette was standing over him, the fire almost dead behind it, the stiff foot prodding him awake. "Catch up the mule," his father said.

When he returned with the mule his father was standing in the black door, the rolled rug over his shoulder. "Ain't you going to ride?" he said.

"No. Give me your foot."

He bent his knee into his father's hand, the wiry, surprising power flowed smoothly, rising, he rising with it, on to the mule's bare back (they had owned a saddle once; the boy could remember it though not when or where) and with the same effortlessness his father swung the rug up in front of him. Now in the starlight they retraced the afternoon's path, up the dusty road rife with honeysuckle, through the gate and up the black tunnel of the drive to the lightless house, where he sat on the mule and felt the rough warp of the rug drag across his thighs and vanish.

"Don't you want me to help?" he whispered. His father did not answer and now he heard again that stiff foot striking the hollow portico with that wooden and clocklike deliberation, that outrageous overstatement of the weight it carried. The rug, hunched, not flung (the boy could tell that even in the darkness) from his father's shoulder, struck the angle of wall and floor with a sound unbelievably loud, thunderous, then the foot again, unhurried and enormous; a light came on in the house and the boy sat, tense, breathing steadily and quietly and just a little fast, though the foot itself did not increase its beat at all, descending the steps now; now the boy could see him.

"Don't you want to ride now?" he whispered. "We kin both ride now," the light within the house altering now, flaring up and sinking. *He's coming down the stairs now,* he thought. He had already ridden the mule up beside the horse block; presently his father was up behind him and he doubled the reins over and slashed the mule across the neck, but before the animal could begin to trot the hard, thin arm came round him, the hard, knotted hand jerking the mule back to a walk.

In the first red rays of the sun they were in the lot, putting plow gear on the mules. This time the sorrel mare was in the lot before he heard it at all, the rider collarless and even bareheaded, trembling, speaking in a shaking voice as the woman in the house had done, his father merely looking up once before stooping again to the hame he was buckling, so that the man on the mare spoke to his stooping back:

"You must realize you have ruined that rug. Wasn't there anybody here, any of your women . . ." he ceased, shaking, the boy watching him, the older brother leaning now in the stable door, chewing, blinking slowly and steadily at nothing apparently. "It cost a hundred dollars. But you never had a hundred dollars. You never will. So I'm going to charge you twenty bushels of corn against your crop. I'll add it in your contract and when you come to the commissary you can sign it. That won't keep Mrs. de Spain quiet but maybe it will teach you to wipe your feet off before you enter her house again."

Then he was gone. The boy looked at his father, who still had not spoken or even looked up again, who was now adjusting the logger-head in the hame.

"Pap," he said. His father looked at him—the inscrutable face, the shaggy brows beneath which the gray eyes glinted coldly. Suddenly the boy went toward him, fast, stopping as suddenly. "You done the best you could!" he cried. "If he wanted hit done different why didn't he wait and tell you how? He won't git no twenty bushels! He won't git none! We'll gether hit and hide hit! I kin watch . . ."

"Did you put the cutter back in that straight stock like I told you?"

"No, sir," he said.

"Then go do it."

That was Wednesday. During the rest of that week he worked steadily, at what was within his scope and some which was beyond it, with an industry that did not need to be driven nor even commanded twice; he had this from his mother, with the difference that some at least of what he did he liked to do, such as splitting wood with the half-size axe which his mother and aunt had earned, or saved money somehow, to present him with at Christmas. In company with the two older women (and on one afternoon, even one of the sisters), he built pens for the shoat and the cow which were a part of his father's contract with the landlord, and one afternoon, his father being absent, gone somewhere on one of the mules, he went to the field.

They were running a middle buster now, his brother holding the plow straight while he handled the reins, and walking beside the straining mule, the rich black soil shearing cool and damp against his bare ankles, he thought *Maybe this is the end of it. Maybe even that twenty bushels that seems hard to have to pay for just a rug will be a cheap price for him to stop forever and always from being what he used to be;* thinking, dreaming now, so that his brother had to speak sharply to him to mind the mule: *Maybe he even won't collect the twenty bushels. Maybe it will all add up and balance and vanish—corn, rug, fire; the terror and grief, the being pulled two ways like between two teams of horses—gone, done with for ever and ever.*

Then it was Saturday; he looked up from beneath the mule he was harnessing and saw his father in the black coat and hat. "Not that," his father said. "The wagon gear." And then, two hours later, sitting in the wagon bed behind his father and brother on the seat, the wagon accomplished a final curve, and he saw the weathered paintless store with its tattered tobacco- and patent-medicine posters and the tethered wagons and saddle animals below the gallery. He mounted the gnawed steps behind his father and brother, and there again was the lane of quiet, watching faces for the three of them to walk through. He saw the man in spectacles sitting at the plank table and he did not need to be told this was a Justice of the Peace; he sent one glare of fierce, exultant, partisan defiance at the man in collar and cravat now, whom he had seen but twice before in his life, and that on a galloping horse, who now wore on his face an expression not of rage but of amazed unbelief which the boy could not have known was at the incredible circumstance of being sued by one of his own tenants, and came and stood against his father and cried at the Justice: "He ain't done it! He ain't burnt . . ."

"Go back to the wagon," his father said.

"Burnt?" the Justice said. "Do I understand this rug was burned too?"

"Does anybody here claim it was?" his father said. "Go back to the wagon." But he did not, he merely retreated to the rear of the room, crowded as that other had been, but not to sit down this time, instead, to stand pressing among the motionless bodies, listening to the voices:

"And you claim twenty bushels of corn is too high for the damage you did to the rug?"

"He brought the rug to me and said he wanted the tracks washed out of it. I washed the tracks out and took the rug back to him."

"But you didn't carry the rug back to him in the same condition it was in before you made the tracks on it."

His father did not answer, and now for perhaps half a minute there was no sound at all save that of breathing, the faint, steady suspiration of complete and intent listening.

"You decline to answer that, Mr. Snopes?" Again his father did not answer. "I'm going to find against you, Mr. Snopes. I'm going to find that you were responsible for the injury to Major de Spain's rug and hold you liable for it. But twenty bushels of corn seems a little high for a man in your circumstances to have to pay. Major de Spain claims it cost a hundred dollars. October corn will be worth about fifty cents. I figure that if Major de Spain can stand a ninety-five-dollar loss on something he paid cash for, you can stand a five-dollar loss you haven't earned yet. I hold you in damages to Major de Spain to the amount of ten bushels of corn over and above your contract with him, to be paid to him out of your crop at gathering time. Court adjourned."

It had taken no time hardly, the morning was but half begun. He thought they would return home and perhaps back to the field, since they were late, far behind all other farmers. But instead his father passed on behind the wagon, merely indicating with his hand for the older brother to follow with it, and crossed the road toward the blacksmith shop opposite, pressing on after his father, overtaking him, speaking, whispering up at the harsh, calm face beneath the weathered hat: "He won't git no ten bushels neither. He won't git one. We'll . . ." until his father glanced for an instant down at him, the face absolutely calm, the grizzled eyebrows tangled above the cold eyes, the voice almost pleasant, almost gentle:

"You think so? Well, we'll wait till October anyway."

The matter of the wagon—the setting of a spoke or two and the tightening of the tires—did not take long either, the business of the tires accomplished by driving the wagon into the spring branch behind the shop and letting it stand there, the mules nuzzling into the water from time to time, and the boy on the seat with the idle reins, looking up the slope and through the sooty tunnel of the shed where the slow hammer rang and where his father sat on an upended cypress bolt, easily, either talking or listening, still sitting there when the boy brought the dripping wagon up out of the branch and halted it before the door.

"Take them on to the shade and hitch," his father said. He did so and returned. His father and the smith and a third man squatting on his heels inside the door were talking, about crops and animals; the boy, squatting too in the ammoniac dust and hoof-parings and scales of rust, heard his father tell a long and unhurried story out of the time before the birth of the older brother even when he had been a professional horsetrader. And then his father came up beside him where he stood before a tattered last year's circus poster on the other side of the store, gazing rapt and quiet at the scarlet horses, the incredible poisings and convolutions of tulle and tights and the painted leers of comedians, and said "It's time to eat."

But not at home. Squatting beside his brother against the front wall, he watched his father emerge from the store and produce from a paper sack a segment of cheese and divide it carefully and deliberately into three with his pocket knife and produce crackers from the same sack. They all three squatted on the gallery and ate, slowly, without talking; then in the store again, they drank from a tin dipper tepid water smelling of the cedar bucket and of living beech trees. And still they did not go home. It was a horse lot this time, a tall rail fence upon and along which men stood and sat and out of which one by one horses were led, to be walked and trotted and then cantered back and forth along the road while the slow swapping and buying went on and the sun began to slant westward, they—the three of them—watching and listening, the older brother with his muddy eyes and his steady, inevitable tobacco, the father commenting now and then on certain of the animals, to no one in particular.

It was after sundown when they reached home. They ate supper by lamplight, then, sitting on the doorstep, the boy watched the night fully accomplish, listening to the whippoorwills and the frogs, when he heard his mother's voice: "Abner! No! No! Oh, God. Oh, God. Abner!" and he rose, whirled, and saw the altered light through the door where a candle stub now burned in a bottle neck on the table and his father, still in the hat and coat, at once formal and burlesque as though dressed carefully for some shabby and ceremonial violence, emptying the reservoir of the lamp back into the five-gallon kerosene can from which it had been filled, while the mother tugged at his arm until he shifted the lamp to the other hand and flung her back, not savagely or viciously, just hard, into the wall, her hands flung out against the wall for balance, her mouth open and in her face the same quality of hopeless despair as had been in her voice. Then his father saw him standing in the door.

"Go to the barn and get that can of oil we were oiling the wagon with," he said. The boy did not move. Then he could speak.

"What . . ." he cried. "What are you . . ."

"Go get that oil," his father said. "Go."

Then he was moving, running, outside the house, toward the stable: this is the old habit, the old blood which he had not been permitted to choose for himself, which had been bequeathed him willy nilly and which had run for so long (and who knew where, battening on what of outrage and savagery and lust) before it came to him. *I could keep on,* he thought. *I could run on and on and never look back, never need to see his face again. Only I can't. I can't,* the rusted can in his hand now, the liquid sploshing in it as he ran back to the house and into it, into the sound of his mother's weeping in the next room, and handed the can to his father.

"Ain't you going to even send a nigger?" he cried. "At least you sent a nigger before!"

This time his father didn't strike him. The hand came even faster than the blow had, the same hand which had set the can on the table with almost excruciating care flashing from the can toward him too quick for him to follow it, gripping him by the back of his shirt and on to tiptoe before he had seen it quit the can, the face stooping at him in breathless and frozen ferocity, the cold, dead voice speaking over him to the older brother who leaned against the table, chewing with that steady, curious, sidewise motion of cows:

"Empty the can into the big one and go on. I'll catch up with you."

"Better tie him up to the bedpost," the brother said.

"Do like I told you," the father said. Then the boy was moving, his bunched shirt and the hard, bony hand between his shoulder-blades, his toes just touching the floor, across the room and into the other one, past the sisters sitting with spread heavy thighs in the two chairs over the cold hearth, and to where his mother and aunt sat side by side on the bed, the aunt's arms about his mother's shoulders.

"Hold him," the father said. The aunt made a startled movement. "Not you," the father said. "Lennie. Take hold of him. I want to see you do it." His mother took him by the wrist. "You'll hold him better than that. If he gets loose don't you know what he is going to do? He will go up yonder." He jerked his head toward the road. "Maybe I'd better tie him."

"I'll hold him," his mother whispered.

"See you do then." Then his father was gone, the stiff foot heavy and measured upon the boards, ceasing at last.

Then he began to struggle. His mother caught him in both arms, he jerking and wrenching at them. He would be stronger in the end, he knew that. But he had no time to wait for it. "Lemme go!" he cried. "I don't want to have to hit you!"

"Let him go!" the aunt said. "If he don't go, before God, I am going there myself!"

"Don't you see I can't!" his mother cried. "Sarty! Sarty! No! No! Help me, Lizzie!"

Then he was free. His aunt grasped at him but it was too late. He whirled, running, his mother stumbled forward on to her knees behind him, crying to the nearer sister: "Catch him, Net! Catch him!" But that was too late too, the sister (the sisters were twins, born at the same time, yet either of them now gave the impression of being, encompassing as much living meat and volume and weight as any other two of the family) not yet having begun to rise from the chair, her head, face, alone merely turned, presenting to him in the flying instant an astonishing expanse of young female features untroubled by any surprise even, wearing only an expression of bovine interest. Then he was out of the room, out of the house, in the mild dust of the starlit road and the heavy rifeness of honeysuckle, the pale ribbon unspooling with terrific slowness under his running feet, reaching the gate at last and turning in, running, his heart and lungs drumming, on up the drive toward the lighted house, the lighted door. He did not knock, he burst in, sobbing for breath, incapable for the moment of speech; he saw the astonished face of the Negro in the linen jacket without knowing when the Negro had appeared.

"De Spain!" he cried, panted. "Where's . . ." then he saw the white man too emerging from a white door down the hall. "Barn!" he cried. "Barn!"

"What?" the white man said. "Barn?"

"Yes!" the boy cried. "Barn!"

"Catch him!" the white man shouted.

But it was too late this time too. The Negro grasped his shirt, but the entire sleeve, rotten with washing, carried away, and he was out that door too and in the drive again, and had actually never ceased to run even while he was screaming into the white man's face.

Behind him the white man was shouting, "My horse! Fetch my horse!" and he thought for an instant of cutting across the park and climbing the fence into the road, but he did not know the park nor how high the vine-massed fence might be and he dared not risk it. So he ran on down the drive, blood and breath roaring; presently he was in the road again though he could not see it. He could not hear either: the galloping mare was almost upon him before he heard her, and even then he held his course, as if the very urgency of his wild grief and need must in a moment more find him wings, waiting until the ultimate instant to hurl himself aside and into the weed-choked roadside ditch as the horse thundered past and on, for an instant in furious silhouette against the stars, the tranquil early summer night sky which, even before the shape of the horse and rider vanished, stained abruptly and violently upward: a long, swirling roar incredible and soundless, blotting the stars, and he springing up and into the road again, running again, knowing it was too late yet still running even after he heard the shot and, an instant later, two shots, pausing now without knowing he had ceased to run, crying "Pap! Pap!", running again before he knew he had begun to run, stumbling, tripping over something and scrabbling up again without ceasing to run, looking backward over his shoulder at the glare as he got up, running on among the invisible trees, panting, sobbing, "Father! Father!"

At midnight he was sitting on the crest of a hill. He did not know it was midnight and he did not know how far he had come. But there was no glare behind him now and he sat now, his back toward what he had called home for four days anyhow, his face toward the dark woods which he would enter when breath was strong again, small, shaking steadily in the chill darkness, hugging himself into the remainder of his thin, rotten shirt, the grief and despair now no longer terror and fear but just grief and despair. *Father. My father*, he thought. "He was brave!" he cried suddenly, aloud but not loud, no more than a whisper: "He was! He was in the war! He was in Colonel Sartoris' cav'ry!" not knowing that his father had gone to that war a private in the fine old European sense, wearing no uniform, admitting the authority of and giving fidelity to no man or army or flag, going to war as Malbrouck[2] himself did: for booty—it meant nothing and less than nothing to him if it were enemy booty or his own.

The slow constellations wheeled on. It would be dawn and then sun-up after a while and he would be hungry. But that would be to-morrow and now he was only cold, and walking would cure that. His breathing was easier now and he decided to get up and go on, and then he found that he had been asleep because he knew it was almost dawn, the night almost over. He could tell that from the whippoorwills. They were everywhere now among the dark trees below him, constant and inflectioned and ceaseless, so that, as the instant for giving over to the day birds drew nearer and nearer, there was no interval at all between them. He got up. He was a little stiff, but walking would cure that too as it would the cold, and soon there would be the sun. He went on down the hill, toward the dark woods within which the liquid silver voices of the birds called unceasing—the rapid and urgent beating of the urgent and quiring heart of the late spring night. He did not look back.

1938

2. Figure in an 18th-century French ballad, "Malbrouck Has Gone to the War," popularly identified with John Churchill, first duke of Marlborough (1650–1722), who rose through the ranks from private to become a famous commander. Despite his military genius, he was often accused of greed and disloyalty.

HART CRANE
1899–1932

Before his suicide at the age of thirty-two, Hart Crane led a life of extremes: he wrote poetry of frequently ecstatic intensity, drank uncontrollably, had bitterly ambivalent relations with his quarreling parents; he relished the comparative erotic freedom of post–World War I Greenwich Village while enduring his literary friends' disapproval of his homosexuality. Born and raised in Ohio, Crane went to New York City in 1917, ostensibly to prepare for college but in fact to investigate the possibility of a literary career. Returning to Cleveland for four years (1919–23), he tried unsuccessfully to enter business as a means of financing an after-hours literary life. During these years he read widely and developed a large circle of intellectual friends and correspondents. He also published some of the poems that made his early reputation: "My Grand-mother's Love Letters" in 1920, "Chaplinesque" in 1921, and "For the Marriage of Faustus and Helen" in 1922. He also began work on the love sequence *Voyages.* By 1923, believing himself ready to succeed as a writer, he moved back to New York City.

His most productive years came between 1923 and 1927. He completed *Voyages* in 1924, published his first collection, *White Buildings,* in 1926, and composed ten of the fifteen poems that were to make up *The Bridge* in 1926. He held occasional jobs, but received most of his support from his parents, friends, and above all from the patronage of a banker, Otto Kahn. Crane defined himself as a follower of Walt Whit-man in the visionary, prophetic, affirmative American tradition, aiming at nothing less than to master the techniques of modernism while reversing its direction—to make it positive, celebratory, and deeply meshed with contemporary American life without sacrificing technical complexity or richness. For him as for the somewhat older William Carlos Williams, Eliot's *The Waste Land* was both threat and model. That poem could become an "absolute impasse," he wrote, unless one could "go *through*" it to a different goal," leaving its negations behind. This was the task he attempted in *The Bridge.*

Crane's practice centered on metaphor—the device that, in his view, represented the difference between poetry and expository prose. He believed that metaphor had preceded logic in the development of human thought and that it still remained the pri-mary mode in which human knowledge was acquired and through which experience was connected to mind. The center of *The Bridge,* for example, is the Brooklyn Bridge—a tangible object transformed metaphorically into the sign of connection, technology, America, history, and the future. The poem, published in 1930, was not particularly well received by the critics; this was a great disappointment to Crane, and even though *Poetry* magazine awarded it a prize and the Guggenheim Foundation gave him a fellowship in the same year, he was perplexed about his future. In Mexico he completed work for a third book, *Key West,* but on the return trip to New York City he jumped overboard and drowned.

The Bridge is a visionary poem made up of fifteen individual sections of varying lengths. It encapsulates a heroic quest, at once personal and epic, to find and enun-ciate "America." Like Walt Whitman's "Song of the Open Road," which also focused on a symbol of expansion and dynamism, *The Bridge* moves westward in imagination from Brooklyn to California. It also goes back into the American past, dwelling on his-torical or legendary figures like Columbus, Pocahontas, and Rip Van Winkle. It moves upward under the guidance of Whitman; down in "The Tunnel" it meets the wander-ing spirit of Edgar Allan Poe. The material bridge stands at the center of all this motion and stands, finally, for the poem and poetry itself. The separate lyrics making up *The Bridge* are arranged like music, with recurring, modulated themes rather than a nar-rative or an expository line. As in most modernist poems, the verse is open and varied, the syntax complicated and often ambiguous, the references often dependent on a per-sonal, sometimes inaccessible train of thought. Like his model Whitman, Crane wrote from the paradoxical, conflicted position of the outsider claiming to speak from and for the very center of America.

The text of the poems included here is that of *Complete Poems of Hart Crane*, edited by Marc Simon (1993).

Chaplinesque[1]

We make our meek adjustments,
Contented with such random consolations
As the wind deposits
In slithered and too ample pockets.

For we can still love the world, who find   5
A famished kitten on the step, and know
Recesses for it from the fury of the street,
Or warm torn elbow coverts.

We will sidestep, and to the final smirk
Dally the doom of that inevitable thumb   10
That slowly chafes its puckered index toward us,
Facing the dull squint with what innocence
And what surprise!

And yet these fine collapses are not lies
More than the pirouettes of any pliant cane;   15
Our obsequies[2] are, in a way, no enterprise.
We can evade you, and all else but the heart:
What blame to us if the heart live on.

The game enforces smirks; but we have seen
The moon in lonely alleys make   20
A grail of laughter of an empty ash can,
And through all sound of gaiety and quest
Have heard a kitten in the wilderness.

                                                                1921, 1926

At Melville's Tomb[1]

Often beneath the wave, wide from this ledge
The dice of drowned men's bones he saw bequeath

---

1. Crane wrote of seeing Charlie Chaplin's film *The Kid* (1921) and said that he aimed "to put in words some of the Chaplin pantomime, so beautiful, and so full of eloquence, and so modern." The film "made me feel myself, as a poet, as being 'in the same boat' with him," Crane wrote.
2. In the double sense of "funeral rites" and "obsequiousness."

1. This poem was published in *Poetry* magazine only after Crane provided the editor, Harriet Monroe, with a detailed explanation of its images. His letter, and Monroe's inquiries and comments, were published with the poem. Crane's detailed comments in the letter are incorporated in the notes to the poem. Herman Melville (1819–1891), American author.

An embassy. Their numbers as he watched,
Beat on the dusty shore and were obscured.[2]

And wrecks passed without sound of bells,   5
The calyx of death's bounty giving back
A scattered chapter, livid hieroglyph,
The portent wound in corridors of shells.[3]

Then in the circuit calm of one vast coil,
Its lashings charmed and malice reconciled,   10
Frosted eyes there were that lifted altars;[4]
And silent answers crept across the stars.

Compass, quadrant and sextant contrive
No farther tides[5] . . . High in the azure steeps
Monody shall not wake the mariner.   15
This fabulous shadow only the sea keeps.

                                                                    1926

From Voyages

I

Above the fresh ruffles of the surf
Bright striped urchins flay each other with sand.
They have contrived a conquest for shell shucks,
And their fingers crumble fragments of baked weed
Gaily digging and scattering.   5

And in answer to their treble interjections
The sun beats lightning on the waves,
The waves fold thunder on the sand;
And could they hear me I would tell them:

2. "Dice bequeath an embassy, in the first place, by being ground (in this connection only, of course) in little cubes from the bones of drowned men by the action of the sea, and are finally thrown up on the sand, having 'numbers' but no identification. These being the bones of dead men who never completed their voyage, it seems legitimate to refer to them as the only surviving evidence of certain messages undelivered, mute evidence of certain things. . . . Dice as a symbol of chance and circumstance is also implied" [Crane's note].
3. "This calyx refers in a double ironic sense both to a cornucopia and the vortex made by a sinking vessel. As soon as the water has closed over a ship this whirlpool sends up broken spars, wreckage, etc., which can be alluded to as livid *hieroglyphs*, making a *scattered chapter* so far as any complete record of the recent ship and crew is concerned. In fact, about as much definite knowledge might come from all this as anyone might gain from the roar of his own veins, which is easily heard (haven't you ever done it?) by holding a shell close to one's ear" [Crane's note]. A calyx is a whorl of leaves forming the outer casing of the bud of a plant.
4. "Refers simply to a conviction that a man, not knowing perhaps a definite god yet being endowed with a reverence for deity—such a man naturally postulates a deity somehow, and the altar of that deity by the very *action* of the eyes *lifted* in searching" [Crane's note].
5. "Hasn't it often occurred that instruments originally invented for record and computation have inadvertently so extended the concepts of the entity they were invented to measure (concepts of space, etc.) in the mind and imagination that employed them, that they may metaphorically be said to have extended the original boundaries of the entity measured? This little bit of 'relativity' ought not to be discredited in poetry now that scientists are proceeding to measure the universe on principles of pure *ratio*, quite as metaphorical, so far as previous standards of scientific methods extended, as some of the axioms in *Job*" [Crane's note].

O brilliant kids, frisk with your dog,   10
Fondle your shells and sticks, bleached
By time and the elements; but there is a line
You must not cross nor ever trust beyond it
Spry cordage of your bodies to caresses
Too lichen-faithful from too wide a breast.   15
The bottom of the sea is cruel.

                                        1923, 1926

III

Infinite consanguinity it bears—
This tendered theme of you that light
Retrieves from sea plains where the sky
Resigns a breast that every wave enthrones;
While ribboned water lanes I wind   5
Are laved and scattered with no stroke
Wide from your side, whereto this hour
The sea lifts, also, reliquary hands.

And so, admitted through black swollen gates
That must arrest all distance otherwise,—   10
Past whirling pillars and lithe pediments,
Light wrestling there incessantly with light,
Star kissing star through wave on wave unto

Your body rocking!
                and where death, if shed,   15
Presumes no carnage, but this single change,—
Upon the steep floor flung from dawn to dawn
The silken skilled transmemberment of song;

Permit me voyage, love, into your hands . . .

                                            1926

V

Meticulous, past midnight in clear rime,
Infrangible and lonely, smooth as though cast
Together in one merciless white blade—
The bay estuaries fleck the hard sky limits.

—As if too brittle or too clear to touch!   5
The cables of our sleep so swiftly filed,
Already hang, shred ends from remembered stars.
One frozen trackless smile . . . What words
Can strangle this deaf moonlight? For we

Are overtaken. Now no cry, no sword   10
Can fasten or deflect this tidal wedge,

Slow tyranny of moonlight, moonlight loved
And changed . . . "There's

Nothing like this in the world," you say,
Knowing I cannot touch your hand and look   15
Too, into that godless cleft of sky
Where nothing turns but dead sands flashing.

"—And never to quite understand!" No,
In all the argosy of your bright hair I dreamed
Nothing so flagless as this piracy.   20

                              But now
Draw in your head, alone and too tall here.
Your eyes already in the slant of drifting foam;
Your breath sealed by the ghosts I do not know:
    Draw in your head and sleep the long way home.   25

                                        1926

From The Bridge

From going to and fro in the earth,
and from walking up and down in it.
          —The Book of Job[1]

To Brooklyn Bridge

How many dawns, chill from his rippling rest
The seagull's wings shall dip and pivot him,
Shedding white rings of tumult, building high
Over the chained bay waters Liberty—

5   *Then, with inviolate curve, forsake our eyes*
As apparitional as sails that cross
Some page of figures to be filed away;
—Till elevators drop us from our day . . .

I think of cinemas, panoramic sleights
10   *With multitudes bent toward some flashing scene*
Never disclosed, but hastened to again,
Foretold to other eyes on the same screen;

And Thee, across the harbor, silver-paced
As though the sun took step of thee, yet left
15   *Some motion ever unspent in thy stride,—*
Implicitly thy freedom staying thee!

1. Satan's answer to Jehovah when asked where he has been (Job 1.7).

Out of some subway scuttle, cell or loft
A bedlamite[2] speeds to thy parapets,
Tilting there momently, shrill shirt ballooning,
20   A jest falls from the speechless caravan.

Down Wall, from girder into street noon leaks,
A rip-tooth of the sky's acetylene;
All afternoon the cloud-flown derricks turn . . .
Thy cables breathe the North Atlantic still.

25   And obscure as that heaven of the Jews,
Thy guerdon . . . Accolade thou dost bestow
Of anonymity time cannot raise:
Vibrant reprieve and pardon thou dost show.

O harp and altar, of the fury fused,
30   (How could mere toil align thy choiring strings!)
Terrific threshold of the prophet's pledge,
Prayer of pariah, and the lover's cry,—

Again the traffic lights that skim thy swift
Unfractioned idiom, immaculate sigh of stars,
35   Beading thy path—condense eternity:
And we have seen night lifted in thine arms.

Under thy shadow by the piers I waited;
Only in darkness is thy shadow clear.
The City's fiery parcels all undone,
40   Already snow submerges an iron year . . .

O Sleepless as the river under thee,
Vaulting the sea, the prairies' dreaming sod,
Unto us lowliest sometime sweep, descend
And of the curveship lend a myth to God.

1927, 1930

From II. Powhatan's Daughter[1]

*   *   *

The River[2]

Stick your patent name on a signboard
brother—all over—going west—young man

2. Insane person, inmate of a hospital for the mentally ill.
1. Powhatan was the Native American chief with whom English settlers in Virginia (1607) had to deal. Pocahontas (1595–1617) was his daughter, whom Crane associated with the American "continent," a "nature symbol" comparable to the "traditional Hertha of ancient Teutonic mythology."
2. Crane wrote the following in a letter: "I'm trying in this part of the poem to chart the pioneer experience of our forefathers—and to tell the story backwards . . . on the 'backs' of hoboes. These hoboes are simply 'psychological ponies' to carry the reader across the country and back to the Mississippi, which you will notice is described as a great River of Time. I also unlatch the door to the pure Indian world which opens out in 'The Dance' section, so the reader is gradually led back in time

Tintex—Japalac—Certain-teed Overalls ads[3]
and lands sakes! under the new playbill ripped
5   in the guaranteed corner—see Bert Williams[4] what?
Minstrels when you steal a chicken just
save me the wing for if it isn't
Erie it ain't for miles around a
Mazda—and the telegraphic night coming on Thomas

*. . . and past
the din and
slogans of
the year—*

10   a Ediford[5]—and whistling down the tracks
a headlight rushing with the sound—can you
imagine—while an EXPRESS makes time like
SCIENCE—COMMERCE AND THE HOLYGHOST
RADIO ROARS IN EVERY HOME WE HAVE THE NORTHPOLE
15   WALLSTREET AND VIRGINBIRTH WITHOUT STONES OR
WIRES OR EVEN RUNning brooks connecting ears
and no more sermons windows flashing roar
breathtaking—as you like it[6] . . . eh?

So the 20th Century—so
20   whizzed the Limited—roared by and left
three men, still hungry on the tracks, ploddingly
watching the tail lights wizen and converge, slipping gimleted and neatly out of sight.

•   •   •   •   •   •   •

The last bear, shot drinking in the Dakotas
25   Loped under wires that span the mountain stream.
Keen instruments,[7] strung to a vast precision
Bind town to town and dream to ticking dream.
But some men take their liquor slow—and count
—Though they'll confess no rosary nor clue—

*to those
whose
addresses
are never
near*

30   The river's minute by the far brook's year.
Under a world of whistles, wires and steam
Caboose-like they go ruminating through
Ohio, Indiana—blind baggage—
To Cheyenne tagging . . . Maybe Kalamazoo.

35   Time's rendings, time's blendings they construe
As final reckonings of fire and snow;
Strange bird-wit, like the elemental gist
Of unwalled winds they offer, singing low
My Old Kentucky Home and *Casey Jones,*
40   *Some Sunny Day.* I heard a road-gang chanting so.

---

to the pure savage world, while existing at the same
time in the present." In the opening lines the image
of a subway is translated into an image of a luxury
express train, the Twentieth Century Limited, traveling from New York City to Chicago.
3. Advertising slogans: trade names of a dye, a varnish, and a brand of overalls.
4. Egbert A. Williams (1876–1922), popular black
minstrel show performer.

5. A combined reference to Thomas Edison
(1847–1931), inventor of the electric lightbulb
(trade name "Mazda"), and Henry Ford (1863–
1947), automobile manufacturer.
6. An echo of Shakespeare's *As You Like It* 2.1.16–
17: "Books in the running brooks, / Sermons in
stones."
7. The telephone and telegraph.

And afterwards, who had a colt's eyes—one said,
"Jesus! Oh I remember watermelon days!" And sped
High in a cloud of merriment, recalled
"—And when my Aunt Sally Simpson smiled," he drawled—
45   "It was almost Louisiana, long ago."
"There's no place like Booneville though, Buddy,"
One said, excising a last burr from his vest,
"—For early trouting." Then peering in the can,
"—But I kept on the tracks." Possessed, resigned,
50   He trod the fire down pensively and grinned,
Spreading dry shingles of a beard. . . .

                  Behind
My father's cannery works I used to see
Rail-squatters ranged in nomad raillery,
55   The ancient men—wifeless or runaway
Hobo-trekkers that forever search
An empire wilderness of freight and rails.
Each seemed a child, like me, on a loose perch,
Holding to childhood like some termless play.
60   John, Jake or Charley, hopping the slow freight
—Memphis to Tallahassee—riding the rods,
Blind fists of nothing, humpty-dumpty clods.

Yet they touch something like a key perhaps.
From pole to pole across the hills, the states
65   —They know a body under the wide rain;   *but who have*
Youngsters with eyes like fjords, old reprobates   *touched her,*
With racetrack jargon,—dotting immensity   *knowing her*
They lurk across her, knowing her yonder breast *without name*
Snow-silvered, sumac-stained or smoky blue—
70   Is past the valley-sleepers, south or west.
—As I have trod the rumorous midnights, too,

And past the circuit of the lamp's thin flame
(O Nights that brought me to her body bare!)
Have dreamed beyond the print that bound her name.
75   Trains sounding the long blizzards out—I heard
Wail into distances I knew were hers.
Papooses crying on the wind's long mane
Screamed redskin dynasties that fled the brain,
—Dead echoes! But I knew her body there,
80   Time like a serpent down her shoulder, dark,
And space, an eaglet's wing, laid on her hair.

Under the Ozarks, domed by Iron Mountain,
The old gods of the rain lie wrapped in pools
Where eyeless fish curvet a sunken fountain   *nor the*
85   And re-descend with corn from querulous crows. *myths of her*
Such pilferings make up their timeless eatage,   *fathers . . .*
Propitiate them for their timber torn
By iron, iron—always the iron dealt cleavage!
They doze now, below axe and powder horn.

90   And Pullman breakfasters glide glistening steel
      From tunnel into field—iron strides the dew—
      Straddles the hill, a dance of wheel on wheel.
      You have a half-hour's wait at Siskiyou,
      Or stay the night and take the next train through.
95   Southward, near Cairo passing, you can see
      The Ohio merging,—borne down Tennessee;
      And if it's summer and the sun's in dusk
      Maybe the breeze will lift the River's musk
      —As though the waters breathed that you might know
100   *Memphis Johnny, Steamboat Bill, Missouri Joe.*
      Oh, lean from the window, if the train slows down,
      As though you touched hands with some ancient clown,
      —A little while gaze absently below
      And hum *Deep River* with them while they go.

105   Yes, turn again and sniff once more—look see,
      O Sheriff, Brakeman and Authority—
      Hitch up your pants and crunch another quid,[8]
      For you, too, feed the River timelessly.

      And few evade full measure of their fate;
110   Always they smile out eerily what they seem.
      I could believe he joked at heaven's gate—
      Dan Midland—jolted from the cold brake-beam.[9]

      Down, down—born pioneers in time's despite,
      Grimed tributaries to an ancient flow—
115   They win no frontier by their wayward plight,
      But drift in stillness, as from Jordan's[1] brow.

      You will not hear it as the sea; even stone
      Is not more hushed by gravity . . . But slow,
      As loth to take more tribute—sliding prone
120   Like one whose eyes were buried long ago
      The River, spreading, flows—and spends your dream.
      What are you, lost within this tideless spell?
      You are your father's father, and the stream—
      A liquid theme that floating niggers swell.

125   Damp tonnage and alluvial march of days—
      Nights turbid, vascular with silted shale
      And roots surrendered down of moraine clays:
      The Mississippi drinks the farthest dale.

      O quarrying passion, undertowed sunlight!
130   The basalt surface drags a jungle grace
      Ochreous and lynx-barred in lengthening might;
      Patience! and you shall reach the biding place!

8. Chunk of chewing tobacco.   death from a train.
9. Structure on a railroad car where hoboes ride.   1. River mentioned frequently in the Bible.
Dan Midland was a legendary hobo who fell to his

Over De Soto's bones the freighted floors
Throb past the City storied of three thrones.[2]
135   Down two more turns the Mississippi pours
(Anon tall ironsides[3] up from salt lagoons)

And flows within itself, heaps itself free.
All fades but one thin skyline 'round . . . Ahead
No embrace opens but the stinging sea;
140   The River lifts itself from its long bed,

Poised wholly on its dream, a mustard glow
Tortured with history, its one will—flow!
—The Passion spreads in wide tongues, choked and slow,
Meeting the Gulf, hosannas silently below.

1930

VII. The Tunnel

To Find the Western path
Right thro' the Gates of Wrath.
        —Blake[1]

Performances, assortments, résumés—
Up Times Square to Columbus Circle lights
Channel the congresses, nightly sessions,
Refractions of the thousand theatres, faces—
5   Mysterious kitchens. . . . You shall search them all.
Someday by heart you'll learn each famous sight
And watch the curtain lift in hell's despite;
You'll find the garden in the third act dead,
Finger your knees—and wish yourself in bed
10   With tabloid crime-sheets perched in easy sight.

        Then let you reach your hat
        and go.
        As usual, let you—also
        walking down—exclaim
15   to twelve upward leaving
        a subscription praise
        for what time slays.

Or can't you quite make up your mind to ride;
A walk is better underneath the L[2] a brisk
20   Ten blocks or so before? But you find yourself

2. New Orleans, at various times under Spanish, French, and English rule. The body of the Spanish explorer Hernándo de Soto (1500–1542) was consigned to the Mississippi River. In 1862 Admiral David G. Farragut (1801–1870) led a Union fleet up the Mississippi from the Gulf and captured New Orleans.
3. Warships.
1. The opening lines of "Morning," by the visionary English poet William Blake (1757–1827).
2. Elevated railway.

Preparing penguin flexions of the arms,—
As usual you will meet the scuttle yawn:
The subway yawns the quickest promise home.

Be minimum, then, to swim the hiving swarms
25   Out of the Square, the Circle burning bright[3]—
Avoid the glass doors gyring at your right,
Where boxed alone a second, eyes take fright
—Quite unprepared rush naked back to light:
And down beside the turnstile press the coin
30   Into the slot. The gongs already rattle.

      And so
      of cities you bespeak
      subways, rivered under streets
      and rivers. . . . In the car
35   the overtone of motion
      underground, the monotone
      of motion is the sound
      of other faces, also underground—

"Let's have a pencil Jimmy—living now
40   at Floral Park
Flatbush—on the fourth of July—
like a pigeon's muddy dream—potatoes
to dig in the field—travlin the town—too—
night after night—the Culver line—the
45   girls all shaping up—it used to be—"

Our tongues recant like beaten weather vanes.
This answer lives like verdigris,[4] like hair
Beyond extinction, surcease of the bone;
And repetition freezes—"What
50   "what do you want? getting weak on the links?
fandaddle daddy don't ask for change—IS THIS
FOURTEENTH? it's half past six she said—if
you don't like my gate why did you
swing on it, why *didja*
55   swing on it
anyhow—"

      And somehow anyhow swing—

The phonographs of hades in the brain
Are tunnels that re-wind themselves, and love
60   A burnt match skating in a urinal—
Somewhere above Fourteenth TAKE THE EXPRESS
To brush some new presentiment of pain—

---

3. An echo of Blake's poem "The Tyger"; also the
lighted sign indicating a subway station.   4. Green coating or stain on copper.

"But I want service in this office SERVICE
I said—after
65   the show she cried a little afterwards but—"

Whose head is swinging from the swollen strap?
Whose body smokes along the bitten rails,
Bursts from a smoldering bundle far behind
In back forks of the chasms of the brain,—
70   Puffs from a riven stump far out behind
In interborough fissures of the mind . . . ?

And why do I often meet your visage here,
Your eyes like agate lanterns—on and on
Below the toothpaste and the dandruff ads?
75   —And did their riding eyes right through your side,
And did their eyes like unwashed platters ride?
And Death, aloft,—gigantically down
Probing through you—toward me, O evermore![5]
And when they dragged your retching flesh,
80   Your trembling hands that night through Baltimore—
That last night on the ballot rounds, did you,
Shaking, did you deny the ticket, Poe?

For Gravesend Manor change at Chambers Street.
The platform hurries along to a dead stop.

85   The intent escalator lifts a serenade
Stilly
Of shoes, umbrellas, each eye attending its shoe, then
Bolting outright somewhere above where streets
Burst suddenly in rain. . . . The gongs recur:
90   Elbows and levers, guard and hissing door.
Thunder is galvothermic[6] here below. . . . The car
Wheels off. The train rounds, bending to a scream,
Taking the final level for the dive
Under the river—
95   And somewhat emptier than before,
Demented, for a hitching second, humps; then
Lets go. . . . Toward corners of the floor
Newspapers wing, revolve and wing.
Blank windows gargle signals through the roar.

100   And does the Daemon take you home, also,
Wop washerwoman, with the bandaged hair?
After the corridors are swept, the cuspidors—
The gaunt sky-barracks cleanly now, and bare,
O Genoese, do you bring mother eyes and hands
105   Back home to children and to golden hair?

---

5. Echoes of "the agate lamp within thy hand" from "To Helen," "Death looks gigantically down" from "The City in the Sea," and the refrain "Nevermore" in "The Raven" —poems by Edgar Allan Poe (1809–1849).

6. I.e., galvanothermic, producing heat by electricity.

Daemon, demurring and eventful yawn!
Whose hideous laughter is a bellows mirth
—Or the muffled slaughter of a day in birth—
O cruelly to inoculate the brinking dawn
110 With antennae toward worlds that glow and sink;—
To spoon us out more liquid than the dim
Locution of the eldest star, and pack
The conscience navelled in the plunging wind,
Umbilical to call—and straightway die!

115 O caught like pennies beneath soot and steam,
Kiss of our agony thou gatherest;
Condensed, thou takest all—shrill ganglia
Impassioned with some song we fail to keep.
And yet, like Lazarus,[7] to feel the slope,
120 The sod and billow breaking,—lifting ground,
—A sound of waters bending astride the sky
Unceasing with some Word that will not die . . . !

•   •   •   •   •   •

A tugboat, wheezing wreaths of steam,
Lunged past, with one galvanic blare stove up the River.
125 I counted the echoes assembling, one after one,
Searching, thumbing the midnight on the piers.
Lights, coasting, left the oily tympanum of waters;
The blackness somewhere gouged glass on a sky.
And this thy harbor, O my City, I have driven under,
130 Tossed from the coil of ticking towers. . . . Tomorrow,
And to be. . . . Here by the River that is East—
Here at the waters' edge the hands drop memory;
Shadowless in that abyss they unaccounting lie.
How far away the star has pooled the sea—
135 Or shall the hands be drawn away, to die?
Kiss of our agony Thou gatherest,
                         O Hand of Fire
                                gatherest—

1927, 1930

7. He was resurrected from the grave by Jesus in John 11.43–44.

ERNEST HEMINGWAY
1899–1961

The narrator in Ernest Hemingway's *A Farewell to Arms,* reflecting on his war experiences, observes at one point, "I was always embarrassed by the words *sacred, glorious,* and *sacrifice* and the expression *in vain.* . . . I had seen nothing sacred, and the things that were glorious had no glory and the sacrifices were like the stockyards at Chicago if nothing was done with the meat except to bury it. There were many words that you could not stand to hear." Hemingway's aim and achievement as a novelist and short-story writer were to convey his concerns in a prose style built from what was left after eliminating all the words one "could not stand to hear." As flamboyant in his personal style as he was severe in his writing, Hemingway became an international celebrity after the publication in 1926 of his first novel, *The Sun Also Rises.* At the time of his death, he was probably the most famous writer in the world.

He was born and raised in Oak Park, Illinois, one of six children. His mother was a music teacher, director of the church choir, and a lover of high culture who had contemplated a career as an opera singer. His father was a successful physician, prone to depression, who enjoyed hunting, fishing, and cooking and who shared in household responsibilities more than most men of his era. The family spent summers at their cottage in northern Michigan, where many of Hemingway's stories are set. After high school, Hemingway took a job on the *Kansas City Star.* When the United States entered the war in 1917, Hemingway was eager to go. An eye problem barred him from the army, so he joined the ambulance corps. Within three weeks he was wounded by shrapnel. After six months in the hospital Hemingway went home as a decorated hero: when wounded, he had carried a comrade more badly hurt than he to safety (see p. 1377). He found readjustment difficult and became increasingly estranged from his family, especially his mother. Years later, when his father committed suicide, Hemingway blamed his mother for that death.

In 1920 he married Hadley Richardson and went to Paris. Supported partly by her money and partly by his journalism, Hemingway worked at becoming a writer. He came to know Gertrude Stein, Sherwood Anderson, Ezra Pound, F. Scott Fitzgerald, and others in the large community of expatriate artistic and literary Americans. Besides reading his manuscripts and advising him, Fitzgerald and Anderson, better known than he, used their influence to get his book of short stories *In Our Time* published in the United States in 1925. In this book, stories about the adolescent Nick Adams as he grows up in northern Michigan alternate with very brief, powerful vignettes of war and crime.

In 1926 his novel *The Sun Also Rises* appeared; it presents the stripped-down "Hemingway style" at its finest. "I always try to write on the principle of the iceberg," he told an interviewer. "There is seven-eighths of it under water for every part that shows." Narrated by Jake Barnes, whose World War I wounds have left him sexually impotent, *The Sun Also Rises* depicts Jake's efforts to live according to a self-conscious code of dignity, of "grace under pressure," in the midst of a circle of self-seeking American and English expatriates in Paris. He finds an ideal in the rich tradition of Spanish peasant life, especially as epitomized in bullfighting and the bullfighter. *The Sun Also Rises* was directly responsible for a surge of American tourism to Pamplona, Spain, where the novel's bullfights are set.

In 1927 Hemingway brought out his second collection of stories, *Men without Women.* Adapting journalistic techniques in telegraphic prose that minimized narrator commentary and depended heavily on uncontextualized dialogue, these stories developed a modern, speeded-up, streamlined style that has been endlessly imitated. His second novel, *A Farewell to Arms,* appeared in 1929. It described a romance between an American army officer, Frederic Henry, and a British nurse, Catherine Barkley. The two run away from war, trying to make "a separate peace," but their idyll is shattered when Catherine dies in childbirth. Hemingway's work has been much criticized for its depictions of women. The wholly good Catherine lives for Frederick Henry alone; and Maria, in his Spanish Civil War novel (*For Whom the Bell Tolls,* 1940), is a fantasy figure of total submissiveness. Characters like Brett Ashley in *The Sun Also Rises* and Pilar in *For Whom the Bell Tolls,* however, are strong, complex figures. Overall, Hemingway identified the rapid change in women's status after World War I and the general blurring of sex roles that accompanied the new sexual freedom as aspects of modernity that men were simultaneously attracted to and found hard to deal with. More recently, especially in light of the themes of some of his posthumously published writings, critics have begun to re-interpret Hemingway's work as preoccupied with the cultural and psychological meanings of masculinity in a way that bespeaks considerable sexual ambivalence.

As Hemingway aged, his interest in exclusively masculine forms of self-assertion and self-definition became more pronounced. War, hunting, and similar pursuits that he had used at first to show men manifesting dignity in the face of certain defeat increasingly became depicted (in his life as well as his writing) as occasions for competitive masculine display and triumph. Soon after the publication of *The Sun Also Rises*, his first marriage broke up; in all he was married four times. In the 1930s and 1940s he adopted the style of life of a celebrity.

In the 1930s two new themes entered his work. One was the decade's ever-present theme of politics. A political loner distrustful of all ideological abstractions, Hemingway was nevertheless drawn into antifascist politics by the Spanish Civil War. In *To Have and Have Not* (1937), the earliest of his political novels, the good characters are working-class people and the antagonists are idle rich. *For Whom the Bell Tolls* draws on Hemingway's experiences in Spain as a war correspondent, celebrating both the peasant antifascists and the Americans who fought on their behalf. Hemingway's opposition to fascism did not, however, keep him from viewing the pro-Loyalist communists, who were also active in the Spanish Civil War, with considerable skepticism. His one play, *The Fifth Column*—which was printed along with his collected stories in 1938 and staged in 1940—specifically blames the communists for betraying the cause.

The second new theme, obviously autobiographical, was that of the successful writer losing his talent in an atmosphere of success, celebrity, and wealth. This is clearly expressed in "The Snows of Kilimanjaro," reprinted here, which also contains passages of his most lyrical and evocative writing as the writer looks back on earlier, happy days living in Paris and skiing in the Austrian Alps. The story also draws on Hemingway's experiences on African hunting safaris and shows the writer blaming his wife for what has happened to him, yet simultaneously recognizing that the fault is his alone.

Hemingway was fiercely anti-Nazi during World War II. As well as working as a war correspondent, work that sent him often to Europe, he used his fishing boat to keep watch for German submarines off the coast of Cuba, where he had a home. After the war ended, he continued his travels and was badly hurt in Africa in October 1953 in the crash of a small plane. He had already published his allegorical fable *The Old Man and the Sea* (1952), in the mass-circulation weekly magazine *Life*; this, his last major work published during his lifetime, won a Pulitzer Prize in 1953 and was central to his winning the Nobel Prize in 1954. The plane crash had damaged his mental and physical health, and he never fully recovered. Subject increasingly to depression and an incapacitating paranoia—afflictions that seem to have run in his family—he was hospitalized several times before killing himself in 1961. Yet it does appear that some of his suspicions about being watched by U.S. government agents may have been justified. Many writers associated with radical causes had dossiers compiled on them by the FBI. Several books have been published posthumously based on the voluminous manuscript collections he left. These include a book of reminiscences about his life in 1920s Paris, *A Moveable Feast* (1964); a novel about literary fame and sexual ambiguity constructed from several unfinished drafts, *Islands in the Stream* (1970); and *The Nick Adams Stories* (1972), a collection that added eight previously unpublished stories to the group.

The text is that of *The Fifth Column and the First Forty-nine Stories* (1938).

The Snows of Kilimanjaro[1]

*Kilimanjaro is a snow covered mountain 19,710 feet high, and is said
to be the highest mountain in Africa. Its western summit is called the
Masai "Ngàje Ngài," the House of God. Close to the western summit
there is the dried and frozen carcass of a leopard. No one has explained
what the leopard was seeking at that altitude.*

"The marvellous thing is that it's painless," he said. "That's how you know
when it starts."

"Is it really?"

"Absolutely. I'm awfully sorry about the odor though. That must bother
you."

"Don't! Please don't."

"Look at them," he said. "Now is it sight or is it scent that brings them like
that?"

The cot the man lay on was in the wide shade of a mimosa tree and as he
looked out past the shade onto the glare of the plain there were three of the
big birds squatted obscenely, while in the sky a dozen more sailed, making
quick-moving shadows as they passed.

"They've been there since the day the truck broke down," he said. "Today's
the first time any have lit on the ground. I watched the way they sailed very
carefully at first in case I ever wanted to use them in a story. That's funny
now."

"I wish you wouldn't," she said.

"I'm only talking," he said. "It's much easier if I talk. But I don't want to
bother you."

"You know it doesn't bother me," she said. "It's that I've gotten so very nervous not being able to do anything. I think we might make it as easy as we
can until the plane comes."

"Or until the plane doesn't come."

"Please tell me what I can do. There must be something I can do."

"You can take the leg off and that might stop it, though I doubt it. Or you
can shoot me. You're a good shot now. I taught you to shoot didn't I?"

"Please don't talk that way. Couldn't I read to you?"

"Read what?"

"Anything in the book bag that we haven't read."

"I can't listen to it," he said. "Talking is the easiest. We quarrel and that
makes the time pass."

"I don't quarrel. I never want to quarrel. Let's not quarrel any more. No
matter how nervous we get. Maybe they will be back with another truck today.
Maybe the plane will come."

"I don't want to move," the man said. "There is no sense in moving now
except to make it easier for you."

"That's cowardly."

"Can't you let a man die as comfortably as he can without calling him
names? What's the use of slanging me?"

"You're not going to die."

---

1. Mount Kilimanjaro is in Tanzania, near the border with Kenya. It is no longer snow covered.

"Don't be silly. I'm dying now. Ask those bastards." He looked over to where the huge, filthy birds sat, their naked heads sunk in the hunched feathers. A fourth planed down, to run quick-legged and then waddle slowly toward the others.

"They are around every camp. You never notice them. You can't die if you don't give up."

"Where did you read that? You're such a bloody fool."

"You might think about some one else."

"For Christ's sake," he said. "That's been my trade."

He lay then and was quiet for a while and looked across the heat shimmer of the plain to the edge of the bush. There were a few Tommies[2] that showed minute and white against the yellow and, far off, he saw a herd of zebra, white against the green of the bush. This was a pleasant camp under big trees against a hill, with good water, and close by, a nearly dry water hole where sand grouse flighted in the mornings.

"Wouldn't you like me to read?" she asked. She was sitting on a canvas chair beside his cot. "There's a breeze coming up."

"No thanks."

"Maybe the truck will come."

"I don't give a damn about the truck."

"I do."

"You give a damn about so many things that I don't."

"Not so many, Harry."

"What about a drink?"

"It's supposed to be bad for you. It said in Black's to avoid all alcohol. You shouldn't drink."

"Molo!" he shouted.

"Yes Bwana."

"Bring whiskey-soda."

"Yes Bwana."

"You shouldn't," she said. "That's what I mean by giving up. It says it's bad for you. I know it's bad for you."

"No," he said. "It's good for me."

So now it was all over, he thought. So now he would never have a chance to finish it. So this was the way it ended in a bickering over a drink. Since the gangrene started in his right leg he had no pain and with the pain the horror had gone and all he felt now was a great tiredness and anger that this was the end of it. For this, that now was coming, he had very little curiosity. For years it had obsessed him; but now it meant nothing in itself. It was strange how easy being tired enough made it.

Now he would never write the things that he had saved to write until he knew enough to write them well. Well, he would not have to fail at trying to write them either. Maybe you could never write them, and that was why you put them off and delayed the starting. Well he would never know, now.

"I wish we'd never come," the woman said. She was looking at him holding the glass and biting her lip. "You never would have gotten anything like this in Paris. You always said you loved Paris. We could have stayed in Paris

2. Familiar name for the Thomson's gazelle of East Africa, smallest of the gazelles.

or gone anywhere. I'd have gone anywhere. I said I'd go anywhere you wanted. If you wanted to shoot we could have gone shooting in Hungary and been comfortable."

"Your bloody money," he said.

"That's not fair," she said. "It was always yours as much as mine. I left everything and I went wherever you wanted to go and I've done what you wanted to do. But I wish we'd never come here."

"You said you loved it."

"I did when you were all right. But now I hate it. I don't see why that had to happen to your leg. What have we done to have that happen to us?"

"I suppose what I did was to forget to put iodine on it when I first scratched it. Then I didn't pay any attention to it because I never infect. Then, later, when it got bad, it was probably using that weak carbolic solution when the other antiseptics ran out that paralyzed the minute blood vessels and started the gangrene." He looked at her. "What else?"

"I don't mean that."

"If we would have hired a good mechanic instead of a half baked kikuyu driver, he would have checked the oil and never burned out that bearing in the truck."

"I don't mean that."

"If you hadn't left your own people, your goddamned Old Westbury, Saratoga, Palm Beach people to take me on—"

"Why, I loved you. That's not fair. I love you now. I'll always love you. Don't you love me?"

"No," said the man. "I don't think so. I never have."

"Harry, what are you saying? You're out of your head."

"No. I haven't any head to go out of."

"Don't drink that," she said. "Darling, please don't drink that. We have to do everything we can."

"You do it," he said. "I'm tired."

Now in his mind he saw a railway station at Karagatch and he was standing with his pack and that was the headlight of the Simplon-Orient[3] cutting the dark now and he was leaving Thrace[4] then after the retreat. That was one of the things he had saved to write, with, in the morning at breakfast, looking out the window and seeing snow on the mountains in Bulgaria and Nansen's Secretary asking the old man if it were snow and the old man looking at it and saying, No, that's not snow. It's too early for snow. And the Secretary repeating to the other girls, No, you see. It's not snow and them all saying, It's not snow we were mistaken. But it was the snow all right and he sent them on into it when he evolved exchange of populations. And it was snow they tramped along in until they died that winter.

It was snow too that fell all Christmas week that year up in the Gauertal, that year they lived in the woodcutter's house with the big square porcelain stove that

---

3. A fast train going from Paris to Constantinople, crossing the Alps into Italy over the Simplon Pass.
4. A region spanning parts of Greece and Turkey,

scene of border wars in 1922 that Hemingway had covered as a war correspondent while living in Paris.

filled half the room, and they slept on mattresses filled with beech leaves, the time the deserter came with his feet bloody in the snow. He said the police were right behind him and they gave him woolen socks and held the gendarmes talking until the tracks had drifted over.

In Schrunz,[5] *on Christmas day, the snow was so bright it hurt your eyes when you looked out from the weinstube and saw every one coming home from church. That was where they walked up the sleigh-smoothed urine-yellowed road along the river with the steep pine hills, skis heavy on the shoulder, and where they ran that great run down the glacier above the Madlener-haus, the snow as smooth to see as cake frosting and as light as powder and he remembered the noiseless rush the speed made as you dropped down like a bird.*

They were snow-bound a week in the Madlener-haus that time in the blizzard playing cards in the smoke by the lantern light and the stakes were higher all the time as Herr Lent lost more. Finally he lost it all. Everything, the skischule money and all the season's profit and then his capital. He could see him with his long nose, picking up the cards and then opening, "Sans Voir."[6] There was always gambling then. When there was no snow you gambled and when there was too much you gambled. He thought of all the time in his life he had spent gambling.

But he had never written a line of that, nor of that cold, bright Christmas day with the mountains showing across the plain that Barker had flown across the lines to bomb the Austrian officers' leave train, machine-gunning them as they scattered and ran. He remembered Barker afterwards coming into the mess and starting to tell about it. And how quiet it got and then somebody saying, "You bloody murderous bastard."

Those were the same Austrians they killed then that he skied with later. No not the same. Hans, that he skied with all that year, had been in the Kaiser-Jägers[7] and when they went hunting hares together up the little valley above the saw-mill they had talked of the fighting on Pasubio and of the attack on Perticara and Asalone and he had never written a word of that. Nor of Monte Corono, nor the Sette Commumi, nor of Arsiero.

How many winters had he lived in the Vorarlberg and the Arlberg? It was four and then he remembered the man who had the fox to sell when they had walked into Bludenz, that time to buy presents, and the cherry-pit taste of good kirsch, the fast-slipping rush of running powder-snow on crust, singing "Hi! Ho! said Rolly!" as you ran down the last stretch to the steep drop, taking it straight, then running the orchard in three turns and out across the ditch and onto the icy road behind the inn. Knocking your bindings loose, kicking the skis free and leaning them up against the wooden wall of the inn, the lamplight coming from the window, where inside, in the smoky, new-wine smelling warmth, they were playing the accordion.

"Where did we stay in Paris?" he asked the woman who was sitting by him in a canvas chair, now, in Africa.

---

5. Alpine ski resort in the western part of Austria.
6. Without seeing (French); a blind opening bet in poker or other gambling games.
7. The Kaiser's Hunters (German); elite Austrian troops. In World War I, Germany and Austria fought against the United Kingdom, France, Italy, and the United States.

"At the Crillon.[8] You know that."

"Why do I know that?"

"That's where we always stayed."

"No. Not always."

"There and at the Pavillion Henri-Quatre in St. Germain. You said you loved it there."

"Love is a dunghill," said Harry. "And I'm the cock that gets on it to crow."

"If you have to go away," she said, "is it absolutely necessary to kill off everything you leave behind? I mean do you have to take away everything? Do you have to kill your horse, and your wife and burn your saddle and your armour?"

"Yes," he said. "Your damned money was my armour. My Swift and my Armour."

"Don't."

"All right. I'll stop that. I don't want to hurt you."

"It's a little bit late now."

"All right then. I'll go on hurting you. It's more amusing. The only thing I ever really liked to do with you I can't do now."

"No, that's not true. You liked to do many things and everything you wanted to do I did."

"Oh, for Christ sake stop bragging, will you?"

He looked at her and saw her crying.

"Listen," he said. "Do you think that it is fun to do this? I don't know why I'm doing it. It's trying to kill to keep yourself alive, I imagine. I was all right when we started talking. I didn't mean to start this, and now I'm crazy as a coot and being as cruel to you as I can be. Don't pay any attention, darling, to what I say. I love you, really. You know I love you. I've never loved any one else the way I love you."

He slipped into the familiar lie he made his bread and butter by.

"You're sweet to me."

"You bitch," he said. "You rich bitch. That's poetry. I'm full of poetry now. Rot and poetry. Rotten poetry."

"Stop it. Harry, why do you have to turn into a devil now?"

"I don't like to leave anything," the man said. "I don't like to leave things behind."

•　　•　　•

It was evening now and he had been asleep. The sun was gone behind the hill and there was a shadow all across the plain and the small animals were feeding close to camp; quick dropping heads and switching tails, he watched them keeping well out away from the bush now. The birds no longer waited on the ground. They were all perched heavily in a tree. There were many more of them. His personal boy was sitting by the bed.

"Memsahib's gone to shoot," the boy said. "Does Bwana want?"

"Nothing."

She had gone to kill a piece of meat and, knowing how he liked to watch the game, she had gone well away so she would not disturb this little pocket

---

8. Luxury hotel in Paris, as is the Henri-Quatre (below).

of the plain that he could see. She was always thoughtful, he thought. On anything she knew about, or had read, or that she had ever heard.

It was not her fault that when he went to her he was already over. How could a woman know that you meant nothing that you said; that you spoke only from habit and to be comfortable? After he no longer meant what he said, his lies were more successful with women than when he had told them the truth.

It was not so much that he lied as that there was no truth to tell. He had had his life and it was over and then he went on living it again with different people and more money, with the best of the same places, and some new ones.

You kept from thinking and it was all marvellous. You were equipped with good insides so that you did not go to pieces that way, the way most of them had, and you made an attitude that you cared nothing for the work you used to do, now that you could no longer do it. But, in yourself, you said that you would write about these people; about the very rich; that you were really not of them but a spy in their country; that you would leave it and write of it and for once it would be written by some one who knew what he was writing of. But he would never do it, because each day of not writing, of comfort, of being that which he despised, dulled his ability and softened his will to work so that, finally, he did no work at all. The people he knew now were all much more comfortable when he did not work. Africa was where he had been happiest in the good time of his life, so he had come out here to start again. They had made this safari with the minimum of comfort. There was no hardship; but there was no luxury and he had thought that he could get back into training that way. That in some way he could work the fat off his soul the way a fighter went into the mountains to work and train in order to burn it out of his body.

She had liked it. She said she loved it. She loved anything that was exciting, that involved a change of scene, where there were new people and where things were pleasant. And he had felt the illusion of returning strength of will to work. Now if this was how it ended, and he knew it was, he must not turn like some snake biting itself because its back was broken. It wasn't this woman's fault. If it had not been she it would have been another. If he lived by a lie he should try to die by it. He heard a shot beyond the hill.

She shot very well this good, this rich bitch, this kindly caretaker and destroyer of his talent. Nonsense. He had destroyed his talent himself. Why should he blame this woman because she kept him well? He had destroyed his talent by not using it, by betrayals of himself and what he believed in, by drinking so much that he blunted the edge of his perceptions, by laziness, by sloth, and by snobbery, by pride and by prejudice,[9] by hook and by crook. What was this? A catalogue of old books? What was his talent anyway? It was a talent all right but instead of using it, he had traded on it. It was never what he had done, but always what he could do. And he had chosen to make his living with something else instead of a pen or a pencil. It was strange, too, wasn't it, that when he fell in love with another woman, that woman should always have more money than the last one? But when he no longer was in

9. Reference to title of a novel by the English writer Jane Austen (1775–1817).

love, when he was only lying, as to this woman, now, who had the most money of all, who had all the money there was, who had had a husband and children, who had taken lovers and been dissatisfied with them, and who loved him dearly as a writer, as a man, as a companion and as a proud possession; it was strange that when he did not love her at all and was lying, that he should be able to give her more for her money than when he had really loved.

We must all be cut out for what we do, he thought. However you make your living is where your talent lies. He had sold vitality, in one form or another, all his life and when your affections are not too involved you give much better value for the money. He had found that out but he would never write that, now, either. No, he would not write that, although it was well worth writing.

Now she came in sight, walking across the open toward the camp. She was wearing jodhpurs and carrying her rifle. The two boys had a Tommie slung and they were coming along behind her. She was still a good-looking woman, he thought, and she had a pleasant body. She had a great talent and appreciation for the bed, she was not pretty, but he liked her face, she read enormously, liked to ride and shoot and, certainly, she drank too much. Her husband had died when she was still a comparatively young woman and for a while she had devoted herself to her two just-grown children, who did not need her and were embarrassed at having her about, to her stable of horses, to books, and to bottles. She liked to read in the evening before dinner and she drank Scotch and soda while she read. By dinner she was fairly drunk and after a bottle of wine at dinner she was usually drunk enough to sleep.

That was before the lovers. After she had the lovers she did not drink so much because she did not have to be drunk to sleep. But the lovers bored her. She had been married to a man who had never bored her and these people bored her very much.

Then one of her two children was killed in a plane crash and after that was over she did not want the lovers, and drink being no anæsthetic she had to make another life. Suddenly, she had been acutely frightened of being alone. But she wanted some one that she respected with her.

It had begun very simply. She liked what he wrote and she had always envied the life he led. She thought he did exactly what he wanted to. The steps by which she had acquired him and the way in which she had finally fallen in love with him were all part of a regular progression in which she had built herself a new life and he had traded away what remained of his old life.

He had traded it for security, for comfort too, there was no denying that, and for what else? He did not know. She would have bought him anything he wanted. He knew that. She was a damned nice woman too. He would as soon be in bed with her as any one; rather with her, because she was richer, because she was very pleasant and appreciative and because she never made scenes. And now this life that she had built again was coming to a term because he had not used iodine two weeks ago when a thorn had scratched his knee as they moved forward trying to photograph a herd of waterbuck standing, their heads up, peering while their nostrils searched the air, their ears spread wide to hear the first noise that would send them rushing into the bush. They had bolted, too, before he got the picture.

Here she came now.

He turned his head on the cot to look toward her. "Hello," he said.

"I shot a Tommy ram," she told him. "He'll make you good broth and I'll have them mash some potatoes with the Klim.[1] How do you feel?"

"Much better."

"Isn't that lovely? You know I thought perhaps you would. You were sleeping when I left."

"I had a good sleep. Did you walk far?"

"No. Just around behind the hill. I made quite a good shot on the Tommy."

"You shoot marvellously, you know."

"I love it. I've loved Africa. Really. If *you're* all right it's the most fun that I've ever had. You don't know the fun it's been to shoot with you. I've loved the country."

"I love it too."

"Darling, you don't know how marvellous it is to see you feeling better. I couldn't stand it when you felt that way. You won't talk to me like that again, will you? Promise me?"

"No," he said. "I don't remember what I said."

"You don't have to destroy me. Do you? I'm only a middle-aged woman who loves you and wants to do what you want to do. I've been destroyed two or three times already. You wouldn't want to destroy me again, would you?"

"I'd like to destroy you a few times in bed," he said.

"Yes. That's the good destruction. That's the way we're made to be destroyed. The plane will be here tomorrow."

"How do you know?"

"I'm sure. It's bound to come. The boys have the wood all ready and the grass to make the smudge.[2] I went down and looked at it again today. There's plenty of room to land and we have the smudges ready at both ends."

"What makes you think it will come tomorrow?"

"I'm sure it will. It's overdue now. Then, in town, they will fix up your leg and then we will have some good destruction. Not that dreadful talking kind."

"Should we have a drink? The sun is down."

"Do you think you should?"

"I'm having one."

"We'll have one together. *Molo, letti dui whiskey-soda!*" she called.

"You'd better put on your mosquito boots," he told her.

"I'll wait till I bathe . . ."

While it grew dark they drank and just before it was dark and there was no longer enough light to shoot, a hyena crossed the open on his way around the hill.

"That bastard crosses there every night," the man said. "Every night for two weeks."

"He's the one makes the noise at night. I don't mind it. They're a filthy animal though."

Drinking together, with no pain now except the discomfort of lying in the one position, the boys lighting a fire, its shadow jumping on the tents, he could feel the return of acquiescence in this life of pleasant surrender. She *was* very good to him. He had been cruel and unjust in the afternoon. She was

---

1. Powdered milk or milk substitute.
2. Fire made to produce a dense smoke, to guide the plane to a landing place.

a fine woman, marvellous really. And just then it occurred to him that he was going to die.

It came with a rush; not as a rush of water nor of wind; but of a sudden evil-smelling emptiness and the odd thing was that the hyena slipped lightly along the edge of it.

"What is it, Harry?" she asked him.

"Nothing," he said. "You had better move over to the other side. To windward."

"Did Molo change the dressing?"

"Yes. I'm just using the boric now."

"How do you feel?"

"A little wobbly."

"I'm going in to bathe," she said. "I'll be right out. I'll eat with you and then we'll put the cot in."

So, he said to himself, we did well to stop the quarrelling. He had never quarrelled much with this woman, while with the women that he loved he had quarrelled so much they had finally, always, with the corrosion of the quarrelling, killed what they had together. He had loved too much, demanded too much, and he wore it all out.

He thought about alone in Constantinople[3] that time, having quarrelled in Paris before he had gone out. He had whored the whole time and then, when that was over, and he had failed to kill his loneliness, but only made it worse, he had written her, the first one, the one who left him, a letter telling her how he had never been able to kill it. . . . How when he thought he saw her outside the Regence one time it made him go all faint and sick inside, and that he would follow a woman who looked like her in some way, along the Boulevard, afraid to see it was not she, afraid to lose the feeling it gave him. How every one he had slept with had only made him miss her more. How what she had done could never matter since he knew he could not cure himself of loving her. He wrote this letter at the Club, cold sober, and mailed it to New York asking her to write him at the office in Paris. That seemed safe. And that night missing her so much it made him feel hollow sick inside, he wandered up past Taxim's, picked a girl up and took her out to supper. He had gone to a place to dance with her afterward, she danced badly, and left her for a hot Armenian slut, that swung her belly against him so it almost scalded. He took her away from a British gunner subaltern after a row. The gunner asked him outside and they fought in the street on the cobbles in the dark. He'd hit him twice, hard, on the side of the jaw and when he didn't go down he knew he was in for a fight. The gunner hit him in the body, then beside his eye. He swung with his left again and landed and the gunner fell on him and grabbed his coat and tore the sleeve off and he clubbed him twice behind the ear and then smashed him with his right as he pushed him away. When the gunner went down his head hit first and he ran with the girl because they heard the M. P.'s coming. They got into a taxi and drove out to Rimmily Hissa along the Bosphorus, and around, and back in the cool night and went to bed and she felt as over-ripe as she looked but

---

3. Now Istanbul, capital of Turkey. In the rest of the paragraph there are references to streets and places in and around the city.

smoother, rose-petal, syrupy, smooth-bellied, big-breasted and needed no pillow under her buttocks, and he left her before she was awake looking blousy enough in the first daylight and turned up at the Pera Palace with a black eye, carrying his coat because one sleeve was missing.

That same night he left for Anatolia and he remembered, later on that trip, riding all day through fields of the poppies that they raised for opium and how strange it made you feel, finally, and all the distances seemed wrong, to where they had made the attack with the newly arrived Constantine officers, that did not know a goddamned thing, and the artillery had fired into the troops and the British observer had cried like a child.

That was the day he'd first seen dead men wearing white ballet skirts and upturned shoes with pompons on them. The Turks had come steadily and lumpily and he had seen the skirted men running and the officers shooting into them and running then themselves and he and the British observer had run too until his lungs ached and his mouth was full of the taste of pennies and they stopped behind some rocks and there were the Turks coming as lumpily as ever. Later he had seen the things that he could never think of and later still he had seen much worse. So when he got back to Paris that time he could not talk about it or stand to have it mentioned. And there in the café as he passed was that American poet with a pile of saucers in front of him and a stupid look on his potato face talking about the Dada movement[4] with a Roumanian who said his name was Tristan Tzara, who always wore a monocle and had a headache, and, back at the apartment with his wife that now he loved again, the quarrel all over, the madness all over, glad to be home, the office sent his mail up to the flat. So then the letter in answer to the one he'd written came in on a platter one morning and when he saw the handwriting he went cold all over and tried to slip the letter underneath another. But his wife said, "Who is that letter from, dear?" and that was the end of the beginning of that.

He remembered the good times with them all, and the quarrels. They always picked the finest places to have the quarrels. And why had they always quarrelled when he was feeling best? He had never written any of that because, at first, he never wanted to hurt any one and then it seemed as though there was enough to write without it. But he had always thought that he would write it finally. There was so much to write. He had seen the world change; not just the events; although he had seen many of them and had watched the people, but he had seen the subtler change and he could remember how the people were at different times. He had been in it and he had watched it and it was his duty to write of it; but now he never would.

"How do you feel?" she said. She had come out from the tent now after her bath.

"All right."

"Could you eat now?" He saw Molo behind her with the folding table and the other boy with the dishes.

"I want to write," he said.

---

4. An international movement in painting, sculpture, and literature that flourished between 1916 and 1922, stressing fantasy, surrealism, and non-sense. The term is a child's cry, chosen because it has no meaning. Tristan Tzara (below) was a leading member of the movement.

"You ought to take some broth to keep your strength up."

"I'm going to die tonight," he said. "I don't need my strength up."

"Don't be melodramatic, Harry, please," she said.

"Why don't you use your nose? I'm rotted half way up my thigh now. What the hell should I fool with broth for? Molo bring whiskey-soda."

"Please take the broth," she said gently.

"All right."

The broth was too hot. He had to hold it in the cup until it cooled enough to take it and then he just got it down without gagging.

"You're a fine woman," he said. "Don't pay any attention to me."

She looked at him with her well-known, well-loved face from *Spur* and *Town and Country*,[5] only a little the worse for drink, only a little the worse for bed, but *Town and Country* never showed those good breasts and those useful thighs and those lightly small-of-back-caressing hands, and as he looked and saw her well known pleasant smile, he felt death come again. This time there was no rush. It was a puff, as of a wind that makes a candle flicker and the flame go tall.

"They can bring my net out later and hang it from the tree and build the fire up. I'm not going in the tent tonight. It's not worth moving. It's a clear night. There won't be any rain."

So this was how you died, in whispers that you did not hear. Well, there would be no more quarrelling. He could promise that. The one experience that he had never had he was not going to spoil now. He probably would. You spoiled everything. But perhaps he wouldn't.

"You can't take dictation, can you?"

"I never learned," she told him.

"That's all right."

There wasn't time, of course, although it seemed as though it telescoped so that you might put it all into one paragraph if you could get it right.

There was a log house, chinked white with mortar, on a hill above the lake. There was a bell on a pole by the door to call the people in to meals. Behind the house were fields and behind the fields was the timber. A line of lombardy poplars ran from the house to the dock. Other poplars ran along the point. A road went up to the hills along the edge of the timber and along that road he picked blackberries. Then that log house was burned down and all the guns that had been on deer foot racks above the open fire place were burned and afterwards their barrels, with the lead melted in the magazines, and the stocks burned away, lay out on the heap of ashes that were used to make lye for the big iron soap kettles, and you asked Grandfather if you could have them to play with, and he said, no. You see they were his guns still and he never bought any others. Nor did he hunt any more. The house was rebuilt in the same place out of lumber now and painted white and from its porch you saw the poplars and the lake beyond; but there were never any more guns. The barrels of the guns that had hung on the deer feet on the wall of the log house lay out there on the heap of ashes and no one ever touched them.

5. Magazines designed for a wealthy audience.

In the Black Forest,[6] after the war, we rented a trout stream and there were two ways to walk to it. One was down the valley from Triberg and around the valley road in the shade of the trees that bordered the white road, and then up a side road that went up through the hills past many small farms, with the big Schwarzwald[7] houses, until that road crossed the stream. That was where our fishing began.

The other way was to climb steeply up to the edge of the woods and then go across the top of the hills through the pine woods, and then out to the edge of a meadow and down across this meadow to the bridge. There were birches along the stream and it was not big, but narrow, clear and fast, with pools where it had cut under the roots of the birches. At the Hotel in Triberg the proprietor had a fine season. It was very pleasant and we were all great friends. The next year came the inflation and the money he had made the year before was not enough to buy supplies to open the hotel and he hanged himself.

You could dictate that, but you could not dictate the Place Contrescarpe[8] where the flower sellers dyed their flowers in the street and the dye ran over the paving where the autobus started and the old men and the women, always drunk on wine and bad marc;[9] and the children with their noses running in the cold; the smell of dirty sweat and poverty and drunkenness at the Café des Amateurs and the whores at the Bal Musette[1] they lived above. The Concierge who entertained the trooper of the Garde Republicaine in her loge, his horsehair-plumed helmet on a chair. The locataire across the hall whose husband was a bicycle racer and her joy that morning at the Cremerie when she had opened L'Auto and seen where he placed third in Paris-Tours, his first big race. She had blushed and laughed and then gone upstairs crying with the yellow sporting paper in her hand. The husband of the woman who ran the Bal Musette drove a taxi and when he, Harry, had to take an early plane the husband knocked upon the door to wake him and they each drank a glass of white wine at the zinc of the bar before they started. He knew his neighbors in that quarter then because they all were poor.

Around that Place there were two kinds; the drunkards and the sportifs. The drunkards killed their poverty that way; the sportifs took it out in exercise. They were the descendants of the Communards[2] and it was no struggle for them to know their politics. They knew who had shot their fathers, their relatives, their brothers, and their friends when the Versailles troops came in and took the town after the Commune and executed any one they could catch with calloused hands, or who wore a cap, or carried any other sign he was a working man. And in that poverty, and in that quarter across the street from a Boucherie Chevaline[3] and a wine co-operative he had written the start of all he was to do. There never was another part of Paris that he loved like that, the sprawling trees, the old white plastered houses painted brown below, the long green of the autobus in that round square, the purple flower dye upon the paving, the sudden drop down the hill of the rue Cardinal Lemoine to the River, and the other way the narrow crowded world of the rue Mouffetard. The street that ran up toward the

---

6. Wooded, mountainous region in southern Germany.
7. Black Forest (German).
8. Square in a working-class neighborhood of Paris.
9. White brandy (French).
1. Dance hall (French).

2. Participants in the 1871 workers' uprising in Paris and the Commune, a local government established on March 18, 1871, but suppressed by the Versailles government two months later.
3. A butcher shop selling horsemeat, once common in poorer neighborhoods throughout Europe.

Pantheon and the other that he always took with the bicycle, the only asphalted street in all that quarter, smooth under the tires, with the high narrow houses and the cheap tall hotel where Paul Verlaine[4] had died. There were only two rooms in the apartments where they lived and he had a room on the top floor of that hotel that cost him sixty francs a month where he did his writing, and from it he could see the roofs and chimney pots and all the hills of Paris.

From the apartment you could only see the wood and coal man's place. He sold wine too, bad wine. The golden horse's head outside the Boucherie Chevaline where the carcasses hung yellow gold and red in the open window, and the green painted co-operative where they bought their wine; good wine and cheap. The rest was plaster walls and the windows of the neighbors. The neighbors who, at night, when some one lay drunk in the street, moaning and groaning in that typical French ivresse[5] that you were propaganded to believe did not exist, would open their windows and then the murmur of talk.

"Where is the policeman? When you don't want him the bugger is always there. He's sleeping with some concierge. Get the Agent." Till some one threw a bucket of water from a window and the moaning stopped. "What's that? Water. Ah, that's intelligent." And the windows shutting. Marie, his femme de menage,[6] protesting against the eight-hour day saying, "If a husband works until six he gets only a little drunk on the way home and does not waste too much. If he works only until five he is drunk every night and one has no money. It is the wife of the working man who suffers from this shortening of hours."

"Wouldn't you like some more broth?" the woman asked him now.

"No, thank you very much. It is awfully good."

"Try just a little."

"I would like a whiskey-soda."

"It's not good for you."

"No. It's bad for me. Cole Porter[7] wrote the words and the music. This knowledge that you're going mad for me."

"You know I like you to drink."

"Oh yes. Only it's bad for me."

When she goes, he thought. I'll have all I want. Not all I want but all there is. Ayee he was tired. Too tired. He was going to sleep a little while. He lay still and death was not there. It must have gone around another street. It went in pairs, on bicycles, and moved absolutely silently on the pavements.

No, he had never written about Paris. Not the Paris that he cared about. But what about the rest that he had never written?

What about the ranch and the silvered gray of the sage brush, the quick, clear water in the irrigation ditches, and the heavy green of the alfalfa. The trail went up into the hills and the cattle in the summer were shy as deer. The bawling and the steady noise and slow moving mass raising a dust as you brought them down in the fall. And behind the mountains, the clear sharpness of the peak in the evening light and, riding down along the trail in the moonlight, bright across

---

4. French Symbolist poet (1844–1896). Hemingway rented and worked in a room in which Verlaine had lived.
5. Drunkenness (French). Because the French drank wine and brandy rather than hard liquor, it was often claimed that there was no real drunkenness among them.
6. Charwoman (French).
7. Popular American song composer (1893–1964).

the valley. Now he remembered coming down through the timber in the dark holding the horse's tail when you could not see and all the stories that he meant to write.

About the half-wit chore boy who was left at the ranch that time and told not to let any one get any hay, and that old bastard from the Forks who had beaten the boy when he had worked for him stopping to get some feed. The boy refusing and the old man saying he would beat him again. The boy got the rifle from the kitchen and shot him when he tried to come into the barn and when they came back to the ranch he'd been dead a week, frozen in the corral, and the dogs had eaten part of him. But what was left you packed on a sled wrapped in a blanket and roped on and you got the boy to help you haul it, and the two of you took it out over the road on skis, and sixty miles down to town to turn the boy over. He having no idea that he would be arrested. Thinking he had done his duty and that you were his friend and he would be rewarded. He'd helped to haul the old man in so everybody could know how bad the old man had been and how he'd tried to steal some feed that didn't belong to him, and when the sheriff put the handcuffs on the boy he couldn't believe it. Then he'd started to cry. That was one story he had saved to write. He knew at least twenty good stories from out there and he had never written one. Why?

"You tell them why," he said.

"Why what, dear?"

"Why nothing."

She didn't drink so much, now, since she had him. But if he lived he would never write about her, he knew that now. Nor about any of them. The rich were dull and they drank too much, or they played too much backgammon. They were dull and they were repetitious. He remembered poor Julian and his romantic awe of them and how he had started a story once that began, "The very rich are different from you and me."[8] And how some one had said to Julian, Yes, they have more money. But that was not humorous to Julian. He thought they were a special glamourous race and when he found they weren't it wrecked him just as much as any other thing that wrecked him.

He had been contemptuous of those who wrecked. You did not have to like it because you understood it. He could beat anything, he thought, because no thing could hurt him if he did not care.

All right. Now he would not care for death. One thing he had always dreaded was the pain. He could stand pain as well as any man, until it went on too long, and wore him out, but here he had something that had hurt frightfully and just when he had felt it breaking him, the pain had stopped.

He remembered long ago when Williamson, the bombing officer, had been hit by a stick bomb some one in a German patrol had thrown as he was coming in through the wire that night and, screaming, had begged every one to kill him. He was a fat man, very brave, and a good officer, although addicted to fantastic shows. But that night he was caught in the wire, with a flare lighting him up and his bowels spilled out into the wire, so when they brought him in, alive, they had to cut him loose. Shoot me, Harry. For Christ sake shoot me. They had

---

8. These are the opening words of "The Rich Boy" by F. Scott Fitzgerald. Hemingway originally used Fitzgerald's name instead of "Julian," but was persuaded to make the change by his editor, Maxwell Perkins.

*had an argument one time about our Lord never sending you anything you
could not bear and some one's theory had been that meant that at a certain time
the pain passed you out automatically. But he had always remembered
Williamson, that night. Nothing passed out Williamson until he gave him all
his morphine tablets that he had always saved to use himself and then they did
not work right away.*

Still this now, that he had, was very easy; and if it was no worse as it went
on there was nothing to worry about. Except that he would rather be in better company.

He thought a little about the company that he would like to have.

No, he thought, when everything you do, you do too long, and do too late,
you can't expect to find the people still there. The people all are gone. The
party's over and you are with your hostess now.

I'm getting as bored with dying as with everything else, he thought.

"It's a bore," he said out loud.

"What is, my dear?"

"Anything you do too bloody long."

He looked at her face between him and the fire. She was leaning back in
the chair and the firelight shone on her pleasantly lined face and he could see
that she was sleepy. He heard the hyena make a noise just outside the range
of the fire.

"I've been writing," he said. "But I got tired."

"Do you think you will be able to sleep?"

"Pretty sure. Why don't you turn in?"

"I like to sit here with you."

"Do you feel anything strange?" he asked her.

"No. Just a little sleepy."

"I do," he said.

He had just felt death come by again.

"You know the only thing I've never lost is curiosity," he said to her.

"You've never lost anything. You're the most complete man I've ever
known."

"Christ," he said. "How little a woman knows. What is that? Your intu-
ition?"

Because, just then, death had come and rested its head on the foot of the
cot and he could smell its breath.

"Never believe any of that about a scythe and a skull,"[9] he told her. "It can
be two bicycle policemen as easily, or be a bird. Or it can have a wide snout
like a hyena."

It had moved up on him now, but it had no shape any more. It simply occupied space.

"Tell it to go away."

It did not go away but moved a little closer.

"You've got a hell of a breath," he told it. "You stinking bastard."

It moved up closer to him still and he could not speak to it, and when it
saw he could not speak it came a little closer, and now he tried to send it away

9. In medieval imagery death is often represented as a skeleton draped in a long cape so that only the skull
shows. He carries a scythe.

without speaking, but it moved in on him so its weight was all upon his chest, and while it crouched there and he could not move, or speak, he heard the woman say, "Bwana is asleep now. Take the cot up very gently and carry it into the tent."

He could not speak to tell her to make it go away and it crouched now, heavier, so he could not breathe. And then, while they lifted the cot, suddenly it was all right and the weight went from his chest.

It was morning and had been morning for some time and he heard the plane. It showed very tiny and then made a wide circle and the boys ran out and lit the fires, using kerosene, and piled on grass so there were two big smudges at each end of the level place and the morning breeze blew them toward the camp and the plane circled twice more, low this time, and then glided down and levelled off and landed smoothly and, coming walking toward him, was old Compton in slacks, a tweed jacket and a brown felt hat.

"What's the matter, old cock?" Compton said.

"Bad leg," he told him. "Will you have some breakfast?"

"Thanks. I'll just have some tea. It's the Puss Moth[1] you know. I won't be able to take the Memsahib. There's only room for one. Your lorry is on the way."

Helen had taken Compton aside and was speaking to him. Compton came back more cheery than ever.

"We'll get you right in," he said. "I'll be back for the Mem. Now I'm afraid I'll have to stop at Arusha to refuel. We'd better get going."

"What about the tea?"

"I don't really care about it you know."

The boys had picked up the cot and carried it around the green tents and down along the rock and out onto the plain and along past the smudges that were burning brightly now, and the grass all consumed, and the wind fanning the fire, to the little plane. It was difficult getting him in, but once in he lay back in the leather seat, and the leg was stuck straight out to one side of the seat where Compton sat. Compton started the motor and got in. He waved to Helen and to the boys and, as the clatter moved into the old familiar roar, they swung around with Compie watching for wart-hog holes and roared, bumping, along the stretch between the fires and with the last bump rose and he saw them all standing below, waving, and the camp beside the hill, flattening now, and the plain spreading, clumps of trees, and the bush flattening, while the game trails ran now smoothly to the dry waterholes, and there was a new water that he had never known of. The zebra, small rounded backs now, and the wildebeeste, big-headed dots seeming to climb as they moved in long fingers across the plain, now scattering as the shadow came toward them, they were tiny now, and the movement had no gallop, and the plain as far as you could see, gray-yellow now and ahead old Compie's tweed back and the brown felt hat. Then they were over the first hills and the wildebeeste were trailing up them, and then they were over mountains with sudden depths of green-rising forest and the solid bamboo slopes, and then the heavy forest again, sculptured into peaks and hollows until they crossed, and hills sloped down and then another plain, hot now, and purple brown, bumpy with

---

1. A small, light airplane seating two people.

heat and Compie looking back to see how he was riding. Then there were other mountains dark ahead.

And then instead of going on to Arusha they turned left, he evidently figured that they had the gas, and looking down he saw a pink sifting cloud, moving over the ground, and in the air, like the first snow in a blizzard, that comes from nowhere, and he knew the locusts were coming up from the South. Then they began to climb and they were going to the East it seemed, and then it darkened and they were in a storm, the rain so thick it seemed like flying through a waterfall, and then they were out and Compie turned his head and grinned and pointed and there, ahead, all he could see, as wide as all the world, great, high, and unbelievably white in the sun, was the square top of Kilimanjaro. And then he knew that there was where he was going.

Just then the hyena stopped whimpering in the night and started to make a strange, human, almost crying sound. The woman heard it and stirred uneasily. She did not wake. In her dream she was at the house on Long Island and it was the night before her daughter's début. Somehow her father was there and he had been very rude. Then the noise the hyena made was so loud she woke and for a moment she did not know where she was and she was very afraid. Then she took the flashlight and shone it on the other cot that they had carried in after Harry had gone to sleep. She could see his bulk under the mosquito bar but somehow he had gotten his leg out and it hung down alongside the cot. The dressings had all come down and she could not look at it.

"Molo," she called, "Molo! Molo!"

Then she said, "Harry, Harry!" Then her voice rising, "Harry! Please, Oh Harry!"

There was no answer and she could not hear him breathing.

Outside the tent the hyena made the same strange noise that had awakened her. But she did not hear him for the beating of her heart.

1936, 1938

THOMAS WOLFE
1900–1938

Thomas Wolfe's writing was diametrically opposed to the suggestive conciseness of such modernist prose writers as F. Scott Fitzgerald and Ernest Hemingway. He wanted to write about America, he said, "not the government, or the Revolutionary War, or the Monroe Doctrine," but rather "the ten million seconds and moments of your life." Elsewhere he said, "I want to write about everything and say all that can be said about each particular." As a result his manuscripts were vast scrawls that had to be shaped into books by his editors and agents.

Wolfe was born in Asheville, North Carolina, the seventh and youngest child of O. W. and Julia Westall Wolfe. His father, who had been married before, was a stonecutter. His mother came from a Carolina mountain family. When Wolfe was about six years old, she opened a boardinghouse a few blocks from the family home. Thereafter, the family divided its time between these two residences. Later, Julia Wolfe began to invest in real estate and between the earnings of the two parents, the family was financially comfortable. All its members were highly individualistic, emotional, and self-expressive; the passionate family drama was both Wolfe's inspiration and his burden. His youth was punctuated by loss as well: his brother Grover died when Wolfe was four, his beloved brother Ben when he was eighteen, and his father when he was twenty-two.

There was no tradition of higher education on either side of the family, but some of Wolfe's teachers persuaded his parents to send him to the University of North Carolina at Chapel Hill. After graduating he took a year of additional study at Harvard University, working with George Pierce Baker, who at that time gave one of the very few courses in playwriting in the nation, the famous "47 Workshop." In 1924 Wolfe moved to New York City, where he taught composition at New York University while trying to write salable plays.

At about this time, Wolfe met and became involved with Aline Bernstein, a successful scene designer for the Neighborhood Playhouse, a New York theater group. She persuaded the young writer to try writing prose fiction, and with her encouragement he turned to the subject of his own life. A three-hundred-thousand-word manuscript—i.e., about a thousand typed pages—titled O Lost made the rounds of several publishers before coming to the attention of Maxwell Perkins at Scribner. Perkins, a leading editor of the day, had made it his life's work to identify major American talents—Fitzgerald and Hemingway were among those he published—and he found in Wolfe a writer who equaled his highest idea of American genius. Reorganized and cut by about a third, the book appeared as Look Homeward, Angel in 1929. Despite the fact that book sales were generally down because of the Great Depression, it was a popular success and made Wolfe a celebrity.

Look Homeward, Angel is an extensive fictional re-creation of Wolfe's youth and of the members of his family; the hero, Eugene Gant, is Wolfe himself. Its picture of the mountain South is a substantial contribution to American regional writing. A sequel, Of Time and the River, came out in 1935 and was even more popular. Wolfe's autobiographical revelations offended some readers, including residents of Asheville and his own family. Only his mother appeared unperturbed by the merciless way in which he had put living people into print. Pro-German statements that he made in the mid-1930s angered many others, and he made numerous enemies. Maxwell Perkins's role came under critical scrutiny—one reviewer going so far as to suggest that Wolfe was only part author of his own books. In distress, Wolfe changed publishers.

In the summer of 1938 Wolfe, before a visit to the West Coast, delivered a crate of manuscript to his new editor, Edward Aswell of Harper's. The crate, he said, contained his next book. What it really contained were thousands of handwritten pages in no particular order. In Seattle, Wolfe contracted a case of pneumonia that developed serious complications. He died of a brain infection in September, and it was left to Aswell to work up two more books from the manuscript material, The Web and the Rock, published in 1939, and You Can't Go Home Again, published in 1940. Although these books have a new hero, George Webber, they continue Wolfe's autobiographical saga. Wolfe's reputation suffered after his death for what was deemed his lack of artistry: his formlessness and prolixity in an age where criticism called for tight structure and verbal economy. Those who admire his work point to his treatment of childhood and adolescence, his depiction of the mountain South, and his romantically nostalgic evocations of lost happiness.

"The Lost Boy" is a segment of the Gant saga, with different names for the characters, that was not used in the novels. It was published as a short story in 1937. As noted, Grover Cleveland Wolfe, Thomas Wolfe's brother, died at the age of eleven when the author-to-be was just four. In 1904 Julia Wolfe took some of the children, including Tom and Grover, to St. Louis, where the World's Fair was being held; there she ran a boardinghouse, the Carolina House, for some months. It was in St. Louis that Grover died of typhoid fever. In "The Lost Boy," Grover is called Robert. The story offers a four-angled view of him: (1) an episode involving Robert and his father, (2) a view of Robert through his mother's eyes, (3) an older sister's account of his illness and death, and (4) the attempt of the author-brother to recapture time and his lost brother by returning years later to the house in St. Louis where they had lived.

The text is from *The Complete Short Stories of Thomas Wolfe* (1987).

The Lost Boy[1]

The light came and went, the booming strokes of three o'clock beat out across the town in thronging bronze, light winds of April blew the fountain out in rainbow sheets, until the plume returned and pulsed, as Robert turned into the Square. He was a child dark-eyed and grave, birthmarked upon his neck—a berry of warm brown—and with a gentle face, perhaps too quiet and listening for his years. The scuffed boy's shoes, the thick-ribbed stockings gartered at the knees, the short knee pants cut straight with three small useless buttons at the side, the sailor blouse, the old cap battered out of shape, perched sideways up on top the raven head—these friendly shabby garments, shaped by Robert, uttered him. He turned and passed along the north side of the Square, and in that moment felt the union of Forever and Now.

Light came and went and came again; the great plume of the fountain pulsed, and the winds of April sheeted it across the Square in rainbow gossamer of spray. The street-cars ground into the Square from every portion of the town's small compass and halted briefly like wound toys in their old quarter-hourly formula of assembled Eight. The courthouse bell boomed out its solemn warning of immediate Three, and everything was just the same as it had always been.

He saw with quiet eyes that haggis[2] of vexed shapes, that hodge-podge of ill-sorted masonries, and he did not feel lost. For "Here," thought Robert, "here's the Square as it has always been—and Papa's shop, the fire department and the city hall, the fountain pulsing with its plume, the drug-store on the corner there, the row of old brick buildings on this side, the people passing and the cars that come and go, the light that comes and changes and that always will come back again, and everything that comes and goes and changes in the Square, and yet will be the same—here," Robert thought, "here is the Square that never changes; here is Robert almost twelve—and here is Time."

For so it seemed to him: small center of his little universe, itself the accidental masonry of twenty years, the chance agglomerate of time and of disrupted strivings, it was for him earth's pivot and the granite core of changelessness, the eternal Place where all things came and passed, the Place that would abide forever and would never change.

The Square walked past him then with steady steps—plume, pulse, and fountain, and the sheeting spray, the open arches of the fire department doors, the wooden stomp of the great hoofs, the casual whiskings of the dry coarse tails. He passed the firetrap of a wiener stand; and the Singer[3] shop, the steel-bright smartness of the new machines, with their swift evocations of the house, the whir, the treadle, and the mounting hum—the vague

1. The text reproduces the story as it appeared in *Redbook* magazine in 1937. The story as collected in *The Hills Beyond* (1941) differs in many particulars from the version that appeared in Wolfe's lifetime.
2. I.e., pudding.
3. Manufacturer of sewing machines.

monotony of women's work. He passed the music-store, the coffined splendor of piano shapes, the deep-toned richness, and the smell of proud dark wood, the stale yet pleasant memory of parlors.

He passed the grocery store then, the gaunt gray horse, the old head leaning to its hitching block; within, the pickle-barrels, the fans, the sultry coffee and the cloven cheese, the musty compost of cool plenty, the delicious All-Smell, and the buttered unction of the grocer with his straw-cuffed sleeves.

He was going past the hardware store now. He always had to stop by places that had shining perfect things in them, and windows full of geometric tools, of hammers, saws, and planing-boards, and strong new rakes and hoes with unworn handles of white perfect wood, stamped hard and vivid with the maker's seal. Ah, how he loved such things as these, strong perfect shapes and pungent smells, the great integrities of use and need, the certitude of this unchanging pattern, set to the grand assurance of the everlasting Square. He turned a corner, and he *was* caught, held. A waft of air, warm, chocolate-laden, filled his nostrils. He tried to pass the white front of the little eight-foot shop; he paused, struggling with conscience; he could not go on. It was the little candy-shop run by old Crocker and his wife. And Robert could not pass.

"Old stingy Crockers!" he thought scornfully. "I'll not go there again. They're so stingy they stop the clocks at night. But—" The maddening fragrance of rich cooking chocolate touched him once again. "I'll just look in the window and see what they've got." He paused a moment, looking with his dark and quiet eyes into the window of the candy shop. His dark eyes rested for a moment on a tray of chocolate drops. Unconsciously he licked his lips. Put one of them upon your tongue and it just melted there like honey. And then the trays full of rich home-made fudge. He looked longingly at the deep body of the chocolate fudge, reflectively at the maple walnut, more critically, yet with longing, at the mints, the nougatines, and all the other tempters.

"Old stingy Crockers!" Robert muttered once again, and turned to go. "I wouldn't go in *there* again."

And yet—he did not go away. "Old stingy Crockers," it was true; still, they did make the best candy in town, the best, in fact, that he had ever tasted.

●   ●   ●

He looked through the window back into the little shop and saw Mrs. Crocker there. A customer had made a purchase, and as Robert looked, he saw Mrs. Crocker, with her little wrenny[4] face, lean over and peer primly at the scales. She had a piece of fudge in her clean bony fingers—and now she broke it, primly, in her little bony hands. She dropped a morsel down into the scales. They weighted down alarmingly, and her thin lips tightened. She snatched a piece of fudge out of the scales and broke it carefully once again. This time the scale wavered, went down very slowly, and came back again. Mrs. Crocker carefully put the reclaimed piece of fudge back in the tray, put the remainder in a paper bag, folded it and gave it to the customer, counted the money carefully, and doled it out into the till.

---

4. Wrenlike; Wolfe's invented word. The wren is a small, wide-eyed, active bird.

Robert stood there, looking scornfully. "Old stingy Crocker—afraid that she might give a crumb away."

He grunted, and again he turned to go. But now Mr. Crocker came out from the little partitioned place behind, bearing a tray of fresh-made candy in his skinny hands. Old man Crocker rocked along the counter to the front and put it down. He was a cripple. One leg was inches shorter than the other, and on this leg there was an enormous thick-soled boot, with a kind of wooden rocker-like arrangement, six inches high at least, to make up for the deficiency of his game right leg. And on this wooden cradle Mr. Crocker rocked along. He was a little pinched and skinny figure of a man with bony hands and meager features, and when he walked, he really rocked along, with a kind of prim and apprehensive little smile, as if he was afraid he was going to lose something.

"Old stingy Crocker," muttered Robert. "Humph! He wouldn't give you *anything.*"

And yet he did not go away. He hung there curiously, peering through the window, with his dark and gentle face now focused and intent, flattening his nose against the glass. Unconsciously he scratched the thick-ribbed fabric of one stockinged leg with the scuffed toe of his old shoe. The fresh warm odor of the new-made fudge had reached him. It was delicious. It was a little maddening. Half-consciously, he began to fumble in one trouser pocket and pulled out his purse, a shabby worn old black one with a twisted clasp. He opened it and prowled about inside.

What he found was not inspiring: a nickel and two pennies and—he had forgotten them—the stamps. He took the stamps out and unfolded them. There were five twos, eight ones, all that remained of the dollar and sixty cents' worth which Reed, the pharmacist, had given him for running errands a week or two before.

"Old Crocker," Robert thought, looked somberly at the grotesque little form and—"Well—" indefinitely—"He's had all the rest of them. He might as well take these."

So, soothing conscience with this sop of scorn, he went into the shop, and pointing with a slightly grimy finger at the fresh-made tray of chocolate fudge, he said: "I'll take fifteen cents' worth of this, Mr. Crocker."

He paused a moment, fighting with embarrassment; then he lifted his dark face and said quietly: "And please, I'll have to give you stamps again."

Mr. Crocker made no answer. He pressed his lips together. Then he got the candy scoop, slid open the door of the glass case, put fudge into the scoop, and rocking to the scales, began to weigh the candy out. Robert watched him as he peered and squinted, watched him purse his lips together, saw him take a piece of fudge and break it into two parts. And then old Crocker broke two parts in two. He weighed, he squinted, he hovered, until it seemed to Robert that by calling *Mrs.* Crocker stingy he had been guilty of a rank injustice. But finally the scales hung there, quivering apprehensively, upon the very hair-line of nervous balance, as if even the scales were afraid that one more move from old man Crocker and they would be undone.

Mr. Crocker took the candy, dumped it into a paper bag, and rocking back along the counter toward the boy, he said: "Where are the stamps?" Robert gave them to him. Mr. Crocker relinquished his claw-like hold on the bag and set it down upon the counter. Robert took the bag and then remembered.

"Mr. Crocker,"—again he felt the old embarrassment that was almost like strong pain,—"I gave you too much," Robert said. "There were eighteen cents in stamps. You—you can just give me three ones back."

Mr. Crocker did not answer for a moment. He was busy unfolding the stamps and flattening them out on top of the glass counter. When he had done so, he peered at them sharply, for a moment, thrusting his scrawny neck forward and running his eye up and down, as a bookkeeper who tots up rows of figures.

Then he said tartly: "I don't like this kind of business. I'm not a post office. The next time you come in here and want anything, you'll have to have the money for it."

Hot anger rose in Robert's throat. His olive face suffused with angry color. His tarry eyes got black and bright. For a moment he was on the verge of saying: "Then why did you take my other stamps? Why do you tell me now, when you have taken all the stamps I had, that you don't want them?"

But he was a quiet, gentle, gravely thoughtful boy, and he had been taught how to respect his elders. So he just stood there looking with his tar-black eyes. Old Man Crocker took the stamps up in his thin, parched fingers, and turning, rocked away down to the till.

He took the twos and laid them in one rounded scallop, then took the ones and folded them and put them in the one next to it. Then he closed the till and started to rock off, down toward the other end. Robert kept looking at him, but Mr. Crocker did not look at Robert. Instead, he began to take some cardboard shapes and fold them into boxes.

In a moment Robert said: "Mr. Crocker, will you give me the three ones, please?"

Mr. Crocker did not answer. But Mrs. Crocker, also folding boxes with her parsley hands, muttered tartly: "Hm! I'd give him nothing!"

Mr. Crocker looked at Robert: "What are you waiting for?"

"Will you give me the three ones, please?" Robert said.

"I'll give you nothing," Mr. Crocker said. "Now you get out of here! And don't you come here with any more of those stamps."

"I should like to know where he gets them, that's what I should like to know," said Mrs. Crocker.

"You get out of here," said Mr. Crocker. "And don't you come back here with any stamps. . . . Where did you get those stamps?" he said.

"That's just what I've been thinking," Mrs. Crocker said.

"You've been coming in here for the last two weeks with stamps," said Mr. Crocker. "I don't like the look of it. Where did you get those stamps?" he said.

"That's what I've been thinking all along," said Mrs. Crocker.

Robert had got white underneath his olive skin. His eyes had lost their luster. They looked like dull, stunned balls of tar. "From Mr. Reed," he said. "I got the stamps from Mr. Reed." He burst out desperately: "Mr. Crocker, Mr. Reed will tell you how I got the stamps. I did some work for Mr. Reed; he gave me those stamps two weeks ago."

"Mr. Reed," said Mrs. Crocker acidly. "I call it mighty funny."

"Mr. Crocker," Robert said, "if you'll just let me have the three ones—"

"You get out of here, boy!" cried Mr. Crocker. "Now don't you come in here again! There's something funny about this whole business! If you can't pay as other people do, then I don't want your trade."

"Mr. Crocker," Robert said again, and underneath the olive skin his face was gray, "if you'll just let me have those three—"

"You get out of here," Mr. Crocker cried, and began to rock forward toward the boy. "If you don't get out—"

"I'd call a policeman, that's what I'd do," Mrs. Crocker said.

Mr. Crocker came rocking up to Robert, took the boy and pushed him with his bony little hands. Robert felt sick and gray down to the hollow pit of his stomach.

"You've got to give me those three ones," he said.

"You get out of here!" shrilled Mr. Crocker. He seized the screen door, pulled it open and pushed Robert out. "Don't you come back in here," he said, pausing for a moment, working thinly at the lips. Then he turned and rocked back in the shop again. Robert stood there on the pavement. And light came and went and came again.

The boy stood there for a moment, and a wagon rattled past. There were some people passing by, but Robert did not notice them. He stood there blindly, in the watches of the sun, but something had gone out of the day.

He felt the soul-sickening guilt that all the children, all the good men of the earth, have felt since time began. And even anger had been drowned out, in the swelling tide of guilt. "There is the Square," thought Robert as before. "This is Now. There is my father's shop. And all of it is as it has always been— save I."

And the Square reeled drunkenly around him, light went in blind gray motes before his eyes, the fountain sheeted out to rainbow iridescence and returned to its proud pulsing plume again. But all the brightness had gone out of day.

The scuffed boots of the lost boy moved and stumbled blindly over. The numb feet crossed the pavement—reached the sidewalk, crossed the plotted central Square—the grass plots, the flower-beds, so soon with red and packed geraniums.

"I want to be alone," thought Robert, "where I can not go near him. Oh, God, I hope he never hears, that no one ever tells him—"

The plume blew out; the iridescent sheet of spray blew over him. He passed through, found the other side and crossed the street. "Oh, God, if Papa ever hears," thought Robert, as his numb feet started up the steps into his father's shop.

He found and felt the steps—the thickness of old lumber twenty feet in length. He saw it all: the iron columns on his father's porch, painted with the dull anomalous black-green that all such columns in this land and weather come to; two angels, fly-specked, and the waiting stones. Beyond and all around, in the stonecutter's shop, cold shapes of white and marble, rounded stone, the limestone base, the languid angel with strong marble hands of love.

He went on down the aisle; the white shapes stood around him. He went on back into the workroom. This he knew—the little cast-iron stove in the left-hand corner, the high, dirty window, looking down across the market square, the rude old shelves, upon the shelves the chisels and a layer of stone dust; an emery wheel with pump tread, and two trestles of coarse wood upon which rested gravestones. At one trestle was a man, at work.

The boy looked numbly, saw the name was *Creasman:* the carved analysis of John, the symmetry of S, the fine finality of *Creasman—November, Nineteen-Three.*

The man looked up and then returned to work. He was a man of fifty-three, immensely long and tall and gaunt. He wore good dark clothes, save he had no coat. He worked in shirt-sleeves with his vest on, a strong watch-chain stretching across his vest; wing collar and black tie, Adam's apple, bony forehead, bony nose, light eyes, gray-green, undeep and cold, and somehow lonely-looking, a striped apron going up around his shoulders, and starched cuffs. And in one hand a tremendous rounded wooden mallet like a butcher's bole; and in his other hand, implacable and cold, the chisel.

"How are you, son?"

He did not look up as he spoke. He spoke quietly, absently. He worked upon the chisel and the wooden mallet as delicately as a jeweler might work upon a watch, except that in the man and the wooden mallet there was power, too.

"What is it, son?" he said.

He moved around the table from the head, and started up on *J* again.

"Papa, I never stole the stamps," said Robert.

The man put down the mallet, laid the chisel down. He came around the trestle.

"What?" he said. And Robert winked his tar-black eyes; they brightened; the hot tears shot out. "I never stole the stamps," he said.

"Hey? What is this?" the man said. "What stamps?"

"That Mr. Reed gave to me, when the other boy was sick and I worked there for three days. . . . And old man Crocker," Robert said, "he took all the stamps. And I told him Mr. Reed had given them to me. And now he owes me three ones—and old man Crocker says—he says—I must have taken them."

"The stamps that Reed gave to you—hey?" the stonecutter said. "The stamps you had—" He wet his great thumb briefly on his lips, strode from his workshop out into the storeroom aisle.

The man came back, cleared his throat, and as he passed the old gray board-partition of his office, he cleared his throat and wet his thumb, and said: "I tell you, now—"

Then he turned and strode up toward the front again and cleared his throat and said: "I tell you, now—" And coming back, along the aisle between the rows of marshaled gravestones, he muttered underneath his breath: "By God, now—"

He took Robert by the hand. They went out flying down along the aisle by all the gravestones, the fly-specked angels waiting there, the wooden steps, across the cobbles and the central plot—across the whole thing, but they did not notice it.

And the fountain pulsed, the plume blew out in sheeted spray and swept across them, and an old gray horse, with a peaceful look about its torn lips, swucked up the cool, the flowing mountain water from the trough as Robert and his father went across the Square.

They went across the Square through the sheeted iridescence of the spray and to the other street and to the candy-shop. The man was dressed in his striped apron still; he was still holding Robert by the hand. He opened the screen door and stepped inside. "Give him the stamps," he said.

Mr. Crocker came rocking forward behind the counter, with a prim and careful look that now was somewhat like a smile. "It was just—" he said.

"Give him the stamps," the man said, and threw some coins down on the counter.

Mr. Crocker rocked away and got the stamps. "I just didn't know—" he said.

The stonecutter took the stamps and gave them to the boy. And Mr. Crocker took the coins.

"It was just that—" Mr. Crocker said, and smiled.

The man in the apron cleared his throat: "You never were a father," the man said. "You never knew the feeling of a child. And that is why you acted as you did. But a judgment is upon you. God has cursed you. He has afflicted you. He has made you lame and childless—and miserable as you are, you will go lame and childless to your grave—and be forgotten!"

And Crocker's wife kept kneading her bony little hands and said imploringly: "Oh, no—oh, don't say that! Please don't say that!"

The stonecutter, the breath still hoarse in him, left the store. Light came again into the day.

"Well, son," he said, and laid his hand on the boy's back. "Now don't you mind."

They walked across the Square, the sheeted spray of iridescent light swept out on them; a horse swizzled at the water-trough.

"Well, son," the gaunt man said again, "now don't you mind."

And he trod his own steps then with his great stride and went back again into his shop.

The lost boy stood upon the Square, close by the porch of his father's shop: light came again into the Square. A car curved in, upon the billboard of the car-end was a poster and some words: "*St. Louis*" and "*Excursion*" and "*The Fair.*"

And light came and went into the Square, and Robert stood there thinking quietly: "Here is the Square that never changes; here is Time."

And light came and went and came again into the Square—but now not quite the same as it had done before. He saw that pattern of familiar shapes, and knew that they were just the same as they had always been. But something had gone out of the day, and something had come in again: out of the vision of those quiet eyes some brightness had been lost; into their vision some deeper color come. He could not say, he did not know through what transforming shadows life had passed within that quarter-hour. He only knew that something had been gained forever—something lost.

As we went down through Indiana—you were too young, child, to remember it, but I always think of all of you, the way you looked that morning, when we went down through Indiana, going to the Fair. All of the apple trees were coming out, and it was April; all of the trees were coming out; it was the beginning of the spring in Indiana, and everything was getting green. Of course we don't have farms at home like those in Indiana. The children had never seen such farms as those and, I reckon, kid-like, had to take it in.

So all of them kept running up and down the aisle—well, no, except for you and *Robert*—*you* were too young; you were just three; I kept you with me. As for Robert: well, I'm going to tell you about that. But the rest of them kept running up and down the aisle and from one window to another. They kept calling out and hollering to each other every time they saw something new. They kept trying to look out on all sides in every way at once, as if they wished they had eyes in the back of their heads. It was the first time any of them had been in Indiana, and I reckon, that, kid-like, it all seemed strange and new.

And so it seemed they couldn't get enough. It seemed they never could be still.

You see, they were excited about going to St. Louis and so curious over everything they saw. They couldn't help it, and they wanted to see everything. But "I'll vow," I said, "if you children don't sit down and rest, you'll be worn to a frazzle before we ever get to see St. Louis and the Fair!"

Except for Robert! He—no sir, not him! Now, boy, I want to tell you—I've raised the lot of you, and if I do say so, there wasn't a numbskull in the lot. But *Robert!* Well, you've all grown up now, all of you have gone away, and none of you are children any more. . . . And of course, I hope that, as the fellow says, you have reached the dignity of man's estate. . . . I suppose you have the judgment of a grown man. . . . But Robert! *Robert* had it, even then!

Oh, even as a child, you know—at a time I was almost afraid to trust the rest of you out of my sight—I could depend on Robert. I could send him anywhere, and I'd always know he'd get back safe, and do exactly what I told him to!

Why, I didn't even have to tell him—you could send that child to market and tell him what you wanted, and he'd come home with *twice* as much as you could get yourself for the same money.

Now you know, I've always been considered a good trader, but *Robert!* Why, it got so finally that your papa said to me: "You'd be better off if you just tell him what you want and leave the rest to him. For," your papa says, "damned if I don't believe he's a better trader than you are. . . . He gets more for the money than anyone I ever saw."

Well, I had to admit it, you know. . . . I had to own up then. . . . Robert, even as a child, was a far better trader than I was. . . . Why, yes, they told it on him all over town, you know. . . . They said all of the market men, all of the farmers, would begin to laugh when they saw him coming. They'd say, "Look out! Here's Robert! Here's one trader you're not going to fool!"

And they were right! . . . *That* child! . . . I'd say: "Robert, suppose you run uptown and see if they've got anything good to *eat* today. Suppose you take this dollar and just see what you can do with it."

Well, sir, that was all that was needed. The minute that you told that child that you depended on his judgment, he'd have gone to the ends of the earth for you—and let me tell you something, he wouldn't *miss*, either!

His eyes would get black as coals—oh, the way that child would look at you, the intelligence and sense in his expression! He'd say, "Yes, *ma'am!* Now don't you worry, Mamma, you leave it all to me—and I'll do *good!*" said Robert.

And he'd be off like a streak of lightning and oh, Lord! As your father said to me, "I've been living in this town for almost thirty years," he said, "and I thought I knew everything there was to know about it—but that child," your papa says, "he knows places that I never heard of!" Oh, he'd go right down there to that place below your papa's shop where the draymen used to park their wagons—or he'd go down there to those old lots on Concord Street where the farmers used to keep their wagons. And child that he was, he'd go right in among them, sir—*Robert* would!—go right in and barter with them like a grown man!

And he'd come home with things he'd bought that would make your eyes stick out. . . . Here he comes one time with another boy, dragging a great bushel basket full of ripe termaters[5] between them. "Why, Robert," I says, "how on earth are we ever going to use them? Why, they'll go bad on us before we're half-way through them." "Well, Mamma," he says, "I know,"—oh, just as solemn as a judge—"but they were the last the man had," he says, "and he wanted to go home, and so I got them for ten cents," he says. "I thought it was a shame to let 'em go, and I figgered what we couldn't eat—why," says Robert, "you could *put up!*" Well, the way he said it, so earnest and so serious, I had to laugh. "But I'll vow," I said, "if you don't beat all!" . . . But that was *Robert* the way he was in *those* days! As everyone said, boy that he was, he had the sense and judgment of a grown man. . . . Child, child, I've seen you all grow up, and all of you were bright enough, but for all-round intelligence, judgment, and general ability, Robert surpassed the whole crowd. . . . I've never seen his equal, and everyone who knew him as a child will say the same.

So that's what I tell them now, when they ask me about all of you. I have to tell the truth. I always said that you were smart enough—but when they come around and brag to me about you, and I reckon how you have got on and have a kind of name—I don't let on to them, I never say a word. Why, yes! Why, here, you know—oh, 'long about a month ago, this feller comes. He said he came from New Jersey, or somewhere up in that part of the country—and he began to ask me all sorts of questions, what you were like when you were a boy and all such stuff as that.

I just pretended to study it all over; then I said, "Well, yes," real serious-like, you know. "Well, yes—I reckon I ought to know a little something about him: he was my child, just the same as all the others were; I brought him up just the the way I brought up all the others. And," I says—oh, just as solemn as you please, "he wasn't a *bad* sort of a boy. Why," I says, "up to the time that he was twelve years old he was just about the same as any other boy—a good average normal sort of fellow."

"Oh," he says. "But didn't you notice something? Didn't you notice how brilliant he was? He must have been more brilliant than the rest!"

"Well, now," I says, and pretended to study that all over, too. "Now let me see. . . . Yes," I says—I just looked him in the eye, as solemn as you please. "I guess he was a fairly bright sort of a boy. I never had no complaints to make of him on that score. He was bright enough," I says. "The only trouble with him was that he was lazy."

"Lazy!" he says—oh, you should have seen the look upon his face, you know—he jumped like someone had stuck a pin in him. "Lazy!" he says, "Why, you don't mean to tell me—"

---

5. Tomatoes.

"Yes," I says, "I was telling him the same thing myself the last time that I saw him. I told him it was a mighty lucky thing for him that he had the gift of gab. Of course, he went off to college and read a lot of books, and I reckon that's where he got this flow of language they say he has. . . . But as I said to him, 'Now look a-here,' I said, 'if you can earn your living doing a light easy class of work like this you do,' I says, 'you're mighty lucky, because none of the rest of your people had any such luck as that. They had to work hard for a living.' "

Oh, I told him, you know. I made no bones about it. And I tell you what— I wish you could have seen his face. It was a study.

"Well," he says, at last, "you've got to admit this, haven't you—he was the brightest boy you had, now wasn't he?"

I just looked at him a moment. I had to tell the truth. I couldn't fool him any longer. "No," I says. "He was a good bright boy—I have no complaint to make about him on that score; but the brightest boy I had, the one that surpassed all the rest of them in sense, and in understanding, and in judgment— the best boy that I had, the smartest boy I ever saw, was—well, it wasn't him," I said. "It was another one."

He looked at me a moment; then he said: "Which boy was that?"

Well, I just looked at him, and smiled. I shook my head. I wouldn't tell him. "I never brag about my own," I said. "You'll have to find out for yourself."

But—I'll have to tell *you:* the best one of the whole lot was—*Robert!*

. . . And when I think of Robert as he was long about that time, I always see him sitting there, so grave and earnest-like, with his nose pressed to the window, as we went down through Indiana in the morning, to the Fair.

So Robert sat beside this gentleman and looked out the window. I never knew the man—I never asked his name—but I tell you what! He was certainly a fine-looking, well-dressed, good substantial sort of man, and I could see that he had taken a great liking to Robert, and Robert sat there looking out, and then turned to this gentleman, as grave and earnest as a grown-up man, and says: "What kind of crops grow here, sir?" Well, this gentleman threw his head back and just ha-ha-ed. "Well, I'll see if I can tell you," says this gentleman, and then, you know, he talked to him, and Robert took it all in, as solemn as you please, and asked this gentleman every sort of question—what the trees were, what was growing there, how big the farms were—all sorts of questions, which this gentleman would answer, until I said: "I'll vow, Robert! You'll bother the very life out of this gentleman."

The gentleman threw his head back and laughed right out. "Now you leave that boy alone. He's all right," he said. "He doesn't bother me a bit, and if I know the answers to his questions, I will answer him. And if I don't know, why, then, I'll tell him so. But he's *all right,*" he said, and put his arm around Robert's shoulders. "You leave him alone. He doesn't bother me a bit."

And I can still remember how he looked, that morning, with his black eyes, his black hair, and with the birthmark on his neck—so grave, so serious, so earnest-like—as he looked out the windows at the apple trees, the farms, the barns, the houses, and the orchards, taking it all in because it was, I reckon, strange and new to him.

It was so long ago, but when I think of it, it all comes back, as if it happened yesterday. And all of you have grown up and gone away, and nothing is the same as it was then. But all of you were there with me that morning, and I guess I should remember how the others looked, but every time I think of it, I still see Robert just the way he was, the way he looked that morning when we went down through Indiana, by the river, to the Fair.

Can you remember how Robert used to look? . . . I mean the birthmark, the black eyes, the olive skin—the birthmark always showed because of those open sailor blouses kids used to wear. . . . But I guess you must have been too young. . . . I was looking at that old photograph the other day—that picture showing all of us before the house in Orchard Street? . . . *You* weren't there. . . . *You* hadn't arrived. . . . You remember how mad you used to get when we used to tell you that you were only a dish-rag hanging out in Heaven, when something happened?

I was looking at that old picture just the other day. There we were. . . . And my God, what is it all about? . . . I mean, when you see the way you were—Mary and Dick and Robert, Bill and all of us—and then—look at us now! Do you ever get to feeling funny? You know what I mean—do you ever get to feeling *queer*?—when you try to figure these things out. . . . You've been to college, and you ought to know the answer. . . . And I wish you'd tell me if you know. . . .

My Lord, when I think sometimes of the way I used to be—the dreams I used to have. . . . Taking singing lessons from Aunt Nell because I felt that some day I was going to have a great career in opera. . . . Can you beat it now? . . . Can you imagine it? . . . *Me!* In grand opera! . . . Now I want to ask you. . . . I'd like to know. . . .

My Lord! When I go uptown and look at all these funny-looking little boys and girls hanging around the drug-store—do you suppose any of them have ambitions the way we did? . . . Do you suppose any of these funny-looking little girls are thinking about a big career in opera? . . . Didn't you ever see that picture of us? It was made before the old house down on Orchard Street, with Papa standing there in his swallow-tail,[6] and Mamma there beside him—and Robert and Dick and Jim, and Mary, Bill, and me, with our feet up on our bicycles.

Well, there I was, and my poor old skinny legs and long white dress, and two pigtails hanging down my back. And all the funny-looking clothes we wore, with the doo-lolly[7] business on them. . . . But I guess you can't remember. You weren't born.

But—well, we were a right nice-looking set of people, if I do say so. And there was 86 the way it used to be, with the front porch, the grape-vines, and the flower-beds before the house. And Miss Martha standing there by Papa with a watch-charm pinned to her waist. . . . I shouldn't laugh, but Miss Martha. . . . Well, Mamma was a pretty woman then—and Papa in his swallow-tail was a good-looking man. Do you remember how he used to get dressed up on Sunday? And how grand he thought he was? And how wonderful that dinky little shop on the Square looked to us! . . . Can you beat it now? . . . Why, we thought that Papa was the biggest man in town and—oh, you can't tell me! You can't tell me! He had his faults, but Papa was a wonderful man. You know he was!

6. Formal coat.　　　　　　　　　　7. Dressy, showy (colloquial).

And there was Jim and Dick and Robert, Mary, Bill, and me lined up there before the house with one foot on our bicycles. . . . And I got to thinking back about it all. It all came back.

Do you remember anything about St. Louis? You were only three or four years old then, but you must remember something. . . . Do you remember how you used to bawl when I would scrub you? How you'd bawl for Robert? . . . Poor kid, you used to yell for Robert every time I'd get you in the tub. He was a sweet kid, and he was crazy about you: he almost brought you up.

That year Robert was working at the Inside Inn out on the Fair Grounds . . . Do you remember the old Inside Inn? That big old wooden thing inside the Fair? . . . And how I used to take you there to wait for Robert when he got through working? . . . And Billy Pelham at the news-stand, how he used to give you a stick of chewing-gum?

They were all crazy about Robert. . . . Everybody liked him. . . . And how proud Robert was of you! . . . Don't you remember how he used to show you off? . . . How he used to take you around and make you talk to Billy Pelham? . . . And Mr. Curtis at the desk? . . . And how Robert would try to make you talk and get you to say, "Robert"? And you couldn't pronounce the "r"— and you'd say *"Wobbut."* Have you forgotten that? . . . You shouldn't forget *that,* because . . . you were a *cute* kid, then . . . Ho-ho-ho-ho-ho. . . . I don't know where it's gone to, but you were a big hit in those days. . . .

And I was thinking of it all the other day: how we used to go and meet Robert there and how he'd take us to the Midway. . . . Do you remember the Midway? The Snake-Eater and the Living Skeleton, the Fat Woman and the Shoot the Chute, the Scenic Railway and the Ferris Wheel? . . . How you bawled the night we took you up on the Ferris Wheel! You yelled your head off. . . . I tried to laugh it off, but I tell you, I was scared myself . . . And how Robert laughed at us and told us there was no danger. . . . My Lord, poor little Robert! He was only twelve years old at the time, but he seemed so grown-up to us. I was two years older, but I thought he knew it all.

It was always that way with him. . . . Looking back now, it sometimes seems that it was Robert who brought us up. He was always looking after us, telling us what to do, bringing us something—some ice-cream or some candy, something he had bought out of the poor little money he'd got at the Inn. . . .

Then I got to thinking of the afternoon we sneaked away from home. . . . Mamma had gone out somewhere. And Robert and I got on the street-car and came downtown. . . . And my Lord, in those days, that was what we called a *trip.* A ride on the street-car was something to write home about in those days. . . . I hear that it's all built up around there now.

So we got on the car and rode the whole way down into the business section of St. Louis. Robert took me into a drug-store and set me up to[8] soda-water. Then we came out and walked around some, down to the Union Station and clear over to the river. . . . And both of us half scared to death at what we'd done and wondering what Mamma would say if she found out.

---

8. Treated me to (slang).

We stayed there till it was getting dark, and we passed by a lunch-room—an old joint with one-armed chairs and people eating at the counter. . . . We read all the signs to see what they had to eat and how much it cost, and I guess nothing on the menu was more than fifteen cents, but it couldn't have looked grander to us if it had been Delmonico's.⁹ . . . So we stood there with our noses pressed against the window, looking in. . . . Two skinny little kids, both of us scared half to death, getting the thrill of a lifetime out of it. . . . You know what I mean? . . . And smelling everything with all our might and thinking how good it all smelled. . . . Then Robert turned to me and whispered, "Come on, Sue. . . . Let's go in. . . . It says fifteen cents for pork and beans. And I've got money," Robert said. "I've got sixty cents."

I was so scared I couldn't speak. . . . I'd never been in a place like that before. . . . But I kept thinking, "Oh, Lord, if Mamma should find out!" . . . Don't you know how it is when you're a kid? It was the thrill of a lifetime. . . . I couldn't resist. So we both went in and ordered pork and beans and a cup of coffee. . . . I suppose we were too frightened at what we'd done really to enjoy anything. We just gobbled it all up in a hurry, and gulped our coffee down. And I don't know whether it was the excitement—I guess the poor kid was already sick when we came in there and didn't know it. But I turned and looked at him, and he was as white as death. . . . And when I asked him what was the matter, he wouldn't tell me. . . . He was too proud. He said he was all right, but I could see that he was sick as a dog. . . . So he paid the bill. . . . It came to forty cents; I'll never forget *that* as long as I live. . . . And sure enough, we no more than got out the door—he'd hardly time to reach the curb—before it all came up. . . .

And the poor kid was so scared and so ashamed. What scared him so was not that he had got sick but that he had spent all that money, and it had come to nothing. And Mamma would find out. . . . Poor kid, he just stood there looking at me and he whispered, "Oh, Sue, don't tell Mamma. She'll be mad if she finds out." Then we hurried home, and he was still white as a sheet when we got there.

Mamma was waiting for us. . . . She looked at us—you know how Miss Martha looks at you, when she thinks you've been doing something that you shouldn't? . . . Mamma said: "Why, where on earth have you two children been?" I guess she was all set to lay us out. Then she took one look at Robert's face. That was enough for her. She said: "Why, child, what in the world—" She was white as a sheet herself. . . . And all that Robert said was "Mamma, I feel sick."

He was sick as a dog. He fell over on the bed, and we undressed him, and Mamma put her hand upon his forehead and came out in the hall—she was so white you could have made a black mark on her face with chalk—and whispered to me:

"Go and get the doctor quick; he's burning up."

And I went running, my pigtails flying, to get Dr. Packer. I brought him back with me. When he came out of Robert's room, he told Mamma what to do, but I don't know if she even heard him.

---

9. A famous and expensive restaurant in New York City.

Her face was white as a sheet. She looked at me and looked right through me. . . . And oh, my Lord, I'll never forget the way she looked, the way my heart stopped and came up in my throat. . . . I was only a skinny little kid of fourteen. But she looked as if she was dying right before my eyes. . . . And I knew that if anything happened to him, she'd never get over it, if she lived to be a hundred.

Poor old Mamma. You know, he always was her eyeballs[1]—you know that, don't you?—Not the rest of us!—No, sir! I know what I'm talking about. It always has been Robert—she always thought more of him than she did of any of the others and—Poor kid! I can see him lying there white as a sheet and remember how sick he was, and how scared I was! . . . I don't know why—all we'd done had been to sneak away from home and go to a lunch-room—but I felt guilty about the whole thing, as if it was my fault. . . .

It all came back to me the other day when I was looking at that picture, and I thought, my God, we were two kids together, and I was only two years older than Robert was. . . . And now I'm forty-six. . . . Can you imagine that—the way we all grow up and change and go away? . . . And my Lord, Robert seemed so grown-up to me even then. He was only a kid; yet he seemed older than the rest of us.

I was thinking of it just the other day, and I wonder what Robert would say now if he could see that picture. For when you look at it, it all comes back—the boarding house, St. Louis and the Fair. . . . And all of it is just the same as it has always been, as if it happened yesterday. . . . And all of us have grown up and gone away. And nothing has turned out the way we thought it would. . . . And all my hopes and dreams and big ambitions have come to nothing.

It's all so long ago, as if it happened in another world. And then it all comes back, as if it happened yesterday. . . . And sometimes I will lie awake at night and think of all the people who have come and gone, and all the things that happened. And hear the trains down by the river, and the whistles and the bell. . . . And how we went to St. Louis back in 1904.

And then I go out into the street and see the faces of the people that I pass. . . . Don't you see something funny in their eyes, as if they were wondering what had happened to them since they were kids—what it was that they had lost? . . . Now am I crazy, or do they look that way to you?

My God, I'd like to find out what is wrong. . . . What has changed since then. . . . And if we have that same queer funny look in our eyes, too. . . . And if it happens to us all, to everyone. . . . Robert and Jim and Dick and me—all standing there before that house on Orchard Street—and then you see the way we were—and how it all gets lost. . . .

The way it all turns out is nothing like the way we thought that it would be. . . . And how it all gets lost, until it seems that it has never happened—that it is something that we dreamed somewhere. . . . You see what I mean now? . . . That it is something that we hear somewhere, that it happened to someone else. . . . And then it all comes back again.

And there you are, two funny, frightened, skinny little kids with their noses pressed against a dirty window thirty years ago. . . . The way it felt, the way it smelled, even the funny smell in that old pantry of our house. And the steps

1. Favorite (slang).

before the house, the way the rooms looked. Those two little boys in sailor suits who used to ride up and down before the house on their tricycles. . . . And the birthmark on Robert's neck. . . . The Inside Inn. . . . St. Louis and the Fair. . . . It all comes back as if it happened yesterday. And then it goes away and seems farther off and stranger than if it happened in a dream.

"This is King's Highway," a man said. I looked and saw that it was just a street. There were some new buildings, and a big hotel; some restaurants, "bar-grill" places of the modern kind, the livid monotone of neon lights, the ceaseless traffic of the motorcars—all this was new, but it was just a street. And I knew that it had always been a street and nothing more. But somehow—I stood there looking at it, wondering what else I had expected to find.

The man kept looking at me, and I asked him if the Fair had been out this way.

"Sure, the Fair was out beyond here," the man said. "Where the park is now. But this street you're looking for? Don't you remember the name of the street or nothing?"

I said I thought the name was Edgemont Street, but that I was not sure. And I said the house was on the corner of this street and another street. And then the man said, "What street was that?" I said I did not know, but that King's Highway was a block or so away and that an interurban line ran past about a block or so from where we lived.

"What line was this?" the man said, and stared at me.

"The interurban line," I said.

Then he stared at me again and finally, "I don't know no interurban line," he said.

I said it was a line that ran behind some houses and that there were board fences there and grass beside the tracks. But somehow I could not say that it was summer in those days and that you could smell the ties, a kind of wooden tarry smell, and feel a kind of absence in the afternoon, after the car had gone. I could not say that King's Highway had not been a street in those days but a kind of road that wound from magic out of some dim land, and that along the way it had got mixed with Tom the Piper's son, with hot cross buns,[2] with all the light that came and went, and with cloud shadows passing on the mountains, with coming down through Indiana in the morning, and the smell of engine smoke, the Union Station, and most of all with voices lost and far and long ago that said, "King's Highway."

I didn't say those things about King's Highway because I looked about me and I saw what King's Highway was. I left him then and went on till I found the place. And again, again, I turned into the street, finding the place where the two corners meet, the huddled block, the turret, and the steps, and paused a moment, looking back, as if the street was Time.

So I waited for a moment for a word, for a door to open, for the child to come. I waited, but no words were spoken; no one came.

Yet all of it was just as it had always been except the steps were lower and the porch less high, the strip of grass less wide than I had thought. A gray-stone front, St. Louis style, three-storied, with a slant slate roof, the side red

2. I.e., Mother Goose nursery rhymes.

brick and windowed, still with the old arched entrance in the center for the doctor's use.

There was a tree in front, a lamp-post, and behind and to the side more trees than I had known there would be. And all the slaty turret gables, all the slaty window gables going into points, the two arched windows, in strong stone, in the front room.

It was all so strong, so solid and so ugly—and so enduring and good, the way I had remembered it, except I did not smell the tar, the hot and caulky dryness of the old cracked ties, the boards of backyard fences and the coarse and sultry grass, and absence in the afternoon when the street-car had gone, and the feel of the hot afternoon, and that everyone was absent at the Fair.

It was a hot day. Darkness had come; the heat hung and sweltered like a sodden blanket in St. Louis. The heat soaked down, and the people sweltered in it; the faces of the people were pale and greasy with the heat. And in their faces was a kind of patient wretchedness, and one felt the kind of desolation that one feels at the end of a hot day in a great city in America—when one's home is far away across the continent, and he thinks of all that distance, all that heat, and feels: "Oh, God, but it's a big country!"

Then he hears the engine and the wheel again, the wailing whistle and the bell, the sound of shifting in the sweltering yard, and walks the street, and walks the street, beneath the clusters of hard lights, and by the people with sagged faces, and is drowned in desolation and no belief.

He feels the way one feels when one comes back, and knows that he should not have come, and when he sees that, after all, King's Highway is—a street; and St. Louis—the enchanted name—a big hot common town upon the river, sweltering in wet dreary heat, and not quite South, and nothing else enough to make it better.

It had not been like this before. I could remember how it got hot in the afternoons, and how I would feel a sense of absence and vague sadness when everyone had gone away. The house would seem so lonely, and sometimes I would sit inside, on the second step of the hall stairs, and listen to the sound of silence and absence in the afternoon. I could smell the oil upon the floor and on the stairs, and see the sliding doors with their brown varnish and the beady chains across the door, and thrust my hand among the beady chains, and gather them together in my arms, and let them clash, and swish with light beady swishings all round me. I could feel darkness, absence, and stained light, within the house, through the stained glass of the window on the stairs, through the small stained glasses by the door, stained light and absence, and vague sadness in the house in a hot mid-afternoon. And all these things themselves would have a kind of life: would seem to wait attentively, to be most living and most still.

Then I would long for evening and return, the slant of light, and feet along the street, the sharp-faced twins in sailor-suits upon their tricycles, the smell of supper and the sound of voices in the house again, and Robert coming from the Fair.

And again, again, I turned into the street, finding the place where two corners meet, turning at last to see if Time was there. I passed the house; some lights were burning in the house; the door was open, and a woman sat upon the porch. And presently I turned and stopped before the house again. I stood looking at it for a moment, and I put my foot upon the step.

Then I said to the woman who was sitting on the porch: "This house—excuse me, but could you tell me, please, who lives here?"

I know my words were strange and hollow and I had not said what I wished to say. She stared at me a moment, puzzled.

Then she said: "I live here. Who are you looking for?"

I said, "Why, I am looking for—There used to be a house—" I said.

The woman was now staring hard at me.

"I used to live here in this house," I said.

She was silent for a moment; then she said: "When was it that you lived here?"

"In 1904."

Again she was silent, looking at me for a moment. Then presently: "Oh. . . . That was the year of the Fair. You were here then?"

"Yes." I now spoke rapidly, with more confidence: "My mother had the house, and we were here for seven months. . . . And the house belonged to Dr. Packer," I went on. "We rented it from him."

"Yes," the woman said, and nodded now. "This was Dr. Packer's house. He's been dead for many years. But this was the Packer house, all right."

"That entrance on the side," I said, "where the steps go up—that was for Dr. Packer's patients. That was the entrance to his office."

"Oh," the woman said, "I didn't know that. I've often wondered what it was. I didn't know what it was for."

"And this big room here in front," I said, "that was the office. And there were sliding doors, and next to it a kind of alcove for his patients."

"Yes, the alcove is still there, only all of it has been made into one room now—and I never knew just what the alcove was for."

"And there were sliding doors on this side, too, that opened on the hall—and a stairway going up upon this side. And halfway up the stairway, at the landing, a little window of stained glass—and across the sliding doors here in the hall a kind of curtain made of strings of beads."

She nodded, smiling. "Yes, it's just the same—we still have the sliding doors and the stained glass window on the stairs. There's no bead curtain any more," she said, "but I remember when people had them. I know what you mean."

"When we were here," I said, "we used the Doctor's office for a parlor—except later on, the last month or two; and then we used it for a bedroom."

"It is a bedroom now," she said. "I rent rooms—all of the rooms upstairs are rented—but I have two brothers and they sleep in this front room."

And we were silent for a moment; then I said, "My brother stayed there, too."

"In the front room?" the woman said.

I answered: "Yes."

She paused a moment; then she said: "Won't you come in? I don't believe it's changed much. Would you like to see?"

I thanked her and said I would, and I went up the steps. She opened the screen door, and I went in.

And it was just the same—the stairs, the hallway, and the sliding doors, the window of stained glass upon the stairs. All of it was just the same except the stained light of absence in the afternoon, and the child who sat there, waiting on the stairs, and something fading like a dream, something coming like a light, something going, passing, fading like the shadows of a wood. And then it would be gone again, fading like cloud shadows in the hills, coming like the vast, the drowsy rumors of the distant enchanted Fair, and coming, going, coming, being found and lost, possessed and held and never captured, like lost voices in the mountains, long ago, like the dark eyes and the quiet face, the dark lost boy, my brother, who himself like shadows, or like absence in the house, would come, would go, and would return again.

The woman took me into the house and through the hall. I told her of the pantry, and I told her where it was and pointed to the place, but now it was no longer there. And I told her of the back yard, and the old board fence around the yard. But the old board fence was gone. And I told her of the carriage-house, and told her it was painted red. But now there was a small garage. And the back yard was still there, but smaller than I thought, and now there was a tree.

"I did not know there was a tree," I said. "I do not remember any tree."

"Perhaps it wasn't there," she said. "A tree could grow in thirty years." And then we came back through the house and paused a moment at the sliding doors.

"And could I see this room?" I said.

She slid the doors back. They slid open smoothly, with a kind of rolling heaviness, as they used to do. And then I saw the room again. It was the same. There was a window to the side, the two arched windows to the front, the alcove and the sliding doors, the fireplace with the tiles of mottled green, the mantel of dark mission wood, a dresser and a bed, just where the dresser and the bed had been so long ago.

"Is this the room?" the woman said. "It hasn't changed?"

I told her it was the same.

"And your brother slept here where my brothers sleep?"

"This was his room," I said.

And we were silent for a moment. Then I turned to go, and said: "Well, thank you. I appreciate your showing me."

The woman said that she was glad and that it was no trouble. And she said, "And when you see your family, you can tell them that you saw the house," she said. "And my name is Mrs. Bell. You can tell your mother that a Mrs. Bell has got the house. And when you see your brother, you can tell him that you saw the room he slept in, and that you found it just the same."

I told her then that he was dead.

The woman was silent for a moment. Then she looked at me and said: "He died here, didn't he? In this room?"

I told her that he did.

"Well, then," she said, "I knew it. I don't know how. But when you told me he was here, I knew it."

I said nothing. In a moment the woman said: "What did he die of?"

"Typhoid."

She looked shocked and troubled, and began involuntarily:

"My two brothers—"

"That was so long ago," I said. "I don't think you need to worry now."

"Oh, I wasn't thinking about that," she said. . . . "It was just hearing that a little boy—your brother—was—was in this room that my two brothers sleep in now—"

"Well, maybe I shouldn't have told you then. But he was a good boy—and if you'd known him, you wouldn't mind."

She said nothing, and I added quickly: "Besides, he didn't stay here long. This wasn't really his room—but the night he came back with my sister, he was so sick—they didn't move him."

"Oh," the woman said, "I see." And in a moment: "Are you going to tell your mother you were here?"

"I don't think so."

"I—I wonder how she feels about this room."

"I don't know. She never speaks of it."

"Oh. . . . How old was he?"

"He was twelve."

"You must have been pretty young yourself."

"I was four."

"And—you just wanted to see the room, didn't you? Is that why you came back?"

"Yes."

"Well"—indefinitely—"I guess you've seen it now."

"Yes, thank you."

"I guess you don't remember much about him, do you? I shouldn't think you would."

"No, not much."

The years dropped off like fallen leaves: the face came back again—the soft dark oval, the dark eyes, the soft brown berry on the neck, the raven hair, all bending down, approaching—the whole ghost-wise, intent and instant, like faces from a haunted wood.

"Now say it: *Robert!*"

"Wobbut."

"No, not *Wobbut: Robert.* . . . Say it."

"Wobbut."

"Ah-h—you *didn't* say it. . . . You said Wobbut: *Robert!* . . . Now say it."

"Wobbut."

"Look, I'll tell you what I'll do if you say it right. . . . Would you like to go down to King's Highway? Would you like Robert to set you up? All right, then. . . . If you say Robert right, I'll take you to King's Highway and set you up to ice-cream. . . . Now say it right: Say *Robert.*"

"Wobbut."

"Ah-h you-u! . . . Old tongue-tie, that's what you are. Some day I'm going to. . . . Well, come on, then. I'll set you up, anyway."

It all came back and faded and was lost again. I turned to go, and thanked the woman, and I said: "Good-bye."

"Well, then, good-bye," the woman said, and we shook hands. "I'm glad if I could show you. I'm glad if—" She did not finish, and at length she said: "Well, then, that was a long time ago. You'll find it all changed now, I guess. It's all built up around here now—way out beyond here, out beyond where the Fair grounds used to be. I guess you'll find it changed," she said.

We could find no more to say. We stood there for a moment on the steps, and shook hands once more.

"Well, then, good-bye."

And again, again, I turned into the street, finding the place where corners meet, turning to look again to see where Time had gone. And all of it was just the same, it seemed that it had never changed since then, except all had been found and caught and captured for forever. And so, finding all, I knew all had been lost.

I knew that I would never come again, and that lost magic would not come again, and that the light that came, that passed and went and that returned again, the memory of lost voices in the hills, cloud shadows passing in the mountains, the voices of our kinsmen long ago, the street, the heat, King's Highway, and the piper's son, the vast and drowsy murmur of the distant Fair—oh, strange and bitter miracle of Time—come back again.

But I knew that it could not come back—the cry of absence in the afternoon, the house that waited and the child that dreamed; and through the thicket of man's memory, from the enchanted wood, the dark eye and the quiet face,—poor child, life's stranger and life's exile, lost, like all of us, a cipher in blind mazes, long ago—my parent, friend, and brother, the lost boy, was gone forever and would not return.

1937, 1987

STERLING BROWN
1901–1989

For much of his long and distinguished career Sterling Brown presented himself to the public mainly as a teacher and scholar of African American folk culture and written literature. During the Harlem Renaissance movement, however, he was also hailed as a technically accomplished and eloquent poet. Rediscovered by younger black poets in the late 1960s, Brown has since been called, to quote the poet Michael S. Harper, "a trustee of consciousness, and a national treasure."

Born in Washington, D.C., and never resident in New York, Brown identified himself with the "New Negro" movement in general rather than with its particular manifestation in Harlem during the 1920s. "The New Negro," he wrote in 1955, "is not to me a group of writers centered in Harlem during the second half of the twenties. Most of the writers were not Harlemites; much of the best writing was not about Harlem, which was the show-window, the cashier's till, but no more Negro America than New York is America." Brown viewed Harlem as the place where African American writing was publicized rather than produced, believing that the cosmopolitan and sophisticated New York writers themselves had not written representatively about, or from the perspective of, ordinary black people. While he himself was well educated and of middle-class background, Brown immersed himself deeply in the full range of African American popular expression—jazz, blues, spirituals, work songs, folk tales—so that his writing could reach beyond his own experience.

Brown's father was the Reverend Sterling Nelson Brown, who had been born a slave but eventually attended Fisk University and Oberlin College and later became professor of religion at Howard University in Washington, D.C. Brown attended the academically oriented Dunbar High School, went to Williams College in 1918, and took a master's degree at Harvard. He won a prize in 1925 for his first nationally published essay—a sketch of the tenor Roland Hayes that appeared in *Opportunity*—and thereby came to the attention of black intellectuals. While teaching at Virginia Seminary and College between 1926 and 1928, he met and married Daisy Turnbull. After brief teaching jobs at Fisk, Lincoln University in Missouri, and Atlanta University, he joined the faculty at Howard University in 1929, where he continued to teach until retirement. His first book, *Outline for the Study of the Poetry of American Negroes* (1931), was a pedagogical supplement to James Weldon Johnson's *Book of American Negro Poetry,* including paper topics, study questions, definitions, and other material. Having published individual poems in magazines and newspapers, Brown brought out a collection of this work called *Southern Road* in 1932. It was highly praised by influential critics, many of whom were especially impressed with Brown's technical virtuosity. Alain Locke, the major theorist of the New Negro movement, believed that the book came very close to his ideal of the "poetic portrayal of Negro folk-life . . . true in both letter and spirit to the idiom of the folk's own way of feeling and thinking." Despite such acclaim, the book did not sell widely—1932 was not a good year for publishing, and the Harlem Renaissance movement had ended abruptly with the onset of the Great Depression in 1929. Brown's planned second book of poems, tentatively called *No Hiding Place* and ready for the press in 1935, was rejected by publishers for economic reasons.

After this setback Brown made little further effort to publish poetry and turned his energies into academic and administrative channels, always retaining his focus on African American culture. From 1936 to 1939 he was Negro affairs editor for the Federal Writers' Project, a government funding source for writers during the Depression years; he also worked on the staff of the "Carnegie-Myrdal Study of the Negro," the basis of a landmark study of race relations, *An American Dilemma,* written by the Swedish sociologists Gunnar Myrdal and Alva Myrdal and published shortly after the end of World War II. *The Negro in American Fiction,* a book of critical essays, and *Negro Poetry and Drama,* a literary history, both appeared in 1938. Together with Ulysses Lee and Arthur P. Davis, Brown edited the important anthology *Negro Caravan* (1941), collecting important examples of African American literature from its folk foundations to 1940. Over the years he published numerous essays, notes, and commentaries on African American literature, the role of blacks in American writing, black folklore, and black music; he was an acknowledged expert on all of these topics.

The civil rights movement of the 1960s motivated him to conduct lectures and poetry readings that brought him and his poetry back into national view. It became clear at this time that Alain Locke's earlier assessment of Brown was only partly true. Although in some sense Brown strove in his poetry to make a literary form appropriate to authentic black folk voices, he saw these voices not as raw folk data but as already artistically self-conscious. Blues, jazz, and spirituals were complex, expressive, culturally sophisticated forms. In addition, Brown deployed his speakers' voices not for the main purpose of celebrating the black folk tradition—though this was certainly part of his aim—but to expose and criticize racial injustice. Both his scholarly writing and his poetry call attention to African American achievements and deplore American racism.

The text of the poems printed here is from *Collected Poems* (1996).

Mister Samuel and Sam

Mister Samuel, he belong to Rotary,
Sam to de Sons of Rest;
Both wear red hats lak monkey men,
An' you cain't say which is de best.

Mister Samuel ride in a Cadillac,   5
Sam ride in a Tin Lizzie Fo'd;
Both spend their jack fo' gas an' oil,
An' both git stuck on de road.

Mister Samuel speak in de Chamber of Commerce,
Sam he speak in ch'uch;   10
Both of 'em talk for a mighty long time,
Widout sayin', Lawd knows, ve'y much.

Mister Samuel deal wid high finance,
Sam deal in a two-bit game;
Mister Samuel crashes, Sam goes broke,   15
But deys busted jes' de same.

Mister Samuel wife speak sof' an' low,
When dey gits in their weekly fight;
Sam catches a broomstick crost his rear,
An' both of 'em's henpecked right.   20

Mister Samuel drinks his Canadian Rye,
Sam drinks his bootleg gin;
Both gits as high as a Georgia pine,
And both calls de doctor in.

Mister Samuel die, an' de folks all know,   25
Sam die widout no noise;
De worl' go by in de same ol' way,
And dey's both of 'em po' los' boys. . . .

1932, 1980

He Was a Man

It wasn't about no woman,
    It wasn't about no rape,
He wasn't crazy, and he wasn't drunk,
    An' it wasn't no shooting scrape,
        He was a man, and they laid him down.   5

He wasn't no quarrelsome feller,
    And he let other folks alone,
But he took a life, as a man will do,
    In a fight for to save his own,
        He was a man, and they laid him down.   10

He worked on his little homeplace
    Down on the Eastern Shore;

He had his family, and he had his friends,
  And he didn't expect much more,
    He was a man, and they laid him down.   15

He wasn't nobody's great man,
  He wasn't nobody's good,
Was a po' boy tried to get from life
  What happiness he could,
    He was a man, and they laid him down.   20

He didn't abuse Tom Wickley,
  Said nothing when the white man curst,
But when Tom grabbed his gun, he pulled his own,
  And his bullet got there first,
    He was a man, and they laid him down.   25

Didn't catch him in no manhunt,
  But they took him from a hospital bed,
Stretched on his back in the nigger ward,
  With a bullet wound in his head,
    He was a man, and they laid him down.   30

It didn't come off at midnight
  Nor yet at the break of day,
It was in the broad noon daylight,
  When they put po' Will away,
    He was a man, and they laid him down.   35

Didn't take him to no swampland,
  Didn't take him to no woods,
Didn't hide themselves, didn't have no masks,
  Didn't wear no Ku Klux hoods,
    He was a man, and they laid him down.   40

They strung him up on Main Street,
  On a tree in the Court House Square,
And people came from miles around
  To enjoy a holiday there,
    He was a man, and they laid him down.   45

They hung him and they shot him,
  They piled packing cases around,
They burnt up Will's black body,
  'Cause he shot a white man down;
    "He was a man, and we'll lay him down."   50

It wasn't no solemn business,
  Was more like a barbecue,
The crackers yelled when the fire blazed,
  And the women and the children too—
    "He was a man, and we laid him down."   55

The Coroner and the Sheriff
　　Said "Death by Hands Unknown."
The mob broke up by midnight,
　　"Another uppity Nigger gone—
　　　　He was a man, an' we laid him down."　　　　　　60

　　　　　　　　　　　　　　　　　　　　　1932, 1980

Master and Man

The yellow ears are crammed in Mr. Cromartie's bin
The wheat is tight sacked in Mr. Cromartie's barn.
The timothy is stuffed in Mr. Cromartie's loft.
The ploughs are lined up in Mr. Cromartie's shed.
The cotton has gone to Mr. Cromartie's factor.　　　　　　5
The money is in Mr. Cromartie's bank.
Mr. Cromartie's son made his frat at the college.
Mr. Cromartie's daughter has got her new car.
The veranda is old, but the fireplace is rosy.
Well done, Mr. Cromartie. Time now for rest.　　　　　　10

Blackened sticks line the furrows that Uncle Ned laid.
Bits of fluff are in the corners where Uncle Ned ginned.
The mules he ploughed are sleek in Mr. Cromartie's pastures.
The hoes grow dull in Mr. Cromartie's shed.
His winter rations wait on the commissary shelves;　　　　　　15
Mr. Cromartie's ledger is there for his service.
Uncle Ned daubs some mortar between the old logs.
His children have traipsed off to God knows where.
His old lady sits patching the old, thin denims;
She's got a new dress, and his young one a doll,　　　　　　20
He's got five dollars. The year has come round.
The harvest is over: Uncle Ned's harvesting,
Mr. Cromartie's harvest. Time now for rest.

　　　　　　　　　　　　　　　　　　　　　1936, 1980

Break of Day

Big Jess fired on the Alabama Central,
Man in full, babe, man in full.
Been throwing on coal for Mister Murphy
From times way back, baby, times way back.

Big Jess had a pleasing woman, name of Mamie,　　　　　　5
Sweet-hipted Mama, sweet-hipted Mame;

Had a boy growing up for to be a fireman,
Just like his pa, baby, like his pa.

Out by the roundhouse Jess had his cabin,
Longside the tracks, babe, long the tracks,   10
Jess pulled the whistle when they high-balled past it
"I'm on my way, baby, on my way."

Crackers craved the job what Jess was holding,
Times right tough, babe, times right tough,
Warned Jess to quit his job for a white man,   15
Jess he laughed, baby, he jes' laughed.

He picked up his lunch-box, kissed his sweet woman,
Sweet-hipted Mama, sweet-hipted Mame,
His son walked with him to the white-washed palings,
"Be seeing you soon, son, see you soon."   20

Mister Murphy let Big Jess talk on the whistle
"So long sugar baby, so long babe";
Train due back in the early morning
Breakfast time, baby, breakfast time.

Mob stopped the train crossing Black Bear Mountain   25
Shot rang out, babe, shot rang out.
They left Big Jess on the Black Bear Mountain,
Break of day, baby, break of day.

Sweet Mame sits rocking, waiting for the whistle
Long past due, babe, long past due.   30
The grits are cold, and the coffee's boiled over,
But Jess done gone, baby he done gone.

1938, 1980

Bitter Fruit of the Tree

They said to my grandmother: "Please do not be bitter,"
When they sold her first-born and let the second die,
When they drove her husband till he took to the swamplands,
And brought him home bloody and beaten at last.
They told her, "It is better you should not be bitter,   5
Some must work and suffer so that we, who must, can live,
Forgiving is noble, you must not be heathen bitter;
These are your orders: you *are* not to be bitter."
And they left her shack for their porticoed house.

They said to my father: "Please do not be bitter,"   10
When he ploughed and planted a crop not his,

When he weatherstripped a house that he could not enter,
And stored away a harvest he could not enjoy.
They answered his questions: "It does not concern you,
It is not for you to know, it is past your understanding,   15
All you need know is: you must not be bitter."

                                                        1939, 1980

LANGSTON HUGHES
1902–1967

Langston Hughes was the most popular and versatile of the many writers connected with the Harlem Renaissance. Along with Zora Neale Hurston, and in contrast to Jean Toomer and Countee Cullen (who wanted to work with the patterns of written literary forms, whether traditional or experimental), he wanted to capture the dominant oral and improvisatory traditions of black culture in written form.

Hughes was born in Joplin, Missouri; and in childhood, since his parents were separated, he lived mainly with his maternal grandmother in Lawrence, Kansas. He did, however, reside intermittently both with his mother in Detroit and Cleveland, where he finished high school and began to write poetry, and with his father, who, disgusted with American racism, had gone to Mexico. Like other poets in this era—T. S. Eliot, Hart Crane, Edgar Lee Masters, and Robert Frost—Hughes had a mother sympathetic to his poetic ambitions and a businesslike father with whom he was in deep, scarring conflict.

Hughes entered Columbia University in 1920 but left after a year. Traveling and drifting, he shipped out as a merchant seaman and worked at a nightclub in Paris (France) and as a busboy in Washington, D.C. All this time he was writing and publishing poetry, chiefly in the two important African American periodicals *Opportunity* and the *Crisis*. Eleven of Hughes's poems were published in Alain Locke's pioneering anthology, *The New Negro* (1925), and he was also well represented in Countee Cullen's 1927 anthology, *Caroling Dusk*. Carl Van Vechten, one of the white patrons of African American writing, helped get *The Weary Blues,* Hughes's first volume of poems, published in 1926. It was in this year, too, that his important essay "The Negro Artist and the Racial Mountain" appeared in the *Nation* (see p. 1511); in that essay Hughes described the immense challenges to be faced by the serious black artist "who would produce a racial art" but insisted on the need for courageous artists to make the attempt. Other patrons appeared: Amy Spingarn financed his college education at Lincoln University (Pennsylvania) and Charlotte Mason subsidized him in New York City between 1928 and 1930. The publication of his novel *Not without Laughter* in 1930 solidified his reputation and sales, enabling him to support himself. By the 1930s he was being called "the bard of Harlem."

The Great Depression brought an abrupt end to much African American literary activity, but Hughes was already a public figure. In the activist 1930s he was much absorbed in radical politics. Hughes and other blacks were drawn by the American Communist Party, which made racial justice an important plank in its platform, promoting an image of working-class solidarity that nullified racial boundaries. He visited the Soviet Union in 1932 and produced a significant amount of radical writing up to the eve of World War II. He covered the Spanish civil war for the *Baltimore Afro-American* in 1937. By the end of the decade he had also been involved in drama and screenplay writing and had begun an autobiography, all the while publishing poetry.

In 1943 he invented the folksy, streetwise character Jesse B. Semple, whose commonsense prose monologues on race were eventually collected in four volumes, and Alberta K. Johnson, Semple's female equivalent, in his series of "Madam" poems.

In the 1950s and 1960s Hughes published a variety of anthologies for children and adults, including *First Book of Negroes* (1952), *The First Book of Jazz* (1955), and *The Book of Negro Folklore* (1958). In 1953 he was called to testify before Senator Joseph McCarthy's committee on subversive activities in connection with his 1930s radicalism. The FBI listed him as a security risk until 1959; and during these years, when he could not travel outside the United States because he would not have been allowed to reenter the country, Hughes worked to rehabilitate his reputation as a good American by producing patriotic poetry. From 1960 to the end of his life he was again on the international circuit.

Within the spectrum of artistic possibilities open to writers of the Harlem Renaissance—drawing on African American rural folk forms; on literary traditions and forms that entered the United States from Europe and Great Britain; or on the new cultural forms of blacks in American cities—Hughes chose to focus his work on modern, urban black life. He modeled his stanza forms on the improvisatory rhythms of jazz music and adapted the vocabulary of everyday black speech to poetry. He also acknowledged finding inspiration for his writing in the work of white American poets who preceded him. Like Walt Whitman he heard America singing, and he asserted his right to sing America back; he also learned from Carl Sandburg's earlier attempts to work jazz into poetry. Hughes did not confuse his pride in African American culture with complacency toward the material deprivations of black life in the United States. He was keenly aware that the modernist "vogue in things Negro" among white Americans was potentially exploitative and voyeuristic; he confronted such racial tourists with the misery as well as the jazz of Chicago's South Side. Early and late, Hughes's poems demanded that African Americans be acknowledged as owners of the culture they gave to the United States and as fully enfranchised American citizens.

The source of the poems printed here is *Collected Poems* (1994).

The Negro Speaks of Rivers

I've known rivers:
I've known rivers ancient as the world and older than the
     flow of human blood in human veins.

My soul has grown deep like the rivers.

I bathed in the Euphrates when dawns were young.
I built my hut near the Congo and it lulled me to sleep.   5
I looked upon the Nile and raised the pyramids above it.
I heard the singing of the Mississippi when Abe Lincoln
     went down to New Orleans, and I've seen its
     muddy bosom turn all golden in the sunset

I've known rivers:
Ancient, dusky rivers.

My soul has grown deep like the rivers.   10

1921, 1926

Mother to Son

Well, son, I'll tell you:
Life for me ain't been no crystal stair.
It's had tacks in it,
And splinters,
And boards torn up,   5
And places with no carpet on the floor—
Bare.
But all the time
I'se been a-climbin' on,
And reachin' landin's,   10
And turnin' corners,
And sometimes goin' in the dark
Where there ain't been no light.
So boy, don't you turn back.
Don't you set down on the steps   15
'Cause you finds it's kinder hard.
Don't you fall now—
For I'se still goin', honey,
I'se still climbin',
And life for me ain't been no crystal stair.   20

1922, 1926

I, Too

I, too, sing America.

I am the darker brother.
They send me to eat in the kitchen
When company comes,
But I laugh,   5
And eat well,
And grow strong.

Tomorrow,
I'll be at the table
When company comes.   10
Nobody'll dare
Say to me,
"Eat in the kitchen,"
Then.

Besides,   15
They'll see how beautiful I am
And be ashamed—

I, too, am America.

1925, 1959

The Weary Blues

Droning a drowsy syncopated tune,
Rocking back and forth to a mellow croon,
   I heard a Negro play.
Down on Lenox Avenue the other night
By the pale dull pallor of an old gas light   5
   He did a lazy sway. . . .
   He did a lazy sway. . . .
To the tune o' those Weary Blues.
With his ebony hands on each ivory key.
He made that poor piano moan with melody.   10
   O Blues!
Swaying to and fro on his rickety stool
He played that sad raggy tune like a musical fool.
   Sweet Blues!
Coming from a black man's soul.   15
   O Blues!
In a deep song voice with a melancholy tone
I heard that Negro sing, that old piano moan—
   "Ain't got nobody in all this world,
   Ain't got nobody but ma self.   20
   I's gwine to quit ma frownin'
   And put ma troubles on de shelf."
Thump, thump, thump, went his foot on the floor.
He played a few chords then he sang some more—
   "I got de Weary Blues   25
   And I can't be satisfied.
   Got de Weary Blues
   And can't be satisfied—
   I ain't happy no mo'
   And I wish that I had died."   30
And far into the night he crooned that tune.
The stars went out and so did the moon.
The singer stopped playing and went to bed.
While the Weary Blues echoes through his head
He slept like a rock or a man that's dead.   35

                              1925

Mulatto

I am your son, white man!

Georgia dusk
And the turpentine woods.
One of the pillars of the temple fell.

   You are my son!   5
   Like hell!

The moon over the turpentine woods.
The Southern night
Full of stars,
Great big yellow stars.   10
    What's a body but a toy?
        Juicy bodies
        Of nigger wenches
        Blue black
        Against black fences.   15
        O, you little bastard boy,
        What's a body but a toy?
The scent of pine wood stings the soft night air.
    What's the body of your mother?
Silver moonlight everywhere.   20

    What's the body of your mother?
Sharp pine scent in the evening air.
        A nigger night,
        A nigger joy,
        A little yellow   25
        Bastard boy.

    Naw, you ain't my brother.
    Niggers ain't my brother.
    Not ever.
    Niggers ain't my brother.   30
The Southern night is full of stars,
Great big yellow stars.
        O, sweet as earth,
        Dusk dark bodies
        Give sweet birth   35
To little yellow bastard boys.

    Git on back there in the night,
    You ain't white.

The bright stars scatter everywhere.
Pine wood scent in the evening air.   40
        A nigger night,
        A nigger joy.

    I am your son, white man!

        A little yellow
        Bastard boy.   45

1927

Song for a Dark Girl

Way Down South in Dixie[1]
    (Break the heart of me)
They hung my black young lover
    To a cross roads tree.

Way Down South in Dixie   5
    (Bruised body high in air)
I asked the white Lord Jesus
    What was the use of prayer.

Way Down South in Dixie
    (Break the heart of me)   10
Love is a naked shadow
    On a gnarled and naked tree.

               1927

Genius Child

This is a song for the genius child.
Sing it softly, for the song is wild.
Sing it softly as ever you can—
Lest the song get out of hand.

Nobody loves a genius child.   5

Can you love an eagle,
Tame or wild?
Can you love an eagle,
Wild or tame?
Can you love a monster   10
Of frightening name?

Nobody loves a genius child.

Kill him—and let his soul run wild!

             1937, 1947

---

1. Last line of "Dixie," the popular minstrel song, probably composed by Daniel D. Emmett (1815–1904).

Visitors to the Black Belt

You can talk about
Across the railroad tracks—
To me it's *here*
On this side of the tracks.

You can talk about   5
Up in Harlem—
To me it's *here*
In Harlem.

You can say
Jazz on the South Side—[1]   10
To me it's hell
On the South Side:

   Kitchenettes
   With no heat
   And garbage   15
   In the halls.

Who're you, outsider?

Ask me who am I.

                                                    1940, 1943

Note on Commercial Theatre

You've taken my blues and gone—
You sing 'em on Broadway
And you sing 'em in Hollywood Bowl,
And you mixed 'em up with symphonies
And you fixed 'em   5
So they don't sound like me.
Yep, you done taken my blues and gone.

You also took my spirituals and gone.
You put me in *Macbeth* and *Carmen Jones*
And all kinds of *Swing Mikados*   10
And in everything but what's about me—
But someday somebody'll
Stand up and talk about me,
And write about me—

---

1. African American neighborhood in Chicago; see also Archibald J. Motley's 1934 painting, *Black Belt* in
the color insert to this volume.

Black and beautiful— 15
And sing about me,
And put on plays about me!

I reckon it'll be
Me myself!

Yes, it'll be me. 20

1940, 1959

Vagabonds

We are the desperate
Who do not care,
The hungry
Who have nowhere
To eat, 5
No place to sleep,
The tearless
Who cannot
Weep.

1941, 1947

Words Like Freedom[1]

There are words like *Freedom*
Sweet and wonderful to say.
On my heart-strings freedom sings
All day everyday.

There are words like *Liberty* 5
That almost make me cry.
If you had known what I know
You would know why.

1943, 1967

Madam and Her Madam

I worked for a woman,
She wasn't mean—
But she had a twelve-room
House to clean.

Had to get breakfast, 5
Dinner, and supper, too—

1. Originally published under the title "Refugee in America."

Then take care of her children
When I got through.

Wash, iron, and scrub,
Walk the dog around—   10
It was too much,
Nearly broke me down.

I said, Madam,
Can it be
You trying to make a   15
Pack-horse out of me?

She opened her mouth.
She cried, Oh, no!
You know, Alberta,
I love you so!   20

I said, Madam,
That may be true—
But I'll be dogged
If I love you!

                                                        1943

Freedom [1][1]

Freedom will not come
Today, this year
    Nor ever
Through compromise and fear.

I have as much right   5
As the other fellow has
    To stand
On my two feet
And own the land.

I tire so of hearing people say,   10
Let things take their course.
Tomorrow is another day.
I do not need my freedom when I'm dead.
I cannot live on tomorrow's bread.

Freedom   15
Is a strong seed
Planted
In a great need.

1. Originally published under the title "Democracy."

I live here, too.
I want freedom   20
Just as you.

                                        1943, 1967

Madam's Calling Cards

I had some cards printed
The other day.
They cost me more
Than I wanted to pay.

I told the man   5
I wasn't no mint,
But I hankered to see
My name in print.

MADAM JOHNSON,
ALBERTA K.   10
He said, Your name looks good
Madam'd that way.

Shall I use Old English
Or a Roman letter?
I said, Use American.   15
American's better.

There's nothing foreign
To my pedigree:
Alberta K. Johnson—
American that's me.   20

                                        1943, 1949

Silhouette

Southern gentle lady,
Do not swoon.
They've just hung a black man
In the dark of the moon.

They've hung a black man   5
To a roadside tree
In the dark of the moon
For the world to see
How Dixie protects
Its white womanhood.   10

> Southern gentle lady,
> Be good!
> Be good!

1944, 1949

Theme for English B

The instructor said,

> *Go home and write*
> *a page tonight.*
> *And let that page come out of you—*
> *Then, it will be true.*   5

I wonder if it's that simple?
I am twenty-two, colored, born in Winston-Salem.
I went to school there, then Durham, then here
to this college on the hill above Harlem.[1]
I am the only colored student in my class.   10
The steps from the hill lead down into Harlem,
through a park, then I cross St. Nicholas,
Eighth Avenue, Seventh, and I come to the Y,
the Harlem Branch Y, where I take the elevator
up to my room, sit down, and write this page: 15

It's not easy to know what is true for you or me
at twenty-two, my age. But I guess I'm what
I feel and see and hear, Harlem, I hear you:
hear you, hear me—we two—you, me, talk on this page.
(I hear New York, too.) Me—who?   20
Well, I like to eat, sleep, drink, and be in love.
I like to work, read, learn, and understand life.
I like a pipe for a Christmas present,
or records—Bessie, bop, or Bach.[2]
I guess being colored doesn't make me *not* like   25
the same things other folks like who are other races.
So will my page be colored that I write?
Being me, it will not be white.
But it will be
a part of you, instructor.   30
You are white—
yet a part of me, as I am a part of you.
That's American.
Sometimes perhaps you don't want to be a part of me.
Nor do I often want to be a part of you.   35

---

1. The City College of the City University of New York; Winston-Salem and Durham are cities in North Carolina.
2. Johann Sebastian Bach (1685–1750), German composer of the Baroque era; Bessie Smith (1894–1937), noted blues singer. "Bop": jazz form developed in Harlem during World War II.

But we are, that's true!
As I learn from you,
I guess you learn from me—
although you're older—and white—
and somewhat more free.   40

This is my page for English B.

1949

KAY BOYLE
1902–1992

Over the course of her long career, Kay Boyle published novels, poetry, and essays, but she remains best known for her short stories. Bridging the gap between high modernism and popular accessibility, her stories of the 1930s and 1940s regularly appeared in respected large-circulation magazines like *Harper's* and the *New Yorker*, where they earned critical respect for their elegant, restrained style and sharp psychological observations.

Boyle was born in St. Paul, Minnesota, to a wealthy family. Her mother, Katherine Evans Boyle, was a volunteer labor activist who took her daughters to the famous Armory show of modernist art in 1913 and read Gertrude Stein aloud to her husband's dinner guests. In 1922 Boyle moved to New York, where she married Richard Brault, a French exchange student. There she attended avant-garde literary open houses that exposed her to the work of writers like Marianne Moore, William Carlos Williams, and John Dos Passos; meanwhile, her own poems and prose started appearing in modernist little magazines. In 1923 she and Brault sailed for France; Boyle would not return to the United States until 1941. As the marriage disintegrated, Boyle became pregnant by another man, Ernest Walsh, who died of tuberculosis before their daughter was born. Boyle's *Wedding Day and Other Stories* appeared in 1930, followed by two novels drawing on her life with Brault and Walsh, *Plagued by the Nightingale* (1931) and *Year Before Last* (1932). Her writing turned from personal toward more political themes in the 1930s. "The White Horses of Vienna," based on Boyle's experience in Austria in the years preceding the Nazi annexation, won the O. Henry Award for best American short story in 1935; her other O. Henry winner, "Defeat" (1941), dramatized the collapse of France under the German attack. Fleeing World War II, Boyle returned to the United States. She went back to postwar Germany as a correspondent for the *New Yorker*, covering the Nuremberg trials of Nazi war criminals. In 1953 she was accused of being a Communist party member by the Loyalty Security Board and investigated by Senator Joseph McCarthy's staff; although she testified that she had never been a Communist, the *New Yorker* dropped her as a correspondent and the large mainstream magazines published much less of Boyle's work than they had previously. Eventually she settled in San Francisco, where she became a teacher at San Francisco State University and continued her writing along with her social activism.

The text of the story printed here is from *Fifty Stories* (1980).

The White Horses of Vienna

I

The doctor often climbed the mountain at night, climbed up behind his own house hour after hour in the dark, and came back to bed long after his two children were asleep. At the end of June he sprained his knee coming down the mountain late. He wrenched it out of joint making his way down with the other men through the pines. They helped him into the house where his wife was waiting and writing letters by the stove, and the agony that he would not mention was marked upon his face.

His wife bound his leg with fresh, wet cloths all through the night, but in the morning the knee was hot with fever. It might be weeks before he could go about again, and there was nothing to do but write to the hospital in Vienna for a student-doctor to come out and take over his patients for a time.

"I'll lie still for a fortnight or so," said the doctor, and he asked his wife to bring him the bits of green wood that he liked to whittle, and his glazed papers and his fancy tag ends of stuff. He was going to busy himself making new personages for his theater, for he could not stay idle for half an hour. The June sun was strong at that height, and the doctor sat on the *Liegestuhl*[1] with his knee bared to the warm light, working like a well man and looking up now and again to the end of the valley where the mountains stood with the snow shining hard and diamond-bright on their brows.

"You'll never sit still long enough for it to do you any good," said the doctor's wife sharply. She was quite a young, beautiful woman, in spite of her two growing sons, and in spite of her husband's ageless, weathered flesh. She was burned from the wind and the snow in winter and burned from the sun at other times of the year; she had straight, long, sunburned limbs, and her dark hair was cut short and pushed behind her ears. She had her nurse's degree from Vienna and she helped her husband in whatever there was to do: the broken bones, the deaths, the births. He even did a bit of dentistry too, when there was need, and she stood by in her nurse's blouse and mixed the cement and porcelain fillings and kept the instruments clean. Or at night, if they needed her, she climbed the mountain with him and the other men, carrying as well a knapsack of candles over her shoulders, climbing through the twig-broken and mossy silence in the dark.

The doctor had built their house himself with the trees cut down from their forest. The town lay in the high valley, and the doctor had built their house above it on the sloping mountainside. There was no real road leading to it: one had to get to him on foot or else on a horse. It was as if the doctor had chosen this place to build so that the village might leave him to himself unless the need were very great. He had come back to his own country after the years as a prisoner of war in Siberia,[2] and after the years of studying in other countries, and the years of giving away as a gift his tenderness and knowledge as he went from one wild place to another. He had studied in cities, but he could not live for long in them. He had come back and bought a piece of land in

---

1. Folding deck chair (German). 2. In World War I.

the Tirol[3] with a pine forest sloping down it, and he built his house there, working throughout the summer months late into the evening with only his two sons and his wife to help him lift the squared, varnished beams into place.

Inside the log walls the doctor made a pure white plaster wall and put his dark-stained bookshelves against it and hung on it his own paintings of Dalmatia[4] and his drawings of the Siberian country. Everything was as neat and clean as wax, for the doctor was a savagely clean man. He had a coarse, reddish, well-scrubbed skin, and the gold hairs sprang out of his scalp, wavy and coarse, and out of his forearms and his muscular, heavy thighs. They would have sprung too around his mouth and along his jaw had he not shaved himself clean every morning. His face was as strong as rock, but it had seen so much of suffering that it had the look of being scarred, it seemed to be split in two, with one side of it given to resolve and the other to compassion.

All of the places that he had been before, Paris and Moscow and Munich and Constantinople, had never left an evil mark. None of the grand places or people had ever done to him what they can do. But merely because of his own strong, humble pride in himself his shirt was always a white one, and of fresh, clean linen no matter what sort of work he was doing. In the summer he wore the short, leather trousers of the country, for he had peasants behind him and he liked to remember that it was so. But the woven stockings that ended just above his calves were perfectly white and the nails of his broad, coarse hands were white. They were spotless, like the nails of a woman's hand.

The day the student doctor arrived from Vienna and walked up from the village, the doctor and his wife were both out in the sun before the house. She had been hanging the children's shirts up on the line to dry, and she came around to the timber piazza, drying her hands in her dress. The doctor was hopping around on one leg like a great, golden, wounded bird; he was hopping from one place to another, holding his wrenched leg off the ground, and seeking the bits of paper and stuff and wood and wire that he needed to make his dolls.

"Let me get the things for you!" his wife cried out. "Why must you do everything for yourself? Why can't you let anyone help you?"

The doctor hopped across to the timber table in the sun and picked up the clown's cap he was making and fitted it on the head of the doll he held in his hand. When he turned around he saw the student-doctor coming up the path. He stood still for a moment, with his leg still lifted up behind him, and then his face cleared of whatever was in it, and he nodded.

"God greet you," he said quietly, and the young man stopped too where he was on the path and looked up at them. He was smiling in his long, dark, alien face, but his city shoes were foul with the soft mud of the mountainside after rain, and the sweat was standing out on his brow because he was not accustomed to the climb.

"Good day," he said, as city people said it. The doctor and his wife stood looking down at him, and a little wave of pallor ran under the woman's skin.

The doctor had caught a very young fox in the spring, and it had now grown to live in the house with them without shyness or fear. The sound of their

---

3. Alpine region of western Austria, bordering Germany, Switzerland, and Italy.

4. Mountainous coastal region of Croatia, known for scenic beauty.

voices and the new human scent on the air brought it forth from the indoor dark of the house. It came out without haste, like a small, gentle dog, with its soft, gray, gently lifted brush and its eyes blinking slowly at the sun. It went daintily down the path toward the stranger, holding its brush just out of the mud of the path, with the black bead of its nose smelling the new smell of this other man who had come.

The young doctor from Vienna leaned over to stroke it, and while his head was down the doctor's wife turned to her husband. She had seen the black, smooth hair on the man's head, and the arch of his nose, and the quality of his skin. She could scarcely believe what she had seen and she must look into her husband's face for confirmation of the truth. But her husband was still looking down the little space toward the stranger. The fox had raised the sharp point of his muzzle and licked the young doctor's hand.

"Is this a dog or a cat?" the young man called up, smiling.

"It's a fox," said the doctor. The young man came up with his hat in his hand and said that his name was Heine and shook hands, and the doctor gave no sign.

"You live quite a way from the village," said the student-doctor, looking back the way he had come.

"You can see the snow mountains from here," said the doctor, and he showed the young man the sight of them at the far end of the valley. "You have to climb this way before you can see them," he said. "They're closed off from the valley."

This was the explanation of why they lived there, and the young man from the city stood looking a moment in silence at the far, gleaming crusts of the everlasting snows. He was still thinking of what he might say in answer when the doctor asked his wife to show Dr. Heine the room that would be his. Then the doctor sat down in the sun again and went on with the work he had been doing.

"What are we going to do?" said his wife's voice in a whisper behind him in a moment.

"What do you mean? About what?" said the doctor, speaking aloud. His crisp-haired head did not lift from his work, and the lines of patience and love were scarred deep in his cheeks as he whittled.

"About *him*," said the doctor's wife in hushed impatience.

"Send one of the boys down for his bag at the station," said the doctor. "Give him a drink of *Apfelsaft*[5] if he's thirsty."

"But don't you see, don't you see what he is?" asked his wife's wild whisper.

"He's Viennese," said the doctor, working.

"Yes, and he's Jewish," said his wife. "They must be mad to have sent him. They know how everyone feels."

"Perhaps they did it intentionally," said the doctor, working carefully with what he had in his hands. "But it wasn't a good thing for the young man's sake. It's harder on him than us. If he works well, I have no reason to send him back. We've waited three days for him. There are people sick in the village."

"Ah," said his wife in anger behind, "we shall have to sit down at table with him!"

---

5. Apple juice (German).

"They recommended him highly," said the doctor gently, "and he seems a very amiable young man."

"Ah," said his wife's disgusted whisper, "they all look amiable! Every one of them does!"

Almost at once there was a tooth to be pulled, and the young wife was there in her white frock with the instruments ready for the new young man. She stood very close, casting sharp looks at Dr. Heine, watching his slender, delicate hands at work, seeing the dark, silky hairs that grew on the backs of them and the black hair brushed smooth on his head. So much had she heard about Jews that the joints of his tall, elegant frame seemed oiled with some special, suave lubricant that was evil, as a thing come out of the Orient,[6] to their clean, Nordic hearts. He had a pale skin, unused to the weather of mountain places, and his skull was lighted with bright, quick, ambitious eyes. But at lunch he had talked simply with them, although they were country people and ignorant as peasants for all he knew. He listened to everything the doctor had told him about the way he liked things done; in spite of his modern medical school and his Viennese hospitals, taking it all in with interest and respect.

"The doctor," said the young wife now, "always stands behind the patient to get at teeth like that."

She spoke in an undertone to Dr. Heine so that the peasant sitting there in the dentist chair with the cocaine slowly paralyzing his jaws might not overhear.

"Oh, yes. Thank you so much," said Dr. Heine with a smile, and he stepped behind the patient. "It's quite true. One can get a better grip that way."

But as he passed the doctor's wife, the tail of his white coat brushed through the flame of the little sterilizing lamp on the table. Nobody noticed that Dr. Heine had caught fire until the tooth was out and the smell of burning cloth filled the clean, white room. They looked about for what might be smoldering in the place, and in another moment the doctor's wife saw that Dr. Heine was burning very brightly: the back of the white jacket was eaten nearly out and the coat within it was flaming. He had even begun to feel the heat on his shirt when the doctor's wife picked up the strip of rug from the floor and flung it about him. She held it tightly around him with her bare, strong arms, and the young man looked back over his shoulder at her, and he was laughing.

"Now I shall lose my job," he said. "The doctor will never stand for me setting fire to myself the first day like this!"

"It's my fault," said the doctor's wife, holding him fast still in her arms. "I should have had the lamp out of the way."

She began to beat his back softly with the palm of her hand, and when she carried the rug to the window, Dr. Heine went to the mirror and looked over his shoulder at the sight of his clothes all burned away.

"My new coat!" he said, and he was laughing. But it must have been very hard for him to see the nice, gray flannel coat that he had bought to look presentable for his first place scalloped black to his shoulders where the fire had eaten its covert way.

6. Here, generic term for lands east of central Europe.

"I should think I could put a piece in," said the doctor's wife, touching the good cloth that was left. And then she bit her lip suddenly and stood back, as if she had remembered the evil thing that stood between them.

II

When they sat down to supper, the little fox settled himself on the doctor's good foot, for the wool of his stocking was a soft bed where the fox could dream a little while. They had soup and the thick, rosy-meated leg of a pig and salt potatoes, and the children listened to their father and Dr. Heine speaking of music, and painting, and books together. The doctor's wife was cutting the meat and putting it on their plates. It was at the end of the meal that the young doctor began talking of the royal, white horses in Vienna,[7] still royal, he said, without any royalty left to bow their heads to, still shouldering into the arena with spirits a man would give his soul for, bending their knees in homage to the empty, canopied loge where royalty no longer sat. They came in, said Dr. Heine in his rich, eager voice, and danced their statuesque dances, their *pas de deux*, their croupade, their capriole.[8] They were very impatient of the walls around them and the bits in their soft mouths, and very vain of the things they had been taught to do. Whenever the applause broke out around them, said Dr. Heine, their nostrils opened wide as if a wind were blowing. They were actresses, with the deep, snowy breasts of prima donnas, these perfect stallions who knew to a breath the beauty of even their mockery of fright.

"There was a maharaja,"[9] said the young doctor, and the children and their father listened, and the young wife sat giving quick, unwilling glances at this man who could have no blood or knowledge of the land behind him; for what was he but a wanderer whose people had wandered from country to country and whose sons must wander, having no land to return to in the end? "There was a maharaja just last year," said Dr. Heine, "who went to the performance and fell in love with one of the horses. He saw it dancing and he wanted to buy it and take it back to India with him. No one else had ever taken a Lippizaner back to his country, and he wanted this special one, the best of them all, whose dance was like an angel flying. So the state agreed that he could buy the horse, but for a tremendous amount of money. They needed the money badly enough, and the maharaja was a very rich man." Oh, yes, thought the young mother bitterly, you would speak about money, you would come here and climb our mountain and poison my sons with the poison of money and greed! "But no matter how high the price was," said Dr. Heine, smiling because all their eyes were on him, "the maharaja agreed to pay it, provided that the man who rode the horse so beautifully came along as well. Yes, the state would allow that too, but the maharaja would have to pay an enormous salary to the rider. He would take him into his employ as the stallion's keeper, and he would have to pay him a salary as big as our own President is paid!" said Dr. Heine, and he ended this with a burst of laughter.

7. Breed of white horses, usually spelled "Lipizzaner," bred by the rulers of Austria from the sixteenth century. After the fall of the Austro-Hungarian monarchy in World War I, a reduced herd was taken over by the Austrian state.
8. Maneuvers performed by the Lipizzaner stallions: "*pas de deux*" (French), a dance for two; "croupade," a high leap bringing the horse's legs underneath its belly; "capriole," a high leap involving an outward kick of the back legs.
9. Indian prince.

"And what then, what then?" said one of the boys as the student-doctor paused to laugh. The whole family was listening, but the mother was filled with outrage. These things are foreign to us, she was thinking. They belong to more sophisticated people, we do not need them here. The Spanish Riding School,[1] the gentlemen of Vienna, they were as alien as places in another country, and the things they cherished could never be the same.

"So it was arranged that the man who rode the horse so well should go along too," said Dr. Heine. "It was finally arranged for a great deal of money," he said, and the mother gave him a look of fury. "But they had not counted on one thing. They had forgotten all about the little groom who had always cared for this special horse and who loved him better than anything else in the world. Ever since the horse had come from the stud farm in Styria, the little groom had cared for him, and he believed that they would always be together, he believed that he would go wherever the horse went, just as he had always gone to Salzburg with the horse in the summer, and always come back to Vienna with it in the wintertime again."

"And so what, what happened?" asked the other boy.

"Well," said the student-doctor, "the morning before the horse was to leave with the maharaja and the rider, they found that the horse had a deep cut on his leg, just above the hoof in front. Nobody could explain how it had happened, but the horse was so wounded that he could not travel then and the maharaja said that he could go on without him and that the trainer should bring the horse over in a few weeks when the cut had healed. They did not tell the maharaja that it might be that the horse could never dance so beautifully again. They had the money and they weren't going to give it back so easily," said Dr. Heine, and to the mother it seemed that their shrewdness pleased his soul. "But when the cut had healed," he went on, "and the horse seemed well enough to be sent by the next boat, the trainer found the horse had a cut on the other hoof, exactly where the other wound had been. So the journey was postponed again, and again the state said nothing to the maharaja about the horse being so impaired that it was likely he could never again fly like an angel. But in a few days the horse's blood was so poisoned from the wound that they had to destroy him."

They all waited, breathless with pain a moment, and then the doctor's wife said bitterly:

"Even the money couldn't save him, could it?"

"No," said Dr. Heine, a little perplexed by her words. "Of course, it couldn't. And they never knew how the cuts had come there until the little groom committed suicide the same day the horse was destroyed. And then they knew that he had done it himself because he couldn't bear the horse to be taken away."

They were all sitting quietly there at the table, with the dishes and remnants of food still before them, when someone knocked at the outside door. One of the boys went out to open it and he came back with the Heimwehr[2]

---

1. Established in 1572 and still in existence, the Spanish Riding School of Vienna trains and exhibits the Lipizzaners in the elaborate gaits and maneuvers of Renaissance horsemanship. Spain supplied several lines of the Lipizzaner breed to Austria.

2. Home guard (German); a paramilitary, quasi-fascist organization active in Austria in the 1920s and 1930s, allied with the right-wing Christian Social party, that promoted extreme nationalism (and, increasingly, anti-Semitism) against both international Marxism and Nazi Germany's interest in annexing Austria.

men following after him, the smooth, little black-and-white cockades lying forward in their caps.

"God greet you," said the doctor quietly when he saw them.

"God greet you," said the Heimwehr men.

"There's a swastika fire burning on the mountain behind you," said the leader of the soldiers. They were not men of the village but men brought from other parts of the country and billeted there as strangers to subdue the native people. "Show us the fastest way up there so we can see that it's put out."

"I'm afraid I can't do that," said the doctor, smiling. "You see, I have a bad leg."

"You can point out to us which way the path goes!" said the leader sharply.

"He can't move," said the doctor's wife, standing straight by the chair. "You have reports on everything. You must know very well that he is injured and has had a doctor come from Vienna to look after the sick until he can get around again."

"Yes," said the leader, "and we know very well that he wouldn't have been injured if he stayed home instead of climbing mountains himself at night!"

"Look here," said the student-doctor, speaking nervously, and his face gone thin and white. "He can't move a step, you know."

"He'll have to move more than a step if they want him at the *Rathaus*[3] again!" said the Heimwehr leader. "There's never any peace as long as he's not locked up!"

The young doctor said nothing after they had gone, but he sat quiet by the window, watching the fires burning on the mountains in the dark. They were blooming now on all the black, invisible crests, marvelously living flowers of fire springing out of the arid darkness, seemingly higher than any other things could grow. He felt himself sitting defenseless there by the window, surrounded by these strong, long-burning fires of disaster. They were all about him, inexplicable signals given from one mountain to another in some secret gathering of power that cast him and his people out, forever out upon the waters of despair.

The doctor's wife and the children had cleared the table, and the doctor was finishing his grasshopper underneath the light. He was busy wiring its wings to its body, and fastening the long, quivering antennae in. The grasshopper was colored a deep, living green, and under him lay strong, green-glazed haunches for springing with his wires across the puppet stage. He was a monstrous animal in the doctor's hands, with his great, glassy, gold-veined wings lying smooth along his back.

"The whole country is ruined by the situation," said the student-doctor, suddenly angry. "Everything is politics now. One can't meet people, have friends on any other basis. It's impossible to have casual conversations or abstract discussions any more. Who the devil lights these fires?"

"Some people light them because of their belief," said the doctor, working quietly, "and others travel around from place to place and make a living lighting them."

"Politics, politics," said the student-doctor, "and one party as bad as another. You're much wiser to make your puppets, *Herr Doktor*.[4] It takes one's

---

3. City Hall (German).
4. Literally, Mr. Doctor, a respectful form of address (German).

mind off things, just as playing cards does. In Vienna we play cards, always play cards, no matter what is happening."

"There was a time for cards," said the doctor, working quietly with the grasshopper's wings. "I used to play cards in Siberia, waiting to be free. We were always waiting then for things to finish with and be over," he said. "There was nothing to do, so we did that. But now there is something else to do."

He said no more, and in a little while the student-doctor went upstairs to bed. He could hear the doctor's wife and the children still washing the dishes and tidying up, their voices clearly heard through the fresh planks of his new-made floor.

Usually in the evening the doctor played the marionette theater for his wife and children, and for whatever friends wanted to come up the mountainside and see. He had made the theater himself, and now he had the new person-ages he had fashioned while nursing his twisted knee, and a week or two after the student-doctor had come he told them at supper that he would give them a show that night.

"The *Bürgermeister* is coming up with his wife and their young sons," he said, "and the *Apotheker*[5] and his nephews sent word that they'd drop in as well."

He moved the little fox from where it was sleeping on the wool sock of his foot, and he hopped on his one good leg across the room. Dr. Heine helped him carry the theater to the corner and set it up where the curtains hung, and the doctor hopped, heavy, and clean, and birdlike, from side to side and behind and before to get the look of the light and see how the curtains drew and fell.

By eight o'clock they were all of them there and seated in the darkened room, the doctor's and the *Bürgermeister*'s boys waiting breathless for the curtain to rise, and the *Apotheker*'s nephews smoking in the dark.

"I think it's marvelous, your husband giving plays like this, keeping the artistic thing uppermost even with times as they are," said Dr. Heine quietly to the doctor's wife. "One gets so tired of the same question everywhere, any-where one happens to be," he said, and she gave him a long, strange, bitter glance from the corners of her eyes.

"Yes," she said. "Yes. I suppose you do think a great deal of art."

"Yes, of course," said Dr. Heine, quite guilelessly. "Art and science, of course."

"Yes," said the doctor's wife, saying the words slowly and bitterly. "Yes. Art and science. What about people being hungry, what about this generation of young men who have never had work in their lives because the factories have never opened since the war? Where do they come in?"

"Yes, that too—" Dr. Heine began, and the whispered dialogue ended.

The curtain had been jerked aside and a wonderful expectancy lay on the air.

The scene before them was quite a simple one: the monstrously handsome grasshopper was sitting in a field, presumably a field, for there were white linen-petaled, yellow-hearted daisies all around him. He was a great, gleam-ing beauty, and the people watching cried out with pleasure. The doctor's

5. Pharmacist (German); *"Bürgermeister"*: mayor.

sons could scarcely wait until the flurry of delight had died and the talking had begun.

There were only two characters in the play, and they were the grasshopper and the clown. The clown came out on the stage and joined him after the grasshopper had done his elegant dance. The dance in itself was a masterpiece of grace and wit, with the music of Mozart playing on the gramophone behind. The children cried with laughter, and Dr. Heine shouted aloud, and the *Bürgermeister* shook with silent laughter. It lifted its legs so delicately, and sprang with such precision this way and that, through the ragged-petaled daisies of the field, that it seemed to have a life of its own in its limbs, separate from and more sensitive than that given it by any human hand. Even the little fox sat watching in fascination, his bright, unwild eyes shining like points of fire in the dark.

"*Wunderbar, wunderschön!*"[6] Dr. Heine called out. "It's really marvelous! He's as graceful as the white horses at Vienna, *Herr Doktor!* That step with the forelegs floating! It's extraordinary how you got it without ever seeing it done!"

And then the little clown came out on the stage. He came through the daisies of the field, a small, dwarfed clown with a sword ten times too big for him girded around his waist and tripping him at every step as he came. He was carrying a bunch of paper flowers and smiling, and there was something very *friseur*[7] about him. He had no smell of the really open country or the roots of things, while the grasshopper was a fine, green-armored animal, strong and perfectly equipped for the life he had to lead.

The clown had a round, human face and he spoke in a faltering human voice, and the grasshopper was the superthing, speaking in the doctor's ringing voice. Just the sound of the doctor's compassionate voice released in all its power was enough to make the guilty and the weak shake in their seats as if it were some accusation made them. It was a voice as ready for honest anger as it was for gentleness.

"Why do you carry artificial flowers?" the grasshopper asked, and the clown twisted and turned on his feet, so ridiculous in his stupidity that the children and all the others watching laughed aloud in the timber room. "Why do you carry artificial flowers?" the grasshopper persisted. "Don't you see that the world is full of real ones?"

"Oh, it's better I carry artificial ones," said the clown in the humorous accent of the country boor, and he tripped on his sword as he said it. "I'm on my way to my own funeral, *nicht?*[8] I want the flowers to keep fresh until I get there."

Everyone laughed very loud at this, but after a little, as the conversation continued between the grasshopper and the clown, Dr. Heine found he was not laughing as loudly as before. It was now evident that the grasshopper, for no conceivable reason, was always addressed as "The Leader," and the humorous little clown was called "Chancellor" by the grasshopper for no reason that he could see. The Chancellor was quite the fool of the piece. The only thing he had to support him was a very ludicrous faith in the power of the Church. The Church was a wonderful thing, the clown kept saying, twisting his poor bouquet.[9]

---

6. Wonderful, beautiful! (German).
7. Like a hairdresser (German, borrowed from French).

8. Am I not? (German).
9. The grasshopper puppet is identified with Adolf Hitler, the clown with Austria's ruler. Austria in

"The cities are full of churches," said the Leader, "but the country is full of God."

The Leader spoke with something entirely different in his voice: he had a wild and stirring power that sent the cold of wonder up and down one's spine. And whatever the argument was, the Chancellor always got the worst of it. The children cried aloud with laughter, for the Chancellor was so absurd, so eternally on his half-witted way to lay his bunch of paper flowers on his own or somebody else's grave, and the Leader was ready to waltz away at any moment with the power of stallion life that was leaping in his limbs.

"I believe in the independence of the individual," the poor humble smiling little clown said, and then he tripped over his sword and fell flat among the daisies. The Leader picked him up with his fragile, lovely forelegs, and set him against the painting of the sky.

"Ow, *mein Gott*,[1] the clouds are giving way!" cried the clown, and the grasshopper replied gently:

"But you are relying upon the heavens to support you. Are you afraid they are not strong enough?"

III

It was one evening in July, and the rain had just drawn off over the mountains. There was still the smell of it on the air, but the moon was shining strongly out. The student-doctor walked out before the house and watched the light bathing the dark valley, rising over the fertile slopes and the pine forests, running clear as milk above the timber line across the bare, bleached rock. The higher one went, the more terrible it became, he thought, and his heart shuddered within him. There were the rocks, seemingly as high as substance could go, but beyond that, even higher, hidden from the sight of the village people but clearly seen from the doctor's house, was the bend of the glacier and beside it were the peaks of everlasting snow. He was lost in this wilderness of cold, lost in a warm month, and the thought turned his blood to ice. He wanted to be indoors, with the warmth of his own people, and the intellect speaking. He had had enough of the bare, northern speech of these others who moved higher and higher as the land moved.

It was then that he saw the little lights moving up from the valley, coming like little beacons of hope carried to him. People were moving up out of the moon-bathed valley, like a little search party come to seek for him in an alien land. He stood watching the slow, flickering movement of their advance, the lights they carried seen far below, a small necklace of men coming to him; and then the utter white-darkness spread unbroken as they entered the wooded places and their lamps were extinguished by the trees.

"Come to me," he was saying within himself, "come to me. I am a young man alone on a mountain. I am a young man alone, as my race is alone, lost here amongst them all."

1934 was governed as a dictatorship by Chancellor Engelbert Dollfuss, a leader of the Austrian nationalist Christian Social party, who suspended democratic elections in fear that the Austrian Nazi party would win a popular majority for merging Austria with Germany. "The Leader," in German "Der Fuhrer," was Hitler's popular title; formally he was also Chancellor of Germany.

1. My God (German).

The doctor and his wife were sitting at work by the table when Dr. Heine came quickly into the room and said:

"There are some men coming up. They're almost here now. They look to me like the Heimwehr come again."

The doctor's wife stood up and touched the side of the timber wall as if something in it would give her fortitude. Then she went to the door and opened it, and in a moment the Heimwehr men came in.

"God greet you," the doctor said as they gathered around the table.

"God greet you," said the Heimwehr leader. "You're wanted at the *Rathaus*," he said.

"My leg isn't good enough to walk on yet," said the doctor quietly. "How will you get me down?"

"This time we brought a stretcher along," said the Heimwehr leader. "We have it outside the door."

The doctor's wife went off to fetch his white wool jacket and to wake the two boys in their beds. Dr. Heine heard her saying:

"They're taking Father to prison again. Now you must come and kiss him. Neither of you is going to cry."

The men brought the stretcher just within the doorway and the doctor hopped over to it and lay down. He looked very comfortable there under the wool rug that his wife laid over him.

"Look here," said Dr. Heine, "why do you have to come after a person at night like this? Do you think the *Herr Doktor* would try to run away from you? What are you up to? What's it all about?"

The Heimwehr leader looked him full in the eyes.

"They got Dollfuss this afternoon," he said. "They shot him in Vienna.[2] We're rounding them all up tonight. Nobody knows what will happen tomorrow."

"Ah, politics, politics again!" cried Dr. Heine, and he was wringing his hands like a woman about to cry. Suddenly he ran out the door after the stretcher and the men who were bearing the doctor away. He felt for the doctor's hand under the cover and he pressed it in his, and the doctor's hand closed over his in comfort. "What can I do? What can I do to help?" he said, and he was thinking of the pure-white horses of Vienna and of their waltz, like the grasshopper's dance across the stage. The doctor was smiling, his cheeks scarred with the marks of laughter in the light from the hurricane lamps that the men were carrying down.

"You can throw me peaches and chocolate from the street," said the doctor. "My wife will show you where we are. She's not a good shot. Her hand shakes too much when she tries. I missed all the oranges she threw me after the February slaughter."[3]

"What do you like best?" Dr. Heine called down after him, and his own voice sounded small and senseless in the enormous night.

"Peaches," the doctor's voice called back from the stretcher. "We get so thirsty . . ."

---

2. Chancellor Dollfuss was assassinated by eight Austrian Nazis on July 25, 1934, as part of an attempted coup.
3. An uprising by Austria's left-wing Social Democrats that began on February 12, 1934, and was suppressed by Dollfuss's ruling Christian Social party and the Heimwehr.

"I'll remember!" said Dr. Heine, his voice calling after the descending lights. He was thinking in anguish of the snow-white horses, the Lippizaners, the relics of pride, the still unbroken vestiges of beauty bending their knees to the empty loge of royalty where there was no royalty any more.

1935

JOHN STEINBECK
1902–1968

Most of John Steinbeck's best writing is set in the region of California that he called home, the Salinas Valley and Monterey peninsula of California, where visitors today will find official remembrances of him everywhere. Steinbeck believed in the American promise of opportunity for all, but believed also that social injustices and economic inequalities had put opportunity beyond reach for many. His work merged literary modernism with literary realism, celebrated traditional rural communities along with social outcasts and immigrant cultures, and endorsed conservative values and radical politics at the same time.

Steinbeck's father managed a flour mill and later became treasurer of Monterey County; his mother, who had taught school before marriage, was active in local civic affairs. Their home was full of books, and Steinbeck read avidly from an early age. After graduating from Salinas High School in 1919, he began to study at Stanford University but took time off for a variety of short-term jobs at local mills, farms, and estates. During this period he developed an abiding respect for people who worked on farms and in factories, and committed his literary abilities to their cause. He left college for good in 1925, having completed less than three years of coursework, and continued his roving life.

With financial help from his father, Steinbeck spent most of 1929 writing. He moved to the seaside town of Pacific Grove, on the Monterey coast, and in 1930 was married (the first of three times). In 1935 he achieved commercial success with his third novel, *Tortilla Flat,* a celebration of the Mexican-American culture of the *"paisanos"* who lived in the Monterey hills. The book favorably contrasted these lusty, idealized types to the valley's respectable, conventional, Anglo-Protestant population. Steinbeck's next novel, *In Dubious Battle* (1936), contrasted the decency of striking migratory farm workers both to the cynicism of landowners and their vigilantes, and to the equal cynicism of Communist labor union organizers who exploit the workers' plight for their own purposes. Sympathy for the underdog appears again in *Of Mice and Men* (1937), a best-selling short novel about two itinerant ranch hands, and yet again in *The Grapes of Wrath* (1939), his most famous and most ambitious novel.

Inspired by the devastating 1930s drought in the southern plains states and the exodus of thousands of farmers from their homes in the so-called Dust Bowl, *The Grapes of Wrath* told the story of the Joad family, who, after losing their land in Oklahoma, migrated westward to California on U.S. Highway 66 looking for, but not finding, a better life. Because of its supposed radicalism, the novel was banned or burned in several states, but even so, it became the nation's number one bestseller and won a Pulitzer Prize in 1940. *Cannery Row* (1940), a local-color novel about workers in the sardine canneries of Monterey, also became a bestseller.

After World War II Steinbeck's work displayed increasing hostility to American culture, whose mass commercialization seemed to him to be destroying individual creativity. "The Leader of the People" expresses his sense that America's heroic times are past and locates value in the story's socially marginal characters—a child, an old man, and a farmhand. His most important later works are *The Wayward Bus* (1947), *East of Eden* (1952), *Sweet Thursday* (1954), and *Travels with Charley in Search of America* (1962), in which he recounts his automobile tour of the United States, taken with his dog. Steinbeck won the Nobel Prize in 1963.

The text is that of *The Red Pony* (1945).

The Leader of the People

On Saturday afternoon Billy Buck, the ranch-hand, raked together the last of the old years' haystack and pitched small forkfuls over the wire fence to a few mildly interested cattle. High in the air small clouds like puffs of cannon smoke were driven eastward by the March wind. The wind could be heard whishing in the brush on the ridge crests, but no breath of it penetrated down into the ranch-cup.

The little boy, Jody, emerged from the house eating a thick piece of buttered bread. He saw Billy working on the last of the haystack. Jody tramped down scuffling his shoes in a way he had been told was destructive to good shoe-leather. A flock of white pigeons flew out of the black cypress tree as Jody passed, and circled the tree and landed again. A half-grown tortoise-shell cat leaped from the bunkhouse porch, galloped on stiff legs across the road, whirled and galloped back again. Jody picked up a stone to help the game along, but he was too late, for the cat was under the porch before the stone could be discharged. He threw the stone into the cypress tree and started the white pigeons on another whirling flight.

Arriving at the used-up haystack, the boy leaned against the barbed wire fence. "Will that be all of it, do you think?" he asked.

The middle-aged ranch-hand stopped his careful raking and stuck his fork into the ground. He took off his black hat and smoothed down his hair. "Nothing left of it that isn't soggy from ground moisture," he said. He replaced his hat and rubbed his dry leathery hands together.

"Ought to be plenty mice," Jody suggested.

"Lousy with them," said Billy. "Just crawling with mice."

"Well, maybe, when you get all through, I could call the dogs and hunt the mice."

"Sure, I guess you could," said Billy Buck. He lifted a forkful of the damp ground-hay and threw it into the air. Instantly three mice leaped out and burrowed frantically under the hay again.

Jody sighed with satisfaction. Those plump, sleek, arrogant mice were doomed. For eight months they had lived and multiplied in the haystack. They had been immune from cats, from traps, from poison and from Jody. They had grown smug in their security, overbearing and fat. Now the time of disaster had come; they would not survive another day.

Billy looked up at the top of the hills that surrounded the ranch. "Maybe you better ask your father before you do it," he suggested.

"Well, where is he? I'll ask him now."

"He rode up to the ridge ranch after dinner. He'll be back pretty soon."

Jody slumped against the fence post. "I don't think he'd care."

As Billy went back to his work he said ominously, "You'd better ask him any-way. You know how he is."

Jody did know. His father, Carl Tiflin, insisted upon giving permission for anything that was done on the ranch, whether it was important or not. Jody sagged farther against the post until he was sitting on the ground. He looked up at the little puffs of wind-driven cloud. "Is it like to rain, Billy?"

"It might. The wind's good for it, but not strong enough."

"Well, I hope it don't rain until after I kill those damn mice." He looked over his shoulder to see whether Billy had noticed the mature profanity. Billy worked on without comment.

Jody turned back and looked at the side-hill where the road from the out-side world came down. The hill was washed with lean March sunshine. Sil-ver thistles, blue lupins and a few poppies bloomed among the sage bushes. Halfway up the hill Jody could see Doubletree Mutt, the black dog, digging in a squirrel hole. He paddled for a while and then paused to kick bursts of dirt out between his hind legs, and he dug with an earnestness which belied the knowledge he must have had that no dog had ever caught a squirrel by digging in a hole.

Suddenly, while Jody watched, the black dog stiffened, and backed out of the hole and looked up the hill toward the cleft in the ridge where the road came through. Jody looked up too. For a moment Carl Tiflin on horseback stood out against the pale sky and then he moved down the road toward the house. He carried something white in his hand.

The boy started to his feet. "He's got a letter," Jody cried. He trotted away toward the ranch house, for the letter would probably be read aloud and he wanted to be there. He reached the house before his father did, and ran in. He heard Carl dismount from his creaking saddle and slap the horse on the side to send it to the barn where Billy would unsaddle it and turn it out.

Jody ran into the kitchen. "We got a letter!" he cried.

His mother looked up from a pan of beans. "Who has?"

"Father has. I saw it in his hand."

Carl strode into the kitchen then, and Jody's mother asked, "Who's the let-ter from, Carl?"

He frowned quickly. "How did you know there was a letter?"

She nodded her head in the boy's direction. "Big-Britches Jody told me."

Jody was embarrassed.

His father looked down at him contemptuously. "He *is* getting to be a Big-Britches," Carl said. "He's minding everybody's business but his own. Got his big nose into everything."

Mrs. Tiflin relented a little. "Well, he hasn't enough to keep him busy. Who's the letter from?"

Carl still frowned on Jody. "I'll keep him busy if he isn't careful." He held out a sealed letter. "I guess it's from your father."

Mrs. Tiflin took a hairpin from her head and slit open the flap. Her lips pursed judiciously. Jody saw her eyes snap back and forth over the lines. "He says," she translated, "he says he's going to drive out Saturday to stay for a lit-tle while. Why, this is Saturday. The letter must have been delayed." She looked at the postmark. "This was mailed day before yesterday. It should have been here yesterday." She looked up questioningly at her husband, and then her face darkened angrily. "Now what have you got that look on you for? He doesn't come often."

Carl turned his eyes away from her anger. He could be stern with her most of the time, but when occasionally her temper arose, he could not combat it.

"What's the matter with you?" she demanded again.

In his explanation there was a tone of apology Jody himself might have used. "It's just that he talks," Carl said lamely. "Just talks."

"Well, what of it? You talk yourself."

"Sure I do. But your father only talks about one thing."

"Indians!" Jody broke in excitedly. "Indians and crossing the plains!"

Carl turned fiercely on him. "You get out, Mr. Big-Britches! Go on, now! Get out!"

Jody went miserably out the back door and closed the screen with elaborate quietness. Under the kitchen window his shamed, downcast eyes fell upon a curiously shaped stone, a stone of such fascination that he squatted down and picked it up and turned it over in his hands.

The voices came clearly to him through the open kitchen window. "Jody's damn well right," he heard his father say. "Just Indians and crossing the plains. I've heard that story about how the horses got driven off about a thousand times. He just goes on and on, and he never changes a word in the things he tells."

When Mrs. Tiflin answered her tone was so changed that Jody, outside the window, looked up from his study of the stone. Her voice had become soft and explanatory. Jody knew how her face would have changed to match the tone. She said quietly, "Look at it this way, Carl. That was the big thing in my father's life. He led a wagon train clear across the plains to the coast, and when it was finished, his life was done. It was a big thing to do, but it didn't last long enough. Look!" she continued, "it's as though he was born to do that, and after he finished it, there wasn't anything more for him to do but think about it and talk about it. If there'd been any farther west to go, he'd have gone. He's told me so himself. But at last there was the ocean. He lives right by the ocean where he had to stop."

She had caught Carl, caught him and entangled him in her soft tone.

"I've seen him," he agreed quietly. "He goes down and stares off west over the ocean." His voice sharpened a little. "And then he goes up to the Horseshoe Club in Pacific Grove, and he tells people how the Indians drove off the horses."

She tried to catch him again. "Well, it's everything to him. You might be patient with him and pretend to listen."

Carl turned impatiently away. "Well, if it gets too bad, I can always go down to the bunkhouse and sit with Billy," he said irritably. He walked through the house and slammed the front door after him.

Jody ran to his chores. He dumped the grain to the chickens without chasing any of them. He gathered the eggs from the nests. He trotted into the house with the wood and interlaced it so carefully in the wood-box that two armloads seemed to fill it to overflowing.

His mother had finished the beans by now. She stirred up the fire and brushed off the stove-top with a turkey wing. Jody peered cautiously at her to see whether any rancor toward him remained. "Is he coming today?" Jody asked.

"That's what his letter said."

"Maybe I better walk up the road to meet him."

Mrs. Tiflin clanged the stove-lid shut. "That would be nice," she said. "He'd probably like to be met."

"I guess I'll just do it then."

Outside, Jody whistled shrilly to the dogs. "Come on up the hill," he commanded. The two dogs waved their tails and ran ahead. Along the roadside the sage had tender new tips. Jody tore off some pieces and rubbed them on his hands until the air was filled with the sharp wild smell. With a rush the dogs leaped from the road and yapped into the brush after a rabbit. That was the last Jody saw of them, for when they failed to catch the rabbit, they went back home.

Jody plodded on up the hill toward the ridge top. When he reached the little cleft where the road came through, the afternoon wind struck him and blew up his hair and ruffled his shirt. He looked down on the little hills and ridges below and then out at the huge green Salinas Valley. He could see the white town of Salinas far out in the flat and the flash of its windows under the waning sun. Directly below him, in an oak tree, a crow congress had convened. The tree was black with crows all cawing at once.

The Jody's eyes followed the wagon road down from the ridge where he stood, and lost it behind a hill, and picked it up again on the other side. On that distant stretch he saw a cart slowly pulled by a bay horse. It disappeared behind the hill. Jody sat down on the ground and watched the place where the cart would reappear again. The wind sang on the hilltops and the puffball clouds hurried eastward.

Then the cart came into sight and stopped. A man dressed in black dismounted from the seat and walked to the horse's head. Although it was so far away, Jody knew he had unhooked the check-rein, for the horse's head dropped forward. The horse moved on, and the man walked slowly up the hill beside it. Jody gave a glad cry and ran down the road toward them. The squirrels bumped along off the road, and a road-runner flirted its tail and raced over the edge of the hill and sailed out like a glider.

Jody tried to leap into the middle of his shadow at every step. A stone rolled under his foot and he went down. Around a little bend he raced, and there, a short distance ahead, were his grandfather and the cart. The boy dropped from his unseemly running and approached at a dignified walk.

The horse plodded stumble-footedly up the hill and the old man walked beside it. In the lowering sun there giant shadows flickered darkly behind them. The grandfather was dressed in a black broadcloth suit and he wore kid congress gaiters[1] and a black tie on a short, hard collar. He carried his black slouch hat in his hand. His white beard was cropped close and his white eyebrows overhung his eyes like mustaches. The blue eyes were sternly merry. About the whole face and figure there was a granite dignity, so that every motion seemed an impossible thing. Once at rest, it seemed the old man would be stone, would never move again. His steps were slow and certain. Once made, no step could ever be retraced; once headed in a direction, the path would never bend nor the pace increase nor slow.

---

1. High-topped shoes, or spats. Grandfather is dressed quite formally, in keeping with his old-fashioned sense of dignity.

When Jody appeared around the bend, Grandfather waved his hat slowly in welcome, and he called, "Why, Jody! Come down to meet me, have you?"

Jody sidled near and turned and matched his step to the old man's step and stiffened his body and dragged his heels a little. "Yes, sir," he said. "We got your letter only today."

"Should have been here yesterday," said Grandfather. "It certainly should. How are all the folks?"

"They're fine, sir." He hesitated and then suggested shyly, "Would you like to come on a mouse hunt tomorrow, sir?"

"Mouse hunt, Jody?" Grandfather chuckled. "Have the people of this generation come down to hunting mice? They aren't very strong, the new people, but I hardly thought mice would be game for them."

"No, sir. It's just play. The haystack's gone. I'm going to drive out the mice to the dogs. And you can watch, or even beat the hay a little."

The stern, merry eyes turned down on him. "I see. You don't eat them, then. You haven't come to that yet."

Jody explained, "The dogs eat them, sir. It wouldn't be much like hunting Indians, I guess."

"No, not much—but then later, when the troops were hunting Indians and shooting children and burning teepees, it wasn't much different from your mouse hunt."

They topped the rise and started down into the ranch-cup, and they lost the sun from their shoulders. "You've grown," Grandfather said. "Nearly an inch, I should say."

"More" Jody boasted. "Where they mark me on the door, I'm up more than an inch since Thanksgiving even."

Grandfather's rich throaty voice said, "Maybe you're getting too much water and turning to pith and stalk. Wait until you head out, and then we'll see."

Jody looked quickly into the old man's face to see whether his feelings should be hurt, but there was no will to injure, no punishing nor putting-in-your-place light in the keen blue eyes. "We might kill a pig," Jody suggested.

"Oh, no! I couldn't let you do that. You're just humoring me. It isn't the time and you know it."

"You know Riley, the big boar, sir?"

"Yes, I remember Riley well."

"Well, Riley ate a hole into that same haystack, and it fell down on him and smothered him."

"Pigs do that when they can," said Grandfather.

"Riley was a nice pig, for a boar, sir. I rode him sometimes, and he didn't mind."

A door slammed at the house below them, and they saw Jody's mother standing on the porch waving her apron in welcome. And they saw Carl Tiflin walking up from the barn to be at the house for the arrival.

The sun had disappeared from the hills by now. The blue smoke from the house chimney hung in flat layers in the purpling ranch-cup. The puff-ball clouds, dropped by the falling wind, hung listlessly in the sky.

Billy Buck came out of the bunkhouse and flung a wash basin of soapy water on the ground. He had been shaving in mid-week, for Billy held Grandfather in reverence, and Grandfather said that Billy was one of the few men of the new generation who had not gone soft. Although Billy was in middle age, Grandfather considered him a boy. Now Billy was hurrying toward the house too.

When Jody and Grandfather arrived, the three were waiting for them in front of the yard gate.

Carl said, "Hello, sir. We've been looking for you."

Mrs. Tiflin kissed Grandfather on the side of his beard, and stood still while his big hand patted her shoulder. Billy shook hands solemnly, grinning under his straw mustache. "I'll put up your horse," said Billy, and he led the rig away.

Grandfather watched him go, and then, turning back to the group, he said as he had said a hundred times before, "There's a good boy. I knew his father, old Mule-tail Buck. I never knew why they called him Mule-tail except he packed mules."

Mrs. Tiflin turned and led the way into the house. "How long are you going to stay, Father? Your letter didn't say."

"Well, I don't know. I thought I'd stay about two weeks. But I never stay as long as I think I'm going to."

In a short while they were sitting at the white oilcloth table eating their supper. The lamp with the tin reflector hung over the table. Outside the dining-room windows the big moths battered softly against the glass.

Grandfather cut his steak into tiny pieces and chewed slowly. "I'm hungry," he said. "Driving out here got my appetite up. It's like when we were crossing. We all got so hungry every night we could hardly wait to let the meat get done. I could eat about five pounds of buffalo meat every night."

"It's moving around does it," said Billy. "My father was a government packer. I helped him when I was a kid. Just the two of us could about clean up a deer's ham."

"I knew your father, Billy," said Grandfather. "A fine man he was. They called him Mule-tail Buck. I don't know why except he packed mules."

"That was it," Bill agreed. "He packed mules."

Grandfather put down his knife and fork and looked around the table. "I remember one time we ran out of meat—" His voice dropped to a curious low sing-song, dropped into a tonal groove the story had worn for itself. "There was no buffalo, no antelope, not even rabbits. The hunters couldn't even shoot a coyote. That was the time for the leader to be on the watch. I was the leader, and I kept my eyes open. Know why? Well, just the minute the people began to get hungry they'd start slaughtering the team oxen. Do you believe that? I've heard of parties that just ate up their draft cattle. Started from the middle and worked toward the ends. Finally they'd eat the lead pair, and then the wheelers. The leader of a party had to keep them from doing that."

In some manner a big moth got into the room and circled the hanging kerosene lamp. Billy got up and tried to clap it between his hands. Carl struck with a cupped palm and caught the moth and broke it. He walked to the window and dropped it out.

"As I was saying," Grandfather began again, but Carl interrupted him. "You'd better eat some more meat. All the rest of us are ready for our pudding."

Jody saw a flash of anger in his mother's eyes. Grandfather picked up his knife and fork. "I'm pretty hungry, all right," he said. "I'll tell you about that later."

When supper was over, when the family and Billy Buck sat in front of the fireplace in the other room, Jody anxiously watched Grandfather. He saw the signs he knew. The bearded head leaned forward; the eyes lost their sternness and looked wonderingly into the fire; the big lean fingers laced themselves on the black knees. "I wonder," he began, "I just wonder whether I ever told you how those thieving Piutes drove off thirty-five of our horses."

"I think you did," Carl interrupted. "Wasn't it just before you went up into the Tahoe country?"

Grandfather turned quickly toward his son-in-law. "That's right. I guess I must have told you that story."

"Lots of times," Carl said cruelly, and he avoided his wife's eyes. But he felt the angry eyes on him, and he said, " 'Course I'd like to hear it again."

Grandfather looked back at the fire. His fingers unlaced and laced again. Jody knew how he felt, how his insides were collapsed and empty. Hadn't Jody been called a Big-Britches that very afternoon? He arose to heroism and opened himself to the term Big-Britches again. "Tell about Indians," he said softly.

Grandfather's eyes grew stern again. "Boys always want to hear about Indians. It was a job for men, but boys want to hear about it. Well, let's see. Did I ever tell you how I wanted each wagon to carry a long iron plate?"

Everyone but Jody remained silent. Jody said, "No. You didn't."

"Well, when the Indians attacked, we always put the wagons in a circle and fought from between the wheels. I thought that if every wagon carried a long plate with rifle holes, the men could stand the plates on the outside of the wheels when the wagons were in the circle and they would be protected. It would save lives and that would make up for the extra weight of the iron. But of course the party wouldn't do it. No party had done it before and they couldn't see why they should go to the expense. They lived to regret it, too."

Jody looked at his mother, and knew from her expression that she was not listening at all. Carl picked at a callus on his thumb and Billy Buck watched a spider crawling up the wall.

Grandfather's tone dropped into its narrative groove again. Jody knew in advance exactly what words would fall. The story droned on, speeded up for the attack, grew sad over the wounds, struck a dirge at the burials on the great plains. Jody sat quietly watching Grandfather. The stern blue eyes were detached. He looked as though he were not very interested in the story himself.

When it was finished, when the pause had been politely respected as the frontier of the story, Billy Buck stood up and stretched and hitched his trousers. "I guess I'll turn in," he said. Then he faced Grandfather. "I've got an old powder horn and a cap and ball pistol down to the bunkhouse. Did I ever show them to you?"

Grandfather nodded slowly. "Yes, I think you did, Billy. Reminds me of a pistol I had when I was leading the people across." Billy stood politely until the story was done, and then he said, "Good night," and went out of the house.

Carl Tiflin tried to turn the conversation then. "How's the country between here and Monterey?[2] I've heard it's pretty dry."

---

2. Peninsula jutting into the Pacific Ocean south of San Francisco.

"It is dry," said Grandfather. "There's not a drop of water in the Laguna Seca.[3] But it's a long pull from '87. The whole country was powder then, and in '61 I believe all the coyotes starved to death. We had fifteen inches of rain this year."

"Yes, but it all came too early. We could do with some now." Carl's eye fell on Jody. "Hadn't you better be getting to bed?"

Jody stood up obediently. "Can I kill the mice in the old haystack, sir?"

"Mice? Oh! Sure, kill them all off. Billy said there isn't any good hay left."

Jody exchanged a secret and satisfying look with Grandfather. "I'll kill every one tomorrow," he promised.

Jody lay in his bed and thought of the impossible world of Indians and buffaloes, a world that had ceased to be forever. He wished he could have been living in the heroic time, but he knew he was not of heroic timber. No one living now, save possibly Billy Buck, was worthy to do the things that had been done. A race of giants had lived then, fearless men, men of a staunchness unknown in this day. Jody thought of the wide plains and of the wagons moving across like centipedes. He thought of Grandfather on a huge white horse, marshaling the people. Across his mind marched the great phantoms, and they marched off the earth and they were gone.

He came back to the ranch for a moment, then. He heard the dull rushing sound that space and silence make. He heard one of the dogs, out in the doghouse, scratching a flea and bumping his elbow against the floor with every stroke. Then the wind arose again and the black cypress groaned and Jody went to sleep.

He was up half an hour before the triangle sounded for breakfast. His mother was rattling the stove to make the flames roar when Jody went through the kitchen. "You're up early," she said. "Where are you going?"

"Out to get a good stick. We're going to kill the mice today."

"Who is 'we'?"

"Why, Grandfather and I."

"So you've got him in it. You always like to have someone in with you in case there's blame to share."

"I'll be right back," said Jody. "I just want to have a good stick ready for after breakfast."

He closed the screen door after him and went out into the cool blue morning. The birds were noisy in the dawn and the ranch cats came down from the hill like blunt snakes. They had been hunting gophers in the dark, and although the four cats were full of gopher meat, they sat in a semi-circle at the back door and mewed piteously for milk. Doubletree Mutt and Smasher moved sniffing along the edge of the brush, performing the duty with rigid ceremony, but when Jody whistled, their heads jerked up and their tails waved. They plunged down to him, wriggling their skins and yawning. Jody patted their heads seriously, and moved on to the weathered scrap pile. He selected an old broom handle and a short piece of inch-square scrap wood. From his pocket he took a shoelace and tied the ends of the sticks loosely together to make a flail. He whistled his new weapon through the air and struck the ground experimentally, while the dogs leaped aside and whined with apprehension.

3. Dry Lagoon (Spanish).

Jody turned and started down past the house toward the old haystack ground to look over the field of slaughter, but Billy Buck, sitting patiently on the back steps, called to him, "You better come back. It's only a couple of minutes till breakfast."

Jody changed his course and moved toward the house. He leaned his flail against the steps. "That's to drive the mice out," he said. "I'll bet they're fat. I'll bet they don't know what's going to happen to them today."

"No, nor you either," Billy remarked philosophically, "nor me, nor anyone."

Jody was staggered by this thought. He knew it was true. His imagination twitched away from the mouse hunt. Then his mother came out on the back porch and struck the triangle, and all thoughts fell in a heap.

Grandfather hadn't appeared at the table when they sat down. Billy nodded at his empty chair. "He's all right? He isn't sick?"

"He takes a long time to dress," said Mrs. Tiflin. "He combs his whiskers and rubs up his shoes and brushes his clothes."

Carl scattered sugar on his mush. "A man that's led a wagon train across the plains has got to be pretty careful how he dresses."

Mrs. Tiflin turned on him. "Don't do that, Carl! Please don't!" There was more of threat than of request in her tone. And the threat irritated Carl.

"Well, how many times do I have to listen to the story of the iron plates, and the thirty-five horses? That time's done. Why can't he forget it, now it's done?" He grew angrier while he talked, and his voice rose. "Why does he have to tell them over and over? He came across the plains. All right! Now it's finished. Nobody wants to hear about it over and over."

The door into the kitchen closed softly. The four at the table sat frozen. Carl laid his mush spoon on the table and touched his chin with his fingers.

Then the kitchen door opened and Grandfather walked in. His mouth smiled tightly and his eyes were squinted. "Good morning," he said, and he sat down and looked at his mush dish.

Carl could not leave it there. "Did—did you hear what I said?"

Grandfather jerked a little nod.

"I don't know what got into me, sir. I didn't mean it. I was just being funny."

Jody glanced in shame at his mother, and he saw that she was looking at Carl, and that she wasn't breathing. It was an awful thing that he was doing. He was tearing himself to pieces to talk like that. It was a terrible thing to him to retract a word, but to retract it in shame was infinitely worse.

Grandfather looked sidewise. "I'm trying to get right side up," he said gently. "I'm not being mad. I don't mind what you said, but it might be true, and I would mind that."

"It isn't true," said Carl. "I'm not feeling well this morning. I'm sorry I said it."

"Don't be sorry, Carl. An old man doesn't see things sometimes. Maybe you're right. The crossing is finished. Maybe it should be forgotten, now it's done."

Carl got up from the table. "I've had enough to eat. I'm going to work. Take your time, Billy!" He walked quickly out of the dining-room. Billy gulped the rest of his food and followed soon after. But Jody could not leave his chair.

"Won't you tell any more stories?" Jody asked.

"Why, sure I'll tell them, but only when—I'm sure people want to hear them."

"I like to hear them, sir."

"Oh! Of course you do, but you're a little boy. It was a job for men, but only little boys like to hear about it."

Jody got up from his place. "I'll wait outside for you, sir. I've got a good stick for those mice."

He waited by the gate until the old man came out on the porch. "Let's go down and kill the mice now," Jody called.

"I think I'll just sit in the sun, Jody. You go kill the mice."

"You can use my stick if you like."

"No, I'll just sit here a while."

Jody turned disconsolately away, and walked down toward the old haystack. He tried to whip up his enthusiasm with thoughts of the fat juicy mice. He beat the ground with his flail. The dogs coaxed and whined about him, but he could not go. Back at the house he could see Grandfather sitting on the porch, looking small and thin and black.

Jody gave up and went to sit on the steps at the old man's feet.

"Back already? Did you kill the mice?"

"No, sir. I'll kill them some other day."

The morning flies buzzed close to the ground and the ants dashed about in front of the steps. The heavy smell of sage slipped down the hill. The porch boards grew warm in the sunshine.

Jody hardly knew when Grandfather started to talk. "I shouldn't stay here, feeling the way I do." He examined his strong old hands. "I feel as though the crossing wasn't worth doing." His eyes moved up the side-hill and stopped on a motionless hawk perched on a dead limb. "I tell those old stories, but they're not what I want to tell. I only know how I want people to feel when I tell them.

"It wasn't Indians that were important, nor adventures, nor even getting out here. It was a whole bunch of people made into one big crawling beast. And I was the head. It was westering and westering. Every man wanted something for himself, but the big beast that was all of them wanted only westering. I was the leader, but if I hadn't been there, someone else would have been the head. The thing had to have a head.

"Under the little bushes the shadows were black at white noonday. When we saw the mountains at last, we cried—all of us. But it wasn't getting here that mattered, it was movement and westering.

"We carried life out here and set it down the way those ants carry eggs. And I was the leader. The westering was as big as God, and the slow steps that made the movement piled up and piled up until the continent was crossed.

"Then we came down to the sea, and it was done." He stopped and wiped his eyes until the rims were red. "That's what I should be telling instead of stories."

When Jody spoke, Grandfather started and looked down at him. "Maybe I could lead the people some day," Jody said.

The old man smiled. "There's no place to go. There's the ocean to stop you. There's a line of old men along the shore hating the ocean because it stopped them."

"In boats I might, sir."

"No place to go, Jody. Every place is taken. But that's not the worst—no, not the worst. Westering has died out of the people. Westering isn't a hunger any more. It's all done. Your father is right. It is finished." He laced his fingers on his knee and looked at them.

Jody felt very sad. "If you'd like a glass of lemonade I could make it for you."

Grandfather was about to refuse, and then he saw Jody's face. "That would be nice," he said. "Yes, it would be nice to drink a lemonade."

Jody ran into the kitchen where his mother was wiping the last of the breakfast dishes. "Can I have a lemon to make a lemonade for Grandfather?"

His mother mimicked—"And another lemon to make a lemonade for you."

"No, ma'am. I don't want one."

"Jody! You're sick!" Then she stopped suddenly. "Take a lemon out of the cooler," she said softly. "Here, I'll reach the squeezer down to you."

1945

COUNTEE CULLEN
1903–1946

More than most poets of the Harlem Renaissance, Countee Cullen valued traditional poetic forms in English—the sonnet, rhymed couplets, and quatrains—over modernist free verse or rhythms suggested by jazz and popular culture. Never one to shy away from controversy, Cullen prefaced his important anthology of African American poetry, *Caroling Dusk* (1927), with the assertion, "As heretical as it may sound, there is the probability that Negro poets, dependent as they are on the English language, may have more to gain from the rich background of English and American poetry than from any nebulous atavistic yearnings toward an African inheritance." Cullen demanded that black poets be considered as American poets, ultimately without any special racial designation. Nevertheless, the titles of his books of poetry—*Color* (1925), *Copper Sun* (1927), *The Ballad of the Brown Girl* (1928)—showed that, like Claude MacKay and Jean Toomer, he felt a responsibility to write about being black even if he did so in modes outside of black folk traditions. Although he clashed with a number of his contemporaries in the Harlem Renaissance, Cullen could also be generous to black writers whose poetics differed from his. What mattered to Cullen was appreciating the full range of black literary writing, a range as great, he insisted, as that found among white poets in English, and resisting every "attempt to corral the ebony muse into some definite mold" to which all black writers should conform.

Although Cullen's birthplace and early years are obscure, he was adopted at some point in his childhood by a Harlem-based minister and given a good education, first in New York public schools and then at New York University, where he received his B.A. in 1925, and at Harvard, where he took an M.A. in 1926. In high school, Cullen earned a city-wide poetry prize for "I Have a Rendezvous with Life," a rejoinder to Alan Seeger's sentimental World War I poem (see p. 1373). His first book of poems, *Color*, appeared in his senior year at college; it established him as the "black Keats," a prodigy.

From 1926 to 1928, Cullen was assistant editor at the important black journal *Opportunity*, for which he also wrote a feature column, "The Dark Tower." In 1928 he married Nina Yolande Du Bois, the daughter of W. E. B. Du Bois, and won a Guggenheim fellowship that took him to Paris and enabled him to complete another book of poems, *The Black Christ* (1929). His marriage quickly disintegrated, however, over Cullen's attraction to men, and the couple was divorced in 1930. Neither *The*

Black Christ nor the novel that followed, *One Way to Heaven* (1932), earned the acclaim of Cullen's earlier books. He spent the last years of his life teaching at New York's Frederick Douglass Junior High School, where his pupils included the future novelist James Baldwin. With the revival of scholarly interest in the Harlem Renaissance, Cullen's distinctive combination of traditionalist poetic skill with acerbic self-questioning on matters of racism and racial identity has once again brought his poetry to critical attention.

Yet Do I Marvel

I doubt not God is good, well-meaning, kind,
And did He stoop to quibble could tell why
The little buried mole continues blind,
Why flesh that mirrors Him must some day die,
Make plain the reason tortured Tantalus   5
Is baited by the fickle fruit, declare
If merely brute caprice dooms Sisyphus[1]
To struggle up a never-ending stair.
Inscrutable His ways are, and immune
To catechism by a mind too strewn   10
With petty cares to slightly understand
What awful brain compels His awful hand.
Yet do I marvel at this curious thing:
To make a poet black, and bid him sing!

                                                        1925

Incident

Once riding in old Baltimore,
    Heart-filled, head-filled with glee,
I saw a Baltimorean
    Keep looking straight at me.

Now I was eight and very small,   5
    And he was no whit bigger,
And so I smiled, but he poked out
    His tongue, and called me, "Nigger."

I saw the whole of Baltimore
    From May until December;   10
Of all the things that happened there
    That's all that I remember.

                                                        1925

---

1. Tantalus and Sisyphus are figures in Greek mythology who were punished in Hades. Tantalus was offered food and water that was then instantly snatched away. Sisyphus had to roll a heavy stone to the top of a hill and, after it rolled back down, repeat the ordeal perpetually.

Heritage

What is Africa to me:
Copper sun or scarlet sea,
Jungle star or jungle track,
Strong bronzed men, or regal black
Women from whose loins I sprang   5
When the birds of Eden sang?
One three centuries removed
From the scenes his fathers loved,
Spicy grove, cinnamon tree,
What is Africa to me?   10

So I lie, who all day long
Want no sound except the song
Sung by wild barbaric birds
Goading massive jungle herds,
Juggernauts[1] of flesh that pass   15
Trampling tall defiant grass
Where young forest lovers lie,
Plighting troth beneath the sky.
So I lie, who always hear,
Though I cram against my ear   20
Both my thumbs, and keep them there,
Great drums throbbing through the air.
So I lie, whose fount of pride,
Dear distress, and joy allied,
Is my somber flesh and skin,   25
With the dark blood dammed within
Like great pulsing tides of wine
That, I fear, must burst the fine
Channels of the chafing net
Where they surge and foam and fret.   30

Africa? A book one thumbs
Listlessly, till slumber comes.
Unremembered are her bats
Circling through the night, her cats
Crouching in the river reeds,   35
Stalking gentle flesh that feeds
By the river brink; no more
Does the bugle-throated roar
Cry that monarch claws have leapt
From the scabbards where they slept.   40
Silver snakes that once a year
Doff the lovely coats you wear,

1. The juggernaut is a sacred Hindu idol dragged on a huge car in the path of which devotees were believed to throw themselves—hence any power demanding blind sacrifice, here spliced with the image of elephants.

Seek no covert in your fear
Lest a mortal eye should see;
What's your nakedness to me?   45
Here no leprous flowers rear
Fierce corollas[2] in the air;
Here no bodies sleek and wet,
Dripping mingled rain and sweat,
Tread the savage measures of   50
Jungle boys and girls in love.
What is last year's snow to me,[3]
Last year's anything? The tree
Budding yearly must forget
How its past arose or set—   55
Bough and blossom, flower, fruit,
Even what shy bird with mute
Wonder at her travail there,
Meekly labored in its hair.
One three centuries removed   60
From the scenes his fathers loved,
Spicy grove, cinnamon tree,
What is Africa to me?

So I lie, who find no peace
Night or day, no slight release   65
From the unremittant beat
Made by cruel padded feet
Walking through my body's street.
Up and down they go, and back,
Treading out a jungle track.   70
So I lie, who never quite
Safely sleep from rain at night—
I can never rest at all
When the rain begins to fall;
Like a soul gone mad with pain   75
I must match its weird refrain;
Ever must I twist and squirm,
Writhing like a baited worm,
While its primal measures drip
Through my body, crying, "Strip!   80
Doff this new exuberance.
Come and dance the Lover's Dance!"
In an old remembered way
Rain works on me night and day.

Quaint, outlandish heathen gods   85
Black men fashion out of rods,
Clay, and brittle bits of stone,

2. The whorl of petals forming the inner envelope of a flower.
3. An echo of the lament "Where are the snows of yesteryear?" from "Grand Testament" by the 15th-century French poet François Villon.

In a likeness like their own,
My conversion came high-priced;
I belong to Jesus Christ,   90
Preacher of humility;
Heathen gods are naught to me.

Father, Son, and Holy Ghost,
So I make an idle boast;
Jesus of the twice-turned cheek[4]   95
Lamb of God, although I speak
With my mouth thus, in my heart
Do I play a double part.
Ever at Thy glowing altar
Must my heart grow sick and falter,   100
Wishing He I served were black,
Thinking then it would not lack
Precedent of pain to guide it,
Let who would or might deride it;
Surely then this flesh would know   105
Yours had borne a kindred woe.
Lord, I fashion dark gods, too,
Daring even to give You
Dark despairing features where,
Crowned with dark rebellious hair,   110
Patience wavers just so much as
Mortal grief compels, while touches
Quick and hot, of anger, rise
To smitten cheek and weary eyes.
Lord, forgive me if my need   115
Sometimes shapes a human creed.
All day long and all night through,
One thing only must I do:
Quench my pride and cool my blood,
Lest I perish in the flood.   120
Lest a hidden ember set
Timber that I thought was wet
Burning like the dryest flax,
Melting like the merest wax,
Lest the grave restore its dead.   125
Not yet has my heart or head
In the least way realized
They and I are civilized.

                                                            1925

---

4. In his Sermon on the Mount (Matthew 5.39), Jesus declared that when struck on the cheek, one should turn the other cheek rather than strike back.

From the Dark Tower[1]

We shall not always plant while others reap
The golden increment of bursting fruit,
Not always countenance, abject and mute,
That lesser men should hold their brothers cheap;
Not everlastingly while others sleep   5
Shall we beguile their limbs with mellow flute,
Not always bend to some more subtle brute;
We were not made eternally to weep.

The night whose sable breast relieves the stark,
White stars is no less lovely being dark,   10
And there are buds that cannot bloom at all
In light, but crumple, piteous, and fall;
So in the dark we hide the heart that bleeds,
And wait, and tend our agonizing seeds.

1927

Uncle Jim

"White folks is white," says uncle Jim;
"A platitude," I sneer;
And then I tell him so is milk,
And the froth upon his beer.

His heart walled up with bitterness,   5
He smokes his pungent pipe,
And nods at me as if to say,
"Young fool, you'll soon be ripe!"

I have a friend who eats his heart
Away with grief of mine,   10
Who drinks my joy as tipplers drain
Deep goblets filled with wine.

I wonder why here at his side,
Face-in-the-grass with him,
My mind should stray the Grecian urn[1]   15
To muse on uncle Jim.

1927

---

1. An allusion to " 'Childe Roland to the Dark Tower Came' " by the British Victorian poet Robert Browning (1812–1889). Cullen also titled his *Opportunity* column after Browning's poem.

1. An allusion to "Ode on a Grecian Urn" by the British Romantic poet John Keats (1795–1821). Cullen was particularly fond of the poetry of Keats.

RICHARD WRIGHT
1908–1960

With the 1940 publication of *Native Son* Richard Wright became the first African American author of a bestseller. *Native Son* is an uncompromising study of an African American underclass youth who is goaded to brutal violence by the oppression, hatred, and incomprehension of the white world. The sensational story disregarded conventional wisdom about how black authors should approach a white reading audience. Bigger Thomas, the main character, embodied everything that such an audience might fear and detest, but by situating the point of view within this character's consciousness Wright forced readers to see the world through Bigger's eyes and thus to understand him. The novel was structured like a hard-boiled detective story, contained layers of literary allusion and symbol, and combined Marxist social analysis with existential philosophy—in brief, it was at once a powerful social statement and a complex work of literary art.

Wright was born near Natchez, Mississippi. When he was five, his father abandoned the family—Wright, his younger brother, and his mother—and for the next ten years Wright was raised by a series of relatives in Mississippi. By 1925, when he went to Memphis on his own, he had moved twenty times. Extreme poverty, a constantly interrupted education that never went beyond junior high school, and the religious fundamentalism of his grandmother, along with the constant experiences of humiliation and hatred in a racially segregated South: all these contributed to Wright's growing sense that the hidden anger of black people was justified and that only by acknowledging and expressing it could they move beyond it. The title of *Native Son* made the point that the United States is as much the country of black as of white; the story showed that blacks had been deprived of their inheritance.

Two years after moving to Memphis, Wright went north to Chicago. There he took a series of odd jobs and then joined the WPA Writers' Project (a government project of the depression years to help support authors) as a writer of guidebooks and as a director of the Federal Negro Theater. He began to study Marxist theory, contributing poetry to leftist literary magazines and joining the Communist party in 1932. By 1935 he had become the center of a group of African American Chicago writers and had started to write fiction. He was influenced by the naturalistic fiction of James T. Farrell, whose study of sociology at the University of Chicago had helped give structure to his popular Studs Lonigan trilogy about working people of Irish descent.

Wright moved to New York in 1937 to write for the New York Writers' Project and as a reporter on the communist *Daily Worker*. In 1938 he published *Uncle Tom's Children*, a collection of four short stories. (An earlier novel, *Lawd Today*, was not published until after his death.) Set in the rural South, the stories center on racial conflict and physical violence. Wright's theme of the devastating effect of relentless, institutionalized hatred and humiliation on the black male's psyche was paramount in all of them.

After *Native Son*, Wright turned to autobiographical writings that eventuated in *Black Boy*, published in 1945. Many consider this to be his best book, and such writers as Ralph Ellison and James Baldwin took it as a model for their own work in the 1950s and 1960s. A communist activist in the early 1940s, Wright became increasingly disillusioned and broke completely with the party in 1944. Visiting France in 1946, he was warmly received by leading writers and philosophers. In 1947 he settled permanently in that country, where he was perceived from the first as one of the important experimental modernist prose writers and was ranked on a level with Hemingway, Fitzgerald, and Faulkner. An existential novel, *The Outsider* (1953), was followed by five more books: two novels and three collections of lectures, travel writings, and sociopolitical commentary. The collection *Eight Men*, from which the story printed here is taken, was the last literary project he worked on, and it appeared the year after his death.

Wright's immersion in Marxist doctrine gave him tools for representing society as divided into antagonistic classes and run for the benefit of the few. But in each of his works he portrays individuals who, no matter how they are deformed and brutalized by oppression and exploitation, retain a transcendent spark of selfhood. Ultimately, it is in this spark that Wright put his faith. His writing from first to last affirmed the dignity and humanity of society's outcasts without romanticizing them, and indicted those who had cast them out. As Ralph Ellison expressed it, Wright's example "converted the American Negro impulse toward self-annihilation and 'going underground' into a will to confront the world" and to "throw his findings unashamedly into the guilty conscience of America."

The text was first published in *Harper's Bazaar* (1939) under the title "Almos' a Man." Under its present title it appeared in *Eight Men* (1961), a posthumous collection of Wright's short fiction.

The Man Who Was Almost a Man

Dave struck out across the fields, looking homeward through paling light. Whut's the use talkin wid em niggers in the field? Anyhow, his mother was putting supper on the table. Them niggers can't understan nothing. One of these days he was going to get a gun and practice shooting, then they couldn't talk to him as though he were a little boy. He slowed, looking at the ground. Shucks, Ah ain scareda them even ef they are biggern me! Aw, Ah know whut Ahma do. Ahm going by ol Joe's sto n git that Sears Roebuck catlog n look at them guns. Mebbe Ma will lemme buy one when she gits mah pay from ol man Hawkins. Ahma beg her t gimme some money. Ahm ol ernough to hava gun. Ahm seventeen. Almost a man. He strode, feeling his long loose-jointed limbs. Shucks, a man oughta hava little gun aftah he done worked hard all day.

He came in sight of Joe's store. A yellow lantern glowed on the front porch. He mounted steps and went through the screen door, hearing it bang behind him. There was a strong smell of coal oil and mackerel fish. He felt very confident until he saw fat Joe walk in through the rear door, then his courage began to ooze.

"Howdy, Dave! Whutcha want?"

"How yuh, Mistah Joe? Aw, Ah don wanna buy nothing. Ah jus wanted t see ef yuhd lemme look at tha catlog erwhile."

"Sure! You wanna see it here?"

"Nawsuh. Ah wans t take it home wid me. Ah'll bring it back termorrow when Ah come in from the fiels."

"You plannin on buying something?"

"Yessuh."

"Your ma lettin you have your own money now?"

"Shucks. Mistah Joe, Ahm gittin t be a man like anybody else!"

Joe laughed and wiped his greasy white face with a red bandanna.

"Whut you plannin on buyin?"

Dave looked at the floor, scratched his head, scratched his thigh, and smiled. Then he looked up shyly.

"Ah'll tell yuh, Mistah Joe, ef yuh promise yuh won't tell."

"I promise."

"Waal, Ahma buy a gun."

"A gun? What you want with a gun?"

"Ah wanna keep it."

"You ain't nothing but a boy. You don't need a gun."

"Aw, lemme have the catlog, Mistah Joe. Ah'll bring it back."

Joe walked through the rear door. Dave was elated. He looked around at barrels of sugar and flour. He heard Joe coming back. He craned his neck to see if he were bringing the book. Yeah, he's got it. Gawddog, he's got it!

"Here, but be sure you bring it back. It's the only one I got."

"Sho, Mistah Joe."

"Say, if you wanna buy a gun, why don't you buy one from me? I gotta gun to sell."

"Will it shoot?"

"Sure it'll shoot."

"Whut kind is it?"

"Oh, it's kinda old . . . a left-hand Wheeler. A pistol. A big one."

"Is it got bullets in it?"

"It's loaded."

"Kin Ah see it?"

"Where's your money?"

"What yuh wan fer it?"

"I'll let you have it for two dollars."

"Just two dollahs? Shucks, Ah could buy tha when Ah git mah pay."

"I'll have it here when you want it."

"Awright, suh. Ah be in fer it."

He went through the door, hearing it slam again behind him. Ahma git some money from Ma n buy me a gun! Only two dollahs! He tucked the thick catalogue under his arm and hurried.

"Where yuh been, boy?" His mother held a steaming dish of black-eyed peas.

"Aw, Ma, Ah just stopped down the road t talk wid the boys."

"Yuh know bettah t keep suppah waitin."

He sat down, resting the catalogue on the edge of the table.

"Yuh git up from there and git to the well n wash yosef! Ah ain feedin no hogs in mah house!"

She grabbed his shoulder and pushed him. He stumbled out of the room, then came back to get the catalogue.

"Whut this?"

"Aw, Ma, it's jusa catlog."

"Who yuh git it from?"

"From Joe, down at the sto."

"Waal, thas good. We kin use it in the outhouse."

"Naw, Ma." He grabbed for it. "Gimme ma catlog, Ma."

She held onto it and glared at him.

"Quit hollerin at me! Whut's wrong wid yuh? Yuh crazy?"

"But Ma, please. It ain mine! It's Joe's! He tol me t bring it back t im termorrow."

She gave up the book. He stumbled down the back steps, hugging the thick book under his arm. When he had splashed water on his face and hands, he groped back to the kitchen and fumbled in a corner for the towel. He bumped into a chair; it clattered to the floor. The catalogue sprawled at his feet. When he had dried his eyes he snatched up the book and held it again under his arm. His mother stood watching him.

"Now, ef yuh gonna act a fool over that ol book, Ah'll take it n burn it up."

"Naw, Ma, please."

"Waal, set down n be still!"

He sat down and drew the oil lamp close. He thumbed page after page, unaware of the food his mother set on the table. His father came in. Then his small brother.

"Whutcha got there, Dave?" his father asked.

"Jusa catlog," he answered, not looking up.

"Yeah, here they is!" His eyes glowed at blue-and-black revolvers. He glanced up, feeling sudden guilt. His father was watching him. He eased the book under the table and rested it on his knees. After the blessing was asked, he ate. He scooped up peas and swallowed fat meat without chewing. Buttermilk helped to wash it down. He did not want to mention money before his father. He would do much better by cornering his mother when she was alone. He looked at his father uneasily out of the edge of his eye.

"Boy, how come yuh don quit foolin wid tha book n eat yo suppah?"

"Yessuh."

"How you n ol man Hawkins gitten erlong?"

"Suh?"

"Can't yuh hear? Why don yuh lissen? Ah ast yu how wuz yuh n ol man Hawkins gittin erlong?"

"Oh, swell, Pa. Ah plows mo lan than anybody over there."

"Waal, yuh oughta keep yo mind on whut yuh doin."

"Yessuh."

He poured his plate full of molasses and sopped it up slowly with a chunk of cornbread. When his father and brother had left the kitchen, he still sat and looked again at the guns in the catalogue, longing to muster courage enough to present his case to his mother. Lawd, ef Ah only had tha pretty one! He could almost feel the slickness of the weapon with his fingers. If he had a gun like that he would polish it and keep it shining so it would never rust. N Ah'd keep it loaded, by Gawd!

"Ma?" His voice was hesitant.

"Hunh?"

"Ol man Hawkins give yuh mah money yit?"

"Yeah, but ain no usa yuh thinking bout throwin nona it erway. Ahm keepin tha money sos yuh kin have cloes t go to school this winter."

He rose and went to her side with the open catalogue in his palms. She was washing dishes, her head bent low over a pan. Shyly he raised the book. When he spoke, his voice was husky, faint.

"Ma, Gawd knows Ah wans one of these."

"One of whut?" she asked, not raising her eyes.

"One of these," he said again, not daring even to point. She glanced up at the page, then at him with wide eyes.

2070 / Richard Wright

"Nigger, is yuh gone plumb crazy?"

"Aw, Ma."

"Git outta here! Don yuh talk t me bout no gun! Yuh a fool!"

"Ma, Ah kin buy one fer two dollahs."

"Not ef Ah knows it, yuh ain!"

"But yuh promised me one."

"Ah don care whut Ah promised! Yuh ain nothing but a boy yit!"

"Ma, ef yuh lemme buy one Ah'll *never* ast yuh fer nothing no mo."

"Ah tol yuh t git outta here! Yuh ain gonna toucha penny of tha money fer no gun! Thas how come Ah has Mistah Hawkins t pay yo wages t me, cause Ah knows yuh ain got no sense."

"But, Ma, we needa gun. Pa ain got no gun. We needa gun in the house. Yuh kin never tell whut might happen."

"Now don yuh try to maka fool outta me, boy! Ef we did hava gun, yuh wouldn't have it!"

He laid the catalogue down and slipped his arm around her waist.

"Aw, Ma, Ah done worked hard alla summer n ain ast yuh fer nothin, is Ah, now?"

"Thas whut yuh spose t do!"

"But Ma, Ah wans a gun. Yuh kin lemme have two dollahs outta mah money. Please, Ma. I kin give it to Pa . . . Please, Ma! Ah loves yuh, Ma."

When she spoke her voice came soft and low.

"What yuh wan wida gun, Dave? Yuh don need no gun. Yuh'll git in trouble. N ef yo pa jus thought Ah let yuh have money t buy a gun he'd hava fit."

"Ah'll hide it, Ma. It ain but two dollahs."

"Lawd, chil, whut's wrong wid yuh?"

"Ain nothing wrong, Ma. Ahm almos a man now. Ah wans a gun."

"Who gonna sell yuh a gun?"

"Ol Joe at the sto."

"N it don cos but two dollahs?"

"Thas all, Ma. Just two dollahs. Please, Ma."

She was stacking the plates away; her hands moved slowly, reflectively. Dave kept an anxious silence. Finally, she turned to him.

"Ah'll let yuh git tha gun ef yuh promise me one thing."

"Whut's tha, Ma?"

"Yuh bring it straight back t me, yuh hear? It be fer Pa."

"Yessum! Lemme go now, Ma."

She stooped, turned slightly to one side, raised the hem of her dress, rolled down the top of her stocking, and came up with a slender wad of bills.

"Here," she said. "Lawd knows yuh don need no gun. But yer pa does. Yuh bring it right back t me, yuh hear? Ahma put it up. Now ef yuh don, Ahma have yuh pa pick yuh so hard yuh won fergit it."

"Yessum."

He took the money, ran down the steps, and across the yard.

"Dave! Yuuuuuh Daaaaave!"

He heard, but he was not going to stop now. "Naw, Lawd!"

The first movement he made the following morning was to reach under his pillow for the gun. In the gray light of dawn he held it loosely, feeling a sense of power. Could kill a man with a gun like this. Kill anybody, black or white.

And if he were holding his gun in his hand, nobody could run over him; they would have to respect him. It was a big gun, with a long barrel and a heavy handle. He raised and lowered it in his hand, marveling at its weight.

He had not come straight home with it as his mother had asked; instead he had stayed out in the fields, holding the weapon in his hand, aiming it now and then at some imaginary foe. But he had not fired it; he had been afraid that his father might hear. Also he was not sure he knew how to fire it.

To avoid surrendering the pistol he had not come into the house until he knew that they were all asleep. When his mother had tiptoed to his bedside late that night and demanded the gun, he had first played possum; then he had told her that the gun was hidden outdoors, that he would bring it to her in the morning. Now he lay turning it slowly in his hands. He broke it, took out the cartridges, felt them, and then put them back.

He slid out of bed, got a long strip of old flannel from a trunk, wrapped the gun in it, and tied it to his naked thigh while it was still loaded. He did not go in to breakfast. Even though it was not yet daylight, he started for Jim Hawkins' plantation. Just as the sun was rising he reached the barns where the mules and plows were kept.

"Hey! That you, Dave?"

He turned. Jim Hawkins stood eying him suspiciously.

"What're yuh doing here so early?"

"Ah didn't know Ah wuz gittin up so early, Mistah Hawkins. Ah wuz fixin t hitch up ol Jenny n take her t the fiels."

"Good. Since you're so early, how about plowing that stretch down by the woods?"

"Suits me, Mistah Hawkins."

"O.K. Go to it!"

He hitched Jenny to a plow and started across the fields. Hot dog! This was just what he wanted. If he could get down by the woods, he could shoot his gun and nobody would hear. He walked behind the plow, hearing the traces creaking, feeling the gun tied tight to his thigh.

When he reached the woods, he plowed two whole rows before he decided to take out the gun. Finally, he stopped, looked in all directions, then untied the gun and held it in his hand. He turned to the mule and smiled.

"Know whut this is, Jenny? Naw, yuh wouldn know! Yuhs jusa ol mule! Anyhow, this is a gun, n it kin shoot, by Gawd!"

He held the gun at arm's length. Whut t hell, Ahma shoot this thing! He looked at Jenny again.

"Lissen here, Jenny! When Ah pull this ol trigger, Ah don wan yuh t run n acka fool now!"

Jenny stood with head down, her short ears pricked straight. Dave walked off about twenty feet, held the gun far out from him at arm's length, and turned his head. Hell, he told himself, Ah ain afraid. The gun felt loose in his fingers; he waved it wildly for a moment. Then he shut his eyes and tightened his forefinger. Bloom! A report half deafened him and he thought his right hand was torn from his arm. He heard Jenny whinnying and galloping over the field, and he found himself on his knees, squeezing his fingers hard between his legs. His hand was numb; he jammed it into his mouth, trying to warm it, trying to stop the pain. The gun lay at his feet. He did not quite know what had happened. He stood up and stared at the gun as though it were a living thing. He gritted his teeth and kicked the gun. Yuh almos broke mah arm! He turned to look for Jenny; she was far over the fields, tossing her head and kicking wildly.

"Hol on there, ol mule!"

When he caught up with her she stood trembling, walling her big white eyes at him. The plow was far away; the traces had broken. Then Dave stopped short, looking, not believing. Jenny was bleeding. Her left side was red and wet with blood. He went closer. Lawd, have mercy! Wondah did Ah shoot this mule? He grabbed for Jenny's mane. She flinched, snorted, whirled, tossing her head.

"Hol on now! Hol on."

Then he saw the hole in Jenny's side, right between the ribs. It was round, wet, red. A crimson stream streaked down the front leg, flowing fast. Good Gawd! Ah wuzn't shootin at tha mule. He felt panic. He knew he had to stop that blood, or Jenny would bleed to death. He had never seen so much blood in all his life. He chased the mule for a half a mile, trying to catch her. Finally she stopped, breathing hard, stumpy tail half arched. He caught her mane and led her back to where the plow and gun lay. Then he stooped and grabbed handfuls of damp black earth and tried to plug the bullet hole. Jenny shuddered, whinnied, and broke from him.

"Hol on! Hol on now!"

He tried to plug it again, but blood came anyhow. His fingers were hot and sticky. He rubbed dirt into his palms, trying to dry them. Then again he attempted to plug the bullet hole, but Jenny shied away, kicking her heels high. He stood helpless. He had to do something. He ran at Jenny; she dodged him. He watched a red stream of blood flow down Jenny's leg and form a bright pool at her feet.

"Jenny . . . Jenny," he called weakly.

His lips trembled. She's bleeding t death! He looked in the direction of home, wanting to go back, wanting to get help. But he saw the pistol lying in the damp black clay. He had a queer feeling that if he only did something, this would not be; Jenny would not be there bleeding to death.

When he went to her this time, she did not move. She stood with sleepy, dreamy eyes; and when he touched her she gave a low-pitched whinny and knelt to the ground, her front knees slopping in blood.

"Jenny . . . Jenny . . ." he whispered.

For a long time she held her neck erect; then her head sank, slowly. Her ribs swelled with a mighty heave and she went over.

Dave's stomach felt empty, very empty. He picked up the gun and held it gingerly between his thumb and forefinger. He buried it at the foot of a tree. He took a stick and tried to cover the pool of blood with dirt—but what was the use? There was Jenny lying with her mouth open and her eyes walled and glassy. He could not tell Jim Hawkins he had shot his mule. But he had to tell something. Yeah, Ah'll tell em Jenny started gittin wil n fell on the joint of the plow. . . . But that would hardly happen to a mule. He walked across the field slowly, head down.

It was sunset. Two of Jim Hawkins' men were over near the edge of the woods digging a hole in which to bury Jenny. Dave was surrounded by a knot of people, all of whom were looking down at the dead mule.

"I don't see how in the world it happened," said Jim Hawkins for the tenth time.

The crowd parted and Dave's mother, father, and small brother pushed into the center.

"Where Dave?" his mother called.

"There he is," said Jim Hawkins.

His mother grabbed him.

"Whut happened, Dave? Whut yuh done?"

"Nothin."

"C mon, boy, talk," his father said.

Dave took a deep breath and told the story he knew nobody believed.

"Waal," he drawled. "Ah brung ol Jenny down here sos Ah could do mah plowin. Ah plowed bout two rows, just like yuh see." He stopped and pointed at the long rows of upturned earth. "Then somethin musta been wrong wid ol Jenny. She wouldn ack right a-tall. She started snortin n kickin her heels. Ah tried t hol her, but she pulled erway, rearin n goin in. Then when the point of the plow was stickin up in the air, she swung erroun n twisted herself back on it . . . She stuck herself n started t bleed. N fo Ah could do anything, she wuz dead."

"Did you ever hear of anything like that in all your life?" asked Jim Hawkins.

There were white and black standing in the crowd. They murmured. Dave's mother came close to him and looked hard into his face. "Tell the truth, Dave," she said.

"Looks like a bullet hole to me," said one man.

"Dave, whut yuh do wid the gun?" his mother asked.

The crowd surged in, looking at him. He jammed his hands into his pockets, shook his head slowly from left to right, and backed away. His eyes were wide and painful.

"Did he hava gun?" asked Jim Hawkins.

"By Gawd, Ah tol yuh tha wu a gun wound," said a man, slapping his thigh.

His father caught his shoulders and shook him till his teeth rattled.

"Tell whut happened, yuh rascal! Tell whut . . ."

Dave looked at Jenny's stiff legs and began to cry.

"Whut yuh do wid tha gun?" his mother asked.

"Whut wuz he doin wida gun?" his father asked.

"Come on and tell the truth," said Hawkins. "Ain't nobody going to hurt you . . ."

His mother crowded close to him.

"Did yuh shoot tha mule, Dave?"

Dave cried, seeing blurred white and black faces.

"Ahh ddinn gggo tt sshooot hher . . . Ah ssswear ffo Gawd Ahh ddin. . . . Ah wuz a-tryin t sssee ef the old gggun would sshoot."

"Where yuh git the gun from?" his father asked.

"Ah got it from Joe, at the sto."

"Where yuh git the money?"

"Ma give it t me."

"He kept worryin me, Bob. Ah had t. Ah tol im t bring the gun right back to me . . . It was fer yuh, the gun."

"But how yuh happen to shoot that mule?" asked Jim Hawkins.

"Ah wuzn shootin at the mule, Mistah Hawkins. The gun jumped when Ah pulled the trigger . . . N fo Ah knowed anythin Jenny was there a-bleedin."

Somebody in the crowd laughed. Jim Hawkins walked close to Dave and looked into his face.

"Well, looks like you have bought you a mule, Dave."

"Ah swear fo Gawd, Ah didn go t kill the mule, Mistah Hawkins!"

"But you killed her!"

All the crowd was laughing now. They stood on tiptoe and poked heads over one another's shoulders.

"Well, boy, looks like yuh done bought a dead mule! Hahaha!"

"Ain tha ershame."

"Hohohohoho."

Dave stood, head down, twisting his feet in the dirt.

"Well, you needn't worry about it, Bob," said Jim Hawkins to Dave's father. "Just let the boy keep on working and pay me two dollars a month."

"Whut yuh wan fer yo mule, Mistah Hawkins?"

Jim Hawkins screwed up his eyes.

"Fifty dollars."

"Whut yuh do wid tha gun?" Dave's father demanded.

Dave said nothing.

"Yuh wan me t take a tree n beat yuh till yuh talk!"

"Nawsuh!"

"Whut yuh do wid it?"

"Ah throwed it erway."

"Where?"

"Ah . . . Ah throwed it in the creek."

"Waal, c mon home. N firs thing in the mawnin git to tha creek n fin tha gun."

"Yessuh."

"Whut yuh pay fer it?"

"Two dollahs."

"Take tha gun n git yo money back n carry it t Mistah Hawkins, yuh near? N don fergit Ahma lam you black bottom good fer this! Now march yosef on home, suh!"

Dave turned and walked slowly. He heard people laughing. Dave glared, his eyes welling with tears. Hot anger bubbled in him. Then he swallowed and stumbled on.

That night Dave did not sleep. He was glad that he had gotten out of killing the mule so easily, but he was hurt. Something hot seemed to turn over inside him each time he remembered how they had laughed. He tossed on his bed, feeling his hard pillow. N Pa says he's gonna beat me . . . He remembered other beatings, and his back quivered. Naw, naw, Ah sho don wan im t beat me tha way no mo. Dam em all! Nobody ever gave him anything. All he did was work. They treat me like a mule, n then they beat me. He gritted his teeth. N Ma had t tell on me.

Well, if he had to, he would take old man Hawkins that two dollars. But that meant selling the gun. And he wanted to keep that gun. Fifty dollars for a dead mule.

He turned over, thinking how he had fired the gun. He had an itch to fire it again. Ef other men kin shoota gun, by Gawd, Ah kin! He was still, listening. Mebbe they all sleepin now. The house was still. He heard the soft breathing of his brother. Yes, now! He would go down and get that gun and see if he could fire it! He eased out of bed and slipped into overalls.

The moon was bright. He ran almost all the way to the edge of the woods. He stumbled over the ground, looking for the spot where he had buried the gun. Yeah, here it is. Like a hungry dog scratching for a bone, he pawed it up. He puffed his black cheeks and blew dirt from the trigger and barrel. He broke it and found four cartridges unshot. He looked around; the fields were filled with silence and moonlight. He clutched the gun stiff and hard in his fingers. But, as soon as he wanted to pull the trigger, he shut his eyes and turned his head. Naw, An can't shoot wid mah eyes closed n mah head turned. With effort he held his eyes open; then he squeezed. *Bloooom!* He was stiff, not breathing. The gun was still in his hands. Dammit, he'd done it! He fired again. *Blooooom!* He smiled. *Blooooom! Blooooom! Click, click.* There! It was empty. If anybody could shoot a gun, he could. He put the gun into his hip pocket and started across the fields.

When he reached the top of a ridge he stood straight and proud in the moonlight, looking at Jim Hawkins' big white house, feeling the gun sagging in his pocket. Lawd, ef Ah had just one mo bullet Ah'd taka shot at tha house. Ah'd like t scare ol man Hawkins jusa little . . . Jusa enough t let im know Dave Saunders is a man.

To his left the road curved, running to the tracks of the Illinois Central. He jerked his head, listening. From far off came a faint *hooof-hoooof; hoooof-hoooof; hoooof-hoooof. . . .* He stood rigid. Two dollahs a mont. Les see now . . . Tha means it'll take bout two years. Shucks! Ah'll be dam!

He started down the road, toward the tracks. Yeah, here she comes! He stood beside the track and held himself stiffly. Here she comes, erroun the ben . . . C mon, yuh slow poke! C mon! He had his hand on his gun; something quivered in his stomach. Then the train thundered past, the gray and brown box cars rumbling and clinking. He gripped the gun tightly; then he jerked his hand out of his pocket. Ah betcha Bill wouldn't do it! Ah betcha. . . . The cars slid past, steel grinding upon steel. Ahm ridin yuh ternight, so hep me Gawd! He was hot all over. He hesitated just a moment; then he grabbed, pulled atop of a car, and lay flat. He felt his pocket; the gun was still there. Ahead the long rails were glinting in the moonlight, stretching away, away to somewhere, somewhere where he could be a man . . .

1939, 1961

CARLOS BULOSAN
1911–1956

Carlos Bulosan was the first, and is still the most important, Filipino-American author, one of the earliest voices in the Asian American literary tradition. Although the lives of Filipinos were always his first concern, his claim that all "who came to the United States as immigrants are Americans too" connects his writing to the rich history of American immigrant literature in general.

Bulosan came from an extremely poor peasant family in the Philippines and had almost no formal education. He arrived in Seattle in 1931, one of thousands of young Filipino men who came for jobs after the Immigrant Act of 1924 excluded the Japanese. Like two older brothers who had emigrated earlier, he worked seasonally from Alaska to southern California—canning fish, planting cauliflower, picking fruit—for low wages in miserable conditions. White Americans had always discriminated against the Asians whose labor underpinned so much West Coast prosperity, but Filipinos were treated with particular brutality and contempt. As Bulosan put it, "In many ways it was a crime to be a Filipino in California."

Within a few years he became active in the dangerous work of organizing migrant farm workers into unions. From 1936 to 1938 he was hospitalized in Los Angeles with tuberculosis; during this time he read widely and began writing poetry. When, during World War II, the Philippines were attacked by the Japanese and Filipinos were allowed to join the U.S. Army, mainland hostility toward them lessened somewhat. Bulosan's first book, a collection of poems titled *Letter for America,* appeared in 1942. He began to publish stories in prestigious magazines like the *New Yorker, Town and Country,* and *Harper's Bazaar. The Laughter of My Father* (1944), sketches of Filipino peasant life, won critical acclaim, as did his powerful memoir, *America Is in the Heart* (1946). Over the years he had many romances with white women but never married. Marriage between whites and Filipinos was, in fact, illegal in the western states during those decades.

Bulosan's writing shifts from oratorical generalization in praise of American ideals to naturalistic, hard-boiled accounts of poverty, exploitation, and prejudice. His stylistic ambivalence well represents his divided feelings. He was in love with an imaginary United States but found that "the terrible truth in America shatters the Filipinos' dream of fraternity."

Many of Bulosan's stories exist in manuscript only and are difficult to date. The text of "Be American" is from *On Becoming Filipino* (1995), edited by E. San Juan Jr.

Be American

It was not Consorcio's fault. My cousin was an illiterate peasant from the vast plains of Luzon. When he came off the boat in San Francisco, he could neither read nor write English or Ilocano, our dialect. I met him when he arrived, and right away he had bright ideas in his head.

"Cousin, I want to be American," he told me.

"Good," I said. "That is the right thing to do. But you have plenty of time. You are planning to live permanently in the United States, are you not?"

"Sure, cousin," he said. "But I want to be American right away. On the boat I say, 'Consorcio stoody Engleesh right away.' Good ideeyas, eh, cousin?"

"It is," I said. "But the first thing for you to do is look for a job."

"Sure, cousin. You have joob for me?"

I did. I took him to a countryman of ours who owned a small restaurant on Kearny Street. He had not done any dishwashing in the Philippines, so he broke a few dishes before he realized that the dishes were not coconut shells that he could flagrantly throw around the place, the way he used to do in his village where coconut shells were plates and carved trunks of trees were platters and his fingers were spoons. He had never seen bread and butter before, so he lost some weight before he realized that he had to eat these basic things like the rest of us, and be an American, which was his own idea in the first place. He had never slept in a bed with a mattress before, so he had to suffer from severe cold before he realized that he had to sleep inside the bed, under the blankets, but not on top of the spread, which was what he had done during his first two weeks in America. And of course he had never worn shoes before, so he had to suffer a few blisters on both feet before he realized that he had to walk lightfooted, easy, and even graceful, but not the way he used to do it in his village, which was like wrestling with a carabao[1] or goat.

All these natural things he had to learn during his first two weeks. But he talked about his Americanization with great confidence.

"You see, cousin," he told me, "I have earned mony quick. I poot the hoot dashes in the sink, wash-wash, day come, day out, week gone—mony! Simple?"

"Fine," I said.

"You know what I done with mony?"

"No."

"I spent all."

"On what?"

"Books. Come see my room."

I went with him to his small room at the back of the restaurant where he was working, near the washrooms. And sure enough, he had lined the four walls of his room with big books. I looked at the titles. He had a cheap edition of the classics, books on science, law and mathematics. He even had some brochures on political and governmental matters. All were books that a student or even a professor would take time to read.

I turned to my cousin. He was smiling with pride.

"Well, I hope these big books will make you an American faster," I told him.

"Sure, cousin. How long I wait?"

"Five years."

"*Five years?*" There was genuine surprise in his dark peasant face. "Too long. I do not wait. I make faster—one year."

"It is the law," I assured him.

"No good law. One year enough for Consorcio. He make good American citizen."

1. Water buffalo, used for plowing on Filipino farms.

"There is nothing you can do about it."

"I change law."

"Go ahead."

"You see, cousin."

But he was puzzled. So I left him. I left San Francisco. When I saw him a year later, he was no longer washing dishes. But he still had the pardonable naivete of a peasant from the plains of Luzon.

"Where are you working now?" I asked him.

"Bakery," he said. "I make da bread. I make da donot. I make da pys."

"Where?"

"Come, cousin. I show you."

It was a small shop, a three-men affair. Consorcio was the handy-boy in the place, scrubbing the floor, washing the pots and pans; and he was also the messenger. The owner was the baker, while his wife was the saleswoman. My cousin lived at the back of the building, near the washrooms. He had a cot in a corner of the dark room. But the books were gone.

"What happened to your books?" I asked him.

He looked sad. Then he said, "I sold, cousin."

"Why?"

"I cannot read. I cannot understand. Words too big and too long."

"You should begin with simple grammar books."

"Those cannot read also. What to do now, cousin?"

"You still want to be an American citizen?"

"Sure."

"Go to night school."

"Is a place like that?"

"Yes."

"No use, cousin. No money."

"The school is free," I told him. "It is for foreign-born people. For adults, so they could study American history."

"Free? I go now."

"The school opens only at night."

"I work night."

"Well, work in the daytime. Look for another job. You still want to be an American, don't you?"

"Sure. But I like boss-man. What to do?"

"Tell him the truth."

"You help me?"

I did. We went to the boss-man. I explained the matter as truthfully as I could and he understood Consorcio's problems. But he asked me to find someone to take the place of my cousin's place, which I did too, so we shook hands around and departed in the best of humor. I helped Consorcio register at the night school, looked for another job for him as janitor in an apartment building. Then I left him, wishing him the best of luck.

I worked in Alaska the next two years. When I returned to the mainland, I made it my duty to pass through San Francisco. But my cousin had left his janitor job and the night school. I could not find his new address, and it seemed that no one knew him well enough in the Filipino community.

I did not think much of his disappearance because we are a wandering people due to the nature of our lowly occupations, which take us from place to place, following the seasons. When I received a box of grapes from a friend, I knew he was working in the grape fields in either Fresno or Delano, depending on the freight mark. When I received a box of asparagus, I knew he was working in Stockton. But when it was a crate of lettuce, he was working in Santa Maria or Salinas, depending on the freight mark again. And in the summertime when I received a large barrel of salmon, I knew he was working in the salmon canneries in Alaska. There were no letters, no post cards—nothing. But these surprising boxes, crates, and barrels that arrived periodically were the best letters in the world. What they contained were lovingly distributed among my city friends. Similarly, when I was in one of my own wanderings, which were done in cities and large towns, I sent my friend or friends unsealed envelopes bursting with the colored pictures of actresses and other beautiful women. I addressed these gifts to poolrooms and restaurants in towns where my friends had lived or worked for a season, because they were bound to go to any of these havens of the homeless wanderer. However, when another curious wanderer opened the envelopes and pilfered the pictures, it was not a crime. The enjoyment which was originally intended for my friends was his and his friends. That is the law of the nomad: finders keepers.

But Consorcio had not yet learned the unwritten law of the nomad. I did not expect him to send me boxes, crates, and barrels from far-away Alaska. So I did not know where I could locate him.

I wandered in and out of Los Angeles the next two years. At the beginning of the third year, when I was talking to the sleeping birds in Pershing Square, I felt a light hand on my shoulders. I was not usually curious about hands, but it was well after midnight and the cops were wandering in and out of the place. So I turned around—and found Consorcio.

I found a new Consorcio. He had aged and the peasant naivete was gone from his face. In his eyes now was a hidden fear. His hands danced and flew when he was talking, and even when he was not talking, as though he were slapping the wind with both hands or clapping with one hand. Have you ever heard the noise of one hand clapping?

That was Consorcio after five years in America. He was either slapping the wind with both hands or clapping with one hand. So I guided him out of the dark park to a lighted place, where we had coffee until the city awoke to give us another day of hope. Of course, I sat in silence for a long time because it was the year of deep silence. And Consorcio sat for a long time too, because by now he had learned to hide in the deep silence that was flung like a mourning cloak across the face of the land. When we talked our sentences were short and punctuated by long silences. So we conversed somewhat like this:

"Been wandering everywhere."

"No job."

"Nothing anywhere."

"Where have you been all these years?"

Silence.

"No finished school?"

Silence.

"Not American citizen yet?"

"You should have told me."

"Told you what?"

"Filipinos can't become American citizens."

"Well, I could have told you. But I wanted you to learn."

"At least I speak better English now."

"This is a country of great opportunity."

Silence.

"No work?"

"No work."

"How long?"

"I have forgotten."

"Better times will come."

"You have a wonderful dream, cousin," he told me and left. He left Los Angeles for a long time. Then, two years later, I received a crate of oranges from him. The freight mark was San Jose. Now I knew he was working and had learned the unwritten law of the wanderers on this troubled earth. So as I ate the oranges, I recalled his last statement: *You have a wonderful dream, cousin. . . .* I had a wonderful dream. But I dreamed it for both of us, for many of us who wandered in silence.

Then the boxes and crates became more frequent. Then a barrel of salmon came from Alaska. And, finally, the letters came. My cousin Consorcio, the one-time illiterate peasant from the vast plains of Luzon, had indeed become an American without knowing it. His letters were full of wondering and pondering about many things in America. Now he realized his naivete when he had landed in San Francisco. But he realized also that he could not ask too much in a strange land. And it was this realization that liberated him from his peasant prison, his heritage, and eventually led him to a kind of work to which he dedicated his time and life until the end.

I was in Oregon when I received a newspaper from Consorcio, postmarked Pismo Beach. It was the first issue of his publication for agricultural workers in California. It was in English. From then on, I received all issues of his publication. For five years it existed defending the workers and upholding the rights and liberties of all Americans, native or foreign-born, so that, as he began to understand the nature of American society, he became more belligerent in his editorials and had to go to jail a few times for his ideas about freedom and peace.

Yes, indeed Consorcio: you have become an American, a real American. And this land that we have known too well is not yet denuded by the rapacity of men. Rolling like a beautiful woman with an overflowing abundance of fecundity and murmurous with her eternal mystery, there she lies before us like a great mother. To her we always return from our prodigal wanderings and searchings for an anchorage in the sea of life; from her we always draw our sustenance and noble thoughts, to add to her glorious history.

But the war came. And the war ended Consorcio's newspaper work and his crusade for a better America. And it ended his life also. When he was brought back from overseas, he knew he would not last long. But he talked the way he had written his editorials, measured sentences that rang like music, great poetry, and soft, soft. He would not shed a tear; but his heart must have been crying, seeing eternal darkness coming toward him, deep, deep in the night of perpetual sleep. Yes, he would not shed a tear; but he must have been crying, seeing that there was so much to do with so little time left. There was in his voice a kindness for me—unhappy, perhaps, that he could not impart what he had learned from his wanderings on this earth: unhappy, also, because he knew that it would take all the people to unmake the unhappiness which had caught up with us. And now, fifteen years after his arrival in San Francisco, he was dying.

And he died. But at least he received his most cherished dream: American citizenship. He did realize later that he had become an American before he received his papers, when he began to think and write lovingly about *our* America. He gave up many things, and finally his own life, to realize his dream.

But Consorcio is not truly dead. He lives again in my undying love for the American earth. And soon, when I see the last winter coming to the last leaf, I will be warm with the thought that another wanderer shall inherit the wonderful dream which my cousin and I had dreamed and tried to realize in America.

1995

Selected Bibliographies

Reference Works and Histories

Chapters on the period may be consulted in the *Columbia Literary History of the United States* (1988), general editor Emory Elliott; the *Columbia History of the American Novel* (1991), general editor Emory Elliot; the *Columbia History of American Poetry* (1993), edited by Jay Parini; *The History of Southern Literature* (1985), edited by Louis D. Rubin et al.; *A Literary History of the American West* (1987); and A. LaVonne Brown Ruoff's *American Indian Literature* (1990). Relevant volumes in the eight-volume *Cambridge History of American Literature* are volume 5, *Poetry and Criticism, 1900–1950* (2003), edited by Sacvan Bercovitch, and volume 6, *Prose Writing, 1910–1950* (2002), edited by Sacvan Bercovitch and Cyrus R. Patell. Other reference works include the *Cambridge Companion to Native American Literature* (2005), edited by Joy Porter and Kenneth Roemer; *A Companion to the Literature and Culture of the American South* (2004), edited by Richard Grey and Owen Robinson; and *An Interethnic Companion to Asian American Literature* (1996), edited by King-Kok Cheung. Reference works dedicated specifically to the period and some of its important movements include *A Companion to Modernist Literature and Culture*, edited by David Bradshaw and Kevin J. H. Dettmar (2006); the *Cambridge Companion to American Modernism* (2005), ed. Walter Kalaidjian; the *Cambridge Companion to the Harlem Renaissance*, edited by George Hutchinson (2006); and *A Companion to Twentieth-Century American Drama* (2005), edited by David Krasner.

For early histories of the period authored by critics who were active in the rise of modernism, see Malcolm Cowley, *Exile's Return* (1951), *After the Genteel Tradition: American Writers, 1910–1930* (1964), and *A Second Flowering: Works and Days of the Lost Generation* (1973); and Edmund Wilson, *The Shores of Light: A Literary Chronicle of the Twenties and Thirties* (1952). Other important early surveys include Alfred Kazin's *On Native Grounds: An Interpretation of Modern American Prose Literature* (1942), Maxwell Geismer's *Writers in Crisis: The American Novel between Two Wars* (1942), Frederick J. Hoffman's *The Twenties: American Writing in the Postwar Decade*, Harold Clurman's *The Fervent Years: The Story of the Group Theatre and the Thirties* (1957), Walter Rideout's *The Radical Novel in the United States, 1900–1954* (1956), Joseph Wood Krutch's *The American Drama Since 1918* (1957), W. M. Frohock's *The Novel of Violence in America* (1957), Daniel Aaron's *Writers on the Left* (1961), Louis D. Rubin's *Writers of the Modern South* (1963), Howard Taubman's *The Making of the American Theater* (1965), Joseph Blotner's *The Modern American Political Novel* (1966), Warren French's *The Social Novel at the End of an Era* (1966), Dale Kramer's

A1

Chicago Renaissance: The Literary Life in the Midwest, 1910–1930 (1966), Brooks Atkinson's *Broadway: Nineteen Hundred to Nineteen Seventy* (1970); Nathan I. Huggins's *Harlem Renaissance* (1971); Hugh Kenner's *The Pound Era* (1971); and Kenner's *A Homemade World: The American Modernist Writers* (1975).

General books on literary and cultural history appearing since 1980 include Marcus Klein's *Foreigners: The Making of American Literature, 1900–1940* (1981), David Levering Lewis's *When Harlem Was in Vogue* (1981), Daniel J. Singal's *The War Within: From Victorian to Modernist Thought in the South 1919–1945* (1982), Shari Benstock's *Women of the Left Bank: Paris 1900–1940* (1986), *Modernism and the Harlem Renaissance* (1987), edited by Houston Baker Jr., Cecilia Tichi's *Shifting Gears: Technology, Literature, Culture in Modernist America* (1987), Joan Shelley Rubin's *The Making of Middlebrow Culture* (1992), Steven Brel's *Independent Intellectuals in the United States, 1910–1945* (1992), Mary Loeffelholz's *Experimental Lives: Women and Literature, 1900–1945* (1992), Michael North's *The Dialect of Modernism: Race, Language and Twentieth-Century Literature* (1994), George Chauncey's *Gay New York: Gender, Urban Culture, and the Making of the Gay Male World, 1980–1940* (1994), George Hutchinson's *The Harlem Renaissance in Black and White* (1995), Cheryl Wall's *Women of the Harlem Renaissance* (1995), Walter Benn Michaels's *Our America* (1995), Ann Douglas's *Terrible Honesty: Mongrel Manhattan in the 1920s* (1995), Ross Posnock's *Color and Culture: Black Writers and the Making of the Modern Intellectual* (1998), William J. Maxwell's *New Negro, Old Left: African-American Writing and Communism between the Wars* (1999), Christine Stansell's *American Moderns: Bohemian New York and the Creation of a New Century* (1999), David G. Nicholls's *Conjuring the Folk: Forms of Modernity in African America* (2000), Michael Szalay's *New Deal Modernism: American Literature and the Invention of the Welfare State* (2000), Edward Pavlic's *Crossroads Modernism: Descent and Emergence in African-American Literary Culture* (2002), Catherine Turner's *Marketing Modernism between the Two World Wars* (2003), Michael Soto's *The Modernist Nation: Generation, Renaissance, and Twentieth-Century American Literature* (2004), and Tim Armstrong's *Modernism: A Cultural History* (2005).

Literary Theory and Criticism

For an introduction to the ideas of literary criticism during the period, see Rene Wellek's *A History of Modern Criticism: American Criticism, 1900–1950*, Vol. 7 (1987) and Vincent B. Leitch's *American Literary Criticism from the 30s to the 80s* (1988). Gordon Hutner's *American Literature, American Culture* (1998) reprints a number of critical statements from the period. Gerald's Graff's *Professing Literature: An Institutional History* (1987), Lawrence H. Schwartz's *Creating Faulkner's Reputation: The Politics of Modern Literary Criticism* (1988), and Mark Jancovich's *The Cultural Politics of the New Criticism* (1994) analyze aspects of American literary criticism in the period and its aftermath.

Theoretical treatments of modernism (often in international perspectives) include Andreas Huyssen's *After the Great Divide: Modernism, Mass Culture, Postmodernism* (1986), Ashadur Eyssteinsson's *The Concept of Modernism*

(1991), Joseph N. Riddel's *The Turning Word: American Literary Modernism and Continental Theory* (1996), Leonard Diepeveen's *The Difficulties of Modernism* (2003), Michael Trask's *Cruising Modernism: Class and Sexuality in American Literature and Social Thought* (2003), Susan McCabe's *Cinematic Modernism: Modernist Poetry and Film* (2005), and Robert Scholes's *Paradoxy of Modernism* (2006).

Criticism of poetry published since 1980 includes Donald E. Stanford's *Revolution and Convention in Modern Poetry* (1983), M. L. Rosenthal and Sally M. Gall's *The Modern Poetic Sequence: The Genius of Modern Poetry* (1984), William Drake's *The First Wave: Women Poets in America, 1914–1945* (1987), Albert Gelpi's *A Coherent Splendor: The American Poetic Renaissance, 1910–1950* (1987), Lisa M. Steinman's *Made in America: Science, Technology, and American Modernist Poets* (1987), Maureen Honey's edited *Shadowed Dreams: Women's Poetry of the Harlem Renaissance* (1989), Cary Nelson's *Repression and Recovery: Modern American Poetry and the Politics of Cultural Memory, 1910–1945* (1989), Elisa New's *Fictions of Form in American Poetry* (1993), Frank Lentricchia's *Modernist Quartet* (1994), Rachel Blau DuPlessis's *Genders, Races, and Religious Cultures in Modern American Poetries, 1908–1934* (2001), Merrill Cole's *The Other Orpheus: A Poetics of Modern Homosexuality* (2003), and Charles Altieri's *The Art of Twentieth-Century American Poetry: Modernism and After* (2006).

Critical studies of fiction published since 1980 include Hazel V. Carby's *Reconstructing Womanhood: The Emergence of the Afro-American Woman Novelist* (1987), Linda Wagner-Martin's *The Modern American Novel, 1914–1945* (1990), J. Gerald Kennedy's *Imagining Paris* (1993), Barbara Foley's *Radical Representations: Politics and Form in U.S. Proletarian Fiction, 1929–41* (1993), David Minter's *A Cultural History of the American Novel* (1994), Laura Hapke's *Daughters of the Great Depression: Women, Work, and Fiction in the American 1930s* (1995), Paula Rabinowitz's *Black and White and Noir: America's Pulp Modernism* (2002), and Christopher Breu's *Hard-Boiled Masculinities* (2005).

Critical studies of drama published since 1980 include C. W. E. Bigsby's *A Critical Introduction to Twentieth-Century American Drama*, Vol. 1, *1900–1940* (1985), Ethan Mordden's *The American Theatre* (1981), Brenda Murphy's *American Realism and American Drama, 1880–1940* (1987), David Krasner's *A Beautiful Pageant: African American Theatre, Drama, and Performance in the Harlem Renaissance, 1910–1927* (2002), and Julia A. Walker's *Expressionism and Modernism in the American Theatre: Bodies, Voices, Words* (2005).

AMERICAN LITERATURE 1914–1945

Sherwood Anderson

There is no collected edition of Anderson's writing. In addition to works mentioned in the author's headnote, Anderson published *The Modern Writer* (1925); *Sherwood Anderson's Notebook* (1925); *Alice and the Lost Novel* (1929); *Nearer the Grass Roots* (1929); *The American Country Fair* (1930); and *Home Town* (1940). The Norton Critical Edition of *Winesburg, Ohio* (1996), edited by Charles E. Modlin and Ray Lewis White, includes background materials and critical essays, as does the edition edited by John H. Ferres (1996). White edited a variorum edition of *Winesburg, Ohio* (1997). *The Letters of Sherwood Anderson* (1953) were edited by Howard Mumford Jones and Walter Rideout. See also *Sherwood Anderson: Selected Letters* (1984), edited by Charles E. Modlin and *Letters to Bab: Sherwood Anderson to Marietta D. Finley, 1916–1933* (1985). Kim Townsend has written *Sherwood Anderson: A Biography* (1987). The first volume of a two-volume biography by Walter Rideout is *Sherwood Anderson: A Writer in America* (2006). For critical commentary see *Sherwood Anderson: A Collection of Critical Essays* (1974), edited by Walter Rideout; *Critical Essays on Sherwood Anderson* (1981), edited by David D. Anderson; *Homage to Sherwood Anderson* (1970), edited by Paul F. Appel; *New Essays on Winesburg, Ohio* (1990), edited by John W. Crowley; Allen Papinchak's *Sherwood Anderson: A Study of the Short Fiction* (1992); Judy Jo Small's *A Reader's Guide to the Short Stories of Sherwood Anderson* (1994); and Ray Lewis White's *Winesburg, Ohio: An Exploration* (1990).

Black Elk

Raymond J. DeMallie's *The Sixth Grandfather: Black Elk's Teachings Given to John Neihardt* (1984) offers the complete texts of the interviews that went into the construction of *Black Elk Speaks* and provides much useful commentary. Further interviews with Black Elk can be found in Joseph Epes Brown's *The Sacred Pipe: Black Elk's Account of the Seven Rites of the Oglala Sioux* (1953). A valuable study is Julian Rice's *Black Elk's Story: Distinguishing Its Lakota Purpose* (1991). Father Michael Steltenkamp's *Black Elk: Holy Man of the Lakota* (1993) may be read alongside Clyde Holler's *Black Elk's Religion: The Sun Dance and Lakota Catholicism* (1995). William Powers's acute essay "When Black Elk Speaks, Everybody Listens" can be found in Christopher Vecsey, ed., *Religion in Native North American* (1990). The Lakota scholar and activist Vine Deloria Jr. has edited *A Sender of Words: Essays in Memory of John G. Neihardt* (1984), which contributes to a fuller understanding of Neihardt's work on his own in addition to his work with Black Elk. Holler edited an essay collection, *The Black Elk Reader* (2000); and Esther Black Elk DeSersa's *Black Elk Lives: Conversations with the Black Elk Family* appeared in 2000 as well.

Kay Boyle

There is currently no full edition of the works of Kay Boyle. Many of her stories are collected in *Fifty Stories* (1980), and there is also a volume of *Collected Poems* (1991). Margaret Atwood introduced *Three Short Novels* (1982). In addition to works mentioned in the author's headnote, Boyle's many published novels include *Gentlemen, I Address You Privately* (1933); *Death of a Man* (1936); *Avalanche* (1944); *His Human Majesty* (1949); *The Seagull on the Step* (1955); *Generation Without Farewell* (1960); and *The Underground Woman* (1975). Elizabeth S. Bell edited *Words That Must Somehow Be Said: Selected Essays of Kay Boyle, 1927–1984*. There are two biographies, Sandra Whipple Spanier's *Kay Boyle: Artist and Activist* (1986) and Joan Mellen's exhaustive *Kay Boyle: Author of Herself* (1994). Elizabeth S. Bell's

Kay Boyle: A Study of the Short Fiction is a useful introduction, as is Marilyn Elkins's *Critical Essays on Kay Boyle* (1997). Thomas Carl Austenfeld's *American Women Writers and the Nazis* (2001) connects Boyle to Katherine Anne Porter, Jean Stafford, and Lillian Hellman.

Sterling Brown

Brown's *Collected Poems*, selected by Michael S. Harper (1989, 1996), includes *Southern Road, No Hiding Place* as well as additional individual poems. *A Son's Return: Selected Essays of Sterling A. Brown* (1996) is edited by Mark A. Sanders. A special issue of the journal *Callaloo*, 5 (1982), contains a bibliography by Robert G. O'Meally along with reminiscences and critical assessments by several scholars; other essays on Brown may be found in issues of the journal *Black American Literature Forum*. Full-length studies are Joanne V. Gabbin's *Sterling A. Brown: Building the Black Aesthetic Tradition* (1985) and Mark A. Sanders's *Afro-Modernist Aesthetics and the Poetry of Sterling A. Brown* (1999). There are discussions of Brown in Stephen Henderson's *Understanding the New Black Poetry* (1973), Jean Wagner's *Black Poetry* (1973), Henry Louis Gates Jr.'s *Figures in Black: Words, Signs, and the "Racial" Self* (1987), Victor Kramer's *The Harlem Renaissance Reconsidered* (1987), and Cary Nelson's *Repression and Recovery* (1989). The fall 1999 issue of *African American Review* has several articles about Brown.

Carlos Bulosan

Bulosan's published works include *The Voice of Bataan* (1943), *The Laughter of My Father* (1944), and *America Is in the Heart* (1946), which was reissued with an introduction by Carey McWilliams in 1973. Compilations drawing on his books, magazine fiction, and manuscripts have been edited and introduced by E. San Juan Jr.; these include *The Philippines Is in the Heart* (1978), *If You Want to Know What We Are: A Carlos Bulosan Reader* (1983), *On Becoming Filipino: Selected Writings of Carlos Bulosan* (1995), and *The Cry and the Dedication* (1995). Two biographical treatments are P. C. Morantte's *Remembering Carlos Bulosan: His Heart Affair with America* (1984) and Susan Evangelista's *Carlos Bulosan and His Poetry: A Biography and Anthology* (1985). San Juan has also written a critical study, *Carlos Bulosan and the Imagination of the Class Struggle* (1972). Rachel C. Lee's *The Americas of Asian American Literature: Gendered Fictions of Nation and Transnation* (1999) includes a chapter on Bulosan.

Willa Cather

Cather's volume of verse, *April Twilights* (1903; rev. 1923; reissued with an introduction by Bernice Slote, 1990), and her collection of essays, *Not under Forty* (1936), supplement the standard edition of her fiction, *The Novels and Stories of Willa Cather* (1937–41). Her tales and novels were published in two volumes by the Library of America with notes by Sharon O'Brien (1987, 1990). A scholarly edition of *My Ántonia* (1994), with background materials, was edited by Charles Mignon with Kari Rounig. Other sources include *Willa Cather on Writing* (1949); *Writings from Willa Cather's Campus Years* (1950), edited by James Shively; and *The Kingdom of Art: Willa Cather's First Principles and Critical Statements* (1967), edited by Bernice Slote. William M. Curtin collected articles and reviews in the two-volume *The World and the Parish* (1970). Personal memoirs include Edith Lewis's *Willa Cather Living* (1953, 2000) and Elizabeth Sergeant's *Willa Cather: A Memoir* (1953, 1992). Janis P. Stout's *A Calendar of the Letters of Willa Cather* (2002) and the biography *Willa Cather: The Writer and Her World* (2000) are worthwhile. *Willa: The Life of Willa Cather* (1982), by Phyllis C. Robinson, is a full-length biography, as is *Willa Cather: A Literary Life* (1987), by James Woodress. Sharon O'Brien's *Willa Cather: The Emerging Voice* (1987) concentrates on Cather's early years.

Critical studies of Cather are David Stouck's *Willa Cather's Imagination* (1975), Marilyn Arnold's *Willa Cather's Short Fiction* (1984) and *Willa Cather: A Reference Guide* (1986), Susan J. Rosowski's *The Voyage Perilous: Willa Cather's Romanticism* (1986), Evelyn Hively's *Sacred Fire: Willa Cather's Novel Cycle* (1994), Sally P. Harvey's *Redefining the American Dream: The Novels of Willa Cather* (1995), Joseph R. Urgo's *Willa Cather and the Myth of American Migration* (1995), Guy Reynolds's *Willa Cather in Context* (1996), O'Brien's *New Essays on My Ántonia* (1999), Ann Roninies's *Willa Cather's Southern Connection* (2000), and Joan Acocella's *Willa Cather and the Politics of Criticism* (2000). Janis P. Stout edited *Willa Cather and Material Culture: Real-World Writing and Writing the Real World* (2005). Also useful are Marilyn Arnold's *A Reader's Companion to the Fiction of Willa Cather* (1993) and John J. Murphy's *My Ántonia: The Road Home* (1989).

Raymond Chandler

The Library of America published Chandler's writings in two volumes: *Stories and Early Novels* (1995) collected pulp stories from 1933–39 as well as the novels *The Big Sleep* (1939), *Farewell, My Lovely* (1940), and *The High Window* (1942); *Later Novels and Other Writings* (1995) included the novels *The Lady in the Lake* (1943), *The Little Sister* (1949), *The Long Goodbye* (1953), and *Playback* (1958). Frank McShane and Tom Hiney edited *The Raymond Chandler Papers: Selected Letters and Nonfiction 1909–1959* (2000). The most recent biography is Tom Hiney's *Raymond Chandler: A Biography* (1997). A collection of interviews with Chandler, *Raymond Chandler Speaking*, was edited by Dorothy Gardiner and Kathrine Sorley Walker (1977). Gene D. Phillips's *Creatures of Darkness: Raymond Chandler, Detective Fiction, and Film Noir* (2000) is the only recent full-length study; William Marling's *The American Roman Noir: Hammett, Cain, and Chandler* (1995) sets Chandler among his American contemporaries. A useful collection of essays is J. K. Van Dover's *The Critical Responses to Raymond Chandler* (1995); see also the essays in a special issue of *Studies in the Novel* devoted to Chandler (fall 2003).

Hart Crane

Marc Simon edited *Complete Poems of Hart Crane* (1993, 2001), the best current text. Also of use is Brom Weber's *The Complete Poems and Selected Letters and Prose of Hart Crane* (1966). Crane's *Collected Poems*, edited by his friend Waldo Frank, appeared in 1933. *Correspondence between Hart Crane and Waldo Frank* (1998) was edited by Steve H. Cook. Other sources of primary and bibliographical material are *My Land, My Friends: The Selected Letters of Hart Crane* (1997), edited by Langdon Hammer and Brom Weber; *Hart Crane: An Annotated Critical Bibliography* (1970), edited by Joseph Schwartz; and *Hart Crane: A Descriptive Bibliography* (1972), edited by Joseph Schwartz and Robert C. Schweik. Gary Lane compiled *A Concordance to the Poems of Hart Crane* (1972). Biographies of Crane are John Unterecker's *Voyager: A Life of Hart Crane* (1969), Paul Mariani's *The Broken Tower: A Life of Hart Crane* (2000), and Clive Fisher's *Hart Crane: A Life* (2002).

Useful earlier studies are R. W. B. Lewis's *The Poetry of Hart Crane* (1967), Monroe K. Spears's *Hart Crane* (1965), R. W. Butterfield's *The Broken Arc: A Study of Hart Crane* (1969), and Hunce Voelcker's *The Hart Crane Voyages* (1967). See also Richard P. Sugg's *Hart Crane's "The Bridge"* (1976), Samuel Hazo's *Smithereened Apart: A Critique of Hart Crane* (1977), Helge Norman Nilsen's *Hart Crane's Divided Vision: An Analysis of "The Bridge"* (1980), Edward Brunner's *Hart Crane and the Making of "The Bridge"* (1984), Thomas E. Yingling's *Hart Crane and the Homosexual Text* (1990), and Brian M. Reed's *Hart Crane: After His Lights* (2006).

Countee Cullen

Cullen's groundbreaking anthology of 1927, *Caroling Dusk*, was reissued in 1993. His poetry volume, *Color*, originally published in 1925, was also reissued in 1993. *My Soul's High Song*, a collection of his writings edited by Gerald Early, appeared in 1991. There is little recent criticism. Earlier work of interest includes Helen J. Dinger's *A Study of Countee Cullen* (1953), Margaret Perry's *A Bio-Bibliography of Countee P. Cullen* (1969), and Blanche E. Ferguson's *Countee Cullen and the*

Negro Renaissance (1966). A recent article is Jeremy Braddock's "The Poetics of Conjecture," in *Callaloo* (fall 2002).

E. E. Cummings

Complete Poems 1904–62, edited by George J. Firmage, was published in 1991. Firmage also edited *Three Plays and a Ballet* (1967). Cummings's prose fiction includes *The Enormous Room* (1922) and *EIMI* (1933). *E. E. Cummings: A Miscellany Revised* (1965), edited by Firmage, contains previously uncollected short prose pieces. *Six Nonlectures* (1953) consists of the talks that Cummings delivered at Harvard in the same year. A gathering of works is *Another E. E. Cummings* (1999), edited by Richard Kostchanetz. *Selected Letters of E. E. Cummings* (1969) was edited by F. W. Dupee and George Stade. George J. Firmage edited *E. E. Cummings: A Bibliography* (1960). Barry Ahearn edited *The Correspondence of Ezra Pound and E. E. Cummings* (1996).

Several of Cummings's earlier individual works have been reedited by Firmage in the Cummings Typescript Editions. These include *Tulips & Chimneys* (1976); *No Thanks* (1978); *The Enormous Room*, including illustrations by Cummings (1978); *ViVa* (1979); *XAIPE* (1979); and *Etcetera*, the unpublished poems (1983).

A biography is *Dreams in the Mirror* (1979, 1994), by Richard S. Kennedy. Early studies include Norman Friedman's *E. E. Cummings: The Growth of a Writer* (1964), Robert E. Wegner's *The Poetry and Prose of E. E. Cummings* (1965), Bethany K. Dumas's *E. E. Cummings: A Remembrance of Miracles* (1974), and Rushworth Kidder's *E. E. Cummings, An Introduction to the Poetry* (1979). See also Cary Lane's *I Am: A Study of E. E. Cummings' Poems* (1976) and Richard S. Kennedy's *E. E. Cummings Revisited* (1994). Norman Friedman edited *E. E. Cummings: A Collection of Critical Essays* (1972).

Hilda Doolittle (H. D.)

The poetry through 1944 has been collected and edited by Louis L. Martz in *Collected Poems 1912–1944* (1983). *Collected Poems of H. D.* was published in 1925. Subsequent volumes of poetry include *Red Rose for Bronze* (1931); the trilogy of war poems *The Walls Do Not Fall* (1944), *Tribute to the Angels* (1945), and *The Flowering of the Rod* (1946); the dramatic monologue *Helen in Egypt* (1961); the major collection of her late poems, *Hermetic Definition* (1972); and the long poem *Vale Ave* (1992). H. D.'s other book-length verse dramas are *Hippolytus Temporizes* (1927) and the translation of Euripides' *Ion* (1937). *Palimpsest* (1926), *Hedylus* (1928), *Bid Me to Live* (1961), *HERmione* (1981), and *Asphodel* (1992), edited by Robert Spoo, compose her major prose fiction. *By Avon River* (1949) celebrates Shakespeare in prose and verse. *Tribute to Freud* (1956) is her account of her psychoanalysis by Freud. Also important are two autobiographical works: *End to Torment* (1979) and *The Gift* (1982, complete edition 1998). Michael Boughn compiled *H. D.: A Bibliography, 1905–1990* (1993). *Richard Aldington and H. D.: The Early Years in Letters* (1992), edited by Caroline Zilboorg, collects correspondence.

Herself Defined: The Poet H. D. and Her World (1984), by Barbara Guest, is a biography, while *H. D.: The Career of That Struggle* (1986), by Rachel Blau DuPlessie, *Psyche Reborn: The Emergence of H. D.* (1981), by Susan S. Friedman, and *H. D.: The Life and Work of an American Poet* (1982), by Janice S. Robinson, combine biography and literary analysis. Among critical books are Gary Barnett's *H. D.: Between Image and Epic, The Mysteries of Her Poetics* (1990), Friedman's *Penelope's Web: Gender, Modernity, and H. D.'s Fiction* (1990), Eileen Gregory's *H. D. and Hellenism* (1997), Diana Collecott's *H. D and Sapphic Modernism* (1999), Georgia Taylor's *H. D. and the Public Sphere of Modernist Women Writers 1913–1946* (2001), and Adalaide Morris's *How to Live/What to Do: H. D.'s Cultural Poetics* (2003).

John Dos Passos

The Library of America reissued *U.S.A.* in a single volume (1997), followed by *Travel Books and Other Writings, 1916–1941* (2003) and *Novels, 1920–1925* (2003). *John Dos Passos, A Reference Guide*, by John Rohrkemper, appeared in 1980. Two biographies are *Dos Passos: A Life*, by Virginia Spencer Carr (1984) and *John Dos Passos: A Twentieth Century Odyssey*, by Townsend Ludlington (1980). *Dos Passos: A Collection of Critical Essays* was edited by Andrew Hook in 1974 and *Dos Passos: The Critical Heritage*, edited by Barry Maine, appeared in 1988 and was reissued in 1997. Useful books include Linda W. Wagner's *Dos Passos: The Artist as American* (1979), Robert C. Rosen's *John Dos Passos: Politics and the Writer* (1981), Donald Pizer's *Dos Passos' U.S.A.: A Critical Study* (1990), Lisa Nanney's *John Dos Passos* (1998), and Janet Casey's *Dos Passos and the Ideology of the Feminine* (1998).

T. S. Eliot

Eliot's poetic works have been collected in *Collected Poems, 1909–1962* (1963) and *The Complete Poems and Plays of T. S. Eliot* (1969). *Inventions of the March Hare: Poems 1909–1917* (1997), edited by Christopher Ricks, contains early, previously unpublished poetry. The indispensable manuscript to *The Waste Land* is in *The Waste Land: A Facsimile and Transcript of the Original Drafts Including the Annotations of Ezra Pound* (1971), edited by Valerie Eliot. Michael North edited a Norton Critical Edition of *The Waste Land* (2001). Important critical writings include *The Use of Poetry and the Use of Criticism* (1933), *Poetry and Drama* (1951), *The Three Voices of Poetry* (1953), *On Poetry and Poets* (1957), and *To Criticize the Critic and Other Writings* (1965). Three volumes of social commentary are *After Strange Gods* (1934), *The Idea of a Christian Society* (1939), and *Notes toward the Definition of Culture* (1948). Valerie Eliot edited *The Letters of T. S. Eliot, Vol. 1: 1898–1922* (1988). J. L. Dawson edited *Concordance to the Complete Poems and Plays of T. S. Eliot* (1995). Good biographies are Peter Ackroyd's *T. S. Eliot: A Life* (1984) and Lyndall Gordon's *T. S. Eliot: An Imperfect Life* (1998, 2000), an updating of her earlier biographies.

Influential earlier studies of Eliot include F. O. Matthiessen's *The Achievement of T. S. Eliot* (rev. 1947), Helen Gardner's *The Art of T. S. Eliot* (1950), Hugh Kenner's *The Invisible Poet* (1959), Northrop Frye's *T. S. Eliot* (1963), and Stephen Spender's *T. S. Eliot* (1976).

Among numerous critical studies are Helen Gardner's *The Composition of Four Quartets* (1978), Derek Traversi's *T. S. Eliot: The Longer Poems* (1976), Louis Menand's *Discovering Modernism: T. S. Eliot and His Context* (1987), Jewel Spears Brooker and Joseph Bentley's *Reading "The Waste Land": Modernism and the Limits of Interpretation* (1990), Brooker's *Mastery and Escape: T. S. Eliot and the Dialectic of Modernism* (1994), A. David Moody's *Thomas Stearns Eliot, Poet* (1994), Anthony Julius's *T. S. Eliot, Anti-Semitism, and Literary Form* (1996), Ronald Schuchard's *Eliot's Dark Angel: Intersections of Life and Art* (2001), and David Chintz's *T. S. Eliot and the Cultural Divide* (2003). Moody also edited the useful *Cambridge Companion to T. S. Eliot* (1994). For collections of critical essays about Eliot, see *T. S. Eliot: A Collection of Criticism* (1974), edited by Linda W. Wagner (1974); *T. S. Eliot: The Modernist in History* (1991), edited by Ronald Bush (1991); *T. S. Eliot, A Voice Descanting: Centenary Essays* (1990), edited by Shyamal Bagchee, and *Gender, Desire, and Sexuality in T. S. Eliot* (2004), edited by Cassandra Laity and Nancy K. Gish. Gareth Reeves's *T. S. Eliot's "The Waste Land"* (1994) is a comprehensive introduction to the poem.

Donald C. Gallup compiled the standard bibliography, *T. S. Eliot: A Bibliography* (rev. 1969).

William Faulkner

The Library of America issued Faulkner's novels in four volumes: *1930–1935* (1985); *1936–1940* (1990); *1942–1954* (1994); and *1957–1962* (1999). In addition to volumes mentioned in the author's headnote are *Early Prose and Poetry* (1962), edited by Carvel Collins (1962); *Dr. Martino and Other Stories* (1934); *Pylon* (1935); *The Unvanquished* (1938); *Intruder in the Dust* (1948); *Knight's Gambit* (1949); *Collected Stories of William Faulkner* (1950);

Requiem for a Nun (1951); *Notes on a Horsethief* (1951); *Big Woods* (1955); and *Essays, Speeches, and Public Letters* (rev. 2004), edited by James B. Meriwether. Transcripts of discussions and interviews with Faulkner include *Faulkner at Nagano* (1956), edited by Robert A. Jelliffe; *Faulkner in the University* (1959), edited by Frederick L. Gwynn and Joseph L. Blotner; *Faulkner at West Point* (1964), edited by Joseph L. Fant and Robert Ashley (1964); and *The Lion in the Garden* (1968), edited by Meriwether and Michael Millgate. Letters are collected in *The Faulkner-Cowley File* (1961), edited by Malcolm Cowley (1961), and *Selected Letters of William Faulkner* (1977), edited by Joseph L. Blotner. Noel Polk has produced editions of several Faulkner novels based on study of the manuscripts. David Minter has published a Norton Critical Edition of *The Sound and the Fury* (1994).

Faulkner: A Biography, 2 vols. (1974), by Blotner has been condensed and updated in *Faulkner* (1984). Two shorter biographies based on Blotner's work are *William Faulkner: His Life and Work* (1980), by David Minter, and *Faulkner: The Transfiguration of Biography* (1979), by Judith Wittenberg.

Comprehensive guides are *Faulkner's World: A Directory of His People and Synopsis of Actions in His Published Works* (1988), by Thomas E. Connolly; *A William Faulkner Encyclopedia* (1999), edited by Robert W. Hamblin and Charles E. Peek; and *William Faulkner A to Z* (2001), edited by A. Nichols Fargnoli and Michael Golay. David Dowling's *William Faulkner* (1989) is a general introduction; another useful introduction is Edmond L. Volpe's *A Reader's Guide to William Faulkner: The Short Stories* (2004). Influential early studies include Cleanth Brooks's *William Faulkner: The Yoknapatawpha Country* (1963) and Hyatt H. Waggoner's *William Faulkner: From Jefferson to the World* (1959). Later studies include John T. Irwin's *Doubling and Incest, Repetition and Revenge: A Speculative Reading of Faulkner* (1975), Thadious M. Davis's *Faulkner's "Negro": Art and the Southern Context* (1983), Eric J. Sundquist's *Faulkner: The House Divided* (1983), Robert Dale Parker's *Faulkner and the Novelistic Imagination* (1985), Warwick Wadlington's *Reading Faulknerian Tragedy* (1987) and *As I Lay Dying: Stories out of Stories* (1992), Stephen M. Ross's *Fiction Inexhaustible Voice: Speech and Writing in Faulkner* (1989), Minrose C. Gwin's *The Feminine and Faulkner: Reading (beyond) Sexual Difference* (1990), André Bleikasten's *The Ink of Melancholy: Faulkner's Novels from "The Sound and the Fury" to "Light in August"* (1990), Richard Moreland's *Faulkner and Modernism: Rereading and Rewriting* (1990), Joel Williamson's *William Faulkner and Southern History* (1993),

Diane Roberts's *Faulkner and Southern Womanhood* (1994), and David Minter's *Faulkner's Questioning Narratives: Fiction of His Major Phase, 1929–42* (2001).

Edited collections of critical essays include Doreen Fowler and Ann J. Abadie's *Faulkner and Race* (1987), Louis J. Budd and Edwin Cady's *On Faulkner* (1989), and Linda Wagner-Martin's *Faulkner: Six Decades of Criticism* (2002).

F. Scott Fitzgerald
Fitzgerald's novels are *This Side of Paradise* (1920), *The Beautiful and Damned* (1922), *The Great Gatsby* (1925), *Tender Is the Night* (1934; rev. 1939; rpt. 1953), and the unfinished *The Last Tycoon* (1941). His collections of stories are *Flappers and Philosophers* (1921), *Tales of the Jazz Age* (1922), *All the Sad Young Men* (1926), and *Taps at Reveille* (1935). Two recent editions of his fiction are the Library of America's *Novels and Stories 1920–1922* (2000) and Matthew J. Bruccoli and Judith Baughman's *Before Gatsby: The First Twenty-Six Stories* (2001). The nine-volume Cambridge Edition of Fitzgerald's works (1991–2006) includes his novels, story collections, and *My Lost City: Personal Essays, 1920–1940* (2005). A satirical play, *The Vegetable, or From Presidents to Postman*, was published in 1923. Among collections of Fitzgerald's writings are *F. Scott Fitzgerald in His Own Time: A Miscellany* (1971), edited by Jackson R. Bryer and Bruccoli, and *Afternoon of an Author* (1957), edited by Arthur Mizener. *The Crack-Up* (1945), edited by Edmund Wilson, collects essays, notebook entries, and letters from the 1930s; youthful work is collected in *F. Scott Fitzgerald: The Princeton Years; Selected Writings, 1914–1920* (1966), edited by Chip Defaa.

The fullest collection of letters is *Correspondence of F. Scott Fitzgerald* (1980), edited by Bruccoli and Margaret M. Duggan. Other volumes of letters are *Dear Scott/Dear Max: The Fitzgerald-Perkins Correspondence* (1971), edited by John Kuehl and Jackson R. Bryer, *As Ever, Scott Fitz* (1972), edited by Bruccoli and Jennifer McCabe Atkinson (letters between Fitzgerald and his literary agent, Harold Ober), and *Dear Scott, Dearest Zelda: The Love Letters of F. Scott and Zelda Fitzgerald* (2002), edited by Jackson R. Bryer and Cathy W. Barks. Fitzgerald's biographies include Bruccoli's *Some Sort of Epic Grandeur: The Life of F. Scott Fitzgerald* (1981), Scott Donaldson's *Fool for Love: F. Scott Fitzgerald, A Biographical Portrait* (1983), James Mellow's *Invented Lives* (1984), Jeffrey Myers's *Scott Fitzgerald* (2000), and Andrew Turnbull's *Scott Fitzgerald* (2001).

Among guides are Mary Jo Tate's *F. Scott Fitzgerald A to Z* (1998), Robert Gale's *An F. Scott Fitzgerald Encyclopedia* (1998), Linda Pelzer's *Student Companion to F. Scott Fitzger-*

ald (2001), and *A Historical Guide to F. Scott Fitzgerald* (2004), edited by Kirk Curnutt. Critical studies include Milton R. Stern's *The Golden Moment: The Novels of F. Scott Fitzgerald* (1970), Brian Way's *F. Scott Fitzgerald and the Art of Social Fiction* (1980), Andrew Hook's *F. Scott Fitzgerald* (1992), and John Kuehl's *F. Scott Fitzgerald, a Study of the Short Fiction* (1991). Among collections of critical essays are *The Short Stories of F. Scott Fitzgerald: New Approaches in Criticism* (1983), edited by Jackson R. Bryer; *New Essays on "The Great Gatsby,"* edited by Bruccoli; *The Cambridge Companion to F. Scott Fitzgerald*, edited by Ruth Prigozy (2001); and *F. Scott Fitzgerald in the Twenty-First Century* (2003), edited by Jackson R. Bryer, Prigozy, and Milton B. Stern.

Robert Frost
The Poetry of Robert Frost (1969) incorporated *Complete Poems* (1949) and Frost's last volume, *In the Clearing* (1962). Eleven early essays on farming, edited by Edward C. Lathem and Lawrance Thompson, appear in *Robert Frost: Farm Poultryman* (1963). The Library of America issued Frost's *Collected Poems, Prose, and Plays* (1995). Important collections of letters appear in *Selected Letters of Robert Frost* (1964), edited by Thompson; *The Letters of Robert Frost to Louis Untermeyer* (1963); and Margaret Anderson, *Robert Frost and John Bartlett: The Record of a Friendship* (1963). His critical essays have been collected in *Selected Prose* (1966), edited by Hyde Cox and Lathem (1966). Conversations and interviews with Frost include Lathem's *Interviews with Robert Frost* (1966), Reginald L. Cook's *The Dimensions of Robert Frost* (1964), Daniel Smythe's *Robert Frost Speaks* (1954), and Louis Mertin's *Robert Frost: Life and Talks—Walking* (1965).

Lawrance Thompson completed two volumes of the authorized biography: *Robert Frost: The Early Years, 1874–1915* (1966) and *Robert Frost: The Years of Triumph, 1915–1938* (1970). The third volume, *Robert Frost, the Later Years*, was completed by Richard Winnick (1976), and Edward C. Lathem produced a shorter version of the biography in *Robert Frost: A Biography* (1981). Other biographies are Jeffrey Meyers's *Robert Frost* (1996) and Jay Parini's *Robert Frost: A Life* (1999). William H. Pritchard in *Frost: A Literary Life Reconsidered* (1984) is interested in the poet's art, not his personal life. James L. Potter's *Robert Frost Handbook* (1980) is a useful guide; Latham produced a concordance to Frost's poetry (1994).

A brief critical introduction is Mordecai Marcus's *The Poems of Robert Frost* (1991). Specialized critical studies are Richard Poirier's *Robert Frost, The Work of Knowing* (1977, reissued with new material in 1990), John C. Kemp's *Robert Frost and New England: The Poet as Regionalist* (1979), George Monteiro's

Robert Frost and the New England Renaissance (1988), Mario D'Avanzo's *A Cloud of Other Poets: Robert Frost and the Romantics* (1990), Judith Oster's *Toward Robert Frost* (1991), George Bagby's *Frost and the Book of Nature* (1993), and Mark Richardson's *Robert Frost: The Poet and His Poetics* (1997). Collections of critical essays include *On Frost* (1991), edited by Edwin H. Cady and Louis J. Budd, and Robert Faggen's *Cambridge Companion to Robert Frost* (2001).

Susan Glaspell

Plays by Susan Glaspell—including *Trifles, The Outside, The Verge,* and *Inheritors*—appeared in 1987. Another collection is *"Lifted Masks" and Other Works* (1993). *Major Novels of Susan Glaspell,* edited by Martha C. Carpenter, was published in 1995. Two biographies are Arthur E. Waterman's *Susan Glaspell* (1966) and Barbara O. Rajkowska's *Susan Glaspell: A Critical Biography* (2000). Critical studies include Marcia Noe's *Susan Glaspell: Voice from the Heartland* (1983), Veronica A. Makowsky's *Susan Glaspell's Century of American Women: A Critical Interpretation of Her Work* (1993), and J. Ellen Gainor's *Susan Glaspell in Context: American Theater, Culture, and Politics, 1915–48* (2001). A collection of critical essays is *Susan Glaspell: Essays on Her Theater and Fiction* (1995), edited by Linda Ben-Zvi.

Ernest Hemingway

There is no collected edition of Hemingway's writings. In addition to works mentioned in the author's headnote, his fiction includes *Today Is Friday* (1926) and *God Rest You Merry Gentlemen* (1933). His tribute to Spain, *The Spanish Earth,* and his play *The Fifth Column* appeared in 1938, the latter in a collection *The Fifth Column and the First Forty-nine Stories.* His journalism has been collected in *The Wild Years* (1962), edited by Gene Z. Hanrahan, and *By-Line: Ernest Hemingway, Selected Articles and Dispatches of Four Decades* (1967), edited by William White. His *Complete Poems* (1992) has been edited by Nicholas Gerogiannis. Audre Hanneman's *Ernest Hemingway: A Comprehensive Bibliography* (1967) is thorough. Scribners published *The Complete Short Stories of Ernest Hemingway* (1987).

The authorized biography is Carlos Baker's *Ernest Hemingway: A Life Story* (1969). Jeffrey Meyers's *Hemingway: A Biography* (1985) and Kenneth S. Lynn's *Hemingway* (1987) are important. Michael Reynolds's detailed volumes include *The Young Hemingway* (1986), *Hemingway: The Paris Years* (1989), *Hemingway: The 1930s* (1997), and *Hemingway: The Final Years* (1999). *The Hemingway Women* (1983), by Bernice Kert, tells about Hemingway's mother, wives, and lovers; *Fame Became of Him: Hemingway as Public Writer* (1984), by John Raeburn, compares the life with the public image.

A Reader's Guide to Ernest Hemingway (1972), by Arthur Waldhorn, and *A Reader's Guide to the Short Stories of Ernest Hemingway* (1989), by Paul Smith, are useful handbooks; Peter B. Messent's *Ernest Hemingway* (1992) is a good overview. For collections of critical essays on Hemingway, see *Ernest Hemingway: Seven Decades of Criticism* (2001), edited by Linda Wagner-Martin; *New Critical Approaches to the Short Stories of Ernest Hemingway* (1991), edited by Jackson J. Benson; *The Cambridge Companion to Hemingway* (1996), edited by Scott Donaldson; and *A Historical Guide to Ernest Hemingway* (2001), edited by Wagner-Martin. Specialized studies include Bernard Oldsey's *Hemingway's Hidden Craft: The Writing of "A Farewell to Arms"* (1979), Wirt Williams's *The Tragic Art of Ernest Hemingway* (1982), and Mark Spilka's *Hemingway's Quarrel with Androgyny* (1990).

Langston Hughes

A fourteen-volume standard edition of Hughes's complete works appeared in 2001 and 2002. Arnold Rampersad and David Roessel edited *The Collected Poems of Langston Hughes* (1994), including *The Weary Blues* (1926), *Fine Clothes to the Jew* (1927), *The Dream Keeper and Other Poems* (1932), *Scottsboro Limited: Four Poems and a Play in Verse* (1932), *Montage of a Dream Deferred* (1951), and *The Panther and the Lash: Poems of our Times* (1967). His short stories were edited by Akiba Sullivan Harper (1996). Faith Berry edited *Good Morning Revolution: Uncollected Social Protest Writings by Langston Hughes* (1973). *Mule Bone* (1991), which he co-authored with Zora Neale Hurston, has been edited with contextual materials by George Houston Pope and Henry Louis Gates Jr. Hughes's autobiographical volumes include *The Big Sea* (1940) and *I Wonder as I Wander* (1956); both were reissued in 1993. Charles H. Nichols edited *Arna Bontemps–Langston Hughes, Letters 1925–1967* (1980).

Early biographies of Hughes include Charlemae Rollins's *Black Troubador: Langston Hughes* (1970) and James S. Haskins's *Always Movin' On: The Life of Langston Hughes* (1976). Faith Berry's *Langston Hughes: Before and Beyond Harlem* (1983, 1995) contains much about Hughes's life to 1940. Arnold Rampersad's two-volume *Life of Langston Hughes*—Vol. I, 1902–1941: *I, Too, Sing America* (1986), and Vol. II, 1941–1967: *I Dream a World* (1988)—is definitive.

Thomas A. Mikolyzk compiled *Langston Hughes: A Bio-Bibliography* (1990). Contemporary reviews were collected by Letitia Dace (1997). Full-length critical studies are Onwuchekwa Jemie's *Langston Hughes: An Introduction to the Poetry* (1976), Richard K. Barksdale's *Langston Hughes: The Poet and His Critics* (1977), Steven C. Tracy's *Langston*

Hughes and the Blues (1988), and R. Baxter Miller's *The Art and Imagination of Langston Hughes* (1989). Essay collections include *Langston Hughes, Black Genius: A Critical Evaluation* (1972), edited by Therman B. O'Daniel; *Langston Hughes: Critical Perspectives Past and Present* (1993), edited by Henry Louis Gates Jr. and K. A. Appiah; *Langston Hughes: The Man, His Art, and His Continuing Influence* (1995), edited by C. James Trotman; and *A Historical Guide to Langston Hughes* (2003), edited by Steven C. Tracy. Peter Mandelik and Stanley Schatt's *A Concordance to the Poetry of Langston Hughes* (1975) is useful.

Zora Neale Hurston

Robert Hemenway's *Zora Neale Hurston, A Literary Biography* (1977) initiated the Hurston revival; her work is mostly available in paperback editions. A recent biography is Valerie Boyd's *Wrapped in Rainbows: The Life of Zora Neale Hurston* (2003). The Library of America published Hurston's writing in two volumes: *Novels and Stories* (1995) and *Folklore, Memoirs, and Other Writings* (1995). Her letters were edited by Carla Kaplan (2002). Book-length studies include Karla C. F. Holloway's *The Character of the Word: The Texts of Zora Neale Hurston* (1987), John Lowe's *Jump at the Sun: Zora Neale Hurston's Cosmic Comedy* (1994), Deborah G. Plant's *Every Tub Must Sit on Its Own Bottom: The Philosophy and Politics of Zora Neale Hurston* (1995), and Margaret Genevieve West's *Zora Neale Hurston and American Literary Culture* (2005). Hurston is linked to other writers in Cheryl A. Wall's *Women of the Harlem Renaissance* (1995), Carla Kaplan's *The Erotics of Talk: Women's Writing and Feminist Paradigms* (1996), and Trudier Harris's *The Power of the Porch: The Storyteller's Craft in Zora Neale Hurston, Gloria Naylor, and Randall Kenan* (1996). Collections of essays are *New Essays on "Their Eyes Were Watching God"* (1990), edited by Michael Awkward; *Zora Neale Hurston: Critical Perspectives Past and Present* (1993), edited by Henry Louis Gates Jr. and K. A. Appiah; and *Critical Essays on Zora Neale Hurston* (1998), edited by Gloria L. Cronin.

Nella Larsen

Larsen's complete fiction, including *Quicksand, Passing,* and three stories, appeared in 1992, edited by Charles R. Larson; this volume was reissued in 2001. The two novels were also made available in 1986, in an edition introduced by Deborah E. McDowell. The Norton Critical Edition of *Passing* (2007), edited by Carla Kaplan, includes critical and historical backgrounds. Biographies are Thadious M. Davis's *Nella Larsen, Novelist of the Harlem Renaissance: A Woman's Life Unveiled* (1994) and George Hutchinson's *In Search of Nella Larsen: A Biography of the Color Line* (2006).

Larsen is also considered in Cheryl A. Wall's *Women of the Harlem Renaissance* (1995). Three critical studies, each connecting Larsen with other African American writers, are Charles R. Larson's *Invisible Darkness: Jean Toomer and Nella Larsen* (1993); Jacquelyn Y. McLendon's *The Politics of Color in the Fiction of Jessie Fauset and Nella Larsen* (1995); and Erika M. Miller's *The Other Reconstruction: Where Violence and Womanhood Meet in the Writings of Wells-Barnett, Grimké, and Larsen* (2000).

Amy Lowell

Lowell's complete poems were published in 1955. Ferris Greenslet, who was her editor at Houghton Mifflin, has written an excellent family chronicle from the first settler to Amy Lowell, *The Lowells and Their Seven Worlds* (1945). Additional biographical material may be found in S. Foster Damon's *Amy Lowell: A Chronicle, with Extracts from Her Correspondence* (1935), and *Florence Ayscough and Amy Lowell: Correspondence of a Friendship* (1945), edited by Harley Farnsworth MacNair. Critical estimates of Lowell include Jean Gould's *Amy: The World of Amy Lowell and the Imagist Movement* (1975), Glenn Richard Ruihley's *The Thorn of a Rose: Amy Lowell Reconsidered* (1975), and Richard Benvenuto's *Amy Lowell* (1985). Mary E. Galvin's *Queer Poetics: Five Modernist Women Writers* (1999) includes Lowell. Adrienne Munich and Melissa Bradshaw edited *Amy Lowell, American Modern* (2004).

Mina Loy

There is no scholarly edition of Loy's writing. Roger L. Conover's edition of *The Lost Lunar Baedeker* (1996) is the fullest collection of Loy's work currently in print; it includes some prose in addition to poetry. Carolyn Burke's *Becoming Mina Loy* (1996) remains the only biography. Virginia M. Kouidis's *Mina Loy: American Modernist Poet* (1980) for many years was the only full-length study. A more recent collection of essays, Maeera Schreiber and Keith Tuma's *Mina Loy: Woman and Poet* (1998), reflects the upsurge in Loy's reputation following Burke's biography. Cristanne Miller's *Cultures of Modernism: Marianne Moore, Mina Loy, and Else Lasker-Schüler* (2005) examines Loy along with other women modernists associated with New York and Berlin.

Edgar Lee Masters

An edition of *Spoon River Anthology* annotated by John E. Hallwas appeared in 1992; uncollected Spoon River poems were edited by Herbert K. Russell in 1991; and Masters's autobiography, *Across Spoon River*, was published with an introduction by Ronald Primeau in 1991. His son, Hardin Wallace Masters, published *Edgar Lee Masters: A Biographical Sketchbook about a Famous American Author*

(1978); the definitive biography is by Russell (2001). A brief general estimate and survey is *Edgar Lee Masters: The Spoon River Poet and His Critics* (1974), by John T. Flanagan. *Beyond Spoon River: The Legacy of Edgar Lee Masters* (1981), by Ronald Primeau, considers Masters's lesser known work.

Claude McKay

Volumes of McKay's poetry include *Songs of Jamaica* (1912), *Constab Ballads* (1912), *Spring in New Hampshire and Other Poems* (1920)—published in England—and *Harlem Shadows* (1922). William J. Maxwell edited the *Complete Poems* (2004), including many poems previously uncollected. Books of prose published in his lifetime include the novels *Home to Harlem* (1928), *Banjo* (1929), and *Banana Bottom* (1933); a short story collection, *Gingertown* (1932, 1991); an autobiography, *A Long Way from Home* (1937), and an essay collection, *Harlem: Negro Metropolis* (1940). Collections brought out after McKay's death include *Selected Poems* (1953), *The Dialect Poetry of Claude McKay* (1972), *The Passion of Claude McKay: Selected Poetry and Prose* (1973); two books of short stories, *Trial By Lynching* (1977) and *My Green Hills of Jamaica* (1979); and an essay collection, *The Negro in America* (1979).

Three good biographies are James R. Giles's *Claude McKay* (1976), Wayne F. Cooper's *Claude McKay: Rebel Sojourner in the Harlem Renaissance* (1987, 1996), and Tyrone Tillery's *Claude McKay: A Black Poet's Struggle for Identity* (1992). A collection of interpretive essays is *Claude McKay: Centennial Studies* (1992), edited by A. L. McLeod. General works with material on McKay include Harold Cruse's still valuable *The Crisis of the Negro Intellectual* (1967), Kenneth Ramchand's *The West Indian Novel and Its Background* (1970; rev. ed. 2004), Nathan I. Huggins's *Harlem Renaissance* (1971), Addison Gayle's *The Way of the New World: The Black Novel in America* (1975), David Levering Lewis's *When Harlem Was in Vogue* (1981), Bernard W. Bell's *The Afro-American Novel and Its Tradition* (1987), and George Hutchinson's *The Harlem Renaissance in Black and White* (1995). Contrasting treatments of McKay's poetry are in Winston James's *A Fierce Hatred of Injustice: Claude McKay's Jamaican Poetry of Rebellion* (2001) and Josh Gosciak's *The Shadowed Country: Claude McKay and the Romance of the Victorians* (2006).

Edna St. Vincent Millay

Millay's *Collected Sonnets* (1941) and *Collected Lyrics* (1943) were followed by *Collected Poems: Edna St. Vincent Millay* (1956), edited by Norma Millay (1956). The Library of America issued *Selected Poems* (2003). Her prose sketches, *Distressing Dialogue,* published under the pseudonym Nancy Boyd, appeared in 1924.

Her three verse plays (*Aria da Capa,* 1920; *The Lamp and the Bell,* 1921; and *Two Slatterns and a King,* 1921) were collected in *Three Plays* (1926). Allan Ross Macdougall edited *Letters of Edna St. Vincent Millay* in 1952. The biographies are Daniel Epstein's *What Lips My Lips Have Kissed* (2001) and Nancy Milford's *Savage Beauty: The Life of Edna St. Vincent* Millay (2001). Essay collections are *Critical Essays on Edna St. Vincent Millay* (1993), edited by William B. Thesing, and *Millay at One Hundred* (1995), edited by Diane P. Freedman.

Marianne Moore

Each collection of Moore's verse excluded some earlier poems while subjecting others to extensive revisions and changes in format. Her separate volumes include *Poems* (1921); *Observations* (1924); *The Pangolin and Other Verse* (1936); *What Are Years?* (1941); *Nevertheless* (1944); *Like a Bulwark* (1956); *O to Be a Dragon* (1959); and *Tell Me, Tell Me* (1966). Collections include *Selected Poems* (1935); *Collected Poems* (1951); and *The Complete Poems of Marianne Moore* (1967, repr. 1981, 1987), which included selections from her translation of *The Fables of La Fontaine* (1954). Grace Shulman's *The Poems of Marianne Moore* (2003) is now the fullest edition. Patricia C. Willis has brought together Moore's published prose in *The Complete Prose of Marianne Moore* (1986). Moore's correspondence with Robert Lowell is published in *Becoming a Poet* (1991), by David Kalstone; her relation to Wallace Stevens is considered by Robin G. Schulze in *The Web of Friendship* (1995). The only biography is *Marianne Moore: A Literary Life* (1990), by Charles Molesworth. Bonnie Costello edited *The Selected Letters of Marianne Moore* (1997). Book-length studies include Bernard F. Engel's *Marianne Moore* (1963, rev. 1989), Costello's *Marianne Moore: Imaginary Possessions* (1982), John M. Slatin's *The Savage's Romance: The Poetry of Marianne Moore* (1986), Grace Shulman's *Marianne Moore: The Poetry of Engagement* (1987), Margaret Holley's *The Poetry of Marianne Moore: A Study in Voice and Value* (1987), Cristanne Miller's *Questions of Authority* (1995), Linda Leanell's *Marianne Moore and the Visual Arts* (1995), and Elisabeth W. Joyce's *Cultural Critique and Abstraction: Marianne Moore and the Avant-Garde* (1998). Essay collections include *Marianne Moore, Woman and Poet* (1990), edited by Patricia Willis, and *Marianne Moore: The Art of a Modernist* (1990), edited by Joseph Parigi. Eugene P. Sheehy and Kenneth A. Lohf compiled *The Achievement of Marianne Moore: A Bibliography, 1907–1957* in 1958, and Craig S. Abbott compiled *Marianne Moore: A Descriptive Bibliography* in 1977. Gary Lane's *A Concordance to the Poems of Marianne Moore* appeared in 1972.

Eugene O'Neill

The Library of America collected O'Neill's plays in three volumes, *Complete Plays 1913–1920*, *Complete Plays, 1920–1931*, and *Complete Plays 1932–1943* (1988). The standard biography of O'Neill is still that of Arthur and Barbara Gelb, *O'Neill* (1962, rev. 2000). Other biographical treatments are Frederic I. Carpenter's *Eugene O'Neill* (1964, rev. 1979), L. Schaeffer's *O'Neill, Son and Artist* (1973, 1990), and Stephen A. Bloch's *Eugene O'Neill: Beyond Mourning and Tragedy* (1999). *The Theatre We Worked For: The Letters of Eugene O'Neill to Kenneth Macgowan* (1982), edited by Jackson R. Bryer, documents O'Neill's attitudes to the theater of his day. Bryer and Travis Bogard edited *Selected Letters of Eugene O'Neill* (1994). *Conversations with Eugene O'Neill* (1990) is edited by Mark W. Estrin. Literary analysis of O'Neill's plays can be found in Bogard's *Contour in Time: The Plays of Eugene O'Neill* (1972, rev. 1987), Michael Manheim's *Eugene O'Neill's New Language of Kinship* (1982), Judith E. Barlow's *Final Acts: The Creation of Three Late O'Neill Plays* (1985), Kurt Eisen's *The Inner Strength of Opposites* (1994; on O'Neill's techniques), Joel Pfister's *Staging Depth: Eugene O'Neill and the Politics of Psychological Discourse* (1995), Donald Gallup's *Eugene O'Neill and His Eleven-Play Cycle* (1998), and Doris Alexander's *Eugene O'Neill's Last Plays: Separating Art from Autobiography* (2005).

Essay collections include *Eugene O'Neill: A Collection of Criticism* (1976), edited by E. Griffin; *Eugene O'Neill's Century* (1991), edited by Richard F. Moorton Jr.; *The Critical Response to Eugene O'Neill* (1993), edited by John H. Houchin; and *The Cambridge Companion to Eugene O'Neill* (1998), edited by Michael Manheim.

Katherine Anne Porter

Primary sources include *Ship of Fools* (1962); *The Collected Stories of Katherine Anne Porter* (1965); *The Collected Essays and Occasional Writings of Katherine Anne Porter* (1970); *The Never-Ending Wrong* (1977), about the Sacco and Vanzetti case; *Letters* (1990), edited by Isabel Bayley; *"This Strange, Old World" and Other Book Reviews by Katherine Anne Porter* (1991), edited by Darlene Harbour Unrue; *Uncollected Early Prose of Katherine Anne Porter* (1993), edited by Ruth M. Alvarez and Thomas F. Walsh; and *Katherine Anne Porter's Poetry* (1996), edited by Unrue.

The first full-scale biography is Joan Givner's *Katherine Anne Porter, A Life* (1982, rev. 1991). Givner also edited *Katherine Anne Porter: Conversations* (1987). *A Bibliography of the Works of Katherine Anne Porter*, edited by Louise Waldrip and Shirley Ann Bauer, appeared in 1969; *Katherine Anne Porter: An Annotated Bibliography* (of criticism) was compiled by Kathryn Hilt and Ruth M. Alvarez (1990).

Critical studies include Jane Krause DeMouy's *Katherine Anne Porter's Women: The Eye of Her Fiction* (1983), Unrue's *Truth and Vision in Katherine Anne Porter's Fiction* (1985), Willene and George Hendrick's *Katherine Anne Porter* (rev. 1988), Thomas F. Walsh's *Katherine Anne Porter and Mexico: The Illusion of Eden* (1992), Robert H. Brinkmeyer's *Katherine Anne Porter's Artistic Development* (1993), Janis P. Stout's *Katherine Anne Porter, A Sense of the Times* (1995), and Mary Titus's *The Ambivalent Art of Katherine Anne Porter* (2005). Unrue edited *Critical Essays on Katherine Anne Porter* (1997).

Ezra Pound

Pound's early poetry, from *A Lume Spento* (1908) through *Ripostes* (1912), is in the authoritative *Collected Early Poems of Ezra Pound* (1976), edited by Michael King. The same volumes, along with later volumes *Hugh Selwyn Mauberley* and *Homage to Sextus Propertius*, are collected in *Personae: The Collected Shorter Poems* (rev. ed. 1949; 2nd rev. ed. 1990). The New Directions edition of *The Cantos* (1993) is definitive. The most important of Pound's critical writings are *The Spirit of Romance* (rev. 1952); *Gaudier-Brzeska: A Memoir* (1916); *Instigations* (1920); *Make It New* (1934); *The ABC of Reading* (1934); *Guide to Kulchur* (1938); and *Patria Mia* (1950). His criticism has been collected in *Literary Essays of Ezra Pound* (1954), edited by T. S. Eliot; *Selected Prose, 1909–1965* (1973), edited by William Cookson (1973); and *Ezra Pound's Poetry and Prose Contributions to Periodicals* (1991), prefaced and arranged by Lea Baechler, A. Walton Litz, and James Longenback in eleven volumes. *Ezra Pound Speaking: Radio Speeches of World War II* (1978), edited by Leonard W. Doob, collects his wartime radio addresses. D. D. Paige edited *The Letters of Ezra Pound, 1907–1941* (1950). Other correspondence is collected in *Ezra Pound and Dorothy Shakespear: Their Letters, 1909–1914* (1984), edited by Omar Pound and A. Walton Litz; *Pound/Lewis: The Letters of Ezra Pound and Wyndham Lewis* (1985), edited by Timothy Materer; *Ezra Pound and James Loughlin* (1994), edited by David M. Gordon; and *Pound/Cummings: The Correspondence of Ezra Pound and E. E. Cummings*, edited by Barry Ahearn. Reviews of Pound are collected in Eric Homberger's *Ezra Pound: The Critical Heritage* (1973, 1997).

James J. Wilhelm's three-volume biography includes *The American Roots of Ezra Pound* (1985), *Ezra Pound in London and Paris, 1908–1925* (1990), and *Ezra Pound: The Tragic Years, 1925–1972* (1994). Also useful are Noel Stock's *The Life of Ezra Pound* (1970, 1982), C.

David Haymann's *Ezra Pound, The Last Rower: A Political Profile* (1976), Humphrey Carpenter's *A Serious Character: The Life of Ezra Pound* (1988), and Wendy Stallard Flory's *The American Ezra Pound* (1989). *The Roots of Treason: Ezra Pound and the Secrets of St. Elizabeth* (1984), by E. Fuller Torrey, focuses on Pound's trial and incarceration.

Hugh Kenner's *The Pound Era* (1972) has been influential. Good introductions are Christine Brooke-Rose's *A ZBC of Ezra Pound* (1971) and James Knapp's *Ezra Pound* (1972). For *The Cantos* see the *Annotated Index to the Cantos of Ezra Pound* (1957) (through Canto LXXXIV), edited by John H. Edwards and William W. Vasse; George Dekker's *The Cantos of Ezra Pound* (1963); Noel Stock's *Reading the Cantos* (1967); Ronald Bush's *The Genesis of Pound's Cantos* (1976); Wilhelm's *The Later Cantos of Ezra Pound* (1977); Lawrence S. Rainey's *Ezra Pound and the Monument of Culture* (1991); Carrol F. Terrill's *A Companion to the Cantos of Ezra Pound* (1993); George Kearn's *Guide to Ezra Pound's Selected Cantos* (1980); Anthony Woodward's *Ezra Pound and "The Pisan Cantos"* (1980); and William Cookson's updated *Guide to the Cantos of Ezra Pound* (2001). *Ezra Pound and Italian Fascism* (1991), by Tim Redman, addresses the poet's politics; as does *Pound in Purgatory: From Economic Realism to Anti-Semitism* (1999), by Leon Surette. Cultural approaches to Pound include Michael Coyle's *Ezra Pound, Popular Genres, and the Discourse of Culture* (1995) and Daniel Tiffany's *Radio Corpse* (1995). Marjorie Perloff's *The Dance of the Intellect* (1996) studies poetry in the Pound tradition. Andrew Gibson edited *Pound in Multiple Perspective: A Collection of Critical Essays* (1993) and Ira B. Nadel edited *The Cambridge Companion to Ezra Pound* (1999).

Edwin Arlington Robinson

Collected Poems of Edwin Arlington Robinson (1921) was enlarged periodically through 1937. In addition to shorter verse, Robinson wrote long narrative poems, including the Arthurian trilogy of *Merlin* (1917), *Lancelot* (1920), and *Tristram* (1927). Other books include *Roman Bartholomew* (1923), *The Man Who Died Twice* (1924), *Cavender's House* (1929), *The Glory of the Nightingales* (1930), *Matthias at the Door* (1931), *Talifer* (1933), *Amaranth* (1934), and *King Jasper* (1935). Ridgely Torrence compiled *Selected Letters* (1940). Denham Sutcliffe edited *Untriangulated Stars: Letters of Edwin Arlington Robinson to Harry de Forest Smith, 1890–1905* (1947). Richard Cary edited *Edwin Arlington Robinson's Letters to Edith Brower* (1968).

There is little recent work on Robinson. Richard Cary documented *The Early Reception of Edwin Arlington Robinson* (1974). Introductions to Robinson's work include Wallace L.

Anderson's *Edwin Arlington Robinson: A Critical Introduction* (1967), Hoyt C. Franchere's *Edwin Arlington Robinson* (1968), and Louis O. Coxe's *Edwin Arlington Robinson: The Life of Poetry* (1969). Ellsworth Barnard edited *Edwin Arlington Robinson: Centenary Essays* (1969). Other collections are *Appreciation of Edwin Arlington Robinson: Twenty-eight Interpretive Essays* (1969), edited by Richard Cary; and *Edwin Arlington Robinson: A Collection of Critical Essays* (1970), edited by Francis Murphy. Richard Hoffpair's *The Contemplative Poetry of Edwin Arlington Robinson, Robert Frost, and Yvor Winters* (2002) links Robinson to other poets.

Carl Sandburg

The Complete Poems of Carl Sandburg (1950) was revised and expanded in 1970. *Breathing Tokens* (1978), edited by Margaret Sandburg, prints unpublished poems. *Billy Sunday and Other Poems* (1993), edited by George and Willene Hendrick, contains some of his unpublished, uncollected, and unexpurgated poems. In addition to eight full-length volumes of poetry, Sandburg wrote a Pulitzer Prize–winning study of Abraham Lincoln: *Abraham Lincoln: The Prairie Years*, 2 vols. (1926), and *Abraham Lincoln: The War Years*, 4 vols. (1939), two collections of journalism and social commentary, *Rootabaga Stories* for children, a novel, and a book of American folk songs. *Fables, Foibles and Foobles* (1988), edited by George Hendrick, is a selection of unpublished humorous pieces. *More Rootabagas* (1993), edited by Hendrick, contains stories for children. *Selected Poems* (1996) was edited by George and Willene Hendrick. *The Letters of Carl Sandburg* (1968, 1988) was edited by Herbert Mitgang. *The Poet and the Dream Girl: The Love Letters of Lilian Steichen and Carl Sandburg* (1987, 1999) was edited by Margaret Sandburg.

Always the Young Strangers (1953) and *Ever the Winds of Chance* (1983), edited by Margaret Sandburg and George Hendrick, are segments of Sandburg's autobiography. A full-scale biography is Penelope Niven's *Carl Sandburg: A Biography* (1991). Critical studies include Richard Crowder's *Carl Sandburg* (1964) and Philip R. Yannella's *The Other Carl Sandburg* (1996).

Gertrude Stein

The Library of America published Stein's writings in two volumes: 1903–32 and 1932–46 (1998). *The Yale Edition of the Unpublished Writings of Gertrude Stein* (1951–58), edited by Carl Van Vechten, contains eight volumes of poetry, prose fiction, portraits, essays, and miscellany. The Norton Critical Edition of *Three Lives and Q.E.D.* (2005), edited by Marianne DeKoven, supplies critical and biographical contexts. Among publications in Stein's lifetime are *Tender Buttons* (1914) and prose fiction, including *Three Lives* (1909), *The Making of Americans* (1925), *Lucy Church Amiably* (1930), *Ida: A Novel* (1941), and *Brewsie and Willie* (1946). *Geography and Plays* (1922), *Operas and Plays* (1932), and *Last Operas and Plays* (1949, 1995), edited by Carl Van Vechten, contain dramatic pieces. Biographical material and portraits of Stein's contemporaries may be found in *The Autobiography of Alice B. Toklas* (1933), *Portraits and Prayers* (1934); *Everybody's Autobiography* (1937), and *Wars I Have Seen* (1945). Other works, including meditations, essays, sketches, and sociolinguistic treatises, are *Useful Knowledge* (1928), *How to Write* (1931), *Lectures in America* (1935), *Narration: Four Lectures by Gertrude Stein* (1935), *What Are Masterpieces* (1940), and *Four in America* (1947). Donald C. Gallup edited *Fernhurst, Q.E.D. and Other Early Writings by Gertrude Stein* (1971) and also a collection of letters to Stein, *The Flowers of Friendship* (1953). Her correspondence with Mabel Dodge Luhan is edited by Patricia R. Everett (1996) and with Thornton Wilder by Edward Burns and Ulla E. Dydo (1996). *Baty Precious Always Shines* (2000), edited by Kay Tarner, has selected love letters written between Stein and her partner, Alice B. Toklas. *Gertrude Stein: An Annotated Bibliography* (1979) was compiled by Maureen R. Liston.

W. G. Rogers's *When This You See Remember Me: Gertrude Stein in Person* (1948) and Alice B. Toklas's *What Is Remembered* (1963) are reminiscences of Stein by friends. Biographies include Howard Greenfield's *Gertrude Stein: A Biography* (1973), James R. Mellow's *Charmed Circle: Gertrude Stein and Company* (1974), Janet Hobhouse's *Everybody Who Was Anybody* (1989), Linda Wagner-Martin's *Favored Strangers: Gertrude Stein and Her Family* (1995), and Brenda Wineapple's *Sister Brother: Gertrude and Leo Stein* (1996).

Critical studies include Robert B. Haas's *A Primer for the Gradual Understanding of Gertrude Stein* (1971), Richard Bridgman's *Gertrude Stein in Pieces* (1970), Wendy Steiner's *Exact Resemblance to Exact Resemblance: The Literary Portraiture of Gertrude Stein* (1978), Marianne DeKoven's *A Different Language: Gertrude Stein's Experimental Writing* (1983), Randa Kay Dubnick's *The Structure of Obscurity: Gertrude Stein, Language, and Cubism* (1984), Lisa Ruddick's *Reading Gertrude Stein: Body, Text, Gnosis* (1990), Bettina L. Knapp's *Gertrude Stein* (1990), Jane P. Bowers's *Gertrude Stein* (1993), Linda Watts's *Gertrude Stein: A Study of the Short Fiction* (1999), Barbara Will's *Gertrude Stein, Modernism, and the Problem of "Genius"* (2000), and Dana Cairns Watson's *Gertrude Stein and the Essence of What Hoppens* (2004). Bruce Kellner edited the useful *Gertrude Stein Com-*

panion (1988). A collection of critical essays, edited by Richard Kostelanetz, is *Gertrude Stein Advanced* (1990).

John Steinbeck
The Library of America issued three volumes of Steinbeck's work, *Novels and Stories 1932–1937* (1994), *The Grapes of Wrath and Other Writings* (1996), and *Novels 1942–1952* (2002). Two biographies are *The True Adventures of John Steinbeck, Writer* (1984), by Jackson J. Benson, and *John Steinbeck* (1995), by Jay Parini. Elaine Steinbeck and Robert Wallsten edited *Steinbeck: A Life in Letters* (1975). Critical studies of Steinbeck include Paul McCarthy's *John Steinbeck* (1980), R. S. Hughes's *Beyond the Red Pony: A Reader's Guide to Steinbeck's Complete Short Stories* (1987), John H. Timmerman's *The Dramatic Landscape of Steinbeck's Short Stories* (1990), and Warren French's *John Steinbeck's Fiction Revisited* (1994). R. David edited *John Steinbeck: A Collection of Critical Essays* (1972); other collections are *Rediscovering Steinbeck* (1989), edited by Cliff Lewis and Carroll Britch; *Critical Essays on Steinbeck's* Grapes of Wrath (1989), edited by John Ditsky; *Short Novels of John Steinbeck* (1990), edited by Jackson J. Benson; *John Steinbeck: The Contemporary Reviews* (1996), edited by Joseph R. McElrath Jr., Jesse S. Crisler, and Susan Shillinglaw; and *Beyond Boundaries: Rereading John Steinbeck* (2002), edited by Shillinglaw and Kevin Hearle.

Wallace Stevens
The Collected Poems of Wallace Stevens was published in 1954. *Opus Posthumous* (1957, rev. 1989) by Milton J. Bates includes previously uncollected poems, plays, and essays. *The Necessary Angel: Essays on Reality and the Imagination* (1951) is Stevens's prose statement on poetry. The Library of America issued his *Collected Poetry and Prose* (1997). Other resources are *Letters of Wallace Stevens* (1966, 1996), edited by Holly Stevens; *The Contemplated Spouse: The Letters of Wallace Stevens to Elsie* (2006), edited by J. Donald Blount; *Concordance to the Poetry of Wallace Stevens* (1963), edited by Thomas Walsh; and *Wallace Stevens: A Descriptive Bibliography* (1973), compiled by J. M. Edelstein.

Joan Richardson's *Wallace Stevens: The Early Years, 1879–1923* (1986) chronicles the poet's youth and her *Wallace Stevens: The Later Years, 1923–1955* (1988) completes the story. Another biography is Tony Sharpe's *Wallace Stevens: A Literary Life* (2000). A. Walton Litz's *Introspective Voyager: The Poetic Development of Wallace Stevens* (1972) traces Stevens's thought and style through his early and middle years. Harold Bloom's *Wallace Stevens: The Poems of Our Climate* (1977) considers intellectual influences on Stevens; Joseph N. Riddle's *The Clairvoyant Eye: The Poetry and Poetics of Wallace Stevens* (1969, 1991) reads many individual poems. Other good full-length studies include Eleanor Cook's *Poetry, Word-Play, and Word-War in Wallace Stevens* (1988), Robert Rehder's *The Poetry of Wallace Stevens* (1988), James Longenbach's *Wallace Stevens: The Plain Sense of Things* (1991), George S. Lensing's *Wallace Stevens: A Poet's Growth* (1991), Daniel Schwarz's *Narrative and Representation in the Poetry of Wallace Stevens* (1993), Alan Filreis's *Modernism from Left to Right* (1994), and Janet McCann's *Wallace Stevens Revisited* (1995). Jacqueline Vaught Brogan's *The Violence Within/The Violence Without: Wallace Stevens and the Emergence of a Revolutionary Poetics* (2003) and Malcolm Woodland's *Wallace Stevens and the Apocalyptic Mode* (2005) consider the relation of Stevens's poetry to war. Albert Gelpi collects essays on the poet in *Wallace Stevens: The Poetics of Modernism* (1990); other collections are *Critical Essays on Wallace Stevens* (1988), edited by Steven Gould Axelrod and Helen Deese, and *Wallace Stevens and the Feminine* (1993), edited by Melita Schaum.

Jean Toomer

Toomer's published works include *Cane* (1923, repr. 1975, pub. also in a Norton Critical Edition, 1988), *Essentials* (1931), *Portage Potential* (1932), and an address, "The Flavor of Man" (1949). His *Collected Poems*, edited by Robert B. Jones and Margery Toomer Latimer, were published in 1988. *A Jean Toomer Reader* (1993), containing previously unpublished writings, was edited by Frederik L. Rusch; Robert B. Jones edited *Selected Essays and Literary Criticism* (1996). Brian Joseph Benson and Mabel Mayle Dillard's *Jean Toomer* (1980); Nellie Y. McKay's *Jean Toomer, Artist: A Study of His Literary Life and Work, 1894–1936* (1984); and Cynthia Earl Kerman and Richard Eldridge's *The Lives of Jean Toomer: A Hunger for Wholeness* (1989) are biographies. Studies include *Jean Toomer and the Terrors of American History* (1998), by Charles Scruggs and Lee Van De Marr, and *Split-Gut Song: Jean Toomer and the Poetics of Modernity* (2005), by Karen Ford Jackson. Essay collections are *Jean Toomer: A Critical Evaluation* (1988), edited by Therman B. O'Daniel, and *Jean Toomer and the Harlem Renaissance*, edited by Geneviève Faber and Michel Faith (2000).

William Carlos Williams

Williams's poems were first collected in three volumes: *Collected Earlier Poems of William Carlos Williams* (1951), *Collected Later Poems of William Carlos Williams* (1950), and *Pictures from Brueghel* (1962). More recent are *The Collected Poems of William Carlos Williams, Vol. 1, 1909–1939* (1996), edited by A. Walton Litz and Christopher MacGowan, and *Vol. 2,*

1939–1962 (1988), edited by MacGowan (1988). *Paterson's* five books, published individually between 1946 and 1958, were issued in one volume in 1963 and reedited by MacGowan (1992). *Kora in Hell*, Williams's volume of prose poetry, is in the collection *Imaginations* (1970), edited by Webster Schott, along with essays, fiction, and creative prose. Williams's short stories are collected in *Make Light of It* (1950) and again, with several additions, in *The Farmers' Daughters* (1961). His novels are *A Voyage to Pagany* (1928), *White Mule* (1937), *In the Money* (1940), and *The Build Up* (1946). His dramatic pieces were published together in *Many Loves and Other Plays* (1961). Important essays are contained in *In the American Grain* (1925, 1940); *Selected Essays of William Carlos Williams* (1954); and *Imaginations* (1970), edited by Webster Schott. Williams's prose also includes *The Autobiography of William Carlos Williams* (1951); a book of recollections dictated to Edith Heal, *I Wanted to Write a Poem* (1958); and *Yes, Mrs. Williams* (1959), a portrait of the poet's mother. J. C. Thirlwall edited *The Selected Letters of William Carlos Williams* (1957). Selections from the Pound–Williams correspondence, edited by Hugh Witemeyer, appeared in 1996. Letters between Williams and Denise Levertov, edited by MacGowan, appeared in 1998. Barry Ahearn edited *The Correspondence of William Carlos Williams and Louis Zukofsky* (2003). *The Humane Particulars: The Collected Letters of William Carlos Williams and Kenneth Burke* (2003) was edited by James H. East. Emily Mitchell Wallace compiled *A Bibliography of William Carlos Williams* (1968). Reed Whittemore's *William Carlos Williams: Poet from Jersey* (1975) is a critical biography, as is Paul Mariani's more detailed *William Carlos Williams: A New World Naked* (1981).

James E. Breslin's *William Carlos Williams: An American Artist* (1970) is a still-useful overview. Other general introductions are Thomas R. Whitaker's *William Carlos Williams* (1989) and Kelli A. Larson's *Guide to the Poetry of William Carlos Williams* (1995). Among specialized studies are Mike Weaver's *William Carlos Williams: The American Background* (1971), Jerome Mazzaro's *William Carlos Williams: The Later Poems* (1973), Joseph N. Riddel's *The Inverted Bell: Modernism and the Counter-Poetics of William Carlos Williams* (1974), Charles Doyle's *William Carlos Williams and the American Poem* (1982), Henry M. Sayre's *The Visual Text of William Carlos Williams* (1983), Kerry Driscoll's *William Carlos Williams and the Maternal Muse* (1987), Ann W. Fisher-Wirth's *William Carlos Williams and Autobiography: The Woods of His Own Nature* (1989), Ron Callan's *William Carlos Williams and Transcendentalism* (1992), T. Hugh Crawford's *Modernism, Medicine, and William Car-*

los Williams (1993), Brian A. Bremen's William Carlos Williams and the Diagnostics of Culture (1993), Peter Halter's The Revolution in the Visual Arts and the Poetry of William Carlos Williams (1994), Donald W. Markos's Ideas in Things (1994), Barry Ahearn's William Carlos Williams and Celebrity (1994), Julio Marzan's The Spanish American Roots of William Carlos Williams (1994), and Stanley Koehler's Countries of the Mind: The Poetry of William Carlos Williams (1998).

Linda Wagner's The Prose of William Carlos Williams (1970) and Robert Coles's William Carlos Williams: The Knack of Survival in America (1975) discuss Williams's prose. For Paterson, see Joel Conarroe's William Carlos Williams' Paterson: Language and Landscape (1970) and Benjamin Sankey's A Companion to William Carlos Williams's Paterson (1971). Paul Mariani's William Carlos Williams: The Poet and His Critics (1975) considers Williams's critical reception, as does William Carlos Williams, The Critical Heritage (1980, 1997), edited by Charles Doyle. Critical Essays on Wallace Stevens was edited by Steven Gould Axelrod and Helen Deese (1988).

Thomas Wolfe

Among primary documents are The Notebooks of Thomas Wolfe (1970), edited by Richard S. Kennedy and P. Reeves; The Autobiography of an American Novelist, by Thomas Wolfe (1983), edited by Leslie Field; The Letters of Thomas Wolfe (1956), edited by Elizabeth Nowell; The Letters of Thomas Wolfe to His Mother (1968), edited by C. Holman and S. Ross; My Other Loneliness: Letters of Thomas Wolfe and Aline Bernstein (1983), edited by Suzanne Stutman; Beyond Love and Loyalty: The Letters of Thomas Wolfe and Elizabeth Nowell (1983), edited by Richard S. Kennedy; and To Loot My Life Clean: The Thomas Wolfe–Maxwell Perkins Correspondence (2000), edited by Matthew Bruccoli. The fullest biography is Look Homeward: A Life of Thomas Wolfe (1987), by David Herbert Donald. A Thomas Wolfe Companion (1987), by John Lane Idol Jr., is informative and useful. John Earl Bassett compiled Thomas Wolfe: An Annotated Critical Bibliography (1996).

There were many critical studies of Wolfe in the 1950s and 1960s. Later books include Carol I. Johnston's Of Time and the Artist (1996) and Robert Taylor Ensign's Lean Down Your Ear upon the Earth, and Listen: Thomas Wolfe's Greener Modernism (2003).

Collections of critical essays are Thomas Wolfe: Three Decades of Criticism (1968), edited by A. Field; Thomas Wolfe: The Critical Reception (1974), edited by P. Reeves; The Loneliness at the Core: Studies in Thomas Wolfe (1975), edited by C. Hugh Holman; and Critical Essays on Thomas Wolfe (1985), edited by John S. Phillipson.

Richard Wright

Wright's fiction includes Uncle Tom's Children (1938), Native Son (1940), The Outsider (1953), and Eight Men (1961). Black Boy (1945) is his autobiography; White Man, Listen! (1957) is an important work of nonfiction. The Library of America has published his writings in two volumes, including an unexpurgated version of Native Son (1991). For a complete bibliography of his writings, see Richard Wright: A Primary Bibliography (1982), compiled by Charles T. Davis and Michel Fabre. A good example of reviews can be found in Richard Wright: The Critical Reception (1978), edited by John M. Reilly; a massive bibliography of Wright criticism around the world has been assembled by Keneth Kinnamon (1988). Kinnamon and Michel Fabre edited Conversations with Richard Wright (1993). The best critical biography is Fabre's The Unfinished Quest of Richard Wright (1993); see also Margaret Walker's Richard Wright, Daemonic Genius (1993) and Hazel Rowley's Richard Wright: The Life and Times (2001). Critical studies include Russell C. Brignano's Richard Wright: An Introduction to the Man and His Works (1970), Kinnamon's The Emergence of Richard Wright (1972), Fabre's Richard Wright: Books and Writers (1990), and Robert Butler's Native Son: The Emergence of a New Black Hero (1991). Abdul R. Jan Mohamed's The Death-Bound-Subject: Richard Wright's Archaeology of Death (2005) is an ambitious theoretical study. Collections of criticism are Yoshinobu Hakutani's Critical Essays on Richard Wright (1982); Richard Wright: Critical Perspectives Past and Present (1993), edited by Henry Louis Gates Jr. and K. A. Appiah; The Critical Response to Richard Wright (1995), edited by Robert J. Butler; Richard Wright: A Collection of Critical Essays (1995), edited by Arnold Rampersad; and Kinnamon's Critical Essays on Richard Wright's Native Son (1997).

PERMISSIONS ACKNOWLEDGMENTS

Sherwood Anderson: "Hands," "Mother," and "Adventure" from WINESBURG, OHIO by Sherwood Anderson, copyright 1919 by B. W. Huebsch. Copyright 1947 by Eleanor Copenhaver Anderson. Used by permission of the publishers, Viking Penguin, a division of Penguin Group (USA), Inc., and Jonathan Cape c/o The Random House Group Ltd.

Kay Boyle: From FIFTY STORIES, copyright © 1980 by Kay Boyle. Reprinted by permission of New Directions Publishing Corp. and Abner Stein.

Sterling Brown: "Mister Samuel and Sam," "He Was a Man," "Master and Man," "Break of Day," "Bitter Fruit of the Tree" from THE COLLECTED POEMS OF STERLING A BROWN, ed. by Michael S. Harper. Copyright © 1980 by Sterling A. Brown. Reprinted by permission of HarperCollins Publishers.

Carlos Bulosan: "Be American" from Carlos Bulosan Papers. ACC 0581-001. Reprinted by permission of Special Collections, Univ. of Washington Libraries.

Willa Cather: "The Novel Démeublé" from NOT UNDER FORTY by Willa Cather, copyright © 1936 by Willa S. Cather, renewed 1964 by Edith Lewis and the City Bank Farmers Trust Co. Used by permission of Alfred A. Knopf, a division of Random House, Inc. MY ÁNTONIA by Willa Cather, Copyright 1918, 1926 by Willa Sibert Cather, © renewed 1946 by Willa Sibert Cather; copyright © renewed 1954 by Edith Lewis. Reprinted by permission of Houghton Mifflin Co. All rights reserved.

Raymond Chandler: "Red Wind" from COLLECTED STORIES by Raymond Chandler, copyright © 2002 by Philip Marlowe BV. Used by permission of Alfred A. Knopf, a division of Random House, Inc., and Ed Victor Ltd.

Hart Crane: "Chaplinesque," "At Melville's Tomb," "Voyages I, III, and V," "The Tunnel," "To Brooklyn Bridge," and "Powhatan's Daughter," from COMPLETE POEMS OF HART CRANE by Hart Crane, ed. by Marc Simon. Copyright 1933, © 1958, 1966 by Liveright Publishing Corporation. Copyright © 1986 by Marc Simon. Used by permission of Liveright Publishing Corporation.

Countee Cullen: "From the Dark Tower," Uncle Jim," "Yet Do I Marvel," "Incident," and "Heritage," from ON THESE I STAND by Countee Cullen. Copyrights held by the Amistad Research Center, Tulane University, administered by Thompson and Thompson, Brooklyn, NY.

E. E. Cummings: "Thy fingers make early flowers of," "in Just-," "O sweet spontaneous," "Buffalo Bill's," "the Cambridge ladies who live in furnished souls," "next to of course god america i,' " "i sing of Olaf glad and big," "somewhere i have never travelled, gladly beyond," "anyone lived in a pretty how town," "my father moved through dooms of love," and "pity this busy monster, manunkind" reprinted from COMPLETE POEMS, 1904–1962, by E. E. Cummings, ed. by George J. Firmage. Copyright 1923, 1925, 1926, 1931, 1935, 1938, 1939, 1940, 1944, 1945, 1946, 1947, 1948, 1949, 1950, 1951, 1952, 1953, 1954, © 1955, 1956, 1957, 1958, 1959, 1960, 1961, 1962, 1963, 1966, 1967, 1968, 1972, 1973, 1974, 1975, 1976, 1977, 1978, 1979, 1980, 1981, 1982, 1983, 1984, 1985, 1986, 1987, 1988, 1989, 1990, 1991 by the Trustees for the E. E. Cummings Trust. Copyright © 1973, 1976, 1978, 1979, 1981, 1983, 1985, 1991 by George James Firmage. "The Enormous Room," a Typescript Edition, with Drawings by the Author, by E. E. Cummings, ed. by George J. Firmage. Copyright © 1978 by the Trustees for the E. E. Cummings Trust. Copyright © 1978 by George James Firmage. Used by permission of Liveright Publishing Corporation.

H. D. (Hilda Doolittle): From COLLECTED POEMS 1912–1944 by H.D. (Hilda Doolittle). Copyright © 1982 by The Estate of Hilda Doolittle. Reprinted by permission of New Directions Publishing Corp. and Carcanet Press Ltd.

John Dos Passos: From THE BIG MONEY from U.S.A. by John Dos Passos. Copyright by Elizabeth H. Dos Passos. Reprinted by permission of Lucy Dos Passos Coggin.

T. S. Eliot: "The Love Song of J. Alfred Prufrock," "Sweeney Among the Nightingales," "Gerontion," and "The Waste Land," reprinted by permission of Faber and Faber Ltd. from COLLECTED POEMS 1909–1962 by T. S. Eliot. "The Hollow Men" and "Journey of the Magi" from COLLECTED POEMS 1909–1962 by T. S. Eliot, copyright 1936 by Harcourt, Inc. and renewed 1964 by T. S. Eliot. "Burnt Norton" from FOUR QUARTETS, copyright 1943 by T. S. Eliot and renewed 1971 by Esme Valerie Eliot. Reprinted by permission of Harcourt, Inc. and Faber and Faber Ltd. "Tradition and the Individual Talent" from SELECTED ESSAYS by T .S. Eliot. Reprinted by permission of Faber & Faber Ltd.

William Faulkner: "As I Lay Dying" and "Barn Burning" from COLLECTED STORIES OF WILLIAM FAULKNER by William Faulkner. Copyright © 1950 by Random House, Inc., and renewed 1977 by Jill Faulkner Summers.

Jessie Redmon Fauset: From THERE IS CONFUSION by Jesse Redmon Fauset. Copyright 1924 by Boni & Liveright, Inc., renewed 1951 by Jesse Redmon Fauset. Used by permission of Liveright Publishing Corp.

F. Scott Fitzgerald: "Babylon Revisited" reprinted by permission of Scribner, an imprint of Simon & Schuster Adult Publishing Group and Harold Ober Associates, Inc., from THE SHORT STORIES OF F. SCOTT FITZGERALD, ed. by Matthew J. Bruccoli. Copyright 1931 by The Curtis Publishing Company. Copyright renewed © 1959 by Frances Scott Fitzgerald Lanahan.

Robert Frost: "The Pasture," "Mowing," "Mending Wall," "The Death of the Hired Man," "Home Burial," "After Apple-Picking," "The Wood-Pile," "The Road Not Taken," "The Oven Bird," "Birches," "Out, Out-" "Fire and Ice," "Nothing Gold Can Stay," "Stopping by Woods on a Snowy Evening," "Departmental," "Desert Places," "Design," "Neither Out Far, Nor in Deep," "Provide, Provide," "The Gift Outright," and "Directive" from THE POETRY OF ROBERT FROST, ed. by Edward Connery Lathem. Copyright 1923, 1930, 1934, 1936, 1939, 1947, 1969 by Henry Holt and Company, copyright 1944, 1951, 1958, 1962 by Robert Frost, copyright 1964, 1967, 1975 by Lesley Frost Ballantine, reprinted by permission of the publishers Henry Holt and Company, LLC and Jonathan Cape c/o The Random House Group Ltd. "The Figure a Poem Makes" from THE SELECTED PROSE OF ROBERT FROST, ed. by Hyde Cox and Edward Connery Lathem. Copyright 1923, 1969 by Henry Holt and Company. Copyright 1951 by Robert Frost. Reprinted by permission of Henry Holt and Company, LLC.

Ernest Hemingway: "The Snows of Kilimanjaro" from THE SHORT STORIES OF ERNEST HEMINGWAY. Copyright 1936 by Ernest Hemingway; copyright renewed © 1964 by Mary Hemingway. Published in Great Britain in THE FIRST 49 STORIES. Reprinted by permission of the publishers, Scribner, an imprint of Simon & Schuster Adult Publishing Group and Jonathan Cape c/o The Random House Group Ltd. Excerpt from letter from Ernest Hemingway to his family (Aug. 18,

"Of Modern Poetry," "Asides on the Oboe," and "The Plain Sense of Things" from THE COLLECTED POEMS OF WAL-LACE STEVENS by Wallace Stevens. Copyright 1954 by Wallace Stevens. Used by permission of Alfred A. Knopf, a division of Random House, Inc. and Faber and Faber Ltd.

Jean Toomer: "Georgia Dusk," "Fern," "Portrait in Georgia," and "Seventh Street" from CANE by Jean Toomer. Copyright 1923 by Boni & Liveright. Copyright renewed 1951 by Jean Toomer. Used by permission of Liveright Publishing Corporation.

William Carlos Williams: From THE COLLECTED POEMS OF WILLIAM CARLOS WILLIAMS 1909–1939, volume I. Copyright © 1938 by New Directions Publishing Corporation and from THE COLLECTED POEMS OF WILLIAM CARLOS WILLIAMS 1939–1962, volume 11. Copyright © 1944, 1953, 1962 by William Carlos Williams. Reprinted by permission of New Directions Publishing Corp. and Carcanet Press Ltd.

Thomas Wolfe: "The Lost Boy" by Thomas Wolfe. Copyright © 1937 by Maxwell Perkins as Executor of the Estate of Thomas Wolfe. Copyright renewed 1969 by Paul Gitlin, C.T.A., Administrator of the Estate of Thomas Wolfe. Reprinted with permission of McIntosh & Otis, Inc.

Richard Wright: "The Man Who Was Almost a Man" from EIGHT MEN by Richard Wright. Copyright © 1961 by Richard Wright. Reprinted by permission of John Hawkins & Associates, Inc.

IMAGE ACKNOWLEDGMENTS

Marsden Hartley, *Portrait of a German Officer*, The Metropolitan Museum of Art, The Alfred Stieglitz Collection, 1949 (49.70.42) Photographed © 1986 The Metropolitan Museum of Art.

Constantin Brâncusi (1876–1957), *Golden Bird*, 1919–20, (pedestal ca. 1922), Bronze, stone and wood, h. 85 3/4 in. (with base). Partial gift of The Arts Club of Chicago, restricted gift of various donors, through prior bequest of Arthur Rubloff, through prior restricted gift of William Hartmann, through prior gifts of Mr. and Mrs. Carter H. Harrison, Mr. and Mrs. Arnold H. Maremont through the Kate Maremont Foundation, Woodruff J. Parker, Mrs. Clive Runnells, Mr. and Mrs. Martin A. Ryerson, and various donors, 1990.88 3/4 view. The Art Institute of Chicago. Photography © The Art Institute of Chicago. © 2006 Artists Rights Society (ARS), New York/ADAGP, Paris.

Charles Sheeler (1883–1965), *River Rouge Plant*, 1932, oil on canvas, 20 x 241/8 in. Whitney Museum of Art, NY, Purchase 32.43.

Archibald J. Motley, *Black Belt*, Hampton University Museum, Hampton, Virginia.

Dorothea Lange, *Towards Los Angeles, 1937*, Library of Congress Prints and Photographs.

Georgia O'Keefe, *From the Faraway, Nearby*, The Metropolitan Museum of Art, Alfred Stieglitz Collection, 1959 (59.204.2). Photographed by Malcolm Varon. © 1984 The Metropolitan Museum of Art.

J. Howard Miller, *We Can Do It!* ("Rosie the Riveter"). Photo: The Granger Collection, NY.

Edward Hopper (1882–1967), *Nighthawks*, 1942, Friends of American Art Collection 1942.51 The Art Institute of Chicago. Photography © The Art Institute of Chicago.

Index